P. C. Wren

P. C. Wren: Adventure Novels & Tales From the Foreign Legion

OK Publishing 2021

P. C. Wren

P. C. Wren: Adventure Novels & Tales From the Foreign Legion

The Wages of Virtue, Cupid in Africa, Snake and Sword, Driftwood Spars...

Published by

MUSAICUM
Books

Advanced Digital Solutions & High-Quality book Formatting
musaicumbooks@okpublishing.info

2021 OK Publishing

ISBN 978-80-272-8077-3

Contents

Novels:	13
SNAKE AND SWORD	15
Part I. The Welding of a Soul	17
Chapter I. The Snake and the Soul	18
Part II. The Searing of a Soul	21
Chapter II. The Sword and the Snake	22
Chapter III. The Snake Appears	29
Chapter IV. The Sword and the Soul	37
Chapter V. Lucille	44
Chapter VI. The Snake's "Myrmidon"	52
Chapter VII. Love—and the Snake	62
Chapter VIII. Troopers of the Queen	72
Chapter IX. A Snake Avenges a Haddock and Lucille Behaves in an Un-Smelliean Manner	83
Chapter X. Much Ado About Almost Nothing—a Trooper	90
Chapter XI. More Myrmidons	97
Part III. The Saving of a Soul	113
Chapter XII. Vultures and Luck—good and Bad	114
Chapter XIII. Found	126
Chapter XIV. The Snake and the Sword	131
Seven Years After	135
Epilogue	136
THE WAGES OF VIRTUE	137
Prologue	139
Chapter I. Soap and Sir Montague Merline	148
Chapter II. A Barrack-Room of the Legion	162
Chapter III. Carmelita Et Cie	172
Chapter IV. The Canteen of the Legion	186
Chapter V. The Trivial Round	194
Chapter VI. Le Cafard and Other Things	208
Chapter VII. The Sheep in Wolf's Clothing	217
Chapter VIII. The Temptation of Sir Montague Merline	230
Chapter IX. The Café and the Canteen	238
Chapter X. The Wages of Sin	248
Chapter XI. Greater Love..	254
Epilogue	266

DRIFTWOOD SPARS	267
Chapter I. The Man	267
Chapter II. The Boy	281
Chapter III. The Woman	304
§ 1. Mr. Grobble	304
§ 2. General Murger	313
§ 3. Sergeant-Major Lawrence-Smith	330
§ 4. Mr. and Mrs. Cornelius Gosling-Green	344
§ 5. Mr. Horace Faggit	353
Chapter IV. "Meet and Leave Again."	357
§ 1	357
§ 2	371
§ 3	376
CUPID IN AFRICA: Or, The Baking of Bertram in Love and War	383
Part I. The Making of Bertram	385
Chapter I. Major Hugh Walsingham Greene	386
Chapter II. Mr. Charles Stayne-Brooker (or Herr Karl Stein-Brücker)	388
Chapter III. Mrs. Stayne-Brooker—and Her Ex-Stepson	390
Part II. The Baking of Bertram By War	391
Chapter I. Bertram Becomes a Man of War	392
Chapter II. And is Ordered to East Africa	399
Chapter III. Preparations	406
Chapter IV. Terra Marique Jactatus	409
Chapter V. Mrs. Stayne-Brooker	417
Chapter VI. Mombasa	419
Chapter VII. The Mombasa Club	424
Chapter VIII. Military and Naval Manœuvres	428
Chapter IX. Bertram Invades Africa	439
Chapter X. M'paga	444
Chapter XI. Food and Feeders	448
Chapter XII. Reflections	455
Chapter XIII. Baking	463
Chapter XIV. The Convoy	468
Chapter XV. Butindi	473
Chapter XVI. The Bristol Bar	478
Chapter XVII. More Baking	484
Chapter XVIII. Trial	489

Chapter XIX. Of a Pudding	494
Chapter XX. Stein-Brücker Meets Bertram Greene—and Death	499
Part III. The Baking of Bertram By Love	505
Chapter I. Mrs. Stayne-Brooker Again	506
Chapter II. Love	509
Chapter III. Love and War	514
Chapter IV. Baked	520
Chapter V. Finis	526
Short Story Collections:	527
STEPSONS OF FRANCE	529
I. Ten Little Legionaries	531
II. À La Ninon De L'Enclos	541
III. An Officer And—a Liar	544
IV. The Dead Hand	551
V. The Gift	558
VI. The Deserter	562
VII. Five Minutes	568
VIII. "Here Are Ladies"	572
IX. The Macsnorrt	577
X. "Belzébuth"	580
XI. The Quest	587
XII. "Vengeance Is Mine..."	594
XIII. Sermons in Stones	597
XIV. Moonshine	602
XV. The Coward of the Legion	605
XVI. Mahdev Rao	610
XVII. The Merry Liars	618
Footnotes	625

Novels:

SNAKE AND SWORD

To
MY WIFE ALICE LUCILLE WREN

Part I
The Welding of a Soul

Chapter I
The Snake and the Soul

When Colonel Matthew Devon de Warrenne, V.C., D.S.O., of the Queen's Own (118th) Bombay Lancers, pinned his Victoria Cross to the bosom of his dying wife's night-dress, in token of his recognition that she was the braver of the twain, he was not himself.

He was beside himself with grief.

Afterwards he adjured the sole witness of this impulsive and emotional act, Major John Decies, never to mention his "damned theatrical folly" to any living soul, and to excuse him on the score of an ancient sword-cut on the head and two bad sun-strokes.

For the one thing in heaven above, on the earth beneath, or in the waters under the earth, that Colonel de Warrenne feared, was breach of good form and stereotyped convention.

And the one thing he loved was the dying woman.

This last statement applies also to Major John Decies, of the Indian Medical Service, Civil Surgeon of Bimariabad, and may even be expanded, for the one thing he ever *had* loved was the dying woman....

Colonel Matthew Devon de Warrenne did the deed that won him his Victoria Cross, in the open, in the hot sunlight and in hot blood, sword in hand and with hot blood on the sword-hand —fighting for his life.

His wife did the deed that moved him to transfer the Cross to her, in darkness, in cold blood, in loneliness, sickness and silence-fighting for the life of her unborn child against an unseen foe.

Colonel de Warrenne's type of brave deed has been performed thousands of times and wherever brave men have fought.

His wife's deed of endurance, presence of mind, self-control and cool courage is rarer, if not unique.

To appreciate this fully, it must be known that she had a horror of snakes, so terrible as to amount to an obsession, a mental deformity, due, doubtless, to the fact that her father (Colonel Mortimer Seymour Stukeley) died of snake-bite before her mother's eyes, a few hours before she herself was born.

Bearing this in mind, judge of the conduct that led Colonel de Warrenne, distraught, to award her his Cross "For Valour".

One oppressive June evening, Lenore de Warrenne returned from church (where she had, as usual, prayed fervently that her soon-expected first-born might be a daughter), and entered her dressing-room. Here her Ayah divested her of hat, dress, and boots, and helped her into the more easeful tea-gown and satin slippers.

"Bootlair wanting ishweets for dinner-table from go-down,[1] please, Mem-Sahib," observed Ayah, the change of garb accomplished.

"The butler wants sweets, does he? Give me my keys, then," replied Mrs. de Warrenne, and, rising with a sigh, she left the dressing-room and proceeded, *via* the dining-room (where she procured some small silver bowls, sweet-dishes, and trays), to the go-down or store-room, situate at the back of the bungalow and adjoining the "dispense-khana" —the room in which assemble the materials and ministrants of meals from the extra-mural "bowachi-khana" or kitchen. Unlocking the door of the go-down, Mrs. de Warrenne entered the small shelf-encircled room, and, stepping on to a low stool proceeded to fill the sweet-trays from divers jars, tins and boxes, with guava-cheese, crystallized ginger, *kulwa*, preserved mango and certain of the more sophisticated sweetmeats of the West.

It was after sunset and the *hamal* had not yet lit the lamps, so that this pantry, a dark room at mid-day, was far from light at that time. But for the fact that she knew exactly where everything was, and could put her hand on what she wanted, she would not have entered without a light.

For some minutes the unfortunate lady stood on the stool.

Having completed her task she stepped down backwards and, as her foot touched the ground, she knew *that she had trodden upon a snake.*

Even as she stood poised, one foot on the ground, the other on the stool, both hands gripping the high shelf, she felt the reptile whipping, writhing, jerking, lashing, flogging at her ankle and instep, coiling round her leg.... And in the fraction of a second the thought flashed through her mind: "If its head is under my foot, or too close to my foot for its fangs to reach me, I am safe while I remain as I am. If its head is free I am doomed-and matters cannot be any the worse for my keeping as I am."

And she kept as she was, with one foot on the stool, out of reach, and one foot on the snake.

And screamed?

No, called quietly and coolly for the butler, remembering that she had sent Nurse Beaton out, that her husband was at polo, that there were none but native servants in the house, and that if she raised an alarm they would take it, and with single heart consider each the safety of Number One.

"Boy!" she called calmly, though the room swam round her and a deadly faintness began to paralyse her limbs and loosen her hold upon the shelf—"Boy! Come here."

Antonio Ferdinand Xavier D'Souza, Goanese butler, heard and came.

"Mem-Sahib?" quoth he, at the door of the go-down.

"Bring a lamp quickly," said Lenore de Warrenne in a level voice.

The worthy Antonio, fat, spectacled, bald and wheezy, hurried away and peremptorily bade the *hamal*[2], son of a jungle-pig, to light and bring a lamp quickly.

The *hamal*, respectfully pointing out to the Bootlair Sahib that the daylight was yet strong and lusty enough to shame and smother any lamp, complied with deliberation and care, polishing the chimney, trimming the wick, pouring in oil and generally making a satisfactory and commendable job of it.

Lenore de Warrenne, sick, faint, sinking, waited...waited...waited...gripping the shelf and fighting against her over-mastering weakness for the life of the unborn child that, even in that awful moment, she prayed might be a daughter.

After many cruelly long centuries, and as she swayed to fall, the good Antonio entered with the lamp. Her will triumphed over her falling body.

"Boy, I am standing on a snake!" said she coolly. "Put the lamp—"

But Antonio did not stay to "put" the lamp; incontinent he dropped it on the floor and fled yelling "Sap! Sap!" and that the Mem-Sahib was bitten, dying, dead-certainly dead; dead for hours.

And the brave soul in the little room waited...waited...waited...gripping the shelf, and thinking of the coming daughter, and wondering whether she must die by snake-bite or fire-unborn-with her unhappy mother. For the fallen lamp had burst, the oil had caught fire, and the fire gave no light by which she could see what was beneath her foot-head, body, or tail of the lashing, squirming snake-as the flame flickered, rose and fell, burnt blue, swayed, roared in the draught of the door-did anything but give a light by which she could see as she bent over awkwardly, still gripping the shelf, one foot on the stool, further prevented from seeing by her loose draperies.

Soon she realized that in any case she could not see her foot without changing her position—a thing she would *not* do while there was hope-and strength to hold on. For hope there was, inasmuch as *she had not yet felt the stroke of the reptile's fangs.*

Again she reasoned calmly, though strength was ebbing fast; she must remain as she was till death by fire or suffocation was the alternative to flight-flight which was synonymous with death, for, as her other foot came down and she stepped off the snake, in that instant it would strike-if it had not struck already.

Meantime-to call steadily and coolly again.

This time she called to the *hamal*, a Bhil, engaged out of compassion, and likely, as a son of the jungle's sons, to be of more courage than the stall-fed butler in presence of dangerous beast or reptile.

"*Hamal*: I want you," she called coolly.

"Mem-Sahib?" came the reply from the lamp-room near by, and the man approached.

"That stupid butler has dropped a lamp and run away. Bring a pail of water quickly and call to the *malli*[3] to bring a pail of earth as you get it. Hasten! —and there is baksheesh," said Mrs. de Warrenne quietly in the vernacular.

Tap and pail were by the door of the back verandah. In a minute the *hamal* entered and flung a pail of water on the burning pool of oil, reducing the mass of blue lambent flames considerably.

"Now *hamal*," said the fainting woman, the more immediate danger confronted, "bring another lamp very quickly and put it on the shelf. Quick! don't stop to fill or to clean it."

Was the pricking, shooting pain the repeated stabbing of the snake's fangs or was it "pins and needles"? Was this deadly faintness death indeed, or was it only weakness?

In what seemed but a few more years the man reappeared carrying a lighted lamp, the which he placed upon a shelf.

"Listen," said Mrs. de Warrenne, "and have no fear, brave Bhil. I have *caught* a snake. Get a knife quickly and cut off its head while I hold it."

The man glancing up, appeared to suppose that his mistress held the snake on the shelf, hurried away, and rushed back with the cook's big kitchen-knife gripped dagger-wise in his right hand.

"Do you see the snake?" she managed to whisper. "Under my foot! Quick! It is moving... moving... moving *out*."

With a wild Bhil cry the man flung himself down upon his hereditary dread foe and slashed with the knife.

Mrs. de Warrenne heard it scratch along the floor, grate on a nail, and crush through the snake.

"Aré!! Dead, Mem-Sahib!! Dead!! See, I have cut off its head! Aré!!!! Wah!! The brave mistress! ——"

As she collapsed, Mrs. de Warrenne saw the twitching body of a large cobra with its head severed close to its neck. Its head had just protruded from under her foot and she had saved the unborn life for which she had fought so bravely by just keeping still.... She had won her brief decoration with the Cross by keeping still. (Her husband had won his permanent right to it by extreme activity.)... Had she moved she would have been struck instantly, for the reptile was, by her, uninjured, merely nipped between instep and floor.

Having realized this, Lenore de Warrenne fainted and then passed from fit to fit, and her child —a boy-was born that night. Hundreds of times during the next few days the same terrible cry rang from the sick-room through the hushed bungalow: "It is under my foot! It is moving... moving... moving... *out!*"

* * *

"If I had to make a prophecy concerning this young fella," observed the broken-hearted Major John Decies, I.M.S., Civil Surgeon of Bimariabad, as he watched old Nurse Beaton performing the baby's elaborate ablutions and toilet, "I should say that he will *not* grow up fond of snakes-not if there is anything in the 'pre-natal influence' theory."

Part II
The Searing of a Soul

Chapter II
The Sword and the Snake

Colonel Matthew Devon De Warrenne, commanding the Queen's Own (118th) Bombay Lancers, was in good time, in his best review-order uniform, and in a terrible state of mind.

He strode from end to end of the long verandah of his bungalow with clank of steel, creak of leather, and groan of travailing soul. As the top of his scarlet, blue and gold turban touched the lamp that hung a good seven feet above his spurred heels he swore viciously.

Almost for the first time in his hard-lived, selfish life he had been thwarted, flouted, cruelly and evilly entreated, and the worst of it was that his enemy was-not a man whom he could take by the throat, but-Fate.

Fate had dealt him a cruel blow, and he felt as he would have done had he, impotent, seen one steal the great charger that champed and pawed there at the door, and replace it by a potter's donkey. Nay, worse-for he had *loved* Lenore, his wife, and Fate had stolen her away and replaced her by a squealing brat.

Within a year of his marriage his wife was dead and buried, and his son alive and-howling. He could hear him (curse him!).

The Colonel glanced at his watch, producing it from some mysterious recess beneath his belted golden sash and within his pale blue tunic.

Not yet time to ride to the regimental parade-ground and lead his famous corps to its place on the brigade parade-ground for the New Year Review and march-past.

As he held the watch at the length of its chain and stared, half-comprehending, his hand-the hand of the finest swordsman in the Indian Army-shook.

Lenore gone: a puling, yelping whelp in her place.... A tall, severe-looking elderly woman entered the verandah by a distant door and approached the savage, miserable soldier. Nurse Beaton.

"*Will* you give your son a name, Sir?" she said, and it was evident in voice and manner that the question had been asked before and had received an unsatisfactory, if not unprintable; reply. Every line of feature and form seemed to express indignant resentment. She had nursed and foster-mothered the child's mother, and-unlike the man-had found the baby the chiefest consolation of her cruel grief, and already loved it not only for its idolized mother's sake, but with the devotion of a childless child-lover.

"The christening is fixed for to-day, Sir, as I have kept reminding you, Sir," she added.

She had never liked the Colonel-nor considered him "good enough" for her tender, dainty darling, "nearly three times her age and no better than he ought to be".

"Name?" snarled Colonel Matthew Devon de Warrenne. "Name the little beast? Call him what you like, and then drown him." The tight-lipped face of the elderly nurse flushed angrily, but before she could make the indignant reply that her hurt and scandalized look presaged, the Colonel added: —

"No, look here, call him *Damocles*, and done with it. The Sword hangs over him too, I suppose, and he'll die by it, as all his ancestors have done. Yes —"

"It's not a nice name, Sir, to my thinking," interrupted the woman, "not for an only name-and for an only child. Let it be a second or third name, Sir, if you want to give him such an outlandish one."

She fingered her new black dress nervously with twitching hands and the tight lips trembled.

"He's to be named Damocles and nothing else," replied the Master, and, as she turned away with a look of positive hate, he added sardonically: —

"And then you can call him 'Dam' for short, you know, Nurse."

Nurse Beaton bridled, clenched her hands, and stiffened visibly. Had the man been her social equal or any other than her master, her pent-up wrath and indignation would have broken forth in a torrent of scathing abuse.

"Never would I call the poor motherless lamb *Dam*, Sir," she answered with restraint.

"Then call him *Dummy!* Good morning, Nurse," snapped the Colonel.

As she turned to go, with a bitter sigh, she asked in the hopeless tone of one who knows the waste of words: —

"You will not repent —I mean relent-and come to the christening of your only son this afternoon, Sir?"

"Good morning, Nurse," observed Colonel Matthew Devon de Warrenne, and resumed his hurried pacing of the verandah.

* * *

It is not enough that a man love his wife dearly and hold her the sweetest, fairest, and best of women-he should tell her so, morning and night.

There is a proverb (the unwisdom of many and the poor wit of one) that says *Actions speak louder than Words*. Whether this is the most untrustworthy of an untrustworthy class of generalizations is debateable.

Anyhow, let no husband or lover believe it. Vain are the deeds of dumb devotion, the unwearying forethought, the tender care, the gifts of price, and the priceless gifts of attentive, watchful guard and guide, the labours of Love-all vain. Silent is the speech of Action.

But resonant loud is the speech of Words and profitable their investment in the Mutual Alliance Bank.

"*Love me, love my Dog?*" Yes-and look to the dog for a dog's reward.

"*Do not show me that you love me-tell me so.*" Far too true and pregnant ever to become a proverb.

Colonel de Warrenne had omitted to tell his wife so-after she had accepted him-and she had died thinking herself loveless, unloved, and stating the fact.

This was the bitterest drop in the bitter cup of the big, dumb, well-meaning man.

And now she would never know....

She had thought herself unloved, and, nerve-shattered by her terrible experience with the snake, had made no fight for life when the unwanted boy was born. For the sake of a girl she would have striven to live-but a boy, a boy can fend for himself (and takes after his father)....

Almost as soon as Lenore Seymour Stukeley had landed in India (on a visit with her sister Yvette to friends at Bimariabad), delighted, bewildered, depolarized, Colonel Matthew Devon de Warrenne had burst with a blaze of glory into her hitherto secluded, narrow life —a great pale-blue, white-and-gold wonder, clanking and jingling, resplendent, bemedalled, ruling men, charging at the head of thundering squadrons —a half-god (and to Yvette he had seemed a whole-god).

He had told her that he loved her, told her once, and had been accepted.

Once! Only once told her that he loved her, that she was beautiful, that he was hers to command to the uttermost. Only once! What could *she* know of the changed life, the absolute renunciation of pleasant bachelor vices, the pulling up short, and all those actions that speak more softly than words?

What could she know of the strength and depth of the love that could keep such a man as the Colonel from the bar, the bridge-table, the race-course and the Paphian dame? Of the love that made him walk warily lest he offend one for whom his quarter of a century, and more, of barrack and bachelor-bungalow life, made him feel so utterly unfit and unworthy? What could she know of all that he had given up and delighted to give up-now that he truly loved a true woman? The hard-living, hard-hearted, hard-spoken man had become a gentle frequenter of his wife's tea-parties, her companion at church, her constant attendant-never leaving the bungalow, save for duty, without her.

To those who knew him it was a World's Marvel; to her, who knew him not, it was nothing at all-normal, natural. And being a man who spoke only when he must, who dreaded the expression of any emotion, and who foolishly thought that actions speak louder than words, he had omitted to tell her daily-or even weekly or monthly-that he loved her; and she had died pitying herself and reproaching him.

Fate's old, old game of Cross Purposes. Major John Decies, reserved, high-minded gentleman, loving Lenore de Warrenne (and longing to tell her so daily), with the one lifelong love of a steadfast nature; Yvette Stukeley, reserved, high-minded gentlewoman, loving Colonel de Warrenne, and longing to escape from Bimariabad before his wedding to her sister, and doing so at the earliest possible date thereafter: each woman losing the man who would have been her ideal husband, each man losing the woman who would have been his ideal wife.

Yvette Stukeley returned to her uncle and guardian, General Sir Gerald Seymour Stukeley, K.C.B., K.C.S.I., at Monksmead, nursing a broken heart, and longed for the day when Colonel de Warrenne's child might be sent home to her care.

Major John Decies abode at Bimariabad, also nursing a broken heart (though he scarcely realized the fact), watched over the son of Lenore de Warrenne, and greatly feared for him.

The Major was an original student of theories and facts of Heredity and Pre-natal Influence. Further he was not wholly hopeful as to the effect of all the *post*-natal influences likely to be brought to bear upon a child who grew up in the bungalow, and the dislike of Colonel Matthew Devon de Warrenne.

Upon the infant Damocles, Nurse Beaton, rugged, snow-capped volcano, lavished the tender love of a mother; and in him Major John Decies, deep-running still water, took the interest of a father. The which was the better for the infant Damocles in that his real father had no interest to take and no love to lavish. He frankly disliked the child-the outward and visible sign, the daily reminder of the cruel loss he so deeply felt and fiercely resented.

Yet, strangely enough, he would not send the child home. Relations who could receive it he had none, and he declined to be beholden to its great-uncle, General Sir Gerald Seymour Stukeley, and its aunt Yvette Stukeley, in spite of the warmest invitations from the one and earnest entreaties from the other.

Nurse Beaton fed, tended, clothed and nursed the baby by day; a worshipping ayah wheeled him abroad, and, by night, slept beside his cot; a devoted sepoy-orderly from the regiment guarded his cavalcade, and, when permitted, proudly bore him in his arms.

Major John Decies visited him frequently, watched and waited, waited and watched, and, though not a youth, "thought long, long thoughts".

He also frequently laid his views and theories on paternal duties before Colonel de Warrenne, until pointedly asked by that officer whether he had no duties of his own which might claim his valuable time.

Years rolled by, after the incorrigible habit of years, and the infant Damocles grew and developed into a remarkably sturdy, healthy, intelligent boy, as cheerful, fearless, impudent, and irrepressible as the heart of the Major could desire-and with a much larger vocabulary than any one could desire, for a baby.

On the fifth anniversary of his birthday he received a matutinal call from Major Decies, who was returning from his daily visit to the Civil Hospital.

The Major bore a birthday present and a very anxious, undecided mind.

"Good morrow, gentle Damocles," he remarked, entering the big verandah adown which the chubby boy pranced gleefully to meet his beloved friend, shouting a welcome, and brandishing a sword designed, and largely constructed, by himself from a cleaning-rod, a tobacco-tin lid, a piece of wood, card-board and wire.

"Thalaam, Major Thahib," he said, flinging himself bodily upon that gentleman. "I thaw cook cut a fowl's froat vis morning. It squorked boofly."

"Did it? Alas, that I missed those pleasing-er-squorks," replied the Major, and added: "This is thy natal day, my son. Thou art a man of five."

"I'm a debble. I'm a *norful* little debble," corrected Damocles, cheerfully and with conviction.

"Incidentally. But you are five also," persisted the senior man.

"It's my birfday to-day," observed the junior.

"I just said so."

"*That* you didn't, Major Thahib. This is a thword. Father's charger's got an over-weach. Jumping. He says it's a dam-nuithanth."

"Oh, that's a sword, is it? And 'Fire' has got an over-reach. And it's a qualified nuisance, is it?"

"Yeth, and the mare is coughing and her *thythe* is a blathted fool for letting her catch cold."

"The mare has a cold and the *syce*⁴ is a qualified fool, is he? H'm! I think it's high time you had a look in at little old England, my son, what? And who made you this elegant rapier? Ochterlonie Sahib or-who?" (Lieutenant Lord Ochterlonie was the Adjutant of the Queen's Greys, a friend of Colonel de Warrenne, an ex-admirer of his late wife, and a great pal of his son.)

"'Tithn't a waper. It'th my thword. I made it mythelf."

"Who helped?"

"Nobody. At leatht, Khodadad Khan, Orderly, knocked the holes in the tin like I showed him-or elthe got the Farrier Thargeant to do it, and thaid *he* had."

"Yes-but who told you how to make it like this? Where did you see a hand-part like this? It isn't like Daddy's sword, nor Khodadad Khan's *tulwar*. Where did you copy it?"

"I didn't copy it.... I shot ten rats wiv a bow-and-arrow last night. At leatht—I don't think I shot ten. Nor one. I don't think I didn't, pwaps."

"But hang it all, the thing's an Italian rapier, by Gad. Some one *must* have shown you how to make the thing, or you've got a picture. It's a *pukka*⁵ mediaeval rapier."

"No it'th not. It'th my thword. I made it.... Have a jolly fight"—and the boy struck an extraordinarily correct fencing attitude-left hand raised in balance, sword poised, legs and feet well placed, the whole pose easy, natural, graceful.

Curiously enough, the sword was held horizontal instead of pointing upward, a fact which at once struck the observant and practised eye of Major John Decies, sometime champion fencer.

"Who's been teaching you fencing?" he asked.

"What ith 'fenthing'? Let'th have a fight," replied the boy.

"Stick me here, Dam," invited the Major, seating himself and indicating the position of the heart. "Bet you can't."

The boy lunged, straight, true, gracefully, straightening all his limbs except his right leg, rigidly, strongly, and the "sword" bent upward from the spot on which the man's finger had just rested.

"Gad! Who *has* taught you to lunge? I shall have a bruise there, and perhaps-live. Who's behind all this, young fella? Who taught you to stand so, and to lunge? Ochterlonie Sahib or Daddy?"

"Nobody. What is 'lunge'? Will you buy me a little baby-camel to play with and teach tricks? Perhaps it would sit up and beg. Do camelth lay eggth? Chucko does. Millions and lakhs. You get a thword, too, and we'll fight every day. Yeth. All day long——"

"Good morning, Sir," said Nurse Beaton, bustling into the verandah from the nursery. "He's as mad as ever on swords and fighting, you see. It's a soldier he'll be, the lamb. He's taken to making that black orderly pull out his sword when he's in uniform. Makes him wave and jab it about. Gives me the creeps-with his black face and white eyes and all. You won't *encourage* the child at it, will you, Sir? And his poor Mother the gentlest soul that ever stepped. Swords! Where he gets his notions *I* can't think (though I know where he gets his language, poor lamb!). Look at *that* thing, Sir! For all the world like the dressed-up folk have on the stage or in pictures."

"You haven't let him see any books, I suppose, Nurse?" asked the Major.

"No, Sir. Never a book has the poor lamb seen, except those you've brought. I've always been in terror of his seeing a picture of a you-know-what, ever since you told me what the effect *might* be. Nor he hasn't so much as heard the name of it, so far as I know."

"Well, he'll see one to-day. I've brought it with me-must see it sooner or later. Might see a live one anywhere-in spite of all your care.... But about this sword-where *could* he have got the idea? It's unlike any sword he ever set eyes on. Besides if he ever *did* see an Italian rapier-and

25

there's scarcely such a thing in India-he'd not get the chance to use it as a copy. Fancy his having the desire and the power to, anyhow!"

"I give it up, Sir," said Nurse Beaton.

"I give it upper," added the Major, taking the object of their wonder from the child.

And there was cause for wonder indeed.

A hole had been punched through the centre of the lid of a tobacco tin and a number of others round the edge. Through the centre hole the steel rod had been passed so that the tin made a "guard". To the other holes wires had been fastened by bending, and their ends gathered, twisted, and bound with string to the top of the handle (of bored corks) to form an ornamental basket-hilt.

But the most remarkable thing of all was that, before doing this, the juvenile designer had passed the rod through a piece of bored stick so that the latter formed a *cross-piece* (neatly bound) within the tin guard-the distinctive feature of the ancient and modern Italian rapiers!

Round this cross-piece the first two fingers of the boy's right hand were crooked as he held the sword-and this is the one and only correct way of holding the Italian weapon, as the Major was well aware!

"I give it most utterly-uppermost," he murmured. "It's positively uncanny. No *uninitiated* adult of the utmost intelligence ever held an Italian-pattern foil correctly yet-nor until he had been pretty carefully shown. Who the devil put him up to the design in the first place, and the method of holding, in the second? Explain yourself, you two-anna[6] marvel," he demanded of the child. "It's *jadu* —black magic."

"Ayah lothted a wupee latht night," he replied.

"Lost a rupee, did she? Lucky young thing. Wish I had one to lose. Who showed you how to hold that sword? Why do you crook your fingers round the cross-piece like that?"

"Chucko laid me an egg latht night," observed Damocles. "He laid it with my name on it-so that cook couldn't steal it."

"No doubt. Look here, where can I get a sword like yours? Where can I copy it? Who makes them? Who knows about them?"

"*I* don't know, Major Thahib. Gunnoo sells 'Fire's' gram to the *methrani* for her curry and chuppatties."

"But how do you know swords are like this? *That* thing isn't a *pukka* sword."

"Well, it'th like Thir Theymour Thtukeley's in my dweam."

"What dream?"

"The one I'm alwayth dweaming. They have got long hair like Nurse in the night, and they fight and fight like anything. Norful good fighters! And they wear funny kit. And their thwords are like vis. _Egg_zackly. Gunnoo gave me a ride on 'Fire,' and he'th a dam-liar. He thaid he forgot to put the warm *jhool* on him when Daddy was going to fwash him for being a dam-fool. I thaid I'd tell Daddy how he alwayth thleepth in it himthelf, unleth he gave me a ride on 'Fire'. 'Fire' gave a *norful* buck and bucked me off. At leatht I think he didn't."

Major Decies' face was curiously intent-as of some midnight worker in research who sees a bright near glimpse of the gold his alchemy has so long sought to materialize in the alembic of fact.

"Come back to sober truth, young youth. What about the dream? Who are they, and what do they say and do?"

"Thir Theymour Thtukeley Thahib tellth Thir Matthew Thahib about the hilt-thwust. (What *is* 'hilt-thwust'?) And Lubin, the thervant, ith a *white* thervant. Why ith he white if he ith a Thahib's 'boy'?"

"Good Gad!" murmured the Major. "I'm favoured of the gods. Tell me all about it, Sonny. Then I'll undo this parcel for you," he coaxed.

"Oh, I don't wemember. They buck a lot by the tents and then Thir Theymour Thtukeley goes and fights Thir Matthew and kills him, and it'th awful lovely, but they dreth up like kids at a party in big collars and silly kit."

26

"Yes, I know," murmured the Major. "Tell me what they say when they buck to each other by the tents, and when they talk about the 'hilt-thrust,' old chap."

"Oh, I don't wemember. I'll listen next time I dweam it, and tell you. Chucko's egg was all brown-not white like those cook brings from the bazaar. He's a dam-thief. Open the parcel, Major Thabib. What's in it?"

"A picture-book for you, Sonny. All sorts of jolly beasts that you'll *shikar* some day. You'll tell me some more about the dream to-morrow, won't you?"

"Yeth. I'll wemember and fink, and tell you what I have finked."

Turning to Nurse Beaton, the Major whispered: —

"Don't worry him about this dream at all. Leave it to me. It's wonderful. Take him on your lap, Nurse, and-er-be *ready*. It's a very life-like picture, and I'm going to spring it on him without any remark-but I'm more than a little anxious, I admit. Still, it's *got* to come, as I say, and better a picture first, with ourselves present. If the picture don't affect him I'll show him a real one. May be all right of course, but I don't know. I came across a somewhat similar case once before-and it was *not* all right. Not by any means," and he disclosed the brilliantly coloured Animal Picture Book and knelt beside the expectant boy.

On the first page was an incredibly leonine lion, who appeared to have solved with much satisfaction the problem of aerial flight, so far was he from the mountain whence he had sprung and above the back of the antelope towards which he had propelled himself. One could almost hear him roar. There was menace and fate in eye and tooth and claw, yea, in the very kink of the prehensile-seeming tail wherewith he apparently steered his course in mid-air. To gaze upon his impressive and determined countenance was to sympathize most fully with the sore-tried Prophet of old (known to Damocles as Dannle-in-the-lines-den) for ever more.

The boy was wholly charmed, stroked the glowing ferocity and observed that he was a *pukka Bahadur*.[7]

On the next page, burning bright, was a tiger, if possible one degree more terrible than the lion. His "fearful cemetery" appeared to be full, judging by its burgeoned bulge and the shocking state of depletion exhibited by the buffalo on which he fed with barely inaudible snarls and grunts of satisfaction. Blood dripped from his capacious and over-furnished mouth.

"Booful," murmured Damocles. "I shall go shooting tigerth to-mowwow. Shoot vem in ve mouth, down ve froat, so as not to spoil ve wool."

Turning over the page, the Major disclosed a most grievous grizzly bear, grizzly and bearish beyond conception, heraldic, regardant, expectant, not collared, fanged and clawed proper, rampant, erect, requiring no supporters.

"You could thtab him wiv a thword if you were quick, while he was doing that," opined Damocles, charmed, enraptured, delighted. One by one, other savage, fearsome beasts were disclosed to the increasingly delighted boy until, without warning, the Major suddenly turned a page and disclosed a brilliant and hungry-looking snake.

With a piercing shriek the boy leapt convulsively from Nurse Beaton's arms, rushed blindly into the wall and endeavoured to butt and bore his way through it with his head, screaming like a wounded horse. As the man and woman sprang to him he shrieked, "It'th under my foot! It'th moving, moving, moving *out*" and fell to the ground in a fit.

Major John Decies arose from his bachelor dinner-table that evening, lit his "planter" cheroot, and strolled into the verandah that looked across a desert to a mountain range.

Dropping into a long low chair, he raised his feet on to the long leg-rest extensions of its arms, and, as he settled down and waited for coffee, wondered why no such chairs are known in the West; why the trunks of the palms looked less flat in the moonlight than in the daylight (in which, from that spot, they always looked exactly as though cut out of cardboard); why Providence had not arranged for perpetual full-moon; why the world looked such a place of peaceful, glorious beauty by moonlight, the bare cruel mountains like diaphanous clouds of tenderest soothing mist, the Judge's hideous bungalow like a fairy palace, his own parched compound like a plot of Paradise, when all was so abominable by day; and, as ever-why his darling, Lenore Stukeley, had had to marry de Warrenne and die in the full flower and promise of her beautiful womanhood.

Having finished his coffee and lighted his pipe (*vice* the over-dry friable cheroot, flung into the garden) the Major then turned his mind to serious and consecutive thought on the subject of her son, his beloved little pal, Dammy de Warrenne.

Poor little beggar! What an eternity it had seemed before he had got him to sleep. How the child had suffered. Mad! Absolutely stark, staring, raving *mad* with sheer terror.... Had he acted rightly in showing him the picture? He had meant well, anyhow. Cruel phrase, that. How cuttingly his friend de Warrenne had observed, "You mean well, doubtless," on more than one occasion. He could make it the most stinging of insults.... Surely he had acted rightly.... Poor little beggar-but he was bound to see a picture or a real live specimen, sooner or later. Perhaps when there was no help at hand.... Would he be like it always? *Might* grow out of it as he grew older and stronger. What would have happened if he had encountered a live snake? Lost his reason permanently, perhaps.... What would happen when he *did* see one, as sooner or later, he certainly must?

What would be the best plan? To attempt gradually to inure him-or to guard him absolutely from contact with picture, stuffed specimen, model, toy, and the real thing, wild or captive, as one would guard him against a fell disease?

Could he be inured? Could one "break it to him gently" bye and bye, by first drawing a wiggly line and then giving it a head? One might sketch a suggestion of a snake, make a sort of dissimilar clay model, improve it, show him a cast skin, stuff it, make a more life-like picture, gradually lead up to a well-stuffed one and then a live one. Might work up to having a good big picture of one on the nursery wall; one in a glass case; keep a harmless live one and show it him daily. Teach him by experience that there's nothing supernatural about a snake-just a nasty reptile that wants exterminating like other dangerous creatures-something to *shikar* with a gun. Nothing at all supernatural....

But this was "super"-natural, abnormal, a terrible devastating agony of madness, inherited, incurable probably; part of mind and body and soul. Inherited, and integrally of him as were the colour of his eyes, his intelligence, his physique.... Heredity... pre-natal influence... breed....

Anyhow, nothing must be attempted yet awhile. Let the poor little chap get older and stronger, in mind and body, first. Brave as a little bull-dog in other directions! Absolutely devoid of fear otherwise, and with a natural bent for fighting and adventure. Climb anywhere, especially up the hind leg of a camel or a horse, fondle any strange dog, clamour to be put on any strange horse, go into any deep water, cheek anybody, bear any ordinary pain with a grin, thrill to any story of desperate deeds—a fine, brave, manly, hardy little chap, and with art extraordinary physique for strength and endurance.

Whatever was to be attempted later, he must be watched, day and night, now. No unattended excursions into the compound, no uncensored picture-books, no juggling snake-charmers.... Yet it *must* come, sooner or later.

Would it ruin his life?

Anyhow, he must never return to India when he grew up, or go to any snake-producing country, unless he could be cured.

Would it make him that awful thing—a coward?

Would it grow and wax till it dominated his mind-drive him mad?

Would succeeding attacks, following encounters with picture or reality, progressively increase in severity?

Her boy in an asylum?

No. He was exaggerating an almost expected consequence that might never be repeated-especially if the child were most carefully and gradually reintroduced to the present terror. Later though-much later on.

Meanwhile, wait and hope: hope and wait....

Chapter III
The Snake Appears

The European child who grows up in India, if only to the age of six or seven years, grows under a severe moral, physical, and mental handicap.

However wise, devoted, and conscientious its parents may be, the evil is great, and remains one of the many heavy costs (or punishments) of Empire.

When the child has no mother and an indifferent father, life's handicap is even more severe.

By his sixth birthday (the regiment being still in Bimariabad owing to the prevalence of drought, famine, and cholera elsewhere) Damocles de Warrenne, knowing the Urdu language and *argot* perfectly, knew, in theory also, more of evil, in some directions, than did his own father.

If the child who grows up absolutely straight-forward, honest, above-board and pure in thought, word, and deed, in England, deserves commendation, what does the child deserve who does so in India?

Understanding every word they spoke to one another, the training he got from native servants was one of undiluted evil and a series of object-lessons in deceit, petty villainy, chicanery, oppression, lying, dishonesty, and all immorality. And yet-thanks to his equal understanding of the words and deeds of Nurse Beaton, Major Decies, Lieutenant Ochterlonie, his father, the Officers of the Regiment, and the Europeans of the station-he had a clear, if unconscious, understanding that what was customary for native servants was neither customary nor possible for Sahibs....

But he knew too much....

He knew what percentage of his or her pay each servant had to hand to the "butler-sahib" monthly-or lose his or her place through false accusation.

He knew why the ayah was graciously exempted from financial toll by this autocrat. He knew roughly what proportion of the cook's daily bill represented the actual cost of his daily purchases. He knew what the door-peon got for consenting to take in the card of the Indian aspirant for an interview with Colonel de Warrenne.

He knew the terms of the arrangements between the head-syce and the grain-dealer, the lucerne-grass seller, the *ghas-wallah*[8] who brought the hay (whereby reduced quantities were accepted in return for illegal gratifications). He knew of retail re-sales of these reduced supplies.

He knew of the purchase of oil, rice, condiments, fire-wood and other commodities from the cook, of the theft (by arrangement) of the poultry and eggs, of the surreptitious milking of the cow, and of the simple plan of milking her-under Nurse Beaton's eye-into a narrow-necked vessel already half full of water.

He knew that the ayah's husband sold the Colonel's soda-water, paraffin, matches, candles, tobacco, cheroots, fruit, sugar, etc., at a little portable shop round the corner of the road, and of the terms on which the *hamal* and the butler supplied these commodities to the ayah for transfer to her good man.

He knew too much of the philosophy, manners, habits, and morals of the dog-boy, of concealed cases of the most infectious diseases in the compound, of the sub-letting and over-crowding of the servants' quarters, of incredible quarrels, intrigues, jealousies, revenges, base villainies and wrongs, superstitions and beliefs.

He would hear the hatching of a plot-an hour's arrangement and wrangle-whereby, through far-sighted activity, perjury, malpractice and infinite ingenuity, the ringleader would gain a *pice* and the follower a *pie* (a farthing and a third of a farthing respectively).

Daily he saw the butler steal milk, sugar, and tea, for his own use; the *hamal* steal oil when he filled the lamps, for sale; the *malli* steal flowers, for sale; the coachman steal carriage-candles; the cook steal a moiety of everything that passed through his hands-every one in that black underworld stealing, lying, back-biting, cheating, intriguing (and all meanwhile strictly and stoutly religious, even the sweeper-descended Goanese cook, the biggest thief of all, purging his Christian soul on Sunday mornings by Confession, and fortifying himself against the temptations of the Evil One at early Mass).

Between these *nowker log*, the servant-people, and his own *jat* or class, the *Sahib-log*, the master-people, were the troopers, splendid Sikhs, Rajputs, Pathans and Punjabis, men of honour, courage, physique, tradition. Grand fighters, loyal as steel while properly understood and properly treated-in other words, while properly officered. (Men, albeit, with deplorably little understanding of, or regard for, Pagett, M.P., and his kind, who yearn to do so much for them.)

These men Damocles admired and loved, though even *they* were apt to be very naughty in the bazaar, to gamble and to toy with opium, bhang, and (alleged) brandy, to dally with houris and hearts'-delights, to use unkind measures towards the good *bunnia* and *sowkar* who had lent them monies, and to do things outside the Lines that were not known in the Officers' Mess.

The boy preferred the Rissaldar-Major even to some Sahibs of his acquaintance-that wonderful old man-at-arms, horseman, *shikarri*, athlete, gentleman. (Yet how strange and sad to see him out of his splendid uniform, in sandals, *dhotie*, untrammelled shirt-tails, dingy old cotton coat and loose *puggri*, undistinguishable from a school-master, clerk, or post-man; so *un*-sahib-like.)

And what a fine riding-master he made for an ambitious, fearless boy-though Ochterlonie Sahib said he was too cruel to be a good *horse*-master.

How *could* people be civilians and live away from regiments? Live without ever touching swords, lances, carbines, saddles?

What a queer feeling it gave one to see the regiment go past the saluting base on review-days, at the gallop, with lances down. One wanted to shout, to laugh-to *cry*. (It made one's mouth twitch and chin work.)

Oh, to *lead* the regiment as Father did-horse and man one welded piece of living mechanism.

Father said you couldn't ride till you had taken a hundred tosses, been pipped a hundred times. A hundred falls! Surely Father had *never* been thrown-it must be impossible for such a rider to come off. See him at polo.

By his sixth birthday Damocles de Warrenne, stout and sturdy, was an accomplished rider and never so happy (save when fencing) as when flogging his active and spirited little pony along the "rides" or over the dusty *maidans* and open country of Bimariabad. To receive a quarter-mile start on the race-course and ride a mile race against Khodadad Khan on his troop-horse, or with one of the syces on one of the Colonel's polo-ponies, or with some obliging male or female early morning rider, was the joy of his life. Should he suspect the competitor of "pulling" as he came alongside, that the tiny pony might win, the boy would lash at both horses impartially.

People who pitied him (and they were many) wondered as to how soon he would break his neck, and remonstrated with his father for allowing him to ride alone, or in charge of an attendant unable to control him.

In the matter of his curious love of fencing Major John Decies was deeply concerned, obtained more and more details of his "dweam," taught him systematically and scientifically to fence, bought him foils and got them shortened. He also interested him in a series of muscle-developing exercises which the boy called his "dismounted squad-dwill wiv'out arms," and performed frequently daily, and with gusto.

Lieutenant Lord Ochterlonie (Officers' Light-Weight Champion at Aldershot) rigged him up a small swinging sand-bag and taught him to punch with either hand, and drilled him in foot-work for boxing.

Later he brought the very capable ten-year-old son of a boxing Troop-Sergeant and set him to make it worth Dam's while to guard smartly, to learn to keep his temper, and to receive a blow with a grin.

(Possibly a better education than learning declensions, conjugations, and tables from a Eurasian "governess".)

He learnt to read unconsciously and automatically by repeating, after Nurse Beaton, the jingles and other letter-press beneath the pictures in the books obtained for him under Major Decies' censorship.

On his sixth birthday, Major John Decies had Damocles over to his bungalow for the day, gave him a box of lead soldiers and a schooner-rigged ship, helped him to embark them and sail them in the bath to foreign parts, trapped a squirrel and let it go again, allowed him to make havoc of his possessions, fired at bottles with his revolver for the boy's delectation, shot a crow or two with a rook-rifle, played an improvised game of fives with a tennis-ball, told him tales, and generally gave up the day to his amusement. What he did *not* do was to repeat the experiment of a year ago, or make any kind of reference to snakes....

A few days later, on the morning of the New-Year's-Day Review, Colonel Matthew de Warrenne once again strode up and down his verandah, arrayed in full review-order, until it should be time to ride to the regimental parade-ground.

He had coarsened perceptibly in the six years since he had lost his wife, and the lines that had grown deepest on his hard, handsome face were those between his eyebrows and beside his mouth-the mouth of an unhappy, dissipated, cynical man....

He removed his right-hand gauntlet and consulted his watch.... Quarter of an hour yet.

He continued the tramp that always reminded Damocles of the restless, angry to-and-fro pacing of the big bear in the gardens. Both father and the bear seemed to fret against fate, to suffer under a sense of injury; both seemed dangerous, fierce, admirable. Hearing the clink and clang and creak of his father's movement, Damocles scrambled from his cot and crept down the stairs, pink-toed, blue-eyed, curly-headed, night-gowned, to peep through the crack of the drawing-room door at his beautiful father. He loved to see him in review uniform-so much more delightful than plain khaki-pale blue, white, and gold, in full panoply of accoutrement, jackbooted and spurred, and with the great turban that made his English face look more English still.

Yes-he would ensconce himself behind the drawing-room door and watch. Perhaps "Fire" would be bobbery when the Colonel mounted him, would get "what-for" from whip and spur, and be put over the compound wall instead of being allowed to canter down the drive and out at the gate....

Colonel de Warrenne stepped into his office to get a cheroot. Re-appearing in the verandah with it in his mouth he halted and thrust his hand inside his tunic for his small match-case. Ere he could use the match his heart was momentarily chilled by the most blood-curdling scream he had ever heard. It appeared to come from the drawing-room. (Colonel de Warrenne never lit the cheroot that he had put to his lips-nor ever another again.) Springing to the door, one of a dozen that opened into the verandah, he saw his son struggling on the ground, racked by convulsive spasms, with glazed, sightless eyes and foaming mouth, from which issued appalling, blood-curdling shrieks. Just above him, on the fat satin cushion in the middle of a low settee, a huge half-coiled cobra swayed from side to side in the Dance of Death.

"It's under my foot-it's moving-moving-moving out," shrieked the child.

Colonel de Warrenne attended to the snake first. He half-drew his sword and then slammed it back into the scabbard. No-his sword was not for snakes, whatever his son might be. On the wall was a trophy of Afghan weapons, one of which was a sword that had played a prominent part on the occasion of the Colonel's winning of the Victoria Cross.

Striding to the wall he tore the sword down, drew it and, with raised arm, sprang towards the cobra. A good "Cut Three" across the coils would carve it into a dozen pieces. No. Lenore made that cushion-and Lenore's cushion made more appeal to Colonel de Warrenne than did Lenore's son. No. A neat horizontal "Cut Two," just below the head, with the deadly "drawing" motion on it, would meet the case nicely. Swinging it to the left, the Colonel subconsciously placed the sword, "resting flat on the left shoulder, edge to the left, hand in front of the shoulder and square with the elbow, elbow as high as the hand," as per drill-book, and delivered a lightning stroke-thinking as he did so that the Afghan *tulwar* is an uncommonly well-balanced, handy cutting-weapon, though infernally small in the hilt.

The snake's head fell with a thud upon the polished boards between the tiger-skins, and the body dropped writhing and twitching on to the settee.

Damocles appeared to be dead. Picking him up, the callous-hearted father strode out to where Khodadad Khan held "Fire's" bridle, handed him to the orderly, mounted, received him again from the man, and, holding him in his strong right arm, cantered to the bungalow of Major John Decies-since it lay on the road to the parade-ground.

Would the jerking hurt the little beggar in his present comatose state? Well, brats that couldn't stand a little jerking were better dead, especially when they screamed and threw fits at the sight of a common snake.

Turning into Major Decies' compound and riding up to his porch, the Colonel saw the object of his search, arrayed in pyjamas, seated in his long cane chair beside a tray of tea, toast, and fruit, in the verandah.

"Morning, de Warrenne," he cried cheerily.

"How's little —" and caught sight of the inanimate child.

"Little coward's fainted after throwing a fit-over a common snake," observed the Colonel coolly.

"Give him here," answered the Major, taking the boy tenderly in his arms, —"and kindly-er-clear out."

He did not wish to strike his friend and senior. How the black rage welled up in his heart against the callous brute who had dared to marry Lenore Seymour Stukeley.

Colonel de Warrenne wheeled his horse without a word, and rode out of Major Decies' life and that of his son.

Galloping to the parade-ground he spoke a few curt words to his Adjutant, inspected the *rissala*, and then rode at its head to the brigade parade-ground where it took up its position on the left flank of the Guns and the Queen's Greys, "sat at ease," and awaited the arrival of the Chief Commissioner at the saluting-base. A British Infantry regiment marched to the left flank of the 118th (Bombay) Lancers, left-turned and stood at ease. Another followed and was followed in turn by Native Infantry Regiments-grand Sikhs in scarlet tunics, baggy black breeches and blue putties; hefty Pathans and Baluchis in green tunics, crimson breeches and high white gaiters, sturdy little Gurkhas in rifle-green, stalwart Punjabi Mahommedans.

The great double line grew and grew, and stood patiently waiting, Horse, Foot, and Guns, facing the sun and a dense crowd of spectators ranked behind the rope-encircled, guard-surrounded saluting-base over which flew the Flag of England.

The Brigadier and his Staff rode on to the ground, were saluted by the mile of troops, and took up their position.

Followed the Chief Commissioner in his state carriage, accompanied by a very Distinguished Guest, and surrounded by his escort. The mile of men again came to attention and the review began. Guns boomed, massed bands played the National Anthem, the crackling rattle of the *feu-de-joie* ran up the front rank and down the rear.

After the inspection and the salutes came the march-past by the regiments.

Now the Distinguished Visitor's wife had told the Chief Commissioner that she "did not want to see the cavalry go past at the gallop as it raised such a dreadful dust". But her maid bungled, her toilette failed, and she decided not to accompany her husband to the Review at all. Her husband, the Distinguished Visitor, *did* desire to see the cavalry go past at the gallop, and so the Chief Commissioner's Distinguished Visitor's wife's maid's bungling had a tremendous influence upon the fate of Damocles de Warrenne, as will be seen.

Passed the massed Guns at the walk, followed by the Cavalry at the walk in column of squadrons and the Infantry in column of companies, each unit saluting the Chief Commissioner by turning "eyes right" as it passed the spot where he sat on horseback surrounded by the civil and military staffs.

Wheeling to the left at the end of the ground the Guns and Cavalry again passed, this time at the trot, while the Infantry completed its circular march to its original position.

Finally the Cavalry passed for the third time, and now at the gallop, an orderly whirlwind, a controlled avalanche of men and horses, with levelled lances, and the hearts of all men were stirred at one of the most stirring sights and sounds in the world — a cavalry charge.

At the head of the leading squadron galloped Colonel de Warrenne, cool, methodical, keeping a distant flag-staff in line with a still more distant church spire, that he might lead the regiment in a perfectly straight line. (Few who have not tried it realize the difficulty of leading a galloping line of men absolutely straight and at true right-angles to the line of their ranks.)

On thundered the squadrons unbending of rank, uncrowded, unopened, squadron-leaders maintaining distance, the whole mass as ordered, shapely, and precisely correct as when at the walk.

Past the saluting-base thundered the squadrons and in full career Colonel de Warrenne's charger put his near fore into ground honey-combed by insect, reptile, or burrowing beast, crashed on its head, rolled like a shot rabbit, and Colonel Matthew Devon de Warrenne lay dead-killed by his own sword.

Like his ancestors of that fated family, he had died by the sword, but unlike them, he had died by the *hilt* of it.

Major John Decies, I.M.S., Civil Surgeon of Bimariabad, executor of the will of the late Colonel de Warrenne and guardian of his son, cabled the sad news of the Colonel's untimely death to Sir Gerald Seymour Stukeley at Monksmead, he being, so far as Major Decies knew, the boy's only male relative in England-uncle of the late Mrs. de Warrenne.

The reply, which arrived in a day or two, appeared from its redundancy and incoherence to be the composition of Miss Yvette Seymour Stukeley, and bade Major Decies either send or bring the infant Damocles to Monksmead *immediately*.

The Major decided to apply forthwith for such privilege-leave and furlough as were due to him, and to proceed to England with the boy. It would be as well that his great-uncle should hear from him, personally, of the matter of the child's mental condition resultant upon the tragedy of his own birth and his mother's death. The Major was decidedly anxious as to the future in this respect-all might be well in time, and all might be very far indeed from well.

Nurse Beaton absolutely and flatly refused to be parted from her charge, and the curious party of three set sail for England in due course.

"Hm! — He's every inch a Stukeley," remarked the General when Damocles de Warrenne was ushered into his presence in the great library at Monksmead. "Hope he's Stukeley by nature too. Sturdy young fella! 'Spose he's vetted sound in wind and limb?"

The Major replied that the boy was physically rather remarkably strong, mentally very sound, and in character all that could be desired. He then did his best to convey to the General an understanding of the psychic condition that must be a cause of watchfulness and anxiety on the part of those who guarded his adolescence.

At dinner, over the General's wonderful Clos Vougeot, the Major again returned to the subject and felt that his words of advice fell upon somewhat indifferent and uncomprehending ears.

It was the General's boast that he had never feed a doctor in his life, and his impression that a sound resort for any kind of invalid is a lethal chamber....

The seven years since the Major had last seen her, seemed to have dealt lightly with the sad-faced, pretty Miss Yvette, gentle, good, and very kind. Over the boy she rhapsodized to her own content and his embarrassment. Effusive endearments and embraces were new to Dam, and he appeared extraordinarily ignorant of the art of kissing.

"Oh, how like his dear Father!" she would exclaim afresh every few minutes, to the Major's slight annoyance and the General's plain disgust.

"Every inch a Stukeley!" he would growl in reply.

But Yvette Seymour Stukeley had prayed for Colonel de Warrenne nightly for seven years and had idealized him beyond recognition. Possibly Fate's greatest kindness to her was to ordain that she should not see him as he had become in fact, and compare him with her wondrous mental image.... The boy was to her, must be, should be, the very image of her life's hero and beloved....

The depolarized and bewildered Damocles found himself in a strange and truly foreign land, a queer, cold, dismal country inhabited by vast quantities of "second-class sahibs," as he termed the British lower middle-class and poor, a country of a strange greenness and orderedness, where there were white servants, strangely conjoined rows of houses in the villages, dangerous-looking fires inside the houses, a kind of tomb-stones on all house-tops, strange horse-drawn vehicles, butlerless and *ghari*[9]-less sahibs, and an utter absence of "natives," sepoys, *byle-gharies*,[10] camels, monkeys, kites, squirrels, bulbuls, *minahs*,[11] mongooses, palm-trees, and temples. Cattle appeared to have no humps, crows to have black heads, and trees to have no fruit. The very monsoon seemed inextricably mixed with the cold season. Fancy the rains coming in the cold weather! Perhaps there was no hot weather and nobody went to the hills in this strange country of strange people, strange food, strange customs. Nobody seemed to have any tents when they left the station for the districts, nor to take any bedding when they went on tour or up-country. A queer, foreign land.

But Monksmead was a most magnificent "bungalow" standing in a truly beautiful "compound" —wherein the very *bhistis*[12] and *mallis* were European and appeared to be second-class sahibs.

Marvellous was the interior of the bungalow with its countless rooms and mountainous stair-cases (on the wall of one of which hung *the Sword* which he had never seen but instantly recognized) and its army of white servants headed by the white butler (so like the Chaplain of Bimariabad in grave respectability and solemn pompousness) and its extraordinary white "ayahs" or maids, and silver-haired Mrs. Pont, called the "house-keeper". Was she a *pukka* Mem-Sahib or a *nowker*[13] or what? And how did she "keep" the house?

A wonderful place-but far and away the most thrilling and delightful of its wonders was the little white girl, Lucille-Damocles' first experience of the charming genus.

The boy never forgot his first meeting with Lucille.

On his arrival at Monksmead he had been "vetted," as he expressed it, by the Burra-Sahib, the General; and then taken to an attractive place called "the school-room" and there had found Lucille....

"Hullo! Boy," had been her greeting. "What's your name?" He had attentively scrutinized a small white-clad, blue-sashed maiden, with curling chestnut hair, well-opened hazel eyes, decided chin, Greek mouth and aristocratic cheek-bones. A maiden with a look of blood and breed about her. (He did not sum her up in these terms at the time.)

"Can you ride, Boy?"

"A bit."

"Can you fight?"

"A bit."

"Can you swim?"

"Not well."

"*I* can-ever so farther. D'you know French and German?"

"Not a word."

"Play the piano?"

"Never heard of it. D'you play it with cards or dice?"

"Lucky dog! It's music. I have to practise an hour a day."

"What for?"

"Nothing... it's lessons. Beastly. How old are you?"

"Seven-er-nearly."

"So'm I —nearly. I've got to be six first though. I shall have a birthday next week. A big one. Have you brought any ellyfunts from India?"

"I've never seen a nellyfunt-only in pictures."

A shudder shook the boy's sturdy frame.

"Why do you go like that? Feel sick?"

"No. I don't know. I seemed to remember something-in a book. I dream about it. There's a nasty blue room with a mud floor. And *Something*. Beastly. Makes you yell out and you can't. You can't run away either. But the Sword dream is lovely."

Lucille appeared puzzled and put this incoherence aside.

"What a baby never to see ellyfunts! I've seen lots. Hundreds. Zoo. Circuses. Persesions. Camels, too."

"Oh, I used to ride a camel every day. There was one in the compound with his *oont-wallah*,[14] Abdul Ghaffr; and Khodadad Khan used to beat the *oont-wallah* on cold mornings to warm himself."

"What's an *oont-wallah*?"

"Don't you *know*? Why, he's just the *oont-wallah*, of course. Who'd graze the camel or load it up if there wasn't one?"

At tea in the nursery the young lady suddenly remarked: —

"I like you, Boy. You're worth nine Haddocks."

This cryptic valuation puzzled Damocles the more in that he had never seen or heard of a haddock. Had he been acquainted with the fowl he might have been yet more astonished.

Later he discovered that the comparison involved the fat boy who sat solemnly stuffing on the other side of the table, his true baptismal name being Haddon.

Yes, Lucille was a revelation, a marvel.

Far quicker of mind than he, cleverer at games and inventing "make believe," very strong, active, and sporting, she was the most charming, interesting, and attractive experience in his short but eventful life.

How he loved to make her laugh and clap her hands! How he enjoyed her quaint remarks, speculations, fairy-tales and jokes. How he yearned to win her approval and admiration. How he strove to please her!

In Lucille and his wonderful new surroundings he soon forgot Major Decies, who returned to live (and, at a ripe old age, to die) at Bimariabad, where had lived and died the woman whom he had so truly and purely loved. The place where he had known her was the only place for him.

On each of his birthdays Damocles received a long fatherly letter and a handsome present from the Major, and by the time he went away to school at Wellingborough, he wondered who on earth the Major might be.

To his great delight Damocles found that he was not doomed to discontinue his riding, fencing, boxing, and "dismounted drill without arms".

General Seymour Stukeley sent for a certain Sergeant Havlan (once a trooper in his own regiment), rough-rider, swordsman, and boxer, now a professional trainer, and bade him see that the boy learned all he could teach him of arms and horsemanship, boxing, swimming, and general physical prowess and skill. Lucille and Haddon Berners were to join in to the extent to which their age and sex permitted.

The General intended his great-nephew to be worthy of his Stukeley blood, and to enter Sandhurst a finished man-at-arms and horseman, and to join his regiment, Cavalry, of course, with nothing much to learn of sword, lance, rifle, revolver, and horse.

Sergeant Havlan soon found that he had little need to begin at the beginning with Damocles de Warrenne in the matter of riding, fencing or boxing, and was unreasonably annoyed thereat.

In time, it became the high ambition and deep desire of Dam to overcome Sergeant Havlan's son in battle with the gloves. As young Havlan was a year his senior, a trained infant prodigy, and destined for the Prize Ring, there was plenty for him to learn and to do.

With foil or sabre the boy was beneath Dam's contempt.

Daily the children were in Sergeant Havlan's charge for riding and physical drill, Dam getting an extra hour in the evening for the more manly and specialized pursuits suitable to his riper years.

He and Lucille loved it all, and the Haddock bitterly loathed it.

Until Miss Smellie came Dam was a happy boy-but for queer sudden spasms of terror of Something unknown; and, after her arrival, he would have been well content could he have been assured of an early opportunity of attending her obsequies and certain of a long-postponed resurrection; well content, and often wildly happy (with Lucille)... but for the curious undefinable fear of Something... Something about which he had the most awful dreams... Something in a blue room with a mud floor. Something that seemed at times to move beneath his foot, making his blood freeze, his knees smite together, the sunlight turn to darkness....

Chapter IV
The Sword and the Soul

One of the very earliest of all Dam's memories in after life-for in a few years he forgot India absolutely-was of *the Sword* (that hung on the oak-panelled wall of the staircase by the portrait of a cavalier), and of a gentle, sad-eyed lady, Auntie Yvette, who used to say: —

"Yes, sonny darling, it is more than two-hundred-and-fifty years old. It belonged to Sir Seymour Stukeley, who carried the King's Standard at Edgehill and died with that sword in his hand... *You* shall wear a sword some day."

(He did-with a difference.)

The sword grew into the boy's life and he would rather have owned it than the mechanical steamboat with real brass cannon for which he prayed to God so often, so earnestly, and with such faith. On his seventh birthday he preferred a curious request, which had curious consequences.

"Can I take the sword to bed with me to-night, Dearest, as it is my birthday?" he begged. "I won't hurt it."

And the sword was taken down from the oak-panelled wall, cleaned, and laid on the bed in his room.

"Promise you will not try to take it out of the sheath, sonny darling," said the gentle, sad-eyed lady as she kissed him "Good night".

"I promise, Dearest," replied the boy, and she knew that she need have no fear.

He fell asleep fondling and cuddling the sword that had pierced the hearts of many men and defended the honour of many ancestors, and dreamed, with far greater vividness and understanding, the dream he had so often dreamt before.

Frequently as he dreamed it during his chequered career, it was henceforth always most vivid and real. It never never varied in the slightest detail, and he generally dreamed it on the night before some eventful, dangerous day on which he risked his life or fought for it.

Of the early dreamings,of course, he understood little, but while he was still almost a boy he most fully understood the significance of every word, act, and detail of the marvellous, realistic dream.

It began with a view of a camp of curious little bell-tents about which strode remarkable, big-booted, long-haired, bedizened men-looking strangely effeminate and strangely fierce, with their feathered hats, curls, silk sashes, velvet coats, and with their long swords, cruel faces, and savage oaths.

Some wore steel breastplates, like that of the suit of armour in the hall, and steel helmets. The sight of the camp thrilled the boy in his dream, and yet he knew that he had seen it all before actually, and in real life-in some former life.

Beside one of a small cluster of tents that stood well apart from the rest sat a big man who instantly reminded the boy of his dread "Grandfather," whom he would have loved to have loved had he been given the chance.

The big man was even more strangely attired than those others who clumped and clattered about the lower part of the camp.

Fancy a great big strong man with long curls, a lace collar, and a velvet coat-like a kid going to a party!

The velvet coat had the strangest sleeves, too-made to button to the elbow and full of slits that seemed to have been mended underneath with blue silk. There was a regular pattern of these silk-mended slits about the body of the coat, too, and funny silk-covered buttons.

On his head the man had a great floppy felt hat with a huge feather —a hat very like one that Dearest wore, only bigger.

One of his long curls was tied with a bow of ribbon-like young Lucille wore-and the boy felt quite uncomfortable as he noted it. A grown man-the silly ass! And, yes! he had actually got lace round the bottoms of his quaint baggy knickerbockers-as well as lace cuffs!

The boy could see it, where one of the great boots had sagged down below the knee.

Extraordinary boots they were, too. Nothing like "Grumper's" riding-boots. They were yellowish in colour, and dull, not nicely polished, and although the square-toed, ugly foot part looked solid as a house, the legs were more like wrinkled leather stockings, and so long that the pulled-up one came nearly to the hip.

Spurs had made black marks on the yellow ankles, and saddle and stirrup-leather had rubbed the legs....

And a sash! Whoever heard of a grown-up wearing a sash? It was a great blue silk thing, wound round once or twice, and tied with a great bow, the ends of which hung down in front.

Of all the Pip-squeaks!

And yet the big man's face was not that of a Pip-squeak —far from it. It was very like Grumper's in fact.

The boy liked the face. It was strong and fierce, thin and clean-cut —marred only, in his estimation, by the funny little tuft of hair on the lower lip. He liked the wavy, rough, upturned moustache, but not that silly tuft. How nice he would look with his hair cut, his lower lip shaved, and his ridiculous silks, velvet, and lace exchanged for a tweed shooting-suit or cricketing-flannels! How Grumper, Father, Major Decies, and even Khodadad Khan and the sepoys would have laughed at the get-up. Nay, they would have blushed for the fellow —a Sahib, a gentleman-to tog himself up so!

The boy also liked the man's voice when he turned towards the tent and called: —

"Lubin, you drunken dog, come hither," a call which brought forth a servant-like person, who, by reason of his clean-shaven face and red nose, reminded the boy of Pattern the coachman.

He wore a dark cloth suit, cotton stockings, shoes that had neither laces nor buttons, but fastened with a kind of strap and buckle, and, queer creature, a big Eton collar!

"Sword and horse, rascal," said the gentleman, "and warn Digby for duty. Bring me wine and a manchet of bread."

The man bowed and re-entered the tent, to emerge a moment later bearing *the Sword*.

How the cut-steel hilt sparkled and shone! How bright and red the leather scabbard-now black, dull, cracked and crumbling. But it was unmistakeably *the* Sword.

It hung from a kind of broad cross-belt and was attached to it by several parallel buckled straps-not like Father's Sam Browne belt at all.

As the gentleman rose from his stool (he must have been over six feet in height) Lubin passed the cross-belt over his head and raised left arm so that it rested on his right shoulder, and the Sword hung from hip to heel.

To the boy it had always seemed such a huge, unwieldy thing. At this big man's side it looked-just right.

Lubin then went off at a trot to where long lines of bay horses pawed the ground, swished their tails, tossed their heads, and fidgeted generally....

From a neighbouring tent came the sounds of a creaking camp-bed, two feet striking the ground with violence, and a prodigious, prolonged yawn.

A voice then announced that all parades should be held in Hell, and that it was better to be dead than damned. Why should gentlemen drill on a fine evening while the world held wine and women?

After a brief space, occupied with another mighty yawn, it loudly and tunefully requested some person or persons unknown to superintend its owner's obsequies.

>"Lay a garland on my hearse
>Of the dismal yew;
>Maidens, willow branches bear;
>Say I died true.
>My love was false, but I was firm
>From my hour of birth.

> Upon my buried body lie
> Lightly, gentle earth...."

"May it do so soon," observed the tall gentleman distinctly.

"What ho, without there! That you, Seymour, lad?" continued the voice. "Tarry a moment. Where's that cursed..." and sounds of hasty search among jingling accoutrements were followed by a snatch of song of which the boy instantly recognized the words. He had often heard Dearest sing them.

> "Drink to me only with thine eyes
> And I will pledge with mine:
> Or leave a kiss within the cup
> And I'll not look for wine.
> The thirst that from the soul doth rise
> Doth ask a drink divine;
> But might I of Jove's nectar sup,
> I would not change for thine."

Lubin appeared, bearing a funny, fat, black bottle, a black cup (both appeared to be of leather), and a kind of leaden plate on which was a small funnily-shaped loaf of bread.

"'Tis well you want none," observed the tall gentleman, "I had asked you to help me crush a flask else," and on the word the singer emerged from the tent.

"Jest not on solemn subjects, Seymour," he said soberly, "Wine may carry me over one more pike-parade.... Good lad.... Here's to thee.... Why should gentlemen drill?...I came to fight for the King, not to...But, isn't this thy day for de Warrenne? Oh, ten million fiends! Plague and pest! And I cannot see thee stick him, Seymour..." and the speaker dashed the black drinking-vessel violently on the ground, having carefully emptied it.

The boy did not much like him.

His lace collar was enormous and his black velvet coat was embroidered all over with yellow silk designs, flowers, and patterns. It was like the silly mantel-borders and things that Mrs. Pont, the housekeeper, did in her leisure time. ("Cruel-work" she called it, and the boy quite agreed.)

This man's face was pink and fair, his hair golden.

"Warn him not of the hilt-thrust, Seymour, lad," he said suddenly. "Give it him first-for a sneering, bullying, taverning, chambering knave."

The tall gentleman glanced at his down-flung cup, raised his eyebrows, and drank from the bottle.

"Such *would* annoy *you*, Hal, of course," he murmured.

A man dressed in what appeared to be a striped football jersey under a leather waistcoat and steel breast-plate, high boots and a steel helmet led up a great horse.

The boy loved the horse. It was very like "Fire".

The gentleman (called Seymour) patted it fondly, stroked his nose, and gave it a piece of his bread.

"Well, Crony Long-Face?" he said fondly.

He then put his left foot in the great box-stirrup and swung himself into the saddle—a very different kind of saddle from those with which the boy was familiar.

It reminded him of Circuses and the Lord Mayor's Show. It was big enough for two and there was a lot of velvet and stuff about it and a fine gold *C.R.* —whatever that might mean-on a big pretty cloth under it (perhaps the gentleman's initials were C.R. just as his own were D. de W. and on some of his things).

The great fat handle of a great fat pistol stuck up on each side of the front of the saddle.

"Follow," said the gentleman to the iron-bound person, and moved off at a walk towards a road not far distant.

"Stap him! Spit him, Seymour," called the pink-faced man, "and warn him not of the hilt-thrust."

As he passed the corner of the camp, two men with great axe-headed spear things performed curious evolutions with their cumbersome weapons, finally laying the business ends of them on the ground as the gentleman rode by.

He touched his hat to them with his switch.

Continuing for a mile or so, at a walk, he entered a dense coppice and dismounted.

"Await me," he said to his follower, gave him the curb-rein, and walked on to an open glade a hundred yards away.

> (It was a perfect spot for Red Indians, Smugglers, Robin Hood, Robinson Crusoe or any such game, the boy noted.)

Almost at the same time, three other men entered the clearing, two together, and one from a different quarter.

"For the hundredth time, Seymour, lad, *mention not the hilt-thrust*, as you love me and the King," said this last one quietly as he approached the gentleman; and then the two couples behaved in a ridiculous manner with their befeathered hats, waving them in great circles as they bowed to each other, and finally laying them on their hearts before replacing them.

"Mine honour is my guide, Will," answered the gentleman called Seymour, somewhat pompously the boy considered, though he did not know the word.

Sir Seymour then began to remove the slashed coat and other garments until he stood in his silk stockings, baggy knickerbockers, and jolly cambric shirt-nice and loose and free at the neck as the boy thought.

He rolled up his right sleeve, drew the sword, and made one or two passes-like Sergeant Havlan always did before he began fencing.

The other two men, meantime, had been behaving somewhat similarly-talking together earnestly and one of them undressing.

The one who did this was a very powerful-looking man and the arm he bared reminded the boy of that of a "Strong Man" he had seen recently at Monksmead Fair, in a tent, and strangely enough his face reminded him of that of his own Father.

He had a nasty face though, the boy considered, and looked like a bounder because he had pimples, a swelly nose, a loud voice, and a swanky manner. The boy disapproved of him wholly. It was like his cheek to resemble Father, as well as to have the same name.

His companion came over to the gentleman called Will, carrying the strong man's bared sword and, bowing ridiculously (with his hat, both hands, and his feet) said: —

"Shall we measure, Captain Ormonde Delorme?"

Captain Delorme then took the sword from Sir Seymour, bowed as the other had done, and handed him the sword with a mighty flourish, hilt first.

It proved to be half an inch shorter than the other, and Captain Delorme remarked that his Principal would waive that.

He and the strong man's companion then chose a spot where the grass was very short and smooth, where there were no stones, twigs or inequalities, and where the light of the setting sun fell sideways upon the combatants-who tip-toed gingerly, and rather ridiculously, in their stockinged feet, to their respective positions. Facing each other, they saluted with their swords and then stood with the right arm pointing downwards and across the body so that the hilt of the sword was against the right thigh and the blade directed to the rear.

"One word, Sir Matthew de Warrenne," said Sir Seymour as they paused in this attitude. "If my point rests for a second on your hilt *you are a dead man.*"

Sir Matthew laughed in an ugly manner and replied: —

"And what is your knavish design now, Sir Seymour Stukeley?"

"My design *was* to warn you of an infallible trick of fence, Sir Matthew. It *now* is to kill you-for the insult, and on behalf of...your own unhappy daughter."

The other yawned and remarked to his friend: —

"I have a parade in half an hour."

"On guard," cried the person addressed, drawing his sword and striking an attitude.

"Play," cried Captain Delorme, doing similarly.

Both principals crouched somewhat, held their swords horizontal, with point to the adversary's breast and hilt drawn back, arm sharply bent-for both, it appeared, had perfected the Art of Arts in Italy.

These niceties escaped the boy in his earlier dreamings of the dream-but the time came when he could name every pass, parry, invitation, and riposte.

The strong man suddenly threw his sword-hand high and towards his left shoulder, keeping his sword horizontal, and exposing the whole of his right side.

Sir Seymour lunged hard for his ribs, beneath the right arm-pit and, as the other's sword swooped down to catch his, twist it over, and riposte, he feinted, cleared the descending sword, and thrust at the throat. A swift ducking crouch let the sword pass over the strong man's head, and only a powerful French circular parry saved the life of Sir Seymour Stukeley.

As the boy realized later, he fought Italian in principle, and used the best of French parries, ripostes, and tricks, upon occasion-and his own perfected combination of the two schools made him, according to Captain Delorme, the best fencer in the King's army. So at least the Captain said to the other second, as they amicably chatted while their friends sought to slay each other before their hard, indifferent-seeming eyes.

To the boy their talk conveyed little-as yet.

The duellists stepped back as the "phrase" ended, and then Sir Seymour gave an "invitation," holding his sword-arm wide to the right of his body. Sir Matthew lunged, his sword was caught, carried out to the left, and held there as Sir Seymour's blade slid inward along it. Just in time, Sir Matthew's inward pressure carried Sir Seymour's sword clear to the right again. Sir Matthew disengaged over, and, as the sudden release brought Sir Seymour's sword springing in, he thrust under that gentleman's right arm and scratched his side.

As he recovered his sword he held it for a moment with the point raised toward Sir Seymour's face. Instantly Sir Seymour's point tinkled on his hilt, and Captain Delorme murmured "Finis" beneath his breath.

Sir Stukeley Seymour's blade shot in, Sir Matthew's moved to parry, and the point of the advancing sword flickered under his hand, turned upward, and pierced his heart.

"Yes," said Captain Delorme, as the stricken man fell, "if he parries outward the point goes under, if he anticipates a feint it comes straight in, and if he parries a lunge-and-feint-under, he gets feint-over before he can come up. I have never seen Stukeley miss when once he rests on the hilt. *Exit* de Warrenne-and Hell the worse for it ——" and the boy awoke.

He kissed the sword and fell asleep again.

One day, when receiving his morning fencing and boxing lessons of Sergeant Havlan, he astonished that warrior (and made a bitter enemy of him) by warning him against allowing his blade to rest on the Sergeant's hilt, and by hitting him clean and fair whenever it was allowed to happen. Also, by talking of "the Italian school of fence" and of "invitations" —the which were wholly outside the fencing-philosophy of the French-trained swordsman. At the age of fifteen the boy was too good for the man who had been the best that Aldershot had known, who had run a *salle d'armes* for years, and who was much sought by ambitious members of the Sword Club.

The Sword, from the day of that newly vivid dream, became to the boy what his Symbol is to the religious fanatic, and he was content to sit and stare at it, musing, for hours.

The sad-eyed, sentimental lady encouraged him and spoke of Knights, Chivalry, Honour, *Noblesse Oblige*, and Ideals such as the nineteenth century knew not and the world will never know again.

"Be a real and true Knight, sonny darling," she would say, "and live to *help*. Help women-God knows they need it. And try to be able to say at the end of your life, 'I have never made a woman weep'. Yes-be a Knight and have 'Live pure, Speak true, Right wrong' on your shield. Be a Round Table Knight and ride through the world bravely. Your dear Father was a great swordsman. You may have the sword down and kiss it, the first thing every morning-and you must salute it every night as you go up to bed. You shall wear a sword some day."

(Could the poor lady but have foreseen!)

She also gave him over-copiously and over-early of her simple, fervent, vague Theology, and much Old and New Testament History, with the highest and noblest intentions-and succeeded in implanting a deep distrust and dislike of "God" in his acutely intelligent mind.

To a prattling baby, *Mother* should be God enough-God and all the angels and paradise in one...(but he had never known a mother and Nurse Beaton had ever been more faithfully conscientious in deed than tenderly loving in manner).

She filled his soul with questionings and his mouth with questions which she could not answer, and which he answered for himself. The questions sometimes appalled her.

If God so loved the world, why did He let the Devil loose in it?

If God could do *anything*, why didn't He lay the Devil out with one hand?

If He always rewarded the Good and punished the Bad, why was Dearest so unhappy, and drunken Poacher Iggulsby so very gay and prosperously naughty?

He knew too that his dead Father had not been "good," for he heard servant-talk, and terrible old "Grandfather" always forgot that "Little Pitchers have Long Ears".

If God always answered devout and faith-inspired prayer, why did He not

1. Save Caiaphas the cat when earnestly prayed for-having been run over by Pattern in the dog-cart, coming out of the stables?

2. Send the mechanical steam-boat so long and earnestly prayed for, with Faith and Belief?

3. Help the boy to lead a higher and a better life, to eat up his crusts and fat as directed, to avoid chivvying the hens, inking his fingers, haunting the stables, stealing green apples in the orchard, tearing his clothes, and generally doing evil with fire, water, mud, stones and other tempting and injurious things?

And was it entirely decent of God to be eternally spying on a fellow, as appeared to be His confirmed habit?

As for that awful heart-rending Crucifixion, was that the sort of thing for a Father to look on at.... As bad as that brutal old Abraham with Isaac his son...were *all* "Good" Fathers like that...?

And nightmare dreams of Hell —a Hell in which there was a *Snake* —wrought no improvement.

And the Bible! How strangely and dully they talked, and what people! That nasty Jacob and Esau business, those horrid Israelites, the Unfaithful Steward; the Judge who let himself be pestered into action; those poor unfortunate swine that were made to rush violently down the steep place into the sea; Ananias and Sapphira. No-not a nice book at all.

The truth is that Theology, at the age of seven, is not commendable-setting aside the question of whether (at any age) Theology is a web of words, ritual, dogma, tradition, invention, shibboleth; a web originally spun by interested men to obscure God from their dupes.

So the boy worshipped Dearest and distrusted and disliked the God she gave him, a big sinister bearded Man who hung spread-eagled above the world, covering the entire roof of the Universe, and watched, watched, watched, with unwinking, all-seeing eye, and remembered with unforgetting, unrelenting mind. Cruel. Ungentlemanly. *Jealous!* Cold.

Also the boy fervently hoped it might never be his lot to go to Heaven —a shockingly dreary place where it was always Sunday and one must, presumably, be very quiet except when singing hymns. A place tenanted by white-robed Angels, unsympathetic towards dirty-faced little sinners who tore their clothes. Angels, cold, superior, unhuggable, haughty, given to ecstatic throes, singers of *Hallelujah* and other silly words-always *praising*.

How he loathed and dreaded the idea of Dearest being an Angel! Fancy sweet Dearest or his own darling Lucille with silly wings (like a beastly goose or turkey in dear old Cook's larder), with a long trumpet, perhaps, in a kind of night-gown, flying about the place, it wasn't decent at all-Dearest and Lucille, whom he adored and hugged-unsympathetic, cold, superior, unhuggable, haughty; and the boy who was very, *very* tender-hearted, would throw his arms round Dearest's neck and hug and hug and hug, for he abhorred the thought of her becoming a beastly angel.

Surely, if God knew His business, Dearest would be always happy and bright and live ever so long, and be ever so old, forty years and more.

And Dearest, fearing that her idolized boy might grow up a man like-well, like "Grumper" had been-hard, quarrelsome, adventurous, flippant, wicked, pleasure-loving, drunken, Godless...redoubled her efforts to Influence-the-child's-mind-for-good by means of the Testaments and Theology, the Covenant, the Deluge, Miracles, the Immaculate Conception, the Last Supper, the Resurrection, Pentecost, Creeds, Collects, Prayers.

And the boy's mind weighed these things deliberately, pondered them, revolted-and rejected them one and all.

Dearest had been taken in....

He said the prayers she taught him mechanically, and when he felt the need of real prayer — (as he did when he had dreamed of the Snake) —he always began, "If you *are* there, God, and *are* a good, kind God"...and concluded, "Yours sincerely, Damocles de Warrenne".

He got but little comfort, however, for his restless and logical mind asked: —

"If God *knows* best and will surely *do* what is best, why bother Him? And if He does not and will not, why bother yourself?"

But Dearest succeeded, at any rate, in filling his young soul with a love of beauty, romance, high adventure, honour, and all physical, mental, and moral cleanliness.

She taught him to use his imagination, and she made books a necessity. She made him a gentleman in soul-as distinct from a gentleman in clothes, pocket, or position.

She gave him a beautiful veneration for woman that no other woman was capable of destroying-though one or two did their best. Then the sad-eyed lady was superseded and her professional successor, Miss Smellie, the governess, finding the boy loved the Sword, asked Grumper to lock it away for the boy's Good.

Also she got Grumper to dismiss Nurse Beaton for impudence and not "knowing her place".

But Damocles entered into an offensive and defensive alliance with Lucille, on whom he lavished the whole affection of his deeply, if undemonstratively, affectionate nature, and the two "hunted in couples," sinned and suffered together, pooled their resources and their wits, found consolation in each other when harried by Miss Smellie, spent every available moment in each other's society and, like the Early Christians, had all things in common.

On birthdays, "high days and holidays" he would ask "Grumper" to let him have the Sword for an hour or two, and would stand with it in his hand, rapt, enthralled, ecstatic. How strange it made one feel! How brave, and anxious to do fine deeds. He would picture himself bearing an unconscious Lucille in his left arm through hostile crowds, while with the Sword he thrust and hewed, parried and guarded.... Who could fear *anything* with the Sword in his hand, the Sword of the Dream! How glorious to die wielding it, wielding it in a good cause...preferably on behalf of Lucille, his own beloved little pal, staunch, clever, and beautiful. And he told Lucille tales of the Sword and of how he loved it!

Chapter V
Lucille

"If you drinks a drop more, Miss Lucy, you'll just go like my pore young sister goed," observed Cook in a warning voice, as Lucille paused to get her second wind for the second draught.

(Lucille had just been tortured at the stake by Sioux and Blackfeet-thirsty work on a July afternoon.)

"And how did she go, Cookie-Bird —*Pop?*" inquired Lucille politely, with round eyes, considering over the top of the big lemonade-flagon as it rose again to her determined little mouth.

"No, Miss Lucy," replied Cook severely. "Pop she did not. She swole...swole and swole."

"You mean 'swelled,' Cookoo," corrected Lucille, inclined to be a little didactic and corrective at the age of ten.

"Well, she were *my* sister after all, Miss Lucy," retorted Cook, "and perhaps I may, or may not, know what she done. *I* say she swole-and what is more she swole clean into a dropsy. All along of drinking water.... *Drops* of water —*Dropsy.*"

"Never drink water," murmured Dam, absentmindedly annexing, and pocketing, an apple.

"Ah, water, but you see this is lemonade," countered Lucille. "Home-made, too, and not-er-gusty. It doesn't make you go — —" and here it is regrettable to have to relate that Lucille made a shockingly realistic sound, painfully indicative of the condition of one who has imbibed unwisely and too well of a gas-impregnated liquor.

"No more does water in my experiants," returned Cook, "and I was not alooding to wulgarity, Miss Lucy, which you should know better than to do such. My pore young sister's systerm turned watery and they tapped her at the last. All through drinking too much water, which lemonade ain't so very different either, be it never so 'ome-made.... Tapped 'er they did-like a carksk, an' 'er a Band of 'Oper, Blue Ribander, an' Sunday Schooler from birth, an' not departin' from it when she grew up. Such be the Ways of Providence," and Cook sighed with protestive respectfulness....

"Tapped 'er systerm, they did," she added pensively, and with a little justifiable pride.

"Were they hard taps?" inquired Lucille, reappearing from behind the flagon. "I hate them myself, even on the funny-bone or knuckles-but on the *cistern!* Ugh!"

"*Hard* taps; they was *silver* taps," ejaculated Cook, "and drawed gallings and gallings-and nothing to laugh at, Master Dammicles, neether.... So don't you drink no more, Miss Lucy."

"I can't," admitted Lucille-and indeed, to Dam, who regarded his "cousin" with considerable concern, it did seem that, even as Cook's poor young sister of unhappy memory, Lucille had "swole"—though only locally.

"Does *beer* make you swell or swole or swellow when you swallow, Cooker?" he inquired; "because, if so, *you* had better be —" but he was not allowed to conclude his deduction, for cook, bridling, bristling, and incensed, bore down upon the children and swept them from her kitchen.

To the boy, even as he fled *via* a dish of tartlets and cakes, it seemed remarkable that a certain uncertainty of temper (and figure) should invariably distinguish those who devote their lives to the obviously charming and attractive pursuit of the culinary art.

Surely one who, by reason of unfortunate limitations of sex, age, ability, or property, could not become a Colonel of Cavalry could still find infinite compensation in the career of cook or railway-servant.

Imagine, in the one case, having absolute freedom of action with regard to raisins, tarts, cream, candy-peel, jam, plum-puddings and cakes, making life one vast hamper, and in the other case, boundless opportunity in the matter of leaping on and off moving trains, carrying lighted bull's-eye lanterns, and waving flags.

One of the early lessons that life taught him, without troubling to explain them, and she taught him many and cruel, was that Cooks are Cross.

"What shall we do now, Dam?" asked Lucille, and added, "Let's raid the rotten nursery and rag the Haddock. Little ass! Nothing else to do. How I *hate* Sunday afternoon.... No work and no play. Rotten."

The Haddock, it may be stated, owed his fishy title to the fact that he once possessed a Wealthy Relative of the name of Haddon. With far-sighted reversionary intent his mother, a Mrs. Berners *née* Seymour Stukeley, had christened him Haddon.

But the Wealthy Relative, on being informed of his good fortune, had bluntly replied that he intended to leave his little all to the founding of Night-Schools for illiterate Members of Parliament, Travelling-Scholarships for uneducated Cabinet Ministers, and Deportment Classes for New Radical Peers. He was a Funny Man as well as a Wealthy Relative.

And, thereafter, Haddon Berners' parents had, as Cook put it, "up and died" and "Grandfather" had sent for, and adopted, the orphan Haddock.

Though known to Dam and Lucille as "The Haddock" he was in reality an utter Rabbit and esteemed as such. A Rabbit he was born, a Rabbit he lived, and a Rabbit he died. Respectable ever. Seen in the Right Place, in the Right Clothes, doing the Right Thing with the Right People at the Right Time.

Lucille was the daughter of Sylvester Bethune Gavestone, the late and lamented Bishop of Minsterbury (once a cavalry subaltern), a school, Sandhurst, and life-long friend of "Grandfather," and husband of "Grandfather's" cousin, Geraldine Seymour Stukeley.

Poor "Grandfather," known to the children as "Grumper," the ferocious old tyrant who loved all mankind and hated all men, with him adoption was a habit, and the inviting of other children to stay as long as they liked with the adopted children, a craze.

And yet he rarely saw the children, never played with them, and hated to be disturbed.

He had out-lived his soldier-contemporaries, his children, his power to ride to hounds, his pretty taste in wine, his fencing, dancing, flirting, and all that had made life bearable-everything, as he said, but his gout and his liver (and, it may be added, except his ferocious, brutal temper).

"Yes.... Let us circumvent, decoy, and utterly destroy the common Haddock," agreed Dam.

The entry into the nursery was an effective night-attack by Blackfeet (not to mention hands) but was spoilt by the presence of Miss Smellie who was sitting there knitting relentlessly.

"Never burst into rooms, children," she said coldly. "One expects little of a boy, but a *girl* should try to appear a Young Lady. Come and sit by me, Lucille. What did you come in for-or rather for what did you burst in?"

"We came to play with the Haddock," volunteered Dam.

"Very kind and thoughtful of you, I am sure," commented Miss Smellie sourly. "Most obliging and benevolent," and, with a sudden change to righteous anger and bitterness, "Why don't you speak the truth?"

"I am speaking the truth, Miss-er-Smellie," replied the boy. "We did come to play with the dear little Haddock-like one plays with a football or a frog. I didn't say we came for Haddock's *good*."

"We needed the Haddock, you see, Miss Smellie," confirmed Lucille.

"How many times am I to remind you that Haddon Berners' name *is* Haddon, Lucille," inquired Miss Smellie. "Why must you always prefer vulgarity? One expects vulgarity from a boy-but a girl should try to appear a Young Lady."

With an eye on Dam, Lucille protruded a very red tongue at surprising length, turned one eye far inward toward her nose, wrinkled that member incredibly, corrugated her forehead grievously, and elongated her mouth disastrously. The resultant expression of countenance admirably expressed the general juvenile view of Miss Smellie and all her works.

Spurred to honourable emulation, the boy strove to excel. Using both hands for the elongation of his eyes, the extension of his mouth, and the depression of his ears, he turned upon the Haddock so horrible a mask that the stricken child burst into a howl, if not into actual tears.

"What's the matter, Haddon?" demanded Miss Smellie, looking up with quick suspicion.

"Dam made a *fathe* at me," whimpered the smitten one.

"Say 'made a grimace' not 'made a face,'" corrected Miss Smellie. "Only God can make *faces*."

Dam exploded.

"At what are you laughing, Damocles?" she asked sternly.

"Nothing, Miss Smellie. What you said sounded rather funny and a little irrevilent or is it irrembrant?"

"Damocles! Should *I* be likely to say anything Irreverent? Should *I* ever dream of Irreverence? What *can* you mean? And never let me see you make faces again."

"I didn't let you see me, Miss Smellie, and only God can make faces —"

"Leave the room at once, Sir, I shall report your impudence to your great-uncle," hissed Miss Smellie, rising in wrath-and the bad abandoned boy had attained his object. Detention in the nursery for a Sunday afternoon was no part of his programme.

Most unobtrusively Lucille faded away also.

"Isn't she a hopeless beast," murmured she as the door closed.

"Utter rotter," admitted the boy. "Let's slope out into the garden and dig some worms for bait."

"Yes," agreed Lucille, and added, "Parse *Smellie,*" whereupon, with one voice and heart and purpose the twain broke into a paean, not of praise —a kind of tribal lay, and chanted: —

"*Smellie* —Very common noun, absurd person, singular back number, tutor gender, objectionable case governed by the word *I*," and so *da capo*.

And yet the poor lady strove to do her duty in that station of life in which it had pleased Providence (or a drunken father) to place her-and to make the children "genteel". Had she striven to win their love instead, her ministrations might have had some effect (other than infinite irritation and bitter dislike).

She was the Compleat Governess, on paper, and all that a person entrusted with the training of young children should not be, in reality. She had innumerable and admirable testimonials from various employers of what she termed "aristocratic standing"; endless certificates that testified unto her successful struggles in Music, Drawing, Needlework, German, French, Calisthenics, Caligraphy, and other mysteries, including the more decorous Sciences (against Physiology, Anatomy, Zoology, Biology, and Hygiene she set her face as subjects apt to be, at times, improper), and an appearance and manner themselves irrefragible proofs of the highest moral virtue.

She also had the warm and unanimous witness of the children at Monksmead that she was a Beast.

To those who frankly realize with open eyes that the student of life must occasionally encounter indelicacies upon the pleasant path of research, it may be revealed, in confidence, that they alluded to Miss Smellie as "Sniffy" when not, under extreme provocation, as "Stinker".

She taught them many things and, prominently, Deceit, Hate, and an utter dislike of her God and her Religion —a most disastrous pair.

Poor old "Grumper"; advertising, he got her, paid her highly, and gave her almost absolute control of the minds, souls, and bodies of his young wards and "grandchildren".

"The best of everything" for them-and they, at the average age of eight, a band of depressed, resentful babes, had "hanged, drawed, and quartered" her in effigy, within a month of coming beneath her stony ministrations.

In appearance Miss Smellie was tall, thin, and flat. Most exceedingly and incredibly flat. Impossibly flat. Her figure, teeth, voice, hair, manner, hats, clothes, and whole life and conduct were flat as Euclid's plane-surface or yesterday's champagne.

To counter-balance the possession, perhaps, of so many virtues, gifts, testimonials, and certificates she had no chin, no eyebrows, and no eyelashes. Her eyes were weak and watery; her spectacles strong and thick; her nose indeterminate, wavering, erratic; her ears large, her teeth irregular and protrusive, her mouth unfortunate and not guaranteed to close.

An ugly female face is said to be the index and expression of an ugly mind. It certainly was so in the case of Miss Smellie. Not that she had an evil or vicious mind in any way-far from it, for she was a narrowly pious and dully conscientious woman. Her mind was ugly as a useful building may be very ugly-or as a room devoid of beautiful furniture or over-crowded with cheap furniture may be ugly.

And her mind was devoid of beautiful thought-furniture, and over-crowded with cheap and ugly furniture of text-book facts. She was an utterly loveless woman, living unloving, and unloved —a terrible condition.

One *could not* like her.

Deadly dull, narrow, pedantic, petty, uninspiring, Miss Smellie's ideals, standards, and aims were incredibly low.

She lived, and taught others to live, for appearances.

The children were so to behave that they might appear "genteel". If they were to do this or that, no one would think they were young ladies or young gentlemen.

"If we were out at tea and you did that, I *should* be ashamed," she would cry when some healthy little human licked its jarnmy fingers, and "*Do* you wish to be considered vulgar or a little gentleman, Damocles?"

Damocles was profoundly indifferent on the point and said so plainly.

They were not to be clean of hand for hygienic reasons-but for fear of what people might "think"; they were not to be honourable, gentle, brave and truthful because these things are fine-but because of what the World might dole out in reward; they were not to eat slowly and masticate well for their health's sake-but by reason of "good manners"; they were not to study that they might develop their powers of reasoning, store their minds, and enlarge their horizons-but that they might pass some infernal examination or other, *ad majorem Smelliae gloriam*; they were not to practise the musical art that they might have a soul-developing aesthetic training, a means of solace, delight, and self-expression —but that they might "play their piece" to the casual visitor to the school-room with priggish pride, expectant of praise; they were not to be Christian for any other reason than that it was the recommended way to Eternal Bliss and a Good Time Hereafter-the whole duty of canny and respectable man being to "save his soul" therefore.

Her charges were skilfully, if unintentionally, trained in hypocrisy and mean motive, to look for low reward and strive for paltry ends-to do what looked well, say what sounded well, to be false, veneered, ungenuine.

And Miss Smellie was giving them the commonly accepted "education" of their class and kind.

The prize product of the Smellie system was the Haddock whose whole life was a pose, a lie, a refusal to see the actual. Perhaps she influenced him more strongly than the others because he was caught younger and was of weaker fibre. Anyhow he grew up the perfect and heartless snob, and by the time he left Oxford, he would sooner have been seen in a Black Maria with Lord Snooker than in a heavenly chariot with a prophet of unmodish garment and vulgar ancestry.

To the finished Haddock, a tie was more than a character, and the cut of a coat more than the cutting of a loving heart.

To him a "gentleman" was a person who had the current accent and waistcoat, a competence, the entree here and there —a goer unto the correct places with the correct people. Manners infinitely more than conduct; externals everything; let the whitening be white and the sepulchre mattered not.

The Haddock had no bloodful vice, but he was unstable as water and could not excel, a moral coward and weakling, a liar, a borrower of what he never intended to return, undeniably and incurably mean, the complete parasite.

From the first he feared and blindly obeyed Miss Smellie, propitiated while loathing her; accepted her statements, standards, and beliefs; curried favour and became her spy and informer.

"What's about the record cricket-ball throw, Dam?" inquired Lucille, as they strolled down the path to the orchard and kitchen-garden, hot-houses, stream and stables, to seek the coy, reluctant worm.

"Dunno," replied the boy, "but a hundred yards wants a lot of doing."

"Wonder if *I* could do it," mused Lucille, picking up a tempting egg-shaped pebble, nearly as big as her fist, and throwing it with remarkably neat action (for a girl) at the first pear-tree over the bridge that spanned the trout-stream.

At, but not into.

With that extraordinary magnetic attraction which glass has for the missile of the juvenile thrower, the orchid-house, on the opposite side of the path from the pear-tree, drew the errant stone to its hospitable shelter.

Through the biggest pane of glass it crashed, neatly decapitated a rare, choice exotic, the pride of Mr. Alastair Kenneth MacIlwraith, head gardener, released from its hold a hanging basket, struck a large pot (perched high in a state of unstable equilibrium), and passed out on the other side with something accomplished, something done, to earn a long repose.

So much for the stone.

The descending pot lit upon the edge of one side of the big glass aquarium, smashed it, and continued its career, precipitating an avalanche of lesser pots and their priceless contents.

The hanging basket, now an unhung and travelling basket, heavy, iron-ribbed, anciently mossy, oozy of slime, fell with neat exactitude upon the bald, bare cranium of Mr. Alastair Kenneth MacIlwraith, head gardener, and dour, irascible child and woman hater.

"Bull's-eye!" commented Dam-always terse when not composing fairy-tales.

"Crikey!" shrieked Lucille. "That's done it," and fled straightway to her room and violent earnest prayer, not for forgiveness but for salvation, from consequences. (What's the good of Saying your Prayers if you can't look for Help in Time of Trouble such as this?)

The face of Mr. Alastair Kenneth MacIlwraith was not pleasant to see as he pranced forth from the orchid-house, brandishing an implement of his trade.

"Ye'll be needing a wash the day, Mon Sandy, and the Sawbath but fower days syne," opined Dam, critically observing the moss-and-mud streaked head, face and neck of the raving, incoherent victim of Lucille's effort.

When at all lucid and comprehensible Mr. MacIlwraith was understood to say he'd give his place (and he twenty-twa years in it) to have the personal trouncing of Dam, that Limb, that Deevil, that predestined and fore-doomed Child of Sin, that —

Dam pocketed his hands and said but: —

"*Havers*, Mon Sandy!"

"I'll tak' the hide fra y'r bones yet, ye feckless, impident —"

Dam shook a disapproving head and said but: —

"*Clavers*, Mon Sandy!"

"I'll *see* ye skelped onny-how — or lose ma job, ye —"

More in sorrow than in anger Dam sighed and said but: —

"*Hoots*, Mon Sandy!"

"I'll go straight to y'r Grandfer the noo, and if ye'r not flayed alive! Aye! I'll gang the noo to Himself——"

"*Wi' fower an twanty men, an' five an' thairrty pipers*," suggested Dam in tuneful song.

Mr. Alastair Kenneth MacIlwraith did what he rarely did-swore violently.

"*Do you think at your age it is right?*" quoted the wicked boy... the exceedingly bad and reprehensible boy.

The maddened gardener turned and strode to the house with all his imperfections on his head and face and neck.

Taking no denial from Butterson, he forced his way into the presence of his master and clamoured for instant retributive justice-or the acceptance of his resignation forthwith, and him twenty-twa years in the ane place.

"Grandfather," roused from slumber, gouty, liverish, ferociously angry, sent for Dam, Sergeant Havlan, and Sergeant Havlan's cane.

"What's the meaning of this, Sir," he roared as Dam, cool, smiling, friendly ever, entered the Sanctum. "What the Devil d'ye mean by it, eh? Wreckin' my orchid-houses, assaultin' my servants, waking me up, annoying ME! Seven days C.B.[15] and bread and water, on each count. What d'ye mean by it, ye young hound? Eh? Answer me before I have ye flogged to death to teach ye better manners! Guilty or Not Guilty? and I'll take your word for it."

"The missile, describing a parabola, struck its subjective with fearful impact, Sir," replied the bad boy imperturbably, misquoting from his latest fiction (and calling it a "parry-bowler," to "Grandfather's" considerable and very natural mystification).

"*What?*" roared that gentleman, sitting bolt upright in astonishment and wrath.

"No. It's _ob_jective," corrected Dam. "Yes. With fearful impact. Fearful also were the words of the Mon Sandy."

"Grandfather" flushed and smiled a little wryly.

"You'd favour *me* with pleasantries too, would you? I'll reciprocate to the best of my poor ability," he remarked silkily, and his mouth set in the unpleasant Stukeley grimness, while a little muscular pulse beat beneath his cheek-bone.

"A dozen of the very best, if you please, Sergeant," he added, turning to Sergeant Havlan.

"Coat off, Sir," remarked that worthy, nothing loath, to the boy who could touch him almost as he would with the foil.

Dam removed his Eton jacket, folded his arms, turned his back to the smiter and assumed a scientific arrangement of the shoulders with tense muscles and coyly withdrawn bones. He had been there before....

The dozen were indeed of the Sergeant's best and he was a master. The boy turned not a hair, though he turned a little pale.... His mouth grew extraordinarily like that of his grandfather and a little muscular pulse beat beneath his cheek-bone.

"And what do you think of *my* pleasantries, my young friend?" inquired Grandfather. "Feeling at all witty *now*?"

"Havlan is failing a bit, Sir," was the cool reply. "I have noticed it at fencing too-Getting old-or beer perhaps. I scarcely felt him and so did not see or feel the point of your joke."

"Grandfather's" flush deepened and his smile broadened crookedly. "Try and do yourself justice, Havlan," he said. "'Nother dozen. 'Tother way."

Sergeant Havlan changed sides and endeavoured to surpass himself. It was a remarkably sound dozen.

He mopped his brow.

The bad boy did not move, gave no sign, but retained his rigid, slightly hunched attitude, as though he had not counted the second dozen and expected another stroke.

"Let that be a lesson to you to curb your damned tongue," said "Grandfather," his anger evaporating, his pride in the stiff-necked, defiant young rogue increasing.

The boy changed not the rigid, slightly hunched attitude.

"Be pleased to wreck no more of my orchid-houses and to exercise your great wit on your equals and juniors," he added.

Dam budged not an inch and relaxed not a muscle.

"You may go," said "Grandfather".... "Well-what are you waiting for?"

"I was waiting for Sergeant Havlan to *begin*," was the reply. "I thought I was to have a second dozen."

With blazing eyes, bristling moustache, swollen veins and bared teeth, "Grandfather" rose from his chair. Resting on one stick he struck and struck and struck at the boy with the other, passion feeding on its own passionate acts, and growing to madness-until, as the head gardener and Sergeant rushed forward to intervene, Dam fell to the ground, stunned by an unintentional blow on the head.

"Grandfather" stood trembling.... "*Quite* a Stukeley," observed he. "Oblige me by flinging his carcase down the stairs."

"'Angry Stookly's mad Stookly' is about right, mate, wot?" observed the Sergeant to the gardener, quoting an ancient local saying, as they carried Dam to his room after dispatching a groom for Dr. Jones of Monksmead.

"Dammy Darling," whispered a broken and tear-stained voice outside Dam's locked and key-less door the next morning, "are you dead yet?"

"Nit," was the prompt reply, "but I'm starving to death, fast."

"I am so glad," was the sobbed answer, "for I've got some flat food to push under the door."

"Shove it under," said Dam. "Good little beast!"

"I didn't know anything about the fearful fracass until tea-time," continued Lucille, "and then I went straight to Grumper and confessed, and he sent me to bed on an empty stummick and I laid upon it, the bed I mean, and howled all night, or part of it anyhow. I howled for your sake, not for the empty stummick. I thought my howls would break or at least soften his hard heart, but I don't think he heard them. I'm sure he didn't, in fact, or I should not have been allowed to howl so loud and long.... Did he blame you with anger as well as injustice?"

"With a stick," was the reply. "What about that grub?"

"I told him you were an innocent unborn babe and that Justice had had a mis-carriage, but he only grinned and said you had got C.B. and dry bread for insilence in the Orderly Room. What is 'insilence'?"

"Pulling Havlan's leg, I s'pose," opined Dam. "What about that *grub*? There comes a time when you are too hungry to eat and then you die. I —"

"Here it is," squealed Lucille, "don't go and die after all my trouble. I've got some thin ice-wafer biscuits, sulphur tablets, thin cheese, a slit-up apple and three sardines. They'll all come under the door-though the sardines may get a bit out of shape. I'll come after lessons and suck some brandy-balls here and breathe through the key-hole to comfort you. I could blow them through the key-hole when they are small too."

"Thanks," acknowledged Dam gratefully, "and if you could tie some up and a sausage and a tart or two and some bread-and-jam and some chicken and cake and toffee and things in a handkerchief, and climb on to the porch with Grumper's longest fishing-rod, you might be able to relieve the besieged garrison a lot. If the silly Haddock were any good he could fire sweets up with a catapult."

"I'd try that too," announced Lucille, "but I'd break the windows. I feel I shall never have the heart to throw a stone or anything again. My heart is broken," and the penitent sinner groaned in deep travail of soul.

"Have you eaten everything, Darling? How do you feel?" she suddenly asked.

"Yes. Hungrier than ever," was the reply. "I like sulphur tablets with sardines. Wonder when they'll bring that beastly dry bread?"

"If there's a sulphur tablet left I could eat one myself," said Lucille. "They are good for the inside and I have wept mine sore."

"Too late," answered Dam. "Pinch some more."

"They were the last," was the sad rejoinder. "They were for Rover's coat, I think. Perhaps they will make your coat hairy, Dam. I mean your skin."

"Whiskers to-morrow," said Dam.

After a pregnant silence the young lady announced: —

"Wish I could hug and kiss you, Darling. Don't you?...I'll write a kiss on a piece of paper and push it under the door to you. Better than spitting it through the key-hole."

"Put it on a piece of *ham*, —more sense," answered Dam.

The quarter-inch rasher that, later, made its difficult entry, pulled fore and pushed aft, was probably the only one in the whole history of Ham that was the medium of a kiss-located and indicated by means of a copying-ink pencil and a little saliva.

Before being sent away to school at Wellingborough Dam had a very curious illness, one which greatly puzzled Dr. Jones of Monksmead village, annoyed Miss Smellie, offended Grumper, and worried Lucille.

Sitting in solitary grandeur at his lunch one Sabbath, sipping his old Chambertin, Grumper was vexed and scandalized by a series of blood-curdling shrieks from the floor above his breakfast-room. Butterson, dispatched in haste to see "who the Devil was being killed in that noisy fashion," returned to state deferentially as how Master Damocles was in a sort of heppipletic fit, and foaming at the mouth. They had found him in the General's study where he had been reading a book, apparently; a big Natural History book.

A groom was galloping for Dr. Jones and Mrs. Pont was doin' her possible.

No. Nothing appeared to have hurt or frightened the young gentleman-but he was distinctly 'eard to shout: *"It is under my foot. It is moving-moving-moving out...."* before he became unconscious.

No, Sir. Absolutely nothing under the young gentleman's foot.

Dr. Jones could shed no light and General Sir Gerald Seymour Stukeley hoped to God that the boy was not going to grow up a wretched epileptic. Miss Smellie appeared to think the seizure a judgment upon an impudent and deceitful boy who stole into his elders' rooms in their absence and looked at their books.

Lucille was troubled in soul for, to her, Damocles confessed the ghastly, terrible, damning truth that he was a Coward. He said that he had hidden the fearful fact for all these years within his guilty bosom and that now it had emerged and convicted him. He lived in subconscious terror of the Snake, and in its presence-nay even in that of its counterfeit presentment-he was a gibbering, lunatic coward. Such, at least, was her dimly realized conception resultant upon the boy's bald, stammering confession.

But how could her dear Dammy be a *coward* —the vilest thing on earth! He who was willing to fight anyone, ride anything, go anywhere, act anyhow. Dammy the boxer, fencer, rider, swimmer. Absurd! Think of the day "the Cads" had tried to steal their boat from them when they were sailing it on the pond at Revelmead. There had been five of them, two big and three medium. Dam had closed the eye of one of them, cut the lip of another, and knocked one of the smaller three weeping into the dust.

They had soon cleared off and flung stones until Dam had started running for them and then they had fled altogether.

Think of the time when she set fire to the curtains. Why, he feared no bull, no dog, no tramp in England.

A coward! Piffle.

And yet he had screamed and kicked and cried-yes *cried* —as he had shouted that it was under his foot and moving out. Rum! *Very* rum!

On the day that Dam left Monksmead for school Lucille wept till she could weep no more. Life for the next few years was one of intermittent streaks of delirious joy and gloomy grief, vacation time when he was at Monksmead and term time when he was at school. All the rest of the world weighed as a grain of dust against her hero, Dam.

Chapter VI
The Snake's "Myrmidon"

For a couple of years and more, in the lower School at Wellingborough, Damocles de Warrenne, like certain States, was happy in that he had no history. In games rather above the average, and in lessons rather below it, he was very popular among his fellow "squeakers" for his good temper, modesty, generous disposition, and prowess at football and cricket.

Then, later, dawned the day when from this comfortable high estate a common adder, preserved in spirits of wine, was the cause of his downfall and Bully Harberth the means of his reinstatement....

One afternoon Mr. Steynker, the Science Master, for some reason and without preliminary mention of his intent, produced a bottled specimen of a snake. He entered the room with the thing under his arm and partly concealed by the sleeve of his gown. Watching him as he approached the master's desk and spoke with Mr. Colfe, the form-master, Dam noted that he had what appeared to be a long oblong glass box of which the side turned towards him was white and opaque.

When Mr. Steynker stepped on to the dais, as Mr. Colfe took up his books and departed, he placed the thing on the desk with the other side to the class....

And there before Dam's starting, staring eyes, fastened to the white back of the tall glass box, and immersed in colourless liquid was the Terror.

He rose, gibbering, to his feet, pale as the dead, and pointed, mopping and mowing like an idiot.

How should a glass box restrain the Fiend that had made his life a Hell upon earth? What did Steynker and Colfe and these others-all gaping at him open-mouthed —know of the Devil with whom he had wrestled deep beneath the Pit itself for ten thousand centuries of horror-centuries whose every moment was an aeon?

What could these innocent men and boys know of the living Damnation that made him pray to die-provided only that he could be *really* dead and finished, beyond all consciousness and fear. The fools!... to think that it was a harmless, concrete thing. It would emerge in a moment like the Fisherman's Geni from the Brass Bottle and grow as big as the world. He felt he was going mad again.

"Help!" he suddenly shrieked. *"It is under my foot. It is moving... moving... moving out."* He sprang to his astounded friend, Delorme, and screamed to him for help-and then realizing that there was *no* help, that neither man nor God could save him, he fled from the room screaming like a wounded horse.

Rushing madly down the corridor, falling head-long down the stone stairs, bolting blindly across the entrance-hall, he fled until (unaware of his portly presence up to the moment when he rebounded from him as a cricket-ball from a net) he violently encountered the Head.

Scrambling beneath his gown the demented boy flung his arms around the massy pillar of the Doctor's leg, and prayed aloud to him for help, between heart-rending screams.

Now it is undeniable that no elderly gentleman, of whatsoever position or condition, loves to be butted violently upon a generous lunch as he makes his placid way to his arm-chair, cigar, book, and ultimate pleasant doze. If he be pompous by profession, precise by practice, dignified as a duty, a monument of most stately correctness and, to small boys and common men, a great and distant, if tiny, God-he may be expected to resent it.

The Doctor did. Almost before he knew what he was doing, he struck the sobbing, gasping child twice, and then endeavoured to remove him by the ungentle application of the untrammelled foot, from the leg to which, limpet-like, he clung.

To Dam the blows were welcome, soothing, reassuring. Let a hundred Heads flog him with two hundred birch-rods, so they could keep him from the Snake. What are mere blows?

Realizing quickly that something very unusual was in the air, the worthy Doctor repented him of his haste and, with what dignity he might, inquired between a bleat and a bellow: —

"What is the matter, my boy? Hush! Hush!"

"The Snake! The Snake!" shrieked Dam. "Save me! Save me! *It is under my foot! It is moving... moving... moving out,*" and clung the tighter.

The good Doctor also moved with alacrity-but saw no snake. He was exceedingly perturbed, between a hypothetical snake and an all too actual lunatic boy.

Fortunately, "Stout" (so called because he was Porter), passing the big doors without, was attracted by the screams.

Entering, he hastened to the side of the agitated Head, and, with some difficulty, untied from that gentleman's leg, a small boy-but not until the small boy had fainted....

When Dam regained consciousness he had a fit, recovered, and found himself in the Head's study, and the object of the interested regard of the Head, Messrs. Colfe and Steynker, the school medico, and the porter.

It was agreed (while the boy fought for his sanity, bit his hand for the reassuring pleasure of physical pain, and prayed for help to the God in whom he had no reason to believe) that the case was "very unusual, very curious, v-e-r-y interesting indeed". Being healthier and stronger than at the time of previous attacks, Dam more or less recovered before night and was not sent home. But he had fallen from his place, and in the little republics of the dormitory and class-room, he was a thing to shun, an outcast, a disgrace to the noble race of Boy.

Not a mere liar, a common thief, a paltry murderer or vulgar parricide-but a COWARD, a blubberer, a baby. Even Delorme, more in sorrow than in anger, shunned his erstwhile bosom-pal, and went about as one betrayed.

The name of "Funky Warren" was considered appropriate, and even the Haddock, his own flesh and blood, and most junior of "squeakers," dared to apply it!....

The infamy of the Coward spread abroad, was talked of in other Houses, and fellows made special excursions to see the cry-baby, who funked a dead snake, a blooming bottled, potted, dead snake, and who had blubbed aloud in his terror.

And Bully Harberth of the Fifth, learning of these matters, revolved in his breast the thought that he who fears dead serpents must, even more, fear living bullies, put Dam upon his list as a safe and pliant client, and thereby (strange instrument of grace!) gave him the chance to rehabilitate himself, clear the cloud of infamy from about his head, and live a bearable life for the rest of his school career....

One wet Wednesday afternoon, as Dam, a wretched, forlorn Ishmael, sat alone in a noisy crowd, reading a "penny horrible" (admirable, stimulating books crammed with brave deeds and noble sentiments if not with faultless English) the Haddock entered the form-room, followed by Bully Harberth.

"That's him, Harberth, by the window, reading a penny blood," said the Haddock, and went and stood afar off to see the fun.

Harberth, a big clumsy boy, a little inclined to fat, with small eyes, heavy low forehead, thick lips, and amorphous nose, lurched over to where Dam endeavoured to read himself into a better and brighter world inhabited by Deadwood Dick, Texas Joe, and Red Indians of no manners and nasty customs.

"I want you, Funky Warren. I'm going to torture you," he announced with a truculent scowl and a suggestive licking of blubber lips.

Dam surveyed him coolly.

Of thick build, the bully was of thicker wit and certainly of no proven courage. Four years older than Dam and quite four inches taller, he had never dreamed of molesting him before. Innumerable as were the stories of his brutalities to the smallest "squeakers" and of his cruel practical jokes on new boys, there were no stories of his fighting, such as there were about Ormond Delorme, of Dam's form, whose habit it was to implore bigger boys of their courtesy to fight him, and to trail his coat where there were "chaws" about.

"I'm going to torture you, Funky. Every day you must come to me and *beg* me to do it. If you don't come and pray for it I'll come to *you* and you'll get it double and treble. If you sneak you'll get it quadru-er-quadrupedal-and also be known as Sneaky as well as Funky. See?" he continued.

"How will you torture me, Harberth, please?" asked Dam meekly, as he measured the other with his eye, noted his puffiness, short reach, and inward tendency of knee.

"Oh! lots of ways," was the reply. "Dry shaves, tweaks, scalpers, twisters, choko, tappers, digs, benders, shinners, windos, all sorts."

"I don't even know what they are," moaned Dam.

"Poor Kid!" sympathized the bully, "you soon will, though. Dry shaves are beautiful. You die dotty in about five minutes if I don't see fit to stop. Twisters break your wrists and you yell the roof off-or would do if I didn't gag you first with a cake of soap and a towel. Tappers are very amusing, too, for me that is-not for you. They are done on the side of your knee with a cricket stump. Wonderful how kids howl when you understand knee-treatment. Choko is good too. Makes you black in the face and your eyes goggle out awful funny. Done with a silk handkerchief and a stick. Windos and benders go together and really want two fellows to do it properly. I hit you in the wind and you double up, and the other fellow un-doubles you from behind-with a cane-so that I can double you up again. Laugh! I nearly died over young Berners. Shinners, scalpers, and tweaks are good too-jolly good!... but of course all this comes after lamming and tunding.... Come along with me...."

"Nit," was Dam's firm but gentle reply, and a little pulse began to beat beneath his cheek bone.

"Oh! Ho!" smiled Master Harberth, "then I'll *begin* here, and when you're broke and blubbing you'll come with me-and get just double for a start."

Dam's spirits rose and he felt almost happy-certainly far better than he had done since the hapless encounter with the bottled adder and his fall from grace. It was a positive, *joy* to have an enemy he could tackle, a real flesh-and-blood foe and tormentor that came upon him in broad daylight and in mere human form.

After countless thousands of centuries of awful nightmare struggling-in which he was bound hand-and-foot and doomed to failure and torture from the outset, the sport, plaything, and victim of a fearful, intangible Horror-this would be sheer amusement and recreation. What could mere man do to *him*, much less mere boy! Why, the most awful torture-chamber of the Holy Inquisition of old was a pleasant recreation-room compared with *any* place where the Snake could enter.

Oh, if the Snake could only be met and fought in the open with free hands and untrammelled limbs, as Bully Harberth could!

Oh, if it could only inflict mere physical pain instead of such agonies of terror as made the idea of any bodily injury-mere cutting, burning, beating, blinding—a trifling nothing-at-all. Anyhow, he could *imagine* that Bully Harberth was the Snake or Its emissary and, since he was indirectly brought upon him by the Snake, regard him as a myrmidon-and deal with him accordingly....

"How do you like this?" inquired that young gentleman as he suddenly seized the seated and unsuspecting Dam by the head, crushed him down with his superior weight and dug cruelly into the sides of his neck, below the ears, with his powerful thumb and fingers. "It is called 'grippers'. You'll begin to enjoy it in a minute."... In a few seconds the pain became acute and after a couple of minutes, excruciating.

Dam kept absolutely still and perfectly silent.

To Harberth this was disappointing and after a time he grew tired. Releasing his impassive victim he arose preparatory to introducing the next item of his programme of tortures.

"How do you like *this*?" inquired Dam rising also-and he smote his tormentor with all his strength beneath the point of his chin. Rage, pain, rebellion, and undying hatred (of the Snake) lent such force to the skilful blow-behind which was the weight and upward spring of his body-that Bully Harberth went down like a nine-pin, his big head striking the sharp edge of a desk with great violence.

He lay still and white with closed eyes. "Golly," shrilled the Haddock, "Funky Warren has murdered Bully Harberth. Hooray! Hooray!" and he capered with joy.

A small crowd quickly collected, and, it being learned from credible eye-witnesses that the smaller boy had neither stabbed the bully in the back nor clubbed him from behind, but had well and truly smitten him on the jaw with his fist, he went at one bound from despised outcast coward to belauded, admired hero.

"You'll be hung, of course, Warren," said Delorme.

"And a jolly good job," replied Dam, fervently and sincerely.

As he spoke, Harberth twitched, moved his arms and legs, and opened his eyes.

Sitting up, he blinked owl-like and inquired as to what was up.

"You are down is what's up," replied Delorme.

"Oh-he's not dead," squeaked the Haddock, and there was a piteous break in his voice.

"What's up?" asked Harberth again.

"Why, Funky-that is to say, Warren-knocked you out, and you've got to give him best and ask for *pax*, or else fight him," said Delorme, adding hopefully, "but of course you'll fight him."

Harberth arose and walked to the nearest seat.

"He hit me a 'coward's poke' when I wasn't looking," quoth he. "It's well known he is a coward."

"You are a liar, Bully Harberth," observed Delorme. "He hit you fair, and anyhow he's not afraid of *you*. If you don't fight him you become Funky Harberth *vice*. Funky Warren-no longer Funky. So you'd better fight. See?" The Harberth bubble was evidently pricked, for the sentiment was applauded to the echo.

"I don't fight cowards," mumbled Harberth, holding his jaw-and, at this meanness, Dam was moved to go up to Harberth and slap him right hard upon his plump, inviting cheek, a good resounding blow that made his hand tingle with pain and his heart with pleasure.

He still identified him somehow with the Snake, and had a glorious, if passing, sensation of successful revolt and some revenge.

He felt as the lashed galley-slave must have felt when, during a lower-deck mutiny, he broke from his oar and sprang at the throat of the cruel overseer, the embodiment and source of the agony, starvation, toil, brutality, and hopeless woe that had thrust him below the level of the beasts (fortunate beasts) that perish.

"Now you've *got* to fight him, of course," said Delorme, and fled to spread the glad tidings far and wide.

"I—I—don't feel well now," mumbled Harberth. "I'll fight him when I'm better," and shambled away, outraged, puzzled, disgusted. What was the world coming to? The little brute! He had a punch like the kick of a horse. The little cad-to *dare*! Well, he'd show him something if he had the face to stand up to his betters and olders and biggers in the ring....

News of the affair spread like wild-fire, and the incredible conduct of the extraordinary Funky Warren-said to be no longer Funky-became the topic of the hour.

At tea, Dam was solemnly asked if it were true that he had cast Harberth from a lofty window and brought him to death's door, or that of the hospital; whether he had strangled him with the result that he had a permanent squint; if he had so kicked him as to break both his thigh bones; if he had offered to fight him with one hand.

Even certain more or less grave and reverend seniors of the upper school took a well-disguised interest in the matter and pretended that the affair should be allowed to go on, as it would do Harberth a lot of good if de Warrenne could lick him, and do the latter a lot of good to reinstate himself by showing that he was not really a coward in essentials. Of course they took no interest in the fight as a fight. Certainly not (but it was observed that Flaherty of the Sixth stopped the fight most angrily and peremptorily when it was over, and that no sign of anger or peremptoriness escaped him until it was over-and he happened to pass behind the gymnasium, curiously enough, just as it started)....

Good advice was showered upon Dam from all sides. He was counselled to live on meat, to be a vegetarian, to rise at 4 a.m. and swim, to avoid all brain-fag, to run twenty miles a day, to rest until the fight, to get up in the night and swing heavy dumb-bells, to eat no pudding, to drink no tea, to give up sugar, avoid ices, and deny himself all "tuck" and everything else that makes life worth living.

He did none of these things-but simply went on as usual, save in one respect.

For the first time since the adder episode, he was really happy. Why, he did not know, save that he was about to "get some of his own back," to strike a blow against the cruel coward Incubus (for he persisted in identifying Harberth with the Snake and in regarding him as a materialization of the life-long Enemy), and possibly to enjoy a brief triumph over what had so long triumphed over him.

If he were at this time a little mad the wonder is that he was still on the right side of the Lunatic Asylum gates.

Mad or not, he was happy-and the one thing wanting was the presence of Lucille at the fight. How he would have loved to show her that he was not really a coward-given a fair chance and a tangible foe.

If only Lucille could be there-dancing from one foot to the other, and squealing. (Strictly *between*, and not during, the rounds, of course.)

"Buck up, Dammy! Ginger for pluck! Never say croak!"

A very large and very informal committee took charge of the business of the fight, and what was alluded to as "a friendly boxing contest between Bully Harberth of the Fifth and de Warrenne-late Funky—" was arranged for the following Saturday afternoon. On being asked by a delegate of the said large and informal committee as to whether he would be trained by then or whether he would prefer a more distant date, Dam replied that he would be glad to fight Harberth that very moment-and thus gained the reputation of a fierce and determined fellow (though erstwhile "funky"—the queer creature).

Those who had been loudest in dubbing him Funky Warrenne were quickest in finding explanations of his curious conduct and explained it well away.

It was at this time that Dam's heart went wholly and finally out to Ormonde Delorme who roundly stated that his father, a bemedalled heroic Colonel of Gurkhas, was "in a blind perishing funk" during a thunderstorm and always sought shelter in the wine cellar when one was in progress in his vicinity.

Darn presented Delorme with his knife and a tiger's tooth forthwith. Saturday came and Dam almost regretted its advent, for, though a child in years, he was sufficiently old, weary, and cynical in spirit to know that all life's fruit contains dust and ashes, that the joys of anticipation exceed those of realization, and that with possession dies desire.

With the fight would end the glorious feeling of successful revolt, and if he overcame one emissary of the Snake there would be a million more to take his place.

And if Providence should be, as usual, on the side of the "big battalions," and the older, taller, stronger, heavier boy should win? Why-then he would bully the loser to his heart's content and the limit of his ingenuity.

Good! Let him! He would fight him every day with the greatest pleasure. A chance to fight the Snake on fair terms was all he asked....

Time and place had been well chosen and there was little likelihood of interference.

Some experienced youth, probably Cokeson himself, had made arrangements as to seconds, time-keeper, judges, and referee; and, though there was no ring of ropes and stakes, a twenty-four-foot square had been marked out and inclosed by forms and benches. Seating was provided for the "officials" and seniors, and two stools for the principals. A couple of bowls of water, sponges, and towels lent a business-like air to the scene.

To his delight, Dam discovered that Delorme was to be his second —a person of sound advice, useful ministrations, and very present help in time of trouble....

Delorme led him to his stool in an angle of the square of benches, bade him spread wide his arms and legs and breathe deeply "for all he was worth, with his eyes closed and his thoughts fixed on jolly things".

Feeling himself the cynosure of neighbouring eyes and able to hear the comments of the crowd, the last part of his second's instructions was a little difficult of strict observation. However, he continued to think of licking Harberth-the "jolliest" thing he could conceive, until his mind wandered home to Lucille, and he enhanced the imaginary jollity by conceiving her present.... "Sturdy little brute," observed a big Fifth Form boy seated with a couple of friends on the bench beside him, "but I'd lay two to one in sovs. (if I had 'em) that he doesn't last a single round with Harberth".

"Disgrace to Harberth if he doesn't eat the kid alive," responded the other.

"Got a good jaw and mouth, though," said the third. "Going to die hard, you'll see. Good little kid."

"Fancy funking a bottled frog or something and fighting a chap who can give him about four years, four inches, and four stone," observed the first speaker.

"Yes. Queer little beast. He knocked Harberth clean out, they say. Perhaps his father has had him properly taught and he can really box. Ever seen him play footer? Nippiest little devil *I* ever saw. Staunch too. Rum go," commented his friend.

Dam thought of Sergeant Havlan and his son, the punching-ball, and the fighting days at Monksmead. Perhaps he could "really" box, after all. Anyhow he knew enough to hit straight and put his weight into it, to guard chin and mark, to use his feet, duck, dodge, and side step. Suppose Harberth knew as much? Well-since he was far stronger, taller, and heavier, the only hope of success lay in the fact that he was connected with the Snake-from whom mere blows in the open would be welcome.

Anyhow he would die or win.

The positive joy of fighting *It* in the glorious day and open air, instead of in the Bottomless Pit-bound, stifled, mad with Fear-none could realize....

Bully Harberth entered the ring accompanied by Shanner, who looked like a Sixth Form boy and was in the Shell.

Harberth wore a thick sweater and looked very strong and heavy.

"If the little kid lasts three rounds with *that*" observed Cokeson to Coxe Major, "he ought to be chaired."

Dam was disposed to agree with him in his heart, but he had no fear. The feeling that *his* brief innings had come-after the Snake had had Its will of him for a dozen years-swallowed up all other feelings.

Coxe Major stepped into the ring. "I announce a friendly boxing contest between Harberth of the Fifth, nine stone seven, and Funky Warren (said to be no longer Funky) of Barton's House, weight not worth mentioning," he declaimed.

"Are the gloves all right," called Cokeson (whose father owned racehorses, was a pillar of the National Sporting Club, and deeply interested in the welfare of a certain sporting newspaper).

"No fault can be found with Warren's gloves," said Shanner, coming over to Dam.

"There's nothing wrong with the gloves here," added Delorme, after visiting Harberth's corner.

This was the less remarkable in that there were no gloves whatsoever.

Presumably the fiction of a "friendly boxing contest" was to be stoutly maintained. The crowd of delighted boys laughed.

"Then come here, both of you," said Cokeson.

The combatants complied.

"Don't hold and hit. Don't butt nor trip. Don't clinch. Don't use knee, elbow, nor shoulder. When I call 'Break away,' break without hitting. If you do any of these things you will be jolly well disqualified. Fight fair and God have mercy on your souls." To Dam it seemed that the advice was superfluous-and of God's mercy on his soul he had had experience.

Returning to their corners, the two stripped to the waist and sat ready, arrayed in shorts and gymnasium shoes.

Seen thus, they looked most unevenly matched, Harberth looking still bigger for undressing and Dam even smaller. But, as the knowing Coxe Major observed, what there was of Dam was in the right place-and was muscle. Certainly he was finely made.

"Seconds out of the ring. *Time!*" called the time-keeper and Dam sprang to his feet and ran at Harberth who swung a mighty round-arm blow at his face as Dam ducked and smote him hard and true just below the breast-bone and fairly on the "mark ".

The bully's grunt of anguish was drowned in howls of "Shake hands!" "They haven't shaken hands!"

"Stop! Stop the fight," shouted Cokeson, and as they backed from each other he inquired with anger and reproach in his voice: —

"Is this a friendly boxing-contest or a vulgar fight?" adding, "Get to your corners and when *Time* is called, shake hands and then begin."

Turning to the audience he continued in a lordly and injured manner: "And there is only *one* Referee, gentlemen, please. Keep silence or I shall stop the fight —I mean-the friendly boxing contest."

As Dam sat down Delorme whispered: —

"Splendid! _In_fighting is your tip. Duck and go for the body every time. He knows nothing of boxing I should say. Tire him-and remember that if he gets you with a swing like that you're out."

"Seconds out of the ring. *Time!*" called the time-keeper and Dam walked towards Harberth with outstretched hand, met him in the middle of the ring and shook hands with great repugnance. As Harberth's hand left Dam's it rose swiftly to Dam's face and knocked him down.

"Shame! Foul poke! Coward," were some of the indignant cries that arose from the spectators.

"Silence," roared the referee. "*Will* you shut up and be quiet.
Perfectly legitimate-if not very sporting."

Dam sprang to his feet, absolutely unhurt, and, if possible, more determined than ever. It was only because he had been standing with feet together that he had been knocked down at all. Had he been given time to get into sparring position the blow would not have moved him. Nor was Harberth himself in an attitude to put much weight behind the blow and it was more a cuff than a punch.

Circling round his enemy, Dam sparred for an opening and watched his style and methods.

Evidently the bully expected to make short work of him, and he carried his right fist as though it were a weapon and not a part of his body.

As he advanced with his right extended, quivering, menacing, and poised for a knock-out blow, his left did not appear in the matter at all.

Suddenly he aimed his fist at Dam like a stone and with great force. Dam side-stepped and it brushed his ear; with his right he smote with all his force upon Harberth's ribs and with his left he drove at his eye as he came up. Both blows were well and truly laid and with good sounding thuds that seemed to delight the audience.

Bully Harberth changed his tactics and advanced upon his elusive opponent with his left in the position of guard and his right drawn back to the arm-pit. Evidently he was going to hold him off with the one and smash him with the other. Not waiting for him to develop his attack, but striking the bully's left arm down with his own left, Dam hit over it with his right and reached his nose and–so curious are the workings of the human mind–thought of Moses striking the rock and bringing forth water.

The sight of blood seemed to distress Harberth and, leaping in as the latter drew his hand across his mouth, Dam drove with all his strength at his mark and with such success that Harberth doubled up and fetched his breath with deep groans. Dam stood clear and waited.

Delorme called out, "You've a right to finish him," and was sternly reproved by the referee.

As Harberth straightened up, Dam stepped towards him, but the bully turned and ran to his stool. As he reached it amid roars of execration the time-keeper arose and cried *"Time!"*

"You had him, you little ass," said Delorme, as he squeezed a sponge of water on Dam's head. "Why on earth didn't you go in and finish him?"

"It didn't seem decent when he was doubled up," replied Dam.

"Did it seem decent his hitting you while you shook hands?" returned the other, beginning to fan his principal with a towel.

"Anyhow he's yours if you go on like this. Keep your head and don't worry about his. Stick to his body till you have a clear chance at the point of his jaw."

"Seconds out of the ring. *Time!*" cried the time-keeper.

This round was less fortunate for the smaller boy. Harberth's second had apparently given him some good advice, for he kept his mark covered and used his left both to guard and to hit.

Also he had learned something from Dam, and, on one occasion as the latter went at his face with a straight left, he dropped the top of his head towards him and made a fierce hooking punch at Dam's body. Luckily it was a little high, but it winded him for a moment, and had his opponent rushed him then, Dam could have done nothing at all.

Just as "Time" was called, Harberth swung a great round-arm blow at Dam which would have knocked him head over heels had not he let his knees go just in time and ducked under it, hitting his foe once again on the mark with all his strength.

"How d'you feel?" asked Delorme as Dam went to his stool.

"Happy," said he.

"Don't talk piffle," was the reply. "How do you feel? Wind all right? Groggy at all?"

"Not a bit," said Dam. "I am enjoying it."

And so he was. Hitherto the Snake had had him bound and helpless. As it pursued him in nightmares, his knees had turned to water, great chains had bound his arms, devilish gags had throttled him, he could not breathe, and he had not had a chance to escape nor to fight. He could not even scream for help. He could only cling to a shelf. *Now* he had a chance. His limbs were free, his eyes were open, he could breathe, think, act, defend himself and *attack*.

"Seconds out of the ring. *Time!*" called the time-keeper and Delorme ceased fanning with the towel, splashed a spongeful of water in Dam's face and backed away with his stool.

Harberth seemed determined to make an end.

He rushed at his opponent whirling his arms, breathing stertorously, and scowling savagely.

Guarding hurt Dam's arms, he had no time to hit, and in ducking he was slow and got a blow (aimed at his chin) in the middle of his forehead. Down he went like a nine-pin, but was up as quickly, and ready for Harberth who had rushed at him in the act of rising, while the referee shouted "Stand clear".

As he came on, Dam fell on one knee and drove at his mark again.

Harberth grunted and placed his hands on the smitten spot.

Judging time and distance well, Dam hit with all his force at the bully's chin and he went down like a log.

Rising majestically, the time-keeper lifted up his voice and counted: *"One-two-three-four-five-six"* —and Harberth opened his eyes, sat up, *"seven-eight-nine"* —and lay down again; and just as Dam was about to leap for joy and the audience to roar their approval-instead of the fatal *"OUT"* the time-keeper called *"Time"*.

Had Dam struck the blow a second sooner, the fight would have been over and he would have won. As it was, Harberth had the whole interval in which to recover. Dam's own luck!

(But Miss Smellie had always said there is no such thing as Luck!) Well-so much the better. *Fighting* the Snake was the real joy, and victory would end it. So would defeat and he must not get cock-a-hoop and careless.

Delorme filled his mouth with water and ejected it in a fine spray over Dam's head and chest. He was very proud of this feat, but, though most refreshing, Dam could have preferred that the water had come from a sprayer.

"Seconds out of the ring, *Time!*" called the referee.

Harberth appeared quite recovered, but he was of a curious colour and seemed tired.

Acting on his second's advice, Dam gave his whole attention to getting at his opponent's body again, and overdid it. As Harberth struck at him with his left, he ducked, and as he was aiming at Harberth's mark, he was suddenly knocked from day into night, from light into darkness, from life into death....

Years passed and Dam strove to explain that the mainspring had broken and that he had heard it click-when suddenly a great black drop-curtain rolled up, while some one snapped back some slides that had covered his ears, and had completely deafened him.

Then he saw Harberth and heard the voice of the time-keeper saying: *"five-six-seven"*.

He scrambled to his knees, *"eight"* swayed and staggered to his feet, collapsed, rose, *"nine"* and was knocked down by Harberth.

The time-keeper again stood up and counted, *"One-two-three"*. But this blow actually helped him.

He lay collecting his strength and wits, breathing deeply and taking nine seconds' rest.

On the word *"nine"* he sprang to his feet and as Harberth rushed in, side-stepped, and, as that youth instinctively covered his much-smitten "mark," Dam drove at his chin and sent him staggering. As he went after him he saw that Harberth was breathing hard, trembling, and swaying on his feet. Springing in, he rained short-arm blows until Harberth fell and then he stepped well back.

Harberth sat shaking his head, looking piteous, and, in the middle of the time-keeper's counting, he arose remarking, "I've had enough"—and walked to his chair.

Bully Harberth was beaten-and Dam felt that the Snake was farther from him than ever it had been since he could remember.

"De Warrenne wins," said Cokeson, and then Flaherty of the Sixth stepped into the ring and stopped the fight with much show of wrath and indignation.

Dam was wildly cheered and chaired and thence-forth was as popular and as admired as he had been shunned and despised.

Nor did he have another Snake seizure by day (though countless terrible nightmares in what must be called his sleep) till some time after he had left school.

When he did, it had a most momentous influence upon his career.

> She is mine! She is mine!
> By her soul divine
> By her heart's pure guile
> By her lips' sweet smile
> She is mine! She is mine.

> Encapture? Aye
> In dreams as fair
> As angel whispers, low and rare,
> In thoughts as pure
> As childhood's innocent allure
> In hopes as bright
> In deeds as white
> As altar lilies, bathed in light.

She is mine! She is mine!
By seal as true
To spirit view
As holy scripture writ in dew,
By bond as fair
To vision rare
As holy scripture writ in air,
By writ as wise to spirit eyes
As holy scripture in God's skies v
She is mine! She is mine!

Elude me? Nay,
Ere earth reclaimed
In joy unveils a Heaven regained,
Ere sea unbound,
Unfretting, rolls in mist-nor sound,
Ere sun and star repentent crash
In scattered ash, across the bar
She is *mine* I She is *mine*!

Chapter VII
Love-and the Snake

Damocles de Warrenne, gentleman-cadet, on the eve of returning from Monksmead to the Military Academy of Sandhurst, appeared to have something on his mind as he sat on the broad coping of the terrace balustrade and idly kicked his heels. Every time he had returned to Monksmead from Wellingborough and Sandhurst, he had found Lucille yet more charming, delightful, and lovable. As her skirts and hair lengthened she became more and more the real companion, the pal, the adviser, without becoming any less the sportsman.

He had always loved her quaint terms of endearment, slang, and epithets, but as she grew into a beautiful and refined and dignified girl, it was still more piquant to be addressed in the highly unladylike (or un-Smelliean) terms that she affected.

Dam never quite knew when she began to make his heart beat quicker, and when her presence began to act upon him as sunshine and her absence as dull cloud; but there came a time when (whether she were riding to hounds in her neat habit, rowing with him in sweater and white skirt, swinging along the lanes in thick boots and tailor-made costume, sitting at the piano after dinner in simple white dinner-gown, or waltzing at some ball-always the belle thereof for him) he *did* know that Lucille was more to him than a jolly pal, a sound adviser, an audience, a confidant, and ally. Perhaps the day she put her hair up marked an epoch in the tale of his affections. He found that he began to hate to see other fellows dancing, skating, or playing golf or tennis with her. He did not like to see men speaking to her at meets or taking her in to dinner. He wanted the blood of a certain neighbouring spring-Captain, a hunter of "flappers" and molester of parlour-maids, home on furlough, who made eyes at her at the Hunt Ball and followed her about all Cricket Week and said something to her which, as Dam heard, provoked her coolly to request him "not to be such a priceless ass". What it was she would not tell Dam, and he, magnifying it, called, like the silly raw boy he was, upon the spring-Captain, and gently requested him to "let my cousin alone, Sir, if you don't mind, or-er —I'll jolly well make you". Dam knew things about the gentleman, and considered him wholly unfit to come within a mile of Lucille. The spring-Captain was obviously much amused and inwardly much annoyed-but he ceased his scarce-begun pursuit of the hoydenish-queenly girl, for Damocles de Warrenne had a reputation for the cool prosecution of his undertakings and the complete fulfilment of his promises. Likewise he had a reputation for Herculean strength and uncanny skill. Yet the gay Captain had been strongly attracted by the beauty and grace of the unspoilt, unsophisticated, budding woman, with her sweet freshness and dignity (so quaintly enhanced by lapses into the slangy, unfettered schoolgirl...). Not that he was a marrying man at all, of course.... Yes-Dam had it weightily on his mind that he might come down from Sandhurst at any time and find Lucille engaged to some other fellow. Girls did get engaged.... It was the natural and obvious thing for them to do. She'd get engaged to some brainy clever chap worth a dozen of his own mediocre self.... Of course she liked him dearly as a pal and all that, an ancient crony and chum-but how should he hope to compete with the brilliant fellers she'd meet as she went about more, and knew them. She was going to have a season in London next year. Think of the kind of chaps she'd run across in Town in the season. Intellectual birds, artists, poets, authors, travellers, distinguished coves, rising statesmen, under-secretaries, soldiers, swells, all sorts. Not much show for him against that lot!

Gad! What a rotten look-out! What a rotten world to be sure! Fancy losing Lucille!... Should he put his fortunes to the touch, risk all, and propose to her. Fellows did these things in such circumstances.... No-hardly fair to try to catch her like that before she had had at least one season, and knew what was what and who was who.... Hardly the clean potato-to take advantage of their long intimacy and try to trap her while she was a country mouse.

It was not as though he were clever and could hope for a great career and the power to offer her the position for which she was fitted. Why, he was nearly bottom of his year at Sandhurst-not a bit brilliant and brainy. Suppose she married him in her inexperience, and then met the right sort of intellectual, clever feller too late. No, it wouldn't be the straight thing and decent at all, to propose to her now. How would Grumper view such a step? What had he to offer her? What was he? Just a penniless orphan. Apart from Grumper's generosity he owned a single five-pound note in money. Never won a scholarship or exam-prize in his life. Mere Public Schools boxing and fencing champion, and best man-at-arms at Sandhurst, with a score or so of pots for running, jumping, sculling, swimming, shooting, boxing, fencing, steeple-chasing and so forth. His total patrimony encashed would barely pay for his Army outfit. But for Grumper's kindness he couldn't go into the Army at all. And Grumper, the splendid old chap, couldn't last very much longer. Why-for many a long year he would not earn more than enough to pay his mess-bills and feed his horses. Not in England certainly.... Was he to ask Lucille to leave her luxurious home in a splendid mansion and live in a subaltern's four-roomed hut in the plains in India? (Even if he could scrape into the Indian army so as to live on his pay-more or less.) Grumper, her guardian, and executor of the late Bishop's will, might have very different views for her. Why, she might even be his heiress-he was very fond of her, the daughter of his lifelong friend and kinsman. Fancy a pauper making up to a very rich girl-if it came to her being that, which he devoutly hoped it would not. It would remove her so hopelessly beyond his reach. By the time he could make a position, and an income visible to the naked eye, he would be grey-haired. Money was not made in the army. Rather was it becoming no place for a poor gentleman but the paradise of rich bounders, brainy little squits of swotters, and commission-without-training nondescripts-thanks to the growing insecurity of things among the army class and gentry generally. If she were really penniless he might-as a Captain-ask her to share his poverty-but was it likely shed be a spinster ten years hence-even if he were a Captain so soon? Promotion is not violently rapid in the Cavalry.... And yet he simply hated the bare thought of life without Lucille. Better to be a gardener at Monksmead, and see her every day, than be the Colonel of a Cavalry Corps and know her to be married to somebody else.... Yes-he would come home one of these times from Sandburst or his Regiment and find her engaged to some other fellow. And what then? Well-nothing-only life would be of no further interest. It was bound to happen. Everybody turned to look at her. Even women gave generous praise of her beauty, grace, and sweetness. Men raved about her, and every male creature who came near her was obviously dpris in five minutes. The curate, plump "Holy Bill," was well known to be fading away, slowly and beautifully, but quite surely, on her account. Grumper's old pal, General Harringport, had confided to Dam himself in the smoking-room, one very late night, that since he was fifty years too old for hope of success in that direction he'd go solitary to his lonely grave (here a very wee hiccup), damn his eyes, so he would, unwed, unloved, uneverything. Very trag(h)ic, but such was life, the General had declared, the one alleviation being the fact that he might die any night now, and ought to have done so a decade ago.

Why, even the little useless snob and tuft-hunter, the Haddock, that tailor's dummy and parody of a man, cast sheep's eyes and made what he called "love" to her when down from Oxford (and was duly snubbed for it and for his wretched fopperies, snobberies, and folly). He'd have to put the Haddock across his knee one of these days.

Then there was his old school pal and Sandhurst senior, Ormonde Delorme, who frequently stayed at, and had just left, Monksmead —fairly dotty about her. She certainly liked Delorme- and no wonder, so handsome, clever, accomplished, and so fine a gentleman. Rich, too. Better Ormonde than another-but, God! what pain even to think of it.... Why had he cleared off so suddenly, by the way, and obviously in trouble, though he would not admit it?...

Lucille emerged from a French window and came swinging across the terrace. The young man, his face aglow, radiant, rose to meet her. It was a fine face-with that look on it. Ordinarily it was somewhat marred by a slightly cynical grimness of the mouth and a hint of trouble in the eyes —a face a little too old for its age.

"Have a game at tennis before tea, young Piggy-wig?" asked Lucille as she linked her arm in his.

"No, young Piggy-wee," replied Dam. "Gettin' old an' fat. Joints stiffenin'. Come an' sit down and hear the words of wisdom of your old Uncle Dammiculs, the Wise Man of Monksmead."

"Come off it, Dammy. Lazy little beast. Fat little brute," commented the lady.

As Damocles de Warrenne was six feet two inches high, and twelve stone of iron-hard muscle, the insults fell but lightly upon him.

"I will, though," she continued. "I shan't have the opportunity of hearing many more of your words of wisdom for a time, as you go back on Monday. And you'll be the panting prey of a gang of giggling girls at the garden party and dance to-morrow.... Why on earth must we muck up your last week-day with rotten 'functions'. You don't want to dance and you don't want to garden-part in the least."

"Nit," interrupted Dam.

"... Grumper means it most kindly but ... we want you to ourselves the last day or two ... anyhow...."

"D'you want me to yourself, Piggy-wee?" asked Dam, trying to speak lightly and off-handedly.

"Of course I do, you Ass. Shan't see you for centuries and months. Nothing to do but weep salt tears till Christmas. Go into a decline or a red nose very likely. Mind you write to me twice a week at the very least," replied Lucille, and added: —

"Bet you that silly cat Amelia Harringport is in your pocket all to-morrow afternoon and evening. *All* the Harringport crowd are coming from Folkestone, you know. If you run the clock-golf she'll *adore* clock-golf, and if you play tennis she'll *adore* tennis.... Can't think what she sees in you...."

"Don't be cattish, Lusilly," urged the young man. "'Melier's all right. It's you she comes to see, of course."

To which, it is regrettable to have to relate, Lucille replied "Rodents".

Talk languished between the young people. Both seemed unwontedly ill at ease and nervous.

"D'you get long between leaving Sandhurst and joining the Corps you're going to distinguish, Dammy?" asked the girl after an uneasy and pregnant silence, during which they had furtively watched each other, and smiled a little uncomfortably and consciously when they had caught each other doing so.

"Dunno. Sure not to. It's a rotten world," replied Dam gloomily. "I expect I shall come back and find you —"

"Of course you'll come back and find me! What do you mean, Dam?" said the girl. She flushed curiously as she interrupted him. Before he could reply she continued: —

"You won't be likely to have to go abroad directly you join your Regiment, will you?"

"I shall try for the Indian Army or else for a British Regiment in India," was the somewhat sullen answer.

"Dam! What ever for?"

"More money and less expenses."

"Dam! You mercenary little toad! You grasping, greedy hog!... Why! I thought...."

Lucille gazed straight and searchingly at her life-long friend for a full minute and then rose to her feet.

"Come to tea," she said quietly, and led the way to the big lawn where, beneath an ancient cedar of Lebanon, the pompous Butterton and his solemn satellite were setting forth the tea "things".

Aunt Yvette presided at the tea-table and talked bravely to two woolly-witted dames from the Vicarage who had called to consult her anent the covering of a foot-stool "that had belonged to their dear Grandmamma".

("Time somebody shot it," murmured Dam to Lucille as he handed her cup.)

Anon Grumper bore down upon the shady spot; queer old Grumper, very stiff, red-faced, dapper, and extremely savage.

Having greeted the guests hospitably and kindly he confined his subsequent conversation to two grunts and a growl.

Lucille and Damocles could not be said to have left the cane-chaired group about the rustic tables and cake-stands at any given moment. Independently they evaporated, after the manner of the Cheshire Cat it would appear, really getting farther and farther from the circle by such infinitely small degrees and imperceptible distances as would have appealed to the moral author of "Little by Little". At length the intervening shrubbery seemed to indicate that they were scarcely in the intimate bosom of the tea-party, if they had never really left it.

"Come for a long walk, Liggy," remarked Dam as they met, using an ancient pet-name.

"Right-O, my son," was the reply. "But we must start off mildly. I have a lovely feeling of too much cake. Too good to waste. Wait here while I put on my clod-hoppers."

The next hour was *the* Hour of the lives of Damocles de Warrenne and Lucille Gavestone-the great, glorious, and wonderful hour that comes but once in a lifetime and is the progenitor of countless happy hours-or hours of poignant pain. The Hour that can come only to those who are worthy of it, and which, whatever may follow, is an unspeakably precious blessing, confuting the cynic, shaming the pessimist, confounding the atheist, rewarding the pure in heart, revealing God to Man.

Heaven help the poor souls to whom that Hour never comes, with its memories that nothing can wholly destroy, its brightness that nothing can ever wholly darken. Heaven especially help the poor purblind soul that can sneer at it, the greatest and noblest of mankind's gifts, the countervail of all his cruel woes and curses.

As they walked down the long sweep of the elm-avenue, the pair encountered the vicar coming to gather up his wife and sister for the evening drive, and the sight of the two fine young people gladdened the good man's heart. He beheld a tall, broad-shouldered, narrow-hipped young man, with a frank handsome face, steady blue eyes, fair hair and determined jaw, a picture of the clean-bred, clean-living, out-door Englishman, athletic, healthy-minded, straight-dealing; and a slender, beautiful girl, with a strong sweet face, hazel-eyed, brown-haired, upright and active of carriage, redolent of sanity, directness, and all moral and physical health.

"A well-matched pair," he smiled to himself as they passed him with a cheery greeting.

For a mile or two both thought much and spoke little, the man thinking of the brilliant, hated Unknown who would steal away his Lucille; the woman thinking of the coming separation from the friend, without whom life was very empty, dull, and poor. Crossing a field, they reached a fence and a beautiful view of half the county. Stopping by mutual consent, they gazed at the peaceful, familiar scene, so ennobled and etherealized by the moon's soft radiance.

"I shall think of this walk, somehow, whenever I see the full moon," said Dam, breaking a long silence.

"And I," replied Lucille.

"I hate going away this time, somehow, more than usual," he blurted out after another spell of silence. "I can't help wondering whether you'll be-the same-when I come back at Christmas."

"Why-how should I be different, Dammy?" asked the girl, turning her gaze upon his troubled face, which seemed to twitch and work as though in pain.

"How?... Why, you might be —"

"Might be what, dear?"

"You might be-engaged."

The girl saw that in the man's eyes to which his tongue could not, or would not, give utterance. As he spoke the word, with a catch in his breath, she suddenly flung her arms round his neck, pressed her lips to his white face, and, with a little sob, whispered: —

"Not unless to you, Dam, darling-there is no other man in the world but you," and their lips met in their first lover's kiss.... Oh, the wonderful, glorious world!... The grand, beautiful old world! Place of delight, joy, wonder, beauty, gratitude. How the kind little stars sang to them and the benign old moon looked down and said: "Never despair, never despond, never fear, God has given you Love. What matters else?" How the man swore to himself that he would be worthy of her, strive for her, live for her; if need be-die for her. How the woman vowed to herself that she would be worthy of her splendid, noble lover, help him, cheer him, watch over him. Oh, if he might only need her some day and depend on her for something in spite of his strength and manhood. How she yearned to do something for him, to give, to give, to give. Their hour lasted for countless ages, and passed in a flash. The world intruded, spoiling itself as always.

"Home to dinner, darling," said the girl at last. "Hardly time to dress if we hurry. Grumper will simply rampage and roar. He gets worse every day." She disengaged herself from the boy's arms and her terribly beautiful, painfully exquisite, trance.

"Give me one more kiss, tell me once more that you love me and only me, for ever, and let us go.... God bless this place. I thank God. I love God-now..." she said.

Dam could not speak at all.

They walked away, hand in hand, incredulous, tremulous, bewildered by the beauty and wonder and glory of Life.

Alas!

As they passed the Lodge and entered the dark avenue, Dam found his tongue.

"Must tell Grumper," he said. Nothing mattered since Lucille loved him like that. She'd be happier in the subaltern's hut in the plains of India than in a palace. If Grumper didn't like it, he must lump it. Her happiness was more important than Grumper's pleasure.

"Yes," acquiesced Lucille, "but tell him on Monday morning when you go. Let's have this all to ourselves, darling, just for a few hours. I believe he'll be jolly glad. Dear old bear, isn't he-really."

In the middle of the avenue Lucille stopped.

"Dammy, my son," quoth she, "tell me the absolute, bare, bald truth. Much depends upon it and it'll spoil everything if you aren't perfectly, painfully honest."

"Right-O," responded Dam. "Go it."

"Am I the very very loveliest woman that ever lived?"

"No," replied Dam, "but I wouldn't have a line of your face changed."

"Am I the cleverest woman in the world?"

"No. But you're quite clever enough for me. I wouldn't have you any cleverer. God forbid."

"Am I absolutely perfect and without flaw-in character."

"No. But I love your faults."

"Do you wish to enshrine me in a golden jewel-studded temple and worship me night and day?"

"No. I want to put you in a house and live with you."

"Hurrah," cried the surprising young woman. "That's *love*, Dam. It's not rotten idealizing and sentimentalizing that dies away as soon as facts are seen as such. You're a man, Dam, and I'm going to be a woman. I loathe that bleating, glorified nonsense that the Reverend Bill and Captain Luniac and poor old Ormonde and people talk when they're 'in love'. *Love!* It's just sentimental idealizing and the worship of what does not exist and therefore cannot last. You love *me*, don't you, Dammy, not an impossible figment of a heated imagination? This will last, dear.... If you'd idealized me into something unearthly and impossible you'd have tired of me in six months or less. You'd have hated me when you saw the reality, and found yourself tied to it for life."

"Make a speech, Daughter," replied Damocles. "Get on a stump and make a blooming speech."

Both were a little unstrung.

"I must wire this news to Delorme," said he suddenly. "He'll be delighted." Lucille made no reply.

As they neared the end of the drive and came within sight of the house, the girl whispered: —

"My own pal, Dammy, for always. And you thought I could be engaged to anyone but *you*. There *is* no one but you in the world, dear. It would be quite empty if you left it. Don't worry about ways and means and things, Dam, I shall enjoy waiting for *you* —twenty years."

He thought of that, later.

On the morrow of that incredible day, Damocles de Warrenne sprang from his bed at sunrise and sought the dew-washed garden below the big south terrace.

The world contained no happier man. Sunrise in a glorious English summer and a grand old English garden, on the day after the Day of Days. He trod on air as he lived over again every second of that wonderful over-night scene, and scarcely realized the impossible truth.

Lucille loved him, as a lover! Lucille the *alter ego*, the understanding, splendid friend; companion in play and work, in idle gaiety and serious consideration; the *bon camarade*, the real chum and pal.

Life was a Song, the world a Paradise, the future a long-drawn Glory.

He would like to go and hold the Sword in his hand for a minute, and-something seemed to stir beneath his foot, and a shudder ran through his powerful frame.

The brightness of the morning was dimmed, and then Lucille came towards him blushing, radiant, changed, and all was well with the world, and God in high heaven.

* * *

After breakfast they again walked in the garden, the truly enchanted garden, and talked soberly with but few endearments though with over-full hearts, and with constant pauses to eye the face of the other with wondering rapture. They came of a class and a race not given to excessive demonstrativeness, but each knew that the other loved-for life.

In the afternoon, guests began to arrive soon after lunch, duties usurped the place of pleasures, and the lovers met as mere friends in the crowd. There was meaning in the passing glances, however, and an occasional hand-touch in the giving of tennis-ball, or tea-cup.

"Half the County" was present, and while the younger fry played tennis, croquet, clock-golf, and bowls, indulged in "mixed cricket," or attempted victory at archery or miniature-rifle shooting, the sedate elders strolled o'er velvet lawns beneath immemorial elms, sat in groups, or took tea by carpet-spread marquees.

Miss Amelia Harringport, seeing Dam with a croquet-mallet in his hand, observed that she *adored* croquet. Dam stated in reply that Haddon Berners was a fearful dog at it, considered there should be a croquet Blue in fact, and would doubtless be charmed to make up a set with her and the curate, the Reverend William Williamson Williams (Holy Bill), and Another. Dam himself was cut off from the bliss of being the Other-did not know the game at all.

Miss Amelia quickly tired of her croquet with the Haddock, Holy Bill and the Vicar's Wife's Sister, who looked straitly after Holy Bill on this and all other occasions. Seeing Dam shepherding a flock of elders to the beautifully-mown putting-tracks radiating from the central circle of "holes" for the putting competition, she informed him that she *adored* putting, so much so that she wanted lessons from him, the local amateur golf-champion.

"I just want a little *personal tuition* from the Champion and I shall be quite a classy putter," she gurgled.

"I will personally tuit," replied Dam, "and when you are tuited we will proceed to win the prize."

Carefully posing the maiden aspirant for putting excellence at the end of the yard-wide velvety strip leading to the green and "hole," Dam gave his best advice, bade her smite with restraint, and then proceeded to the "hole" to retrieve the ball for his own turn. Other couples did "preliminary canters" somewhat similarly on the remaining spokes of the great wheel of the putting "clock".

The canny and practised Amelia, who had designs upon the handsome silver prize as well as upon the handsome Damocles, smote straight and true with admirable judgment, and the ball sped steadily down the track direct for the "hole," a somewhat large and deep one.

"By Jove! Magnificent!" cried Dam, with quick and generous appreciation of the really splendid putt. "You'll hole out in one this time, anyhow." As the slowing ball approached the "hole" he inserted his hand therein, laughing gaily, to anticipate the ball which with its last grain of momentum would surely reach it and topple in.

Then the thing happened!

As he put his hand to the grass-encircled goal of the maiden's hopes and ball, its gloomy depths appeared to move, swirl round, rise up, as a small green snake uncoiled in haste and darted beneath Dam's approaching upturned hand, and swiftly undulated across the lawn.

With a shriek that momentarily paralysed the gay throng, turned all eyes in his direction, and brought the more cool and helpful running to the spot, Dam fell writhing, struggling, and screaming to the ground.

"The SNAKE! The SNAKE!" he howled, while tears gushed from his eyes and he strove to dig his way into the ground for safety.

"There it goes!" squealed the fair Amelia pointing tragically. Ladies duly squeaked, bunched their skirts tightly, jumped on chairs or sought protection by the side of stalwart admirers.

Men cried "Where?" and gathered for battle. One sporting character emitted an appalling "View Halloo" and there were a few "Yoicks" and "Gone Aways" to support his little solecism. Lucille, rushing to Dam, encountered the fleeing reptile and with a neat stroke of her putter ended its career.

"It's all right, old chap," sneered Haddon Berners, as the mad, convulsed, and foaming Dam screamed: "*It's under my foot. It's moving, moving, moving out,*" and doubled up into a knot.

"Oh no, it isn't," he continued. "Lucille has killed it. Nothing to be terrified about.... Oh, chuck it, man! Get up and blow your nose...." He was sent sprawling on his back as Lucille dropped by Dam's side and strove to raise his face from the grass.

"Come off it, Dam! You're very funny, we know," adjured the sporting character, rather ashamed and discomfortable at seeing a brother man behaving so. There are limits to acting the goat-especially with wimmin about. Why couldn't Dam drop it?...

Lucille was shocked and horrified to the innermost fibres of her being. Her dignified, splendid Dam rolling on the ground, shrieking, sobbing, writhing.... Ill or well, joke or seizure, it was horrible, unseemly.... Why couldn't the gaping fools be obliterated?...

"Dam, dear," she whispered in his ear, as she knelt over the shuddering, gasping, sobbing man. "What is it, Dam? Are you ill? Dam, it's Lucille.... The snake is quite dead, dear. I killed it. Are you joking? Dam! *Dam!*"...

The stricken wretch screamed like a terrified child.

"Oh, won't somebody fetch Dr. Jones if he's not here yet," she wailed, turning to the mystified crowd of guests. "Get some water quickly, somebody, salts, brandy, anything! Oh, *do* go away," and she deftly unfastened the collar of the spasm-wracked sufferer. "Haddon," she cried, looking up and seeing the grinning Haddock, "go straight for Dr. Jones. Cycle if you're afraid of spoiling your clothes by riding. Quick!"

"Oh, he'll be all right in a minute," drawled the Haddock, who did not relish a stiff ride along dusty roads in his choicest confection. "He's playing the fool, I believe-or a bit scared at the ferocious serpent."

Lucille gave the youth a look that he never forgot, and turned to the sporting person.

"You know the stables, Mr. Fellerton," she said. "Would you tell Pattern or somebody to send a man for Dr. Jones? Tell him to beat the record."

The sporting one sprinted toward the shrubbery which lay between the grounds and the kitchen-gardens, beyond which were the stables.

Most people, with the better sort of mind, withdrew and made efforts to recommence the interrupted games or to group themselves once more about the lawns and marquees.

Others remained to make fatuous suggestions, to wonder, or merely to look on with feelings approaching awe and fascination. There was something uncanny here —a soldier and athlete weeping and screaming and going into fits at the sight of a harmless grass-snake, probably a mere blind worm! Was he a hysterical, neurotic coward, after all—a wretched decadent?

Poor Lucille suffered doubly-every pang, spasm, and contortion that shook and wrung the body of her beloved, racked her own frame, and her mind was tortured by fear, doubts, and agony. "Oh, please go away, dear people," she moaned. "It is a touch of sun. He is a little subject to slight fits-very rarely and at long intervals, you know. He may never have another." A few of the remaining onlookers backed away a little shamefacedly. Others offered condolences while inwardly scoffing at the "sun" explanation. Did not de Warrenne bowl, bat, or field, bare-headed, throughout the summer's day without thinking of the sun? Who had heard of the "fits" before? Why had they not transpired during the last dozen years or so? "Help me carry him indoors, somebody," said the miserable, horrified Lucille. That would get rid of the silly staring "helpers" anyhow-even if it brought matters to the notice of Grumper, who frankly despised and detested any kind of sick person or invalid.

What would he say and do? What had happened to the glowing, glorious world that five minutes ago was fairy-land and paradise? Was her Dam a wretched coward, afraid of things, screaming like a girl at the sight of a common snake, actually terrified into a fit? Better be a pick-pocket than a.... Into the thinning, whispering circle came General Sir Gerald Seymour Stukeley, apoplectically angry. Some silly fool, he understood, had fainted or something-probably a puling tight-laced fool of a woman who starved herself to keep slim. People who wanted to faint should stay and do it at home-not come creating disturbances and interruptions at Monksmead garden-parties....

And then he saw a couple of young men and Lucille striving to raise the recumbent body of a man. The General snorted as snorts the wart-hog in love and war, or the graceful hippopotamus in the river.

"What the Devil's all this?" he growled. "Some poor fella fainted with the exertions of putting?" A most bitter old gentleman.

Lucille turned to him and his fierce gaze fell upon the pale, contorted, and tear-stained face of Dam.

The General flushed an even deeper purple, and the stick he held perpendicularly slowly rose to horizontal, though he did not raise his hand.

He made a loud but wholly inarticulate sound.

Haddon Berners, enjoying himself hugely, volunteered the information.

"He saw a little grass-snake and yelled out. Then he wept and fainted. Coming round now. Got the funks, poor chap."

Lucille's hands closed (the thumbs correctly on the knuckles of the second fingers), and, for a moment, it was in her heart to smite the Haddock on the lying mouth with the straight-from-the-shoulder drive learned in days of yore from Dam, and practised on the punching-ball with great assiduity. Apparently the Haddock realized the fact for he skipped backward with agility.

"He is ill, Grumper dear," she said instead. "He has had a kind of fit. Perhaps he had sunstroke in India, and it has just affected him now in the sun...."

Grumper achieved the snort of his life.

It may have penetrated Dam's comatose brain, indeed, for at that moment, with a moan and a shudder, he struggled to a sitting posture.

"The Snake," he groaned, and collapsed again.

"What the Devil!" roared the General. "Get up, you miserable, whining cur! Get indoors, you bottle-fed squalling workhouse brat! Get out of it, you decayed gentlewoman!"... The General bade fair to have a fit of his own.

Lucille flung herself at him.

"Can't you see he's very ill, Grumper? Have you no heart at all? Don't be so cruel...and... stupid."

The General gasped.... Insults!...From a chit of a girl!... "Ill!" he roared. "What the Devil does he want to be ill for now, here, to-day? I never..."

Dam struggled to his feet with heroic efforts at self-mastery, and stood swaying, twitching, trembling in every limb, and obviously in an agony of terror.

"The Snake!" he said again.

"Ha!" barked General Stukeley. "Been fighting forty boa-constrictors, what? Just had a fearful struggle with five thousand fearful pythons, what? There'll be another Victoria Cross in your family soon, if you're not careful."

"You are an unjust and cruel old man," stormed Lucille, stamping her foot at the hitherto dread Grumper. "He is ill, I tell you! You'll be ill yourself someday. He had a fit. He'll be all right in a minute. Let him go in and lie down. It wasn't the snake at all. There wasn't any snake-where he was. He is just ill. He has been working too hard. Let him go in and lie down."

"Let him go to the Devil," growled the infuriated General, and turned to such few of the guests as had not displayed sufficient good sense and good taste to go elsewhere and resume their interrupted games, tea, or scandal, to remark: —

"I really apologize most sincerely and earnestly for this ridiculous scene. The boy should be in petticoats, apparently. I hope he won't encounter a mouse or a beetle to-night. Let's all-er-come and have a drink."

Lucille led her shaking and incoherent lover indoors and established him on a sofa, had a fire lit for him as he appeared to be deathly cold, and sat holding his clammy hand until the arrival of Dr. Jones.

As well as his chattering teeth and white frozen lips would allow, he begged for forgiveness, for understanding. "He wasn't really wholly a coward in essentials."...

The girl kissed the contorted face and white lips passionately. Dr. Jones prescribed bed and "complete mental and bodily rest". He said he would "send something," and in a cloud of wise words disguised the fact that he did not in the least know what to do. It was not in his experience that a healthy young Hercules, sound as a bell, without spot or blemish, should behave like an anaemic, neurotic girl....

Dam passed the night in the unnameable, ghastly hell of agony that he knew so well and that he wondered to survive.

In the morning he received a note from Sir Gerald Seymour Stukeley. It was brief and clear: —"Sandhurst is scarcely the place for a squealing coward, still less the Army. Nor is there room for one at Monksmead. I shall not have the pleasure of seeing you before you catch the 11.15 train; I might say things better left unsaid. I thank God you do not bear our name though you have some of our blood. This will be the one grain of comfort when I think that the whole County is gibing and jeering. No-your name is no more Seymour Stukeley than is your nature. If you will favour my Solicitors with your address, they will furnish you with an account of your patrimony and such balance thereof as may remain-if any. But I believe you came to England worth about fifty pounds-which you have probably spent as pocket-money. I beg of you to communicate with me or my household in no way whatsoever.

"G.S.S."

Hastily dressing, Dam fled from the house on foot, empty handed and with no money but a five-pound note legitimately his own private property. On his dressing-table he left the cheque given to him by his "grandfather" for ensuing Sandhurst expenses. Hiding in the station waiting-room, he awaited the next train to London-with thoughts of recruiting-sergeants and the Guards. From force of habit he travelled first-class, materially lessening his five pounds. In the carriage, which he had to himself, he sat stunned. He was rather angry than dismayed and appalled. He was like the soldier, cut down by a sabre-slash or struck by a bullet, who, for a second, stares dully at the red gash or blue hole-waiting for the blood to flow and the pain to commence.

He was numbed, emotionally dead, waiting the terrible awakening to the realization that he had *lost Lucille*. What mattered the loss of home, career, friends, honour—mere anti-climax to glance at it.

Yesterday!... To-day!

What was Lucille thinking? What would she do and say? Would she grow to hate the coward who had dared to make love to her, dared to win her love!

Would she continue to love him in spite of all?

I shall enjoy waiting twenty years for you, she had said yesterday, and *The world would be quite empty if you left it*. What would it be while he remained in it a publicly disgraced coward? A coward ridiculed by the effeminate, degenerate Haddock, who had no soul above club-ribbons, and no body above a Piccadilly crawl!

Could she love him in spite of all? She was great-hearted enough for anything. Perhaps for anything but that. To her, cowardice must be the last lowest depths of degradation. Anyhow he had done the straight thing by Grumper, in leaving the house without any attempt to let her know, to say farewell, to ask her to believe in him for a while. If there had been any question as to the propriety of his trying to become engaged to her when he was the penniless gentleman-cadet, was there any question about it when he was the disgraced out-cast, the publicly exposed coward?

Arrived at the London terminus he sought a recruiting-sergeant and, of course, could not find one.

However, Canterbury and Cavalry were indissolubly connected in his mind, and it had occurred to him that, in the Guards, he would run more risk of coming face to face with people whom he knew than in any other corps. He would go for the regiment he had known and loved in India (as he had been informed) and about which he had heard much all his life. It was due for foreign service in a year or two, and, so far as he knew, none of its officers had ever heard of him. Ormonde Delorme was mad about it, but could not afford its expensive mess. Dam had himself thought how jolly it would be if Grumper "came down" sufficiently handsomely for him to be able to join it on leaving Sandhurst. He'd join it *now*!

He hailed a hansom and proceeded to Charing Cross, whence he booked for the noble and ancient city of Canterbury.

Realizing that only one or two sovereigns would remain to him otherwise, he travelled in a third-class carriage for the first time in his hitherto luxurious life. Its bare discomfort and unpleasant occupants (one was a very malodorous person indeed, and one a smoker of what smelt like old hats and chair-stuffing in a rank clay pipe) brought home to him more clearly than anything had done, the fact that he was a homeless, destitute person about to sell his carcase for a shilling, and seek the last refuge of the out-of-work, the wanted-by-the-police, the disgraced, and the runaway.

That carriage and its occupants showed him, in a blinding flash, that his whole position, condition, outlook, future, and life were utterly and completely changed.

He was Going Under. Had anybody else ever done it so quickly?...

He went Under, and his entrance to the Underworld was through the great main-gates of the depot of the Queen's Own (2nd) Regiment of Heavy Cavalry, familiarly known as the Queen's Greys.

Chapter VIII
Troopers of the Queen

Glimpses of Certain "Poor Devils" and the Hell They Inhabited

The Queen's Own (2nd) Regiment of Heavy Cavalry (The Queen's Greys) were under orders for India and the influence of great joy. That some of its members were also under the influence of potent waters is perhaps a platitudinous corollary.

..."And phwat the Divvle's begone of me ould pal Patsy Flannigan, at all, at all?" inquired Trooper Phelim O'Shaughnessy, entering the barrack-room of E Troop of the Queen's Greys, lying at Shorncliffe Camp. "Divvle a shmell of the baste can I see, and me back from furlough-leaf for minnuts. Has the schamer done the two-shtep widout anny flure, as Oi've always foretould? Is ut atin' his vegetables by the roots he now is in the bone-orchard, and me owing the poor bhoy foive shillin'? Where is he?"

"In 'orsepittle," laconically replied Trooper Henry Hawker, late of Whitechapel, without looking up from the jack-boot he was polishing.

"Phwat wid?" anxiously inquired the bereaved Phelim.

"Wot wiv'? Wiv' callin' 'Threes abaht' after one o' the Young Jocks,"[16] was the literal reply.

"Begob that same must be a good hand wid his fisties-or was it a shillaleigh?" mused the Irishman.

"Eld the Helliot belt in Hinjer last year, they say," continued the Cockney. "*Good?* Not'arf. I wouldn't go an' hinsult the bloke for the price of a pot. No. 'Erbert 'Awker would not. (Chuck us yore button-stick, young 'Enery Bone.) *Good?* 'E's a 'Oly Terror-and I don't know as there's a man in the Queen's Greys as could put 'im to sleep-not unless it's Matthewson," and here Trooper Herbert Hawker jerked his head in the direction of Trooper Damocles de Warrenne (*alias* D. Matthewson) who, seated on his truckle-bed, was engaged in breathing hard, and rubbing harder, upon a brass helmet from which he had unscrewed a black horse-hair plume.

Dam, arrayed in hob-nailed boots, turned-up overalls "authorized for grooming," and a "greyback" shirt, looked indefinably a gentleman.

Trooper Herbert Hawker, in unlaced gymnasium shoes, "leathers," and a brown sweater (warranted not to show the dirt), looked quite definably what he was, a Commercial Road ruffian; and his foreheadless face, greasy cow-lick "quiff" (or fringe), and truculent expression, inspired more disgust than confidence in the beholder.

His reference to Dam as the only likely champion of the Heavy Cavalry against the Hussar was a tribute to the tremendous thrashing he had received from "Trooper D. Matthewson" when the same had become necessary after a long course of unresented petty annoyance. Hawker was that very rare creature, a boaster, who made good, a bully of great courage and determination, and a loud talker, who was a very active doer; and the battle had been a terrible one.

The weary old joke of having a heavy valise pulled down on to one's upturned face from the shelf above, by means of a string, as one sleeps, Dam had taken in good part. Being sent to the Rough-Riding Sergeant-Major for the "Key of the Half Passage" by this senior recruit, he did not mind in the least (though he could have kicked himself for his gullibility when he learned that the "Half Passage" is not a place, but a Riding-School manoeuvre, and escaped from the bitter tongue of the incensed autocrat-called untimely from his tea! How the man had *bristled*. Hair, eyebrows, moustache, buttons even-the Rough-Riding Sergeant-Major had been rough indeed, and had done his riding rough-shod over the wretched lad).

Being instructed to "go and get measured for his hoof-picker" Dam had not resented, though he had considered it something of an insult to his intelligence that Hawker should expect to "have" him so easily as that. He had taken in good part the arrangement of his bed in such a way that it collapsed and brought a pannikin of water down with it, and on to it, in the middle of a cold night. He had received with good humour, and then with silent contempt, the names of "Gussie the Bank Clurk," references to "broken-dahn torfs" and "tailor's bleedn' dummies," queries as to the amount of "time" he had got for the offence that made him a "Queen's Hard Bargain," and various the other pleasantries whereby Herbert showed his distaste for people whose accent differed from his own, and whose tastes were unaccountable.

Dam had borne these things because he was certain he could thrash the silly animal when the time came, and because he had a wholesome dread of the all-too-inevitable military "crimes" (one of which fighting is-as subversive of good order and military discipline).

It had come, however, and for Dam this exotic of the Ratcliffe Highway had thereafter developed a vast admiration and an embarrassing affection. It was a most difficult matter to avoid his companionship when "walking-out" and also to avoid hurting his feelings.

It was a humiliating and chastening experience to the man, who had supported himself by boxing in booths at fairs and show-grounds, to find this "bloomin' dook of a 'Percy,'" this "lah-de-dar 'Reggie'" who looked askance at good bread-and-dripping, this finnicky "Clarence" without a "bloody" to his conversation, this "blasted, up-the-pole[17] 'Cecil'"—a man with a quicker guard, a harder punch, a smarter ring-craft, a better wind, and a tougher appetite for "gruel" than himself.

The occasion was furnished by a sad little experience.

Poor drunken Trooper Bear (once the Honourable MacMahon FitzUrse), kindliest, weakest, gentlest of gentlemen, had lurched one bitter soaking night (or early morning) into the barrack-room, singing in a beautiful tenor: —

"Menez-moi" dit la belle,
"A la rive fidèle
Où l'on aime toujours."
... —"Cette rive ma chère
On ne la connait guère
Au pays des amours."....

Trooper Herbert Hawker had no appreciation for Theophile Gautier-or perhaps none for being awakened from his warm slumbers.

"'Ere! stow that blarsted catawaulin'," he roared, with a choice selection from the Whitechapel tongue, in which he requested the adjectived noun to be adverbially "quick about it, too".

With a beatific smile upon his weak handsome face, Trooper Bear staggered toward the speaker, blew him a kiss, and, in a vain endeavour to seat himself upon the cot, collapsed upon the ground.

"You're a...." (adverbially adjectived noun) shouted Hawker. "You ain't a man, you're a...."

"[Greek: skias hovar havthropos]"..."Man is the dream of a shadow," suggested Bear dreamily with a hiccup....

"D'yer know where you *are*, you..." roared Hawker.

"Dear Heart, I am in hell," replied the recumbent one, "but by the Mercy of God I'm splendidly drunk. Yes, hell. '*Lasciate ogni speranza,*' sweet Amaryllis. I am Morag of the Misty Way. *Mos'* misty. Milky Way. Yesh. Milk Punchy Way."...

"I'll give you all the *punch* you'll want, in abaht two ticks if you don't chuck it-you blarsted edjucated flea," warned Hawker, half rising.

Dam got up and pulled on his cloak preparatory to helping the o'er-taken one to bed, as a well-aimed ammunition boot took the latter nearly on the ear.

Struggling to his feet with the announcement that he was "the King's fair daughter, weighed in the balance and found-devilish heavy and very drunk," the unhappy youth lurched and fell upon the outraged Hawker-who struck him a cruel blow in the face.

At the sound of the blow and heavy fall, Dam turned, saw the blood-and went Stukeley-mad. Springing like a tiger upon Hawker he dragged him from his cot and knocked him across it. In less than a minute he had twice sent him to the boards, and it took half-a-dozen men on either side to separate the combatants and get them to postpone the finish till the morning. That night Dam dreamed his dream and, on the morrow, behind the Riding-School, and in fifteen rounds, became, by common consent, champion bruiser of the Queen's Greys-by no ambition of his own.

And so-as has been said-Trooper Henry Hawker ungrudgingly referred Trooper Phelim O'Shaughnessy to him in the matter of reducing the pride of the Young Jock who had dared to "desthroy" a dragoon.

Trooper Phelim O'Shaughnessy-in perfect-fitting glove-tight scarlet stable-jacket (that never went near a stable, being in fact the smart shell-jacket, shaped like an Eton coat, sacred to "walking-out" purposes), dark blue overalls with broad white stripe, strapped over half-wellington boots adorned with glittering swan-neck spurs, a pill-box cap with white band and button, perched jauntily on three hairs-also looked what he was, the ideal heavy-cavalry man, the swaggering, swashbuckling trooper, *beau sabreur*, good all round and all through....

The room in which these worthies and various others (varying also in dress, from shirt and shorts to full review-order for Guard) had their being, expressed the top note and last cry-or the lowest note and deepest groan-of bleak, stark utilitarianism. Nowhere was there hint or sign of grace and ornament. Bare deal-plank floor, bare white-washed walls, plank and iron truckle beds, rough plank and iron trestle tables, rough plank and iron benches, rough plank and iron boxes clamped to bedsteads, all bore the same uniform impression of useful ugliness, ugly utility. The apologist in search of a solitary encomium might have called it clean-save around the hideous closed stove where muddy boots, coal-dust, pipe-dottels, and the bitter-end of five-a-penny "gaspers"[18] rebuked his rashness.

A less inviting, less inspiring, less home-like room for human habitation could scarce be found outside a jail. Perhaps this was the less inappropriate in that a jail it was, to a small party of its occupants-born and bred to better things.

The eye was grateful even for the note of cheer supplied by the red cylindrical valise on the shelf above each cot, and by the occasional scarlet tunic and stable-jacket. But for these it had been, to the educated eye, an even more grim, grey, depressing, beauty-and-joy-forsaken place than it was....

Dam (*alias* Trooper D. Matthewson) placed the gleaming helmet upon his callous straw-stuffed pillow, carefully rubbed the place where his hand had last touched it, and then took from a peg his scarlet tunic with its white collar, shoulder-straps and facings. Having satisfied himself that to burnish further its glittering buttons would be to gild refined gold, he commenced a vigorous brushing-for it was now his high ambition to "get the stick" —in other words to be dismissed from guard-duty as reward for being the best-turned-out man on parade.... As he reached up to his shelf for his gauntlets and pipe-clay box, Trooper Phelim O'Shaughnessy swaggered over with much jingle of spur and playfully smote him, netherly, with his cutting whip.

"What-ho, me bhoy," he roared, "and how's me natty Matty-the natest foightin' man in E Troop, which is sayin' in all the Dhraghoons, which is sayin' in all the Arrmy! How's Matty?"

"Extant," replied Dam. "How's Shocky, the biggest liar in the same?"

As he extended his hand it was noticeable that it was much smaller than the hand of the smaller man to whom it was offered. "Ye'll have to plug and desthroy the schamin' divvle that strook poor Patsy Flannigan, Matty," said the Irishman. "Ye must bate the sowl out of the baste before we go to furrin' parts. Loife is uncertain an' ye moight never come back to do ut, which the Holy Saints forbid-an' the Hussars troiumphin' upon our prosprit coorpses. For the hanner an' glory av all Dhraghoons, of the Ould Seconds, and of me pore bed-ridden frind, Patsy Flannigan, ye must go an' plug the wicked scutt, Matty darlint."

"It was Flannigan's fault," replied Dam, daubing pipe-clay on the huge cuff of a gauntlet which he had drawn on to a weird-looking wooden hand, sacred to the purposes of glove-drying.

"He got beastly drunk and insulted a better man than himself by insulting his Corps-or trying to. He called a silly lie after a total stranger and got what he deserved. He shouldn't seek sorrow if he doesn't want to find it, and he shouldn't drink liquor he can't carry."

"And the Young Jock beat Patsy when drunk, did he?" murmured O'Shaughnessy, in tones of awed wonder. "I riverince the man, for there's few can beat him sober. Knocked Patsy into hospital an' him foightin' dhrunk! Faith, he must be another Oirish gintleman himself, indade."

"He's a Scotchman and was middle-weight champion of India last year," rejoined Dam, and moistened his block of pipe-clay again in the most obvious, if least genteel, way.

"Annyhow he's a mere Hussar and must be rimonsthrated wid for darin' to assault and batther a Dhraghoon-an' him dhrunk, poor bhoy. Say the wurrud, Matty. We'll lay for the spalpeen, the whole of E Troop, at the *Ring o' Bells*, an' whin he shwaggers in like he was a Dhraghoon an' a sodger, ye'll up an' say *'Threes about'* an' act accordin' subsequint, an' learn the baste not to desthroy an' insult his betthers of the Ould Second. Thread on the tail of his coat, Matty...."

"If I had anything to do with it at all I'd tread on Flannigan's coat, and you can tell him so, for disgracing the Corps.... Take off your jacket and help with my boots, Shocky. I'm for Guard."

"Oi'd clane the boots of no man that ud demane himself to ax it," was the haughty reply of the disappointed warrior. "Not for less than a quart at laste," he amended.

"A quart it is," answered Dam, and O'Shaughnessy speedily divested himself of his stable-jacket, incidentally revealing the fact that he had pawned his shirt.

"You have got your teeth ready, then?" observed Dam, noting the underlying bareness-and thereby alluded to O'Shaughnessy's habit of pawning his false teeth after medical inspection and redeeming them in time for the next, at the cost of his underclothing-itself redeemed in turn by means of the teeth. Having been compelled to provide himself with a "plate" he invariably removed the detested contrivance and placed it beside him when sitting down to meals (on those rare occasions when he and not his "uncle" was the arbiter of its destinies)....

A young and important Lance-Corporal, a shocking tyrant and bully, strode into the room, his sword clanking. O'Shaughnessy arose and respectfully drew him aside, offering him a "gasper". They were joined by a lean hawk-faced individual answering to the name of Fish, who said he had been in the American navy until buried alive at sea for smiling within sight of the quarter-deck.

"Yep," he was heard to say to some statement of O'Shaughnessy's. "We'll hatch a five-bunch frame-up to put the eternal kibosh on the tuberous spotty-souled skunklet. Some. We'll make him wise to whether a tippy, chew-the-mop, bandy-legged, moke-monkey can come square-pushing, and with his legs out, down *this* side-walk, before we ante out. Some."

"Ah, Yus," agreed the Lance-Corporal. "Damned if I wouldn't chawnce me arm[19] and go fer 'im meself before we leave-on'y I'm expectin' furver permotion afore long. But fer that I'd take it up meself"—and he glanced at Dam.

"Ketch the little swine at it," remarked Trooper Herbert Hawker, as loudly as he dared, to his "towny," Trooper Henry Bone. "'Chawnst 'is arm!' It's 'is bloomin' life 'e'd chawnce if that Young Jock got settin' abaht 'im. Not 'arf!" and the exotic of the Ratcliffe Highway added most luridly expressed improprieties anent the origins of the Lance-Corporal, his erstwhile enemy and, now, superior officer, in addition.

"That's enough," said Dam shortly.

"Yep. Quit those low-browed sounds, guttermut, or I'll get mad all over," agreed Fish, whose marvellous vocabulary included no foul words. There was no need for them.

"Hi halso was abaht ter request you not to talk beastial, Mr. 'Erbert 'Awker," chimed in Trooper "Henery" Bone, anxious to be on the side of the saints. "Oo'd taike you to be the Missin' Hair of a noble 'ouse when you do such —'Missin' Hair!' *Missin' Link* more like," he added with spurious indignation.

The allusion was to the oft-expressed belief of Trooper Herbert Hawker, a belief that became a certainty and subject for bloodshed and battle after the third quart or so, that there was a mystery about his birth.

There was, according to his reputed papa....

The plotters plotted, and Dam completed the burnishing of his arms, spurs, buckles, and other glittering metal impedimenta (the quantity of which earned the Corps its barrack-room soubriquet of "the Polish Its"), finished the flicking of spots of pipe-clay from his uniform, and dressed for Guard.

Being ready some time before he had to parade, he sat musing on his truckle-bed.

What a life! What associates (outside the tiny band of gentlemen-rankers). What cruel awful *publicity* of existence-that was the worst of all. Oh, for a private room and a private coat, and a meal in solitude! Some place of one's own, where one could express one's own individuality in the choice and arrangement of property, and impress it upon one's environment.

One could not even think in private here.

And he was called a *private* soldier! A grim joke indeed, when the crying need of one's soul was a little privacy.

A *private* soldier!

Well-and what of the theory of Compensations, that all men get the same sum-total of good and bad, that position is really immaterial to happiness? What of the theory that more honour means also more responsibility and worry, that more pay also means more expenses and a more difficult position, that more seniority also means less youth and joy-that Fate only robs Peter to pay Paul, and, when bestowing a blessing with one hand, invariably bestows a curse with the other?

Too thin.

Excellent philosophy for the butterfly upon the road, preaching contentment to the toad, who, beneath the harrow, knows exactly where each tooth-point goes. Let the butterfly come and try it.

What a life!

Not so bad at first, perhaps, for a stout-hearted, hefty sportsman, during recruit days when everything is novel, there is something to learn, time is fully occupied, and one is too busy to think, too busy evading strange pit-falls, and the just or (more often) unjust wrath of the Room Corporal, the Squadron Orderly Sergeant, the Rough-Riding Corporal, the Squadron Sergeant-Major, the Rough-Riding Sergeant-Major, the Regimental Sergeant-Major, the Riding-Master.

But when, to the passed "dismissed soldier," everything is familiar and easy, weary, flat, stale and unprofitable?

The (to one gently nurtured) ghastly food, companions, environment, monotony-the ghastly ambitions!

Fancy an educated gentleman's ambitions and horizon narrowed to a good-conduct "ring," a stripe in the far future (and to be a Lance-Corporal with far more duty and no more pay, in the hope of becoming a Corporal-that comfortable rank with the same duty and much more pay, and little of the costly gold-lace to mount, and heavy expenses to assume that, while putting the gilt on, takes it off, the position of Sergeant); and, for the present, to "keep off the peg," not to be "for it," to "get the stick," for smartest turn-out, to avoid the Red-Caps,[20] to achieve an early place in the scrimmage at the corn-bin and to get the correct amount of two-hundred pounds in the corn-sack when drawing forage and corn; to placate Troop Sergeants, the Troop Sergeant-Major and Squadron Sergeant-Major; to have a suit of mufti at some safe place outside and to escape from the branding searing scarlet occasionally; possibly even the terrible ambition to become an Officer's servant so as to have a suit of mufti as a right, and a chance of becoming Mess-Sergeant and then Quarter-Master, and perhaps of getting an Honorary Commission without doing a single parade or guard after leaving the troop!...

What a life for a man of breeding and refinement!...Fancy having to remember the sacred and immeasurable superiority of a foul-mouthed Lance-Corporal who might well have been your own stable-boy, a being who can show you a deeper depth of hell in Hell, wreak his dislike of you in unfair "fatigues," and keep you at the detested job of coal-drawing on Wednesdays; who can achieve a "canter past the beak"[21] for you on a trumped-up charge and land you in the "digger,"[22] who can bring it home to you in a thousand ways that you are indeed the toad beneath the harrow. Fancy having to remember, night and day, that a Sergeant, who can perhaps just spell and cypher, is a monarch to be approached in respectful spirit; that the Regimental Sergeant-Major, perhaps coarse, rough, and ignorant, is an emperor to be approached with fear and trembling; that a Subaltern, perhaps at school with you, is a god not to be approached at all. Fancy looking forward to being "branded with a blasted worsted spur," and, as a Rough-Riding Corporal, receiving a forfeit tip from each young officer who knocks off his cap with his lance in Riding-School....

Well! One takes the rough with the smooth-but perceives with great clearness that the (very) rough predominates, and that one does not recommend a gentleman to enlist, save when a Distinguished Relative with Influence has an early Commission ready in his pocket for him.

Lacking the Relative, the gently-nurtured man, whether he win to a Commission eventually or not, can only do one thing more rash than enlist in the British Army, and that is enlist in the French Foreign Legion.

Discipline for soul and body? The finest thing in all the world-in reason. But the discipline of the tram-horse, of the blinded bullock at the wheel, of the well-camel, of the galley-slave — meticulous, puerile, unending, unchanging, impossible...? Necessary perhaps, once upon a time-but hard on the man of brains, sensibility, heart, and individuality.

Soul and body? Deadly for the soul-and fairly dangerous for the body in the Cavalry Regiment whose riding-master prefers the abominable stripped-saddle training to the bare-backed....

Dam yawned and looked at the tin clock on the shelf above the cot of the Room Corporal. Half an hour yet.... Did time drag more heavily anywhere in the world?...

His mind roamed back over his brief, age-long life in the Queen's Greys and passed it in review.

The interview with the Doctor, the Regimental Sergeant-Major, the Adjutant, the Colonel-the Oath on the Bible before that dread Superman.... How well he remembered his brief exordium —"Obey your Superiors blindly; serve your Queen, Country, and Regiment to the best of your ability; keep clean, don't drink, fear God, and-most important of all-take care of your horse. *Take care of your horse*, d'ye hear?"

Also the drawled remark of the Adjutant afterwards, "Ah-what-ah-University?" —his own prompt reply of "Whitechapel, sir," and the Adjutant's approving "Exactly.... You'll get on here by good conduct, good riding, and good drill-not by-ah-good accent or anything else."

How well he remembered the strange depolarized feeling consequent upon realizing that his whole worldly possessions consisted in three "grey-back" shirts, two pairs of cotton pants, two pairs of woollen socks, a towel; a hold-all containing razor, shaving-brush, spoon, knife and fork, and a button-stick; a cylindrical valise with hair-brush, clothes-brush, brass-brush, and boot-brushes; a whip, burnisher, and dandy-brush (all three, for some reason, to be paid for as part of a "free" kit); jack-boots and jack-spurs, wellington-boots and swan-neck box-spurs, ammunition boots; a tin of blacking and another of plate powder; blue, white-striped riding-breeches, blue, white-striped overalls, drill-suit of blue serge, scarlet tunic, scarlet stable-jacket, scarlet drill "frock," a pair of trousers of lamentable cut "authorized for grooming," brass helmet with black horse-hair plume, blue pill-box cap with white stripe and button, gauntlets and gloves, sword-belt and pouch-belt, a carbine and a sword. Also of a daily income of one loaf, butter, tea, and a pound of meat (often uneatable), and the sum of one shilling and twopence subject to a deduction of threepence a day "mess-fund," fourpence a month for delft, and divers others for library, washing, hair-cutting, barrack-damages, etc.

Yes, it had given one a strange feeling of nakedness, and yet of a freedom from the tyranny of things, to find oneself so meagrely and yet so sufficiently endowed.

Then, the strange, lost, homeless feeling that Home is nothing but a cot and a box in a big bare barrack-room, that the whole of God's wide Universe contains no private and enclosed spot that is one's own peculiar place wherein to be alone-at first a truly terrible feeling.

How one envied the Rough-Riding Sergeant-Major his Staff Quarters-without going so far as to envy the great Riding-Master his real separate and detached house!

No privacy-and a scarlet coat that encarnadined the world and made its wearer feel, as he so often thought, like a live coal glowing bright in Hell.

Surely the greatest of all an officer's privileges was his right of mufti, his daily escape from the burning cloth.

"Why does not the British officer wear his uniform always?" writes the perennial gratuitous ass to the Press, periodically in the Silly Season.... Dam could tell him.

Memories...!

Being jerked violently from uneasy slumber and broken, vivid dreams at 5 a.m., by the thunderous banging of the Troop Sergeant's whip on the table, and his raucous roar of "Tumble out, you lazy swine, before you get sunstroke! Rise and shine! Rise and shine, you tripe-hounds!"... Broken dreams on a smelly, straw-stuffed pillow and lumpy straw-stuffed pallet, dreams of *"Circle and cha-a-a-a-a-a-nge" "On the Fore-hand, Right About" "Right Pass, Shoulder Out" "Serpentine" "Order Lance" "Trail Lance" "Right Front Thrust"* (for the front rank of the Queen's Greys carry lances); dreams of riding wild mad horses to unfathomable precipices and at unsurmountable barriers....

Memories...!

His first experience of "mucking out" stables at five-thirty on a chilly morning-doing horrible work, horribly clad, feeling horribly sick. Wheeling away intentionally and maliciously overpiled barrows to the muck-pits, upsetting them, and being cursed.

Being set to water a notoriously wild and vicious horse, and being pulled about like a little dog at the end of the chain, burning into frozen fingers.

Not much of the glamour and glow and glory left!

Better were the interesting and amusing experiences of the Riding-School where his trained and perfected hands and seat gave him a tremendous advantage, an early dismissal, and some amelioration of the roughness of one of the very roughest experiences in a very rough life.

Even he, though, knew what it was to have serge breeches sticking to abraded bleeding knees, to grip a stripped saddle with twin suppurating sores, and to burrow face-first in filthy tan *via* the back of a stripped-saddled buck-jumper. How he had pitied some of the other recruits, making their first acquaintance with the Trooper's "long-faced chum" under the auspices of a pitiless, bitter-tongued Rough-Riding Sergeant-Major! *Rough!* What a character the fellow was! Never an oath, never a foul word, but what a vocabulary and gift of invective, sarcasm and cruel stinging reproof! A well-educated man if not a gentleman. "Don't dismount again, Muggins-or is it Juggins? —without permission" when some poor fellow comes on his head as his horse (bare of saddle and bridle) refuses at a jump. "Get up (and SIT BACK) you-you-hen, you pierrot, you *Aard Vark,* you after-thought, you refined entertainer, you pimple, you performing water-rat, you mistake, you *byle*, you drip, you worm-powder.... What? You think your leg's broken? Well —*you've got another*, haven't you? Get up and break that. Keep your neck till you get a stripped saddle and no reins.... Don't embrace the horse like that, you pawn-shop, I can hear it blushing.... Send for the key and get inside it.... Keep those fine feet forward. Keep them *forward* (and SIT BACK), Juggins or Muggins, or else take them into the Infantry-what they were meant for by the look of them. Now then-over you go without falling if I have to keep you here all night.... Look at *that*" (as the poor fellow is thrown across the jump by the cunning brute that knows its rider has neither whip, spurs, saddle nor reins). "What? The *horse* refuse? One of *my* horses *refuse? If the man'll jump, the horse'll jump.* (All of you repeat that after me and don't forget it.) No. It's the *man* refuses, not the poor horse. Don't you know the ancient proverb 'Faint heart ne'er took fair jump'....? What's the good of coming here if your heart's the size of your eye-ball instead of being the size of your fist? *Refuse?*

Put him over it, man. *Put* him over-SIT BACK and lift him, and *put* him over. I'll give you a thousand pounds if he refuses *me*...."

Then the day when poor bullied, baited, nervous Muggins had reached his limit and come to the end of his tether-or thought he had. Bumped, banged, bucketed, thrown, sore from head to foot, raw-kneed, laughed at, lashed by the Rough-Riding Sergeant-Major's cruel tongue, blind and sick with dust and pain and rage, he had at last turned his horse inward from his place in the ride to the centre of the School, and dismounted.

How quaintly the tyrant's jaw had dropped in sheer astonishment, and how his face had purpled with rage when he realized that his eyes had not deceived him and that the worm had literally turned-without orders.

Indian, African, and Egyptian service, disappointment, and a bad wife had left Rough-Riding Sergeant-Major Blount with a dangerous temper.

Poor silly Muggins. He had been Juggins indeed on that occasion, and, as the "ride" halted of its own accord in awed amazement, Dam had longed to tell him so and beg him to return to his place ere worse befell....

"I've 'ad enough, you bull-'eaded brute," shouted poor Muggins, leaving his horse and advancing menacingly upon his (incalculably) superior officer, "an' fer two damns I'd break yer b — — jaw, I would. You..."

Even as the Rough-Riding Corporal and two other men were dragging the struggling, raving recruit to the door, *en route* for the Guard-room, entered the great remote, dread Riding-Master himself.

"What's this?" inquired Hon. Captain Style, Riding-Master of the Queen's Greys, strict, kind-hearted martinet.

Salute, and explanations from the Rough-Riding Sergeant-Major.

Torrent of accusation and incoherent complaint and threat from the baited Muggins.

"Mount that horse," says the Riding-Master.

"I'll go to Clink first," gasps Muggins. "I'll go to 'Ell first."

"No. *Afterwards,*" replies the Riding-Master and sends the Rough-Riding Corporal for the backboard-dread instrument of equestrian persuasion.

Muggins is forcibly mounted, put in the lunging ring and sent round and round till he throws himself off at full gallop and lies crying and sobbing like a child-utterly broken.

Riding-Master smiles, allows Muggins to grow calmer, accepts his apologies and promises, shows him he has had his Hell *after*, as promised, and that it is a better punishment than one that leaves him with a serious "crime" entry on his Defaulter's Sheet for life.... That vile and damning sheet that records the youthful peccadilloes and keeps it a life-long punishment after its own severe punishment.... To the Rough-Riding Sergeant-Major he quietly remarks: "No good non-com *makes* crimes...and don't forget that the day of riding-school brutality is passing. You can carry a man further than you can kick him."

And the interrupted lesson continues.

"Sit *back* and you can't come off. Nobody falls off backwards."...

Poor "Old Sit-Back"! (as he was called from his constant cry) —after giving that order and guarantee daily for countless days-was killed in the riding-school by coming off backwards from the stripped saddle of a rearing horse —(which promptly fell upon him and crushed his chest) — that had never reared before and would not have reared then, it was said, but for the mysterious introduction, under its saddle, of a remarkably "foreign" body.

Memories...!

How certain old "Sit-Back" had been that Dam was a worthless "back-to-the-Army-again" when he found him a finished horseman, an extraordinarily expert swordsman, and a master of the lance.

"You aren't old enough for a 'time-expired,'" he mused, "nor for a cashiered officer. One of the professional 'enlist-desert-and-sell-me-kit,' I suppose. Anyhow you'll do time for one of the three if *I* don't approve of ye.... You've been in the Cavalry before. Lancer regiment, too.

Don't tell *me* lies...but see to it that I'm satisfied with your conduct. Gentlemen-rankers are better in their proper place —*Jail*."...

None the less it had given Dam a thrill of pride when, on being dismissed recruit-drills and drafted from the reserve troop to a squadron, the Adjutant had posted him to E Troop, wherein were congregated the seven other undoubted gentlemen-rankers of the Queen's Greys (one of whom would one day become a peer of the realm and, meantime, followed what he called "the only profession in the world" in discomfort for a space, the while his Commission ripened).

To this small band of "rankers" the accession of the finest boxer, swordsman, and horseman in the corps, was invaluable, and helped them notably in their endeavour to show that there are exceptions to all rules, and that a gentleman *can* make a first-class trooper. At least so "Peerson" had said, and Dam had been made almost happy for a day.

Memories...!

His first walk abroad from barracks, clad in the "walking-out" finery of shell-jacket and overalls, with the jingle of spurs and effort at the true Cavalry swagger, or rather the first attempt at a walk abroad, for the expedition had ended disastrously ere well begun. Unable to shake off his admirer, Trooper Herbert Hawker, Dam had just passed the Main Guard and main gates in the company of Herbert, and the two recruits had encountered the Adjutant and saluted with the utmost smartness and respect....

"What the Purple Hell's that thing?" had drawled the Adjutant thereupon-pointing his whip at Trooper Henry Hawker, whose trap-like mouth incontinent fell open with astonishment. "It's got up in an imitation of the uniform of the Queen's Greys, I do believe!...It's not a rag doll either.... It's a God-forsaken undertaker's mute in a red and black shroud with a cake-tin at the back of its turnip head and a pair of chemises on its ugly hands.... Sergeant of the Guard!... Here!"

"Sir?" and a salute of incredible precision from the Sergeant of the Guard.

"What the name of the Devil's old Aunt is *this* thing? What are you on Guard for? To write hymns and scare crows-or to allow decayed charwomen to stroll out of barracks in a dem parody of your uniform? Look at her! Could turn round in the jacket without taking it off. Room for both legs in one of the overalls. Cap on his beastly neck. Gloves like a pair of... *Get inside you*!...Take the thing in with a pair of tongs and bury it where it won't contaminate the dung-pits. Burn it! Shoot it! Drown it! D'ye hear?...And then I'll put you under arrest for letting it pass...."

It had been a wondrously deflated and chapfallen Herbert that had slunk back to the room of the reserve troop, and perhaps his reputation as a mighty bruiser had never stood him in so good stead as when it transpired that an Order had been promulgated that no recruit should leave barracks during the first three months of his service, and that the names of all such embryos should be posted in the Main Guard for the information of the Sergeant....

Memories...!

His first march behind the Band to Church....

The first Review and March Past....

His first introduction to bread-and-lard....

His wicked carelessness in forgetting-or attempting to disregard-the law of the drinking-troughs. "So long as one horse has his head down no horse is to go." There had been over a score drinking and he had moved off while one dipsomaniac was having a last suck.

His criminal carelessness in not removing his sword and leaving it in the Guard-room, when going on sentry after guard-mounting —"getting the good Sergeant into trouble, too, and making it appear that *he* had been equally criminally careless ".

The desperate quarrel between Hawker and Bone as to whether the 10th Hussars were called the "Shiny Tenth" because of their general material and spiritual brilliance, or the "Chainy Tenth" because their Officers wore pouch-belts of gold chain-mail.... The similar one between Buttle and Smith as to the reason of a brother regiment being known as "The Virgin Mary's

Body-guard," and their reluctant acceptance of Dam's dictum that they were both wrong, it having been earned by them in the service of a certain Maria Theresa, a lady unknown to Messrs. Buttle and Smith.... Dam had found himself developing into a positive bully in his determination to prevent senseless quarrelling, senseless misconduct, senseless humourless foulness, senseless humourless blasphemy, and all that unnecessary, avoidable ugliness that so richly augmented the unavoidable....

Memories...!

Sitting throughout compulsory church, cursing and mutinous of heart, because after spending several hours of the Day of Rest in burnishing and pipe-claying, blacking and shining ("Sunday spit an' polish"), he was under orders for sharp punishment-because at the last moment his tunic had been fouled by a passing pigeon! When would the Authorities realize that soldiers are still men, still Englishmen (even if they have, by becoming soldiers, lost their birthright of appeal to the Law of the Land, though not their amenability to its authority), and cease to make the Blessed Sabbath a curse, the worst day of the week, and to herd angry, resentful soldiers into church to blaspheme with politely pious faces? Oh, British, British, Pharisees and Humbugs-make Sunday a curse, and drive the soldier into church to do his cursing-make it the chief day of dress "crimes" and punishments, as well as the busiest day, and force the soldier into church to Return Thanks....

The only man in the world flung into church as though into jail for punishment! Shout it in the Soldier's ear, *"You are not a Man, you are a Slave,"* on Sundays also, on Sundays louder than usual.... And when he has spent his Sunday morning in extra hard labour, in suffering the indignity of being compulsorily marched to church, and very frequently of having been punished because it is a good day on which a Sergeant may decide that he is not sufficiently cleanly shaved or his boots of minor effulgence-then let him sit and watch his hot Sunday dinner grow stone cold before the Colonel stalks through the room, asks a perfunctory question, and he is free to fall to.

"O Day of Rest and Gladness, O Day of Joy most Bright...."

Yah!

A pity some of the energy that went to making the annual 20,000 military "criminals" out of honest, law-abiding, well-intending men could not go to harassing the Canteen instead of the soldier (whom the Canteen swindles right and left, and whence *he* gets salt-watery beer, and an "ounce" of tobacco that will go straight into his pipe in one "fill" —no need to wrap it up, thank you) and discovering how handsome fortunes, as well as substantial "illegal gratifications," are made out of his much-stoppaged one-and-tuppence-a-week.

Did the Authorities really yearn to _dis_courage enlistment and to _en_courage desertion and "crime"? When would they realize that making "crimes," and manufacturing "criminals" from honest men, is *not* discipline, is *not* making soldiers, is *not* improving the Army-is *not* common ordinary sanity and sense? When would they break their dull, unimaginative, hide-bound —no, tape-bound —souls from the ideas that prevailed before (and murdered) the Crimean Army.... The Army is not now the sweepings of the jails, and more in need of the wild-beast tamer than of the kind firm teacher, as once it was. How long will they continue to suppose that you make a fine fighting-man, and a self-reliant, intelligent soldier, by treating him as a depraved child, as a rightless slave, as a mindless automaton, and by encouraging the public (whom he protects) to regard him as a low criminal ruffian to be classed with the broad-arrowed convict, and to be excluded from places where any loafing rotten lout may go.... When would a lawyer-ridden Army Council realize that there is a trifle of significance in the fact that there are four times as many soldier suicides as there are civilian, and that the finest advertisement for the dwindling Army *is the soldier*. To think that sober men should, with one hand spend vast sums in lying advertisements for the Army, and with the other maintain a system that makes the soldier on furlough reply to the question "Shall I enlist, mate?" with the words "Not while you got a razor to cut yer throat".... Ah, well, common sense would reach even the Army some day, and the soldier be treated and disciplined as a man and a citizen-and perhaps, when it did, and the soldier gave a better description of his life, the other citizen, the smug knave who despises him while he shelters behind him, will become less averse from having his own round shoulders straightened, his back flattened and his muscles developed as he takes his part in the first fundamental elementary duty of a citizen-preparation for the defence of hearth and home.... Lucille! Well...Thank God she could not see him and know his life. If *she* had any kindness left for him she would suffer to watch him eating well-nigh uneatable food, grooming a horse, sweeping a stable, polishing trestle-legs with blacklead, scrubbing floors, sleeping on damp straw, carrying coals, doing scullion-work for uneducated roughs, being brow-beaten, bullied, and cursed by them in tight-lipped silence-not that these things troubled him personally-the less idle leisure for thought the better, and no real man minds physical hardship-there is no indignity in labour *per se* any more than there is dignity....

"'Ere, Maffewson, you bone-idle, moonin' waster," bawled the raucous voice of Lance-Corporal Prag, and Dam's soaring spirit fell to earth.

The first officer to whom Trooper Matthewson gave his smart respectful salute as he stood on sentry-duty was the Major, the Second-in-Command of the Queen's Greys, newly rejoined from furlough, —a belted Earl, famous for his sporting habit of riding always and everywhere without a saddle-who, as a merry subaltern, had been Lieutenant Lord Ochterlonie and Adjutant of the Queen's Greys at Bimariabad in India. There, he had, almost daily, taken upon his knee, shoulder, saddle, or dog-cart, the chubby son of his polo and pig-sticking exemplar, Colonel Matthew Devon de Warrenne.

The sentry had a dim idea that he had seen the Major somewhere before.

Chapter IX
A Snake Avenges a Haddock and Lucille Behaves in an Un-Smelliean Manner

Finding himself free for the afternoon, and the proud possessor of several shillings, "Trooper Matthewson" decided to walk to Folkestone, attend an attractively advertised concert on the pier, and then indulge in an absolutely private meal in some small tea-room or confectioner's shop.

Arrayed in scarlet shell-jacket, white-striped overalls, and pill-box cap, he started forth, carrying himself as though exceeding proud to be what he was, and wondering whether a swim in the sea, which should end somewhere between Shorncliffe and Dieppe (and end his troubles too), would not be a better pastime.

Arrived at the Folkestone pier, Dam approached the ticket office at the entrance and tendered his shilling to the oily-curled, curly-nosed young Jew who sat at the receipt of custom.

"Clear out o' this," said Levi Solomonson.

"I want a ticket for the concert," said Dam, not understanding.

"Would you like a row o' stalls to sprawl your dirty carcase on?... Outside, I tell yer, Tommy Atkins, this ain't a music-'all nor yet a pub. Soldiers *not* "'alf-price to cheap seats' nor yet full-price—nor yet for ten pound a time. Out yer go, lobster."

The powerful hand of Damocles de Warrenne approached the window and, for a second, Mr. Levi Solomonson was in danger-but only for a second. Dam was being well-broken-in, and quickly realized that he was no longer a free British citizen entitled to the rights of such so long as he behaved as a citizen should, but a mere horrible defender of those of his countrymen, who were averse from the toils and possible dangers of self-defence. It was brought home to him, then and there, with some clearness, that the noble Britons who (perhaps) "never never will be slaves," have a fine and high contempt for those whose life-work is to save them from that distressing position; that the noble Briton, while stoutly (and truly Britishly) refusing to hear of universal service and the doing by each man of his first duty to the State, is informed with a bitter loathing of those who, for wretched hire and under wretched conditions, perform those duties for him. Dam did not mind, though he did not enjoy, doing housemaid's work in the barrack-room, scrubbing floors, blackleading iron table-legs and grates, sweeping, dusting, and certain other more unpleasant menial tasks; he did not mind, though he did not like, "mucking-out" stables and scavenging; he could take at their proper value the insults of ignorant boors set in authority over him; he could stand, if not enjoy, the hardships of the soldier's life-but he did *not* see why his doing his duty in that particular sphere-an arduous, difficult, and frequently dangerous sphere-should earn him the united insult of the united public! Why should an educated and cultured man, a gentleman in point of fact, be absolutely prohibited from hearing a "classical" concert because he wore the Queen's uniform and did that most important and necessary work which the noble Briton is too slack-baked, too hypocritically genteel, too degenerate, to perform, each man for himself?

In a somewhat bitter frame of mind the unfortunate young man strolled along the Leas and seated himself on a public bench, honestly wondering as he did so, whether he were sufficiently a member of the great and glorious public to have a right to do it while wearing the disgraceful and disgracing garb of a Trooper of the Queen.... Members of that great and glorious public passed him by in rapid succession. Narrow-chested youths of all classes, and all crying aloud in slack-lipped silence for the drill-sergeant to teach them how to stand and walk; for the gymnasium-instructor to make them, what they would never be, *men*; for some one to give them an aim and an ideal beyond cigarettes, socks, and giggling "gels" or "gals" or "garls" or "gyurls" or "gurrls" according to their social sphere. Vast-stomached middle-aged men of all classes, and all crying aloud in fat-lipped silence of indulgence, physical sloth, physical decay before physical prime should have been reached, of mental, moral, and physical decadence from the great Past incredible, and who would one and all, if asked, congratulate themselves on living in these glorious modern times of 'igh civilization and not in the dark, ignorant days of old.

(Decidedly a bitter young man, this.)

> Place Mister Albert Pringle, Insurance Agent; Mister Peter Snagget, Grocer; Mister Alphonso Pumper, Rate Collector; Mister Bill 'Iggins, Publican; Mister Walter Weed, Clerk; Mister Jeremiah Ramsmouth, Local Preacher; Mr. 'Ookey Snagg, Loafer; Mister William Guppy, Potman-place them beside Hybrias, Goat-herd; Damon, Shepherd; Phydias, Writer; Nicarchus, Ploughman; Balbus, Bricklayer; Glaucus, Potter; Caius, Carter; Marcus, Weaver; Aeneas, Bronze-worker; Antonius, Corn-seller; Canidius, Charioteer-and then talk of the glorious modern times of high civilization and the dark ignorant days of old!...

And as he sat musing thus foolishly and pessimistically, who should loom upon his horizon but-of all people in the world-the Haddock, the fishy, flabby, stale, unprofitable Haddock! Most certainly Solomon in all his glory was not arrayed like this. A beautiful confection of pearly-grey, pearl-buttoned flannel draped his droopy form, a pearly-grey silk tie, pearl-pinned, encircled his lofty collar, pearly-grey silk socks spanned the divorcing gap 'twixt beautiful grey kid shoes and correctest trousers, a pearly-grey silk handkerchief peeped knowingly from the cuff of his pearly-grey silk shirt by his pearly-grey kid glove, and his little cane was of grey lacquer, and of pearl handle. One could almost have sworn that a pearl-grey smile adorned the scarce-shut mouth of the beautiful modern product of education and civilization, to carry on the so well-devised colour-scheme to the pearly-grey grey-ribboned soft hat.

The Haddock's mind wandered not in empty places, but wrestled sternly with the problem —*would* it not have been better, after all, perhaps, to have worn the pearly-grey spats (with the pearl buttons) instead of relying on the pearly-grey socks alone? When one sat down and modestly protruded an elegant foot as one crossed one's legs and gently drew up one's trouser (lest a baggy knee bring black shame), one could display both-the spat itself, *and*, above it, the sock. Of course! To the passer-by, awe-inspired, admiring, stimulated, would then have been administered the double shock and edification. While gratefully observing the so-harmonizing grey spat and grey shoe he would have noted the Ossa of grey silk sock piled upon that Pelion of ultra-fashionable foot-joy! Yes. He had acted hastily and had erred and strayed from the Perfect Way-and a cloud, at first no bigger than a continent or two, arose and darkened his mental sky.

But what of the cloud that settled upon him, black as that of the night's Plutonian shore, a cloud much bigger than the Universe, when a beastly, awful, ghastly, common private soldier arose from a seat —a common seat for which you do not pay a penny and show your selectitude- arose, I say, from a beastly common seat and SEIZED HIM BY THE ARM and remarked in horrible, affected, mocking tones: —

"And how's the charming little Haddock, the fourpenny, common breakfast Haddock?"

Yes, in full sight of the Leas of Folkestone, and the nobility, gentry, shopmen, nurse-girls, suburban yachtsmen, nuts, noisettes, bath-chairmen and all the world of rank and fashion, a common soldier took the pearly-grey arm of *the* Haddon Berners as he took the air and walked abroad to give the public a treat. And proved to be his shameful, shameless, disgraced, disgraceful, cowardly relative, Damocles de Warrenne!

The Haddock reeled, but did not fall.

On catching sight of the beautiful young man, Dam's first impulse was to spring up and flee, his second to complete the work of Mr. Levi Solomonson of the pier concert and see for himself, once again, how he was regarded by the eyes of all right-minded and respectable members of society, including those of a kinsman with whom he had grown up.

Yes, in his bitterness of soul, and foolish youthful revolt against Fate, he was attracted by the idea of claiming acquaintance with the superb Haddock in his triumphant progress, take him by the arm, and solemnly march him the whole length of the Leas! He would, by Jove! *He did*.

Confronting the resplendent languid loafer, he silkily observed, as he placed his cutting-whip beneath his left arm and extended his white cotton-gloved right hand: —

"And how's the charming little Haddock, the fourpenny, common breakfast Haddock?"

Had it been Ormonde Delorme, any friend of Monksmead days, any school or Sandhurst acquaintance, had it been any other relative, had it been Lucille, he would have fled for his life, he would have seen his hand paralysed ere he would have extended it, he would have been struck dumb rather than speak, he would have died before he would have inflicted upon them the indignity of being seen in the company of a common soldier. But the Haddock! 'twould do the Haddock a world of good; the Haddock who had mocked him as he fought for sanity and life on the lawn at Monksmead-the Haddock who "made love" to Lucille.

The Haddock affected not to see the hand.

"I —er-don't —ah-know you, surely, do I?" he managed to mumble as he backed away and turned to escape.

"Probably not, dear Haddock," replied the embittered desperate Dam, "but you're going to. We're going for a walk together."

"Are you-ah-dwunk, fellow? Do you suppose I walk with-ah —*soldiers?*"

"I don't, my Fish, but you're going to now-if I have to carry you. And if I have to do that I'll slap you well, when I put you down!"

"I'll call a policeman and give you in charge if you dare molest me. What do you-ah-desire? Money?... If you come to my hotel this evening —" and the hapless young man was swung round, his limp thin arm tucked beneath a powerful and mighty one, and he was whirled along at five miles an hour in the direction of the pier, gasping, feebly struggling, and a sight to move the High Gods to pity.

"To the pier, my Haddock, and then back to the turnpike gate, and if you let a yell, or signal a policeman, I'll twist your little neck. Fancy our Haddock in a vulgar street row with a common soldier and in the Police Court! Step it out, you worm!"

Then the agonized Haddock dropped pretence.

"Oh, Dam, I'm awf'ly sorry. I apologize, old chap. *Let up* —I say-this is *awful*.... Good God, here's Lady Plonk, the Mayor's wife!"

"You shall introduce me, Lovely One-but no, we mustn't annoy ladies. You must *not* go trying to introduce your low companions-nay, relations-to Lady Plonkses. Step out-and look happy."

"Dam-for God's sake, let me go! I didn't know you, old chap. I swear I didn't. The disgrace will kill me. I'll give you —"

"Look here, wee Fish, you offer me money again and I'll —I'll undress you and run away with your clothes. I will, upon my soul."

"I shall call to this policeman," gasped the Haddock.

"And appear with your low-class *relation* in Court? Not you, Haddock. I'd swear you were my twin brother, and that you wouldn't pay me the four pence you borrowed of me last week."

And the cruel penance was inflicted to the last inch. Near the end the Haddock groaned: "Here's Amelia Harringport-Oh! my God," and Dam quickly turned his face unto the South and gazed at the fair land of France. He remembered that General Harringport dwelt in these parts.

At the toll-gate Dam released the perspiration-soaked wretch, who had suffered the torments of the damned, and who seemed to have met every man and woman whom he knew in the world as he paraded the promenade hanging lovingly to the arm of a common soldier! He thought of suicide and shuddered at the bare idea.

"Well, I'm awf'ly sorry to have to run away and leave you now, dear Haddock. I might have taken you to all the pubs in Folkestone if I'd had time. I might have come to your hotel and dined with you. You *will* excuse me, won't you? I *must* go now. I've got to wash up the tea things and clean the Sergeant's boots," said Dam, cruelly wringing the Haddock's agonized soft hand, and, with a complete and disconcerting change, added, "And if you breathe a word about having seen me, at Monksmead, or tell Lucille, *I'll seek you out, my Haddock*, and-we will hold converse with thee". Then he strode away, cursing himself for a fool, a cad, and a deteriorated, demoralized ruffian. Anyhow, the Haddock would not mention the appalling incident and give him away.

Nemesis followed him.

Seeking a quiet shop in a back street where he could have the long-desired meal in private, he came to a small taxidermist's, glanced in as he passed, and beheld the pride and joy of the taxidermist's heart—a magnificent and really well-mounted boa-constrictor, and fell shrieking, struggling, and screaming in the gutter.

That night Damocles de Warrenne, ill, incoherent, and delirious, passed in a cell, on a charge of drunk and disorderly and disgracing the Queen's uniform.

Mr. Levi Solomonson had not disgraced it, of course.

"If we were not eating this excellent bread-and-dripping and drinking this vile tea, what would you like to be eating and drinking, Matthewson?" asked Trooper Nemo (formerly Aubrey Roussac d'Aubigny of Harrow and Trinity).

"Oh,... a little real turtle," said Dam, "just a lamina of *sole frite*, a trifle of *vol au vent à la financière*, a breast of partridge, a mite of *paté de fois gras*, a peach *à la Melba*, the roe of a bloater, and a few fat grapes —"

"'Twould do. 'Twould pass," sighed Trooper Burke, and added, "I would suggest a certain Moselle I used to get at the Byculla Club in Bombay, and a wondrous fine claret that spread a ruby haze of charm o'er my lunch at the Yacht Club of the same fair city. A *'Mouton Rothschild* something,' which was cheap at nine rupees a small bottle on the morrow of a good day on the Mahaluxmi Racecourse." (It was strongly suspected that Trooper Burke had worn a star on his shoulder-strap in those Indian days.)

"It's an awful shame we can't all emerge from the depths and run up to Town to breathe the sweet original atmosphere for just one night before we leave old England," put in Trooper Punch Peerson (son of a noble lord) who would at that moment have been in the Officers' Mess but for a congenital weakness in spelling and a dislike of mathematics. "Pity we can't get 'leaf,' and do ourselves glorious at the Carlton, and 'afterwards'. We could change at my Governor's place into borrowed, stolen, and hired evening-kit, paint the village as scarlet as Sin or a trooper's jacket, and then come home, like the Blackbird, to tea. I am going, and if I can't get 'leaf' I shall return under the bread in the rations-cart. Money's the root of all (successful) evil."

Trooper Punch Peerson was a born leader of men, a splendid horseman and soldier, and he had the Army in his ardent, gallant blood and bones; but how shall a man head a cavalry charge or win the love and enthusiastic obedience of men and horses when he is weak in spelling and has a dislike of mathematics?

However, he was determined to follow in the footsteps of his ancestors, to serve his country in spite of her, and his Commission was certain and near. Meanwhile he endeavoured to be a first-class trooper, had his uniform made of officers' materials in Bond Street by his father's famous tailor, and "got the stick" with ease and frequency.

"We're not all gilded popinjays (nor poppin' bottles)," observed a young giant who called himself Adam Goate, and had certainly been one in the days when he was Eugene Featherstonthwaite. "All very well for you to come to the surface and breathe, seeing that you'll be out of it soon. You're having nothing but a valuable experience and a hardening. You're going through the mill. We've got to *live* in it. What's the good of our stirring everything up again? Dam-silly of a skinned eel to grow another skin, to be skinned again.... No, 'my co-mates and brothers in exile,' what I say is—you can get just as drunk on 'four-'arf' as on champagne, and a lot cheaper. Ask my honourable friend, Bear."

(Trooper Bear gave a realistic, but musical hiccup.)

"Also, to the Philosopher, bread-and-dripping is as interesting and desirable prog as the voluble-varied heterogeny of the menu at the Carlton or the Ritz—'specially when you've no choice."

"Hear, hear," put in Dam.

"Goatey ol' Goate!" said Trooper Bear with impressive solemnity. "Give me your hand, Philossiler. I adore dripping. I'ss a (hic) mystery. (No, I don' want both hands," as Goate offered his right to Bear's warm embrace.) I'm a colliseur of Dripping. I understan' it. I write odes to it. Yesh. A basin of dripping is like a Woman. 'Strornarillily. You never know what's beneath fair surface.... Below a placid, level, unrevealing surface there may be-nothing...and there may be a rich deposit of glorious, stimulating, piquant *essence*."

"Oh, shut up, Bear, and don't be an Ass," implored Trooper Burke (formerly Desmond Villiers FitzGerald)..."but I admit, all the same, there's lots of worse prog in the Officers' Mess than a crisp crust generously bedaubed with the rich jellified gravy that (occasionally) lurks like rubies beneath the fatty soil of dripping."

"Sound plan to think so, anyway," agreed Trooper Little (*ci devant* Man About Town and the Honourable Bertie Le Grand). "Reminds me of a proverb I used to hear in Alt Heidelberg, 'What I have in my hand is best'."

"Qui' sho," murmured Trooper Bear with a seraphic smile, "an' wha' I have in my 'place of departed *spirits*,' my tummy, is better. Glor'us mixshure. Earned an honest penny sheven sheparate times cleaning the 'coutrements of better men...'an look at me for shevenpence' ..." and he slept happily on Dam's shoulder.

In liquor, Trooper Bear was, if possible, gentler, kinder, and of sweeter disposition than when sober; wittier, more hopelessly lovable and disarming. These eight men-the "gentlemen-rankers" of the Queen's Greys, made it a point of honour to out-Tommy "Tommy" as troopers, and, when in his company, to show a heavier cavalry-swagger, a broader accent, a quiffier "quiff," a cuttier cutty-pipe, a smarter smartness; to groom a horse better, to muck out a stall better, to scrub a floor better, to spring more smartly to attention or to a disagreeable "fatigue," and to set an example of Tomminess from turning out on an Inspection Parade to waxing a moustache.

Trooper Bear professed to specialize as a model in the carrying of liquor "like a man and a soldier". When by themselves, they made it a point of honour to behave and speak as though in the clubs to which they once belonged, to eat with washen hands and ordered attire, to behave at table and elsewhere with that truest of consideration that offends no man willingly by mannerism, appearance, word or act, and which is the whole Art of Gentility.

They carefully avoided any appearance of exclusiveness, but sought every legitimate opportunity of united companionship, and formed a "mess" of eight at a table which just held that number, and on a couple of benches each of which exactly fulfilled the slang expression "room for four Dragoons on a form".

It was their great ambition to avoid the reproach of earning the soubriquet "gentleman-ranker," a term that too often, and too justly, stinks in the nostrils of officer, non-commissioned officer, and man (for, as a rule, the "gentleman-ranker" is a complete failure as a gentleman and a completer one as a ranker).

To prove a rule by a remarkably fine exception, these eight were among the very smartest and best troopers of one of the smartest and best Corps in the world-and to Damocles de Warrenne, their "Society of the Knights of the dirty Square Table" was a Rock and a Salvation in the midst of a howling sea of misery —a cool pool in a searing branding Hell.

Trooper Bear's brief nap appeared to have revived him wonderfully.

"Let us, like the Hosts of Midian, prowl around this happy Sabbeth eve, my dear," quoth he to Dam, "and, like wise virgins, up and smite them, when we meet the Red-Caps.... No, I'm getting confused. It's they up and smite us, when we've nothing to tip them.... I feel I could be virtuous in your company-since you never offer beer to the (more or less) fatherless and widowed-and since I'm stony. How *did* you work that colossal drunk, Matty, when you came home on a stretcher and the Red-Caps said you '*was the first-classest delirious-trimmings as ever was, aseein' snakes somethink 'orrible,*' and in no wise to be persuaded '*as 'ow there wasn't one underyer bloomin' foot the 'ole time*'. Oh you teetotallers!"

Dam shuddered and paled. "Yes, let's go for as long a walk as we can manage, and get as far from this cursed place as time allows," he replied.

His hair was still short and horribly hacked from the prison-crop he had had as a preliminary to "168 hours cells," for "drunk and disorderly".

"I'll come too," announced the Honourable Bertie.

"Yes," chimed in Trooper Adam Goate, "let's go and gladden the eyes, if not the hearts of the nurse-maids of Folkestone."

"Bless their nurse-maidenly hearts," murmured Trooper Bear. "One made honourable proposals of marriage to me, quite recently, in return for my catching the runaway hat of her young charge.... Come on." And in due course the four derelicts set forth with a uniformity of step and action that corresponded with their uniformity of dress.

"Let's take the Lower Road," said Dam, as they reached the western limit of the front at Folkestone. "I fear we rather contaminate the pure social air of the Upper Road and the fashionable promenade."

"Where every prospect pleases and only man, in the Queen's uniform, is vile," observed Trooper Bear.

Dam remembered afterwards that it was he who sought the quiet Lower Road-and he had good reason to remember it. For suddenly, a fashionably dressed and beautiful young girl, sitting alone in a passing private victoria, stood up, called "Stop! Stop!" to the coachman, and ere the carriage well came to a standstill, sprang out, rushed up to the double file of soldiers, and flung her arms around the neck of the outside one of the front rank.

With a cry of "Oh, *Dam*! Oh, *Dammy!*"—a cry that mightily scandalized a serious-minded policeman who stood monumentally at the corner-she kissed him again and again!

Troopers Bear, Goate, and Little, halting not in their stride, glancing not unto the right hand nor unto the left hand, speaking no word, and giving no sign of surprise, marched on in perfect silence, until Trooper Bear observed to the world in general "The lady was *not* swearing. His *name* must be Dam-short for Damon or Pythias or Iphigenia or something which we may proceed to forget.... Poor old chappie-no wonder he's taking to secret drinking. *I* should drink, myself. *Poor* chap!" and Trooper Goate, heaving a sympathetic sigh, murmured also "Poor chap!"

But Trooper Little, once the Hon. Bertie Le Grand, thought "Poor *lady!*"

* * *

The heart of Damocles de Warrenne bounded within him, stood still, and then seemed like to burst.

"Oh, *Lucille*! Oh, darling!" he groaned, as he kissed her fiercely and then endeavoured to thrust her from him. "Jump into your carriage quickly. *Lucille* —Don't...*Here* ...! Not *here*.... People are looking... *You*...! A common soldier.... Let me go. Quick.... Your carriage.... Some one may —"

"Let you *go*, darling...! Now I have found you.... If you say another word I'll serve you as you served the Haddock. I'll hang on to your arm right along the Leas. I'll hang round your neck and scream if you try to run away. This is poetic justice, darling. Now you know how our Haddock felt. *No* —I *won't* leave go of your sleeve. Where shall we go, dearest darling Dammy. Dare you drive up and down the Front with me in Amelia Harringport's sister's young man's mother's victoria? oh, my *darling* Dam...." and Lucille burst into happy tears.

"Go up that winding path and I'll follow in a minute. There will be secluded seats."

"And you'll bolt directly I leave go of you?...I —"

"No, darling, God knows I should if I were a man, but I can't, *I can't*. Oh, Lucille!"

"Stay here," cried the utterly fearless, unashamed girl to the unspeakably astounded coachman of the mother of the minor Canon who had the felicity of being Amelia Harringport's sister's young man, and she strode up the pathway that wound, tree-shaded, along the front of the gently sloping cliff.

In the utter privacy of a small seat-enclosing, bush-hidden half-cave, Damocles de Warrenne crushed Lucille to his breast as she again flung her arms around his neck.

"Oh, Lucille, how *could* you expose yourself to scandal like that; I ought to be hung for not taking to my heels as you came, but I could not believe my eyes, I thought I was going mad again," and he shivered.

"What should I have cared if every soul in the world who knows me had arranged himself and herself in rows and ranks to get a good view? I'd have done the same if Grumper had been beside me in the carriage. What is the rest of the World to me, beside *you*, darling?... Oh, your *poor* hair, and what is that horrid scar, my dearest? And you are a '2 Q.G.' are you, and how soon may you marry? I'm going to disappear from Monksmead, now, just like you did, darling, and I'm coming here and I'm going to be a soldier's wife. Can I live with you in your house in barracks, Dammy, or must I live outside, and you come home directly your drill and things are finished?"

Dam groaned aloud in hopeless bitterness of soul.

"Lucille-listen," said he. "I earn one-and tuppence a day. I may not marry. If you were a factory-girl or a coster-woman I would not drag you down so. Apart from that, I am unfit to marry any decent woman. I am-what you know I am.... I have-fits. I am not-sound-normal—I may go m...."

"Don't be a pure priceless Ass, darling. You are my own splendid hero-and I am going to marry you, if I have to *be* a factory-girl or a coster-woman, and I am going to live either with you or near you. You want looking after, my own boy. I shall have some money, though, when I am of age. When may I run away from Monksmead, darling?"

"Lucille," groaned the miserable man. "Do you think that the sight of you in the mire in which I wallow would make me happier? Can't you realize that I'm ruined and done-disgraced and smashed? Lucille, I am not sane at times.... The SNAKE... *Do* you love me, Lucille? Then if so, I beg and implore you to forget me, to leave me alone, to wait awhile and then marry Delorme or some sane, wholesome *man* —who is neither a coward nor a lunatic nor an epileptic. Lucille, you double and treble my misery. I *can't* bear it if I see you. Oh, why didn't you forget me and do the right and proper thing? I am unfit to touch you! I am a damned scoundrel to be here now," and leaping up he fled like a maddened horse, bounded down the slope, sprang into the road, nor ceased to run till he fell exhausted, miles away from the spot whereon he had suffered as he believed few men had done before.

    And thus and thus we women live!
    With none to question, none to give
    The Nay or Aye, the Aye or Nay
    That might smoothe half our cares away.
    O, strange indeed! And sad to know
    We pitch too high and doing so,
    Intent and eager not to fall,
    We miss the low clear note of call.
    Why is it so? Are we indeed
    So like unto the shaken reed?
    Of such poor clay? Such puny strength?
    That e'en throughout the breadth and length
    Of purer vision's stern domain
    We bend to serve and serve in vain?
    To some, indeed, strange power is lent
    To stand content. Love, heaven-sent,
    (For things or high or pure or rare)
    Shows likest God, makes Life less bare.
    And, ever and anon there stray
    In faint far-reaching virèlay
    The songs of angels, Heav'nward-found,
    Of little children, earthward-bound.

Chapter X
Much Ado About Almost Nothing —a Trooper

Mr. Ormonde Delorme, Second Lieutenant of the 34th Lancers, sat in his quarters at Aldershot, reading and re-reading with mingled feelings a letter from the woman he loved.

It is one thing to extract a promise from The Woman that she will turn to you for help if ever your help should be needed (knowing that there could be no greater joy than to serve her at any cost whatsoever, though it led to death or ruin), but it is quite another thing when that help is invited for the benefit of the successful rival!

To go to the world's end for Lucille were a very small matter to Ormonde Delorme-but to go across the road for the man who had won her away, was not.

For Dam *had* won her away from him, Delorme considered, inasmuch as he had brought him to Monksmead, time after time, had seen him falling in love with Lucille, had received his confidences, and spoken no warning word. Had he said but "No poaching, Delorme," nothing more would have been necessary; he would have kept away thenceforth, and smothered the flame ere it became a raging and consuming fire. No, de Warrenne had served him badly in not telling him plainly that there was an understanding between him and his cousin, in letting him sink more and more deeply over head and ears in love, in letting him go on until he proposed to Lucille and learnt from her that while she liked him better than any man in the world but one-she did not love him, and that, frankly, yes, she *did* love somebody else, and it was hopeless for him to hope....

He read the letter again: —

"My Dear Ormonde,

"This is a begging letter, and I should loathe to write it, under the circumstances, to any man but such a one as you. For I am going to ask a great deal of you and to appeal to that nobleness of character for which I have always admired you and which made you poor Dam's hero from Lower School days at Wellingborough until you left Sandhurst (and, alas! quarrelled with him-or rather with his memory-about me). That was a sad blow to me, and I tell you again as I told you before, Dam had not the faintest notion that *I* cared for *him* and would not have told me that he cared for me had I not shown it. Your belief that he didn't trouble to warn you because he had me safe is utterly wrong, absurd, and unjust.

"When you did me the great honour and paid me the undeserved and tremendous compliment of asking me to marry you, and I told you that I could not, and *why* I could not, I never dreamed that Dam could care for me in that way, and I knew that I should never marry any one at all unless he did.

"And on the same occasion, Ormonde, you begged me to promise that if ever you could serve me in any way, I would ask for your help. You were a dear romantic boy then, Ormonde, and I loved you in a different way, and cried all night that you and I could not be friends without thought of love, and I most solemnly promised that I would turn to you if I ever needed help that you could give. (Alas, I thought to myself then that nobody in the world could do anything for me that Dam could not do, and that I should never need help from others while he lived.)

"I want your help, Ormonde, and I want it for Dam-and me.

"You have, of course, heard some garbled scandal about his being driven away from home and cut off from Sandhurst by grandfather. I need not ask if you have believed ill of him and I need not say he is absolutely innocent of any wrong or failure whatever. He is *not* an effeminate coward, he is as brave as a lion. He is a splendid hero, Ormonde, and I want you to simply strangle and kill any man who says a word to the contrary.

"When he left home, he enlisted, and Haddon Berners saw him in uniform at Folkestone where he had gone from Canterbury (cricket week) to see Amelia Harringport's gang. Amelia whose sister is to be the Reverend Mrs. Canon Mellifle at Folkestone, you know, met the wretched Haddon being rushed along the front by a soldier and nearly died at the sight-she declares he was weeping!

"Directly she told me I guessed at once that he had met Dam and either insulted or cut him, and that poor Dam, in his bitter humour and self-loathing had used his own presence as a punishment and had made the Haddock walk with him! Imagine the company of Damocles de Warrenne being anything but an ennobling condescension! Fancy Dam's society a horrible injury and disgrace! To a thing like Haddon Berners!

"Well, I simply haunted Folkestone after that, and developed a love for Amelia Harringport and her brothers that surprised them-hypocrite that I am! (but I was punished when they talked slightingly of Dam and she sneered at the man whom she had shamelessly pursued when all was well with him. She 'admires' Haddon now.)

"At last I met him on one of my week-end visits-on a Sunday evening it was-and I simply flew at him in the sight of all respectable, prayer-book-displaying, before-Church-parading, well-behaved Folkestone, and kissed him nearly to death.... And can you believe a woman could be such a *fool*, Ormonde-while carefully noting the '2 Q.G.' on his shoulder-straps, I never thought to find out his *alias* —for of course he hides his identity, thinking as he does, poor darling boy, that he has brought eternal disgrace on an honoured name —a name that appears twice on the rolls of the V.C. records.

"Ormonde, were it not that it would *increase* his misery and agony of mind I would run away from Monksmead, take a room near the Queen's Greys barracks, and haunt the main gates until I saw him again. He should then tell me how to communicate with him, or I would hang about there till he did. I'd marry him 'off the strength' and live (till I am 'of age') by needlework if he would have me. But, of course, he'd *never* understand that I'd be happier, and a better woman, in a Shorncliffe lodging, as a soldier's wife, than ever I shall be here in this dreary Monksmead-until he is restored and re-habilitated (is that the word? I mean-comes into his own as a brave and noble gentleman who never did a mean or cowardly action in his life).

"And he is *so* thin and unhappy looking, Ormonde, and his poor hands are in such a state and his beautiful hair is all hacked about and done like a soldier's, all short except for a long piece brushed down his forehead and round to his cap-oh, dreadful...and he has a scar on his face! No wonder Amelia never recognized him. Oh, *do* help me, Ormonde. I *must* find out how to address him. I dare not let them know there is a *D. de Warrenne* in the regiment-and he'd never get it either-he's probably Smith or Jones or Robinson now. If some horrid Sergeant called out 'Trooper D. de Warrenne,' when distributing letters, Dam would never answer to the name he thinks he has eternally disgraced, and disgrace it further by dragging it in the mire of the ranks. How *can* people be such snobs? Isn't a good private a better man than a bad officer? Why should there be any 'taint' about serving your country in any capacity?

"How *can* I find him, Ormonde, unless you help me? I could pay a servant to hang about the barracks until he recognized Dam-but that would be horrible for the poor boy. He'd deny it and say the man was mad, I expect-and it would be most unpleasant and unfair to Dam to set some one to find out from his comrades what he calls himself. If he chooses to hide from what he thinks is the chance of further disgracing his people, and suffers what he does in order to remain hidden, shall *I* be the one to do anything to show him up and cause him worse suffering-expose him to a servant?

"How *can* I get him a letter that shall not have his name on it? If I wrote to his Colonel or the Adjutant and enclosed a letter with just 'Dam' on it they'd not know for whom it was meant-and I dare not tell them his real name.

"Could you get a letter to him, Ormonde, without letting him know that you know he is a private soldier, and without letting a soul know his real name?

"I do apologize for the length of this interminable letter, but if you only knew the *relief* it is to me to be doing something that may help him, and to be talking, or rather writing about him, you would forgive me.

"His name must not be mentioned here. Think of it!

"Oh, if it only would not make him *more* unhappy, I would go to him this minute, and refuse ever to leave him again.

"Does that sound unmaidenly, Ormonde? I don't care whether it does or not, nor whether it *is* or not. I love him, and he loves me. I am his *friend*. Could I stay here in luxury if it would make him happier to marry me? Am I a terribly abandoned female? I told Auntie Yvette just what I had done, and though it simply saved her life to know he had not committed suicide (I believe she *worshipped* father) —she seemed mortally shocked at me for behaving so. I am not a bit ashamed though. Dam is more important than good form, and I had to show him in the strongest possible way that he was dearer to me than ever. If it *was* 'behaving like a servant-girl' —all honour to servant-girls, I think...considering the circumstances. You should have seen his face before he caught sight of me. Yes —*and* after, too. Though really I think he suffered more from my kissing him-in uniform, in the street-than if I had cut him. It would be only for the minute though... it *must* comfort him *now*, and always, to think that I love him so (since he loves *me* —and always has done). But what I must know before I can sleep peacefully again is the name by which he goes in the '2 Q.G's.,' so that I can write and comfort him regularly, send him things, and make him buy himself out when he sees he has been foolish and wicked in supposing that he has publicly disgraced himself and his name and us. And I'm going to make Grandfather's life a misery, and go about skinny and ragged and weeping, and say: '*This* is how you treat the daughter of your dead friend, you wicked, cruel, unjust old man,' until he relents and sends for Dam and gets him into the Army properly.... But I am afraid Dam will think it his silly duty to flee from me and all my works, and hide himself where the names of de Warrenne and Stukeley are unknown and cannot be disgraced.

"I rely on you, Ormonde,

"Your ashamed grateful friend,

"Lucille Gavestone."

Second Lieutenant Delorme rang the bell.

"Bradshaw," he said, as his soldier-servant appeared. "And get me a telegraph form."

"Yussir," said Private Billings, and marched to the Mess ante-room purposefully, with hope in his heart that Mr. Delorme 'ad nothink less than a 'alf dollar for the telegram and would forgit to arx for the chainge, as was his occasional praiseworthy procedure.

Mr. Delorme, alas, proved to have a mean and vulgar shilling, the which he handed to Private Billings with a form containing the message: —

"Can do. So cheer up. Writing his adjutant, pal of mine. Coming over Saturday if get leave. Going Shorncliffe if necessary. Leave due. Dam all right. Will blow over. Thanks for letting me help."

"'Fraid they don' give no tick at the Telegraft Orfis, Sir," observed Private Billings, who, as quondam "trained observer" of his troop, had noted the length of the telegram and the shortness of the allowance therefor.

"What the deuce...?"

"This is more like a 'alf-dollar job, Sir," he groaned, waving the paper, "wot wiv' the haddress an' all."

"Oh-er-yes, bit thick for a bob, perhaps; here's half a sov...."

"*That's* more like "*Eres to yer*,' Mr. D——" remarked the good man-outside the door. "And don't yer werry about trifles o' chainge. Be a gent!"

* * *

Lucille read and re-read the telegram in many ways.

"Can do so. Cheer up. Writing his adjutant. Pal of mine coming over Saturday. If get leave going Shorncliffe if necessary leave due Dam. All right will blow over thanks." No, *that* wouldn't do.

(What a pity people *would* not remember when writing telegrams that the stops and capitals they put are ignored by the operators.)

At last, the wish being father to the thought, she decided it to be "Can do" (she knew that to be a navy expression). "So cheer up. Writing. His adjutant a pal of mine. Coming over Saturday if I get leave. Going Shorncliffe if necessary. Leave due. Dam all right. Will blow over. Thanks for letting me help." Which was not far wrong.

Dear old Ormonde! She knew he would not fail her-although he had been terribly cut up by her rejection of his suit and by his belief that Dam had let him haunt her in the knowledge that she was his own private property, secured to him.

* * *

Having dispatched his telegram and interviewed his Adjutant, Captain, and Colonel, Mr. Delorme sat him down and wrote to Lieutenant the Honourable Reginald Montague Despencer, Adjutant of the Queen's Greys:—

"My Dear Monty,

"At the Rag. the other day, respectfully dining with my respected parent, I encountered, respectfully dining with his respected parent, your embryo Strawberry Leaf, old 'Punch Peerson'. (Do you remember his standing on his head on the engine at Blackwater Station when he was too 'merry' to be able to stand steady on his feet?) I learnt that he is still with you and I want him to do something for me. He'll be serious about it if *you* speak to him about it-and I am writing to him direct. I'm going to send you a letter (under my cover), and on it will be one word 'Dam' (on the envelope, of course). I want you to give this to Punch and order him to show it privately to the *gentlemen-rankers* of the corps till one says he recognizes the force of the word (pretty forceful, too, what!) and the writing. To this chap he is to give it. Be good to your poor 'rankers,' Monty, I know one damned hard case among them. No fault of *his*, poor chap. I could say a lot-surprise you-but I mustn't. It's awfully good of you, old chap. I know you'll see it through. It concerns as fine a gentleman as ever stepped and *the* finest woman!

"Ever thine,

"O. Delorme."

"Look here, my lambs-or rather, Black Sheep," quoth Trooper Punch Peerson one tea-time to Troopers Bear, Little, Goate, Nemo, Burke, Jones, and Matthewson, "I suppose none of you answers to the name of '*Dam*'?"

No man answered, and Trooper Peerson looked at the face of no man, nor any one at any other.

"No. I thought not. Well, I have a letter addressed in that objurgatory term, and I am going to place it beneath my pillow before I go out to-night. If it is there when I come in I'll destroy it unopened. 'Nuff said,' as the lady remarked when she put the mop in her husband's mouth. Origin of the phrase 'don't chew the mop,' I should think," and he babbled on, having let his unfortunate friends know that for one of them he had a letter which might be received by the addressed without the least loss of his anonymity.

Dam's heart beat hard and seemed to swell to bursting. He felt suffocated.

"Quaint superscription," he managed to observe. "How did you come by it?" and then wished he had not spoken.... Who but the recipient could be interested in its method of delivery? If anyone suspected him of being "Dam" would they not at once connect him with the notorious Damocles de Warrenne, ex-Sandhurst cadet, proclaimed coward and wretched neurotic decadent before the pained, disgusted eyes of his county, kicked out by his guardian...a disgrace to two honoured names...."The Adjer handed it over. Thought *I* was the biggest Damn here, I suppose," Trooper Peerson replied without looking up from his plate. "Practical silly joke I should think. No one here with such a l_oath_some, name as *Dam*, of course," but Trooper Punch Peerson had his philosophic "doots". He, like others of that set, had heard of a big chap who was a marvel at Sandhurst with the gloves, sword, horse, and other things, and who had suddenly and marvellously disappeared into thin air leaving no trace behind him, after some public scandal or other.... But that was no concern of Trooper Punch Peerson, gentleman....

With a wary eye on Peerson, Dam lay on his bed, affecting to read a stale and dirty news-sheet. He saw him slip something beneath his pillow and swagger out of the barrack-room. Anon no member of the little band of gentleman-rankers was left. Later, the room was empty, save for a heavily snoring drunkard and a busy polisher who, at the shelf-table at the far end of the room, laboured on his jack-boots, hissing the while, like a groom with a dandy-brush.

Going to Peerson's bed, Dam snatched the letter, returned to his own, and flung himself down again-his heart pumping as though he had just finished a mile race. *Lucille had got a letter to him somehow.* Lucille was not going to drop him yet-in spite of having seen him a red-handed, crop-haired, "quiff"-wearing, coarse-looking soldier.... Was there another woman in the world like Lucille? Would any other girl have so risen superior to her breeding, and the teachings of Miss Smellie, as to do what she thought right, regardless of public scandal...? But he must not give her the opportunity of being seen talking to a soldier again-much less kissing one. Not that she would want to kiss him again like that. That was the kiss of welcome, of encouragement, of proof that she was unchanged to him-her first sight of him after the *débâcle*. It was the unchecked impulse of a noble heart-and the action showed that Miss Smellie had been unable to do it much harm with her miserable artificialities and stiflings of all that is natural and human and right.... Should he read the letter at once or treasure it up and keep it as a treat in store? He would hold it in his hand unopened and imagine its contents. He would spin out the glorious pleasure of possession of an unopened letter from Lucille. He could, of course, read it hundreds of times-but he would then soon know it by heart, and although its charm and value would be no less, it would merge with his other memories and become a memory itself. He did not want it to become a memory too soon.

The longer it remained an anticipation, the more distant the day when it became a memory....

With a groan of "Oh, my brain's softening and I'm becoming a sentimentalist," he opened the letter and read Lucille's loving, cheering-yet agonizing, maddening-words: —

"My Own Darling Dam,

"If this letter reaches you safely you are to sit down at once and write to me to tell me how to address you by post in the ordinary way. If you don't I shall come and haunt the entrance to the Lines and waylay you. People will think I am a poor soul whom you have married and deserted, or whom you won't marry. *I'll* show up your wicked cruelty to a poor girl! How would you like your comrades to say 'Look out, Bill, your pore wife's 'anging about the gates' and to have to lie low-and send out scouts to see if the coast was clear later on? Don't you go playing fast and loose with *me*, master Dam, winning my young affections, making love to me, kissing me-and then refusing to marry me after it all! I don't want to be too hard on you (and I am reasonable enough to admit that one-and-two a day puts things on a smaller scale than I have been accustomed to in the home of my fathers-or rather uncles, or perhaps uncles-in-law), and like the kind Tailor whom the Haddock advertises (and like the unkind Judge before whom he'll some day come for something) I will 'give you time'. But it's only a respite, Mr. de Warrenne. You are not going to trifle with my young feelings and escape altogether. I have my eye on you-and if I respect your one-and-twopence a day *now*, it is on the clear understanding that you share my Little All on the day I come of age. I will trust you once more, although you *have* treated me so-bolting and hiding from your confiding fiancée.

"So write and tell me what you call yourself, so that I can write to you regularly and satisfy myself that you are not escaping me again. How *could* you treat a poor trusting female so-and then when she had found you again, and was showing her delight and begging to be married and settled in life-to rush away from her, leaving her and her modest matrimonial proposals scorned and rejected! For shame, Sir! I've a good mind to come and complain to your Colonel and ask him to make you keep your solemn promises and marry me....

"Now look here, darling, nonsense aside —I solemnly swear that if you don't buy yourself out of the army on the day I come of age (or before, if you will, and can) I will really come and make you marry me and I will live with you as a soldier's wife. If you persist in your wrong-headed notion of being a 'disgrace' (*you*!) then we'll just adopt the army as a career, and we'll go through all the phases till you get a Commission. I hope you won't take this course-but if you do, you'll be a second Hector Macdonald and retire as Lieutenant-General Sir Damocles de Warrenne (K.C.B., K.C.M.G., K.C.S.I., D.S.O., and, of course, V.C.), having confessed to an *alias*. It will be a long time before we should be in really congenial society, that way, darling, but I'm sure I should enjoy every hour of it with you, so long as I felt I was a comfort and happiness to you. And when you got your Commission I should not be a social drag upon you as sometimes happens. Nor before it should I be a nuisance and hindrance to you and make you wish you were 'shut of the curse of a soldier'. I could 'rough it' as well as you and, besides, there would *be* no 'roughing it' where you were, for me. It is *here* that I am 'roughing it,' sitting impotent and wondering what is happening to you, and whether that terrible illness ever seizes you, and whether you are properly looked after when it does.

"Now, just realize, dearest Dam —I said I would wait twenty years for you, if necessary. I would and I will, but don't make me do it, darling. Realize how happy I should be if I could only come and sew and cook and scrub and work for you. Can you understand that life is only measurable in terms of happiness and that *my* happiness can only be where *you*, are? If you weren't liable to these seizures I could bear to wait, but as it is, I can't. I beg and beseech you not to make me wait till I am of age, Dam. There's no telling what may happen to you and I just can't bear it. *I'm coming*, if I don't hear from you, and I can easily do something to compel you to marry me, if I come. You are *not* going to bear this alone, darling, so don't imagine it. We're not going to keep separate shops after all these years, just because you're ill with a trouble of some kind that fools can't understand.

"Now write to me at once and put me in a position to write to you in the ordinary way-or look out for me! I'm all ready to run away, all sorts of useful things packed-ready to come and be a soldier's girl.

"You know that I *do* what I think I'll do-you spoke of my 'steel-straight directness and sweet brave will' in the poem you were making about me, you poor funny old boy, when you vanished, and which I found in your room when I went there to cry, (Oh, *how* I cried when I found your odds and ends of verse about me there —I really did think my heart was 'broken' in actual fact.) Don't make me suffer any more, darling. I'm sure your Colonel will be sweet about it and give us a nice little house all to ourselves, now he has seen what a splendid soldier you are. If you stick to your folly about 'disgrace' I need not tell him our names and Grumper couldn't take me away from you, even if he ever found out where we were.

"I could go on writing all night, darling, but I'll only just say again *I am going to marry you and take care of you, Dam, in the army or out of it.*

"Your fiancee and friend,

"Lucille Gavestone."

Dam groaned aloud.

"Four o' rum 'ot, is wot *you* want, mate, for that," said the industrious self-improver at the shelf-table. "Got a chill on yer stummick on sentry-go in the fog an' rine las' night.... I'd give a 'ogs'ead to see the bloke who wrote in the bloomin' Reggilashuns *'nor must bloomin' sentries stand in their blasted sentry-boxes in good or even in moderate-weather'* a doin' of it 'isself in 'is bloomin' 'moderate weather' with water a runnin' down 'is back, an' 'is feet froze into a puddle, an' the fog a chokin' of 'im, an' 'is blighted carbine feelin' like a yard o' bad ice-an' then find the bloomin' winder above 'is bed been opened by some kind bloke an' 'is bed a blasted swamp...Yus-you 'ave four o' rum 'ot and you'll feel like the bloomin' 'Ouse o' Lords. Then 'ave a Livin'stone Rouser." "Oh, shut up," said Dam, cursing the Bathos of Things and returning to the beginning of Lucille's letter.

* * *

In his somewhat incoherent reply, Dam assured Lucille that he was in the rudest health and spirits, and the particular pet of his Colonel who inquired after his health almost daily with tender solicitude; that he had exaggerated his feeling on That Evening when he had kissed Lucille as a lover, and begged forgiveness; that marriage would seriously hamper a most promising military career; that he had had no recurrence of the "fit" (a mere touch of sun); that it would be unkind and unfair of Lucille to bring scandal and disgrace upon a rising young soldier by hanging about the Lines and making inquiries about him with a view to forcing him into marriage, making him keep to a bargain made in a rash, unguarded moment of sentimentality; that, in any case, soldiers could not marry until they had a certain income and status, and, if they did so, it was no marriage and they were sent to jail; that his worst enemy would not do anything to drag him out once again into the light of publicity, and disgrace his family further, now that he had effectually disappeared and was being forgotten; and that he announced that he was known as Trooper Matthewson (E Troop, The Queen's Greys, Cavalry Lines, Shorncliffe) to prevent Lucille from keeping her most unladylike promise of persecuting him.

Lucille's next letter was shorter than the first.

"My Darling Dam,

"Don't be such a *priceless* Ass. Come off it.
"Your own

"Lucille

"P.S.—Write to me properly at once-or expect me on Monday."

He obeyed, poured out his whole heart in love and thanks and blessings, and persuaded her that the one thing that could increase his misery would be her presence, and swore that he would strain every nerve to appear before her at the earliest possible moment a free man with redeemed name-provided he could persuade himself he was not *a congenital lunatic, an epileptic, a decadent-could cure himself of his mental disease....*

Chapter XI
More Myrmidons

The truly busy man cannot be actively and consciously unhappy. The truly miserable and despondent person is never continuously and actively employed. Fits of deep depression there may be for the worker when work is impossible, but, unless there be mental and physical illness, sleep is the other anaesthetic, refuge-and reward.

The Wise thank God for Work and for Sleep-and pay large premia of the former as Insurance in the latter.

To Damocles de Warrenne-to whom the name "Trooper Matthewson" now seemed the only one he had ever had-the craved necessity of life and sanity was *work*, occupation, mental and physical labour. He would have blessed the man who sentenced him to commence the digging of a trench ten miles long and a yard deep for morning and evening labour, and to take over all the accounts of each squadron, for employment in the heat of the day. There was no man in the regiment so indefatigable, so energetic, so persevering, so insatiable of "fatigues," so willing and anxious to do other people's duty as well as his own, so restless, so untiring as Trooper Matthewson of E Troop. For Damocles de Warrenne was in the Land of the Serpent and lived in fear. He lived in fear and feared to live; he thought of Fear and feared to think. He turned to work as, but for the memory of Lucille, he would have turned to drink: he laboured to earn deep dreamless sleep and he dreaded sleep. Awake, he could drug himself with work; asleep, he was the prey-the bound, gagged helpless, abject prey-of the Snake. The greediest glutton for work in the best working regiment in the world was Trooper Matthewson-but for him was no promotion. He was, alas, "unreliable" —apt to be "drunk and disorderly," drunk to the point of "seeing snakes" and becoming a weeping, screaming lunatic —a disgusting spectacle. And, when brought up for sentence, would solemnly assure the Colonel that he was *a total abstainer*, and stick to it when "told-off" for adding impudent lying to shameful indulgence and sickening behaviour. No promotion for that type of waster while Colonel the Earl of A——— commanded the Queen's Greys, nor while Captain Daunt commanded the squadron the trooper occasionally disgraced.

But he had his points, mark you, and it was a thousand pities that so fine a soldier was undeniably subject to attacks of *delirium tremens* and unmistakeably a secret drinker who might at any time have a violent outburst, finishing in screams, sobs, and tears. A *most* remarkable case! Who ever heard of a magnificent athlete-regimental champion boxer and swordsman, admittedly as fine and bold a horseman and horse-master as the Rough-Riding Sergeant-Major or the Riding-Master himself-being a sufficiently industrious secret-drinker to get "goes" of "d.t.," to drink till he behaved like some God-and-man-forsaken wretch that lives on cheap gin in a chronic state of alcoholism. He had his points, and if the Brigadier had ever happened to say to the Colonel: "Send me your smartest, most intelligent, and keenest man to gallop for me at the manoeuvres," or the Inspector of Army Gymnasia had asked for the regiment's finest specimen, or if one representative private soldier had to be sent somewhere to uphold the credit and honour of the Queen's Greys, undoubtedly Trooper Matthewson would have been chosen.

What a splendid squadron-sergeant major, regimental sergeant-major, yea, what a fine officer he would have made, had he been reliable. But there, you can't have an officer, nor a non-com., either, who lies shrieking and blubbering on the floor *coram publico*, and screams to God and man to save him from the snakes that exist only in his own drink-deranged mind. For of course it can only be Drink that produces "Snakes"! Yes, it is only through the ghastly alcohol-tinted glasses that you can "see snakes" —any fool knows *that*.

And the fools of the Queen's Greys knew it, and hoped to God that Matthewson would "keep off it" till after the Divisional Boxing Tournament and Assault-at-Arms, for, if he did, the Queen's Greys would certainly have the Best Man-at-Arms in the Division and have a mighty good shot at having the Heavy-Weight All-India Champion, since Matthewson had challenged the Holder and held an absolutely unbroken record of victories in the various regimental and inter-regimental boxing tournaments in which he had taken part since joining the regiment. And he had been "up against some useful lads" as Captain Chevalier, the president and Maecenas of the Queen's Greys' boxing-club, expressed it. Yes, Matthewson had his points and the man who brought the Regiment the kudos of having best Man-at-Arms and Heavy-Weight Champion of India would be forgiven a lot.

And Damocles de Warrenne blessed the Divisional Boxing Tournament, Assault-at-Arms, and, particularly, the All-India Heavy-Weight Championship.

Occupation, labour, anodyne.... Work and deep Sleep. Fighting to keep the Snake at bay. No, fighting to get away from it-there was no keeping it at bay-nothing but shrieking collapse when It came....

From parade ground to gymnasium, from gymnasium to swimming-bath, from swimming-bath to running-track, from running-track to boxing-ring, from boxing-ring to gymnasium again. Work, occupation, forgetfulness. Forget the Snake for a little while-even though it is surely lurking near-waiting, waiting, waiting; nay, even beneath his very foot and *moving*....

Well, a man can struggle with himself until the Thing actually appears in the concrete, and he goes mad-but Night! Oh, God grant deep sleep at night-or wide wakefulness *and a light*. Neither Nightmare nor wakefulness *in the dark*, oh, Merciful God.

Yes, things were getting worse. *He was going mad.* MAD. Desert-and get out of India somehow?

Never! No gentleman "deserts" anything or anybody.

Suicide-and face God unafraid and unashamed?

Never! The worst and meanest form of "deserting".

No. Stick it. And live to work-work to live. And strive and strive and strive to obliterate the image of Lucille-that sorrow's crown of sorrow.

And so Trooper Matthewson's course of training was a severe one and he appeared to fear rest and relaxation as some people fear work and employment.

His favourite occupation was to get the ten best boxers of the regiment to jointly engage in a ten-round contest with him, one round each. He would frequently finish fresher than the tenth man. Coming of notedly powerful stock on both sides, and having been physically *educated* from babyhood, Dam, with clean living and constant training, was a very uncommon specimen. There may have been one or two other men in the regiment as well developed, or nearly so; but when poise, rapidity, and skill were taken into account there was no one near him. Captain Chevalier said he was infinitely the quickest heavy-weight boxer he had ever seen-and Captain Chevalier was a pillar of the National Sporting Club and always knew the current professionals personally when he was in England. In fact, with the enormous strength of the best heavy-weight, Dam combined the lightning rapidity and mobility of the best feather-weight.

His own doubt as to the result of his contest with the heavy-weight Champion of India arose from the fact that the latter was a person of much lower nervous development, a creature far less sensitive to shock, a denser and more elementary organism altogether, and possessed of a far thicker skull, shorter jaw, and thicker neck. Dam summed him up thus with no sense of contemptuous superiority, but with a plain recognition of the facts that the Champion was a fighting machine, a dull, foreheadless, brutal gladiator who owed his championship very largely to the fact that he was barely sensible to pain, and impervious to padded blows. It was said that he had never been knocked out in all his boxing-career, that the kick of a horse on his chin would not knock him out, that his head was solid bone, and that the shortness of his jaw and thickness of his neck absolutely prevented sufficient leverage between the point of the jaw and the spinal cord for the administration of the shock to the *medulla oblongata* that causes the necessary ten-seconds' unconsciousness of the "knock-out".

He was known as the Gorilla by reason of his long arms, incredible strength, beauty, and pleasing habits, and he bore the reputation of a merciless and unchivalrous opponent and one who needed the strictest and most experienced refereeing. It would be a real terrific fight, and that was the main thing to Dam, though he would do his very utmost to win, for the credit of the Queen's Greys, and would leave no stone unturned to that end. He regretted that he could not get leave and go to Pultanpur to see the Champion box, and learn something of his style and methods when easily defending his title in the Pultanpur tournament. And when the Tournament and Assault-at-Arms were over he must find something else to occupy him by day and tire him before night. Meanwhile life was bearable, with the fight to come-except for sentry-go work. That was awful, unspeakable, and each time was worse than the last. Sitting up all night in the guard-room under the big lamp, and perhaps with some other wakeful wretch to talk to, was nothing. That was well enough-but to be on a lonely post on a dark night... well-he couldn't do it much longer.

Darkness and the Snake that was always coming and never came! To prowl round and round some magazine, store, or boundary-stone with his carbine at the "support," or to tramp up and down by the horse-lines, armed only with his cutting-whip; to stand in a sentry-box while the rain fell in sheets and there was no telling what the next flash of lightning might reveal-that was what would send him to a lunatic's padded cell.

To see the Snake by day would give him a cruel, terrible fit-but to be aware of it in the dark would be final-and fatal to his reason (which was none too firmly enthroned). No, he had the dreadful feeling that his reason was none too solidly based and fixed. He had horrible experiences, apart from the snake-nightmares, nowadays. One night when he awoke and lay staring up at his mosquito-curtain in the blessed light of the big room-lamp (always provided in India on account of rifle thieves) he had suddenly felt an overwhelming surge of fear. He sat up. God!—he was in a marble box! These white walls and roof were not mosquito-netting, they were solid marble! He was in a tomb. He was buried alive. The air was growing foul. His screams would be absolutely inaudible. He screamed, and struck wildly at the cold cruel marble, and found it was soft, yielding netting after all. But it was a worse horror to find that he had thought it marble than if he had found it to be marble. He sprang from his cot.

"I am going mad," he cried.

"Goin'?... *Gorn*, more like," observed the disrobing room-corporal. "Why donchew keep orf the booze, Maffewson? You silly gapin' goat. Git inter bed and shut yer 'ead-or I'll get yew a night in clink, me lad-and wiv'out a light, see?"

Corporal Prag knew his victim's little weakness and grinned maliciously as Dam sprang into bed without a word.

The Stone Jug without a gleam of light! Could a man choke himself with his own fingers if the worst came to the worst? The Digger and Stygian darkness-now —*when he was going mad*! Men could not be so cruel.... But they'd say he was drunk. He would lie still and cling with all his strength and heart and soul to sanity. He would think of That Evening with Lucille-and of her kisses. He would recite the Odes of Horace, the Aeneid, the Odyssey as far as he could remember them, and then fall back on Shakespeare and other English poets. Probably he knew a lot more Greek and Latin poetry (little as it was) than he did of English....

Corporal Prag improved the occasion as he unlaced his boots. "Bloomin' biby! Afraid o' the dark! See wot boozin' brings yer to. Look at yer! An' look at *me*. Non-c'misshn'd orficer in free an' a 'arf years from j'inin'. Never tasted alc'ol in me life, an' if any man offud me a glarse, d'ye know what I'd *dew*?"

"No, Corporal, I'd like to hear," replied Dam. (Must keep the animal talking as long as possible for the sake of human company. He'd go mad at once, perhaps, when the Corporal went to bed.)

"I'd frow it strite in 'is faice, I would," announced the virtuous youth. A big boot flopped heavily on the floor.

"I daresay you come of good old teetotal stock," observed Dam, to make conversation. Perhaps the fellow would pause in his assault upon the other boot and reply-so lengthening out the precious minutes of diversion. Every minute was a minute nearer dawn....

"*Do* yer? Well, you're bloomin' well wrong, Maffewson, me lad. My farver 'ad a bout every Saturday arternoon and kep' it up all day a Sund'y, 'e did-an' in the werry las' bout 'e ever 'ad 'e bashed 'is ole woman's 'ead in wiv' a bottle."

"And was hanged?" inquired Dam politely and innocently, but most tactlessly.

"Mind yer own b — — business," roared Corporal Prag. "Other people's farvers wasn't gallows-birds if yourn was. 'Ow'd you look if I come and punched you on the nose, eh? Wot 'ud you do if I come an' set abaht yer, eh?"

"Break your neck," replied Dam tersely.

"Ho, yus. *And* wot 'ud yew say when I calls the guard and they frows you into clink? Without no light, Trooper Maffewson!"

Dam shuddered.

Corporal Prag yet further improved the occasion, earning Dam's heartfelt blessing.

"Don't you fergit it, Trooper Maffewson. I'm yore sooperier orficer. You *may* be better'n me in the Ring, praps, or with the sword (Dam could have killed him in five minutes, with or without weapons), but if I 'olds up my little finger *you* comes to 'eel-or other'ow you goes ter clink. 'Ung indeed! You look after yer own farver an' don' pass remarks on yer betters. Why! You boozin' waster, I shall be Regimental Sargen' Majer when you're a bloomin' discharged private wiv an 'undred *'drunks*' in red on yer Defaulter's Sheet. Regimental Sarjen' Majer! I shall be an Orficer more like, and walk acrost the crossin' wot *you're* asweepin', to me Club in bloomin' well Pickerdilly! Yus. This is the days o' ? *Demockerycy*, me lad. 'Good Lloyd George's golden days' as they sing-and steady fellers like me is goin' to ave C'missh'ns-an' don' you fergit it! Farver 'ung indeed!"

"I'm awf'ly sorry, Corporal, really," apologized Dam. "I didn't think...."

"No, me lad," returned the unmollified superior, as he stooped to the other boot, "if you was to think more an' booze less you'd do better.... 'Ow an' where you gets 'old of it, beats me. I've seed you in delirium trimmings but I ain't never seed you drinkin' nor yet smelt it on yer. You're a cunnin' 'ound in yer way. One o' them beastly secret-drinkin' swine wots never suspected till they falls down 'owlin' blue 'orrors an' seem' pink toadses. Leastways it's snakes *you* sees. See 'em oncte too orfen, you will.... See 'em on p'rade one day in front o' the Colonel. Fall orf yer long-face an get trampled-an' serve yer glad.... An' now shut yer silly 'ed an' don' chew the mop so much. Let me get some sleep. *I* 'as responsibilities *I* do...."

A crossing outside a Club! More likely a padded cell in a troopship and hospital until an asylum claimed him.

In the finals, "Sword versus Sword Dismounted," Dam had a foeman worthy of his steel.

A glorious chilly morning, sunrise on a wide high open *maidan*, rows of tents for the spectators at the great evening final, and crowds of officers and men in uniform or gymnasium kit. On a group of chairs sat the Divisional General, his Colonel on the Staff, and Aide-de-Camp; the Brigadier-General, his Brigade-Major, and a few ladies, wives of regimental colonels, officers, and leading Civilians.

Semi-finals of Tent-pegging, Sword v. Sword Mounted, Bayonet-fighting, Tug-of-War, Fencing, and other officers' and men's events had been, or were being, contested.

The finals of the British Troops' Sword *v.* Sword Dismounted, was being reserved for the last, as of supreme interest to the experts present, but not sufficiently spectacular to be kept for the evening final "show," when the whole of Society would assemble to be thrilled by the final Jumping, Driving, Tent-pegging, Sword *v.* Sword Mounted, Bayonet-fighting, Sword *v.* Lance, Tug-of-War, and other events for British and Indian officers and men of all arms.

It was rumoured that there was a Sergeant of Hussars who would give Trooper Matthewson a warm time with the sabre. As the crowd of competitors and spectators gathered round the sabres-ring, and chairs were carried up for the Generals, ladies, and staff, to witness the last and most exciting contest of the morning's meeting, a Corporal-official of the Assault-at-Arms Executive Committee called aloud, "Sergeant O'Malley, 14th Hussars, get ready," and another fastened a red band to the Sergeant's arm as he stepped forward, clad in leather jacket and leg-guards and carrying the heavy iron-and-leather head-guard necessary in sabre combats, and the blunt-edged, blunt-pointed sabre.

Dam approached him.

"Don't let my point rest on your hilt, Sergeant," he said.

"What's the game?" inquired the surprised and suspicious Sergeant.

"My little trick. I thrust rather than cut, you know," said Dam.

"I'll watch it, me lad," returned Sergeant O'Malley, wondering whether Dam were fool or knave.

"Trooper Matthewson, get ready," called the Corporal, and Dam stepped into the ring, saluted, and faced the Sergeant.

A brief direction and caution, the usual preliminary, and the word—

"On guard—*Play*" and Dam was parrying a series of the quickest cuts he had ever met. The Sergeant's sword flickered like the tongue of a—*Snake*. Yes-of a *Snake*! and even as Dam's hand dropped limp and nerveless, the Sergeant's sword fell with a dull heavy thud on his head-guard. The stroke would have split Dam's head right neatly, in actual fighting.

"Stop," shouted the referee. "Point to Red."

"On guard—*Play*"

But if the Sergeant's sword flickered like the tongue of a snake-why then Dam must be fighting the Snake. *Fighting the Snake* and in another second the referee again cried "Stop!" And added, "Don't fight savage, White, or I'll disqualify you".

"I'm awf'ly sorry," said Dam, "I thought I was fighting the Sn——"

"Hold your tongue, and don't argue," replied the referee sternly.

"On Guard—*Play*."

Ere the Sergeant could move his sword from its upward-inclined position Dam's blade dropped to its hilt, shot in over it, and as the Sergeant raised his forearm in guard, flashed beneath it and bent on his breast.

"Stop," cried the referee. "Point to White. Double"—two marks being then awarded for the thrust hit, and one for the cut.

"On guard—*Play*."

Absolutely the same thing happened again within the next half-second, and Dam had won the British Troops' Sword *v.* Sword Dismounted, in addition to being in for the finals in Tent-pegging, Sword *v.* Sword Mounted, Jumping (Individual and By Sections), Sword *v.* Lance, and Tug-of-War.

"Now jest keep orf it, Matthewson, and sweep the bloomin' board," urged Troop-Sergeant-Major Scoles as Dam removed his fencing-jacket, preparatory to returning to barracks. "You be Best Man-at-arms in the Division and win everythink that's open to British Troops Mounted, and git the 'Eavy-Weight Championship from the Gorilla-an' there'll be some talk about promotion for yer, me lad."

"Thank you, Sergeant," replied Dam. "I am a total abstainer."

"Yah! *Chuck* it," observed the Sergeant-Major.

Of no interest to Women nor modern civilized Men.

The long-anticipated hour had struck, the great moment had arrived, and (literally) thousands of British soldiers sat in a state of expectant thrill and excited interest, awaiting the appearance of the Gorilla (Corporal Dowdall of the 111th Battery, Royal Garrison Artillery-fourteen stone twelve) and Trooper Matthewson (Queen's Greys-fourteen stone) who were to fight for the Elliott Belt, the Motipur Cup, and the Heavy-Weight Championship of India.

The Boxing Tournament had lasted for a week and had been a huge success. Now came the *pièce de resistance, the* fight of the Meeting, the event for which special trains had brought hundreds of civilians and soldiers from neighbouring and distant cantonments. Bombay herself sent a crowded train-load, and it was said that a, by no means small, contingent had come from Madras. Certainly more than one sporting patron of the Great Sport, the Noble Art, the Manly Game, had travelled from far Calcutta. So well-established was the fame of the great

Gorilla, and so widely published the rumour that the Queen's Greys had a prodigy who'd lower his flag in ten rounds-or less.

A great square of the grassy plain above Motipur had been enclosed by a high canvas wall, and around a twenty-four foot raised "ring" (which was square) seating accommodation for four thousand spectators had been provided. The front rows consisted of arm-chairs, sofas, and drawing-room settees (from the wonderful stock of Mr. Dadabhoy Pochajee Furniturewallah of the Sudder Bazaar) for the officers and leading civilians of Motipur, and such other visitors as chose to purchase the highly priced reserved-seat tickets.

Not only was every seat in the vast enclosure occupied, but every square inch of standing-room, by the time the combatants entered the arena.

A few dark faces were to be seen (Native Officers of the pultans[23] and rissal[24] of the Motipur Brigade), and the idea occurred to not a few that it was a pity the proceedings could not be witnessed by every Indian in India. It would do them good in more ways than one.

Although a large number of the enormously preponderating military spectators were in the khaki kit so admirable for work (and so depressing, unswanksome and anti-enlistment for play, or rather for walking-out and leisure), the experienced eye could see that almost every corps in India furnished contingents to the gathering. Lancers, dragoons, hussars, artillery, riflemen, Highlanders, supply and transport, infantry of a score of regiments, and, rare sight away from the Ports, a small party of Man-o'-War's-men in white duck, blue collars, and straw hats (huge, solemn-faced men who jested with grimmest seriousness of mien and insulted each other outrageously). Officers in scarlet, in dark blue, in black and cherry colour, in fawn and cherry colour, in pale blue and silver, in almost every combination of colours, showed that the commissioned ranks of the British and Indian Services were well represented, horse, foot, guns, engineers, doctors, and veterinary surgeons-every rank and every branch. On two sides of the roped ring, with its padded posts, sat the judges, boxing Captains both, who had won distinction at Aldershot and in many a local tournament. On another side sat the referee, *ex*-Public-Schools Champion, Aldershot Light-Weight Champion, and, admittedly, the best boxer of his weight among the officers of the British Army. Beside him sat the time-keeper. Overhead a circle of large incandescent lamps made the scene as bright as day.

"Well, d'you take it?" asked Seaman Jones of Seaman Smith. "Better strike while the grog's 'ot. A double-prick o' baccy and a gallon o' four-'arf, evens, on the Griller. I ain't never 'eard o' the Griller till we come 'ere, and I never 'eard o' t'other bloke neether-but I 'olds by the Griller, cos of 'is name and I backs me fancy afore I sees 'em. —Loser to 'elp the winner with the gallon."

"Done, Bill," replied the challenged promptly, on hearing the last condition. (He could drink as fast as Bill if he lost, and he could borrer on the baccy till it was wore out.) "Got that bloomin' 'igh-falutin' lar-de-dar giddy baccy-pouch and yaller baccy you inwested in at Bombay?" he asked. "Yus, 'Enery," replied William, diving deeply for it.

"Then push it 'ere, an' likewise them bloomin' 'igh-falutin' lar-de-dar giddy fag-papers you fumble wiv'. Blimey! ain't a honest clay good enough for yer now? I knows wots the matter wiv *you*, Billy Jones! You've got a weather-heye on the Quarter Deck you 'ave. You fink you're agoin' to be a blighted perishin' orficer you do! Yus, you flat-footed matlot-not even a blasted tiffy you ain't, and you buys a blighted baccy-pouch and yaller baccy and fag-pipers, like a Snottie, an' reckons you's on the 'igh road to be a bloomin' Winnie Lloyd Gorgeous Orficer. 'And 'em 'ere-fore I'm sick. Lootenant, —Gunnery Jack, —Number One, —Commerdore!"

"Parding me, 'Enery Smiff," returned William Jones with quiet dignity. "In consequents o' wot you said, an' more in consequents o' yore clumsy fat fingers not been used to 'andlin' dellikit objex, and most in consequents o' yore been a most ontrustable thief, I will perceed to roll you a fag meself, me been 'ighly competent so fer to do. Not but wot a fag'll look most outer place in *your* silly great ugly faice."

The other sailor watched the speaker in cold contempt as he prepared a distinctly exiguous, ill-fed cigarette.

"Harthur Handrews," he said, turning to his other neighbour, "'Ave yew 'appened to see the Master Sail-maker or any of 'is mermydiuns 'ere-abahts, by any chawnst?"

"Nope. 'An don' want. Don' wan' see nothink to remind me o'

Ther blue, ther fresh, ther *hever* free,
Ther blarsted, beastly, boundin' sea.

Not even your distressin' face and dirty norticle apparile. Why do you arksk sich silly questchings?"

"Willyerm Jones is amakin' a needle for 'im."

"As 'ow?"

"Wiv a fag-paper an' a thread o' yaller baccy. 'E's makin' a bloomin' needle," and with a sudden grab he possessed himself of the pouch, papers, and finished product of Seaman Jones's labours and generosity.

Having pricked himself severely and painfully with the alleged cigarette, he howled with pain, cast it from him, proceeded to stick two papers together and to make an uncommonly stout, well-nourished, and bounteous cigarette.

"I 'fought I offered you to make yourself a cigarette, 'Enery," observed the astounded owner of the *materia nicotina*.

"I grabbed for to make myself a cigarette, Willyerm," was the pedantically correct restatement of Henry.

"Then why go for to try an' mannyfacter a bloomin' banana?" asked the indignant victim, whose further remarks were drowned in the roars of applause which greeted the appearance from the dressing-tents of the Champion and the Challenger.

Dam and Corporal Dowdall entered the ring from opposite corners, seated themselves in the chairs provided for them, and submitted themselves to the ministrations of their respective seconds.

Trooper Herbert Hawker violently chafed Dam's legs, Trooper Bear his arms and chest, while Trooper Goate struggled to force a pair of new boxing-gloves upon his hands, which were scientifically bandaged around knuckles, back, and wrist, against untimely dislocations and sprains.

Clean water was poured into the bowls which stood behind each chair, and fresh resin was sprinkled over the canvas-covered boards of the Ring.

Men whose favourite "carried their money" (and each carried a good deal) anxiously studied that favourite's opponent.

The Queen's Greys beheld a gorilla indeed, a vast, square, long-armed hairy monster, with the true pugilist face and head.

"Wot a werry ugly bloke," observed Seaman Arthur Andrews to Seaman Henry Smith. "'E reminds me o' Hadmiral Sir Percy 'Opkinton, so 'e do. P'raps 'e's a pore relation."

"Yus," agreed Seaman Smith. "A crost between our beloved 'Oppy an' ole Bill Jones 'ere. Bill was reported to 'ave 'ad a twin brother-but it was allus serposed Bill ate 'im when 'e wasn' lookin'."

The backers of Corporal Dowdall were encouraged at seeing a man who looked like a gentleman and bore none of the traditional marks of the prize-fighter. His head was not cropped to the point of bristly baldness, his nose was unbroken, his eyes well opened and unblackened, his ears unthickened, his body untattooed. He had the white skin, small trim moustache, high-bred features, small extremities, and general appearance and bearing of an officer.

Ho, G'rilla Dowdall would make short work of *that* tippy young toff.
Why, look at him!

And indeed it made you shudder to think of that enormous ferocity, that dynamic truculence, doing its best to destroy you in a space twenty-four feet square.

Let the challenger wait till G'rilla put his fighting face on-fair terrifyin'.

Not an Artilleryman but felt sure that the garrison-gunner would successfully defend the title and "give the swankin' Queen's Greys something to keep them *choop*[25] for a bit. Gettin' above 'emselves they was, becos' this bloke of theirs had won Best Man-at-Arms and had the nerve to challenge G'rilla Dowdall, R.G.A."

Even the R.H.A. admitted the R.G.A. to terms of perfect equality on that great occasion.

But a few observant and experienced officers, gymnasium instructors, and ancient followers of the Noble Art were not so sure.

"Put steel-and-whalebone against granite and I back the former," said Major Decoulis to Colonel Hanking; "other things being equal of course-skill and ring-craft. And I hear that No. 2—the Queen's Greys' man-is unusually fast for a heavy-weight."

"I'd like to see him win," admitted the Colonel. "The man looks a gentleman. *Doesn't* the other look a Bill Sykes, by Jove!"

The Staff Sergeant Instructor of the Motipur Gymnasium stepped into the ring.

"Silence, please," he bawled. "Fifteen-round contest between Corporal Dowdall, 111th Battery, Royal Garrison Artillery, Heavy-Weight Champion of Hindia, fourteen twelve (Number 1—on my right 'and) and Trooper Matthewson, Queen's Greys, fourteen stun (Number 2—on my left 'and). Please keep silence durin' the rounds. The winner is Heavy-Weight Champion of Hindia, winner of the Motipur Cup and 'older of the Elliott Belt. All ready there?"

Both combatants were ready.

"Come here, both of you," said the referee.

As he arose to obey, Dam was irresistibly reminded of his fight with Bully Harberth and smiled.

"Nervous sort o' grin on the figger-'ead o' the smaller vessel, don't it," observed Seaman Smith.

"There wouldn't be no grin on *your* fat face at all," returned Seaman Jones. "It wouldn't be there. You'd be full-steam-ahead, bearings 'eated, and showin' no lights, for them tents-when you see wot you was up against."

The referee felt Dam's gloves to see that they contained no foreign bodies in the shape of plummets of lead or other illegal gratifications. (He had known a man fill the stuffing-compartments of his gloves with plaster of Paris, that by the third or fourth round he might be striking with a kind of stone cestus as the plaster moulded with sweat and water, and hardened to the shape of the fist.)

As he stepped back, Dam looked for the first time at his opponent, conned his bruiser face and Herculean body, and, with a gasp and shudder, was aware that a huge tattooed serpent reared its head in the centre of his vast chest while smaller ones encircled the mighty biceps of his arms. He clutched the rope and leant trembling against the post as the referee satisfied himself (with very great care in this case) of the innocence of the Gorilla's gloves.

"I know you of old, Dowdall," he said, "and I shall only caution you once mind. Second offence-and out you go."

Corporal Dowdall grinned sheepishly. He appeared to think that a delicate and gentlemanly compliment had been paid to his general downiness, flyness, and ring-craft,—the last of which, for Corporal Dowdall, included every form of foul that a weak referee would pass, an inexperienced one misunderstand, or a lazy one miss. Major O'Halloran, first-class bruiser himself, was in the habit of doing his refereeing inside the ring and within a foot or two of the principals, where he expected foul play.

As the Major cautioned the Gorilla, Dam passed his hand wearily across his face, swallowed once or twice and groaned aloud.

It was *not* fair. Why should the Snake be allowed to humiliate him before thousands of spectators? Why should It be brought here to shame him in the utmost publicity, to make him fail his comrades, disgrace his regiment, make the Queen's Greys a laughing-stock?

But-he had fought an emissary of the Snake before-and he had won. This villainous-looking pugilist was perhaps *the Snake Itself in human form*—and, see, he was free, he was in God's open air, no chains bound him, he was not gagged, this place was not a pit dug beneath the Pit itself! This was all tangible and real. He would have fair play and be able to defend himself. This was not a blue room with a mud floor. Nay, he would be able to attack-to fight, fight like a wounded pantheress for her cubs. This accursed Snake in Human Form would only be able to use puny fists. Mere trivial human fists and human strength. Everything would be on the human plane. It would be unable to wrap him in its awful coils and crush and crush the soul and life and manhood out of him, as it did at night before burrowing its way ten million miles below the floor of Hell with him, and immuring him in a molten incandescent tomb where he could not even scream or writhe.

"Get to your corners," said the referee, and Dam returned to his place with a cruel smile upon his compressed lips. By the Merciful Living God he had the Snake Itself delivered unto him in human form-to do with as he could. Oh, that It might last out the fifteen times of facing him in his wrath, his pent-up vengeful wrath at a ruined life, a dishonoured name and *a lost Lucille!*

When would they give the word for him to spring upon it and batter it lifeless to the ground?

"Don't grind yer silly teeth like that," whispered Hawker, his grim ugly face white with anxiety and suspense (for he loved Damocles de Warrenne as the faithfullest of hounds loves the best of masters). "You're awastin' henergy all the time."

"God! if they don't give the word in a minute I shall be unable to hold off It," replied Dam wildly.

"That's the sperrit, Cocky," approved Hawker, "but donchew fergit you gotter larst fifteen bloomin' rahnds. 'Taint no kindergarters. '*E*'ll stick it orlrite, an' you'll avter win on *points* — —"

"Seconds out of the Ring," cried the time-keeper, staring at his watch.

"Don't get knocked out, dear boy," implored Trooper Bear. "Fight to win on points. You *can't* knock him out. I'm going to pray like hell through the rounds — —"

"*Time*" barked the time-keeper, and, catching up the chair as Dam rose, Trooper Bear dropped down from the boards of the ring to the turf, where already crouched Hawker and Goate, looking like men about to be hanged.

The large assembly drew a deep breath as the combatants approached each other with extended right hands-Dam clad in a pair of blue silk shorts, silk socks and high, thin, rubber-soled boots, the Gorilla in an exiguous bathing-garment and a pair of gymnasium shoes.

Dam a picture of the Perfect Man, was the taller, and the Gorilla, a perfect Caliban, was the broader and had the longer reach. Their right hands touched in perfunctory shake, Dam drew back to allow the Snake to assume sparring attitude, and, as he saw the huge shoulders hunch, the great biceps rise, and the clenched gloves come to position, he assumed the American "crouch" attitude and sprang like a tiger upon the incarnation of the utter Damnation and Ruin that had cursed his life to living death.

The Gorilla was shocked and pained! The tippy pink-and-white blasted rookie was "all over him" and he was sent staggering with such a rain of smashing blows as he had never, never felt, nor seen others receive. The whole assembly of soldiers, saving the Garrison Artillerymen, raised a wild yell, regardless of the referee's ferocious expostulations (in dumb-show) and even the ranks of the Horse-Gunners could scarce forbear to cheer. The Queen's Greys howled like fiends and Hawker, unknown to himself, punched the boards before him with terrific violence. Never had anything like it been seen. Matthewson was a human whirlwind, and Dowdall had not had a chance to return a blow. More than half the tremendous punches, hooks and infighting jabs delivered by his opponent had got home, and he was "rattled". A fair hook to the chin might send him down and out at any moment.

Surely never had human being aimed such an unceasing, unending, rain of blows in the space of two minutes as had Trooper Matthewson. His arms had worked like the piston rods of an express engine-as fast and as untiringly. He had taken the Gorilla by surprise, had rushed him, and had never given him a fraction of time in which to attack. Beneath the rain of sledge-hammer blows the Gorilla had shrunk, guarding for dear life. Driven into a corner, he cowered down, crouched beneath his raised arms, and allowed his face to sink forward. Like a whirling piece of machinery Dam's arm flew round to administer the *coup-de-grace*, the upper cut, that would lay the Snake twitching and unconscious on the boards.

The Gorilla was expecting it.

As it came, his bullet head was jerked aside, and as the first swung harmlessly up, he arose like a flash, and, as he did so, his mighty right shot up, took Darn on the chin and laid him flat and senseless in the middle of the ring.

The Gorilla breathed heavily and made the most of the respite. He knew it must be about "Time," and that he had not won. If it wasn't "Time," and the cub arose he'd knock him to glory as he did so. Yes, the moment the most liberal-minded critic could say he was just about on his feet, he'd give him a finisher that he'd bear the mark of. The bloomin' young swine had nearly "had" him-him, the great G'rilla Dowdall, about to buy himself out with his prize-money, and take to pugilism as a profession.

"One-two-three-four," counted the timekeeper amid the most deathly silence, and, as he added, *"five-six-Time,"* a shout arose that was heard for miles.

Trooper Matthewson was saved-if his seconds could pull him round in time.

At sound of the word "Time," the seconds leapt into the ring. Hawker and Bear rushed to the prostrate Dam, hauled him to his feet, and dragged him to the chair which Goate had placed ready. As he was dropped into it, a spongeful of icy water from Goate's big sponge brought Dam to consciousness.

"Breave for all y'r worf," grunted Hawker, as he mightily swung a big bath-towel in swift eddies, to drive refreshing air upon the heaving, panting body of his principal.

Bear and Goate applied massaging hands with skilled violence.

"By Jove, I thought you had him," panted Goate as he kneaded triceps and biceps. "And then I thought he had you. It's anybody's fight, Matty-but *don't* try and knock him out. You couldn't do it with an axe."

"No," agreed Bear. "You've got to keep on your feet and win on points."

"I've got to kill *the Snake*," hissed Dam, and his seconds glanced at each other anxiously.

He felt that nothing could keep him from victory. He was regaining his faith in a just Heaven, now that the Snake had been compelled to face him in the puny form of a wretched pugilist. Some one had said something about an axe. It would be but fair if he had an axe, seeing that hitherto the Snake had had him utterly defenceless while exercising its own immeasurable and supernatural powers, when torturing him to its heart's content for endless aeons. But-no-since it was here in human form and without weapons, *he* would use none, and would observe the strictest fairness in fight, just as he would to a real human enemy.

"Abaht that there little bet, 'Enery," observed Seaman Jones, "I fink we'll alter of it. I don't wish to give no moral support to this 'ere Griller. T'other bloke's only jus' fresh from the Novice Class, I reckon, jedgin' by 'is innercent young faice, an' e's aputtin' up the werry best fight as ever I see. We'll chainge it like this 'ere. We backs the 'orse-soldier to win, and, if he *do*, we drinks a gallon between us. If 'e don't, we drinks *two* fer to console 'im, an' drahn sorrer, wot?"

"So it are, Will'm," agreed Henery. "Then we wins *either* way! *You* got a 'ead fer logger-rhythms. Oughter been a bloomin' bookie. They 'as to be big an' ugly ——"

"Seconds out of the Ring," called the referee, and a hush fell upon the excited throng.

Bear and Goate dropped to the ground, Hawker splashed water all over Dam's body and, as he rose on the word *"Time"* snatched away the chair and joined his colleagues, who crouched with faces on a level with the boards.

"Oh, buck him up, good Lord, and put ginger in his short-arm work, and O Lord, take care of his chin and mark," prayed Trooper Bear, with deep and serious devoutness.

No need to shake hands this bout-not again till the fifteenth, noted Dam, as he arose and literally leapt at his opponent with a smashing drive of his right and a feint of his left which drew the Gorilla's guard and left his face exposed. The Gorilla received Dam's full weight and full strength, and, but for the ropes, would have been knocked among the spectators.

A tremendous yell went up, led by the Queen's Greys.

As the tautening of the ropes swayed the Gorilla inward again, Dam delivered a brace of lightning strokes that, though they did not find the chin, staggered and partly stunned him, and, ere he could pull himself together, Dam was inside his guard, almost breast to breast with him, and raining terrific blows, just above the belt. Left, right, left, right, and no chance for the Gorilla to get his own hands up for a couple of seconds, and, when he could, and drove an appalling blow at Dam's chin, it was dodged and he received a cross-counter that shook him. He must sham weariness and demoralization, lead the tippy rookie on to over-confidence and then land him clean over the ropes. A sullen rage grew in the Gorilla's heart. He wasn't doing himself justice. He wasn't having a fair show. This blasted half-set pink and white recruit hadn't given him time to settle down. A fifteen-round contest shouldn't be bustled like *this!* The bloke was more like a wild-cat than a sober heavyweight boxer.

He received a heavy blow in the face and, as he shook his head with an evil grin, according to his custom when well struck, he found it followed practically instantaneously by another. The swab was about the quickest thing that ever got into a ring. He was like one of these bloomin', tricky, jack-in-the-box featherweights, instead of a steady lumbering "heavy". And the Gorilla allowed himself to be driven to a corner again, and let his head sink forward, that the incautious youth might again put all his strength into an upper-cut, miss as the other dodged, and be at the mercy of the Gorilla as the errant fist completed its over-driven swing.

But Damocles de Warrenne fought with his brain as well as his strength and skill. He had learnt a lesson, and no dull-witted oaf of a Gorilla was going to have him like that twice. As the Gorilla cowered and crouched in simulated defeat and placed his face to tempt the *coup de grace* which he would see swinging up, and easily dodge, Dam swiftly side-stepped and summoning every ounce of strength, rage, and mad protesting frenzy against the life-long torturing tyrant, he delivered a Homeric blow at the champion's head, beside and behind the ear. (Since he was indestructible by the ordinary point-of-the-chin knock-out, let him make the best of that fearful blow upon the base of the brain and spinal cord, direct.)

Experienced men said it was the heaviest blow they had ever seen struck with the human fist. It was delivered slightly downward, coolly, at measured distance, with change from left foot to right in the act of delivery, and with the uttermost strength of a most powerful athlete in perfect training-and Hate Incarnate lent the strength of madness to the strength of training and skill.

THUD!—and the Gorilla dropped like a log.

"*One-two-three-four-five-six-seven* —" counted the time-keeper, as men scarcely breathed in the dead silence into which the voice cut sharply —"*eight* —" and, in perfect silence, every man of those thousands slowly rose to his feet —"*nine-OUT!*" and such a roar arose as bade fair to rend the skies. "*Outed*" *in two rounds!* Men howled like lunatics, and the Queen's Greys behaved like very dangerous lunatics. Hawker flung his arms round Dam and endeavoured to raise him on his shoulders and chair him unaided. Bear and Goate got each a hand and proceeded to do their best to crush it.

Seamen Jones and Smith exchanged a chaste kiss.

Damocles de Warrenne was the hero of the Queen's Greys. Best Man-at-Arms in the Division, winner in Sword v. Sword Mounted and Dismounted, Tent-pegging, Sword v. Lance, and Individual Jumping, and in the winning teams for Tug-of-War, Section Jumping, and Section Tent-pegging!

"Give him a trial as Corporal then, from the first of next month, sir, if there's no sign of anything wrong during the week," agreed Captain Daunt, talking him over with the Colonel, after receiving through Troop-Sergeant-Major Scoles a petition to promote the man.

Within twenty-four hours of his fight with the Gorilla, Dam found himself on sentry-go over what was known in the Regiment as "the Dead 'Ole"—which was the mortuary, situated in a lonely, isolated spot beyond a nullah some half-furlong from the Hospital, and cut off from view of human habitation by a belt of trees.

On mounting guard that evening, the Sergeant of the Guard had been informed that a corpse lay in the mortuary, a young soldier having been taken ill and having died within a few hours, of some disease of a distinctly choleraic nature.

"I'll tell *you* orf for that post, Matthewson," said the Sergeant. "P'raps you'll see ghosties there, for a change," for it was customary to mount a sentry over "the Dead 'Ole" when it contained an occupant, and one of the sentry's pleasing duties was to rap loudly and frequently upon the door throughout the night to scare away those vermin which are no respecters of persons when the persons happen to be dead and the vermin ravenous.

"I'm not afraid of ghosts, Sergeant," replied Dam-though his heart sank within him at the thought of the long lonely vigil in the dark, when he would be so utterly at the mercy of the Snake-the Snake over whom he had just won a signal victory, and who would be all the more vindictive and terrible in consequence. Could he keep sane through the lonely darkness of those dreadful hours? Perhaps-if he kept himself in some severe physical agony. He would put a spur beneath his tight-drawn belt and next to his skin, he would strike his knee frequently with the "toe of the butt" of his carbine, he would put pebbles in his boots, and he would cause cramp in his limbs, one after the other. Any kind of pain would help.

* * *

It must be quarter of an hour since he had rapped on the mortuary door and sent his messages of prohibition to mouse, rat, bandicoot, civet-cat, wild-cat or other vermin intruder through the roof-ventilation holes. He would knock again. A strange thing this-knocking at a dead man's door in the middle of the night. Suppose the dead man called "Come in!" It would be intensely interesting, but in no wise terrifying or horrible. Presumably poor young Trooper Priddell was no more dangerous or dreadful in the spirit than he had been in the flesh.... Fortunate young man! Were he only on sentry-go outside the peaceful mortuary and Damocles de Warrenne stretched on the bier within, to await the morrow and its pomp and ceremony, when the carcass of the dead soldier would receive honours never paid to the living, sentient man, be he never so worthy, heroic, virtuous and deserving. Oh, to be lying in there at rest, to be on the other side of that closed door at peace!...

To-morrow that poor dead yokel's body would receive a "Present Arms" (as though he were an armed party commanded by an Officer) from the Guard, which the sentry would turn out as the coffin passed the Guard-room. For the first and last time in his life, he would get a *"Present Arms"*. It wouldn't be in his *life* though. For the first and last time in his death? That didn't sound right either. Anyhow he would get it, and lots of strange, inexplicable, origin-forgotten rites would be observed over this piece of clay-hitherto so cheaply held and roughly treated.

Queer! As "Trooper Priddell" he was of no account. As a piece of fast-decaying carrion he would be the centre of a piece of elaborate ceremonial! His troop would parade in full dress and (save for a firing-party of twelve who would carry carbines) without arms. A special black horse would be decked out with a pall of black velvet and black plumes. Across this horse the spurred jackboots of the dead man would be slung with toes pointing to the rear. Two men, wearing black cloaks, would lead the horse by means of new handkerchiefs passed through the bridoon rings of its bridle, handkerchiefs which would become their perquisites and *memento mori*.

With crape-draped drums, the band, in silence, would lead the troop to the mortuary where would await it a gun-carriage with its six horses and coffin-supporting attachment. Here the troop would break ranks, file into the mortuary and bare-headed take, each man, his last look at the face of the dead as he lay in his coffin. The lid would then be screwed on, the troop would form a double line, facing inward, the firing-party would "present arms," and six of the dead man's more particular pals, or of his "townies," would bear the coffin out and place it upon the gun-carriage. It would then be covered with a Union Jack and on it would be placed the helmet, sword, and carbine of the deceased trooper, the firing-party standing meanwhile, leaning on their reversed carbines, with bowed heads.

As the melancholy procession formed up for its march to the graveyard, the smallest and junior men would take front place, the bigger and senior men behind them, non-commissioned officers would follow, and subalterns and captain last of all. In stepping off from the halt, all would step off with the right foot instead of with the left. Apparently the object was to reverse ordinary procedure to the uttermost-which would but be in keeping with the great reversal of showing honour to such an unhonoured thing as a private soldier-one of the despised and rejected band that enable the respectable, wealthy, and smug to remain so; one of the "licentious soldiery" that have made, and that keep, the Empire of which the respectable wealthy and smug are so proud.

At the "slow march," and in perfect silence until beyond hearing by the inmates of the Hospital, the cortege would proceed. Anon the band would call heaven and earth to mourn with the sonorous dreadful strains of the Dead March; whereafter the ordinary "quick march" would bring the funeral party to the cemetery, in sight of which the "slow march" would be resumed, and the Chaplain, surpliced, book-bearing, come forth to put himself at its head, leading the way to the grave-side where, with uncovered heads, the mourners would listen to the impressive words with feelings varying as their education, religion, temperament, and-digestion-impelled.

At the close of the service, the firing-party in their places, six on either side of the grave, would fire three volleys into the air, while the band breathed a solemn dirge.

And-perhaps most impressively tragic touch of all-the party would march briskly off to the strains of the liveliest air in the whole repertoire of the band.

Why should John Humphreyville Priddell-doubtless scion of the great Norman houses of Humphreyville and Paradelle, who shared much of Dorsetshire between them from Domesday Book to Stuart downfall-have been born in a tiny village of the Vale of Froom in "Dorset Dear," to die of cholera in vile Motipur? Was some maid, in barton, byre, or dairy, thinking of him but now-with an ill-writ letter in her bosom, a letter beginning with *"I now take up my pen to right you these few lines hopping they find you the same which they now leave me at present"* according to right tradition and proper custom, and continuing to speak of homesick longings, dreams of furlough, promotion, marrying "on the strength," and retirement to green fair Dorset Dear on a Sergeant-Major's pension?

What was the meaning of it all? Was it pure chance and accident-or had a Living, Scheming, Purposeful Deity a great wise object in this that John Humphreyville Priddell should have been born and bred and nurtured in the Vale of Froom to be struck from lusty life to a death of agony in a few hours at Motipur in the cruel accursed blighted land of Ind?

Well, well! —high time to rap again upon the door, the last door, of John Humphreyville Priddell, Trooper, ex-dairyhand, decaying carrion, —and scare from his carcass such over-early visitants as anticipated....

How hollowly the blows re-echoed. Did they strike muffled but murderous upon the heart of the thousand-league distant dairymaid, or of the old cottage-mother whose evenings were spent in spelling out her boy's loving letters-that so oft covered a portion of his exiguous pay?...

Was that a scuttling within? Quite probably. It might be-rats, it might be a bandicoot; it could hardly be a jackal; it might be a SNAKE, —and Trooper Matthewson's carbine clattered to the ground and his knees smote together as he thought the word. Pulling himself together he hastily snatched up his carbine with a flush of shame at the slovenly unsoldierly "crime" of dropping it. He'd be dropping his arms on parade next! But it *might be a snake* —for he had certainly heard the sound of a movement of some sort. The strong man felt faint and leant against the mortuary wall for a moment.

Oh, that the wretched carbine were a sword! A man could feel a *man* with a sword in his hand. He could almost face the Snake, even in Snake form, if he had a sword...but what is a carbine, even a loaded Martini-Henry carbine with its good soft man-stopping slug? There are no traditions to a carbine-nothing of the Spirit of one's Ancestors in one —a vile mechanic thing of villainous saltpetre. How should the Snake fear that? Now a sword was different. It stood for human war and human courage and human deeds from the mistiest past, and behind it must be a weight of human wrath, feats, and tradition that must make even the Snake pause. Oh, for his sword-if the Snake came upon him when he had but this wretched carbine he would probably desert his post, fling the useless toy from him, and flee till he fell blind and fainting on the ground.... And what would the Trooper of the Queen get who deserted his sentry-post, threw away his arms and fled-and explained in defence that he had seen a snake? Probably a court-martial would give him a spell of Military Prison. Yes—*Jail*.... What proportion of truth could there be in the firmly-held belief of the men that "crimes" are made so numerous and so inevitable, to the best-meaning and most careful, because there exist a great Military Prison System and a great Military Prison personnel-and that "criminals" are essential to the respective proper inhabitation and *raison d'être* thereof-that unless a good supply of military "criminals" were forthcoming there might have to be reductions and curtailments-loss of snug billets.... Certainly soldiers got years of imprisonment for "crimes" for which civilians would get reprimands or nominal fines, and, moreover, when a man became a soldier he certainly lost the elementary fundamental rights guaranteed to Englishmen by Magna Charta-among them the right of trial by his peers....

Would poor Priddell mind if he did not knock again? If it were the Snake it could do Priddell no harm now-he being happily dead-whereas, if disturbed, it might emerge to the utter undoing-mind, body, and soul-of Trooper Matthewson. It would certainly send him to Jail or Lunatic Asylum-probably to both in due succession, for he was daily getting worse in the matter of the Snake.

No-it was part of his orders, on this sentry-post, to knock at the door, and he would do his duty, Snake or not. He had always tried to do his duty faithfully and he would continue....

Once more to knock at a dead man's door....

Bump, Bump: Bump, Bump: Bump, Bump.

"You'll soon be at rest, Priddell, old chap-and I wish I could join you," called Dam, and it seemed to his excited brain that *a deep hollow groan replied.*

"By Jove! He's not dead," coolly remarked the man who would have fled shrieking from a harmless blind-worm, and, going round to the back of the building, he placed his carbine against the wall and sprang up at a kind of window-ledge that formed the base of a grated aperture made for purposes of ventilation. Slowly raising his body till his face was above the ledge, he peered into the dimly moonlit cell and then dropped to the ground and, catching up his carbine, sprinted in the direction of the Hospital Guard-room.

There arrived, he shouted for the Corporal of the Guard and was quickly confronted by Corporal Prag.

"Wot the devil you deserted yore".... he began.

"Get the key of the mortuary, send for the Surgeon, and come at once," gasped Dam as soon as he could speak. *"Priddell's not dead.* Must be some kind of catalepsy. Quick, man"....

"Catter wot? You drunken 'og," drawled the Corporal. "Catter_waulin' *more like it. Under arrest you goes, my lad. Now you* 'ave_ done it. 'Ere, 'Awker, run down an' call up the Sergeant o' the Guard an' tell 'im Maffewson's left 'is post. 'E'll 'ave to plant annuvver sentry. Maffewson goes ter clink."

"Yes-but send for the Surgeon and the key of the mortuary too," begged Dam. "I give you fair warning that Priddell is alive and groaning and off the bier—"

"Pity *you* ain't 'off the beer' too," said the Corporal with a yawn.

"Well-there are witnesses that I brought the report to you. If Priddell is found dead on the ground to-morrow you'll have to answer for manslaughter."

"'Ere, *chuck* it you snaike-seeing delirying trimmer, *will* yer! Give anyone the 'orrers to listen to yer! When Priddell is wrote off as 'Dead' 'e *is* dead, whether 'e likes it or no," and he turned to give orders to the listening guard to arrest Trooper Matthewson.

The Sergeant of the Guard arrived at the "double," followed by Trooper Bear carrying a hurricane-lamp.

"What's the row?" panted the Sergeant. "Matthewson on the booze again?"

"I report that there is a living man in the mortuary, Sergeant," replied Dam. "Priddell is not dead. I heard him groan, and I scrambled up to the grating and saw him lying on the ground by the door."

"Well, you'll see yerself groanin' an' lyin' on the ground in the Digger, now," replied the Sergeant, and, as much in sorrow as in anger, he added, "An' *you*'re the bloke I signed a petition for his permotion are yer? At it agin a'ready!"

"But, good Heavens, man, can't you see I'm as sober as you are, and much less excited? Can't you send for the key of the mortuary and call the doctor? The poor chap may die for your stupidity."

"You call *me* a 'man' again, my lad, an' I'll show you what a Sergeant can do fer them as 'e don't like! As fer 'sober'—I've 'ad enough o' you 'sober'. W'y, in two ticks you may be on the ground 'owlin' and bellerin' and squealin' like a Berkshire pig over the blood-tub. *Sober*! Yus—I seen you at it."

"Why on earth can't you come and *prove* I'm drunk or mad," besought Dam. "Open the mortuary and prove I'm wrong-and then put me under arrest. Call the Surgeon and say the sentry over the mortuary reports the inmate to be alive—*he* has heard of catalepsy and comatose collapse simulating death if *you* haven't."

"Don' use sech 'orrible languidge," besought the respectable Corporal Prag.

"Ho, yus! *I*'m agoin' to see meself whipt on the peg fer turnin' out the Surgin from 'is little bed in the middle o' the night-to come an' 'ave a look at the dead corpse 'e put in orders fer the Dead 'Ole, ain't I? Jest becos the champion snaike-seer o' E Troop's got 'em agin, wot?"

Corporal Prag laughed merrily at the wit of his superior.

Turning to Bear, whom he knew to be as well educated as himself, Dam remarked: —

"Poor chap has rallied from the cholera collapse and could probably be saved by stimulants and warmth. This suspended animation is common enough in cholera. Why, the Brahmins have a regular ritual for dealing with cases of recovery on the funeral pyre-purification after defilement by the corpse-washers or something of the sort. These stupid oafs are letting poor Priddell die—"

"What! you drunken talkin' parrot," roared the incensed Sergeant. "'Ere, sling 'is drunken rotten carkis—"

"What's the row here?" cut in a quiet curt voice. "Noise enough for a gang of crows——"

Surgeon-Captain Blake of the Royal Army Medical Corps had just left the Hospital, having been sent for by the night Nursing Sister. The men sprang to attention and the Sergeant saluted.

"Drunk sentry left 'is post, Sir," he gabbled. "'Spose the Dead 'Ole-er-Morshuerry, that is, Sir, got on 'is nerves. 'E's given to secret boozin', Sir——"

"Excuse me, Sir," broke in Dam, daring to address an Officer unbidden, since a life was at stake, "I am a total abstainer and Trooper Priddell is not dead. It must have been cataleptic trance. I heard him groan and I climbed up and saw him lying on the ground."

"This man's not drunk," said Captain Blake, and added to himself, "and he's an educated man, and a cultured, poor devil."

"Oh, that's how 'e goes on, Sir, sober as a judge you'd say, an' then nex' minnit 'e's on the floor aseein' blue devils an' pink serpents——"

"The man's dying while we talk, Sir," put in Dam, whose wrath was rising. (If these dull-witted ignorant louts could not tell a drunken man from a sober, nor realize that a certified dead man may *not* be dead, surely the doctor could.)

The Sergeant and the Corporal ventured on a respectful snigger.

"Bring me that lamp," said Captain Blake, and Trooper Bear raised it to his extended hand. Lifting it so that its light shone straight in Dam's face the doctor scanned the latter and examined his eyes. This was not the face of a drunkard nor was the man in any way under the influence of liquor now. Absurd! Had he fever? Was he of deranged intellect? But, alas, the light that shone upon Dam's face also shone upon Captain Blake's collar and upon the badge of his Corps which adorned it-and that badge is a serpent entwining a rod.

It was the last straw! Dam had passed through a most disturbing night; he had kept guard in the lonely Snake-haunted darkness, guard over a mortuary in which lay a corpse; he had had to keep knocking at the corpse's door, his mind had run on funerals, he had thought he heard the dead man groan, he believed he had seen the dead man moving, he had wrestled with thick intelligences who held him drunk or mad while precious moments passed, and he had had the Snake before his mental vision throughout this terrible time-and here was another of its emissaries *wearing its badge*, an emissary of high rank, an Officer-Emissary!...Well, he was in the open air, thank God, and could put up a fight as before.

Like a panther he sprang upon the unfortunate officer and bore him to the ground, with his powerful hands enclosing the astounded gentleman's neck, and upon the couple sprang the Sergeant, the Corporal, and the Hospital Guard, all save the sentry, who (disciplined, well-drilled man!) brought his carbine to the "order" and stood stiffly at "attention" in a position favourable for a good view of the proceedings though strictly on his beat.

Trooper Bear, ejaculating "Why do the heathen rage furiously together," took a running jump and landed in sitting posture on the heap, rolled off, and proceeded to seize every opportunity of violently smiting his superior officers, in his apparent zeal to help to secure the dangerous criminal-lunatic. Thoughts of having just *one* punch at a real Officer (if only a non-combatant still a genuine Commissioned Officer) flashed across his depraved mind.

It was a Homeric struggle. Captain Blake was himself an old Guy's Rugger three-quarter and no mean boxer, and the Sergeant, Corporal, and Guard, were all powerful men, while Dam was a Samson further endowed with the strength of undeniable madness. When at length he was dragged from Captain Blake's recumbent form, his hands torn from that officer's throat, and the group stood for a second panting, Dam suddenly felled Corporal Prag with such a blow as had been the undoing of the Gorilla, sent Sergeant Wotting head over heels and, ere the Guard could again close with him, drove his fist into the face of the supposed myrmidon of the Snake and sprang upon his body once more....

It was some time before seven strong men could pinion him and carry him on a stretcher to the Guard-room, and, of those seven strong men, only Trooper Bear bore no mark of serious damage. (Trooper Bear had struck two non-commissioned officers with great violence, in his misdirected zeal, and one Commissioned Officer-though only playfully and for the satisfaction of being able to say that he had done so.) That night, half dead, wholly mad, bruised and bleeding, Damocles de Warrenne lay in the dark cell awaiting trial on a charge of assaulting an Officer, striking his superior officers, resisting the Guard, deserting his sentry-post, and being drunk and disorderly.

* * *

"What'll he get, d'you think?" sadly asked Trooper Goate of Trooper Hawker.

"Two stretch 'ard laiber and discharged from the Army wiv' iggernerminny," groaned Trooper Hawker. "Lucky fer 'im floggin's erbolished in the British Army."

* * *

When the mortuary door was unlocked next morning a little force was required to open it, some obstacle apparently retarding its inward movement. The obstacle proved to be the body, now certainly the dead body, of Trooper Priddell who had died with his fingers thrust under the said door.[26]

Part III
The Saving of a Soul

Chapter XII
Vultures and Luck-good and Bad

To the strongest and sanest mind there is something a small trifle disturbing, perhaps, in riding silently hour after hour on a soft-footed camel over soft sand in a silent empty land through the moonlit silent night, beside an overland-telegraph wire on every individual post of which sits a huge vulture!...Just as the sun set, a fiery red ball, behind the distant mountains, Damocles de Warrenne, gentleman-at-large, had caught sight of what he had sought in the desert for some days, the said overland telegraph, and thereby saved himself from the highly unpleasant death that follows prolonged deprivation of water. He had also saved his camel from a little earlier death, inasmuch as he had decided to probe for the faithful creature's jugular vein and carotid artery during the torturing heats of the morrow and prolong his life at its expense. (Had he not promised Lucille to do his best for himself?)

The overland telegraph pointed absolutely straight to the border city of Kot Ghazi and, better still, to a river-bed which would contain pools of water, thirty miles this side of it, at a spot a few miles from which stood a lost lone dak-bungalow on Indian soil —a dak-bungalow whereat would be waiting a *shikarri* retainer, and such things as tea, fuel, potted foods, possibly fresh meat, and luxury of luxuries, a hot bath....

And, with a sigh of relief, he had wheeled his camel under the telegraph wires after a glance at the stars and brief calculation as to whether he should turn to left or right. (He did not want to proceed until he collapsed under the realization that he was making for the troubled land of Persia.)

Anyhow, without knowing where he was, he knew he was on the road to water, food, human companionship (imagine Abdul Ghani a human companion! —but he had not seen a human face for three weeks, nor heard nor uttered a word), and safety, after suffering the unpleasant experience of wandering in circles, lost in the most inhospitable desert on the earth. Vultures! He had not realized there were so many in the world. Hour after hour, a post at every few yards, and on every post a vulture —a vulture that opened its eyes as he approached, regarded him from its own point of view-that of the Eater whose life is an unending search for Meat-calculatingly, and closed them again with a sigh at his remaining vigorousness.

He must have passed hundreds, thousands, —had he died of thirst in actual fact and was he doomed to follow this line through this desert for evermore as a punishment for his sins? No-much too mild a punishment for the God of Love to inflict, according to the Chaplain. This would be Eternal Bliss compared with the Eternal Fire. He must be still alive...Was he mad, then, and *imagining* these unending bird-capped posts? If not mad, he soon would be. Why couldn't they say something-mannerless brutes! Should he swerve off and leave the telegraph line? No, he had starved and suffered the agonies of thirst for nearly a week-and, if he could hang on all night, he might reach water tomorrow and be saved. Food was a minor consideration and if he could drink a few gallons of water, soak his clothes in it, lie in it, —he could carry on for another day or two. Nearly as easy to sprawl face-downward on a camel-saddle as on the ground-and he had tied himself on. The camel would rub along all right for days with camel-thorn and similar dainties.... No, better not leave the line. Halt and camp within sight of it till the morning, when the brutes would fly away in search of food? No...might find it impossible to get going again, if once man and beast lay down now...Ride as far as possible from the line, keeping it in sight? No...if he fell asleep the camel would go round in a circle again, and he'd wake up a dozen miles from the line, with no idea of direction and position. Best to carry straight on. The camel would stick to the line so long as he was left exactly on it...think it a road...He could sleep without danger thus. He would shut his eyes and not see the vultures, for if he saw a dozen more he knew that he would go raving mad, halt the camel and address an impassioned appeal to them to *say something-*for God's sake to *say something.* Didn't they know that he had been in solitary confinement in a desert for three weeks or three centuries (what is time?) without hearing a sound or seeing a living thing-expecting the SNAKE night and day, and, moreover, that he was starving, dying of thirst, and light-headed, and that he was in the awful position of choosing between murdering the camel that had stood by him-no, under him-all that fearful time, and breaking his word to Lucille-cheating and deceiving Lucille. Then why couldn't they *say* something instead of sitting there in their endless millions, mile after billions of miles, post after billions of trillions of posts-menacing, watchful, silent, silent as the awful desert, silent as the SNAKE.... This would not do... he must think hard of Lucille, of the Sword, of his Dream, his Dream that came so seldom now. He would repeat Lucille's last letter, word for word: —

"My Darling,

"It is over, thank God-Oh, thank God-and you can leave the army at once and become a 'gentleman' in position as well as in fact. Poor old Grumper died on Saturday (as I cabled) and before he died he became quite another man-weak, gentle and anxious to make any amends he could to anybody. For nearly a week he was like this, and it was a most wonderful and pathetic thing. He spent most of the time in telling me, General Harringport, Auntie Yvette or the Vicar, about wicked things he had done, cruelties, meannesses, follies-it was most distressing, for really he has been simply a strong character with all the faults of one-including, as we know too well, lack of sympathy, hardness, and sometimes savage cruelty, which, after all, was only the natural result of the lack of sympathy and understanding.

"As he grew weaker he grew more sympathetic with illness and suffering, I suppose, for he sent for me in the middle of the night to say that he had suddenly remembered Major Decies' story about your probably being subject to fits and seizures in certain circumstances, and that he was coming to the conclusion that he had been hasty and unjust and had unmercifully punished you for no fault whatever. He said 'I have punished him for being punished. I have added my injustice to that of Fate. Write to him that I ask his pardon and confess my fault. Tell him I'll make such reparation as I can,' and oh, Dam-he leaves *you* Monksmead, and *me* his money, on the understanding that we marry as soon as any physician, now living in Harley Street, says that you are fit to marry (I must write it I suppose) without fear of our children being epileptic, insane, or in any way tainted. If none of them will do this, I am to inherit Monksmead and part of the money and you are to have a part of the money. If we marry *then*, we lose everything and it goes to Haddon Berners. Mr. Wyllis, who has been his lawyer and agent for thirty years, is to take you to Harley Street (presumably to prevent your bribing and corrupting the whole of the profession there residing).

"Come at once, Darling. If the silly old physicians won't certify, why-what *does* it matter? I am going to let lodgings at Monksmead to a Respectable Single Man (with board) and Auntie Yvette will see that he behaves himself.

"Cable what boat you start by and I'll meet you at Port Said. I don't know how I keep myself sitting in this chair. I could turn head over heels for joy! (And poor Grumper only just buried and his Will read!) He didn't lose quite all his grim humour in that wonderful week of softening, relenting and humanizing. What do you think he solemnly gave and bequeathed to the poor Haddock? His *wardrobe*!!! And nothing else, but if the Haddock wears only Grumper's clothes, including his boots, shirts, ties, collars and everything else, for one full and complete year, and wears absolutely nothing else, he is to have five thousand pounds at the end of it-and he is to begin on the day after the funeral! And even at the last poor Grumper was a foot taller and a foot broader (not to mention *thicker*) than the Haddock! It appears that he systematically tried to poison Grumper's mind against you-presumably with an eye on this same last Will and Testament. He hasn't been seen since the funeral. I wonder if he is going to try to win the money by remaining in bed for a year in Grumper's pyjamas!

"Am I not developing 'self-control and balance'? Here I sit writing news to you while my heart is screaming aloud with joy, crying 'Dam is coming home. Dam's troubles are over. Dam is saved!' Because if you are ever so 'ill,' Darling, there is nothing on earth to prevent your coming to your old home at once-and if we can't marry we can be pals for evermore in the dear old place of our childhood. But of *course* we can marry. Hurry home, and if any Harley Street doctor gives you even a doubtful look, throw him up his own stairs to show how feeble you are, or tie his poker round his neck in a neat bow, and refuse to undo it until he apologizes. I'm sure you could! *'Ill'* indeed! If you can't have a little fit, on the rare occasions when you see a snake, without fools saying you are ill or dotty or something, it is a pity! Anyhow there is one small woman who understands, and if she can't marry you she can at any rate be your inseparable pal-and if the Piffling Little World likes to talk scandal, in spite of Auntie Yvette's presence-why it will be amusing. Cable, Darling! I am just bursting with excitement and joy-and fear (that something may go wrong at the last moment). If it saved a single day I should start for Motipur myself at once. If we passed in mid-ocean I should jump overboard and swim to your ship. Then you'd do the same, and we should 'get left,' and look silly.... Oh, what nonsense I am talking-but I don't think I shall talk anything else again-for sheer joy!

"You can't write me a lot of bosh *now* about 'spoiling my life' and how you'd be ten times more miserable if I were your wife. Fancy —a soldier to-day and a 'landed proprietor' to-morrow! How I wish you were a *landed* traveller, and were in the train from Plymouth-no, from Dover and London, because of course you'd come the quickest way. Did my cable surprise you very much?

"I enclose fifty ten-pound notes, as I suppose they will be quicker and easier for you to cash than those 'draft' things, and they'll be quite safe in the insured packet. Send a cable at once, Darling. If you don't I shall imagine awful things and perhaps die of a broken heart or some other silly trifle.

"Mind then: —Cable to-day; Start to-morrow; Get here in a fortnight-and keep a beady eye open at Port Said and Brindisi and places-in case there has been time for me to get there. Au revoir. Darling Dam,

"Your

"Lucille

"Three cheers! And a million more!"

* * *

Yes, a long letter, but he could almost say it backwards. He couldn't be anything like mad while he could do that?... How had she received his answer-in which he tried to show her the impossibility of any decent man compromising a girl in the way she proposed in her sweet innocence and ignorance. Of course *he*, a half-mad, epileptic, fiend-ridden monomaniac-nay, dangerous lunatic, —could not *marry*. Why, he might murder his own wife under some such circumstances as those under which he attacked Captain Blake. (Splendid fellow Blake! Not every man after such a handling as that would make it his business to prove that his assailant was neither drunk, mad, nor criminal-merely under a hallucination. But for Blake he would now be in jail, or lunatic asylum, to a certainty. The Colonel would have had him court-martialled as a criminal, or else have had him out of the regiment as a lunatic. Nor, as a dangerous lunatic, would he have been allowed to buy himself out when Lucille's letter and his money arrived. Blake had got him into the position of a perfectly sober and sane person whose mind had been temporarily upset by a night of horror-in which a coffin-quitting corpse had figured, and so he had been able to steer between the cruel rocks of Jail and Asylum to the blessed harbour of Freedom.)

Yes-in spite of Blake's noble goodness and help, Dam knew that he was *not* normal, that he *was* dangerous, that he spent long periods on the very border-line of insanity, that he stood fascinated on that border-line and gazed far into the awful country beyond-the Realms of the Mad....

Marry! Not Lucille, while he had the sanity left to say "No"!

As for going to live at Monksmead with her and Auntie Yvette-it would be an even bigger crime. Was it for *him* to make *Lucille* a "problem" girl, a girl who was "talked about," a by-word for those vile old women of both sexes whose favourite pastime is the invention and dissemination of lies where they dare, and of even more damaging head-shakes, lip-pursings, gasps and innuendoes where they do not?

Was it for *him* to get *Lucille* called "The Woman Who Did," by those scum of the leisured classes, and "That peculiar young woman," by the better sort of matron, dowager and chaperone,—make her the kind of person from whose company careful mothers keep their innocent daughters (that their market price may never be in danger of the faintest depreciation when they are for sale in the matrimonial market), the kind of woman for whom men have a slightly and subtly different manner at meet, hunt-ball, dinner or theatre-box? Get Lucille "talked about"?

No-setting aside the question of the possibility of living under the same roof with her and conquering the longing to marry.

No-he had some decency left, tainted as he doubtless was by his barrack-room life.

Tainted of course.... What was it he had heard the senior soldierly-looking man, whom the other addressed as "General," say concerning some mutual acquaintance, at breakfast in the dining-car going up to Kot Ghazi?

"Yes, poor chap, was in the ranks-and no man can escape the barrack-room taint when he has once lived in it. Take me into any Officers' Mess you like-say 'There is a promoted gentleman-ranker here,' and I'll lay a thousand to one I spot him. Don't care if he's the son of a Dook-nor yet if he's Royal, you can spot him alright...."

Pleasant hearing for the "landed proprietor," whom a beautiful, wealthy and high-bred girl proposed to marry!

Tainted or not, in that way-he was *mentally* tainted, a fact beside which the other, if as true as Truth, paled into utterest insignificance.

No-he had taken the right line in replying to Lucille that he was getting worse mentally, that no doctor would dream of "vetting" him "sound," that he was not scoundrel enough to come and cause scandal and "talk" at Monksmead, and that he was going to disappear completely from the ken of man, wrestle with himself, and come to her and beg her to marry him directly he was better-sufficiently better to "pass the doctor," that is. If, meanwhile, she met and loved a man worthy of her, such a man as Ormonde Delorme, he implored her to marry him and to forget the wholly unworthy and undesirable person who had merely loomed large upon her horizon through the accident of propinquity...

(He could always disappear again and blow out such brains as he possessed, if that came to pass, he told himself.)

Meanwhile letters to the Bank of Bombay would be sent for, at least once a year-but she was not to write-she was to forget him. As to searching for him-he had not quite decided whether he would walk from Rangoon to Pekin or from Quetta to Constantinople-perhaps neither, but from Peshawur to Irkutsk. Anyhow, he was going to hide himself pretty effectually, and put himself beyond the temptation of coming and spoiling her life. Sooner or later he would be mad, dead, or cured. If the last-why he would make for the nearest place where he could get news of her-and if she were then happily married to somebody else-why-why-she *would* be happy, and that would make him quite happy...

Had the letter been quite sane and coherent-or had he been in a queer mental state when he wrote it?...

He opened his eyes, saw a vulture within a few yards of him, closed them again, and, soon after, fell into an uneasy slumber as the camel padded on at a steady seven miles an hour unurged-save by the *smell* of pure clear water which was still a score of miles distant....

When Damocles de Warrenne awoke, he was within a few hundred yards of the nearly dry River Helnuddi, where, failing occasional pools, the traveller can always procure water by digging and patiently awaiting the slow formation of a little puddle at the bottom of the hole.

For a minute he halted. Should he dig while he had strength, or should he turn to the left and follow the river-bed until he came to a pool-or could go no farther? Perhaps he would be too weak to dig, though, by that time.... Remarkable how eager to turn to the left and get on, the camel was-considering how tired he must be-perhaps he could smell distant water or knew of a permanent pool hereabouts. Well, let that decide it....

An hour later, as the camel topped a rise in the river-bank, a considerable pool came into view, tree-shaded, heron-haunted, too incredibly beautiful and alluring for belief. Was it a mirage?...

A few minutes later, Damocles de Warrenne and his camel were drinking, and a few hours later entered the dreary featureless compound of a wretched hovel, which, to the man at least, was a palatial and magnificent asylum (no, not *asylum* —of all words) —refuge and home-the more so that a camel knelt chewing in the shade of the building, and a man, Abdul Ghani himself, lay slumbering in the verandah....

"You understand, then," said Dam in the vernacular, to the malodorous, hideous, avaricious Abdul who reappeared from Kot Ghazi a few days later, "you return here again, one week from to-day, bringing the things written down on this paper, from the shop of Rustomji at Kot Ghazi. Here you wait until I come. If I find there is truth in your *khubbar*[27] of ibex you will be rewarded... Why don't I take you? Because I want to be alone. Set out now for Kot Ghazi. I may return here to-night, and I may not return for days. Do not come until one whole week has passed . . . You are certain they were ibex you saw, and within four koss of here-only yesterday ? "

Abdul swore by the hilt of his knife and the beard of the Prophet If the Sahib doubted him and found them not, Abdul the honest, truthful, innocent, and impeccable, could take the Sahib to the very spot where they had passed the night, leaving the usual signs of their presence- Strange, for ibex to come within fifty miles of civilization ? Perhaps, but who knoweth the mind of the ibex or the Will of Allah, and moreover Abdul was a poor man, the Sahib being his Father and Mother. Conclusively, why should Abdul lie, in this particular, since the Sahib was already paying him by the day?

Had his luck turned at last ? It almost looked like it-for surely that was a record head-anything from fifty to sixty inches! The head was still the property of the ibex who carried it, of course, but still, is was something even to be in sight of a magnificent pair of horns like that-after a fortnight of toil and hardship that would make a coal-miner strike for ever.

The beast, seen through field-glasses, looked a mere appanage of his great curving, tapering horns. He seemed to stand under them as a train under a railway-arch. And he was absolutely unsuspicious, quite accessible, up wind and within a hundred yards of good cover. Damocles de Warrenne heaved a sigh of pure contentment as he returned his field-glasses to their case ere he unstrapped it and laid it on the ground with his water-bottle, haversack, and coat-preparatory to the long and painful crawl and wriggle which should bring him within shot of his quarry.

First he must creep on hands and knees down a watercourse away from the ibex. Then he must go on his stomach for half a mile, behind a low ridge, to where he could turn to the right and climb above the beast, going with infinite care from rock to rock and cactus to cactus. Arrived on the plateau, he would have to steal on tip-toe to the bushes, crawl through them, and then do a last stomach-wriggle to the rock from behind which he could get a shot

He took from his haversack, and slipped on, a pair of loose gloves with leather palms, and started. It was not so bad in the watercourse, in spite of sore knees and roasted neck. The rifle was the trouble. He must either go "on three legs" or put the rifle on the ground, beneath the hand that held it, every time he moved forward. He determined to have a sling attached to it, next time, and carry it on his back, Yes, and then it would bump against rocks, or slip round with a crash, and give him away. Better carry it in the hand-but it was cruel on the wrist.

A stone fell and clattered. Dam shrank, cringed, and shut his eyes-as one expecting a heavy blow. *Ah-h-h-h* —had the beast bolted? With the slowness of an hour-hand he raised his head above the bank of the watercourse until his eye cleared the edge. *No* —still there. After a painful crawl that seemed to last for hours, he reached the point where the low ridge ran off at right-angles, crept behind it, and lay flat on his face, to rest and recover breath. He was soaked in perspiration from head to foot, giddy with sun and unnatural posture, very sore as to elbows and knees, out of breath, trembling-and entirely happy. The half-mile crawl, with the greater part of his body on the burning ground, and the rifle to shuffle steadily along without noise or damage, was the equivalent of a hard day's work to a strong man. At the end of it he lay gasping and sick, aching in every limb, almost blind with glare and over-exertion, weary to death-and entirely happy. Thank God he would be able to stand up in a moment and rest behind a big cactus. Then he would have a spell of foot-work for a change, and, though crouching double, would not be doing any crawling until he had crossed the plateau and reached the bushes.

The upward climb was successfully accomplished with frequent halts for breath, behind boulders. On the plateau all that was required was silence. The ibex could not see him up there. In his rubber-soled khaki-coloured shoes he could almost run, but it was a question whether a drink of cold water would not be worth more than all the ibexes in the world.

He tip-toed rapidly across the level hill-top, reached the belt of low bushes, dropped, and lay to recover breath before resuming the painful and laborious crawling part of his journey. Was it possible to tap one's tongue against one's teeth and hear the noise of it as though it were made of wood? It seemed so. Was this giddiness and dimness of vision sunstroke? What would he give to have that fly (that had followed him for hundreds of thousands of miles that morning) between his fingers?

Last lap! There was the rock, and below it must be the quarry-if it had not fled. He must keep that rock between himself and his prey and he must get to it without a sound. It would be easy enough without the rifle. Could he stick it through his belt and along his back, or trail it behind him? What nonsense! He must be getting a touch of sun. Would these stones leave marks of burns on his clothes? Surely he could smell himself singeing. Enough to explode the rifle... The big rock at last! A rest and then a peep, with infinite precaution. Dam held his breath and edged his face to the corner of the great boulder. Moving imperceptibly, he peeped... *No ibex!* ... He was about to spring up with a hearty malediction on his luck when he perceived a peculiar projection on a large stone some distance down the hill. It moved-and Dam dropped back. It must be the top of the curve of one of the horns of the ibex and the animal must be lying down.... What to do? It might lie for hours and he himself might go to sleep. It might get up and depart at any moment without coming into the line of fire-without being seen indeed. Better continue the stalk and hope to get a standing shot, or, failing that, a running one.

It looked a nasty descent, since silence was essential-steep, slippery, and strewn with round stones. Anyhow, he could go down on his feet, which was something to be thankful for, as it was agony to put a knee or elbow to the ground. He crept on.

Surely his luck was changing, for here he was, within fifty yards of a stone behind which lay an unsuspecting ibex with a world's-record head. Hullo! a nasty little precipice! With a nastily sloping shelf at the bottom too, eight feet away-and then another little precipice and another sloping shelf at its base.

Better lay the rifle on the edge, slip over, hang by the hands, grab it with one, and then drop the intervening few inches. Rubber soles would play their part here! Damn this giddiness-touch of sun, no doubt. Damocles de Warrenne knelt on the edge of the eight-foot drop, turned round, swayed, fell, struck the sloping ledge, rolled off it, fell, struck the next sloping ledge, fell thirty feet-arousing an astounded ibex *en route* —and landed in a queer heap on a third shelf, with a few broken ribs, a dislocated shoulder, broken ankles, and a fractured thigh.

A vulture, who had been interested in his proceedings for some time, dropped a few thousand feet and had a look. What he saw decided him to come to earth. He perched on a rock and waited patiently. He knew the symptoms and he knew the folly of taking risks. A friend or two joined him-each, as he left his place in the sky, being observed and followed by a brother who was himself in turn observed and followed by another who brought others....

One of the hideous band had drawn quite near and was meditating rewarding his own boldness with a succulent eye, when Dam groaned and moved. The pretty birds also moved and probably groaned in spirit-but they didn't move far.

What was that Miss Smellie had been so fond of saying? "There is no such thing as 'luck,' Damocles. All is ordered for the best by an all-seeing and merciful Providence." Yes. No doubt.

What was that remark of his old friend, "Holy Bill"?

"What do you mean by 'luck,' Damocles? All that happens is ordained by God in His infinite mercy." Yes.

Holy Bill had never done a day's work in his life nor missed a meal-save when bilious from overeating....

A pity the infinite mercy didn't run to a little water! It would have been easy for the all-seeing and merciful Providence to move him to retain his water-bottle when starting the stalk-if it were necessary to the schemes of the Deity to have him smashed like a dropped egg.... What agony a human being could endure!...

Not even his rifle at hand with its means of speedy death. He might live for days and then be torn alive by those accursed vultures. One mighty effort to turn on his back and he would breathe easier-but that would bring his eyes to the sun-and the vultures.... Had he slept or fainted? How long had he lain there?... Chance of being found? Absolutely none. Shikarri would have visited the dak-bungalow a week ago. Camel left below on the plain-and it would wander miles from where he left it when it grew hungry. Even if Abdul and an organized search-party were after him *now* they might as well be searching for a needle in a hay-stack. No one knew which of the thousand gullies he had ascended and no one could track camel-pads or flat rubber soles over bare solid rock, even if given the starting-point. No-he had got to die of thirst, starvation, and vultures, barring miracles of luck-and he had *never* had any good luck-for luck existed, undoubtedly, in spite of mealy-mouthed platitude-makers and twaddle about everything being pre-arranged and ordained with care and deliberation by a kind paternal Providence.

And what luck he had had-all his life! Born fated!

Had he fainted again or slept? And could he hear the tinkle of ice against the sides of a tall thin tumbler of lemonade, or was it the sound of a waterfall of clear, cold water close by? Were the servants asleep, or was the drink he had ordered being prepared?... No-he was dying in agony on a red-hot rock, surrounded by vultures and probably watched by foxes, jackals and hyenas. And a few yards away were the rifle that would have put him out of his misery, and the water-bottle that would have alleviated his pain-to the extent, at any rate, of enabling him to think clearly and perhaps scribble a few words in blood or something, somehow, for Lucille... Lucille! Would the All-Merciful let him see her once again for a moment in return for an extra thousand years of Hell or whatever it was that unhappy mortals got as a continuation of the joys of this gay world? Could he possibly induce the vultures to carry him home-if he pledged himself to feed them and support their progeny? They could each have a house in the compound. It would pay them far better than eating him now. Did they understand Pushtoo or was it Persian? Certainly not Hindustani and Urdu. People who came shooting alone in the desert and mountains, where vultures abounded, should learn to talk Vulture and pass the Higher Standard in that tongue. But even if they understood him they might be unwilling to serve a coward. *Was* he a coward? Anyhow he lay glued with his own blood to the spot he would never leave-unless the vultures could be bribed. Useless to hope anything of the jackals. He had hunted too many foxes to begin now to ask favours. Besides they could only drag, and he had been dragged once by a horse. Quite enough for one lifetime. But he had never injured a vulture. Pity he had no copy of Grimm or Anderson with him-they contained much useful information about talking foxes, obliging birds, and other matters germane to the occasion. If he could only get them to apply it, a working-party of vultures and jackals certainly had the strength to transport him a considerable distance-alternately carrying and dragging him. The big bird, stalking nearer, was probably the *macuddam* or foreman. Would it be at all possible for vultures to bring water? He would be very willing to offer his right hand in return for a little water. The bird would be welcome to eat it off his body if it would give him a drink first. Did not ravens bring meat to the prophet Elijah? Intelligent and obliging birds. Probably cooked it, too. But water was more difficult to carry, if easier to procure.

How close they were coming and how they watched with their horrible eyes-and pretended not to watch!...

Oh, the awful, unspeakable agony! Why was he alive again? Was his chest full of terribly rusty machinery that would go on when it ought to stop for want of oil?...If pain is punishment for sin, as placid stall-fed Holy Bill held (never having suffered any), then Damocles de Warrenne must have been the prince of sinners. Oh God! a little drop of water! Rivers of it flowing not many miles away!

Monsoons of it falling recently! A water-bottle full a few yards distant-and he must die for want of a drop...What a complete circle the vultures made on the rocks and stunted trees of the sloping hill-side. Oh, for a revolver! A man ought to carry one on shikar expeditions. One would give him a chance of life when under a tiger or panther-and a chance of decent death in a position such as this. Where had he read that vultures begin on the eyes of their prey? Without awaiting its death either, so long as it could not defend itself. There were other depraved gustatory preferences, too, if he remembered rightly-He would have an opportunity of testing the accuracy of the statement-though not of assuring its author as to its correctness.

Water...Water...Water...

Had he fainted again, that the vultures were so much nearer?...Why should he be a second Prometheus? Had he not had suffering enough in his life, without having more in his death?... If the sending of a little water were too obvious a miracle, was it too much to ask that his next fainting and collapse might last long enough for the vultures to get to work, make a beginning, and an end?

Surely that would not be too great a miracle, since he had lain for years on a red-hot rock with blood in his mouth and his body wrecked like a smashed egg. He must be practically dead. Perhaps if he held his laboured breath and closed his eyes they *would* begin, and he would have the strength to keep still when they did so. That would be the quickest way. Once they started, it would not be long before his bones were cleaned. No possible ghost of a chance of being saved. Probably no human foot had been on these particular rocks since human feet existed. Nor would he ever again have the strength to drag his shattered body to where the rifle lay. Only a few yards away lay speedy happy release.

"No such thing as luck, Damocles."

Perhaps the vultures thought otherwise.

Colonel John Decies, still of Bimariabad, but long retired on pension from the Indian Medical Service, was showing his mental and physical unfitness for the service of the Government that had ordered his retirement, by devoting himself at the age of fifty-nine to aviation-aviation in the interests of the wounded on the battlefield. What he wanted to live to see was a flying stretcher-service of the Royal Army Medical Corps that should flash to and fro at the rate of a hundred miles an hour between the rear of the firing-line and the field hospital and base hospital in aeroplanes built especially for the accommodation of wounded men-an officer of the Corps accompanying each in the dual capacity of surgeon and potential pilot. When he allowed his practical mind to wander among the vast possibilities of the distant future, he dreamed of bigger and bigger aeroplanes until they became fully equipped flying hospitals themselves, and removed the wounded from the danger zone to the nearest salubrious spot for their convalescence. Meanwhile, he saw no reason why the more powerful biplanes should not carry an operating-table and all surgical accessories, a surgeon, and two or three wounded men who could not be made sitting-up cases.

To Colonel John Decies it seemed that if soldiers schemed to adapt the flying-machine to purposes of death and destruction, doctors might do the same to purposes of life and salvation. Think of the difference between being jolted for hours in a bullock-cart in the dust and heat and being borne through the air without jerk or jar. Think of the hundreds of men who, in the course of one campaign, would be saved from the ghastly fate of lying unfound, unseen by the stretcher-bearers, to starve to death, to lie weltering in their blood, to live through days of agony....

He was making quite a name for himself by his experiments at the Kot Ghazi flying-school and by his articles and speeches on the formation and training of a R.A.M.C. flying branch. Small beginnings would content him (provided they were intended to lead to great developments)—an aeroplane at first, that could carry one or two special cases to which the ordinary means of transport would be fatal, and that could scour the ground, especially in the case of very broken terrain and hill-country, for overlooked cases, wounded men unable to move or call, and undiscovered by the searchers.

He was hard at work on the invention of a strong collapsible operating-table (that could readily be brought into use in the field and also be used in aerial transport) and a case for the concentration of equipment-operation instruments, rubber gloves, surgical gauntlets, saline infusion apparatus, sterilizer, aseptic towels, chloroform, bandages, gauze, wool, sponges, drainage-tubing, inhaler, silk skeins, syringes, field tourniquets, waterproof cloth, stethoscope-everything, and the whole outfit, table and all, weighing forty pounds. This would be an improvement on the system of having to open half a dozen medical and surgical cases when operating on the line of march, cases requiring the most expert repacking after use...

* * *

Perhaps it was a sign of advancing years and weakening mind that this fine specimen of a fine service felt that, when flying some thousands of feet above the earth, he was nearer to Lenore in Heaven. All his science and sad experience had failed to deprive him of a sub-conscious belief in an actual place "above," a material Hereafter beyond the sky, and, when clouds cut him off from sight of the earth, he had a quaint, half-realized feeling of being in the ante-room of the Great House of many mansions, wherein dwelt Lenore.

Yes, when flying, Colonel John Decies felt that he was nearer to the woman he had lost nearly a quarter of a century before. In one sense he may have been so, for he was a very reckless airman, and never in greater danger than when engaged in what he called "ground-scouring" among the air-current haunted, mist-haunted mountains of the Border. He anticipated an early Border-war and realized that here would be a great opportunity for a keen-sighted and iron-nerved medical airman to locate, if not to pick up, overlooked wounded. Here, too, would be a double need of such service in a country where "the women come out to cut up what remains"! Imagine, too, cavalry reconnaissances and bad casualties a score of miles from medical help...

Whether it brought him nearer in any sense to Lenore de Warrenne, it brought him nearer to her son, on one of those hundred-mile circular "scours" which he practised when opportunity offered, generally accompanied by a like-minded officer of the R.A.M.C., to which Corps he had become a kind of unofficial and honorary instructor in "First- Aid Flying" at the Kot Ghazi flying-school, situate in the plains at the foot of the "Roof of the World".

"Hullo!" said Colonel John Decies to himself—"vultures! I suppose they might be referred to in my manual as a likely guide to the wounded. Good idea. 'The flying casualty-scout should always take note of the conduct of vultures, noting the direction of flight if any are seen dropping to earth. These birds may prove invaluable guides. A collection of them on the ground may indicate a wounded man who may be alive.'..."

The Colonel was thinking of his *magnum opus*, "The Aeroplane and the Surgeon, in War," wherewith he lived laborious days at Bimariabad in the intervals of testing, developing, and demonstrating his theories at Kot Ghazi.

Turning his head, he shouted to Surgeon-Captain Digby-Soames, R.A.M.C., his passenger and pupil: —

"Vultures on the left-front or starboard bow. 'Invariable battle-field sign of wounded man. Note spot if unable to land and rescue. Call up stretcher-party by signal—*Vide* page 100 of Decies' great work,' what?"

"By Jove, it is a wounded man," replied Captain Digby-Soames, who was using field-glasses. "Damned if it isn't a Sahib, too! Out shikarring and sprained his ankle, I suppose. Dead, I'm afraid. Poor devil!"

"Vultures aren't *at work*, anyhow," commented Colonel Decies. "Can't land anywhere hereabouts, and I'm afraid 'calling up the stretcher party' isn't in the game here."

"Nothing nearer than Kot Ghazi and that's a good thirty miles," replied Captain Digby-Soames as the aeroplane hovered and slowly sank.

"Let's see all we can and then find the nearest landing-place. Search all round for any sign of a tent or encampment. There may be a dak-bungalow somewhere down in the plains, too. The river-bed down on the right there, marks the border."

Captain Digby-Soames "scoured" earnestly with his glasses.

"Camel on the port-bow, at the foot of the hills," he announced. "What may be a dak-bungalow several miles away...a white square dot, anyhow...Camel saddled up, kneeling...His, no doubt. Wonder where his shikarri is —"

As the aeroplane approached, the disappointed vultures departed, misliking the size, shape and sounds of the strange fowl. As it passed over him, and the Major shouted, Dam opened his eyes.

This must be pretty well the end-when he heard the voice of some one he knew well, and saw a flying-machine just above him. He would see blocks of ice and cascades of cold water in a moment, doubtless, and hear Lucille calling.

A flying-machine in Ghazistan! The voice of an old, old friend to whom he could not, for the moment, give a name...Why couldn't the cowardly brutes of vultures begin their business, and end his? What was that familiar voice calling: —

"Hold on a bit, we'll soon be with you! Don't give up. We can't land just here. If we drop anything can you crawl and get it?"

"He opened his eyes," said Captain Digby-Soames, "but I doubt if he's conscious. He must have come a frightful cropper. You can see there's a compound fracture of the right femur from here, and one of his feet is fairly pointing backwards. Blood from the mouth, too. Anyhow he's alive. Better shoot him if we can't shift him — —"

"We'll *get* him all right. This is a Heaven-sent 'problem' and we'll solve it-and I'll quote it in my 'manual'. Quite war-conditions. Very badly wounded man-inaccessible position-stretcher-parties all out of sight-aeroplane can't land for any first-aid nor to pick up the casualty — *excellent* problem and demonstration. That oont[28] will simplify it, though. Look here —I'll drop down and land you by it, and then come here again and hover. You bring the beast up-you'll be able to ride most of the way if you zig-zag, and lead him most of the rest. Then you'll have to carry the casualty to the oont and bring him down."

The aeroplane swooped down and grounded gently within a hundred yards of the kneeling camel, who eyed it with the cold and superciliious disdain of his kind.

"Tell you what," said Colonel Decies, "when I get up there again, have a good squint and see if you think you can locate the spot for yourself from below. If you can, I'll come down again and we'll both go up on the oont. Bring the poor beggar down much better if one of us can hold him while the other drives the camel. It's no Grand Trunk Road, by Jove."

"Right-O," acquiesced Captain Digby-Soames. "If I can get a clear bearing to a point immediately below where you hover, I'll lie flat on the ground as an affirmative signal. If there's no good landmark I'll stay perpendicular, what?"

"That's it," said Colonel Decies, and, with a swift run and throbbing whirr, the aeroplane soared from the ground and rose to where, a thousand feet from the plain, lay the mangled "problem". As it came to a halt and hovered[29] (like a gigantic dragon-fly poised on its invisibly-rapid wings above a pool), the junior officer's practised eye noted a practicable gully that debouched on a level with, and not far from, the ledge over which the aeroplane hung, and that a stunted thorn-tree stood below the shelf and two large cactus bushes on its immediate left. Having taken careful note of other landmarks and glanced at the sun, he lay on the ground at full length for a minute and then arose and approached the camel, who greeted him with a bubbling snarl. On its great double saddle were a gun-cover and a long cane, while from it dangled a haversack, camera, cartridge-case, satchel, canvas water-bag, and a cord-net holdall of odds and ends.

Obviously the "problem's" shikar-camel. Apparently he was out without any shikarri, orderly, or servant—a foolish thing to do when stalking in country in which a sprained ankle is more than a possibility, and a long-range bullet in the back a probability anywhere on that side of the border.

The aeroplane returned to earth and grounded near by. Stopping the engine Colonel Decies climbed out and swung himself into the rear seat of the camel saddle. Captain Digby-Soames sprang into the front one and the camel lurched to its feet, and was driven to the mouth of the gully which the Captain had noted as running up to the scene of the tragedy.

To and fro, in and out of the gully, winding, zig-zagging, often travelling a hundred yards to make a dozen, the sure-footed and well-trained beast made its way upward.

"Coming down will be joy," observed the Colonel. "I'd sooner be on a broken aeroplane in a cyclone."

"Better hop off here, I should think," said Captain Digby-Soames anon. "We can lead him a good way yet, though. Case of divided we stand, united we fall. Let him fall by himself if he wants to," and at the next reasonably level spot the camel was made to kneel, that his riders might descend. Slithering down from a standing camel is not a sport to practise on a steep hillside, if indulged in at all.

Another winding, scrambling climb and the head of the nullah was reached.

"Have to get the beast kneeling when we climb down to him with the casualty," opined the Colonel. "Better get him down here, I think. Doesn't seem any decent place farther on," and the camel was brought to an anchor and left to his own devices.

"By Jove, the poor beggar *has* come a purler," said Captain Digby-Soames, as the two bent over the apparently unconscious man.

"Ever seen him at Kot Ghazi or Bimariabad?" inquired Colonel Decies.

"No," said the Captain, "never seen him anywhere. Why-have you?"

"Certainly seen him somewhere-trying to remember where. I thought perhaps it might have been at the flying-school or at one of the messes. Can't place him at all, but I'll swear I've met him."

"Manoeuvres, perhaps," suggested the other, "or 'board ship."

"Extraordinary thing is that I feel I *ought* to know him well. Something most familiar about the face. I'm afraid it's a bit too late to-Broken ribs-fractured thigh-broken ankles-broken arm-perforated lungs-not much good trying to get him down, I'm afraid. He might linger for days, though, if we decided to stand by, up here. A really first-class problem for solution-we're in luck," mused Colonel Decies, making his rapid and skilful examination. "Yes, we must get him down, of course-after a bit of splinting."

"And then the real 'problem' will commence, I suppose," observed Captain Digby-Soames. "You couldn't put him into my seat and fly him to Kot Ghazi while I dossed down with the camel and waited for you to come for me. And it wouldn't do to camel him to that building which looks like a dak-bungalow."

"No. I think you'll have to stand by while I fly to Kot Ghazi and bring the necessary things for a temporary job, and then return and try to guide an ambulance waggon here. Oh, for an aeroplane-ambulance! This job brings it home to you pretty clearly, doesn't it? Or I might first go and have a look at the alleged dak-bungalow and see if we could possibly run him over there on a charpoy[30] or an improvised camel-stretcher. It'll be a ghastly job getting down. I don't know that you hadn't better stick to him up here while I go straight back for proper splints and bandages and so forth, and bring another chap too...Where the devil have I seen him before? I shall forget my own name next."

The Colonel pondered a moment.

"Look here," he decided. "This case is urgent enough to justify a risky experiment. He's been here a devil of a time and if he's not in a *pukka* hospital within the next few hours it's all up with him. He's going to have the distinction of being the first casualty removed to hospital by flying-machine. I'll tie him on somewhere. We'll splint him up as well as possible, and then make him into a blooming cocoon with the cord, and whisk him away."

"Pity we haven't a few planks," observed Captain Digby-Soames. "We could make one big splint of his whole body and sling him, planks and all, underneath the aeroplane."

"Well, you start splinting that right leg on to the left and stiffen the knees with something (you'll probably be able to get a decent stick or two off that small tree), and shove the arm inside his leather legging. We've two pairs of putties you can bandage with, and there are *puggries* on all three *topis*. Probably his gun's somewhere about, for another leg-splint, too. I'll get down to the machine for the cord and then I'll skirmish around for anything in the nature of poles or planks. I can get over to that hut and back before you've done. It'll be the camelling that'll kill him."

At the distant building the Colonel found an abandoned broken-wheeled bullock-cart, from which he looted the bottom-boards, which were planks six feet long, laid upon, but not fastened to, the framework of the body of the cart. From the compound of the place (an ancient and rarely-visited dak-bungalow, probably the most outlying and deserted in India) he procured a bamboo pole that had once supported a lamp, the long leg-rests of an old chair, and two or three sticks, more or less serviceable for his purpose.

Returning to the camel, he ascended to where his passenger and pupil awaited him. Over his shoulder he bore the planks, pole and sticks that the contemptuous but invaluable camel had borne to a point a few yards below the scene of the tragedy.

"Good egg," observed the younger man. "We'll do him up in those like a mummy."

"Yes," returned the Colonel, "then carry him to the oont and bind him along one side of the saddle, and then lead the beast down. Easily sling him on to the machine, and there we are. Lucky we've got the coil of cord. Fine demonstration for the Kot Ghazi fellers! Show that the thing can be done, even without the proper kind of 'plane and surgical outfit. What luck we spotted him—or that he fell just in our return track!"

"Doubtless he was born to that end," observed the Captain, who was apt to get a little peevish when hungry and tired.

And when the Army Aeroplane *Hawk* returned from its "ground-scouring for casualties" trip, lo, it bore, beneath and beside the pilot and passenger, a real casualty slung in a kind of crude coffin-cradle of planks and poles, a casualty in whose recovery the Colonel took the very deepest interest, for was he not a heaven-sent case, born to the end that he might be smashed to demonstrate the Colonel's theories? But no credit was given to the vultures, without whom the "casualty" would never have been found.

Chapter XIII
Found

Colonel John Decies, I.M.S. (retired), visiting the Kot Ghazi Station Hospital, whereof his friend and pupil, Captain Digby-Soames, was Commandant, scanned the temperature chart of the unknown, the desperately injured "case," retrieved by his beloved flying-machine, who, judging by his utterances in delirium, appeared to be even worse damaged in spirit than he was in body.

"Very high again last night," he observed to Miss Norah O'Neill of the Queen Alexandra Military Nursing Sisterhood.

"Yes, and very violent," replied Miss O'Neill. "I had to call two orderlies and they could hardly hold him. He appeared to think he was fighting a huge snake or fleeing from one. He also repeatedly screamed: 'It is under my foot! It is moving, moving, moving *out*.'"

"*Got it*, by God!" cried the Colonel, suddenly smiting his forehead with violence. "*Of course!* Fool! Fool that I am! Merciful God in Heaven —*it's her boy* —and *I* have saved him! *Her boy!* And I've been cudgelling my failing addled brains for months, wondering where I had seen his face before. He's my godson, Sister, and I haven't set eyes on him for the last-nearly twenty years!"

Miss Norah O'Neill had never before seen an excited doctor in a hospital ward, but she now beheld one nearly beside himself with excitement, joy, surprise, and incredulity. (It is sad to have to relate that she also heard one murmuring over and over again to himself, "Well, I am damned".)

At last Colonel John Decies announced that the world was a tiny, small place and a very rum one, that it was just like *The Hawk* to be the means of saving *her* boy of all people, and then took the patient's hand in his, and sat studying his face, in wondering, pondering silence.

To Miss Norah O'Neill this seemed extraordinarily powerful affection for a mere *godson*, and one lost to sight for twenty years at that. Yet Colonel Decies was a bachelor and, no, the patient certainly resembled him in no way whatsoever. The tiny new-born germ of a romance died at once in Miss O'Neill's romantic heart-and yet, had she but known, here was a romance such as her soul loved above all things-the son of the adored dead mistress discovered *in extremis*, and saved, by the devout platonic lover, the life-long lover, and revealed to him by the utterance of the pre-natally learnt words of the dead woman herself!

Yes-how many times through those awful days had Decies heard that heart-rending cry! How cruelly the words had tortured him! And here, they were repeated twenty years on-for the identification of the son by the friend!

That afternoon Colonel Decies dispatched a cablegram addressed to a Miss Gavestone, Monksmead, Southshire, England, and containing the words, "Have found him, Kot Ghazi, bad accident, doing well, Decies," and by the next mail Lucille, with Aunt Yvette and a maid, left Port Said, having travelled overland to Brindisi and taken passage to Egypt by the *Osiris* to overtake the liner that had left Tilbury several days before the cable reached Monksmead. And in Lucille's largest trunk was an article the like of which is rarely to be found in the baggage of a young lady-nothing more nor less than an ancient rapier of Italian pattern!...

To Lucille, who knew her lover so well, it seemed that the sight and feel of the worshipped Sword of his Ancestors must bring him comfort, self-respect, memories, thoughts of the joint youth and happiness of himself and her.

She knew what the Sword had been to him, how he had felt a different person when he held its inspiring hilt, how it had moved him to the telling of his wondrous dream and stories of its stirring past, how he had revered and loved it...surely it must do him good to have it? If he were stretched upon a bed of sickness, and it were hung where he could see it, it *must* help him. It would bring diversion of thought, cheer him, suggest bright memories-perhaps give him brave dreams that would usurp the place of bad ones.

If he were well or convalescent it might be even more needful as a tonic to self-respect, a reminder of high tradition, a message from dead sires. Yes, surely it must do him good where she could not. If there were any really insurmountable obstacle to their-their —union-the Sword could still be with him always, and say unceasingly: "Do not be world-beaten, son of the de Warrennes and Stukeleys. Do not despair. Do not be fate-conquered. Fight! Fight! Look upon me not as merely the symbol of struggle but as the actual Sword of your actual Fathers. Fight Fate! Die fighting-but do not live defeated" —but of course her hero Dam needed no such exhortations. Still-the Sword must be a comfort, a pleasure, a hope, an inspiration, a symbol. When she brought it him he would understand. Swords were to sever, but *the* Sword should be a link —a visible bond between them, and between them again and their common past.

To her fellow-passengers Lucille was a puzzling enigma. What could be the story of the beautiful, and obviously wealthy, girl with the anxious, preoccupied look, whose thoughts were always far away, who took no interest in the pursuits and pastimes usual to her sex and age on a long sea voyage; who gave no glance at the wares of local vendors that came aboard at Port Said and Aden; who occupied her leisure with no book, no writing, no conversation, no deck-games; and who constantly consulted her watch as though impatient of the slow flight of time or the slow progress of the ship?

Many leading questions were put to Auntie Yvette, but, dearly as she would have liked to talk about her charge's romantic trouble, her tongue was tied and she dreaded to let slip any information that might possibly lead to a train of thought connecting Lucille, Dam, and the old half-forgotten scandal of the outcast from Monksmead and Sandhurst. If her beloved nephew foolishly chose to hide his head in shame when there was no shame, it was not for those who loved him best to say anything which might possibly lead to his discovery and identification.

While cordially polite to all men (including women) Lucille was found to be surrounded by an impenetrable wall of what was either glass or ice according to the nature of the investigator. Those who would fain extend relationship beyond that of merest ephemeral ship-board acquaintanceship (and the inevitabilities of close, though temporary, daily contact), while admitting that her manner and manners were beautiful, had to admit also that she was an extremely difficult young person "to get to know". A gilt-edged, bumptious young subalternknut, who commenced the voyage apoplectically full of self-admiration, self-confidence, and admiring wonder at his enormous attractiveness, importance, and value, finished the same in a ludicrously deflated condition-and a quiet civilian, to whom the cub had been shamefully insolent, was moved to present him with a little poem of his composition commencing "There was a puppy caught a wasp," which gave him the transient though salutary gift of sight of himself as certain others saw him....

Even the Great Mrs. "Justice" Spywell (her husband was a wee meek joint-sessions-judge) was foiled in her diligent endeavours, and those who know the Great Mrs. "Justice" Spywell will appreciate the defensive abilities of Lucille. To those poor souls, throughout the world, who stand lorn and cold without the charmed and charming circle of Anglo-Indiandom, it may be explained that the Great Mrs. "Justice" Spywell was far too Great to be hampered by silly scruples of diffidence when on the track of information concerning the private affairs of lesser folk-which is to say other folk.

When travelling abroad she is THE Judge's Wife; when staying at Hill Stations she is The JUDGE'S Wife, and when adorning her proper sphere, her native heath of Chota Pagalabad, she is The Judge's WIFE. As she is the Senior Lady of all Chota Pagalabad she, of course, always (like Mary) Goes In First at the solemn and superior dinner parties of that important place, and is feared, flattered, and fawned upon by the other ladies of the station, since she can socially put down the mighty from their seat and exalt the humble and meek and them of low degree (though she would not be likely to touch the last-named with a pair of tongs, socially speaking, of course). And yet, such is this queer world, the said lesser ladies of the famous mofussil station of Chota Pagalabad are, among themselves, agreed *nemine contradicente* that the Great Mrs. "Justice" Spywell is a vulgar old frump ("country-bred to say the least of it"), and call her The First Seven Sister. This curious and unsyntactically expressed epithet alludes to the fact that she and six other "ladies" of like instincts meet daily for tea and scandal at the Gymkhana and, for three solid hours, pull to pieces the reputations of all and sundry their acquaintances, reminding the amused on-looker, by their voices, manner, and appearance, of those strange birds the *Sat Bai* or Seven Sisters, who in gangs of seven make day hideous in their neighbourhood...

"Are you going to India to be married, my dear child?" she asked Lucille, before she knew her name.

"I really don't know," replied Lucille.

"You are not actually engaged, then?"

"I really don't know."

"Oh, of course, if you'd rather keep your own counsel, pray do so," snapped the Great Lady, bridling.

"Yes," replied Lucille, and Mrs. Spywell informed her circle of stereotypes that Lucille was a stupid chit without a word to say for herself, and an artful designing hussy who was probably an adventuress of the "fishing-fleet".

To Auntie Yvette it appeared matter of marvel that earth and sky and sea were much as when she last passed that way. In quarter of a century or so there appeared to be but little change in the Egyptian and Arabian deserts, in the mountains of the African and Arabian coasts, of the Gulf of Suez, in the contours of the islands of the Red Sea, and of Aden, whilst, in mid-ocean, there was absolutely no observable difference between then and now. Wonderful indeed!

This theme, that of what was going on at Monksmead, and that of what to do when Dam was recaptured, formed the bulk of her conversation with her young companion.

"What will you *do*, dear, when we *have* found the poor darling boy?" she would ask.

"Take him by the ear to the nearest church and marry him," Lucille would reply; or —"Stick to him like a leech for evermore, Auntie"; or —"Marry him when he isn't looking, or while he's asleep, if he's ill-or by the scruff of his neck if he's well...."

(What a pity the Great Mrs. "Justice" Spywell could not hear these terrible and unmaidenly sentiments! An adventuress of the "fishing-fleet" in very truth!)

And with reproving smile the gentle spinster would reply: —

"My *dear!* Suppose anyone overheard you, what *would* they think?"

Whereunto the naughty girl would answer: —

"The truth, Auntie-that I'm going to pursue some poor young man to his doom. If Dam were a leper in the gutter, begging his bread, I would marry him in spite of himself-or share the gutter and bread in-er-guilty splendour. If he were a criminal in jail I would sit on the doorstep till he came out, and do the same dreadful thing. I'm just going to marry Dam at the first possible moment-like the Wild West 'shoot on sight' idea. I'm going to seize him and marry him and take care of him for the rest of his life. If he never had another grief, ache, or pain in the whole of his life, he must have had more than ten times his share already. Anyhow whether he'll marry me or whether he won't —in his stupid quixotic ideas of his 'fitness' to do so —I'm never going to part from him again."

And Auntie Yvette would endeavour to be less shocked than a right-minded spinster aunt should be at such wild un-Early-Victorian sentiments.

* * *

Come, this was a better sort of dream! This was better than dreaming of prison-cells, lunatic asylums, tortures by the Snake, lying smashed on rocks, being eaten alive by vultures, wandering for aeons in red- hot waterless deserts, and other horrors. However illusory and tantalizing, this was at least a glorious dream, a delirium to welcome, a wondrous change indeed-to seem to be holding the hand of Lucille while she gazed into his eyes and, from time to time, pressed her lips to his forehead. A good job most of the bandages were gone or she could hardly have done that, even in a dream. And how wondrously *real!* Her hand felt quite solid, there were tears trickling down her cheeks, tears that sometimes dropped on to his own hand with an incredible effect of actuality. It was even more vivid than his Sword-dream which was always so extraordinarily realistic and clear. And there, yes, by Jove, was dear old Auntie Yvette, smiling and weeping simultaneously. Such a dream was the next best thing to reality-save that it brought home to one too vividly what one had lost. Pain of that kind was nevertheless a magnificent change from the other ghastly nightmares, of the wholly maleficent kind. This was a kindly, helpful pain....It is so rare to see the faces of our best-beloved in dreams...Sleep was going to be something other than a procession of hideous nightmares then...

"I believe he knew me, Auntie," whispered Lucille. "Oh, when will Colonel Decies come back. I want him to be here when he opens his eyes again. He would know at a glance whether he were in his right mind and knew me."

"I am certain he did, dear," replied Auntie Yvette. "I am positive he smiled at you, and I believe he knew me too."

"I *won't* believe I have found him too late. It *couldn't* be true," wept the girl, overstrained and unstrung by long vigils, heart-sick with hope deferred, as she turned to her companion.

"Lucille! Is it real?" came a feeble whisper from the bed-and Lucille, in the next moments, wondered if it be true that joy cannot kill...

* * *

A few weeks later, Damocles de Warrenne sat on the verandah of the Grand Imperial Hotel Royal of Kot Ghazi, which has five rooms and five million cockroaches, and stared blankly into the moonlit compound, beyond which stretched the bare rocky plain that was bounded on the north and west by mighty mountains, on the east by a mighty river, and on the south by the more mighty ocean, many hundreds of miles away.

He had just parted from Auntie Yvette and Lucille-Lucille whose last words as she turned to go to her room had been: —

"Now, understand, Dammy, what you want now is a sea-voyage, a sea-voyage to England and Monksmead. When we have got you absolutely right, Mr. Wyllis shall show you as a specimen of the Perfect Man in Harley Street-and *then*, Dammy..." and his burning kisses had closed her mouth.

Was he scoundrel enough to do it? Had he deteriorated to such a depth of villainy? Could he let that noblest and finest flower of womanhood marry a —dangerous lunatic, a homicidal maniac who had nearly killed the man who proved to be almost his greatest benefactor? Could he? Would the noble-hearted Decies frankly say that he was normal and had a right to marry? He would not, and no living man was better qualified to give an opinion on the case of Damocles de Warrenne than the man who was a foster-father to him in childhood, and who brought him into the world in such tragic circumstances. Decies had loved his mother, Lenore de Warrenne. Would he have married *her* in such circumstances? Would he have lived under the same roof with her permanently-knowing how overpowering would be the temptation to give way and marry her, knowing how scandal would inevitably arise? A thousand times No. Was there *no* gentlemanliness left in Damocles de Warrenne that he should even contemplate the doing of a deed at which his old comrades-in-arms, Bear, Burke, Jones, Little, Goate, Nemo and Peerson would stand aghast, would be ready to kick him out of a decent barrack-room —and the poor demented creature called for a "boy," and ordered him to send, at once, for one Abdul Ghani who would, as usual, be found sleeping beside his camels in the market-place...

Anon the gentle Abdul came, received certain instructions, and departed smiling till his great yellow fangs gleamed in the moonlight beneath the bristling moustache, cut back from the lips as that of a righteous Mussulman *shikarri* and *oont-wallah* should be.

Damocles de Warrenne's brain became active with plots and plans for escape-escape from himself and the temptation which he must avoid by flight, since he felt he could not conquer it in fight.

He must disappear. He must die—die in such a way that Lucille would never suppose he had committed suicide. It was the only way to save himself from so awful a crime and to save her from himself.

He would start just before dawn on Abdul's shikar camel, be well away from Kot Ghazi by daylight and reach the old deserted dak-bungalow, that no one ever used, by evening. There Abdul would come to him with his *bhoja-oont*[31] bringing the usual supplies, and on receipt of them he would dismiss Abdul altogether and disappear again into the desert, this time for good. Criminal lunatics and homicidal maniacs are better dead, especially when they are tempted beyond their strength to marry innocent, beautiful girls who do not understand the position.

Chapter XIV
The Snake and the Sword

The dak-bungalow again at last! But how terribly dreary, depressing, and horrible it looked *now* —the hut that had once seemed a kind of heaven on earth to the starving wanderer. Then, Lucille was thousands of miles away (geographically, and millions of miles away in imagination). Now, she was but thirty miles away-and it was almost more than human endurance could bear.... Should he turn back even now, ride straight to Kot Ghazi, fall at her feet and say: "I can struggle no longer. Come back to Monksmead-and let what will be, be. I have no more courage."

And go mad, one day, and kill her? Keep sane, and sully her fair name? On to the hovel. Rest for the night, and, at dawn, strike into the desert and there let what will be, be.

Making the camel kneel, Damocles de Warrenne removed its saddle, fastened its rein-cord tightly to a post, fed it, and then detached the saddle-bags that hung flatly on either side of the saddle frame, as well as a patent-leather sword-cover which contained a sword of very different pattern from that for which it had been made.

Entering the hut, of which the doors and windows were bolted on the outside, he flung open the shutters of the glassless windows, lit a candle, and prepared to eat a frugal meal. From the saddlebags he took bread, eggs, chocolate, sardines, biscuits and apples. With a mixture of permanganate of potash, tea and cold water from the well, if the puddle at the bottom of a deep hole could be so termed, he made a drink that, while drinkable by one who has known worse, was unlikely to cause an attack upon an enfeebled constitution, of cholera, enteric, dysentery or any other of India's specialities. What would he not have given for a clean whisky-and-soda in the place of the nauseating muck-but what should be the end of a man who, in his position, turned to *alcohol* for help and comfort? "The last state of that man..."

After striking a judicious balance between what he should eat for dinner and what he should reserve for breakfast, he fell to, ate sparingly, lit his pipe, and gazed around the wretched room, of which the walls were blue-washed with a most offensive shade of blue, the bare floor was frankly dry mud and dust, the roof was bare cob-webbed thatch and rafter, and the furniture a rickety table, a dangerous-looking cane-bottomed settee and a leg-rest arm-chair from which some one had removed the leg-rests. Had some scoundrelly *oont-wallah* pinched them for fuel? (No, Damocles, an ex-Colonel of the Indian Medical Service "pinched" them for splints.) A most depressing human habitation even for the most cheerful and care-free of souls, a terrible place for a man in a dangerous mental state of unstable equilibrium and cruel agony.... Only thirty miles away-and a camel at the door. *Lucille* still within a night's ride. Lucille and absolute joy.... The desert and certain death —a death of which she must be assured, that in time she might marry Ormonde Delorme or some such sound, fine man. Abdul must find his body-and it must be the body not of an obvious suicide, but of a man who, lost in the desert, had evidently travelled in circles, trying to find his way to the hut he had left, on a shooting expedition. Yes-he knew all about travelling in circles-and what he had done in ignorance (as well as in agony and horror), he would now do intentionally and with grim purpose. Hard on the poor camel!... Perhaps he could manage so that it was set free in time to find its way back somehow. It would if it were loosed within smell of water.... He must die fairly and squarely of hunger and thirst-no blowing out of brains or throat-cutting, no trace of suicide; just lost, poor chap, and no more to be said.... Death of *thirst* —in that awful desert —*again* —No! God in Heaven he had faced the actual pangs of it once, and escaped-he could *not* face it again-he wasn't strong enough... and the unhappy man sprang to his feet to rush from the room and saddle-up the camel for-Life and Lucille-and then his eye fell on the Sword, the Sword of his Fathers, brought to him by Lucille, who had said, "Have it with you always, Dearest. It can *talk* to you, as even I can not...."

He sat down and drew it from the incongruous modern case and from its scabbard. Ha! What did it say but "*Honour*!" What was its message but "Do the right thing. Death is nothing-Honour is everything. Be worthy of your Name, your Traditions, your Ancestors —"

He would die.

Let him die that Lucille's honour, Lucille's happiness, Lucille's welfare, might live-and he kissed the hilt of the Sword as he had so often done in childhood. Having removed boots, leggings and socks, he lay down on the settee-innocent of bedding and pillows, pulled over him the coat that had been rolled and strapped trooper-fashion behind the saddle and fell asleep....

And dreamed that he was shut naked in a tiny cell with a gigantic python upon whose yard-long fangs he was about to be impaled and, as usual, awoke trembling and bathed in perspiration, with dry mouth and throbbing head, sickness, and tingling extremities.

The wind had got up and had blown out the candle which should have lasted till dawn!...

As he lay shaking, terrified (uncertain as to whether he were a soul in torment or a human being still alive), and debating as to whether he could get off the couch, relight the candle, and close the windward window, he heard a sound that caused his heart to miss a beat and his hair to rise on end. A strange, dry rustle merged in the sound of paper being dragged across the floor, and he knew that he *was* shut in with a snake, shut up in a *blue room*, cut off from the matches on the table, and doomed to lie and await the Death he dreaded more than ten thousand others-or, going mad, to rush upon that Death.

He was shut in with the SNAKE. At last it had come for him in its own concrete form and had him bound and gagged by fascination and fear-in the Dark, the awful cruel Dark. No more mere myrmidons. *The SNAKE ITSELF.*

He tried to scream and could not. He tried to strike out at an imaginary serpent-head, huge as an elephant, that reared itself above him-and could not.

He could not even draw his bare foot in under the overcoat. And steadily the paper dragged across the floor...Was it approaching? Was it progressing round and round by the walls? Would the Snake find the bed and climb on to it? Would it coil round his throat and gaze with-luminescent eyes into his, and torture him thus for hours ere thrusting its fangs into his brain? Would it coil up and sleep upon his body for hours before doing so, knowing that he could not move? Here were his Snake-Dreams realized, and in the actual flesh he lay awake and conscious, and could neither move nor cry aloud!

In the Dark he lay bound and gagged, in a blue-walled room, and the Snake enveloped him with its Presence, and he could in no wise save himself.

Oh, God, why let a sentient creature suffer thus? He himself would have shot any human being guilty of inflicting a tithe of the agony on a pariah dog. There could *be* no God!... and then the beams of the rising moon fell upon the blade of the Sword, making it shine like a lamp, and, with a roar as of a charging lion, Damocles de Warrenne sprang from the bed, seized it by the hilt, and was aware, without a tremor, of a cobra that reared itself before him in the moonlight, swaying in the Dance of Death.

With a mere flick of the sword he laid the reptile twitching on the floor-and for a few minutes was madder with Joy than ever in his life he had been with Fear.

For Fear was gone. The World of Woe had fallen from his shoulders. The Snake was to him but a wretched reptile whose head he would crush ere it bruised his heel. He was sane-he was safe-he was a Man again, and ere many days were past he would be the husband of Lucille and the master of Monksmead.

"Oh, God forgive me for a blind, rebellious worm," he prayed. "Forgive me, and strike not this cup from my lips. You would not punish the blasphemy of a madman? I *cannot* pray in ordered forms, but I beg forgiveness for my hasty cry 'There is on God'..." and then pressed the Sword to his lips-the Sword that, under God, had overthrown the Snake for ever, saved his reason-and given him Lucille....

With the Sword in his hand he lay on the bed once more, and slept the sweet, dreamless sleep of a healthy, happy child. In the morning, when he awoke, his eyes fell upon the still living cobra that appeared to watch him with the hate of a baffled Lucifer as it lay broken-backed, impotent, and full of vicious fury.

Rising, Damocles de Warrenne stepped across to the reptile, and, with a quick snatch, seized it behind the head and raised it from the ground. Staring into its baleful, evil-looking eyes, he remarked: —

"Well, mine ancient enemy and almost victor! I'm not of a particularly vengeful disposition, but I fancy a few of your brethren have got to die before I leave India. Why, you poor wretched worm, you miserable maggot, —to think what I have *suffered*" and he angrily dashed it on the ground and spurned it with his foot.

"Easy to do that when your back's broken, you think?" he continued. "Right-O, my lad, wait till I find your mate, and we'll see. Hand to hand, no weapons-my quickness and strength against his quickness and venom. Snakes! The paltriest things that crawl"—and he kicked the reptile into a corner and burst into song as he busied himself about preparations for washing, food for himself and the camel, and —*return*. After enough food to hearten them both for the thirty-mile journey he would go as fast as camel's legs could move to Lucille and the announcement that would send her frantic with joy. He would take her in his arms-then they would waltz for an hour to keep themselves from behaving like lunatics.... Fear was dead! The SNAKE was dead-killed by the SWORD, the Sword that Lucille had brought, and thereby saved him! Madness was dead! Joy, Peace, Sanity, Health were come-the wedding-bells were trembling to burst into peals of joyous announcement.

He would, for Lucille's sake and the names of de Warrenne and Stukeley, show whether he was a Coward or a snake-fearing Lunatic, an epileptic, an unfit-to-marry monstrosity and freak. He would show the Harley Street physicians how much he feared snakes, and would challenge them to an undertaking which would give them food for thought before acceptance.... Where were his boots? He must fly to Lucille!...

And then the galloping hoofs of a horse were heard thudding towards the hut, and, hastening to the door, he saw Lucille whipping a lathered horse.

Rushing towards her he shouted: —

"Will you marry me to-morrow? Will you marry me to-day, Lucille?" and, as she pulled her horse in, he darted back into the room and reappeared twirling a twitching cobra by its tail, and laughing uproariously....

Lucille appeared to be about to faint as he dropped it, seized her in his arms, and said: —

"Darling, I am cured! I have not the slightest fear of snakes. The Sword has saved me. I am a Man again."

He told her all as she sat laughing and sobbing for joy and the dying snake lay at their feet.

In her heart of hearts Lucille determined that the wedding should take place immediately, so that if this were but a temporary respite, the result of the flash of daring inspired by the Sword, she would have the right to care for him for the rest of his life... She would ——

"Look!" she suddenly shrieked, and pointed to where, in the doorway, cutting them off from escape, was the mate of the cobra that lay mangled before them. Had the injured reptile in some way called its mate-or were they regular inhabitants of this deserted hut?

It was Lucille's first experience of cobras and she shuddered to see the second-evidently comprehending, aggressive, vengeful-would it spring from there... and the Sword lay on the bed, out of reach.

Dam arose with a laugh, picked up his heavy boot as he did so, and, all in one swift movement, hurled it at the half-coiled swaying creature, with the true aim of the first-class cricketer and trained athlete; then, following his boot with a leap, he snatched at the tail of the coiling, thrashing reptile and "cracked" the snake as a carter cracks a whip-whereafter it dangled limp and dead from his hand! Lucille shrieked, paled, and sprang towards him.

"Oh, Dam!" she cried, "how *could* you!"

"Pooh, Kiddy," he replied. "I'm going to invite the Harley Street cove to have a match at that-and I'm going to give a little exhibition of it on the lawn at Monksmead-to all the good folk who witnessed my disgrace.... What's a snake after all? It's *my* turn now;" and Lucille's heart was at rest and very thankful. This was not a temporary "cure". Oh, thank God for her inspiration anent the Sword... Thank God, thank God!...

Seven Years After

A beautiful woman, whose face is that of one whose soul is full of peace and joy, passes up the great staircase of the stately mansion of Monksmead. Slowly, because her hand holds that of a chubby youth of five, a picture of sturdy health, strength and happiness. They pass beneath an ancient Sword and the boy wheels to the right, stiffens himself, brings his heels together, and raises a fat little hand to his forehead in solemn salute. The journey is continued without remark until they reach the day nursery, a big, bright room of which a striking feature is the mural decoration in a conventional pattern of entwined serpents, the number of brilliant pictures of snakes, framed and hung upon the walls, and two glass cases, the one containing a pair of stuffed cobras and the other a finely-mounted specimen of a boa-constrictor (which had once been the pride of the heart of a Folkestone taxidermist).

"Go away, Mitthis Beaton," says the small boy to a white-haired but fresh-looking and comely old dame; "I'se not going to bed till Mummy hath tolded me about ve bwacelet again."

"But I've told you a *thousand* times, Dammykins," says the lady.

"Well, now tell me ten hundred times," replies the young man coolly, and attempts to draw from the lady's wrist a huge and remarkable bracelet.

This uncommon ornament consists of a great ruby-eyed gold snake which coils around the lady's arm and which is pierced through every coil by a platinum, diamond-hilted sword, an exact model of the Sword which hangs on the staircase.

"You tell *me*, Sonny, for a change," suggests the lady.

"Velly well," replies the boy.... "Vere was once a Daddy and a hobberell gweat Thnake always bovvered him and followed him about and wouldn't let him gone to thleep and made him be ill like he had eaten too much sweets, and the doctor came and gave him lotths of meddisnin. Then he had to wun away from the Thnake, but it wunned after him, and it wath jutht going to kill him when Mummy bwoughted the Thword and Daddy killed the Thnake all dead. And I am going to have the Thword when I gwow up, but vere aren't any more bad Thnakes. They is all good now and Daddy likes vem and I likes vem. Amen."

"*I* never said *Amen*, when I told you the story, Sonny," remarks the lady.

"Well you can, now I have tolded you it," permits her son. "It means *bus*[32] —all finished. Mitthis Beaton thaid tho. And when I am as big as Daddy I'm going to be the Generwal of the Queenth Gweyth and thay '*Charge!*' and wear the Thword."

Lucille de Warrenne here smothers conversation in the manner common to worshipping mothers whose prodigies make remarks indicative of marvellous precocity, in fact absolutely unique intelligence.

Epilogue

Is it well, O my Soul, is it well?
In silent aisles of sombre tone
Where phantoms roam, thou dwell'st apart
In drear alone.
Where serpents coil and night-birds dart
Thou liest prone, O Heart, my Heart,
In dread unknown.
O Soul of Night, surpassing fair,
Guide this poor spirit through the air,
And thus atone...

This sad Soul, searching for the light....
O Soul of Night, enstarréd bright,
Shine over all.
Enforce thy right to fend for us
Extend thy power to fight for us
Raise thou night's pall.
Ensteep our minds in loveliness
In all sweet hope and godliness
Give guard o'er all...
This brave Soul striving in stern fight....

Thou soul of Night, thou spirit-elf,
Rise up and bless.
Help us to cleanse in holiness
Show how to dress in saintliness
Our weary selves,
Expurge our deeds of earthiness
Expunge desires of selfliness
Rise up and bless...
This strong Soul dying in such plight....

. . . . .

Night gently spreads her wings and flies
Star-laden, wide across the skies.
My Soul, new strong,
So late enstained with earthly dust
So long estranged in wander-lust
Gives praise and song,
Strives to create in morning light
The starry wonders of the night

In praise and song...

This strong Soul praising in new right.
It is well, O my Soul, it is well....

THE WAGES OF VIRTUE

To
THE CHARMINGEST WOMAN

"Vivandière du régiment,

C'est Catin qu'on me nomme;
Je vends, je donne, je bois gaiment,
Mon vin et mon rogomme;
J'ai le pied leste et l'oeil mutin,
Tintin, tintin, tintin, r'lin tintin,
Soldats, voilà Catin!
"Je fus chère à tous nos héros;

Hélas! combien j'en pleure,
Ainsi soldats et généraux
Me comblaient à tout heure
D'amour, de gloire et de butin,
Tintin, tintin, tintin, r'lin tintin
D'amour, de gloire et de butin,
Soldats, voilà Catin!"

BÉRANGER.

Prologue

Lord Huntingten emerged from his little green tent, and strolled over to where Captain Strong, of the Queen's African Rifles, sat in the "drawing-room." The drawing-room was the space under a cedar fir and was furnished with four Roorkee chairs of green canvas and white wood, and a waterproof ground-sheet.

"I do wish the Merlines would roll up," he said. "I want my dinner."

"Not dinner time yet," remarked Captain Strong. "Hungry?"

"No," answered Lord Huntingten almost snappishly. Captain Strong smiled. How old Reggie Huntingten always gave himself away! It was the safe return of Lady Merline that he wanted.

Captain Strong, although a soldier, the conditions of whose life were almost those of perpetual Active Service, was a student--and particularly a student of human nature. Throughout a life of great activity he found, and made, much opportunity for sitting in the stalls of the Theatre of Life and enjoying the Human Comedy. This East African shooting-trip with Lord Huntingten, Sir Montague, and Lady Merline, was affording him great entertainment, inasmuch as Huntingten had fallen in love with Lady Merline and did not know it. Lady Merline was falling in love with Huntingten and knew it only too well, and Merline loved them both. That there would be no sort or kind of "dénouement," in the vulgar sense, Captain Strong was well and gladly aware--for Huntingten was as honourable a man as ever lived, and Lady Merline just as admirable. No saner, wiser, nor better woman had Strong ever met, nor any as well balanced. Had there been any possibility of "developments," trouble, and the usual fiasco of scandal and the Divorce Court, he would have taken an early opportunity of leaving the party and rejoining his company at Mombasa. For Lord Huntingten was his school, Sandhurst and lifelong friend, while Merline was his brother-in-arms and comrade of many an unrecorded, nameless expedition, foray, skirmish, fight and adventure.

"Merline shouldn't keep her out after dusk like this," continued Lord Huntingten. "After all, Africa's Africa and a woman's a woman."

"And Merline's Merline," added Strong with a faint hint of reproof. Lord Huntingten grunted, arose, and strode up and down. A fine upstanding figure of a man in the exceedingly becoming garb of khaki cord riding-breeches, well-cut high boots, brown flannel shirt and broad-brimmed felt hat. Although his hands were small, the arms exposed by the rolled-up shirtsleeves were those of a navvy, or a blacksmith. The face, though tanned and wrinkled, was finely cut and undeniably handsome, with its high-bridged nose, piercing blue eyes, fair silky moustache and prominent chin. If, as we are sometimes informed, impassivity and immobility of countenance are essential to aspirants for such praise as is contained in the term "aristocratic," Lord Huntingten was not what he himself would have described as a "starter," for never did face more honestly portray feeling than did that of Lord Huntingten. As a rule it was wreathed in smiles, and brightly reflected the joyous, sunny nature of its owner. On those rare occasions when he was angered, it was convulsed with rage, and, even before he spoke, all and sundry were well aware that his lordship was angry. When he did speak, they were confirmed in the belief without possibility of error. If he were disappointed or chagrined this expressive countenance fell with such suddenness and celerity that the fact of so great a fall being inaudible came as a surprise to the observant witness. At that moment, as he consulted his watch, the face of this big, generous and lovable man was only too indicative of the fact that his soul was filled with anxiety, resentment and annoyance. Captain Strong, watching him with malicious affection, was reminded of a petulant baby and again of a big naughty boy who, having been stood in the corner for half an hour, firmly believes that the half-hour has long ago expired. Yes, he promised himself much quiet and subtle amusement, interest and instruction from the study of his friends and their actions and reactions during the coming weeks. What would Huntingten do when he realised his condition and position? Run for his life, or grin and bear it? If the former, where would he go? If, living in Mayfair and falling in love with your neighbour's wife, the correct thing is to go and shoot lions in East Africa, is it, conversely, the correct thing to go and live in Mayfair if, shooting lions in East Africa, you fall in love with your neighbour's wife? Captain Strong smiled at his whimsicality, and showed his interesting face at its best. A favourite remark of his was to the effect that the world's a queer place, and life a queer, thing. It is doubtful whether he realised exactly how queer an example of the fact was afforded by his being a soldier in the first place, and an African soldier in the second. When he was so obviously and completely cut out for a philosopher and student (with relaxations in the direction of the writing of Ibsenical-Pinerotic plays and Shavo-Wellsian novels), what did he in that galley of strenuous living and strenuous dying? Further, it is interesting to note that among those brave and hardy men, second to none in keenness, resourcefulness and ability, Captain Strong was noted for these qualities.

A huge Swahili orderly of the Queen's African Rifles, clad in a tall yellow tarboosh, a very long blue jersey, khaki shorts, blue puttees and hobnail boots, approached Captain Strong and saluted. He announced that Merline *Bwana* was approaching, and, on Strong's replying that such things did happen, and even with sufficient frequency to render the widest publication of the fact unnecessary, the man informed him that the *macouba Bwana Simba* (the big Lion Master) had given his bearer orders to have the approach of Merline *Bwana* signalled and announced.

Turning to Huntingten, Strong bade that agitated nobleman to be of good cheer, for Merline was safe--his *askaris* were safe--his pony was safe, and it was even reported that all the dogs were safe.

"Three loud cheers," observed his lordship, as his face beamed ruddily, "but, to tell you the truth, it was of *Lady* Merline I was thinking....You never know in Africa, you know...."

Captain Strong smiled.

Sir Montague and Lady Merline rode into camp on their Arab ponies a few minutes later, and there was a bustle of Indian and Swahili "boys" and bearers, about the unlacing of tents, preparing of hot baths, the taking of ponies and guns, and the hurrying up of dinner.

While Sir Montague gave orders concerning the *enyama*[33] for the *safari* servants and porters, whose virtue had merited this addition to their *posho*[34] Lady Merline entered the "drawing-room," and once again gladdened the heart of Lord Huntingten with her grace and beauty. He struck an attitude, laid his hand upon his heart, and swept the ground with his slouch hat in a most gracefully executed bow. Lady Merline, albeit clad in brief khaki shooting-costume, puttees, tiny hobnail boots, and brown pith helmet, returned the compliment with a Court curtsey.

Their verbal greeting hardly sustained the dignity of the preliminaries.

"How's Bill the Lamb?" quoth the lady.

"How's Margarine?" was the reply.

Their eyes interested Captain Strong more than their words.

(Lady Merline's eyes were famous; and, beautiful as Strong had always realised those wonderful orbs to be, he was strongly inclined to fancy that they looked even deeper, even brighter, even more beautiful when regarding the handsome sunny face of Lord Huntingten.)

Sir Montague Merline joined the group.

"Hallo, Bill! Hallo, Strong!" he remarked. "I say, Strong, what's *marodi*, and what's *gisi* in Somali?"

"Same as *tembo* and *mbogo* in Swahili," was the reply.

"Oh! Elephant and buffalo. Well, that one-eyed Somali blighter with the corrugated forehead, whom Abdul brought in, says there are both--close to Bamania over there--about thirteen miles you know."

"He's a liar then," replied Captain Strong.

"Swears the elephants went on the tiles all night in a *shamba*[35] there, the day before yesterday."

"Might go that way, anyhow," put in Lord Huntingten. "Take him with us, and rub his nose in it if there's nothing."

"You're nothing if not lucid, Bill," said Lady Merline. "I'm off to change," and added as she turned away, "I vote we go to Bamania anyhow. There may be lemons, or mangoes, or bananas or something in the *shamba*, if there are no elephants or buffaloes."

"Don't imagine you are going upsetting elephants and teasing buffaloes, young woman," cried "Bill" after her as she went to her tent. "The elephants and buffaloes of these parts are the kind that eat English women, and feeding the animals is forbidden...."

It occurred to Captain Strong, that silent and observant man, that Lady Merline's amusement at this typical specimen of the Huntingten humour was possibly greater than it would have been had he or her husband perpetrated it.

"Dinner in twenty minutes, Monty," said he to Sir Montague Merline and departed to his tent.

"I say, Old Thing, dear," observed Lord Huntingten to the same gentleman, as, with the tip of his little finger, he "wangled" a soda-water bottle with a view to concocting a whiskey-and-soda. "We won't let Marguerite have anything to do with elephant or buffalo, will we?"

"Good Lord, no!" was the reply. "We've promised her one pot at a lion if we can possibly oblige, but that will have to be her limit, and, what's more, you and I will be one each side of her when she does it."

"Yes," agreed the other, and added, "Expect I shall know what nerves are, when it comes off, too."

"Fancy 'nerves' and the *Bwana Simba*," laughed Sir Montague Merline as he held out his glass for the soda.... "Here's to Marguerite's first lion," he continued, and the two men solemnly drank the toast.

Sir Montague Merline struck a match for his pipe, the light illuminating his face in the darkness which had fallen in the last few minutes. The first impression one gathered from the face of Captain Sir Montague Merline, of the Queen's African Rifles, was one of unusual gentleness and kindliness. Without being in any way a weak face, it was an essentially friendly and amiable one--a soldierly face without any hint of that fierce, harsh and ruthless expression which is apparently cultivated as part of their stock-in-trade by the professional soldiers of militarist nations. A physiognomist, observing him, would not be surprised to learn of quixotic actions and a reputation for being "such an awful good chap--one of the best-hearted fellers that ever helped a lame dog over a stile." So far as such a thing can be said of any strong and honest man who does his duty, it could be said of Sir Montague Merline that he had no enemies. Contrary to the dictum that "He who has no enemies has no friends" was the fact that Sir Montague Merline's friends were all who knew him. Of these, his best and closest friend was his wife, and it had been reserved for Lord Huntingten unconsciously to apprise her of the fact that she was this and nothing more. Until he had left his yacht at Mombasa a few weeks before, on the invitation of Captain Strong (issued with their cordial consent) to join their projected shooting trip, Lady Merline had fondly imagined that she knew what love was, and had thought herself a thoroughly happy and contented woman. In a few days after his joining the party it seemed that she must have loved him all her life, and that there could not possibly be a gulf of some fifteen years between then and the childish days when he was "Bill the Lamb" and she the unconsidered adjunct of the nursery and schoolroom, generally addressed as "Margarine." Why had he gone wandering about the world all these years? Why had their re-discovery of each other had to be postponed until now? Why couldn't he have been at home when Monty came wooing and ... When Lady Merline's thoughts reached this point she resolutely switched them off. She was doing a considerable amount of switching off, these last few days, and realised that when Lord Huntingten awoke to the fact that he too must practise this exercise, the shooting trip would have to come to an untimely end. As she crouched over the tiny candle-lit mirror on the *soi-disant* dressing-table in her tent, while hastily changing for dinner that evening, she even considered plausible ways and possible means of terminating the trip when the inevitable day arrived.

She was saved the trouble.

As they sat at dinner a few minutes later, beneath the diamond-studded velvet of the African sky--an excellent dinner of clear soup, sardines, bustard, venison, and tinned fruit--Strong's orderly again appeared in the near distance, saluting and holding two official letters in his hand. These, it appeared, had just been brought by messenger from the railway-station some nineteen miles distant.

Captain Strong was the first to gather their import, and his feeling of annoyance and disappointment was more due to the fact of the interruption of his interesting little drama than to the cancellation of his leave and return to harness.

"Battle, Murder and Sudden Death!" he murmured. "I wish people wouldn't kill people, and cause other people to interfere with the arrangements of people.... Our trip's bust."

"What is it?" asked Lady Merline.

"Mutiny and murder down Uganda way," replied her husband, whose letter was a duplicate. "I'm sorry, Huntingten, old chap," he added, turning to his friend. "It's draw stumps and hop it, for Strong and me. We must get to the railway to-morrow--there will be a train through in the afternoon.... Better luck next time."

Lord Huntingten looked at Lady Merline, and Lady Merline looked at her plate.

2

Down the narrowest of narrow jungle-paths marched a small party of the Queen's African Rifles. They marched, perforce, in single file, and at their head was their white officer. A wiser man would have marched in the middle, for the leading man was inevitably bound to "get it" if they came upon the enemy, and, albeit brave and warlike men, negroes of the Queen's African Rifles (like other troops) fight better when commanded by an officer. A "point" of a sergeant and two or three men, a couple of hundred yards in front, is all very well, but the wily foe in ambush knows quite enough to take, as it were, the cash and let the credit go--to let the "point" march on, and to wait for the main body.

Captain Sir Montague Merline was well aware of the unwisdom and military inadvisability of heading the long file, but did it, nevertheless. If called upon to defend his conduct, he would have said that what was gained by the alleged wiser course was more than lost, inasmuch as the confidence of the men in so discreet a leader would not be, to say the least of it, enhanced. The little column moved silently and slowly through the horrible place, a stinking swamp, the atmosphere almost unbreatheable, the narrow winding track almost untreadable, the enclosing walls of densest jungle utterly unpenetrable--a singularly undesirable spot in which to be attacked by a cunning and blood-thirsty foe of whom this was the "native heath."

Good job the beggars did not run to machine guns, thought Captain Merline; fancy one, well placed and concealed in one of these huge trees, and commanding the track. Stake-pits, poisoned arrows, spiked-log booby-traps, and poisoned needle-pointed snags neatly placed to catch bare knees, and their various other little tricks were quite enough to go on with. What a rotten place for an ambush! The beggars could easily have made a neat clearing a foot or two from the track, and massed a hundred men whose poisoned arrows, guns, and rifles could be presented a few inches from the breasts of passing enemies, without the least fear of discovery. Precautions against that sort of thing were utterly impossible if one were to advance at a higher speed than a mile a day. The only possible way of ensuring against flank attack was to have half the column out in the jungle with axes, hacking their way in line, ahead of the remainder. They couldn't do a mile a day at that rate. That "point" in front was no earthly good, nor would it have been if joined by Daniel Boone Burnham and Buffalo Bill. The jungle on either side might as well have been a thirty-foot brick wall. Unless the enemy chose to squat in the middle of the track, what could the "point" do in the way of warning?--and the enemy wouldn't do that. Of course, an opposing column might be marching toward them along the same path, but, in that case, except at a sudden bend, the column would see them as soon as the "point." Confound all bush fighting--messy, chancy work. Anyhow, he'd have ten minutes' halt and send Ibrahim up a tree for a look round.

Captain Merline put his hand to the breast pocket of his khaki flannel shirt for his whistle, with a faint short blast on which he would signal to his "point" to halt. The whistle never reached his lips. A sudden ragged crash of musketry rang out from the dense vegetation on either side, and from surrounding trees which commanded and enfiladed the path. More than half the little force fell at the first discharge, for it is hard to miss a man with a Snider or a Martini-Henry rifle at three yards' range. For a moment there was confusion, and more than one of those soldiers of the Queen, it must be admitted, fired off his rifle at nothing in particular. A burly sergeant, bringing up the rear, thrust his way to the front shouting an order, and the survivors of the first murderous burst of fire crouched down on either side of the track and endeavoured to force their way into the jungle, form a line on either side, and fire volleys to their left, front and right. Having made his way to the head of the column, Sergeant Isa ibn Yakub found his officer shot through the head, chest and thigh.... A glance was sufficient. With a loud click of his tongue he turned away with a look of murderous hate on his ebony face and the lust of slaughter in his rolling yellow eye. He saw a leafy twig fall from a tree that overhung the path and crouched motionless, staring at the spot. Suddenly he raised his rifle and fired, and gave a hoarse shout of glee as a body fell crashing to the ground. In the same second his tarboosh was spun from his head and the shoulder of his blue jersey torn as by an invisible claw. He too wriggled into the undergrowth and joined the volley-firing, which, sustained long enough and sufficiently generously and impartially distributed, must assuredly damage a neighbouring foe and hinder his approach. Equally assuredly it must, however, lead to exhaustion of ammunition, and when the volley-firing slackened and died away, it was for this reason. Sergeant Isa ibn Yakub was a man of brains and resource, as well as of dash and courage. Since the enemy had fallen silent too, he would emerge with his men and collect the ammunition from their dead and wounded comrades. He blew a number of short shrill blasts on the whistle which, with the stripes upon his arm, was the proudest of his possessions.

The ammunition was quickly collected and the worthy Sergeant possessed himself of his dead officer's revolver and cartridges.... The next step? ... If he attempted to remove his wounded, his whole effective force would become stretcher-bearers and still be inadequate to the task. If he abandoned his wounded, should he advance or retire? He would rather fight a lion or three Masai than have to answer these conundrums and shoulder these responsibilities.... He was relieved of all necessity in the matter of deciding, for the brooding silence was again suddenly broken by ear-piercing and blood-curdling howls and a second sudden fusillade, as, at some given signal, the enemy burst into the track both before and behind the column. Obviously they were skilfully handled and by one versed in the art of jungle war. The survivors of the little force were completely surrounded--and the rest was rather a massacre than a fight. It is useless to endeavour to dive into dense jungle to form a firing line when a determined person with a broad-bladed spear is literally at your heels. Sergeant Isa ibn Yakub did his utmost and fought like the lion-hearted warrior he was. It is some satisfaction to know that the one man who escaped and made his way to the temporary base of the little columns to tell the story of the destruction of this particular force, was Sergeant Isa ibn Yakub.

One month later a Lieutenant was promoted to Captain Sir Montague Merline's post, and, twelve months later, Lord Huntingten married his wife.

Captain Strong of the Queen's African Rifles, home on furlough, was best man at the wedding of the handsome and popular Lord Huntingten with the charming and beautiful Lady Merline.

3

At about the same time as the fashionable London press announced to a more or less interested world the more or less important news that Lady Huntingten had presented her lord and master with a son and heir, a small *safari* swung into a tiny African village and came to a halt. The naked Kavarondo porters flung down their loads with grunts and duckings, and sat them down, a huddled mass of smelly humanity. From a litter, borne in the middle of the caravan, stepped the leader of the party, one Doctor John Williams, a great (though unknown) surgeon, a medical missionary who gave his life and unusual talents, skill and knowledge to the alleviation of the miseries of black humanity. There are people who have a lot to say about missionaries in Africa, and there are people who have nothing to say about Dr. John Williams because words fail them. They have seen him at work and know what his life is--and also what it might be if he chose to set up in Harley Street.

Doctor John Williams looked around at the village to which Fate brought him for the first time, and beheld the usual scene--a collection of huts built of poles and grass, and a few superior dwelling-places with thatched walls and roofs. A couple of women were pounding grain in a wooden mortar; a small group of others was engaged in a kind of rude basket weaving under the porch of a big hut; a man seated by a small fire had apparently "taken up" poker work, for he was decorating a vase-shaped gourd by means of a red-hot iron; a gang of tiny naked piccaninnies, with incredibly distended stomachs, was playing around a...

What?

Dr. John Williams strode over to the spot. A white man, or the ruin of a sort of a white man, was seated on a native stool and leaning against the bole of one of the towering palms that embowered, shaded, concealed and enriched the little village. His hair was very long and grey, his beard and moustache were long and grey, his face was burnt and bronzed, his eyes blue and bright. On his head were the deplorable ruins of a khaki helmet, and, for the rest, he wore the rags and remains of a pair of khaki shorts. Dr. John Williams stood and stared at him in open-mouthed astonishment. He arose and advanced with extended hand. The doctor was too astounded to speak, and the other could not, for he was dumb. In a minute it was obvious to the new-comer that he was more--that he was in some way "wanting."

From the headman of the villagers, who quickly gathered round, he learned that the white man had been with them for "many nights and days and seasons," that he was afflicted of the gods, very wise, and as a little child. Why "very wise" Dr. John Williams failed to discover, or anything more of the man's history, save that he had simply walked into the village from nowhere in particular and had sat under that tree, all day, ever since. They had given him a hut, milk, corn, cocoanut, and whatever else they had. Also, in addition to this propitiation, they had made a minor god of him, with worship of the milder sorts. Their wisdom and virtue in this particular had been rewarded by him with a period of marked prosperity; and undoubtedly their crops, their cattle, and their married women had benefited by his benevolent presence....

When Doctor John Williams resumed his journey he took the dumb white man with him, and, in due course, reached his own mission, dispensary and wonderful little hospital a few months later. Had he considered that there was any urgency in the case, and the time-factor of any importance, he would have abandoned his sleeping-sickness tour, and gone direct to the hospital to operate upon the skull of his foundling. For this great (and unknown) surgeon, upon examination, had decided that the removal of a bullet which was lodged beneath the scalp and in the solid bone of the top of the man's head was the first, and probably last, step in the direction of the restoration of speech and understanding. Obviously he was in no pain, and he was not mad, but his brain was that of a child whose age was equal to the time which had elapsed since the wound was caused. Probably this had happened about a couple of years ago, for the brain was about equal to that of a two-year-old child. But why had the child not learned to talk? Possibly the fact that he had lived among negroes, since his last return to consciousness, would account for the fact. Had he been shot in the head and recovered among English people (if he were English) he would probably be now talking as fluently as a two-year-old baby....

The first few days after his return to his headquarters were always exceedingly busy ones for the doctor. The number of things able to "go wrong" in his absence was incredible, and, as he was the only white man resident in a district some ten thousand square miles in area, the accumulation of work and trouble was sufficient to appal most people. But work and trouble were what the good doctor sought and throve on....One piece of good news there was, however, in the tale of calamities. A pencilled note, scribbled on a leaf of a military pocket-book, informed him that his old friend Strong, of the Queen's African Rifles, had passed through his village three weeks earlier, and would again pass through, on his return, in a week's time. Having made a wide détour to see his friend, Strong was very disappointed to learn of his absence, and would return by the same devious route, in the hope of better luck....

Good! A few days of Strong's company would be worth a lot. A visit from any white man was something; from a man of one's own class and kind was a great thing; but from worldly-wise, widely-read, clever old Strong! ...Excellent!...

4

Captain Strong, of the Queen's African Rifles, passed from the strong sunlight into the dark coolness of Doctor John Williams' bungalow side by side with his host, who was still shaking him by the hand, in his joy and affection. Laying his riding-whip and helmet on a table he glanced round, stared, turned as white as a sunburnt man may, ejaculated "Oh, my God!" and seized the doctor's arm. His mouth hung open, his eyes were starting from his head, and it was with shaking hand that he pointed to where, in the doctor's living-room, sat the dumb and weak-witted foundling.

Doctor Williams was astounded and mightily interested.

"What's up, Strong?" he asked.

"B--b--b--but he's *dead!*" stammered Strong with a gasp.

"Not a bit of it, man," was the reply, "he's as alive as you or I. He's dumb, and he's dotty, but he's alive all right....What's wrong with you? You've got a touch of the sun..." and then Captain Strong was himself again. If Captain Sir Montague Merline, late of the Queen's African Rifles, were alive, it should not be Jack Strong who would announce the fact....

Monty Merline? ...Was that vacant-looking person who was rising from a chair and bowing to him, his old pal Merline? ...Most undoubtedly it was. Besides--there on his wrist and forearm was the wonderfully-tattooed snake....

"How do you do?" he said. The other bowed again, smiled stupidly, and fumbled with the buttons of his coat....Balmy!...

Strong turned and dragged his host out of the room.

"Where's he come from?" he asked quickly. "Who is he?"

"Where he came from last," replied the doctor, "is a village called, I believe, Bwogo, about a hundred and twenty miles south-east of here. How he got there I can't tell you. The natives said he just walked up unaccompanied, unbounded, unpursued. He's got a bullet or something in the top of his head and I'm going to lug it out. And then, my boy, with any luck at all, he'll very soon be able to answer you any question you like to put him. Speech and memory will return at the moment the pressure on the brain ceases."

"Will he remember up to the time the bullet hit him, or since, or both?" asked Strong.

"All his life, up to the moment the bullet hit him, certainly," was the reply. "What happened since will, at first, be remembered as a dream, probably. If I had to prophesy I should say he'd take up his life from the second in which the bullet hit him, and think, for the moment, that he is still where it happened. By-and-by, he'll realise that there's a gap somewhere, and gradually he'll be able to fill it in with events which will seem half nightmare, half real."

"Anyhow, he'll be certain of his identity and personal history and so forth?" asked Strong.

"Absolutely," said the surgeon. "It will be precisely as though he awoke from an ordinary night's rest.... It'll be awfully interesting to hear him give an account of himself.... All this, of course, if he doesn't die under the operation."

"I hope he will," said Strong.

"What *do* you mean, my dear chap?"

"I hope he'll die under the operation."

"Why?"

"He'll be better dead.... And it will be better for three other people that he should be dead.... Is he likely to die?"

"I should say it's ten to one he'll pull through all right.... What's it all about, Strong?"

"Look here, old chap," was the earnest reply. "If it were anybody else but you I shouldn't know what to say or do. As it's *you*, my course is clear, for you're the last thing in discretion, wisdom and understanding.... But don't ask me his name.... I know him.... Look here, it's like this. His wife's married again.... There's a kid.... They're well known in Society.... Awful business.... Ghastly scandal.... Shockin' position." Captain Strong took Doctor John Williams by the arm. "Look here, old chap," he said once again. "Need you do this? It isn't as though he was 'conscious,' so to speak, and in pain."

"Yes, I must do it," replied the doctor without hesitation, as the other paused.

"But why?" urged Strong. "I'm absolutely certain that if M-—, er--that is--this chap--could have his faculties for a minute he would tell you not to do it.... You'll take him from a sort of negative happiness to the most positive and acute unhappiness, and you'll simply blast the lives of his wife and the most excellent chap she's married.... She waited a year after this chap 'died' in--er--that last Polar expedition--as was supposed.... Think of the poor little kid too.... And there's estates and a ti-— so on...."

"No good, Strong. My duty in the matter is perfectly clear, and it is to the sick man, as such."

"Well, you'll do a damned cruel thing ... er--sorry, old chap, I mean *do* think it over a bit and look at it from the point of view of the unfortunate lady, the second husband, and the child.... And of the chap himself.... By God! He won't thank you."

"I look at it from the point of view of the doctor and I'm not out for thanks," was the reply.

"Is that your last word, Williams?"

"It is. I have here a man mentally maimed, mangled and suffering. My first and only duty is to heal him, and I shall do it."

"Right O!" replied Strong, who knew that further words would be useless. He knew that his friend's intelligence was clear as crystal and his will as firm, and that he accepted no other guide than his own conscience....

As the three men sat in the moonlight that night, after dinner, Captain Strong was an uncomfortable man. That tragedy must find a place in the human comedy he was well aware. It had its uses like the comic relief--but for human tragedy, undilute, black, harsh, and dreadful, he had no taste. He shivered. The pretty little comedy of Lord Huntingten and Sir Montague and Lady Merline, of two years ago, had greatly amused and deeply interested him. This tragedy of the same three people was unmitigated horror.... Poor Lady Merline! He conjured up her beautiful face with the wonderful eyes, the rose-leaf complexion, the glorious hair, the tender, lovely mouth--and saw the life and beauty wiped from it as she read, or heard, the ghastly news ... bigamy ... illegitimacy....

The doctor's "bearer" came to take the patient to bed. He was a remarkable man who had started life as a ward-boy in Madras. He it was who had cut the half-witted white man's hair, shaved his beard and dressed him in his master's spare clothes. When the patient was asleep that night, he was going to endeavour to shave the top of his head without waking him, for he was to be operated on, in the morning....

"Yes, I fully understand and I give you my solemn promise, Strong," said the doctor as the two men rose to go in, that night. "The moment the man is sane I will tell him that he is not to tell me his name, nor anything else until he has heard what I have to say. I will then break it to him--using my own discretion as to how and when--that he was reported dead, that his will was proved, that his widow wore mourning for a year and then married again, and had a son a year later....I undertake that he shall not leave this house, *knowing that*, unless he is in the fullest possession of his faculties and able to realise with the utmost clearness *all* the bearings of the case and *all* the consequences following his resumption of identity. And I'll let him hide here for just as long as he cares to conceal himself--if he wishes to remain 'dead' for a time."

"Yes...And as I can't possibly stay till he recovers, nor, in fact, over to-morrow without gross dereliction of duty, I will leave a letter for you to give him at the earliest safe moment....I'll tell him that I am the only living soul who knows his name as well as his secret. He'll understand that no one else will know this--from me."

As he sat on the side of his bed that night, Captain Strong remarked unto his soul, "Well--one thing--if I know Monty Merline as well as I think, 'Sir Montague Merline' died two years ago, whatever happens....And yet I can't imagine Monty committing suicide, somehow. He's a chap with a conscience as well as the soul of chivalry....Poor, poor, old Monty Merline!..."

Chapter I
Soap and Sir Montague Merline

Sir Montague Merline, second-class private soldier of the First Battalion of the Foreign Legion of France, paused to straighten his back, to pass his bronzed forearm across his white forehead, and to put his scrap of soap into his mouth--the only safe receptacle for the precious morsel, the tiny cake issued once a month by Madame La République to the Legionary for all his washing purposes. When one's income is precisely one halfpenny a day (paid when it has totalled up to the sum of twopence halfpenny), one does not waste much, nor risk the loss of valuable property; and to lay a piece of soap upon the concrete of *Le Cercle d'Enfer* reservoir, is not so much to risk the loss of it as to lose it, when one is surrounded by gentlemen of the Foreign Legion. Let me not be misunderstood, nor supposed to be casting aspersions upon the said gentlemen, but their need for soap is urgent, their income is one halfpenny a day, and soap is of the things with which one may "decorate oneself" without contravening the law of the Legion. To steal is to steal, mark you (and to deserve, and probably to get, a bayonet through the offending hand, pinning it to the bench or table), but to borrow certain specified articles permanently and without permission is merely, in the curious slang of the Legion, "to decorate oneself."

Contrary to what the uninitiated might suppose, *Le Cercle d'Enfer*–the Circle of Hell--is not a dry, but a very wet place, it being, in point of fact, the *lavabo* where the Legionaries of the French Foreign Legion stationed in Algeria at Sidi-bel-Abbès, daily wash their white fatigue uniforms and occasionally their underclothing.

Oh, that *Cercle d'Enfer*! I hated it more than I hated the *peloton des hommes punis, salle de police, cellules*, the "Breakfast of the Legion," the awful heat, monotony, flies, Bedouins; the solitude, hunger, and thirst of outpost stations in the south; I hated it more than I hated *astiquage*, *la boîte*, the *chaussettes russes*, hospital, the terrible desert marches, sewer-cleaning fatigues, or that villainous and vindictive ruffian of a *cafard*-smitten *caporal* who systematically did his very able best to kill me. Oh, that accursed *Cercle d'Enfer*, and the heart-breaking labour of washing a filthy alfa-fibre suit (stained perhaps with rifle-oil) in cold water, and without soap!

Only the other day, as I lay somnolent in a long chair in the verandah of the Charmingest Woman (she lives in India), I heard the regular *flop, flop, flop* of wet clothes, beaten by a distant *dhobi* upon a slab of stone, and at the same moment I smelt wet concrete as the *mali* watered the maidenhair fern on the steps leading from Her verandah to the garden. Odours call up memories far more distinctly and readily than do other sense-impressions, and the faint smell of wet concrete, aided as it was by the faintly audible sound of wet blows, brought most vividly before my mind's eye a detailed picture of that well-named Temple of Hygiea, the "Circle of Hell." Sleeping, waking, and partly sleeping, partly waking, I saw it all again; saw Sir Montague Merline, who called himself John Bull; saw Hiram Cyrus Milton, known as The Bucking Bronco; saw "Reginald Rupert"; the infamous Luigi Rivoli; the unspeakable Edouard Malvin; the marvellous Mad Grasshopper, whose name no one knew; the truly religious Hans Djoolte; the Russian twins, calling themselves Mikhail and Feodor Kyrilovitch Malekov; the terrible Sergeant-Major Suicide-Maker, and all the rest of them. And finally, waking with an actual and perceptible taste of soap in my mouth, I wished my worst enemy were in the *Cercle d'Enfer*, soapless, and with much rifle-oil, dust, leather marks and wine stains on his once-white uniform--and then I thought of Carmelita and determined to write this book.

For Carmelita deserves a monument (and so does John Bull), however humble.... To continue....

Sir Montague Merline did not put his precious morsel of soap into his pocket, for the excellent reason that there was no pocket to the single exiguous garment he was at the moment wearing--a useful piece of material which in its time played many parts, and knew the service of duster, towel, turban, tablecloth, polishing pad, tea-cloth, house-flannel, apron, handkerchief, neckerchief, curtain, serviette, holder, fly-slayer, water-strainer, punkah, and, at the moment, nether garment. Having *cached* his soup and having observed "*Peste!*" as he savoured its flavour, he proceeded to pommel, punch, and slap upon the concrete, the greyish-white tunic and breeches, and the cotton vest and shirt which he had generously soaped before the hungry eyes of numerous soapless but oathful fellow-labourers, who less successfully sought that virtue which, in the Legion, is certainly next to, but far ahead of, mere godliness.

In due course, Sir Montague Merline rinsed his garments in the reservoir, wrung them out, bore them to the nearest clothes-line, hung them out to dry, and sat himself down in their shadow to stare at them unwaveringly until dried by the fierce sun--the ancient enemy, for the moment an unwilling friend. To watch them unwaveringly and intently because he knew that the turning of his head for ten seconds might mean their complete and final disappearance--for, like soap, articles of uniform are on the list of things with which a Legionary may "decorate" himself, if he can, without incurring the odium of public opinion. (He may steal any article of equipment, clothing, kit, accoutrement, or general utility, but his patron saint help him and Le Bon Dieu be merciful to him, if he be caught stealing tobacco, wine, food, or money.)

Becoming aware of the presence of Monsieur le Légionnaire Edouard Malvin, Sir Montague Merline increased the vigilance of his scrutiny of his pendent property, for ce cher Edouard was of pick-pockets the very prince and magician; of those who could steal the teeth from a Jew while he sneezed and would steal the scalp from their grandmamma while she objected.

"Ohé! Jean Boule, lend me thy soap," besought this stout and dapper little Austrian, who for some reason pretended to be a Belgian from the Congo. "This cursed alfa-fibre gets dirtier the more you wash it in this cursed water," and he smiled a greasy and ingratiating grin.

Without for one second averting his steady stare from his clothes, the Englishman slowly removed the soap from his mouth, expectorated, remarked *"Peaudezébie,"*[36] and took no further notice of the quaint figure which stood by his side, clad only in ancient red Zouave breeches and the ingratiating smile.

"Name of a Name! Name of the Name of a Pipe! Name of the Name of a Dirty Little Furry Red Monkey!" observed Monsieur le Légionnaire Edouard Malvin as he turned to slouch away, twirling the dripping grey-white tunic.

"Meaning me?" asked Sir Montague, replacing the soap in its safe repository and preparing to rise.

"But no! But not in the least, old cabbage. Thou hast the *cafard*. Mais oui, tu as le cafard," replied the Belgian and quickened his retreat.

No, the grey Jean Boule, so old, so young, doyen of Légionnaires, so quick, strong, skilful and enduring at *la boxe*, was not the man to cross at any time, and least of all when he had *le cafard*, that terrible Legion madness that all Legionaries know; the madness that drives them to the cells, to gaol, to the Zephyrs, to the firing-party by the open grave; or to desertion and death in the desert. The grey Jean Boule had been a Zephyr of the Penal Battalions once, already, for killing a man, and Monsieur Malvin, although a Legionary of the Foreign Legion, did not wish to die. No, not while Carmelita and Madame la Cantinière lived and loved and sold the good Algiers wine at three-halfpence a bottle....No, bon sang de sort!

M. le Légionnaire Malvin returned to the dense ring of labouring perspiring washers, and edged in behind a gigantic German and a short, broad, burly Alsatian, capitalists as joint proprietors of a fine cake of soap.

Sacré nom de nom de bon Dieu de Dieu de sort! Dull-witted German pigs might leave their soap unguarded for a moment, and, if they did not, might be induced to wring some soapy water from their little pile of washing, upon the obstinately greasy tunic of the good M. Malvin.

Légionnaire Hans Schnitzel, late of Berlin, rinsed his washing in clean water, wrung it, and took it to the nearest drying line. Légionnaire Alphonse Dupont, late of Alsace, placed his soap in the pocket of the dirty white fatigue-uniform which he wore, and which he would wash as soon as he had finished the present job. Immediately, Légionnaire Edouard Malvin transferred the soap from the side pocket of the tunic of the unconscious Légionnaire Alphonse Dupont to that of his own red breeches, and straightway begged the loan of it.

"*Merde!*" replied Dupont. "Nombril de Belzébutt! I will lend it thee *peaudezébie*. Why should I lend thee soap, *vieux dégoulant*? Go decorate thyself, *sale cochon*. Besides 'tis not mine to lend."

"And that is very true," agreed M. Malvin, and sauntered toward Schnitzel, who stood phlegmatically guarding his drying clothes. In his hand was an object which caused the eyebrows of the good M. Malvin to arch and rise, and his mouth to water--nothing less than an actual, real and genuine scrubbing-brush, beautiful in its bristliness. Then righteous anger filled his soul.

"Saligaud!" he hissed. "These pigs of filthy Germans! Soap *and* a brush. Sacripants! Ils me dégoutant à la fin."

As he regarded the stolid German with increasing envy, hatred, malice and all uncharitableness, and cast about in his quick and cunning mind for means of relieving him of the coveted brush, a sudden roar of wrath and grief from his Alsatian partner, Dupont, sent Schnitzel running to join that unfortunate man in fierce and impartial denunciations of his left-hand and right-hand neighbours, who were thieves, pigs, brigands, dogs, Arabs, and utterly *merdant* and *merdable*. Bursting into the fray, Herr Schnitzel found them, in addition, *bloedsinnig* and *dummkopf* in that they could not produce cakes of soap from empty mouths.

As the rage of the bereaved warriors increased, more and more Pomeranian and Alsatian patois invaded the wonderful Legion-French, a French which is not of Paris, nor of anywhere else in the world save La Légion. As Dupont fell upon a laughing Italian with a cry of "Ah! zut! Sacré grimacier," Schnitzel spluttered and roared at a huge slow-moving American who regarded him with a look of pitying but not unkindly contempt....

"Why do the 'eathen rage furious *to*gether and *im*agine a vain thing?" he enquired in a slow drawl of the excited "furriner," adding "Ain't yew some *schafs-kopf*, sonny!" and, as the big German began to whirl his arms in the windmill fashion peculiar to the non-boxing foreigner who meditates assault and battery, continued--

"Now yew stop *zanking* and playing *versteckens* with me, yew pie-faced Squarehead, and be *schnell* about it, or yew'll git my goat, see? *Vous obtiendrez mon chèvre*, yew perambulating *prachtvoll bierhatte*," and he coolly turned his back upon the infuriated German with a polite, if laborious, "Guten tag, mein Freund."

Mr. Hiram Cyrus Milton (late of Texas, California, the Yukon, and the "main drag" generally of the wild and woolly West) was exceeding proud of his linguistic knowledge and skill. It may be remarked, en passant, that his friends were even prouder of it.

At this moment, le bon Légionnaire Malvin, hovering for opportunity, with a sudden *coup de savate* struck the so-desirable scrubbing-brush from the hand of Herr Schnitzel with a force that seemed like to take the arm from the shoulder with it. Leaping round with a yell of pain, the unfortunate German found himself, as Malvin had calculated, face to face with the mighty Luigi Rivoli, to attack whom was to be brought to death's door through that of the hospital.

Snatching up the brush which was behind Schnitzel when he turned to face Rivoli, le bon M. Malvin lightly departed from the vulgar scuffle in the direction of the drying clothes of Herren Schnitzel and Dupont, the latter, last seen clasping, with more enthusiasm than love, a wiry Italian to his bosom. The luck of M. Malvin was distinctly in, for not only had he the soap and a brush for the easy cleansing of his own uniform, but he had within his grasp a fresh uniform to wear, and another to sell; for the clothing of ce bon Dupont would fit him to a marvel, while that of the pig-dog Schnitzel would fetch good money, the equivalent of several litres of the thick, red Algerian wine, from a certain Spanish Jew, old Haroun Mendoza, of the Sidi-bel-Abbès ghetto.

Yes, the Saints bless and reward the good Dupont for being of the same size as M. Malvin himself, for it is a most serious matter to be short of anything when showing-down kit at kit-inspection, and that thrice accursed Sacré Chien of an *Adjudant* would, as likely as not, have spare white trousers shown-down on the morrow. What can a good Légionnaire do, look you, when he has not the article named for to-morrow's *Adjudant's* inspection, but "decorate himself"? Is it easy, is it reasonable, to buy new white fatigue-uniform on an income of one halfpenny per diem? Sapristi, and Sacré Bleu, and Name of the Name of a Little Brown Dog, a litre of wine costs a penny, and a packet of tobacco three-halfpence, and what is left to a gentleman of the Legion then, on pay-day, out of his twopence-halfpenny, nom d'un pétard? As for ce bon Dupont, he must in his turn "decorate" himself. And if he cannot, but must renew acquaintance with *la boîte* and *le peloton des hommes punis*, why--he must regard things in their true light, be philosophical, and take it easy. Is it not proverbial that "Toutes choses peut on souffrir qu'aise"? And with a purr of pleasure, a positive licking of chops, and a murmur of "Ah! Au tient frais," he deftly whipped the property of the embattled Legionaries from the line, no man saying him nay. For it is not the etiquette of the Legion to interfere with one who, in the absence of its owner, would "decorate" himself with any of those things with which self-decoration is permissible, if not honourable. Indeed, to Sir Montague Merline, sitting close by, and regarding his proceedings with cold impartial eye, M. Malvin observed--

"'Y a de bon, mon salop! I have heard that le bon Dieu helps those who help themselves. I do but help myself in order to give le bon Dieu the opportunity He doubtless desires. I decorate myself incidentally. Mais oui, and I shall decorate myself this evening with a p'tite ouvrière and to-morrow with une réputation d'ivrogne," and he turned innocently to saunter with his innocent bundle of washing from the *lavabo*, to his *caserne*. Ere he had taken half a dozen steps, the cold and quiet voice of the grey Jean Boule broke in upon the resumed day-dreams of the innocently sauntering M. Malvin.

"Might one aspire to the honour of venturing to detain for a brief interview Monsieur le Légionnaire Edouard Malvin?" said the soft metallic voice.

"But certainly, and without charge, mon gars," replied that gentleman, turning and eyeing the incomprehensible and dangerous Jean Boule, *à coin de l'oeil*.

"You seek soap?"

"I do," replied the Austrian "Belgian" promptly. The possession of one cake of soap makes that of another no less desirable.

"Do you seek sorrow also?"

"But no, dear friend. 'J'ai eu toutes les folies.' In this world I seek but wine, woman, and peace. Let me avoid the 'gros bonnets' and lead my happy tumble life in peaceful obscurity. A modest violet, I. A wayside flow'ret, a retiring primrose, such as you English love."

"Then, cher Malvin, since you seek soap and not sorrow, let not my little cake of soap disappear from beneath the polishing-rags in my sack. The little brown sack at the head of my cot, cher Malvin. Enfin! I appoint you guardian and custodian of my little cake of soap. But in a most evil hour for le bon M. Malvin would it disappear. Guard it then, cher Malvin. Respect it. Watch over it as you value, and would retain, your health and beauty, M. Malvin. And when *I* have avenged *my* little piece of soap, the true history of the last ten minutes will deeply interest those earnest searchers after truth, Legionaries Schnitzel and Dupont. Depart in peace and enter upon your new office of Guardian of my Soap! Vous devez en être joliment fier."

"Quite a speech, in effect, mon drôle," replied the stout Austrian as he doubtfully fingered his short beard *au poinçon*, and added uneasily, "I am not the only gentleman who 'decorates' himself with soap."

"No? Nor with uniforms. Go in peace, Protector of my Soap."

And smiling wintrily M. Malvin winked, broke into the wholly deplorable ditty of "Pére Dupanloup en chemin de fer," and pursued his innocent path to barracks, whither Sir Montague Merline later followed him, after watching with a contemptuous smile some mixed and messy fighting (beside the apparently dead body of the Legionary Schnitzel) between an Alsatian and an Italian, in which the Italian kicked his opponent in the stomach and partly ate his ear, and the Alsatian used his hands solely for purpose of throttling.

Why couldn't they stand up and fight like gentlemen under Queensberry rules, or, if boxing did not appeal to them, use their sword-bayonets like soldiers and Legionaries--the low rooters, the vulgar, rough-and-tumble gutter-scrappers....

Removing his almost dry washing from the line, Sir Montague Merline marched across to his barrack-block, climbed the three flights of stone stairs, traversed the long corridor of his

Company, and entered the big, light, airy room wherein he and twenty-nine other Legionaries (one of whom held the very exalted and important rank of *Caporal*) lived and moved and had their monotonous being.

Spreading his tunic and breeches on the end of the long table he proceeded to "iron" them, first with his hand, secondly with a tin plate, and finally with the edge of his "quart," the drinking-mug which hung at the head of his bed ready for the reception of the early morning *jus*, the strong coffee which most effectively rouses the Legionary from somnolence and most ineffectively sustains him until midday.

Anon, having persuaded himself that the result of his labours was satisfactory, and up to Legion standards of smartness--which are as high as those of the ordinary *piou-piou* of the French line are low--he folded his uniform in elbow-to-finger-tip lengths, placed it with the *paquetage* on the shelf above his bed, and began to dress for his evening walk-out. The Legionary's time is, in theory, his own after 5 p.m., and the most sacred plank in the most sacred platform of all his sacred tradition is his right to promenade himself at eventide and listen to the Legion's glorious band in the Place Sadi Carnot.

Having laid his uniform, belt, bayonet, and képi on his cot, he stepped across to the next but one (the name-card at the head of which bore the astonishing legend "Bucking Bronco, No. 11356. Soldat 1ère Classe), opened a little sack which hung at the head of it, and took from it the remains of an ancient nail-brush, the joint property of Sir Montague Merline, alias Jean Boule, and Hiram Cyrus Milton, alias Bucking Bronco, late of Texas, California, Yukon, and "the main drag" of the United States of America.

Even as Sir Montague's hand was inserted through the neck of the sack, the huge American (who had been wrongfully accused and rashly attacked by Legionary Hans Schnitzel) entered the barrack-room, caught sight of a figure bending over his rag-sack, and crept on tiptoe towards it, his great gnarled fists clenched, his mouth compressed to a straight thin line beneath his huge drooping moustache, and his grey eyes ablaze. Luckily Sir Montague heard the sounds of his stealthy approach, and turned just in time. The American dropped his fists and smiled.

"Say," he drawled, "I thought it was some herring-gutted weevil of a Dago or a Squarehead shenannikin with my precious jools. An' I was jest a'goin' ter plug the skinnamalink some. Say, Johnnie, if yew hadn't swivelled any, I was jest a'goin' ter slug yew, good an' plenty, behind the yeer-'ole."

"Just getting the tooth-nail-button-boot-dandy-brush, Buck," replied Sir Montague. "How are you feeling?"

"I'm feelin' purty mean," was the reply. "A dirty Squarehead of a dod-gasted Dutchy from the Farterland grunted in me eye, an' I thought the shave-tail was fer rough-housin', an' I slugged him one, just ter start 'im gwine. The gosh-dinged piker jest curled up. He jest wilted on the floor."

The Bucking Bronco, in high disgust, expectorated and then chid himself for forgetting that he was no longer on the free soil of America, where a gentleman may spit as he likes and be a gentleman for a' that and a' that.

"I tell yew, Johnnie," he continued, "he got me jingled, the lumberin' lallapaloozer! There he lay *an'* lay--and then some. 'Git up, yew rubberin' rube,' I ses, 'yew'll git moss on your teeth if yew lie so quiet; git up, an' deliver the goods,' I ses, 'I had more guts then yew when I was knee high to a June bug.' Did he arise an' make good? *I* should worry. Nope. Yew take it from Uncle, that bonehead is there yit, an' afore I could make him wise to it thet he didn't git the bulge on Uncle with *thet* bluff, another Squarehead an' a gibberin' Dago put up a dirty kind o' scrap over his body, gougin' and kickin' an' earbitin' an' throttlin', an' a whole bunch o' boobs jined in an' I give it up an' come 'ome." And the Bucking Bronco sat him sadly on his bed and groaned.

"Cheer up, Buck, we'll all soon be dead," replied his comrade, "don't *you* go getting cafard," and he looked anxiously at the angry-lugubrious face of his friend. "What's the *ordre du jour* for walking-out dress to-day?" he added. "Blue tunic and red trousers? Or tunic and white? Or *capote*, or what?"

"It was tunic an' white yesterday," replied the American, "an' I guess it is to-day too."

"It's my night to howl," he added cryptically "Let's go an' pow-wow Carmelita ef thet fresh gorilla Loojey Rivoli ain't got 'er in 'is pocket. I'll shoot 'im up some day, sure...."

A sudden shouting, tumult, and running below, and cries of "Les bleus! Les bleus!" interrupted the Bronco's monologue and drew the two old soldiers to a window that overlooked the vast, neat, gravelled barrack-square, clean, naked, and bleak to the eye as an ice-floe.

"Strike me peculiar," remarked the Bucking Bronco. "It's another big gang o' tenderfeet."

"A draft of rookies! Come on--they'll all be for our Company in place of those *poumpists*,[37] and there may be something Anglo-Saxon among them," said Legionary John Bull, and the two men hastily flung their capotes over their sketchy attire and hurried from the room, buttoning them as they went.

Like Charity, the Legionary's overcoat covers a multitude of sins--chiefly of omission--and is a most useful garment. It protects him from the cold dawn wind, and keeps him warm by night; it protects him from the cruel African sun, and keeps him cool by day, or at least, if not cool, in the frying-pan degree of heat, which is better than that of the fire. He marches in it without a tunic, and relies upon it to conceal the fact when he has failed to "decorate" himself with underclothing. Its skirts, buttoned back, hamper not his legs, and its capacious pockets have many uses. Its one drawback is that, being double-breasted, it buttons up on either side, a fact which has brought the grey hairs of many an honest Legionary in sorrow to the cellules, and given many a brutal and vindictive Sergeant the chance of that cruelty in which his little tyrant soul so revels. For, incredible as it may seem to the lay mind, the ingenious devil whose military mind concocts the ordres du jour, changes, by solemn decree, and almost daily, the side upon which the overcoat is to be buttoned up.

Clattering down the long flights of stone stairs, and converging across the barrack-square, the Legionaries came running from all directions, to gaze upon, to chaff, to delude, to sponge upon, and to rob and swindle the "Blues"–the recruits of the *Légion Étrangère*, the embryo *Légionnaires d'Afrique*.

In the incredibly maddeningly dull life of the Legion in peace time, the slightest diversion is a god-send and even the arrival of a batch of recruits a most welcome event. To all, it is a distraction; to some, the hope of the arrival of a fellow-countryman (especially to the few English, Americans, Danes, Greeks, Russians, Norwegians, Swedes, and Poles whom cruel Fate has sent to La Légion). To some, a chance of passing on a part of the brutality and tyranny which they themselves suffer; to some, a chance of getting civilian clothes in which to desert; to others, an opportunity of selling knowledge of the ropes, for litres of canteen wine; to many, a hope of working a successful trick on a bewildered recruit--the time-honoured villainy of stealing his new uniform and pretending to buy him another *sub rosa* from the dishonest quartermaster, whereupon the recruit buys back his own original uniform at the cost of his little all (for invariably the alleged substitute-uniform costs just that sum of money which the poor wretch has brought with him and augmented by the compulsory sale of his civilian kit to the clothes-dealing harpies and thieves who infest the barrack-gates on the arrival of each draft).

As the tiny portal beside the huge barrack-gate was closed and fastened by the Corporal in charge of the squad of "blues" (as the French army calls its recruits[38]), the single file of derelicts halted at the order of the Sergeant of the Guard, who, more in sorrow than in anger, weighed them and found them wanting.

"Sweepings," he summed them up in passing judgment. "Foundlings. Droppings. Crumbs. Tripe. Accidents. Abortions. Cripples. Left by the tide. Blown in by the wind. Born pékins.[39] Only one man among them, and he a pig of a Prussian--or perhaps an Englishman. Let us hope he's an Englishman...."

In speaking thus, the worthy Sergeant was behaving with impropriety and contrary to the law and tradition of the Legion. What nouns and adjectives a non-commissioned officer may use wherewith to stigmatise a Legionary, depend wholly and solely upon his taste, fluency and vocabulary. But it is not etiquette to reproach a man with his nationality, however much a matter for reproach that nationality may be.

"Are you an Englishman, most miserable *bleu?*" he suddenly asked of a tall, slim, fair youth, dressed in tweed Norfolk-jacket, and grey flannel trousers, and bearing in every line of feature and form, and in the cut and set of his expensive clothing, the stamp of the man of breeding, birth and position.

"By the especial mercy and grace of God, I am an Englishman, Sergeant, thank you," he replied coolly in good, if slow and careful French.

The Sergeant smiled grimly behind his big moustache. Himself a cashiered Russian officer, and once a gentleman, he could appreciate a gentleman and approve him in the strict privacy of his soul.

"*Slava Bogu!*" he roared. "Vile *bleu*! And now by the especial mercy and grace of the Devil you are a Légionnaire--or will be, if you survive the making...." and added *sotto voce*, "Are you a degraded dog of a broken officer? If so, you can claim to be appointed to the *élèves caporaux* as a non-commissioned officer on probation, if you have a photo of yourself in officer's uniform. Thus you will escape all recruit-drill and live in hope to become, some day, Sergeant, even as I," and the (for a Sergeant of the Legion) decent-hearted fellow smote his vast chest.

"I thank you, Sergeant," was the drawled reply. "You really dazzle me--but *I* am not a degraded dog of a broken officer."

"*Gospodi pomilui!*" roared the incensed Sergeant. "Ne me donnez de la gabatine, pratique!" and, for a second, seemed likely to strike the cool and insolent recruit who dared to bandy words with a Sergeant of the Legion. His eyes bulged, his moustache bristled, and his scarlet face turned purple as he literally showed his teeth.

"Go easy, old chap," spoke a quiet voice, in English, close beside the Englishman. "That fellow can do you to death if you offend him," and the recruit, turning, beheld a grey-moustached, white-haired elderly man, bronzed, lined, and worn-looking--a typical French army *vielle moustache*–an "old sweat" from whose lips the accents of a refined English gentleman came with the utmost incongruity.

The youth's face brightened with interest. Obviously this old dear was a public-school, or 'Varsity man, or, very probably, an *ex*-British officer.

"Good egg," quoth he, extending a hand behind him for a surreptitious shake. "See you anon, what?"

"Yes, you'll all come to the Seventh Company. We are below strength," said Legionary John Bull, in whose weary eyes had shone a new light of interest since they fell upon this compatriot of his own caste and kidney.

A remarkably cool and nonchalant recruit--and surely unique in the history of the Legion's "blues" in showing absolutely no sign of privation, fear, stress, criminality, poverty, depression, anxiety, or bewilderment!

"Now, what'n hell is he doin' in thet bum outfit?" queried the Bucking Bronco of his friend John Bull, who kept as near as possible to the Englishman whom he had warned against ill-timed causticity of humour.

"He's some b'y, thet b'y, but he'd better quit kickin'. He's a way-up white man I opine. What's 'e a'doin' in this joint? He's a gay-cat and a looker. He's a fierce stiff sport. He has sand, some--sure. Yep," and Mr. Hiram Cyrus Milton checked himself only just in time from defiling the immaculate and sacred parade-ground, by "signifying in the usual manner" that he was mentally perturbed, and himself in these circumstances of expectoration-difficulty by observing that the boy was undoubtedly "some" boy, and worthy to have been an American citizen had he been born under a luckier star--or stripe.

"I can't place him, Buck," replied the puzzled John Bull, his quiet voice rendered almost inaudible by the shouts, howls, yells and cries of the seething mob of Legionaries who swarmed round the line of recruits, assailing their bewildered ears in all the tongues of Europe, and some of those of Asia and Africa.

"He doesn't look hungry, and he doesn't look hunted. I suppose he is one of the few who don't come here to escape either starvation, creditors, or the Law. And he doesn't look desperate like the average turned-down lover, ruined gambler, deserted husband, or busted bankrupt.... Wonder if he's come here in search of 'Romance'?"

"Wal, ef he's come hyar for his health an' amoosement he'd go to Hell to cool himself, or ter the den of a grizzly b'ar fer gentle stimoolation and recreation. Gee whiz! Didn't he fair git ole Bluebottle's goat? He sure did git nixt him."

"Bit of a contrast to the rest of the gang, what?" remarked John Bull, and indeed the truth of his remark was very obvious.

"Ain't they a outfit o' dodgasted hoboes an' bindlestiffs!" agreed his friend.

Straight as a lance, thin, very broad in the shoulders and narrow of waist and hip; apparently as clean and unruffled as when leaving his golf-club pavilion for a round on the links; cool, self-possessed, haughty, aristocratic and clean-cut of feature, this Englishman among the other recruits looked like a Derby winner among a string of equine ruins in a knacker's yard; like a panther among bears--a detached and separated creature, something of different flesh and blood. Breed is a very remarkable thing, even more distinctive than race, and in this little band of derelicts was another Englishman, a Cockney youth who had passed from street-arab and gutter-snipe, *via* Reformatory, to hooligan, coster and soldier. No man in that collection of wreckage from Germany, Spain, Italy, France, and the four corners of Europe looked less like the tall recruit than did this brother Englishman.

To Sir Montague Merline, fallen and shattered star of the high social firmament, the sight of him was as welcome as water in the desert, and he thanked Fate for having brought another Englishman to the Legion--and one so debonair, so fine, so handsome, cool and strong.

"There's Blood there," he murmured to himself.

"His shoulders hev bin drilled somewheres, although he's British," added the Bucking one. "Yep. He's one o' the flat-backed push."

"I wonder if he can be a cashiered officer. He's drilled as you say....If he has been broke for something it hasn't marked him much. Nothing hang-dog there," mused Legionary John Bull.

"Nope. He's a blowed-in-the-glass British aristocrat," agreed the large-minded Hiram Cyrus, "and I opine an ex-member of the commishunned ranks o' the British Constitootional Army. He ain't niver bin batterin' the main-stem for light-pieces like them other hoodlums an' toughs an' smoudges. Nope. He ain't never throwed his feet fer a two-bit poke-out....Look at that road-kid next 'im! Ain't he a peach? I should smile! Wonder the medicine-man didn't turn down some o' them chechaquos...."

And, truly, the draft contained some very queer odd lots. By the side of the English gentleman stood a big fat German boy in knicker-bockers and jersey, bare-legged and wearing a pair of button-boots that had belonged to a woman in the days when they still possessed toe-caps. Pale face, pale hair, and pale eyes, conspired to give him an air of terror--the first seeming to have the hue of fright, the second to stand *en brosse* with fear, and the last to bulge like those of a hunted animal.

Presumably M. le Médicin-Major must have been satisfied that the boy was eighteen years of age, but, though tall and robust, he looked nearer fifteen--an illusion strengthened, doubtless, by the knickerbockers, bare calves, and button-boots. If he had enlisted in the Foreign Legion to avoid service in the Fatherland, he had quitted the frying-pan for a furnace seven times heated. Possibly he hoped to emulate Messieurs Shadrach, Meshach, and Abed-Nego. In point of fact, he was a deserter (driven to the desperate step of fleeing across the French frontier by a typical Prussian non-commissioned officer), and already wishing himself once more *zwei jahriger* in the happy Fatherland.

Already, to his German soul and stomach, the lager-bier of Munich, the sausage, *zwieback*, and *kalte schnitzel* of home, seemed things of the dim and distant past, and unattainable future.

Next to him stood a gnarled and knotted Spaniard, whose face appeared to be carven from his native mahogany, and whose ragged clothing--grimy, oily, blackened--proclaimed him wharf-side coal-heaver, dock-rat, and longshoreman. What did he among the Legion's blues? Was it lack of work, was it slow starvation? Or excess of temper and a quick blow with a coal-shovel upon the head of an enemy in some Marseilles coal-barge--that had brought him to Sidi-bel-Abbès in the sands of Africa?

By his side slouched a dark-faced, blunt-featured Austrian youth, whose evil-looking mouth was unfortunately in no wise concealed by a sparse and straggling moustache, laboriously pinched into two gummed spikes, and whose close-set eyes were not in harmony of focus. His dress appeared to be that of a lower-class clerk, ill-fitting black cloth of lamentable cut, the type of suit that, in its thousands, renders day horrible in European and American cities, and is, alas, spreading to many Asiatic. His linen was filthy, his crinkly hair full of dust, his boots cracked and shapeless. He looked what he was--an absconding Viennese tout who had had a very poor time of it. He proved to be a highly objectionable and despicable scoundrel.

His left-hand neighbour was a weedy, olive-faced youth, wearing a velvet tam-o'-shanter cap, and a brown corduroy suit, of which the baggy, peg-top trousers fitted tightly at the ankles over pearl-buttoned spring-side patent boots. He had long fluffy brown hair, long fluffy brown beard, whiskers, and moustache! long filthy finger nails, and no linen. Apparently a French student of the Sorbonne, or artist from The Quarter, overwhelmed by some terrible cataclysm, some *affaire* of the heart, the pocket, or *l'honneur*.

Beside this gentleman, whose whole appearance was highly offensive to the prejudiced insular eye of the Englishman, stood a typical *Apache*--a horrible-looking creature whose appalling face showed the cunning of the fox, the ferocity of the panther, the cruelty of the wolf, the treachery of the bear, the hate of the serpent, and the rage of the boar. Monsieur l'Apache had evidently chosen the Legion as a preferable alternative to the hulks and the chain-gang--Algeria rather than Noumea. He lived to doubt the wisdom of his choice.

Beside him, and evidently eyeing him askance, stood two youths as extraordinarily similar as were ever twins in this world. Dark, slightly "rat-faced," slender, but decidedly athletic looking.

"Cheer up, *golubtchik*! If one cannot get *vodka* one must drink *kvass*," whispered one.

"All right, Fedia," replied the other. "But I am so hungry and tired. What wouldn't I give for some good hot tea and *blinni*!"

"We're bound to get something of some sort before long--though it won't be *zakuska*. Don't give way on the very threshold now. It is our one chance, or I would not have brought you here, Olichka."

"Ssh!" whispered back the other. "Don't call me that here, Feodor."

"Of course not, Mikhail, stout fellow," replied Feodor, and smote his companion on the back.

Regarding them, sharp-eyed, stood the Cockney, an undersized, narrow-chested, but wiry-looking person--a typical East End sparrow; impudent, assertive, thoroughly self-reliant, tenacious, and courageous; of the class that produces admirable specimens of the genus "Tommy."

In curious contrast to his look of *gamin* alertness was that of his neighbour, a most stolid, dull and heavy-looking Dutchman, whose sole conversational effort was the grunt "*Verstaan nie*," whenever addressed. Like every other member of the draft he appeared "to feel his position" keenly, and distinctly to deplore it. Such expression as his bovine face possessed, suggested that Algerian sun and sands compared unfavourably with Dutch mists and polders, and the barrack-square of the Legion with the fat and comfortable stern of a Scheldt canal boat.

Square-headed, flat-faced Germans, gesticulating Alsatians and Lorraines, fair Swiss, and Belgians, with a sprinkling of Italians, swarthy Spaniards, Austrians and French, made up the remainder of the party, men whose status, age, appearance, bearing, and origins were as diverse as their nationalities levelled by a common desperate need (of food, or sanctuary, or a fresh start in life), and united by a common filthiness, squalor, and dejection--a gang powerless in the bonds of hunger and fear, delivered bound into the relentless, grinding mills of the Legion.

And thus, distinguished and apart, though in their midst, stood the well-dressed Englishman, apparently calm, incurious, with equal mind; his linen fresh, his face shaven, his clothing uncreased, his air rather that of one who awaits the result of the footman's enquiry as to whether Her Ladyship is "at home" to him.

More and more, the heart of Sir Montague Merline warmed to this young man of his own race and class, with his square shoulders, flat back, calm bearing, and hard high look. He approved and admired his air and appearance of being a Man, a Gentleman, and a Soldier. Had he a son, it was just such a youth as this he would have him be.

"Any 'Murricans thar?" suddenly bawled the Bucking Bronco.

"Nao," replied the Cockney youth, craning forward. "But I'm Henglish--which is better any d'y in the week, ain't it?"

The eye of the large American travelled slowly and deliberately from the crown of the head to the tip of the toe of the Cockney, and back. He then said nothing--with some eloquence.

"Say, ma honey, yew talk U.S. any?" queried a gigantic Negro, in the uniform of the Legion (presumably recruited in France as a free American citizen of Anglo-Saxon speech), addressing himself to the tall Englishman. "Youse ain't Dago, nor Dutchie, nor French. Cough it up, Bo, right hyar ef youse U.S."

The eyes of the young Englishman narrowed slightly, and his naturally haughty expression appeared to deepen toward one of contempt and disgust. Otherwise he took no notice of the Negro, nor of his question.

Remarking, "Some poah white trash," the Negro turned to the next man with the same query.

Cries in various tongues, such as "Anybody from Spain?" "Anyone from Vienna?" "Any Switzers about?" and similar attempts by the crowding, jostling Legionaries to discover a compatriot, and possibly a "towny," evoked gleams and glances of interest from the haggard, wretched eyes of the "blues," and, occasionally, answering cries from their grim and grimy lips.

A swaggering, strutting Sergeant emerged from the neighbouring regimental offices, roared "*Garde à vous*," brought the recruits to attention, and called the roll. As prophesied by Legionary John Bull, the whole draft was assigned to the Seventh Company, recently depleted by the desertion, en masse, of a *cafard*-smitten German *escouade*, or section, who had gone "on pump," merely to die in the desert at the hands of the Arabs--several horribly tortured, all horribly mangled.

Having called the roll, this Sergeant, not strictly following the example of the Sergeant of the Guard, looked the draft over more in anger than in sorrow.

"Oh, Name of the Name of Beautiful Beelzebub," bawled he, "but what have we here? To *drill* such worm-casts! Quel métier! Quel chien d'un métier! Stand up, stand up, oh sons of Arab mothers and pariah dogs," and then, feigning sudden and unconquerable sickness, he turned upon the Corporal in charge with a roar of--

"March these sacred pigs to their accursed sties."

As the heterogeneous gang stepped off at the word of command, "*En avant. Marche!*" toward the Quartermaster's store of the Seventh Company, it was clear to the experienced eye that the great majority were "Back to the army again," and were either deserters, or men who had already put in their military service in the armies of their own countries.

In the store-room they were endowed by the *Fourrier-Sergent*, to the accompaniment of torrential profanity, with white fatigue-uniforms, night-caps, rough shirts, harsh towels, and scraps of soap. From the store-room the squad was "personally conducted" by another, and even more terrible, Sergeant to a washing-shed beyond the drill-ground, and bidden to soap and scour itself, and then stand beneath the primitive shower-baths until purged and clean as never before in its unspeakable life.

As they neared the washing-shed, the bare idea of ablutions, or the idea of bare ablutions, appeared to strike consternation, if not positive terror, into the heart of at least one member of the squad, for the young Russian who had been addressed by his twin as Mikhail suddenly seized the other's arm and said with a gasp--

"Oh, Fedichka, how can I? Oh Fedia, Fedia, what shall I do?"

"We must trust in God, and use our wits, Olusha. I will..."

But a roar of "Silence, Oh Son of Seven Pigs," from the Sergeant, cut him short as they reached the shed.

"Now strip and scrub your mangy skins, you dogs. Scrape your crawling hides until the floor is thick in hog-bristles and earth, oh Great-grandsons of Sacréd Swine," he further adjured the wretched "blues," with horrible threats and fearful oaths.

"Wash, you mud-caked vermin, wash, for the carcase of the Legionary must be as spotless as the Fame of the Legion, or the honour of its smartest Sergeant--Sergeant Legros," and he lapped his bulging chest lest any Boeotian present should be ignorant of the identity of Sergeant Legros of the Legion.

Walking up and down before the doorless stalls in which the naked recruits washed, Sergeant Legros hurled taunts, gibes, insults, and curses at his charges, stopping from time to time to give special attention to anyone who had the misfortune to acquire his particular regard. Pausing to stare at the tall Englishman in affected disgust at the condition of his brilliant and glowing skin, he enquired--

"Is that a vest, disclosed by scrubbing and the action of water? Or is it your hide, pig?" And was somewhat taken aback by the cool and pleasant reply,

"No, that is not a new, pink silk vest that you see, Sergeant, it really is my own skin--but many thanks for the kind compliment, none the less."

Sergeant Legros eyed the recruit with something dimly and distantly akin to pity. Mad as a March hare, poor wretch, of course--it could not be intentional impudence--and the Sergeant smiled austerely--he would probably die in the cells ere long, if *le cafard* did not send him to the Zephyrs, the firing-platoon, or the Arabs. Mad to begin with! Ho! Ho! What a jest!--and the Sergeant chuckled.

But what was this? Did the good Sergeant's eyes deceive him? Or was there, in the next compartment, a lousy, lazy "blue" pretending to cleanse his foul and sinful carcase without completely stripping? The young Russian, Mikhail, standing with his back to the doorway, was unenthusiastically washing the upper part of his body.

Sergeant Legros stiffened like a pointer, at the sight. Rank disobedience! Flagrant defiance of orders, coupled with the laziest and filthiest indifference to cleanliness! This vile "blue" would put the Legion's clean shirt and canvas fatigue-suit on an indifferently washen body, would he? Let him wait until he was a Legionary, and no longer a recruit--and he should learn something of the powers of the Sergeant Legros.

"Off with those trousers, thou mud-caked flea-bitten scum," he thundered, and then received perhaps the greatest surprise of a surprising life. For, ere the offending recruit could turn, or obey, there danced forth from the next cubicle, with a wild whoop, his exact double, who, naked as he was born, turned agile somersaults and Catherine-wheels past the astounded Sergeant, down the front of the bathing-shed, and round the corner.

"Sacré Nom de Nom de Bon Dieu-de-Dieu!" ejaculated Sergeant Legros, and rubbed his eyes. He then displayed a sample of the mental quickness of the trained Legionary in darting to the neighbouring corner of the building instead of running down the entire front in the wake of the vanished acrobat.

Dashing along the short side-wall, Sergeant Legros turned the corner and beheld the errant lunatic approaching in the same literally revolutionary manner.

On catching sight of the Sergeant, the naked recruit halted, and broke into song and dance, the latter being of that peculiarly violent Cossack variety which constrains the performer to crouch low to earth and fling out his legs, alternately, straight before him.

For the first time in his life, words failed Sergeant Legros. For some moments he could but stand over the dancer and gesticulate and stutter. Rising to his feet with an engaging smile--.

"Ça va mieux, mon père?" observed the latter amiably.

Seizing him by arm and neck, the apoplectic Sergeant Legros conducted this weird disciple of Terpsichore back to his cubicle, while his mazed mind fumbled in the treasure-house of his vocabulary, and the armoury of his weapons of punishment.

Apparently there was method, however, in the madness of Feodor Kyrilovitch Malekov, for a distinct look of relief and satisfaction crossed his face as, in the midst of a little crowd of open-mouthed, and half-clothed recruits, he caught sight of his brother in complete fatigue-uniform.

Gradually, and very perceptibly the condition of Sergeant Legros improved. His halting recriminations and imprecations became a steady trickle, the trickle a flow, the flow a torrent, and the torrent an overwhelming deluge. By the time he had almost exhausted his vocabulary and himself, he began to see the humorous and interesting aspect of finding two lunatics in one small draft. He would add them to his collection of butts. Possibly one, or both of them, might even come to equal the Mad Grasshopper in that rôle. Fancy more editions of La Cigale--who had provided him with more amusement and opportunities for brutality than any ten sane Legionaries!

"Now, do great and unmerited honour to your vile, low carcases by putting on the fatigue-uniform of the Legion. Gather up your filthy civilian rags, and hasten," he bawled.

And when the, now wondrously metamorphosed, recruits had all dressed in the new canvas uniforms, they were marched to a small side gate in the wall of the barrack-square, and ordered to sell immediately everything they possessed in the shape of civilian clothing, including boots and socks. Civilian clothing is essential to the would-be deserter, and La Légion does not facilitate desertion.

That the unfortunate recruits got the one or two francs they did receive was solely due to the absence of a "combine" among the scoundrelly Arabs, Greeks, Spanish Jews, Negroes, and nondescript rogues who struggled for the cast-off clothing. For the Englishman's expensive suit a franc was offered, and competition advanced this price to four. For the sum of five francs he had to sell clothes, hat, boots, collar, tie, and underclothing that had recently cost him over fifty times as much. That he felt annoyed, and that, in spite of his apparent nonchalance, his temper was wearing thin, was evidenced by the fact that a big Arab who laid a grimy paw upon his shoulder and snatched at his bundle, received the swift blow of dissuasion--a sudden straight-left in the eye, sending him flying--to the amusement and approval of the sentry whose difficult and arduous task it was to keep the scrambling, yelling thieves of old-clo' dealers from invading the barrack-square, and repentant recruits from quitting it.

When the swindle of the forced sale was complete, and several poor wretches had parted with their all for a few *sous*, the gate was shut and the weary squad marched to the offices of the Seventh Company that each man's name and profession might be entered in the Company Roll, and that he might receive his *matricule* number, the number which would henceforth hide his identity, and save him the trouble of retaining a personality and a name.

To Colour-Sergeant Blanc, the tall English youth, like most Legionaries, gave a *nom d'emprunt*, two of his own names, Reginald Rupert. He concealed his surname and sullied the crystal truth of fact by stating that his father was the Commander-in-Chief of the Horse Marines of Great Britain and Inspector-General of the Royal Naval Horse Artillery; that he himself was by profession a wild-rabbit-tamer, and by conviction a Plymouth Rock--all of which was duly and solemnly entered in the great tome by M. Blanc, a man taciturn, *très boutonné*, and of no imagination.

Whatever the recruit may choose to say is written down in the Company lists, and should a recruit wax a little humorous, why--the Legion will very soon cure him of any tendency to humour. The Legion asks no questions, answers none, takes the recruit at his own valuation, and quickly readjusts it for him. Reconducted to the Store-room of the Seventh Company, the batch of recruits, again to the accompaniment of a fusillade of imprecations, and beneath a torrential deluge of insults and oaths, was violently tailored by a number of non-commissioned officers, and a fatigue-party of Légionnaires.

To "Reginald Rupert," at any rate, the badges of rank worn by the non-commissioned officers were mysterious and confusing--as he noted a man with one chevron giving peremptory orders in loud tone and bullying manner to a man who wore two chevrons. It also puzzled him that the fat man, who was evidently the senior official present, was addressed by the others as *"chef,"* as though he were a cook. By the time he was fitted out with kit and accoutrement, he had decided that the "chef" (who wore two gold chevrons) was a Sergeant-Major, that the men wearing one gold chevron were Sergeants, and that those wearing two red ones were Corporals; and herein he was entirely correct.

Every man had to fit (rather than be fitted with) a red képi having a brass grenade in front; a double-breasted, dark blue tunic with red facings and green-fringed red epaulettes; a big blue greatcoat, or *capote*; baggy red breeches; two pairs of boots; two pairs of linen spats, and a pair of leather gaiters. He also received a long blue woollen cummerbund, a knapsack of the old British pattern, a bag of cleaning materials, belts, straps, cartridge-pouches, haversack, and field flask.

To the fat Sergeant-Major it was a personal insult, and an impudence amounting almost to blasphemy, that a képi, or tunic should not fit the man to whom it was handed. The idea of adapting a ready-made garment to a man appeared less prominent than that of adapting a ready-made man to a garment.

"What!" he roared in Legion French, to the fat German boy who understood not a word of the tirade. "What? Nom d'un pétard! Sacré Dieu! The tunic will not easily button? Then contract thy vile body until it will, thou offspring of a diseased pig and a dead dog. I will fit thee to that tunic, and none other, within the week. Wait! But wait--till thou has eaten the Breakfast of the Legion once or twice, fat sow...."

A gloomy, sardonic Legionary placed a képi upon the crisply curling hair of Reginald Rupert. It was miles too big--a ludicrous extinguisher. The Englishman removed it, and returned it with the remark, "Ça ne marche pas, mon ami."

"Merde!" ejaculated the liverish-looking soldier, and called Heaven to witness that he was not to blame if the son of a beetle had a walnut for a head.

Throwing the képi back into the big box he fished out another, banged it on Rupert's head, and was about to bring his open hand down on the top of it, when he caught the cold but blazing eye of the recruit, and noticed the clenched fist and lips. Had the Legionary's right hand descended, the recruit's left hand would have risen with promptitude and force.

"If that is too big, let the sun boil thy brains and bloat thy skull till it fits, and if it be too small, sleep in it," he remarked sourly, and added that thrice-accursed "blues" were creatures of the kind that ate their young, encumbered the earth, polluted the air, loved to *faire Suisse*,[40] and troubled Soldiers of the Legion who might otherwise have been in the Canteen, or at Carmelita's--instead of being the valets of sons of frogs, nameless excrescences....

"Too small," replied Rupert coolly, and flung the cap into the box. "Valet? I should condole with a crocodile that had a clumsy and ignorant yokel like you for a valet," he added, in slow and careful French as he tried on a third cap, which he found more to his liking.

The old Legionary gasped.

"Il m'enmerde!" he murmured, and wiped his brow. He, Jules Duplessis, Soldat 1ère Classe, with four years' service and the *medaille militaire*, had been outfaced, browbeaten, insulted by a miserable "blue." What were the World and La Légion coming to? *"Merde!"*

While trying on his tunic, Rupert saw one of the Russians hand to the other the tunic and trousers which he had tried on. Apparently being as alike as two pins in every respect they had adopted the labour-saving device of one "fitting on" for both.

Having put on the képi, Mikhail bundled up the uniform, struck an attitude with arms akimbo, and inquired of the other--

"Do I look *very* awful in this thing, Fedia?"

"Shut up, you little fool," replied Feodor, with a quick frown. "Try and look more like a *mujik* in *maslianitza*,[41] and less like a young student at private theatricals. You're a Legionary now."

When, at length, the recruits had all been fitted into uniforms, and were ready to depart, they were driven forth with the heart-felt curse and comprehensive anathema of the Sergeant-Major--

"Sweep the room clear of this offal, Corporal," quoth he. "And if thou canst make a Légionnaire's little toe out of the whole draft--thou shalt have the Grand Cross of the Legion of Honour--I promise it."

"*En avant. Marche!*" bawled the Corporal, and the "blues" were led away, up flights of stairs, and along echoing corridors to their future home, their new quarters. A Légionnaire, carrying a huge earthenware jug, encountering them outside the door thereof, gave them their first welcome to the Legion.

"Oh thrice-condemned souls, welcome to Hell," he cried genially, and kicking open the door of a huge room, he liberally sprinkled each passing recruit, murmuring as he did so--

"Le diable vous bénisse."

Chapter II
A Barrack-Room of the Legion

The room which Reginald Rupert entered, with a dozen of his fellow "blues," was long and lofty, painfully orderly, and spotlessly clean. Fifteen cots were exactly aligned on each long side, and down the middle of the floor ran long wooden tables and benches, scoured and polished to immaculate whiteness. Above each bed was a shelf on which was piled a very neat erection of uniforms and kit. To the eye of Rupert (experienced in barrack-rooms) there was interesting novelty in the absence of clothes-boxes, and the presence of hanging-cupboards suspended over the tables from the ceiling.

Evidently the French authorities excelled the English in the art of economising space, as nothing was on the floor that could be accommodated above it. In the hanging cupboards were tin plates and cups and various utensils of the dinner-table.

The Englishman noted that though the Lebel rifles stood in a rack in a corner of the room, the long sword-bayonets hung by the pillows of their owners, each near a tin quart-pot and a small sack.

On their beds, a few Légionnaires lay sleeping, or sat laboriously polishing their leatherwork--the senseless, endless and detested *astiquage* of the Legion--or cleaning their rifles, bayonets, and buttons. Whatever else the Légionnaire is, or is not, he is meticulously clean, neat, and smart, and when his day's work is done (at four or five o'clock) he must start a half-day's work in "making *fantasie*"–in preparation for the day's work of the morrow.

Rising from his bed in the corner as the party entered, Legionary John Bull approached the Corporal in charge of the room and suggested that the English recruit should be allotted the bed between his own and that of Légionnaire Bronco, as he was of the same mother-tongue, and would make quicker progress in their hands than in those of foreigners. As the Corporal, agreeing, indicated the second bed from the window, to Rupert, and told him to take possession of it and make his *paquetage* on the shelf above, the Cockney recruit pushed forward:

"'Ere, I'm Henglish too! I better jine these blokes."

"Qu'est-ce-qu'il dit, Jean Boule?" enquired the Corporal.

On being informed, Corporal Achille Martel allotted the fourth bed, that on the other side of the Bucking Bronco, to Recruit Higgins with an intimation that the sooner he learnt French, and ceased the use of barbarous tongues the better it would be for his welfare. The Corporal then assigned berths to the remaining recruits, each between those of two old soldiers, of whom the right-hand man was to be the new recruit's guide, philosopher and friend, until he, in his turn, became a prideful, full-blown Legionary.

The young Russian who had given his name as Mikhail Kyrilovitch Malekov observed that the card at the head of the cot on his right-hand bore the inscription: "Luigi Rivoli, No. 13874, Soldat 2ième Classe."

As he stood, irresolute, and apparently in great anxiety and perturbation, nervously opening and shutting a cartridge-pouch, his face suddenly brightened as his twin entered the room and intercepted the departing Corporal.

"*Mille pardons*, Monsieur," he said, saluting smartly and respectfully. "But I earnestly and humbly request that you will permit me to inhabit this room in which is my brother. As we reached this door another *sous-officier* took me and the remainder to the next room when twelve had entered here....Alas! My brother was twelfth, and I thirteenth," he added volubly. "Look you, Monsieur, he is my twin, and we have never been separated yet. We shall get on much faster and better, helping each other, and be more credit to you and your room, *petit père*."

"Sacré Dieu, and Name of a Purple Frog! Is this a scurvy and lousy beggar, whining for alms at a mosque door? And am I a God-forsaken and disgusting *pékin* that you address me as 'Monsieur'? Name of a Pipe! Have I no rank? Address me henceforth as Monsieur le Caporal, thou kopeck-worth of Russian."

"Oui, oui; milles pardons, Monsieur le Caporal. But grant me this favour and I and my brother will be your slaves."

"Va t'en, babillard! Rompez, jaseur!" snarled the Corporal.

But the Russian, true to type, was tenacious. Producing a five-franc piece he scratched his nose therewith, and dropping the wheedling and suppliant tone, asked the testy Corporal if he thought it likely Messieurs les Caporaux of the Seventh Company could possibly be induced to drink the health of so insignificant an object as Recruit Feodor Kyrilovitch Malekov.

"Corporals do not drink with Légionnaires," was the answer, "but doubtless Corporal Gilles of the next room will join me in a drink to the health of a worthy and promising 'blue,'" and, removing his képi, he stretched his gigantic frame and yawned hugely as the Russian dexterously, and apparently unnoticed, slipped the coin into the képi. Having casually examined the lining of his képi, Monsieur le Caporal Martel replaced it on his head, and with astounding suddenness and ferocity pounced upon an ugly, tow-haired German, and with a shout of "Out, pig! Out of my beautiful room! Thy face disfigures it," he hunted him forth and bestowed him upon the neighbouring Corporal, M. Auguste Gilles, together with a promise of ten bottles of Madame la Cantinière's best, out of the thirty-and-five which the Russian's five-franc piece would purchase.

In a moment the Russian had opened negotiations with the Spaniard who had taken the bed next but one to that of Mikhail.

Like all educated Russians, Feodor Kyrilovitch was an accomplished linguist, and, while speaking French and English idiomatically, could get along very comfortably in Spanish, Italian, and German.

A very few minutes enabled him to make it clear to the Spaniard that an exchange of beds would do him no harm, and enrich him by a two-franc piece.

"No hay de que, Señor. Gracias, muchas gracias," replied the Spaniard. "En seguida, con se permiso," and transferred himself and his belongings to the berth vacated by the insulted and dispossessed German.

Meanwhile, Reginald Rupert, with soldierly promptitude, lost no time in setting about the brushing and arrangement of his kit, gathering up, as he did so, the pearls of local wisdom that fell from the lips of his kindly mentor, whose name and description he observed to be "Légionnaire John Bull, No. 11867, Soldat 2ième Classe."

Having shown his pupil the best and quickest way of folding his uniform in elbow-to-finger-tip lengths, and so arranging everything that he could find it in the dark, and array himself *en tenue de campagne d'Afrique* in ten minutes without a light, he invited him to try his own hand at the job.

"Now you try and make that '*paquetage* of the Legion,'" observed the instructor, "and the sooner you learn to make it quickly, the better. As you see, you have no chest for your kit as you had in the British Army, and so you keep your uniform on your shelf, *en paquetage*, for tidiness and smartness, without creases. The Légionnaire is as *chic* and particular as the best trooper of the crackest English cavalry-corps. We look down on the *piou-piou* from a fearful height, and swagger against the *Chasseur d'Afrique* himself. I wish to God we had spurs, but there's no cavalry in the Legion--though there are kinds of Mounted-Rifle Companies on mules, down South. I miss spurs damnably, even after fourteen years of foot-slogging in the Legion. You can't really swagger without spurs--not that the women will look at a Legionary in any case, or the men respect him, save as a fighter. But you can't swing without spurs."

"No," agreed Rupert, "I was just thinking I should miss them, and it'll take me some time to get used to a night-cap, a neck-curtained képi, a knapsack, and a steel bayonet-scabbard."

"You'll appreciate the first when you sleep out, and the second when you march, down South. The nights are infernally cold, and the days appallingly hot--and yet sunstroke is unknown in the Legion. Some put it down to wearing the overcoat to march in. The steel scabbard is bad--noisy and heavy. The knapsack is the very devil on the march, but it's the one and only place in the world in which you can keep a photo, letter, book, or scrap of private property, besides spare uniform and small kit. You'll soon learn to pack it, to stow underclothing in the haversack, and to know the place for everything, so that you can get from bed to barrack-square, fully equipped and accoutred in nine minutes from the bugle....And don't, for Heaven's sake, lose anything, for a spiteful N.C.O. can send you to your death in Biribi--that's the Penal Battalion--by running you in two or three times for 'theft of equipment.' Lost kit is regarded as stolen kit, and stolen kit is sold kit (to a court-martial), and the penalty is six months with the Zephyrs. It takes a good man to survive that....If you've got any money, try and keep a little in hand, so that you can always replace missing kit. The fellows here are appalling thieves--of uniform. It is regarded as a right, natural and proper thing to steal uniforms and kit, and yet we'd nearly kill a man who stole money, tobacco, or food. The former would be 'decorating' yourself, the latter disgracing yourself. We've some queer beasts here, but we're a grand regiment."

The disorderly heap of garments having become an exceedingly neat and ingenious little edifice, compact, symmetrical, and stable, Rupert's instructor introduced the subject of that bane of the Legionary's life--the eternal *astiquage*, the senseless and eternal polishing of the black leather straps and large cartridge-pouches.

"This stuff looks as though it had been left here by the Tenth Legion of Julius Cæsar, rather than made for the Foreign Legion," he remarked. "Let's see what we can make of it. Watch me do this belt, and then you can try the cartridge-cases. Don't mind firing off all the questions you've got to ask, meanwhile."

"Thanks. What sort of chaps are they in this room?" asked Rupert, seating himself on the bed beside his friendly preceptor, and inwardly congratulating himself on his good luck in meeting, on the threshold of his new career, so congenial and satisfactory a bunk-mate.

"Very mixed," was the reply. "The fellow on the other side of your berth is an American, an *ex*-U.S.A. army man, miner, lumber-jack, tramp, cow-boy, bruiser, rifle and revolver trick-shooter, and my very dear friend, one of the whitest men I ever met, and one of the most amusing. His French conversation keeps me alive by making me laugh, and he's learning Italian from a twopenny dictionary, and a Travellers' Phrase Book, the better to talk to Carmelita. The next but one is a Neapolitan who calls himself Luigi Rivoli. He used to be a champion Strong Man, and music-hall wrestler, acrobat, and juggler. Did a bit of lion-taming too, or, at any rate, went about with a show that had a cageful of mangy performing lions. He is not really very brave though, but he's a most extraordinary strong brute. Quite a millionaire here too, for Carmelita gives him a whole franc every day of his life."

"What made him enlist then?" asked Rupert, carefully watching the curious *astiquage* methods, so different from the pipe-clay to which he was accustomed.

"This same girl, and she's worth a thousand of Rivoli. It seems she pretended to turn him down, and take up with some other chap to punish Rivoli after some lover's quarrel or other, and our Luigi in a fit of jealous madness stabbed the other chap in the back, and then bolted and enlisted in the Legion, partly to pay her out, but chiefly to save himself. He was doing a turn at a *café-chantant* over in Algiers at the time. Of course, Carmelita flung herself in transports of grief, repentance, and self-accusation upon Luigi's enormous bosom, and keeps him in pocket-money while she waits for him. She followed him, and runs a *café* for Légionnaires here in Sidi-bel-Abbès. She gets scores of offers from our Non-coms., and from Frenchmen of the regular army stationed in Sidi, and her *café* is a sort of little Italian club. My friend, the Bucking Bronco, proposes to her once a week, but she remains true to Luigi, whom she intends to marry as soon as he has done his time. The swine's carrying on at the same time with Madame la Cantinière, who is a widow, and whose canteen he would like to marry. Between the two women he has a good time, and, thanks to Carmelita's money, gets all his work done for him. The brute never does a stroke. Pays substitutes for all fatigues and corvées, has his kit and accoutrements polished, and his clothes washed. Spends the balance of Carmelita's money at the Canteen, ingratiating himself with Madame! Keeps up his great strength with extra food too. He is a Hercules, and, moreover, seems immune from African fever and *le cafard*, which is probably due to his escaping three-parts of the work done by the average penniless. And he's as nasty as he is strong."

"What's his particular line of nastiness--besides cheating women I mean?" asked Rupert, who already knew only too well how much depends on the character, conduct, manners, and habits of room-mates with whom one is thrown into daily and nightly intimate contact, year after year, without change, relief, or hope of improvement.

"Oh, he's the Ultimate Bounder," replied the other, as he struck a match and began melting a piece of wax with which to rub his leather belt. "He's the Compleat Cad, and the Finished Bully. He's absolute monarch of the rank-and-file of the Seventh Company by reason of his vast wealth, and vaster strength. Those he does not bribe he intimidates. Remember that the Wages of Virtue here is one halfpenny a day as opposed to the Wages of Sin which is rather worse than death.

"Think of the position of a man who has the income of all in this room put together, in addition to the run of his best girl's own *café*. What with squaring Non-coms., hiring substitutes, and terrorising 'fags,' he hasn't done a stroke, outside parades of course, since he joined--except hazing recruits, and breaking up opponents of his rule."

"How does he fight?" asked Rupert.

"Well, wrestling's his *forte*–and he can break the back of any man he gets his arms round--and the rest's a mixture of boxing, ju-jitsu, and *la savate*, which, as you know, is kicking. Yes, he's a dirty tighter, though it's precious rarely that it comes to what you could call a fight. What I'm waiting for is the most unholy and colossal turn-up that's due to come between him and Buck sooner or later. It's bound to come, and it'll be a scrap worth seeing. Buck has been a professional glove-man among other things, and he holds less conservative views than I do, as to what is permissible against an opponent who kicks, clinches, and butts.... No, fighting's apt to be rather a dirty business here, and, short of a proper duel, a case of stand face to face and do all you can with all Nature's weapons, not forgetting your teeth....'*C'est la Légion.*'"

"How disgustin'!" murmured the young man. "Will this bird trouble me?"

"He will," answered the other, "but I'll take a hand, and then Buck will too. He hates Luigi like poison, and frequently remarks that he has it in for him when the time comes, and Luigi isn't over anxious to tackle him, though he hankers. Doesn't understand him, nor like the look in his eye. Buck is afraid of angering Carmelita if he 'beats up' Rivoli.... Yes, I dare say Buck and I can put the gentle Neapolitan off between us."

Reginald Rupert stiffened.

"I beg that you will in no way interfere," he observed coldly. "I should most strongly resent it."

The heart of the old soldier warmed to the youth, as he contrasted his slim boyish grace with the mighty strength, natural and developed, of the professional Strong Man, Wrestler, and Acrobat--most tricky, cunning, and dangerous of relentless foes.

"You keep clear of Luigi Rivoli as long as you can," he said with a kindly smile. "And at least remember that Buck and I are with you. Personally, I'm no sort of match for our Luigi in a rough-and-tumble nowadays, should he compel one. But he has let me alone since I told him with some definiteness that he would have to defend himself with either lead or steel, if he insisted on trouble between him and me."

"There now," he continued, rising, "now try that for yourself on a cartridge-pouch.... First melt the wax a bit, with a match--and don't forget that matches are precious in the Legion as they're so damned dear--and rub it on the leather as I did. Then take this flat block of wood and smooth it over until it's all evenly spread. And then rub hard with the coarse rag for an hour or two, then harder with the fine rag for about half an hour. Next polish with your palm, and then with the wool. Buck and I own a scrap of velvet which you can borrow before Inspection Parades, and big shows--but we don't use it extravagantly of course....

"Well, that's the *astiquage* curse, and the other's washing white kit without soap, and ironing it without an iron. Of course, Madame la République couldn't give us glazed leather, or khaki webbing--nor could she afford to issue one flat-iron to a barrack-room, so that we could iron a white suit in less than a couple of hours.... The devil of it is that it's all done in our 'leisure' time when we're supposed to be resting, or recreating.... Think of the British 'Tommy' in India

165

with his *dhobi*, his barrack-sweeper, his table-servant, and his *syce*–or his share in them. If we did nothing in the world but our daily polishing, washing and ironing, we should be busy men. However! '*C'est la Legion!*' And one won't live for ever....You won't want any help with the rifle and bayonet, I suppose?"

"No, thanks, I've 'had some,' though I haven't handled a Lebel before," and Reginald Rupert settled down to work while Legionary John Bull proceeded with his toilet.

"Anything else you want to know?" enquired the latter, as he put a final polish upon his gleaming sword-bayonet. "You know enough not to cut your rifle-sling stropping your razor on it....Don't waste your cake of soap making a candlestick of it. Too rare and precious here."

"Well, thanks very much; the more you tell me, the better for me, if it's not troubling you, Sir."

John Bull paused and looked at the recruit.

"Why do you call me 'Sir'?" he enquired.

"Why? ...Because you are senior and a Sahib, I suppose," replied the youth.

"Thanks, my boy, but don't. I am just Légionnaire John Bull 11867, Soldier of the Second Class. You'll be a soldier of the First Class, and my senior in a few months, I hope....I suppose you've assumed a *nom de guerre* too," replied the other, making a mental note that the recruit had served in India. He had already observed that he pointed his toes as he walked, and had a general cavalry bearing.

"Yes, I gave part of my own name; I'm 'Reginald Rupert' now. Didn't see why I should give my own. I've only come to have a look round and learn a bit. Very keen on experiences, especially military ones."

"Merciful God!" ejaculated John Bull softly. "Out for experiences! You'll get 'em, here."

"Keen on seein' life, y'know," explained the young man.

"Much more likely to see death," replied the other. "Do you realise that you're in for five years--and that no money, no influence, no diplomatic representations, no extradition can buy, or beg, or drag you out; and that by the end of five years, if alive, you'll be lucky if you're of any use to the Legion, to yourself, or to anyone else? I, personally, have had unusual luck, and am of unusual physique. I re-enlisted twice, partly because at the end of each five years I was turned loose with nothing in the world but a shapeless blue slop suit--partly for other reasons...."

"Oh! I've only come for a year, and shall desert. I told them so plainly at the enlistment bureau, in Paris," was the ingenuous reply.

The old Legionary smiled.

"A good many of our people desert, at least once," he said, "when under the influence of *le cafard*–especially the Germans. Ninety-nine per cent come to one of three ends--death, capture, or surrender. Death with torture at the hands of the Arabs; capture, or ignominious return and surrender after horrible sufferings from thirst, starvation and exposure."

"Yes; I heard the Legion was a grand military school, and a pretty warm thing, and that desertion was a bit of a feat, and no disgrace if you brought it off--so I thought I'd have a year of the one, and then a shot at the other," replied the young man coolly. "Also, I was up against it somewhat, and well--you know--seeking sorrow."

"You've come to the right place for it then," observed Legionary John Bull, sheathing his bayonet with a snap, as the door banged open...."Ah! Enter our friend Luigi," he added as that worthy swaggered into the room with an obsequious retinue, which included le bon Légionnaire Edouard Malvin, looking very smart and dapper in the uniform of Légionnaire Alphonse Dupont of the Eleventh Company.

"Pah! I smell 'blues'! Disgusting! Sickening!" ejaculated Légionnaire Luigi Rivoli in a tremendous voice, and stood staring menacingly from recruit to recruit.

Reginald Rupert, returning his hot, insolent glare with a cold and steady stare, beheld a huge and powerful-looking man with a pale, cruel face, coarsely handsome, wherein the bold, heavily lashed black eyes were set too close together beneath their broad, black, knitted brows, and the little carefully curled black moustache, beneath the little plebeian nose, hid nothing of the over-ripe red lips of an over-small mouth.

"Corpo di Bacco!" he roared in Italian and Legion French. "The place reeks of the stinking 'blues.' Were it not that I now go *en ville* to dine and drink my Chianti wine (none of your filthy Algerian slops for Luigi Rivoli), and to smoke my *sigaro estero* at my *café*, I would fling them all down three flights of stairs," and, like his companions, he commenced stripping off his white uniform. Having bared his truly magnificent arms and chest, he struck an attitude, ostentatiously contracted his huge right biceps, and smote it a resounding smack with the palm of his left hand.

"Aha!" he roared, as all turned to look at him.

"Disgustin' bounder," remarked Reginald Rupert very distinctly, as, with a second shout of "Aha!" Rivoli did the same with the left biceps and right hand, and then bunched the vast *pectoralis major* muscles of his chest.

"Magnifique:" cried Légionnaire Edouard Malvin, who was laying out his patron's uniform from his *paquetage*, preparatory to helping him to dress.

"As thou sayest, my *gallo*, 'C'est magnifique,'" replied Luigi Rivoli, and for five minutes contracted, flexed, and slapped the great muscles of his arms, shoulders, and chest.

"Come hither--thou little bambino Malvin, thou Bad Wine, thou Cattevo Vino Francese, and stand behind me....What of the back? Canst thou see the 'bull's head' as I set the *trapezius*, *rhomboideus*, and *latissimus dorsi* muscles?"

"As clearly as I see your own head, Main de Fer," replied the Austrian in affected astonishment and wonder. "It is the World's Most Wonderful Back! Why, were Maxick and Saldo, Hackenschmidt, the three Saxons, Sandow--yea--Samson and Hercules themselves here, all would be humiliated and envious."

"Aha!" again bawled Rivoli, "thou art right, *piccolo porco*," and, sinking to a squatting position upon his raised heels, he rose and fell like a jack-in-the-box for some time, before rubbing and smiting his huge thighs and calves to the accompaniment of explosive shouts. Thereafter, he fell upon his hands and toes, and raised and lowered his stiffened body a few dozen times.

The display finished, he enquired with lordly boredom: "And what are the absurd orders for walking-out dress to-night. Is it blue and red, or blue and white, or overcoats buttoned on the left--or what?"

"Tunic and red, Hercule, and all ready, as you see," replied Malvin, and he proceeded to assist at the toilet of the ex-acrobat, the plutocrat and leader of the rank-and-file of the Seventh Company by virtue of his income of a franc a day, and his phenomenal strength and ferocity.

Turning round that Malvin might buckle his belt and straighten his tunic, the great man's foot touched that of Herbert Higgins (late of Hoxton and the Loyal Whitechapel Regiment) who had been earnestly endeavouring for the past quarter of an hour to follow the instructions of the Bucking Bronco--instructions given in an almost incomprehensible tongue, of choice American and choicer French compact.

Profound disgust, deepening almost to horror, was depicted on the face of the Italian as he bestowed a vicious, hacking kick upon the shin of the offending "blue."

"Body of Bacchus, what is this?" he cried. "Cannot I move without treading in *vidanges*? Get beneath the bed and out of my sight, *cauchemar!*"

But far from retreating as bidden, the undersized Cockney rose promptly to his feet with a surprised and aggrieved look upon his face, hitherto expressive only of puzzled bewilderment.

"'Ere! 'Oo yer fink you're a kickin' of?" he enquired, adding with dignity, "I dunno' 'oo yer fink you *are*. I'm 'Erb 'Iggins, I am, an' don't yer fergit it."

That Mr. Herbert Higgins stood rubbing his injured shin instead of flying at the throat of the Italian, was due in no wise to personal fear, but to an utter ignorance of the rank, importance, and powers of this "narsty-lookin' furriner." He might be some sort of an officer, and to "dot 'im one" might mean lingering gaol, or sudden death. Bitterly he regretted his complete ignorance of the French tongue, and the manners and customs of this strange place. Anyhow, he could give the bloke some lip in good old English.

"Bit too 'andy wiv yer feet, ain't yer? Pretty manners, I *don't* fink! 'Manners none, an' customs narsty's' abart your mark, ain't it?"

But ere he could proceed with further flowers of rhetoric, and rush in ignorance upon his fate, the huge hand of the American fell upon his shoulder from behind and pressed him back upon his cot.

"Hello, Loojey dear! Throwin' bouquets to yerself agin, air yew? Gittin' fresh agin, air yew, yew greasy Eye-talian, orgin-grindin', ice-cream-barrer-pushin', back-stabbin', garlic-eatin', street-corner, pink-spangled-tights ackerobat," he observed in his own inimitable vernacular, as he unwound his long blue sash preparatory to dressing for the evening.

"Why don't yew per*chase* a barrel-orgin an' take yure dear pal Malvin along on it? Snakes! I guess I got my stummick full o' yew an' Mon-seer Malvin some. I wish yew'd kiss yureself goodbye, Loojey. Yew fair git my goat, yew fresh gorilla! *Oui, vous gagnez mon chevre proprement.*"

"*Qu'est-ce qu'il dit?*" asked Rivoli, his contemptuously curled lips baring his small, even teeth.

"Keskerdee? Why, yep! We uster hev a bunch o' dirty little' keskerdees' at the ol' Glowin' Star mine, way back in Californey when I was a road-kid. Keskerdees!—so named becos they allus jabbered 'Keskerdee' when spoke to. We uster use their heads fer cleanin' fryin'-pans. 'Keskerdee' is Eye-talian--a kind o' sorter low French," observed the Bucking Bronco.

It is to be feared that his researches into the ethnological and etymological truths of the European nations were limited and unprofitable, in spite of the fact that (like all other Legionaries of any standing) he spoke fluent Legion French on everyday military matters, and studied Italian phrases for the benefit of Carmelita. The Bucking Bronco's conversational method was to express himself idiomatically in the American tongue, and then translate it literally into the language of the benighted foreigner whom he honoured at the moment.

The Italian eyed the American malevolently, and, for the thousandth time, measured him, considered him, weighed him as an opponent in a boxing-wrestling-kicking match, remembered his uncanny magic skill with rifle and revolver, and, for the thousandth time, postponed the inevitable settlement, misliking his face, his mouth, his eye, and his general manner, air, and bearing.

"Give some abominable 'bleu' the honour of lacing the boots of Luigi Rivoli," he roared, turning with a contemptuous gesture from the American and the Cockney, to his henchman, Malvin. Fixing his eye upon the swarthy, spike-moustached Austrian, who sat at the foot of the bed opposite his own, he added:

"Here, dog, the privilege is thine. Allez schieblos"[42] and thrust out the unlaced boots that Malvin had pulled on to his feet.

The Austrian, squatting dejected, with his head between his fists, affected not to understand, and made no move.

"*Koom. Adji inna. Balek! fahesh beghla,*"[43] adjured the Italian, airing his Arabic, and insulting his intended victim by addressing him as though he were a native.

The Austrian did not stir.

"Quick," hissed the Italian, and pointed to his boots that there might be no mistake.

The Austrian snarled.

"Bring it to me," said the great man, and, in a second, the recruit was run by the collar of his tunic, his ears, his twisted wrists, his woolly hair, and by a dozen willing hands, to the welcoming arms of the bully.

"Oh, thou deserter from the *Straf Bataillon*,"[44] growled the latter. A sudden grab, a swift twist, and the Austrian was on his face, his elbows meeting and overlapping behind his back, and his arms drawn upward and backward. He shrieked.

A quick jerk and he was on his feet, and then swung from the ground face downward, his wrists behind him in one of Rivoli's big hands, his trouser-ends in the other. Placing his foot in the small of the Austrian's back, the Italian appeared to be about to break the spine of his victim, whose screams were horrible to hear. Dashing him violently to the ground, Rivoli re-seated himself, and thrust forward his right foot. Groaning and gasping, the cowed Austrian knelt to his task, but, fumbling and failing to give satisfaction, received a kick in the face.

Reginald Rupert dropped the cartridge-pouch which he was polishing, and stepped forward, only to find himself thrust back by a sweep of the American's huge arm, which struck him in the chest like an iron bar, and to be seized by Légionnaire John Bull who quietly remarked:

"Mind your own business, recruit.... *C'est la Légion!*"

No one noticed that the Russian, Mikhail, was white and trembling, and that his brother came and led him to the other end of the room.

"Bungler! *Polisson! Coquin!* Lick the soles of my boots and go," cried Rivoli, and, as the lad hesitated, he rose to his feet.

Cringing and shrinking, the wretched "blue" hastened to obey, thrust forth his tongue, and, as the boot was raised, obediently licked the nether surface and the edges of the sole until its owner was satisfied.

"Austria's proper attitude to Italy," growled the bully. "Now lick the other...."

Le Légionnaire Luigi Rivoli might expect prompt obedience henceforth from le Légionnaire Franz Joseph Meyer.

Standing in the ring of amused satellites was the evil-looking *Apache*, a deeply interested spectator of this congenial and enjoyable scene. His hang-dog face caught the eye of the Italian.

"Come hither, thou *blanc-bec*," quoth he. "Come hither and show this *vaurien* how to lace the boots of a gentleman."

The Apache obeyed with alacrity, and, performing the task with rapidity and skill, turned to depart.

"A nimble-fingered sharper," observed the Italian, and, rising swiftly, bestowed a shattering kick upon the retreating Frenchman. Recovering his balance after the sudden forward propulsion, the *Apache* wheeled round like lightning, bent double, and flew at his assailant. Courage was his one virtue, and he was the finest exponent of the art of butting in all the purlieus and environs of Montmartre, and had not only laid out many a good bourgeois, but had overcome many a rival, by this preliminary to five minutes' strenuous kicking with heavy boots. If he launched himself--a one-hundred-and-fifty pound projectile--with his hard skull as battering-ram, straight at the stomach of his tormentor, that astounded individual ought to go violently to the ground, doubled up, winded and helpless. A score of tremendous kicks would then teach him that an *Apache* King (and he, none other than Tou-Tou Boil-the-Cat, *doyen* of the heroes of the Rue de Venise, Rue Pirouette, and Rue des Innocents, *caveau*-knight and the beloved of the beauteous Casque d'Or) was not a person lightly to be trifled with.

But if Monsieur Tou-Tou Boil-the-Cat was a *Roi des Apaches*, Luigi Rivoli was an acrobat and juggler, and, to mighty strength, added marvellous poise, quickness and skill.

"*Ça ne marche pas, gobemouche*," he remarked, and, at the right moment, his knee shot up with tremendous force and crashed into the face of the butting *Apache*. For the first time the famous and terrible attack of the King of the Paris hooligans had failed. When the unfortunate monarch regained his senses, some minutes later, and took stock of his remaining teeth and features, he registered a mental memorandum to the effect that he would move along the lines of caution, rather than valour, in his future dealings with the Légionnaire Luigi Rivoli--until his time came.

"*Je m'en souviendrai*," said he....

An interesting object-lesson in the effect, upon a certain type of mind, of the methods of the Italian was afforded by the conduct of a Greek recruit, named Dimitropoulos. Stepping forward with ingratiating bows and smiles, as the unfortunate M. Tou-Tou was stretched senseless on the floor, he proclaimed himself to be the best of the *lustroi* of the city of Corinth, and begged for the honour and pleasure of cleaning the boots of Il Signor Luigi Rivoli.

Oh, but yes; a *lustros* of the most distinguished, look you, who had polished the most eminent boots in Greece at ten *leptas* a time. Alas! that he had not all his little implements and sponges, his cloth of velvet, his varnish for the heel. Had he but the tools necessary to the true artist in his profession, the boots of Il Illustrissimo Signor should be then and thenceforth of a brightness dazzling and remarkable.

As he gabbled, the Greek scrubbed at Rivoli's boots with a rag and the palm of his hand. Evidently the retinue of the great man had been augmented by one who would be faithful and true while his patron's strength and money lasted. As, at the head of his band of henchmen and parasites, the latter hero turned to leave the barrack-room with a shout of "*Allons, mes enfants d'Enfer,*" he bent his lofty brow upon, cocked his ferocious eye at, and turned his haughty regard toward the remaining recruits, finishing with Reginald Rupert:

"I will teach useful tricks to you little dogs later," he promised. "You shall dance me the *rigolboche*, and the *can-can*," and swaggered out....

"Nice lad," observed Rupert, looking up from his work--and wondered what the morrow might bring forth. There should be a disappointed Luigi, or a dead Rupert about, if it came to interference and trouble.

"Sure," agreed Légionnaire Bronco, seating himself on the bed beside his beloved John Bull. "He's some stiff, that guy, an' I allow it'll soon be up ter me ter *con*duct our Loojey ter the bone-orchard. He's a plug-ugly. He's a ward-heeler. Land sakes! I wants ter punch our Loojey till Hell pops; an' when it comes ter shootin' I got Loojey skinned a mile--sure thing. *J'ai Loojey écorché un mille....* Nope, there ain't 'nuff real room fer Looje an' me in Algery--not while Carmelita's around....

"Say, John," he continued, turning to his friend, "she up an' axed me las' night ef he ever went ter the Canteen an' ef Madam lar Canteenair didn't ever git amakin' eyes at her beautiful Looje! Yep! It *is* time Loojey kissed hisself good-bye."

"Oh? What did you tell her?" enquired John Bull. "There is no doubt the swine will marry the Canteen if he can. More profitable than poor little Carmelita's show. He *is* a low stinker, and she's one of the best and prettiest and pluckiest little women who ever lived.... She's so *débrouillarde.*"

"Wot did I say? Wal, John, wot I ses was--'Amakin' eyes at yure Loojey, my dear.' I ses, 'Madam lar Canteenair is a woman with horse-sense an' two eyes in 'er 'ead. She wouldn't look twice at a boastin', swankin', fat-slappin', back-stabbin', dime-show ackerobat,' I ses. 'Yure Loojey flaps 'is mouth too much. *Il frappe sa bouche trop,*' I ses. But I didn't tell her as haow 'e's amakin' up ter Madam lar Canteenaire all his possible. She wouldn't believe it of 'im. She wouldn't even believe that 'e *goes* ter the Canteen. I only ses: 'Yure Loojey's a leary lipper so don't say as haow I ain't warned yer, Carmelita honey,' I ses--an' I puts it inter copper-bottomed Frencho langwago also. Yep!"

"What did Carmelita say?" asked John Bull.

"Nix," was the reply. "It passes my com*pre*hension wot she sees in that fat Eye-talian ice-cream trader. Anyhaow, it's up ter Hiram C. Milton ter git upon his hind legs an' *fer*bid the bangs ef she goes fer ter marry a greasy orgin-grinder ... serposin' he don't git Madam lar Canteenair," and the Bucking Bronco sighed deeply, produced some strong, black Algerian tobacco, and asked High Heaven if he might hope ever again to stuff some real Tareyton Mixture (the best baccy in the world) into his "guley-brooley"--whereby Legionary John Bull understood him to mean his *brûle-gueule*, or short pipe--and relapsed into lethargic and taciturn apathy.

"How would you like a prowl round?" asked John Bull, of Rupert.

"Nothing better, thank you, if you think I could pass the Sergeant of the Guard before being dismissed recruit-drills."

"Oh, that'll be all right if you are correctly dressed. Hop into the tunic and red breeches and we'll try it. You're free until five-thirty to-morrow morning, and can do some more at your kit when we return. We'll go round the barracks and I'll show you the ropes before we stroll round Sidi-bel-Abbès, and admire the wonders of the Rue Prudon, Rue Montagnac, and Rue de Jerusalem. Our band is playing at the Military Club to-night, and the band of the Première Légion Étrangère is the finest band in the whole world--largely Germans and Poles. We are allowed to listen at a respectful distance. We'll look in at the *Village d'Espagnol*, the *Mekerra*, and the *Faubourg des Palmiers* another time, as they're out of bounds. Also the *Village Négre* if you like, but if we're caught there we get a month's hard labour, if not solitary confinement and starvation in the foul and stinking *cellules*–because we're likely to be killed in the *Village Négre*."

"Let's go there now," suggested Rupert eagerly, as he buttoned his tunic.

"No, my boy. Wait until you know what *cellule* imprisonment really is, before you risk it. You keep out of the *trou* just as long as you can. It's different from the Stone Jug of a British regiment--very. Don't do any *rabiau*[45] until you must. We'll be virtuous to-night, and when you must go out of bounds, go with me. I'll take you to see Carmelita this evening at the Café de la Légion, and we'll look in on Madame la Cantinière, at the Canteen, before the Last Post at nine o'clock.... Are you coming, Buck?"

And these three modern musketeers left the *chambrée* of their *caserne* and clattered down the stone stairs to the barrack-square.

Chapter III
Carmelita Et Cie

"Those boots comfortable?" asked John Bull as they crossed the great parade-ground.

"Wonderfully," replied Rupert. "I could do a march in them straight away. Fine boots too."

"Yes," agreed the other. "That's one thing you can say for the Legion kit, the boots are splendid--probably the best military boots in the world. You'll see why, before long."

"Long marches?"

"Longest done by any unit of human beings. Our ordinary marches would be records for any other infantry, and our forced marches are incredible--absolute world's records. They call us the '*Cavalerie à pied*' in the Service, you know. One of the many ways of killing us is marching us to death, to keep up the impossible standard. Buck, here, is our champion."

"Waal, yew see--I strolled crost Amurrica ten times," apologised the Bronco, "ahittin' the main drag, so I oughter vamoose some. Yep! I can throw me feet *con*siderable."

"I've never been a foot-slogger myself," admitted Rupert, "but I've Mastered a beagle pack, and won a few running pots at school and during my brief 'Varsity career. What are your distances?"

"Our minimum, when marching quietly out of barracks and back, without a halt is forty kilometres under our present Colonel, who is known in the Legion as The Marching Pig, and we do it three or four times a week. On forced marches we do anything that is to be done, inasmuch as it is the unalterable law of the Legion that all forced marches must be done in one march. If the next post were forty miles away or even fifty, and the matter urgent, we should go straight on without a halt, except the usual 'cigarette space,' or five minutes in every hour, until we got there. I assure you I have very often marched as much as six hundred kilometres in fifteen days, and occasionally much more. And we carry the heaviest kit in the world--over a hundred-weight, in full marching order."

"What is a kilometre?" asked the interested Rupert.

"Call it five furlongs."

"Then an ordinary day's march is about thirty miles without a halt, and you may have to do four hundred miles straight off, at the rate of twenty-five consecutive miles a day? Good Lord above us!"

"Yes, my own personal record is five hundred and sixty miles in nineteen days, without a rest day--under the African sun and across sand...."

"I say--what's *this* game?" interrupted Rupert, as the three turned a corner and entered a small square between the rear of the *caserne* of the Fourth Company and the great barrack-wall--a square of which all exits were guarded by sentries with fixed bayonets. Round and round in a ring at a very rapid quick-step ran a dismal procession of suffering men, to the monotonously reiterated order of a Corporal--

"A droit, *droit*. A droit, *droit*. A droit, *droit*."

Their blanched, starved-looking faces, glazed eyes, protruding tongues and doubled-up bodies made them a doleful spectacle. On each man's back was a burden of a hundred pounds of stones. On each man's emaciated face, a look of agony, and on the canvas-clad back of one man, a great stain of wet blood from a raw wound caused by the cutting and rubbing of the stone-laden knapsack. Each man wore a fatigue-uniform, filthy beyond description.

"Why the hell can't they be set ter sutthin' useful--hoein' pertaties, or splittin' rails, or chewin' gum--'stead o' that silly strain-me-heart and break-me-sperrit game on empty stummicks twice a day?" observed the Bucking Bronco.

Every panting, straining, gasping wretch in that pitiable *peloton des hommes punis* looked as though his next minute must be his last, his next staggering step bring him crashing to the ground. What could the dreadful alternative be, the fear of which kept these suffering, starving wretches on their tottering, failing legs? Why would they *not* collapse, in spite of Nature? Fear of the Legion's prison? No, they were all serving periods in the Legion's prison already, and twice spending three hours of each prison-day in this agony. Fear of the Legion's Hospital? Yes, and of the Penal Battalion afterwards.

"What sort of crimes have they committed?" asked Rupert, as they turned with feelings of personal shame from the sickening sight.

"Oh, all sorts, but I'm afraid a good many of them have earned the enmity of some Non-com. As a rule, a man who wants to, can keep out of that sort of thing, but there's a lot of luck in it. One gets run in for a lost strap, a dull button, a speck of rust on rifle or bayonet, or perhaps for being slow at drill, slack in saluting, being out of bounds, or something of that sort. A Sergeant gives him three days' confinement to barracks, and enters it in the *livre de punitions*. Very likely, the Captain, feeling liverish when he examines the book, makes it eight days' imprisonment. That's not so bad, provided the Commander of the Battalion does not think it might be good for discipline for him to double it. And that again is bearable so long as the Colonel does not think the scoundrel had better have a month--and imprisonment, though only called 'Ordinary Arrest,' carries with it this beastly *peloton de chasse*. Still, as I say, a good man and keen soldier can generally keep fairly clear of *salle de police* and *cellule*."

"So Non-coms. can punish off their own bat, in the Legion, can they?" enquired Rupert as they strolled toward the main gate.

"Yes. The N.C.O. is an almighty important bird here, and you have to salute him like an officer. They can give extra corvée, confinement to barracks, and up to eight days' *salle de police*, and give you a pretty bad time while you're doing it, too. In peace time, you know, the N.C.O.s run the Legion absolutely. We hardly see our officers except on marches, or at manoeuvres. Splendid soldiers, but they consider their duty is to lead us in battle, not to be bothered with us in peace. The N.C.O.s can do the bothering for them. Of course, we're pretty frequently either demonstrating, or actually fighting on the Southern, or the Moroccan border, and then an officer's job is no sinecure. They are real soldiers--but the weak spot is that they avoid us like poison, in barracks."

"We're mostly foreigners, of course," he continued, "half German, and not very many French, and there's absolutely none of that mutual liking and understanding which is the strength of the British Army....And naturally, in a corps like this, they've got to be severe and harsh to the point of cruelty. After all, it's not a girls' school, is it? But take my advice, my boy, and leave the Legion's punishment system of starvation, over-work, and solitary confinement outside your 'experiences' as much as possible...."

"I say--what a ghastly, charnel-house stink," remarked the recipient of this good advice, as the trio passed two iron-roofed buildings, one on each side of the closed main-entrance of the barracks. "I noticed it when I first came in here, but I was to windward of it I suppose. It's the bally limit. Poo-o-oh!"

"Yes, you live in that charming odour all night, if you get *salle de police* for any offence, and all day as well, if you get 'arrest' in the regimental lock-up--except for your two three-hour turns of *peloton des hommes punis*. It's nothing at this distance, but wait until you're on sentry-go in one of those barrack-prisons. There's a legend of a runaway pig that took refuge in one, gave a gasp, and fell dead....Make Dante himself envious if he could go inside. The truth of that Inferno is much stranger than the fiction of his."

"Yep," chimed in the American. "But what gits my goat every time is *cellules*. Yew squats on end in a dark cell fer the whole of yure sentence, an' yew don't go outside it from start to finish, an' thet may be thirty days. Yew gits a quarter-ration o' dry bread an' a double ration of almighty odour. 'Nuff ter raise the roof, but it don't do it. No exercise, no readin', no baccy, no nuthin'. There yew sits and there yew starves, an' lucky ef yew don't go balmy...."

"I hope we get you past the Sergeant of the Guard," interrupted John Bull. "Swank it thick as we go by."

The cold eye of the Sergeant ran over the three Legionaries as they passed through the little side wicket without blazing into wrath over any lack of smartness and *chic* in their appearance.

"One to you," said John Bull, as they found themselves safe in the shadow of the Spahis' barracks outside. "If you had looked too like a recruit he'd have turned you back, on principle...."

To Reginald Rupert the walk was full of interest, in spite of the fact that the half-vulgar, half-picturesque Western-Eastern appearance of the town was no novelty. He had already seen all that Sidi-bel-Abbès could show, and much more, in Algiers, Tangiers, Cairo, Alexandria, Port Said, and Suez. But, with a curious sense of proprietorship, he enjoyed listening to the distant strains of the band--their "own" band. To see thousands of Legionaries, Spahis, Turcos, Chasseurs d'Afrique, Sapeurs, Tirailleurs, Zouaves, and other French soldiery, from their own level, as one of themselves, was what interested him. Here was a new situation, here were new conditions, necessities, dangers, sufferings, relationships. Here, in short, were entirely new experiences....

"This is the Rue Prudon," observed John Bull. "It separates the Military goats on the west, from the Civil sheep on the east. Not that you'll find them at all 'civil' though....Reminds me of a joke I heard our Captain telling the Colonel at dinner one night when I was a Mess Orderly. A new man had taken over the Grand Hotel, and he wrote to the Mess President to say he made a speciality of dinner-parties for Military and *Civilised* officers! Bit rough on the Military, what?"

Having crossed the Rue Prudon rubicon, and invaded the Place de Quinconces with its Palais de Justice and prison, the Promenade Publique with its beautiful trees, and the Rue Montagnac with its shops and life and glitter, the three Legionaries quitted the quarter of electric arc-lights, brilliant cafés, shops, hotels, aperitif-drinking citizens, promenading French-women, newspaper kiosks, loitering soldiers, shrill hawkers of the *Echo d'Oran*, white-burnoused Arabs (who gazed coldly upon the hated Franswazi, and bowed to officials with stately dignity, arms folded on breast), quick-stepping Chasseurs, scarlet-cloaked Spahis, and swaggering Turcos, crossed the Place Sadi Carnot, and made for the maze of alleys, slums, and courts (the quarter of the Spanish Jews, town Arabs, *hadris*, *odjar*-wearing women, Berbers, Negroes, half-castes, semi-Oriental scum, "white trash," and Legionaries), in one of which was situated Carmelita's Café de la Légion.

§2

La Belle Carmelita, black-haired, red-cheeked, black-eyed, red-lipped, lithe, swift, and graceful, sat at the receipt of custom. Carmelita's Café de la Légion was for the Legion, and had to make its profits out of men whose pay is one halfpenny a day. It is therefore matter for little surprise that it compared unfavourably with Voisin's, the Café de la Paix, the Pré Catalan, Maxim's, the Café Grossenwahn, the Das Prinzess Café, the restaurants of the Place Pigalle, Le Rat Mort, or even Les Noctambules, Le Cabaret de l'Enfer, the Chat Noir, the Elysée Montmartre, and the famous and infamous *caveaux* of Le Quartier--in the eyes of those Legionaries who had tried some, or all, of these places.

However, it had four walls, a floor, and a roof; benches and a large number of tables and chairs, many of which were quite reliable. It had a bar, it had Algerian wine at one penny the bottle, it had *vert-vert* and *tord-boyaud* and *bapédi* and *shum-shum*. It had really good coffee, and really bad cigarettes. It had meals also--but above all, and before all, it had a welcome. A welcome for the Legionary. The man to whose presence the good people of Sidi-bel-Abbès (French petty officials, half-castes, Spanish Jews, Arabs, clerks, workmen, shopkeepers, waiters, and lowest-class bourgeoisie) took exception at the bandstand, in the Gardens, in the Cafés, in the very streets; the man from the contamination of whose touch the very cocottes, the demi-mondaines, the joyless *filles de joie*, even the daughters of the pavement; drew aside the skirts of their dingy finery (for though the Wages of Virtue are a halfpenny a day for the famous Legion, the Wages of Sin are more for the infamous legion); the man at whom even the Goums, the Arab *gens-d'armes* shouted as at a pariah dog, this man, the Soldier of the Legion, had a welcome in Carmelita's Café. There were two women in all the world who would endure to breathe the same air as the sad Sons of the Legion--Madame la Cantinière (official *fille du régiment*) and Carmelita. Is it matter for wonder that the Legion's sons loved them--particularly Carmelita, who, unlike Madame, was under no obligation to shed the light of her countenance upon them? Any man in the Legion might speak to Carmelita provided he spoke as a gentleman should speak to a lady--and did not want to be pinned to her bar by the ears, and the bayonets of his indignant brothers-in-arms--any man who might speak to no other woman in the world outside the Legion. (Madame la Cantinière is inside the Legion, *bien entendu*, and always married to it in the person of one of its sons.) She would meet him as an equal for the sake of her beautiful, wonderful, adored Luigi Rivoli, his brother-in-arms. Perhaps one must be such an outcast that the sight of one causes even painted lips to curl in contemptuous disdain; such a *thing* that one is deterred from entering decent Cafés, decent places of amusement and decent boulevards; so low that one is strictly doomed to the environment of one's prison, or the slums, and to the society of one's fellow dregs, before one can appreciate the attitude of the Sons of the Legion to Carmelita. They revered her as they did not revere the Mother of God, and they, broken and crucified wretches, envied Luigi Rivoli as they did not envy the repentant thief absolved by Her Son.

She, Carmelita, welcomed *them*, Legionaries! It is perhaps comprehensible if not excusable, that the attitude of Madame la Cantinière was wholly different, that she hated Carmelita as a rival, and with single heart, double venom and treble voice, denounced her, her house, her wine, her coffee, and all those *chenapans* and *sacripants* her clients.

"*Merde!*" said Madame la Cantinière. "That which makes the slums of Naples too hot for it, is warm indeed! Naples! Ma foi! Why Monsieur Le Bon Diable himself must be reluctant when his patrol runs in a *prisonnier* from Naples to the nice clean guard-room and *cellules* in his Hell ... Naples! ... La! La!..." which was unkind and unfair of Madame, since the very worst she knew of Carmelita was the fact that she kept a Café whereat the Legionaries spent their half-pence. It is not (rightly or wrongly) in itself an indictable offence to be a Neapolitan.

So the Legion loved Carmelita, Madame la Cantinière hated her, the Bucking Bronco worshipped her, John Bull admired her, le bon M. Edouard Malvin desired her, and Luigi Rivoli owned her--body, soul and cash-box--what time he sought to do the same for Madame la Cantinière whose body and cash-box were as much larger than those of Carmelita as her soul was smaller.

Between two fools one comes to the ground--sometimes--but Luigi intended to come to a bed of roses, and to have a cash-box beneath it. One of the fools should marry and support him, preferably the richer fool, and meantime, oh the subtlety, the cleverness, the piquancy--of being loved and supported by both while marrying neither! Many a time as he lay on his cot while a henchman polished the great cartridge-pouches (that earned the Legion the sobriquet of "the Leather-Bellies" from the Russians in the Crimea), the belts, the buttons, the boots, and the rifle and bayonet of the noble Luigi, while another washed his fatigue uniforms and underclothing, that honourable man would chuckle aloud as he saw himself frequently cashing a ten-franc piece of Carmelita's at Madame's Canteen, and receiving change for a twenty-franc piece from the fond, yielding Madame. Ten francs too much, a sigh too many, and a kiss too few--for Madame did not kiss, being, contrary to popular belief with regard to vivandières in general, and the Legion's vivandière in particular, of rigid virtue, oh, but yes, of a respectability profound and colossal--during "vacation." Her present vacation had lasted for three months, and Madame felt it was time to replace le pauvre Etienne Baptiste--cut in small pieces by certain Arab ladies. Madame was a business woman, Madame needed a husband in her business, and Madame had an eye for a fine man. None finer than Luigi Rivoli, and Madame had never tried an Italian. Husbands do not last long in the Legion, and Madame had had three French, one Belgian, and one Swiss (seriatim, *bien entendu*). No, none finer in the whole Legion than Rivoli. None, nom de Dieu! But a foreign husband may be a terrible trial, look you, and an Italian is a foreigner in a sense that a French-speaking Belgian or Swiss is not. No, an

Italian is not a Frenchman even though he be a Légionnaire. And there were tales of him and this vile shameless creature from Naples, who decoyed les braves Légionnaires from their true and lawful Canteen to her noisome den in the foul slums, there to spend their hard-earned sous on her poisonous red-ink wine, her muddy-water coffee, and her--worse things. Yes, that cunning little fox le Légionnaire Edouard Malvin had thrown out hints to Madame about this Neapolitan *ragazza*–but then, ce bon M. Malvin was himself a suitor for Madame's hand--as well as a most remarkable liar and rogue. Perhaps 'twould be as well to accept ce beau Luigi at once, marry him immediately, and see that he spent his evenings helping in the Canteen bar, instead of gallivanting after Neapolitan hussies of the bazaar. Men are but men--and sirens are sirens. What would you? And Luigi so gay and popular. Small blame that he should stray when Madame was unkind or coy....Yes, she would do it, if only to spite this Neapolitan cat.... But--he was a foreigner and something of a rogue--and incredibly strong. Still, Madame had tamed more than one recalcitrant husband by knocking the bottom off an empty bottle and stabbing him in the face with it. And however strong one's husband might be, he must, like Sisera, sleep sometimes.

The beautiful Luigi would hate to be awakened with a bottomless bottle, and would not need it more than once....And the business soul of scheming, but amorous Madame, much troubled, still halted between two opinions--while the romantic and simple soul of loving little Carmelita remained steadfast, and troubled but little. Just a little, because the fine *gentilhomme*, Légionnaire Jean Boule, and the great, kind Légionnaire Bouckaing Bronceau, and certain others, seemed somehow *to warn her* against her Luigi; seemed to despise him, and hint at treachery. She did not count the sly Belgian (or Austrian) Edouard Malvin. The big stupid Americano was jealous, of course, but Il Signor Inglese was not and he was--oh, like a Reverend Father--so gentle and honest and good. But no, her Luigi could not be false, and the next Légionnaire who said a word against him should be forbidden Le Café de la Légion, ill as it could afford to lose even halfpenny custom--what with the rent, taxes, *bakshish* to gens-d'armes, service, cooking, lighting, wine, spirits, coffee, and Luigi's daily dinner, Chianti and franc pocket-money....If only that franc could be increased--but one must eat, or get so thin--and the great Luigi liked not skinny women. What was a franc a day to such a man as Luigi, her Luigi, strongest, finest, handsomest of men?–and but for her he would never have been in this accursed Legion. Save for her aggravating wickedness, he would never have stabbed poor Guiseppe Longigotto and punished her by enlisting. How great and fine a hero of splendid vengeance! A true Neapolitan, yet how magnanimous when punishment was meted! He had forgiven--and forgotten--the dead Guiseppe, and he had forgiven her, and he accepted her miserable franc, dinner and Chianti wine daily. Also he had allowed her--miserable ingrate that she had been to annoy him and make him jealous--to find the money that had mysteriously but materially assisted in procuring the perpetual late-pass that allowed him to remain with her till two in the morning, long after all the other poor Légionnaires had returned to their dreadful barracks. Noble Luigi! Yet there were people who coupled his name with that of wealthy Madame la Cantinière in the barrack yonder.

She had overheard Légionnaires doing it, here in her own Café, though they had instantly and stoutly denied it when accused, and had looked furtive and ashamed. Absurd, jealous wretches, whose heads Luigi could knock together as easily as she could click her castanets....

Almost time that the Légionnaires began to drop in for their litre and their *tasse*–and Carmelita rose and went to the door of the Café de la Légion and looked down the street toward the Place Sadi Carnot. One of three passing Chasseurs d'Afrique made a remark, the import of which was not lost on the Italian girl though the man spoke in Paris slum argot.

"If Monsieur would but give himself the trouble to step inside and sit down for a moment," said Carmelita in Legion-French, "Monsieur's question shall be answered by Luigi Rivoli of La Legion. Also he will remove Monsieur's pretty uniform and scarlet *ceinturon* and will do for Monsieur what Monsieur's mamma evidently neglected to do for Monsieur when Monsieur was a dirty little boy in the gutter....Monsieur will not come in as he suggested? Monsieur will not wait a minute? No? Monsieur is a very wise young gentleman...."

An Arab Spahi swaggered past and leered.

"*Sabeshad zareefeh chattaha,*" said he, "*saada atinee.*"

"*Roh! Imshi!*" hissed Carmelita and Carmelita's hand went to her pocket in a significant manner, and Carmelita spat.

A Greek ice-cream seller lingered and ogled.

"*Bros!*" snapped Carmelita with a jerk of her thumb in the direction in which the young person should be going.

A huge Turco, with a vast beard, brought his rolling swagger to a halt at her door and made to enter.

"*Destour!*" said the tiny Carmelita to the giant, pointed to the street and stared him unwaveringly in the eye until, grinning sheepishly, he turned and went.

Carmelita did not like Turcos in general, and detested this one in particular. He was too fond of coming when he knew the Café to be empty of Légionnaires.

An old Spanish Jew paused in his shuffle to ask for a cigarette.

"*Varda!*" replied Carmelita calmly, with the curious thumb-jerking gesture of negation, distinctive of the uneducated Italian.

A most cosmopolitan young woman, and able to give a little of his own tongue to any dweller in Europe and to most of those in Northern Africa. Not in the least a refined young woman, however, and her many accomplishments not of the drawing-room. Staunch, courageous, infinitely loving, utterly honest, loyal, reliable, and very self-reliant, she was, upon occasion, it is to be feared, more emphatic than delicate in speech, and more uncompromising than ladylike in conduct. She was not *une maîtresse vierge*, and her standards and ideals were not those of the Best Suburbs. You see, Carmelita had begun to earn her own living at the unusually early age of three, and earned it in coppers on a dirty rug, on a dirtier Naples quay, for a decade or so, until at the age of fourteen, or fifteen, she, together with her Mamma, her reputed Papa, her sister and her brother, performed painful acrobatic feats on the edge of the said quay for the delectation of the passengers of the big North German Lloyd and other steamers that tied up thereat for purposes of embarkation and debarkation, and for the reception of coal and the discharge of cargo.

At the age of fifteen, Carmelita, most beautiful of form and coarsely beautiful of face, of perfect health, grace, poise, and carriage, fell desperately in love with the great Signor Carlo Scopinaro, born Luigi Rivoli, a star of her own firmament but of far greater magnitude.

Luigi Rivoli, one of a troupe of acrobats who performed at the Naples Scala, Vésuvie, and Variétés, meditating setting up on his own account as Strong Man, Acrobat, Juggler, Wrestler, Dancer, and Professor of Physical Culture, was, to the humble "tumbler" of the quay, as the be-Knighted Actor-Manager of a West End Theatre to the last joined chorus girl, or walking-lady on his boards. And yet the great Signor Carlo Scopinaro, born Luigi Rivoli, meditating desertion from his troupe and needing an "assistant," deigned to accept the services and whole-souled adoration of the girl who was as much more skilful as she was less powerful than he.

When, in her perfect, ardent, and beautiful love, her reckless and uncounting adoration, she gave herself, mind, body and soul, to her hero and her god, he accepted the little gift "without prejudice"–as the lawyers say. "Without prejudice" to Luigi's future, that is.

During their short engagement at the Scala--terminated by the Troupe's earnest endeavour to assassinate the defaulting and defalcating Luigi, and her family's endeavour to maim Carmelita for setting up on her own account, and deserting her loving "parents"–it was rather the girl whom the public applauded for her wonderful back-somersaults, contortions, hand-walking, Catherine-wheels, trapeze-work, and dancing, than the man for his feats with dumb-bells of doubtful solidity, his stereotyped ball-juggling, his chain-breaking, and weight-lifting, his muscle-slapping and *Ha!* shouting, his posturing and grimacing, and his issuing of challenges to wrestle any man in the world for any sum he liked to name, and in any style known to science.

And, when engagements at the lower-class halls and cafés of Barcelona, Marseilles, Toulon, Genoa, Rome, Brindisi, Venice, Trieste, Corinth, Athens, Constantinople, Port Said, Alexandria, Messina, Valetta, Algiers, Oran, Tangiers, or Casa Blanca were obtained, it was always, and obviously, the girl, rather than the man, who decided the proprietor or manager to engage them, and who won the applause of his patrons.

When times were bad, as after Luigi's occasional wrestling defeats and during the bad weeks of Luigi's typhoid, convalescence, and long weakness at Marseilles, it was Carmelita, the humbler and lesser light, who (the Halls being worked out) tried desperately to keep the wolf from the door by returning to the quay-side business, and, for dirty coppers, exhibiting to passengers, coal-trimmers, cargo-workers, porters and loafers, the performances that had been subject of signed contracts and given on fine stages in beautiful music-halls and *cafés*, to refined and appreciative audiences. Incidentally the girl learned much French (little knowing how useful it was to prove), as well as smatterings of Spanish, Greek, Turkish, English and Arabic.

So Carmelita had "assisted" the great Luigi in the times of his prosperity and had striven to maintain him in eclipse, by quay-side, public-house, workmen's dinner-hour, low *café*, backyard, gambling-den, and wine-shop exhibitions of her youthful skill, grace, agility, and beauty--and had failed to make enough by that means. To the end of her life poor Carmelita could never, never forget that terrible time at Marseilles, try as she might to thrust it into the background of her thoughts. For there, ever there, in the background it remained, save when called to cruel prominence by some mischance, or at rare intervals by the noble Luigi himself, when displeased by some failure on the part of Carmelita. A terrible, terrible memory, for Carmelita's nature was essentially virginal, delicate, and of crystal purity. Where she loved she gave all--and Luigi was to Carmelita as much her husband as if they had been married in every church they had passed, in every cathedral they had seen, and by every *padre* they had met....

A terrible, terrible memory.... But Luigi's life was at stake and what true woman, asked Carmelita, would not have taken the last step of all (when every other failed) to raise the money necessary for doctors, medicine, delicacies, food, fuel, and lodging? If, by thrusting her right hand into the fire, Carmelita could have burnt away those haunting and corroding Marseilles memories, then into the fire her right hand would have been thrust. Yet, side by side with the self-horror and self-disgust was no remorse nor repentance. If, to-morrow, Luigi's life could only thus again be saved, thus saved should it be, as when at Marseilles he lay convalescent but dying for lack of the money wherewith to buy the delicacies that would save him.... Luigi's life always, and at any time, before Carmelita's scruples and shrinkings.

In return, Luigi had been kind to her and had often spoken of matrimony--some day--in spite of what she had done at Marseilles when he was too ill to look after her, and provide her with all she needed. Once even, when they were on the crest of a great wave of prosperity, Luigi had gone so far as to mention her seventeenth birthday as a possibly suitable date for their wedding. That had been a great and glorious time, though all too short, alas! and the sequel to a brilliant scheme devised by that poor dear Guiseppe Longigotto in the interests of his beloved and adored friend Carmelita. Poor Guiseppe! He had deserved as Carmelita was the first to admit, something better, than a stab in the back from Luigi Rivoli, for the idea had been wholly and solely his, until the great Roman sporting Impresario had taken it up and developed it. First there was a tremendous syndicate-engineered campaign of advertisement, which let all Europe know that *Il Famoso e Piu Grande Professors Carlo Scopinaro*, Champion Wrestler of Europe, America and Australia, would shortly meet the Egregious Egyptian, or Conquering Copt, Champion Wrestler of Africa and Asia, in Rome, and wrestle him in the Graeco-Roman style, for the World's Championship and ten thousand pounds a side. (Yes actually and authoritatively *diecimila lire sterline*.) From every hoarding in Rome, Venice, Milan, Turin, Genoa, Florence, Naples, Brindisi, and every other town in Italy, huge posters called your attention to the beauties and marvels of the smiling face and mighty form of the great Carlo Scopinaro; to the horrors and terrors of the scowling face and enormous carcase of the dreadful Conquering Copt. (To positively none but Luigi, Guiseppe, and the renowned Roman Impresario was it known that the Conquering Copt was none other than Luigi's old pal, Abdul Hamid, chucker-out at a Port Said music-hall, and most modest and retiring of gentlemen--until this greatness of Champion Wrestler of Africa and Asia was suddenly thrust upon him, and he was summoned from Port Said to Rome to be coached by Luigi in the arts and graces of realistic stage-wrestling, and particularly in those of life-like and convincing defeat after a long and obviously terrible struggle.) ...Excitement was splendidly engineered, the newspapers of every civilised country and of Germany advertised the epoch-making event, speculated upon its result, and produced interesting articles on such questions as, *"Should a Colour-Line be drawn in Wrestling?"* and, *"Is Scopinaro the White Hope?"* A self-advertising reverend Nonconformist announced his intention in the English press of proceeding to Rome to create a disturbance at the Match. He got himself frequently interviewed by specimens of the genus, "Our representative," and the important fact that he was a Conscientious Objector to all forms of sport was brought to the notice of the Great British Public.

The struggle was magnificently staged and magnificently acted. Every spectator in the vast theatre, no matter whether he had paid one hundred lire or a paltry fifty centesimi for his seat, felt that he had had his money's worth. In incredibly realistic manner the White Hope of Europe and the Champion of Africa and Asia struck attitudes, cried *"Ha!"*, snatched at each other, stamped, straddled, pushed, pulled, embraced, slapped, jerked, hugged, tugged, lugged, and lifted each other with every appearance of fearful exertion, dauntless courage, fierce determination and unparalleled skill for one crowded hour of glorious life, during which the house went mad, rose at them to a man, and, with tears and imprecations, called upon the Italian to be worthy of his country and upon the Conquering Copt to be damned.

Few scenes in all the troubled history of Rome can have equalled, for excitement, that which ensued when the White Hope finally triumphed, the honour of Europe in general was saved, and that of Italy in particular illuminated with a blaze of glory.

Anyhow, what was solid fact, with no humbug about it, was that Luigi received the renowned Roman Impresario's fervid blessing and five hundred pounds, while the complacent Abdul received blessings equally fervid, though a less enthusiastic cheque. Both gentlemen were then provided by the kind Impresario with single tickets to the most distant spot he could induce them to name.

For Carmelita, the days following that on which her Luigi won the great World's Championship match, were a glorious time of expensive dinners, fine apartments, and beautiful clothes; a time of being *café* and music-hall patrons instead of performers; of being entertained instead of entertaining. The joy of Carmelita's life while the five hundred pounds lasted was to sit in a stage-box, proud and happy, beside her noble Luigi, and criticise the various "turns" upon the stage. Never an evening performance, nor a matinée did they miss, and Luigi drank a quart of champagne at lunch, and another at dinner. Luigi must keep his strength up, of course, and the soothing influence of innumerable Havana cigars was not denied to his nerves.

And then, just as the five hundred pounds was finished, a wretched Russian (quickly followed by an American, two Russians, a Turk, a Frenchman, and an Englishman) publicly challenged Luigi in the press of Europe, to wrestle for the Championship of the World in any style he liked, for any amount he liked, when and where he liked--and that branch of his profession was closed to Luigi--for these men were giants and terrors, arranging no "crosses," stern fighters, and out for fame, money, genuine sport, and the real Championship.

Then had come a time of poverty, straits, mean shifts and misery, followed by Luigi's job as a "tamer" of tame lions. This post of lion-tamer to a cageful of mangy, weary lions, captive-born, pessimistic, timid and depressed, had been secured by Guiseppe Longigotto, and handed over to Luigi (on its proving safe and satisfactory), in the interests of Guiseppe's adored and hungry Carmelita. Arrayed in the costume worn by all the Best Lion-tamers, Luigi looked a truly noble figure, as, with flashing eyes and gleaming teeth, he cracked the whip and fired the revolver that induced the bored and disgusted lions to amble round the cage, crouching and cringing in humility and fear. That insignificant little rat, Guiseppe, was far more in the picture, of course, as fiddler to the show, than he was in his original role of tamer of the lions. Followed a bad time along the African coast, culminating, at Algiers, in poor Guiseppe's impassioned pleadings that Carmelita would marry him (and, leaving this dreadful life of the road, live with him and his beautiful violin on the banked proceeds of his great Wrestling Championship scheme), Luigi's jealousy, his overbearing airs of proprietorship, his drunken cruelty, his presuming on her love and obedience to him until she sought to give him a fright and teach him a lesson, his killing of the poor, pretty musician, and his flight to Sidi-bel-Abbès....

To Sidi-bel-Abbès also fled Carmelita, and, with the proceeds of Guiseppe's dying gift to her, eked out by promises of many things to many people, such as Jew and Arab lessors and landlords, French dealers, Spanish-Jew jobbers and contractors, and Negro labourers, contrived to open La Café de la Légion, to run it with herself as proprietress, manageress, barmaid, musician, singer, actress, and *danseuse*, and to make it pay to the extent of a daily franc, bottle of Chianti, and a macaroni, polenta, or spaghetti meal for Luigi, and a very meagre living for herself. When in need of something more, Carmelita performed at matinées at the music-hall and at private stances in Arab and other houses, in the intervals of business. When professional dress would have rendered her automatic pistol conspicuous and uncomfortable, Carmelita carried a most serviceable little dagger in her hair. Also she let it be known among her patrons of the Legion that she was going to a certain house, garden, or *café* at a certain time, and might be there enquired for if unduly delayed. Carmelita knew the seamy side of life in Mediterranean ports, and African littoral and hinterland towns, and took no chances....

And by-and-by her splendid and noble Luigi would marry her, and they would go to America--where that little matter of manslaughter would never crop up and cause trouble--and live happily ever after.

So, faithful, loyal, devoted, Carmelita might be; generous, chaste, and brave, Carmelita might be--but alas! not refined, not genteel, not above telling a Chasseur d'Afrique what she thought of him and his insults; not above spitting at a leering, gesture-making Spahi. No lady....

"Ben venuti, Signori!" cried Carmelita on catching sight of Il Signor Jean Boule and the Bucking Bronco. "Soyez le bien venu, Monsieur Jean Boule et Monsieur Bronco. Che cosa posso offrirvi?" and, as they seated themselves at a small round table near the bar, hastened to bring the wine favoured by these favoured customers--the so gentle English Signor, *gentilhomme*, (doubtless once a *milord*, a *nobile*), and the so gentle, foolish Americano, so slow and strong, who looked at her with eyes of love, kind eyes, with a good true love. No *milordino* he, no *piccol Signor* (but nevertheless a good man, a *uomo dabbéne*, most certainly...)

Reginald Rupert was duly presented as Légionnaire Rupert, with all formality and ceremony, to the Madamigella Carmelita, who ran her bright, black eye over him, summed him up as another *gentiluomo*, an obvious *gentilhomme*, pitied him, and wondered what he had "done."

Carmelita loved a "gentleman" in the abstract, although she loved Luigi Rivoli in the concrete; adored aristocrats in general, in spite of the fact that she adored Luigi Rivoli in particular. To her experienced and observant young eye, Légionnaire Jean Boule and this young *bleu* were of the same class, the *aristocratico* class of *Inghilterra*; birds of a feather, if not of a nest. They might be father and son, so alike were they in their difference from the rest. So different even from the English-speaking Americano, so different from her Luigi. But then, her Luigi was no mere broken aristocrat; he was the World's Champion Wrestler and Strong Man, a great and famous Wild Beast Tamer, and--her Luigi.

"Buona sera, Signor," said Carmelita to Rupert. "Siete venuto per la via di Francie?" and then, in Legion-French and Italian, proceeded to comment upon the new recruit's appearance, his *capetti riccioluti* and to enquire whether he used the *calamistro* and *ferro da ricci* to obtain the fine crisp wave in his hair.

Not at all a refined and ladylike maiden, and very, very far from the standards of Surbiton, not to mention Balham.

Reginald Rupert (to whom love and war were the two things worth living for), on understanding the drift of the lady's remarks, proposed forthwith "to cross the bar" and "put out to see" whether he could not give her a personal demonstration of the art of hair-curling, but--

"*Non vi pigliate fastidio*," said Carmelita. "Don't trouble yourself Signor Azzurro--Monsieur Bleu. And if Signor Luigi Rivoli should enter and see the young Signor on my side of the bar--Luigi's side of the bar--why, one look of his eye would so make the young Signor's hair curl that, for the rest of his life, the *calamistro*, the curling-tongs, would be superfluous."

"Yep," chimed in the Bucking Bronco. "I guess as haow it's about time yure Loojey's bright eyes got closed, my dear, an' I'm goin' ter bung 'em both up one o' these fine days, when I got the cafard. Yure Loojey's a great lady-killer an' recruit-killer, we know, an' he can talk a tin ear on a donkey. I say *Il parlerait une oreille d'etain sur un âne*. Yure Loojey'd make a hen-rabbit git mad an' bark. I say *Votre Loojey causer ait une lapine devenir fou et écorcer*. I got it in fer yure Loojey. I say *Je l'ai dans pour votre Loojey....Comprenny? Intendete quel che dico?*" and the Bucking Bronco drank off a pint of wine, drew his tiny, well-thumbed French dictionary from one pocket and his "Travellers' Italian Phrase-book" from another, cursed the Tower of Babel, and all foreign tongues, and sought words wherewith to say that it was high time for Luigi Rivoli "to quit beefin' aroun' Madam lar Canteenair, to wipe off his chin considerable, to cease being a sticker, a sucker, and a skinamalink girl-sponging meal-and-money cadger; and to quit tellin' stories made out o' whole cloth,[46] that cut no ice with nobody except Carmelita."

This young lady gathered that, as usual, the poor, silly jealous Americano was belittling and insulting her Luigi, if not actually threatening him. *Him*, who could break any Americano across his knee. With a toss of her head and a contemptuous "Invidioso! Scioccone!" for the Bronco, a flick on the nose with the *krenfell* flower from her ear for Rupert, a blown kiss for *Babbo* Jean Boule, Carmelita flitted away, going from table to table to minister to the mental, moral, and physical needs of her other devoted Légionnaires as they arrived--men of strange and dreadful lives who loved her then and there, who remembered her thereafter and elsewhere, and who sent her letters, curios, pressed flowers and strange presents from the ends of the earth where flies the *tricouleur*, and the Flag of the Legion--in Tonkin, Madagascar, Senegal, Morocco, the Sahara--in every Southern Algerian station wherever the men of the Legion tramped to their death to the strains of the regimental march of "*Tiens, voilà du boudin.*"

"Advise me, Mam'zelle," said a young Frenchman of the Midi, rising to his feet with a flourish of his képi and a sweeping bow, as Carmelita approached the table at which he and three companions sat, "Advise me as to the investment of this wealth, fifty centimes, all at once. Shall it be five glorious green absinthes or five *chopes* of the wine of Algiers?--or shall I warm my soul with burning bapédi...?"

"Four bottles of wine is what you want for André, Raoul, Léon, and yourself," was the reply. "Absinthe is the mamma and the papa and all the ancestors of *le cafard* and you are far too young and tender for bapédi. It mingles not well with mother's milk, that...."

In the extreme corner of the big, badly-lit room, a Legionary sat alone, his back to the company, his head upon his folded arms. Passing near, on her tour of ministration, Carmelita's quick eye and ear perceived that the man was sobbing and weeping bitterly. It might be the poor Grasshopper passing through one of his terrible dark hours, and Carmelita's kind heart melted with pity for the poor soul, smartest of soldiers, and maddest of madmen.

Going over to where he sat apart, Carmelita bent over him, placed her arm around his neck, and stroked his glossy dark hair.

"*Pourquoi faites-vous Suisse, mon pauvre?*" she murmured with a motherly caress. "What is it? Tell Carmelita." The man raised his face from his arms, smiled through his tears and kissed the hand that rested on his shoulder. The handsome and delicate face, the small, well-kept hands, the voice, were those of a man of culture and refinement.

"*I ja nai ka!*--How delightful!" he said. "You will make things right. I am to be made *machibugiyo*, governor of the city to-morrow, and I wish to remain a Japanese lady. I do not want to lay aside the *suma-goto* and *samisen* for the *wakizashi* and the *katana*—the lute for the dagger and sword. I don't want to sit on a *tokonoma* in a *yashiki* surrounded by *karo*...."

"No, no, no, mon cher, you shall not indeed. See le bon Dieu and le bon Jean Boule will look after you," said Carmelita, gently stroking his hot forehead and soothing him with little crooning sounds and caresses as though he had really been the child that, in mind and understanding, he was.

John Bull, followed by Rupert, unobtrusively joined Carmelita. Seating himself beside the unhappy man, he took his hands and gazed steadily into his suffused eyes.

"Tell me all about it, Cigale," said he. "You know we can put it right. When has Jean Boule failed to explain and arrange things for you?"

The madman repeated that he dreaded to have to sit on the raised dais of the Palace of a Governor of a City surrounded by officials and advisers.

"I know I should soon be involved in a *kataki-uchi* with a neighbouring clan, and have to commit hara-kiri if I failed to keep the Mikado's peace. It is terrible. You don't know how I long to remain a lady. I want silk and music and cherry-blossom instead of steel and blood," and again he laid his head upon his arms and continued his low, hopeless sobbing.

Reginald Rupert's face expressed blank astonishment at the sight of the weeping soldier.

"What's up?" he said.

Légionnaire John Bull tapped his forehead.

"Poor chap will behave *more Japonico* for the rest of the day now. I fancy he's been an attaché in Japan. You don't know Japanese by any chance? I have forgotten the little I knew."

Rupert shook his head.

"Look here, Cigale," said John Bull, raising the afflicted man and again fixing the steady, benign gaze upon his eyes, "why are you making all this trouble for yourself? You know I am the Mikado and All-powerful! You have only to appeal to me and the Shogun must release you. Of course you can remain a Japanese lady--and I'll tell you what, ma chère, ma petite fille Japonaise, not only shall you remain a lady, but a lady of the old school and of the days before the accursed Foreign Devils came in to break down ancient customs. I promise it. To-morrow you shall shave off your eyebrows and paint them in two inches above your eyes. I promise it. More. Your teeth shall be lacquered black. Now cease these ungrateful repinings, and be a happy maiden once again. By order of the Mikado!"

Once again the voice and eye, and the gentle wise sympathy and comprehension of ce bon Jean Boule had succeeded and triumphed. The madman, falling at his feet, knelt and bowed three times, his forehead touching the ground, in approved geisha fashion.

"And now you've got to come and lie down, or you won't be fit for the eyebrow-shaving ceremony to-morrow," said Carmelita, and led him to a broad, low divan, which made a cosy, if dirty, corner remote from the bar.

"That's as extraordinary a case as ever I came across," remarked John Bull to Rupert as they rejoined the Bucking Bronco, who was talking to the Cockney and the Russian twins, "as mad as any lunatic in any asylum in the world, and yet as absolutely competent and correct in every detail of soldiering as any soldier in the Legion. He is the Perfect Private Soldier--and a perfect lunatic. Most of the time, off parade that is, he thinks he's a grasshopper, and the rest of the time he thinks he's of some remarkably foreign nationality, such as a Zulu, an Eskimo, or a Chinaman. I should very much like to know his story. He must have travelled pretty widely. He has certainly been an officer in the Belgian Guides (their Officers' Mess is one of the most exclusive and aristocratic in the world, as you know) and he has certainly been a Military Attaché in the East. He is perfectly harmless and a most thorough gentleman, poor soul....Yes, I should greatly like to know his story," and added as he poured out a glass of wine, "but we don't ask men their 'stories' in the Legion...."

Carmelita returned to her high seat by the door of her little room behind the bar--the door upon the outside of which many curious regards had oftentimes been fixed.

Carmelita was troubled. Why did not Luigi come? Were his duties so numerous and onerous nowadays that he had but a bare hour for his late dinner and his bottle of Chianti? Time was, when he arrived as soon after five o'clock as a wash and change of uniform permitted. Time was, when he could spend from early evening to late night in the Café de la Légion, outstaying the latest visitors. And that time was also the time when Madame la Cantinière was not a widow--the days before Madame's husband had been sliced, sawn, snapped, torn, and generally mangled by certain other widows--of certain Arabs--away to the South. This might be coincidence of course, and yet--and yet--several Légionnaires who had no axe to grind and who were not jealous of Luigi's fortune, had undoubtedly coupled his name with that of Madame....

"An' haow did yew find yure little way to our dope-joint hyar?" the Bucking Bronco enquired of Mikhail Kyrilovitch, as he did the honours of Carmelita's "joint" to the three *bleus* who had entered while John Bull was talking to the Grasshopper.

"Well, since you arx, we jest ups an' follers you, old bloke, when yer goes aht wiv these two uvver Henglish coves," replied the Cockney.

The American regarded him with the eye of large and patient tolerance. He preferred the Russians, particularly Mikhail, and rejoiced that they spoke English. It would have been too much to have attempted to add a working knowledge of Russian to his other linguistic stores. Nevertheless, he would, out of compliment to their nationality, produce such words of their strange tongue as he could command. It might serve to make them feel more at home like.

"I'm afraid I can't ask yew moojiks ter hev a little caviare an' wodky, becos' Carmelita is out of it....But there's cawfy in the sammy-var I hev no doubt," he said graciously.

The Russians thanked him, and Feodor pledging him in a glass of absinthe, promised to teach him the art of concocting *lompopo*, while Mikhail quietly sipped his glass of sticky, sweet Algerian wine.

Restless Carmelita joined the group, and her friend Jean Boule introduced the three new patrons.

"Prahd an' honoured, Miss, I'm shore," said the Cockney. "'Ave a port-an'-lemon or there-abahts?"

But Carmelita was too interested in the startling similarity of the twins to pay attention to the civilities and blandishments of the Cockney, albeit he surreptitiously wetted his fingers with wine and smoothed his smooth and shining "cowlick" or "quiff" (the highly ornamental fringe which, having descended to his eyebrows, turned aspiringly upward).

"*Gemello*," she murmured, turning from Feodor and his cheery greeting to Mikhail, who responded with a graceful little bow, suddenly terminated and changed to a curt nod, like that given by Feodor. As Carmelita continued her direct gaze, a dull flush grew and mantled over his face.

"*Cielo*! But how the boy blushes! Now is it for his own sins, or mine, I wonder?" laughed Carmelita, pointing accusingly at poor Mikhail's suffused face.

"Gawdstreuth! Can't 'e blush," remarked Mr. Higgins.

The dull flush became a vivid, burning blush under Carmelita's pointing finger, and the regard of the amused Legionaries.

"Corpo di Bacco!" laughed the teasing girl. "A blushing Legionary! The dear, sweet, good boy. If only *I* could blush like that. And he brings his blushes to Madame la République's Legion. Well, it is not *porta vasi a Samo!*"[47]

"Never mind, Sonny," said the American soothingly, "there's many a worse stunt than blushin'. I uster use blushes considerable meself--when I was a looker 'bout yure age." He translated.

Carmelita's laughter pealed out again at the idea of the blushing American. Feodor's laughter mingled with Carmelita's, but sounded forced.

"Isn't it funny?" he remarked. "My brother has always been like that, but believe me, Padrona, I could not blush to save my life."

"Si, si," laughed Carmelita. "You have sinned and he has blushed--all your lives, is it not so--le pauvre petit?" and saucily rubbed the side of Mikhail's crimson face with the backs of her fingers--and looked unwontedly thoughtful as he jerked his head away with a look of annoyance.

"La, la, la!" said Carmelita. "Musn't he be teased then?..."

"Come, Signora," broke in Feodor again, "you're making him blush worse than ever. Such kindness is absolutely wasted. Now I..."

"No, *you* wouldn't blush with shame and fright, no, nor yet with innocence, would you, Signor Feodor? *E un peccato!*" replied the girl, and lightly brushed his cheek as she spoke.

The good Feodor did not blush, but the look of thoughtfulness deepened on Carmelita's face.

To the finer perceptions of John Bull there seemed to be something strained and discomfortable in the atmosphere. Carmelita had fallen silent, Feodor seemed annoyed and anxious, Mikhail frightened and anxious, and Mr. 'Erb 'Iggins of too gibing a humour.

"You are making me positively jealous, Signora Carmelita, and leaving me thirsty," he said, and with a small repentant squeal Carmelita flitted to the bar.

"Would you like a biscuit too, Signor Jean Boule?" she called, and tossed one across to him as she spoke. John Bull neatly caught the biscuit as it flew somewhat wide. Carmelita, like most women, could not throw straight.

"*Tiro maestro,*" she applauded, and launched another at the unprepared Mikhail with a cry of "Catch, *goffo.*" Instinctively, he "made a lap" and spread out his hands.

"*Esattamente!*" commented Carmelita beneath her breath and apparently lost interest in the little group....

A quartet of Legionaries swaggered into the *café* and approached the bar--Messieurs Malvin, Borges, Bauer and Hirsch, henchmen and satellites of Luigi Rivoli--and saluted to Carmelita's greeting of "Buona sera, Signori...."

"Bonsoir, M. Malvin," added she to the dapper, low-bowing Austrian, whose evil face, with its close-set ugly eyes, sharp crooked nose, waxed moustache, and heavy jowl, were familiar to her as those of one of Luigi's more intimate followers. "Where is Signor Luigi Rivoli to-night? He has no guard duty?"

"No, mia signora--er--that is--yes," replied Malvin in affected discomfort. "He is--ah--on duty."

"On duty in the Canteen?" asked Carmelita, flushing.

"What do I know of the comings and goings of the great Luigi Rivoli?" answered Malvin. "Doubtless he will fortify himself with a litre of wine at Madame's bar in the Canteen before walking down here."

"Luigi Rivoli drinks no sticky Algerian wine," said Carmelita angrily and her eyes and teeth flashed dangerously. "He drinks Chianti from Home. He never enters her Canteen."

"Ah! So?" murmured Malvin in a non-committal manner. And then Carmelita's anxiety grew a little greater--greater even than her dislike and distrust of M. Edouard Malvin, and she did what she had never done before. She voiced it to him.

"Look you, Monsieur Malvin, tell me the truth. I will not tell my Luigi that you have accused him to me, or say that you have spoken ill of him behind his back. Tell me the truth. *Is* he in the Canteen? Tell me, cher Monsieur Malvin."

"Have I the double sight, bella Carmelita? How should I know where le Légionnaire Rivoli may be?" fenced the soi-disant Belgian, who desired nothing better than to win the woman from the man--and toward himself. Failing Madame la Cantinière and the Legion's Canteen, what better than Carmelita and the Café de la Légion for a poor hungry and thirsty soldier? If the great Luigi must win the greater prize let the little Malvin win the lesser. To which end let him curry favour with La Belle Carmelita--just as far as such a course of action did not become premature, and lead to a painful interview with an incensed Luigi Rivoli.

"Tell me the truth, cher Monsieur Malvin. Where is my Luigi?" again asked Carmelita pleadingly.

"*Donna e Madonna*," replied the good M. Malvin, with piteous eyes, broken voice, and protecting hand placed gently over that of Carmelita which lay clenched upon the zinc-covered bar. "What shall I say? Luigi Rivoli is a giant among men--I, a little fat *deboletto*, a *sparutello* whom the great Luigi could kill with one hand. Though I love Carmelita, I fear Luigi. How shall I tell of his doings with that husband-seeking *puttana* of the Canteen; of his serving behind the bar, helping her, taking her money, drinking her wine (wine of Algiers); of his passionate and burning prayers that she will marry him? How can I, his friend, tell of those things? But oh! Carmelita, my poor honest heart is wrung..." and le bon Monsieur Malvin paused to hope that his neck also would not be wrung as the result of this moving eloquence.

For a moment Carmelita's eyes blazed and her hands and her little white teeth clenched. Mother of God! if Luigi played her false after all she had done for him, after all she had given him--given *for* him!...But no, it was unthinkable....This Malvin was an utter knave and liar, and would fool her for his own ends--the very man *fare un pesce d'Aprile a qualcuno*. He should see how far his tricks succeeded with Carmelita of the Legion, the chosen of Carlo Scopinaro! And yet...and yet...She would ask Il Signor Jean Boule again. He would never lie. He would neither backbite Luigi Rivoli, nor stand by and see Carmelita deceived. Yes, she would ask Jean Boule, and then if he *too* accused Luigi she would find some means to see and hear for herself.... Trust her woman's wit for that. And meantime this serpent of a Malvin...

"*Se ne vada!*" she hissed, whirling upon him suddenly, and pointed to the door. Malvin slunk away, by no means anxious to be present at the scene which would certainly follow should Luigi enter before Carmelita's mood had changed. He would endeavour to meet and delay him....

"What do yew say to acontinuin' o' this hyar gin-crawl?" asked the Bucking Bronco of Rupert. "Come and see our other pisen-joint and Madame lar Cantenair."

"Anything you like," replied Rupert.

"Let's go out when they do," said Mikhail quickly, in Russian, to Feodor.

"All right, silly Olka," was the whispered reply.

"Silly Fedka, to call me Olka," was the whispered retort. "You're a pretty *budotchnik*,[48] aren't you?"

"Yus," agreed Mr. 'Erb Higgins, nodding cordially to Rupert, and bursting into appropriate and tuneful song--

> "Come where the booze is cheaper,
> Come where the pots 'old more,
> Come where the boss is a bit of a joss,
>
> Ho! come to the pub next door."

Evidently a sociable and expansive person, easily thawed by a *chope* of cheap wine withal; neither standoffish nor haughty, for he thrust one friendly arm through that of Jean Boule, and another round the waist of Reginald Rupert. Let it not be supposed that it was under the influence of liquor rather than of sheer, expansive geniality that 'Erb proposed to walk *a braccetto*, as Carmelita observed, with his new-found friends....

As the party filed out of the *café*, Mikhail Kyrilovitch, who was walking last of the party, felt a hand slip within his arm to detain him. Turning, he beheld Carmelita's earnest little face near his own. In his ear she whispered in French--

"I have your secret, little one--but have no fear. Should anyone else discover it, come to Carmelita," and before the astonished Mikhail could reply she was clearing empty glasses and bottles from their table.

Chapter IV
The Canteen of the Legion

From the Canteen, a building in the corner of the barrack-square, proceeded sounds of revelry by night.

"Blimey! Them furriners are singin' 'Gawd save the Queen' like bloomin' Christians," remarked 'Erb as the little party approached the modest Temple of Bacchus.

"No, they are Germans singing '*Heil dir im Sieges-Kranz*,' replied Feodor Kyrilovitch in English.

"And singing it most uncommonly well," added Legionary John Bull.

"Fancy them 'eathens pinchin' the toon like that," commented 'Erb. "They oughtn't to be allowed...Do they 'old concerts 'ere? I dessay they'd like to 'ear some good Henglish songs...."

Reginald Rupert never forgot his first glimpse of the Canteen of the Legion, though he entered it hundreds of times and spent hundreds of hours beneath its corrugated iron roof. Scores of Legionaries, variously clad in blue and red or white sat on benches at long tables, or lounged at the long zinc-covered bar, behind which were Madame and hundreds of bottles and large wine-glasses.

Madame la Vivandière de la Légion was not of the school of "Cigarette." Rupert failed to visualise her with any clearness as leading a cavalry charge (the *Drapeau* of La France in one hand, a pistol in the other, and her reins in her mouth), inspiring Regiments, advising Generals, softening the cruel hearts of Arabs, or "saving the day" for La Patrie, in the manner of the vivandière of fiction. Madame had a beady eye, a perceptible moustache, a frankly downy chin, two other chins, a more than ample figure, and looked, what she was, a female camp-sutler. Perhaps Madame appeared more Ouidaesque on the march, wearing her official blue uniform as duly constituted and appointed *fille du régiment*. At present she looked...However, the bow of Reginald Rupert, together with his smile and honeyed words, were those of Mayfair, as he was introduced by Madame's admired friend ce bon Jean Boule, and he stepped straight into Madame's experienced but capacious heart. Nor was the brightness of the image dulled by the ten-franc piece which he tendered with the request that Madame would supply the party with her most blushful Hippocrene. 'Erb, being introduced, struck an attitude, his hand upon his heart. Madame coughed affectedly.

"Makes a noise like a 'igh-class parlour-maid bein' jilted, don' she?" he observed critically.

Having handed a couple of bottles and a large glass to each member of the party, by way of commencement in liquidating the coin, she returned to her confidential whispering with Monsieur le Légionnaire Luigi Rivoli (who lolled, somewhat drunk, in a corner of the bar) as the group seated itself at the end of a long table near the window.

It being "holiday," that is, pay-day, the Canteen was full, and most of its patrons had contrived to emulate it. A very large number had laid out the whole of their *décompté*—every farthing of two-pence halfpenny--on wine. Others, wiser and more continent, had reserved a halfpenny for tobacco. In one corner of the room an impromptu German glee party was singing with such excellence that the majority of the drinkers were listening to them with obvious appreciation. With hardly a break, and with the greatest impartiality they proceeded from part-song to hymn, from hymn to drinking-song, from drinking-song to sentimental love-ditty. Finally *Ein feste burg ist unser Gott* being succeeded by *Die Wacht am Rhein* and *Deutschland über Alles*, the French element in the room thought that a little French music would be a pleasing corrective, and with one accord, if not in one key, gave a spirited rendering of the Marseillaise, followed by--

> "Tiens, voilà du boudin
> Tiens, voilà du boudin
> Tiens, voià du boudin
>
> Pour les Alsaciens, les Suisses, et les Lorraines,
> Four les Belges il n'y en a plus

Car ce sont des tireurs du flanc..." etc., immediately succeeded by--

"As-tu vu la casquette
La casquette
Du Père Bougeaud," etc.

As the ditty came to a close a blue-jowled little Parisian--quick, nervous, and alert--sprang on to a table, and with a bottle in one hand, and a glass in the other, burst into the familiar and favourite--

"C'est l'empereur de Danemark
Qui a dit a sa moitié
Depuis quelqu' temps je remarque

Que tu sens b'en fort les pieds..." etc.
"C'est la reine Pomaré

Qui a pour tout tenue
Au milieu de l'été..."

the song being brought to an untimely end by reason of the parties on either side of the singer's table entering into a friendly tug-of-war with his feet as rope-ends. As he fell, amid howls of glee and the crashing of glass, the Bucking Bronco remarked to Rupert--

"Gwine ter be some rough-housin' ter-night ef we're lucky," but ere the mêlée could become general, Madame la Cantinière, descending from her throne behind the bar, bore down upon the rioters and rated them soundly--imbeciles, fools, children, vauriens, and *sales cochons* that they were. Madame was well aware of the fact that a conflagration should be dealt with in its earliest stages and before it became general.

"This is really extraordinarily good wine," remarked Rupert to John Bull.

"Yes," replied the latter. "It's every bit as good at three-halfpence a bottle as it is at three-and-six in England, and I'd advise you to stick to it and let absinthe alone. It does one no harm, in reason, and is a great comfort. It's our greatest blessing and our greatest curse. Absinthe is pure curse--and inevitably means 'cafard.'"

"What is this same 'cafard' of which one hears so much?" asked Rupert.

"Well, the word itself means 'beetle,' I believe, and sooner or later the man who drinks absinthe in this climate feels the beetle crawling round and round in his brain. He then does the maddest things and ascribes the impulse to the beetle. He finally goes mad and generally commits murder or suicide, or both. That is one form of *cafard*, and the other is mere fed-up-ness, a combination of liverish temper, boredom and utter hatred and loathing of the terrible ennui of the life."

"Have you had it?" asked the other.

"Everyone has it at times," was the reply, "especially in the tiny desert-stations where the awful heat, monotony, and lack of employment leave one the choice of drink or madness. If you drink you're certain to go mad, and if you don't drink you're sure to. Of course, men like ourselves--educated, intelligent, and all that--have more chance than the average 'Tommy' type, but it's very dangerous for the highly strung excitable sort. He's apt to go mad and stay mad. We only get fits of it."

"Don't the authorities do anything to amuse and employ the men in desert stations, like we do in India?" enquired the younger man.

"Absolutely nothing. They prohibit the *Village Négre* in every station, compel men to lie on their cots from eleven till four, and do nothing at all to relieve the maddening monotony of drill, sentry-go and punishment. On the other hand, *cafard* is so recognised an institution that punishments for offences committed under its influence are comparatively light. It takes different people differently, and is sometimes comic--though generally tragic."

"I should think you're bound to get something of the sort wherever men lead a very hard and very monotonous life, in great heat," said Rupert.

"Oh yes," agreed John Bull. "After all *le cafard* is not the private and peculiar speciality of the Legion. We get a very great deal of madness of course, but I think it's nearly as much due to predisposition as it is to the hard monotonous life....You see we are a unique collection, and a considerable minority of us must be more or less queer in some way, or they wouldn't be here."

Rupert wondered why the speaker was "here" but refrained from asking.

"Can you classify the recruits at all clearly?" he asked.

"Oh yes," was the reply. "The bulk of them are here simply and solely for a living; hungry men who came here for board and lodging. Thousands of foreigners in France have found themselves down on their uppers, with their last sou gone, fairly on their beam-ends and their room-rent overdue. To such men the Foreign Legion offers a home. Then, again, thousands of soldiers commit some heinous military 'crime' and desert to the Foreign Legion to start afresh. We get most of our Germans and Austrians that way, and not a few French who pretend to be Belgians to avoid awkward questions as to their papers. We get Alsatians by the hundred of course, too. It is their only chance of avoiding service under the hated German. They fight for France, and by their five years' Legion-service earn the right to naturalisation also. There are a good many French, too, who are 'rehabilitating' themselves. Men who have come to grief at home and prefer the Legion to prison. Then there is undoubtedly a wanted-by-the-police class of men who have bolted from all parts of Europe and taken sanctuary here. Yes, I should say the out-of-works, deserters, runaways and Alsatians make up three parts of the Legion."

"And what is the other part?"

"Oh, keen soldiers who have deliberately chosen the Legion for its splendid military training and constant fighting experience--romantics who have read vain imaginings and figments of the female mind like 'Under Two Flags'; and the queerest of Queer Fish, oddments and remnants from the ends of the earth...." A shout of "Ohé, Grasshopper!" caused him to turn.

In the doorway, crouching on his heels, was the man they had left lying on the settee at Carmelita's. Emitting strange chirruping squeaks, turning his head slowly from left to right, and occasionally brushing it from back to front with the sides of his "forelegs," the Grasshopper approached with long, hopping bounds.

"And that was once an ornament of Chancelleries and Courts," said John Bull, as he rose to his feet. "Poor devil! Got his *cafard* once and for all at Aïn Sefra. There was a big grasshopper or locust in his *gamelle* of soup one day....I suppose he was on the verge at the moment. Anyhow, he burst into tears and has been a grasshopper ever since, except when he's a Jap or something of that sort....He's a grasshopper when he's 'normal' you might say."

Going over to where the man squatted, the old Legionary took him by the arm. "Come and sit on my blade of grass and drink some dew, Cigale," said he.

Smiling up brightly at the face which he always recognised as that of a sympathetic friend, the Grasshopper arose and accompanied John Bull to the end of the long table at which sat the Englishmen, the Russians, and the American....

Yet more wine had made 'Erb yet more expansive, and he kindly filled his glass and placed it before the Grasshopper.

"'Ere drink that hup, Looney, an' I'll sing yer a song as'll warm the cockles o' yer pore ol' 'eart," he remarked, and suiting the action to the word, rose to his feet and, lifting up his voice, delivered himself mightily of that song not unknown to British barrack-rooms--

> "A German orficer crossin' the Rhine
> 'E come to a pub, an' this was the sign
> Skibooo, skibooo,
>
> Skibooo, skiana, skibooo."

The raucous voice and unwonted British accents (for Englishmen are rare in the Legion) attracted some attention, and by the time 'Erb had finished with the German officer and commenced upon "'Oo's that aknockin' on the dawer," he was well across the footlights and had the ear and eye of the assembly. Finding himself the cynosure of not only neighbouring but distant eyes, 'Erb mounted the table and "obliged" with a clog-dance and "double-shuffle-breakdown" to the huge delight of an audience ever desiring a new thing. Stimulated by rounds of applause, and by the cheers and laughter which followed the little Parisian's cry of "Vive le goddam biftek Anglais," 'Erb burst into further Barrack-room Ballads unchronicled by, and probably quite unknown to, Mr. Kipling, and did not admit the superior claims of private thirst until he had dealt faithfully with "The Old Monk," "The Doctor's Boy," and the indiscreet adventure of Abraham the Sailor with the Beautiful Miss Taylor....

"Some boy, that *com*patriot o' yourn, John," remarked the Bucking Bronco, "got a reg'lar drorin' room repertory, ain't 'e?" and the soul of 'Erb was proud within him, and he drank another pint of wine.

"Nutthink like a little--*hic*-'armony," he admitted modestly, "fer making a *swarry* sociable an' 'appy. Wot I ses is--*hic*-wot I ses is--*hic*-wot I ses is--*hic*...."

"It is so, sonny, and that's almighty solemn truth," agreed the Bucking Bronco.

"Wot I ses is--*hic*-" doggedly repeated 'Erb.

"Right again, sonny.... He knows what 'e's sayin' all right," observed the American, turning to the Russians.

"Wot I ses is--*hic*-" repeated 'Erb dogmatically....

"'*Hic jacet!*' Monsieur would say, perhaps?" suggested Feodor.

'Erb turned upon the last speaker with an entirely kindly contempt.

"Don't yer igspose yer *hic*-norance," he advised. "You're a foreiller. You're a neathen. You're a pore *hic*-norant foreiller. Wot I was goin' ter say was..." But 'Erb lost the thread of his discourse. "Wisht me donah wos 'ere," he confided sadly to Mikhail Kyrilovitch, wept with his arm about Mikhail's waist, his head upon Mikhail's shoulder, and anon lapsed into dreams. Feodor roused the somnolent 'Erb with the offer of another bottle of wine, and changed places with Mikhail. 'Erb accepted this tribute to the attractiveness of his personality with modesty, and with murmured words, the purport of which appeared to be that Feodor was a discriminating heathen.

As the evening wore on, the heady wine took effect. The fun, which had been fast and furious, grew uproarious. Dozens of different men were singing as many different songs, several were merely howling in sheer joyless glee, many were dancing singly, others in pairs, or in fours; one, endeavouring to clamber on to the bar and execute a *pas seul*, was bodily lifted and thrown half-way down the room by the fighting-drunk Luigi Rivoli. It was noticeable that, as excitement waxed, the use of French waned, as men reverted to their native tongues. It crossed the mind of Rupert that a blindfolded stranger, entering the room, might well imagine himself to be assisting at the building of the Tower of Babel. A neighbouring party of Spaniards dropping their guttural, sibilant Legion-French (with their *ze* for *je*, *zamais* for *jamais*, and *zour* for *jour*) with one accord broke into their liquid Spanish and *Nombre de Dios* took the place of *Nom de Dieu*, as their saturnine faces creased into leathery smiles. Evidently the new recruit who sat in their midst was paying his footing with the few francs that he had brought with him, or obtained for his clothes, for each of the party had four bottles in solemn row before him, and it was not with the clearest of utterance that the recruit solemnly and portentously remarked, as he drained his last bottle--

"Santissima Maria! Wine is the tomb of memory, but he who sows in sand does not reap fish," the hearing of which moved his neighbour to drop his empty bottles upon the ground with a tear, and a farewell to them--

"Vaya usted con Dios. Adios." He then turned with truculent ferocity and a terrific scowl upon the provider of the feast and growled--"*Sangre de Cristo!* thou peseta-less burro, give me a cigarillo or with the blessing and aid of el Eterno Padre I will cut thy throat with my thumb-nail. Hasten, perro!"

With a grunt of "Cosas d'Espafia," the recruit removed his képi, took a cigarette therefrom and placed it in the steel-trap mouth of his *amigo*, to be rewarded with an incredibly sweet and sunny smile and a "Bueno! Gracias, Senor José...."

Letting his eye roam from this queer band of ex-muleteers, brigands and smugglers to another party who were wading in the wassail, it needed not the loud "Donnerwetters!" and rambling reminiscent monologue of a fat brush-haired youth (on the unspeakable villainies of der Herr Wacht-meister whose wicked *schadenfreude* had sent good men to this *schweinerei* of a Legion, and who was only fit for the military-train or to be decapitated with his own *pallasch*) to label them Germans enjoying a *kommers*. Their stolid, heavy bearing, their business-like and somewhat brutish way of drinking in great gulps and draughts--as though a distended stomach rather than a tickled palate was the serious business of the evening, if not the end and object of life--together with their upturned moustaches, piggish little eyes, and tow-coloured bristles, proclaimed them sons of Kultur.

Rupert could not forbear a smile at the heavy, philosophical gravity with which the speaker, ceasing his monologue, heaved a deep, deep sigh and delivered the weighty dictum that a *schoppen* of the beer of Munich was worth all the wine of Algiers, and the Hofbrauhaus worth all the vineyards and canteens of Africa.

It interested him to notice that among all the nationalities represented, the French were by far the gayest (albeit with a humour somewhat *macabre*) and the Germans the most morose and gloomy. He was to learn later that they provided by far the greatest number of deserters, that they were eternally grumbling, notably bitter and resentful, and devoid of the faintest spark of humour.

His attention was diverted from the Germans by a sudden and horrible caterwauling which arose from a band of Frenchmen who suddenly commenced at the tops of their voices to howl that doleful dirge the "Hymne des Pacifiques." Until they had finished, conversation was impossible.

"Not all foam neither, Miss, please," murmured the sleeping 'Erb in the comparative silence which followed the ending of this devastating chant.

"What's the penalty here for drunkenness?" asked Rupert of John Bull.

"Depends on what you do," was the reply. "There's no penalty for drunkenness, as such, so long as it leads to no sins of omission nor commission.... The danger of getting drunk is that it gives such an opportunity to any Non-com. who has a down on you. When he sees his man drunk, he'll follow him and give him some order, or find him some *corvée*, in the hope that the man will disobey or abuse him--possibly strike him. Then it's Biribi for the man, and a good mark, as well as private vengeance, for the zealous Sergeant, who is again noted as a strong disciplinarian....I'm afraid it's undeniably true that nothing helps promotion in the non-commissioned ranks so much as a reputation for savage ferocity and a brutal insatiable love of punishing. A knowledge of German helps too, as more than half the Legion speaks German, but harsh domineering cruelty is the first requisite, and a Non-commissioned Officer's merit is in direct proportion to the number of punishments he inflicts. Our Sergeant-Major, for example, is known as the 'Suicide-maker,' and is said to be very proud of the title. The number of men he has sent to their graves direct, or *via* the Penal Battalions, must be enormous, and, so far as I can see, he has attained his high and exceedingly influential position simply and solely by excelling in the art of inventing crimes and punishing them severely--for he is a dull uneducated peasant without brains or ability. It is this type of Non-com., the monotony, and the poverty, that make the Legion such a hell for anyone who is not dead keen on soldiering for its own sake...."

"I'm very glad you're keen," he added.

"Oh, rather. I'm as keen as mustard," replied Rupert, "and I was utterly fed up with peace-soldiering and poodle-faking. I have done Sandhurst and had a turn as a trooper in a crack cavalry corps. I wanted to have a look-in at the North-west Frontier Police in Canada after this, and then the Cape Mounted Rifles. I shan't mind the hardships and monotony here if I can get some active service, and feel I am learning something. I have a few thousand francs, too, at the *Crédit Lyonnais*, so I shan't have to bear the poverty cross."

"A few thousand francs, my dear chap!" observed John Bull, smiling. "Croesus I A few thousand francs will give you a few hundred fair-weather friends, relief from a few hundred disagreeable corvées, and duties; give you wine, tobacco, food, medicine, books, distractions-- almost anything but escape from the Legion's military duties as distinguished from the menial. There is nowhere in the world where money makes so much difference as in the Legion--simply because nowhere is it so rare. If among the blind the one-eyed is king, among Legionaries he who has a franc is a bloated plutocrat. Where else in the world is tenpence the equivalent of the daily wages of twenty men--twenty soldier-labourers? Yes, a few thousand francs will greatly alleviate your lot in the Legion, or expedite your departure when you've had enough--for it's quite hopeless to desert without mufti and money."

"I'll leave some in the bank then, against the time I feel I've had enough.... By the way, if you or your friend--er--Mr. Bronco at any time.... If I could be of service ... financially..." and he coloured uncomfortably.

To offer money to this grave, handsome gentleman of refined speech and manners was like tipping an Ambassador, or offering the "price of a pot" to your Colonel, or your Grandfather.

"What do you mean by *corvée* and the Legion's menial duties, and soldier-labourers?" he continued hurriedly to change the subject.

"Yesterday," replied Sir Montague Merline coolly, "I was told off as one of a fatigue-party to clean the congested open sewers of the native gaol of Sidi-bel-Abbès. While I and my brothers-in-arms (some of whom had fought for France, like myself, in Tonkin, Senegal, Madagascar, and the Sahara) did the foulest work conceivable, manacled Negro and Arab criminals jeered at us, and bade us strive to give them satisfaction. Having been in India, you'll appreciate the situation. Natives watching white 'sweepers' labouring on their behalf."

"One can hardly believe it," ejaculated Rupert, and his face froze with horror and indignation.

"Yes," continued the other. "I reflected on the dignity of labour, and remembered the beautiful words of John Bright, or John Bunyan, or some other Johnnie about, 'Who sweeps a room as unto God, makes himself and the action fine.' I certainly made myself very dirty.... The Legionaries are the labourers, scavengers, gardeners, builders, road-makers, street-cleaners, and general coolies of any place in which they are stationed. They are drafted to the barracks of the Spahis and Turcos--the Native Cavalry and Infantry--to do jobs that the Spahis and Turcos would rather die than touch; and, of course, they're employed for every kind of work to which Government would never dream of setting French regulars. I have myself worked (for a ha'penny a day) at wheeling clay, breaking stones, sawing logs, digging, carrying bricks, hauling trucks, shovelling sand, felling trees, weeding gardens, sweeping streets, grave-digging, and every kind of unskilled manual corvée you can think of--in addition, of course, to the daily routine-work and military training of a soldier of the Legion--which is three times as arduous as that of any other soldier in the world."

"Sa--a--ay, John," drawled the Bucking Bronco, rousing himself at last from the deep brooding reverie into which he had plunged in search of mental images and memories of Carmelita, "give yure noo soul-affinity the other side o' the medal likewise, or yew'll push him off the water-waggon into the absinthe-barrel."

"Well," continued John Bull, "you can honestly say you belong to the most famous, most reckless, most courageous regiment in the world; to the regiment that has fought more battles, won more battles, lost more men and gained more honours, than any in the whole history of war. You belong to the Legion that never retreats, that dies--and of whose deaths no record is kept.... It is the last of the real Mercenaries, the Soldiers of Fortune, and if France sent it to-morrow to such a task that five thousand men were wastefully and vainly killed, not a question would be asked in the Chamber, nor the Press: nothing would be said, nothing known outside the War Department. We exist to die for France in the desert, the swamp, or the jungle, by bullet or disease--in Algeria, Morocco, Sahara, the Soudan, West Africa, Madagascar, and Cochin

China--in doing what her regular French and Native troops neither could nor would do. We are here to die, and it's the duty of our officers to kill us--more or less usefully. To kill us for France, working or fighting...."

"'Ear, 'ear, John!" applauded the Bucking Bronco. "Some orator, ain't he?" he observed with pride, turning to Mikhail who had been following the old Legionary with parted lips and shining eyes. "Guess ol' John's some stump-speecher as well as a looker....Go it, ol' section-boss, git on a char," and he smote his beloved John resoundingly upon the back.

John Bull, despite his years and grey hairs, blushed painfully.

"Sorry," he grunted.

"But indeed, Monsieur speaks most interestingly and with eloquence. Pray continue," said Mikhail with diffident earnestness.

John Bull looked still more uncomfortable.

"Do go on," said Rupert.

"Oh, that's all," replied John Bull...."But we are the cheapest labourers, the finest soldiers, the most dangerous, reckless devils ever gathered together....The incredible army--and there's anything from eight to twelve thousand of us in Africa and China, and nobody but the War Minister knows the real number. You're a ha'penny hero now, my boy, and a ha'penny day-labourer, and you're not expected to wear out in less than five years--unless you're killed by the enemy, disease, or the Non-coms."

"Have you ever regretted coming here?" asked Rupert, and could have bitten his tongue as he realised he had asked a personal and prying question.

"Well, I have re-enlisted twice," parried the other, "and that is a pretty good testimonial to La Légion. I have had unlimited experience of active service of all kinds, against enemies of all sorts except Europeans, and I hope to have that--against Germany[49] –before I've done."

"But what about all the Germans in the Legion, in that case?" enquired Rupert.

"Oh, they wouldn't be sent," was the reply. "They'd all go to the Southern Stations, and the Moroccan border, or to Madagascar and Tonkin. Of course, the Alsatians and Lorraines would jump for joy at the chance."

Conversation at this point again became more and more difficult in the increasing din, which was not diminished as 'Erb awoke, yawned, stated that he had a mouth like the bottom of a parrot's cage, that he was thoroughly blighted, and indeed blasted, produced a large mouth-organ, and rendered "Knocked 'em in the Old Kent Road," with enthusiastic soul and vigorous lungs.

Roused to a pinnacle of joyous enthusiasm and yearning for emulation, not only the little Parisian, but the whole party of Frenchmen leapt upon their table with wild whoops, and commenced to dance, some the *carmagnole*, some the *can-can*, some the cake-walk, and others the *bamboula*, the *chachuqua*, or the "*singe-sur-poele.*" Glasses and bottles crashed to the ground, and Legionaries with them. A form broke.

Above the stamping, howling, smashing, and crashing, Madame's shrill screams rang clear, as she mingled imprecations and commands with lamentations that Luigi Rivoli had departed. Pandemonium increased to "*tohuwabohu.*" Louder wailed the mouth-organ, louder bawled the Frenchmen, louder screamed Madame, loudest of all shrilled the "Lights Out" bugle in the barrack-square--and peace reigned. In a minute the room was empty, silent and dark, as the clock struck nine.

§2

"You'll be awakened by yells of '*Au jus*' from the garde-chambre at about five to-morrow," said John Pull to Rupert as they undressed. "As soon as you have swallowed the coffee he'll pour into your mug from his jug, hop out and sweep under your bed. The room-orderly has got to sweep out the room and be on parade as soon as the rest, and it's impossible unless everybody sweeps under his own bed and leaves the orderly to do the rest."

"What about food?" asked the other, who had the healthy appetite of his years and health.

"Oh--plain and sufficient," was the answer. "Good soup and bread; hard biscuit twice a week; and wine every other day--monotonous of course. Meals at eleven o'clock and five o'clock only....By the way unless your feet are fairly tough, you'd better wear *chaussettes russes* until they harden--strips of greasy linen bound round, you know. The skin will soon toughen if you pour *bapédi*, or any other strong spirit into your boots, and you can tallow your feet before a long march. Having no socks will seem funny at first, but in time you come to hate the idea of them. Much less cleanly really, and the cause of all blisters."

Rupert looked doubtful, and thought of his silk-sock bills. Even as a trooper he had always kept one silk pair to put on after the bath which followed a long march. (There are few things so refreshing as the vigorous brushing of one's hair and the putting of silk socks on to bathed feet after a heavy day.)

"Good night, and Good Luck in the Legion," added John Bull as he lay down.

"Good night--and thanks awfully, sir, for your kindness," replied Rupert, and vainly endeavoured to compose himself to sleep on his bed which consisted of a straw-stuffed mattress, a straw-stuffed pillow, and two thin raspy blankets....

Mikhail Kyrilovitch sat on his bed whispering with his brother, about the medical examination of recruits which would take place on the morrow.

"Well, we can only hope for the best," said Feodor at last, "and they all say the same thing--that it is generally the merest formality. The Médecin-Major looks at your face and teeth and asks if you are healthy. It's not like what Ivan and I went through in Paris....They wouldn't have two searching medical examinations unless there appeared to be signs of weakness, I should think."

When the room was wrapped in silence and darkness the latter arose.

"Good night, *golubtchik*," he whispered, "and when your heart fails you, remember Marie Spiridinoff--and be thankful you are here rather than There."

Mikhail shuddered.

Anon, every soul in the room was awakened by the uproarious entrance of the great Luigi Rivoli supported by Messieurs Malvin, Borges and Bauer, all very drunk and roaring *"Brigadier vous avez raison,"* a song which tailed off into an inane repetition of--

>"Si le Caporal savait ça
>Il dirait 'nom de Dieu,'"

in the midst of which the great man collapsed upon his bed, while, with much hiccupping laughter and foul jokes, his faithful satellites contrived to remove his boots and leave him to sleep the sleep of the just and the drunken....

Anon the Dutch youth, Hans Djoolte, sat up and looked around. All was quiet and apparently everyone was asleep. The conscience of Hans was pricking him--he had said his prayers lying in bed, and that was not the way in which he had been taught to say them by his good Dutch mother, whose very last words, as she died, had been, "Say your prayers each night, my son, wherever you may be."

Hans got out of bed, knelt him down, and said his prayers again. Thenceforward, he always did so as soon as he had undressed, regardless of consequences--which at first were serious. But even the good Luigi Rivoli, in time, grew tired of beating him, particularly when the four English-speaking occupants of the *chambrée* intimated their united disapproval of Luigi's interference. The most startling novelty, by repetition, becomes the most familiar commonplace, and the day, or rather the night, arrived when Hans Djoolte could pray unmolested....Occupants of less favoured *chambrées* came to see the sight. The *escouade* indeed became rather proud of having two authentic lunatics....

Chapter V
The Trivial Round

As he had done almost every night for the last twenty-five years, Sir Montague Merline lay awake for some time, thinking of his wife.

Was she happy? Of course she was. Any woman is happy with the man she really loves.

Did she ever think of him? Of course she did. Any woman thinks, at times, of the man in whose arms she has lain. No doubt his photo stood in a silver frame on her desk or piano. Huntingten would not mind that. Nothing petty about Lord Huntingten--and he had been very fond of "good old Merline," "dear old stick-in-the-mud," as he had so often called him.

Of course she was happy. Why shouldn't she be? Although Huntingten was poor as English peers go, there was enough for decent quiet comfort--and Marguerite had never been keen on making a splash. She had not minded poverty as Lady Merline.... She was certainly as happy as the day was long, and it would have been the damnedest cruelty and caddishness to have turned up and spoilt things. It would have wrecked her life and Huntingten's too....

Splendid chap, Huntingten--so jolly clever and original, so full of ideas and unconventionality...."How to be Happy though Titled." ... "How to be a Man though a Peer." ... "Efforts for the Effete," and Sir Montague smiled as he thought of the eccentric peer's pleasantries.

Yes, she'd be happy enough with that fine brave big sportsman with his sunny face and merry laugh, his gentle and kindly ways, his love of open-air life, games, sport, and all clean strenuous things. Of course she was happy.... Did she ever think of him? ... Were there any more children? ... (And, as always, at this point, Sir Montague frowned and sighed.)

How he would love a little girl of hers, if she were very, very like her--and how he would hate a boy if he were like Huntingten. No--not hate the boy--hate the idea of her having a boy who was like Huntingten. But how she would love the boy....

What would he not give to see her! Unseen himself, of course. He hoped he would not get *cafard* again, when next stationed in the desert. It had been terrible, unspeakably terrible, to feel that resolution was weakening, and that when it failed altogether, he would desert and go in search of her.... Suppose that, with madman's cunning, and with madman's strength, he should be successful in an attempt to reach Tunis--the only possible way for a deserter without money--and should live to reach her, or to be recognised and proclaimed as the lost Sir Montague Merline. Her life in ruins and her children illegitimate--nameless bastards.... It was a horribly disturbing thought, that under the influence of *cafard* his mind might lose all ideas and memories and wishes except the one great longing to see her again, to clasp her in his arms again, to have and to hold.... Well--he had a lot to be thankful for. So long as Cyrus Hiram Milton was his bunk-mate it was not likely to happen. Cyrus would see that he did not desert, penniless and mad, into the desert. And now this English boy had come--a man with the same training, tastes, habits, haunts and *clichés* as himself. Doubtless they had numbers of common acquaintances. But he must be wary when on that ground. Possibly the boy knew Lord and Lady Huntingten.... After all it's a very small world, and especially the world of English Society, clubs, Services, and sport.... This boy would be a real *companion*, such as dear old Cyrus could never be, best of friends as he was. He would make a hobby of the boy, look after him, live his happy past again in talking of London, Sandhurst, Paris, racing, golf, theatres, clubs, and all the lost things whose memories they had in common. The boy might perhaps have been at Winchester too.... Thank Heaven he had come! It would make all the difference when *cafard* conditions arose again. Of course he'd get promoted *Soldat première classe* before long though, and then *Caporal*. Corporals may not walk and talk with private soldiers. Yes--the boy would rise and leave him behind. Just his luck.... Might he not venture to accept promotion now--after all these years, and rise step by step with him? No, better not. Thin end of the wedge. Once he allowed himself to be *Soldat première classe* he'd be accepting promotion to *Caporal* and *Sergent* before he knew it. The temptation to go on to *Chef* and *Adjudant* would be overwhelming, and when offered a commission (and the return to the life of an officer and gentleman) would be utterly irresistible. Then would come the very thing to prevent which he had buried himself alive in this hell of a Legion--recognition and then the public scandal of his wife's innocent bigamy, and her children's illegitimacy. As an officer he would meet foreign officers and visitors to Algeria. His portrait might get into the papers. He might have to go to Paris, or Marseilles, and run risks of being recognised. No--better to put away temptation and take no chance of the evil thing. Poor little Marguerite! Think of the cruel shattering blow to her. It would kill her to give up Huntingten in addition to knowing her children to be nameless, unable to inherit title or estates....No--unthinkable! Do the thing properly or not at all....But it was hell to be a second-class soldier all the time, and never be exempt from liability to sentry-duty, guards, fatigues, filthy corvées and punishment at the hands of Non-coms. seeking to acquire merit by discovering demerit....And he could have had a commission straight away, when he got his bit of *ferblanterie*[50] in Tonkin and again in Dahomey. They knew he could speak German and had been an officer....It had been a sore temptation--but, thank God, he had conquered it and not run the greatly enhanced risk of discovery. He ought really to have committed suicide directly he learned that she was married. No business to be alive--let alone grumbling about promotion. Moreover, if any living soul on this earth discovered that he was alive he must not only die, but let his wife have proof that he really was dead, this time. Then she and Huntingten could re-marry as the first ceremony was null and void, and the children be legitimatised....Of course there would be more children--they loved each other so....

As things were, his being alive did the Huntingtens no harm. It was the *knowledge* of his existence that would do the injury--both legal and personal....No harm, so long as it wasn't known. They were quite innocent in the sight of le bon Dieu, and so long as neither they, nor anyone else, knew--nothing mattered so far as they were concerned....

But fourteen years as a second-class soldier of the Legion! ...And what was he to do at the end of the fifteenth? They would not re-enlist him. He would get a pension of five hundred francs a year--twenty pounds a year--and he had got the cash "bonus" given him when he won the *médaille militaire*. Where could he hide again? Perhaps he could get a job as employed-pensioner of the Legion--such as sexton at the graveyard or assistant-cook, or Officers'-Mess servant? ...Otherwise he'd find himself one fine morning at the barracks-gates, dressed in a suit of blue sacking from the Quartermaster's store, fitting him where it touched him; a big flat tam-o'-shanter sort of cap; a rough shirt, and a blue cravat "to wind twice round the neck"; a pair of socks (for the first time in fifteen years), and a decent pair of boots. He'd have his papers, a free pass to any part of France he liked to name, a franc a day for the journey thereto, and his week's pay.

And what good would the papers and pass be to him--who dared not leave the shelter of the all-concealing Legion? ...Surely it would be safe for him to return to England, or at any rate to go to France or some other part of Europe? Why not to America or the Colonies? No, nowhere was safe, and nothing was certain. Besides, how was he to get there? His pass would take him to any part of France, and nowhere else. A fine thing--to hide in the Legion for fifteen years, actually to survive fifteen years of a second-class soldier's life in the Legion, and then to risk rendering it all useless! One breath of rumour--and Marguerite's life was spoilt....Discovery--and it was ruined, just when her children (if she had any more) were on the threshold of their careers....Well, life in the Legion was remarkably uncertain, and there still remained a year in which all problems might be finally solved by bullet, disease, or death in some other of the many forms in which it visited the step-sons of France....Where was old Strong now?...

Legionary John Bull fell asleep.

Meanwhile, a few inches from him, Reginald Rupert had found himself unusually and unpleasantly wakeful. It had been a remarkably full and tiring day, and as crowded with new experiences as the keenest experience-seeker could desire....He was very glad he had come. This was going to be a good toughening man's life, and real soldiering. He would not have missed it for anything. It would hold a worthy place in the list of things which he had done and been, the list that, by the end of his life, he hoped would be a long and very varied one. By the time "the governor" died (and he trusted that might not happen for another forty years) he hoped to have been in many armies and Frontier Police forces, to have been a sailor, a cowboy, a big-game hunter, a trapper, an explorer and prospector, a gold-miner, a war correspondent, a gumdigger, and many other things in many parts of the world, in addition to his present record of Public-school, Sandhurst, 'Varsity man, British officer, trooper, and French Légionnaire. He hoped to continue to turn up in any part of the world where there was a war.

What Reginald, like his father, loathed and feared was Modern Society life, and in fact all modern civilised life as it had presented itself to his eyes--with its incredibly false standards, values and ideals, its shoddy shams and vulgar pretences, its fat indulgences, slothfulness and folly.

To him, as to his father (whose curious mental kink he had inherited), the world seemed a dreadful place in which drab, dull folk followed drab, dull pursuits for drab, dull ends. People who lived for pleasure were so occupied and exhausted in its pursuit that they got no pleasure. People who worked were so closely occupied in earning their living that they never lived. He did not know which class he disliked more--the men who lived their weary lives at clubs, grandstands, country-house parties, Ranelagh and Hurlingham, the Riviera, the moors, and the Yacht Squadron; or those who lived dull laborious days in offices, growing flabby and grey in pursuit of the slippery shekel.

The human animal seemed to him to have become as adventurous, gallant, picturesque and gay as the mole, the toad, and the slug. An old tomcat on a backyard fence seemed to him to be a more independent, care-free, self-respecting and gentlemanly person than his owner, a man who, all God's wide world before him, was, for a few monthly metal discs, content to sit in a stuffy hole and copy hieroglyphics from nine till six--that another man might the quicker amass many dirty metal discs and a double chin. To Reginald, the men of even his own class seemed travesties and parodies of a noble original, in that they were content to lead the dreadful lives they did--killing tame birds, knocking little balls about the place, watching other people ride races, rushing around in motors, sailing sunny seas in luxury and safety, seeing foreign lands only from their best hotels, poodle-faking and philandering, doing everything but anything--pampered, soft, useless; each a most exact and careful copy of his neighbour. Reginald loved, and excelled at, every form of sport, and had been prominent in the playing-fields at Winchester, Sandhurst and Oxford, but he could not live by sport alone, and to him it had always been a means and not an end, a means to health, strength, skill and hardihood--the which were to be applied--not to *more* games--but to the fuller living of life. The seeds of his father's teaching had fallen on most receptive and fertile soil, and their fruit ripened not the slower by reason of the fact that his father was his friend, confidant, hero and model....He could see him now as he straddled mightily on the rug before the library fire, in his pink and cords, his spurred tops splashed with mud, and grey on the inner sides with the sweat of his horse....

"Brown-paper prisons for poor men, and pink-silk cages for rich--that's Life nowadays, my boy, unless you're careful....Get hold of Life, don't let Life get hold of you. Take the family motto for your guidance in actual fact. *'Be all, see all.'* Try to carry it out as far as humanly possible. *Live* Life and live it in the World. Don't live a thousandth part of Life in a millionth part of the World, as all our neighbours do. When you succeed me here and marry and settle down, be able to say you've seen everything, done everything, been everything....Be a gentleman, of course, but one can be a man as well as being a gentleman--gentility is of the heart and conduct and manners--not of position and wealth and rank. What's the good of seeing one little glimpse of life out of one little window--whether it's a soldier's window (which is the best of windows), or a sailor's, or a lawyer's, parson's, merchant's, scholar's, sportsman's, landowner's, politician's, or any other....And go upwards and downwards too, my boy. Tramps, ostlers, costermongers and soldiers are a dam' sight more interestin' than kings--and a heap more human. A chap who's only moved in one plane of society isn't educated--not worth listening to..." and much more to the same effect--and Rupert smiled to himself as he thought of how his father had advised him not to "waste" more than a year at Sandhurst, another at Oxford, and another in an Officers' Mess, before setting forth to see real life, and real men living it hard and to the full, in the capitals and the corners of the earth.

"How the dear old boy must have worshipped mother--to have married and settled down, at forty," he reflected, "and what a beauty she must have been. She's lovely now," and again his rather hard face softened into a smile as he thought of the interview in which he told her of his intention to "chuck" his commission and go and do things and see things. Little had he known that she had fully anticipated and daily expected the declaration which he feared would be a "terrible blow" to her....Did she expect him to be anything else than the son of his father and his eccentric and adventurous House?

"I wouldn't have you be anything but a chip of the old block, my darling boy. You're of age and your old mother isn't going to be a millstone round your neck, like she's been round your father's. Only one woman can have the right to be that, and you will give her the right when you marry her....Your family really ought not to marry."

"Mother, Mother!" he had protested, "and 'bring up our children to do the same,' I suppose?"

She had been bravely gay when he went, albeit a little damp of eye and red of nose....Really he was a lucky chap to have such a mother. She was one in a thousand and he must faithfully do his utmost to keep his promise and go home once a year or thereabouts--also "to take care of his nails, not crop his hair, change damp socks, and wear wool next his skin...." Want a bit of doin' in the Legion, what! Good job the poor darling couldn't see Luigi Rivoli breaking up recruits, or Sergeant Legros superintending the ablutions of her Reginald. What would she think of this galley and his fellow galley-slaves--of 'Erb, the *Apache*, Carmelita, the Grasshopper, and the drunkards of the Canteen? The Bucking Bronco would amuse her, and she'd certainly be interested in John Bull, poor old chap....What could his story be, and why was he here? Was there a woman in it? ...Probably. He didn't look the sort of chap who'd "done something." Poor devil! ...Yes, her big warm heart would certainly have a corner for John Bull. Had she not been well brought up by her husband and son in the matter of seeing a swan in every goose they brought home? Yes, he'd repay John Bull's kindness to the full when he left the Legion. He should come straight to Elham Old Hall and his mother should have the chance, which she would love, of thanking and, in some measure, repaying the good chap. He wouldn't tell him exactly who they were and what they were, lest he should pretend that fifteen years of Legion life had spoilt him for *la vie de château*, and refuse to visit them....He'd like to know his story. What *could* be the cause of a man like him leading this ha'penny-a-day life for fourteen years? Talk of paper prisons and silken cages--this was a prison of red-hot stone. Fancy this the setting for the best years of your life, and he sat up and looked round the moonlit room.

Next to him lay the Bucking Bronco, snoring heavily, his moustache looking huge and black in the moonlight that made his face appear pale and fine....A strong and not unkindly face, with its great jutting chin and square heavy jaw.

'Erb lay on the neighbouring cot, his hands clasped above his head as he slept the sleep of the just and innocent, for whom a night of peaceful slumber is the meet reward of a well-spent day. His pinched and cunning little face was transfigured by the moonlight, and the sleeping Herbert Higgins looked less the vulgar, street-bred guttersnipe than did the waking "'Erbiggins" of the day.

Beyond him lay the mighty bulk of Luigi Rivoli, breathing stertorously in drunken slumber as he sprawled, limb-scattered, on his face, fully dressed, save for his boots....

What an utter swine and cad--reflected Reginald--and what would happen when he selected him for his attentions? Of course, the Neapolitan had ten times his strength and twice his weight--but there would have to be a fight--or a moral victory for the recruit. He would obey no behests of Luigi Rivoli, nor accept any insults nor injuries tamely. He would land the cad one of the best, and take the consequences, however humiliating or painful. And he'd do it every time too, until he were finally incapacitated, or Luigi Rivoli weary of the game. Evidently the brute had some sort of respect for the big American and for John Bull. He should learn to have some for "Reginald Rupert," too, or the latter would die in the attempt to teach it.

The prospect was not alluring though, and the Austrian and the *Apache* had received sharp and painful lessons on the folly of defying or attacking Luigi Rivoli. Still--experiences, dangers, difficulties and real, raw, primitive life were what his family sought--and here were some of them. Yes, he was ready for Il Signor Luigi Rivoli....

In the next bed lay the Russian, Mikhail. Queer, shy chap. What a voice, and what a complexion for a recruit of the Foreign Legion! How extraordinarily alike he and his brother were, and yet there was a great difference between their respective voices and facial expressions....Another queer story there. They looked like students....Probably involved in some silly Nihilist games and had to bolt for their lives from the Russian police or from Nihilist confederates, or both. It was nice to see how the manlier brother looked after the other. He seemed to be in a perpetual state of concern and anxiety about him.

Beyond the Russian recruit lay the mad Legionary known as the Grasshopper. What a pathetic creature--an ex-officer of one of the most aristocratic corps in Europe. In fact he must be a nobleman or he could not have been in the Guides. Must be of an ancient family moreover. Besides, he was so very obviously of *ceux qui ont pris la peine de naître*. What could his story be? Fancy the man being a really first-class soldier on parade, manoeuvres, march, or battlefield, and an obvious lunatic at the same time....Poor devil!...

Next to him was the other Russian, and then Edouard Malvin, the nasty-looking cad who appeared to be Rivoli's chief toady. His neighbour was the fat and dull-looking Dutch lad (who was to display such unusual and enviable moral courage)....

Footsteps resounded without, and the Room-Corporal entered with a clatter. Turning down his blanket, as though expecting to find something beneath it, he disclosed some bottles, a few packets of tobacco and cigarettes, and a little heap of coins.

"Bonheur de Dieu vrai!" he ejaculated. "'Y'a de bon!" and examined the packets for any indication of their orientation. "'Les deux Russes,'" he read, and broke into a guinguette song. Monsieur le Caporal loved wine and was *un ramasseur de sous*. These Russians were really worthy and sensible recruits, and, though they should escape none of their duties, they should be regarded with a tolerant and non-malicious eye by Monsieur le Caporal. No undue share of corvées should be theirs....No harm in their complimenting their good Caporal and winning his approval--but, on the other hand, no bribery and corruption. Mais non--c'est tout autre chose!

As the Corporal disrobed, the Grasshopper rose from his cot, crouched, and hopped towards him.

The Corporal evinced no surprise.

"Monsieur le Caporal," quoth the Grasshopper. "How can a Cigale steer a gunboat? ...I ask you....How can I possibly dip the ensign from peak to taffrail, cat the anchor or shoot the sun, by the pale glimmer of the binnacle light? ...And I have, for cargo, the Cestus of Aphrodite...."

"And *I* have, for cargo, seven bottles of good red wine--beneath my Cestus of Corporal--so I can't tell you, Grasshopper," was the reply...."Va t'en! ...You go and ask Monsieur le bon Diable--and tell him his old *ami* Caporal Achille Martel sent you....Go on--*allez schteb' los*–and let me sleep...."

The Grasshopper hopped to the door and out into the corridor....

Rupert fell asleep....

As John Bull had prophesied, he was awakened by yells of *"Au jus! Au jus! Au jus!"* from the garde-chambre, the room-orderly on duty, as he went from cot to cot with a huge jug.

Each sleepy soul roused himself sufficiently to hold out the tin mug which hung at the head of his bed, and to receive a half-pint or so of the "gravy"–which proved to be really excellent coffee. For his own part, Rupert would have been glad of the addition of a little milk and sugar, but he had swallowed too much milkless and sugarless tea (from a basin) in the British Army, to be concerned about such a trifle....

"Good morning. Put on the white trousers and come downstairs with me," said John Bull, as he also swallowed his coffee. "Be quick, or you won't get a chance at the lavatory. There's washing accommodation for six men when sixty want it....Come on."

As he hurried from the room, Rupert noticed that Corporal Martel lay comfortably in bed while the rest hurriedly dressed. From time to time he mechanically shouted: "Levez-vous, mes enfants...." "Levez-vous, assassins...." "Levez-vous, scélérats...."

After each of his shouts came, in antistrophe, the anxious yell of the garde-chambre (who had to sweep the room before parade) of "Balayez au-dessous vos lits!"

Returning from his hasty and primitive wash, Rupert noticed that the Austrian recruit was lacing Rivoli's boots, while the *Apache*, grimacing horribly behind his back, brushed the Neapolitan down, Malvin superintending their labours.

"Shove on the white tunic and blue sash," said John Bull to his protégé--"and you'll want knapsack, cartridge-belt, bayonet and rifle.... Bye-bye! I must be off. You'll have recruit-drills separate from us for some time.... See you later...."

§3

Légionnaire Reginald Rupert soon found that French drill methods of training differed but little from English, though perhaps more thorough and systematically progressive, and undoubtedly better calculated to develop initiative.

It did not take the Corporal-Instructor long to single him out as an unusually keen and intelligent recruit, and Rupert was himself surprised at the pleasure he derived from being placed as Number One of the *escouade* of recruits, after a few days. His knowledge of French helped him considerably, of course, and on that first morning he had obeyed the Corporal's roar of "*Sac à terre,*" "*A gauche,*" "*A droit,*" "*En avant, marche,*" "*Pas gymnastique,*" or "*Formez les faisceaux,*" before the majority of the others had translated them. He also excelled in the eating of the "Breakfast of the Legion," which is nothing more nor less than a terribly punishing run, in quick time, round and round the parade-ground. By the time the Corporal called a halt, Rupert, who was a fine runner, in the pink of condition, was beginning to feel that he had about shot his bolt, while, with one or two exceptions, the rest of the squad were in a state of real distress, gasping, groaning, and coughing, with protruding eyeballs and faces white, green, or blue. During the brief "cigarette halt," he gazed round with some amusement at the prostrate forms of his exhausted comrades.

The Russian, Feodor, seemed to be in pretty well as good condition as himself--in striking contrast to Mikhail, whose state was pitiable, as he knelt doubled up, drawing his breath in terrible gasps, and holding his side as though suffering agonies from "stitch."

'Erb was in better case, but he lay panting as though his little chest would burst.

"Gawdstrewth, matey," he grunted to M. Tou-tou Boil-the-Cat, "I ain't run so much since I last see a copper."

The *Apache*, green-faced and blue-lipped, showed his teeth in a vicious snarl, by way of reply. Absinthe and black cigarettes are a poor training-diet.

The fat Dutch lad, Hans Djoolte, appeared to be in extremis and likely to disappear in a pool of perspiration. The gnarled-looking Spaniard drew his breath with noisy whoops, and stout Germans, Alsatians, Belgians and Frenchmen gave the impression of persons just rescued from drowning or suffocation by smoke. Having finished his cigarette, the Corporal ran to the far side of the parade-ground, raised his hand with a shout, and cried, "*A moi.*"

"Well run, *bleu*," he observed to Rupert, who arrived first.

Before the "breakfast" half-hour was over, he was thoroughly tired, and more than a little sorry for some of the others. M. Tou-tou Boil-the-Cat was violently sick; the plump Dutchman was soaked from head to foot; many a good, stout Hans, Fritz and Carl wished he had never been born; and Mikhail Kyrilovitch distinguished himself by falling flat in a dead faint, to the contemptuous and outspoken disgust of the Corporal.

It was indeed a kill-or-cure training, and, in some cases, bade fair to kill before it cured. One drill-manoeuvre interested Rupert by its novelty and yet by its suggestion of the old Roman *testudo*. On the order *"A genoux,"* all had to fall on their knees and every man of the squad, not in the front rank, to thrust his head well under the knapsack of the man in front of him. Since, under service conditions, knapsacks would be stuffed with spare uniforms and underclothing, and covered with tent-canvas, blanket, spare boots, fuel or a cooking-pot, excellent head-cover was thus provided against shrapnel and shell-fragments, and from bullets from some of such rifles as are used by the Chinese, African, Madagascan, and Arab foes of the Legion. Interested or not, it was with unfeigned thankfulness that, at about eleven o'clock, Rupert found himself marching back to barracks and heard the *"Rompez"* command of dismissal outside the *caserne* of his Company. Hurrying up to the *chambrée* he put his Lebel in the rack, his knapsack and belts on the shelf above his bed, and lay down to get that amount of rest without which he felt he could not face breakfast.

"Hallo, Rupert! Had a gruelling?" enquired John Bull, entering and throwing off his accoutrements. "They make you earn your little bit of corn, don't they? You feel it less day by day though, and soon find you can do it without turning a hair. Not much chance of a chap with weak lungs or heart surviving the 'Breakfast of the Legion,' for long. You see the point of the training when you begin the desert marches."

"Quite looking forward to it," said Rupert.

"It's better looking back on it, on the whole," rejoined the other grimly.... "Feel like breakfast?" he added in French, remembering that the more his young friend spoke in that tongue the better.

"Oh, I'm all right. What'll it be?"

"Well, not *bec-fins* and *pêche Melba* exactly. Say a mug of bread-soup, containing potato and vegetables and a scrap of meat. Sort of Irish stew."

"*Arlequins* at two sous the plate, first, for me, please," put in M. Tou-tou Boil-the-Cat, whose small compact frame seemed to have recovered its normal elasticity and vigour.

As he spoke, the voice of a kitchen-orderly was raised below in a long-drawn howl of *"Soupe! A la Soupe!"* Turning with one accord to the garde-chambre the Legionaries bawled *"Soupe!"* as one man, and like an arrow from a bow, the room-orderly sped forth, to return a minute later bearing the soup-kettle and a basket of loaves of grey bread. Tin plates and utensils were snatched from the hanging-cupboards, and mugs from their hooks on the wall and the Legionaries seated themselves on the benches that ran down either side of the long table.

"Fraid you'll have to stand out, Rupert, being a recruit," said John Bull. "There's only room for twenty at this table."

"Of course. Thanks," was the reply, and the speaker betook himself to his bed, and sat him down with his mug and crust.

With cheerful sociability, 'Erb had already seated himself at table, and was beating a loud tattoo with mug and plate as he awaited the administrations of the soup-laden Ganymede.

Suddenly the expansive and genial smile faded on 'Erb's happy face, as he felt himself seized by the scruff of his neck and the seat of his trousers, and raised four feet in the air.... For a second he hovered, descended a foot and was then shot through the air with appalling violence to some distant corner of the earth. Fortunately for 'Erb, that corner contained a bed and he landed fairly on it.... The Legionary Herbert Higgins in the innocence of his ignorance had occupied the Seats of the Mighty, had sat him down in the place of Luigi Rivoli--and Luigi had removed the insect.

"Gawd love us!" said 'Erb. " 'Oo'd a' thought it?" as he realised that he was still in barracks and had only travelled from the table to a cot, a distance of some six feet....

Mikhail Kyrilovitch lay stretched on his bed, too exhausted to eat. It interested and rather touched Rupert to see how tenderly the other Russian half raised him from the bed, coaxed him with soup and, failing, produced a bottle of wine from behind the *paquetage* on his shelf, and induced him to drink a little....

"Potato fatigue after this, Rupert," said John Bull as he came over to the recruit, and offered him a cigarette. "Ghastly stuff you'll find this black Algerian tobacco, but one gets used to it.

It's funny, but when I get a taste of any of the tobaccos from Home, I find my palate so ruined that I don't enjoy it. Seems acrid and strong though it's infinitely milder...."

The Kitchen-Corporal thrust his head in at the door of the *chambrée*, roared *"Aux palates"* and vanished. Trooping down to the kitchen, the whole Company stood in a ring and solemnly peeled potatoes. Here, at any rate, Mikhail Kyrilovitch distinguished himself among the recruits, for not only was his the first potato to fall peeled into the bucket, but his peel was the thinnest, his output the greatest. Standing next to him, Rupert noticed how tiny were his hands and wrists, and how delicate his nails.

"Apparently this is part of regular routine and not a corvée," he remarked.

"Mais oui, Monsieur," replied Mikhail primly.

"Great tip to get cunning at dodging extra fatigues when you're a soldier," continued Rupert.

"Mais oui, Monsieur," replied Mikhail primly.

"Expect they'll catch us wretched recruits on that lay until we get artful."

"Mais oui, Monsieur," replied Mikhail primly.

What a funny shy lad he was, with his eternal "Mais oui, Monsieur"... Perhaps that was all the French he knew!...

"Do you think the medical-examination will be very--er--searching, Monsieur?" asked Mikhail.

So he did know French after all. What was he trembling about now?

"Shouldn't think so. Why? You're all right, aren't you? You wouldn't have passed the doctor when you enlisted, otherwise."

"Non, Monsieur."

"Where did you enlist?"

"At Paris, Monsieur."

"So did I; Rue St. Dominique. LIttle fat cove in red breeches and a white tunic. I suppose you had the same chap?"

"Er--oui, Monsieur."

"I suppose he overhauled you very thoroughly? ...Wasn't it infernally cold standing stark naked in that beastly room while he punched you about?"

"Oh!–er--oui, Monsieur. Oh, please let us ... Er--wasn't that running dreadful this morning?"...

"I say, Monsieur Rupaire, do you think we shall have the same 'breakfast' every morning?" put in Feodor Kyrilovitch. "It'll be the death of my brother here, if we do. He never was a runner."

"'Fraid so, during recruits' course," replied Rupert, and added: "I noticed a great difference between you and your brother."

"Oh, it's only just in that respect," was the reply. "I've always been better winded than he.... Illness when he was a kid....Lungs not over strong...."

Even as he had prophesied, an Orderly-Sergeant swooped down upon them as the potato-fatigue finished, and, while the old Legionaries somehow melted into thin air and vanished like the baseless fabric of a vision, the recruits were captured and commandeered for a barrack-scavenging corvée which kept them hard at work until it was time to fall in for "theory."

This Rupert discovered to be instruction in recognition of badges of rank, and, later, in every sort and kind of rule and regulation; in musketry, tactics, training and the principles and theory of drill, entrenchment, scouting, skirmishing, and every other branch of military education.

At two o'clock, drill began again, and lasted until four, at which hour Monsieur le Médicin-Major held the medical examination, the idea of which seemed so disturbing to Mikhail Kyrilovitch. It proved to be the merest formality--a glance, a question, a caution against excess, and the recruits were passed and certified as *bon pour le service* at the rate of twenty to the quarter-hour. They were, moreover, free for the remainder of the day (provided they escaped all victim-hunting Non-coms., in search of corvée-parties) with the exception of such hours as might be necessary for labours of *astiquage* and the *lavabo*.

On returning to the *chambrée*, Rupert found his friend John Bull awaiting him.

"Well, Rupert," he cried cheerily, "what sort of a day have you had? Tired? We'll get 'soupe' again shortly. I'll take you to the *lavabo* afterwards, and show you the ropes. Got to have your white kit, arms and accoutrements all *klim-bim*, as the Germans say, before you dress and go out, or else you'll have to do it in the dark."

"Yes, thanks," replied Rupert. "I'll get straight first. I hate 'spit and polish' after Lights Out. What'll the next meal be?"

"Same as this morning--the eternal 'soupe.' The only variety in food is when dog-biscuit replaces bread....Nothing to grumble at really, except the infernal monotony. Quantity is all right--in fact some fellows save up a lot of bread and biscuit and sell it in the town. (Eight days *salle de police* if you're caught.) But sometimes you feel you could eat anything in the wide world except Legion 'soupe,' bread and biscuit...."

After the second and last meal of the day, at about five o'clock, Rupert was introduced to the *lavabo* and its ways--particularly its ways in the matter of disappearing soap and vanishing "washing"–and, his first essay in laundry-work concluded, returned with Legionary John Bull and the Bucking Bronco for an hour or two of leather-polishing, accoutrement-cleaning and "Ironing" without an iron.

The room began to fill and was soon a scene of more or less silent industry. On his bed, the great Luigi Rivoli lay magnificently asleep, while, on neighbouring cots and benches, his weapons, accoutrements, boots and uniform received the attentions of Messieurs Malvin, Meyer, Tou-tou Boil-the-Cat, Dimitropoulos, Borges, Bauer, Hirsch, and others, his henchmen.

Anon the great man awoke, yawned cavernously, ejaculated "*Dannazione*" and sat up. One gathered that the condition of his mouth was not all that it might be, and that his head ached. Even he was not exempt from the penalties incurred by lesser men, and even he had to recognise the fact that a next-morning follows an evening-before. Certain denizens of the *chambrée* felt, and looked, uneasy, but were reassured by the reflection that there was still a stock of *bleus* unchastened, and available for the great man's needs and diversion. Rising, he roared "*Oho!*", smacked and flexed his muscles according to his evening ritual, and announced that a recruit might be permitted to fetch him water.

Feodor Kyrilovitch unobtrusively changed places with his brother Mikhail, whose bed was next to that of the bully.

"Here, dog," roared the Neapolitan, and brought his "quart" down with a right resounding blow upon the bare head of Feodor. Without a word the Russian took the mug and hurried to the nearest lavatory. Returning he handed it respectfully to Rivoli, and pointing into it said in broken Italian--

"There would appear to be a mark on the bottom of the Signor's cup."

The great man looked--and smiled graciously as he recognised a gold twenty-franc piece. "A thoroughly intelligent recruit," he added, turning to Malvin who nodded and smiled drily. It entered the mind of le bon Légionnaire Malvin that this recruit should also give an exhibition of his intelligence to le bon Légionnaire Malvin.

"Where's that fat pig from Olanda who can only whine '*Verstaan nie*' when he is spoken to?" enquired Rivoli, looking round. "Let me see if I can 'Verstaan' him how to put my boots on smartly."

But, fortunately for himself, the Dutch recruit, Hans Djoolte, was not present.

"Not there?" thundered the great man, on being informed. "How dare the fat calf be not there? Let it be known that I desire all the recruits of this room to be on duty from 'Soupe' till six, or later, in case I should want them. Let them all parade before me now."

Some sheepishly grinning, some with looks of alarm, some under strong protest, all the recruits with one exception, "fell in" at the foot of the Italian's bed. Some were dismissed as they came up; the two Russians, as having paid their footing very handsomely; the *Apache*, and Franz Josef Meyer, as having been properly broken to bit and curb; the Greek, as a declared admirer and slave; and one or two others who had already wisely propitiated, or, to their sorrow, encountered less pleasantly, the uncrowned king of the Seventh Company. The remainder received tasks, admonitions and warnings, the which were received variously, but without open defiance.

"The attitude of le Légionnaire 'Erbiggins was characteristic. Realising that he had not a ghost of a chance of success against a man of twice his weight and thrice his strength, he took the leggings which were given him to clean and returned a stream of nervous English, of which the pungent insults and vile language accorded but ill with the bland innocence of his face, and the deferential acquiescence of his manner.

"Ain't yew goin' ter jine the merry throng?" asked the Bucking Bronco of Reginald Rupert, upon hearing that recruit reply to Malvin's order to join the line, with a recommendation that Malvin should go to the devil.

"I am not," replied Rupert.

"Wal, I guess we'll back yew up, sonny," said the American with an approving smile.

"I shall be glad if you will in no way interfere," returned the Englishman.

"Gee-whillikins!" commented the Bucking Bronco.

John Bull looked anxious. "He's the strongest man I have ever seen," he remarked, "besides being a professional wrestler and acrobat."

Malvin again approached, grinning maliciously.

"Il Signor Luigi Rivoli would be sorry to have to come and fetch you, English pig," said he. "Sorry for you, that is. Do you wish to find yourself *au grabat*,[51] you scurvy, mangy, lousy cur of a recruit? ...What reply shall I take Il Signor Luigi Rivoli?"

"*That!*" replied the Englishman, and therewith smote the fat Austrian a most tremendous smack across his heavy blue jowl with the open hand, sending him staggering several yards. Without paying further attention to the great man's ambassador, he strode in the direction of the great man himself, with blazing eyes and clenched jaw.

"You want me, do you?" he shouted at the astonished Luigi, who was rising open-mouthed from his bed; and, putting the whole weight of his body behind the blow, drove most skilfully and scientifically straight at the point of his jaw.

It must be confessed that the Italian was taken unawares, and in the very act of getting up, so that his hands were down, and he was neither standing nor sitting.

He was down and out, and lay across his bed stunned and motionless.

Into the perfect silence of the *chambrée* fell the voice of the Bucking Bronco. Solemnly he counted from one to ten, and then with a shout of "OUT!" threw his képi to the roof and roared "*Hurrah!*" repeatedly.

"Il ira loin," remarked Monsieur Tou-tou Boil-the-Cat, viewing Rupert's handiwork with experienced, professional eye.

Exclamatory oaths went up in all the languages of Europe.

"Il a fait de bon boulet," remarked a grinning greybeard known as "Tant-de-Soif" to the astounded and almost awe-stricken crowd.

But le Légionnaire Jean Boule looked ahead.

"You've made two bad enemies, my boy, I'm afraid....What about when he comes round?"

"I'll give him some more, if I can," replied Rupert. "Don't interfere, anyhow."

"Shake, sonny," said the Bucking Bronco solemnly. "An' look at hyar. Let's interfere, to the extent o' makin' thet cunning coyote fight down in the squar'....Yew won't hev no chance--so don't opine yew will--but yew'll hev' more chance than yew will right hyar....Yew want space when you roughhouses with Loojey. Once he gits a holt on yew--yure monica's up. Savvy?"

"Thanks," replied the Englishman. "Right-ho! If he won't fight downstairs, tell him he can take the three of us."

"Fower, matey. Us fower Henglishmen agin' 'im an' 'is 'ole bleedin' gang," put in 'Erb. "'E's a bloke as wants takin' dahn a peg....Too free wiv' hisself....Chucks 'is weight abaht too much....An' I'll tell yer wot, Cocky. Keep a heye on that cove as you giv' a smack in the chops."

"Sure thing," agreed the Bucking Bronco, and turned to the Belgian who stood ruefully holding his face and looking as venomous as a broken-backed cobra, added: "Yew look at hyar, Mounseer Malvin, my lad. Don't yew git handlin' yure Rosalie[52] any dark night. Yew try ter *zigouiller*[53] my pal Rupert, an' I'll draw yure innards up through yure mouth till yew look like half a pound of dumplin' on the end of half a yard of macaroni. Twiggez vous? *Je tirerai vos gueutes à travers votre bouche jusqu'à vous resemblez un demi-livre de ponding au bout d'un demi-yard de macaroni....* Got it?..."

Rivoli twitched, stirred, and groaned. It was interesting to note that none of his clients and henchmen offered any assistance. The sceptre of the great man swayed in his hand. Were he beaten, those whom he ruled by fear, rather than by bribery, would fall upon him like a pack of wolves. The hands of Monsieur Tou-tou Boil-the-Cat twitched and he licked his lips.

"*Je m'en souviendrai*," he murmured.

Rivoli sat up.

"Donna e Madonna!" he said. "Corpo di Bacco!" and gazed around. "What has happened?..." and then he remembered. "A minute," he said. "Wait but a minute--and then bring him to me."

Obedience and acquiescence awoke in the bosoms of his supporters. The great Luigi was alive and on his throne again. The Greek passed him a mug of water.

"Yes, wait but a moment, and then just hand him to me.... One of you might go over to the hospital and say a bed will be wanted shortly," he added. "And another of you might look up old Jules Latour down at the cemetery and tell him to start another grave."

"You're coming to me, for a change, Rivoli," cut in Rupert contemptuously. "You're going to fight me down below. There's going to be a ring, and fair play. Will you come now, or will you wait till to-morrow? I can wait if you feel shaken."

"Plug the ugly skunk while he's rattled, Bub," advised the American, and turning to the Italian added, "Sure thing, Loojey. Ef yew ain't hed enuff yew kin tote downstairs and hev' a five-bunch frame-up with the b'y. Ef yew start rough-housin' up hyar, I'll take a hand too. I would anyhaow, only the b'y wants yew all to himself.... Greedy young punk."

"I will kill him and eat him *now*," said the Italian rising magnificently. Apparently his splendid constitution and physique had triumphed completely, and it was as though the blow had not been struck.

"Come on, b'ys," yelped the American, "an' ef thet Dago don't fight as square as he knows haow, I'll pull his lower jaw off his face."

In a moment the room was empty, except for Mikhail Kyrilovitch, who sat on the edge of his brother's bed and shuddered.

Clattering down the stairs and gathering numbers as it went, the party made for the broad space, or passage, between high walls near the back entrance of the Company's *caserne*, a safe and secluded spot for fights. As they went along, John Bull gave good advice to his young friend.

"Remember he's a wrestler and a savate man," he said, "and that public opinion here recognises the use of both in a fight--so you can expect him to clinch and kick as well as butt."

"Right-o!" said Rupert.

A large ring was formed by the rapidly growing crowd of spectators, a ring, into the middle of which the Bucking Bronco stepped to declare that he would rearrange the features, as well as the ideas, of any supporter of Luigi Rivoli who in any way interfered with the fight.

The two combatants stripped to the waist and faced each other. It was a pleasant surprise to John Bull to notice that his friend looked bigger "peeled," than he did when dressed. (It is a good test of muscular development.) Obviously the youth was in the pink of condition and had systematically developed his muscles. But for the presence of Rivoli, the arms and torso of the Englishman would have evoked admiring comments. As it was, the gigantic figure of the Italian dwarfed him, for he looked what he was--a professional Strong Man whose stock-in-trade was his enormous muscles and their mighty strength.... It was not so much a contrast between David and Goliath as between Apollo and Hercules.

The Italian assumed his favourite wrestling attitude with open hands advanced; the Englishman, the position of boxing.

The two faced each other amidst the perfect silence of the large throng.

As, to the credit of human nature, is always the case, the sentiment of the crowd was in favour of the weaker party. No one supposed for a moment that the recruit would win, but he was a "dark horse," and English--of a nation proverbially dogged and addicted to *la boxe*.... He might perhaps be merely maimed and not killed.... For a full minute the antagonists hung motionless, eyeing each other warily. Suddenly the Italian swiftly advanced his left foot and made a lightning grab with his left hand at the Englishman's neck. The latter ducked; the great arm swung, harmless, above his head, and two sharp smacks rang out like pistol-shots as the Englishman planted a left and right with terrific force upon the Italian's ribs. Rivoli's gasp was almost as audible as the blows. He sprang back, breathing heavily.

John Bull moistened his Lips and thanked God. Rupert circled round his opponent, sparring for an opening. Slowly ... slowly ... almost imperceptibly, the Italian's head and shoulders bent further and further back. What the devil was he doing?--wondered the Englishman--getting his head out of danger? Certainly his jaw was handsomely swollen.... Anyhow he was exposing his mark, the spot where the ribs divide. If he could get a "right" in there, with all his weight and strength, Il Signor Luigi Rivoli would have to look to himself in the ensuing seconds. Rupert made a spring. As he did so, the Italian's body turned sideways and leant over until almost parallel with the ground, as his right knee drew up to his chest and his right foot shot out with the force of a horse's kick. It caught the advancing Englishman squarely on the mouth, and sent him flying head over heels like a shot rabbit. The Italian darted forward--and so did the Bucking Bronco.

"Assez!" he shouted. "Let him get up." At this point his Legion French failed him, and he added in his own vernacular, "Ef yew think yu're gwine ter kick him while he's down, yew've got another think comin', Loojey Rivoli," and barred his path.

John Bull raised Rupert's head on to his knee. He was senseless and bleeding from mouth and nose.

Pushing his way through the ring, came 'Erb, a mug of water in one hand, a towel in the other. Filling his mouth with water, he ejected a fine spray over Rupert's face and chest, and then, taking the towel by two corners of a long side, flapped it mightily over the prostrate man.

The latter opened his eyes, sat up, and spat out a tooth.

"Damned kicking cad," he remarked, on collecting his scattered wits and faculties.

"No Queensberry rules here, old chap," said John Bull.

"You do the sime fer 'im, matey. Kick 'is bleedin' faice in.... W'y carn't 'e fight like a man, the dirty furriner?" and turning from his ministrations to where the great Luigi received the congratulations of his admiring supporters, he bawled with the full strength of his lungs: "Yah! you dirty furriner!" and crowned the taunt by putting his fingers to his nose and emitting a bellowing *Boo-oo-oo!* of incredibly bull-like realism. "If I wasn't yer second, matey, I'd go an' kick 'im in the stummick naow, I would," he muttered, resuming his labour of love.

Rupert struggled to his feet.

"Give me the mug," he said to 'Erb, and washed out his mouth. "How long 'time' is observed on these occasions?" he asked of John Bull.

"Oh, nothing's regular," was the reply. "'Rounds' end when you fall apart, and 'time' ends when both are ready.... You aren't going for him again, are you?"

"I'm going for him as long as I can stand and see," was the answer. 'Erb patted him on the back.

"Blimey! You're a White Man, matey," he commended. "S'welp me, you are!"

"Seconds out of the ring," bawled the Bucking Bronco, and unceremoniously shoved back all who delayed.

A look of incredulity spread over the face of the Italian. Could it be possible that the fool did not know that he was utterly beaten and abolished? ... He tenderly felt his jaw and aching ribs....

It was true. The Englishman advanced upon him, the light of battle in his eyes, and fierce determination expressed in the frown upon his white face. His mouth bore no expression--it was merely a mess.

A cheer went up from the spectators.

A recruit asking for it *twice*, from Luigi Rivoli!

That famous man, though by no means anxious, was slightly perplexed. There was something here to which he was not accustomed. It was the first time in his experience that this had happened. Few men had defied and faced him once--none had done it twice. This, in itself was bad, and in the nature of a faint blow to his prestige.... He had tried a grapple--with unfortunate results; he had tried a kick--most successfully, and he would try another in a moment. Lest his opponent should be warily expecting it, he would now administer a battering-ram butt. He crouched forward, extending his open hands as though to grapple, and, suddenly ducking his head, flung himself forward, intending to drive the breath from his enemy's body and seize him by the throat ere he recovered.

Lightly and swiftly the Englishman side-stepped and, as he did so, smote the Italian with all his strength full upon the ear--a blow which caused that organ to swell hugely, and to "sing" for hours. Rivoli staggered sideways and fell. The Englishman stood back and waited. Rivoli arose as quickly as he fell, and, with a roar of rage, charged straight at the Englishman, who drove straight at his face, left and right, cutting his knuckles to the bone. Heavy and true as were the blows, they could not avail to stop that twenty-stone projectile, and, in a second, the Italian's arms were round him. One mighty hug and heave, and his whole body, clasped as in a vice to that of the Italian, was bent over backward in a bow.

"Thet's torn it," groaned the American, and dashed his képi upon the ground. "Fer two damns I'd..."

John Bull laid a restraining hand upon his arm.

"Go it, Rupert," bawled 'Erb, dancing in a frenzy of excitement. "Git 'is froat.... Swing up yer knee.... Kick 'im."

"Shut up," snapped John Bull. "He's not a hooligan...."

One of Rupert's arms was imprisoned in those of the Italian. True to his training and standards, he played the game as he had learnt it, and kept his free right hand from his opponent's throat. With his failing strength he rained short-arm blows on the Italian's face, until it was turned sideways and crushed against his neck and shoulder.

John Bull mistook the bully's action.

"If you bite his throat, I'll shoot you, Rivoli," he shouted, and applauding cheers followed the threat.

The muscles of Rivoli's back and arms tightened and bunched as he strained with all his strength. Slowly but surely he bent further over, drawing the Englishman's body closer and closer in his embrace.

To John Bull, the seconds seemed years. Complete silence reigned. Rupert's blows weakened and became feeble. They ceased. Rivoli bent over further. As Rupert's right arm fell to his side, the Italian seized it from behind. His victim was now absolutely powerless and motionless. John Bull was reminded of a boa-constrictor which he had once seen crush a deer. Suddenly the Italian's left arm was withdrawn, his right arm continuing to imprison Rupert's left while his right hand retained his grip of the other. Thrusting his left hand beneath the Englishman's chin he put all his colossal strength into one great effort--pushing the head back until it seemed that the neck must break, and at the same time contracting his great right arm and bending himself almost double. He then raised his opponent and dashed him to the ground....

Reginald Rupert recovered consciousness in the Legion's Hospital.

A skilful, if somewhat brutal, surgeon soon decided that his back was not broken but only badly sprained. On leaving hospital, a fortnight later, he did eight days *salle de police* by way of convalescence.

On return to duty, he found himself something of a hero in the Seventh Company, and decidedly the hero of the recruits of his *chambrée*.

Disregarding the earnest entreaties of John Bull and the reiterated advice of the Bucking Bronco, and of the almost worshipping 'Erb--he awaited Luigi Rivoli on the evening after his release and challenged him to fight.

The great man burst into explosive laughter--laughter almost too explosive to be wholly genuine.

"Fight you, whelp! Fight you, *whelp!*" he scoffed. "*Why* should I fight you? Pah! Out of my sight--I have something else to do."

"Oh have you? Well, don't forget that I have nothing else to do, any time you feel like fighting. See?" replied the Englishman.

The Italian again roared with laughter, and Rupert with beating heart and well-concealed sense of mighty relief, returned to his cot to work.

It was noticeable that Il Signor Luigi Rivoli invariably had something else to do, so far as Rupert was concerned, and molested him no more.

Chapter VI
Le Cafard and Other Things

For Légionnaire Reginald Rupert the days slipped past with incredible rapidity, and, at the end of six months, this adaptable and exceedingly keen young man felt himself to be an old and seasoned Legionary, for whom the Depôt held little more in the way of instruction and experience.

His thoughts began to turn to Foreign Service. When would he be able to volunteer for a draft going to Tonkin, Madagascar, Senegal, or some other place of scenes and experiences entirely different from those of Algeria? When would he see some active service--that which he had come so far to see, and for which he had undergone these hardships and privations?

Deeply interested as he was in all things military, and anxious as he was to learn and become the Compleat Soldier, he found himself beginning to grow very weary of the trivial round, the common task, of Life in the Depôt. Once he knew his drill as an Infantryman, he began to feel that the proportion of training and instruction to that of corvée and fatigues was small. He had not travelled all the way to Algiers to handle broom and wheelbarrow, and perform non-military labours at a wage of a halfpenny per day. Of course, one took the rough with the smooth and shrugged one's shoulders with the inevitable "Que voulez-vous? C'est la Légion," but, none the less, he had had enough, and more than enough, of Depôt life.

He sometimes thought of going to the *Adjudant-Major*, offering to provide proofs that he had been a British officer, and claiming to be placed in the class of *angehende corporale* (as he called the *élèves Caporaux* or probationary Corporals) with a view to promotion and a wider and different sphere of action.

There were reasons against this course, however. It would, very probably, only result in his being stuck in the Depôt permanently, as a Corporal-Instructor--the more so as he spoke German. Also, it was neither quite worth while, nor quite playing the game, as he did not intend to spend more than a year in the Legion and was looking forward to his attempt at desertion as his first real Great Adventure.

He had heard horrible stories of the fate of most of those who go "on pump," as, for no discoverable reason, the Legionary calls desertion. In every barrack-room there hung unspeakably ghastly photographs of the mangled bodies of Legionaries who had fallen into the hands of the Arabs and been tortured by their women. He had himself seen wretched deserters dragged back by Goums,[54] a mass of rags, filth, blood and bruises; their manacled hands fastened to the end of a rope attached to an Arab's saddle. Inasmuch as the captor got twenty-five francs for returning a deserter, alive or dead, he merely tied the wounded, or starved and half-dead wretch to the end of a rope and galloped with him to the nearest outpost or barracks. When the Roumi[55] could no longer run, he was quite welcome to fall and be dragged.

Rupert had also gathered a fairly accurate idea of the conditions of life--if "life" it can be called--in the Penal Battalions.

Yes, on the whole, desertion from the Legion would be something in the nature of an adventure, when one considered the difficulties, risks, and dangers, which militated against success, and the nature of the punishment which attended upon failure. No wonder that desertion was regarded by all and sundry as being a feat of courage, skill and endurance to which attached no slightest stigma of disgrace! One gathered that most men "made the promenade" at some time or other--generally under the influence of *le cafard* in some terrible Southern desert-station, and were dealt with more or less leniently (provided they lost no articles of their kit) in view of the fact that successful desertion from such places was utterly impossible, and only attempted by them "while of unsound mind." Only once or twice, in the whole history of the Legion, had a man got clear away, obtained a camel, and, by some miracle of luck, courage and endurance, escaped death at the hands of the Arabs, thirst, hunger, and sunstroke, to reach the Moroccan border and take service with the Moors--who are the natural and hereditary enemies of the Touaregs and Bedouins.

Yes, he had begun to feel that he had certainly come to the end of a period of instruction and experience, and was in need of change to fresh fields and pastures new. Vegetating formed no part of his programme of life, which was far too short, in any case, for all there was to see and to do....

Sitting one night on his cot, and talking to the man for whom he now had a very genuine and warm affection, he remarked--

"Don't you get fed up with Depôt life, Bull?"

"I have been fed up with life, Depôt and otherwise, for over twenty years," was the reply.... "Don't forget that life here in Sidi is a great deal better than life in a desert station in the South. It is supportable anyhow; there--it simply isn't; and those who don't desert and die, go mad and die. The exceptions, who do neither, deteriorate horribly, and come away very different men.... Make the most of Sidi, my boy, while you are here, and remember that foreign service, when in Tonkin, Madagascar, or Western Africa, inevitably means fever and dysentery, and generally broken health for life....Moreover, Algeria is the only part of the French colonial possessions in which the climate lets one enjoy one's pipe."

That very night, shortly after the *caserne* had fallen silent and still, its inmates wrapped in the heavy sleep of the thoroughly weary, an alarm-bugle sounded in the barrack-square, and, a minute later, non-commissioned officers hurried from room to room, bawling, *"Aux armes! Aux armes! Aux armes!"* at the top of their voices.

Rupert sat up in his bed, as Corporal Achille Martel began to shout, *"Levez-vous donc. Levez-vous! Faites le sac! Faites le sac! En tenue de Campagne d'Afrique."*

"'Ooray!" shrilled 'Erb. "Oo-bloomin'-ray."

"Buck up, Rupert," said John Bull. "We've got to be on the barrack-square in full 'African field equipment' in ten minutes."

The *chambrée* became the scene of feverish activity, as well as of delirious excitement and joy. In spite of it being the small hours of the morning, every man howled or whistled his own favourite song, without a sign of that liverish grumpiness which generally accompanies early-morning effort. The great Luigi's slaves worked at double pressure since they had to equip their lord and master as well as themselves. Feodor Kyrilovitch appeared to pack his own knapsack with one hand and that of Mikhail with the other, while he whispered words of cheer and encouragement. The Dutch boy, Hans Djoolte, having finished his work, knelt down beside his bed and engaged in prayer. Speculation was rife as to whether France had declared war on Morocco, or whether the Arabs were in rebellion, for the hundredth time, and lighting the torch of destruction all along the Algerian border.

In ten minutes from the blowing of the alarm-bugle, the Battalion was on parade in the barrack-square, every man fully equipped and laden like a beast of burden. One thought filled every mind as the ammunition boxes were brought from the magazine and prised open. *What would the cardboard packets contain?* A few seconds after the first packet had been torn open by the first man to whom one was tossed, the news had spread throughout the Battalion.

Ball-Cartridge!

The Deity in that moment received the heartfelt fervid thanks of almost every man in the barrack-square, for ball-cartridge meant active service--in any case, a blessed thing, whatever might result--the blessing of death, of promotion, of decorations, of wounds and discharge from the Legion. The blessing of change, to begin with.

There was one exception however. When Caporal Achille Martel "told off" Légionnaire Mikhail Kyrilovitch for orderly-duty to the *Adjudant Vaguemestre*,[56] duty which would keep him behind in barracks, that Legionary certainly contrived to conceal any disappointment that he may have felt.

A few minutes later the Legion's magnificent band struck up the Legion's march of *"Tiens, voilà du boudin,"* and the Battalion swung out of the gate, past the barracks of the Spahis, through the quiet sleeping streets into the main road, and so out of the town to which many of them never returned.

In the third row of fours of the Seventh Company marched the Bucking Bronco, John Bull, Reginald Rupert, and Herbert Higgins. In the row in front of them, Luigi Rivoli, Edouard Malvin, the Grass hopper, and Feodor Kyrilovitch. In the front row old Tant-de-Soif, Franz Josef Meyer, Tou-tou Boil-the-Cat, and Hans Djoolte. In front of them marched the four drummers. At the head of the Company rode Captain d'Armentières, beside whom walked Lieutenant Roberte.

Marching "at ease," the men discussed the probabilities and possibilities of the expedition. All the signs and tokens to be read by experienced soldier-eyes, were those of a long march and active service.

"It'll be a case of 'best foot foremost' a few hours hence, Rupert, I fancy," remarked John Bull. "I shouldn't be surprised if we put up thirty miles on end, with no halt but the 'cigarette spaces.'"

"Sure thing," agreed the Bucking Bronco. "I got a hunch we're gwine ter throw our feet some, to-day. We wouldn't hev' hiked off like this with sharp ammunition and made out get-away in quarter of an hour ef little Johnnie hadn't wanted the doctor. Well, I'm sorry fer the b'ys as ain't good mushers... Guess we shan't pound our ears[57] before we wants tew, this trip."

Marching along the excellent sandy road through the cool of the night, under a glorious moon, with the blood of youth, and health, and strength coursing like fire through his veins, it was difficult for Rupert to realise that, within a few hours, he would be wearily dragging one foot after the other, his rifle weighing a hundredweight, his pack weighing a ton, his mouth a lime-kiln, his body one awful ache. He had had some pretty gruelling marches before, but this was the first time that the Battalion had gone out on a night alarm with ball-cartridge, and every indication of it being the "real thing."

On tramped the Legion.

Anon there was a whistle, a cry of *Halt!* and there was a few minutes' rest. Men lit cigarettes; some sat down; several fumbled at straps and endeavoured to ease packs by shifting them. Malvin made his master lie down after removing his pack altogether. It is a pack well worth removing--that of the Legion--save when seconds are too precious to be thus spent, and you consider it the wiser plan to fall flat and lie from the word *"Halt!"* to the word *"Fall in!"* The knapsack of black canvas is heavy with two full uniforms, underclothing, cleaning materials and sundries. Weighty tent-canvas and blankets are rolled round it, tent-supports are fastened at the side, firewood, a cooking-pot, drinking-mug and spare boots go on top.

Attached to his belt the Legionary carries a sword-bayonet with a steel scabbard, four hundred rounds of ammunition in his cartridge-pouches, an entrenching tool, and his "sac." Add his rifle and water-bottle, and you have the most heavily laden soldier in the world. He does not carry his overcoat--he wears it, and is perhaps unique in considering a heavy overcoat to be correct desert wear. Under his overcoat he has only a canvas shirt and white linen trousers (when *en tenue de campagne d'Afrique*), tucked into leather gaiters. Round his waist, his blue sash--four yards of woollen cloth--acts as an excellent cholera-belt and body-support. The linen neckcloth, or couvre-nuque, buttoned on to the white cover of his képi, protects his neck and ears, and, to some extent, his face, and prevents sunstroke....

The Battalion marched on through the glorious dawn, gaily singing *"Le sac, ma foi, toujours au dos,"* and the old favourite marching songs *"Brigadier," "L'Empereur de Danmark," "Père Bugeaud,"* and *"Tiens, voilà du boudin."* Occasionally a German would lift up his splendid voice and soon more than half the battalion would be singing--

> "Trinken wir noch ein Tröpfchen
> Aus dem kleinen Henkeltöpfchen."

or *Die Wacht am Rhein* or the pathetic *Morgenlied*.

At the second halt, when some eight miles had been covered, there were few signs of fatigue, and more men remained standing than sat down. As the long column waited by the side of the road, a small cavalcade from the direction of Sidi-bel-Abbès overtook it. At the head rode a white-haired, white-moustached officer on whose breast sparkled and shone that rare and glorious decoration, the Grand Cross of the Legion of Honour.

"That's the Commander-in-Chief in Algeria," said John Bull to Rupert. "That settles it: we're out for business this time, and I fancy you'll see some Arab-fighting before you are much older.... Feet going to be all right, do you think?"

"Fine," replied Rupert. "My boots are half full of tallow, and I've got a small bottle of bapédi in my sack...."

On tramped the Legion.

The day grew hot and packs grew heavy. The Battalion undeniably and unashamedly slouched. Many men leant heavily forward against their straps, while some bent almost double, like coal-heavers carrying sacks of coal. Rifles changed frequently from right hand to left. There was no singing now. The only sound that came from dry-lipped, sticky mouths was an occasional bitter curse. Rupert began to wonder if his shoulder straps had not turned to wires. His arms felt numb, and the heavy weights, hung about his shoulders and waist, caused a feeling of constriction about the heart and lungs. He realised that he quite understood how people felt when they fainted....

By the seventh halt, some forty kilometres, or twenty-seven miles lay behind the Battalion. At the word *Halt!* every man had thrown himself at full length on the sand, and very few wasted precious moments of the inexorably exact five minutes of the rest-period in removing knapsacks. Hardly a man spoke; none smoked.

On tramped the Legion.

Gone was all pretence of smartness and devil-may-care humour--that queer *macabre* and bitter humour of the Legion. Men slouched and staggered, and dragged their feet in utter hopeless weariness. Backs rounded more and more, heads sank lower, and those who limped almost outnumbered those who did not. A light push would have sent any man stumbling to the ground.

As the whistle blew for the next halt, the Legion sank to the ground with a groan, as though it would never rise again. As the whistle blew for the advance the Legion staggered to its feet as one man....Oh, the Legion marches! Is not its motto, *"March or Die"*? The latter it may do, the former it must. The Legion has its orders and its destination, and it marches. If it did not reach its destination at the appointed time, it would be because it had died in getting there.

On tramped the Legion.

With horrible pains in its blistered shoulders, its raw-rubbed backs, its protesting, aching legs and blistered heels and toes, the Legion staggered on, a silent pitiable mass of suffering. Up and down the entire length of the Battalion rode its Colonel, "the Marching Pig." Every few yards he bawled with brazen throat and leathern lungs: "March or die, my children! March or die!" And the Legion clearly understood that it must march or it must die. To stagger from the ranks and fall was to die of thirst and starvation, or beneath the *flissa* of the Arab.

Legionary Rupert blessed those "Breakfasts of the Legion" and the hard training which achieved and maintained the hard condition of the Legionary. Sick, giddy, and worn-out as he felt, he knew he could keep going at least as long as the average, and by the time the average man had reached the uttermost end of his tether, the end of their march must be reached. After all, though they were Legionaries whose motto was "March or Die," they were only human beings--and to all human effort and endeavour there is a limit. He glanced at his comrades. The Bucking Bronco swung along erect, his rifle held across his shoulder by the muzzle, and his belt, with all its impedimenta, swinging from his right hand. He stared straight ahead and, with vacant mind and tireless iron body, "threw his feet."

Beside him, John Bull looked very white and worn and old. He leant heavily against the pull of his straps and marched with his chest bare. On Rupert's left, 'Erb, having unbuttoned and unbuckled everything unbuttonable and unbuckleable, slouched along, a picture of slack unsoldierliness and of dauntless dogged endurance. Suddenly throwing up his head he screamed from parched lips, "Aw we dahn'earted?" and, having painfully swallowed, answered his own strident question with a long-drawn, contemptuous "Ne--a--ow." Captain d'Armentières, who knew England and the English, looked round with a smile...."Bon garçon," he nodded.

On the right of the second row of fours marched Luigi Rivoli, in better case than most, as the bulk of his kit was now impartially distributed among Malvin, Meyer, Tou-tou and Tant-de-Soif. (The power of money in the Legion is utterly incredible.) Feodor Kyrilovitch was carrying the Grasshopper's rifle--and that made a mighty difference toward the end of a thirty-mile march.

At the end of the next halt, the Grasshopper declared that he could not get up....At the command, "Fall in!" the unfortunate man did not stir.

"Kind God! What *shall* I do?" he groaned. It was his first failure as a soldier.

"Come on, my lad," said John Bull sharply. "Here, pull off his kit," he added and unfastened the Belgian's belt. Between them they pulled him to his feet and dragged him to his place in the ranks. John Bull took his pack, the Bucking Bronco his belt and its appurtenances, and Feodor his rifle. His eyes were closed and he sank to the ground.

"Here," said Rupert to 'Erb. "Get in his place and let him march in yours beside me. We'll hold him up."

"Give us yer rifle, matey," replied 'Erb, and left Rupert with hands free to assist the Grasshopper.

With his right arm round the Belgian's waist, he helped him along, while John Bull insisted on having the poor fellow's right hand on his left shoulder.

On tramped the Legion.

Before long, almost the whole weight of the Grasshopper's body was on Rupert's right arm and John Bull's left shoulder.

"Stick to it, my son," said the latter from time to time, "we are sure to stop at the fifty-kilometre stone."

The Belgian seemed to be semiconscious, and did not reply. His feet began to drag, and occasionally his two comrades bore his full weight for a few paces. Every few yards Feodor looked anxiously round. These four, in their anxiety for their weaker brother, forgot their own raw thighs, labouring lungs, inflamed eyes, numbed arms and agonising feet.

Just as the Colonel rode by, the Grasshopper's feet ceased to move, and dragged lifeless along the ground.

Rupert stumbled and the three fell in a heap, beneath the Colonel's eye.

"Sacré Baptême!" he swore--the oath he only used when a Legionary fell out on the march--"March or die, accursed pigs."

Rupert and John Bull staggered to their feet, but the Grasshopper lay apparently lifeless. The Colonel swore again, and shouted an order. The Grasshopper was dragged to the side of the road, and a baggage-cart drove up. A tent-pole was thrust through its sides and tied securely. To this pole the Belgian was lashed, the pole passing across the upper part of his back and under his arms, which were pulled over it and tied together. If he could keep his feet, well and good. If he could not, he would hang from the pole by his arms (as an athlete hangs from a parallel-bar in a gymnasium, before revolving round and round it).

On tramped the Legion.

Before long, the Grasshopper's feet dragged in the dust as he drooped inanimate, and then hung in the rope which lashed him to the pole.

At the fifty-fifth kilometre, thirty-five miles from Sidi-bel-Abbès, the command to halt was followed by the thrice-blessed God-sent order:

"*Campez!*"

Almost before the words, "*Formez les faisceaux*" were out of the Company-Commanders' mouths, the men had piled arms. Nor was the order "*Sac à terre*" obeyed in any grudging spirit. In an incredibly short space of time the jointed tent-poles and canvas had been removed from the knapsacks. Corporals of sections had stepped forward, holding the tent-poles above their heads, marking each Company's tent-line, and a city of small white tents had come into being on the face of the desert. A few minutes later, cooking-trenches had been dug, camp-fires lighted and water, containing meat and macaroni, put on to boil.

A busy and profitable hour followed for Madame la Cantinière, who, even as her cart stopped, had set out her folding tables, benches and bar for the sale of her Algerian wine. Her first customer was the great Luigi, who, thanks to Carmelita's money, could sit and drink while his employees did his work. The fly in the worthy man's ointment was the fact that his Italian dinner and Italian wine were thirty-five miles behind him at Carmelita's café. Like ordinary men, he must, to-night and for many a night to come, content himself with the monotonous and meagre fare of common Legionaries. However--better half a sofa than no bed; and he was easily prime favourite with Madame.... This would be an excellent chance for consolidating his position with her, winning her for his bride, and apprising Carmelita, from afar, of the fact that he was now respectably settled in life. Thus would a disagreeable scene be avoided and, on the return of the Battalion to Sidi-bel-Abbès, he would give the Café de la Légion a wide berth.... Could he perhaps *sell* his rights and goodwill in the *café* and Carmelita to some Legionary of means? One or two of his own *chambrée* seemed to have money--the Englishman; the Russians.... Better still, sell out to Malvin, Tou-tou, Meyer, or some other penniless toady and *make him pay a weekly percentage* of what he screwed out of Carmelita. Excellent! And if the scoundrel did not get him enough, he would supplant him with a more competent lessee.... Meanwhile, to storm Madame's experienced and undecided heart. Anyhow, if she wouldn't have Luigi she shouldn't have anyone else....

There was, that evening, exceeding little noise and movement, and "the stir and tread of armed camps." As soon as they had fed--and, in many cases, before they had fed--the soldiers lay on their blankets, their heads on their knapsacks and their overcoats over their bodies.

Scarcely, as it seemed to Rupert, had they closed their eyes, when it was time to rise and resume their weary march. At one o'clock in the morning, the Battalion fell in, and each man got his two litres of water and strict orders to keep one quarter of it for to-morrow's cooking purposes. If he contributed no water to the cooking-cauldron he got no cooked food.

On tramped the Legion.

Day after day, day after day, it marched, and, on the twelfth day from Sidi-bel-Abbès, had covered nearly three hundred and fifty miles. Well might the Legion be known in the Nineteenth Division as the *Cavalerie à pied*.

§2

Life for the Seventh Company of the First Battalion of the Legion in Aïnargoula was, as John Bull had promised Rupert, simply hell. Not even the relief of desert warfare had broken the cruel monotony of desert marches and life in desert stations--stations consisting of red-hot barracks, and the inevitable filthy and sordid *Village Négre*. Men lived--and sometimes died--in a state of unbearable irritation and morose savagery. Fights were frequent, suicide not infrequent, and murders not unknown. *Cafard* reigned supreme. The punishment-cells were overcrowded night and day, and abortive desertions occurred with extraordinary frequency.

The discontent and sense of wasted time, which had begun to oppress Rupert at Sidi-bel-Abbès, increased tenfold. To him and to the Bucking Bronco (who daily swore that he would desert that night, and tramp to Sidi-bel-Abbès to see Carmelita) John Bull proved a friend in need. Each afternoon, during that terrible time between eleven and three, when the incredible heat of the barrack-room made it impossible for any work to be done, and the men, by strict rule, were compelled to lie about on their cots, it was John Bull who found his friends something else to think about than their own sufferings and miseries.

A faithful coadjutor was 'Erb, who, with his mouth-organ and Jew's-harp, probably saved the reason, or the life, of more than one man. 'Erb seemed to feel the heat less than bigger men, and he would sit cross-legged upon his mattress, evoking tuneful strains from his beloved instruments when far stronger men could only lie panting like distressed dogs. Undoubtedly the three Englishmen and the American exercised a restraining and beneficial influence, inasmuch as they interfered as one man (following the lead of John Bull, the oldest soldier in the room) whenever a quarrel reached the point of blows, in their presence.... Under those conditions of life and temper a blow is commonly but the prelude to swift homicide.

One terrible afternoon, as the Legionaries lay on their beds, almost naked, in that stinking oven, the suddenness of these tragedies was manifested. It was too hot to play *bloquette* or *foutrou*, too hot to sing, too hot to smoke, too hot to do anything, and the hot bed positively burnt one's bare back. The Bucking Bronco lay gasping, his huge chest rising and falling with painful rapidity. John Bull was showing Rupert a wonderfully and beautifully Japanese-tattooed serpent which wound twice round his wrist and ran up the inner side of his white forearm, its head and expanded hood filling the hollow of his elbow. Rupert, who would have liked to copy it, was wondering how its brilliant colours had been achieved and had remained undimmed for over thirty-five years, as John Bull said was the case, it having been done at Nagasaki when he was a midshipman on the *Narcissus*. It was too hot even for 'Erb to make music and he lay fanning himself with an ancient copy of the *Echo d'Oran*. It was too hot to sleep, save in one or two cases, and these men groaned, moaned and rolled their heads as they snored. It was too hot to quarrel--almost. But not quite. Suddenly the swift *zweeep* of a bayonet being snatched from its steel scabbard hissed through the room, and all eyes turned to where Legionary Franz Josef Meyer flashed his bayonet from his sheath and, almost in the same movement, drove it up through the throat of the Greek, Dimitropoulos, and into his brain.

"Take that, you scum of the Levant," he said, and then stared, wide-eyed and open-mouthed, at his handiwork. There had been bad blood between the men for some time, and for days the Austrian had accused the Greek of stealing a piece of his wax. Some taunt of the dead man had completed the work of *le cafard*....

That night Meyer escaped from the cells--and his body, three days later, was delivered up in return for the twenty-five francs paid for a live or dead deserter. It would perhaps be more accurate to say that parts of his body were brought in--sufficient, at any rate, for identification.

He had fallen into the hands of the Arabs.

To give the Arabs their due, however, they saved the situation. Just when Legionary John Bull had begun to give up hope, and nightly to dread what the morrow might bring forth for his friends and himself, the Arabs attacked the post. The strain on the over-stretched cord was released and men who, in another day, would have been temporarily or permanently raving madmen, were saved.

The attack was easily beaten off and without loss to the Legionaries, firing from loopholes and behind stone walls.

On the morrow, a reconnaissance toward the nearest oasis discovered their camp and, on the next day, a tiny punitive column set forth from Aïnargoula--the Legionaries as happy, to use Rupert's too appropriate simile, as sand-boys. Like everybody else, he was in the highest spirits. Gone was the dark shadow of *le cafard* and the feeling that, unless something happened, he would become a homicidal maniac and run amuck.

Here was the "real thing." Here was that for which he had been so long and so drastically trained--desert warfare. He thrilled from head to foot with excitement, and wondered whether the day would bring forth one of the famous and terrible Arab cavalry charges, and whether he would have his first experience of taking part in the mad and fearful joy of a bayonet charge. Anyhow, there was a chance of either or both.

The Company marched on at its quickest, alternating five minutes of swift marching with five minutes of the *pas gymnastique*, the long, loping stride which is the "double" of the Legion.

Far ahead marched a small advance-guard; behind followed a rear-guard, and, well out on either side, marched the flankers. Where a sandy ridge ran parallel with the course of the Company, the flankers advanced along the crest of it, that they might watch the country which lay beyond. This did not avail them much, for, invariably, such a ridge was paralleled by a similar one at no great distance. To have rendered the little Company absolutely secure against sudden surprise-attack on either flank, would have necessitated sending out the majority of the force for miles on either side. Rupert, ever keen and deeply interested in military matters, talked of this with John Bull, who agreed with him that, considerable as the danger of such an attack was, it could not be eliminated.

"Anyhow," concluded he, "we generally get something like at least five hundred yards' margin and if the Arabs can cut us up while we have that--they deserve to. Still, it's tricky country I admit, with all these *wadis* and folds in the ground, as well as rocks and ridges."

On marched the Company, and reached an area of rolling sand-hills, and loose heavy sand under foot.

The day grew terribly hot and the going terribly heavy. As usual, all pretence and semblance of smart marching had been abandoned, and the men marched in whatever posture, attitude or style seemed to them best....

...It came with the suddenness of a thunderclap on a fine day, at a moment when practically everything but the miseries of marching through loose sand in the hottest part of one of the hottest days of the year had faded from the minds of the straining, labouring men.

A sudden shout, followed by the firing of half a dozen shots, brought the column automatically to a halt and drew all eyes to the right.

From a wide shallow *wadi*, or a fold in the ground, among the sand-hills a few hundred yards away, an avalanche of *haik* and *djellab*-clad men on swift horses suddenly materialised and swept down like a whirlwind on the little force. Behind them, followed a far bigger mass of camel-riders howling "*Ul-Ul-Ullah-Akbar!*" as they came. Almost before the column had halted, a couple of barks from Lieutenant Roberte turned the Company to the right in two ranks, the front rank kneeling, the rear rank standing close up behind it, with bayonets fixed and magazines charged...Having fired their warning shots, the flankers were running for their lives to join the main body. The Company watched and waited in grave silence. It was Lieutenant Roberte's intention that, when the Arabs broke and fled before the Company's withering blast of lead, they should leave the maximum number of "souvenirs" behind them. His was the courage and nerve that is tempered and enhanced by imperturbable coolness. He would let the charging foe gallop to the very margin of safety for his Legionaries. To turn them back at fifty yards would be much more profitable than to do it at five hundred.

Trembling with excitement and the thrilling desire for violent action, Rupert knelt between John Bull and the Bucking Bronco, scarcely able to await the orders to fire and charge. Before any order came he saw a sight that for a moment sickened and shook him, a sight which remained before his eyes for many days. Corporal Auguste Gilles, who was commanding the flankers, either too weary or too ill to continue his sprint for comparative safety, turned and faced the thundering rush of the oncoming Arab *harka*, close behind him. Kneeling by a prickly pear or cactus bush he threw up his rifle and emptied his magazine into the swiftly rushing ranks that were almost upon him. As he fired his last shot, an Arab, riding ahead of the rest, lowered his lance and, with a cry of "*Kelb ibn kelb,*"[58] bent over towards him. Springing to his feet the Corporal gamely charged with his bayonet. There can be only one end to such a combat when the horseman knows his weapon. The Corporal was sent flying into the cactus, impaled upon the Arab's lance, and, as it was withdrawn as the horseman swept by, the horrified Rupert saw his comrade stagger to his feet and totter forward--tethered to the cactus by his own entrails. Happily, a second later, the sweep of an Arab *flissa* almost severed his head from his shoulders....

The Company stood firm and silent as a rock, the shining bayonets still and level. Just as it seemed to Rupert that it must be swept away and every man share the fate of that mangled lump of clay in front (for there is no more nerve-shaking spectacle than cavalry charging down upon you like a living avalanche or flood) one word rang out from Lieutenant Roberte.

When the crashing rattle (like mingled, tearing thunder and the wild hammer of hail upon a corrugated iron roof), ceased as magazines were emptied almost simultaneously, the Arabs were in flight at top speed, leaving two-thirds of their number on the plain; and upon the fleeing *harka* the Company made very pretty shooting--for the Legion shoots as well as it marches.

When the "Cease Fire" whistle had blown, Rupert remarked to John Bull--

"No chance for a bayonet charge, then?" to which the old soldier replied--

"No, my son, that is a pleasure to which the Arab does not treat us, unless we surprise his sleeping *douar* at dawn...."

The Arabs having disappeared beyond the horizon, the Company camped and bivouacked on the battlefield, resuming its march at midnight. As Lieutenant Roberte feared and expected, the oasis which was surrounded and attacked at dawn, was found to be empty.

The Company marched back to Aïnargoula and, a few days later, returned to Sidi-bel-Abbès.

Chapter VII
The Sheep in Wolf's Clothing

Légionnaire John Bull sat on the edge of his cot at the hour of *astiquage*. Though his body was in the *chambrée* of the Seventh Company, his mind, as usual, was in England, and his thoughts, as usual, played around the woman whom he knew as Marguerite, and the world as Lady Huntingten.

What *could* he do next year when his third and last period of Legion service expired? Where could he possibly hide in such inviolable anonymity that there was no possible chance of any rumour arising that the dead Sir Montague Merline was in the land of the living? ... How had it happened that he had survived the wounds and disease that he had suffered in Tonkin, Madagascar, Dahomey, and the Sahara--the stake-trap pit into which he had fallen at Nha-Nam--the bullet in his neck from the Malagasy rifle--the hack from the *coupe-coupe* which had split his collar-bone in that ghastly West African jungle--the lance-thrust that had torn his arm from elbow to shoulder at Elsefra?

It was an absolute and undeniable fact that the man who desired to die in battle could never do it; while he who had everything to live for, was among the first to fall. If they went South again to-morrow and were cut up in a sudden Arab *razzia*, he would be the sole survivor. But if a letter arrived on the previous day, stating that Lord Huntingten was dead leaving no children, and that Lady Huntingten had just heard of his survival and longed for his return--would he survive that fight? Most certainly not.

What to do at the end of the fifteenth year of his service? His face had been far too well known among the class of people who passed through Marseilles to India and elsewhere--who winter on the Riviera, who golf at Biarritz, who recuperate at Vichy or Aix, who go to Paris in the Spring; and who, in short, are to be found in various parts of France at various times of the year--for him to dream of using the Legion's free pass to any part of France. The risk might be infinitesimal, but it existed, and he would run no risk of ruining Marguerite's life, after more than twenty-five years.

She must be over forty-five now.... Had time dealt kindly with her? Was she as beautiful as ever? Sure to be. Marguerite was of the type that would ripen, mature, and improve until well on into middle life. Who was the eminent man who said that a woman was not interesting until she was forty?...

What would he not give for a sight of Marguerite? It would be easy enough, next year. Only next year--and it was a thousand to one, a million to one, against anyone recognising him if he were well disguised and thoroughly careful. Just one sight of Marguerite--after more than twenty-five years! Had he not made sacrifices enough? Might he not take *that* much reward for half a lifetime of life in death--a lifetime which his body dragged wretchedly and wearily along among the dregs of the earth, while his mind haunted the home of his wife, a home in which another man was lord and master. Was it much to ask--one glimpse of his wife after twenty-seven years of renunciation?

"Miserable, selfish cur!" he murmured aloud as he melted a piece of wax in the flame of a match. "You would risk the happiness of your wife, your old friend, and their children--all absolutely innocent of wrong--for the sake of a minute's self-indulgence.... Be ashamed of yourself, you whining weakling...."

It had become a habit of Légionnaire John Bull to talk to himself aloud, when alone--a habit he endeavoured to check as he had recently, on more than one occasion, found himself talking aloud in the company of others.

Having finished the polishing of his leather-work, he took his Lebel rifle from the rack and commenced to clean it. As he threw open the chamber, he paused, the bolt in his right hand, the rifle balanced in his left. Someone was running with great speed along the corridor toward the room. What was up? Was it a case of *Faites le sac*? Would the head of an excited and delighted Legionary be thrust in at the door with a yell of--"*Aux armes! Faites le sac*"?

The door burst open and in rushed Mikhail Kyrilovitch, bare-headed, coatless, with staring eyes and blanched cheeks.

"Save me, save me, Monsieur," he shrieked, rushing towards the old Legionary. "Save me--*I am a woman....*"

"Good God!" ejaculated Legionary John Bull, involuntarily glancing from the face to the flat chest of the speaker.

"I am a girl," sobbed the *soi-disant* Mikhail...."I am a girl....And that loathsome beast Luigi Rivoli has found me out....He's coming....He chased me....What shall I do? What *shall* I do? Poor Feodor...."

As Légionnaire Luigi Rivoli entered the room, panting slightly with his unwonted exertions, the girl crouched behind John Bull, her face in her hands, her body shaken by deep sobs. It had all happened so quickly that John Bull found himself standing with his gun balanced, still in the attitude into which he had frozen on hearing the running feet without.

So it had come, had it--and he was to try conclusions with Luigi Rivoli at last? Well, it should be no inconclusive rough-and-tumble. Perhaps this was the solution of his problem, and might settle, once and for all, the question of his future?

"Ho-ho! Ho-ho!" roared the Neapolitan, "she's your girl, is she, you *aristocratico Inglese*? Ho-ho! You are *faisant Suisse* are you? Ho-ho! Your own private girl in the very *chambrée*! Corpo di Bacco! You shall learn the penalty for breaking the Legion's first law of share-and-share-alike. Get out of my way, *cane Inglese*."

John Bull closed the breech of his rifle, and pointed the weapon at Rivoli's broad breast.

"Stand back," he said quietly. "Stand back, you foul-mouthed scum of Naples, or I'll blow your dirty little soul out of your greasy carcase." He raised his voice slightly. "Stand back, you dog, do you hear?" he added, advancing slightly towards his opponent.

Luigi Rivoli gave ground. The rifle might be loaded. You never knew with these cursed, quiet Northerners, with their cold, pale eyes....The rifle might be loaded....Rivoli was well aware that every Legionary makes it his business to steal a cartridge sooner or later, and keeps it by him for emergencies, be they of suicide, murder, self-defence, or desertion....The Englishman had been standing in the attitude of one who loads a rifle at the moment of his entrance. Perhaps his girl had told him of the discovery and assault, and he had been loading the rifle to avenge her.

"Listen to me, Luigi Rivoli," said John Bull, still holding the rifle within a foot of the Italian's breast. "Listen, and I'll tell you what you are. Then I will tell the Section what you are, when they come in....Then I will tell the whole Company....Then I will stand on a table in the Canteen and shout it, night after night....This is what you are. You are a coward. A *coward*, d'you hear?--a miserable, shrinking, frightened coward, who dare not fight...."

"Fight! *Iddio*! *Fight*! Put down that rifle and I'll tear you limb from limb. Come down into the square and I will break your back. Come down now--and fight for the girl."

"...A trembling, frightened coward who dare not fight, and who calls punching, and hugging and kicking 'fighting.' I challenge you to fight, Luigi Rivoli, with rifles--at one hundred yards and no cover; or with revolvers, at ten paces; or with swords of any sort or kind--if it's only sword-bayonets. Will you fight, or will you be known as *Rivoli the Coward* throughout both Battalions of the Legion?"

Rivoli half-crouched for a spring, and straightway the rifle sprang to the Englishman's shoulder, as his eyes blazed and his fingers fell round the trigger. Rivoli recoiled.

"I don't want to shoot you, unarmed, Coward," he said quietly. "I am going to shoot you, or stab you, or slash you, in fair fight--or else you shall kneel and be christened *Rivoli the Coward* on the barrack square....I've had enough of you, and so has everybody--unless it's your gang of pimps....Now go. Go on--get out....Go on--before I lose patience. Clear out--and make up your mind whether you will fight or be christened."

"Oh, I'll fight you--you mangy old cur. You are brave enough with a loaded rifle, eh? Mother of Christ! I'll send you where the birds won't trouble you....Shoot me in the back as I go, Brave

Man with a Gun"–and Luigi Rivoli departed, in a state of horrid doubt and perturbation....This cursed Englishman meant what he said....

Legionary John Bull lowered his rifle with a laugh, and became aware of the fact that the Russian girl was hugging his leg in a way which would have effectually hampered him in the event of a struggle, and which made him feel supremely ridiculous.

"Get up, *petite*," he said bending over her, as she lay moaning and weeping. "It's all right--he's gone. He won't trouble you again, for I am going to kill him. Come and lie on your bed and tell me all about it....We must make up our minds as to what will be the best thing to do.... Rivoli will tell everybody."

He helped the girl to her feet, partly led and partly carried her to her bed, and laid her on it.

Holding his lean brown hand between her little ones, in a voice broken and choked with sobs, she told him something of her story--a sad little story all too common.

The listener gathered that the two were children of a prominent revolutionary who had disappeared into Siberia, after what they considered a travesty of a trial. They had been students at the University of Moscow, and had followed in their father's political footsteps from the age of sixteen. Their youth and inexperience, their fanatical enthusiasm, and their unselfish courage, had, in a few years, brought them to a point at which they must choose between death or the horrors of prison and Siberia on the one hand, and immediate flight, and most complete and utter evanishment on the other. When his beloved twin sister had been chosen by the Society as an "instrument," Feodor's heart had failed him. He had disobeyed the orders of the Central Committee; he had coerced the girl; he had made disclosures.

They had escaped to Paris. Before long it had been a question as to whether they were in more imminent and terrible danger from the secret agents of the Russian police or from those of the Nihilists. The sight of the notice, *"Bureau de recruitment. Engagements volontaires,"* over the door of a dirty little house in the Rue St. Dominique had suggested the Légion Etrangère, and a possible means of escape and five years' safety.

But the Medical Examination?...

Accompanied by a fellow-fugitive who was on his way to America, Feodor had gone to the Bureau and they had enlisted, passed the doctor, and received railway-passes to Marseilles, made out in the names of Feodor and Mikhail Kyrilovitch; sustenance money; and orders to proceed by the night train from the Gare de Lyons and report at Fort St. Jean in the morning, if not met at the station by a Sergeant of the Legion. Their compatriot had handed his travelling warrant to the girl (dressed in a suit of Feodor's) ind had seen the twins off at the Gare de Lyons with his blessing....

Monsieur Jean Boule knew the rest, and but for this hateful, bestial Luigi Rivoli, all might have been well, for she was very strong, and had meant to be very brave. Now, what should she do; what *should* she do? ...And what would poor Feodor say when he came in from corvée and found that she had let herself get caught like this at last? ...What could they do?

And indeed, Sir Montague Merline did not know what a lady could do when discovered in a *chambrée* of a *caserne* of the French Foreign Legion in Sidi-bel-Abbès. He did not know in the least. There was first the attitude of the authorities to consider, and then that of the men. Would a Court Martial hold that, having behaved as a man, she should be treated as one, and kept to her bargain, or sent to join the Zephyrs? Would they imprison her for fraud? Would they repatriate her? Would they communicate with the Russian police? Or would they just fling her out of the barrack-gate and let her go? There was probably no precedent, whatever, to go upon.

And supposing the matter were hushed up in the *chambrée*, and the authorities never knew-- would life be livable for the girl? Could he, and Rupert, the Bucking Bronco, Herbert Higgins, Feodor, and perhaps one or two of the more decent foreigners, such as Hans Djoolte, and old Tant-de-Soif, ensure her a decent life, free from molestation and annoyance? No, it couldn't be done. Life would be rendered utterly impossible for her by gross animals of the type of Rivoli, Malvin, the *Apache*, Hirsch, Bauer, Borges, and the rest of Rivoli's sycophants. It was sufficiently ghastly, and almost unthinkable, to imagine a woman in that sink when nobody dreamed she was anything but what she seemed. How could one contemplate a woman, who was *known* to be a woman, living her life, waking and sleeping, in such a situation? The more devotedly her bodyguard shielded and protected her, the more venomously determined would the others be to annoy, insult and injure her in a thousand different ways. It would be insupportable, impossible....But of course it could not be kept from the authorities for a week. What was to be done?

As he did his utmost to soothe the weeping girl, clumsily patting her back, stroking her hands, and murmuring words of comfort and promises of protection, Merline longed for the arrival of Rupert. He wanted to take counsel with another English gentleman as to the best thing to be done for this unfortunate woman. He dared not leave her weeping there alone. Anybody might enter at any moment. Rivoli might return with the choicest scoundrels of his gang....Why did not the Bucking Bronco turn up? When he and Rupert arrived there would be an accession of brawn and of brains that would be truly welcome.

Curiously enough, Sir Montague Merline's insular Englishness had survived fourteen years of life in a cosmopolitan society, speaking a foreign tongue in a foreign land, with such indestructible sturdiness that it was upon the Anglo-Saxon party that he mentally relied in this strait. He had absolutely forgotten that it was the girl's own brother who was her natural protector, and upon whom lay the onus of discovering the solution of this insoluble problem and extricating the girl from her terrible position.

What could he do? It was all very well to say that the three Englishmen and the American would protect her, that night, by forming a sentry-group and watching in turn--but how long could that go on? It would be all over the barracks to-morrow, and known to the authorities a few hours later. Oh, if he could only do her up in a parcel and post her to Marguerite with just a line, *"Please take care of this poor girl.–Monty."* Marguerite would keep her safe enough....But thinking nonsense wasn't helping. He would load his rifle in earnest, and settle scores with Luigi Rivoli, once and for all, if he returned with a gang to back him. Incidentally, that would settle his own fate, for it would mean a Court Martial at Oran followed by a firing-party, or penal servitude in the Zephyrs, and, at his age, that would only be a slower death.

All very well for him and Rivoli, but what of the girl? ...What ghastly danger it must have been that drove them to such a dreadful expedient. Truly the Legion was a net for queer fish. Poor, plucky little soul, what could he do for her?

Never since he wore the two stars[59] of a British Captain had he longed, as he did at that moment, for power and authority. If only he were a Captain again, Captain of the Seventh Company, the girl should go straight to his wife, or some other woman. Suddenly he rose to his feet, his face illuminated by the brilliance of the idea which had suddenly entered his mind.

"Carmelita!" he almost shouted to the empty room. He bent over the crying girl again, and shook her gently by the shoulder.

"I have it, little one," he said. "Thank God! Yes--it's a chance. I believe I have a plan. Carmelita! Let's get out of this at once, straight to the Café de la Legion. Carmelita has a heart of gold...."

The girl half sat up. "She may be a kind girl--but she's Luigi Rivoli's mistress," she said. "She would do anything he ordered."

"Carmelita considers herself Rivoli's wife," replied the Englishman, "and so she would be, if he were not the biggest blackguard unhung. Very well, he can hardly go to the woman who is practically his wife and say, 'Hand over the woman you are hiding.'"

"When a woman loves a man she obeys him," said the girl, and added with innocent naïveté, "And I will obey you, Monsieur Jean Boule....Anyhow, it is a hope--in a position which is hopeless."

"Get into walking-out kit quickly," urged the old soldier, "and see the Sergeant of the Guard has no excuse for turning you back. The sooner we're away the better....I wish Rupert and the

Bronco would roll up....If you can get to Carmelita's unseen, and change back into a girl, you could either hide with Carmelita for a time, or simply desert in feminine apparel."

"And Feodor?" asked the Russian. "Will they shoot him? I can't leave..."

"Bother Feodor," was the quick reply. "One soldier is not responsible because another deserts. Let's get you safe to Carmelita's, and then I'll find Feodor and tell him all about it."

Hiram Cyrus Milton, entering the room bare-footed and without noise, was not a little surprised to behold a young soldier fling his arms about the neck of the eminently staid and respectable Legionary John Bull, with a cry of--

"Oh, may God reward you, kind good Monsieur."

"Strike me blue and balmy," ejaculated the Bucking Bronco. "Ain't these gosh-dinged furriners a bunch o' boobs? Say, John, air yew his long-lost che-ild? It's a cinch. Where's that dod-gasted boy 'Erb fer slow music on the jewzarp? ...Or is the lalapaloozer only a-smellin' the roses on yure damask cheek?"

"Change quickly, *petite*," said John Bull to the girl as he pushed her from him, and turned to the American.

"Come here, Buck," said he, taking the big man's arm and leading him to the window.

"Don't say as haow yure sins hev' come home to roost, John? Did yew reckernise the puling infant by the di'mond coronite on the locket, or by the strawberry-mark in the middle of its back? Or was his name wrote on the tail of his little shirt? Put me next to it, John. Make me wise to the secret mystery of this 'ere drarmer."

The Bucking Bronco was getting more than a little jealous.

"I will, if you will give me a chance," replied John Bull curtly. "Buck, that boy's a girl. Rivoli has found her out and acted as you might expect. I suppose he spotted her in the wash-house or somewhere. She rushed to me for protection, and the game's up. I am going to take her to Carmelita."

The big American stared at his friend with open mouth.

"Yew git me jingled, John," he said slowly. "Thet little looker a *gal*? Is this a story made out of whole cloth,[60] John?"

"Get hold of it, Buck, quickly," was the reply. "The two Russians are political refugees. Their number was up, in Russia, and they bolted to Paris. Same in Paris--and they made a dash for here. Out of the frying-pan into the fire. This one's a girl. Luigi Rivoli knows, and it will be all over the barracks before to-night. She rushed straight to me, and I am going to see her through. If you can think of anything better than taking her to Carmelita, say so."

"I'll swipe the head off'n Mister Lousy Loojey Rivoli," growled the American. "God smite me ef I don't. Thet's torn it, thet has....The damned yaller-dog Dago....Thet puts the lid on Mister Loojey Rivoli, thet does."

"*I'm* going to deal with Rivoli, Buck," said John Bull.

"He'd crush yew with a b'ar's hug, sonny; he'd bust in yure ribs, an' break yure back, an' then chuck yew down and dance on yew."

"He won't get the chance, Buck; it's not going to be a gutter-scrap. When he chased the girl in here I challenged him to fight with bullet or steel, and told him I'd brand him all over the shop till he was known as 'Rivoli the Coward,' or fought a fair and square duel....Let's get the girl out of this, and then we'll put Master Luigi Rivoli in his place once and for all."

"Shake!" said the Bucking Bronco, extending a huge hand.

"Seen Rupert lately?" asked the Englishman.

"Yep," replied the other. "He's a-settin' on end a-rubberin' at his pants in the lavabo."

"Good! Go and fetch him quick, Buck."

The American sped from the room without glancing at the girl, returning a minute or two later with Rupert. The two men hurried to their respective cots and swiftly changed from fatigue-dress into blue and red.

"If Carmelita turns us down, let's all three desert and take the girl with us," said Rupert to John Bull. "I have plenty of money to buy mufti, disguises, and railway tickets. She would go as a woman of course. We could be a party of tourists. Yes, that's it, English tourists. Old Mendoza would fit us out--at a price."

"Thanks," was the reply. "We'll get her out somehow....She'd stand a far better chance alone though, probably. If suspicion fell on one of us they'd arrest the lot."

"Say," put in the American. "Ef she can do the boy stunt, I reckon as haow her brother oughter be able ter do the gal stunt ekally well. Ef Carmelita takes her in, and fits her out with two of everything, her brother could skedaddle and jine her, and put on the remainder of the two-of-everything; then they ups and goes on pump as the Twin Sisters Golightly, a-tourin' of the Crowned Heads of Yurrup, otherwise, as The Twin Roosian Bally-Gals Skiporfski...."

"Smart idea," agreed Rupert. "I hope Carmelita takes her in. What the devil shall we do with her if she won't? She can't very well spend the night here after Luigi has put it about.... And what's her position with regard to the authorities? Is it a case of Court Martial or toss for her in the Officers' Mess, or what?"

"Don't know, I'm sure. Haven't the faintest idea," replied John Bull. "If only Carmelita turns up trumps...."

"Seenyoreena Carmelita is the whitest little woman as ever lived," growled the American. "She's a blowed-in-the-glass heart-o'-gold. Yew can put yure shirt on Carmelita....Yew know what I mean--yure bottom dollar....Ef it wasn't fer that filthy Eye-talian sarpint, she'd jump at the chance of giving this Roosian gal her last crust....I don't care John whether you shoot him up or nit. I'm gwine ter slug him till Hell pops. Let him fight his dirtiest an' damnedest--I'll see him and raise him every time, the double-dealin' gorilla...."

"I am ready, Monsieur," said the girl Olga to John Bull. "But I do not want you, Monsieur, nor these other gentlemen, to make trouble for yourselves on my account....I have brought this on myself, and there is no reason why you..."

"Oh, shucks! Come on, little gal," broke in the Bucking Bronco. "We'll see yew through. We ain't Loojeys...."

"Of course, we will. We shall be only too delighted," agreed Rupert. "Don't you worry."

"Pull yourself together and swagger all you can," advised John Bull. "It might ruin everything if the Sergeant of the Guard took it into his head to turn you back. I wonder if we had better go through in a gang, or let you go first? If we are all together there is less likelihood of excessive scrutiny of any one of us, but on the other hand it may be remembered that you were last seen with us three, and that might hamper our future usefulness....Just as well Feodor isn't here.... Tell you what, you and I will go out together, and I'll use my wits to divert attention from you if we are stopped. The others can come a few minutes later, or as soon as someone else has passed."

"That's it," agreed Rupert; "come on."

With beating hearts, the old soldier and the young girl approached the little side door by the huge barrack-gates. Close by it stood the Sergeant of the Guard. Their anxiety increased as they realised that it was none other than Sergeant Legros, one of the most officious, domineering and brutal of the Legion's N.C.O.'s. Luck was against them. He would take a positive delight in standing by that door the whole evening and in turning back every single man whose appearance gave him the slightest opportunity for fault-finding, as well as a good many whose appearance did not.

As they drew near and saluted smartly, the little piggish eyes of Sergeant Legros took in every detail of their uniform. The girl felt the blood draining from her cheeks. What if they had made a mistake? What if red trousers and blue tunic should be wrong, and the *ordre du jour* should be white trousers and blue tunic or capote? What if she had a button undone or her bayonet on the wrong side? What if Sergeant Legros should see, or imagine a speck upon her tunic? ...Had she been under his evil gaze for hours? Was the side of the Guard House miles in length? ...Thank God, they were through the gate and free. Free for the moment, and if the good God were merciful she was free for ever from the horrors and fears of that terrible place. Could anything worse befall her? Yes, there were worse places for a girl than a barrack-room of the French Foreign Legion. There was a Russian prison--there was the dark prison-van and warder--there was the journey to Siberia--there was Siberia itself. Yes, there were worse places than that she had just left--until her secret was discovered. A thousand times worse. And she thought of her friend, that poor girl who had been less fortunate than she. Poor, poor Marie! Would she herself be sent back to Russia to share Marie's fate, if these brave Englishmen and Carmelita failed to save her? What would become of Feodor? ...Did this noble Englishman, with the gentle face, love this girl Carmelita? ...Might not Carmelita's house be a very trap if the loathsome Italian brute owned its owner?...

"Let's stroll slowly now, my dear," said John Bull, "and let the others overtake us. The more the merrier, if we should run into Rivoli and his gang, or if he is already at Carmelita's. I don't think he will be. I fancy he puts in the first part of his evening with Madame la Cantinière, and goes down to Carmelita's later for his dinner....If he should be there I don't quite see what line he can take in front of Carmelita. He could hardly molest you in front of the woman whom he pretends he is going to marry, and I don't see on what grounds he could raise any objection to her befriending you....It's a deuced awkward position--for the fact that I intend to kill Rivoli, if I can, hardly gives me a claim on Carmelita. She loves the very ground the brute treads on, you know, and it would take me, or anybody else, a precious long time to persuade her that the man who rid the world of Luigi Rivoli would be her very best friend....He's the most noxious and poisonous reptile I have ever come across, and I believe she is one of the best of good little women....It is a hole we're in. We've got to see Carmelita swindled and then jilted and broken-hearted; or we've got to bring the blackest grief upon her by saving her from Rivoli."

"Do *you* love her too, Monsieur?" asked Olga.

"Good Heavens, no!" laughed the Englishman. "But I have a very great liking and regard for her, and so has my friend Rupert. It is poor old Buck who loves her, and I am really sorry for him. It's bad enough to love a woman and be unable to win her, but it must be awful to see her in the power of a man whom you know to be an utter blackguard....Queer thing, Life....I suppose there is some purpose in it....Here they come," he added, looking round.

"Who's gwine ter intervoo Carmelita, and put her wise to the sitooation?" asked the Bucking Bronco as he and Rupert joined the others. "Guess yew'd better, John. Yew know more Eye-talian and French than we do, an', what's more, Carmelita wouldn't think there was any '*harry-air ponsey*'–or is it '*double-intender*'–ef the young woman is interdooced, as sich, by yew."

"All right," replied John Bull. "I'll do my best--and we must all weigh in with our entreaties if I fail."

"Yew'll do it, John. I puts my shirt on Carmelita every time...."

Le Café de la Légion was swept and garnished, and Carmelita sat in her *sedia pieghevole*[61] behind her bar, awaiting her evening guests.

It was a sadder-looking, thinner, somewhat older-looking Carmelita than she who had welcomed Rupert and his fellow *bleus* on the occasion of their first visit to her *café*. Carmelita's little doubt had grown, and worry was bordering upon anxiety--for Luigi Rivoli was Carmelita's life, and Carmelita was not only a woman, but an Italian woman, and a Neapolitan at that. Far better than life she loved Luigi Rivoli, and only next to him did she love her own self-respect and virtue. As has been said before, Carmelita considered herself a married woman. Partly owing to her equivocal position, partly to an innate purity of mind, Carmelita had a present passion for "respectability" such as had never troubled her before.

And Luigi was causing her grief and anxiety, doubt and care, and fear. For long she had fought it off, and had stoutly refused to confess it even to herself, but day by day and night by night, the persistent attack had worn down her defences of Hope and Faith until at length she stood face to face with the relentless and insidious assailant and recognised it for what it was--Fear. It had come to that, and Carmelita now frankly admitted to herself that she had fears for the faith, honesty and love of the man whom she regarded as her husband and knew to be the father of the so hoped-for *bambino*....

Could it be possible that the man for whom she had lived, and for whom she would at any time have died, her own Luigi, who, but for her, would be in a Marseilles graveyard, her own husband--was laying siege to fat and ugly Madame la Cantinière, because her business was a more profitable one than Carmelita's? It could not be. Men were not devils. Men did not repay women like that. Not even ordinary men, far less her Luigi. Of course not--and besides, there was the Great Secret.

For the thousandth time Carmelita found reassurance, comfort and cheer in the thought of the Great Secret, and its inevitable effect upon Luigi when he knew it. What would he say when he realised that there might be another Luigi Rivoli, for, of course, it would be a boy--a boy who would grow up another giant among men, another Samson, another Hercules, another winner of a World's Championship.

What would he do in the transports of his joy? How his face would shine! How heartily he would agree with her when she pointed out that it would be as well for them to marry now before the *bambino* came. No more procrastination now. What a wedding it should be, and what a feast they would give the brave *soldati*! Il Signor Jean Boule should have the seat of honour, and the Signor Americano should come, and Signor Rupert, and Signor 'Erbiggin, and the poor Grasshopper, and the two Russi (ah! what of that Russian girl, what would be her fate? It was wonderful how she kept up the deception. Poor, poor little soul, what a life--the constant fear, the watchfulness and anxiety. Fancy eating and drinking, walking, talking and working, dressing and undressing, waking and sleeping among those men--some of them such dreadful men). Yes, it should be a wedding to remember, without stint of food or drink--*un pranzo di tre portate* with *i maccheroni* and *la frittate d'uova* and the best of *couscous*, and there should be *vino Italiano*–they would welcome a change from the eternal *vino Algerino*....

Four Legionaries entered, and Carmelita rose with a smile to greet them. There was no one she would sooner see than Il Signor Jean Boule and his friends--since it was not Luigi who entered.

"*Che cosa posso offrirve?*" she asked. (Although Carmelita spoke Legion French fluently one noticed that she always welcomed one in Italian, and always counted in that language.)

"I want a quiet talk with you, carissima Carmelita," said John Bull. "We are in great trouble, and we want your help."

"I am glad," replied Carmelita. "Not glad that you are in trouble, but glad you have come to me."

"It is about Mikhail Kyrilovitch," said the Englishman.

"I thought it was," said Carmelita.

"Don't think me mad, Carmelita," continued John Bull, "but listen. Mikhail Kyrilovitch is a *girl*."

"Don't think me mad, Signor Jean Boule," mimicked Carmelita, "but listen. I have known Mikhail Kyrilovitch was a girl from the first evening that she came here."

The Englishman's blue eyes opened widely in surprise, as he stared at the girl. "How?" he asked.

"Oh, in a dozen ways," laughed Carmelita. "Hands, voice, manner. I stroked her cheek, it was as soft as my own, while her twin brother's was like sand-paper. When she went to catch a biscuit she made a 'lap,' as one does who wears a skirt, instead of bringing her knees together as a man does....And what can I do for Mademoiselle Mikhail?"

"You can save her, Carmelita, from I don't know what dangers and horrors. She has been found out, and what her fate would be at the tender mercies of the authorities on the one hand, and of the men on the other, one does not like to think. The very least that could happen to her is to be turned into the streets of Sidi-bel-Abbès."

"Do the officers know yet?" asked Carmelita. "Who does know? Who found her out?"

"Luigi Rivoli found her out," replied John Bull.

"And sent her to me?" asked Carmelita. "I am glad he..."

"He did not send her to you," interrupted the Englishman gravely.

"What did he do?" asked Carmelita quickly.

"I will tell you what he did, Carmelita, as kindly as I can.... He forgot he was a soldier, Carmelita; he forgot he was an honest man; he forgot he was your--er--*fidanzato*, your *sposo*, Carmelita...."

Carmelita went very white.

"Tell me, Signor," she said quickly. "Did you have to protect this Russian wretch from Luigi?"

"I did," was the reply. "Why do you speak contemptuously of the girl? She is as innocent as--as innocent as you are, Carmelita."

"I hate her," hissed Carmelita...."Did Luigi kiss her? What happened? Did he...?"

The Englishman put his hand over Carmelita's little clenched fist as it lay on the bar.

"Listen, little one," he said. "You are one of the best, kindest and bravest women I have known. I am certain you are going to be worthy of yourself now. So is Rupert, so is Monsieur Bronco. He has been blaming us bitterly when we have even for a moment wondered whether you would save this girl. He is worth a thousand Rivolis, and loves you a thousand times better than Rivoli ever could. Don't disappoint him and us, Carmelita. Don't disappoint us *in yourself*, I mean.... What has the girl done that you should hate her?"

"Did Luigi kiss her?" again asked Carmelita.

"He did not," was the reply. "He behaved..."

"And he could not, of course, while she was with me, could he?" said Carmelita.

"Exactly," smiled the Englishman. "Take her in now, little woman, and lend her some clothes until we can get some things bought or made for her."

"Clothes cost francs, Signor Jean," was the practical reply of the girl, who had grown up in a hard school. "I can give her food and shelter, and I can lend her my things, but I have no francs for clothes."

"Rupert will find whatever is necessary for her clothes and board and lodging, and for her ticket too. She shan't be with you long, cara Carmelita, nor in Sidi-bel-Abbès."

Carmelita passed from behind the bar and went over to the table at which sat Rupert, the American, and the girl Olga. Putting her arm around the neck of the last, Carmelita kissed her on the cheek.

"Come, little one," she said. "Come to my bed and sleep. You shall be as safe as if in the Chapel of the Mother of God," and, as the girl burst into tears, led her away.

John Bull joined his friends as the two women disappeared through the door leading to Carmelita's room.

"Well, thank God for that," he said as he sat down, and wiped his forehead. "What's the next step?"

"Find the other little Roosian guy, an' put him wise to what's happened to sissy, I guess," replied the American.

"Yes," agreed Rupert. "It's up to him to carry on now, with any sort or kind of help that we can give him.... Where did he go after parade, I wonder?"

"The gal got copped for a wheel-barrer corvée--they was goin' scavengin' round the officers' houses and gardens I think--an' he took her place.... He'd be back by dark an' start washin' hisself," opined the American.

"Better get back at once then," said John Bull.

"I feel a most awful cad," he added.

"What on earth for?" asked Rupert.

"About Carmelita," was the reply. "I've got her help under false pretences. If I had told her that I was going to fight a serious duel with her precious Luigi, she'd never have taken that girl in. If I don't fight him now, he'll make my life utterly unlivable....I wish to God Carmelita could be brought to see him as he is and to understand that the moment the Canteen will have him, he is done with the Café.... I wish Madame la Cantinière would take him and settle the matter. Since it has got to come, the sooner the better. I should really enjoy my fight with him if he had turned Carmelita down, and she regarded me as her avenger instead of as the destroyer of her happiness."

"One wouldn't worry about Madame la Cantinière's feelings if one destroyed her young man or her latest husband, I suppose?" queried Rupert with a smile.

"Nope," replied the American. "Nit. Not a damn. Nary a worry. You could beat him up, or you could shoot him up, and lay your last red cent that Madam lar Canteenair would jest say, '*Mong Jew! C'est la Legion*' and look aroun' fer his doo and lorful successor....Let's vamoose, b'ys, an' rubber aroun' fer the other Roosian chechaquo."

The three Legionaries quitted le Café de la Légion and made their way back to their *caserne*.

"I'll look in the *chambrée*," said John Bull as they entered the barrack-square. "You go to the lavabo, Rupert, and you see if he is in the Canteen, Buck. Whoever finds him had better advise him to let Luigi Rivoli alone, and make his plans for going on pump. Tell him I think his best line would be to see Carmelita and arrange for him and his sister to get dresses alike, and clear out boldly by train to Oran, as girls. After that, they know their own business best, but I should recommend England as about the safest place for them."

"By Jove! I could give him a letter to my mother," put in Rupert. "Good idea. My people would love to help them--especially as they could tell them all about me."

"Gee-whiz! That's a brainy notion," agreed the Bucking Bronco. "Let 'em skin out and make tracks for yure Old-Folk-at-Home. It's a cinch."

Legionary John Bull found Legionary Feodor Kyrilovitch sitting on his cot polishing "Rosalie," as the soldier of France terms his bayonet. Several other Legionaries were engaged in *astiquage* and accoutrement cleaning. For the thousandth time, the English gentleman realised that one of the most irksome and maddening of the hardships and disabilities of the common soldier's life is its utter lack of privacy.

"Bonsoir, cher Boule," remarked Feodor Kyrilovitch, looking up as the English approached. "Have you seen my brother? He appears to have come in and changed and gone out without me."

Evidently the boy was anxious.

"Your brother is at Carmelita's," replied John Bull, and added: "Come over to my bed and sit beside me with your back to the room. I want to speak to you."

"Don't be alarmed," he continued as they seated themselves. "Your brother is absolutely all right."

The Russian gazed anxiously at the kindly face of the man whom he had instinctively liked and trusted from the first.

"Your brother is quite all right," continued the Englishman, "but I am afraid you will have to change your plans."

"Change our plans, Monsieur Boule?"

"Yes," replied the older man, as he laid his hand on Feodor's knee with a reassuring smile. "You will have to change your plans, for Mikhail can be Mikhail no longer."

The Russian bowed his head upon his hands with a groan.

"My poor little Olusha," he whispered.

"Courage, mon brave," said John Bull, patting him on the back. "We have a plan for you. As soon as your sister was discovered, we took her to Carmelita, with whom she will be quite safe for a while. Our idea is that she and Carmelita make and buy women's clothes for both of you, and that you escape as sisters. Since she made such a splendid boy, you ought to be able to become a fairly convincing girl. Légionnaire Mikhail Kyrilovitch will be looked for as a man--probably in uniform. By the time the hue and cry is over, and he is forgotten, everything will be ready for both of you, then one night you slip into Carmelita's café and, next day, two café-chantant girls who have been visiting Carmelita, walk coolly to the station and take train for Oran.... Rivoli can't tell on them and still keep in with Carmelita. He'll have to help--or pretend to."

Feodor Kyrilovitch was himself again--a cool and level-headed conspirator, accustomed to weighing chances, taking risks and facing dangers.

"Thanks, mon ami," he said. "I believe I owe you my sister's salvation....There will be difficulties, and there are risks--but it is a plan."

"Seems fairly hopeful," replied the other. "Anyhow, we could think of nothing better."

"We might get to Oran," mused Feodor; "but where we can go from there, God knows. We daren't go to Paris again, and I doubt if we have a hundred and fifty roubles between us....And we dare not write to friends in Russia."

"We've thought of that too, my boy," interrupted the Englishman. "My friend Rupert has money in the Credit Lyonnais, here in the town. He says he will be only too delighted to lend you enough to get you to England, and write a letter for you to take to his people. He says his mother will welcome you with open arms as coming from him....From what he has said to me about her at different times, I imagine her to be one of the best--and the best of Englishwomen are the best of women, let me tell you."

"And the best of Englishmen are the best of men," replied Feodor, seizing the old Legionary's hand and kissing it fervently--to the latter gentleman's consternation and utter discomfort.

"Don't be an ass," he replied in English...."Clear out now, and go and have a talk with Carmelita. You can trust her absolutely. Give her what money you've got, and she'll poke around in the ghetto for clothes. She'll know lots of the Spanish Jew dealers and cheap *couturières*, if old Mendoza hasn't what she wants. Meanwhile, Rupert will draw some money from the *banque*."

The Russian rose to his feet.

"But how can I thank you, Monsieur? How can I repay Monsieur Rupert for his kindness?"

"Don't thank me, and repay Rupert by visiting his mother and waxing eloquent over his marvellous condition of health, happiness and prosperity. Tell her he is having a lovely time in a lovely place with lovely people."

"You joke, Monsieur, how *can* I repay you all?"

"Well, I'll tell you, my son--by getting your sister clear of this hell and safe into England."

The Russian struck himself violently on the forehead and turned away.

A minute later Rupert entered the *chambrée*.

"He's not in the lavabo," he announced.

"No, it's all right. I found him here. He has just gone down to Carmelita's....Let's go over to the Canteen, I want to meet the gentle Luigi Rivoli there."

On the stairs they encountered the Bucking Bronco, who was told that Feodor had been found and informed.

"Our Loojey's in the road-house," he announced, "layin' off ter Madam....I wish she'd deliver the goods ef she's gwine ter. Then we could git next our Loojey without raisin' hell with Carmelita."

"Is the Canteen fairly full?" asked John Bull.

"Some!" replied the Bucking Bronco.

"Then I'm going over to seek sorrow," said the other.

"Yure not goin' ter git fresh, an' slug the piker any, air yew, John?" enquired the American anxiously.

"No, Buck," was the reply. "I'm only going to make an interestin' announcement," and, turning to Rupert, he advised him not to identify himself with any proceedings which might ensue.

"You are hardly complimentary, Bull," commented Rupert resentfully....

As the three entered the Canteen, which was rapidly filling up, they caught sight of Rivoli lolling against the bar in his accustomed corner, and whispering confidentially to Madame, during her intervals of leisure. Pushing his way through the throng John Bull, closely followed by his two friends, approached the Neapolitan. His back was towards them. The American, whose face wore an ugly look, touched Rivoli with his foot.

"Makin' yure sweet self agreeable as usual, Loojey, my dear?" he enquired, and proceeded with the difficult task of making himself both sarcastic and intelligible in the French language. The Italian wheeled round with a scowl at the sound of the voice he hated.

John Bull stepped forward.

"I have come for your answer, Rivoli," he said quietly. "I wish to know when and with what weapons you would prefer to fight me. Personally, I don't care in the least what they are, so long as they're fatal."

A ring of interested listeners gathered round. The Neapolitan laughed contemptuously.

"Weapons!" he growled. "A *fico* for weapons. I'll twist your neck and break your back, if you trouble me again."

"Very good," replied the Englishman. "Now listen, bully. We have had a little more than enough of you. You take advantage of your strength to terrorise men who are not street acrobats, and professional weight-lifters. Now *I* am going to take advantage of this, to terrorise *you*," and he produced a small revolver from his pocket. "Now choose. Try your blackguard-rush games and get a bullet through your skull, or fight me like a man with any weapon you prefer."

An approving cheer broke from the quickly increasing audience. The Italian moistened his lips and glared round.

"Mais oui," observed Madame with cool impartiality, "but that is a fair offer."

As though stung by her remark, the Italian threw himself into wrestling attitude and extended his arms. John Bull moved only to extend his pistol-arm, and Luigi Rivoli recoiled. Strangling men who could not wrestle was one thing, being shot was quite another. The thrice-accursed English dog had got him nicely cornered. To raise a hand to him was to die--better to face his enemy, himself armed than unarmed. Better still to catch him unarmed and stamp the life out of him. He must temporise.

"Ho-ho, Brave Little Man with a Pistol," he sneered. "Behold the English hero who fears the bare hands of no man--while he has a revolver in his own."

"You miss the point, Rivoli," was the reply. "I want nothing to do with you bare-handed. I want you to choose any weapon you like to name," and turning to the deeply interested crowd he raised his voice a little:

"Gentlemen of the Legion," he said, "I challenge le Légionnaire Luigi Rivoli of the Seventh Company of the First Battalion of La Légion Etrangère to fight me with whatever weapon he prefers. We can use our rifles; he can have the choice of the revolvers belonging to me and my friend le Légionnaire Bouckaing Bronceau; we can use our sword-bayonets; we can get sabres from the Spahis; or it can be a rifle-and-bayonet fight. He can choose time, place, and weapon--and, if he will not fight, let him be known as *Rivoli the Coward* as long as he pollutes our glorious Regiment."

Ringing and repeated cheers greeted the longest public speech that Sir Montague Merline had ever made.

A bitter sneer was frozen on Rivoli's white face.

"*Galamatias!*" he laughed contemptuously, but the laugh rang a little uncertain.

Madame la Cantinière was charmed. She felt she was falling in love with ce brave Jean Boule *au grand galop*. This was a far finer man, and a far more suitable husband for a hard-working Cantinière than that lump of a Rivoli, with his pockets always *pleine de vide* and his mouth always full of *langue vert*. A trifle on the elderly side perhaps, but aristocrat *au bout des ongles*. Yes, decidedly grey as to the hair, but then, how nice to be an old man's darling!–and Madame simpered, bridled and tried to blush.

"Speak up thou, Rivoli," she cried sharply. "Do not stand there like a *blanc bec* before a Sergeant-Major. Speak, *bécasse*–or speak not again to me."

The Neapolitan darted a glance of hatred at her.

"Peace, fat sow," he hissed, and added unwisely--"You wag your beard too much."

In that moment vanished for ever all possibility of Madame's trying an Italian husband. "Sow" may be a term of endearment, but no gentleman alludes to beards in the presence of a lady whose chin does not betray her sex.

Turning to his enemy, Rivoli struck an attitude and pointed to the door.

"Go, dig your grave *ci-devant*," he said portentously, "and I will kill you beside it, within the week."

"Thanks," replied the Englishman, and invited his friends to join him in a litre....

The barracks of the First Battalion of the Foreign Legion hummed and buzzed that night, from end to end, in a ferment of excitement over the two tremendous items of most thrilling and exciting news, to wit, that there was among them a sheep in wolf's clothing--a girl in uniform--and, secondly, that there was a duel toward, a duel in which no less a person than the great Luigi Rivoli was involved.

Cherchez la femme was the game of the evening; and the catch-word of the wits on encountering any bearded and grisled *ancien* in corridor *chambrée*, canteen, or staircase, was--

"Art *thou* the girl, petite?"

The wrinkled old grey-beard, Tant-de-Soif, was christened Bébé Fifinette, provided with a skirt improvised from a blanket, and subjected to indignities.

Chapter VIII
The Temptation of Sir Montague Merline

Il Signor Luigi Rivoli strode forth from the Canteen in an unpleasant frame of mind.

"Curse the Englishman!" he growled. "Curse that hag behind the bar. Curse that Russian *ragazza*. Curse that thrice-damned American...."

In fact--curse everybody and everything. And among them, Il Signor Luigi Rivoli cursed Carmelita for not making a bigger financial success of her Café venture, and saving a Neapolitan gentlemen from the undignified and humiliating position of having to lay siege to a cursed fat French *bitche*, to get a decent living.... What a fool he'd been that evening! He had lost ground badly with Madame, and he had lost prestige badly with the Legionaries. He must regain both as quickly as possible.... That accursed English devil must meet with an accident within the week. It would not be the first time by hundreds that a Légionnaire had been stabbed in the back for his sash and bayonet in the *Village Négre* and alleys of the Ghetto.... A little job for Edouard Malvin, or Tou-tou Boil-the-Cat. Yes, a knife in the back would settle the Englishman's hash quite effectually, and it would be the simplest thing in the world to leave his body in one of those places to which Legionaries are forbidden to go--for the very reason that they are likely to remain in them for ever.... Curse that old cow of the Canteen! Had he offended her beyond hope of reconciliation? The Holy Saints forbid, for the woman was positively wealthy. Well, he must bring the whole battery of his blandishments to bear and make one mighty effort to win her fortune, hand and heart--in fact, he would give her an ultimatum and settle things, one way or the other, for Carmelita was beginning to show distinct signs of restiveness. Curse Carmelita! He was getting very weary of her airs and jealousies--a franc a day did not pay for it all. As soon as things were happily settled with Madame he would be able to sell his rights and goodwill in Carmelita and her Café. But one must not be precipitate. There must be no untimely killing of geese that laid golden eggs. Carmelita must be kept quiet until Madame's affair was settled. 'Twas but a clumsy fool that would lose both the substance and the shadow--both the Canteen and the Café. If Madame returned an emphatic and final No, to his ultimatum, the Café must suffice until something better turned up. Luigi Rivoli and an unaugmented halfpenny a day would be ill partners, and agree but indifferently....

Revolving these things in his heart, the gentle Luigi became conscious of a less exalted organ, and bethought him of dinner, Chianti, and his cigar. He turned in the direction of the Café de la Légion, his usual excellent appetite perhaps a trifle dulled and blunted by uncomfortable thoughts as to what might happen should this grey English dog survive the week, in spite of the attentions of Messieurs Malvin, Tou-tou, et Cie. The choice between facing the rifle or revolver of the Company marksman, or of being branded for ever as *Rivoli the Coward* was an unpleasant one.... Should he choose steel and have a dagger-fight with sword-bayonets? No, he absolutely hated cold steel, and his mighty strength would be almost as useless to him as in a shooting-duel. Suppose he selected sword-bayonets, to be used as daggers--held his in his left hand, seized his enemy's right wrist, broke his arm, and then made a wrestle of it after all? He could strangle him or break his back with ease. And suppose he missed his snatch at the Englishman's wrist? The devil's bayonet would be through his throat in a second! ...But why these vain and discomforting imaginings? Ten francs would buy a hundred bravos in the *Village Négre* and slums, if Malvin failed him....

He turned into Carmelita's alley and entered the Café.

Carmelita, whose eyes had rarely left the door throughout the evening, saw him as he entered, and her face lit up as does a lantern when the wick is kindled. Here was her noble and beautiful Luigi. Away with all wicked doubts and fears. Even the good Jean Boule was prejudiced against her Luigi She would now hear his version of the discovery of the Russian girl. How amused he would be to know that she had guessed Mikhail's secret long ago.

Rivoli passed behind the bar. Carmelita held open the door of her room, and having closed it behind him, turned and flung her arms round his neck.

"Marito amato!" she murmured as she kissed him again and again. How could she entertain these doubts of her Luigi in his absence? She was a wicked, wicked girl, and undeserving of her fortune in having so glorious a mate. She decided to utter no reproaches and ask no questions concerning the discovery of the Russian girl. She would just tell him that she had taken her in and that she counted on his help in keeping the girl's secret and getting her away.

"Beloved and beautiful Luigi of my heart," she said, as she placed a steaming dish of macaroni before him, "I want your help once more. That poor, foolish, little Mikhail Kyrilovitch has come and told me he is in trouble, and begged my help. Fancy his thinking he could lead the life that my Luigi leads--that of a soldier of France's fiercest Regiment. Poor little fool....Guess where he is at this moment, Luigi."

With his mouth full, the noble Luigi intimated that he knew not, cared not, and desired not to know.

"I will tell my lord," murmured Carmelita, bending over his lordship's huge and brawny shoulder, and kissing the tip of the ear into which she whispered, "He is in my bed."

Luigi had to think quickly. How much had the Russian girl told of what had happened in the wash-house? Nothing, or Carmelita would not be in this frame of mind. What did Carmelita know? Did she know that *he* knew? He sprang to his feet with an oath, and a well-assumed glare of ferocity. He raised his fist above his head, and by holding his breath, contrived to induce a dark flush and raise the veins upon his forehead.

"In your bed, *puttana*?" he hissed. (Carmelita was overjoyed, Luigi was angered and jealous. Where there is jealousy, there is love! Of course, Luigi loved her as he had always done. How dared she doubt it? Throwing her arms around his neck with a happy laugh, she reassured her ruffled mate until he permitted himself to calm down and resume his interrupted meal. Jean Boule had lied to her! Luigi knew nothing!...) She went to the bar.

Curse this Russian anarchist! But for her he would not have been in danger of losing Madame, nor of finding a violent death. Curse Carmelita, the stupid fool, for harbouring her. What should he do? What could he say? If he thwarted Carmelita's plan, she would think he desired the Russian wench for himself, and fly into a rage. She would be a very fiend from hell if she were jealous! A pretty pass he would be brought to if both Canteen and Café were closed to him! He had better walk warily here, until he had ascertained the exact amount of damage he had done by his most unwise allusion to Madame's whiskers. (Never tell a cross-eyed man he squints.) But he must get even with this Russian she-devil who had thwarted him in the lavatory, struck him across the face, humiliated him before the Englishman, ruined his prestige with his comrades and Madame, and brought him to the brink of an abyss of danger....He had an idea....When Carmelita came into the room again from the bar, she should have the shock of her life, and the Russian *puttana*, another. Also the over-clever Jean Boule should learn that the race is not always to the slow, nor the battle to the weak....Carmelita entered. Picking up his képi, he extended his arms, and with a smile of lofty sadness, bade her come and kiss him while she might....

While she might! Carmelita turned pale, and Doubt again reared its horrid head. Was this his way of beginning some tale concerning separation? Some tale in which Madame la Cantinière's name would appear sooner or later? By the Blessed Virgin and the Holy Bambino, she would tear the eyes from Luigi Rivoli's head, before they should look on that French *meretrice* as his wife.

"While I may? Why do you say that, Luigi?" she asked in a dead voice.

The ruffian felt uncomfortable as he watched those great, black eyes blazing in the pinched, blanched face, and realised that there were depths in Carmelita that he had not sounded--and would be ill-advised to sound. What a devil she looked! Luigi Rivoli would do well to eat no food to which Carmelita had had access, when once she knew the truth. Luigi Rivoli would do well to watch warily, and, move quickly, should Carmelita's hand go to the dagger in her garter when he told her that he was thinking of settling in life. In fact it was a question whether his life would be safe, so long as Carmelita was in Sidi-bel-Abbès, and he was the husband of

Madame! Another idea! *Madre de Dios*! A brilliant one. Denounce Carmelita for aiding and abetting a deserter! Two birds with one stone--Carmelita jailed and deported, and the Russian recaptured--Luigi Rivoli rid of a danger from the one, and gratified by a vengeance on the other! As these thoughts flashed through the Italian's evil mind, he maintained his pose, and gently and sadly shook his head.

"While you may, indeed, my Carmelita," he murmured, and produced the first of his brilliant ideas. "While you may. Do not think I reproach you, Carmelita, for you have acted but in accordance with the dictates of your warm young heart in taking in this girl. How were *you* to know that this would involve me in a duel to the death with the finest shot in the Nineteenth Division, the most famous marksman in the army of Africa?"

"What?" gasped Carmelita.

"What I say, my poor girl," was the reply, uttered with calm dignity. "Your English friend, this Jean Boule, who fears to meet me face to face, and man to man, with Nature's weapons, has forced a quarrel on me over this Russian girl. He challenged me in the Canteen this night, and I, who could break him like a dried stick, must stand up to be shot by him, like a dog.... I do not blame *you*, Carmelita. How were you to know?..."

Carmelita suddenly sat down.

"I do not understand," she whispered and sat agape.

"The Englishman owns this girl...."

"He brought her here," Carmelita interrupted, nodding her head.

"Ha! I guessed it....Yes, he owns her, and when I discovered the shameless *puttana's* sex he drew a pistol on me, an innocent, unarmed man....Did he tell you it was I who found the shameful hussy out? What could I do against him empty-handed? ...And now I must fight him--and he can put a bullet where he will....So kiss me, while you may, Carmelita."

With a low cry the girl sprang into his arms.

"My love! My love! My husband!" she wailed, and Luigi hoped that she would release her clasp from about his neck in time for him to avoid suffocation....Curse all women--they were the cause of nine-tenths of the sorrows of mankind. But one could not do without them....Suddenly Carmelita started back, and clapped her hands with a cry of glee. "The Holy Virgin be praised! I have it! I have it! Unless Légionnaire Jean Boule confesses his fault and begs my Luigi's pardon--out into the gutter goes his Russian mistress," and Carmelita pirouetted with joy.... Thank God! Thank God! Here was a solution, and she embraced her lover again and again. Luigi's face was wreathed in smiles. *Excellente*! That would do the trick admirably, and the thrice-accursed, and ten-times-too-clever English *aristocratico* should publicly apologise, if he wished to save his mistress....Yes, that would be very much pleasanter than a mere stab-in-the-back revenge, as well as safer. There is always some slight risk, even in Sidi-bel-Abbès, about arranging a murder, and blackmail is always unpleasant--for the blackmailed. Ho-ho! Ho-ho! Only to think of the cold and haughty Englishman publicly apologising and begging Luigi, of his mercifulness, to cancel the duel. *Corpo di Bacco*, he should do it on his knees. "Rivoli the Coward," forsooth, and what of "Jean Boule the Coward," after this? ...Yes; Jean Boule defeated, the Russian girl denounced when clear of Carmelita's Café, if Madame proved unkind, and denounced in the Café together with Carmelita if Madame accepted him. He himself need not appear personally in the matter at all. And when Carmelita was jailed or deported, and the Russian girl sent to Biribi, or turned into a *figlia del reggimento*, the Englishman should still get it in the back one dark night--and Signor Luigi Rivoli would wax fat behind Madame's bar, until his five years' service was completed and he could live happy ever after, upon the earnings of Madame....

Stroking her hair, he smiled superior upon Carmelita.

"A clever thought, my little one," he murmured, "and bravely meant, but your Luigi's days are numbered. Would that proud, cold *aristocratico* eat the words he shouted before half the Company? No! He will leave the girl to shift for herself."

Carmelita's face fell.

"Do not say so," she begged. "No! No! He would not do that. You know how these English treat women. You know the sort of man this Jean Boule is," and for a moment, involuntarily, Carmelita contrasted her Luigi with Il Signor Jean Boule in the matter of their chivalry and honour, and ere she could thrust the thought from her mind, she had realised the comparison to be unfavourable to her lover.

"Luigi," she said, "I feel it in my heart that, since the Englishman has said that he will save his mistress, he will do it at any cost whatsoever to himself.... Go, dearest Luigi, go now, and I will send to him, and say I must see him at once. He will surely come, thinking that I send on behalf of this Russian fool."

And with a last vehement embrace and burning kiss, she thrust him before her into the bar and watched him out of the Café.

Le Légionnaire Jean Boule was not among the score or so of Legionaries who sat drinking at the little tables, nor were either of his friends. Whom could she send? Was that funny English *ribaldo*, Légionnaire Erbiggin, there? ...No....Ah!–There sat the poor Grasshopper. He would do. She made her way with laugh and jest and badinage to where he sat, *faisant Suisse* as usual.

"Bonsoir, cher Monsieur Cigale," she said. "Would you do me a kindness?"

The Grasshopper rose, thrust his hands up the sleeves of his tunic as far as his elbows, bowed three times, and then knelt upon the ground and smote it thrice with his forehead. Rising, he poured forth a torrent of some language entirely unknown to Carmelita.

"Speak French or Italian, cher Monsieur Cigale," she said.

"A thousand pardons, Signora," replied the Grasshopper. "But you will admit it is not usual for a Mandarin of the Highest Button to speak French. I was saying that the true kindness would be your allowing me to do you a kindness. May I doom your *wonk*[62] of an enemy to the death of the Thousand Cuts?"

"Not this evening, dear Mandarin, thank you," replied Carmelita; "but you can carry a message of the highest military importance. It is well known that you are a soldier of soldiers, and have never yet failed in any military duty."

The Mandarin bowed thrice.

"Will you go straight and find le Légionnaire Jean Boule of your Company, and tell him to come to me at once. Say Carmelita sent you and tell him you have the countersign:–'Our Ally, Russia, is in danger!'"

"I am honoured and I fly," was the reply. "I will send no official of the Yamen, but go myself. Should the Po Sing, they of the Hundred Names, the [Greek: *hoi polloi*], beset my path I will cry, '*Sha! Sha!*–Kill! Kill!–and scatter them before me. Should the *kwei tzu*, the Head Dragon from Hell, or the Military Police (and they are *tung yen* you know--of the same race and tarred with the same brush) impede me, they too shall die the death of the Wire Net," and the Grasshopper placed his képi on his head.

Carmelita knew that John Bull would be with her that evening, and that the risk of eight days' *salle de police*, for being out after tattoo, would not deter him.

In a fever of anxiety, impatience, hope and fear, Carmelita paced up and down behind her bar, like a panther in its cage. One thought shone brightly on the troubled turmoil of her soul. Luigi loved her still; Luigi so loved her that he had been ready to strike her dead as the tide of jealousy surged in his soul. That was the sort of love that Carmelita understood. Let him take her by the throat until she choked--let him seize her by the hair and drag her round the room--let him stab her in the breast, so it be for jealousy. Better Luigi's knife in Carmelita's throat than Luigi's lips on Madame's face. Thank God! Luigi had suffered those pangs--on hearing of a Russian boy in her room--that she herself had suffered on hearing Malvin and the rest couple Luigi's name with Madame's. Thank God! that Luigi knew jealousy even as she did herself. Where there is jealousy, there is love....

And then Carmelita struck her forehead with her clenched fists and laid her head upon her folded arms with a piteous groan. Luigi had been acting. Luigi had *pretended* that jealousy of the Russian. Luigi knew Mikhail Kyrilovitch was a girl--he had fooled her, and once again doubt raised its cruel head in Carmelita's poor distracted mind. "Oh Luigi! Luigi!" she sobbed beneath her breath. And then again a ray of comfort--the *bambino*. Merciful Mother of God grant that it might be true, and that her bright and golden hopes were based on more solid foundation than themselves. Why had she not told him that evening? But no, she was glad she hadn't. She would keep the wonderful secret until such moment as it really seemed to her that it should be produced as the gossamer fairy chain, weightless but unbreakable, that should bind them together, then and forever, in its indissoluble bonds. Yes, she must force herself to believe devoutly and implicitly in the glorious and beautiful secret, and she must treasure it up as long as possible and whisper it in Luigi's ear if it should ever seem that, for a moment, her Luigi strayed from the path of justice and honesty to his unwedded wife.

Faith again triumphed over Doubt.

These others were jealous of her Luigi, or mistook his natural and beautiful politeness to Madame, for overtures and love-making. Could not her Luigi converse with, and smile upon, Madame la Cantinière without setting all their idle and malicious tongues clacking and wagging? As for this Russian wretch, Luigi had given her no more thought than to the dust beneath his feet, and she should go forth into the gutter, in Carmelita's night-shift, before her protector should injure a hair of Luigi's head. She was surprised at Jean Boule, but there--men were all alike, all except her Luigi, that is. How deceived she had been in the kindly old Englishman! ... Fancy coming to her with their cock-and-bull story....

The voice of the man of whom she was thinking broke in upon her reverie.

"What is it, little one? Nothing wrong about Olga?"

"Come in here, Signor Jean Boule," said Carmelita, and led the way into her room.

The Englishman involuntarily glanced round the little sanctum into which no man save Luigi Rivoli had been known to penetrate, and noted the clean tablecloth, the vase with its bunch of krenfell and oleander flowers, the tiny, tidy dressing table, the dilapidated chest of drawers, bright oleographs, cheap rug, crucifix and plaster Madonna--a room still suggestive of Italy.

Turning, Carmelita faced the Englishman and pointed an accusing finger at his face, her great black eyes staring hard and straight into the narrowed blue ones.

"Signor Jean Boule," she said, "you have played a trick on me; you have deceived me; you have killed my faith in Englishmen--yes, in all men--except my Luigi. Why did you bring your mistress to me and beg my help while you knew you meant to kill my husband, because he had found you out? Oh, Monsieur Jean Boule--but you have hurt me so. And I had thought you like a father--so good a man, yes, like a holy padre, a *prête*. Oh, Signor Jean Boule, are you like those others, loving wickedly, killing wickedly? Are there *no* good honest men--except my Luigi?..."

The Englishman shifted uncomfortably from foot to foot, twisting his képi in his fingers, a picture of embarrassment and misery. How could he persuade this girl that the man was a double-dealing, villainous blackguard? And if he could do so, why should he? Why destroy her faith and her happiness together? If this hound failed in his attempt upon the celibacy of Madame, he would very possibly marry the girl, and, in his own interests, treat her decently. Apparently he had kept her love for years--why should she not go on worshipping the man she believed her lover to be, until the end? But no, it was absurd. How should Luigi Rivoli ever treat a woman decently? Sooner or later he was certain to desert her. What would Carmelita's life be when Luigi Rivoli had the complete disposal of it? Sooner or later she must know what he was, and better sooner than later. A thousand times better that she should find him out now, while there was a risk of his marrying her.... It would be a really good deed to save Carmelita from the clutches of Luigi Rivoli. Stepping toward her, he laid his hands upon the girl's shoulders and gazed into her eyes with that look which he was wont to fasten upon the Grasshopper to soothe and influence him.

"Listen to me, Carmelita," he said, "and be perfectly sure that every word I say to you is absolutely true....I did not know that Mikhail Kyrilovitch was a woman more than half an hour before you did. I only knew it when she rushed to me for protection from Luigi Rivoli, who had discovered her and behaved to her like the foul beast he is. I have challenged him to fight me in the only way in which it is possible for me to fight him, and I mean to kill him. I am going to kill him partly for your sake, partly for my own, and partly for that of every wretched recruit and decent man in the Company."

Carmelita drew back.

"Coward!" she hissed. "You only dare face my Luigi with a gun in your hand."

"I am not a coward, Carmelita. It is Rivoli who is the coward. He is by far the strongest man in the Regiment, and is a professional wrestler. He trades on this to bully and terrorise all who do not become his servants. He is a brutal ruffian, and he is a coward, for he would do anything rather than meet me in fair fight. He is only a *risquetout* where there are no weapons and the odds are a hundred to one in his favour.... If I hear one more word about my trading on my marksmanship, he shall fight me with revolvers across a handkerchief. Besides, I have told him he can choose any weapon in the world."

"And now hear *me*," replied Carmelita, "and I would say it if it were my last word. Either you take all that back and apologise to my Luigi, or out into the night goes this Russian girl," and she pointed with the dramatic gesture of the excited Southerner to the *bassourab*-cloth which screened off the little inner chamber which was just big enough to hold Carmelita's bed.

The Englishman started.

"You don't mean that, Carmelita!" he asked anxiously.

The girl laughed bitterly, cruelly.

"Do you think a thousand Russians would weigh with me against one hair of my husband's head?" she answered. "Give me your solemn promise now and here, or I will do more than throw her out, I will denounce her. I will give her to the Turcos and Spahis. I will have her dragged to the Village Négre."

"Hush! Carmelita. I am ashamed of you. Are you mad?" said John Bull sternly.

"I am sorry," was the reply. "Yes, I *am* mad, Signor Jean Boule. I am being driven mad by this horrible plot against my Luigi. Why are you all his enemies? It is because you are jealous of him and because you fear him--but you shall not hurt him. This, at least, I say and mean: Take the Russian girl away with you now, or promise me you will never fight my husband with lead or steel."

"I cannot promise it, Carmelita. I have challenged Rivoli publicly and must fight him. To draw out now would brand me as a coward, would make him twice the bully he is, and would be a cruelty to you.... You ask too much, you ask an impossibility. I must make some other plan for Olga Kyrilovitch."

Carmelita staggered, and stared open-mouthed. She could not believe her ears.

"What?" she gasped.

"The girl must go elsewhere," repeated the Englishman. Carmelita appeared to be about to faint. Could he mean it? Was it possible? Was her brilliant plan failing?

"Will you lend the girl some clothes?" asked John Bull.

"Most certainly will I not," she whispered.

"Then please go and tell her to dress again in uniform," was the answer, as he pointed to the uniform lying folded on a chair.

"And will you ruin her chance of escape, Signor Jean Boule?" asked Carmelita. "Is *that* how Englishmen treat women who throw themselves on their mercy? Do you put your own vengeance before her safety and honour and life?"

"No, Carmelita, I do not," answered the man. "I am in a terrible position, and am going to choose the lesser of two evils. It is better that I take the girl away and help her brother to desert with her, than let Rivoli wreck your life, break your heart, and doubly regain the bully's prestige and power to make weaker comrades' lives a misery and a burden. He, at any rate, shall be the cause of no more suicides."

Carmelita flung herself upon the hideous horsehair couch and burst into a torrent of hysterical tears. What could she say to this hard, cold man? What could she do? What *could* she do?

John Bull, suffering acutely as he had ever suffered in his life, stood silent, and wondered how far the wish was father to the thought that, in this ghastly dilemma, it was his duty to stand firm in his attitude toward Rivoli. For once, the thing he longed to do was the right thing to do, and the course which he would loathe to follow was the wrong course for him to pursue. Olga Kyrilovitch had brought her fate upon herself, and he had no more responsibility to her than the common duty of lending a helping hand to a neighbour in trouble. Had there been no other consideration, he would have helped her to the utmost of his power, without counting cost or risk. When it came to a clear choice between saving Carmelita, protecting recruits, making a stand for self-respect and decency, and redeeming his own word and honour and reputation on the one hand, and, on the other hand, helping this rash and lawless Russian girl, there could be no hesitation.

Carmelita sprang to her feet.

"I will denounce her," she cried. "I will throw open those shutters and scream and scream until there is a crowd, and they shall have her in her nightdress. *Now* will you spare my husband?"

"You'll do nothing of the kind," answered John Bull calmly. "You know you would regret it all the days of your life. Is this Italian hospitality, womanliness, and honour? Be ashamed of yourself, to talk so. Be fair. Be just. Who needs protection most--your bully, or this wretched girl?" and here Legionary John Bull showed more than his wonted wisdom in dealing with women. Stepping up to Carmelita he seized her by the shoulders and shook her somewhat sharply, saying as he did so, "And understand once and for all, little fool, I keep my promise to Luigi Rivoli--whatever you do."

In return for her shaking, the surprising Carmelita smiled up into the old soldier's face, and clasped her hands behind his head.

"Monsieur Jean Boule," she said, "I think I would have loved my father like I love you--but how you try to hide the soft, kind heart with the hard, cruel face!" and Carmelita gave John Bull the first kiss he had received for over a quarter of a century.

He pushed her from him roughly. Carmelita was glad. This was a thousand times better than that glacial immobility. This meant that he was moved.

"Save Olga's life, Babbo," she whispered coaxingly. "Save Olga and make me happy. Don't ruin two women for fear men should not think you brave. Who doubts the courage of the man who wears the *médaille*? The man who had the courage to challenge Luigi Rivoli can have the courage to withdraw it if it suits him."

"The man who killed Luigi Rivoli would be your best friend, Carmelita," was the reply, "and Olga Kyrilovitch must be saved in some other way. I must keep my word. It is due to others as well as to myself that I do so."

The two regarded each other without realising that it was across an abyss of immeasurable width and unfathomable depth. He was a man, she was a woman; he a Northerner, she a Southerner. To him honour came first; and without love there could be, she thought, neither honour nor happiness nor life itself.

How should these two understand each other, these two whose souls spoke languages differing as widely as those spoken by their tongues? The woman understood and appreciated the rectitude and honour of the man as little as he realised and fathomed the depth and overwhelming intensity of her love and devotion.

Carmelita now made a great mistake and took a false step--a mistake which turned to her advantage and a false step which led whither she so yearned to go. For Luigi's sake she played the temptress. In defence of her virtue let it be said that, as once before, she believed that her Luigi's life was actually at stake; in defence of her judgment, let it be remembered that she had grown up in a hard school, and had reason to believe that no man does something for nothing where a woman is concerned. She advanced with her bewitching smile, took the Englishman's face between her hands, drew his head down and kissed him upon the lips.

The Englishman blushed as he returned her kiss, and laughed to find himself blushing as the thought struck him that he might have had a daughter older than Carmelita. The girl misunderstood the kiss and smile. Alas! all men were alike in one thing and the best were like the worst. She put her lips to his ear and whispered....

John Bull drew back. Placing his hands upon the girl's shoulders, he gazed into her eyes. Carmelita blushed painfully, and dropped her eyes before the man's searching stare. She heaved a sobbing sigh. Yes, all alike, all had their price--and any pretty woman could pay it. All alike--even grey-haired, kind old Babbo Jean Boule, who looked as though he might be her grandfather.

She felt his hand beneath her chin, raising her face to his. Again he gazed into her eyes and slowly shook his head.

"And is this what men and Life have taught you, Carmelita?" he said....

A horrid fear gripped Carmelita's heart. Could she be wrong? Could she have offered herself in vain? Could this man's pride and hatred be so great that the bribe was not enough?

"And you would do this--*you*, Carmelita; for that filthy blackguard?"

"I would do anything for my Luigi. Sell me his life and I will pay you now, the highest price a woman can. Kiss me on the lips, dear Monsieur Jean, and I will trust you to keep your part of the bargain--never to fight nor attack my Luigi with a weapon in your hand. Kiss me! Kiss me!"

The Englishman drew the pleading girl to him and kissed her on the forehead. She flung her arms around his neck in a transport of joy and relief.

"You will sell me my Luigi's life?" she cried. "Oh praise and thanks to the Mother of God. You *will*?"

"I will *give* you your Luigi's life," said Sir Montague Merline, and went out.

Chapter IX
The Café and the Canteen

As the door closed behind the departing John Bull, the heavy *purdah* between the sitting-room and the tiny side-chamber or alcove in which was Carmelita's bed, was pushed aside, and Olga Kyrilovitch, barefooted and dressed in night attire belonging to Carmelita, entered the room. On the sofa lay Carmelita sobbing, her hands pressed over her eyes.

Looking more boy-like than ever, with her short hair, the Russian girl advanced noiselessly and shook Carmelita sharply by the shoulder.

"You fool," she hissed between clenched teeth. "You stupid fool. You blind, stubborn, hopeless *fool*!" Carmelita sat up. This was language she could understand, and a situation with which she could deal.

"Yes?" she replied without resentment, "and why?"

"Those two men.... Compare them... I heard every word--I could not help it. I could not come out--I should not have been safe, even with you here, with that vile, filthy Italian in the room, nor could I come, for shame, like this, while the Englishman was here.... *Why did you let him say he does not love me?*" and the girl burst into tears. Carmelita stared.

"Oho! you love him, do you?" quoth she.... "Then if you know what love is, why do you abuse the man *I* love?"

The girl raised her impassioned tear-stained face to Carmelita's.

"Will nothing persuade you, little fool?" she cried, "that that Italian beast no more loves you than--than Jean Boule loves me--that he is playing with you, that he is battening on you, and that, the moment the fat Canteen woman accepts him, he will marry her and you will see him no more? Why should Jean Boule lie to you? Why should the American? Why should I?--Ask any Legionary in Sidi."

Carmelita clenched her little fist and appeared to be about to strike the Russian girl.

"Stop!" continued Olga, and pointed to the uniform which lay folded on the chair. "See! Prove your courage and prove us all liars if you can. Put on that uniform, disguise yourself, and go to the Canteen any night in the week. If your Rivoli is not there behind the bar, hand-in-glove with Madame, turn me into the street--or leave me at the mercy of your Rivoli. There now...."

"*I will*," said Carmelita, and then screamed and laughed, laughed and screamed, as her overwrought nerves and brain gave way in a fit of hysterics.

When she recovered, Olga Kyrilovitch discovered that the seed which she had sown had taken root, and that it was Carmelita's unalterable intention to pay a visit to the Canteen on the very next evening.

"For my Luigi's own sake I will spy upon him," she said, "and to prove all his vile accusers wrong. When I have done it I will confess to him with tears and throw myself at his feet. He shall do as he likes with me.... But he will understand that it was only to disprove these lies that I did it, and not because I for one moment doubted him."

But doubt him Carmelita did. As soon as her decision was taken and announced, she allowed Olga to talk on as she pleased, and insensibly came to realise that at the bottom of her heart she knew John Bull to be incapable of deceiving her. Why should he? Why should all the Legionaries, except Rivoli's own hirelings, take up the same attitude towards him? Why should there be no man to speak well of him save such men as Borges, Hirsch, Bauer, Malvin, and the others, all of whom carried their vileness in their faces? As her doubts and fears increased, so did her wrath and excitement, until she strode up and down the little room like a caged pantheress, and Olga feared for her sanity and her own safety. And then again, Love would triumph, and she would beat her breast and wildly reproach herself for her lack of faith, and overwhelm Olga with a deluge of vituperation and accusation.

At length came the relief of quiet weeping, and, having whispered to Olga her Great Secret, or rather her hopes of having one to tell, she sobbed herself to sleep on the girl's shoulder, to dream of the most wonderful of *bambinos*.

Meanwhile, John Bull spent one of the wretchedest evenings of a wretched life. Returning to his *chambrée* to find himself hailed and acclaimed "hero," he commenced at once, with his usual uncompromising directness and simplicity, to inform all and sundry, who mentioned the subject, that there would be no duel. It hurt him most of all to see the face of his friend Rupert fall and harden, as he informed him that he could not fight Rivoli after all. On his explaining the position to him, Reginald Rupert, decidedly shocked, remarked--

"*Your* business, of course," and privately wondered whether *les beaux yeux* of Carmelita, or of Olga, had shed the light in which his friend had come to see things so differently. Surely, Carmelita's best friend would be the person who saved her from Rivoli; and, if it were really Olga whom Bull were considering, there were more ways of killing a cat than choking it with melted butter. Anyhow, he didn't envy John Bull, nor yet the weaker vessels of the Seventh Company. What would John Bull do, if, on hearing of his change of mind, Rivoli simply took him and put him across his knee? Would his promise to Carmelita sustain him through that or similar indignities? After all, a challenge is a challenge; and some people would consider that the prior engagement to Rivoli could not in honour be cancelled afterwards by an engagement with Carmelita or anybody else.

No. To the young mind of Rupert this was not "the clean potato," and he was disappointed in his friend. As they undressed, in silence, an idea struck him, and he turned to that gentleman.

"I say, look here, Bull, old chap," quoth he. "You'll of course do as you think best in the matter, and so shall I. I'm going to challenge Rivoli myself. I shall follow your admirable example and challenge him publicly, and I shall add point to it by wasting a litre of wine on his face, which I shall also smack with what violence I may. I am not Company Marksman like you, but, as Rivoli knows, I am a First Class shot. I shall say I have been brooding over his breaking my back, and now want to fight him on even terms."

A look of pain crossed the face of the old soldier.

"Rupert," he said, rising and laying his hand on his friend's shoulder, "you'll do nothing of the kind....Not, that is, if you value my friendship in the least, or have the slightest regard for me. Do you not understand that I have given Carmelita my word that I will neither fight Rivoli with a weapon in my hand, nor attack him with one? Would she not instantly and naturally suppose that I had got you to do it *for* me? ...Would anything persuade her to the contrary?"

"Is he to go unpunished then? Is he to ride roughshod over us all? He'll be ten times worse than before. You know he'll ascribe your withdrawal to cowardice--and so will everybody else," was the reply.

"They will," agreed John Bull.

"What's to be done then?"

"I don't know, but I'll tell you what is not to be done. No friend of mine is to challenge Rivoli to a duel."

The Bucking Bronco entered.

"Say, John," he drawled, "I jest bin and beat up Mister Mounseer Malvin, I hev'. 'Yure flappin' yure mouth tew much,' I ses. '*Vous frappez votre bouche trop*,' I ses. 'Yew come off it, me lad,' I ses. 'Yew jes' wipe off yure chin some. *Effacez votre menton*,' I ses. Then I slugs him a little one."

"What was it all about, Buck?" enquired Rupert.

"Do yew know what the little greasy tin-horn of a hobo was waggin' his chin about? Sed as haow yew was *a-climbin' down and a-takin' back the challenge to our Loojey*! I told him ef he didn't wipe off his chin and put some putty on his gas-escape I'd do five-spot in Biribi fer him. 'Yes, Mounseer Malvin,' I ses when I'd slugged him, 'I'll git the *as de pique*[63] on my collar for yew!' ...'*It's true*,' he snivelled. '*It's true*,' and lays on the groun' so as I shan't slug him agin. So

I comes away--not seein' why I should do the two-step on nuthin' at the end of a rope for a dod-gasted little bed-bug like Mounseer Malvin."

"It *is* true, Buck," replied John Bull.

"Well then, I wisht I'd stayed and plugged him some more," was the remarkable reply.

"Rivoli told Carmelita about the duel, and I've promised her I'd let him go," continued John Bull.

"Then yure a gosh-dinged fool, John," said the Bucking Bronco. "Yew ain't to be trusted where wimmin's about. It would hev' bin the best day's work yew ever done fer Carmelita ef you'd let daylight through thet plug-ugly old bluff. He'll lie ter her from Revelley to Taps[64] until old Mother Canteen takes him into her shebang fer good--and then as like as not, he'll put Carmelita up at auction.... There'll be no holding our Loojey now, John. I should smile. Anybody as thinks our Loojey'll make it easy fer yew has got another think comin'. It's a cinch. He'll give yew a dandy time, John. What's a-bitin' yew anyway?"

"Carmelita," was the reply.

"I allow the right stunt fer eny pal o' Carmelita's is ter fill our Loojey up with lead as you perposed ter do.... Look at here, John. *I'll* do it. I could hit all Loojey's buttons with my little gun, one after the other, at thirty yards--and I'd done it long ago, but I know'd it meant the frozen mit fer mine from Carmelita, and I wasn't man enuff ter kill him fer Carmelita's good and make my name mud to her fer keeps."

"Same thing now, Buck," was the answer. "Challenge Luigi, and you can never set foot in the Café de la Légion again. If you killed him--it would be Carmelita's duty in life to find you and stab you."

"Sure thing, John--an' what about yew? Ef our Looj was to be 'Rivoli the Coward' ef he wouldn't fight, who's to be 'coward' now? ...Yew've bitten off more'n yew can chew."

"Anyhow, Buck, if you're any friend of mine--you'll let Rivoli alone. *Qui facit per alium facit per se*, and that's Dutch for 'I might as well kill Rivoli with my own hand as kill him through yours.'"

The Bucking Bronco broke into song--

"But serpose an' serpose,
Yure Hightaliand lad shouldn't die?
Nor the bagpipes shouldn't play o'er him
Ef I punched him in the eye!"

chanted he, as he placed his beloved "gun"–an automatic pistol--under his pillow. "I'll beat him up, Johnnie. Fer Carmelita's sake I ain't shot him up, an' fer her sake and yourn I won't shoot him up now, but the very first time as he flaps his mouth about this yer dool, I'll beat him up--and there'll be *some* fight," and the Bucking Bronco dived into his "flea-bag."

The next day the news spread throughout the *caserne* of the First Battalion of the Legion that the promised treat was off, the duel between the famous Luigi Rivoli and the Englishman, John Bull, would not take place, the latter, in spite of the publicity and virulence of his challenge, having apologised.

The news was ill received. In the first place the promise of a brilliant break in the monotony of Depôt life was broken. In the second place, the undisputed reign of a despotic and brutal tyrant would continue and grow yet heavier and more insupportable; while, in the third place, it was not in accordance with the traditions of the Legion that a man should fiercely challenge another in public, and afterwards apologise and withdraw. Italian shares boomed and shot sky-high, while John Bulls became a drug in the market.

That evening the Bucking Bronco, for the first time in his life, received a message from Carmelita, a message which raised him to the seventh heaven of expectation and hope, while the sanguine blood coursed merrily through his veins.

Carmelita wanted him. At five o'clock without fail, Carmelita would expect him at the Café. She needed his help and relied upon him for it.... *Gee*-whillikins! She should have it.

At half-past five that evening, the Bucking Bronco entered le Café de la Légion and stared in amazement at seeing a strange Legionary behind Carmelita's bar. He was a small, slight man in correct walking-out dress--a blue tunic, red breeches and white spats. His képi was pulled well down over a small, intelligent face, the most marked features of which were very broad black eyebrows, and a biggish dark moustache. The broad chin-strap of the képi was down, and pressed the man's chin up under the large moustache beneath which the strap passed. The soldier had a squint and the Bucking Bronco had always experienced a dislike and distrust of people so afflicted.

"An' what'n Hell are *yew* a-doin' thar, yew swivel-eyed tough?" he enquired, and repeated his enquiry in Legion French.

The Legionary laughed--a ringing peal which was distinctly familiar.

"Don't yew git fresh with me, Bo, or I'll come roun' thar an' improve yure squint till you can see in each ear-'ole," said the American, trying to "place" the man.

Again the incongruous tinkling peal rang out and the Bucking Bronco received the shock of his life as Carmelita's voice issued through the big moustache. Words failed him as he devoured the girl with his eyes.

"Dear Monsieur Bouckaing Bronceau," said she. "Will you walk out to-night with the youngest recruit in the Legion?"

The Bronco still stared agape.

"I am in trouble," continued Carmelita, "and I turn to you for help."

The light of hope shone in the American's eyes.

"Holy Poker!" said he. "God bless yure sweet eyes, fer sayin' so, Carmelita. But why *me*? Have yew found yure Loojey out, at last? Why me?"

"I turn to you for help, Monsieur Bronco," said the girl, "because you have told me a hundred times that you love me. Love gives. It is not always asking, asking, asking. Now give me your help. I want to get at the truth. I want to clear a good and honest man from a web of lies. Take me to the Canteen with you to-night. They say my Luigi goes there to see Madame la Cantinière. They say he flirts and drinks with her, that he helps her there, and serves behind her bar. They even dare to say that he asks her to marry him...."

"It's true," interrupted the Bucking Bronco.

"Very well--then take me there now. My Luigi has sworn to me a hundred times that he never sets foot in Madame's Canteen, that he would not touch her filthy Algerian wine--my Luigi who drinks only the best Chianti from Home. Take me there and prove your lies. Take me now, and either you and your friends, or else Luigi Rivoli, shall never cross my threshold again." Carmelita's voice was rising, tears were starting to her eyes, and her bosom rose and fell as no man's ever did.

"Easy, honey," said the big American. "Ef yure gwine ter carry on right here, what'll you do in the Canteen when yew see yure Loojey right thar doin' bar-tender fer the woman he's a-doin' his damnedest to marry?"

"*Do?*" answered Carmelita in a low tense voice. "Do? I would be cold as ice. I would be still and hard as one of the statues in my own Naples. All Hell would be in my breast, but a Hell of frozen fire do you understand, and I would creep away. Like a silent spirit I would creep away--but I would be a spirit of vengeance. To Monsieur Jean Boule would I go and I would say, 'Kill him! Kill him! For the love of God and the Holy Virgin and the Blessed Bambino, *kill* him--and let me come and stamp upon his face.' That is what I would say, Monsieur Bronco."

The American covered the girl's small brown hand with his huge paw.

"Carmelita, honey," he whispered. "Don't go, little gel--don't go. May I be struck blind and balmy right hyar, right naow, ef I tell you a word of a lie. Every night of his life he's thar, afore he comes down hyar with lies on his lips to yew. Don't go. Take my word fer it, an' John Bull's word, and young Rupert's word. They're White Men, honey, they wouldn't lie ter yew. Believe what we tell yew, and give ole John Bull back his promise, an' let him shoot-up this low-lifer rattlesnake...."

"I will see with my own eyes," said Carmelita--adding with sound feminine logic, "and if he's not there to-night, I'll know that you have all lied to me, and that he never was there--and never, never, never again shall one of you enter my house, or my Legionaries shall nail you by the ears to the wall with their bayonets....Shame on me, to doubt my Luigi for a moment."

The American gave way.

"Come on then, little gel," he said. "P'raps it's fer the best."

§2

Entering the Canteen that evening for his modest litre, 'Erb caught sight of his good friend, the Bucking Bronco, seated beside a Legionary whom 'Erb did not know. The American beckoned and 'Erb emitted a joyous sound to be heard more often in the Ratcliffe Highway than in the wilds of Algeria. Apparently his pal's companion was, or had been, in funds, for his head reposed upon his folded arms.

"Wotto, Bucko!" exclaimed the genial 'Erb. "We a-goin' to ketch this pore bloke's complaint? Luvvus! Wish I got enuff to git as ill as wot 'e is."

"Sit down t'other side of him, 'Erb," responded the American. "We may hev' to help the gay-cat to bed. He's got a jag. Tight as a tick--an' lef me in the lurch with two-francs' worth to drink up."

"Bless 'is 'eart," exclaimed 'Erb. "I dunno wevver 'e's a-drinkin' to drahn sorrer or wevver he's a-drinkin' to keep up 'is 'igh sperrits--but he shan't say as 'ow 'Erb 'Iggins didn't stand by 'im to the larst--the larst boll' I mean," and 'Erb filled the large glass which the American reached from the bar.

"'Ere's 'ow, Cocky," he shouted in the ear of the apparently drunken man, giving him a sharp nudge in the ribs with his elbow.

The drunken man gasped at the blow, gave a realistic hiccough and murmured: "A votre santé, Monsieur."

"Carn't the pore feller swaller a little more, Buck?" enquired 'Erb with great concern. "Fency two francs--an' he's 'ad ter giv' up! ...Never mind, Ole Cock," he roared again in the ear of the drunkard, "p'raps you'll be able ter go ahtside in a minnit an' git it orf yer chest. Then yer kin start afresh. See? ...'Ope hon, 'ope hever....'Sides," he added, as a cheering afterthought, "It'll tiste as good a-comin' up as wot it did a-goin' dahn." He then blew vinously into his mouth-organ and settled down for a really happy evening.

A knot of Legionaries, friends of Rivoli, stood at the bar talking with Madame.

"Here he comes," said one of them, leaning with his back against the bar. "Ask him."

Luigi Rivoli strode up, casting to right and left the proud glances of the consciously Great.

"Bonsoir, ma belle," quoth he to Madame. "And how is the Soul of the Soul of Luigi Rivoli?"

The drunken man, sitting between the Bucking Bronco and le Légionnaire 'Erbiggin, moved his head. He lay with the right side of it upon his folded arms and his flushed face toward the bar. His eyes were apparently closed in sottish slumber.

Madame la Cantinière fixed Rivoli with a cold and beady eye. (She "wagged her beard" too much, did she? Oho!)

"And since when have I been the Soul of the Soul of Luigi Rivoli?" she enquired.

"Can you ask it, My Own?" was the reply. "Did not the virgin fortress of my heart capitulate to the trumpet of your voice when first its musical call rang o'er its unsealed walls?"

"Pouf!" replied Madame, bridling....(What a way he had with him, and what a fine figure of a man he was, but "*beards*" quotha!) Raising the flap of the zinc-covered bar, Luigi, as usual, passed within and poured himself a bumper of wine. Raising the glass--

"To the brightest eyes and sweetest face that I ever looked upon," he toasted, and drank.

Madame simpered. Her wrath had, to some extent, evaporated.... Not that she would ever *dream* of marrying him. No! that "beard" would be ever between them. No! No! He had dished himself finally. He had, as it were, hanged himself in that beard as did Absalom in the branches of a tree. The price he should pay for that insult was the value of her Canteen and income. There was balm and satisfaction in the thought. Still--until his successor were chosen, or rather, the successor of the late-lamented, so cruelly, if skilfully, carved by those *sacrépans* and *galopins* of Arabs--the assistance of the big man as waiter and chucker-out should certainly not be refused. By no means.

"And what is this tale I hear of you and le Légionnaire Jean Boule?" enquired Madame. "They say that the Neapolitan trollop of Le Café de la Légion (*sous ce nom-là!*) has begged your life of him."

The drunken man slowly opened his eyes and Rivoli put down his glass with a fierce frown.

"And who invented that paltry, silly lie?" he asked, and laughed scornfully. Madame pointed a fat forefinger at the Bucking Bronco who leant, head on fist, regarding Rivoli with a sardonic smile.

"Sure thing, Loojey. I'm spreadin' the glad joyous tidin's, as haow yure precious life has been saved, all over the whole caboodle," and proceeded to translate.

"Oh, is *that* the plot?" replied the Italian. "Is *that* the best lie the gang of you could hatch? Corpo di Bacco! It's a poor one. Couldn't the lot of you think of a likelier tale than that?"

The Bucking Bronco opined as haow thar was nuthin' like the trewth.

"Look you," said the Italian to Madame, and the assembled loungers. "This grey English cur--pot-valiant--comes yapping at me, being in his cups, and challenges me, *me*, Luigi Rivoli, to fight. I say: 'Go dig your grave, dog,' and he goes. I have not seen him since, but on all hands I hear that he has arranged with this strumpet of the Café to say that she has begged my life of him," and Luigi Rivoli roared with laughter at the idea. "Now listen you, and spread this truth abroad....Madame will excuse me," and he turned with his stage bow to Madame.... "I am no plaster saint, I am a Légionnaire. Sometimes I go to this Café--I admit it," and again turning to Madame, he laid his hand upon his heart. "Madame," he appealed, "I have no home, no wife, no fireside to which to be faithful....And as I honestly admit I visit this Café. The girl is glad of my custom and possibly a little honoured--of that I would say nothing....Accidents will happen to the bravest and most skilful of men in duels. The girl begged me not to fight. 'You are my best customer,' said she, 'and the handsomest of all my patrons,' and carried on as such wenches do, when trade is threatened. 'Peace, woman,' said I, 'trouble me not, or I go to Zuleika across the way.' ... She then took another line. 'Look you, Signor,' said she, 'this old fool, Boule, comes to me when he has money; and he drinks here every night. Spare his miserable carcase for what I make out of it,' and with a laugh I gave the girl my franc and half-promise....Still, what is one's word to a wanton? I may shoot the dog yet, if he and his friends be not careful how they lie."

The drunken man had turned his face on to his arms. No one but the American and 'Erb noticed that his body was shaken convulsively. Perhaps with drunken laughter?

"Tole yer so, Cocky," bawled 'Erb in his ear. "You'll be sick as David's sow in a minnit, 'an' we'll all git blue-blind, paralytic drunk,'" and rising to his feet 'Erb lifted up his voice in song to the effect that--

> "White wings they never grow whiskers,
> They kerry me cheerily over the sea
> To ye Banks and Braes o' Bonny Doon
> Where we drew 'is club money this mornin'.
> Witin' to 'ear the verdict on the boy in the prisoner's dock
> When Levi may I menshun drew my perlite attenshun
> To the tick of 'is grandfarver's clock.
> Ninety years wivaht stumblin', Tick, Tick, Tick,–
> Ninety years wivaht grumblin', gently does the trick,

> When it stopped short, never to go agine
> Till the ole man died.
> An' ef yer wants ter know the time, git yer 'air cut."

For the moment 'Erb was the centre of interest, though not half a dozen men in the room understood the words of what the vast majority supposed to be a wild lament or dirge.

John Bull entered the Canteen, and 'Erb was forgotten. All near the counter, save the drunken man, watched his approach. He strode straight up to the oar, his eyes fixed on Rivoli.

"I wish to withdraw my challenge to you," he said in a clear voice. "I am not going to fight you after all."

"*But, Mother of God, you are!*" whispered the drunken man.

"Oho!" roared Rivoli. "Oho!" and exploded with laughter. "Sober to-night are you, English boaster? And how do you know that I will not fight you, *flaneur?*"

"That rests with you, of course," was the reply.

"Oho, it does, does it, Monsieur Coup Manqué? And suppose I decide *not* to fight you, but to punish you as little barking dogs should be punished? By the Wounds of God you shall learn a lesson, little vur...."

The drunken man moved, as though to spring to his feet, but the big American's arm flung round him pressed him down, as he lurched his huge body drunkenly against him, pinning him to the table.

"'Ere," expostulated 'Erb. "'E wants ter be sick, I tell yer. Free country ain't it, if 'e *is* a bloomin' Legendary....Might as well be a bleed'n drummerdary if 'e carn't be sick w'en 'e wants to....'Ope 'e ain't got seven stummicks, eny'ow," he added as an afterthought, and again applied himself to the business of the evening.

John Bull turned, without a word, and left the Canteen. The knot about the bar broke up and Luigi was alone with Madame save for two drunken men and one who was doing his best to achieve that blissful state.

"Have you forgiven me, Beloved of my Soul?" asked Rivoli of Madame, as she mopped the zinc surface of the bar.

"No," snapped Madame. "I have not."

"Then do it now, my Queen," he implored. "Forgive me, and then do one other thing."

"What is that?" enquired Madame.

"Marry me," replied Rivoli, seizing Madame's pudgy fist.

The eyes of the drunken man were on him, and the American watching, thought of the eyes of the snake that lies with broken back watching its slayer. There was death and the hate of Hell in them, and while he shuddered, his heart sang with hope.

"Marry me, Véronique," he repeated. "Have pity on me and end this suspense. See you, I grow thin," and he raised his mighty arms in a pathetic gesture.

Madame glanced at the poor man's stomach. There was no noticeable *maigreur*.

"And what of the Neapolitan hussy and your goings on in the Café de la Légion?" she asked.

"To Hell with the *putain*," he almost shouted. "I am like other men--and I have been to her dive like the rest. Marry me and save me from this loose irregular soldier's life. Do you think I would stray from *thee*, Beloved, if thou wert mine?"

"Not twice," said Madame.

"Then away with this jealousy," replied the ardent Luigi. "Let me announce our nuptials here and now, and call upon my comrades-in-arms to drink long life and happiness to my beauteous bride--whom they all so chastely love and revere. Come, little Star of my Soul! Come, carissima, and I will most solemnly swear upon the Holy Cross that never, never, never again will I darken the doors of the *casse-croûte* of that girl of the Bazaar. I swear it, Véronique--so help me God and all the Holy Saints--your husband will die before he will set foot in Carmelita's brothel."

"Come," said the drunken man, with a little piteous moan. "Could you carry me out, Signor? I am going to faint."

The Bucking Bronco gathered Carmelita up in his arms and strode toward the door.

"'Ere 'old on," ejaculated 'Erb. "'Arf a mo'! I'll tike 'is 'oofs...."

"Stay whar yew are, 'Erb," said the American sternly, over his shoulder.

"Right-o, ole bloke," agreed 'Erb, always willing to oblige. "Right-o! Shove 'im in 'is kip[65] while I 'soop 'is bare."[66]

Outside, the Bucking Bronco set Carmelita down upon a bench in a dark corner and chafed her hands as he peered anxiously into her face.

"Pull yureself together, honey," he urged. "Don't yew give way yit. Yew've gotter walk past the Guard ef I carries yew all the rest of the way."

The broken-hearted girl could only moan. The American racked his brains for a solution of the difficulty and wished John Bull and Rupert were with him. It would be utterly hopeless to approach the gate with the girl in his arms. What would happen if he could not get her out that night? Suddenly the girl rose to her feet. Pride had come to her rescue.

"Come, Monsieur Bronco," she said in a dead, emotionless voice. "Let me get home," and began to walk like an automaton. Slipping his arm through hers, the American guided and supported her, and in time, Carmelita awoke from a terrible dream to find herself at home. The Russian girl, in some clothing and a wrap of Carmelita's, admitted them at the back door.

"Get her some brandy," said the Bucking Bronco. "Shall I open the Caffy and serve fer yew, Carmelita, ma gel?" he asked.

Before he could translate his question into Legion French, Carmelita had understood, partly from his gestures. She shook her head.

Olga Kyrilovitch looked a mute question at the American. He nodded slightly. Carmelita caught the unspoken communication between the two.

"Yes," she said, turning to Olga, "you were right....They were all right. And I was wrong.... He is the basest, meanest scoundrel who ever betrayed a woman. I do not realise it yet--I am stunned....And I am punished too. I shall die or go mad when I understand....And I want to be alone. Go now, dear Signor Orso Americano, and take my love and this message to Signor Jean Boule. *I kiss his boots in humility and apology, and if he will kill this Rivoli for me I will be his slave for life.*"

"Let me kill him fer yew, Carmelita," begged the American as he turned to go, and then paused as his face lit up with the brightness of an idea. "No," he said. "Almighty God! I got another think come. I'll come an' see yew to-morrow, Carmelita--and make yew a *proposal* about Mounseer Loojey as'll do yew good." At the door he beckoned to the Russian girl.

"Look at hyar, Miss Mikhail," he whispered. "Stand by her like a man to-night. Nuss her, and coddle her and soothe her. You see she don't do herself no harm. Yew hev' her safe and in her right mind in the mornin'--an' we'll git yew and yure brother outer Sidi or my name ain't Hyram Cyrus Milton."

§3

That night was one of the most unforgettable of all the memorable nights through which Olga Kyrilovitch ever lived in the course of her adventurous career. For it was the only night during which she was shut up with a violent and dangerous homicidal maniac. In addition to fighting for her own life, the girl had, at times, to fight for that of her assailant, and she deserved well of the Bucking Bronco. Nature at length asserted herself and Carmelita collapsed. She slept, and awoke in the middle of the next day as sane as a person can be, every fibre of whose being yearns and tingles with one fierce obsession. Even to the experienced Russian girl, the wildness of the Neapolitan revenge-passion was an alarming revelation.

"Though I starve or go mad, I cannot eat nor sleep till I have spat on his dead face," were the only words she answered to Olga's entreaty that she would take food. But she busied herself about her daily tasks with pinched white face, pinched white lips, and cavernous black brooding eyes.

"Rivoli's next meal here will be his last," thought Olga Kyrilovitch, and shuddered.

Terrible and unfathomable as was Carmelita's agony of mind, she insisted on carrying out the programme for the escape of the two Russians fixed for that day, and Olga salved a feeling of selfishness by assuring herself that anything which took the girl's thoughts from her own tragedy was for her good.

That afternoon, Feodor Kyrilovitch made his unobtrusive exit from the Legion and was admitted by his sister at the back door of the Café. In his pocket was a letter enclosed in a blank envelope. On an inner envelope was the following name and address: *"Lady Huntingten, Elham Old Hall, Elham, Kent, England."*

By the five-thirty train two flighty females--one blonde, the other brunette--were seen off from the little Sidi-bel-Abbès station of the Western Algerian Railway, which runs from Tlemcen to Oran, by Mademoiselle Carmelita of the Café de la Légion. Their conversation and playful badinage with the guard of Légionnaires, which is always on duty at the platform gate, were frivolous and unedifying. Sergeant Boulanger, as gallant to women as he was ferocious to men, vowed to his admired Carmelita that it broke his heart to announce that he feared he could not allow her two friends to proceed on their journey until--Carmelita's white face seemed to go a little whiter--they had both given him a chaste salute. On hearing this, one of the girls fled squealing to the train, while the other, with very real blushes and unfeigned reluctance, submitted her face to partial burial beneath the vast moustache of the amorous Sergeant.... As the ramshackle little train crawled out of the station, this girl said to the one who had fled: "You *were* a sneak to bolt like that, Feodor," and received the somewhat cryptic reply--

"My dear Olga, and where should we both be now if his lips had felt the bristles around mine? ...You don't suppose that a double shave, twice over, makes a man's face like a girl's, do you?...."

These two young females found Lady Huntingten all, and more than all, her son had prophesied. When Feodor and Olga Kyrilovitch left the hospitable roof of Elham Old Hall, she parried their protestations of gratitude with the statement that she was fully repaid and over-paid, for anything she had been able to do for them, by the pleasure of talking with friends of her son, friends who had actually been with him but a few days before, and who so fully bore out the statements contained in his letter to the effect that he was in splendid health and having a splendid time.

On returning to her Café, Carmelita found the Bucking Bronco, John Bull, Reginald Rupert, 'Erbiggins, and several other Légionnaires awaiting admittance. Having opened her bar and mechanically ministered to her customers' needs, the unsmiling, broken-looking Carmelita, all of whose vitality and energy seemed concentrated in her burning eyes beckoned to the American and led him into her room Gripping his wrist with her cold hand, and almost shaking him in her too-long suppressed frenzy:

"Have you told Jean Boule?" she asked. "When will he kill him? Where? Quick, tell me! I must be there. I must see him do it....Oh! He will die too quickly....It is too good a death for such a reptile....It is no punishment....Why should he not suffer some thousandth part of what *I* suffer?"

"Look at hyar, Carmelita, honey," interrupted the American, putting his arm round the little heaving shoulders as he mentally translated what he must first say in his own tongue. "Thet's jest whar the swine would git the bulge on yew. Why shouldn't he git a glimpse o' sufferin', sech as I had ter sit an' see yew git, las' night? ...An' I gits it in the think-box las' night, right hyar. Listen, ma honey. *I'm gwine ter beat him up*, right naow, right hyar, in yure Caffy--an' before yure very eyes. In front of all his bullies an' all the guys he's beat up, I'll hev' him on his knees a-blubberin' an' a-prayin' fer mercy....Then he shall lick yure boots, little gel, same as he makes recruits lick his. Then he shall grovel on the ground an' beg an' pray yew to marry him, and at that insult yew shall ask me to put him across my knee and irritate his pants with my belt--an' then throw him neck and crop, tail over tip, in the gutter! Termorrer John Bull smacks his face on the barrack-square an' tells him he was only playin' with him about lettin' him off that dool."

When Carmelita clearly understood the purport of this remarkable speech she put her arms around the Bucking Bronco's neck.

"Dear Signor Orso Americano," she whispered. "Humiliate him to the dust before his comrades, bring him grovelling to my feet, begging me to marry him--and I will be your wife.... Blind, blind, unnameable *fool* that I have been--to think this dog a god and you a rough barbarian....Forgive me, Signor....I could kill myself."

The Bucking Bronco folded the woman in his arms. Suddenly she struggled free, thrust him from her, and, falling into a chair, buried her face in her arms and burst into tears. Standing over her the Bucking Bronco awkwardly patted her back with his huge hand.

"Do yew good, ma gel," he murmured over and over again. "Nuth'n like a good cry for a woman....Git it over naow, and by'n-by show a smilin' face an' a proud one fer Loojey Rivoli to see fer the las' time."

"The *bambino*," wailed the girl. "The *bambino*."

"*What?*" exclaimed the Bucking Bronco.

Rising, the girl looked the man in the face and painfully but bravely stammered out what had been her so-wonderful Secret, and the hope of her life.

The Bucking Bronco again folded Carmelita in his arms.

Chapter X
The Wages of Sin

It was soon evident that the word had been passed round that there would be "something doing" at the Café de la Légion that evening. Never before had its hospitable roof covered so large an assembly of guests. Though it was not exactly what could be called "a packed house," it was far from being a selected gathering of the special friends of Il Signor Luigi Rivoli. To Legionaries John Bull, Reginald Rupert and 'Erb 'Iggins it was obvious that the Bucking Bronco had been at some pains to arrange that the spectators of whatever might befall that evening, were men who would witness the undoing of Luigi Rivoli--should that occur--with considerable equanimity. Scarcely a man there but had felt at some time the weight of his brutal fist and the indignity of helpless obedience to his tyrannous behest. Of one thing they were sure--whatever they might, or might not behold, they would see a Homeric fight, a struggle that would become historic in the annals of la Légion. The atmosphere was electric with suppressed excitement and a sense of pleasurable expectation.

In a group by the bar, lounged the Bucking Bronco and the three Englishmen with a few of their more immediate intimates, chiefly Frenchmen, and members of their *escouade*. Carmelita, a brilliant spot of colour glowing on either cheek, busied herself about her duties, flitting like a butterfly from table to table. Never had she appeared more light-hearted, gay, and *insouciante*. But to John Bull, who watched her anxiously, it was clear that her gaiety was feverish and hectic, her laughter forced and hysterical.

"Reckon 'e's got an earthly, matey?" asked 'Erb of Rupert. "'E'll 'ave ter scrag an' kick, same as Rivoli, if 'e don't want ter be counted aht."

"I'd give a hundred pounds to see him win, anyhow," was the reply. "I expect he'll fight the brute with his own weapons. He'll go in for what he calls 'rough-housing' I hope.... No good following Amateur Boxing Association rules if you're fighting a bear, or a Zulu, or a Fuzzy-wuzzy, or Luigi Rivoli...."

And that was precisely the intention of the American, whose fighting had been learnt in a very rough and varied school. When earning his living as a professional boxer, he had given referees no more than the average amount of trouble; and in the ring, against a clean fighter, had put up a clean fight. A tricky opponent, resorting to fouls, had always found him able to respond with very satisfying tricks of his own--"and then some." But the Bucking Bronco had also done much mixed fighting as a hobo[67] with husky and adequate bulls[68] in many of the towns of the free and glorious United States of America, when guilty of having no visible means of support; with exasperated and homicidal shacks[69] on most of that proud country's railways, when "holding her down," and frustrating their endeavours to make him "hit the grit"; with terrible and dangerous lumber-jacks in timber camps when the rye whiskey was in and all sense and decency were out; with cow-punchers and ranchers, with miners, with Bowery toughs, and assorted desperadoes.

To-night, when he stood face to face with Luigi Rivoli, he intended to do precisely what his opponent would do, to use all Nature's weapons and every device, trick, shift and artifice that his unusually wide experience had taught him.

He knew, and fully admitted, that, tremendously powerful and tough as he himself was, Rivoli was far stronger. Not only was the Italian a born Strong Man, but he had spent his life in developing his muscles, and it was probable that there were very few more finely developed athletes on the face of the earth. Moreover, he was a far younger man, far better fed (thanks to Carmelita), and a trained professional wrestler. Not only were his muscles of marvellous development, they were also trained and educated to an equally marvellous quickness, skill and poise. Add to this the fact that the man was no mean exponent of the arts of *la savate* and *la boxe*, utterly devoid of any scruples of honour and fair-play, and infused with a bitter hatred of the American--and small blame accrues to the latter for his determination to meet the Italian on his own ground.

As he stood leaning against the bar, his elbows on it and his face toward the big room, it would have required a very close observer to note any signs of the fact that he was about to fight for his life, and, far more important, for Carmelita, against an opponent in whose favour the odds were heavy. His hard strong face was calm, the eyes level and steady, and, more significant, the hands and fingers quiet and reposeful. Studying his friend, John Bull noticed the absence of any symptoms of excitement, nervousness, or anxiety. There was no moistening of lips, no working of jaw muscles, no change of posture, no quickening of speech. It was the same old Buck, large, lazy, and lethargic, with the same humorous eye, the same measured drawl, the same quaint turn of speech. In striking contrast with the immobility of the American, was the obvious excitement of the Cockney.

"It'll be an 'Ellova fight," he kept on saying. "Gawdstreuth, it'll be an 'Ellova fight," and bitterly regretted the self-denying ordinance which he had passed upon himself to the effect that no liquor should wet his lips till all was o'er....

Luigi Rivoli, followed as usual by Malvin, Tou-tou Boil-the-Cat, Borges, Hirsch and Bauer, strode into the Café. He was accustomed to attracting attention and to the proud consciousness of nudges, glances and whisperings wherever he went. Not for nothing is one the strongest and most dangerous man in the Foreign Legion. But to-night he was aware of more than usual interest as silence fell upon the abnormally large gathering in Carmelita's Café. He at once ascribed it to the widespread interest in the public challenge he had received from John Bull to a *duel à l'outrance* and the rumour that the Englishman had as publicly withdrawn it. He felt that fresh lustre had been added to his brilliant name.... Carmelita *had* been useful there, and had delivered him from a very real danger, positively from the fangs of a mad dog. Very useful. What a pity it was that he could not marry Madame, and run Carmelita. Might she not be brought to consent to some such arrangement? Not even when she found she could have him in no other way? ... Never!

Absolutamente ... Curse her.... Well, anyhow, there were a few more francs, dinners, and bottles of Chianti. One must take what one can, while one can--and after all the Canteen was worth ten Cafés. Madame had been very kind to-night and would give her final answer to-morrow. That had been a subtle idea of his, telling her that, unless she married him, she should marry no one, and remain a widow all the days of her life, for he'd break the back of any man who so much as looked at her. That had given the old sow something to think about. Ha! Ha!...

As he entered, John Bull was just saying to the Bucking Bronco, "Don't do it, Buck. I know all about that

> 'Thrice-armed is he who hath his quarrel just,
> But four times is he who gets his blow in fust.'

But thrice is quite enough, believe me, old chap. You've no need to descend to such a trick as hitting him unawares, by way of starting the fight."

"Is this my night ter howl, John, or yourn? Whose funeral is it?"

..."Fight him by his own methods if you like, Buck--but don't put yourself in the wrong for a start.... You'll win all right, or I shall cease to believe in Eternal Justice of Things."

It had been the purpose of the Bucking Bronco to lessen the odds against himself, to some extent, by intimating his desire to fight, with a shattering blow which should begin, and, at the same time, half win the battle.

Rivoli approached.

Ha! There was that cursed Englishman, was he? Well, since he had given his promise to Carmelita and was debarred from a duel, he should repeat his apology of last night before this large assembly. Moreover, he would now be free to handle this English dog--to beat and torture and torment him like a new recruit. Bull's hands would be tied as far as weapons were concerned by his promise to Carmelita.... The dog was leaning against the flap of the bar which he would have to raise to pass through to his dinner. Should he take him by the ears and rub his face in the liquor-slops on the bar, or should he merely put him on the ground and wipe his feet on him?

Better not perhaps, there was that thrice-accursed American *scelerato* and that indestructible young devil Rupert, who had smitten his jaw and ribs so vilely, and wanted to fight again directly he had left hospital and *salle de police*. The Devil smite all Englishmen....His wrath boiled over, his arm shot out and he seized John Bull by the collar, shook him, and slung him from his path.

And then the Heavens fell.

With his open, horny palm, the Bucking Bronco smote the Italian as cruelly stinging a slap as ever human face received. But for his friend's recent behest, he would have struck with his closed fist, and the Italian would have entered the fight, if not with a broken jaw, at least with a very badly "rattled" head.

"*Ponk!*" observed 'Erb, dancing from foot to foot in excitement and glee.

"Ah--h--h!" breathed Carmelita,

The Italian recovered his balance and gathered himself for a spring.

"No you don't," shouted Rupert, and the three Englishmen simultaneously threw themselves in front of him, at the same time calling on the spectators to make a ring.

In a moment, headed by Tant-de-Soif, the Englishmen's friends commenced pulling chairs, tables and benches to the walls of the big room. Old Tant-de-Soif had never received a sou or a drink from the bully, though many and many a blow and bitter humiliation. Long he had served and long he had hated. He felt that a great hour had struck.

The scores and scores of willing hands assisting, the room was quickly cleared.

"This American would die, it appears, poor madman," observed M. Malvin ingratiatingly to Carmelita.

"I do not think he will die," replied the girl. "But I think that anyone who interferes with him will do so."

The eyes of the good M. Malvin narrowed. Lay the wind in that quarter? The excellent Luigi was found out, was he? Well, there might be a successor....

Meantime the Italian had removed and methodically folded his tunic and canvas shirt. A broad belt sustained his baggy red breeches.

So it had come, had it? Well, so much the better. This American had been the fly in the ointment of his comfort too long. Why had he not strangled the insolent, or broken his back long ago? He would break him now, once and for all--maim him for life if he could; at least make a serious hospital case of him.

Bidding Malvin mount guard over his discarded garments, Rivoli stepped forth Into the middle of the large cleared space, flexing and slapping his muscles. Having done so, he looked round the crowded sides of the room for the usual applause. To his surprise none followed. He gazed about him again. Was this a selected audience? It was certainly not the audience he would have selected for himself. It appeared to consist mostly of *miserabile* whom he had frequently had to punish for insubordination and defiance of his orders. They should have a demonstration, that evening, of the danger of defying Luigi Rivoli.

As the American stepped forward John Bull caught his sleeve. "Take off your tunic, Buck," he said in surprise.

"Take off nix," replied the American.

"But he'll get a better hold on you," remonstrated his friend.

"I should worry," was the cryptic reply, as the speaker unbuttoned the upper part of his tunic and pushed his collar well away from his neck at the back.

"'E'll cop 'old of 'im wiv that coller, an' bleed'n well strangle 'im," said 'Erb to Rupert.

"Fancy that now, sonny," said the Bucking Bronco, with an exaggerated air of surprise, and stepped into the arena.

Complete silence fell upon the room as the two antagonists faced each other.

Nom de nom de bon Dieu de Dieu! Why had not le Légionnaire Bouckaing Bronceau stripped? Was it sheer bravado? How could he, or any other living man, afford to add to the already overwhelming risks when fighting the great Luigi Rivoli?...

The Bucking Bronco got his "blow in fust" after all, and, as his friend had prophesied, was glad that it had not been a "foul poke"–taking his opponent unawares.

"Come hither, dog, and let me snap thy spine," growled the Italian as the Bucking Bronco faced him. As he spoke, he thrust his right hand forward, as though to seize the American in a wrestling-hold. With a swift snatch the latter grabbed the extended hand, gave a powerful jerking tug and released it before his enemy could free it and fasten upon him in turn. The violent pull upon his arm swung the Italian half left and before he could recover his balance and regain his position, the Bucking Bronco had let drive at the side of his face with all his weight and strength. It was a terrific blow and caught Rivoli on the right cheek-bone, laying the side of his face open.

Only those who have seen--or experienced--it, know the effect of skilled blows struck by hands unhampered by boxing gloves.

The Italian reeled and, like the skilled master of ringcraft that he was, the Bucking Bronco gave him no time in which to recover. With a leap he again put all his strength, weight, and skill behind a slashing right-hander on his enemy's face, and, as he raised his arms, a left-hander on his ribs. Had any of these three blows found the Italian's "point" or "mark," it is more than probable that the fight would have been decided. As it was, Rivoli was only shaken--and exasperated to the point of madness....

Wait till he got his arms round the man! ...Corpo di Bacco! But wait! Let him wait till he got his hand on that collar that the rash fool had left undone and sticking out so temptingly?

Ducking swiftly under a fourth blow, he essayed to fling his arms round the American's waist. As the mighty arms shot out for the deadly embrace, the Bucking Bronco's knee flew up with terrific force, to smash the face so temptingly passed above it. Like a flash the face swerved to the left, the knee missed it, and the American's leg was instantly seized as in a vice.

The spectators held their breath. Was this the end? Rivoli had him! Could there be any hope for him?

There could. This was "rough-housin'"–and at "rough-housin'" the Bucking Bronco had had few equals. He suddenly thought of one of *the* fights of his life--at 'Frisco, with the bucko mate of a hell-ship on which he had made a trip as fo'c's'le-hand, from the Klondyke. The mate had done his best to kill him at sea, and the Bucking Bronco had "laid for him" ashore as the mate quitted the ship. It had been "some" fight and the mate had collared his leg in just the same way. He would try the method that had then been successful....He seized the Italian's neck with both huge hands, and, with all his strength, started to throttle him--his thumbs on the back of his opponent's neck, his fingers crushing relentlessly into his throat. Of course Rivoli would throw him--that was to be expected--but that would not free Rivoli's throat. Not by any manner of means. With a fair and square two-handed hold on the skunk's throat, it would be no small thing to get that throat free again while there was any life left in its proprietor....

With a heave and a thrust, the Italian threw the Bucking Bronco heavily and fell heavily upon him. The latter tightened his grip and saw his enemy going black in the face....Swiftly Rivoli changed his hold. While keeping one arm round the American's leg, at the knee, he seized his foot with the other hand and pressed it backward with all his gigantic strength. As the leg bent back, he pressed his other arm more tightly into the back of the knee. In a moment the leg must snap like a carrot, and the American knew it--and also that he would be lame for life if his knee-joint were thus rent asunder. It was useless to hope that Rivoli would suffocate before the leg broke...Nor would a dead Rivoli be a sufficient compensation for perpetual lameness. Never to walk nor ride nor fight....A lame husband for Carmelita....Loosing his hold on his antagonist's throat, he punched him a paralysing blow on the muscle of the arm that was bending his leg back, and then seized the same arm by the wrist with both hands, and freed his foot....A deadlock....They glared into each other's eyes, mutually impotent, and then, by tacit mutual consent, released holds, rose, and confronted each other afresh.

So far, honours were decidedly with the American, and a loud spontaneous cheer arose from the spectators. "Vive le Bouckaing Broncean!" was the general sentiment.

Carmelita sat like a statue on her high chair--lifeless save for her terrible eyes. Though her lips did not move, she prayed with all the fervour of her ardent nature.

Breathing heavily, the antagonists faced each other like a pair of half-crouching tigers.... Suddenly Rivoli kicked. Not the horizontal kick of *la savate* in which the leg is drawn up to the chest and the foot shot out sideways and parallel with the floor, so that the sole strikes the object flatly--but in the ordinary manner, the foot rising from the ground, to strike with the toe. The Bucking Bronco raised his right foot and crossed his right leg over his left, so that the Italian's rising shin met his own while the rising foot met nothing at all. Had the kick been delivered fully, the leg would have broken as the shin was suddenly arrested while the foot met nothing. (This is the deadliest defence there is against a kicker, other than a savatist.) But so fine was the poise and skill of the professional acrobat, that, in full flight, he arrested the kick ere it struck the parrying leg with full violence. He did not escape scot-free from this venture, however, for, even as he raised his leg in defence, the Bucking Bronco shot forth his right hand with one of the terrible punches for which Rivoli was beginning to entertain a wholesome respect. He saved his leg, but received a blow on the right eye which he knew must, before long, cause it to close completely. He saw red, lost his temper and became as an infuriated bull. As he had done under like circumstances with the Légionnaire Rupert, he rushed at his opponent with a roar, casting aside wisdom and prudence in the madness of his desire to get his enemy in his arms. He expected to receive a blow in the face as he sprang, and was prepared to dodge it by averting his head. With an agility surprising in so big a man, the Bucking Bronco ducked below the Italian's outstretched arms and, covering his face with his bent left arm, drove at his antagonist's "mark" with a blow like the kick of a horse. The gasping groan with which the wind was driven out of Rivoli's body was music to the Bucking Bronco's ears. He knew that, for some seconds, his foe, be he the strongest man alive, was at his mercy. Springing erect he punched with left and right at his doubled-up and gasping enemy, his arms working like piston-rods and his fists falling like sledge-hammers. The cheering became continuous as Rivoli shrank and staggered before that rain of terrific blows. Suddenly he recovered, drew a deep breath and flung his arms fairly round the Bucking Bronco's waist.

Corpo di Bacco! He had got him!...

Clasping his hands behind the American, he settled his head comfortably down into that wily man's neck, and bided his time. He had got him.... He would rest and wait until his breathing was more normal. He would then tire the *scelerato* down ... tire him down ... and then...

This was his programme, but it was not that of the Bucking Bronco, or not in its entirety. He realised that "Loojey had the bulge on him." For the moment it was "Loojey's night ter howl." He would take a rest and permit Loojey to support him, also he would feign exhaustion and distress. It was a pity that it was his right arm that was imprisoned in the bear-hug of the wrestler. However, nothing much could happen so long as he kept his back convex.

Seconds, which seemed like long minutes, passed.

Suddenly the Italian made a powerful effort to draw him closer and decrease the convexity of his arched back. He resisted the constriction with all his strength, but realised that he had been drawn slightly inward.

Again a tremendous tensing of mighty muscles, again a tremendous heave in opposition, and again he was a little nearer.

The process was repeated. Soon the line of his back would be concave instead of convex. That would be the beginning of the end. Once he bent over backward there would be no hope; he would finally drop from the Italian's grasp with a sprained or broken back, to receive shattering kicks in the face, ribs and stomach, before Rivoli jumped upon him with both feet and twenty stone weight. For a moment he half regretted having so stringently prohibited any sort or kind of interference in the fight, whatever happened, short of Rivoli's producing a weapon. But only for a moment. He would not owe his life to the intervention of others, after having promised Carmelita to beat him up and bring him grovelling to her feet. He had been winning so far.... He *would* win.... As the Italian again put all his force into an inward-drawing hug, the American, for a fraction of a second, resisted with all his strength and then suddenly did precisely the opposite. Shooting his feet between the straddled legs of his adversary, he flung his left arm around his head, threw all his weight on to it and brought himself and Rivoli crashing heavily to the ground. As the arms of the latter burst asunder, the Bucking Bronco had time to seize his head and bang it twice, violently, upon the stone floor.

Both scrambled to their feet.

It had been a near thing. He must not get into that rib-crushing hug again, for the trick would not avail twice. Like a springing lion, Rivoli was on him. Ducking, he presented the top of his head to the charge and felt the Italian grip his collar. With an inarticulate cry of glee he braced his feet and with tremendous force and speed revolved his head and shoulders round and round in a small circle, the centre and axis of which was Rivoli's hand and forearm. The first lightning-like revolution entangled the tightly-gripping hand, the second twisted and wrenched the wrist and arm, the third completed the terrible work of mangling disintegration. In three seconds the bones, tendons, ligaments, and tissue of Rivoli's right hand and wrist were broken, wrenched and torn. The bones of the forearm were broken, the elbow and shoulder-joints were dislocated. Tearing himself free, the American sprang erect and struck the roaring, white-faced Italian between the eyes and then drove him before him, staggering backward under a ceaseless rain of violent punches. Drove him back and back, even as the bully put his uninjured left hand behind him for the dagger concealed in the hip pocket of his baggy trousers, and sent him reeling, stumbling and half-falling straight into the middle of his silent knot of jackals, Malvin, Borges, Hirsch, Bauer, and Tou-tou Boil-the-Cat. Against these he fell. Malvin was seen to put out his hands to stop him, Borges and Hirsch closed in on him to catch him, Bauer pressed against Malvin, Tou-tou Boil-the-Cat stooped with a swift movement. With a grunt Rivoli collapsed, his knees gave way and, in the middle of the dense throng, he slipped to the ground. As the Bucking Bronco thrust in, and the crowd pressed back, Rivoli lay on his face in the cleared space, a knife in his left hand, another in his back.

He never moved nor spoke again, but M. Tou-tou Boil-the-Cat did both.

As he left the Café he licked his lips, smiled and murmured: *"Je m'en ai souvenu."*

Chapter XI
Greater Love..

At the bottom of the alley, le bon Légionnaire Tou-tou Boil-the-Cat encountered Sergeant Legros....A bright idea! ...Stepping up to the worthy Sergeant, he saluted, and informed him that, passing the notorious Café de la Légion, a minute since, he had heard a terrible *tohuwabohu* and, looking in, had seen a crowd of excited Legionaries fighting with knives and side-arms. He had not entered, but from the door had seen at least one dead man upon the ground.

The worthy Sergeant's face lit up as he smacked his lips with joy. Ah, ha! here were punishments....Here were crimes....Here were victims for *salle de police* and *cellules*....Fodder for the *peloton des hommes punis* and the Zephyrs....Here was distinction for that keen disciplinarian, Sergeant Legros.

"*V'la quelqu'un pour la boîte*," quoth he, and betook himself to the Café at the *pas gymastique*.

§2

At the sight of the knife buried in the broad naked back of the Italian, the silence of horror fell upon the stupefied crowd.

Nombril de Belzébuth! How had it happened?

Sacré nom de nom de bon Dieu de Dieu de Dieu de sort! Who had done it? Certainly not le Légionnaire Bouckaing Bronceau. Never for one second had the Légionnaire Rivoli's back been toward him. Never for one instant had there been a knife in the American's hand. Yet there lay the great Luigi Rivoli stabbed to the heart. There was the knife in his back. *Dame*!

Men's mouths hung open stupidly, as they stared wide-eyed. Gradually it grew clear and obvious. Of course--he had been knocked backwards into that group of his jackals, Malvin, Borges, Hirsch and Bauer, and one of them, who hated him, had been so excited and uplifted by the sight of his defeat that he had turned upon him. Yes, he had been stabbed by one of those four.

"Malvin did it. I saw him," ejaculated Tant-de-Soif. He honestly thought he had--or thought he thought so. "God bless him," he added solemnly.

He had many a score to settle with M. Malvin, but he could afford to give him generous praise--since he was booked for the firing-party beside the open grave, or five years *rabiau* in Biribi. It is not every day that one's most hated enemies destroy each other....

"Wal! I allow thet's torn it," opined the Bucking Bronco as he surveyed his dead enemy.

Carmelita came from behind the bar and down the room. What was happening? Why had the fight stopped? She saw the huddled heap that had been Rivoli....She saw the knife--and thought she understood. This was as things should be. This was how justice and vengeance were executed in her own beloved Naples. Il Signor Americano was worthy to be a Neapolitan, worthy to inherit and transmit *vendetta*. How cruelly she had misjudged him in thinking him a barbarian....

"*Payé*," she cried, turning in disgust from the body, and threw her arms round the Bucking Bronco's neck, as the Sergeant burst in at the door. Sergeant Legros was in his element. Not only was there here a grand harvest of military criminals for his reaping, but here was vengeance--and vengeance and cruelty were the favourite food of the soul of Sergeant Legros. Here was a grand opportunity for vengeance on the Italian trollop who had, when he was a private Legionary, not only rejected his importunities with scorn, but had soundly smacked his face withal. Striding forward, as soon as he had roared, "*Attention!*" he seized Carmelita roughly by the arm and shook her violently, with a shout of: "To your kennel, *prostituée*." Whereupon the Bucking Bronco felled his superior officer to the ground with a smashing blow upon the jaw, thereby establishing an indisputable claim to life-servitude in the terrible Penal Battalions.

Among the vices of vile Sergeant Legros, physical cowardice found no place. Staggering to his feet, he spat out a tooth, wiped the blood from his face, drew his sword-bayonet, and rushed at the American intending to kill him forthwith, in "self-defence." At the best of times Sergeant Legros looked, and was, a dangerous person--but the blow had made him a savage, homicidal maniac. The Bucking Bronco was dazed and astonished at what he had done. Circumstances had been too strong for him. He had naturally been in an abnormal state at the end of such a fight, and in no condition to think and act calmly when his adored Carmelita was insulted and assaulted.... What had he done? This meant death or penal servitude from the General Court Martial at Oran. He had lost her in the moment of winning her, and he dropped his hands as the Sergeant flew at him with the sword-bayonet poised to strike. No--he would fight.... He would make his get-away.... He would skin out and Carmelita should join him.... He would fight... Too late! ... The bayonet was at his throat.... Crash! ... Good old Johnny! ... That had been a near call. As the maddened Legros was in the act to thrust, Legionary John Bull had struck him on the side of the head with all his strength, sending him staggering, and had leapt upon him to secure the bayonet as they went crashing to the ground. As they struggled, Legionary Rupert set his foot heavily on the Sergeant's wrist and wrenched the bayonet from his hand.

The problem of Sir Montague Merline's future was settled and the hour for Reginald Rupert's desertion had struck.

An ominous growl had rumbled round the room at the brutal words and action of the detested Legros, and an audible gasp of consternation had followed the Bucking Bronco's blow. Sacré Dieu! Here were doings of which ignorance would be bliss--and there was a rush to the door, headed by Messieurs Malvin, Borges, Hirsch and Bauer.

Several Legionaries, as though rooted to the spot by a fearful fascination, or by the hope of seeing Legros share the fate of Rivoli, had stood their ground until John Bull struck him and Rupert snatched the bayonet as though to kill him. Then, with two exceptions, this remainder fled. These two were Tant-de-Soif and the Dutchman, Hans Djoolte; the former, absolutely unable to think of flight and the establishment of an *alibi* while the man who had made his life a hell was fighting for his own life; the latter, clear of conscience, honestly innocent and wholly unafraid. Staring round-eyed, they saw Sergeant Legros mightily heave his body upward, his head pinned to the ground by 'Erb 'Iggins, his throat clutched by Légionnaire Jean Boule, his right hand held down by Légionnaire Rupert. Again he made a tremendous effort, emitted a hideous bellowing sound and then collapsed and lay curiously still. Meanwhile, Carmelita had closed and fastened the doors and shutters of the Café and was turning out the lamps. Within half a minute of the entrance of the Sergeant, the Café was closed and in semi-darkness.

"The bloomin' ol' fox is shammin' dead," panted 'Erb, and removed his own belt. "'Eave 'im up and shove this rahnd 'is elbers while 'e's a-playin' 'possum. Shove yourn rahnd 'is legs, Buck," he added.

While still lying perfectly supine, the Sergeant was trussed like a fowl.

"Naow we gotter hit the high places. We gotter vamoose some," opined the Bucking Bronco, as the four arose, their task completed. They looked at each other in consternation. Circumstances had been too much for them. Fate and forces outside themselves had whirled them along in a spate of mischance, and cast them up, stranded and gasping. Entering the place with every innocent and praiseworthy intention, they now stood under the shadow of the gallows and the gaol. With them in that room was a murdered man, and an assaulted, battered and outraged superior....

The croaking voice of Tant-de-Soif broke the silence. *"Pour vous,"* quoth he, *"il n'y a plus que l'Enfer."*

"Shut up, you ugly old crow," replied Reginald Rupert, "and clear out.... Look here, what are you going to do about it? What are you going to say?"

"I?" enquired Tant-de-Soif. "Le Légionnaire Djoolte and I have seen each other in the Bar de Madagascar off the Rue de Daya the whole evening. We have been here *peaudezébie*. Is it not, my Djoolte? Eh, *mon salop?*"

But the sturdy Dutch boy was of a different moral fibre.

"I have not been in the Bar de Madagascar," replied he, in halting Legion French. "I have been in le Café de la Légion the whole evening and seen all that happened."

"'E's a-seekin' sorrer. 'E wants a fick ear," put in 'Erb in his own vernacular.

"If my evidence is demanded, I saw a fair fight between the Légionnaire Bouckaing Bronceau and le Légionnaire Luigi Rivoli. I then saw le Légionnaire Luigi Rivoli fall dead, having been stabbed by either le Légionnaire Malvin or le Légionnaire Bauer, if it were not le Légionnaire Hirsch, or le Légionnaire Borges. I believe Malvin stabbed him while these three held him, but I do not know. I then saw le Sergent Legros enter and assault and abuse Mam'zelle Carmelita. I then saw him fall as though someone had struck him and he then attempted to murder le Légionnaire Bronco with his Rosalie. I then saw some Légionnaires tie him up....That is the evidence that I shall give if I give any at all. I may refuse to answer, but I shall tell no lies."

"That is all right," said the Bucking Bronco. "Naow yew git up an' yew git--an' yew too, Tant-de-Soif, and tell the b'ys ter help Carmelita any they can, ef Legros gits 'er inter trouble an' gits 'er Caffy shut....An' when yew gits the Gospel truth orf yure chest, Fatty, yew kin say, honest Injun, as haow I tol' yew, thet me an' John Bull was a-goin' on pump ter Merocker, an' Mounseers Rupert an' 'Erb was a-goin' fer ter do likewise ter Toonis. Naow git," and the two were hustled out of the Café.

"Now," said John Bull, taking command, "we've got to be quick, as it's just possible the news of what's happened may reach the picket and you may be looked for before you're missing. First thing is Carmelita, second thing's money, and third thing's plan of campaign....Is Carmelita in any danger over this?"

"Don't see why she should be," said Rupert. "It's not her fault that there was a fight in her Café. It has never been in any sense a 'disorderly house,' and what happened, merely happened here."

"Yep," agreed the Bucking Bronco. "But I'm plum' anxious. I'm sure tellin' yew, I don't like ter make my gitaway an' leave her hyar. But we can't take a gal on pump."

"Arx the young lidy," suggested 'Erb, and with one consent they went to the bar, leaning on which Carmelita was sobbing painfully. The strain and agony of the last twenty-four hours had been too much and she had broken down. As they passed the two silent bodies, 'Erb stopped and bent over Sergeant Legros, remarking: "Knows 'ow ter lie doggo, don't 'e--the ol' cunnin'-chops?" He fell silent a moment, and then in a very different voice ejaculated, "Gawds-treuth 'e's *mort*, 'e is. 'E's *tué*."

John Bull and Reginald Rupert looked at each other, and then turned back quietly to where the Sergeant was lying.

"Cerebral hemorrhage," suggested John Bull. "I struck him on the side of the head."

"'Eart failure," suggested 'Erb. "I set on 'is 'ead till 'is 'eart stopped, blimey!"

"Apple Plexy, I opine," put in the Bucking Bronco. "All comes o' gittin' excited, don't it?"

"He certainly made himself perfectly miserable when I took his bayonet away," admitted Legionary Rupert.

"Anyhow, it's a fair swingin' job nah, wotever it was afore," said 'Erb. Whatever the cause and whosesoever the hand, Sergeant Legros was undoubtedly dead. They removed the belts, straightened his limbs, closed his eyes and 'Erb placed the dead man's képi over the face, bursting as he did so into semi-hysterical song--

> "Ours is a 'appy little 'ome,
> I wisht I was a kipper on the foam,
> There's no carpet on the door,
> There's no knocker on the floor,
> Oo! Ours is a 'appy little 'ome."

"Shut that damned row," said Legionary Rupert.

"Carmelita, honey," said the Bucking Bronco, stroking the hair of the weeping girl. "Yew got the brains. Wot'll we do? Shall we stop an' look arter ye? Will yew come on pump with us? Will yew ketch the nine-fifteen ter Oran? Yew could light out fer the railroad *de*-pot right now--or will yew stick it out here, an' see ef they takes away yure licence? They couldn't do nuthin' more....Give it a name, little gal--we've gotter hike quick, ef we ain't a-goin' ter stay."

Carmelita controlled herself with an effort and dried her eyes. Not for nothing had her life been what it had.

"You must all go at once," she said unhesitatingly. "Take Signor Rupert's money and make for Mendoza's in the Ghetto. He'll sell you mufti and food. Change, and then run, all night, along the railway. Lie up all day, and then run all night again. Then take different trains at different wayside stations, one by one, and avoid each other like poison in Oran; and leave by different boats on different days. I shall stay here. After trying for some hours to revive Legros, I shall send for the picket. You will be far from Sidi then. I shall give the Police all information as to the fight, and as to the murder of *that*, by Malvin; and shall conceal nothing of Legros' murderous attempt upon the Légionnaire Bouckaing Bronceau and of his death by *apoplessia*....They will see he has no wound....This will give weight and truth to my evidence to the effect that it was a fair, clean fight and that no blame attaches to le Légionnaire Bouckaing Bronceau....Where am I to blame?...No, you can leave me without fear. Also will I give evidence to having heard you plotting to make the promenade in different directions and to avoid the railway and Oran...."

The Bucking Bronco was overcome with admiration.

"Ain't that horse-sense?" he ejaculated.

Laying her hands upon his shoulders, Carmelita looked him in the eyes.

"And when you write to me to join you also, dear Americano, I will come," she said. "I, Carmelita, have said it....Now that *that* is dead, I shall be able to save some money. Write to me when you are safe, and I will join you wherever you are--whether it be Napoli or Inghilterra or America."

"God bless ye, little gal," growled the American, folding her in his arms, and for the first time of his life being on the verge of an exhibition of weakness. "We'll make our gitaway all right, an' we couldn't be no use ter yew in prison hyar....I'll earn or steal some money ter send yer, Carmelita, honey."

"I can help you there," put in Legionary Rupert.

"You and your loose cash are the *deus ex machina*, Rupert, my boy," said John Bull...."But for you, the Russians would hardly have got away so easily, and now a few pounds will make all the difference between life and death to Buck and Carmelita, not to mention yourself and 'Erb."

"I am very fortunate," said Rupert, gracefully. "By the way, how much have we left Carmelita?" he added.

"Exactly seven hundred francs, Monsieur," she replied. "Monsieur drew one thousand, he will remember, and the Russians after all, needed only three hundred in addition to their own roubles."

"What are you going to do, 'Erb?" asked John Bull. "You haven't committed yourself very deeply you know. Legros can't give evidence against you and I doubt whether Tant-de-Soif or Djoolte will....I don't suppose any of the others noticed you, but there's a risk--and ten years of Dartmoor would be preferable to six months in the Penal Battalions. What shall you do?"

"Bung orf," replied 'Erb. "I'm fair fed full wiv Hafrica. Wot price the Ol' Kent Road on a Sat'day night!"

"Then seven hundred francs will be most ample for three of you, to get mufti, railway tickets and tramp-steamer passages from Oran to Hamburg."

"Why three?" asked Rupert.

"You, Buck and 'Erb," replied John Bull.

"Oh, I see. You have money for your own needs?" observed Rupert in some surprise.

"I'm not going," announced John Bull.

"*What?*" exclaimed four voices simultaneously, three in English and one in French.

"I'm not going," he reiterated, "for several reasons.... To begin with, I've nowhere to go. Secondly, I don't want to go. Thirdly, I did not kill Legros," and, as an inducement to the Bucking Bronco to agree with his wishes, he added, "and fourthly, I may be able to be of some service to Carmelita if only by supporting her testimony with my evidence at the trial--supposing that I am arrested."

"Come off it, old chap," said Rupert. "There are a hundred men whose testimony will support Carmelita's."

"Wot's bitin' yew naow, John?" asked the Bucking Bronco. "Yew know it's a plum' sure thing as haow it'll come out thet yew slugged Legros in the year-'ole when we man-handled him. Won't that be enuff ter give yew five-spot in Biribi?"

"Yus. Wot cher givin' us, Ole Cock?" expostulated 'Erb. "Wot price them blokes Malvin, an' Bower, an' Borjis, an' 'Ersh? Fink they'll shut their 'eads? An' wot price that bloomin' psalm-smitin', Bible-puncher of a George Washington of a Joolt? Wot price ole Tarntderswoff? Git 'im in front of a court martial an' 'e wouldn't jabber, would 'e? Not arf, 'e wouldn't. I *don't* fink."

"And don't talk tosh, my dear chap, about having nowhere to go, please," said Rupert. "You're coming home with me of course. My mother will love to have you."

"Thanks awfully, but I'm afraid I can't go to England," was the reply. "I must..."

"*Garn*," interrupted 'Erb. "I'm wanted meself, but I'm a-goin' ter chawnst it. No need ter 'ang abaht Scotland Yard.... I knows lots o' quiet juggers. 'Sides, better go where it's a risk o' bein' pinched than stop where it's a dead cert.... Nuvver fing. You ain't goin' ter be put away fer wot you done, Gawd-knows-'ow-many years ago. That's all blowed over, long ago. Why you've bin 'ere pretty nigh fifteen year, ain't yer? Talk sinse, Ole Cock--ain't yer jest said yer'd raver do a ten stretch in Portland than 'arf a one in Biribi?"

John Bull and Reginald Rupert smiled at each other.

"Thanks awfully, Rupert," said the former, "but I can't go to England." Turning to the Cockney he added, "You're a good sort, Herbert, my laddie--but I'm staying here."

"Shucks," observed the American with an air of finality, and turning to Carmelita requested her to fetch the nuggets, the spondulicks, the dope--in short, the wad. Carmelita disappeared into her little room and returned in a few moments with a roll of notes.

"Well, good-bye, my dear old chap," said John Bull, taking the American's hand. "You understand all I can't say, don't you? ... Good-bye."

"Nuthin' doin', John," was the answer.

"Hurry him off, Carmelita, we've wasted quite time enough," said John Bull, turning to the girl. "If he doesn't go now and do his best for himself, he doesn't love you. Do clear him out. It's death or penal servitude if he's caught. He struck Legros before Legros even threatened him--and Legros is dead."

"You hear what Signor Jean Boule says. Are you going?" said Carmelita, turning to the American.

"No, my gal. I ain't," was the prompt reply. "How can I, Carmelita? ... I'm his pal.... Hev' I got ter choose between yew an' him?"

"Of course you have," put in John Bull. "Stay here and you will never see her again. It won't be a choice between me and her then; it'll be between death and penal servitude."

The Bucking Bronco took Carmelita's face between his hands.

"Little gal," he said, "I didn't reckon there was no such thing as 'love,' outside books, ontil I saw yew. Life wasn't worth a red cent ontil yew came hyar. Then every time I gits inter my bunk, I thinks over agin every word I'd said ter yew thet night, an' every word yew'd said ter me. An' every mornin' when I gits up, I ses, 'I shall see Carmelita ter-night,' an' nuthin' didn't jar me so long as that was all right. An' when I knowed yew wasn't fer mine, because yew loved Loojey Rivoli, then I ses, '*Hell!*' An' I didn't shoot 'im up because I see how much yew loved him. An' I put up with him when he uster git fresh, because ef I'd beat 'im up yew'd hev druv me away from the Caffy, an' life was jest Hell, 'cause I knowed 'e was a low-lifer reptile an' yew'd never believe it....An' now yew've found 'im out, an' he's gorn, an' yure mine--an' it's too late....Will yew think I don't love yew, little gal? ...Don't tell me ter go or I might sneak off an' leave John in the lurch."

"You can't help me, Buck," put in John Bull. "I shall be all right. Who'll you benefit by walking into gaol?"

The American looked appealingly at the girl, and his face was more haggard and anxious than when he was fighting for his life.

"This is my answer, Signor Bouckaing Bronceau," spake Carmelita. "Had you gone without Signor Jean Boule, I should not have followed you. Now I have heard you speak, I trust you for ever. Had you deserted your friend in trouble, you would have deserted me in trouble. If Signor Jean Boule will not go, then you must stay, for he struck Legros to save your life, as you struck him to avenge me. Would *I* run away while you paid for that blow?..."

Carmelita then turned with feminine wiles upon John Bull.

"Since Signor Jean Boule will not go on pump," she continued, "you must stay and be shot, or sent to penal servitude, and I must be left to starve in the gutter."

Sir Montague Merline came to the conclusion that after all the problem of his immediate future was not settled.

"Very well," said he, "come on. We'll cut over to Mendoza's and go to earth. As soon as he has rigged us out, we'll get clear of Sidi."

(He could always give himself up when they had to separate and he could help them no more. Yes, that was it. He would pretend that he had changed his mind and when they had to separate he would pretend that he was going to continue his journey. He would return and give himself up. Having told the exact truth with regard to his share in the matter, he would take his chance and face whatever followed.)

"*A rivederci*, Carmelita," said he and kissed her.

"*Mille grazie*, Signor," replied Carmelita. "*Buon viaggio*," and wept afresh.

"So-long, Miss," said 'Erb. "Are we dahn'arted? *Naow!*"

Carmelita smiled through her tears at the quaint English *ribaldo*, and brought confusion on Reginald Rupert by the warmth of her thanks for his actual and promised financial help....

"We'd better go separately to Mendoza's," said John Bull. "Buck had better come last. I'll go first and bargain with the old devil. We shan't be missed until the morning, but we needn't exactly obtrude ourselves on people."

He went out, followed a few minutes later by Rupert and 'Erb.

Left alone with Carmelita, the Bucking Bronco picked her up in his arms and held her like a baby, as with haggard face and hoarse voice he tried to tell her of his love and of his misery in having to choose between losing her and leaving her. Having arranged with her that he should write to her in the name of Jules Lebrun from an address which would not be in France or any of her colonies, the Bucking Bronco allowed himself to be driven from the back door of the Café. Carmelita's last words were--

"Good-bye, *amato*. When you send for me I shall come, and you need not wait until you can send me money."

§3

The good Monsieur Mendoza, discovered in a dirty unsavoury room, at the top of a broken winding staircase of a modestly unobtrusive, windowless house, in a dirty unsavoury slum of the Ghetto, was exceedingly surprised to learn that le Légionnaire Jean Boule had come to *him*, of all people in the world, for assistance in deserting.

The surprise of le bon Monsieur Mendoza was in itself surprising, in view of the fact that the facilitation of desertion was his profession. Still, there it was, manifest upon his expressive and filthy countenance, not to mention his expressive and filthy hands, which waggled, palms upward, beside his shrugged shoulders, as he gave vent to his pained astonishment, not to say indignation, at the Legionary's suggestion....He was not that sort of man....Besides, how did he know that Monsieur le Légionnaire had enough?...

John Bull explained patiently to le bon Monsieur Mendoza, of whose little ways he knew a good deal, that he had come to him because he was subterraneously famous in the Legion as the fairy god-papa who could, with a wave of his wand, convert a uniformed Légionnaire into a most convincing civilian. Further, that he was known to be wholly reliable and incorruptibly honest in his dealings with those who could afford to be his god-sons.

All of which was perfectly true.

(Monsieur Mendoza did not display a gilt-lettered board upon the wall of his house, bearing any such inscription as "*Haroun Mendoza, Desertion Agent. Costumier to Poumpistes and All who make the Promenade. Desertions arranged with promptitude and despatch. Perfect Disguises a Speciality. Foreign Money Changed. Healthy Itineraries mapped out. Second-hand Uniforms disposed of. H.M.'s Agents and Interpreters meet All Trains at Oran; and Best Berths secured on all Steamers. Convincing Labelled Luggage Supplied. Special Terms for Parties....*" nor advertise in the *Echo d'Oran*, for it would have been as unnecessary as unwise....)

All very well and all very interesting, parried Monsieur Mendoza, but while compliments garlic no *caldo*, shekels undoubtedly make the mule to go. Had le bon Légionnaire shekels?

No, he had not, but they would very shortly arrive.

"And how many shekels will arrive?" enquired the good Monsieur Mendoza.

"Sufficient unto the purpose," was the answer, and then the bargaining began. For the sum of fifty francs the Jew would provide one Legionary with a satisfactory suit of clothes. The hat, boots, linen and tie consistent with each particular suit would cost from thirty to forty francs extra....Say, roughly, a hundred francs for food and complete outfit, per individual. The attention of the worthy Israelite was here directed to the incontrovertible fact that he was dealing, not with the Rothschild brothers, but with four Legionaries of modest ambition and slender purse. To which, M. Mendoza replied that he who supped with the Devil required not only a long, but a golden spoon. In the end, it was agreed that, for the sum of three hundred francs, four complete outfits should be provided.

The next thing was the production and exhibition of the promised disguises. Would M. Mendoza display them forthwith, that they might be selected by the time that the other clients arrived?

"*Si, si,*" said M. Mendoza. "*Ciertamente. Con placer.*" It was no desire of M. Mendoza that any client should be expected *comprar a ciegas*–to buy a pig in a poke. No, *de ningun modo*....

Shuffling into an inner room, the old gentleman returned, a few minutes later, laden with a huge bundle of second-hand clothing.

"Will you travel as a party--say two tourists and their servants? Or as a party of bourgeoisie interested in the wine trade? Or--say worthy artisans or working men returning to Marseilles? ... What do you say to some walnut-juice and haiks--wild men from the *Tanezrafet*? One of you a Negro, perhaps (pebbles in the nostrils), carrying an *angareb* and a bundle. I could let you have some *hashish*....I could also arrange for camels--it's eighty miles to Oran, you know....Say, three francs a day, per camel, and *bakshish* for the men....Not *meharis* of course, but you'll be relying more on disguise than speed, for your escape...."

"No," interrupted John Bull. "It only means more trouble turning into Europeans again at Oran. We want to be four obvious civilians, of the sort who could, without exciting suspicion, take the train at a wayside station."

"What nationalities are you?" enquired the Jew.

"English," was the reply.

"Then take my advice and don't pretend to be French," said the other, and added, "Are any of the others gentlemen?"

Sir Montague Merline smiled.

"One," he said.

"Then you and that other had better go as what you are--English gentlemen. If you are questioned, do not speak too good French, but get red in the face and say, 'Goddam' ... Yes, I think one of you might have a green veil round his hat.... the others might be horsey or seamen.... Swiss waiters.... Music-hall artistes.... Or German touts, bagmen or spies.... Father Abraham! That's an idea! To get deported as a German spy! Ha, ha!" There was a knock at the door....

"Escuche!" he whispered with an air of mystery, and added, *"Quien esta ahi?"*

"It's the Lord Mayor o' Lunnon, Ole Cock," announced 'Erb as he entered. "Come fer a new set of robes an' a pearly 'at."

"That one can go either as a dismissed groom, making his way back to England, or an out-of-work Swiss waiter," declared Mendoza, as his artist eye and ear took in the details of 'Erb's personality.

A great actor and actor manager had been lost in le bon M. Mendoza, and he enjoyed the work of adapting disguises according to the possibilities of his clients, almost as much as he enjoyed wrangling and bargaining, for their last sous. A greedy and grasping old scoundrel, no doubt, but once you entrusted yourself to M. Mendoza you could rely upon his performing his part of the bargain with zeal, honesty, and secrecy.

The two Legionaries divested themselves of their uniforms and put on the clothes handed to them.

Another knock, and Rupert came in.

"Hallo, Willie Clarkson," said he to Mendoza, who courteously replied with a *"Buenas tardes, señor."*

"That one will be an English caballero," he observed.

"Thought I should never get here," said Rupert. "Got into the wrong rabbit-warren," and took off his tunic.

The Jew did not "place" the Bucking Bronco immediately upon his entrance, but studied him carefully, for some minutes, before announcing that he had better shave off his moustache and be a Spanish fisherman, muleteer, or sailor. If questioned, he might tell some tale, in execrable French, of a wife or daughter kidnapped at Barcelona and traced to a Tlemcen brothel. He should rave and be violent and more than a little drunk....

And could the worthy M. Mendoza supply a couple of good revolvers with ammunition?

"Si, si," said M. Mendoza. *"Ciertamente. Con placer.* A most excellent one of very large calibre and with twenty-eight rounds of ammunition for forty francs, and another of smaller calibre and longer barrel, but with, unfortunately, only eleven rounds for thirty-five francs...."

"Keep your right hand in your pocket, each of you," said M. Mendoza as they parted, "or you'll respectfully salute the first Sergeant you meet...."

§4

The two Englishmen, in light summer suits, one wearing white buckskin boots, the other light brown ones, both carrying gloves and light canes, attracted no second glance of attention as they strolled along the boulevard, nor would anyone have suspected the vehement beating of their hearts as they passed the Guard at the gate in the fortification walls.

Similarly innocent of appearance, was an ordinary-looking and humble little person who shuffled along, round-shouldered, shrilly whistling "Viens Poupoule, viens Poupoule, viens."

Nor more calculated to arouse suspicion in the breast of the most observant Guard, was the big, slouching, blue-jowled Spaniard, who rolled along with his *béret* over one eye, and his cigarillo pendent from the corner of his mouth. The distance separating these from the two English gentlemen lessened as the latter, leaving the main promenades, passed through a suburb and, turning to the right, followed a quiet country road, which led to a railway station.

Making a wide détour and avoiding the station, the four, marching parallel with the railway line, headed north for Oran.

So far, so good. They were clear of Sidi-bel-Abbès and they were free. Free, but in the greatest danger. The next thing was to get clear of Africa and from beneath the shadow of the tri-couleur.

"*Free!*" said Rupert, as the other two joined him and John Bull, and drew a long, deep breath, as of relief.

"Not a bit of it, Rupert," said John Bull. "It's merely a case of a good beginning and a sporting chance."

"Anyhow, well begun's half done, Old Thing. I feel like a boy let out of school," and he began to sing--

> "Si tu veux
> Faire mon bonheur,
> Marguerite, Marguerite,
>
> Si tu veux
> Faire mon bonheur,
> Marguerite, donne-moi ton coeur,

You'll have to sing that, Buck, and put 'Carmelita' for 'Marguerite,'" he added.

"Business first," interrupted John Bull. "This is the programme. We'll go steady all night at the 'quick' and the 'double' alternately, and five minutes' rest to the hour. If we can't do thirty miles by daylight, we're no Legionaries. Sleep all day to-morrow, in the shadow of a boulder, or trees....By the way, we mustn't fetch up too near Les Imberts or we might be seen by somebody while we're asleep. Les Imberts is about thirty miles from Sidi, I believe. To-morrow night, we'll do another thirty miles and that'll bring us to Wady-el-hotoma. From there I vote we go independently by different trains...."

"That's it," agreed Rupert. "United for defence--separated for concealment. We'd better hang together as far as Wady-what-is-it, in case a Goum patrol overtakes us."

"Why not bung orf from this 'ere Lace Imbear?" enquired 'Erb. "Better'n doin' a kip in the desert, and paddin' the 'oof another bloomin' night. I'm a bloomin' gennelman naow, Ole Cock. I ain't a lousy Legendary."

"Far too risky," replied John Bull. "We should look silly if Corporal Martel and a guard of men from our own *chambrée* were on the next train, shouldn't we? Whichever of us went into the station would be pinched. The later we hit the line the better, though on the other hand we can't hang about too long. We're between the Devil and the Deep Sea--station-guards and mounted patrols."

It occurred to the Bucking Bronco that his own best "lay" would be an application of the art of "holding her down." In other words, waiting outside Sidi-bel-Abbès railway station until the night train pulled out, and jumping on to her in the darkness and "decking her"–in other words, climbing on to the roof and lying flat. As a past-master in "beating an overland," he could do this without the slightest difficulty, leaving the train as it slowed down into stations and making a détour to pick it up again as it left. Before daylight he could leave the train altogether and book as a passenger from the next station (since John strongly advised against walking into Oran by road, as that was the way a penniless Legionary might be expected to arrive). By that means he would arrive at Oran before they were missed at roll-call in the morning. Should he, by any chance, be seen and "ditched" by what he called the "brakemen" and "train-crew," he would merely have "to hit the grit," and wait for the next train. Yes, that's what he would do if he were alone--but the four of them couldn't do it, even if they possessed the necessary nerve, skill and endurance--and he wasn't going to leave them.

"Come on, boys, *en avant, marche*," said John Bull, and they started on their thirty-mile run, keeping a sharp look-out for patrols, and halting for a second to listen for the sound of hoofs each time they changed from the *pas gymnastique* to the quick march. Galloping hoofs would mean a patrol of Arab gens-d'armes, the natural enemies of the *poumpiste*, the villains who make a handsome bonus on their pay by hunting white men down like mad dogs and shooting them, as such, if they resist. (It is not for nothing that the twenty-five francs reward is paid for the return of a deserter *"dead* or alive.")

On through the night struggled the little band, keeping as far from the railway as was possible without losing its guidance. When a train rolled by in the distance, the dry mouth of the Bucking Bronco almost watered, as he imagined himself "holding her down," "decking her," "riding the blind," or perhaps doing the journey safely and comfortably in a "side-door Pullman" (or goods-waggon).

Before daylight, the utterly weary and footsore travellers threw themselves down to sleep in the middle of a collection of huge boulders that looked as though they had been emptied out upon the plain from a giant sack. During the night they had passed near many villages and had made many détours to avoid others which lay near the line, as well as farms and country houses, surrounded by their fig, orange and citron trees, their groves of date-palms, and their gardens. For miles they had travelled over sandy desert, and for miles through patches of cultivation, vineyards and well-tilled fields. They had met no one and had heard nothing more alarming than the barking of dogs. Now they had reached an utterly desert spot, and it had seemed to the leader of the party to be as safe a place as they would find in which to sleep away the day. It was not too near road, path, building, or cultivation, so far as he could tell, and about a mile from the railway. The cluster of great rocks would hide them from view of any possible wayfarer on foot, horseback, or camel, and would also shelter them from the rays of the sun. He judged that they were some two or three miles from Les Imberts station, and four or five from the village of that name.

The next trouble would be water. They'd probably want water pretty badly before they got it. Perhaps it would rain. That would give them water, but would hardly improve the chances of himself and Rupert as convincing tourists. Thank Heaven they had a spare clean collar each, anyhow. Good old Mendoza. What an artist he was!...

John Bull fell asleep.

§5

"Look, my brothers! Behold!" cried "Goum" Hassan ibn Marbuk, an hour later, as he reined in his horse and pointed to where the footprints of four men left a track and turned off into the desert. "Franzwazi--they wear boots. It is they. Allah be praised. A hundred francs for us, and death for four Roumis. Let us kill the dogs."

Turning his horse from the road, he cantered along the trail of the footsteps, followed by his two companions.

"Allah be praised!" he cried again. "But our Kismet is good. Had it been but five minutes earlier it would have been too dark to notice them."

"The footprints lead into that el Ahagger," he added later, pointing to the group of great boulders.

The three men drew their revolvers and rode in among the rocks. The leading Arab gave a cry of joy and covered Rupert, who was nearest to him. As the Arab shouted, John Bull awoke and, even as he opened his eyes, yelled *"Aux armes!"* at the top of his voice. (He had shouted those words and heard them shouted, off and on, for fifteen years.) As he cried out, Hassan ibn Marbuk changed his aim from Rupert to John Bull and fired. The report of the revolver was instantly followed by three others in the quickest succession. John Bull's cry had awakened the Bucking Bronco and that wary man had slept with his "gun" in his hand. A second after Hassan ibn Marbuk fired, the Bucking Bronco shot him through the head, and then with lightning rapidity and apparently without aim, fired at the other two "Goums" who were behind their leader. Not for nothing had the Bucking Bronco been, for a time, trick pistol-shot in a Wild West show. Hassan ibn Marbuk fell from his saddle, the second Arab hung over his horse's neck, and the third, after a convulsive start, drooped and slowly bent backward, until he lay over the high crupper of his saddle.

"Arabs ain't no derned good with guns," remarked the Bucking Bronco, as he rose to his feet, though it must, in justice, be admitted that the leading Arab had decidedly screened the view, and hampered the activity of the other two as he emerged from the little gully between two mighty rocks.

"Gawd luvvus," said 'Erb, sitting up and rubbing his eyes. "Done in three coppers in a bloomin' lump!"

The Bucking Bronco secured the horses.

"I say," said Rupert, who was bending over Sir Montague Merline, "Bull's badly hit."

"Ketch holt, quick," cried the Bucking Bronco, holding out to 'Erb the three reins which he had drawn over the horses' heads. He threw himself down beside his friend and swore softly, as his experienced eye recognised the unmistakable signs.

"Is he dying?" whispered Rupert.

"His number's up," groaned the American.

"Done in by a copper!" marvelled 'Erb, and, putting his arm across his face, he leaned against the nearest horse and sobbed.... He was a child-like person, and, without knowing it, had come to centre all his powers of affection on John Bull.

The dying man opened his eyes. "Got it where the chicken got the axe," he whispered. "Good-bye, Buck.... See you in the ... Happy Hunting Grounds ... I hope."

The Bucking Bronco looked at Rupert.

"Carmelita put thisyer brandy in my pocket, Rupert," he said producing a medicine bottle. "Shall I dope him?"

He coughed and swallowed, his mouth and chin twitched and worked, and tears trickled down his face.

"Can't do much harm," said Rupert, and took the bottle from the American's shaking hand.

The brandy revived the mortally wounded man.

"Good-bye, Rupert," he said. "I advise you to go straight down to Les Imberts station ... and take the next train.... There will be a patrol ... after this patrol ... before long. You can't lie up here for long now.... Buck might take a horse and gallop for it.... Lie up somewhere else.... And ride to Oran to-night.... 'Erb should go as Rupert's servant ... or by a different train.... Remember Mendoza's tips."

The stertorous, wheezy breathing was painfully interrupted by a paroxysm of coughing.

"Much pain, old chap?" asked the white-faced Rupert, as he wiped the blood from his friend's lips.

"No," whispered Sir Montague Merline. "I am dead ... up to ... the heart.... Expanding bullet.... Lungs ... and spine ... I ... ex- ... pect. Shan't be ... long."

"Anything I can do--any message or anything?" asked Rupert.

The dying man closed his eyes.

The Bucking Bronco was frankly blubbering. Turning to the dead "Goum" who had shot his friend, he swore horribly, and deplored that the man was dead and beyond the reach of his further vengeance. He fell instantly silent as his stricken friend spoke again.

"If you ... get ... to Eng ... land, Rupert ... will ... you go ... to ... my wife? She's Lady..." he whispered.

"Yes--Lady ... *who?*" asked Rupert eagerly.

"NO," continued the dying man, in a stronger voice, as he opened his eyes. "I never ... had ... a ... wife."

Silence again.

"Why *Marguerite* ... My ... darling ... girl. *Darling* ... at ... last. *Marguerite.*"

Sir Montague Merline's problem was solved, and the last of his wages paid....

§6

The Honourable Reginald Rupert Huntingten never forgot the hour that followed. The three broken-hearted men buried their friend in a shallow, sandy grave and piled a cairn of rocks and stones above the spot. It gave them a feeling akin to pleasure to realise that every minute devoted to this labour of love, lessened their chance of escape.

Their task accomplished, they shook hands and parted--the Bucking Bronco incapable of speech. Before he rode away, Huntingten thrust a piece of paper into his hand, upon which he had scribbled: "*R. R. Huntingten, Elham Old Hall, Elham, Kent,*" and said, "Wire me there. Or--better still, come--and we'll arrange about Carmelita."

The Bucking Bronco rode away in the cool of the morning.

Having settled by the toss of a coin whether he or 'Erb should attempt the next train, he gave that grief-stricken warrior the same address and invitation.

With a crushing hand-clasp they parted, and Huntingten, with a light and jaunty step, and a sore and heavy heart, set forth for the station of Les Imberts to put his nerve and fortune to the test.

Epilogue

"Well, good night, my own darling Boy," said the beautiful Lady Huntingten, as she lit her candle from that of her son, by the table in the hall. "Don't keep Father up all night, if he and General Strong come to your bedroom."

"Good night, dearest," replied he, kissing her fondly.

Setting down her candlestick, she took him by the lapels of his coat as though loth to let him out of her sight and part with him, even for the night.

"Oh, but it is good to have you again, darling," she murmured, gazing long at his bronzed and weather-beaten face. "You won't go off again for a long, long time, will you? And we must keep your promise to that wholly delightful 'Erb, if it's humanly possible. But I really cannot picture him as a discreet and silent-footed valet....I simply loved him and the Bucking Bronco. I don't know which is the more precious and priceless....I do so wonder whether he'll be happy with his Carmelita....I shall love seeing her."

"Yes, 'Erb and Buck are great birds," replied her son, "but poor old John Bull was the chap."

"Poor man, how awful--with freedom in sight....You knew nothing of his story?" she asked.

"Absolutely nothing, dearest. All I know about him is that he was one of the very best. Funny thing, y' know, Mother--I simply lived with that chap, night and day, for a year, and know no more about him than just that. That, and his marks--and by Jove, he'd got some....Simply a mass of scars, beginning with the crown of his head, where was a hole you could have laid your thumb in. Been about a bit, too; fought in China, Madagascar, West Africa, the Sahara and Morocco, in the Legion. Certainly been in the British Army--in Africa, too. I fancy he'd been a sailor as well--anyhow he'd been in Japan and got the loveliest bit of tattooing I ever set eyes on. Wonderful colours--snake winding round his wrist and up his forearm. Thing looked alive though it had been done for over thirty years. Nagasaki, I think he said...." He yawned hugely. "But here I am rambling on about a person you never saw, and keeping you up," he added. He bent to kiss his mother again.

"Mother!--*darling*! Don't you feel well? Here, I'll get you a little brandy."

Lady Huntingten was clutching at the edge of the table, and staring at her son, white-lipped. Her face looked drawn and suddenly old.

"No, no," she said. "Come back. I--sometimes--a little..." and she sat down on the oak settle beside the table.

"The heat ..." she continued incoherently. "There, I'm all right now. Tell me some more about this--John Bull....He *is* dead? ...You buried him yourself, you said."

"Yes, poor old chap, it was awful."

"And he gave you no messages for his people? He did not tell you his real name?"

"No. Nothing. He's taken his story with him. The last words he said were 'Will you go and tell my wife, Lady...' and there he pulled himself up, and said he never had a wife. But he had, I'm sure--and he called to her by her Christian name. As he died, he cried out, '*At last--my darling--*'"

"*Marguerite*," whispered Lady Huntingten.

DRIFTWOOD SPARS

The Stories Of A Man, A Boy, A Woman, And Certain Other People Who Strangely Met Upon The Sea Of Life

> "Like driftwood spars which meet and pass
> Upon the boundless ocean-plain,
> So on the sea of life, alas!
> Man nears man, meets, and leaves again"

—MATTHEW ARNOLD

To
THE MEMORY OF MY BELOVED WIFE

Chapter I
The Man

(Mainly concerning the early life of John Robin Ross-Ellison.)

Truth is stranger than fiction, and many of the coincidences of real life are truly stranger than the most daring imaginings of the fictionist.

Now, I, Major Michael Malet-Marsac, happened at the moment to be thinking of my dear and deeply lamented friend John Ross-Ellison, and to be pondering, for the thousandth time, his extraordinary life and more extraordinary death. Nor had I the very faintest notion that the Subedar-Major had ever heard of such a person, much less that he was actually his own brother, or, to be exact, his half-brother. You see I had known Ross-Ellison intimately as one only can know the man with whom one has worked, soldiered, suffered, and faced death. Not only had I known, admired and respected him —I had loved him. There is no other word for it; I loved him as a brother loves a brother, as a son loves his father, as the fighting-man loves the born leader of fighting-men: I loved him as Jonathan loved David. Indeed it was actually a case of "passing the love of women" for although he killed Cleopatra Dearman, the only woman for whom I ever cared, I fear I have forgiven him and almost forgotten her.

But to return to the Subedar-Major. "Peace, fool! Art blind as Ibrahim Mahmud the Weeper," growled that burly Native Officer as the zealous and over-anxious young sentry cried out and pointed to where, in the moonlight, the returning reconnoitring-patrol was to be seen as it emerged from the lye-bushes of the dry river-bed.

A recumbent comrade of the outpost sentry group sniggered.

My own sympathies were decidedly with the sentry, for I had fever, and "fever is another man". In any case, hours of peering, watching, imagining and waiting, for the attack that will surely come-and never comes-try even experienced nerves.

"And who was Ibrahim the Weeper, Subedar-Major Saheb?" I inquired of the redoubtable warrior as he joined me.

"He was my brother's enemy, Sahib," replied Mir Daoud Khan Mir Hafiz Ullah Khan, principal Native Officer of the 99th Baluch Light Infantry and member of the ruling family of Mekran Kot in far Kubristan.

"And what made him so blind as to be for a proverb unto you?"

"Just some little drops of water, Sahib, nothing more," replied the big man with a smile that lifted the curling moustache and showed the dazzling perfect teeth.

It was bitter, bitter cold-cold as it only can be in hot countries (I have never felt the cold in Russia as I have in India) and the khaki flannel shirt, khaki tunic, shorts and putties that had seemed so hot in the cruel heat of the day as we made our painful way across the valley, seemed miserably inadequate at night, on the windy hill-top. Moreover I was in the cold stage of a go of fever, and to have escaped sunstroke in the natural oven of that awful valley at mid-day seemed but the prelude to being frost-bitten on the mountain at midnight. Subedar-Major Mir Daoud Khan Mir Hafiz Ullah Khan appeared wholly unaffected by the 100° variation in temperature, but then he had a few odd stone of comfortable fat and was bred to such climatic trifles. He, moreover, knew not fever, and, unlike me, had not experienced dysentery, malaria, enteric and pneumonia fairly recently.

"And had the hand of your brother anything to do with the little drops of water that made Ibrahim the Weeper so blind?" I asked.

"Something, Sahib," replied Mir Daoud Khan with a laugh, "but the hand of Allah had more than that of my brother. It is a strange story. True stories are sometimes far stranger than those of the bazaar tale-tellers whose trade it is to invent or remember wondrous tales and stories, myths, and legends."

"We have a proverb to that effect, Mir Saheb. Let us sit in the shelter of this rock and you shall tell me the story. Our eyes can work while tongue and ear play-or would you sleep?"

"*Nahin*, Sahib! Am I a Sahib that I should regard night as the time wholly sacred to sleep and day as the time when to sleep is sin? I will tell the Sahib the tale of the Blindness of Ibrahim Mahmud the Weeper, well knowing that he, a truth-speaker, will believe the truth spoken by his servant. To no liar would it seem possible.

"Know then, Sahib, that this brother of mine was not my mother's son, though the son of my father (Mir Hafiz Ullah Khan Mir Faquir Mahommed Afzul Khan), who was the youngest son of His Highness the Jam Saheb of Mekran Kot in Kubristan. And he, my father, was a great traveller, a restless wanderer, and crossed the Black Water many times. To Englistan he went, and without crossing water he also went to the capital of the Amir of Russia to say certain things, quietly, from the King of Islam, the Amir of Afghanistan. To where the big Waler horses come from he also went, and to where they take the camels for use in the hot and sandy northern parts."

"Yes, Australia" I remarked.

"Without doubt, if the Sahib be pleased to say it. And there, having taken many camels in a ship that he might sell them at a profit, he wedded a white woman —a woman of the race of the Highland soldiers of Englistan, such as are in this very Brigade."

"Married a Scotchwoman?"

"Without doubt. Of a low caste-her father being a drunkard and landless (though grandson of a Lord Sahib), living by horses and camels menially, out-casted, a jail-bird. Formerly he had carried the mail through the desert, a fine rider and brave man, but *sharab*[70] had loosened the thigh in the saddle and palsied hand and eye. On hearing this news, the Jam Saheb was exceeding wroth, for he had planned a good marriage for his son, and he arranged that the woman should die if my father, on whom be Peace, brought her to Mekran Kot. 'Tis but desert and mountain, Sahib, with a few big *jagirs*[71] and some villages, a good fort, a crumbling tower, and a town on the Caravan Road-but the Jam Saheb's words are clearly heard and for many miles.

"Our father, however, was not so foolish as to bring the woman to his home, for he knew that Pathan horse-dealers, camel-men, and traders would have taken the truth, and more than the truth, concerning the woman's social position to the gossips of Mekran Kot. And, apart from the fact that her father was a drunkard, landless, a jail-bird, out-casted by his caste-fellows, no father loves to see his son marry with a woman of another community, nor with any woman but her with whose father he has made his arrangements.

"So my father, bringing the fair woman, his wife, by ship to Karachi, travelled by the *rêlwêy terain* to Kot Ghazi and left her there in India, where she would be safe. There he left her with her *butcha*,[72] my half-brother, and journeyed toward the setting sun to look upon the face of his father the Jam Saheb. And the Jam Saheb long turned his face from him and would not look upon him nor give him his blessing-and only relented when my father took to himself another wife, my mother, the lady of noble birth whom the Jam Saheb had desired for him-and sojourned for a season at Mekran Kot. But after I was born of this union (I am of pure and noble descent) his heart wearied, being with the fair woman at Kot Ghazi, for whom he yearned, and with her son, his own son, yet so white of skin, so blue of eye, the fairest child who ever had a Pathan father. Yea, my brother was even fairer than I, who, as the Huzoor knoweth, have grey eyes, and hair and beard that are not darkly brown.

"So my father began to make journeys to Kot Ghazi to visit the woman his first wife, and the boy his first-born. And she, who loved him much, and whom he loved, prevailed upon him to name my brother after *her* father as well as after himself, the child's father (as is our custom) and so my brother was rightly called Mir Jan Rah-bin-Ras el-Isan Ilderim Dost Mahommed Mir Hafiz Ullah Khan."

"And what part of that is the name of his mother's father?" I asked, for the Subedar-Major's rapid utterance of the name conveyed nothing of familiar English or Scottish names to my mind.

"Jan Rah-bin-Ras el-Isan," replied Mir Daoud Khan; "that was her father's name, Sahib."

"Say it again, slowly."

"Jan Rah-bin-Ras el-Isan."

"I have it! Yes, but *what*? —John Robin Ross-Ellison? Good God! But *I* knew a John Robin Ross-Ellison when *I* was a Captain. He was Colonel of the Corps of which I was Adjutant, in fact-the Gungapur Volunteer Rifles.... By Jove! That explains a lot. *John Robin Ross-Ellison!*"

I was too incredulous to be astounded. It *could* not be.

"*Han*[73] Sahib, *bé shak!*[74] Jan Rah-bin-Ras el-Isan Ilderim Dost Mahommed Mir Hafiz Ullah Khan was his name. And his mother called him Jan Rah-bin-Ras el-Isan and his father, Mir Hafiz Ullah Khan, called him Ilderim Dost Mahommed."

"H'm! A Scotch Pathan, brought up by an Australian girl in India, would be a rare bird-and of rare possibilities naturally," I murmured, while my mind worked quickly backward.

"My brother was unlike us in some things, Sahib. He was fond of the *sharab* called 'Whisky' and of dogs; he drank smoke from the cheroot after the fashion of the Sahib-log and not from the hookah nor the *bidi*;[75] he wore boots; he struck with the clenched fist when angered; and never did he squat down upon his heels nor sit cross-legged upon the ground. Yet he was true Pathan in many ways during his life, and he died as a Pathan should, concerning his honour (and a woman). Yea-and in his last fight, ere he was hanged, he killed more men with his long Khyber knife, single-handed against a mob, than ever did lone man before with cold steel in fair fight."

Then it was so. And the Subedar-Major was John Robin Ross-Ellison's brother!

"He may have been foolishly kind to women, servants and dogs, and of a foolish type of honour that taketh not every possible advantage of the foe-but he was very brave, Huzoor, a strong enemy, and when he began he made an end, and if that same honour were affronted he killed his man. And yet he did not kill Ibrahim Mahmud the Weeper, who surely earned his death twice, and who tried to kill him in a manner most terrible to think of. No, he did not-but it shall be told.... And the white woman prevailed upon our father to make her man-child a Sahib and to let him go to the *maktab*[76] and *madressah-tul-Islam*[77] at Kot Ghazi, to learn the clerkly lore that gives no grip to the hand on the sword-hilt and lance-shaft nor to the thighs in the saddle, no skill to the fingers on the reins, no length of sight to the eye, no steadiness to the rifle and the lance, no understanding of the world and men and things. But our father corrected all this, that the learning might do him no harm, for oft-times he brought him to Mekran Kot (where my mother tried to poison him), and he took him across the Black Water and to Kabul and Calcutta and showed him the world. Also he taught him all he knew of the horse, the rifle, the sword, and the lance-which was no small matter. Thus, much of the time wasted at school was harmless, and what the boy lost through the folly of his mother was redeemed by the wisdom of his father. Truly are our mothers our best friends and worst enemies. Why, when I was but a child my mother gave me money and bade me go prove-but I digress. Well, thus my brother grew up not ignorant of the things a man should know if he is to be a man and not a *babu*, but the woman, his mother, wept sore whenever he was taken from her, and gave my father trouble and annoyance as women ever do. And when, at last, she begged that the boy might enter the service of the Sirkar as a wielder of the pen in an office in Kot Ghazi, and strive to become a leading *munshi*[78] and then a Deputy-Saheb, a *babu* in very fact, my father was wroth, and said the boy would be a warrior-yea, though he had to die in his first skirmish and ere his beard were grown. Then the woman wept and wearied my father until it seemed better to him that she should die and, being at peace, bring peace. No quiet would he have at Mekran Kot from my mother and his father, the Jam Saheb, while the woman lived, nor would she herself allow him quiet at Kot Ghazi. And was she not growing old and skinny moreover? And so he sent my brother to Mekran Kot-and the woman died, without scandal. So my brother dwelt thenceforward in Mekran Kot, knowing many things, for he had passed a great *imtahan*[79] at Bombay and won a *sertifcut*[80] thereby, whereof the Jam Saheb was very pleased, for the son of the Vizier had also gone to a *madresseh* and won a *sertifcut*, and it was time the pride of the Vizier and his son were abated.

"Now the son of the Vizier, Mahmud Shahbaz, was Ibrahim-and a mean mangy pariah cur this Ibrahim Mahmud was, having been educated, and he hated my brother bitterly by reason of the *sertifcut* and on account of a matter concerning a dancing-girl, one of those beautiful fat Mekranis, and, by reason of his hatred and envy and jealousy, my mother made common cause with him, she also desiring my brother's death, in that her husband loved this child of another woman, an alien, his first love, better than he loved hers. But *I* bore him no ill-will, Huzoor. I loved him and admired his deeds.

"Many attempts they made, but though my mother was clever and Ibrahim Mahmud and his father the Vizier were unscrupulous, my brother was in the protection of the Prophet. Moreover he was much away from Mekran Kot, being, like our father, a great traveller and soon irked by whatever place he might be in. And, one time, he returned home, having been to Germany on secret service (a thing he often did before he became a Sahib) and to France and Africa on a little matter of rifles for Afghanistan and the Border, and spoke to us of that very Somaliland to which this very *pultan*, the 99th Baluch Light Infantry, went in 1908 (was it?), and how the English were losing prestige there and would have to send troops or receive *boondah*[81] and the blackened face from him they called the Mad Mullah. And yet another time he returned from India bringing a Somali boy, a black-faced youth, but a good Mussulman, whom, some time before, he had known and saved from death in Africa, and now had most strangely encountered again. And this Somali lad-who was not a *hubshi*, a Woolly One, not a Sidi[82] slave-saved my brother's life in his turn. I said he was not a slave-but in a sense he was, for he asked nothing better than to sit in the shadow of my brother throughout his life; for he loved my brother as the Huzoors' dogs love their masters, yea-he would rather have had blows from my brother than gold from another. He it was who saved Mir Jan Rah-bin-Ras el-Isan from the terrible death prepared for him by Ibrahim Mahmud. It was during this visit to Mekran Kot that Mahmud Shahbaz, the Vizier, announced that he was about to send his learned son, the dog Ibrahim, to Englistan to become English-made first-class Pleader-what they called —'*Barishtar-at-Lar*' is it not, Sahib?"

"That's it, Mir Saheb," replied I, sitting alert with chattering teeth and shivering ague-stricken body. "Barrister-at Law.... Sit as close to me as you can, for warmth.... Hark! Is that a signal?" as a long high wavering note rose from the dry river-bed before us and wailed lugubriously upon the night, rising and falling in mournful cadence.

"'Twas a genuine jackal-cry, Huzoor. One can always tell the imitation if jackals have sung one's lullaby from birth-though most Pathans can deceive white ears in the matter.... Well, this made things no pleasanter, for Ibrahim crowed like the dung-hill cock he was, and boasted loudly. Also my mother urged him to do a deed ere he left Mekran Kot for so long a sojourn in Belait.[83] And to her incitements and his own inclination and desires was added that which made revenge and my brother's death the chiefest things in all the world to Ibrahim Mahmud, and it happened thus.... But do I weary the Sahib with my babble?"

"Nay-nay-far from it, Mir Saheb," replied I. "The sentry of talk challenges the approaching skirmishers of sleep. The thong of narrative drives off the dogs of tedium. Tell on." And in point of fact I was now too credulous to be anything but astounded.... *John Robin Ross-Ellison!*

"Well, one day, my brother and I went forth to shoot sand-grouse, tuloor,[84] chikor,[85] chinkara[86] and perchance ibex, leaving behind this black body-servant Moussa Isa, the Somali boy, because he was sick. And it was supposed that we should not return for a week at the least. But on the third day we returned, my brother's eyes being inflamed and sore and he fearing blindness if he remained out in the desert glare. This is a common thing, as the Sahib knoweth, when dust and sun combine against the eyes of those who have read over-many books and written over-much with the steel pen upon white paper, and my brother was somewhat prone to this trouble in the desert if he exhausted himself with excessive *shikar* and-other matters. And this angered him greatly. Yet it was all ordained by Allah for the undoing of that unclean dog Ibrahim Mahmud-for, returning and riding on his white camel (a far-famed pacer of speed and endurance) under the great gateway of the Jam's fort-high enough for a camel-rider to pass unstooping and long enough for a *rêlwêy*-tunnel-he came upon Mahmud Ibrahim and his friends and followers (for he had many such, who thought he might succeed his father as Vizier) doing a thing that enraged my brother very greatly. Swinging at the end of a cord tied to his hands, which were bound behind his back, was the boy Moussa Isa the Somali, apparently dead, for his eyes were closed and he gave no sign of pain as Ibrahim's gang of pimps, panders, bullies and *budmashes*[87] kept him swinging to and fro by blows of *lathis*[88] and by kicks, while Ibrahim and his friends, at a short distance, strove to hit the moving body with stones. I suppose the agony of hanging forward from the arms, and the blows of staff and stone, had stunned the lad-who had offended Ibrahim, it appeared, by preventing him from entering my brother's house-probably to poison his water-*lotah*[89] and *gurrah*[90] —at the door of which he, Moussa Isa, lay sick. My brother, Mir Jan, sprang from his camel without waiting for the driver to make it kneel, and going up to Ibrahim, he struck him with his closed, but empty, hand. Not with the slap that stings and angers, he struck him, but with the thud that stuns and injures, upon the mouth, removing certain of his teeth, —such being his anger and his strength. Rising from the ground and plucking forth his knife, Ibrahim sprang at my brother who, unarmed, straightway smote him senseless, and that is talked of in Mekran Kot to this day. Yea-senseless. Placing the thumb upon the knuckles of the clenched fingers, he smote at the chin of Ibrahim, and laid him, as one dead, upon the earth. Straight to the front from the shoulder and not downwards nor swinging sideways he struck, and it was as though Ibrahim had been shot. The Sahib being English will believe this, but many Baluchis and Pathans do not. They cannot believe it, though to me Subedar-Major Mir Daoud Khan Mir Hafiz Ullah Khan of the 99th Baluch Light Infantry of the Army of the King Emperor of India, they pretend that they do, when I tell of that great deed.... Then my brother loosed Moussa Isa with his own hand, saying that even as he had served Ibrahim Mahmud so would he serve any man who injured a hair of the head of his body-servant. And Moussa Isa clave to my brother yet the more, and when a great Sidi slave entered the room of my brother by night, doubtless hired by Ibrahim Mahmud to slay him, Moussa Isa, grappling with him, tore out his throat with his teeth, though stabbed many times by the Sidi, ere my brother could light torch or wick to tell friend from foe. Whether he were thief or hired murderer, none could say-least of all the Sidi when Moussa Isa, at my brother's bidding, loosed his teeth from the man's throat. But all men held that it was the work of Ibrahim, for, on recovering his senses that day of the blow, he had walked up to my brother Mir Jan and said: —

"'For that blow will I have a great revenge, O Jan Rah-bin-Ras el-Isan Ilderim Dost Mahommed Mir Hafiz Ullah Khan, descendant of Mirs and of *mlecca* dogs, this year or next year, or ten years hence, or when thou art old, or upon thy first-born. By the sacred names of God, by the Beard of the Prophet, by the hilt and blade of this my knife, and by the life of my oldest son, I swear to have a vengeance on thee that shall turn men pale as they whisper it. *And may Allah smite me blind* if I do not unto thee a thing of which children yet unborn shall speak with awe.'

"Thus spake Ibrahim, son of Mahmud, for though a dog, a mangy pariah cur, he was still a Pathan.

"But my brother laughed in his face and said but 'It would seem that I too have tortured a slave' whereat Ibrahim repeated again 'Yea —*may Allah smite me blind!*'

"And something of this coming to the ears of our father, now heir to the Jam of Mekran Kot, as his brothers were dead (in the big Border War they died), he prayed the Jam Saheb to hasten the departure of the Vizier's cub, and also told the Vizier that he would surely cut out his tongue if aught befell Mir Jan. So the Vizier sent Ibrahim to Kot Ghazi on business of investing moneys-wrung by knavery, doubtless, from litigant suitors, candidates, criminals, and the poor of Mekran Kot. And shortly after, the Jam Saheb heard of a new kind of gun that fires six of the fat cartridges such as are used for the shooting of birds, without reloading; and he bade Mir Jan who understood all things, and the ways of the European gun-shop at Kot Ghazi, to hasten forthwith and procure him a couple, and if none were in Kot Ghazi to send a *tar*[91] to Bombay for them, or even, if necessary, to Englistan, though at a cost of two rupees a word. With such a gun the Jam hoped to get better *shikar* when sitting on his camel and circling round the foolish crouching grouse or *tuloor*, and firing at them as they sat. He thought he might fire twice or thrice at them sitting, and again twice or thrice at the remnant flying, and perchance hit some on the wing, after the wonderful manner of the Sahibs. So he sent my brother, knowing him to be both clever and honest and understanding the speech and ways of the English most fully.

"Now it is many days' journey, Sahib, across the desert and the mountains, from Mekran Kot in Kubristan to Kot Ghazi in India, but at Kot Ghazi is a fine bungalow, the property of the Jam Saheb, and there all travellers from his house may sojourn and rest after their long and perilous travel.

"Taking me and Mir Abdul Haq and Mir Hussein Ali and many men and servants, among whom was the body-servant, the boy Moussa Isa Somali, he set forth, a little depressed that we heard not the cry of the partridge in the fields of Mekran Kot as we started-not exactly a bad omen, but lacking a good one. And sure enough, ere we won to Kot Ghazi, his eyes became red and inflamed, very sore and painful to use. So, he put the tail of his *puggri*[92] about his face and rode all day from sun-rise to sun-set in darkness, his camel being driven by Abdulali Gulamali Bokhari-the same who later rose to fame and honour as an outlaw and was hanged at Peshawar after a brave and successful career. And being arrived, in due course, at Kot Ghazi, before entering the bungalow belonging to the Jam Saheb, he knelt his camel at the door of the shop of a European *hakim* —in English a —er —"

"Chemist, Mir Saheb," I suggested.

"Doubtless, since your honour says it-of a *kimmish*, and entering, to the Eurasian dog therein said in English, of which he knew everything (and taught me much, as your honour knows), 'Look you. I need lotion for my eyes, eye medicine, and a bath for them' and the man mixed various waters and poured them into a blue bottle with red labels, very beautiful to see, and wrote upon it. Also he gave my brother a small cup of glass, shaped like the mouth of the *pulla* fish or the eye-socket of a man. And my brother, knowing what to do, used the things then and there, to the wonder of Abdul Haq and Hussein Ali, pouring the liquor into the glass cup, and holding it to his eyes, and with back-thrown head washing the eye and soothing it.

"'Shahbas!'[93] quoth he. 'It is good,' and anon we proceeded to the gun-shop and then to the bungalow belonging to the Jam Saheb. And lo and behold, here we discovered the dog Ibrahim Mahmud, and my brother twisted the knife of memory in the wound of insult by ordering him to quit the room he occupied and seek another, since Mir Jan intended the room for his body-servant, Moussa Isa Somali-the servant of a Mir being more deserving of the room than the son of a Vizier! This was unwise, but my brother's heart was too great to fear (or to fathom) the guile of such a serpent as Ibrahim.

"And when he had bathed and prayed, eaten and drunk and rested, my brother again anointed his eyes with the liquid-which though only like water, was strong to soothe and heal. And our servants and people watched him doing this with wonder and admiration, and the news of it spread to the servants of Ibrahim Mahmud, who told their master of this cleverness of Mir Jan, —and Ibrahim, after a while, sent a message and a present to my brother, humbling himself, and asking that he too might see this thing.

"And Mir Jan, perhaps a little proud of his English ways, sat upon his *charpai*,[94] and bathed his eyes in the little bath, until, wearying of the trouble of pouring back the liquid into the bottle, he would press the bottle itself to his eye and throw back his head. So his eyes were quickly eased of pain, and in the evening we all went forth to enjoy.

"On his return to the room, Mir Jan flung himself, weary, upon his *charpai* and Moussa Isa lay across the doorway.

"In the morning my brother awoke and sitting on the *charpai*, took up the blue bottle, drew the cork, and raised the bottle towards his eyes. As he did this, Moussa Isa entered, and knowing not why he did so, sprang at his master and dashed the bottle from his hand. It fell to the ground but broke not, the floor being *dhurrie*[95]-covered.

"In greatest amazement Mir Jan glanced from Moussa Isa to the bottle, clenching his hand to strike the boy-when behold! the very floor bubbled and smoked beneath the touch of the liquid as it ran from the bottle. By the Beard of the Prophet, that stone floor bubbled and smoked like water and the *dhurrie* was burnt! Snatching up the bottle my brother dropped drops from it upon the blade of his knife, upon the leather of his boots, upon paint and brass and clothing-and behold it was liquid fire, burning and corroding all that it touched! To me he called, and, being shown these things, I could scarce believe-and then I cried aloud 'Ibrahim Mahmud! Thine enemy!... Oh, my brother, —thine eyes!' and I remembered the words of Ibrahim, *'a vengeance that shall turn men pale as they whisper it —a thing of which children yet unborn shall speak with awe'* and we rushed to his room, —to find it empty. He and his best camel and its driver were gone, but all his people and servants and *oont-wallahs*[96] were in the *serai*,[97] and said they knew not where he was, but had received a *hookum*[98] over-night to set out that day for Mekran Kot. And, catching up a pariah puppy, I re-entered the house and dropped one drop from the blue bottle into its eye. Sahib, even *I* pitied the creature and slew it quickly with my knife. And it was this that Ibrahim Mahmud had intended for the blue eyes of my beautiful brother. This was the vengeance of which men should speak in whispers. Those who saw and heard that puppy would speak of it in whispers indeed-or not at all. I felt sick and my fingers itched to madness for the throat of Ibrahim Mahmud. Had I seen him then, I would have put out his eyes with my thumbs. Nay—I would have used the burning liquid upon him as he had designed it should be used by my brother.

"Hearing Mir Jan's voice, I hurried forth, and found that his white pacing-camel was already saddled and that he sat in the front seat, prepared to drive. 'Up, Daoud Khan' he cried to me 'we go a-hunting' —and I sprang to the rear saddle even as the camel rose. 'Lead on, Moussa Isa, and track as thou hast never tracked before, if thou wouldst live,' said he to the Somali, a noted *paggi*,[99] even among the Baluch and Sindhi *paggis* of the police at Peshawar and Kot Ghazi. 'I can track the path of yesterday's bird through the air and of yesterday's fish through the water,' answered the black boy; 'and I would find this Ibrahim by smell though he had blinded *me*,' and he led on. Down the Sudder Bazaar he went unfaltering, though hundreds of feet of camels, horses, bullocks and of men were treading its dust. As we passed the shop of the European *hakim*, yes, the *kimmish*, my brother leapt down and entering the shop asked questions. Returning and mounting he said to me: "Tis as I thought. Hither he came last night, and, saying he was science-knowing failed B.Sc., demanded certain acids, that, being mixed, will eat up even gold-which no other acid can digest, nor even assail...."

"*Aqua Regia*, or vitriol, I believe," I murmured, still marvelling... *Ross-Ellison!*

"Doubtless, if your honour is pleased to say so. 'He must have poured these acids into the bottle while we were abroad last night,' continued my brother. 'Oh, the dog! The treacherous dreadful dog!...'Twas in a good hour that I saved Moussa Isa,' and indeed I too blessed that Somali, so mysteriously moved by Allah to dash the bottle from my brother's hand.

"'Think you that Ibrahim Mahmud bribed Moussa and that he repented as he saw you about to anoint your eyes with the acid?' I asked of my brother.

"'Nay-Moussa was with me until I returned,' replied he, 'and returning, I put the bottle beneath my pillow. Besides, Ibrahim had fled ere we returned to the bungalow. Moreover, Moussa would lose his tongue ere he would tell me a lie, his eyes ere he would see me suffer, his hand ere he would take a bribe against me. No-Allah moved his heart-rewarding me for saving his life at the risk of mine own, when he lay beneath a lion, —or else it is that the black dog hath the instincts of a dog and knows when evil threatens what it loves.' And indeed it is a wonderful thing and true; and Moussa Isa never knew how he knew, but said his arm moved of itself and that he wondered at himself as he struck the bottle from his master's hand. And, in time, we left the city and followed the road and found that Ibrahim was fleeing to Mekran Kot, doubtless to be far away when the thing happened, and also to get counsel and money from his father and my mother, should suspicion fall on him and flight be necessary. And anon even untrained eyes could see where he had left the Caravan Road and taken the shorter route whereby camels bearing no heavy load could come by steeper passes and dangerous tracks in shorter time to Mekran Kot, provided the rider bore water sufficient-for there was no oasis nor well. 'Enough, Moussa Isa, thou mayest return, I can track the camel of Ibrahim now that he hath left the road,' quoth my brother, breaking a long silence; but Moussa Isa, panting as he ran before, replied: 'I come, Mir Saheb. I shall not fall until mine eyes have beheld thy vengeance-in which perchance, *I* may take a part. He called me "*Hubshi*".'

"'He hath many hours' start, Moussa,' said my brother, 'and his camel is a good one. He will not halt and sleep for many hours even though he suppose me dead!'

"'I can run for a day; for a day and a night I can run,' replied the Somali, 'and I can run until the hour of thy vengeance cometh. He called *me* "Hubshi"'... and he ran on.

"Sahib, for the whole of that day he ran beside the fast camel, my brother drawing rein for no single minute, and when, at dawn, I awoke from broken slumber in the saddle, Moussa Isa was running yet! And then we heard the cry of the partridge and knew that our luck was good.

"'He may have left the track,' quoth my brother soon after dawn, 'but I think he is making for Mekran Kot, to get money and documents and to escape again ere news of his deed-or the suspicion of him-reaches the Jam Saheb. We may have missed him, but I could not halt and wait for daylight. He cannot be far ahead of us now. This camel shall live on milk and meal and wheaten bread, finest *bhoosa*[100] and chosen young green shoots, and buds, and leaves-and he shall have a collar of gold with golden bells, and reins of silk, and hanging silken tassels, and he shall — —" and then Moussa Isa gave a hoarse scream and pointed to the sky-line above which rose a wisp of smoke.

"'It is he,' said my brother, and within the hour we beheld the little bush-tent of Ibrahim Mahmud (made with cloths thrown over a bent bush) and his camel, near to which, his *oont-wallah* Suleiman Abdulla had kindled a fire and prepared food. (Later this liar swore that he made the fire smoke with green twigs to guide the pursuit, —a foolish lie, for he knew not what Ibrahim had done, nor anything but that his master hastened.)

"Moussa Isa staggered to where Ibrahim Mahmud lay asleep, looked upon his face, and fell, seeming to be about to die.

"Making a little *chukker*[101] round, my brother drove the camel between Suleiman and the tent and made it kneel.

"'*Salaam aleikoum*,¹⁰² Mir Saheb,' said Suleiman, and my brother replied: —

"'Salaam. Tend thou my camel and prepare food for me, and my brother, and my servant. And if thou wouldst not hang in a pig's skin, be wise and wary, and keep eyes, ears, and mouth closed.' And we drank water.

"Then, treading softly, we went to the tent where Ibrahim Mahmud slept and sat us down where we could look upon his face. There he slept, Sahib, peacefully, like a little child! —having left Mir Jan to die the death 'whereof men should speak with awe,' as he had threatened.

"We sat beside him and watched. Saying nothing, we sat and watched. An hour passed and an hour again. For another hour without moving or speaking we sat and Moussa Isa joined us and watched.

"'Twas sweet, and I licked my lips and hoped he might not wake for hours, although I hungered. The actual revenge is very, very sweet, Sahib, but does it exceed the joy of watching the enemy as he lies wholly at your mercy, lies in the hollow of your hand and is your poor foolish plaything, —knave made fool at last? Like statues we sat, moving not our eyes from his face, and we were very happy.

"Then, suddenly, he awoke and his eyes fell on my brother-and he shrieked aloud, as the hare shrieks when hound or jackal seize her; as the woman shrieks when the door goes down before the raiders and the thatch goes up in flame.

"Thus he shrieked.

"We moved not.

"'Why cryest thou, dear brother?' asked Mir Jan in a soft, sweet voice.

"'I —I —thought thou wast a spirit, come to —' he faltered, and my brother answered: —

"'And why should *I* be a spirit, my brother? Am I not young and strong?'

"'I dreamed,' quavered Ibrahim.

"'I too have had a dream,' said my brother.

"''Twas but a dream, Mir Jan. I will arise and prepare some —' replied Ibrahim, affecting ease of manner but poorly, for he had no real nerve.

"'Thou wilt not arise yet, Ibrahim Mahmud,' murmured my brother gently.

"'Why?'

"'Because thine eyes are somewhat wearied and I purpose to wash them with my magic water,' and as he held up the blue bottle with the red label Ibrahim screamed like a girl and flung himself forward at my brother's feet, shrieking and praying for mercy: —

"'*No, No!*' he howled; 'not *that!* Mercy, O kingly son of Kings! I will give thee —"

"'Nay, my brother, —what is this?' asked Mir Jan softly, with kind caressing voice. 'What is all this? I do but propose to bathe thine eyes with this same magic water wherewith I bathed mine own, the day before yesterday. Thou didst see me do it-thou didst watch me do it.'

"'Mercy-most noble Mir! Have pity, 'twas not I. Mercy!' he screamed.

"'But, Ibrahim, dear brother' expostulated Mir Jan, 'why this objection to my magic water? It gave me great relief and my eyes were quickly healed. Thine own need care-for see-water gushes from them even now.'

"The dog howled-like a dog-and offered lakhs of rupees.

"'But surely, my brother, what gave me relief will give thee relief? Thou knowest how my eyes were soothed and healed, and that it is a potent charm, and surely *it is not changed?*' Mir Jan Rah-bin-Ras el-Isan was all Pathan then, Sahib, whatever he may have been at other times. I could not have played more skilfully with the dog myself.

"At last, turning to Moussa Isa he said: —

"'Our brother seemeth distraught, and perchance will do himself some injury if he be not tended with care and watched over. Bind him, to make sure that he hurt not himself in this strange madness that hath o'ertaken him, making him fancy harm even in this healing balm.

Bind him tightly.' And at that, the treacherous, murderous dog found his manhood for a moment and made to spring to his feet and fight, but as he tried to rise, Moussa Isa kicked him in the face and fell upon him.

"'Shall I serve thee as I served thy *Hubshi* hireling, thy Sidi slave?' he grunted and showed his sharp strong teeth.

"'Perchance 'twould cure him of his madness if we bled the poor soul a little,' cooed my brother, putting his hand to his cummerbund where was his long Afghan knife, and Ibrahim Mahmud lay still. Picking up his big, green turban from beside his rug, I bound his arms to his sides and then, going forth, got baggage-cords from the *oont-wallah* and likewise his *puggri*, and Moussa Isa bound his feet and hands and knees.

"Then my brother called Suleiman Abdulla the *oont-wallah*, and bade Moussa Isa sleep-which he did with his knife in his hand, having bound his foot to that of Ibrahim.

"'Look, thou dog,' said Mir Jan to Suleiman, 'should this rat-flea escape, thy soul and thy body shall pay, for I will put out thine eyes with glowing charcoal and hang thee in the skin of a pig, if I have to follow thee to Cabul to do it-yea, to Balkh or Bokhara. See to it.' And Suleiman put his head upon my brother's feet, poured dust upon it and said 'So be it, Mir Saheb. Do this and more if he escape,' and we slept awhile.

"Anon we awoke, ate, drank and smoked, my brother smoking the cheroots of the Sahib-log and I having to be content with the *bidis* of Suleiman as there was no hookah.

"And when we had rested we went and sat before the face of Ibrahim and gazed upon him long, without words.

"And he wept. Like a woman he wept, and said 'Slay me, Mir Saheb, and have done. Slay me with thy knife.'

"But my brother replied softly and sweetly: —

"'What wild words are these, Ibrahim? Why should I slay thee? Some matter of a quarrel there was concerning thy torturing of my servant-but I am not of them that bear grudges and nurse hatred. In no anger slay thee with my knife? Why should I injure thee? I do most solemnly swear, Ibrahim, that I will do thee no wilful hurt. I will but anoint thine eyes with the contents of this bottle just as I did anoint my own. Why should I slay thee or do thee hurt?'

"And I chuckled aloud. He was all Pathan then, Sahib, and handling his enemy right subtly.

"And Ibrahim wept yet more loudly and said again: —

"'Slay me and have done.' Then my brother gave him the name by which he was known ever after, saying: —

"'Why should I slay thee, *Ibrahim, the Weeper?*' and he produced the bottle and held it above that villain's face.

"His screams were music to me, and in the joy of his black heart Moussa Isa burst into some strange chant in his own Somali tongue.

"'Nay, our friends must hear thy eloquence and songs, Ibrahim,' said my brother, after he had held the bottle tilted above the face of the Weeper for some minutes. "Twere greedy to keep this to ourselves.'

"Again and again that day my brother would say: 'Nay —I cannot wait longer. Poor Ibrahim's weeping eyes must be relieved at once,' and he would produce the bottle, uncork it, and hold it over Ibrahim's face as he writhed and screamed and twisted in his bonds.

"'What ails thee, Ibrahim the Weeper?' he would coo. 'Thou knowest it is a soothing lotion. Didst thou not see me use it on mine own eyes?' Yea, he was true Pathan then, and I loved him the more.

"A hundred times that day he did thus and enjoyed the music of Ibrahim's screams, and by night the dog was a little mad. So, lest we defeat ourselves and lose something of the sport our souls loved, we left him in peace that night, if 'peace' it is to know that the dreadful death you have prepared for another now overhangs you. Moussa Isa kept watch through the night. And in the morning came Abdul Haq and Hussein Ali and the servants and *oont-wallahs*, save a few who had been sent with laden camels by the Caravan Road. And, when all had eaten and rested, my brother held *durbar*,[103] having placed Ibrahim Mahmud in the midst, bound, and looking like one who has long lain upon a bed of sickness.

"This *durbar* proceeded with the greatest solemnity and no man smiled when my brother said: 'And now, touching the matter of my beloved and respected Ibrahim Mahmud, son of our grandfather's Vizier,—the learned Ibrahim, who shortly goeth (perhaps) across the black water to Englistan to become a great and famous pleader,—can any suggest the cause of the strange and distressing madness that hath come upon him so suddenly? For, behold, I have to keep him bound lest he do himself an injury, and constantly he crieth, "Kill me, Mir Saheb, kill me with thy knife and make an end." And when I go to bathe his poor eyes, so sore and red with weeping, behold he shrieketh like the *rêlwêy terain* at Peshawar and weepeth like a woman.'

"And Abdul Haq spoke and said: 'Is it so indeed, Mir Saheb?' And my brother said: 'It is so;' and Hussein Ali said: 'Is it so indeed, Mir Saheb?' And my brother said 'It is so;' and all men said the same thing gravely and my brother made the same answer.

"Sahib, I shall never forget the joy of that *durbar* with Ibrahim the Weeper there, like a trapped rat, in the midst, looking from face to face for mercy.

"'Yea-it is so. It is indeed so,' again said my brother when all had asked. 'You shall see-and hear. Behold I will drop but one drop of my soothing lotion into each of his eyes!'...and he turned to Ibrahim the Weeper, with the uncorked bottle in his hand-the bottle from which came forth smoke, though it was cold. But Ibrahim rolled screaming, and strove to thrust his face into the ground. 'It is strange indeed,' mused Abdul Haq, stroking his beard, while none smiled. 'Strange, in every truth. But thou hast not dropped the drops, Mir Saheb. Perchance he will arise and thank thee and be cured of this madness when he feels the healing anointment that so benefited thine own eyes. Oh, the cleverness of these European *hakims*,' and he raised hands and eyes in wonder as he sighed piously.

"'Yea-perchance he will,' agreed my brother and bade Moussa Isa hold him by the ears with his face to the sky while the *oont-wallahs* kept him on his back. And Ibrahim's body heaved up those four strong men as it bent like a bow and bucked like a horse, while my brother removed the cork once again.

"His shrieks delighted my soul.

"'Tis a marvellous mystery to me,' sighed my brother. 'He knows how innocent and healing are these waters and yet he refuses them. He saw me use them on my own eyes-and surely the medicine is unchanged?' And he balanced the bottle sideways above the face of his enemy and allowed the devilish acid to well up and impend upon the very edge of the neck of the bottle, as he murmured: 'But a single drop for each eye! More I cannot spare-to-day. Perchance a drop for each ear to-morrow, and one for his tongue on the next day-if his madness spare him to us for so long.'

"Then, as Ibrahim, foaming, shrieked curses and cried aloud to Allah and Mohammed his Prophet, he said: 'Nay, this is ingratitude. He shall not have them to-day at all, but shall endure without them till sunrise to-morrow. Take him yonder, and lay him on that flat rock, bareheaded in the sun, that his tears may be dried for him.'...

"Yea! I found no fault with my brother then, Sahib.

"He was a master in his revenge. And the *durbar* murmured its applause, and praised and thanked my brother. Not one of them but had suffered at the hands of Mahmud Shahbaz, his father, the Vizier, or at the insolent hands of this his own son.... Then Mir Jan called to Moussa Isa, his body-servant, and said unto him:—

"'Hear, Moussa Isa, and make no tiny error if thou wouldst see to-morrow's sun and go to Paradise anon. Feed that carrion well and pretend to be filled with the pity that is the child of avarice. Ask what he will give thee to help him to escape. Affect to haggle long, and speak much of the difficulties and dangers of the deed. At length agree to put him on my fast camel this night at moon-rise, if thou art left as his guard and we are wrapt in slumber. Play thy part well, and show thy remorse at cheating thy master-even for a lakh[104] of rupees-yea, and show fear of what will happen to thee, and pretend distrust of him. At length succumb again, and as the moon just shows above the mountains untie his bonds and do thus and thus —' and he whispered instructions while a light shone in the eyes of Moussa Isa, the Somali, and a smile played about his mouth.

"And Mir Jan told the matter that night to all and gave instructions.

"Moussa Isa meanwhile did everything as he was bid and, while we ate, he carried his own food to the Weeper, as though secretly.

"Long and merrily we feasted, pretending to drink to excess of the forbidden *sharab*, singing and behaving like toddy-laden coolies, and in time we staggered to our carpets, put on our *poshteens*,[105] pulled rugs over our heads and slept-not.

"From under his rug my brother kept watch. Shortly after, Moussa Isa arose from beside Ibrahim the Weeper and crawled like a snake to where the camels knelt in a ring, and there he saddled the swift white camel of Mir Jan, and I heard its bubbling snarl as he made it rise, and led it over near to where Ibrahim lay. There he made it kneel again, and, throwing the nose-rope over its head, he laid the loop thereof, with his stick, on the front seat of the saddle. This done, he crept back to Ibrahim Mahmud and feigned sleep awhile. Anon, none stirring, he began to untie with his teeth and knife-point the cords that bound the captive, and when, at length, the man was free, Moussa chafed his stiffened arms and legs, his hands and feet.

"When, after a time, Ibrahim tried to rise, he fell again and again, and the moon not yet having risen above the mountains, the avaricious-seeming Moussa again massaged and chafed the limbs of the villain Ibrahim, who earnestly prayed Moussa Isa to lay him on the saddle as he was-and depart ere some sleeper awoke. But Moussa said 'twould be vain to start until Ibrahim could sit in the saddle and hold on, and he continued to rub his arms and legs.

"But when the edge of the moon shone above the mountain, Moussa placed the arm of Ibrahim around his neck, put his arm round Ibrahim's body, and staggered with him to where the racing-camel knelt. After a few steps the strength of Ibrahim seemed to return, and, by the time they reached the camel, he could totter on his feet and stand without help. With some difficulty Moussa hoisted him into the rear saddle. Having done so, he thrust the stirrups upon his feet and commenced to unwind his puggri.

"'Mount, mount!' whispered Ibrahim.

"'Nay, I must tie thee on,' replied Moussa Isa and, knotting one end of the *puggri* to the back of the saddle, he passed it twice round Ibrahim and tied the other end near the first. This done, and Ibrahim being in a frantic fever of haste and fear and hope, Moussa Isa commenced to bargain, Ibrahim agreeing to every demand and promising even more.

"'Anything! anything!' he shrieked beneath his breath. 'Bargain as we go. You cannot ask too much. I and my father will strip ourselves for thee.'...And having tortured him awhile, Moussa sprang into the saddle and brought the camel to its feet-as my brother's voice said, softly and sweetly: —

"'Wouldst thou leave us, O Ibrahim, my friend?' and my own chimed in: —

"'Could'st thou leave us, O Ibrahim, my brother's friend?' and the voice of Abdul Haq followed with: —

"'Shouldst thou leave us, O Ibrahim, my cousin's friend?' and Hussein Ali's voice added: —

"'Do not leave us, O Ibrahim, my friend's friend.' Like the wolf-pack, every other voice in the camp in turn implored: —

"'Never leave us, O Ibrahim, our master's friend.'

"'Go! go!' shrieked Ibrahim, kicking with his heels at the camel's sides and striking at Moussa Isa, as that obedient youth, raising his stick, caused the camel to bound forward, and drove it, swiftly trotting-to where my brother lay, and there made it kneel again....

"Dost thou sleep, Huzoor?"

"Nay, Mir Saheb," I replied, "nor would I till your tale be done and I have seen the return of another reconnoitring-patrol. We might then take turns.... Nay, I will not sleep at all. 'Tis too near dawn-when things are wont to happen in time of war."

Little did the worthy Subedar-Major guess how, or why, his tale enthralled me.

"I have nearly done, Sahib.... On the morrow my brother said: 'To-day I will make an end. After the evening prayer let all assemble and behold the anointing of the eyes of Ibrahim the Weeper with the same balm that he intended to be applied to mine.' And during the day men drove strong stakes deep into the ground, the distance between them being equal to the width of Ibrahim's head, which they measured-telling him why. Also pegs were driven into the ground convenient for the fastening of his hands and feet, and stones were collected as large as men could carry.

"And, after evening prayer and prostration we took Ibrahim, and forcing his head between the stakes so that he could not turn it, we tied his hands and feet to the pegs and weighted his body with the stones, being careful to do him no injury and to cause no such pain as might detract from the real torture, and lessen his punishment.

"And then Mir Jan stood over him with the bottle and said, softly and sweetly: —

"'Ibrahim, my friend, thou didst vow upon me a vengeance, the telling of which should turn men pale, because I struck thee for torturing my servant. And now I return good for thine evil, for I take pity on thy weeping eyes and heal them. These several days thou hast refused this benefaction with floods of tears, and sobs and screams. Now, behold, and see how foolish thou hast been,' and he spilt a drop from the bottle, so that it fell near the face of Ibrahim, but not on it.

"And I was amazed to see that the stone upon which the drop fell did not bubble and boil. This prolongation and refinement of the torture I could appreciate and enjoy-but why did not the acid affect the stone? 'Twas as though mere cold water had fallen upon it. Nor was the bottle smoking as always hitherto.

"And even as I wondered, my brother quickly stooped and dashed some of the contents of the bottle in the eyes of Ibrahim the Weeper.

"With a shriek that pierced our ear-drums and must have been heard for many kos,[106] Ibrahim writhed and jerked so that the stones were thrown from his body and the pegs that held his feet and hands were torn from the ground. The stakes holding his head firmly, he flung his body over until his head was beneath it and then back again, and screamed like a wounded horse. At last he wrenched his head free, and, holding his hands to his face-which appeared to be in no way injured-leapt up and ran round and round in circles, until he was seized, and, by my brother's orders, his hands were torn from his face.

"And behold, his eyes and face were unmarked and uninjured, and the liquid that dripped upon his clothing made no mark and did no hurt.

"'*Blind*,' he shrieked,' I am *blind!* O Merciful Allah, my eyes!' and he fell, howling.

"'Now that is very strange,' said my brother, 'for I threw pure, plain, cold water in his face. See me drink of the remainder!' and he drank from the bottle, and so did I, in fear and wonder. Cold, pure, fair water it was, and nothing else!

"But Ibrahim the Weeper was blind. Stone blind to his dying day and never looked upon the sun again. Little drops of water had struck him blind. Nay, the Hand of Allah had struck him blind-him who had cried: '*May Allah strike me blind* if I do not unto thee a thing of which children yet unborn shall speak with awe". He had tried to do such a thing and God had struck him blind-though my brother, who was very learned, spoke of self-suggestion, and of imagination being sometimes strong enough to make the imagined come to pass. (He told of a man who died for no reason, on a certain day at a certain hour, because his father had done so and he believed that *he* would also. But more likely it was witchcraft and he was under a curse.)

"Howbeit, little drops of pure water blinded Ibrahim the Weeper. And there the foreign blood of my poor brother showed forth. He could not escape the taint and was weak. At the last moment he had wavered and, like a fool, had forgiven his enemy."

"Was he a Christian?" I asked (and had often wondered in the past).

"*Nahin*, Sahib! He was a Mussulman, my father having had him taught with special care by a holy *moulvie*,[107] by reason of the fact that his mother had had him sprinkled with holy water by her priests and had taught him the tenets of the Christian faith-doubtless a high and noble one since your honour is of it."

"He had been taught the Christian doctrines, then?"

"Without doubt, Sahib. Throughout his childhood; in the absence of his father. And doubtless this aided his foreign blood in making him act thus foolishly."

"Doubtless," I agreed, with a smile.

"Yea, at the last moment he had put his vengeance from him and behaved like a weak fool, throwing away the acid, cleaning the bottle and filling it with pure water. He had intended to give Ibrahim a fright (and also the opprobrious title of *the Weeper*), to teach him a lesson and to let him go-provided he swore on the Q'ran never to return to Mekran Kot when he left for England.... Such a man was my poor brother. But the hand of Allah intervened and Ibrahim the Weeper lived and died stone blind.... A strange man that poor brother of mine, strong save when his foreign blood and foreign religion arose like poison within him and made him weak.... There was the case of the English Sergeant Larnce-Ishmeet whom he spared and sent into the English lines in the little Border War."

"Lance-Sergeant Smith? What regiment?" I asked.

"I know not, Sahib, save that it was a British Infantry Regiment. (He was not Lance-Sergeant Ishmeet but Sergeant Larnce-Ishmeet.) We...I mean...they...slew many of a Company that was doing rear-guard and their officers being slain and many men also, a Sergeant took them off with great skill. Section by section, from point to point he retired them, and our...their... triumphant joy at the capture and slaughter of the Company was changed to gnashing of teeth-for we lost many and the Company retired safely on the main body. But we got the Sergeant, badly wounded, and my brother would not have him slain. Rather he showed him much honour and had him borne to Mekran Kot, and when he was healed he took him to within sight of the outermost Khyber fort and set him free.... Yet was he not an enemy, Sahib, taken in war? Strange weaknesses had my poor brother...."

"I knew a Sergeant-Major Lawrence-Smith," I remarked, as light dawned on me after pondering "Larnce-Ishmeet." "He shot himself at Duri some time ago."

"He was a brave man," said Mir Daoud Khan. "Peace be upon him."

"And what became of your brother?" I asked, although I knew only too well-alas!

"He left Mekran Kot when I did, Sahib, for our father died, the old Jam Saheb was poisoned, and we had to flee or die. I never saw him again for he made much money (out of rifles), travelled widely, and became a Sahib (and I followed the *pultan*[108]). But he died as a Pathan should-for his honour. In Gungapur jail they hanged him (after the failure of the foolish attempt by some seditious Sikhs and Punjabis and Bengalis at a second Great Killing) and I do not care to speak of that thing even to —"

A sputter of musketry broke out in the thick vegetation of the river-bed, crackled and spread, as Subedar-Major Mir Daoud Khan (once against the civilized, brave and distinguished officer) and I sprang to our feet and hurried to our posts — I, even at that moment, thinking how small a World is this, and how long is the long arm of Coincidence. Here was I, while waiting for what then seemed almost certain death, hearing from the lips of his own brother, the early history of the remarkable, secretive and mysterious man whom I had loved above all men, and whose death had been the tragedy of my life.

Chapter II
The Boy

(Mainly concerning the early life of Moussa Isa Somali.)

Moussa Isa Somali never stole, lied, seduced, cheated, drank, swore, gambled, betrayed, slandered, blasphemed, nor behaved meanly nor cowardly-but, alas! he had personal and racial Pride.

It is written that Pride is the sin of Devils and that by it, Lucifer, Son of the Morning, fell.

If it be remembered that he fell for nine days, be realized that he must have fallen with an acceleration of velocity of thirty-two feet per second, each second, and be conceded that he weighed a good average number of pounds, some idea will be formed of the violence of the concussion with which he came to earth.

In spite of the terrible warning provided by so great a smash there yet remain people who will argue that it is better to fall through Pride than to remain unfallen through lack of it. By Pride, *Pride* is meant of course-not Conceit, Snobbishness and Bumptiousness, which are all very damnable, and signs of a weak, base mind. One gathers that Lucifer, Son of the Morning, was not conceited, snobbish, nor bumptious. Nor was Moussa, son of Isa, Somali-but, like Lucifer, Son of the Morning, Devil, he fell, through Pride, and came to a Bad End.

One has known people who have owned to a sneaking liking and unwilling admiration for Lucifer, Son of the Morning-people of the same sort as those who find it difficult wholly to revere the prideless Erect when comparing them with the prideful Fallen-and, for the life of me, I cannot help a sneaking liking and unwilling admiration for Moussa Isa Somali, who fell through Pride.

There was something fine about him, even as there was about Lucifer, Son of the Morning, and one cannot avoid feeling that if both did not get more of hard luck and less of justice than some virtuous people one knows, they certainly cut a better figure. Of course it is a mistake to adopt any line of action that leads definitely to the position of Under-Dog, and to fight when you cannot win. It is not Prudent, and Prudence leads to Favour, Success, Decorations, and the Respect of Others if not of yourself. It is also to be remembered that whether you are a Wicked Rebel or a Noble True-Hearted Patriot depends very largely on whether you succeed or fail.

All of which is mere specious and idle special pleading on behalf of Moussa Isa, a sinful murderous Somali....

Most of the memories of Moussa Isa centred round scars. When I say "memories of Moussa Isa" I mean Moussa Isa's own memories, for there are no memories concerning him. The might, majesty, dominion and power of the British Empire were arrayed against him, and the Empire's duly appointed agents hanged him by the neck until he was dead-at an age when some people are yet at school, albeit he had gathered in his few years of life a quantity and quality of experience quite remarkable.

'Twas a sordid business, and yet Moussa Isa died, like many very respectable and highly belauded folk, from the early Christians in Italy to the late Christians in Armenia, for a principle and an idea.

He was black, he was filthy, he was savage, ignorant and ugly-but he had his Pride, both personal and racial, for he was a Somali. A Somali, mark you, not a mere *Hubshi* or Woolly One, not a common Nigger, not a low and despicable person-worshipping idols, eating human flesh, grubs, roots and bark-the "black ivory" of Arabs.

If you called Moussa Isa a Hubshi, he either killed you or marked you down for death, according to circumstances.

Had Moussa Isa lived a few centuries earlier, been of another colour, and swanked around in painful iron garments and assorted cutlery, he would have been highly praised for his fine and proper spirit. Poet, bard, and troubadour would have noted and published his quickness on the point of honour. Moussa would have been set to music and have become a source of income to the gifted. He would have become a Pillar of the Order of Knighthood and an Ornament of the Age of Chivalry. A wreath of laurels would have encircled his brow-instead of a rope of hemp encircling his neck.

For such fine, quick, self-respecting Pride, such resentment of insult, men have become Splendid Figures of the Glorious Past.

Autres jours autres moeurs.

How many people called him *Hubshi*, we know not; but we know, from his own lips, of the killing of some few. Of the killing of others he had forgotten, for his memory was poor, save for insult and kindness. And, having caught and convicted him in one or two cases the appointed servants of the British Empire first "reformed" and then slew him in their turn-thus descending to his level without his excuse of private personal insult and injury....

The scars on Moussa Isa's face with the hole in his ear were connected with one of his very earliest memories-or one of his very earliest memories was connected with the scars on his face and the hole in his ear —a memory of jolting along on a camel, swinging upside-down, while a strong hand grasped his foot; of seeing his father rush at his captor with a long, broad-bladed spear, of being whirled and flung at his father's head; and of seeing his father's intimate internal economy seriously and permanently disarranged by the two-handed sword of one of the camel rider's colleagues (who flung aside a heavy gun which he had just emptied into Moussa's mamma) as his father fell to the ground under the impact and weight of the novel missile. Though Moussa was unaware, in his abysmal ignorance, of the interesting fact, the great two-handed sword so effectually wielded by the supporter of his captor, was exactly like that of a Crusader of old. It was like that of a Crusader of old, because it was a direct lineal descendant of the swords of the Crusaders who had brought the first specimens to the country, quite a good many years previously. Indeed some people said that a few of the swords owned by these Dervishes were real, original, Crusaders' swords, the very weapons whose hilts were once grasped by Norman hands, and whose blades had cloven Paynim heads in the name of Christianity and the interests of the Sepulchre. I do not know-but it is a wonderfully dry climate, and swords are there kept, cherished, and bequeathed, even more religiously than were the Stately Homes of England in that once prosperous land, in the days before park, covert, pleasaunce, forest, glade, dell, and garden became allotments, and the spoil of the "Working"-man.

Picked up after the raid and pursuit with a faceful of gravel, sand, dirt, and tetanus-germs, Moussa Isa, orphan, was flung on a pile of dead Somali spearmen and swordsmen, of horses, asses, camels, negroes, (old) women and other cattle-and, crawling off again, received kicks and orders to clean and polish certain much ensanguined weapons sullied with the blood of his near and distant relatives. Thereafter he was recognized by the above-mentioned swordsman, and accorded the privilege of removing his own father's blood from the great two-handed sword before alluded to —a task of a kind that does not fall to many little boys. So willingly and cheerfully did Moussa perform his arduous duty (arduous because the blood had had time to dry, and dried blood takes a lot of removing from steel by one unprovided with hot water) that the Arab swordsman instead of blowing off the child's head with his long and beautiful gun, damascened of barrel, gold-mounted of lock, and pearl-inlaid of stock, allowed him to rim for his life that he might die a sporting death in hot blood, doing his devilmost. (These were not slavers but avengers of enmity to the Mad Mullah and punishers of friendship to the English.)

"How much law will you give me, O Emir?" asked the child.

"Perhaps ten yards, dog, perhaps a hundred, perhaps more.... Run!"

"*You* could hit me at a thousand yards, O Emir," was the reply. "Let me die by a shot that men will talk about...."

"Run, yelping dog," growled the Arab with a sardonic smile.

And Moussa ran. He also bounded, shied, dodged, ducked, swerved, dropped, crawled, zig-zagged and generally gave his best attention to evading the shot of the common fighting-man whom he had propitiatorily addressed as "*Emir*," though a mere wearer of a single fillet of camel-hair cord around his *haik*. Like a naval gunner-the Arab laid his gun and waited till the sights "came on," fired, and had the satisfaction of seeing the child fling up his arms, leap into the air and fall twitching to the ground. Good shot! The twitches and the last convulsive spasm were highly artistic and creditable to the histrionic powers of Moussa Isa, shot through the ear, and inwardly congratulating himself that he had yet a chance. But then he had had wide opportunity for observation, and plenty of good models, in the matter of sudden-death spasms and twitches, so the credit is the less. Anyhow, it deceived experienced Arab eyes at a hundred yards, and the performance may therefore be classed as good. To the reflective person it will be manifest that Moussa's reverence for the sanctity of human life received but little encouragement or development from the very beginning....

Returning refugees, a few days later, found Moussa very pleased-with himself and very displeased with uncooked putrid flesh. Being exceedingly poor and depressed as a result of the Mad Mullah's vengeful *razzia*, they sold Moussa Isa, friendless, kinless orphan, and once again cursed the false English who made them great promises in the Mahdi's troublous day, and abandoned them to the Mad Mullah and his Dervishes as soon as the Mahdi was happily dead.

The Mad Mullah they could understand; the English they could not. For the Mad Mullah they had no blame whatsoever; for the English they had the bitterest blame, the deepest hatred and the uttermost contempt. Who blames the lion for seeking and slaying his prey? Who defends the unspeakable creature that throws its friends and children to the lion-in payment of its debts and in cancellation of its obligations to those friends and children? In discussing the raid on their way to market with Moussa Isa, they mentioned the name of the Mad Mullah with respect and fear. When they mentioned the English they expectorated and made a gesture too significant to be particularized. And the tom-toms once again throbbed through the long nights, sending (by a code that was before Morse) from village to village, from the sea to the Nile, from the Nile to the Niger and the Zambesi, from the Mediterranean to the Cape, the news that once more the Mad Mullah had flouted that failing and treacherous race, the English, and slaughtered those who lived within their gates, under the shadow of their flag and the promise of their protection.

Ere Moussa Isa got his next prominent scar, the signal-drums throbbed out the news that the gates were thrown open, the flag hauled down, and the promises shamefully broken. That the representatives of the failing treacherous race now stood huddled along the sea-shore in fear and trembling, while those who had helped them in their trouble and had believed their word were slaughtered by the thousand; that the country was the home of fire and sword, the oasis-fields yielding nothing but corpses, the wells choked with dead...red slaughter, black pestilence, starvation, misery and death, where had been green cultivation, fenced villages, the sound of the quern and the well-wheel, the song of women and the cry of the ploughman to his oxen. News and comments which did nothing to lessen the pride and insolence of the Jubaland tribesmen, of the Wak tribesmen, of the bold Zubhier sons of the desert, nor to strike terror to the hearts of the murderers of Captain Aylmer and Mr. Jenner, of slave-traders, game-poachers, raiders, wallowers in slaughter....

Another very noticeable and remarkable scar broke the fine lines and smooth contours of Moussa's throat and another memory was as indelibly established in his mind as was the said scar on his flesh.

At any time that he fingered the horrible ridged cicatrice, he could see the boundless ocean and the boundless blue sky from a wretched cranky canoe-shaped boat, in which certain Arab, Somali, Negro, and other gentlemen were proceeding all the way from near Berbera to near Aden with large trustfulness in Allah and with certain less creditable goods. It was a long, unwieldy vessel which ten men could row, one could steer with a broad oar, and a small three-cornered sail could keep before the wind.

But the various-clad crew of this cranky craft were gentlemen all, who, beyond running up the string-tied sail to the clothes-prop mast, or taking a trick at the wheel-another clothes-prop with a large disc of wood at the water-end, were far above work.

Trusting in Allah and Mohammed his Prophet is a lot easier than rowing a lineless, blunt-nosed, unseaworthy boat beneath a tropical sun. So they trusted in God, and permitted Moussa Isa, slave-boy, to do all that it was humanly possible for him to do.

Moussa did all that was expected of him, but not so Allah and Mohammed his Prophet.

The gentle breeze that (sometimes) carries you steadily over a glassy sea straight up the forty-fifth meridian of east longitude from Berbera to Aden in the month of October, failed these worthy trustful Argonauts, and they were becalmed.

But Time is made for slaves, and the only slave upon the Argosy was Moussa Isa, and so the becalming was neither here nor there. The cargo would keep (if kept dry) for many a long day-and the greater the delay in delivery, the greater the impatience of the consignees and their willingness to pay even more than the stipulated price-its weight in silver *per* rifle. But food is made for men as well as slaves, and if you, in your noble trustfulness, resolutely decline to reduce your daily rations, there must, with mathematical certitude of date, arrive the final period to any given and limited supply. Though banking wholly with Heaven in the matter of their own salvation from hunger, the Argonauts displayed mere worldly wisdom in the case of Moussa Isa and gave him the minimum of food that might be calculated to keep within him strength adequate to his duties of steering, swarming up the mast, baling, cooking, massaging the liver of the Leading Gentleman, and so forth. And in due course, the calm continuing, these pious and religious voyagers came to the bitter end of their water, their rice, their *dhurra*, their dates-and all (except the salt and coffee which formed part of the ostensible, bogus cargo) that they had, as they too-slowly drifted into the track of those vessels that enter and leave the strait of Bab-el-Mandeb, the Gate of Tears, the tears of the starving, drowning, ship-wrecked and castaway.

Salt *per se* is a poor diet, and, for the making of potable coffee, fresh water is very necessary.

Some of the Argonauts were, as has been said, Negro gentlemen. On the third day of absolute starvation, one had an Idea and made a suggestion.

The Leading Gentleman entertained it with an open mind and without enthusiasm.

The Tanga tout acclaimed it as a divine inspiration.

The one-eyed Moor literally smiled upon it. As his eye was single and his body therefore full of light, he saw the beauty of the notion at once. Had it been full of food instead, we may charitably suppose he would not have remarked: —

"A pity we did not feed him up better".

For the suggestion concerned Moussa Isa and food-Moussa Isa as food, in point of fact. The venerable gentle-looking Arab, whose face beamed effulgent with benevolence and virtue, murmured: —

"He will have but little blood, the dog. None of it must be-er —*wasted* by the-ah-butcher."

The huge man with the neat geometrical pattern of little scars, perpendicular on the forehead, horizontal on the cheeks and in concentric circles on the chest (done with loving care and a knife, in his infancy, by his papa) said only "*Ptwack*" as he chewed a mouthful of coffee-beans and hide. It may have been a pious ejaculation or a whole speech in his own peculiar vernacular. It was a tremendous smacking of tremendous lips, and the expression which overspread his speaking countenance was of gusto, appreciative, and such as accords with lip-smacking.

But a very fair man (very fair beside the Negroes, Somalis, Arabs and others our little black and brown brothers), a man with grey-blue eyes, light brown hair and moustache, and olive complexion, said to the originator of the Idea in faultless English, if not in faultless taste "You damned swine".

A look of profoundest disgust overspread his handsome young face, a face which undoubtedly lent itself to very clear expression of such feelings as contempt, disgust and scorn, an unusual face, with the thin high-bridged nose of an English aristocrat, the large eyes and pencilled black brows of an Indian noble, the sallow yet cheek-flushed complexion of an Italian peasant-girl, and the firm lips, square jaw, and prominent chin of a fighting-man. It was essentially an English face in expression, and essentially foreign in detail; a face of extraordinary contradictions. The eyes were English in colour, Oriental in size and shape; the mouth and chin English in mould and in repose, Oriental in mobility and animation; the whole countenance English in shape, Oriental in complexion and profile —a fine, high-bred, strong face, upon which played shadows of cruelty, ferocity, diabolical cunning; a face admired more quickly than liked, inspiring more speculation than trust.

The same duality and contradiction were proclaimed in the hands-strong, tenacious, virile hands; small, fine, delicate hands; hands with the powerful and purposeful thumb of the West; hands with the supple artistic fingers and delicate finger-nails of the East.

And the man's name was in keeping with hands and face, with mind, body, soul, and character, for, though he would not have done so, he could have replied to the query "What is your name?" with "My name? Well, in full, it is John Robin Ross-Ellison Ilderim Dost Mahommed Mir Hafiz Ullah Khan, and its explanation is my descent from General Ross-Ellison, Laird of Glencairn, and from Mir Faquir Mahommed Afzul Khan, Jam of Mekran Kot".

In Piccadilly, wearing the garb of Piccadilly, he looked an Englishman of the English.

In Abdul Rehman Bazaar, Cabul, wearing the garb of Abdul Rehman Bazaar, he looked a Pathan of Pathans. In the former case, rather more sunburnt than the average lounger in Piccadilly; in the latter, rather fairer than the average Afghan and Pathan loafer in Abdul Rehman Bazaar.

"Walking down Unter den Linden in Berlin, with upturned moustache, he looked a most Teutonic German.

"You observed, my friend?" queried the Leading Gentleman (whose father was the son of a Negro-Arab who married, or should have married, a Jewess captured near Fez, and whose mother was the daughter of a Tunisian Turk by a half-bred Negress of Timbuctoo).

"I observed," replied the fair young man in the mongrel Arabic-Swahili *lingua franca* of the Red Sea and East African littorals "that it is but natural for dogs to prey upon dogs."

"There are times when the lion is driven to prey upon dogs, my dear son," interposed the mild-eyed, benevolent-looking Arab —a pensive smile on his venerable face.

"Yes-when he is old, mangy, toothless and deserving of nothing better, my dear father," replied the fair young man, and his glances at the white beard, scanty locks and mumbling mouth of the ancient gentleman had an unpleasantly personal quality. To the casual on-looker it would have seemed that an impudent boy deliberately insulted a harmless benevolent old gentleman. To the fair young man, however, it was well known that the old gentleman's name was famous across Northern and Eastern Africa for monstrous villainy and fiendish cruelty-the name of the worst and wickedest of those traders in "black ivory," one of whose side-lines is frequently gun-running. Also he knew that the benevolent-looking old dear was desirous that the Leading Gentleman, his partner, should join with him in a little scheme (a scheme revealed by one Moussa Isa, eaves-dropper) to give the fair young man some inches of steel instead of the pounds of Teutonic gold due for services (and rifles) rendered, when they should reach the quiet spot on the northern shore of the Persian Gulf where certain bold caravan-leaders would await them and their precious cargo —a scheme condemned by the Leading Gentleman on the grounds of the folly of killing the goose that laid the golden eggs. But then the wealthy Arab patriarch was retiring from the risky business (already nearly ruined and destroyed by English gun-boats) after that trip, and the Leading Gentleman was not. Thus it was that the attitude of the fair young man toward Sheikh Abou ben Mustapha Muscati did not display that degree of respect that his grey hairs and beautiful old face would appear to deserve.

The French-speaking Moslem Berber *ex*-Zouave, from Algiers, suggested that Moussa Isa, a slave, was certainly not fitting food for gentlemen who fight, hunt, travel, poach elephants, deal in "black ivory," run guns, and generally lead a life too picturesque for an over-"educated," utilitarian and depressing age-but what would you? "One eats-but yes, one eats, or one ceases to live, and one does not wish to cease to live-and therefore one eats" and he cocked a yellow and appraising eye at Moussa Isa. The sense of the meeting appeared to be that though one would not have chosen this particular animal, necessity knows no rule-and if the throat be cut while the animal be alive, one may eat of the flesh and break the Law by so much the less. Moussa Isa must be *halalled*.[109] But the fair young man drawing a Khyber knife with two feet of blade, observed that it was now likely that there would be a plethora of food, as he would most assuredly cut the throat of any throat-cutter.

Moussa Isa regarded him with the look often seen in the eye of an intelligent dog.

The venerable Arab smiled meaningly at the Leading Gentleman, and the Tanga tout asked if all were to hunger for the silly scruples of one. "If the fair-faced Sheikh did not wish to eat of Moussa, none would urge it. Live and let live. The gentlemen were hungry;..." but the fair young man unreasonably replied, "Then let them eat *thee* since they can stomach carrion," and for the moment the subject dropped-largely because the fair young man was supposed always to carry a revolver, which was not a habit of his good colleagues. It was another evidence of his strange duality that revolver and knife were (rare phenomenon) equally acceptable to him, though in certain environment the pistol rather suggested itself to his left hand, while in others his right hand went quite unconsciously to his long knife.

In the present company no thought of the fire-arm entered his head-this was a knifing, back-stabbing outfit;—none here who stood up to shoot and be shot at in fair fight....

The Leading Gentleman looked many times and hard at Moussa Isa during the second day of his own starvation, which was the third of that of his companions and the fourth of Moussa's. The Leading Gentleman, who was as rich as he was ragged and dirty, wore a very beautiful knife, which (though it reposed in a gaudy sheath of yellow, green and blue beads, fringed with a dependent filigree, or lace work, of similar beads with tassels of cowrie-shells) hailed from Damascus and had a handle of ivory and gold, and an inlaid blade on which were inscribed verses from the Q'ran.

Moussa Isa knew the pattern of it well by the close of day. The Leading Gentleman took that evening to sharpening the already sharp blade of the knife. As he sharpened it on his sandal and the side of the boat, and tried its edge on his thumb, he regarded the thin body of Moussa Isa very critically.

His look blended contempt, anticipation, and anxiety.

He broke a long brooding silence with the remark: —

"The little dog will be thinner still, to-morrow "—a remark which evoked from the fair youth the reply: "And so will you".

Perhaps truth covered and excused a certain indelicacy and callousness in the statement of the Leading Gentleman, albeit the fair young man appeared annoyed at it. His British blood and instincts became predominant when the killing and eating of a fellow-creature were on the *tapis* —the said fellow-creature being on it at the same time.

A colleague from Dar-es-Salaam, who had an ear and a half, three teeth, six fingers, innumerable pockmarks and a German accent, said, "He will have little fat," and there was bitterness in his tone. As a business man he realized a bad investment of capital. The food in which they had wallowed should have gone to the fattening of Moussa Isa. Also a fear struck him.

"He'll jump overboard in the night-the ungrateful dog. Tie him up," and he reached for a coil of cord.

"He will not be tied up," observed the fair youth in a quiet, obstinate voice.

"See, my friend," said the Leading Gentleman, "it is a case of one or many. Better *that* one," and he pointed to Moussa Isa, "than another," and he looked meaningly at the fair young man.

"And yet, I know not," murmured the venerable Arab, "I know not. We are not in the debt of the slave. We *are* in the debt of the Sheikh. It would cancel all obligations if the Sheikh from the North preferred to offer himself as —"

The young man's long knife flashed from its sheath as he sprang to his feet. "Let us eat monkey, if eat we must," he cried, pointing to the Arab-and, even as he spoke, the huge man with the scars, flinging his great arms around the youth's ankles, partly rose and neatly tipped him overboard. He had long hated the fair man.

Straightway, unseen by any, as all eyes were on the grey-eyed youth and his assailant, Moussa Isa cast loose the *toni*[110] that nestled beneath the stern of the larger boat. He was about to shout that he had done so when he realised that this would defeat his purpose, and also that the fair Sheikh was still under water.

"Good," murmured the old Arab, "now brain him as he comes up-and secure his body."

But the fair youth knew better than to rise in the immediate neighbourhood of the boat. Swimming with the ease, grace and speed of a seal, he emerged with bursting lungs a good hundred yards from where he had disappeared. Having breathed deeply he again sank, to re-appear at a point still more distant, and be lost in the gathering gloom.

"He is off to Cabul to lay his case before the Amir," observed the elderly Arab with grim humour.

"Doubtless," agreed the Leading Gentleman, "he will swim the 2000 miles to India, and then up the Indus to Attock." And added, "But, bear witness all, if the young devil turn up again some day, that *I* had no quarrel with him.... A pity! A pity!...Where shall we find his like, a Prank among the Franks, an Afghan among Afghans, a Frenchman in Algiers, a nomad robber in Persia, a Bey in Cairo, a Sahib in Bombay-equally at home as gentleman or tribesman? Where shall we find his like again as gatherer of the yellow honey of Berlin and as negotiator in Marseilles (where the discarded Gras breech-loaders of the army grow) and in Muscat? Woe! Woe!"

"Or his like for impudence to his elders, harshness in a bargain, cunning and greed?" added the benevolent-looking Arab, who had gained a handsome sum by the murder.

"For courage," corrected the Leading Gentleman, and with a heavy sigh, groaned. "We shall never see him more-and he was worth his weight to me annually in gold."

"No, you won't see him again," agreed the Arab. "He'll hardly swim to Aden-apart from the little matter of sharks.... A pity the sharks should have so fair a body-and we starve!" and he turned a fatherly benevolent eye on Moussa Isa-whom a tall slender black Arab, from the hills about Port Sudan, of the true "fuzzy-wuzzy" type, had seized in his thin but Herculean arms as the boy rose to spring into the *toni* and paddle to the rescue of his benefactor.

The Dar-es-Salaam merchant threw Fuzzy Wuzzy a coil of cord and Moussa Isa (who struggled, kicked, bit and finding resistance hopeless, screamed, "Follow the boat, Master," as he lay on his back), was bound to a cracked and salt-encrusted beam or seat that supported, or was supported by, the cracked and salt-encrusted sides of the canoe-shaped vessel.

Although very, very hungry, and perhaps as conscienceless and wicked a gang as ever assembled together on the earth or went down to the sea in ships, there was yet a certain reluctance on the part of some of the members to revert to cannibalism, although all agreed that it was necessary.

Among the reluctant-to-commence were those who had no negro blood. Among the ready-to-commence, the full-blooded negroes were the most impatient.

Although very hungry and rather weak they were in different case from that of European castaway sailors, in that all were inured to long periods of fasting, all had crossed the Sahara or the Sus, lived for days on a handful of dates, and had tightened the waist-string by way of a meal. Few of them ever thought of eating between sunrise and sunset. The lives of the negroes were alternations of gorging and starving, incredible repletion and more incredible fasting; devouring vast masses of hippopotamus-flesh to-day, and starving for a week thereafter; pounds of prime meat to-day, gnawing hunger and the weakness of semi-starvation for the next month.

"At sunrise," said the Leading Gentleman finality.

Good! That left the so-desirable element of chance. It left opportunity for change of programme inasmuch as sunrise might disclose help in the shape of a passing ship. The matter would rest with Heaven, and pious men might lay them down to sleep with clear conscience, reflecting that, should it be the Will of Allah that His servants should not eat of this flesh, other would be provided; should other not be provided it was clearly the Will of Allah that His servants should eat of this flesh! Excellent-there would be a meal soon after sunrise.

And the Argonauts laid them down to sleep, hungry but gratefully trustful, trustfully grateful. But Moussa Isa watched the wondrous lustrous stars throughout the age-long, flash-short night and thought of many things.

Had the splendid, noble Sheikh from the North heard his cry and had he found the *toni*? How far had he swum ere his strength gave out or, with sudden swirl, he was dragged under by the man-eating shark? Would he remove his long cotton shirt, velvet waistcoat and baggy cotton trousers? The latter would present difficulties, for the waist-string would tangle and the water would swell the knot and prevent the drawing of string over string.

Moreover, the garments, though very baggy, were tight round the ankles. Would he cast off his beautiful yard-long Khyber knife? It would go to his heart to do that, both for the sake of the weapon itself and because he would have to go to his death unavenged, seized by a shark without giving it its death-wound. Had he heard and would he follow the boat in the moonlight, find the *toni* and escape? Could he swim to Aden? They had said not-even leaving sharks out of consideration, and indeed it must be forty or fifty miles away. Judging by their progress they must have done about one hundred and fifty miles since they embarked at the lonely spot on the Berbera coast for the other lonely spot on the Aden coast, where certain whisperings with certain mysterious camel-riders would preface their provisioning for the voyage along the weary Hadramant coast to the Ras el Had and Muscat-just a humble boat-load of poor but honest toilers and tradesmen, interested in dried fish, dates, the pearl-fishery and the pettiest trading. No, he would never reach land, wonderful swimmer as he was. He would be lost in the sea as is the Webi Shebeyli River in the sands of the South, unless he followed the drifting boat and found the *toni*. Otherwise, he might be picked up, but he would have to keep afloat all night to do that, unless he had the extraordinary luck to be seen by dhow or ship before dark. That could hardly be, unless the same ship or dhow were visible from their own boat, and none had been seen.

No, he must be dead-and Moussa Isa would shortly follow him. How he wished he could have given his life to save him. Had he known, he would have cried out, "Let them eat me, O Master," and prevented him from risking his life. If he should get the chance of striking one blow for his life in the morning he would bestow it upon the scar-faced beast who had tripped the fair Sheik overboard. If he could strike two he would give the second to the old Arab who flogged women and children to death with the *kourbash*,[111] as an amusement, and whose cruelties were famous in a cruel land; the old Evil who hated, and plotted the death of, the fair Sheikh, with the leader of the expedition in order that they might divide his large share of the gun-running proceeds and German subsidy. If he could strike a third blow it should be at the filthy Hubshi of the Aruwimi, the low degraded Woolly One from the dark Interior (of human sacrifice, cannibalism and ju-ju) who had proposed eating him. Yes-if he could grab the leader's knife and deal three such stabs as the Sheikh dealt the lion, at these three, he could die content. But this was absurd! They would *halal* him first, of course, and unbind him afterwards.... They might unbind him first though, so as to place him favourably with regard to-economy. They would use the empty army-ration tin, shining there like silver in the moonlight, the tin with which he had done so much weary baling. Doubtless the leader and the Arab would share its contents. He grudged it them, and hoped a quarrel and struggle might arise and cause it to be spilt.

An unpleasant death! Without cowardice one might dislike the thought of having one's throat cut while one's hands were bound and one watched the blood gushing into an old army-ration tin. Perhaps there would be none to gush-and a good job too. Serve them right. Could he cut his wrists on a nail or a splinter or with the cords, and cheat them, if there were any blood in him now. He would try. Yes, an unpleasant death. No one, no true Somali, that is, objected to a prod in the heart with a shovel-headed spear, a thwack in the head with a hammered slug, a sweep at the neck with a big sword-but to have a person sawing at your throat with weak and shaking hands is rotten....

One quite appreciated that masters must eat and slaves must die, and the religious necessity for cutting the throat while the animal is alive, according to the Law-and there was great comfort in the fact that the leader's knife was inscribed with verses of the Q'ran and would probably be used for the job. (The leader liked jobs of that sort.) Countless it would confer distinction in Paradise upon one already distinguished as having died to provide food for a band of right-thinking, religious-minded gentlemen, who, even in such terrible straits, forgot not the Law nor omitted the ceremonies....

Where now was the fair-faced master who so resembled the English but was so much braver, fiercer, so much more staunch? Though fair as they, and knowing their speech, he could not be of a race that led whole tribes to trust in them, called them "Friendlies" and then forsook them; came to them in the day of trouble asking help, and then scuttled away and deserted their allies, leaving them to face alone the Power whose wrath and vengeance their help-giving had provoked. Yet there were good men among them-there was Kafil[112] Bey for example. Kafil Bey whose last noble fight he had witnessed. If the fair-faced Sheikh had any of the weak English blood in his veins it must be of such a man as Kafil Bey.

Was he still swimming? Had he been picked up? Was he shark's food? To think that *he* should have come to his death over such a thing as a slave boy (albeit a Somali and no Hubshi).

This was an Emir indeed.

An idea!...He called aloud: "Are you there, Master? The *toni* is loose and must be near," again and again, louder and louder. Perhaps he was following and would hear. Again, louder still.

The one-eyed man, disturbed by the cry, stirred, threw his arms abroad, stretched, and put his foot on the mouth of a neighbour lying head-to-foot beside him. The neighbour snored loudly and turned his face sideways under the foot. He had slept standing jammed against the wall in the Idris of Omdurman, one of the most terrible jails of all time, and a huge foot on his face was a matter of no moment.

The Tanga tout suddenly emitted a scream, a blood-curdling scream, and immediately scratched his ribs like a monkey.... Moussa Isa held his peace.

Anon the scar-faced man turned over, moving others.

Could it be near dawn already, and were his proprietors waking up? He could see no change in the East, no paling of the lustrous stars. Was it an hour ago or eight hours ago that the night had fallen? Had he an hour to live or a night? Would he ever see Berbera again, steer a boat down its deep inlet, gaze upon its two lighthouses, its fort, hospital, barracks, piers, warehouses, bazaars; drive a camel along by its seven miles of aqueduct, look down from the hills upon this wonderful and mighty metropolis, greater and grander than Jibuti, Zeyla, Bulhar and Karam, surely the greatest and most marvellous port and city of the world, ere driving on through the thorn-bush and acacia-jungle into the vast waterless Haud? Would he ever again see the sun rise in the desert, smell the smoke of the camel-dung cooking-fires.... What was that? The sky was paling in the East, growing grey, a rose-pink flush on the horizon-dawn and death were at hand.

Before the heralds of the sun, the moon slowly veiled her face with lightest gossamer while the weaker stars fled. The daily miracle and common marvel proceeded before the tired eyes of the bound slave; the rim of the sun appeared above the rim of the sea; the moon more deeply veiled her face from the fierce red eye, and gracefully and gradually retired before the advance of the usurping conqueror-and the slave seemed to hear the fat croaking voice of the leader saying, "At sunrise".

Broad day and all but he asleep. Well-it had come at last. When would they awake? Was the toni anywhere near?

The man with the geometrical pattern of scars on his face and chest suddenly sat bolt upright like a released spring, yawned, looked at the sky and the limp sail, and then at Moussa Isa. As his eye fell upon the boy he smiled copiously, protruded a very red tongue between very white teeth, and licked huge blue-black lips. He leaned over and awakened the Leading Gentleman. Then he pointed to the Victim. Both watched the horizon where, beyond distant Bombay and China, the sun was appearing, rising with the rapidity of the minute hand of a big clock. Neither looked to the West.

The child knew that when the sun had risen clear of the sea, he might look upon it for a minute or two-and no more. A puff of wind fanned his cheek; the sail filled and drew. The boat moved through the water and the one-eyed gentleman, arising and treading upon the out-lying tracts of the sleepers, stumbled to the rudder, which was tied with coconut-fibre to an upright stake. The breeze strengthened and there was a ripple of water at the bows. Was he saved?

The one-eyed person looked more disappointed than pleased, and observed to the Leading Gentleman: "We cannot live to Aden, though the wind hold. We must eat," and he regarded the figure of Moussa Isa critically, appraisingly, with mingled favour and disfavour. His expressive countenance seemed to say, "He is food-but he is poor food".

Nevertheless an unmistakable look of relief overspread his face as the Leading Gentleman replied with conviction, "We must eat...." and added, "This is but a dawn-breeze and will not take us half a mile".

"Then let us eat forthwith," said the one-eyed man, and he fairly beamed upon Moussa Isa, doubtless with the said light of which his body was full, in consequence of his singleness of vision. The whole party was by this time awake and Moussa Isa the cynosure of neighbouring eyes. The Leading Gentleman drew his beautiful knife from its tawdry sheath and gave it a last loving strop on his horny palm.

Willing hands dragged the head of Moussa Isa across the beam and willing bodies sat upon him, that he might not waste time, and something more precious, by thoughtless wriggling, delaying breakfast. The Leading Gentleman crawled to an advantageous position, and having bowed in prayer, sawed away industriously.

Moussa Isa wished to shriek to him that he was a fool and a bungler; that throats were not to be cut in that fashion, with hackings and sawing at the gullet. Knew the clumsy fumbler nothing of big blood-vessels?... but he could not speak.

"*That* is not the way," said the benevolent-looking old Arab. "Stab, man, stab under the ear-don't cut... not there, anyhow."

The Leading Gentleman tried the other side of the double-edged blade, continuing obstinately, and Moussa Isa contrived a strange sound which died away on a curious bubbling note and he grew faint.

Suddenly the one-eyed individual at the rudder screamed aloud, and disturbed the Leading Gentleman's earnest endeavour to prevent waste. Not from sensibility did the one-eyed scream, nor on account of his growing conviction that the Leading Gentleman was getting more than his share, but because, as all realized upon looking up, a great ship was bearing down upon them from the West.

So intent had all been upon the preparation of breakfast that the steamer was almost audible when seen.

Good! Here came water, rice, bread, sugar, flour, and perhaps meat, for poor castaways, and probably money-from kindly lady-passengers, this last, for the ship was obviously a liner. The wretched Moussa Isa's carcase was now superfluous-nay dangerous, and must be disposed of at once, for Europeans are most kittle cattle. They will exterminate your tribe with machine-guns, gin, small-pox, and still nastier things, but they are fearfully shocked at a bit of killing on the part of others. They call it murder. And though they will well-nigh depopulate a country themselves, they will wax highly indignant if any of the survivors do a little slaying, even if they kill but a miserable slave, like this Somali dog.

Heave him overboard.

No. Ships carry the "far-eye," the magic instrument that makes the distant near, that brings things from miles away to within a few yards. Doubtless telescopes were on them already. Keep in a close group round the body, smuggle it under the palm-mats and make believe to have been trying to kindle a fire in an old kerosine-oil tin.... Signals of distress appeared and Moussa Isa disappeared. The great steamer approached, slowed down, and came to a standstill beside the boat of the starving castaways. From her cliff-like side the passengers, crowding the rails of her many decks, looked down with interest upon a prehistoric craft in which lay a number of poor emaciated blacks and Arabs, clad for the most part in scanty cotton rags. These poor creatures feebly extended skinny hands and feebly raised quavering voices, as they begged for water and a little rice, only water and a little rice in the name of Allah the Merciful, the Compassionate. Their tins, lotahs and goat-skins were filled, bags of rice, bread and flour were lowered to them; a box of sugar and a packet of biscuit were added; and a gentle little rain of coins fell as though from Heaven.

Kodaks clicked, clergymen beamed, ladies said, "How sweetly picturesque-poor dears"; the Captain murmured, "Damnedest scoundrels unhung-but can't leave 'em to starve"; the "poor dears" smiled largely and ate wolfishly; Moussa Isa bled, and the great steamer resumed her way.

"Pat" Brighte (she was Cleopatra Diamond Brighte who married Colonel Dearman of the Gungapur Volunteer Bines) found she had got a splendid snap-shot when her films were developed at Gungapur. A little later she got another when the look-out saw, and a boat picked up, a man who was lying in a little dug-out or *toni*. When able to speak, he told the *serang*[113] of the lascars that he was the sole survivor of a bunder-boat which had turned turtle and sunk. He understood nothing but Hindustani.... Miss Brighte pitied the poor wretch but thought he looked rather horrid....

The hearts of the castaways were filled with contentment as their stomachs were filled with food, and so busily did they devote themselves to eating, drinking, and sleeping that they forgot all about Moussa Isa beneath the palm-mats.

When they chanced upon him he was just alive, and his wound was closed. The attitude in which he had been dumped down upon the cargo (the ostensible and upper strata thereof, consisting of hides and salt, with a hint of ostrich-feathers, coffee, frankincense and myrrh) had favoured his chance of recovery, for, thanks to a friendly bundle, his head was pressed forward to his chest and the lips of the gaping wound in his throat were shut.

Moussa Isa was tougher than an Indian chicken.

Near Aden his proprietors were captured by an officious and unsympathetic police (Moussa was sent to what he dreamed to be Heaven and later perceived to be a hospital) and while they went to jail, a number of bristly-haired Teutonic gentlemen at the Freidrichstrasse, Arab gentlemen at Muscat, and Afghan gentlemen at Cabul, were made to exercise the virtue of patience. So the would-be murderers of John Robin Ross-Ellison Ilderim Dost Mahommed unintentionally saved him from jail, but never received his acknowledgments....

Discharged from the hospital, Moussa became his own master, a gentleman at large, and, for a time, prospered in the coal-trade.

He steered a coal-lighter that journeyed between the shore and the ships.

One day he received a blow, a curse, and an insult, from the *maccudam* or foreman of the gang that worked in the boat which he steered. Neither blows nor curses were of any particular account to Moussa, but this man Sulemani, a nondescript creature of no particular race, and only a man in the sense that he was not a woman nor a quadruped, had called him *"Hubshi"* Woolly One. Had called Moussa Isa of the Somal a *Hubshi*, as though he had been a common black nigger. And, of course, it was intentional, for even this eater of dogs and swine and lizards knew the great noble, civilized and cultured Somal, Galla, Afar and Abyssinian people from niggers. Even an English hide-and-head-buying tripper and *soi-disant* big-game hunter knew a Zulu from a Hottentot, a Masai from a Wazarambo, and a Somali from a Nigger!

The only question was as to *how* the scoundrel should be killed, for he was large and strong, and never far from a shovel, crow-bar, boat-hook or some weapon. Not much hope of being able to fasten on his throat like a young leopard on a dibatag, kudu or impala buck.

As Moussa sat behind him at the tiller, he would regard the villain's neck with interest, his fat neck, just below and behind the big ear.

If he only had a knife-such as the beauty that once cut his throat-or even a scrap of iron or of really hard pointed wood, honour could be satisfied and a stain removed from the scutcheon of Moussa Isa of the Somal race, insulted.

One lucky night he got his next scar, the fine one that ornamented his cheek-bone, and a really serviceable weapon of offence against the offender Sulemani.

On this auspicious night, a festive English sailor flung a bottle at him, in merry sport, as he passed beneath the verandah of the temple of Venus and Bacchus in which the sailor sprawled. It struck him in the face, broke against his cheek-bone, and provided him with a new scar and a serviceable weapon, a dagger, convenient to handle and deadly to slay. The bottle-neck was a perfect hilt and the long tapering needle-pointed spire of glass projecting from it was a perfect blade-rightly used, of course. Only a fool would attempt a heart-stab with such a dagger, as it would shatter on the ribs, leaving the fool to pay for his folly. But the neck-stab—for the big blood-vessels—oho! And Moussa Isa licked his chops just as he had seen the black-maned lion do in his own fatherland; just as did the lion from whom the fair Sheikh had saved him.

Toward the sailor, Moussa felt no resentment for the assault that had laid him bleeding in the gutter. Had he called him "*Hubshi*" it would have been a different matter-perhaps very different for the sailor. Moussa Isa regarded curses, cruelties, blows, wounds, attempts at murder, as mere natural manifestations of the attitude of their originators, and part of the inevitable scheme of things. Insults to his personal and racial Pride were in another category altogether.

Yes-the bottle must have been thus usefully broken by the hand of the Supreme Deity himself, prompted by Moussa's own particular and private *kismet*, to provide Moussa with the means of doing his duty by himself and his race, in the matter of the dog who had likened a long-haired, ringletty-haired aquiline-nosed, thin-lipped son of the Somals to a Woolly One—a black beast of the jungle!

Our young friend had never heard of the historical glass-bladed daggers of the *bravos* of Venice, but he saw at a glance, as he rose to his feet and stared at the bottle, that he could do his business (and that of the foreman) with the fortunately-shaped fragment, and eke leave the point of the weapon in the wound for future complications if the blow failed of immediate fatal effect.

He bided his time....

One black night Moussa Isa sat on the stern of his barge holding to a rope beneath the high wall of the side of the P. & O. liner, *Persia*, in shadow and darkness undispelled by the flickering flare of a brazier of burning fuel, designed to illuminate the path of panting, sweating, coal-laden coolies up and down narrow bending planks, laid from the lighter to the gloomy hole in the ship's side.

The hot, still air was thick with coal-dust and the harmless necessary howls of the hundreds of sons of Ham, toiling at high pressure.

In the centre of a vast, silent circle of mysterious lamp-spangled sea and shore, and of star-spangled sky, this spot was Inferno, an offence to the brooding still immensity.

And suddenly Moussa Isa was dimly conscious of his enemy, of him who had insulted the great Somal race and Moussa Isa. On the broad edge of the big barge Sulemani stood, before, and a foot below him, in the darkness, yelling directions, threats, promises and encouragement to his gang. If only there had been a moon or light by which he could see to strike! Suddenly the edge of a beam of yellow light from a port-hole struck upon Sulemani's neck, illuminating it below and behind his ear. Mrs. "Pat" Dearman, homeward bound, had just entered her cabin and switched on the electric light. (When last she passed Aden she had been Miss Cleopatra Diamond Brighte, bound for Gungapur and the bungalow of her brother.)

It was Mrs. Pat Dearman's habit to read a portion of the Scriptures nightly, ere retiring to rest, for she was a Good Woman and considered the practice to be not only a mark of, but essential to, goodness.

Doubtless the Powers of Evil smiled sardonically when they noted that the light which she evoked for her pious exercise lit the hand of Moussa Isa to murder, providing opportunity.

Moussa Isa weighed chances and considered. He did not want to bungle it and lose his revenge and his life too. Would he be seen if he struck now? The light fell on the very spot for the true infallible death-stroke. Should he strike now, here, in the midst of the yelling mob?

Rising silently, Moussa drew his dagger of glass from beneath his only garment, aimed at the patch of light upon the fat neck, and struck. Sulemani lurched, collapsed, and fell between the lighter and the ship without an audible sound in that dim pandemonium.

Even as the "dagger" touched flesh, the light was quenched, Mrs. Pat Dearman having realized that the stuffy, hot cabin was positively uninhabitable until the port-hole could be opened, after coaling operations were completed.

Moussa Isa reseated himself, grabbed the rope again, and with clear conscience, duty done, calmly awaited that which might follow.

Nothing followed. None had seen the deed, consummated in unrelieved gloom; the light had failed most timely....

The next person who mortally affronted Moussa Isa, committing the unpardonable sin, was a grievously fat, foolish Indian Mohammedan youth whose father supported four wives, five sons, six daughters and himself in idleness and an Aden shop.

It was a remarkably idle and unobtrusive shop and yet money flowed into it without stint, mysteriously and unostentatiously, the conduits of its flow being certain modest and retiring Arab visitors in long brown or white *haiks*, with check cotton head-dresses girt with ropes of camel-hair, who collogued with the honest tradesman and departed as silently and unobtrusively as they came....

One of them, strangely enough, ejaculated "*Himmel*" and "*Donnerwetter*" as often as "*Bismillah*" and "*Inshallah*" when he swore.

The very fat son of this secretive house in an evil hour one inauspicious evening took it upon him to revile and abuse his father's servant, one Moussa Isa, an African boy, as he performed divers domestic duties in the exiguous "compound" of the dwelling-place and refused to do the fat youth's behest ere completing them.

"Haste thee at once to the bazaar, thou dog," screamed the fat youth.

"Later on," replied Moussa Isa, using the words that express the general attitude of the East.

"Now, dog. Now, Hubshi, or I will beat thee."

"I will kill *you*," replied Moussa Isa, and again bided his time.

"Hubshi, Hubshi, Hubshi," goaded the misguided fat one.

His Kismet led the youth, some weeks later, to lay him down and sleep in the shade of the house upon some broad flagstones. Here Moussa found him and regretted the loss of his glass-dagger, —last seen in the neck of a foreman of coal-coolies toppling into the dark void between a barge and a ship, —but remembered a big heavy stone used to facilitate the scaling of the compound wall.

Staggering with it to the spot where the fat youth lay slumbering peacefully, Moussa Isa, in the sight of all men (who happened to be looking), dashed it upon his fez-adorned head, and established the hitherto disputable fact that the fat youth had brains.

To the Magistrate, Moussa Isa offered neither excuse nor prayer.

Explanation he vouchsafed in the words: —

"He called *me*, Moussa Isa of the Somali, a *Hubshi!*"

Being of tender years and of insignificant stature he was condemned to flogging and seven years in a Reformatory School. He was too juvenile for the Aden Jail. The Reformatory School nearest to Aden is at Duri in India, and thither, in spite of earnest prayers that he might go to hard labour in Aden Jail like a man and a Somali, was Moussa Isa duly transported and therein incarcerated.

At the Duri Reformatory School, Moussa Isa was profoundly miserable, most unhappy, and deeply depressed by a sense of the very cruellest injustice.

For here they simply did not know the difference between a Somal and a woolly-haired dog of a negro. They honestly did not know that there was a difference. To them, a clicking Bushman was as a Nubian, an earth-eating Kattia as a Kabyle, a face-cicatrized, tooth-sharpened cannibal of the Aruwimi as a Danakil, —a *Hubshi* as a Somal. They simply did not know. To them all Africans were *Hubshis* (just as to an English M.P. all the three or four hundred millions of Indians are Bengali babus). They meant no insult; they knew no better. All Africans were black niggers and every soul in the place, from Brahmin to Untouchable, looked down upon the African, the Black Man, the Nigger, the Cannibal, the *Hubshi*, sent from Africa to defile their Reformatory and destroy their caste.

Here, the proud self-respecting Moussa, jealous champion of the honour of his, to him, high and noble race, found himself a god-send to the Out-castes, the Untouchables, the Depressed Classes, Mangs, Mahars, and Sudras, —they whose touch, nay the touch of whose very shadow, is defilement! For, at last, they, too, had some one to look down upon, to despise, to insult. After being the recipients-of-contempt as naturally and ordainedly as they were breathers-of-air, they at last could apply a salve, and pass on to another the utter contempt and loathing which they themselves received and accepted from the Brahmins and all those of Caste. They had found one lower than themselves. *Moussa Isa of the Somali* was the out-cast of out-casts, the pariah of pariahs, prohibited from touching the untouchables, one of a class depressed below the depressed classes-in short a *Hubshi!*

Even a broad-nosed, foreheadless, blubber-lipped aborigine from the hill-jungles objected to his presence!

In the small, self-contained, self-supporting world of the Reformatory, it was Moussa Isa against the World. And against the World he stood up.

It had to learn the difference between a Somali and a *Hubshi* at any cost-the cost of Moussa's life included.

What added to the sorrow of the situation was the realization of how charming and desirable a retreat the place was in itself, —apart from its ignorant and stupid inhabitants.

Expecting a kind of torture-house wherein he would be starved, sweated, thrashed by brutal *kourbash*-wielding overseers, he found the most palatial and comfortable of clubs, a place of perfect peace, safety, and ease, where one was kindly treated by those in authority, sumptuously fed, luxuriously lodged, and provided with pleasant occupation, attractive amusements and reasonable leisure.

He had always heard and believed that the English were mad, and now he knew it.

As a punishment for murder he had got a birching that merely tickled him, and a free ticket to seven years' board, lodging, clothing, lighting, medical care, instruction and diversion!

Wow!

Were it not for the presence of the insolent, ignorant, untravelled, inexperienced, soft-living, lily-livered dogs of inhabitants, the place was the Earthly Paradise. They were the crocodile in the ointment.

A young Brahmin, son of a well-paid Government servant, and incarcerated for forgery and theft, was his most annoying persecutor. He was at great pains to expectorate and murmur "*Hubshi*" in accents of abhorrent contempt, whenever Moussa Isa chanced between the wind and his nobility.

The first time, Moussa replied with pitying magnanimity and all reasonableness: —

"I am not a *Hubshi*, but a Somali, which is quite different-even as a lion is different from a jackal or a man from an ape".

To which the Brahmin replied but: —

"*Hubshi*," and pointed out that there was danger of Moussa Isa's shadow touching him, if Moussa were not careful.

"I must kill you if you call me *Hubshi*, understanding that I am of the Somals," said Moussa Isa.

"*Hubshi*," would the Brahmin reply and loudly bewail his evil Luck which had put him in the power of the accursed Feringhi Government—a Government that compelled a Brahmin to breathe the same air as a filthy negro dog, a Woolly One of Africa, barely human and most untouchable, a living Contamination... and Moussa cast about for a weapon.

His first opportunity arose when he found the Brahmin, who was in the book-binding and compositor department, working one day in the same gardening-gang with himself.

He had but a watering-can by way of offensive weapon, but good play can be made with a big iron watering-can wielded in the right spirit and the right hand.

Master Brahmin was feebly tapping the earth with a kind of single-headed pick, and watching him, Moussa Isa saw that, in a quarter of an hour or so, he might plausibly and legitimately pass within a yard or two of this his enemy, as he went to and fro between the water-tap and the strip of flower-border that he was sprinkling.... Would they hang him if he killed the Brahmin, or would they feebly flog him again and give him a longer sentence (that he be supported, fed, lodged, clothed and cared for) than the present seven years?

There was no foretelling what the mad English would do. Sometimes they acquitted a criminal and gave him money and education, and sometimes they sent him to far distant islands in the South and there housed and fed him free, for life; and sometimes they killed him at the end of a rope.

Doubtless Allah smote the English mad to prevent them from stealing the whole world.... If they were not mad they would do so and enslave all other races-except their conquerors, the Dervishes, of course.... It was like the lying hypocrites to call the Great Mullah "the Mad Mullah" knowing themselves to be mad, and being afraid of their victorious enemy who had driven them out of Somaliland to the coast forts....

Oh, if they would only treat him, Moussa Isa, as an adult, and send him to the Aden Jail to hard labour. There folk knew a Somali from a *Hubshi*; a gentleman of Afar and Galla stock, of Arab blood, Moslem tenets, and Caucasian descent, from a common nigger, a low black Ethiopian, an eater of men and insects, a worshipper of idols and *ju-ju*.

In Aden, men knew a Somali from a *Hubshi* as surely as they knew an Emir from a mere Englishman.

Here, in benighted, ignorant, savage India, the Dark Continent indeed, men knew not what a Somali was, likened him to a Negro, ranked him lower than a Hindu even-called him a *Hubshi* in insolent ignorance. If only the beautiful Reformatory were in Berbera, and tenanted by Africans.

Better Aden Jail a thousand times than Duri Reformatory.

What a splendid joke if the dog of a Brahmin who persistently insulted him-even after he had been shown his error and ignorance-should be the unwitting means of his return to Aden-where a Somali gentleman is recognized. There is no harm about a Jail as such. Far from it. A jail is a wise man's paradise provided by fools. You have excellent and plentiful food, a roof against the sun, unfailing water supply, clothing, interesting occupation, and safety-protection from your enemies. No man harries you, you are not chained, you are not tortured; you have all that heart can desire. Freedom?...What *is* Freedom? Freedom to die of thirst in the desert? Freedom to be disembowelled by the Great Mullah? Freedom to be sold as a slave into Arabia or Persia? Freedom to be the unfed, unpaid, well-beaten property of gun-runners in the Gulf, or of Arab *safari* ruffians and "black-ivory" men? Freedom to be left to the hyaena when you broke down on the march? Freedom to die of starvation when you fell sick and could not carry coal? Thanks.

If the mad English provided beautiful refuges, and made the commission of certain crimes the requisite qualification for admission, let wise men qualify.

Take this Reformatory-where else could a little Somali boy get such safety, peace, food, and sumptuous luxury; everything the heart could desire, in return for doing a little gardening? Even a house to himself as though he were the honoured, favourite son of some chief.

To Moussa Isa, the dark and dingy cell with its bare stone walls, mud floor, grated aperture and iron door was a fine safe house; its iron bed-frame with cotton-rug-covered laths and stony pillow, a piece of wanton luxury; its shelf, stool and utensils, prideful wealth. If only the place were in Africa or Aden! Well, Aden Jail would do, and if the Brahmin's death led to his being sent there as a serious and respectable murderer, it would be a real case of two enemies on one spear-an insult avenged and a most desired re-patriation achieved.

That would be subtilty, —at once washing out the insult in the Brahmin's blood and getting sent whither his heart turned so constantly and fondly. They had treated him as a juvenile offender because he was so small and young, and because the killing of the fat Mussulman was his first offence, as they supposed. Surely they would recognize that he was a man when he had killed his second enemy-especially if he told them about Sulemani. What in the name of Allah did they want, to constitute a real sound criminal, fit for Aden Jail, if three murders were not enough? Well, he would go on killing until they did have enough, and were obliged to send him to Aden Jail. There he would behave beautifully and kill nobody until they wanted to turn him out to starve. Then, since murder was the requisite qualification, he would murder to admiration. He knew they could not send him over the way to the Duri Jail, since he belonged to Aden, had been convicted there, and only sent to the Duri Reformatory because Aden boasted no such institution....

Yes. The Brahmin's corpse should be the stepping-stone to higher things and the place where people knew a Somali from a Negro.

If only he were in the carpentry department with Master Brahmin, where there were axes, hammers, chisels, knives, saws, and various pointed instruments. Fancy teaching the young gentleman manners and ethnology with an axe! However, after one or two more journeys between the tap and the flower-bed, he would pass within striking-distance of the dog as he worked his slow way along the tract of earth he was supposed to be digging up with the silly short-handled pick.

Should he try and seize the pick and give him one on the temple with it? No, the Brahmin would scream and struggle and the overseer would be on Moussa Isa in a single bound. He must strike a sudden blow in the act of passing.

A few more journeys to the water-tap....
Now! "*Hubshi*," eh?
Halting beside the crouching Brahmin youth, Moussa Isa swung up the heavy watering-can by the spout and aimed a blow with all his strength at the side of his enemy's head. He designed to bring the sharp strong rim of the base behind the ear with the first blow, on the temple with the second, and just anywhere thereafter, if time permitted of a thereafter.

But the aggravating creature tossed his head as Moussa, with a grunt of energy, brought the vessel down, and the rim merely struck the top of the shaven skull. Another-harder. Another-with frenzied strength and the force of long-suppressed rage and sense of wrong.

And then Moussa was knocked head over heels and sat upon by the overseer in charge of the garden-gang, while the Brahmin twitched convulsively on the ground. He was by no means dead, however, and the sole immediate results, to Moussa, were penal diet, solitary confinement in his palatial cell, a severe sentence of corn-grinding with the heavy quern, and most joyous recollections of the sound of the water-can on the pate of the foe.

"I have still to kill you, of course," he whispered to his victim, the next time they met, and the Brahmin went in terror of his life. He was a very clever young person and had passed an astounding number of examinations in the course of his brief career. But he was not courageous, and his "education" had given him skill in nothing practical, except in penmanship, which skill he had devoted to forgery.

"Why did you violently commit this dastardish deed, and assault the harmless peaceful Brahmin?" asked the Superintendent, a worthy and voluble babu, and then translated the question into debased Hindustani.

"He called me *Hubshi*, and I will kill him," replied Moussa.

"Oho! and you kill everyone who calls you *Hubshi*, do you, Master African?"

"I do. I wish to go to Aden Jail for attempting murder. It will be murder if I am kept here where none knows a man from a dog."

"Oho! And you would kill even *me*, I suppose, if I called you *Hubshi*."

"Of course! I will kill you in any case if I am not sent to Aden Jail."

The babu decided that it was high time for some other institution to shelter this touchy and truculent person, and that he would lay the case before the next weekly Visitor and ask for it to be submitted to the Committee at their ensuing monthly meeting.

The Visitor of the week happened to be the Educational Inspector. "Wants to leave India, does he?" said the Inspector, looking Moussa over as he heard the statement of the Superintendent. "I admire his taste. India is a magnificent country to leave."

The Educational Inspector, a very keen, thoughtful and competent educationist, was a disappointed man, like so many of his Service. He felt that he had, for quarter of a century, strenuously woven ropes of sand. When his liver was particularly sluggish he felt that for quarter of a century he had worked industriously, not at a useless thing, but at an evil thing—a terrible belief.

Moreover, after quarter of a century of faithful labour and strict economy, he found himself with a load of debt, broken health, and a cheaply educated family of boys and girls to whom he was a complete stranger-merely the man who found the money and sent it Home, visiting them from time to time at intervals of four or five years. India had killed his wife, and broken him.

He had had what seemed to him to be bitter experience also. An individual, notoriously slack and incompetent, ten years his junior, had been promoted over his head, because he was somebody's cousin and the kind of fatuous ass that only labours industriously in drawing-rooms and at functions, recuperating by slacking idly in offices and at duties—a paltry but paying game much practised by a very small class in India.

Another individual, by reason of his having come to India two boats earlier than the Inspector, drew Rs. 500 a month more than he did, this being the Senior Inspector's Allowance. That he was reported on as lazy, eccentric, and irregular, made no difference to the fact that he was a fortnight senior to, and therefore worth Rs. 500 a month more than, the next man. The recipient regarded the extra trifle (£400 a year) as his bare right and merest due. The Inspector regarded it as an infamous piece of injustice and folly that for fifteen years the whole of this sum should go to a lazy fool because he happened to set sail from England on a certain date, and not a fortnight later. So he loathed and detested India where he had had bad luck, bad health and what he considered bad treatment, and sympathized with the desire of Moussa Isa.

"Why do you want to go back to Aden?" he inquired in the *lingua franca* of the Indian Empire, of Moussa whose heart beat high with hope.

"Because here, where there are no lions, wolves think a lion is a dog; here where there are no men, asses think a man is a monkey. I am a Somal, and these ignorant camels think I am a negro—a filthy Hubshi."

"And you tried to kill another boy because he called you 'Hubshi,' eh?"

"I did, Sahib, and I will kill him yet if I be not sent to Aden. If that fail I will kill myself also."

"Stout fella," commented the Inspector in his own vernacular, and added, musing aloud:—

"You'll come to the gallows through possessing pride, self-respect and determination, my lad. You're behind the times-or rather you maintain a spirit for which Civilization has no use. You must return to the Wilds of the Earth or else you must be content to become good, grubby, and grey, dull and dejected, sober and sorrowful, respectable and unenterprising-like me; and you must cultivate fat, propriety, smugness and the Dead Level.... What, you young Devil! You'd have self-respect and pride, would you; be quick upon the point of honour, eh? revive the duello, what? Get thee to a —er-less civilized and respectable age or place...in other words, Mr. Toshiwalla, bring the case before the Committee of Visitors. I'll put up a note to the effect that he had better be sent back to Aden. This is a Reformatory, and there's nothing very reformatory about keeping him to plan murder and suicide because he has been (quite unjustifiably) transported as well as flogged and imprisoned. Yes, we'll consider the case. Meanwhile, keep a sharp eye on him-and give him all the corn-grinding he can do. Sweat the Original Sin out of him...and see he does not secrete any kind of weapon."

Accordingly was Moussa segregated, and to the base women's-work of corn-grinding in the cook-house, wholly relegated. It was hard, soul-breaking work, ignoble and degrading, but he drew two crumbs of comfort from the bread of affliction. He was developing his arm-muscles and he was literally watering the said bread of affliction with the sweat of labour. As the heavy drops trickled from chin and nose into the meal around the grindstone, it pleased Moussa Isa to reflect that his enemy should eat of it. Since the shadow of Moussa was pollution to these travesties of men and warriors, let them have a little concrete pollution also. But in the cook-house, while arm and soul wearied together, one heavy day of copper sky and brazen earth, first eye and then foot, fell upon a piece of tin, the lid of some empty milk-tin or like vessel. The prehensile toes gathered in the trove, the foot gently rose and the fingers of the pendant left hand secured the disc, while the body swayed with the strenuous circlings of the right hand chat revolved the heavy upper millstone.

That night, immediately after being locked in his cell, that there might be the fullest time for bleeding to death, he slashed and slashed while strength lasted at wrist and abdomen-but without succeeding in penetrating the abdominal wall and reaching the viscera.

This effected his transfer to the Reformatory hospital and underlined the remark of the Inspector in the Visitors' Book to the effect that one Moussa Isa would commit suicide or murder, if kept at Duri, and would certainly not be "reformed" in any way. In hospital, Major Jackson of the Royal Army Medical Corps, a Visitor of the Duri Jail, paying his periodical visits, grew interested in the sturdy bright boy and soon came to like him for his directness, cheery courage, and refreshing views. When the boy was convalescent he took him on the surrounding Duri golf-links as his caddie in his endless games with his poor friend Sergeant-Major Lawrence-Smith, *ex*-gentleman.

Moussa was grateful and, fingering the scar on his throat, likened Major Jackson to his hero, the fair Sheikh who had saved him from the lion and had lost his life through intervening on Moussa's behalf in the boat. But *he* was not mad like these English. He would not, with infinite earnestness, seriousness and mingled joy at success and grief at failure, have pursued a little white ball with a stick, mile after mile, knocking it with infinite precautions, every now and then, into a little hole, and taking it out again.

No, *his* idea of sport across country with an iron-shod stick would rather have been lion-hunting with an assegai (yet, curiously enough, one, Robin Ross-Ellison, lived to play more than one game of golf with Major Jackson on these same Duri Links). To see this adult white man behaving so, *coram publico*, made Moussa bitterly ashamed for him.

And, as the sun set, Moussa Isa earned a sharp rebuke for inattentive slacking, as he stood sighing his soul to where it sank in the West over Aden and Somaliland.... Wait till his chance of escape arrived; he would journey straight for the sunset, day after day, until he reached a sea-shore. There he would steal a canoe and paddle and paddle straight for the sunset, day after day, until he reached a sea-shore again. That would be Africa or Arabia, and Moussa Isa would be where a Somal is known from a *Hubshi*.... Should he make a bolt for it now? No, too weak, and not fair to this kind Sahib who had healed him and sympathized with him in the matter of the ignorance and impudence of those who misnamed a son of the Somals.... In due course, the Committee of Visitors met at the Reformatory one morning, and found on the agenda paper *inter alia* the case of Moussa Isa, a murderer from Aden, his attempt at murder and suicide, and his prayer to be sent to Aden Jail.

On the Committee were the Director of Public Instruction, the Collector, the Executive Engineer, the Superintendent of Duri Jail, the Educational Inspector, the Cantonment Magistrate, Major Jackson of the Royal Army Medical Corps, and a number of Indian gentlemen. To the

Chairman's inquiries Moussa Isa made the usual replies. He had been mortally affronted and had endeavoured to avenge the insult. He had tried to do his duty to himself-and to his enemy. He had been put to base women's-work as a punishment for defending his honour and he had tried to take his life in despair. Was there *no* justice in British lands? What would the Sahib himself do if his honour were assailed? If one rose up and insulted him and his race? Called him baboon, born of baboons, for example? Or had the Sahib no honour? Why should he have been transported when he was not sentenced to transportation? What had he done but defend his honour and avenge insults? Unless he were now tried for murder and suicide, and sentenced to hard labour in Aden Jail, he would go on murdering until they did send him there. If they said, "Well, you shan't go there, whatever you do," he would kill himself. If he could get no sort of weapon he would starve himself (he did not in his ignorance quote the gentle and joyous Pankhurst family) or hold his breath. So they had better send him, and that was all he had got to say about it.

"Send him for trial before the City Magistrate and recommend that he go to Aden Jail at once, before he hurts somebody else," said the native members of the Committee. "Why should we be troubled with the off-scourings of Aden?"

"Certainly not," opined the Collector of Duri. A pretty state of affairs if every criminal were to be allowed to select his own place of punishment, and to terrorize any penitentiary that had the misfortune to lack favour in his sight. Let the boy be well flogged for the assault and attempted suicide, and then let him rejoin the ordinary gangs and classes. It was the Superintendent's duty to watch his charges and keep discipline in what was, after all, a school.

"Sir, he is one violent and dangerous character and will assault the peaceful and mild. Yea-he may even attack *me*," objected the babu.

"Are we to understand that you admit your inability to maintain order in this Reformatory?" inquired the Director of Public Instruction from the Chair.

Anything but that. They were to understand, on the contrary, that the babu was respectfully a most unprecedented disciplinarian.

"You don't expect cock angels in a Reformatory, y' know," said the engineer, suddenly awaking to light a fat black cheroot. "Got to use the-ah-strong hand; —on their-ah —*you* know," and he resumed his slumbers, puffing mechanically and unconsciously at his cheroot.

So Moussa Isa was flogged and sent back to gardening, lessons and drawing.

Yes-the Somali was taught drawing. Not mere utilitarian drawing-to-scale and making plans and elevations, but "freehand"-drawing, the reproducing of meaningless twirly curves and twiddly twists from symmetrical conventional "copies". He copied copies and drew lines-but never copied things, nor drew things. In time he could, with infinite labour, produce a copy of a flat "copy" that a really observant eye could identify with the original, but had you asked him to draw his foot or the door of the room, his desk, his watering-can or book, he would probably have replied, "*They* are not drawing-copies," and would have laughed at your absurd joke. No, he was not taught to draw *things*, nor to give expression to impression.

And he had a special warder all to himself, who watched him as a cat watches a mouse. However, warders cannot prevent looks and smiles, and whenever Moussa Isa saw the Brahmin youth, he gave a peculiar look and a meaning smile. It was borne in upon the clever young man that the Hubshi looked at his neck, below his ear, when he smiled that dreadful smile.

Sometimes a significant gesture accompanied the meaning smile. For Moussa Isa had decided, upon the rejection of his prayer by the Committee, to wait until he was a little older and bigger, more like a proper criminal and less of a wretched little "juvenile offender," and then to qualify, by murder, for the Aden Jail-with the unoffered help of the Brahmin boy.

Allah would vouchsafe opportunity, and when he did so, Moussa Isa, his servant, would seize it. Doubtless it would come as soon as he was big enough to receive the privileges of an adult and serious criminal. Anyhow, the insult would be properly punished and the honour of the Somal race avenged....

Came the day when certain of the sinful inhabitants of the Duri Reformatory were to be conducted to a neighbouring Government High School, a centre for the official Drawing Examinations for the district, there to sit and be examined in the gentle art of Art.

To this end they had been trained in the copying of lines and in the painting of areas of conventional shape, not that they might be made to observe natural form, express themselves in reproduction, render the inner outer, originate, articulate... but that they might pass an examination in copying unnatural things in impossible colours. Thus it came to pass that, in the big hall of this school, divers of the Reformed found themselves copying, and colouring the copy of, a curious picture pinned to a blackboard-the picture of a floral wonder unknown to Botany, possessed of delicate mauve leaves, blue-veined, shaped some like the oak-leaf and some like the ivy; of long slender blades like those of the iris, but of tenderest pink; of beautiful and profusely chromatic blossoms, reminding one now of the orchid, now of the sunflower and anon of the forget-me-not; and likewise of clustering fulgent fruit.

And at the back of all these budding artists and blossoming jail-birds, and in the same small desk sat the Brahmin youth and-Oh Merciful Allah!—Moussa Isa, Somali.

The native gentleman in charge of the party from the Duri Reformatory had duly escorted his charges into the hall, handed them over to Mr. Edward Jones, the Head of the High School, and been requested to wait outside with similar custodians of parties. (Mr. Edward Jones had known very strange things to happen in Examination Halls to which the friends and supporters of candidates had access during the examination.)

To Mr. Edward Jones the thus deserted Brahmin boy made frantic and piteous appeal.

"Oh, Sir," prayed he, "let me sit somewhere else and not beside this African."

"You'll stay where you are," replied Mr. Edward Jones, suspicious of the appeal and the appellant. If the fat glib youth objected to the African on principle, Mr. Edward Jones would be glad, metaphorically speaking, to rub his Brahminical nose in it. If this were not his reason, it was, doubtless, one even less creditable. Mr. Edward Jones had been in India long enough to learn to look very carefully for the motive.

Moussa Isa licked his chops once again, and, as Mr. Jones turned away, the unhappy Brahmin cried in his anguish of soul: —

"Oh, Sir! Watch this African carefully."

"All will be watched carefully," was the suspicious and cold reply.

Moussa smiled broadly upon his erstwhile contemptuous and insulting enemy, and began to consider the possibilities of a long and well-pointed lead-pencil as a means of vengeance. Pencils were intended for marking fair surfaces-might one not be used on this occasion for the cleaning of a sullied surface, that of a besmirched honour?

One insulter of the Somal race had died by the stab of a piece of broken bottle. Might not another die by the stab of a lead-pencil?

Doubtful. Very risky. The stabbing and piercing potentialities of a lead pencil are not yet properly investigated, tabulated, established and known. It would be a pity to do small damage and incur a heavy corn-grinding punishment. He might never get another chance of vengeance either, if he bungled this one.

Well, there were three hours in which to decide... and Moussa Isa commenced to draw, pausing, from time to time, to smile meaningly at the Brahmin, and to lick his chops suggestively. Anon he rested from his highly uninteresting and valueless labours, laid his pencil on the desk, and gazed around in search of inspiration in the matter of the best method of dealing with his enemy.

His eye fell upon a picture of a lion that ornamented the wall of the hall; he stiffened like a pointer and fingered some scars on his right arm. He had never seen a picture of a lion before and, for a fraction of a second, he was shocked and alarmed-and then, while his body sat in an Indian High School hall, his spirit flew to an East African desert, and there sojourned awhile.

Moussa Isa was again the slave of an ivory-poaching, hide-poaching, specimen-poaching, slave-dealing gang of Arabs, Negroes, and Portuguese half-castes, led by a white man of the Teutonic persuasion. He could feel the smiting heat, see the scrub, jungle, and sand shimmering and dancing in the heat haze. He could see the line of porters, bales on heads, the Arabs on horseback, the white man in a litter swinging from a long bamboo pole beneath which half a dozen Swahili loped along. He could see the velvet star-gemmed night and the camp-fires, smell the smoke and the savoury odours of the cooking, hear the sudden shrieks and yells that followed the roar of the springing lion, feel the crushing crunch of its great teeth in his arm as it seized him from beside the nearest fire and stood over him.... Yes, that was the night when the fair Sheikh from the North had showed the mettle of his pastures and bound Moussa Isa to him for ever in the bonds of worshipping gratitude and love. For, while others shrieked, yelled, fled, flung burning brands and spears, or fired hasty, unaimed, ineffectual shots, the fair Sheikh from the North had sprung at the lion as it stood over Moussa Isa and driven his knife into its eye, and as it smote him to the earth, buried its fangs in his shoulder and started to drag him away, had stabbed upward between the ribs, giving it a second death-blow, transfixing its heart. Thus it was he had earned the name by which he was known from Zanzibar to Berbera, "He-who-slays-lions-with-the-knife," had earned the envy and hatred of the fat white man and the Arabs, the boundless admiration of the Swahili askaris, hunters and porters, and the deep dog-like affection of Moussa Isa....

And then Moussa's spirit returned to his body and he saw but the picture of a lion on a High School wall. He commenced to draw again and suddenly had an inspiration. Deliberately he broke the point of his pencil and, rising, marched up to the dais, whereon, at a table, sat Mr. Edward Jones.

Mr. Edward Jones had been shot with bewildering suddenness from Cambridge quadrangles into the Indian Educational Service. Of India he knew nothing, of education he knew less, but boldly took it upon him to combine the two unknowns for the earning of his living. If wise and beneficent men offered him a modest wage for becoming a professor and exponent of that which he did not know, he had no objection to accepting it; but there were people who wondered why it should be that, out of forty million English people, Mr. Edward Jones should be the chosen one to represent England to the youth of Duri, and asked whether there were no keen, strictly conscientious, sporting, strong Englishmen available; no enthusiastic educational experts left in all the British Isles, that Mr. Edward Jones of all people had come to Duri?

"What do you want?" he asked (how he hated these poverty-stricken, smelly, ignoble creatures. Why was he not a master at Eton, instead of at Duri High School. Why wouldn't somebody give him a handsome income for looking handsome and standing around beautifully-like these aide-de-camp Johnnies and "staff" people. Since there was nothing on earth he could do well, he ought to have been provided with a job in which he could look well).

"May I borrow the Sahib's knife?" asked Moussa Isa, "I have broken my pencil and cannot draw." Mr. Edward Jones picked up the penknife that lay on his desk, the cheap article of restricted utility supplied to Government Offices by the Stationery Department, and handed it to Moussa Isa. Even as he took it with respectful salaam, Moussa Isa summed up its possibilities. Blade two inches long, sharp-pointed, handle six inches long, wooden; not a clasp knife, blade immovable in handle. It would do-and he turned to go to his seat and presumably to sharpen his pencil.

Idly watching the boy and thinking of other things, Jones saw him try the point of the knife on his thumb, walk up behind the other occupant of his desk, his Brahmin neighbour, seize that neighbour by the hair, push his head sharp over on to the shoulder, and plunge the knife into his neck; seat himself, and commence to draw with the unfortunate Brahmin's pencil.

Jones sprang to his feet and rushed to the spot, to find that he had not been dreaming. No-on the back seat drooped a boy bleeding like a stuck pig and another industriously drawing, his face illuminated by a smile of contentment.

Jones pressed his thumbs into the neck of the sufferer, as he called to an assistant-supervisor to run to the hospital for Dr. Almeida, hoping to be able to close the severed jugular from which welled an appalling stream of blood.

"It is quite useless, Sahib," observed Moussa, "nor can a doctor help. When one has got it *there*, he may give his spear to his son and turn his face to the wall. That dog will never say '*Hubshi*' to a Somal again."

"Catch hold of that boy," said Mr. Edward Jones to another assistant-supervisor who clucked around like a perturbed hen.

"Fear not, Sahib, I shall not escape. I go to Aden Jail," said Moussa cheerfully-but he pondered the advisability of attempting escape from the Reformatory should he be sentenced to be hanged. It had always seemed an impossibility, but it would be better to attempt the impossible than to await the rope. But doubtless they would say he was too small and light to hang satisfactorily, and would send him to Aden. Thanks, Master Brahmin, realize as you die that you have greatly obliged your slayer....

* * *

"Now you will most certainly be hanged to death by rope and I shall be rid of troublesome fellow," said the Superintendent to Moussa Isa when that murderous villain was temporarily handed over to him by the police-sepoy to whom he had been committed by Mr. Jones.

"I have avenged my people and myself," replied Moussa Isa, "even as I said, I go to Aden Jail-where there are *men*, and where a Somal is known from a Hubshi"

"You go to hang-across the road there at Duri Gaol," replied the babu, and earnestly hoped to find himself a true prophet. But though the wish was father to the thought, the expression thereof was but the wicked uncle, for it led to the undoing of the wish. So convinced and convincing did the babu appear to Moussa Isa, that the latter decided to try his luck in the matter of unauthorized departure from the Reformatory precincts. If they were going to hang him (for defending and purging his private and racial honour), and not send him to Aden after all, he might as well endeavour to go there at his own expense and independently. If he were caught they could not do more than hang him; if he were not caught he would get out of this dark ignorant land, if he had to walk for a year....

When he came to devote his mind to the matter of escape, Moussa Isa found it surprisingly easy. A sudden dash from his cell as the door was incautiously opened that evening, a bound and scramble into a tree, a leap to an out-house roof, another scramble, and a drop which would settle the matter. If something broke he was done, if nothing broke he was within a few yards of six-foot-high crops which extended to the confines of the jungle, wherein were neither police, telegraph offices, railways, roads, nor other apparatus of the enemy. Nothing broke-Duri Reformatory saw Moussa Isa no more. For a week he travelled only by night, and thereafter boldly by day, getting lifts in *bylegharies*,[114] doing odd jobs, living as the crows and jackals live when jobs were unavailable, receiving many a kindness from other wayfarers, especially those of the poorer sort, but always faring onward to the West, ever onward to the setting sun, always to the sea and Africa, until the wonderful and blessed day when he believed for a moment that he was mad and that his eyes and brain were playing him tricks.... After months and months of weary travel, always toward the setting sun, he had arrived one terrible evening of June at a wide river and a marvellous bridge —a great bridge hung by mighty chains upon mightier posts which stood up on either distant bank. It was a *pukka* road, a Grand Trunk Road suspended in the air across a river well-nigh great as Father Nile himself.

On the banks of this river stood an ancient walled city of tall houses separated by narrow streets, a city of smells and filth, wherein there were no Sahibs, few Hindus and many Mussulmans. In a mud-floored miserable *mussafarkhana*,[115] without its gates, Moussa Isa slept, naked, hungry and very sad-for he somehow seemed to have missed the sea. Surely if one kept on due westward always to the setting sun, one reached the sea in time? The time was growing long, however, and he was among a strange people, few of whom understood the Hindustani he had learnt at Duri. Luckily they were largely Mussulmans. Should he abandon the setting sun and take to the river, following it until it reached the sea? He could take ship then for Africa by creeping aboard in the darkness, and hiding himself until the ship had started.... There might be no city at the mouth of the river when he got there. It might never reach the sea. It might just vanish into some desert like the Webi-Shebeyli in Somaliland. No, he would keep on toward the West, crossing the great bridge in the morning. He did so, and turned aside to admire the railway-station of the Cantonment on the other side of the river, to get a drink, and to see a train come in, if happily such might occur.

Ere he had finished rinsing his mouth and bathing his feet at the public water-standard on the platform, the whistle of a distant train charmed his ears and he sat him down, delighted, to enjoy the sights and sounds, the stir and bustle, of its arrival and departure. And so it came about that certain passengers by this North West Frontier train were not a little intrigued to notice a small and very black boy suddenly arise from beside the drinking-fountain and, with a strange hoarse scream, fling himself at the feet of a young Englishman (who in Norfolk jacket and white flannel trousers strolled up and down outside the first-class carriage in which he was travelling to Kot Ghazi from Karachi), and with every sign of the wildest excitement and joy embrace and kiss his boots....

Moussa Isa was convinced that he had gone mad and that his eyes and brain were playing him tricks.

Mr. John Robin Ross-Ellison (also Mir Ilderim Dost Mahommed Mir Hafiz Ullah Khan when in other dress and other places) was likewise more than a little surprised-and certainly a little moved, at the sight of Moussa Isa and his wild demonstrations of uncontrollable joy.

"Well, I'm damned!" said he in the *rôle* of Mr. John Robin Ross-Ellison. "Rum little devil. Fancy your turning up here." And in the *rôle* of Mir Ilderim Dost Mahommed Mir Hafiz Ullah Khan added in debased Arabic: "Take this money, little dog, and buy thee a *tikkut* to Kot Ghazi. Get into this train, and at Kot Ghazi follow me to a house."

To the house Moussa Isa followed him and to the end of his life likewise, visiting *en route* Mekran Kot, among other places, and encountering one, Ilderim the Weeper, among other people (as was told to Major Michael Malet-Marsac by Ross-Ellison's half-brother, the Subedar-Major.)

Chapter III
The Woman

(And Augustus Grabble; General Murger; Sergeant-Major Lawrence-Smith; Mr. and Mrs. Cornelius Gosling-Green; Mr. Horace Faggit; as well as a reformed JOHN ROBIN ROSS-ELLISON.)

§ 1. Mr. Grobble

There was something very maidenly about the appearance of Augustus Clarence Percy Marmaduke Grobble. One could not imagine him doing anything unfashionable, perspiry, rough or rude; nor could one possibly imagine him doing anything ruthless, fine, terrible, strong or difficult.

One expected his hose to be of the same tint as his shirt and handkerchief, his dress-trousers to be braided, his tie to be delicate and beautiful, his dainty shoes to be laced with black silk ribbon, —but one would never expect him to go tiger-shooting, to ride a gay and giddy young horse, to box, or to do his own cooking and washing in the desert or jungle.

Augustus had been at College during that bright brief period of the attempted apotheosis of the dirty-minded little Decadent whose stock in trade was a few Aubrey Beardsley drawings, a widow's-cruse-like bottle of Green Chartreuse, an Oscar Wilde book, some dubious blue china, some floppy ties, an assortment of second-hand epigrams, scent and scented tobacco, a *nil admirari* attitude and long weird hair.

Augustus had become a Decadent —a silly harmless conventionally-unconventional Decadent. But, as Carey, a contemporary Rugger blood, coarsely remarked, he hadn't the innards to go far wrong.

It was part of his cheap and childish ritual as a Decadent to draw the curtains after breakfast, light candles, place the flask of Green Chartreuse and a liqueur-glass on the table, drop one drip of the liquid into the glass, burn a stinking pastille of incense, place a Birmingham "god" or an opening lily before him, ruffle his hair, and sprawl on the sofa with a wicked French novel he could not read-hoping for visitors and an audience.

If any fellow dropped in and, very naturally, exclaimed, "What the devil *are* you doing?" he would reply: —

"Wha'? Oh, sunligh'? Very vulgar thing sunligh'. Art is always superior to Nature. You love the garish day being a gross Philistine, wha'? Now I only live at night. Glorious wicked nigh'. So I make my own nigh'. Wha'? Have some Green Chartreuse-only drink fit for a Hedonist. I drink its colour and I taste its glorious greenness. Ichor and Nectar of Helicon and the Pierian Spring. I loved a Wooman once, with eyes of just that glowing glorious green and a soul of ruby red. I called her my Emerald-eyed, Ruby-souled Devil, and we drank together deep draughts of the red red Wine of Life — —"

Sometimes the visitor would say: "Look here, Grobb, you ought to be in the Zoo, you know. There's a lot there like you, all in one big cage," or similar words of disapproval.

Sometimes a young fresher would be impressed, especially if he had been brought up by Aunts in a Vicarage, and would also become a Decadent.

During vac. the Decadents would sometimes meet in Town, and See Life —a singularly uninteresting and unattractive side of Life (much more like Death), and the better men among them-better because of a little sincerity and pluck-would achieve a petty and rather sordid "adventure" perhaps.

Augustus had no head for Mathematics and no gift for Languages, while his Classics had always been a trifle more than shaky. History bored him-so he read Moral Philosophy.

There is a somewhat dull market for second-hand and third-class Moral Philosophy in England, so Augustus took his to India. In the first college that he adorned his classes rapidly dwindled to nothing, and the College Board dispensed with the services of Augustus, who passed on to another College in another Province, leaving behind him an odour of moral dirtiness, debt, and decadence. Quite genuine decadence this time, with nothing picturesque about it, involving doctors' bills, alimony, and other the fine crops of wild-oat sowing.

At Gungapur he determined to "settle down," to "turn over a new leaf," and laid a good space of paving-stone upon his road to reward.

He gave up the morning nip, docked the number of cocktails, went to bed before two, took a little gentle exercise, met Mrs. Pat Dearman-and (like Mr. Robin Ross-Ellison, General Miltiades Murger and many another) succumbed at once.

Mrs. Pat Dearman had come to India (as Miss Cleopatra Diamond Brighte) to see her brother, Dickie Honor Brighte, at Gungapur, and much interested to see, also, a Mr. Dearman whom, in his letters to her, Dickie had described as "a jolly old buster, simply full of money, and fairly spoiling for a wife to help him blew it in." She had not only seen him but had, as she wrote to acidulous Auntie Priscilla at the Vicarage, "actually married him after a week's acquaintance-fancy! —the last thing in the world she had ever supposed...etc." (Auntie Priscilla had smiled in her peculiarly unpleasant way as the artless letter enlarged upon the strangeness of her ingenuous niece's marrying the rich man about whom her innocent-minded brother had written so much.)

Having thoroughly enjoyed a most expensive and lavish honeymoon, Mrs. Pat Dearman had settled down to make her good husband happy, to have a good time and to do any amount of Good to other people-especially to young men-who have so many temptations, are so thoughtless, and who easily become the prey of such dreadful people and such dreadful habits.

Now it is to be borne in mind that Mrs. Dearman's Good Time was marred to some extent by her unreasoning dislike of all Indians, a dislike which grew into a loathing hatred, born and bred of her ignorance of the language, customs, beliefs and ideals of the people among whom she lived, and from whom her husband's great wealth sprang.

To Augustus-fresh from very gilded gold, painted lilies and highly perfumed violets-she seemed a vision of delight, a blessed damozel, a living Salvation.

"Incedit dea aperta," he murmured to himself, and wondered whether he had got the quotation right. Being a weak young gentleman, he straightway yearned to lead a Beautiful Life so as to be worthy to live in the same world with her, and did it-for a little while. He became a teetotaller, he went to bed at ten and rose at five-going forth into the innocent pure morning and hugging his new Goodness to his soul as he composed odes and sonnets to Mrs. Pat Dearman. So far so excellent-but in Augustus was no depth of earth, and speedily he withered away. And his reformation was a house built upon sand, for, even at its pinnacle, it was compatible with the practising of sweet and pure expressions before the glass, the giving of much time to the discovery of the really most successful location of the parting in his long hair, the intentional entangling of his fingers with those of the plump and pretty young lady (very brunette) in Rightaway & Mademore's, what time she handed him "ties to match his eyes," as he requested.

It was really only a change of pose. The attitude now was: "I, young as you behold me, am old and weary of sin. I have Passed through the Fires. Give me beauty and give me peace. I have done with the World and its Dead Sea Fruit. There is no God but Beauty, and Woman is its Prophet." And he improved in appearance, grew thinner, shook off a veritable Old Man of the Sea in the shape of a persistent pimple which went ill with the Higher Aestheticism, and achieved great things in delicate socks, sweet shirts, dream ties, a thumb ring and really pretty shoes.

In the presence of Mrs. Pat Dearman he looked sad, smouldering, despairing and Fighting-against-his-Lower-Self, when not looking Young-but-Hopelessly-Depraved-though-Yearning-for-Better-Things. And he flung out quick epigrams, sighed heavily, talked brilliantly and wildly, and then suppressed a groan. Sometimes the pose of, "Dear Lady, I could kiss the hem of your garment for taking an interest in me and my past-but it is too lurid for me to speak of it, or for you to understand it if I did," would appear for a moment, and sometimes that of, "Oh, help me-or my soul must drown. Ah, leave me not. If I have sinned I have suffered, and in your hands lie my Heaven and my Hell." Such shocking words were never uttered of course-but there are few things more real than an atmosphere, and Augustus Clarence could always get his atmosphere all right.

And Mrs. Pat Dearman (who had come almost straight from a vicarage, a vicar papa and a vicarish aunt, to an elderly, uxorious husband and untrammelled freedom, and knew as much of the World as a little bunny rabbit whom its mother has not brought yet out into the warren for its first season), was mightily intrigued.

She felt motherly to the poor boy at first, being only two years his junior; then sisterly; and, later, very friendly indeed.

Let it be clearly understood that Mrs. Pat Dearman was a thoroughly good, pure-minded woman, incapable of deceiving her husband, and both innocent and ignorant to a remarkable degree. She was the product of an unnatural, specialized atmosphere of moral supermanity, the secluded life, and the careful suppression of healthy, natural instincts. In justice to Augustus Clarence also it must be stated that the impulse to decency, though transient, was genuine as far as it went, and that he would as soon have thought of cutting his long beautiful hair as of thinking evil in connection with Mrs. Pat Dearman.

Yes, Mrs. Pat Dearman was mightily intrigued-and quickly came to the conclusion that it was her plain and bounden duty to "save" the poor, dear boy-though from *what* she was not quite clear. He was evidently unhappy and obviously striving-to-be-Good —and he had such beautiful eyes, dressed so tastefully, and looked at one with such a respectful devotion and regard, that, really-well, it added a tremendous savour to life. Also he should be protected from the horrid flirting Mrs. Bickker who simply lived to collect scalps.

And so the friendship grew and ripened-quickly as is possible only in India. The evil-minded talked evil and saw harm where none existed, proclaiming themselves for what they were, and injuring none but themselves. (Sad to say, these were women, with one or two exceptions in favour of men-like the Hatter-who perhaps might be called "old women of the male sex," save that the expression is a vile libel upon the sex that still contains the best of us.) Decent people expressed the belief that it would do Augustus a lot of good-much-needed good; and the crystallized male opinion was that the poisonous little beast was uncommon lucky, but Mrs. Pat Dearman would find him out sooner or later.

As for Mr. (or Colonel) Dearman, that lovable simple soul was grateful to Augustus for ex-isting-as long as his existence gave Mrs. Dearman any pleasure. If the redemption of Augustus interested her, let Augustus be redeemed. He believed that the world neither held, nor had held, his wife's equal in character and nobility of mind. He worshipped an image of his own creation in the shape of Cleopatra Dearman, and the image he had conceived was a credit to the single-minded, simple-hearted gentleman.

Naturally he did not admire Augustus Clarence Percy Marmaduke Grobble (learned in millinery; competent, as modes varied, to discuss harem, hobble, pannier, directoire, slit, or lamp-shade skirts, berthes, butterfly-*motif* embroideries, rucked ninon sleeves, chiffon tunics, and similar mysteries of the latest fashion-plates, with a lady undecided).

Long-haired men put Dearman off, and he could not connect the virile virtues with large bows, velvet coats, scent, manicure, mannerisms and meandering.

But if Augustus gave his wife any pleasure-why Augustus had not lived wholly in vain. His attitude to Augustus was much that of his attitude to his wife's chocolates, fondants, and crys-tallized violets —"Not absolutely nourishing and beneficial for you, Dearest; —but harmless, and I'll bring you a ton with pleasure".

Personally he'd as soon go about with his wife's fat French poodle as with Augustus, but so long as either amused her-let the queer things flourish.

Among the nasty-minded old women who "talked" was the Mad Hatter.

"Shameful thing the way that Dearman woman throws dust in her husband's eyes!" said he, while sipping his third Elsie May at the club bar. "He should divorce her. I would, to-morrow, if I were burdened with her."

A knee took him in the small of the back with unnecessary violence and he spun round to demand instant apology from the clumsy....

He found himself face to face with one John Robin Ross-Ellison newly come to Gungapur, a gentleman of independent means but supposed to be connected with the Political Department or the Secret Service or something, who stared him in the eyes without speaking while he poised a long drink as though wondering whether it were worth while wasting good liquor on the face of such a thing as the Hatter.

"You'll come with me and clear the dust from Dearman's eyes at once," said he at last. "Made your will all right?"

The Hatter publicly apologised, then and there, and explained that he had, for once in his life, taken a third drink and didn't know what he was saying.

"If your third drink brings out the real man, I should recommend you to stick to two, Bonnett," said the young man, and went away to cogitate.

Should he speak to Dearman? No. He didn't want to see so good a chap hanged for a thing like the Bonnett. Should he go and slap Augustus Grobble hard and make him leave the station somehow? No. Sure to be a scandal. You can no more stop a scandal than a locust-cloud or a fog. The best way to increase it is to notice it. What a horrid thing is a scandal-monger —exhaling poison. It publishes the fact that it is poisonous, of course-but the gas is not enjoyable.

Well, God help anybody Dearman might happen to hear on the subject! Happily Mr. (or Colonel) Dearman heard nothing, for he was a quiet, slow, jolly, red-haired man, and the wrath of a slow, quiet, red-haired man, once roused, is apt to be a rather dangerous thing. Also Mr. Dearman was singularly elephantine in the blundering crushing directness of his methods, and his idea of enough might well seem more than a feast to some.

And Mr. Dearman suffered Augustus gladly, usually finding him present at tea, frequently at dinner, and invariably in attendance at dances and functions.

Augustus was happy and Good-for Augustus. He dallied, he adored, he basked. For a time he felt how much better, finer, more enjoyable, more beautiful, was this life of innocent communion with a pure soul-pure, if just a little insipid, after the real spankers he had hitherto affected.

He was being saved from himself, reformed, helped, and all the rest of it. And when privileged to bring her pen, her fan, her book, her cushion, he always kissed the object with an appearance of wishing to be unseen in the act. It was a splendid change from the Lurid Life and the mean adventure. Piquant.

Unstable as water he could not excel nor endure, however, even in dalliance; nor persevere even when adopted as the *fidus Achates* of a good and beautiful woman-the poor little weathercock. He was essentially weak, and weakness is worse than wickedness. There is hope for the strong bad man. He may become a strong good one. Your weak man can never be that.

There came a lady to the Great Eastern Hotel where Augustus lived. Her husband's name, curiously enough, was Harris, and wags referred to him as *the* Mr. Harris, because he had never been seen-and like Betsey Prig, they "didn't believe there was no sich person". And beyond doubt she was a spanker.

Augustus would sit and eye her at meals-and his face would grow a little less attractive. He would think of her while he took tea with Mrs. and Mr. Dearman, assuring himself that she was certainly a stepper, a stunner, and, very probably, —thrilling thought —a wrong 'un.

Without the very slightest difficulty he obtained an introduction and, shortly afterwards, decided that he was a man of the world, a Decadent, a wise Hedonist who took the sweets of every day and hoped for more to-morrow.

Who but a fool or a silly greenhorn lets slip the chances of enjoyment, and loses opportunities of experiences? There was nothing in the world, they said, to compare with War and Love. Those who wanted it were welcome to the fighting part, he would be content with the loving rôle. He would be a Dog and go on breaking hearts and collecting trophies. What a milk-and-water young ass he had been, hanging about round good, silly, little Mrs. Dearman, denying himself champagne at dinner-parties, earning opprobrium as a teetotaller, going to bed early like a bread-and-butter flapper, and generally losing all the joys of Life! Been behaving like a *backfisch*. He read his Swinburne again, and unearthed from the bottom of a trunk some books that dealt with the decadent's joys,—poets of the Flesh, and prosers of the Devil, in his many weary forms.

Also he redoubled his protestations (of undying, hopeless, respectful devotion and regard) to Mrs. Dearman, until she, being a woman, therefore suspected something and became uneasy.

One afternoon he failed to put in an appearance at tea-time, though expected. He wrote that he had had a headache. Perhaps it was true, but, if so, it had been borne in the boudoir of the fair spanker whose husband may or may not have been named Harris.

As his absences from the society of Mrs. Dearman increased in frequency, his protestations of undying gratitude and regard for her increased in fervour.

Mrs. Dearman grew more uneasy and a little unhappy.

Could she be losing her influence for Good over the poor weak boy? Could it be-horrible thought-that he was falling into the hands of some nasty woman who would flirt with him, let him smoke too many cigarettes, drink cocktails, and sit up late? Was he going to relapse and slip back into that state of wickedness of some kind, that she vaguely understood him to have been guilty of in the unhappy past when he had possessed no guardian angel to keep his life pure, happy and sweet, as he now declared it to be?

"Where's your young friend got to lately?" inquired her husband one day.

"I don't know, John," she replied, "he's always missing appointments nowadays," and there was a pathetic droop about the childish mouth.

"Haven't quarrelled with him, or anything, have you, Pat?"

"No, John dear. It would break his heart if I were unkind to him-or it would have used to. I mean it used to have would. Oh, you know what I mean. Once it would have. No, I have not been unkind to him-it's rather the other way about, I think!"

Rather the other way about! The little affected pimp unkind to Mrs. Dearman! Mr. (or Colonel) Dearman made no remark-aloud.

Augustus came to tea next day and his hostess made much of him. His host eyed him queerly. Very.

Augustus felt uncomfortable. Good Heavens! Was Dearman jealous? The man was not going to cut up jealous at this time of day, surely! Not after giving him the run of the house for months, and allowing him to take his wife everywhere-nay, encouraging him in every way. Absurd idea!

Beastly disturbing idea though-Dearman jealous, and on your track! A rather direct and uncompromising person, red-haired too. But the man was absolutely fair and just, and he'd never do such a thing as to let a fellow be his wife's great pal, treat him as one of the family for ages, and then suddenly round on him as though he were up to something. No. Especially when he was, if anything, cooling off a bit.

"He was always most cordial-such a kind chap,—when I was living in his wife's pocket almost," reflected Augustus, "and he wouldn't go and turn jealous just when the thing was slacking off a bit."

But there was no doubt that Dearman was eyeing him queerly....

"Shall we go on the river to-morrow night, Gussie?" said Mrs. Dearman, "or have a round of golf, or what?"

"Let's see how we feel to-morrow," replied Augustus, who had other schemes in view. "Sufficient unto the day is the joy thereof," and he escorted Mrs. Dearman to the Gymkhana, found her some nice, ladies' pictorials, said, "I'll be back in a minute or two,"—and went in search of Mrs. "Harris".

"Well," said that lady, "been a good little boy and eaten your bread and butter nicely? Have a Lyddite cocktail to take the taste away. So will I."...

"Don't forget to book the big punt," said the Siren an hour or so later.

"I'll be ready for you about five."

Augustus wrote one of his charming little notes on his charming little note-paper that evening.

"Kind and Gracious Ladye,

"Pity me. Pity and love me. To-morrow the sun will not shine for your slave, for he will not see it. I am unable to come over in the evening. I stand 'twixt love and duty, and know you would counsel duty. Would the College and all its works were beneath the ocean wave! Think of me just once and I shall survive till the day after. Oh, that I could think your disappointment were but one thousandth part of mine. I live but for Thursday.

"Ever your most devoted loving slave,

"Gussie"

Mrs. Dearman wept one small tear, for she had doubted his manner when he had evaded making the appointment, and was suspicious. Mr. Dearman entered and noted the one small tear ere it trickled off her dainty little nose.

She showed him the note.

Mr. (or Colonel) Dearman thought much. What he said was "Hm!"

"I suppose he has got to invigilate at some horrid examination or something," she said, but she did not really suppose anything of the kind. Even to her husband she could not admit the growing dreadful fear that the brand she had plucked from the burning was slipping from her hand-falling back into the flames.

At a dinner-party that night a woman whom she hated, and wrote down an evil-minded scandal-monger and inventor and disseminator of lies, suddenly said to her, "Who *is* this Mrs. Harris, my dear?"

"How should I know?" replied Mrs. Dearman.

"Oh, I thought your young friend Mr. Grobble might have told you-he seems to know her very well," answered the woman sweetly.

That night Mr. Dearman heard his wife sobbing in bed. Going to her he asked what was the matter, and produced eau-de-Cologne, phenacetin, smelling-salts and sympathy.

She said that nothing at all was the matter and he went away and pondered. Next day he asked her if he could row her on the river as he wanted some exercise, and Augustus was not available to take her for a drive or anything.

"I should love it, John dear," she said. "You row like an ox," and John, who had been reckoned an uncommon useful stroke, felt that a compliment was intended if not quite materialized.

Mrs. Pat Dearman enjoyed the upstream trip, and, watching her husband drive the heavy boat against wind and current with graceful ease, contrasted him with the puny, if charming, Augustus-to the latter's detriment. He was so safe, so sound, so strong, reliable and true. But then he never needed any protection, care and help. It was impossible to "mother" John. He loved her devotedly and beautifully but one couldn't pretend he leaned on her for moral help. Now Augustus did need her or he had done so-and she did so love to be needed. *Had* done so? No-she would put the thought away. He needed her as much as ever and loved her as devotedly and honourably.... The boat was turned back at the weir and, half an hour later, reached the Club wharf.

"I want to go straight home without changing, Pat; do you mind? I'll drop you at the Gymkhana if you don't want to get home so early," said Dearman, as he helped his wife out.

"Won't you change and have a drink first, John?" she replied. "You must be thirsty."

"No. I want to go along now, if you don't mind."

He did want to-badly. For, rowing up, he had seen something which his wife, facing the other way, could not see.

Under an over-hanging bush was a punt, and in the punt were Augustus and the lady known as Mrs. Harris.

The bush met the bank at the side toward his wife, but at the other side, facing Dearman, there was an open space and so he had seen and she had not. Returning, he had drawn her attention to something on the opposite bank. This had been unnecessary, however, as Augustus had effected a change of venue without delay. And now he did not want his wife to witness the return of the couple and learn of the duplicity of her snatched Brand.

(He'd "brand" him anon!)

* * *

Augustus Clarence Percy Marmaduke Grobble sat in the long cane chair in his sitting-room, a glass beside him, a cigarette between his lips, a fleshly poet in his hand, and a reminiscent smile upon his flushed face.

She undoubtedly was a spanker. Knew precisely how many beans make five. A woman of the world, that. Been about. Knew things. Sort of woman one could tell a good story to-and get one back. Life! Life! Knew it up and down, in and out. Damn reformation, teetotality, the earnest, and the strenuous. Good women were unmitigated bores, and he.... A sharp knock at the door.

"*Kon hai?*"[116] he called. "*Under ao.*"[117]

The door opened and large Mr. Dearman walked in. He bore a nasty-looking malacca cane in his hand-somewhat ostentatiously.

"Hullo, Dearman!" said Augustus after a decidedly startled and anxious look. "What is it? Sit down. I'm just back from College. Have a drink?"

Large Mr. Dearman considered these things *seriatim*.

"I will sit down as I want a talk with you. You are a liar in the matter of just being back from College. I will not have a drink." He then lapsed into silence and looked at Augustus very straight and very queerly, while bending the nasty malacca suggestively. The knees of Augustus smote together.

Good God! It had come at last! The thrashing he had so often earned was at hand. What should he do? What *should* he do!

Dearman thought the young man was about to faint.

"Fine malacca that, isn't it?" he asked.

"Ye-yes!"

"Swishy, supple, tough."

"Ye-yes!" (How could the brute be such a fool as to be jealous now-now when it was all cooling off and coming to an end?)

"Grand stick to thrash a naughty boy with, what?"

"Ye-yes! —Dearman, I swear before God that there is nothing between me and ——"

"Shut up, you infernal God-forsaken cub, or I shall have to whip you. I——"

"Dearman, if you are jealous of me——"

"Better be quiet and listen, or *I* shall get cross, and *you'll* get hurt.... You have given us the pleasure of a great deal of your company this year, and I have come to ask you——"

"Dearman, I have not been so much lately, and I—"

"That's what I complain of, my young friend."

"What?"

"That's what I complain of! I have come to protest against your making yourself almost necessary to me, in a sense, and then-er-deserting me, in a sense."

"You are mocking me, Dearman. If you wish to take advantage of my being half your size and strength to assault me, you — —"

"Not a bit of it, my dear Augustus. I am in most deadly earnest, as you'll find if you are contumacious when I make my little proposition. What I say is this. *I* have grown to take an interest in you, Augustus. *I* have been very kind to you and tried to make a better man of you. *I* have been a sort of mother to you, and you have sworn devotion and gratitude to me. *I* have reformed you somewhat, and you have admitted to me that I have made another man of you, Augustus, and that you love me for it, you love *me* with a deep Platonic love, my Augustus, and-don't you forget it."

"I admit that your wife — —"

"Don't you mention my wife, Augustus, or you and I and that malacca will have a period of great activity. I was saying that *I* am disappointed in you, Augustus, and truly grieved to find you so shallow and false. I asked you to take me on the river to-night and you lied to me and took a very different type of-er-person. Such meanness and ingratitude fairly get me, Augustus. Now I never *asked* you to run after me and come and swear I had saved your dirty little soul alive, but since you did it, Augustus, and *I* have come to take a deep interest in saving the thing-why, you've got to stick it, Augustus-and if you don't —why, then I'll make you, my dear."

"Dearman, your wife has been the noblest friend — —"

"*Will* you come off it, Augustus? I don't want to be cruel. Now look here. *I* have got accustomed to having you about the house and employing you in those funny little ways in which you are a useful little animal. I am under no delusion as to the value of that Soul of yours-but, such as it is, *I* am determined to save it. So just you bring it round to tea to-morrow, as usual; and don't you ever be absent again without my permission. You began the game and I'll end it-when I think fit. Grand malacca that."

"Dearman, I will always — —"

"'Course you will. See you at tea to-morrow, Gussie. If ever my wife hears of this I'll kill you painfully. Bye-Bye."

Augustus was present at tea next day, and, thenceforth, so regular was he that Mrs. Dearman found, first, that she had been very foolish in thinking that her Brand was slipping back into the fire and, later, that Gussie was a bore and a nuisance.

One day he said in the presence of John: —

"I can't keep that golf engagement on Saturday, dear lady, I have to attend a meeting of the Professors, Principal and College Board".

"Have you seen my malacca cane, Pat," said Dearman. "I want it."

"But I really have!" said Augustus, springing up.

"Of course you have," replied Dearman. "What *do* you mean?"

* * *

"John dear," remarked Mrs. Dearman one day, "I wish you could give Gussie a hint not to come quite so often. I have given him some very broad ones during the last few months, but he won't take them. He would from you, I expect."

"Tired of the little bounder, Pat?"

"Oh, sick and tired. He bores me to tears. I wish he were in Government Service and could be transferred. A Government man's always transferred as soon as he has settled to his job. I can't forbid him the house, very well, but I *wish* he'd realize how weary I am of his poses and new socks."

* * *

311

Augustus Clarence Percy Marmaduke Grobble sat in the long cane chair in his sitting-room, a look of rebellious discontent upon his face. What could he do? Better chuck his job and clear out! The strain was getting awful. What a relentless, watchful brute Dearman was! To him entered that gentleman after gently tapping at the chamber door.

"Gussie," said he, "I have come to say that I think you weary me. I don't want you to come and play with me any more. *But* be a nice good boy and do me credit. I have brought you this malacca as a present and a memento. I have another, Gussie, and am going to watch you, so be a real credit to me."

And Gussie was.

So once again a good woman redeemed a bad man-but a trifle indirectly perhaps.

Then came General Miltiades Murger and Mr. John Robin Ross-Ellison to be saved.

During intervals in the salvation process, Mr. John Robin Ross-Ellison vainly endeavoured to induce Mr. Augustus Clarence Percy Marmaduke Grobble to lend his countenance, as well as the rest of his person, to the European Company of the Gungapur Fusilier Volunteer Corps which it was the earnest ambition of Ross-Ellison to raise and train and consolidate into a real and genuine defence organization, with a maxim-gun, a motor-cycle and car section, and a mounted troop, and with, above all, a living and sturdy *esprit-de-corps*. Such a Company appeared to him to be the one and only hope of regeneration for the ludicrous corps which Colonel Dearman commanded, and to change the metaphor, the sole possible means of leavening the lump by its example of high standards and high achievement.

To Augustus, however, as to many other Englishmen, the idea was merely ridiculous and its parent simply absurd.

The day dawned when Augustus, like the said many other Englishmen, changed his mind. In his, and their defence, it may be urged that they knew nothing of the activities of a very retiring but persevering gentleman, known to his familiars as Ilderim the Weeper, and that they had grown up in the belief that all England's fighting and defence can be done by a few underpaid, unconsidered, and very vulgar hirelings.

Perish the thought that Augustus and his like should ever be expected to do the dirty work of defending themselves, their wives, children, homes and honour.

§ 2. General Murger

In a temporary Grand Stand of matchboarding and canvas *tout Gungapur* greeted Mrs. Pat Dearman, who was quite At Home, ranged itself, and critically inspected the horses, or the frocks, of its friends, according to its sex.

Around the great ring on to which the Grand Stand looked, Arab, Pathan, and other heathen raged furiously together and imagined many vain things. Among them unobtrusively moved a Somali who listened carefully to conversations, noted speakers, and appeared to be collecting impressions as to the state of public opinion-and of private opinion. Particularly he sought opportunities of hearing reference to the whereabouts and doings of one Ilderim the Weeper. In the ring were a course of stiff jumps, lesser rings, the judges' office, a kind of watch-tower from which a strenuous fiend with a megaphone bawled things that no living soul could understand, and a number of most horsily-arrayed gentlemen, whose individual status varied from General and cavalry-colonel to rough rider, troop sergeant-major and stud groom.

I regret to add that there was also a Lady, that she was garbed for riding in the style affected by mere man, and that she swaggered loud-voiced, horsey, slapping a boot.

Let men thank the good God for womanly women while such be-and appreciate them.

Behind the Grand Stand were massed the motor-cars and carriages of Society, as well as the Steward of the Gungapur Club, who there spent a busy afternoon in eating ices and drinking Cup while his myrmidons hurried around, washed glasses, squeezed lemons, boiled water and dropped things. Anon he drank ices and ate Cup (with a spoon) and was taken deviously back to his little bungalow behind the Club by the Head Bootlaire Saheb (or butler) who loved and admired him.

Beyond the big ring ran the river, full with the summer rains, giving a false appearance of doing much to cool the air and render the afternoon suitable to the stiff collars and "Europe" garments of the once sterner sex.

A glorious sea-breeze did what the river pretended to do. Beneath the shade of a clump of palms, scores of more and less valuable horses stamped, tossed heads, whisked tails and possibly wondered why God made flies, while an equal number of *syces* squatted, smoked pungent *bidis*, and told lies.

Outside a tent, near by, sat a pimply youth at a table bearing boxes of be-ribboned labels, number-inscribed, official, levelling.

These numbers corresponded with those attached to the names of the horses in the programme of events, and riders must tie one round each arm ere bringing a horse up for judgment when called on.

Certain wretched carping critics alleged that this arrangement was to prevent the possibility of error on the part of the Judges, who, otherwise, would never know whether a horse belonged to a General or a Subaltern, to a Member of Council or an Assistant Collector, to a Head of a Department or a wretched underling-in short to a personage or a person.

You find this type of doubter everywhere-and especially in India where official rank is but the guinea stamp and gold is brass without it.

Great, in the Grand Stand, was General Miltiades Murger. Beside Mrs. Dearman, most charming of hostesses, he sate, in the stage of avuncular affection, and told her that if the Judges knew their business his hunter would win the Hunter-Class first prize and be "Best Horse in the Show" too.

As to his charger, his hack, his trapper, his suitable-for-polo ponies, his carriage-horses he did not worry; they might or might not "do something," but his big and beautiful hunter-well, he hoped the Judges knew their business, that was all.

"Are you going to show him in the ring yourself, General?" asked Mrs. Dearman.

"And leave your side?" replied the great man in manner most avuncular and with little reassuring pats upon the lady's hand. "No, indeed. I am going to remain with you and watch Rissaldar-Major Shere Singh ride him for me. Finest horseman in India. Good as myself. Yes, I *hope* the Judges for Class XIX know their business. I imported that horse from Home and he cost me over six thousand rupees."

Meanwhile, it may be mentioned, evil passions surged in the soul of Mr. John Robin Ross-Ellison as he watched the General, and witnessed his avuncular pattings and confidential whisperings. Mr. Ross-Ellison had lunched with the Dearmans, had brought Mrs. Dearman to the Horse Show, and was settling down, after she had welcomed her guests, to a delightful, entrancing, and thrilling afternoon with her-to be broken but while he showed his horse-when he had been early and utterly routed by the General. The heart of Mr. Ross-Ellison was sore within him, for he loved Mrs. Dearman very devotedly and respectfully.

He was always devotedly in love with some one, and she was always a nice good woman.

When she, or he, left the station, his heart died within him, life was hollow, and his mouth filled with Dead Sea fruit. The world he loved so much would turn to dust and ashes at his touch. After a week or so his heart would resurrect, life would become solid, and his mouth filled with merry song. He would fall in love afresh and the world went very well then.

At present he loved Mrs. Dearman-and hated General Miltiades Murger, who had sent him for a programme and taken his seat beside Mrs. Dearman. There was none on the other side of her-Mr. Ross-Ellison had seen to that-and his prudent foresight had turned and rent him, for he could not plant a chair in the narrow gangway.

He wandered disconsolately away and instinctively sought the object of the one permanent and unwavering love of his life-his mare "Zuleika," late of Balkh.

Zuleika was more remarkable for excellences of physique than for those of mind and character. To one who knew her not, she was a wild beast, fitter for a cage in a Zoo than for human use, a wild-eyed, screaming man-eating she-devil; and none knew her save Mr. John Robin Ross-Ellison, who had bought her unborn. (He knew her parents.)

"If you see an ugly old cove with no hair and a blue nose come over here for his number, just kick his foremost button, *hard*," said Mr. Ross-Ellison to her as he gathered up the reins and, dodging a kick, prepared to mount. This was wrong of him, for Zuleika had never suffered any harm at the hands of General Miltiades Murger, "'eavy-sterned amateur old men" he quoted in a vicious grumble.

A wild gallop round the race-course did something to soothe the ruffled spirit of Mr. Ross-Ellison and nothing to improve Zuleika's appearance-just before she entered the show-ring.

On returning, Mr. Ross-Ellison met the Notable Nut (Lieutenant Nottinger Nutt, an ornament of the Royal Horse Artillery), and they talked evil of Dignitaries and Institutions amounting to high treason if not blasphemy, while watching the class in progress, with young but gloomy eyes.

"I don't care what _any_body says," observed the Notable Nut. "You read the lists of prize-winners of all the bally horse-shows ever held here and you'll find 'em all in strict and decorous order of owner's rank. 'Chargers. First Prize —*Lieutenant-General* White's "Pink Eye". Second Prize —*Brigadier-General* Black's "Red Neck". Third Prize —*Colonel* Brown's "Ham Bone". Highly commended —*Major* Green's "Prairie Oyster". Nowhere at all —*Second-Lieutenant* Blue's "Cocktail,"' —and worth all the rest put together. I tell you I've seen horse after horse change hands after winning a First Prize as a General's property and then win nothing at all as a common Officer's or junior civilian's, until bought again by a Big Pot. Then it sweeps the board. I don't for one second dream of accusing Judges of favouritism or impropriety any kind, but I'm convinced that the glory of a brass-bound owner casts a halo about his horse that dazzles and blinds the average rough-rider, stud-groom and cavalry-sergeant, and don't improve the eyesight of some of their betters, when judging."

"You're right, Nutty," agreed Mr. Ross-Ellison. "Look at that horse 'Runaway'. Last year it won the First Prize as a light-weight hunter, First Prize as a hack, and Highly Commended as a charger-disqualified from a prize on account of having no mane. It then belonged to a Colonel of Dragoons. This year, with a mane and in, if possible, better condition, against practically the same horses, it wins nothing at all. This year it belongs to a junior in the P.W.D. one notices."

"Just what I say," acquiesced the aggrieved Nut, whose rejected horse had been beaten by another which it had itself beaten (under different ownership) the previous year. "Fact is, the judges should be absolutely ignorant as to who owns the horses. They mean well enough, but to them it stands to reason that the most exalted Pots own the most exalted horses. Besides, is it fair to ask a troop sergeant-major to order his own Colonel's horse out of the ring, or the General's either? They ought not to get subordinates in at all. Army Veterinary Colonels from other Divisions are the sort of chaps you want, and some really knowledgeable unofficial civilians-and, as I say, to be in complete ignorance as to ownership. No man to ride his own horse-and none of these bally numbers to prevent the Judges from thinking a General's horse belongs to a common man, and from getting the notion that a subaltern's horse belongs to a General."

"Yes" mused Mr. Ross-Ellison, "and another thing. If you want to get a horse a win or a place in the Ladies' Hack class-get a pretty girl to ride it. They go by the riders' faces and figures entirely.... Hullo! Class XIX wanted. That's me and Zuleika. Come and tie the labels on my arms like a good dog."

"Right O. But you haven't the ghost of a little look in," opined the Nut. "Old Murger has got a real corking English hunter in. A General will win as usual-but he'll win with by far the best horse, for once in the history of horse-shows."

Dismounting and handing their reins to the syces, the two young gentlemen strolled over to the table where presided he of the pimples and number-labels.

A burly Sikh was pointing to the name of General Miltiades Murger and asking for the number printed thereagainst.

The youth handed Rissaldar-Major Shere Singh two labels each bearing the number 99. These, the gallant Native Officer proceeded to tie upon his arms-putting them upside down, as is the custom of the native of India when dealing with anything in any wise reversible.

Mr. Ross-Ellison approached the table, showed his name on the programme and asked for his number —66.

"Tie these on," said he returning to his friend. "By Jove-there's old Murger's horse," he added —"what a magnificent animal!"

Looking up, the Nut saw Rissaldar-Major Shere Singh mounting the beautiful English hunter-and also saw that he bore the number 66. Therefore the labels handed to him were obviously 99, and as 99 he tied on the 66 of Mr. Ross-Ellison —who observed the fact.

"I am afraid I'm all Pathan at this moment," silently remarked he unto his soul, and smiled an ugly smile.

"Not much good my entering Zuleika against *that* mare," he said aloud. "It must have cost just about ten times what I paid for her. Never mind though! We'll show up-for the credit of civilians," and he rode into the ring-where a score of horses solemnly walked round and round the Judges and in front of the Grand Stand....

General Murger brought Mrs. Dearman a cup of tea, and, having placed his *topi*[118] in his chair, went, for a brandy-and-soda and cheroot, to the bar behind the rows of seats.

On his return he beheld his superb and expensive hunter behaving superbly and expensively in the expert hands of Rissaldar-Major Shere Singh.

He feasted his eyes upon it.

Suddenly a voice, a voice he disliked intensely, the voice of Mr. Dearman croaked fiendishly in his ear: "Why, General, they've got your horse numbered wrongly!"

General Miltiades Murger looked again. Upon the arm of Rissaldar-Major Shere Singh was the number 66.

Opening his programme with trembling fingers he found his name, his horse's name, and number 99!

He rose to his feet, stammering and gesticulating. As he did so the words: —

"Take out number 66," were distinctly borne to the ears of the serried ranks of the fashionable in the Grand Stand. Certain military-looking persons at the back abandoned all dignity and fell upon each other's necks, poured great libations, danced, called upon their gods, or fell prostrate upon settees.

Others, seated among the ladies, looked into their bats as though in church.

"Has Ross-Ellison faked it?" ran from mouth to mouth, and, "He'll be hung for this".

A minute or so later the Secretary approached the Grand Stand and announced in stentorian tones:

"First Prize-General Murger's *Darling*, Number 99".

While behind him upon Zuleika, chosen of the Judges, sat and smiled Mr. John Robin Ross-Ellison, who lifted his voice and said: "Thanks-No! —This horse is *mine* and is named *Zuleika*." He looked rather un-English, rather cunning, cruel and unpleasant-quite different somehow, from his ordinary cheery, bright English self.

* * *

"Old" Brigadier General Miltiades Murger was unique among British Generals in that he sometimes resorted to alcoholic stimulants beyond reasonable necessity and had a roving and a lifting eye for a pretty woman. In one sense the General had never taken a wife-and, in another, he had taken several. Indeed it was said of him by jealous colleagues that the hottest actions in which he had ever been engaged were actions for divorce or breach of promise, and that this type of imminent deadly breach was the kind with which he was best acquainted. Also that he was better at storming the citadel of a woman's heart than at storming anything else.

No eminent man is without jealous detractors.

As to the stimulants, make no mistake and jump to no hasty conclusions. General Murger had never been seen drunk in the whole of his distinguished and famous (or as the aforesaid colleagues called it, egregious and notorious) career.

On the other hand, the voice of jealousy said he had never been seen sober either. In the words of envy, hatred, malice and all uncharitableness it declared that he had been born fuddled, had lived fuddled, and would die fuddled. And there were ugly stories.

Also some funny ones-one of which concerns the, Gungapur Fusilier Volunteer Corps and Colonel Dearman, their beloved but shortly retiring (and, as some said, their worthy) Commandant.

Mr. Dearman was a very wealthy (and therefore popular), very red haired and very patriotic mill-owner who tried very hard to be proud of his Corps, and, without trying, was immensely proud of his wife.

As to the Corps-well, it may at least be said that it would have followed its beloved Commandant anywhere (that was neither far nor dangerous), for every one of its Officers, except Captain John Robin Ross-Ellison, and the bulk of its men, were his employees.

They loved him for his wealth and they trusted him absolutely-trusted him not to march them far nor work them much. And they were justified of their faith.

Several of the Officers were almost English-though Greeks and Goa-Portuguese predominated, and there was undeniably a drop or two of English blood in the ranks, well diffused of course. Some folk said that even Captain John Robin Ross-Ellison was not as Scotch as his name.

On guest-nights in the Annual Camp of Exercise (when the Officers' Mess did itself as well as any Mess in India-and only took a few hundred rupees of the Government Grant for the purpose)

Colonel Dearman would look upon the wine when it was bubbly, see his Corps through its golden haze, and wax so optimistic, so enthusiastic, so rash, as roundly to state that if he had five hundred of the Gungapur Fusiliers, with magazines charged and bayonets fixed, behind a stout entrenchment or in a fortified building, he would stake his life on their facing any unarmed city mob you could bring against them. But these were but post-prandial vapourings, and Colonel Dearman never talked nor thought any such folly when the Corps was present to the eye of flesh.

On parade he saw it for what it was —a mob of knock-kneed, sniffling lads with just enough strength to suck a cigarette; anaemic clerks, fat cooks, and loafers with just enough wind to last a furlong march; huge beery old mechanics and ex-"Tommies," forced into this coloured galley as a condition of their "job at the works "; and the non-native scum of the city of Gungapur-which joined for the sake of the ammunition-boots and khaki suit.

There was not one Englishman who was a genuine volunteer and not half a dozen Parsis. Englishmen prefer to join a corps which consists of Englishmen or at least has an English Company. When they have no opportunity of so doing, it is a little unfair to class them with the lazy, unpatriotic, degenerate young gentlemen who have the opportunity and do not seize it. Captain Ross-Ellison was doing his utmost to provide the opportunity-with disheartening results.

However-Colonel Dearman tried very hard to be proud of his Corps and never forgave anyone who spoke slightingly of it.

As to his wife, there was, as stated, no necessity for any "trying". He was immensely and justly proud of her as one of the prettiest, most accomplished, and most attractive women in the Bendras Presidency.

Mrs. "Pat" Dearman, *née* Cleopatra Diamond Brighte, was, as has been said, consciously and most obviously a Good Woman. Brought up by a country rector and his vilely virtuous sister, her girlhood had been a struggle to combine her two ambitions, that of being a Good Woman with that of having a Good Time. In the village of Bishop's Overley the former had been easier; in India the latter. But even in India, where the Good Time was of the very best, she forgot not the other ambition, went to church with unfailing regularity, read a portion of the Scriptures daily; headed subscription lists for the myriad hospitals, schools, widows'-homes, work-houses, Christian associations, churches, charitable societies, shelters, orphanages, rescue-homes and other deserving causes that appeal to the European in India; did her duty by Colonel Dearman, and showed him daily by a hundred little bright kindnesses that she had not married him for his great wealth but for his-er-his-er-not exactly his beauty or cleverness or youthful gaiety or learning or ability-no, for his Goodness, of course, and because she loved him-loved him for the said Goodness, no doubt. No, she never forgot the lessons of the Rectory, that it is the Whole Duty of Man to Save his or her Soul, but remembered to be a Good Woman while having the Good Time. Perhaps the most industriously pursued of all her goodnesses was her unflagging zealous labour in Saving the Souls of Others as well as her own Soul-the "Others" being the young, presentable, gay, and well-placed men of Gungapur Society.

Yes, Mrs. Pat Dearman went beyond the Rectory teachings and was not content with personal salvation. A Good Woman of broad altruistic charity, there was not a young Civilian, not a Subaltern, not a handsome, interesting, smart, well-to-do, well-in-society, young bachelor in whose spiritual welfare she did not take the deepest personal interest. And, perhaps, of all such eligible souls in Gungapur, the one whose Salvation she most deeply desired to work out (after she wearied of the posings and posturings of Augustus Grobble) was that of Captain John Robin Ross-Ellison of her husband's corps-an exceedingly handsome, interesting, smart, well-to-do, well-in-society young bachelor. The owner of this eligible Soul forebore to tell Mrs. Pat Dearman that it was bespoke for Mohammed the Prophet of Allah-inasmuch as *almost* the most entrancing, thrilling and delightful pursuit of his life was the pursuit of soul-treatment at the hands, the beautiful tiny white hands, of Mrs. Pat Dearman. Had her large soulful eyes penetrated this subterfuge, he would have jettisoned Mohammed forthwith, since, to him, the soul-treatment was of infinitely more interest and value than the soul, and, moreover, strange as it may seem, this Mussulman English gentleman had received real and true Christian teaching at his mother's knee. When Mrs. Pat Dearman took him to Church, as she frequently did, on Sunday evenings, he was filled with great longings-and with a conviction of the eternal Truth and Beauty of Christianity and the essential nobility of its gentle, unselfish, lofty teachings. He would think of his mother, of some splendid men and women he had known, especially missionaries, medical and other, at Bannu and Poona and elsewhere, and feel that he was really a Christian at heart; and then again in Khost and Mekran Kot, when carrying his life in his hand, across the border, in equal danger from the bullet of the Border Police, Guides, or Frontier Force cavalry-outposts and from the bullet of criminal tribesmen, when a devil in his soul surged up screaming for blood and fire and slaughter; during the long stealthy crawl as he stalked the stalker; during the wild, yelling, knife-brandishing rush; as he pressed the steady trigger or guided the slashing, stabbing Khyber knife, or as he instinctively *hallaled* the victim of his *shikar*, he knew he was a Pathan and a Mussulman as were his fathers.

But whether circumstances brought his English blood to the surface or his Pathan blood, whether the day were one of his most English days or one of his most Pathan days, whether it were a day of mingled and quickly alternating Englishry and Pathanity he now loved and supported Britain and the British Empire for Mrs. Dearman's sake. Often as he (like most other non-officials) had occasion to detest and desire to kick the Imperial Englishman, championship of England and her Empire was now his creed. And as there was probably not another England-lover in all India who had his knowledge of under-currents, and forces within and without, he was perhaps the most anxiously loving of all her lovers, and the most appalled at the criminal carelessness, blind ignorance, fatuous conceit, and folly of a proportion of her sons in India.

Knowing what he knew of Teutonic intrigue and influence in India, Ceylon, Afghanistan, Aden, Persia, Egypt, East Africa, the Straits Settlements, and China, he was reminded of the men and women of Pompeii who ate, drank, and were merry, danced and sang, pursued pleasure and the nimble denarius, while Vesuvius rumbled.

Constantly the comparison entered his mind.

He had sojourned with Indian "students" in India, England, Germany, Geneva, America and Japan, and had belonged to the most secret of societies. He had himself been a well-paid agent of Germany in both Asia and Africa; and he had been instrumental in supplying thousands of rifles to Border raiders, Persian bandits, and other potential troublers of the *pax Britannica*. He now lived half his double life in Indian dress and moved on many planes; and to many places where even he could not penetrate unsuspected, his staunch and devoted slave, Moussa Isa, went observant. And all that he learnt and knew, within and without the confines of Ind, *by itself* disturbed him, as an England-lover, not at all. Taken in conjunction with the probabilities of a great European War it disturbed him mightily. As mightily as unselfishly. To him the dripping weapon, the blazing roof, the shrieking woman, the mangled corpse were but incidents, the unavoidable, unobjectionable concomitants of the Great Game, the game he most loved (and played upon every possible occasion)—War.

While, with one half of his soul, John Robin Ross-Ellison might fear internal disruption, mutiny, rebellion and civil war for what it might bring to the woman he loved, with the other half of his soul, Mir Ilderim Dost Mahommed Mir Hafiz Ullah Khan dwelt upon the joys of battle, of campaigning, the bivouac, the rattle of rifle-fire, the charge, the circumventing and slaying of the enemy, as he circumvents that he may slay. Thus, it was with no selfish thought, no personal dread, that he grew, as said, mightily disturbed at what he knew of India whenever he saw signs of the extra imminence of the Great European Armageddon that looms upon the horizon, now near, now nearer still, now less near, but inevitably there, plain to the eyes of all observant, informed and thoughtful men.[119]

What really astounded and appalled him was the mental attitude, the mental condition, of British "statesmen," who (while a mighty and ever-growing neighbour, openly, methodically, implacably prepared for the war that was to win her place in the sun) laboured to reap votes by sowing class-hatred and devoted to national "insurance" moneys sorely needed to insure national *existence*.

To him it was as though hens cackled of introducing time-and-labour-saving incubators while the fox pressed against the unfastened door, smiling to think that their cackle smothered all other sounds ere they reached them or the watch-dog.

Yes-while England was at peace, all was well with India; but let England find herself at war, fighting for her very existence... and India might, in certain parts, be an uncomfortable place for any but the strong man armed, as soon as the British troops were withdrawn-as they, sooner or later, most certainly would be. Then, feared Captain John Robin Ross-Ellison of the Gungapur Fusiliers, the British Flag would, for a terrible breathless period of stress and horror, fly, assailed but triumphant, wherever existed a staunch well-handled Volunteer Corps, and would flutter down into smoke, flames, ruin and blood, where there did not. He was convinced that, for a period, the lives of English women, children and men; English prosperity, prestige, law and order; English rule and supremacy, would in some parts of India depend for a time upon the Volunteers of India. At times he was persuaded that the very continuance of the British Empire might depend upon the Volunteers of India. If, during some Black Week (or Black Month or Year) of England's death-struggle with her great rival she lost India (defenceless India, denuded of British troops), she would lose her Empire, —be the result of her European war what it might. And knowing all that he knew, he feared for England, he feared for India, he feared for the Empire. Also he determined that, so far as it lay in the power of one war-trained man, the flag should be kept flying in Gungapur when the Great European Armageddon commenced, and should fly over a centre, and a shelter, for Mrs. Dearman, and for all who were loyal and true.

That would be a work worthy of the English blood of him and of the Pathan blood too. God! he would show some of these devious, subterranean, cowardly swine what war *is*, if they brought war to Gungapur in the hour of India's danger and need, the hour of England and the Empire's danger and need.

And Captain John Robin Ross-Ellison (and still more Mir Ilderim Dost Mahommed Mir Hafiz Ullah Khan), obsessed with the belief that a different and more terrible 1857 would dawn with the first big reverse in England's final war with her systematic, slow, sure, and certain rival, her deliberate, scientific, implacable rival, gave all his thoughts, abilities and time to the enthralling, engrossing game of Getting Ready.

Perfecting his local system of secret information, hearing and seeing all that he could with his own Pathan ears and eyes, and adding to his knowledge by means of those of the Somali slave, he also learnt, at first hand, what certain men were saying in Cabul and on the Border-and what those men say in those places is worth knowing by the meteorologist of world-politics. The pulse of the heart of Europe can be felt very far from that heart, and as is the wrist to the pulse-feeling doctor, is Afghanistan and the Border to the head of India's Political Department; as is the doctor's sensitive thumb to the doctor's brain, is the tried, trusted and approven agent of the Secret Service to the Head of all the Politicals.... What chiefly troubled Captain John Robin Ross-Ellison of the Gungapur Fusiliers was the shocking condition of those same Fusiliers and the blind smug apathy, the fatuous contentment, the short memories and shorter sight, of the British Pompeians who were perfectly willing that the condition of the said Fusiliers should remain so.

Clearly the first step towards a decently reliable and efficient corps in Gungapur was the abolition of the present one, and, with unformulated intentions towards its abolition, Mr. Ross-Ellison, by the kind influence of Mrs. Dearman, joined as a Second Lieutenant and speedily rose to the rank of Captain and the command of a Company. A year's indefatigable work convinced him that he might as well endeavour to fashion sword-blades from leaden pipes as to make a fighting unit of his gang of essentially cowardly, peaceful, unreliable, feeble nondescripts. That their bodies were contemptible he would have regarded as merely deplorable, but there was no spirit, no soul, no tradition-nothing upon which he could work. "Broken-down tapsters and serving-men" indeed, in Cromwell's bitter words, and to be replaced by "men of a spirit".

They must go-and make way for men-if indeed *men* could be found, men who realized that even an Englishman owes something to the community when he goes abroad, in spite of his having grown up in a land where honourable and manly National Service is not, and those who keep him safe are cheap hirelings, cheaply held....

On the arrival of General Miltiades Murger he sat at his feet as soon as, and whenever, possible; only to discover that he was not only uninterested in, but obviously contemptuous of, volunteers and volunteering. When, at the Dearmans' dinner-table, he endeavoured to talk with the General on the subject he was profoundly discouraged, and on his asking what was to happen when the white troops went home and the Indian troops went to the Border, or even to Europe, as soon as England's inevitable and final war broke out, he was also profoundly snubbed.

When, after that dinner, General Miltiades Murger made love to Mrs. Dearman on the verandah, he also made an enemy, a bitter, cruel, and vindictive enemy of Mr. Ross-Ellison (or rather of Mir Ilderim Dost Mahommed Mir Hafiz Ullah Khan).

Nor did his subsequent victory at the Horse Show lessen the enmity, inasmuch as Mrs. Dearman (whom Ross-Ellison loved with the respectful platonic devotion of an English gentleman and the fierce intensity of a Pathan) took General Miltiades Murger at his own valuation, when that hero described himself and his career to her by the hour. For the General had succumbed at a glance, and confided to his Brigade-Major that Mrs. Dearman was a dooced fine woman and the Brigade-Major might say that he said so, damme.

As the General's infatuation increased he told everybody else also-everybody except Colonel Dearman-who, of course, knew it already.

He even told Jobler, his soldier-servant, promoted butler, as that sympathetic and admiring functionary endeavoured to induce him to go to bed without his uniform.

At last he told Mrs. Dearman herself, as he saw her in the rosy light that emanated from the fine old Madeira that fittingly capped a noble luncheon given by him in her honour.

He also told her that he loved her as a father-and she besought him not to be absurd. Later he loved her as an uncle, later still as a cousin, later yet as a brother, and then as a man.

She had laughed deprecatingly at the paternal affection, doubtfully at the avuncular, nervously at the cousinly, angrily at the brotherly,—and not at all at the manly.

In fact-as the declaration of manly love had been accompanied by an endeavour to salute what the General had called her damask-cheek—she had slapped the General's own cheek a resounding blow....

"Called you 'Mrs. Darlingwoman,' did he!" roared Mr. Dearman upon being informed of the episode. "Wished to salute your damask cheek, did he! The boozy old villain! Damask cheek! *Damned* cheek! Where's my dog-whip?"... but Mrs. Dearman had soothed and restrained her lord for the time being, and prevented him from insulting and assaulting the "aged roué"—who was years younger, in point of fact, than the clean-living Mr. Dearman himself.

But he had shut his door to the unrepentant and unashamed General, had cut him in the Club, had returned a rudely curt answer to an invitation to dinner, and had generally shown the offender that he trod on dangerous ground when poaching on the preserves of Mr. Dearman. Whereat the General fumed.

Also the General swore that he would cut the comb of this insolent money-grubbing civilian.

Further, he intimated his desire to inspect the Gungapur Fusiliers "on Saturday next".

Not the great and terrible Annual Inspection, of course, but a preliminary canter in that direction.

Doubtless, the new General desired to arrive at a just estimate of the value of this unit of his Command, and to allot to it the place for which it was best fitted in the scheme of local defence and things military at Gungapur.

Perhaps he desired to teach the presumptuous upstart, Dearman, a little lesson....

The Brigade Major's demy-official letter, bearing the intimation of the impending visitation-fell as a bolt from the blue and smote the Colonel of the Gungapur Fusiliers a blow that turned his heart to water and loosened the tendons of his knees.

The very slack Adjutant was at home on leave; the Sergeant-Major was absolutely new to the Corps; the Sergeant-Instructor was alcoholic and ill; and there was not a company officer, except the admirable Captain John Robin Ross-Ellison, competent to drill a company as a separate unit, much less to command one in a battalion. And Captain John Robin Ross-Ellison was away on an alleged *shikar*-trip across the distant Border. Colonel Dearman knew his battalion-drill. He also knew his Gungapur Fusiliers and what they did when they received the orders of those feared and detested evolutions. They walked about, each man a law unto himself, or stood fast until pushed in the desired direction by blasphemous drill-corporals.

Nor could any excuse be found wherewith to evade the General. It was near the end of the drill-season, the Corps was up to its full strength, all the Officers were in the station-except Captain Ross-Ellison and the Adjutant. And the Adjutant's absence could not be made a just cause and impediment why the visit of the General should not be paid, for Colonel Dearman had with some difficulty, procured the appointment of one of his Managers as acting-adjutant.

To do so he had been moved to describe the man as an "exceedingly smart and keen Officer," and to state that the Corps would in no way suffer by this temporary change from a military to a civilian adjutant, from a professional to an amateur.

Perhaps the Colonel was right-it would have taken more than that to make the Gungapur Fusiliers "suffer".

And all had gone exceeding well up to the moment of the receipt of this terrible demi-official, for the Acting-Adjutant had signed papers when and where the Sergeant-Major told him, and had saluted the Colonel respectfully every Saturday evening at five, as he came on parade, and suggested that the Corps should form fours and march round and round the parade ground, prior to attempting one or two simple movements-as usual.

No. It would have to be-unless, of course, the General had a stroke before Saturday, or was smitten with *delirium tremens* in time. For it was an article of faith with Colonel Dearman since the disgraceful episode-that a "stroke" hung suspended by the thinnest of threads above the head of the "aged roué" and that, moreover, he trembled on the verge of a terrible abyss of alcoholic diseases —a belief strengthened by the blue face, boiled eye, congested veins and shaking hand of the breaker of hearts. And Colonel Dearman knew that he must not announce the awful fact until the Corps was actually present-or few men and fewer Officers would find it possible to be on parade on that occasion.

Saturday evening came, and with it some five hundred men and Officers-the latter as a body, much whiter-faced than usual, on receipt of the appalling news.

"Thank God I have nothing to do but sit around on my horse," murmured Major Pinto.

"Don't return thanks yet," snapped Colonel Dearman. "You'll very likely have to drill the battalion" —and the Major went as white as his natural disadvantages permitted.

Bitterly did Captain Trebizondi regret his constant insistence upon the fact that he was senior Captain-for he was given command of "A" Company, the post of honour and danger in front of all, and was implored to "pull it through" and not to stand staring like an owl when the Colonel said the battalion would advance; or turn to the left when he shouted "In succession advance in fours from the right of Companies".

And in the orderly-room was much hurried consulting of Captain Ross-Ellison's well-trained subaltern and of drill-books; and a babel of such questions as: "I say, what the devil do I do if I'm commanding Number Two and he says 'Deploy outwards'? Go to the right or left?"

More than one gallant officer was seen scribbling for dear life upon his shirt-cuff, while others, to the common danger, endeavoured to practise the complicated sword-brandishment which is consequent upon the order "Fall out the Officers".

Colonel Dearman appealed to his brothers-in-arms to stand by him nobly in his travail, but was evidently troubled by the fear that some of them would stand by him when they ought to march by him. Captain Petropaulovski, the acting-adjutant, endeavoured to moisten his parched lips with a dry tongue and sat down whenever opportunity offered.

Captain Euxino Spoophitophiles was seen to tear a page from a red manual devoted to instruction in the art of drill and to secrete it as one "palms" a card-if one is given to the palming of cards. Captain Schloggenboschenheimer was heard to promise a substantial *trink-geld*, *pour-boire*, or vot-you-call-tip to Sergeant-Instructor Progg in the event of the latter official remaining mit him and prompting him mit der-vord-to-say ven it was necessary for him der-ting-to-do.

Too late, Captain Da Costa bethought him of telephoning to his wife (to telephone back to himself imploring him to return at once as she was parlous ill and sinking fast), for even as he stepped quietly toward the telephone-closet the Sergeant-Major bustled in with a salute and the fatal words: —

"'Ere's the General, Sir!"

"For God's sake get on parade and play the man this day," cried Colonel Dearman, as he hurried out to meet the General, scoring his right boot with his left spur and tripping over his sword *en route*.

* * *

The General greeted the Colonel as a total stranger, addressed him as "Colonel," and said he anticipated great pleasure from this his first visit to the well-known Gungapur Fusiliers. He did, and he got it.

Dismounting slowly and heavily from his horse (almost as though "by numbers") the General, followed by his smart and dapper Brigade-Major and the perspiring Colonel Dearman, strode with clank of steel and creak of leather, through the Headquarters building and emerged upon the parade-ground where steadfast stood seven companies of the Gungapur Fusilier Volunteers in quarter column-more or less at "attention".

"'Shun!" bawled Colonel Dearman, and those who were "at ease" 'shunned, and those who were already 'shunning took their ease.

"'*Shun!*" again roared the Colonel, and those who were now in that military position relinquished it-while those who were not, assumed it in their own good time.

As the trio drew nigh unto the leading company, Captain Trebizondi, coyly lurking behind its rear rank, shrilly screamed, "'A' Gompany! Royal Salutes! Present Arrrrms!" while a volunteer, late a private of the Loyal Whitechapel Regiment, and now an unwilling member of this corps of auxiliary troops, audibly ejaculated through one corner of his mobile mouth: —

"Don't you do nothink o' the sort!" and added a brief orison in prejudice of his eyesight.

Certain of "A's" stalwarts obeyed their Captain, while others took the advice of the volunteer-who was known to have been a man of war in the lurid past, and to understand these matters.

Lieutenant Toddywallah tugged valiantly at his sword for a space, but finding that weapon coy and unwilling to leave its sheath, he raised his helmet gracefully and respectfully to the General. His manner was always polished.

"What the devil are they doing?" inquired the General.

"B," "C," "D," "E," "F," and "G" Companies breathed hard and protruded their stomachs, while Sergeant-Instructor Progg deserved well of Captain Schloggenboschenheimer by sharply tugging his tunic-tail as he was in the act of roaring: —

"*Gomm*—!" the first syllable of the word "Company," with a view to bestowing a royal salute likewise. Instead, the Captain extended the hand of friendship to the General as he approached. The look of *nil admirari* boredom slowly faded from the face of the smart and dapper Brigade-Major, and for a while it displayed quite human emotions.

Up and down and between the ranks strode the trio, the General making instructive and interesting comments from time to time, such as: —

"Are your buttons of metal or bone, my man? Polish them and find out."

"What did you cook in that helmet?"

"Take your belt in seven holes, and put it where your waist was."

"Are *you* fourteen years old yet?"

"Personally I don't care to see brown boots, patent shoes nor carpet slippers with uniform."

"And when were you ninety, my poor fellow?"

"Get your belly out of my way."

"Put this unclean person under arrest or under a pump, please, Colonel."

"Can you load a rifle unaided?" and so forth.

The last-mentioned query "Can you load a rifle unaided?" addressed to a weedy youth of seventeen who stood like a living mark-of-interrogation, elicited the reply: —

"Nossir".

"Oh, really! And what *can* you do?" replied the General sweetly.

"Load a rifle Lee-Metford," was the prompt answer.

The General smiled wintrily, and, at the conclusion of his peregrination, remarked to Colonel Dearman: —

"Well, Colonel, I can safely say that I have never inspected a corps quite like yours" —an observation capable of various interpretations-and intimated a desire to witness some company drill ere testing the abilities of the regiment in battalion drill.

"Let the rear company march out and go through some movements," said he.

"Why the devil couldn't he have chosen Ross-Ellison's company," thought Colonel Dearman, as he saluted and lifted up his voice and cried aloud: —

"Captain Rozario! March 'G' Company out for some company-drill. Remainder-stand *easy.*"

Captain Rozario paled beneath the bronze imparted to his well-nourished face by the suns of Portugal (or Goa), drew his sword, dropped it, picked it up, saluted with his left hand and backed into Lieutenant Xenophontis of "F" Company, who asked him vare the devil he was going to-hein?...

To the first cold stroke of fright succeeded the hot flush of rage as Captain Rozario saw the absurdity of ordering him to march his company out for company drill. How in the name of all the Holy Saints could he march his company out with six companies planted in front of him? Let them be cleared away first. To his men he ejaculated: —

"Compannee——!" and they accepted the remark in silence.

The silence growing tense he further ejaculated "Ahem!" very loudly, without visible result or consequence. The silence growing tenser, Colonel Dearman said encouragingly but firmly: —

"*Do* something, Captain Rozario".

Captain Rozario did something. He drew his whistle. He blew it. He replaced it in his pocket.

Nothing happening, he took his handkerchief from his sleeve, blew his nose therewith and dropped it (the handkerchief) upon the ground. Seven obliging volunteers darted forward to retrieve it.

"May we expect the evolutions this evening, Colonel?" inquired General Murger politely.

"We are waiting for you to move off, Captain Rozario," stated Colonel Dearman.

"Sir, how can I move off with *oll* the rest in my front?" inquired Captain Rozario reasonably.

"Form fours, right, and quick march," prompted the Sergeant-Major, and Captain Rozario shrilled forth:

"Form right fours and march quick," at the top of his voice.

Many members of "G" Company turned to their right and marched towards the setting-sun, while some turned to their left and marched in the direction of China.

These latter, discovering in good time that they had erred, hurried to rejoin their companions- and "G" Company was soon in full swing if not in fours....

There is a limit to all enterprise and the march of "G" Company was stayed by a high wall. Then Captain Rozario had an inspiration.

"About turn," he shrieked-and "G" Company about turned as one man, if not in one direction.

The march of "G" Company was stayed this time by the battalion into which it comfortably nuzzled.

Again Captain Rozario seized the situation and acted promptly and resourcefully.

"Halt!" he squeaked, and "G" Company halted-in form an oblate spheroid.

Some of its members removed their helmets and the sweat of their brows, some re-fastened bootlaces and putties or unfastened restraining hooks and buttons. One gracefully succumbed to his exertions and fainting fell, with an eye upon the General.

"Interestin' evolution," remarked that Officer. "Demmed interestin'. May we have some more?"

"Get on, Captain Rozario," implored Colonel Dearman. "Let's see some company-drill."

"One hundred and twenty-five paces backward march," cried Captain Rozario after a brief calculation, and "G" Company reluctantly detached itself from the battalion, backwards.

"Turn round this away and face to me," continued the gallant Captain, "and then on the left form good companee."

The oblate spheroid assumed an archipelagic formation, melting into irregularly-placed military islands upon a sea of dust.

"*Oll* get together and left dress, please," besought Captain Rozario, and many of the little islands amalgamated with that on their extreme right while the remainder gravitated to their left-the result being two continents of unequal dimensions.

As Captain Rozario besought these disunited masses to conjoin, the voice of the General was heard in the land —

"Kindly order that mob to disperse before it is fired on, will you, Colonel? They can go home and stay there," said he.

Captain Rozario was a man of sensibility and he openly wept.

No one could call this a good beginning-nor could they have called the ensuing battalion-drill a good ending.

"Put the remainder of the battalion through some simple movements if they know any," requested the General.

Determined to retrieve the day yet, Colonel Dearman saluted, cleared his throat terrifically and shouted: "'Tallish, 'shun!" with such force that a nervous man in the front rank of "A" Company dropped his rifle and several "presented" arms.

Only one came to the "slope," two to the "trail" and four to the "shoulder".

Men already at attention again stood at ease, while men already at ease again stood at attention.

Disregarding these minor *contretemps*, Colonel Dearman clearly and emphatically bellowed: —

"The battalion will advance. In succession, advance in fours from the left of companies —"

"Why not tell off the battalion-just for luck?" suggested General Murger.

"Tell off the battalion," said Colonel Dearman in his natural voice and an unnaturally crest-fallen manner.

Captain Trebizondi of "A" Company glared to his front, and instead of replying "Number One" in a loud voice, held his peace-tight.

But his lips moved constantly, and apparently Captain Trebizondi was engaged in silent prayer.

"Tell off the battalion," bawled the Colonel again.

Captain Trebizondi's lips moved constantly.

"*Will* you tell off the dam battalion, Sir?" shouted the Colonel at the enrapt supplicant.

Whether Captain Trebizondi is a Mohammedan I am not certain, but, if so, he may have remembered words of the Prophet to the effect that it is essential to trust in Allah absolutely, and expedient to tie up your camel yourself, none the less. Captain Trebizondi was trusting in Allah perchance-but he had not tied up his camel; he had not learnt his drill.

And when Colonel Dearman personally and pointedly appealed to him in the matter of the battalion's telling-off, he turned round and faced it and said —

"Ah-battalion-er —" in a very friendly and persuasive voice.

Then a drill corporal took it upon him to bawl *Number One* as Captain Trebizondi should have done, some one shouted *Number Two* from "B" Company, the colour-sergeant of "C" bawled *Number Three* and then, with ready wit, the Captains of "D," "E," and "F" caught up the idea, and the thing was done.

So far so good.

And the Colonel returned to his first venture and again announced to the battalion that it would advance in succession and in fours from the left of companies.

It bore the news with equanimity and Captain Trebizondi visibly brightened at the idea of leaving the spot on which he had suffered and sweated-but he took no steps in the matter personally.

He tried to scratch his leg through his gaiter.

"'A' Company going this evening?" inquired the General. "Wouldn't hurry you, y'know, but —I dine at nine."

Captain Trebizondi remembered his parade-manners and threw a chest instead of a stomach.

The jerk caused his helmet to tilt forward over his eyes and settle down slowly and firmly upon his face as a fallen cliff upon the beach beneath.

"The Officer commanding the leading company appears to be trying to hide," commented General Murger.

Captain Trebizondi uncovered his face —a face of great promise but no performance.

"*Will* you march your company off, sir," shouted Colonel Dearman, "the battalion is waiting for you."

With a look of reproachful surprise and an air of "Why couldn't you say so?" the harassed Captain agitated his sword violently as a salute, turned to his company and boomed finely: —

"March off!"

The Company obeyed its Commander.

Seeing the thing so easy of accomplishment Captains Allessandropoulos, Schloggenboschen-heimer, Da Costa, Euxino, Spoophitophiles and José gave the same order and the battalion was in motion-marching to its front in quarter-column instead of wheeling off in fours.

Unsteadily shoulder from shoulder,

Unsteadily blade from blade,

Unsteady and wrong, slouching along,

Went the boys of the old brigade.

"Halt," roared Colonel Dearman.

"Oh, don't halt 'em," begged General Murger, "it's the most entertainin' show I have ever seen."

The smart and dapper Brigade-Major's mouth was open.

Major Pinto and Captain-and-Acting-Adjutant Petropaulovski forgot to cling to their horses with hand and heel and so endangered their lives.

The non-commissioned officers of the permanent staff commended their souls to God and marched as men in a dream.

On hearing the Colonel's cry of "Halt" many of the men halted. Not hearing the Colonel's cry of "Halt" many of the men did not halt.

In two minutes the battalion was without form and void.

In ten minutes the permanent staff had largely re-sorted it and, to a great extent, re-formed the original companies.

Captain José offered his subaltern, Lieutenant Bylegharicontractor, a hundred rupees to change places with him.

Offer refused, with genuine and deep regret, but firmly.

"Shall we have another try, Colonel," inquired General Murger silkily. "Any amount of real initiative and originality about this Corps. But I am old-fashioned enough to prefer drill-book evolutions on the barrack-square, I confess. Er-let the Major carry on as it is getting late."

Colonel Dearman's face flushed a rich dark purple. His eyes protruded till they resembled those of a crab. His red hair appeared to flame like very fire. His lips twitched and he gasped for breath. Could he believe his ears. *"Let the Major carry on as it is getting late!"* Let him step into the breach "as it is getting late!" Let the more competent, though junior, officer take over the command "as it is getting late". Ho!—likewise Ha! This aged roué, this miserable wine-bibbing co-respondent, with his tremulous hand and boiled eye, thought that Colonel Dearman did not know his drill, did he? Wanted the wretched and incompetent Pinto to carry on, did he?—as it was getting late.

Good! Ha! Likewise Ho! "Let Pinto carry on as it was getting late!"

Very well! *If it cost Colonel Dearman every penny he had in the world he would have his revenge on the insolent scoundrel.* He might think he could insult Colonel Dearman's wife with impunity, he might think himself entitled to cast ridicule on Colonel Dearman's Corps-but "let the Major carry on as it is getting late!" By God that was too much!—That was the last straw that breaks the camel's heart-and Colonel Dearman would have his revenge or lose life, honour, and wealth in the attempt.

Ha! and, moreover, *Ho*!

The Colonel knew his battalion-drill by heart and backwards. Was it *his* fault that his officers were fools and his men damn-fools?

Major Pinto swallowed hard, blinked hard, and breathed hard. Like the
Lady of Shallott he felt that the curse had come upon him.

"Battalion will advance. Quick march," he shouted, as a safe beginning. But the Sergeant-Major had by this time fully explained to the sweating Captain Trebizondi that he should have given the order "Form fours. Left. Right wheel. Quick march," when the Colonel had announced that the battalion would advance "in succession from the left of companies".

Like lightning he now hurled forth the orders. "Form fours. Left. Right wheel. Quick march.", and the battalion was soon under way with one company in column of fours and the remaining five companies in line....

Time cures all troubles, and in time "A" Company was pushed and pulled back into line again.

The incident pleased Major Pinto as it wasted the fleeting minutes and gave him a chance to give the only other order of which he was sure.

"That was *oll* wrong," said he. "We will now, however, oll advance as 'A' Company did. The arder will be 'Battalion will advance. In succession, advance in fours from the right of companees.' Thenn each officer commanding companees will give the arder 'Form fours. Right. Left wheel. Quick march' one after *thee* other."

And the Major gave the order.

To the surprise of every living soul upon the parade-ground the manoeuvre was correctly executed and the battalion moved off in column of fours. And it kept on moving. And moving. For Major Pinto had come to the end of his tether.

"*Do* something, man," said Colonel Dearman with haughty scorn, after some five minutes of strenuous tramping had told severely on the *morale* of the regiment.

And Major Pinto, hoping for the best and fearing the worst, lifted up his voice and screamed: —

"On the right *form battalion!*"

Let us draw a veil.

The adjective that General Murger used with the noun he called the Gungapur Fusiliers is not to be printed.

The address he made to that Corps after it had once more found itself would have led a French or Japanese regiment to commit suicide by companies, taking the time from the right. A Colonel of Romance Race would have fallen on his sword at once (and borrowed something more lethal had it failed to penetrate).

But the corps, though not particularly British, was neither French nor Japanese and was very glad of the rest while the General talked. And Colonel Dearman, instead of falling on his sword, fell on General Murger (in spirit) and swore to be revenged tenfold.

He would have his own back, cost what it might, or his name was not Dearman-and he was going Home on leave immediately after the Volunteer Annual Camp of Exercise, just before General Murger retired....

"I shall inspect your corps in camp," General Murger had said, "and the question of its disbandment may wait until I have done so."

Disbandment! The question of the *disbandment* of the fine and far-famed Fusiliers of Gungapur could wait till then, could it? Well *and* good! Ha! and likewise Ho!

On Captain John Robin Ross-Ellison's return from leave, Colonel Dearman told that officer of General Murger's twofold insult-to Colonel Dearman's wife and to Colonel Dearman's Corps. On hearing of the first, Captain Ross-Ellison showed his teeth in a wolfish and ugly manner, and, on hearing of the second, propounded a scheme of vengeance that made Colonel Dearman grin and then burst into a roar of laughter. He bade Captain Ross-Ellison dine with him and elaborate details of the scheme.

* * *

To rumours of General Murger's failing health and growing alcoholism Colonel Dearman listened with interest-nay, satisfaction. Stories of seizures, strokes and "goes" of *delirium tremens* met with no rebuke nor contradiction from him-and an air of leisured ease and unanxious peacefulness pervaded the Gungapur Fusiliers. If any member had thought that the sad performance of the fatal Saturday night and the winged words of General Murger were to be the prelude to period of fierce activity and frantic preparation, he was mistaken. It was almost as though Colonel Dearman believed that General Murger would not live to carry out his threat.

The corps paraded week by week, fell in, marched round the ground and fell out again. There was no change of routine, no increase of work, no stress, no strain.

All was peace, the corps was happy, and in the fullness of time (and the absence of the Adjutant) it went to Annual Camp of Exercise a few miles from Gungapur. And there the activities of Captain John Robin Ross-Ellison and a large band of chosen men were peculiar. While the remainder, with whom went Colonel Dearman, the officers, and the permanent staff, marched about in the usual manner and enjoyed the picnic, these others appeared to be privately and secretly rehearsing a more specialized part-to the mystification and wonder of the said remainder.

Even on the great day, the day of the Annual Inspection, this division was maintained and the "remainder" were marched off to the other side of the wood adjacent to the Camp, some couple of hours before the expected arrival of the General, who would come out by train.

The arrangement was that the horses of the General and the Brigade-Major should await those officers at the camp station, and that, on arrival, they would be mounted by their owners who would then ride to the camp, a furlong distant. Near the camp a mounted orderly would meet the General and escort him to the spot where the battalion, with Colonel Dearman at its head, would be drawn up for his inspection.

A large bungalow, used as the Officers' Mess, a copse, and a hillock completely screened the spot used as the battalion parade-ground, from the view of one approaching the Camp, and the magnificent sight of the Gungapur Fusiliers under arms would burst upon him only when he rounded the corner of a wall of palms, cactus, and bamboos, and entered by a narrow gap between it and a clump of dense jungle.

* * *

General Murger was feeling distinctly bad as he sat on the edge of his bed and viewed with the eye of disfavour the *choti hazri*[120] set forth for his delectation.

As he intended to inspect the Volunteers in the early morning and return to a mid-day breakfast, the *choti hazri* was substantial, though served on a tray in his bedroom.

The General yawned, rubbed his eyes and grunted.

"Eggs be demmed," said he.

"Toast be demmed," he said.

"Tea be demmed," he shouted.

"*Paté de fois gras* be demmed," shouted he.

"Jobler! Bring me a bottle of beer," he roared.

"No, bring me a brandy-cocktail," roared he.

For the brandy-cocktail the General felt better for a time but he wished, first, that his hand would not shake in such a way that hair-brushing was difficult and shaving impossible; secondly, that the prevailing colour of everything was not blue; thirdly, that he did not feel giddy when he stood up; fourthly, that his head did not ache; fifthly, that his mouth would provide some other flavour than that of a glue-coated copper coin; sixthly, that things would keep still and his boots cease to smile at him from the corner; seventhly, that he had not gone to the St. Andrew's dinner last night, begun on *punch à la Romaine*, continued on neat whisky in *quaichs* and finished on port, liqueurs, champagne and haphazard brandy-and-sodas, whisky-and-sodas, and any old thing that was handy; and eighthly, that he had had a quart of beer instead of the brandy-cocktail for *choti hazri*.

But that could easily be remedied by having the beer now. The General had the beer and soon wished that he hadn't, for it made him feel very bad indeed.

However, a man must do his dooty, ill or well, and when the Brigade-Major sent up to remind the General that the train went at seven, he was answered by the General himself and a hint that he was officious. During the brief train-journey the General slumbered.

On mounting his horse, the General was compelled to work out a little sum.

If one has four fingers there must be three inter-finger spaces, eh? Granted. Then how the devil are four reins to go into three places between four fingers, eh? Absurd idea, an' damsilly. However, till the matter was referred to the War Office and finally settled, one could put two reins between two fingers or pass one outside the lill' finger, what? But the General hated compromises.... The mounted orderly met the General, saluted and directed him to the entrance to the tree-encircled camp and parade-ground.

At the entrance, the General, leading, reined in so sharply as to throw his horse on its haunches-his mouth fell open, his mottled face went putty-coloured, and each hair that he possessed appeared to bristle.

He uttered a deep groan, rubbed his eyes, emitted a yell, wheeled round and galloped for dear life, with a cry, nay a scream, of "*I've got 'em at last*," followed by his utterly bewildered but ever-faithful Brigade-Major, who had seen nothing but foliage, scrub, and cactus. To Gungapur the General galloped without drawing rein, took to his bed, sent for surgeon and priest-and became a teetotaller.

And what had he seen?

The affair is wrapped in mystery.

The Brigade-Major says nothing because he knows nothing, as it happens, and the Corps declared it was never inspected. Father Ignatius knows what the General saw, or thinks he saw, and so does the Surgeon-General, but neither is in the habit of repeating confessions and confidences. What Jobler, at the keyhole, understood him to say he had seen, or thought he had seen, is not to be believed.

Judge of it.

"I rode into the dem place and what did I behold? A dem pandemonium, Sir, a pantomime — a lunatic asylum, Sir-all Hell out for a Bank Holiday, I tell you. There was a battalion of Red Indians, Negroes, Esquimaux, Ballet Girls, Angels, Sweeps, Romans, Sailors, Pierrots, Savages, Bogeymen, Ancient Britons, Bishops, Zulus, Pantaloons, Beef-eaters, Tramps, Life-Guards, Washerwomen, Ghosts, Clowns and God-knows-what, armed with jezails, umbrellas, brooms, catapults, pikes, brickbats, *kukeries*,[121] pokers, clubs, axes, horse-pistols, bottles, dead fowls, polo-sticks, assegais and bombs. They were commanded by a Highlander in a bum-bee tartan kilt, top-hat and one sock, with a red nose a foot long, riding on a rocking horse and brandishing a dem great cucumber and a tea-tray made into a shield. There was a thundering great drain-pipe mounted on a bullock-cart and a naked man, painted blue, in a cocked-hat, laying an aim and firing a penny-pistol down the middle of it and yelling 'Pip!'

"There was a chauffeur in smart livery on an elephant, twirling a steering-wheel on its neck for dear life, and tooting a big motor-horn.. There was a fat man in a fireman's helmet and pyjamas, armed with a peashooter, riding a donkey backwards-and the moke wore two pairs of trousers!...As I rubbed my poor old eyes, the devil in command howled 'General salaam. Pre_-sent_-legs' —and every fiend there fell flat on his face and raised his right leg up behind —I tell you, Sir, I fled for my life, and-no more liquor for me."...

When ex-Colonel Dearman heard any reference to this mystery he roared with laughter-but it was the Last Muster of the fine and far-famed Gungapur Fusiliers, as such.

The Corps was disbanded forthwith and re-formed on a different basis (of quality instead of quantity) with Lieutenant-Colonel John Robin Ross-Ellison, promoted, in command-he having caught the keen eye of that splendid soldier and gentleman Lieutenant-General Sir Arthur Barnet, K.C.V.O., K.C.S.I. (G.O.C., XVIth Division), as being the very man for the job of re-organizing the Corps, and making it worth its capitation-grant.

"If I could get Captain Malet-Marsac as Adjutant and a Sergeant-Major of whom I know (used to be at Duri-man named Lawrence-Smith) I'd undertake to show you something, Sir, in a year or two," said Lieutenant-Colonel Ross-Ellison.

"Malet-Marsac you can certainly have," replied Sir Arthur Barnet. "I'll speak to your new Brigadier. If you can find your Lawrence-Smith we'll see what can be done."...

And Lieutenant-Colonel Ross-Ellison wrote to Sergeant-Major Lawrence-Smith of the Duri Volunteer Rifles to know if he would like a transfer upon advantageous terms, and got no reply.

As it happened, Lieutenant-Colonel Ross-Ellison, in very different guise, had seen Sergeant Lawrence-Smith extricate and withdraw his officerless company from the tightest of tight places (on the Border) in a manner that moved him to large admiration. It had been a case of "and even the ranks of Tuscany" on the part of Mir Jan Rah-bin-Ras el-Isan Ilderim Dost Mahommed.... Later he had encountered him and Captain Malet-Marsac at Duri.

§ 3. Sergeant-Major Lawrence-Smith

Mrs. Pat Dearman was sceptical.

"Do you mean to tell me that *you*, a man of science, an eminent medical man, and a soldier, believe in the supernatural?"

"Well, you see, I'm 'Oirish' and therefore unaccountable," replied Colonel Jackson (of the Royal Army Medical Corps), fine doctor, fine scholar, and fine gentleman.

"And you believe in haunted houses and ghosts and things, do you? *Well!*"

The salted-almond dish was empty, and Mrs. Dearman accused her other neighbour, Mr. John Robin Ross-Ellison. Having already prepared to meet and rebut the charge of greediness he made passes over the vessel and it was replenished.

"Supernatural!" said she.

"Most," said he.

She prudently removed the dish to the far side of her plate-and Colonel Jackson emptied it.

Not having prepared to meet the request to replenish the store a second time, it was useless for Mr. Ross-Ellison to make more passes when commanded so to do.

"The usual end of the 'supernatural,'" observed Mrs. Dearman with contempt.

"Most usual," said he.

"More than 'most,'" corrected Mrs. Dearman. "It is the invariable end of it, I believe. Just humbug and rubbish. It is either an invention, pure and simple, or else it is perfectly explicable. Don't you think so, Colonel Jackson?"

"Not always," said her partner. "Now, will you, first, believe my word, and, secondly, find the explanation-if I tell you a perfectly true 'supernatural' story?"

"I'll certainly believe your word, Colonel, if you're serious, and I'll try and suggest an explanation if you like," replied Mrs. Dearman.

"Same to me, Mrs. Dearman?" asked Mr. Ross-Ellison. "I've had 'experiences' too-and can tell you one of them."

"Same to you, Mr. Ross-Ellison," replied Mrs. Dearman, and added: "But why only one of them?"

Mr. Ross-Ellison smiled, glanced round the luxuriously appointed table and the company of fair women and brave men-and thought of a far-distant and little-known place called Mekran Kot and of a phantom cavalry corps that haunted a valley in its vicinity.

"Only one worth telling," said he.

"Well, —first case," began Colonel Jackson, "I was once driving past a cottage on my way home from College (in Ireland), and I saw the old lady who lived in that cottage come out of the door, cross her bit of garden, go through a gate, scuttle over the railway-line and enter a fenced field that had belonged to her husband, and which she (and a good many other people) believed rightly belonged to her.

"'There goes old Biddy Maloney pottering about in that plot of ground again,' thinks I. 'She's got it on the brain since her law-suit.' I knew it was Biddy, of course, not only because of her coming out of Biddy's house, but because it was Biddy's figure, walk, crutch-stick, and patched old cloak. When I got home I happened to say to Mother: 'I saw poor old Biddy Maloney doddering round that wretched field as I came along'.

"'What?' said my mother, 'why, your father was called to her, as she was dying, hours ago, and she's not been out of her bed for weeks.' When my father came in, I learned that Biddy was dead an hour before I saw her-before I left the railway station in fact! What do you make of that? Is there any 'explanation'?"

"Some other old lady," suggested Mrs. Dearman.

330

"No. There was nobody else in those parts mistakable for Biddy Maloney, and no other old woman was in or near the house while my father was there. We sifted the matter carefully. It was Biddy Maloney and no one else."

"Auto-suggestion. Visualization on the retina of an idea in the mind. Optical illusion," hazarded Mrs. Dearman.

"No good. I hadn't realized I was approaching Biddy Maloney's cottage until I saw her coming out of it and I certainly hadn't thought of Biddy Maloney until my eye fell upon her. And it's a funny optical illusion that deceives one into seeing an old lady opening gates, crossing railways and limping away into fenced fields."

"H'm! What was the other case?" asked Mrs. Dearman, turning to Mr. Ross-Ellison.

"That happened here in India at a station called Duri, away in the Northern Presidency, where I was then-er-living for a time. On the day after my arrival I went to call on Malet-Marsac to whom I had letters of introduction-political business-and, as he was out, but certain to return in a minute or two from Parade, I sat me down in a comfortable chair in the verandah ———"

"And went to sleep?" interrupted Mrs. Dearman.

"'I *nevah* sleep,'" quoted Mr. Ross-Ellison, "and I had no time, if any inclination. Scarcely indeed had I seated myself, and actually while I was placing my *topi* on an adjacent stool, a lady emerged from a distant door at the end of the verandah and walked towards me. I can tell you I was mighty surprised, for not only was Captain Malet-Marsac a lone bachelor and a misogynist of blameless life, but the lady looked as though she had stepped straight out of an Early Victorian phonograph-album. She had on a crinoline sort of dress, a deep lace collar, spring-sidey sort of boots, mittens, and a huge cameo brooch. Also she had long ringlets. Her face is stamped on my memory and I could pick her out from a hundred women similarly dressed, or her picture from a hundred others...."

"What did you do?" asked Mrs. Dearman, whose neglected ice-pudding was fast being submerged in a pink lake of its own creation.

"Do? Nothing. I grabbed my *topi*, stood up, bowed-and looked silly."

"And what did the lady do?"

"Came straight on, taking no notice whatsoever of me, until she reached the steps leading into the porch and garden.... She passed down these and out of my sight.... That is the plain statement of an actual fact. Have you any 'explanation' to offer?"

"Well-what about a lady staying there, unexpectedly and unbeknownst (to the station), trying on a get-up for a Fancy Dress Ball. Going as 'My ancestress' or something?" suggested Mrs. Dearman.

"Exactly what I told myself, though I *knew* it was nothing of the kind.... Well, five minutes later Malet-Marsac rode up the drive and we were soon fraternizing over cheroots and cold drinks.... As I was leaving, an idea struck me, and I saw a way to ask a question-which was burning my tongue, —without being too rudely inquisitive.

"By the way,' said I, 'I fear I did not send in the right number of visiting cards, but they told me there was no lady here, so I only sent in one-for you.'

"'There *is* no lady here,' he replied, eyeing me queerly. 'What made you think you had been misinformed?'

"'Well,' said I bluntly, 'a lady came out of the end room just now, walked down the verandah, and went out into the garden. You'd better see if anything is missing as she's not an inhabitant!'

"'No-there won't be anything missing,' he replied. 'Did she wear a crinoline and a general air of last century?'

"'She did,' said I.

"'Our own private ghost,' was the answer-and it was the sort of statement I had anticipated. Now I solemnly assure you that at that time I had never heard, read, nor dreamed that there was a 'ghost' in this bungalow, nor in Duri-nor in the whole Northern Presidency for that matter....

"'What's the story?' I asked, of course.

"'Mutiny. 1857,' said Malet-Marsac. 'Husband shot on the parade-ground. She got the news and marched straight to the spot. They cut her in pieces as she held his body in her arms. Lots of people have seen her-anywhere between that room and the parade-ground.'

"'Then you have to believe in ghosts-in Duri, or how do you account for it?' I asked.

"'I don't bother my head,' he replied. 'But I have seen that poor lady a good many times. And no one told me a word about her until after I had seen her.'"

And then Mrs. Dearman suddenly rose, as her hostess "caught" the collective female eye of the table.

"Was all that about the 'ghosts' of the old Irishwoman and the Early Victorian Lady true, you fellows?" asked John Bruce, the Professor of Engineering, after coffee, cigars and the second glass of port had reconciled the residue or sediment to the departure of the sterner sex.

"Didn't you hear me say my story was true?" replied Colonel Jackson brusquely. "It was absolutely and perfectly true."

"Same here," added Mr. Ross-Ellison.

"Then on two separate occasions you two have seen what you can only believe to be the ghosts of dead people?"

"On one occasion I have, without any possibility of error or doubt, seen the ghost of a dead person," said Colonel Jackson.

"Have you ever come across any other thoroughly substantiated cases of ghost-seeing —cases which have really convinced you, Colonel?" queried Mr. Ross-Ellison —being deeply interested in the subject by reason of queer powers and experiences of his own.

"Yes. Many in which I fully believe, and one about which I am *certain*. A very interesting case-and a very cruel tragedy."

"Would you mind telling me about it?" asked Mr. Ross-Ellison.

"Pleasure. More —I'll give you as interesting and convincing a 'human document' about it as ever you read, if you like."

"I shall be eternally grateful," replied the other.

"It was a sad and sordid business. The man, whose last written words I'll give you to read, was a Sergeant-Major in the Volunteer Rifles (also at Duri where I was stationed, as you know) and he was a gentleman born and bred, poor chap." ["Lawrence-Smith," murmured Mr. John Robin Ross-Ellison with an involuntary movement of surprise. His eyebrows rose and his jaw fell.] "Yes, he was that rare bird a gentleman-ranker who remained a gentleman and a ranker- and became a fine soldier. He called himself Lawrence-Smith and owned a good old English name that you'd recognize if I mentioned it-and you'd be able to name some of his relatives too. He was kicked out of Sandhurst for striking one of the subordinate staff under extreme provocation. The army was in his blood and bones, and he enlisted."

"Excuse me," interrupted Mr. Ross-Ellison, "you speak of this Sergeant-Major Lawrence-Smith in the past tense. Is he dead then?"

"He is dead," replied Colonel Jackson. "Did you know him?"

"I believe I saw him at Duri," answered Mr. Ross-Ellison with an excellent assumption of indifference. "What's the story?"

"I'll give you his own tale on paper-let me have it back-and, mind you, every single word of it is Gospel truth. The man was a *gentleman*, an educated, thoughtful, sober chap, and as sane as you or I. I got to know him well-he was in hospital, with blood-poisoning from panther-bite, for a time-and we became friends. Actual friends, I mean. Used to play golf with him. (You remember the Duri Links.) In mufti, you'd never have dreamed for a moment that he was not a Major or a Colonel. Army life had not coarsened him in the slightest, and he kept some lounge-suits and mess-kit by Poole. Many a good Snob of my acquaintance has left my house under the impression that the Lawrence-Smith he had met there, and with whom he had been hail-fellow-well-met, was his social equal or superior.

"He simply was a refined and educated gentleman and that's all there is about it. Well-you'll read his statement-and, as you read, you may tell yourself that I am as convinced of its truth as I am of anything in this world.... He was dead when I got to him."

"The stains, on the backs of some of the sheets and on the front of the last one, are-blood stains...."

And at this point their host suggested the propriety of joining the ladies....

Colonel Jackson gave Mr. Ross-Ellison a "lift" in his powerful motor as far as his bungalow, entered, and a few minutes later emerged with a long and fat envelope.

"Here you are," said he. "I took it upon myself to annex the papers as I was his friend. Let's have 'em back. No need for me to regard them as 'private and confidential' so far as I can see, poor chap. Good-night."

Having achieved the haven of loose Pathan trousers and a muslin shirt (worn over them) in the privacy of his bed-room, Mr. Ross-Ellison, looking rather un-English, sat on a camp-cot (he never really liked chairs) and read, as follows, from a sheaf of neatly-written (and blood-stained) sheets of foolscap.

* * *

I have come to the point at which I decide to stop. I have had enough.
But I should like to ask one or two questions.

1. Why has a man no right to quit a world in which he no longer desires to live? 2. Why should Evil be allowed to triumph? 3. Why should people who cannot see spirit forms be so certain that such do not exist, when none but an ignorant fool argues, "I believe in what I can see"?

With regard to the first question I maintain that a man has a perfect right to "take" the life that was "given" him (without his own consent or desire), provided it is not an act of cowardice nor an evasion of just punishment or responsibility. I would add-provided also that he does not, in so doing, basely desert his duty, those who are in any way dependent on him, or those who really love him.

I detest that idiotic phrase "while of unsound mind". I am as sound in mind as any man living, but because I end an unbearable state of affairs, and take the only step I can think of as likely to give me peace —I shall be written down mad. Moreover should I fail-in my attempt to kill myself (which I shall not) I should be prosecuted as a criminal!

To me, albeit I have lived long under strict discipline and regard true discipline as the first essential of moral, physical, mental, and social training, to me it seems a gross and unwarrantable interference with the liberty of the individual-to deny him sufficient captaincy of his soul for him to be free to control it at the dictates of his conscience, and to keep it Here or to send it There as may seem best. Surely the implanted love of life and fear of death are sufficient safeguards without any legislation or insolent arrogant interference between a man and his own ego? Anyhow, such are my views, and in perfect soundness of mind and body, after mature reflection and with full confidence in my right so to do, I am about to end my life here.

As to the second question, "Why should Evil be allowed to triumph?" I confess that my mind cannot argue in a circle and say, "You are born full of Original Sin, and if you sin you are Damned" —a vicious circle drawn for me by the gloomy, haughty, insincere and rather unintelligent young gentleman whom I respectfully salute as Chaplain, and who regards me and every other non-commissioned soldier as a Common, if not Low, person.

He would not even answer my queries by means of the good old loop-hole, "It is useless to appeal to Reason if you cannot to Faith" and so beg the question. He said that things *were* because the Lord said they were, and that it was impious to doubt it. More impious was it, I gathered, to doubt him, and to allude to Criticisms he had never read.

His infallible "proof" was "It is in the Bible".

Possibly I shall shortly know why an Omnipotent, Omniscient, Impeccable Deity allows this world to be the Hell it is, even if there be no actual Hell for the souls of his errant Creatures (in spite of the statements of the Chaplain who appears to have exclusive information on the subject, inaccessible to laymen, and to rest peacefully assured of a Real Hell for the wicked, — nonconforming, and vulgar).

At present I cannot understand and I do not know-though I am informed and infused with a burning and reverent desire to understand and to know-why Evil should be allowed to triumph, as in my own case, as well as in those of millions of others, it does. And thirdly, why does the man who would never deny beauty in a poem or picture because he failed to see it while others did, deny that immaterial forms of the dead exist, because he has never seen one, though others have?

I know of so many many men who would blush to be called "I-believe-what-I-see men," who yet laugh to scorn the bare idea of the materialization and visualization of visitants from the spirit world, because they have never seen one. I have so often met the argument, "The ghost of a man I might conceive-but I can *not* conceive the appearance of the ghost of a pair of trousers or of a top-hat," offered as though it were unanswerable. Surely the spirit, aura, shade, ghost, soul, ego-what you will-can permeate and penetrate and pervade clothing and other matter as well as flesh?

Well, once again, I do not know,—and yet I have seen, not once but repeatedly, not by moonlight in a churchyard, but under the Indian sun on a parade-ground, the ghost of a man *and of all his accoutrements, —of a rifle, of a horse and all a horse's trappings.*

I have been a teetotaller for years, I have never had sunstroke and I am as absolutely sane as ever a man was.

And further I am in no sense remorseful, repentant, or "dogged by the spectre of an evil deed".

I killed Burker intentionally. Were he alive again I would kill him again. I punished him myself because the law could not punish him as he deserved, and I in no way regret or deplore my just and judicial action. There are deeds a gentleman must resent and punish-with the extreme penalty. No, it is in no sense a case of the self-tormented wretch driven mad by the awful hallucinations of his guilty, unhinged mind. I am no haunted murderer pursued by phantoms and illusions, believing himself always in the presence of his victim's ghost.

All people who have read anything, have read of the irresistible fascination that the scene of the murder has for the murderer, of the way in which the victim "haunts" the slayer, and of how the truth that "murder will out" is really based on the fact that the murderer is his own most dangerous accuser by reason of his life of terror, remorse, and terrible hallucination.

My case is in no wise parallel.

I am absolutely without fear, regret, remorse, repentance, dread or terror in the matter of my killing Sergeant Burker. Exactly how and why I killed him, and how and why I am about to kill myself, I will now set forth, without the slightest exaggeration, special pleading or any other deviation from the truth....

I am to my certain knowledge the eighth consecutive member of my family, in the direct line, to follow the profession of arms, but am the first to do so without bearing a commission. My father died young in the rank of Captain, my grandfather led his own regiment in the Crimea, my great-grandfather was a Lieutenant-General, and, if I told you my real name, you could probably state something that he did at Waterloo.

I went to Sandhurst and I was expelled from Sandhurst-very rightly and justly-for an offence, or rather the culminating offence of a series of offences, that were everything but mean, dishonest or underhand. I was wild, hasty, undisciplined and I was lost for want of a father to thrash me as a boy, and by possession of a most loving and devoted mother who worshipped, spoiled-and ruined me.

I enlisted under an assumed name in my late father's (and grandfather's) old Regiment of Foot and quickly rose to the rank of Sergeant-Major.

I might have had a commission in South Africa but I decided that I preferred ruling in hell to serving in heaven, and declined to be a grey-haired Lieutenant and a nuisance to the Officers' Mess of the Corps I would not leave until compelled.

In time I *was* compelled and I became Sergeant-Major of the Volunteer Rifle Corps here and husband of a —well —*de mortuis nil nisi bonum*.

Why I married I don't know.

The English girl of the class from which soldiers are drawn never attracted me in the very least, and I simply could not have married one, though a paragon of virtue and compendium of housewifely qualities.

Admirable and pretty as Miss Higgs, Miss Bloggs, or Miss Muggins might be, my youthful training prevented my seeing beyond her fringe, finger-nails, figure, and aspirates, to her solid excellences; —and from sergeants'-dances I returned quite heart-whole and still unplighted to the Colonel's cook. But Dolores De Souza was different.

There was absolutely nothing to offend the most fastidious taste in her speech, appearance, or manners. She was convent-bred, accomplished, refined, gentle, worthless and wicked. The good Sisters of the Society of the Broken Heart had polished the exterior of the Eurasian orphan very highly-but the polish was a thin veneer on very cheap and unseasoned wood.

It is a strange fact that, while I could respect the solid virtues of the aspirateless Misses Higgs, Bloggs or Muggins, I could never have married one of them; yet, while I knew Dolores to be a heartless flirt, and more than suspected her to be of most unrigid principle, I was infatuated with her dark beauty, her grace, her wiles and witchery-and asked her to become my wife.

The good Sisters of the Society of the Broken Heart had taught Dolores to sing beautifully, to play upon the piano and the guitar, to embroider, to paint mauve roses on pink tambourines and many other useful arts, graces and accomplishments-but they had not taught her *practical* morality nor anything of cooking, marketing, plain sewing, house-cleaning or anything else of house-keeping. However, having been bred as I had been bred, I could take the form and let the substance go, accept the shapely husks and shout not for the grain, and prefer a pretty song, and a rose in black hair over a shell-like ear, to a square meal. I fear the average Sergeant-Major would have beaten Dolores within a week of matrimony, but I strove to make loss, discomfort, and disappointment a discipline, —and music, silk dresses and daintiness an aesthetic re-training to a barrack-blunted mind.

In justice to Dolores I should make it clear that she was not of the slatternly, dirty, lazy, half-breed type that pigs in a *peignoir* from twelve to twelve and snores again from midnight to midday. She was trim and dainty, used good perfume or none, rose early and went in the garden, loathed cheap and showy trash whether in dress, jewellery, or furniture; and was incapable of wearing fine shoes over holey stockings or a silk gown over dirty linen. No-there was nothing to offend the fastidious about Dolores, but there was everything to offend the good house-keeper and the moralist.

Frequently she would provide no dinner in order that we might be compelled to dine in public at a restaurant or a hotel, a thing she loved to do, and she would often send out for costly sweets and pastry, drink champagne (very moderately, I admit), and generally behave as though she were the wife of a man of means.

And she was an arrant, incorrigible, shameless flirt.

Well —I do not know that a virtuous vulgar dowd is preferable to a wicked winsome witch of refined habits and person, and I should probably have gone quietly on to bankruptcy without any row or rupture, but for Burker. Having been bred in a "gentle" home I naturally took the attitude of "as you please, my dear Dolores" and refrained from bullying when quiet indication of the inevitable end completely failed. Whether she intended to act in a reasonable manner and show some wifely traits when my £250 of legacy and savings was quite dissipated I do not know. Burker came before that consummation.

A number of gentlemen joined the Duri Volunteer Corps and formed a Mounted Infantry troop, and, though I am a good horseman, I was not competent to train the troop, as I had never enjoyed any experience of mounted military work of any kind. So Sergeant Burker, late of the 54th Lancers, was transferred to Duri as Instructor of the Mounted Infantry Troop. Naturally I did what I could to make him comfortable and, till his bungalow was furnished after a fashion, gave him our spare room.

Sergeant Barker was the ideal Cavalryman and the ideal breaker of hearts,—hearts of the Mary-Ann and Eliza-Jane order.

He was a black-haired, blue-eyed Irishman with a heart as black as his hair, and language as blue as his eye—a handsome, plausible, selfish, wicked devil with scarcely a virtue but pride and high courage. I disliked him at first sight, and Dolores fell in love with him equally quickly, I am sure.

I don't think he had a solitary gentlemanly instinct.

Being desirous of learning Mounted Infantry work, I attended all his drills, riding as troop-leader, and, between close attention to him and close study of the drill-book, did not let the gentlemen in the ranks know that, in the beginning, I knew as little about it as they did.

And an uncommonly good troop he soon made of it, too.

Of course it was excellent material, all good riders and good shots, and well horsed.

Burker and I were mounted by the R.H.A. Battery here, and the three drills we held, weekly, were seasons of delight to a horse-lover like myself.

Now the horse I had was a high-spirited, powerful animal, and he possessed the trait, very common among horses, of hating to be pressed behind the saddle. Turning to look behind while "sitting-easy" one day I rested my right hand on his back behind the saddle and he immediately lashed out furiously with both hind legs. I did not realize for the moment what was upsetting him-but quickly discovered that I had only to press his back to send his hoofs out like stones from a sling. I then remembered other similar cases and that I had also read of this curious fact about horses-something to do with pressure on the kidneys I believe.

One day Burker was unexpectedly absent and I took the drill, finding myself quite competent and *au fait*.

The same evening I went to my wife's wardrobe, she being out, to try and find the keys of the sideboard. I knew they frequently reposed in the pocket of her dressing-gown.

In the said pocket they were-and so was a letter in the crude large handwriting of Sergeant Burker.

I did not read it, but I did not see the necessity of a correspondence between my wife and such a man as I knew Sergeant Burker to be. They met often enough, in all conscience, to say what they might have to say to each other.

At dinner I remarked casually: "I shouldn't enter into a correspondence with Burker if I were you, Dolly. His reputation isn't over savoury and —" but, before I could say more, my wife was literally screaming with rage, calling me "Spy," "Liar," "Coward," and demanding to know what I insinuated and of what I accused her. I replied that I had accused her of nothing at all, and merely offered advice in the matter of correspondence with Burker. I explained how I had come to find the letter and stated that I had not read it.

"Then how do you know that we —" she began, and suddenly stopped.

"That you-what?" I inquired.

"Nothing," she said.

At the next Sergeants' Dance at the Institute I did not like Burker's manner to my wife at all. It was-well, amorous, and tinged with a shade of proprietorship. I distinctly heard him call her "Dolly," and equally distinctly saw an expressively affectionate look in her eyes as he hugged her in the waltzes-whereof they indulged in no less than five.

My position was awkward and unpleasant. I loathe a row or a scene unspeakably-though I delight in fighting when that pastime is legitimate-and I was brought into daily contact with the ruffian and I disliked him intensely.

I was very averse from the course of forbidding him the house and thus insulting my wife by implication-since she obviously enjoyed his society-and descending to pit myself against the greasy cad in a struggle for a woman's favour, and that woman my own wife. Nor could I conscientiously take the line of, "If she desires to go to the Devil let her," for a man has as much responsibility for his wife as for his children, and it is equally his duty to guide and control her and them. Women may vote and may legislate for men-but on men they will ever depend and rely.

No, the position of carping, jealous husband was one that I could not fill, and I determined to say nothing, do nothing and be watchful-watchful, that is, to avoid exposing her to temptation. I did my best, but I was away from home a good deal, visiting the out-station detachments of the Corps.

Then, one day, the wretched creature I called "butler" came to me with an air of great mystery and said: "Sahib, Sergeant Burker Sahib sending Mem Sahib bundle of flowers and *chitti*[122] inside and diamond ring yesterday. His boy telling me and I seeing. He often coming here too when Sahib out. Both wicked peoples."

I raised my hand to knock his lies down his throat-and dropped it. They were not lies, I knew, and the fellow had been faithful to me for many years and-the folly of childish human vanity —I felt he knew I was a "gentleman," and I liked him for it.

I paid him his wages then and there, gave him a present and a good testimonial and discharged him. He wept real tears and shook with sobs of grief-easy grief, but very genuine.

When Dolores came home from the Bandstand I said quietly: "Show me the jewellery Burker sent you, Dolly. I am very much in earnest, so don't bluster."

She seemed about to faint and looked very frightened-perhaps my face was more expressive than a gentleman's should be.

"It was only a little thing for my birthday," she whined. "Can't I keep it? Don't be a tyrant or a fool."

"Your next birthday or your last?" I asked. "Please get it at once. We'll settle matters quietly and finally."

I fear the poor girl had visions of the doorstep and a closed door. Two, perhaps, for I am sure Burker would not have taken her in if I had turned her out, and she may have thought the same.

It was a diamond ring, and the scoundrel must have given a couple of months' pay for it-if he had paid for it at all. I thrust aside the sudden conviction that Burker's own taste could not have been responsible for its choice and that it was selected by my wife.

"Why should he give you this, Dolores?" I asked. "Will you tell me or must I go to him?" And then she burst into tears and flung herself at my feet, begging for mercy.

Mercy!

Qui s'excuse s'accuse.

What should I do?

To cast her out was to murder her soul quickly and her body slowly, and I could foresee her career with prophetic eye and painful clearness.

And what could the Law do for me?

Publish our shame and perhaps brand me that wretched thing-the willingly deceived and complaisant husband.

What could I do by challenging Burker?

He was a champion man-at-arms, a fine boxer, and a younger, stronger man, I should merely experience humiliation and defeat. What *could* I do?

If I said, "Go and live with your Burker," I should be committing a bigger crime than hers, for if he did take her in, it would not be for long.

I sat the night through, pondered the question carefully, looked at it from all points of view and-decided that Burker must die. Also that he must not drag me to jail or the scaffold as he went to his doom. If I shot him and was punished, Dolores would become a —well, as I have said, her soul would die quickly and her body slowly. I had married Dolores and I must do what lay in my power to protect Dolores. But I simply could not kill the hound in some stealthy secret manner and wait for the footsteps of warrant-armed police for the rest of my life.

What could I do? Or rather-for the question had narrowed to that-how could I kill him?

And as the sun struck upon my eyes at dawn, an idea struck upon my mind.

I would leave it to Fate and if Fate willed it so, Burker should die.

If Burker stood behind my charger, Fate sat with down-turned thumb.

I would not seek the opportunity-but, by God, I would take it if it offered.

If it did not, I would go to Burker and say to him quietly: "Burker, you must leave this station at once and never see or communicate with my wife in any way. Otherwise I have to kill you, Burker-to execute you, you understand."...

A native syce from the Artillery lines led my charger into the little compound of my tiny bungalow.

Having buckled on my belt I went out, patted him, and gave him a lump of sugar. He nuzzled me for more, and, as he did so, I placed my hand on his back, behind the saddle, and pressed. He lashed out wildly.

I then trotted across the *maidan*[123] to the Volunteer Headquarters and parade-ground.

Several gentlemen of the Mounted Infantry were waiting about, some standing by their horses, some getting bandoliers, belts, and rifles, some cantering their horses round the ground.

Sergeant Burker strode out of the Orderly Boom.

"Morning, Smith," said he. "How's the Missus?"

I looked him in the eye and made no reply.

He laughed, as jeering, evil, and caddish a laugh as I have ever heard. I almost forgot my purpose and had actually turned toward the armoury for a rifle and cartridge when I remembered and controlled my rage.

If I shot him, then and there, I must go to the scaffold or to jail forthwith, and Dolores must inevitably go to a worse fate. Had I been sure that she could have kept straight, Burker would have been shot, then and there.

"Fall in," he shouted, but did not mount his horse.

The gentlemen assembled with their horses and faced him in line, dismounted, I in front of the centre of the troop. How clearly I can see every feature and detail of that morning's scene, and hear every word and sound.

"Tell off by sections," commanded Burker.

"One, two, three, four-one, two, three, four...."

There were exactly six sections.

"Flanks of sections, proof."

"Section leaders, proof."

"Centre man, proof."

"Prepare to mount."

"Mount."

"Sections right."

"Sections left."

The last two words were the last words Burker ever spoke. Passing on foot along the line of mounted men, to inspect saddlery, accoutrements, and the adjustment of rifle-buckets and slings, he halted immediately behind me, where I sat on my charger in front of the centre of the troop.

I could not have placed him more exactly with my own hands. *Fate sat with down-pointing thumb.*

Turning round, as though to look at the troop, I rested my hand on my horse's back-just behind the saddle-and pressed hard. He lashed out with both hoofs and Sergeant Burker dropped-and never moved again.

The base of his skull was smashed like an egg, and his back was broken like a dry stick....

The terrible accident roused wide sympathy with the unfortunate man, the local reporter used all his adjectives, and a military funeral was given to the soldier who had died in the execution of his duty.

On reaching home, after satisfying myself at the Station Hospital that the man was dead, I said to my poor, pale and red-eyed wife: —

"Dolores, Sergeant Burker met with an accident this morning on parade. He is dead. Let us never refer to him again."

She fainted.

I spent that night also in meditation, questioning myself and examining my soul-with every honest endeavour to be not a self-deceiver.

I came to the conclusion that I had acted rightly and in the only way in which a gentleman could act. I had snatched Dolores from his foul clutches, I had punished him without depriving Dolores of my protection, and I had avenged the stain on my honour.

"You have committed a treacherous cowardly murder," whispered the Fiend in my ear.

"You are a liar," I replied. "I did not fear the man and I took this course solely on account of Dolores. I was strong enough to accept this position-and to risk the accusation of murder, from my conscience, from the Devil, or from man."

Any doubt I might otherwise have had was forestalled and inhibited by the obvious Fate that placed Burker in the one spot favourable to my scheme of punishment.

God had willed it?

God had not prevented it.

Surely God was consenting unto it....

And Dolores? I would forgive her and offer her the choice of remaining with me or leaving me and receiving a half of my income and possessions-both alternatives being contingent upon good conduct.

At dawn I prepared tea for her, and entered our bedroom. Dolores had wound a towel round her neck, twisted the ends tightly-and suffocated herself.

She had been dead for hours....

At the police inquiry, held the same day, I duly lied as to the virtues of the "deceased," and the utter impossibility of assigning any reason for the rash and deplorable act. The usual smug stereotyped verdict was pronounced, and, in addition to expressing their belief that the suicide was committed "while of unsound mind," the officials expressed much sympathy with the bereaved husband.

Dolores was buried that evening and I returned to an empty house.

I believe opinion had been divided as to whether I was callous or "stunned" —but the sight of her little shoes caused pains in my throat and eyes. Had Burker been then alive I would have killed him with my hands-and teeth. Yes, teeth.

I spent that night in packing every possession and trace of Dolores into her boxes, and then in trying to persuade myself that I should have acted differently.

I could not do so. I had acted for the best-so let God who gave me free-will, intelligence, conscience and opportunity, approve the deed or take the blame.

And let God remember how that opportunity came so convincingly-so impellingly-and if He would judge me and ask for my defence I would ask him who sent Burker here, and who placed him on that fatal spot?

Does God sit only in judgment?

Does God calmly watch His creatures walking blindfold to the Pit-struggling to tear away the bandage as they walk? Can He only judge, and can He never help?

"Pray?"

Is God a petty-minded "jealous" God to be propitiated like the gods of the heathen? Must we continually ask, or, not asking, not receive?

And if we know not to ask aright and to demand the best and highest?

Cannot the well-fed, well-read, well-paid Chaplain give advice?

"*God knoweth best. Ask unceasingly. Pray always.*"

Why? —if. He knows best, is All Merciful, All Powerful?

"Praise?"

Is God a child, a savage, a woman? Shall I offer adulation that would sicken *me*.

"*God is our Father which art in heaven.*"

Would I have my son praise me to my face continually-or at all. Would I compel him to pester me with demands for what he desired, —good, bad and indifferent?

And would I give him what he asked regardless of what was best for him-or say, "If you ask not, you receive not?" Give me a God finer and greater and juster and nobler than myself-something higher than the Chaplain's jealous, capricious, inconsequent and illogical God. Anthropomorphism!

Is there a God at all?

I shall soon know.

If so —

Oh Thou, who man of baser earth didst make
And ev'n with Paradise devised the Snake,
For all the Sin the face of wretched man
Is black with-Man's forgiveness give-and take!

At dawn I said aloud: —

"This Chapter is closed. The story of Burker and Dolores is written. I may now strive to forget."

I was wrong.

Major Jackson of the R.A.M.C. came to see me soon after daylight. He gave me an opiate and I slept all that day and night. I went on parade next morning, fresh, calm, and cool-and saw *Burker riding toward the group of gentlemen who were awaiting the signal to "fall in"*.

I say I was fresh, calm, and cool.

I was.

And there was Burker-looking exactly as in life, save for a slight nebulosity, a very faint vagueness of outline, and a hint of transparency.

I had been instructed by the Adjutant to assume the post of Instructor (as the end of the Mounted Infantry drill season was near) —and I blew the "rally" on my whistle as many of the gentlemen were riding about, and shouted the command: "Fall in".

Twenty living men and one dead faced me, twenty dismounted and one mounted. I called the corporal in charge of the armoury.

"How many on parade?" I asked.

He looked puzzled, counted, and said: —

"Why-twenty, ain't there?"

I numbered the troop.

Twenty-and Burker.

"Tell off by sections."

Five sections-and Burker.

"Sections right."

A column of five sections-and Burker, in the rear.

I called out the section-leader of Number One section.

"Are the sections correctly proved?" I asked, and added: "Put the troop back in line and tell-off again".

"Five sections, correct," he reported.

I held that drill, with five sections of living men, and a single file of dead, who manoeuvred to my word.

When I gave the order "With Numbers Three for action dismount," or "Right-hand men, for action dismount," Burker remained mounted. When I dismounted the whole troop, Burker remained mounted. Otherwise he drilled precisely as Number Twenty-one would have drilled in a troop of twenty-one men.

Was I frightened? I do not know.

At first my heart certainly pounded as though it would leap from my body, and I felt dazed, lost, and shocked.

I think I *was* frightened-not of Burker so much as of the unfamiliar, the unknown, the impossible.

How would you feel if your piano suddenly began to play of itself? You would be alarmed and afraid probably, not frightened of the piano, but of the fact.

A door could not frighten you-but you would surely be alarmed at its persistently opening, each time you shut, locked, and bolted it, if it acted thus.

Of Burker I had no fear-but I was perturbed by the *fact* that the dead could ride with the living.

When I gave the order "Dismiss" at the end of the parade Burker rode away, as he had always done, in the direction of his bungalow.

Returning to my lonely house, I sat me down and pondered this appalling event that had come like a torrent, sweeping away familiar landmarks of experience, idea, and belief. I was conscious of a dull anger against Burker and then against God.

Why should He allow Burker to haunt me?...

Why should Evil triumph?...

Was I haunted? Or was it, after all, but a hallucination-due to grief, trouble, and the drug of the opiate?

I sat and brooded until I thought I could hear the voices of Burker and
Dolores in converse.

This I knew to be hallucination, pure and simple, and I went to see my friend (if he will let me call him what he is in the truest and highest sense) Major Jackson of the R.A.M.C.

He took me for a long ride, kept me to dinner, and manufactured a job for me —a piece of work that would occupy and tire me.

He assured me that the Burker affair was pure hallucination and staked his professional reputation that the image of Burker came upon my retina from within and not from without. "The shock of the deaths of your wife and your friend on consecutive days has unhinged you, and very naturally so," he said.

Of course I did not tell him that I had killed Burker, though I should have liked to do so. I felt I had no right to put him in the position of having to choose between denouncing me and condoning a murder-compounding a felony.

Nor did I see any reason for confessing to the Police what I had done (even though Dolores was dead) and finishing my career on the scaffold.

One owes something to one's ancestors as well as to oneself. Well, perhaps it was a hallucination. I would wait.

At the next drill Burker was present and rode as Number Three in Section
Six.

As there were twenty-three (living) on parade I ordered Number Twenty-three to ride as Number Four of his section and leave a blank file.

Burker rode in that blank file and drilled so, throughout-save that he would not dismount.

Once, as the troop rode in column of sections, I fell to the rear and, coming up behind, struck with all my might at that slightly nebulous figure, with its faint vagueness of outline and hint of transparency.

My heavy cutting-whip whistled-and touched nothing. I was as one who beats the air. Section Six must have thought me mad.... Twice again the dead man drilled with the living, and each time I described what happened to Major Jackson.

"It is a persistent hallucination," said he; "you must go on leave."

"I won't run from Burker, nor from a hallucination," I replied.

Then came the end.

At the next drill, twenty-one gentlemen were present and Number Twenty-one, the Sessions Judge of Duri, a Scot, kept staring with looks of amazement and alarm at Burker, who rode as Number Four on his flank, making an odd file into a skeleton section. I was certain that he saw Burker.

As the gentlemen "dismissed" after parade, the Judge rode up to me and, with a white face, demanded: —

"Who the devil was that rode with me as Number Twenty-four? It was-it was-like-Sergeant Burker."

"It *was* Sergeant Burker, Sir," said I.

"I knew it was," he replied, and added: "Man, you and I are fey."

"Will you tell Major Jackson of this, Sir?" I begged. "He knows I have seen Burker's ghost here before, and tells me it is a hallucination."

"I'll go and see him now." he replied. "He is an old friend of mine, and-he's a damned good doctor. Man-you and I are fey." He rode to where his trap, with its spirited cob, was awaiting him, dismounted and drove off.

As everybody knows, Mr. Blake of the Indian Civil Service, Sessions Judge of Duri, was thrown from his trap and killed. It happened five minutes after he had said to me, with a queer look in his eyes, and a queer note in his voice, "Man! you and I are fey".... So it is no hallucination and I am haunted by Burker's ghost. Very good. I will fight Burker on his own ground.

My ghost shall haunt Burker's ghost-or I shall be at peace.

Though the religion of the Chaplain has failed me, the religion of my Mother, taught to me at her knee, has implanted in me an ineradicable belief in the ultimate justice of things, and the unquenchable hope of "somehow good".

I am about to go before my Maker or to obliteration and oblivion. If the former, I am prepared to say to Him: "You made me a man. I have played the man. I look to you for justice, and that is-compensation and not 'forgiveness'. Much less is it punishment. You have treated me ill and given me no help. You have bestowed free-*will* without free-*dom*. Compensate me or know Yourself unjust."

To a servant or child who spoke so to me and with equal reason, I would reply: —

"Compensation is due to you and not 'forgiveness' —much less punishment," and I would act accordingly.... Why should I cringe to God-and why should He love a cringer more than I do?

God help Men and Women-and such Children as are doomed to grow up to be Men and Women.

As I finish this sentence I shall put my revolver in my mouth and seek Justice or Peace....

* * *

"Bad luck," murmured Mr. Robin Ross-Ellison, "that was the man of all men for me! A gentleman, wishful to die.... That is the sort that *does* things when swords are out and bullets fly. Seeks a gory grave and gets a V.C. instead. He and Mike Malet-Marsac and I would have put a polish on the new Gungapur Fusiliers.... Rough luck...."

He was greatly disappointed, for his experiences in the bazaars, market-places, secret-meeting houses, and the bowers of Hearts' Delights, —the Rialtos of Gungapur (he disguised, now as an Afghan horse-dealer, now as a sepoy, now as a Pathan money-lender, again as a gold-braided, velvet waistcoated, swaggering swashbuckler from the Border) —his experiences were disquieting, were such as to make him push on preparations, perfect plans, and work feverishly at the "polishing" of his re-organized Corps.

Also the reports of his familiar, a Somali yclept Moussa Isa, were disquieting, disturbing to a lover of the Empire who foresaw the Empire at war in Europe.

Moussa Isa also knew that there was talk among Pathan horse-dealers and *budmashes* of the coming of one Ilderim the Weeper, a mullah of great influence and renown, and talk, moreover, among men of other race, of a Great Conspiracy.

Moussa was bidden to take service as a mill-coolie in one of Colonel Dearman's mills, and to report on the views and attitude of the thousands who laboured therein. This he did and there learnt many interesting facts.

§ 4. Mr. and Mrs. Cornelius Gosling-Green

It was Sunday-and therefore John Bruce, the Engineering College Professor, was exceptionally busy. On a-week-day he only had to deliver his carefully prepared lectures, interview students, read and return essays, take the chair at meetings of college societies, coach one or two "specialists," superintend the games on the college gymkhana ground, interview seekers after truth and perverters of the same, write letters on various matters of college business, visit the hostel, set question papers and correct answers, attend common-room meetings, write articles for the college magazine and papers for the Scientific, Philosophical, Shakespearean, Mathematical, Debating, Literary, Historical, Students', Old Boys', or some other "union" and, if God willed, get a little exercise and private study at his beloved "subject" and invention, before preparing for the morrow.

On Sundays, the thousand and one things crowded out of the programme were to be cleared up, his home mail was to be written, and then arrears of work had to be attacked.

At four o'clock he addressed Roy Pittenweem and Mrs. MacDougall, his dogs, and said: —

"There's a bloomin' bun-snatch somewhere, you fellers, don't it?". Though a Professor and one of the most keen and earnest workmen in India, his own college blazers were not quite worn out, and Life, the great Artist, had not yet done much sketching on the canvas of his face-in spite of his daily contact with the Science Professor, William Greatorex Bonnett, B.A., widely known as the Mad Hatter, the greatest of whose many great achievements is his avoidance of death at the hands of his colleagues and acquaintance.

Receiving no reply beyond a wink and a waggle, he dropped his blue pencil, rose, and went to the table sacred to litter; and from a wild welter of books, pipes, papers, golf-balls, hats, cigar-boxes, dog-collars, switches, cartridges and other sediment, he extracted a large gilt-edged card and studied it without enthusiasm or bias.

"Large coat of arms," he murmured —"patience-no —a pay-sheet on a monument asking for time; item a hand, recently washed; ditto, a dickey bird-possibly pigeon plucked proper or gull argent; guinea-pig regardant and expectant; supporters, two bottliwallahs rampant. Crest, a bum-boat flottant, and motto '*Cinq-cento-percentum*'. All done in gold. Likewise in gold and deboshed gothic, the legend 'Sir and Lady Fuggilal Potipharpar, At Home. To meet Mr. and Mrs. Cornelius Gosling-Green, M.P. Five p.m. C.T.'...Now what the devil, Roy Pittenweem, *is* C.T.? Is it 'Curious Time' or 'Cut for Trumps' or a new decoration for gutter plutocrats? It *might* mean 'Calcutta Time,' mightn't it, as the egregious Phossy and his gang would have it? Well, we'll go and look upon the Cornmealious Gosling-Green, M.P.'s, and chasten our soul from sinful pride-ain't it, Mrs. MacDougall?" and the Professor strolled across to the Sports Club for a cup of tea.

In the midst of cheery converse with a non-moral and unphilosophic Professor of Moral Philosophy, a fat youth of the name of Augustus Grobble whose life was one long picturesque pose, he sprang to his feet, remarking: "I go, Augustus, I am bidden to behold some prize Gosling-Greens or something, at 5 p.m., D.V. or D.T. or C.T. or L.S.D. or otherwise. Perhaps it was S.T. which means 'Standard Time,' and as I said, I go, Augustus."

Augustus Grobble was understood to return thanks piously....

"Taxi, Sahib?" inquired the messenger-boy at the door.

"Go to," said the Professor. "Also go call me a *tikka-gharri*[124] and select a *very* senior horse, blind, angular, withered, wilted, and answering to the name, most obviously, of Skin-and-Grief—lest I be taken by the Grizzly-Goslings for a down-trodden plutocrat and a brother-and not seen for the fierce and 'aughty oppressor that I am."

"Sahib?"

"*Tikka-gharri lao*,[125] you lazy little 'ound! Don't I speak plain English?" The Professor made it a practice to "rot" when not working-hoping thus even in India to retain sanity and the broad and wholesome outlook, for he was a very short-tempered person, easily roused to dangerous wrath.

A carriage, upholding a pony who, in return, spasmodically moved the carriage which gave evidence of having been where moths break through and steal, lumbered into the Club garden, and the Professor, imploring the jehu not to let the pony "die on him" in the Hibernian sense of the expression, gingerly entered.

"Convey me to the gilded Potipharparian 'alls, Arthur," said he.

"Sahib?"

"Why *don't* you listen? *Palangur Hill ki pas*[126] And don't forget you've to get me there at 5 p.m. C.T. or S.T. —I leave it to you, partner."

On arrival, the Professor concluded that if he had arrived at 5 p.m. C.T. he ought to have come at 5 p.m. S.T., or vice versa; as what he termed 'the show' was evidently about over. Fortune favours all sorts of people.

His hostess, who looked as though she had come straight out of the Bible *via* Bond Street, and his host, who looked as though he had never come out of Petticoat Lane at all, both accused him of being unable to work out the problem of "Find Calcutta Time given the Standard Time," and he professed to be proud to be able to acknowledge the truth of the compliment.

"Come and be presented to Meester and Meesers Carneelius Garsling-Green, M.P.," said the lady, waddling before him; and her husband echoed: —

"Oah, yess. Come and be presented to Meester and Meesers Garsling-Green," waddling after him.

Mr. Cornelius Gosling-Green, M.P., proved to be a tall, drooping, melancholy creature, with "Dundreary" whiskers, reach-me-down suit of thick cloth, wrong kind of tie, thickish boots, and no presence. Without "form" and void.

Mrs. Cornelius Gosling-Green was a Severe Person, tiny, hard-featured and even more garrulous than her husband, who watched her anxiously and nervously as he answered any question put in her presence....

"And, oh, why, *why* are not you Mohammedans *loyal?*" said Mrs. Cornelius Gosling-Green, to a magnificent-looking specimen of the Mussulman of the old school-stately, venerable, courteous and honourable-who stood near, looking as though he wondered what the devil he was doing in that galley.

Turning from his friend, Mir Ilderim Dost Mahommed Mir Hafiz Ullah Khan, a fine Pathan, "Loyal, Madam! *Loyal!* Believe me we Mohammedans are most intensely and devotedly loyal," he replied. "You have indeed been misled. Though you are only spending a month in India for collecting the materials for your book or pamphlet, you must really learn *that* much. We Mohammedans are as loyal as the English themselves. —More loyal than some in fact," he added, with intent. The Pathan smiled meaningly.

"Ah, that's just it. I mean 'Why aren't you Mohammedans *loyal to poor India?*'"

The man turned and left the marquee and the garden without another word.

"Poor *bleeding* India," corrected the Professor.

"And are *you* a friend and worker for India?" continued the lady, turning to him and eyeing him with severity.

"I am. I do my humble possible in my obscure capacity, Mrs. Grisly-Gosling," he replied. "I *beg* your pardon, Mrs. Grossly-Grin——that is-er-Gosling-Green, I *should* say."

Be sure your sins will find you out. Through wilful perversion of the pleasing name the Professor had rendered himself incapable of enunciating it.

"And what do *you* do for India, —write, speak, organize, subscribe or what?" asked the lady with increasing severity.

"I work."

"In what capacity?"

"I am a professor at the Government Engineering College, here in Gungapur."

"O-h-h-h-h! You're one of the overpaid idlers who bolster up the Bureaucracy and batten on the....'"

"Allow me to assure you that I neither bolster, batten, nor bureau, Mrs. Grizzling—I mean *Gosling* Green. Nor do I talk through my hat. I——" the Professor was beginning to get angry and to lose control.

"Perhaps you are one of us in disguise—a Pro-Native?"

"I am intensely Pro-Native."

The tall Pathan stared at the Professor.

"Oh, *good!* I *beg* your pardon! Cornelius, this gentleman is a Government professor and is *with us!*" said this female of the M.P. species.

"That's right," gushed the Gosling. "We want a few in the enemy's camp both to spy out their weakness and to embarrass them. Now about this University business. I am going to take it up. That history affair now! *Scandalous! I cannot* tell you what a wave of indignation swept over England when that syllabus was drawn up. Nothing truly *Liberal* about the whole course, much less Radical. I at once said: '*I* will see this righted. *I* will go to India, and *I* will beard the....'"

"I think it was *I* who said it, Cornelius," remarked his much better half, coldly.

"Yes, my dear Superiora, yes. Now with your help I think we can do something, Professor. Good. This *is* providential. We shall be able to embarrass them now! Will you write me——"

"You are going a little too fast, I think," said the Professor. "I am a 'Pro-Native' and a servant of the Pro-Native Government of India. As such, I don't think I can be of any service to twenty-one-day visitors who wish to 'embarrass' the best friends of my friends the Natives, even supposing I were the sort of gentle Judas you compliment me by imagining me. I——"

"You distinctly say you are Pro-Native and then——"

"I repeat I am intensely Pro-Native, and so are the Viceroy, the Governors, the entire Civil Service, the Educational Service, the Forest Service, the P.W.D., the Medical Service, the Army, and every other Service and Department in India as well as every decent man in India. We are *all* Pro-Native, and all doing our best in our respective spheres, in spite of a deal of ignorant and officious interference and attempted 'embarrassment' at the hands of the self-seeking, the foolish, the busy-body, the idle-not to mention the vicious. What a *charming* day it is. I have so enjoyed the honour of meeting you."

* * *

"Well, my Scroobious Bird! And have they this day roasted in India such a Gosling as shall never be put out?" inquired the non-moral and unphilosophic Professor of Moral Philosophy, a little later.

"No, my Augustus," was the reply. "It's a quacking little gosling, and won't lead to any great commotion m the farm-yard. Nasty little bird-like a *sat-bai* or whatever they call those appalling things 'seven-sister' birds, aren't they, that chatter and squeak all day."

"Have a long drink and tell us all about it," replied Mr. Augustus Clarence Percy Marmaduke Grobble.

"Oh, same old game on the same old stage. Same old players. Leading lady and gent changed only. Huge great hideous bungalow, like a Goanese wedding-cake, in a vast garden of symmetrically arranged blue and red glazed 'art' flower-pots. Lofty room decorated with ancestral portraits done by Mr. Guzzlebhoy Fustomji Paintwallah; green glass chandeliers and big blue and white tin balls; mauve carpet with purple azure roses; wall-paper, bright pink with red lilies and yellow cabbages; immense mouldy mirrors, and a tin alarm clock. Big crowd of all the fly-blown rich knaves of the place who have got more than they want out of Government or else haven't got enough. Only novelty was a splendid Pathan chap, got-up in English except for the conical cap and puggri. Extraordinarily like Ross-Ellison, except that he had long black Pathan hair on his shoulders. Been to England; barrister probably, and seemed the most viciously seditious of the lot. Silly ignorant Goslings in the middle saying to Brahmins, 'And you are Muscleman, aren't you, or are you a Dhobi?' and to Parsis, 'I suppose you High Caste gentlemen have to bathe *every* day?' shoving their awful ignorance under the noses of everybody, and inquiring after the healths of the 'chief wives'. Silly fatuous geese! —and then talking the wildest piffle about the 'burning question of the hour' and making the seditious rotters groan at their ineptitude and folly, until they cheer them up sudden-like with a bit of dam' treason and sedition they ought to be jailed for. *Jailed*. I nearly threw a fit when the old geezer, in a blaze of diamonds and glory, brought up old Phossy and presented him to the Gander, and he murmured: —

"'My *deah* friend,' as Phossy held on to his paw in transports, 'to think of their casting *you* into jail,' and old Mother Potiphar squeaked: *'Oh, this is not the forger of that name-but the eminent politeecian'*. But poor Gosly had thought he had been a political prisoner! Meant no offence. And then some little squirt of an editor primed him with lies about the University and the new syllabus, and straightway the Gander tried to get me on the 'embarrass the Government' lay, and talked as though he knew all about it. 'I'll get some of the ladies of my committee sent out here as History-lecturers at your University,' says he. 'They'll teach pure Liberal History and inculcate true ideas of liberty and self-government.' I wanted to go outside and be ill. Good old 'Paget M.P.'—takes up a 'Question' and writes a silly pamphlet on it and thinks he's said the last word. —Written thousands. —Don't matter so long as he does it in England. —Just the place for him nowadays. —But when he feels he's shoved out of the lime-light by a longer-haired Johnny, it's rough luck that he should try and get back by spending his blooming committee's money coming here and deludin' the poor seditionist and seducin' your Hatter from his allegiance to his salt.... Awful old fraud really-no ability whatever. Came to my college to spout once, in my time. Lord! Still he was a guest, and we let him go. Run by his missus really, I think. Why can't she stop at home and hammer windows? They say she went and asked the Begum of Bhopal to join her in a 'mission and crusade'. Teach the Zenana Woman and Purdah Lady to Come Forth instead of Bring Forth. Come Forth and smash windows. Probably true. Silly Goslings. Drop 'em.... What did you think of our bowling yesterday? With anything like a wicket your College should be...."

* * *

Entering his lonely and sequestered bungalow that evening Mir Ilderim Dost Mahommed changed his Pathan dress for European dining-kit, removed his beard and wig, and became Mr. Robin Ross-Ellison. After dinner he wrote to the eminent Cold weather Visitor to India, Mr. Cornelius Gosling-Green, as follows—

"Dear Sir,

"As I promised this afternoon, when you graciously condescended to honour me with your illuminating conversation, I enclose the papers which I guaranteed would shed some light on certain aspects of Indian conditions, and which I consider likely to give you food for thought.

"As I was myself educated in India, was brought up to maturity with Indian students, and have lived among them in many different places, I may claim to know something about them. As a class they are gentle, affectionate, industrious, well-meaning and highly intelligent. They are the most malleable of human metal, the finest material for the sculptor of humanity, the most impressionable of wax. In the right hands they can be moulded to anything, by the right leader led to any height. And conversely, of them a devil can make fiends. By the wrong leader they can be led down to any depth.

"The crying need of India is noble men to make noble men of these fine impressionable youths. Read the enclosed and take it that the writer (who wrote this recently in Gungapur Jail) is typical of a large class of misled, much-to-be-pitied youths, wrecked and ruined and destroyed-their undoing begun by an unspeakably false and spurious educational ideal, and completed by the writings, and the spoken words of heartless unscrupulous scoundrels who use them to their own vile ends.

"Read, Sir, and realize how truly noble, useful and beautiful is your great work of endeavouring to embarrass our wicked Government, to weaken its prestige here and in England, to encourage its enemies, to increase discontent and unrest, to turn the thoughts of students to matters political, and, in short, to carry on the good work of the usual Self-advertising Visitation M.P.

"Humbly thanking your Honour, and wishing your Honour precisely the successes and rewards that your Honour deserves,

"I remain,

"The dust of your Honour's feet,

"Ilderim Dost Mahommed."

And Mr. Cornelius Gosling-Green, M.P., read as follows:—

...And so I am to be hanged by the neck till I am dead, am I? And for a murder which I never committed, and in the perpetration of which I had no hands? Is it, my masters? I trow so. But I can afford to spit-for I did commit a murder, nevertheless, a beautiful secret murder that no one could possibly ever bring to my home or cast in my tooth.

"Well, well! Hang me and grin in sleeve-and I will laugh on other side of face while dancing on nothing-for if you think you are doing me in eye, I know I have done you in eye!

"Yes. *I* murdered Mr. Spensonly, the Chief Secretary of the Nuddee River Commission.

"As the Latin-and-Greeks used to say, '*Solo fesit*'!

"You think Mr. Spensonly died of plague? So he did. And who caused him to have plague? In short, who *plagued* him? (Ha! Ha! An infinite jest!) You shall know all about it and about, as Omar says, for I am going now to write my autobiography of myself, as all great so-called Criminals have done, for the admiration of mankind and the benefit of posterity. And my fellow-brothers and family-members shall proudly publish it with my photo-that of a great Patriot Hero and second Mazzini, Robespierre, Kossuth, Garibaldi, Wallace, Charlotte Corday, Kosciusko, and Mr. Robert Bruce (of spider fame).

"And I shall welcome death and embrace the headsman ere making last speech and dying confession. Having long desired to know what lies Beyond, I shall make virtue of necessity and seize opportunity (of getting to know) to play hero and die garnish.

"Not like the Pathan murderer who walked about in front of condemned cell with Koran balanced on head, crying to his Prophet to save him, and defying Englishes to touch him. Of course they cooked his geese, Koran or not. One warder does more than many Prophets in Gungapur Jail. (He! He! Quite good epigram and nice cynicality of educated man.) The degraded and unpolished fellow decoyed two little girls into empty house to steal their jewellery, and cut off fingers and noses and ears to get rings and nose-jewels and ear-drops, and left to die. Holy Fakir, gentleman of course! Pooh! and Bah! for all holy men. I give spurnings to them all for fools, knaves, or hypocrites. There are no gods any more for educated gentleman, except himself, and that's very good god to worship and make offering to (Ha! Ha! What a wit will be lost to the silly world when it permits itself to lose me.)

"Well, to return to the sheep, as the European proverb has it. I was born here in Gungapur, which will also have honour of being my death-and-cremation place, of poor but honest parent on thirty rupees a mensem. He was very clever fellow and sent five sons to Primary School, Middle School, High School and Gungapur Government College at cost of over hundred rupees a month, all out of his thirty rupees a mensem. He always used proverb 'Politeness lubricates wheels of life and palm also,' and he obliged any man who made it worth his while. But he fell into bad odours at hands of Mr. Spensonly owing to folly of bribing-fellow sending cash to office and the letter getting into Mr. Spensonly's post-bag and opening by mistake.

"But the Sahib took me up into his office to soften blow to progenitor and that shows he was a bad man or his luck would not have been to take me in and give chance to murder him.

"My good old paternal parent made me work many hours each night, and though he knew nothing of the subjects he could read English and would hear all my lessons and other brothers', and we had to say Skagger Rack, Cattegat, Scaw Fell and Helvellyn, and such things to him, and he would abuse us if we mis-arranged the figures and letters in $CaH2O2$ and $H2SO4$ and all those things in bottles. Before the Matriculation Examination he made a Graduate, whom he had got under his thumb-nail, teach us all the answers to all the back questions in all subjects till we knew them all by heart, and also made us learn ten long essays by heart so as to make up the required essay out of parts of them. He nearly killed my brother by starvation (saving food as well as punishing miscreant) for failing-the only one of us who ever failed in any examination-which he did by writing out all first chapter of Washington Irving for essay, when the subject was 'Describe a sunrise in the Australian back-blocks'. As parent said, he could have used 'A moonlight stroll by the sea-shore' and change the colour from silver to golden. But the fool was ill-so ill that he tried to kill himself and had not the strength. He said he would rather go to the missionaries' hell, full of Englishes, than go on learning *Egbert, Ethelbald, Ethelbert, Ethelwulf, Ethelred, Alfred, Edward the Elder, Edred, Edwy, Edgar, Ethelred the Unready*, and *If two triangles have two sides of the one equal to two angles of the other each to each and the sides so subtended equal then shall the bases or fourth sides be equal each to each or be isosceles.*

"Well, the progenitor kept our noses in the pie night and day and we all hated the old papa piously and wished he and we and all teachers and text-books were burned alive.

"But we were very much loved by everybody as we were so learned and clever, and whenever the Collector or anybody came to School, the Head Master used to put one of us in each room and call on us to answer questions and recite and say capes and bays without the map, and other clever things; and when my eldest brother left I had to change coat with another boy and do it twice sometimes, in different rooms.

"Sometimes the Educational Inspector himself would come, but then nothing could be done, for he would not ask questions that were always asked and were in the book, like the teachers and Deputy Inspectors did, but questions that no one knew and had to be thought out then and there. That is no test of Learning-and any fool who has not troubled to mug his book by heart might be able to answer such questions, while the man who had learnt every letter sat dumb.

"I hated the school and the books I knew by heart, but I loved Mr. Ganeshram Joshibhai. He was a clever cunning man, and could always tweak the leg of pompous Head Master when he came to the room, and had beautiful ways of cheating him when he came to examine-better than those of the other teachers.

"Before we had been with him a month he could tell us things while being examined, and no one else knew he was doing it. The initial letters of each word made up the words he wanted to crib to us, and when he scratched his head with the right hand the answer was 'No,' while with the left hand it was 'Yes'. And the clever way he taught us sedition while teaching us History, and appearing to praise the English!

"He would spend hours in praising the good men who rebelled and fought and got Magnum Charter and disrespected the King and cheeked the Government and Members of Council. We knew all about Oliver Cromwell, Hampden, Pim, and those crappies, and many a boy who had never heard of Wolsey and Alfred the Great knew all about Felton the jolly fine patriot who stabbed the Member of Council, Buckingham Esquire, in back.

"We learnt whole History book at home and he spent all History lessons telling us about Plots, all the English History Plots and foreign too, and we knew about the man who killed Henry of Navarre, as well as about the killing of French and American Presidents of to-day. He showed always why successful plots succeeded and the others failed. And he gave weeks to the American Independence War and the French Revolution.

"And all the Indian History was about the Mutiny and how and why it failed, when he was not showing us how the Englishes have ruined and robbed India, and comparing the Golden Age of India (when no cow ever died and there was never famine, plague, police nor taxes) with the miserable condition of poor bleeding India to-day.

"He was a fine fellow and so clever that we were almost his worshippers. But I am not writing his autobiography but my own, so let him lapse herewith into posterity and well-merited oblivious.

"At the College when we could work no longer, we who had never learnt crickets and tennis and ping-pongs, would take a nice big lantern with big windows in four sides of it, and sit publicly in the middle of the grass at the Gardens (with our books for a blind) and make speech to each other about Mother India and exhort each other to join together in a secret society and strike a blow for the Mother, and talk about the heroes who had died on the scaffolding for her, or who were languishing in chokey and do *poojah* to their photos. But the superior members did no *poojah* to anything. Then came the Emissary in the guise of a holy man (and I thought it the most dangerous disguise he could have assumed, for I wonder the police do not arrest every sannyasi and fakir on suspicion) and brought us the Message. And he took us to hear the blind Mussulman they call Ilderim the Weeper.

"All was ready and nothing lacked but the Instrument.

"Would any of us achieve eternal fame and undying glory by being the next Instrument?

"We wouldn't. No jolly fear, and thanks awfully.

"But we agreed to make a strike at the College and to drop a useless Browning pistol where it would be found, and in various other ways to be unrestful. And one of us, whom the Principal would not certify to sit for his F.E. and was very stony hard-up, joined the Emissary and went away with him to be a Servant and perhaps an Instrument later on (if he could not get a girl with a good dowry or a service of thirty rupees a mensem), he was so hungry and having nothing for belly.

"Yes, as Mr. Ganeshram Joshibhai used to say, that is what the British Government does for you-educates you to be passed B.A. and educated gent., and then grudges to give you thirty rupees a mensem and expects you to go searching for employment and food to put in belly! Can B.A. work with hands like *maistri*?

"Then there came the best of all my friends, a science-knowing gentleman who gave all his great talents to bomb. And the cream of all the milky joke was that he had learnt all his science free, from Government, at school and college, and he not only used his knowledge to be first-class superior anarchist but he got chemicals from Government own laboratory.

"His brother was in Government Engineering College and between them they did much-for one could make the bomb and the other could fill it.

"But they are both to be hanged at the same time that I am, and I do not grudge that I am to be innocently hanged for their plot and the blowing up of the *bhangi* by mistake for the Collector, for I have long aspired to be holy martyr in Freedom's sacred cause and have photo in newspapers and be talked about.

"Besides, as I have said, I am not being done brown, as I murdered Mr. Spensonly, the Engineer.

"How I hated him!
"Why should he be big and strong while I am skinny and feeble-owing to night-and-day burning midnight candle at both ends and unable to make them meet?

"Besides did he not bring unmerited dishonour on grey hairs of poor old progenitor by finding him out in bribe-taking? Did he not bring my honoured father's aforesaying grey hairs in sorrow to reduced pension?

"Did he not upbraid and rebuke, nay, reproach me when I made grievous little errors and backslippers?

"A thousand times Yea.

"But I should never have murdered him had I not caught the Plague, so out of evil cometh good once more.

"The Plague came to Gungapur in its millions and we knew not what to do but stood like drowning man splitting at a straw.

"Superstitious Natives said it was the revenge of Goddess Kali for not sacrificing, and superstitious Europeans said it was a microbe created by their God to punish unhygienic way of living.

"Knowing there are no gods of any sort I am in a position to state that it was just written on our foreheads.

"To make confusion worse dumbfounded the Government of course had to seize horns of dilemma and trouble the poor. They had all cases taken to hospital and made segregation and inspection camps. They disinfected houses and burnt rags and even purdah women were not allowed to die in bosom of family. Of course police stole lakhs of rupees worth of clothes and furniture and said it was infected. And many good men who were enemies of Government were falsely accused of being plague-stricken and were dragged to hospital and were never seen again.

"Terrible calamities fell upon our city and at last it nearly lost me myself. I was seized, dragged from my family-bosom, cast into hospital and cured. And in hospital I learned from fellow who was subordinate-medical that rats get plague in sewers and cesspools and when they die of it their fleas must go elsewhere for food, and so hop on to other rat and give that poor chap plague too, by biting him with dirty mouths from dead rat, and then he dies and so *in adfinitum*, as the poet has it. But suppose no other rat is handy, what is poor hungry flea to do? When you can't get curry, eat rice! When flea can't get rat he eats man-turns to nastier food. (He! He!)

"So when flea from plague-stricken rat jumps on to man and bites him, poor fellow gets plague —*bus*.[127]

"Didn't friends and family-members skeddaddle and bunk when they saw rat after I told them all that! But I didn't care, I had had plague once, and one cannot get it twice. Not one man in thousand recovers when he has got it, but I did. Old uneducated fool maternal parent did lots of thanks-givings and *poojah* because gods specially attentive to me-but I said 'Go to, old woman. It was written on forehead.'

"And when I returned to work, one day I had an idea-an idea of how to punish Mr. Spensonly for propelling honoured parent head first out of job, and idea for striking blow at British prestige. We had our office in private bungalow in those days before new Secretariat was built, and it was unhealthy bungalow in which no one would live because they died.

"Mr. Spensonly didn't care, and he had office on top floor, but bottom floor was clerks' office who went away at night also. Now it was my painful duty to go every morning up to his office-room and see that peon had put fresh ink and everything ready and that the *hamal* had dusted properly. So it was not long before I was aware that all the drawers were locked except the top right-hand drawer, and that was not used as there was a biggish hole in the front of it where the edge was broken away from the above, some miscreant having once forced it open with tool.

"And verily it came to pass that one day, entering my humble abode-room, I saw a plague-rat lying suffering from *in extremis* and about to give up ghost. But having had plague I did not trouble about the fleas that would leave his body when it grew stiff and cold, in search of food. Instead I let it lie there while my food was being prepared, and regretted that it was not beneath the chair of some enemy of mine who had not had plague, instead of beneath my own...that of Mr. Spensonly for example!...

"It was Saturday night. I returned to the office that evening, knowing that Mr. Spensonly was out; and I went to his office-room with idle excuse to the peon sitting in verandah-and in my pocket was poor old rat kicking bucket fast.

"Who was to say *I* put deceasing rat in the Sahib's table-drawer just where he would come and sit all day-being in the habit of doing work on Sunday the Christian holy day (being a man of no religion or caste)? What do I know of rats and their properties when at death's front door?

"Cannot rat go into a Sahib's drawer as well as into poor man's? If he did no work on Sunday very likely the fleas would remain until Monday, the rat dying slowly and remaining warm and not in *rigour mortuis*. Anyhow when they began to seek fresh fields and pastures new, being fed up with old rat-or rather not able to get fed up enough, they would be jolly well on the look out, and glad enough to take nibble even at an Englishman! (He! He!) So I argued, and put good old rat in drawer and did slopes. On Monday, Mr. Spensonly went early from office, feeling feverish; and when I called, as in duty bound, to make humble inquiries on Tuesday, he was reported jolly sickish with Plague-and he died Tuesday night. I never heard of any other Sahib dying of Plague in Gungapur except one missionary fellow who lived in the native city with native fellows.

"So they can hang me for share in bomb-outrage and welcome (though I never threw the bomb nor made it, and only took academic interest in affair as I told the Judge Sahib) —for I maintain with my dying breath that it was I who murdered Mr. Spensonly and put tongue in cheeks when *Gungapur Gazette* wrote column about the unhealthy bungalow in which he was so foolish as to have his office. When I reflect that by this time to-morrow I shall be Holy Martyr I rejoice and hope photo will be good one, and I send this message to all the world —

"'Oh be....'"

* * *

Neither Mr. nor Mrs. Gosling-Green, M.P., liked this Pathan gentleman so well after reading his letter and enclosure. Before long they liked him very much less-although they did not know it-which sounds cryptic.

§ 5. Mr. Horace Faggit

"Fair cautions, ain't they, these bloomin' niggers," observed Mr. Horace Faggit, as the train rested and refreshed itself at a wayside station on its weary way to distant Gungapur.

Colonel Wilberforce Wriothesley, of the 99th Baluch Light Infantry, apparently did not feel called upon to notice the remark of Horace, whom he regarded as a Person.

"Makes you proud to think you are one of the Ruling Rice to look at the silly blighters, don't it?" he persisted.

"No authority on rice," murmured the Colonel, without looking up from his book.

Stuffy old beggar he seemed to the friendly and genial Horace, but Horace was too deeply interested in India and Horace to be affected by trifles.

For Mr. Horace Faggit had only set foot in his Imperial Majesty the King Emperor's Indian Empire that month, and he was dazed with impressions, drunk with sensations, and uplifted with pride. Was he not one of the Conquerors, a member of the Superior Society, one of the Ruling Race, and, in short, a Somebody?

The train started again and Horace sank back upon the long couch of the unwonted first-class carriage, and sighed with contentment and satisfaction.

How different from Peckham and from the offices of the fine old British Firm of Schneider, Schnitzel, Schnorrer & Schmidt! A Somebody at last—after being office-boy, clerk, straphanger, gallery-patron, cheap lodger, and paper-collar wearer. A Somebody, a Sahib, an English gent., one of the Ruling and Upper Class after being a fourpenny luncher, a penny-'bus-and-twopenny—tuber, a waverer 'twixt Lockhart and Pearce-and-Plenty.

For him, now, the respectful salaam, precedence, the first-class carriage, the salutes of police and railway officials, hotels, a servant (elderly and called a "Boy"), cabs (more elderly and called "gharries"), first-class refreshment and waiting rooms, a funny but imposing sun-helmet, silk and cotton suits, evening clothes, deference, regard and prompt attention everywhere. Better than Peckham and the City, this! My! What tales he'd have to tell Gwladwys Gwendoline when he had completed his circuit and returned.

For Mr. Horace Faggit, plausible, observant, indefatigably cunning, and in business most capable ("No bloomin' flies on 'Orris F." as he would confidently and truthfully assure you) was the first tentative tentacle advanced to feel its way by the fine old British Firm of Schneider, Schnitzel, Schnorrer & Schmidt, in the mazy markets of the gorgeous Orient, and to introduce to the immemorial East their famous jewellery and wine of Birmingham and Whitechapel respectively; also to introduce certain exceeding-private documents to various gentlemen of Teutonic sympathies and activities in various parts of India-documents of the nature of which Horace was entirely ignorant.

And the narrow bosom of Horace swelled with pride, as he realized that, here at least, he was a Gentleman and a Sahib.

Well, he'd let 'em know it too. Those who did him well and pleased him should get tips, and those who didn't should learn what it was to earn the displeasure of the Sahib and to evoke his wrath. And he would endeavour to let all and sundry see the immeasurable distance and impassable gulf that lay between a Sahib and a nigger-of any degree whatsoever.

This was the country to play the gentleman in and no error! You *could* fling your copper cash about in a land where a one-and-fourpenny piece was worth a hundred and ninety-two copper coins, where you could get a hundred good smokes to stick in your face for about a couple of bob, and where you could give a black cabby sixpence and done with it. Horace had been something of a Radical at home (and, indeed, when an office-boy, a convinced Socialist), especially when an old-age pension took his lazy, drunken old father off his hands, and handsomely rewarded the aged gentleman for an unswervingly regular and unbroken career of post-polishing and pub-pillaring. But now he felt he had been mistaken. Travel widens the horizon and class-hatred is only sensible and satisfactory when you are no class yourself. When you have got a position you must keep it up-and being one of the Ruling Race was a position undoubtedly. Horace Faggit *would* keep it up too, and let 'em see all about it.

The train entered another station and drew in from the heat and glare to the heat and comparative darkness.

Yes, he would keep up his position as a Sahib haughtily and with jealousy, —and he stared with terrible frown and supercilious hauteur at what he mentally termed a big, fat buck-nigger who dared and presumed to approach the carriage and look in. The man wore an enormous white turban, a khaki Norfolk jacket, white jodhpore riding-breeches that fitted the calf like skin, and red shoes with turned-up pointed toes. His beard was curled, and his hair hung in ringlets from his turban to his shoulders in a way Horace considered absurd. Could the blighter be actually looking to see whether there might be room for him, and meditating entry? If so Horace would show him his mistake. Pretty thing if niggers were to get into First-Class carriages with Sahibs like Horace!

"'Ere! What's the gaime?" he inquired roughly. "Can't yer see this is Firs-Class, and if you got a Firs-Class ticket, can't yer see there's two Sahibs 'ere? Sling yer 'ook, *sour*.[128] Go on, *jao!*"[129]

The man gave no evidence of having understood Horace.

"Sahib!" said he softly, addressing Colonel Wilberforce Wriothesley.

The Colonel went on reading.

"*Jao*, I tell yer," repeated Horace, rather proud of his grasp of the vernacular. "Slope, *barn-shoot*."[130]

"Sahib!" said the man again.

The Colonel looked up and then sprang to his feet with outstretched hand.

"*Bahut salaam*,[131] Subedar Major Saheb," he cried, and wrung the hand of the "big fat buck-nigger" (who possessed the same medal-ribbons that he himself did) as he poured forth a torrent of mingled Pushtu, Urdu, and English while the Native Officer alternately saluted and pressed the Colonel's hand to his forehead in transports of pure and wholly disinterested joy.

"They told me the Colonel Sahib would be passing through this week," he said, "and I have met all the trains that I might look upon his face. I am weary of my furlough and would rejoin but for my law-suit. Praise be to Allah that I have met my Colonel Sahib," and the man who had five war decorations was utterly unashamed of the tear that trickled.

"How does my son, Sahib?" he asked in Urdu.

"Well, Subedar Major Saheb, well. Worthily of his father-whose place in the *pultan* may he come to occupy."

"Praise be to God, Sahib! Let him no more seek his father's house nor look upon his father's face again, if he please thee not in all things. And is there good news of Malet-Marsac Sahib, O Colonel Sahib?" Then, with a glance at Horace, he asked: "Why does this low-born one dare to enter the carriage of the Colonel Sahib and sit? Truly the *rêlwêy terain* is a great caste-breaker! Clearly he belongs to the class of the *ghora-log*, the common soldiers."...

"'Oo was that, —a Rajah?" inquired the astounded Horace, as the train moved on.

"One of the people who keep India safe for you bagmen," replied the Colonel, who was a trifle indignant on behalf of the insulted Subedar Major Mir Daoud Khan Mir Hafiz Ullah Khan of the 99th Baluch Light Infantry.

"No doubt he thought I was another officer," reflected Horace. "They think you're a gent, if you chivvy 'em."

At Umbalpur Colonel Wilberforce Wriothesley left the train and Mr. Faggit had the carriage to himself-for a time.

And it was only through his own firmness and proper pride that he had it to himself for so long, for at the very next station a beastly little brute of a black man actually tried to get in-in with *him*, Mr. Horace Faggit of the fine old British Firm of Schneider, Schnitzel, Schnorrer & Schmidt, manufacturers of best quality Birmingham jewellery and "importers" of a fine Whitechapel wine.

But Horace settled *him* all right and taught him to respect Sahibs. It happened thus. Horace lay idly gazing at the ever-shifting scene of the platform in lordly detachment and splendid isolation, when, just as the train was starting, a little fat man, dressed in a little red turban like a cotton bowler, a white coat with a white sash over the shoulder, a white apron tucked up behind, pink silk socks, and patent leather shoes, told his servant to open the door. Ere the stupefied Horace could arise from his seat the man was climbing in! The door opened inwards however, and Horace was in time to give it a sharp thrust with his foot and send the little man, a mere Judge of the High Court, staggering backwards on to the platform where he sprawled at full length, while his turban, which Horace thought most ridiculous for a grown man, rolled in the dust. Slamming the door the "Sahib" leant out and jeered, while the insolent presumptuous "nigger" wiped the blood from his nose with a corner of the *dhoti* or apron-like garment (which Horace considered idiotic if not improper)....

But Homer nodded, and-Horace went to sleep.

When he awoke he saw by the dim light of the screened roof-lamp that he was not alone, and that on the opposite couch a *native* had actually made up a bed with sheets, blankets and pillow, undressed himself, put on pyjamas and gone to bed! Gord streuth, he had! He'd attend to him in the morning-though it would serve the brute right if Horace threw him out at the next station-without his kit. But he looked rather large, and Mercy is notoriously a kingly attribute.

In the morning Mir Jan Rah-bin-Ras el-Isan Mir Ilderim Dost Mahommed of Mekran Kot, Gungapur, and the world in general, awoke, yawned, stretched himself and arose.

He arose to some six feet and three inches of stature, and his thin pyjamasuit was seen to cover a remarkably fine and robustious figure-provided with large contours where contours are desirable, and level tracts where such are good. As he lay flat back again, Horace noted that his chest rose higher than his head and the more southerly portion of his anatomy, while the action of clasping his hands behind his neck brought into prominence a pair of biceps that strained their sleeves almost to bursting. He was nearly as fair as London-bred Horace, but there were his turbanned conical hat, his curly toed shoes, his long silk coat, his embroidered velvet waistcoat and other wholly Oriental articles of attire. Besides, his vest was of patterned muslin and he had something on a coloured string round his neck.

"What are you doing 'ere?" demanded Horace truculently, as this bold abandoned "native" caught his eye and said "Good-morning".

"At present I am doing nothing," was the reply, "unless passive reclining may count as being something. I trust I do not intrude or annoy?"

"You do intrude and likewise you do annoy also. I ain't accustomed to travel with blacks, and I ain't agoing to have you spitting about 'ere. You got in when I was asleep."

"You were certainly snoring when I got in, and I was careful not to awaken you-but not on account of any great sensation of guilt or fear. I assure you I have no intention of spitting or being in any way rude, unmannerly, or offensive. And since you object to travelling with 'blacks' I suggest-that you leave the carriage."

Did Horace's ears deceive him? Did he sleep, did he dream, and were visions about? *Leave the carriage*?

"Look 'ere," he shouted, "you keep a civil tongue in your 'ead. Don't you know I am a gentleman? What do you mean by getting into a first-class carriage with a gentleman and insulting 'im? Want me to throw you out before we reach a station? Do yer?"

"No, to tell you the truth I did not realize that you are a gentleman-and I have known a great number of English gentlemen in England and India, and generally found them mirrors of chivalry and the pink of politeness and courtesy. And I hope you won't try to throw me out either in a station or elsewhere for I might get annoyed and hurt you."

What a funny nigger it was! What did he mean by "mirrors of chivalry". Talked like a bloomin' book. Still, Horace would learn him not to presoom.

The presumptuous one retired to the lavatory; washed, shaved, and reappeared dressed in full Pathan kit. But for this, there was nothing save his very fine physique and stature to distinguish him from an inhabitant of Southern Europe.

Producing a red-covered official work on Mounted Infantry Training, he settled down to read. Horace regretted that India provided not his favourite *Comic Cuts and Photo Bits.*

"May I offer you a cigarette and light one myself?" said the "black" man in his quiet cultured voice.

"I don't want yer fags-and I don't want you smoking while I got a empty stummick," replied the Englishman.

Anon the train strolled into an accidental-looking station with an air of one who says, "Let's sit down for a bit-what?" and Horace sprang to the window and bawled for the guard.

"'Ere-ask this native for 'is ticket," he said, on the arrival of that functionary. "Wot's 'e doing in 'ere with *me?*"

"Ticket, please?" said the guard —a very black Goanese.

The Pathan produced his ticket.

"Will you kindly see if there is another empty first-class carriage, Guard?" said he.

"There iss one next a'door," replied the guard.

"Then you can escape from your unpleasant predicament by going in there, Sir," said the Pathan.

"I shall remine where I ham," was the dignified answer.

"And so shall I," said the Pathan.

"Out yer go," said the bagman, rising threateningly.

"I am afraid I shall have to put you to the trouble of ejecting me," said the Pathan, with a smile.

"I wouldn't bemean myself," countered Horace loftily, and didn't.

"One often hears of the dangerous classes in India," said the Pathan, as the train moved on again. "You belong to the most dangerous of all. You and your kind are a danger to the Empire and I have a good mind to be a public benefactor and destroy you. Put you to the edge of the sword-or rather of the tin-opener," and he pulled his lunch-basket from under the seat.

"Have some chicken, little Worm?" he continued, opening the basket and preparing to eat.

"Keep your muck," replied Horace.

"No, no, little Cad," corrected the strange and rather terrible person; "you are going to breakfast with me and you are going to learn a few things about India-and yourself."

And Horace did....

"Where are you going?" asked the Pathan person later.

"I'm going to work up a bit o' trade in a place called Gungerpore," was the reply of the cowed Horace.

But in Gungapur Horace adopted the very last trade that he, respectable man, ever expected to adopt-that of War.

Chapter IV
"Meet and Leave Again."

"So on the sea of life, Alas!
Man nears man, meets and leaves again."

§ 1

It had come. Ross-Ellison had proved a true prophet (and was to prove himself a true soldier and commander of men).

Possibly the most remarkable thing about it was the quickness and quietness, the naturalness and easiness with which it had come. A week or two of newspaper forecast and fear, a week or two of recrimination and feverish preparation, an ultimatum-England at war. The navy mobilized, the army mobilizing, auxiliaries warned to be in readiness, overseas battalions, batteries and squadrons recalled, or re-distributed, reverses and "regrettable incidents," —and outlying parts of India (her native troops massed in the North or doing garrison-duty overseas) an archipelago of safety-islands in a sea of danger; Border parts of India for a time dependent upon their various volunteer battalions for the maintenance, over certain areas, of their civil governance, their political organization and public services.

In Gungapur, as in a few other Border cities, the lives of the European women, children and men, the safety of property, and the continuance of the local civil government depended for a little while upon the local volunteer corps.

Gungapur, whose history became an epitome of that of certain other isolated cities, was for a few short weeks an intermittently besieged garrison, a mark for wandering predatory bands composed of *budmashes* outlaws, escaped convicts, deserters, and huge mobs drawn from that enormous body of men who live on the margin of respectability, peaceful cultivator today, bloodthirsty dacoit to-morrow, wielders of the spade and mattock or of the *lathi* and *tulwar*[132] according to season, circumstance, and the power of the Government; recruits for a mighty army, given the leader and the opportunity-the hour of a Government's danger.

As had been pointed out, time after time, in the happy and happy-go-lucky past, the practical civilian seditionist and active civilian rebel is more fortunately situated in India than is his foreign brother, in that his army exists ready to hand, all round him, in the thousands of the desperately poor, devoid of the "respectability" that accompanies property, thousands with nothing to lose and high hopes of much to gain, heaven-sent material for the agitator.

Thanks to the energy of Colonel John Robin Ross-Ellison, his unusual organizing ability, his personality, military genius and fore-knowledge of what was coming, Gungapur suffered less than might have been expected in view of its position on the edge of a Border State of always-doubtful friendliness, its large mill-hand element, and the poverty and turbulence of its general population.

The sudden departure of the troops was the sign for the commencement of a state of insecurity and anxiety which quickly merged into one of danger and fear, soon to be replaced by a state of war.

From the moment that it was known for certain that the garrison would be withdrawn, Colonel Ross-Ellison commenced to put into practice his projected plans and arrangements. On the day that Mr. Dearman's coolies (after impassioned harangues by a blind Mussulman fanatic known as Ibrahim the Weeper, a faquir who had recently come over the Border to Gungapur and attained great influence; and by a Hindu professional agitator who had obtained a post at the mills in the guise of a harmless clerk) commenced rioting, beat Mr. Dearman to death with crowbars, picks, and shovels, murdered all the European and Eurasian employees, looted all that was worth stealing, and, after having set fire to the mills, invaded the Cantonment quarter, burning, murdering, destroying, —Colonel Ross-Ellison called out his corps, declared martial law, and took charge of the situation, the civil authorities being dead or cut off in the "districts".

The place which he had marked out for his citadel in time of trouble was the empty Military Prison, surrounded by a lofty wall provided with an unassailable water-supply, furnished with cook-houses, infirmary, work-shop, and containing a number of detached bungalows (for officials) in addition to the long lines of detention barracks.

As soon as his men had assembled at Headquarters he marched to the place and commenced to put it in a state of defence and preparation for a siege.

While Captain Malet-Marsac and Captain John Bruce (of the Gungapur Engineering College) slaved at carrying out his orders in the Prison, other officers, with picked parties of European Volunteers, went out to bring in fugitives, to commandeer the contents of provision and grain shops, to drive in cattle, to seize cooks, sweepers and other servants, to shoot rioters and looters in the Cantonment area, to search for wounded and hidden victims of the riot, to bury corpses, extinguish fires, penetrate to European bungalows in the city and in outlying places, to publish abroad that the Military Prison was a safe refuge, to seize and empty ammunition shops and toddy shops, to mount guards at the railway-station, telegraph office, the banks, the gate-house of the great Jail, the Treasury and the Kutcherry,[133] and generally, to use their common sense and their rifles as the situation demanded.

Day by day external operation became more restricted as the mob grew larger and bolder, better armed and better organized, daily augmented and assisted from without. The last outpost which Colonel Ross-Ellison withdrew was the one from the railway-station, and that was maintained until it was known that large bridges had been blown up on either side and the railway rendered useless. In the Jail gate-house he established a strong guard under the Superintendent, and urged him to use it ruthlessly, to kill on the barest suspicion of mutiny, and to welcome the first opportunity of giving the sharpest of lessons.

In this matter he set a personal example and behaved, to actual rioters, with what some of his followers considered unnecessary severity, and what others viewed as wise war-ending firmness.

When remonstrated with by Mr. Cornelius Gosling-Green (caught, alas! with his admirable wife in this sudden and terrible maelstrom), for shooting, against the Prison wall, a squad of armed men caught by night and under more than suspicious circumstances, within Cantonment limits, he replied curtly and rudely:—

"My good little Gosling, I'd shoot *you* with my own hand if you failed me in the least particular-so stick to your drill and hope to become a Corporal before the war is over".

The world-famous Mr. Cornelius Gosling-Green, M.P., hoping to become a Corporal! Meanwhile he was less—a private soldier, doing four hard drills a day-not to mention sentry-go and fatigues. Like Augustus Clarence Percy Marmaduke Grobble, he grumbled bitterly-but he obeyed, having been offered the hard choice of enrolment or exclusion.

"I'll have no useless male mouths here," had said Colonel Ross-Ellison.
"Enroll or clear out and take your chance. I'll look after your wife."

"But, my dear Sir...."
"'Sir' without the 'my dear,' please."
"I was about to say that I could-ah-assist, advise, sit upon your councils, give you the benefit of my-er-experience,..." the Publicist had expostulated.
"Experience of war?"
"No-er —I ——"
"Enroll or clear out-and when you have enrolled remember that you are under martial law and in time of war."

A swift, fierce, masterful man, harsh and ruthless making war without kid gloves-that it might end the sooner and be the longer remembered by the survivors. The flag was to be kept flying in Gungapur, the women and children were to be saved, all possible damage was to be inflicted on the rebels and rioters, more particularly upon those who led and incited them. The

Gosling-Greens and Grobbles who could not materially assist to this end could go, those who could thwart or hinder this end could die.

Gleams of humour enlivened the situation. Mrs. Gosling-Green (*née* a Pounding-Pobble, Superiora Pounding-Pobble, one of the Pounding-Pobbles of Putney) was under the orders, very much under the orders, of the wife of the Sergeant-Major, and early and plainly learnt that good woman's opinion that she was a poor, feckless body and eke a fushionless, not worth the salt of her porridge—a lazy slut withal.

Among the "awkward squads" enrolled when rioting broke out and the corps seized the old Prison, were erstwhile grave and reverend seniors learning to "stand up like a man an' look prahd o' yourself" at the orders of the Sergeant-Major. Among them were two who had been Great Men, Managers signing *per* and *pro*, Heads of Departments, almost Tin Gods, and one of them, alas, was at the mercy of a mere boy whom he had detested and frequently "squashed" in the happy days of yore. The mere boy (a cool, humorous, and somewhat vindictive person, one of the best subalterns of the Corps and especially chosen by Colonel Ross-Ellison when re-organizing the battalion after its disbandment) was giving his close attention to the improvement of his late manager, a pompous, dull and silly bureaucrat, even as his late manager had done for him.

"Now, Private Bulliton," he would urge, "*do* learn which is your right hand and which is your left. And *do* stand up.... No-don't drop your rifle when you are told to 'shoulder'. *That's* better-we shall make something of you yet. Head up, man, head up! Try and look fierce. Look at Private Faggit-he'll be a Sergeant yet"...and indeed Private Horace Faggit was looking very fierce indeed, for he desired the blood of these interfering villains who were hindering the development of the business of the fine old British firm of Messrs. Schneider, Schnitzel, Schnorrer & Schmidt and the commissions of their representative. Also he felt that he was assisting at the making of history. 'Orace in a bloomin' siege-Gorblimey!—and he, who had never killed anything bigger than an insect in his life, lusted to know how it felt to shove your bayonet into a feller or shoot 'im dead at short rynge. So Horace drilled with alacrity and zest, paid close attention to aiming-instruction and to such visual-training and distance-judging as his officer, Captain John Bruce, could give him, and developed a military aptitude surprising to those who had known him only as Horace Faggit, Esquire, the tried and trusted Representative of the fine old British Firm of Schneider, Schnitzel, Schnorrer & Schmidt.

To Captain Malet-Marsac, an unusually thoughtful, observant and studious soldier, it was deeply interesting to see how War affected different people how values changed, how the Great became exceeding small, and the insignificant person became important. By the end of the first month of what was virtually the siege of the Military Prison, Horace Faggit, late office-boy, clerk, and bagman, was worth considerably more than Augustus Grobble, late Professor of Moral Philosophy; Cornelius Gosling-Green, late Publicist; Edward Jones, late (alleged) Educationist, of Duri formerly; and a late Head of a Department,—all rolled into one—a keen, dapper, self-reliant soldier, courageous, prompt, and very bloodthirsty.

As he strolled up and down, supervising drills, went round the sentry-posts by night, or marched at the head of a patrol, Captain Malet-Marsac would reflect upon the relativity of things, the false values of civilization, and the extraordinary devitalising and deteriorating results of "education". When it came to vital issues, elementals, stark essential manhood,—then the elect of civilization, the chosen of education, weighed, was found not only wanting but largely negligible. Where the highly "educated" was as good as the other he was so by reason of his games and sports, his *shikar*, or his specialized training-as in the case of the engineers and other physically-trained men.

Captain John Bruce, for example, Professor of Engineering, was a soldier in a few weeks and a fine one. In time of peace, a quiet, humorous, dour and religious-minded man, he was now a stern disciplinarian and a cunning foe who fought to kill, rejoicing in the carnage that taught a lesson and made for earlier peace. The mind that had dreamed of universal brotherhood and the Oneness of Humanity now dreamed of ambushes, night-attacks, slaughterous strategy and magazine-fire on a cornered foe.

Surely and steadily the men enclosed behind the walls of the old Prison rose into the ranks of the utterly reliable, the indefatigable, the fearless and the fine, or sank into those of the shifty, unhearty, unreliable, and unworthy-save the few who remained steadily mediocre, well-meaning, unsoldierly, fairly trustworthy—a useful second line, but not to be sent on forlorn hopes, dangerous reconnoitring, risky despatch-carrying, scouting, or ticklish night-work. One siege is very like another-and Ross-Ellison's garrison knew increasing weariness, hunger, disease and casualties.

Mrs. Dearman's conduct raised Colonel Ross-Ellison's love to a burning, yearning devotion, and his defence of Gungapur became his defence of Mrs. Dearman. For her husband she appeared to mourn but little-there was little time to mourn-and, for a while, until sights, sounds and smells became increasingly horrible, she appeared almost to enjoy her position of Queen of the Garrison, the acknowledged Ladye of the Officers and men of the Corps. Until she fell sick herself, she played the part of amateur Florence Nightingale right well, going regularly with a lamp-the Lady with the Lamp-at night through the hospital ward. Captain John Bruce was the only one who was not loud in her praises, though he uttered no dispraises. He, a dour and practical person, thought the voyage with the Lamp wholly unnecessary and likely to awaken sleepers to whom sleep was life; that lint-scraping would have been a more useful employment than graciousness to the poor wounded; that a woman, as zealous as Mrs. Dearman looked, would have torn up dainty cotton and linen confections for bandages instead of wearing them; that the Commandant didn't need all the personal encouragement and enheartenment that she wished to give him-and many other uncomfortable, cynical, and crabby thoughts. Captain Malet-Marsac loved her without criticism.

Mrs. Cornelius Gosling-Green, after haranguing all and sundry, individually and collectively, on the economic unsoundness, the illogic, and the unsocial influence of War, took to her bed and stayed there until she found herself totally neglected. Arising and demanding an interview with the Commandant, she called him to witness that she entered a formal protest against the whole proceedings and registered her emphatic——until the Commandant, sending for Cornelius (whose duties cut him off, unrepining, from his wife's society), ordered him to remove her, silence her, beat her if necessary-and so save her from the unpleasant alternative of solitary confinement on bread and water until she could be, if not useful, innocuous.

Many a poor woman of humble station proved herself (what most women are) an uncomplaining, unconsidered heroine, and more than one "subordinate" of mixed ancestry and unpromising exterior, a brave devoted man. As usual, what kept the flag flying and gave ultimate victory to the immeasurably weaker side was the spirit, the personality, the force, the power, of one man.

To Captain Malet-Marsac this was a revelation. Even to him, who knew John Robin Ross-Ellison well, and had known and studied him for some time at Duri and elsewhere, it was a wonderful thing to see how the quiet, curious, secretive man (albeit a fine athlete, horseman and adventurous traveller) stepped suddenly into the fierce light of supreme command in time of war, a great, uncompromising, resourceful ruler of men, skilful strategist and tactician, remarkable both as organizer, leader, and personal fighter.

Did he *ever* sleep? Night after night he penetrated into the city disguised as a Pathan (a disguise he assumed with extraordinary skill and which he strengthened by a perfect knowledge of many Border dialects as well as of Pushtoo), or else personally led some night attack, sally, reconnaissance or foraging expedition. Day after day he rode out on Zuleika with the few mounted men at his command, scouting, reconnoitring, gleaning information, attacking and slaughtering small parties of marauders as occasion offered.

From him the professional soldier, his adjutant, learned much, and wondered where his Commandant had learned all he had to teach. Captain Malet-Marsac owned him master, his military as well as his official superior, and grew to feel towards him as his immediate followers felt toward Napoleon-to love him with a devoted respect, a respecting devotion. He recognized in him the born guerrilla leader-and more, the trained guerrilla leader, and wondered where on earth this strange civilian had garnered his practical military knowledge and skill.

Wherever he went on foot, especially when he slipped out of the Prison for dangerous spy-work among the forces of the mutineers, rebels, rioters and *budmashes* of the city, he was followed by his servant, an African, concerning whom Colonel Ross-Ellison had advised the servants of the Officers' Mess to be careful and also to bear in mind that he was not a *Hubshi*. Only when the Colonel rode forth on horseback was he separated from this man who, when the Colonel was in his room, invariably slept across the door thereof.

On night expeditions, the Somali would be disguised, sometimes as a leprous beggar, as stable-boy, again as an Arab, sometimes as a renegade sepoy from a Native Border Levy, sometimes as a poor fisherman, again as a Sidi boatman, he being, like his master, exceptionally good at disguises of all kinds, and knowing Hindustani, Arabic, and his native Somal dialect.

He was an expert bugler, and in that capacity stuck like a burr to the Colonel by day, looking very smart and workmanlike in khaki uniform and being of more than average usefulness with rifle and bayonet. Not until after the restoration of order did Mr. Edward Jones, formerly of the Duri High School, long puzzled as to where he had seen him before, realize who he was.

* * *

In a low dark room, dimly lighted that evening by wick-and-saucer *butties*, squatted, lay, sat, stood and sprawled a curious collection of scoundrels. The room was large, and round the four sides of it ran a very broad, very low, and very filthy divan, intended for the rest and repose of portly *bunnias*,[134] *seths*,[135] brokers, shopkeepers and others of the commercial fraternity, what time they assembled to chew pan and exchange lies and truths anent money and the markets. A very different assembly now occupied its greasy lengths *vice* the former habitués of the *salon*, now dispersed, dead, robbed, ruined, held to ransom, or cruelly blackmailed.

In the seat of honour (an extra cushion), sat the blind faquir who, with his clerkly colleague, had set the original match to the magazine by inciting the late Mr. Dearman's coolies. Apparently a relentless, terrible fanatic and bitter hater of the English, for his councils were all of blood and fire, rapine and slaughter, he taunted his hearers with their supine cowardice in that the Military Prison still held out, its handful of defenders still manned its walls, nay, from time to time, made sallies and terrible reprisals upon a careless ill-disciplined enemy.

"Were I but as other men! Had I but mine eyes!" he screamed, "I would overwhelm the place in an hour. Hundreds to one you are-and you are mocked, robbed, slaughtered."

A thin-faced, evil-looking, squint-eyed Hindu whose large, thick, gold-rimmed goggles accorded ill with the sword that lay athwart his crossed legs, addressed him in English.

"Easy to talk, Moulvie. Had you your sight you could perhaps drill and arm the mob into an army, eh? Find them repeating rifles and ammunition, find them officers, find them courage? Is it not? Yes."

"Hundreds to one, Babu," grunted the blind man, and spat.

"I would urge upon this august assemblee," piped a youthful weedy person, "that recreemination is not argument, and that many words butter no parsneeps, so to speak. We are met to decide as to whether the treasure shall be removed to Pirgunge or still we keep it with us here in view of sudden sallies of foes. I hereby beg to propose and my honourable friend Mister ——"

"Sit down, crow," said the blind faquir unkindly and there was a snigger. "The treasure will be removed at once-this night, or I will remove myself from Gungapur with all my followers-and go where deeds are being done. I weary of waiting while pi-dogs yelp around the walls they cannot enter. Cowards! Thousands to one-and ye do not kill two of them a day. Conquer and slay them? Nay-rather must our own treasure be removed lest some night the devil, in command there, swoop upon it, driving ye off like sheep and carrying back with him ——"

"Flesh and blood cannot face a machine-gun, Moulvie," said the squint-eyed Hindu. "Even *your* holy sanctity would scarcely protect you from bullets. Come forth and try to-morrow."

"Nor can flesh and blood-such flesh and blood as Gungapur provides-surround the machine-gun and rush upon it from flank and rear of course," replied the blind man. "Do machine guns fire in all directions at once? When they ran the accursed thing down to the market-place and fired it into the armed crowd that listened to my words, could ye not have fled by other streets to surround it? Had all rushed bravely from all directions how long would it have fired? Even thus, could more have died than did die? Scores they slew-and retired but when they could fire no longer.... And ye allowed it to go because a dozen men stood between it and you — —," and again the good man spat.

"I do not say 'Sit down, crow' for thou art already sitting," put in a huge, powerful-looking man, arrayed in a conical puggri-encircled cap, long pink shirt over very baggy peg-top trousers, and a green waistcoat, "but I weary of thy chatter Blind-Man. Keep thy babble for fools in the market-place, where, I admit, it hath its uses. Remain our valued and respected talker and interfere not with fighting men, nor criticize. And say not 'The treasure will be removed this night,' nor anything else concerning command. *I* will decide in the matter of the treasure and I prefer to keep it here under mine hand...."

"Doubtless," sneered the blind man. "Under thy hand-until, in the end, it be found to consist of boxes of stones and old iron. Look you-the treasure goes to-night or *I* go, and certain others go with me. And suppose I change my tune in the market-place, Havildar Nazir Ali Khan, and say certain words concerning *thee* and thy designs, give hints of treachery-and where is the loud-mouthed Nazir Ali Khan?..." and his blind eyes glared cold ferocity at the last speaker who handled his sword and replied nothing.

The secret of the man's power was clear.

"The treasure will be removed to night," he repeated and a discussion of times, routes, escort and other details followed. A dispute arose between the big man addressed as Havildar Nazir Ali Khan and a squat broad-shouldered Pathan as to the distance and probable time that a convoy, moving at the rate of laden bullock-carts, would take in reaching Pirgunge.

The short thick-set Pathan turned for confirmation of his estimate to another Pathan, grey-eyed but obviously a Pathan, nevertheless.

"I say it is five *kos* and the carts should start at moonrise and arrive before the moon sets."

"You are right, brother," replied the grey-eyed Pathan, who, for his own reasons, particularly desired that the convoy should move by moonlight. This individual had not spoken hitherto in the hearing of the blind faquir, and, as he did so now, the blind man turned sharply in his direction, a look of startled surprise and wonder on his face.

"Who spoke?" he snapped.

But the grey-eyed man arose, yawned hugely, and, arranging his puggri and straightening his attire, swaggered towards the door of the room, passed out into a high-walled courtyard, exchanged a few words with the guardian of a low gateway, and emerged into a narrow alley where he was joined by an African-looking camel-man.

The blind man, listening intently, sat motionless for a minute and then again asked sharply: —

"Who spoke? Who spoke?"

"Many have spoken Pir Saheb," replied the squat Pathan.

"Who said '*You are right, brother,*' but now? Who? Quick!" he cried.

"Who? Why, 'twas one of us," replied the squat Pathan. "Yea, 'twas Abdulali Habbibullah, the money-lender. I have known him long...."

"Let him speak again," said the blind man.

"Where is he? He has gone out, I think," answered the other.

"Call him back, Hidayetullah. Take others and bring him back. I must hear his voice again," urged the faquir.

"He will come again, Moulvie Saheb, he is often here," said the short man soothingly. "I know him well. He will be here to-morrow."

"See, Hidayetullah," said the blind faquir "when next he comes, say then to me, 'May I bring thee tobacco, Pir Saheb,' if he be sitting near, but say 'May I bring thee tobacco, Moulvie Saheb,' if he be sitting afar off. If this, speak to him across the room that I may hear his voice in answer, and call him by his name, Abdulali Habbibullah. And if I should, on a sudden, cry out 'Hold the door,' do thou draw knife and leap to the door...."

"A *spy*, Pir Saheb?" asked the interested man.

"That I shall know when next I hear his voice-and, if it be he whom I think, thou shalt scrape the flesh from the bones of his face with thy knife and put his eyeballs in his mouth. But he must not die. Nay! Nay!"

The Pathan smiled.

"Thou shalt hear his voice, Pir Saheb," he promised.

* * *

An hour later the African-looking camel-man and the Pathan approached the gates of the Military Prison and at a distance of a couple of hundred yards the African imitated the cry of a jackal, the barking of a dog and the call of the "Did-ye-do-it" bird.

Approaching the gate he whispered a countersign and was admitted, the gate being then held open for the Pathan who followed him at a distance of a hundred yards. Entering Colonel Ross-Ellison's room the Pathan quickly metamorphosed himself into Colonel Ross-Ellison, and sent for his Adjutant, Captain Malet-Marsac.

"Fifty of the best, with fifty rounds each, to parade at the gate in half an hour," he said. "Bruce to accompany me, you to remain in command here. All who can, to wear rubber-soled shoes, others to go barefoot or bandage their boots with putties over cardboard or paper. No man likely to cough or sneeze is to go. Luminous-paint discs to be served out to half a dozen. No rations, no water,—just shirts, shorts and bandoliers. Nothing white or light-coloured to be worn. Put a strong outpost, all European, under Corporal Faggit on the hill, and double all guards and sentries. Shove sentry-groups at the top of the Sudder Bazaar, West Street and Edward Road.—*You* know all about it.... I've got a good thing on. There'll be a lot of death about to-night, if all goes well."

Half an hour later Captain Bruce called his company of fifty picked men to "attention" as Colonel Ross-Ellison approached, the gate was opened and an advance-guard of four men, with four flankers, marched out and down the road leading to the open country. Two of these wore each a large tin disc painted with luminous paint fastened to his back. When these discs were only just visible from the gate a couple more disc-adorned men started forth, and before their discs faded into the darkness the remainder of the party "formed fours" and marched after them, all save a section of fours which followed a couple of hundred yards in the rear, as a rear-guard. In silence the small force advanced for an hour, passed some cross-roads, and then Colonel Ross-Ellison, who had joined the advance-guard, signalled a halt and moved away by himself to the right of the road.

In the shadow of the trees, the moon having risen, Captain Bruce ordered his men to lie down, announcing in a whisper that he would have the life of anyone who made a sound or struck a match. This was known to be but half in jest, for the Captain was a good disciplinarian and a man of his word.

Save for the occasional distant bark of the village-dogs, the night was very still. Sitting staring out into the moon-lit hazy dusk in the direction in which his chief had disappeared, Captain John Bruce wondered if he were really one of a band of armed men who hoped shortly to pour some two and a half thousand bullets into other men, really a soldier fighting and working and starving that the Flag might fly, really a primitive fighting-man with much blood upon his hands and an earnest desire for more-or whether he were not a respectable Professor who would shortly wake, beneath mosquito-curtains, from a very dreadful dream. How thin a veneer was this thing called Civilization, and how unchanged was human nature after centuries and centuries of— —

363

Colonel Ross-Ellison appeared.

"Bring twenty-five men and follow me. Hurry up," he said quietly, and, a minute later, led the way from the high-road across country. Five minutes marching brought the party, advancing in file, to the mouth of a nullah which ran parallel with the road. Along this, Colonel Ross-Ellison led them, and, when he gave the signal to halt, it was seen that they were behind a high sloping bank within fifty yards of the high-road.

"Now," said the Colonel to Captain John Bruce, "I'm going to leave you here. Let your men lie below the top of the bank and if any man looks over, till your command 'Up and fire,' kick his face in. You will peep through that bit of bush and no one else will move. Do nothing until I open fire from the other side. The moment I open fire, up your lot come and do the same. Magazine, of course. The moon will improve as it rises more. You'll fix bayonets and charge magazines now. I expect a pretty big convoy-and before very long. Probably a mob all round a couple of *bylegharies*[136] and a crowd following-everybody distrusting every one, as it is treasure, looted from all round. Don't shoot the bullocks, but I particularly want to kill a blind bloke who may be with 'em, so if we charge, barge in too, and look out for a blinder and don't give him any quarter-give him half instead-half your sword. He's a ringleader-and I want him for auld lang syne too, as it happens. He doesn't look blind at all, but he would be led.... Any questions?"

"No, Sir. I'm to hide till you fire. Then fire, magazine, and charge if you do. A blind man to be captured if possible. The bullocks not to be shot, if possible."

"Eight O. Carry on," and the Colonel strode back to where the remaining twenty-five waited, under a Sergeant. These he placed behind an old stone wall that marked the boundary of a once-cultivated patch of land, some forty yards from the road, to which the ground sloped sharply downwards.

A nice trap if all went well.

All went exceeding well.

Within an hour and a half of the establishment of the ambush, the creaking of ungreased wheels was heard and the loud nasal singing of some jovial soul. Down the silent deserted road came three bullock-carts piled high with boxes and escorted by a ragged regiment of ex-sepoys, ex-police, mutineers, almost a battalion from the forces of the wild Border State neighbouring Gungapur. A small crowd of variously armed uniformless men preceded the escort and carts, while a large one followed them.

No advance-guard nor flanking-parties guaranteed the force from ambush or attack.

Suddenly, as the carts crossed a long culvert and the escort perforce massed on to the road, instead of straggling on either side beneath the trees, a voice said coolly in English "Up and fire," and as scores of surprised faces turned in the direction of the voice the night was rent with the crash of fifty rifles pouring in magazine fire at the rate of fifteen rounds a minute. Magazine fire at less than fifty yards, into a close-packed body of men. Scarcely a hundred shots were returned and, by the time a couple of thousand rounds had been fired (less than three minutes), and Colonel Boss-Ellison had cried "Ch-a-a-a-r-ge" there was but little to charge and not much for the bayonet to do. Of the six bullocks four were uninjured.

"Load as many boxes as you can on two carts, and leave half a dozen men to bring them in. They'll have to take their chance. We must get back *ek dum*,"[137] said Colonel Ross-Ellison.

Even as he spoke, the sound of distant firing fell upon the ears of the party and the unmistakable stammer-hammer racket of the maxim.

"They're attacked, by Jove," he cried. "I thought it likely. There may have been an idea that we should know something of this convoy and go for it. All ready? Now a steady double. We'll double and quick-march alternately. Double *march*."

* * *

Near the Military Prison was a low conical hill, bare of vegetation and buildings, a feature of the situation which was a constant source of anxiety to Colonel Ross-Ellison, for he realized that life in the beleaguered fortress would be very much harder, and the casualty rate very much higher, if the enemy had the sense to occupy it in strength and fire down into the Prison. Against this contingency he always maintained a picket there at night and a special sentry to watch it by day, and he had caused deep trenches to be dug and a covered way made in the Prison compound, so that the fire-swept area could be crossed, when necessary, with the minimum of risk. Until the night of the convoy-sortie, however, the enemy had not had the ordinary common sense to grasp the fact that the hill was the key of the situation and to seize it.

"Bloomin' cold up 'ere, Privit Greens, wot?" observed Corporal Horace Faggit to the famous Mr. Cornelius Gosling-Green, M.P., in kindly and condescending manner, as he placed him back to back with Private Augustus Grobble on the hill-top. "But you'll keep awake all the better for that, me lad.... Now you other four men can go to sleep, see? You'll lie right close up agin the feet o' Privits Greens an' Grabbles, and when they've done their two hours, they'll jes' give two o' you a kick and them two'll rise up an' take their plaices while they goes to sleep. Then them two'll waike 'tother two, see? An' if hannyone approaches, the sentry as is faicin' 'im will 'olleraht 'Alt! 'Oo comes there?' an' if the bloke or blokes say, 'Friend,' then 'e'll say 'Hadvance one an' give the countersign,' and if he can't give no countersign, then blow 'is bleedin' 'ead off, see?... Now *I* shall visit yer from time to time, an' let me find you spry an' smart with yer, '*Alt,*' '*Oo comes there?* see? An' if either sentry sees anythink suspicious down below there-let 'im send the other sentry across fer me over in the picket there, see? 'E'll waike up the others meanwhile an' they'll all watch out till I comes and gives orders, see? An' if you're attacked afore I come, then retire firing. Retire on the picket, see? We won't shoot yer. Don't make a bloomin' blackguard-rush for the picket though. Jest retire one by one firin' steady, see? Now I'm goin' back to the picket. Ow! an' don' fergit the reconnoitrin' patrol. Don' go an' shoot at 'em as they comes back. 'Alt 'em for the countersign as they comes out, and 'alt 'em fer it agin as they comes in, see? Right O. Now you keep yer eyes skinned, Greens and Grobbles."

Private Cornelius Gosling-Green, M.P., had never looked really impressive even on the public platform in over-long frock-coat and turned-down collar. In ill-fitting khaki, ammunition boots, a helmet many sizes too big, and badly-wound putties, he looked an extremely absurd object. Private Augustus Grobble looked a little more convincing, inasmuch as his fattish figure filled his uniform, but the habit of wearing his helmet on the back of his neck and a general congenital unmilitariness of habit and bearing, operated against success.

Two unhappier men rarely stood back to back upon a lonely, windy hill-top. Both were very hungry, very sleepy and very cold, both were essentially men of peace, and both had powerful imaginations-especially of horrors happening to their cherished selves.

Both were dealers in words; neither was conversant with things, facts, deeds, and all that lay outside their inexpressibly artificial and specialized little spheres. Each had been "educated" out of physical manliness, self-reliance, courage, practical usefulness, adaptability, "grit" and the plain virile virtues.

Cornelius burned with a peevish indignation that he, writer of innumerable pamphlets, speaker at innumerable meetings, organizer of innumerable societies, compiler of innumerable statistics, author of innumerable letters to the press, he, husband of the famous suffragist worker, speaker, organizer and leader, Superiora Gosling-Green (a Pounding-Pobble of the Pounding-Pobbles of Putney), that he, Cornelius Gosling-Green, Esq., M.P., should be stuck there like a common soldier, with a heavy and dangerous gun and a nasty sharp-pointed bayonet, to stand and shiver while others slept. To stand, too, in a horribly dangerous situation... he had a good mind to resign in protest, to take his stand upon his inalienable rights as a free Englishman. Who should dare to coerce a Gosling-Green, Member of Parliament, of the Fabian Society, and a hundred other "bodies". His Superiora did all the coercing he wanted and more too. He would enter a formal protest and tender his resignation. He had always, hitherto, been able to protest and resign when things did not go as he wished.

He yawned, and again.

"I can see as well sitting or kneeling as I can standing," he remarked to Private Augustus Grobble.

"It is a great physiological truth," replied Augustus, and they both sat down, leaning against each other for warmth and support, back to back.

The soul of Augustus was filled with a melancholy sadness and a gentle woe. To think that he, the loved of many beautiful Wimmin should be suffering such hardships and running such risks. How his face was falling in and how the wrinkles were gathering round his eyes. Some of the beautiful and frail, of whom he thought when he gave his usual toast after dinner, "To the Wimmin who have loved me," would hardly recognize the fair boy over whom they had raved, whose poems they had loved, whose hair, finger-nails, eyes, ties, socks and teeth they had complimented.. A cruel, cruel waste. But how rather romantic-the war-worn soldier! He who knew his Piccadilly, Night Clubs, the theatres, the haunts of fair women and brave men, standing, no-sitting, on a lonely hill-top watching, watching, the lives of the garrison in his hands.... He would return to those haunts, bronzed, lined, hardened-the man from the edge of the Empire, from the back of Beyond, the man who had Done Things-and talk of camp-fires, the trek, the Old Trail, smells of sea and desert and jungle, and the man-stifled town,... battle,... brave deeds... unrecognized heroism... a medal... perhaps the... and the nodding head of Augustus settled upon his chest.

His deep breathing and occasional snores did not attract the attention of Private Gosling-Green, as Private Gosling-Green was sound asleep. Nor did they awaken the weary four who made up the sentry group-Edward Jones, educationist; Henry Grigg, barber; Walter Smith, shopman; Reginald Ladon Gurr, Head of a Department-and whose right it was to sleep so long as two of the six watched.

* * *

"Let there be no mistake then," said the burly Havildar Nazir Ali Khan to one Hidayetulla, squat thick-set Pathan, "at the first shot from the hill your party, ceasing to crawl, will rush upon the picket, and mine will swoop upon the gate bearing the tins of kerosene oil, the faggots and the brushwood. All those with guns will fire at the walls save the Border State company who will reserve their fire till the gate is opened or burnt down. The dogs within must either open it to extinguish the fire, or it must burn. On their volley, all others will charge for the gate with knife and sword. Do thou win the hill-top and keep up a heavy fire into the Prison. There will be Lee-Metford rifles and ammunition there ready for thy taking-ha-ha!"

"And if we are seen and fired on as we stalk the picket on the hill?"

"Then their first shot will, as I said, be the signal for your rush and ours. Understandest thou?"

"I understand. 'Tis a good plan of the blind Moulvie's."

"Aye! He can *plan*,—and talk. We can go and be shot, and be blamed if his plans miscarry," grumbled the big man, and added, "How many have you?"

"About forty," was the reply, "and all Khost men save seven, of whom four are Afghans of Cabul, two are Punjabis, and one a Sikh."

"Is it three hours since the treasure started? That was the time the Moulvie fixed for the attack."

"It must be, perhaps," replied the other. "Let us begin. But what if the hill be not held, or if we capture it with the knife, none firing a shot?"

"Then get into good position, make little sungars where necessary, and, all being ready, open fire into the Prison compound.... At the first shot-whatever be thy luck-we shall rush in our thousands down the Sudder Bazaar, West Street and Edward Street, and do as planned. Are thy forty beneath the trees beyond the hill?"

"They are. I join them now," and the squat broad-shouldered figure rolled away with swinging, swaggering gait.

Suddenly Private Augustus Grobble started from deep sleep to acutest wide-eyed consciousness and was aware of a man's face peering over a boulder not twenty yards from him —a hideous hairy face, surmounted by a close-fitting skull-cap that shone greasy in the moonlight. The blood of Augustus froze in his veins, he held his breath, his heart shook his body, his tongue withered and dried. He closed his eyes as a wave of faintness swept over him, and, as he opened them again, he saw that the man was crawling towards him, and that between his teeth was a huge knife. The terrible Pathan, the cruel dreadful stalker, the slashing disemboweller was upon him! —and with a mighty effort he sprang to his feet and fled for his life down the hill in the direction of the Prison. His sudden movements awoke Private Green, who, in one scared glance, saw a number of terrible forms arising from behind boulders and rushing silently and swiftly towards him and his flying comrade. Leaping up he fled after Grabble, running as he had never run before, and, even as he leapt clear of the sleeping group, the wave of Pathans broke upon it and with slash and stab assured it sound sleep for ever, all save Edward Jones, who, badly wounded as he was, survived (to the later undoing of Moussa Isa, murderer of a Brahmin boy).

Of the four Pathans who had surprised the sentry group, one, with a passing slash that rearranged the face of Reginald Ladon Gurr, sped on after the flying sentries. But that the man was short and stout of build and that the fugitives had a down-hill start, both would have died that night. As it was, within ten seconds, a tremendous sweep of the heavy blade of the long Khyber knife caused Private Gosling-Green to lose his head completely and for the last time. Augustus Grobble, favoured of fortune for the moment, took flying leaps that would have been impossible to him under other circumstances, bounded and ran unstumbling, gained the shadow of the avenue of trees, and with bursting breast sped down the road, reached the gate, shouted the countersign with his remaining breath, and was dragged inside by Captain Michael Malet-Marsac.

"Well?" inquired he coldly of the gasping terrified wretch.

When he could do so, Augustus sobbed out his tale.

"Bugler, sound the alarm!" said the officer. "Sergeant of the Guard put this man in the guard-room and keep him under arrest until he is sent for," and, night-glasses in hand, he climbed one of the ladders leading to the platform erected a few feet below the top of the well-loopholed wall, just as a shot was fired and followed by others in rapid succession on the hill whence Grobble had fled.

The shot was fired by Corporal Horace Faggit and so were the next four as he rapidly emptied his magazine at the swiftly charging Pathans who rose out of the earth on his first shot at the man he had seen wriggling to the cover of a stone. As he fired and shouted, the picket-sentry did the same, and, within a minute of Horace's first shot, ten rifles were levelled at the spot where the rushing silent fiends had disappeared. Within thirty yards of them were at least half a dozen men-and not a glimpse of one to be seen.

"I got one, fer keeps, any'ow," said Horace in the silence that followed the brief racket; "I see 'im drop 'is knife an' fall back'ards...."

Perfect silence-and then...*bang*...and a man standing beside
Horace grunted, coughed, and scuffled on the ground.

"Get down! Get down! You fools," cried Horace, who was himself standing up. "Wha's the good of a square sungar if you stands up in it? All magazines charged? It's magazine-fire if there's a rush."....

Silence.

"Fire at the next flash, all of yer," he said, "an' look out fer a rush." Adding, "Bli' me —'ark at 'em dahn below," as a burst of fire and a pandemonium of yells broke out.

A yellow glare lit the scene, flickered on the sky, and even gave sufficient light to the picket on the hill-top to see a wave of wild, white-clad, knife-brandishing figures surge over the edge of the hill and bear down upon them, to be joined, as they passed, by those who had sunk behind stones at the picket's first fire.

"Stiddy," shrilled Horace. "Aim stiddy at the b——s. *Fire*," and again the charging line vanished.

"Gone to earf," observed Horace in the silence. "Nah look aht for flashes an' shoot at 'em...."

Bang! and Horace lost a thumb and a portion of his left cheek, which was in line with his left thumb as he sighted his rifle.

Before putting his left hand into his mouth he said, a little unsteadily: —

"If I'm knocked aht you go on shootin' at flashes and do magazine-fire fer rushes. If they gets in 'ere, we're tripe in two ticks."

Then he fainted for a while, came to, and felt much better. "Goo' job it's the left fumb," he observed as he strove to re-charge his magazine. The dull thud of bullet into flesh became a frequent sound. The last observation that Horace made to the remnant of his men was: —

"Bli' me! they're all rahnd us now-like flies rahnd a fish-barrer. Dam' swine!..."

* * *

Firing steadily at the advancing mobs the street-end pickets retired on the Prison and were admitted as the surging crowds amalgamated, surrounded the walls, and opened a desultory fire at the loopholes and such of the defenders as fired over the coping from ladders.

One detachment, with some show of military discipline and uniform, arrayed itself opposite the gate and a couple of hundred yards from it, lining the ditch of the road, and utilizing the cover and shadow of the trees. Suddenly a large party, mainly composed of Mahsuds, and headed by a very big powerful man, made a swift rush to the gate, each man bearing a bundle of faggots or a load of cut brushwood, save two or three who bore vessels of kerosene oil. With reckless courage and daring, they ran the gauntlet of the loopholes and the fire from the wall-top, piled their combustibles against the wooden gate, poured gallons of kerosene over the heap, set fire to it, and fled.

The leaping flames spread and shot forth licking tongues and, in a few minutes, the pile was a roaring crackling furnace.

The mob grew denser and denser toward the gate side of the Prison, leaving the remaining portions of the perimeter thinly surrounded by those who possessed firearms and had been instructed to shoot at loopholes and at all who showed themselves over the wall. It was noticeable to Captain Malet-Marsac that the ever-increasing mob opposite the fire left a clear front to the more-or-less uniformed and disciplined body that had taken up a position commanding the gate.

That was the game was it? Burn down the gate, pour in a tremendous fire as the gate fell, and then let the mob rush in and do its devilmost....

What was happening on the hill-top? The picket must be holding whatever force had attacked it, for no shots were entering the Prison compound and the only casualties were among those at the loopholes and on the ladders and platforms round the walls. How long would the gate last? Absolutely useless to attempt to pour water on the fire. Even if it were not certain death to attempt it, one might as well try to fly, as to quench that furnace with jugs and *chatties*[138] of water.

There was nothing to be done. Every man who could use a rifle was at loophole or embrasure, ammunition was plentiful, all non-combatants were hidden. Every one understood the standing-orders in case of such an emergency....

The gate was on fire. It was smoking on the inner side, warping, cracking, little flames were beginning to appear tentatively, and disappear again.

"*Now* bugler!" said Captain Malet-Marsac, and Moussa Isa's *locum tenens* blew his only call — a series of long loud G's.... The gate blazed, before long it would fall.... A hush fell upon the expectant multitude without, the men of the more-or-less uniformed and disciplined party raised their rifles, a big burly man bawled orders....

With a crash and leaping fountain of sparks the gate fell into the dying fire, a mighty roar burst from the multitude, and a crashing fusillade from the rifles of the uniformed men....

As their magazine-fire slackened, dwindled to a desultory popping, and ceased, the mob with a howl of triumph surged forward to the gaping gateway, trampled and scattered the glowing remnants of the fire, swarmed yelling through, and-found themselves face to face with a stout semicircular rampart of stone, earth and sandbags, which, loopholed, embrasured and strongly manned, spanned the gateway in a thirty-yard arc. From the centre of it, pointing at the entrance, looked the maxim gun.

"*Fire*," shouted a voice, and in a minute the place was a shambles. Before Maxim and Lee-Metford were too hot to touch, before the baffled foe fell back, those who surged in through the gate climbed, not over a wall of dead, but up on to a platform of dead, a plateau through which ran a valley literally blasted out by the ceaseless maxim-fire....

And, as the less fanatical, less courageous, less bloodthirsty withdrew and gathered without and to one side, where they were safe from that terrible fire-belching rampart that was itself like the muzzle of some gigantic thousand-barrelled machine-gun, they were aware, in their rear, of a steady tramp of running feet and of the orders:—

"From the centre *extend*! At the enemy in front; fixed sights; *fire*," and of a withering hail of bullets.

Colonel Ross-Ellison had arrived in the nick of time. It was a "crowning mercy" indeed, the beginning of the end, and when (a few days later), over a repaired bridge, came a troop-train, gingerly advancing, the battalion of British troops that it disgorged at Gungapur Road Station found disappointingly little to do in a city of women, children, and eminently respectable innocent, householders.

* * *

On the hill-top, at dawn, Colonel Ross-Ellison and Captain Malet-Marsac found all that was left of the picket and sentry-group, —of the latter, three mangled corpses, the headless deserter, and a just-living man, horribly slashed. It was Moussa Isa Somali who improvised a stretcher and lifted this poor fellow on to it and tended him with the greatest solicitude and faithful care. Was he not Jones Sahib who at Duri gave him the knife wherewith he cleansed his honour and avenged his insulted People?

Of the picket, nine lay dead and one dying. Of the dead, one had his lower jaw neatly and cleanly removed by a bullet. Two had bled to death.

"'Ullo, Guvner!" whispered Corporal Horace Faggit through parched cracked lips. "We kep' 'em orf. We 'eld the bleedin' fort," and the last effect of the departing mind upon the shot-torn, knife-slashed body was manifested in a gasping, quavering wail of—

"'Owld the Fort fer Hi am comin'"

Jesus whispers still.

"'Owld the Fort fer Hi am comin,'"

—By Thy graice we will.

Each of these corpses Moussa Isa carried reverently down to the Prison that they might be "buried darkly at dead of night" with the other heroes, in softer ground without the walls —a curious funeral in which loaded rifles and belted maxim played their silent part. Apart from the honoured dead was buried the body of Private Augustus Grabble, shot against the Prison wall by order of Colonel Ross-Ellison for cowardice in the face of the enemy and desertion of his post. So was that of Private Green, deserter also. After the uninterrupted ceremony, Moussa Isa, in the guise of an ancient beggar, lame, decrepit, and bandaged with foul rags, sought the city and the news of the bazaar.

Limping down the lane in which stood the tall silent house that his master often visited, he saw three men emerge from the well-known low doorway.

Two approached him while one departed in the opposite direction. One of these two held the arm of the other.

"I must hear his voice again. I have not heard his voice again," urged this one insistently to the other.

"Nay-but I have heard thine, thou Dog!" said Moussa Isa to himself, and turning, followed.

In a neighbouring bazaar the man who seemed to lead the other left him at the entrance to a mosque—a dark and greasy entry with a short flight of stone steps.

As he set his foot upon the lowest of these, a hand fell upon the neck of the man who had been led, and a voice hissed:—

"*Salaam! O Ibrahim the Weeper!* Salaam! A '*Hubshi*' would speak with thee...." and another hand joined the first, encircling his throat....

"Art thou dead, Dog?" snarled Moussa Isa, five minutes later....

Moussa Isa never boasted (if he realized the fact) that the collapse of the revolt and mutiny in Gungapur, before the arrival of troops, was due as much to the death of its chief ringleader and director, the blind faquir, as to the disastrous repulse of the great assault upon the Military Prison.

§ 2

It had gone. Nothing remained but to clear up the mess and begin afresh with more wisdom and sounder policy. It was over, and, among other things now possible, Colonel John Robin Ross-Ellison might ask the woman he loved whether she could some day become his wife. He had saved her life, watched over her, served her with mind and body, lived for her. And she had smiled upon him, looked at him as a woman looks at the man she more than likes, had given him the encouragement of her smiles, her trust, affectionate greeting on return from danger, prayers that he would be "careful" when he went forth to danger.

He believed that she loved him, and would, after a decent interval, even perhaps a year hence, marry him.

And then he would abandon the old life and ways, become wholly English and settle down to make her life a happy walk through an enchanted valley. He would take her to England and there, far from all sights, sounds and smells of the East, far from everything wild, turbulent, violent, crush out all the Pathan instincts so terribly aroused and developed during the late glorious time of War. He would take himself cruelly in hand. He would neither hunt nor shoot. He would eat no meat, drink no alcohol, nor seek excitement. He would school himself until he was a quiet, domesticated English country-gentleman —respectable and respected, fit husband for a delicately-bred English gentlewoman. And if ever his hand itched for the knife-hilt, his finger for the trigger, his cheek for the rifle-butt, his nostrils for the smell of the cooking-fires, his soul for the wild mountain passes, the mad gallop, the stealthy stalk-he would live on cold water until the Old Adam were drowned.

He *would* be worthy of her-and she should never dream what blood was on his hands, what sights he had looked on, what deeds he had done, what part he had played in wild undertakings in wild places. English would he be to the back-bone, to the finger tips, to the marrow; a quiet, clean, straight-dealing Englishman of normal tastes, habits, and life.

Strange if, with all his love of fighting, he could not fight (and conquer) himself. Yes-his last great fight should be with himself.... He would call, to-day, at the bungalow to which Mrs. Dearman, prior to starting for Home, had removed as soon as the carefully-guarded Cantonment area was pronounced absolutely safe as a place of residence for the refugees who had been besieged in the old Military Prison.

She would be sufficiently "straight" in her bungalow, by this time, to permit of a formal mid-day call being a reasonable and normal affair....

"Good-morning, Preserver of Gungapur," said Mrs. Dearman brightly; "have the Victoria Cross and the Distinguished Service Order materialized yet-or don't they give them to Volunteers? What a shame if they don't!"

"I want something far more valuable and desirable than those, Mrs. Dearman," said Colonel Ross-Ellison as he took the extended hand of his hostess, who was a picture of coolness and health.

"Oh? —and-what is that?" she asked, seating herself on a big settee with her back to the light.

"You," was the direct and uncompromising reply of the man who had been leading a remarkably direct and uncompromising life for several years.

Mrs. Dearman trembled, flushed and paled.

"What *do* you mean?" she managed to say, with a fine affectation of coolness, unconcern, and indifference.

"I mean what I say," was the answer. "I want *you*. I cannot live without you. I want to take care of you. I want to devote my life to making you happy. I want to make you forget this terrible experience and tragedy. You are lonely and I worship you. I want you to marry me-when you can-later-and let me serve you for the rest of my life. Make me the happiest and proudest man in the world and I will strive to be the noblest."

He was very English then-in his fine passion. He took her hand and it was not withdrawn. He bent to look in her eyes, she smiled, and in a second was in his embrace, strained to his breast, her lips crushed by his.

For a minute he could not speak.

"I cannot believe it," he whispered at length. "Is this a dream?"

"You are a very concrete dream-dear," said Mrs. Dearman, re-arranging crushed and disarranged flowers at her breast, blushing and laughing shyly.

The man was filled with awe, reverence and a deep longing for worthiness.

The woman felt happy in the sense of safety, of power, of pride in the love of so fine a being.

"And how long have you loved me?" she murmured.

"Loved you, Cleopatra? Dearest —I have loved you from the moment my eyes first fell on you.... Poor salt-encrusted, weary, bloodshot eyes they were too," he added, smiling, reminiscent.

"What do you mean?" asked Mrs. Dearman, puzzled.

"Ah —I have a secret to tell you —a confession that will open those beautiful eyes wide with surprise. I first saw you when you *were* Cleopatra Brighte."

"Good gracious!" ejaculated Mrs. Dearman in great surprise. "When_ever_ when?"

"I'll tell you," said the man, smiling fondly. "You have my photograph. You took it yourself-on board the 'Malaya'."

"I?" said Mrs. Dearman. "What *are* you talking about?"

"About you, dearest, and the time when I first saw you-and fell in love with you; —love at first sight, indeed."

"But I never photographed you on board ship. I never saw you on a ship. I met you first here in Gungapur."

"Do you remember the 'Malaya' stopping to pick up a shipwrecked sailor, a castaway, in a little dug-out canoe, somewhere in the Indian Ocean, when you were first coming out to India? But of course you do-you have the snap-shot in your collection...."

"Why-yes —I remember, of course-but that was a horrid, beastly *native*. The creature could only speak Hindustani. He was the sole survivor of the crew of some dhow or bunder-boat, they said.... He lived and worked with the Lascars till we got to Bombay. Yes...."

"I was that native," said Colonel Ross-Ellison.

"*You*," whispered Mrs. Dearman. "*You*," and scanned his face intently.

"Yes. I. I *am* half a native. My father was a Pathan. He ——"

"*What?*" asked the woman hoarsely, drawing away. "*What? What* are you saying?"

"I am half Pathan-my father was a Pathan and my mother an Australian squatter's daughter."

"*Go*," shrieked Mrs. Dearman, springing to her feet. "*Go.* You wretch! You mean, base liar! To cheat me so! To pretend you were a gentleman. Leave my house! Go! You horrible —*mongrel* —you——. To take me in your arms! To make love to me! To kiss me! Ugh! I could die for shame! I could *die* ——"

The face of the man grew terrible to see. There was no trace of the West in it, no sign of English ancestry, the face of a mad, blood-mad Afghan.

"*We will both die*," he gasped, and took her by the throat.

* * *

A few minutes later a Pathan in the dirty dress of his race fled from Colonel Ross-Ellison's bungalow in Cantonments and took the road to the city.

Threading his way through its tortuous lanes, alleys, slums and bazaars he reached a low door in the high wall that surrounded an almost windowless house, knocked in a particular manner, parleyed, and was admitted.

The moment he was inside, the custodian of the door slammed, locked and bolted it, and then raised an outcry.

"Come," he shouted in Pushtoo. "The Spy! The Feringhi! The Pushtoo-knowing English dog, that Abdulali Habbibullah," and he drew his Khyber knife and circled round Ross-Ellison.

A clatter of heavy boots, the opening of wooden "windows" that looked inward on to the high-walled courtyard, and in a minute a throng of Pathans and other Mussulmans entered the compound from the house-some obviously aroused from heavy slumber.

"It is he," cried one, a squat, broad-shouldered fellow, as they stood at gaze, and long knives flashed.

"Oho, Spy! Aha, Dog! For what hast thou come?" asked one burly fellow as he advanced warily upon the intruder, who backed slowly to the angle of the high walls.

"To die, Hidayetullah. To die, Nazir Ali Khan. To die slaying! Come on!" was the reply, and in one moment the speaker's Khyber knife flashed from his loose sleeve into the throat of the nearest foe.

As he withdrew it, the door-keeper slashed at his abdomen, missed by a hair's-breadth, raised his arm to save his neck from a slash, and was stabbed to the heart, the knife held dagger-wise. Another Pathan rushing forward, with uplifted knife held as a sword, was met by a sudden low fencing-lunge and fell with a hideous wound, and then, whirling his weapon like a claymore in an invisibly rapid Maltese cross of flashing steel, the man who had been Ross-Ellison drove his enemies before him, whirled about, and established himself in the opposite corner, and spat pungent Border taunts at the infuriated crowd.

"Come on, you village curs, you landless cripples, you wifeless sons of burnt fathers! Come on! Strike for the credit of your noseless mothers! Run not from me as your wives ran from you-to better men! Come on, you sweepers, you swine-herds, you down-country street-scrapers!" and they came on to heart's content, steel clashed on steel and thudded on flesh and bone.

"Get a rifle," cried one, lying bleeding on the ground, striving to rise while he held his right shoulder to his neck with his partly severed left hand. As he fainted the shoulder gaped horribly.

"Get a cannon," mocked Ross-Ellison. "Get a cannon, dogs, against one man," and again, whirling the great jade-handled knife, long as a short sword, he rushed forward and the little mob gave ground before the irresistible claymore-whirl, the unbreakable Maltese cross described by the razor-edge and needle-point.

"It is a devil," groaned a man, as his knife and his hand fell together to the ground, and he clapped his turban on the stump as a boy claps his hat upon some small creature that he would capture.

The madman whirled about in the third corner and, as he ceased the wild whirl, ducked low and lunged, lessening the number of his enemies by one. This lunge was a new thing to men who could only slash and stab, a new thing and a terrible, for it could not be parried save by seizing the blade and losing half a hand.

"Come on, you growing maidens! Come on, grandmothers! Come on, you cleaners of pig-skins, you washers of dogs! Come on!" and as he shouted, the door crashed down and a patrol of British soldiers, attracted by the noise, and delayed by the stout door, burst into the courtyard.

"At the henemy in front, fixed sights," shouted the corporal in charge. And added an order not to be found in the drill-book: "Blow 'em to 'ell if they budges."

In the hush of surprise his voice arose, addressing the fighters: "*Bus*[139] you bleedin' soors,[140]" said Corporal Cook. "*Bus*; and you *dekho*[141] 'ere. If any of you *jaos*[142] from where 'e is, I'll *pukkaro*[143] 'im and give 'im a punch in the *dekho*."

And, as bayonets rose breast-high and fingers curled lovingly round triggers, every knife but that of Ross-Ellison disappeared as by magic, and the Corporal beheld a little crowd of innocent men endeavouring to secure a dangerous lunatic at the risk of their lives-terrible risk, as the bodies of five dead and dying men might testify.

"I give myself up to you as a murderer, Corporal," said he who had been Colonel John Robin Ross-Ellison. "I am a murderer. If you will take me before your officer I will confess and give details."

"I'm agoin' to take you bloomin' well all," replied the surprised Corporal. "Chuck down that there beastly carvin' knife. You seem a too 'andy cove wiv' it."

At the Corporal's order of, "Prod 'em all up agin that wall and shoot any bloke as moves 'and or 'oof," the party of panting, bleeding and perspiring ruffians was lined up, relieved of its weapons, and duly marched to the guard-room.

Here, one of the gang (later identified as the man who had been known as John Robin Ross-Ellison, and who insisted that he was a Baluchi) declared that he had just murdered Mrs. Dearman in her drawing-room and made a full statement—a statement found to be only too true, its details corroborated by a trembling *hamal* who had peeped and listened, as all Indian servants peep and listen.

* * *

Duly tried, all members of the gang received terms of imprisonment (largely a prophylactic measure), save the extraordinary English-speaking Baluchi, who had long imposed, it was said, upon Gungapur Society in the days before that Society had disappeared in the cataclysm.

A few days before the date fixed for the execution of this very remarkable desperado, Captain Michael Malet-Marsac, Adjutant of the Gungapur Volunteer Corps, received two letters dated from Gungapur Jail, one covering the other. The covering letter ran:—

"My Dear Malet-Marsac,

"I forward the enclosed. Should you desire to attend the execution you could accompany the new City Magistrate, Wellson, who will doubtless be agreeable.

"Yours sincerely,

"A. RANALD, Major I.M.S."

The accompaniment was from John Robin Ross-Ellison Mir Ilderim Dost Mahommed Mir Hafiz Ullah Khan.

"My Dear Old Friend,

"For the credit of the British I am pretending to be a Baluchi. I am not a Baluchi and I hope to die like a Briton-at any rate like a man. I have been held responsible for what I did when I was not responsible, and shall be killed in cold blood by sane people, for what I did in hot blood when quite as mad as any madman who ever lived. I don't complain—I _ex_plain. I want you to understand, if you can, that it was not your friend John Ross-Ellison who did that awful deed. It was a Pathan named Ilderim Dost Mahommed. And yet it was I." ["Poor chap is mad!" murmured the bewildered and horrified reader who had lived in a kind of nightmare since the woman he loved had been murdered by the man he loved. "The strain of the war has been too much for him. He must have had sunstroke too." He read on, with misty sight.]

"And it is I who will pay the penalty of Ilderim Dost Mahommed's deed. As I say, I do not complain, and if the Law did not kill me I would certainly kill myself-to get rid of Ilderim Dost Mahommed.

"I have thought of doing so and cheating the scaffold, but have decided that Ilderim will get his deserts better if I hang, and I may perhaps get rid of him, thus, for ever.

"Will you come? I would not ask it of any living soul but you, and I ask it because your presence would show me that you blindly believe that it was not John Robin Ross-Ellison who killed poor Mrs. Dearman, and that would enable me to die quite happy. Your presence would also be a great help to me. It would help me to feel that, whatever I have lived, I die a Briton-that if I could not live without Ilderim Dost Mahommed I can die without him. But this must seem lunatic wanderings to you.

"I apologize for writing to you and I hesitated long. At length I said, 'I will tell him the truth-that the deed was not done by Ross-Ellison and perhaps he will understand, and come'. Mike —*John Robin Ross-Ellison did not murder Mrs. Dearman.*

"Your distracted and broken-hearted ex-friend,

"J.R. Ross-Ellison"

"He *was* 'queer' at times," said Captain Michael Malet-Marsac. "There was a kink somewhere. The bravest, coolest, keenest chap I ever met, the finest fighting-man, the truest comrade and friend, —and from time to time something queer peeped out, and one was puzzled.... Madness in the family, I suppose.... Poor devil, poor, poor devil!" and Captain Malet-Marsac stamped about and swore, for his eyes tingled and his chin quivered.

§ 3

Captain Michael Malet-Marsac alighted from his horse at the great gate of the Gungapur Jail, loosed girths, slid stirrup irons up the leathers to the saddle, and handed his reins to the orderly who had ridden behind him.

"Walk the horses up and down," said he, for both were sweating and the morning was very cold. Perhaps it was the cold that made Captain Michael Malet-Marsac's strong face so white, made his teeth chatter and his hands shake. Perhaps it was the cold that made him feel so sick, and that weakened the tendons of his knees so that he could scarcely stand-and would fain have thrown himself upon the ground.

With a curious coughing sound, as though he swallowed and cleared his throat at the same moment, he commenced to address another order or remark to the mounted sepoy, choked, and turned his back upon him.

Striding to the gate, he struck upon it loudly with his hunting-crop, and turning, waved the waiting orderly away.

Not for a king's ransom could he have spoken at that moment. He realized that something which was rising in his throat must be crushed back and swallowed before speech would be possible. If he tried to speak before that was done-he would shame his manhood, he would do that which was unthinkable in a man and a soldier. What would happen if the little iron wicket in the great iron door in the greater wooden gates opened before he had swallowed the lump in his throat, had crushed down the rising tumult of emotion, and a European official, perhaps Major Ranald himself, spoke to him? He must either refuse to answer, and show himself too overcome for speech-or he must-good God forbid it-burst into tears. He suffered horribly. His skin tingled and he burnt hotly from head to foot.

And then-he swallowed, his will triumphed-and he was again as outwardly self-possessed and nonchalant as he strove to appear.

He might tremble, his face might be blanched and drawn, he might feel physically sick and almost too weak and giddy to stand, but he had swallowed, he had triumphed over the rising flood that had threatened to engulf him, and he was, outwardly, himself again. He could go through with it now, and though his face might be ghastly, his lips white, his hand uncertain, his gait considered and careful, he would be able to chat lightly, to meet Ross-Ellison's jest with jest-for that Ross-Ellison would die jesting he knew....

Why did not the door open? Had his knock gone unheard? Should he knock again, louder? And then his eye fell upon the great iron bell-pull and chain, and he stepped towards it. Of course-one entered a place like this on the sonorous clanging of a deep-throated bell that roused the echoes of the whole vast congeries of buildings encircled by the hideous twelve-foot wall, unbroken save by the great gatehouse before which he stood insignificant. As his shaking hand touched the bell-pull he suddenly remembered, and withdrew it. He was to meet the City Magistrate outside the jail and enter with him. He could gain admittance in no other way.

He looked at his watch. Seventeen minutes to seven. Wellson should be there in a minute-he had said, "At the jail-entrance at 6.45". God send him soon or the new-found self-control might weaken and a rising tide creep up and up until it submerged his will-power again.

With an effort he swallowed, and turning, strode up and down on a rapid, mechanical sentry-go.

A guard of police-sepoys emerged from a neighbouring guard-room and "fell in" under the word of command of an Inspector. They were armed with Martini-Henry rifles and triangular-bladed bayonets, very long. Their faces looked cruel, the stones of the gate-house and main-guard looked cruel, the beautiful misty morning looked cruel.

Would that damned magistrate never come? Didn't he know that Malet-Marsac was fighting for his manhood and terribly afraid? Didn't he know that unless he came quickly Malet-Marsac would either leap on his horse and ride it till it fell, or else lose control inside the jail and either burst into tears, faint, or-going mad-put up a fight for his friend there in the jail itself, snatch weapons, get back to back with him and die fighting then and there-or, later, on the same scaffold? His friend-by whose side he had fought, starved, suffered, triumphed-his poor two-natured friend....

Could not one of these cursed clever physicians, alienists, psychologists, hypnotists-whatever they were-have cut the strange savagery and ferocity out of the splendid John Robin Ross-Ellison?...

A buffalo passed, driven by a barely human lout. The lout was free-the brainless, soulless bovine lout was free in God's beautiful world-and Ross-Ellison, soldier and gentleman, lay in a stone cell, and in quarter of an hour would dangle by the neck in a pit below a platform-perhaps suffering unthinkable agonies-who could tell?... His old friend and commandant —

Would Wellson never come? What kept the fellow? It was disgraceful conduct on the part of a public servant in such circumstances. Think what an eternity of mental suffering each minute must now be to Ross-Ellison! What was he doing? What were they doing to him? *Could* the agony of Ross-Ellison be greater than that of Malet-Marsac? It must be a thousand times greater. How could that tireless activity, that restless initiative, that cool courage, that unfathomable ingenuity be quenched in a second? How could such a wild free nature exist in a cell, submit to pinioning, be quietly led like a sheep to the slaughter? He who so loved the mountain, the wild desert, the ocean, the free wandering life of adventure and exploration.

Would Wellson never come? It must be terribly late. Could they have hanged Ross-Ellison already? Could he have gone to his death thinking his friend had failed him; had passed by, like the Levite, on the other side; had turned up a sanctimonious nose at the letter of the Murderer; had behaved as some "friends" do behave in time of trouble?

Could he have died thinking this? If so, he must now know the truth, if the Parsons were right, those unconvincing very-human Parsons of like passions, and pretence of unlike passions. Could his friend be dead, his friend whom he had so loved and admired? And yet he was a murderer-and he had murdered... *her*....

Captain Michael Malet-Marsac leant against a tree and was violently sick.

Curse the weak frail body that was failing him in his hour of need! It had never failed him in battle nor in athletic struggle. Why should it weaken now. He *would* see his friend, and bear himself as a man, to help him in his dreadful hour.

Would that scoundrel never come? He was the one who should be hanged.

A clatter of hoofs behind, and Malet-Marsac turned to see the City Magistrate trot across the road from the open country. He drew out his watch accusingly and as a torrent of reproach rose to his white parched lips, he saw that the time-was exactly quarter to seven.

"Morning, Marsac," said the City Magistrate as he swung down from the saddle. "You're looking precious blue about the gills."

"Morning, Wellson," replied the other shortly.

To the City Magistrate a hanging was no more than a hair-cut, a neither pleasing nor displeasing interlude, hindering the doing of more strenuous duties; a nuisance, cutting into his early-morning report-writing and other judicial work. He handed his reins to an obsequious sepoy, eased his jodhpores at the knee, and rang the bell.

The grille-cover slid back, a dusky face appeared behind the bars and scrutinized the visitors, the grille was closed again and the tiny door opened. Malet-Marsac stepped in over the foot-high base of the door-way and found himself in a kind of big gloomy strong-room in which were native warders and a jailer with a bunch of huge keys. On either side of the room was an office. Following Wellson to a large desk, on which reposed a huge book, he wrote his name, address, and business, controlling his shaking hand by a powerful effort of will.

This done, and the entrance-door being again locked, bolted, and barred, the jailer led the way to another pair of huge gates opposite the pair through which they had entered, and opened a similar small door therein. Through this Malet-Marsac stepped and found himself, light-dazzled, in the vast enclosure of Gungapur Jail, a small town of horribly-similar low buildings, painfully regular streets, soul-stunning uniformity, and living death.

"'Morning, Malet-Marsac," said Major Ranald of the Indian Medical Service, Superintendent of the jail. "You look a bit blue about the gills, what?"

"'Morning, Ranald," replied Malet-Marsac, "I *am* a little cold."

Was he really speaking? Was that voice his? He supposed so.

Could he pretend to gaze round with an air of intelligent interest? He would try.

A line of convicts, clad in a kind of striped sacking, stood with their backs to a wall while a native warder strode up and down in front of them, watching another convict placing brushes and implements before them. Suddenly the warder spoke to the end man, an elderly stalwart fellow, obviously from the North. The reply was evidently unsatisfactory, perhaps insolent, for the warder suddenly seized the grey beard of the convict, tugged his head violently from side to side, shook him, and then smote him hard on either cheek. The elderly convict gave no sign of having felt either the pain or the indignity, but gazed straight over the warder's head. Of what was he thinking? Of what might be the fate of that warder were he suddenly transported to the wilds of Kathiawar, to lie at the mercy of his late victim and the famous band of outlaws whom he had once led to fame —a fame as wide as Ind?

There was something fine about the old villain, once a real Robin Hood, something mean about the little tyrant.

Had Ranald seen the incident? No, he stood with his back to a buttress looking in the opposite direction. Did he always stand with a wall behind him in this terrible place? How could he live in it? A minute of it made one sick if one were cursed with imagination. Oh, the horror of the prison system-especially for brave men, men with a code of honour of their own-possibly sometimes a higher code than that of the average British politician, not to mention the be-knighted cosmopolitan financier, friend of princes and honoured of kings.

Could not men be segregated in a place of peace and beauty and improved, instead of being segregated in a dull hell and crushed? What a home of soulless, hopeless horror!... And his friend was here.... Could he contain himself?... He must say something.

"Do you always keep your back to a wall when standing still, in here?" he asked of Major Ranald.

"I do," was the reply, "and I walk with a trustworthy man close behind me." "Would you like to go round, sometime?" he added.

"No, thank you," said Malet-Marsac. "I would like to get as far away as possible and stay there."

Major Ranald laughed.

"Wouldn't like to visit the mortuary and see a post-mortem?"

"No, thank you."

"What about the Holy One?" put in the City Magistrate. "Did you 'autopsy' him? A pleasure to hang a chap like him."

"Yes, the brute. I'll show you his neck vertebrae presently if you like. Kept 'em as a curiosity. An absolute break of the bone itself. People talk about pain, strangulation, suffocation and all that. Nothing of the sort. Literally breaks the neck. Not mere separation of the vertebrae you know. I'll show you the vertebra itself-clean broken...."

Captain Malet-Marsac swayed on his feet. What should he do? A blue mist floated before his eyes and a sound of rushing waters filled his ears. Was he fainting? He must *not* faint, and fail his friend. And then, the roar of the waters was pierced and dominated by the voice of that friend saying—

"Hul_lo_! old bird. Awf'ly good of you to turn out, such a beastly cold morning."

John Robin Ross-Ellison had come round an adjacent corner, a European warder on either side of him and another behind him, all three, to their credit, as white as their white uniforms and helmets. On his head was a curious bag-like cap.

Ross-Ellison appeared perfectly cheerful, absolutely natural, and without the slightest outward and visible sign of any form of perturbation.

"'Morning, Ranald," he continued. "Sorry to be the cause of turning you out in the cold. Gad! *isn't* it parky. Hope you aren't going to keep me standing. If I might be allowed I'd quote unto you the words which a pretty American girl once used when I asked if I might kiss her —'*Wade right in, Bub!*'"

"'Fraid I can't 'wade in' till seven o'clock-er-Ross-Ellison," answered the horribly embarrassed Major Ranald. "It won't be long."

"Right O, I was only thinking of your convenience. *I'm* all right," said the remarkable criminal, about to suffer by the Mosaic law at the hands of Christians, to receive Old Testament mercy from the disciples of the New, to be done-by as he had done.

An Indian clerk, salaaming, joined the group, and prepared to read from an official-looking document.

"Read," said Major Ranald, and the clerk in a high sing-song voice, regardless of punctuation, read out the charge, conviction and death-warrant of the man formerly calling himself John Robin Ross-Ellison, and now professing and confessing himself to be a Baluchi. Having finished, the clerk smiled as one well pleased with a duty well performed, salaamed and clacked away in his heelless slippers.

"It is my duty to inquire whether you have anything to say or any last request to make," said Major Ranald to the prisoner.

"Well, I've only to say that I'm sorry to cause all this fuss, y' know-and, well, yes, I *would* like a smoke," replied the condemned man, and added hastily: "Don't think I want to delay things for a moment though-but if there is time...."

"It is four minutes to seven," said Major Ranald, "and tobacco and matches are not supposed to be found in a Government Jail."

Ross-Ellison winked at the Major and glanced at a bulge on the right side of the breast of the Major's coat.

At this moment the warder standing behind the condemned man seized both his wrists, drew them behind him and fastened them with a broad, strong strap.

"H'm! That's done it, I suppose," said the murderer. "Can't smoke without my hands. Queer idea too-never thought of it before. Can't smoke without hands.... Rather late in life to realize it, what?"

"Oh, yes, you can," said the Major, drawing his big silver cheroot-case from his pocket and selecting a cheroot. Placing it between the prisoner's lips he struck a match and held it to the end of the cigar. Ross-Ellison drew hard and the cigar was lit. He puffed luxuriously and sighed.

"Gad! That's good," he said, "May some one do as much for you, old chap, when *you* come to be-er-no, I don't mean that, of course.... Haven't had a smoke for weeks. Yes-you can smoke without hands after all-but not for long without feeling the inconvenience. I used to know an American (wicked old gun-running millionaire he was, Cuba way, and down South too) who could change his cigar from one corner of his mouth right across to the other with his tongue. Fascinatin' sight to watch...."

Captain Malet-Marsac swallowed continuously, lest he lose the faculty of swallowing-and be choked.

Major Ranald looked at his watch.

"Two minutes to seven. Come on," he said, and took the cheroot from the prisoner's mouth.

"Good-bye, Mike," said that person to the swallowing fainting wretch. "Don't try and say anything. I know exactly what you feel. Sorry we can't shake hands," and he stepped off in the wake of Major Ranald, closely guarded by three warders.

The City Magistrate and Captain Malet-Marsac followed. At Major Ranald's knock, the small inner door of the gate-house was opened and the procession filed through it into the strong room where the warders stood to attention. Having re-fastened the door, the jailer opened the outer one and the procession passed out of the jail into the blessed free world, the world that might be such a place of wonder, beauty, delight, health and joy, were man not educated to materialism, false ideals, false standards, and blind strife for nothing worth.

The sepoy-guard stood in a semicircle from the gate-house to the entrance to a door-way in the jail-wall. Ross-Ellison took his last look at the sky, the distant hills, the trees, God's good world, and then turned into the doorless door-way with his jailers, and faced the scaffold in a square, roofless cell. The warder behind him drew the cap down over his face, and he was led up a flight of shallow stairs on to a platform on which was a roughly-chalked square where two hinged flaps met. As he stood on this spot the noose of the greased rope was placed round his neck by a warder who then looked to Major Ranald for a sign, received it, and pulled over a lever which withdrew the bolts supporting the hinged flaps. These fell apart, Ross-Ellison dropped through the platform, and Christian Society was avenged.

Without a word, Captain Malet-Marsac strode, as in a dream, to his horse, rode home, and, as in a dream, entered his sanctum, took his revolver from its holster and loaded it.

Laying it on the table beside him, he sat down to write a few words to the Colonel of his regiment, Colonel Wilberforce Wriothesley of the 99th Baluch Light Infantry, and to send his will to a brother-officer whom he wished to be his executor.

This done, he took up the revolver, placed the muzzle in his mouth, the barrel pointing upward, and pulled the trigger.

Click!

And nothing more.

A tiny, nerve-shattering, world-shaking, little universe-rocking *click* —and nothing more.

A bad cartridge. He remembered complaints about the revolver ammunition from the Duri Small Arms Ammunition Factory. Too long in stock.

Should he try the same one again, or go on to the next? Probably get better results from the first, as the cap would be already dented by the concussion. He took the muzzle of the big revolver from his aching mouth and, releasing the chamber, spun it round.... He would place it to his temple this time. Holding one's mouth open was undignified. He raised the revolver-and John Bruce burst into the room. He had seen Malet-Marsac ride by, and knew where he had been.

"Half a second!" he shouted. "News! Do that afterwards."

"What is it?" asked Malet-Marsac, taken by surprise.

"Put that beastly thing in the drawer while I tell you, then. It might go off. I hate pistols," said Bruce.

Malet-Marsac obeyed. Bruce was a man to be listened to, and what had to be done could be done when he had gone. If it were some last piece of duty or service, it should be seen to.

"It is this," said Bruce. "You are a liar, a forger, a thief, a dirty pickpocket, a coward, a seller of secrets to Foreign Powers," and, ere the astounded soldier could speak, John Bruce sprang at him and tried to knock him out. "Take that you greasy cad-and fight me if you dare," he shouted as the other dodged his punch.

Malet-Marsac sprang to his feet, furious, and returned the blow. In a second the men were fighting fiercely, coolly, murderously.

Bruce was the bigger, stronger, more scientific, and there could be but one result, given ordinary luck. It was a long, severe, and punishing affair.

"Time," gasped Malet-Marsac at length, and dropped his hands. "Get-breath-fight-decently-time —'nother round-after," and as he spoke Bruce knocked him down and out, proceeding instantly to tie his feet with the punkah-cord and his hands with two handkerchiefs and a pair of braces. This done, he carried him into his bedroom, and laid him on the bed, and sprinkled his face with water.

Malet-Marsac blinked and stirred.

"Awful sorry, old chap," said Bruce at length. "I thought it the best plan. Will you give me your word to chuck the suicide idea, or do you want some more?"

"You damned fool! I...." began the trussed one.

"Yes, I know-but I solemnly swear I won't untie you, nor let anybody else, until you've promised."

Malet-Marsac swore violently, struggled valiantly and, anon, slept.

When he awoke, ten hours later, he informed Bruce, sitting by the bed, that he had no intention of committing suicide....

Years later, as a grey-haired Major, he learnt, from the man's own brother, the story of the strange hero who had fascinated him, and of whose past he had known nothing-save that it had been that of a *man*.

CUPID IN AFRICA: Or, The Baking of Bertram in Love and War

"Ex Africa semper aliquid novi"
"And the son shall take his father's spear

And he shall avenge his father" . . . .

—*Askari Song*

Part I
The Making of Bertram

Chapter I
Major Hugh Walsingham Greene

There never lived a more honourable, upright, scrupulous gentleman than Major Hugh Walsingham Greene, and there seldom lived a duller, narrower, more pompous or more irascible one.

Nor, when the Great War broke out, and gave him something fresh to do and to think about, were there many sadder and unhappier men. His had been a luckless and unfortunate life, what with his two wives and his one son; his excellent intentions and deplorable achievements; his kindly heart and harsh exterior; his narrow escapes of decoration, recognition and promotion.

At cards he was *not* lucky-and in love he . . . well-his first wife, whom he adored, died after a year of him; and his second ran away after three months of his society. She ran away with Mr. Charles Stayne-Brooker (elsewhere the Herr Doktor Karl Stein-Brücker), the man of all men, whom he particularly and peculiarly loathed. And his son, his only son and heir! The boy was a bitter disappointment to him, turning out badly —a poet, an artist, a musician, a wretched student and "intellectual," a fellow who won prizes and scholarships and suchlike by the hatful, and never carried off, or even tried for, a "pot," in his life. Took after his mother, poor boy, and was the first of the family, since God-knows-when, to grow up a dam' civilian. Father fought and bled in Egypt, South Africa, Burma, China, India; grandfather in the Crimea and Mutiny, great-grandfather in the Peninsula and at Waterloo, ancestors with Marlborough, the Stuarts, Drake-scores of them: and this chap, *his* son, *their* descendant, a wretched creature of whom you could no more make a soldier than you could make a service saddle of a sow's ear!

It was a comfort to the Major that he only saw the nincompoop on the rare occasions of his visits to England, when he honestly did his best to hide from the boy (who worshipped him) that he would sooner have seen him win one cup for boxing, than a hundred prizes for his confounded literature, art, music, classics, and study generally. To hide from the boy that the pæans of praise in his school reports were simply revolting-fit only for a feller who was going to be a wretched curate or wretcheder schoolmaster; to hide his distaste for the pale, slim beauty, which was that of a delicate girl rather than of the son of Major Hugh Walsingham Greene. . . . Too like his poor mother by half-and without one quarter the pluck, nerve, and "go" of young Miranda Walsingham, his kinswoman and playmate. . . . Too dam' virtuous altogether. . . .

Gad! If this same Miranda had only been a boy, his boy, there would have been another soldier to carry on the family traditions, if you like!

But this poor Bertram of his . . .

His mother, a Girton girl, and daughter of a Cambridge Don, had prayed that her child might "take after" *her* father, for whom she entertained a feeling of absolute veneration. She had had her wish indeed-without living to rejoice in the fact.

* * *

When it was known in the cantonment of Sitagur that Major Walsingham Greene was engaged to Prudence Pym, folk were astonished, and a not uncommon comment was "Poor little girl!" in spite of the fact that the Major was admitted by all to be a most honourable and scrupulous gentleman. Another remark which was frequently made was "Hm! Opposites attract. What?"

For Prudence Pym was deeply religious, like her uncle, the Commissioner of the Sitagur Division; she was something of a blue-stocking as became her famous father's daughter; she was a musician of parts, an artist of more than local note, and was known to be writing a Book. So that if "oppositeness" be desirable, there was plenty of it-since the Major considered attendance at church to be part and parcel of drill-and-parade; religion to be a thing concerning which no gentleman speaks and few gentlemen think; music to be a noise to be endured in the drawing-room after dinner for a little while; art to be the harmless product of long-haired fellers with shockin' clothes and dirty finger-nails; and books something to read when you were absolutely reduced to doing it-as when travelling. . . .

When Prudence Walsingham Greene knew that she was to have a child, she strove to steep her soul in Beauty, Sweetness and Light, and to feed it on the pure ichor of the finest and best in scenery, music, art and literature. . . .

Entered to her one day-pompous, pleased, and stolid; heavy, dull, and foolish-the worthy Major as she sat revelling in the (to her) marvellous beauties of Rosetti's *Ecce Ancilla Domini*. As she looked up with the sad mechanical smile of the disappointed and courageous wife, he screwed his monocle into his eye and started the old weary laceration of her feelings, the old weary tramplings and defilements of tastes and thoughts, as he examined the picture wherewith she was nourishing (she hoped and believed) the æsthetic side of her unborn child's mind.

"Picture of a Girl with Grouse, what?" grunted the Major.

"With a . . . ? There is no bird? I don't . . . ?" stammered Prudence who, like most women of her kind, was devoid of any sense of humour.

"Looks as though she's got a frightful grouse about somethin', *I* should say. The young party on the bed, I mean," continued her spouse. "'Girl with the Hump' might be a better title p'r'aps-if you say she hasn't a grouse," he added.

"*Hump?*"

"Yes. Got the hump more frightfully about something or other—p'r'aps because the other sportsman's shirt's caught alight. . . . Been smokin', and dropped his cigar. . . ."

"It is an angel shod with fire," moaned Prudence as she put the picture into its portfolio, and felt for her handkerchief. . . .

A little incident, a straw upon the waters, but a straw showing their steady flow toward distaste, disillusionment, dislike, and hopeless regret. The awful and familiar tragedy of "incompatibility of temperament," of which law and priests in their wisdom take no count or cognizance, though counting trifles (by comparison) of infidelity and violence as all important.

And when her boy was born, and named Bertram after her father, Dr. Bertram Pym, F.R.S., she was happy and thankful, and happily and thankfully died.

* * *

In due course the Major recovered from his grief and sent his son home to his place, Leighcombe Abbey, where dwelt his elderly spinster relative, Miss Walsingham, and her niece, Miranda Walsingham, daughter of General Walsingham, his second cousin. Here the influence of prim, gentle, and learned Miss Walsingham was all that his mother would have desired, and in the direction of all that his father loathed-the boy growing up bookish, thoughtful, and more like a nice girl than a human boy. Him Miranda mothered, petted, and occasionally excoriated, being an Amazonian young female of his own age, happier on the bare back of a horse than in the seats of the learned.

Chapter II
Mr. Charles Stayne-Brooker (or Herr Karl Stein-Brücker)

When it was known in the cantonment of Hazarigurh that Major Hugh Walsingham Greene was engaged to Dolly Dennison, folk were astonished, and a not uncommon comment was "Poor old Walsingham Greene," in spite of the fact that the young lady was very beautiful, accomplished and fascinating.

Here also another remark, that was frequently heard, was that opposites attract, for Dolly was known to be seventeen, and the Major, though not very much more than twice her age, looked as old as her father, the Sessions Judge, and *he* looked more like the girl's grandfather than her father.

It was agreed, however, that it was no case of kidnapping, for Dolly knew her way about, knew precisely how many beans made five, and needed no teaching from her grandmother as to the sucking of eggs, or anything else. For Dolly, poor child, had put her hair up and "come out" at the age of fifteen-in an Indian cantonment!

Little more need be said to excuse almost anything she might do or be. Motherless, she had run her father's hospitable house for the last two years, as well as her weak and amiable father; and when Major Walsingham Greene came to Hazarigurh he found this pitiable spoilt child (a child who had never had any childhood) the *burra mem-sahib* of the place, in virtue of her position as the head of the household of the Senior Civilian. With the manners, airs, and graces of a woman of thirty, she was a blasé and world-weary babe —"fed up" with dances, gymkhanas, garden parties, race meetings and picnics; and as experienced and cool a hand at a flirtation as any garrison-hack or station-belle in the country. Dolly knew the men with whom one flirts but does not marry, and the men one marries but with whom one does not flirt.

Mr. Charles Stayne-Brooker was the pride of the former; Major Walsingham Greene *facile princeps* of the latter. Charles was the loveliest, daringest, wickedest flirt you *ever* —and Hugh was a man of means and position, with an old Tudor "place" in Dorset. So Charles for fun-and Hugh for matrimony, just as soon as he suggested it. She hoped Hugh would be quick, too, for Charles had a terrible fascination and power over her. She had been frightened at herself one moonlight picnic, frightened at Charles's power and her own feelings-and she feared the result if Hugh (who was most obviously of a coming-on disposition), dallied and doubted. If Hugh were not quick, Charles would get her-for she preferred volcanoes to icebergs, and might very easily forget her worldly wisdom and be carried off her feet some night, as she lurked in a *kala jugga* with the daring, darling wicked Charles-whose little finger was more attractive and mysterious than the Major's whole body. Besides-the Major was a grey-haired widower, with a boy at school in England and *so* dull and prosperous. . . .

But, ere too late, the Major proposed and was accepted. Charles was, or affected to be, ruined and broken-hearted, and the wedding took place. The Major was like a boy again-for a little while. And Dolly felt like a girl taken from an hotel in Mentone and immured in a convent in Siberia.

For Major Hugh Walsingham Greene would have none of the "goings-on" that had made Dolly's father's bungalow the centre of life and gaiety for the subalterns and civilian youth of Hazarigurh; whilst Mr. Charles Stayne-Brooker, whom he detested as a flamboyant bounder, he cut dead. He also bade Dolly remove the gentleman's name finally and completely from her visiting-list, and on no account be "at home" when he called. All of which Dolly quite flatly and finally refused to do.

* * *

Mr. Charles Stayne-Brooker (or the Herr Doktor Karl Stein-Brücker, as he was at other times and in other places) was a very popular person wherever he went-and he went to an astonishing number of places. It was wonderful how intimate he became with people, and he became intimate with an astonishing number and variety of people. He could sing, play, dance, ride and take a hand at games above the average, and *talk* —never was such a chatter-box—on any subject under the sun, especially on himself and his affairs. And yet, here again, it was astonishing how little he said, with all his talk and ingenious chatter. Everybody knew all about dear old Charlie-and yet, did they know anything at all when it came to the point? In most of the places in which he turned up, he seemed to be a sort of visiting manager of a business house-generally a famous house with some such old-fashioned British name as Schneider and Schmidt; Max Englebaum and Son; Plügge and Schnadhorst; Hans Wincklestein and Gartenmacher; or Grosskopf and Dümmelmann. In out-of-the-way places he seemed to be just a jolly globe-trotter with notions of writing a book on his jolly trip to India. Evidently he wanted to know something of the native of India, too, for when not in large commercial centres like Calcutta, Madras, Bombay or Colombo, he was to be found in cantonments where there were Native Troops. He loved the Native Officer and cultivated him assiduously. He also seemed to love the Bengali amateur politician, more than some people do. . . . Often a thoughtful and observant official was pleased to see an Englishman taking such a friendly interest in the natives, and trying to get to know them well at first hand—a thing far too rare. . . .

There were people, however-such as Major Walsingham Greene-who affected to detect something of a "foreign" flavour about him, and wrote him down as a flashy and bounderish outsider.

Certainly he was a great contrast to the Major, whose clipped moustache, bleak blue eye, hard bronzed face and close-cut hair were as different as possible from Mr. Stayne-Brooker's waxed and curled moustache over the ripe red mouth; huge hypnotic and strange black eyes; pink and white puffy face, and long dark locks. And then again, as has been said, Mr. Stayne-Brooker was only happy when talking, and the Major only happy (if then) when silent.

On sight, on principle, and on all grounds, the latter gentleman detested the jabbering, affected, over-familiar, foreign-like fellow, and took great pleasure in ordering his bride, on their return from the ten-days-leave honeymoon, to cut him dead and cut him out-of her life.

And, alas, his bride seemed to take an even greater pleasure in defying her husband on this, and certain other, points; in making it clear to him that she fully and firmly intended "to live her own life" and go her own way; and in giving copious and convincing proof of the fact that she had never known "discipline" yet, and did not intend to make its acquaintance now.

Whereupon poor Major Walsingham Greene, while remaining the honourable, upright and scrupulous gentleman that he was, exhibited himself the irascible, pompous fool that he also was, and by his stupid and overbearing conduct, his "*That's enough! Those are my orders,*" and his hopeless mishandling of the situation, drove her literally into the arms of Mr. Charles Stayne-Brooker, with whom the poor little fool disappeared like a beautiful dream.

* * *

When his kind heart got the better of his savage wrath and scourged pride, the Major divorced her, and the Herr Doktor (who particularly needed an English wife in his profession of Secret Agent especially commissioned for work in the British Empire) married her, broke her heart, dragged her down into the moral slime in which he wallowed, and, on the rare occasions of her revolt and threat to leave him, pointed out that ladies who were divorced once for leaving their husbands *might* conceivably have some excuse, but that the world had a very hard name for those who made a habit of it. . . . And then there was her daughter to consider, too. *His* daughter, alas! but also hers.

Chapter III
Mrs. Stayne-Brooker —and Her Ex-Stepson

From Hazarigurh Mr. Charles Stayne-Brooker went straight to Berlin, became the Herr Doktor Stein-Brücker once more, and saw much of another and more famous Herr Doktor of the name of Solf. He then went to South Africa and thence to England, where his daughter was born. Having placed her with the family of an English clergyman whose wife "accepted" a few children of Anglo-Indians, he proceeded to America and Canada, and thence to Vladivostok, Kïaou-Chiaou, Hong Kong, Shanghai, and Singapore; then to the Transvaal by way of Lourenzo Marques and to German East Africa. And every step of the way his wife went with him-and who so English, among Englishmen, as jolly Charlie Stayne-Brooker, with his beautiful English wife? . . . What he did, save interviewing stout gentlemen (whose necks bulged over their collars, whose accents were guttural, and whose table-manners were unpleasant) and writing long letters, she did not know. What she did know was that she was a lost and broken woman, tied for life to a base and loathsome scoundrel, by her yearning for "respectability," her love for her daughter, and her utter dependence for food, clothing and shelter upon the man whom, in her mad folly, she had trusted. By the time they returned to England *via* Berlin, the child, Eva, was old enough to go to an expensive boarding-school at Cheltenham, and here Mrs. Stayne-Brooker had to leave her when her husband's "duties" took him, from the detailed study of the Eastern Counties of England, to Africa again. Here he seemed likely to settle at last, interesting himself in coffee and rubber, and spending much of his time in Mombasa and Nairobi, as well as in Dar-es-Salaam, Tabora, Lindi and Zanzibar.

***

Meanwhile, Major Hugh Walsingham Greene, an embittered and disappointed man, withdrew more and more into his shell, and, on each successive visit to Leighcombe Priory, more and more abandoned hope of his son's "doing any good" in life. He was the true grandson of that most distinguished scholar, Dr. Bertram Pym, F.R.S., of Cambridge University, and the true son of his mother. . . . What a joy the lad would have been to these two, with his love of books and his unbroken career of academic successes, and what a grief he was to his soldier father, with his utter distaste for games and sports and his dislike of all things military.

Useless it was for sweet and gentle Miss Walsingham to point to his cleverness and wisdom, or for Amazonian and sporting Miranda Walsingham hotly to defend him and rail against the Major's "unfairness" and "stupid prejudice." Equally useless for the boy to do his utmost to please the man who was to him as a god. . . .

When the Major learned that his son had produced the Newdigate Prize Poem, won the Craven and the Ireland Scholarships, and taken his Double First-he groaned. . . .

Brilliant success at Oxford? What is *Oxford*? He would sooner have seen him miserably fail at Sandhurst and enlist for his commission. . . .

Finally the disappointing youth went to India as private secretary and travelling companion to the great scientist, Sir Ramsey Wister, his father being stationed at Aden.

***

Then came the Great War.

Part II
The Baking of Bertram By War

Chapter I
Bertram Becomes a Man of War

Mr. Bertram Greene, emerging from the King Edward Terminus of the Great Indian Railway at Madrutta, squared his shoulders, threw out his chest, and, so far as he understood the process and could apply it, strode along with the martial tread and military swagger of all the Best Conquerors.

From khaki helmet to spurred brown heel, he was in full panoply of war, and wore a dangerous-looking sword. At least, to the ignorant passer-by, it appeared that its owner was in constant danger of being tripped up by it. Bertram, however, could have told him that he was really in no peril from the beastly thing, since a slight pressure on the hilt from his left elbow kept the southern end clear of his feet.

What troubled him more than the sword was the feeling of constriction and suffocation due to the tightness of the belts and straps that encompassed him about, and the extreme heat of the morning. Also he felt terribly nervous and unaccustomed, very anxious as to his ability to support the weight of his coming responsibility, very self-distrustful, and very certain that, in the full active-service kit of a British Officer of the Indian Army, he looked a most frightful ass.

For Mr. Bertram Greene had never before appeared on this, or any other stage, in such a part; and the change-from a quiet modest civilian, "bashful, diffident and shy," to what his friends at dinner last night had variously called a thin red hero, a licentious soldiery, a brutal mercenary, a hired assassin, a saviour of his Motherland, a wisp of cannon-fodder, a pup of the bull-dog breed, a curly-headed hero, a bloody-minded butcher, and one who would show his sword to be as mighty as his pen-was overwhelmingly great and sudden. When any of the hundreds of hurrying men who passed him looked at him with incurious eyes, he felt uncomfortable, and blushed. He knew he looked an ass, and, far worse, that whatever he might look, he actually was—a fraud, and a humbug. Fancy him, Bertram Greene, familiarly known as "Cupid," the pale-faced "intellectual," the highbrowed hero of the class-room and examination-hall, the winner of scholarships and the double-first, guilty of a thin volume of essays and a thinner one of verse-just fancy him, the studious, bookish sedentary, disguised as a soldier, as a leader of men in the day of battle, a professional warrior! . . . He who had never played games was actually proposing to play the greatest Game of all: he who had never killed an animal in his life was going to learn to kill men: he who had always been so lacking in self-reliance was going to ask others to rely on him!

And, as his spirits sank lower, Bertram held his head higher, threw back his shoulders further, protruded his chest more, and proceeded with so firm a tread, and so martial a demeanour, that he burst into profuse and violent perspiration.

He wished he could take a taxi, but even had there been one available, he knew that the Native Infantry Lines almost adjoined the railway terminus, and that he had to cross a grass *maidan* [144] on foot.

Thank heaven it was not far, or he would arrive looking as though he had come by sea-swimming. A few more steps would take him out of this crowd of students, clerks, artisans, and business-men thronging to their schools, colleges, offices, shops, mills, and works in Madrutta. . . . What did they talk about, these queer "city men" who went daily from the suburbs to "the office," clad in turbans, sandals, *dhoties*, [145] and cotton coats? Any one of these bare-legged, collarless, not *very* clean-looking worthies might be a millionaire; and any one of them might be supporting a wife and large family on a couple of pounds a month. The vast majority of them were doing so, of course. . . . Anyhow, none of them seemed to smile derisively when looking at him, so perhaps his general appearance was more convincing than he thought.

But then, short as had been his sojourn in India, he had been in the country long enough to know that the native does not look with obvious derision upon the European, whatever may be the real views and sentiments of his private mind-so there was no comfort in that. . . . Doubtless the Colonel and British officers of the regiment he was about to join would not put themselves to the trouble of concealing their opinions as to his merits, or lack of them, as soon as those opinions were conceived. . . . Well, there was one thing Bertram Greene could do, and would do, while breath was in his body-and that was his very best. No one can do more. He might be as ignorant of all things military as a babe unborn: he might be a simple, nervous, inexperienced sort of youth with more culture and refinement than strength of character and decision of mind: he might be a bit of an ass, whom other fellows were always ragging and calling "Cupid" —but, when the end came, none should be able to say that he had failed for want of doing his utmost, and for lack of striving, with might and main, to learn *how* to do his duty, and then to do it to the limit of his ability.

A couple of British soldiers, privates of the Royal Engineers, came towards him on their way to the station. Bertram attempted the impossible in endeavouring to look still more inflexibly and inexorably martial, as he eyed them hardily. Would they look at him and smile amusedly? If so, what should he do? He might be a fool himself, but-however farcically-he bore the King's Commission, and it had got to be respected and saluted by all soldiers. The men simultaneously placed their swagger-sticks beneath their left arms, and, at three paces' distance, saluting smartly and as one man, maintained the salute until they were three paces beyond him.

Bertram's heart beat high with pride and thankfulness. He would have liked to stop and shake hands with the men, thanking them most sincerely. As it was, he added a charming and friendly smile to the salute which he gave in acknowledgment of theirs.

He passed on, feeling as though he had drunk some most stimulating and exhilarating draught. He had received his first salute! Moreover, the men had looked most respectfully, nay, almost reverentially, if with a certain stereotyped and bovine rigidity of stare, toward the officer they so promptly and smartly honoured. He would have given a great deal to know whether they passed any contemptuous or derisive comment upon his appearance and bearing. . . . In point of fact, Scrounger Evans had remarked to Fatty Wilkes, upon abandoning the military position of the salute: "Horgustus appears to 'ave 'ad a good night at bridge, and took a few 'undreds orf Marmadook an' Reginald. Wot?"

Whereunto Fatty had murmured:

"Jedgin' by 'is 'appy liddle smile," as he sought the smelly stump of a cigarette in its lair behind his spreading shady ear.

Enheartened, but perspiring, Bertram strode on, and crossed the broad grass *maidan*, at the far side of which he could see the parallel streets of the Native Infantry Lines, where lay the One Hundred and Ninety-Ninth Regiment, to which he had been ordered to report himself "forthwith." Yesterday was but crowded, excited yesterday, terminating in a wild farewell dinner and an all-night journey. *To-day* was "forthwith." . . . What would to-morrow be? Perhaps the date of the termination of his career in the Indian Army-if the Colonel looked him over, asked him a few questions, and then said: "Take away this bauble!" or "Sweep this up!" or words to that effect. He had heard that Colonels were brief, rude, and arbitrary persons, sometimes very terrible. . . . Approaching the end of the first long row of the mud buildings of the Native Infantry Lines, Bertram beheld a sentry standing outside his sentry-box, in the shade of a great banyan tree. The man was clad in khaki tunic, shorts and puttees, with a huge khaki turban, from which protruded a fringed scrap of blue and gold; hob-nailed black boots, and brown belt and bandolier. His bare knees, his hands and face were very far from being black; in fact, were not even brown, but of a pale wheat-colour.

The thoughts of Private Ilderim Yakub were far away, and his eyes beheld a little *sungar-*enclosed watch-tower that looked across a barren and arid valley of solid rock. In the low, small doorway sat a fair-faced woman with long plaits of black hair, and, at her feet, crawled a tiny naked boy . . . and then the eyes of Private Ilderim Yakub beheld a British officer, in full war-paint and wearing his sword, bearing down upon him. By Allah the Compassionate and the Beard of the Prophet! He had been practically asleep at his post, and this must certainly be the Orderly Officer Sahib or the Adjutant Sahib, if not the Colonel Sahib himself! Possibly even the "Gineraal" Sahib (from the neighbouring Brigade Headquarters) having a quiet prowl round. It must be *somebody*, or he wouldn't be "in drill order with sword," and marching straight for the guard-room.

Private Ilderim Yakub (in the days when he had been a —well —a scoundrelly border-thief and raider) had very frequently been in situations demanding great promptitude of thought and action; and now, although at one moment he had been practically asleep and his wits wool-gathering in the Khost Valley, the next moment he had sprung from his box, yelled "*Guard turn out!*" with all the strength of his leathern lungs and brazen throat, and had then frozen to the immobility of a bronze statue in the attitude of the salute.

In response to his shout, certain similarly clad men arose from a bench that stood outside a large thatched, mud-built hut, another, wearing a red sash and three white stripes on the sleeve of his tunic, came hurrying from within it, and the party, with promptitude and dispatch, "fell in," the Sergeant (or Havildar) beside them.

"Guard!" roared that bearded worthy, "'*Shun*! *Present* arms!" and, like the sentry, the Sergeant and the Guard stood as bronze statues to the honour and glory of Second-Lieutenant Bertram Greene-the while that gentleman longed for nothing more than that the ground might open and swallow him up.

What on earth ought he to do? Had he not read in his newly purchased drill-book that the Guard only turned out for Emperors or Field-Marshals, or Field Officers or something? Or was it only for the Colonel or the Officer of the Day? It most certainly was not for stray Second-Lieutenants of the Indian Army Reserve. Should he try to explain to the Sergeant that he had made a mistake, and that the Guard was presenting arms to the humblest of God's creatures that wore officer's uniform? Should he "put on dog" heavily and "inspect" the Guard? Should he pretend to find fault? No! For one thing he had not enough Hindustani to make himself intelligible. (But it was a sign that a change was already coming over Bertram, when he could even conceive such a notion, and only dismiss it for such a reason.)

What *should* he do, in these distressingly painful circumstances?

Should he absolutely ignore the whole lot of them, and swagger past with a contemptuous glance at the fool Sergeant who had turned the Guard out? . . . It wasn't *his* fault that the wretched incident had occurred. . . . *He* hadn't made the mistake, so why should he be made to look a fool? It would be the others who'd look the fools, if he took not the slightest notice of their silly antics and attitude-striking. . . (Heavens! How they'd made the perspiration trickle again, by putting him in this absurd and false position.) . . . Yes-he'd just go straight past the lot of them as if they didn't exist. . . . No-that would be horribly rude, to say the least of it. They were paying him a military compliment, however mistakenly, and he must return it. Moreover-it wasn't the Sergeant-fellow's fault. The sentry had shouted to the Guard, and the Sergeant had naturally supposed that one of those Great Ones, for whom Guards turn out, was upon them.

Should he march past with a salute, as though he were perfectly accustomed to such honours, and rather bored with them? Unless he were near enough for them to see the single "pip" on his shoulder-strap, they would never know they had made a mistake. (He would hate them to feel as horribly uncomfortable as he did.)

And if he did, where should he go? He must find the Officers' Lines, and go to the Officers' Mess and inquire for the Colonel. Besides, this was *his* regiment; he was attached to it, and these men would all see him again and know who and what he was. . . .

Of course-he would do the correct and natural thing, and behave as though he were merely slightly amused at the sentry's not unnatural mistake and its results. . . . With a smart salute to the Guard, Bertram smiled upon the puzzled, imperturbable and immobile Havildar, with the remark:

"*Achcha*, [146]Sergeant. Guard, dismiss *karo*" [147]—upon hearing which barbarous polyglot of English and Hindustani, the Non-Commissioned Officer abandoned his rigid pose and roared, with extreme ferocity, in the very ears of the Sepoys:

"Guard! *Order-r ar-r-rms.* Stannat *eashe.* Dees*mees!*" and with another salute, again turned to Bertram to await his further pleasure.

"*Ham Colonel Sahib mangta. Kither hai?*" [148] said that gentleman, and the intelligent Havildar gathered that this young and strange Sahib "wanted" the Colonel. He smiled behind his vast and bushy beard at the idea of sending a message of the "Hi! you-come here! You're wanted" description to that Great One, and pictured the meeting that would ensue if the Colonel Sahib came hastily, expecting to find the Commander-in-Chief-in-India awaiting him.

No-since the young Sahib wanted the Colonel, he had better go and find him. Calling to a young Sepoy who was passing on some fatigue duty, he bade him haste away, put on his tunic, tuck his long khaki shirt inside his shorts, and conduct the Sahib to the Adjutant Sahib's office. (That would be quite in order; the Adjutant Sahib could decide as to the wisdom of "wanting" the Colonel Sahib at this-or any other-hour of the day; and responsibility would be taken from the broad, unwilling shoulders of Havildar Afzul Khan Ishak.)

An uncomfortable five minutes followed. Bertram, longing with all his soul to say something correct, natural, and pleasant, could only stand dumb and unhappy, while the perspiration trickled; the Havildar stood stiffly at attention and wondered whether the Sahib were as old as his son, Private Mahommed Afzul Khan, new recruit of the One Hundred and Ninety-Ninth; and the Guard, though dismissed, stood motionless in solemn row beside the bench (on which they would sit as soon as the Sahib turned his back), and, being Indian Sepoys, emptied their minds of all thought, fixed their unseeing gaze upon Immensity and the Transcendental Nothingness-of-Non-existent-Non-entity-in-Oblivion, and tried to look virtuous.

Returning and saluting, the young Sepoy wheeled about and plodded heavily down the road, walking as though each hob-nailed boot weighed a ton. But pride must suffer pain, and not for worlds would this young man (who had, until a few months ago, never worn anything heavier than a straw-plaited sandal as he "skipped like a young ram" about his native hill-tops) have been without these tokens of wealth and dignity. What he would have liked, had the Authorities been less touchy about it, would have been to wear them slung about his neck, plain for all to admire, and causing their owner no inconvenience.

Following his guide through the lines of mud huts, saluted every few yards by passing Sepoys and by groups who sat about doorways and scrambled to their feet as he passed, Bertram found himself in a broad sandy road, lined by large stone European bungalows, which ran at right-angles across the ends of the Sepoys' lines. Each bungalow stood in a large compound, had a big lawn and flower-gardens in front of it, and was embowered in palm-trees. Turning into the garden of the largest of these, the young Sepoy pointed to the big house, ejaculated: "Arfeecers' Mess, Sahib," saluted, performed a meticulously careful "about turn," the while his lips moved as though he were silently giving himself the necessary orders for each movement, and solemnly marched away.

A pair of large old-fashioned cannon and a white flagstaff gave the place an important and official appearance. Beyond the big porch stretched to left and right a broad and deep verandah, in the shady recesses of which Bertram could see a row of chairs wherein lay khaki-clad figures, their feet, raised upon the long leg-rests, presented unitedly and unanimously towards him. Indeed, as he advanced with beating heart and sense of shy discomfort, all that he could see of the half-dozen gentlemen was one dozen boot-soles backed by a blur of khaki. Up to the time he had reached the flight of steps, leading up from the drive to the verandah, no one had moved. Mounting the steps, and coming to the level of the recumbent figures, ranged along the rear wall of the verandah and on each side of an open door, the unhappy Bertram, from this new standpoint, saw that the face of each officer was hidden behind a newspaper or a magazine.... Profound silence reigned as he regarded the twelve boot-soles, each crossed by a spur-chain, and the six newspapers.

Another embarrassing and discomfortable situation. What should he do? Should he cough-as the native does when he wishes to attract your attention, or to re-affirm his forgotten presence? It seemed a rather feeble and banal idea. Should he pretend he had not seen the six stalwart men lying there in front of his nose, and shout: "*Qui hai!*" as one does to call an invisible servant? And suppose none of them moved, and a Mess servant came-he had no card to send in. He couldn't very well tell the man to announce in stentorian voice and the manner of a herald: "Behold! Second-Lieutenant Bertram Greene, of the Indian Army Reserve, standeth on the threshold!" And supposing the man did precisely this and *still* nobody moved, *what* a superlative ass the said Second-Lieutenant Bertram Greene would feel! . . . But could he feel a bigger ass than he did already-standing there in awkward silence beneath the stony regard, or disregard, of the twelve contemptuous boot-soles? . . .

Should he walk along the row of them, giving each alternate foot a heavy blow? That would make them look up all right. . . . Or should he seize a couple of them and operate them in the manner of the young lady in the Railway Refreshment Rooms or the Village Inn, as she manipulates the handles of the beer-engine? The owners of the two he grabbed and pulled would come from behind their papers fast enough. . . . Bertram moved, and his sword clanked sharply against a pillar. None of the readers had looked up at the sound of footsteps-they were resting from the labours of breakfast, and footsteps, as such, are of no interest. But, strange to say, at the sound of a sword clanking, they moved as one man; six papers were lowered and six pairs of eyes stared at the unhappy Bertram. After three seconds of penetrating scrutiny, the six papers rose again as one, as though at the sound of the ancient and useful military order, "*As you were.*"

Major Fordinghame beheld a very good-looking boy, who appeared to be taking his new sword and revolver for a walk in the nice sunshine and giving the public a treat. He'd hardly be calling on the Mess dressed up in lethal weapons. Probably wanted the Adjutant or somebody. He was quite welcome to 'em. . . . These "planter" cheroots were extraordinarily good at the price. . . . Lieutenant and Quartermaster Macteith wondered who the devil *this* was. Why did he stick there like a stuck pig and a dying cod-fish? Still-if he wanted to stick, let him stick, by all means. Free country. . . . Captain Brylle only vaguely realised that he was staring hard at some bloke or other-he was bringing all the great resources of his brain to bear upon a joke in the pink paper he affected. It was so deep, dark and subtle a joke that he had not yet "got" it. Bloke on the door-mat. What of it? . . . Captain Tavner had received a good fat cheque that morning; he was going on ten days' leave to-morrow; he had done for to-day; and he had had a bottle of beer for breakfast. *He* didn't mind if there were a rhinoceros on the doorstep. Doubtless someone would take it into the Mess and give it a drink. . . . Cove had got his sword on-or was it two swords? Didn't matter to him, anyway. . . .

Captain Melhuish idly speculated as to whether the chap would be "calling" at so early an hour of the morning. It was the Mess President's business, anyhow. . . . Why the sword and revolver? And mentally murmuring: "Enter-one in armour," Captain Melhuish, the *doyen* of the famous Madrutta Amateur Dramatic Society, returned to his perusal of *The Era*. . . . Lieutenant Bludyer didn't give a damn, anyhow. . . . And so none of these gentlemen, any one of whom would have arisen, had he been sitting there alone, and welcomed Bertram hospitably, felt it incumbent upon him to move, and the situation resumed what Bertram privately termed its formerness.

Just as he had decided to go to the nearest reader and flatly request him to arise and direct him to the Colonel, another officer came rushing from the room whose open doorway faced the porch. In his mouth was a quill pen, and in his hands were papers.

"Lazy perishers!" he remarked as he saw the others, and added: "Come along, young Macteith," and was turning to hurry down the verandah when Bertram stepped forward.

"Excuse me," he said, "d'you think I could see the Colonel? I have been ordered to report to this regiment."

"You *could* see the Colonel," replied this officer, "but I shouldn't, if I were you. I'd see the Adjutant. Much pleasanter sight. I'm the Adjutant. Come along to my office," and he led the way down the verandah, across a big whitewashed room, simply furnished with a table, a chair, and a punkah, to a smaller room, furnished with two of each of the above-mentioned articles.

Dropping the pen and papers upon the table, the Adjutant wheeled round upon Bertram, and, transfixing him with a cold grey eye, said, in hollow voice and tragic tones:

"Do not trifle with me, Unhappy Boy! Say those blessed words again-or at once declare them false. . . . *Did* I hear you state that you have been ordered to join this corps-or did I not?"

"You did, sir," smiled Bertram.

"Shake," replied the Adjutant. "God bless you, gentle child. For two damns, I'd fall on your neck. I love you. Tell me your honoured name and I'll send for my will. . . ."

"I'm glad I'm welcome," said the puzzled and astonished Bertram; "but I'm afraid I shan't be very useful. I am absolutely ignorant-you see, I've not been a soldier for twenty-four hours yet. . . . Here's the telegram I got yesterday," and he produced that document.

"Good youth," replied Captain Murray. "I don't give a tinker's curse if you're deaf, dumb, blind and silly. You are my deliverer. I love you more and more. I've been awaiting you with beating heart-lying awake for you, listening for your footprints. Now you come — *I* go."

"What-to the Front?" said Bertram.

"You've guessed it in once, fair youth. East Africa for little Jock Murray. We are sending a draft of a hundred men to our link battalion there-awfully knocked about they've been-and I have it, straight from the stable, that I'm the lad that takes them. . . . They go in a day or two. . . . I was getting a bit anxious, I can tell you-but my pal in the Brigade Office said they were certain to send a Reserve man here and relieve me. . . . Colonel *will* be pleased-he never *says* anything but '*H'm!*' but he'll bite your ear if you don't dodge."

"I suppose he'll simply hate losing an experienced officer and getting me," said Bertram, apprehensively.

"He'll make himself perfectly miserable," was the reply, "but nothing to what he'll make you. I'm the Adjutant, you see, and there'll be a bit of a muddle until my successor has picked up all the threads, and a bit of extra bother for the Colonel. . . . Young Macteith'll have to take it on, I expect. . . . He'll bite your other ear for that. . ." and Murray executed a few simple steps of the *can-can*, in the joy of his heart that the chance of his life had come. No one but himself knew the agonies of mind that he had suffered, as he lay awake at night realising that the war might he a short one, time was rushing on, and hundreds of thousands of men had gone to fight-while he still sat in an office and played C.O.'s lightning conductor. A usually undemonstrative Scot, he was slightly excited and uplifted by this splendid turn of Fortune's wheel. Falling into a chair, he read the telegram:

To Second-Lieutenant Bertram Greene, A.A.A.

You have been appointed to Indian Army Reserve of Officers with rank of Second-Lieutenant, and are ordered to report forthwith to O.C. One Hundred and Ninety-Ninth Regiment, Madrutta. A.A.A. Military Secretary.

"Any relation to Major Walsingham Greene?" enquired Murray.

"Son," replied Bertram, "and nephew of General Walsingham."

"Not your fault, of course," observed Murray. "Best to make a clean breast of these things, though. . . . Had any sort of military training?" he added.

"Absolutely none whatever. Soon after war broke out I felt I was a disgrace to my family-they are all soldiers-and I thought of going home and enlisting. . . . Then I thought it was a pity if nearly twenty years of expensive education had fitted me for nothing more useful than what any labourer or stable-boy can do-and I realised that I'm hardly strong enough to be of much good in the trenches during a Belgian winter —I've been there-so I wrote to my father and my uncle and told them I'd like to get into the Indian Army Reserve of Officers. I thought I might soon learn enough to be able to set free a better man, and, in time, I might possibly be of some good-and perhaps go to the Frontier or something. . . ."

"Goo' *boy*," said the merry Murray. "I could strain you to my bosom."

"Then I received some papers from the Military Secretary, filled them up, and returned them with a medical certificate. I bought some kit and ordered a uniform, and studied the drill-book night and day. . . . I got that wire yesterday-and here I am."

"I love you, Bertram," repeated the Adjutant.

"I feel a dreadful fraud, though," continued the boy, "and I am afraid my uncle, General Walsingham, thinks I am 'one of the Greenes' in every way, whereas I'm a most degenerate and unworthy member of the clan. Commonly called 'Cupid' and 'Blameless Bertram,' laughed at . . . . Really he is my father's cousin-but I've always called him 'Uncle,'" he added ingenuously.

"Well-sit you there awhile and I'll be free in a bit. Then I'll take you round the Lines and put you up to a few things. . . ."

"I should be most grateful," replied Bertram.

Macteith entered and sat him down at the other desk, and for half an hour there was a *va et vient* of orderlies, clerks, Sepoys and messengers, with much ringing of the telephone bell.

When he had finished his work, Murray kept his promise, gave Bertram good advice and useful information, and, before tiffin, introduced him to the other officers-who treated him with cordial friendliness. The Colonel did not appear at lunch, but Bertram's satisfaction at the postponement of his interview was somewhat marred by a feeling that Lieutenant Macteith eyed him malevolently and regarded his advent with disapproval.

Chapter II
And is Ordered to East Africa

That afternoon the Adjutant very good-naturedly devoted to assisting Bertram to remedy his utter nakedness and ashamedness in the matter of necessary campaigning kit. Taking him in his dog-cart to the great Madrutta Emporium, he showed him what to buy, and, still better, what not to buy, that he might be fully equipped, armed and well prepared, as a self-supporting and self-dependent unit, provided with all he needed and nothing he did not need, that he might go with equal mind wheresoever Fate-or the Military Secretary-might suddenly send him.

After all, it was not very much —a very collapsible camp-bed of green canvas, hardwood and steel; a collapsible canvas washstand to match; a collapsible canvas bath (which was destined to endanger the blamelessness of Blameless Bertram's language by providing more collapses than baths); a canteen of cooking utensils; a green canvas valise which contained bedding, and professed to be in itself a warm and happy home from home, even upon the cold hard ground; and a sack of similar material, provided with a padlock, and suitable as a receptacle for such odds and ends of clothing and kit as you might choose to throw in it.

"Got to remember that, if you go on active service, your stuff may have to be carried by coolies," said the Adjutant. "About forty pounds to a man. No good trying to make one big package of your kit. Say, one sack of spare clothing and things; one bundle of your bed, bath, and washing kit; and the strapped-up valise and bedding. If you had to abandon one of the three, you'd let the camp-bed, bath and wash-stand go, and hang on to the sleeping-valise and sack of underclothes, socks, boots, spare uniform and sundries," and much other good advice.

To festoon about Cupid's person, in addition to his sword, revolver, water-bottle and haversack, he selected a suitable compass, map-case, field-glasses, ammunition-pouch, whistle and lanyards, since his earnest and anxious protégé desired to be fitted out fully and properly for manœuvres, and as though for actual active service.

Assurance being received that his purchases would be forthwith despatched to the Adjutant's bungalow, Bertram drove back to the Mess with that kindly officer, and gratefully accepted his invitation to dine with him, that night, at the famous Madrutta Club.

"What about kit, though?" enquired Bertram. "I've only got what I stand up in. I left all my —"

"That's all right," was the reply. "Everybody's in khaki, now we're mobilised-except the miserable civilians," he added with a grin, whereat Bertram, the belted man of blood, blushed and smiled.

At dinner Bertram sat respectfully silent, collecting the pearls of wisdom that fell from the lips of his seniors, fellow-guests of the Adjutant. And his demeanour was of a gravity weighty and serious even beyond his wont, for was he not now a soldier among soldiers, a uniformed, commissioned, employed officer of His Majesty the King Emperor, and attached to a famous fighting regiment? Yes—a King's Officer, and one who might conceivably be called upon to fight, and perhaps to die, for his country and for those simple Principles for which his country stood.

He was a little sorry when some of his bemedalled fellow-guests joked on solemn and sacred subjects, and spoke a little slightingly of persons and principles venerable to him; but he comforted and consoled himself with the recollection and reflection that this type of man so loathed any display, or even mention, of sentiment and feeling, that it went to the opposite extreme, and spoke lightly of things weighty, talked ribaldly of dignitaries, and gave a quite wrong impression as to its burning earnestness and enthusiasm.

After dinner, when the party broke up for bridge, billiards or the bar, he sat on, listening with all his ears to the conversation of the Adjutant and an officer, who seemed exceedingly well informed on the subject of the battle of Tanga, in German East Africa, concerning which the general public knew nothing at all.

Murray noticed his intelligent and attentive silence, and counted it for righteousness unto the boy, that he could "keep his head shut," at any rate. . . .

And next day The Blow fell!

For poor Captain and Adjutant Murray, of the Hundred and Ninety-Ninth Infantry, it dawned like any ordinary day, and devoid of baleful omens.

There was nothing ominous about the coming of the tea, toast, and oranges that "Abdul the Damned," his bearer, brought into the big, bare and comfortless room (furnished with two camp-beds, one long chair, one *almirah* [149] and a litter on the floor) in which he and Bertram slept.

Early morning parade passed off without unusual or untoward event.

Breakfast was quite without portent, omen, or foreshadow of disaster. The Colonel's silence was no more eloquent than usual, the Major's remarks were no ruder, the Junior Subaltern's no sillier, and those of the other fellows were no more uninteresting than upon other days; and all unconscious of his fate the hapless victim strayed into his office, followed by his faithful and devoted admirer, Second-Lieutenant Bertram Greene, who desired nothing better than to sit at his feet and learn. . . .

And then it came!

It came in the shape of a telegram from the Military Secretary, and, on the third reading of the fair-writ type, Murray had to realise that the words undoubtedly and unmistakably were:

To O.C. 199th Infantry, A.A.A.

Second-Lieutenant Greene, I.A.R., to proceed to Mombasa forthwith in charge of your draft of one hundred P.M.'s and one Native Officer, by s.s. Elymas to-morrow and report to O.C., One Hundred and Ninety-Eighth immediately. A.A.A. Military Secretary, Delhi.

He read it through once again and then laid it on his table, leant his head on his hand and felt physically faint and sick for a moment. He had not felt quite as he did then more than three or four times in the whole of his life. It was like the feeling he had when he received the news of his mother's death; when his proposal of marriage to the one-and-only girl had been rejected; when he had been bowled first ball in the Presidency Match, and when he had taken a toss from his horse at the Birthday Parade, as the beast, scared at the *feu-de-joie*, had suddenly bucked and bounced like an india-rubber ball. . . . He handed the telegram to Bertram without comment.

That young gentleman read it through, and again. He swallowed hard and read it once more. His hand shook. He looked at the Adjutant, who noticed that he had turned quite pale.

"Got it?" enquired Murray. "Here, sit down." He thought the boy was going to faint.

"Ye-e-s. I—er-think so," was the reply. "*I* am to take the draft from the Hundred and Ninety-Ninth to the Hundred and Ninety-Eighth in East Africa! . . . Oh, Murray, I *am* sorry-for you. . . . And I am so utterly inadequate and incompetent. . . . It is cruel hard luck for you. . . ."

The Adjutant, a really keen, good soldier, said nothing. There was nothing to say. He felt that his life lay about him in ruins. At the end of the war-which might come anywhere now that Russia had "got going"—he would be one of the few professional soldiers without active service experience, without a medal or decoration of any sort whatever. . . . Children who had gone straight from Sandhurst to the Front would join this very battalion, after the war, with their honours thick upon them-and when he, the Adjutant, tried to teach them things, they'd smile and say: "We-ah!—didn't do it like that at the Marne and Ypres. . . ." He could go straight away and shoot himself then and there. . . . And this pink civilian baby! This "Cupid"! No, there was nothing to say-apart from the fact that he could not trust himself to speak.

For minutes there was complete silence in the little office. Bertram was as one in a dream—a dream which was partly sweet and partly a nightmare. *He* to go to the Front to-morrow? To go on Active Service? He whom fellows always ragged, laughed at, and called Cupid and Blameless Bertram and Innocent Ernest? To go off from here in sole charge of a hundred of these magnificent fighting-men, and then to be an officer in a regiment that had been fighting for weeks and had already lost a third of its men and a half of its officers, in battle? He, who had never fired a gun in his life; never killed so much as a pheasant, a partridge, a grouse or a rabbit; never suffered so much as a tooth-extraction —to shoot at his fellow-men, to risk being horribly mangled and torn! . . . Yes-but what was that last compared with the infinitely greater horror, the unspeakable ghastliness of being *inadequate*, of being too incapable and inexperienced to do his duty to the splendid fellows who would look to him, the White Man, their Officer, for proper leadership and handling?

To fail them in their hour of need. . . . He tried to moisten dry lips with a dry tongue.

Oh, if only he had the knowledge and experience of the Adjutant-he would then change places with no man in the world. Why had the England that had educated him so expensively, allowed him to grow up so hopelessly ignorant of the real elemental essentials of life in the World-As-It-Is? He had been brought up as though the World were one vast Examination Hall, and nothing else. Yes-he had been prepared for examinations all his life, not prepared for the World at all. Oh, had he but Murray's knowledge and experience, or one-tenth part of it-he would find the ability, courage, enthusiasm and willingness all right.

But, as it was, who was *he*, Bertram Greene, the soft-handed sedentary, the denizen of libraries and lecture-rooms, the pale student, to dare to offer to command, control and guide trained and hardy men of war? What had he (brought up by a maiden "aunt"!) to do with arms and blood, with stratagems and ambuscades, with gory struggles in unknown holes and corners of the Dark Continent? Why, he had never shouted an order in his life; never done a long march; never administered a harsh reprimand; never fired a revolver nor made a pass with a sword. (If only he *had* had more to do with such "passes" and less with his confounded examination passes-he might feel less of an utter fraud now.) At school and at Oxford he had been too delicate for games, and in India, too busy, and too interested in more intellectual matters, for shikar, sport and hunting. He had just been "good old Blameless Bertram" and "our valued and respected Innocent Ernest," and "our pretty pink Cupid" —more at home with antiquarians, ethnologists, Orientalists and scientists than with sportsmen and soldiers. . . .

The fact was that Civilisation led to far too much specialisation and division of labour. Why shouldn't fellows be definitely trained and taught, physically as well as mentally? Why shouldn't every man be a bit of an artisan, an agriculturalist, a doctor, and a soldier, as well as a mere wretched book-student? Life is not a thing of books. . . .

Anyhow, in the light of this telegram, it was pretty clear that his uncle, General Sir Hugh Walsingham, K.C.S.I., had described him more optimistically than accurately when forwarding his application for admission to the Indian Army Reserve of Officers, to the Military Secretary. . . . Another awful thought-suppose he let Uncle Hugh down badly. . . . And what of his father? . . .

Well-there was one thing, he would do his absolute utmost, his really ultimate best; and no one could do more. But, oh, the fathomless profundity of his ignorance and inexperience! Quite apart from any question of leading men in battle, how could he hope to avoid incurring their contempt on the parade-ground? They'd see he was an Ass, and a very ignorant one to boot, before he had been in front of them for five minutes. . . . One thing-he'd know that drill-book absolutely by heart before long. His wretched examination training would stand him in good stead there, at any rate. . . .

"Must tell the Colonel," said Murray suddenly, and he arose and left the office.

A few minutes later the Quartermaster, Lieutenant Macteith, entered. Instead of going to his desk and settling down to work, he took a powerful pair of field-glasses from their case on Murray's table and carefully examined Bertram through them.

Bertram coloured, and felt quite certain that he did not like Macteith at all.

Reversing the glasses, that gentleman then examined him through the larger end.

"Oh, my God!" he ejaculated at last, and then feigned unconquerable nausea.

He had heard the news, and felt personally injured and insulted that this miserable half-baked rabbit should be going on Active Service while Lieutenant and Quartermaster Macteith was not.

An orderly entered, saluted, and spoke to him in Hindustani.

"Colonel wants you," he said, turning to Bertram, as the orderly again saluted, wheeled about, and departed. "He wants to strain you to his breast, to clasp your red right hand, to give you his photograph and beg for yours-or else to wring your neck!" And as Bertram rose to go, he added: "Here-take this pen with you."

"What for?" asked Bertram.

"To write something in his autograph-album and birthday-book—he's sure to ask you to," was the reply.

Bertram turned and departed, depressed in spirit. He hated anyone to hate him, and he had done Macteith no harm. But in spite of his depression, he was aware of a wild little devil of elation who capered madly at the back of his brain. This exuberant little devil appeared to be screaming joyous war-whoops and yelling: "*Active Service!* . . . *You are going to see service and to fight!* . . . *You will have a war-medal and clasps!* . . . *You are going to be a real war-hardened and experienced soldier!* . . . *You are going to be a devil of a fellow!* . . . *Whoop and dance, you Ass!* . . . *Wave your arms about, and caper!* . . . *Let out a loud yell, and do a fandango!* . . ." But in the Presence of the Colonel, Bertram declined to entertain the little devil's suggestions, and he neither whooped nor capered. He wondered, nevertheless, what this cold monument of imperturbability would do if he suddenly did commence to whoop, to caper and to dance before him. Probably say "H'm!"—since that was generally reported to be the only thing he ever said. . . .

Marching into the room in which the Colonel sat at his desk, Bertram halted abruptly, stood at attention stiffly, and saluted smartly. Then he blushed from head to foot as he realised that he had committed the ghastly *faux pas*, the horrible military crime, of saluting bare-headed. He could have wept with vexation. To enter so smartly, hearing himself like a trained soldier-and then to make such a Scarlet Ass of himself! . . . The Colonel gazed at him as at some very repulsive and indescribable, but very novel insect.

". . . And I'll make a list of the cooking-pots and other kit that they'll have to take for use on board, sir, and give it to Greene with a letter to Colonel Rock asking him to have them returned here," the Adjutant was saying, as he laid papers before the Colonel for signature.

"H'm!" said the Colonel.

"I have ordered the draft to parade at seven to-morrow, sir," he continued, "and told the Bandmaster they will be played down to the Docks. . . . Greene can take them over from me at seven and march them off. I have arranged for the kits to go down in bullock-carts beforehand. . . ."

"H'm!" said the Colonel.

"I'll put Greene in the way of things as much as possible to-day," went on the Adjutant. "I'll go with him and get hold of the cooking-pots he'll take for the draft to use on board-and then I'd better run down and see the Staff Embarkation Officer with him, about his cabin and the men's quarters on the *Elymas*, and. . ."

"H'm!" said the Colonel, and taking up his cane and helmet, departed thence without further remark.

". . . And—I hope you'll profit by every word you've heard from the Colonel, my lad," the Adjutant concluded, turning ferociously upon Bertram. "Don't stand there giggling, flippant and indifferent—a perfect picture of the Idle Apprentice, I say," and he burst into a peal of laughter at the solemn, anxious, tragic mask which was Bertram's face.

"No," he added, as they left the room. "Let the Colonel's wise and pregnant observations sink into your mind and bring forth fruit. . . . Such blossoming, blooming flowers of rhetoric *oughter* bring forth fruit in due season, anyhow. . . . Come along o' me."

Leaving the big Mess bungalow, the two crossed the *maidan*, wherein numerous small squads of white-clad recruits were receiving musketry-instruction beneath the shady spread of gigantic banyans. The quickly signalled approach of the dread Adjutant-Sahib galvanised the Havildar and Naik instructors to a fearful activity and zeal, which waned not until he had passed from sight. In one large patch of shade the Bandmaster-an ancient Pathan, whose huge iron-rimmed spectacles accorded but incongruously with his fierce hawk face, ferocious curling white moustache and beard, and bemedalled uniform-was conducting the band's tentative rendering of "My Bonnie is over the Ocean," to Bertram's wide-eyed surprise and interest. Through the Lines the two officers made a kind of Triumphal Progress, men on all sides stiffening to "attention" and saluting as they passed, to where, behind a cook-house, lay nine large smoke-blackened cooking-pots under a strong guard.

"There they are, my lad," quoth the hitherto silent Adjutant. "Regard them closely, and consider them well. Familiarise yourself with them, and ponder."

"Why?" asked Bertram.

"For in that it is likely that they, or their astral forms, will haunt your thoughts by day, your dreams by night. Your every path through life will lead to them," answered the Adjutant.

"What have I got to do with them?" enquired Bertram, with uncomfortable visions of adding the nine big black cauldrons to his kit.

"Write about them," was the succinct reply.

"To whom?" was the next query.

"Child," said the Adjutant solemnly, "you are young and ignorant, though earnest. To you, in your simplicity and innocence—

'A black cooking-pot by a cook-house door
A black cooking-pot is, and nothing more,'

as dear William Wordsworth so truly says in his *Ode on the Imitations of Immorality*, is it-or is it in '*Hark how the Shylock at Heaven's gate sings*'? I forget.... But these are *much* more. Oh, very much."

"How?" asked the puzzled but earnest one.

"*How?* ... Why they are the subject-matter, from this moment, of a Correspondence which will be still going on when your children's grandchildren are doddering grey-beards, and you and I are long since swept into the gulf of well-deserved oblivion. *Babus* yet unborn will batten on that Correspondence and provide posts for their relatives unnumbered as the sands of the seashore, that it may be carried on unfailing and unflagging. As the pen drops from their senile palsied hands they will see the Correspondence take new lease of life, and they will turn their faces to the wall, smile, and die happy."

"I am afraid I don't really understand," admitted Bertram.

"*Do* you think Colonel Rock will return these pots? Believe me, he will not. He will say, '*A pot in the hand is worth two in the bush-country*,' or else '*What I have I hold*,' or '*Ils suis, ils reste*'—being a bit of a scholar like-or perhaps he'll just swear he bought 'em off a man he went to see about a dog, just round the corner, at the pub. I don't know about *that*—but return them he will not...."

"But if I say they belong to Colonel Frost and that he wants them back-and that I promised to make it clear to him that Colonel Frost desires their immediate return," protested Bertram, who visualised himself between the anvil of Colonel Rock and the hammer of Colonel Frost.

"Why then he'll probably say they now 'belong to Colonel Rock and that he *doesn't* want them to go back, and that you must promise to make it clear to Colonel Frost that he desires *his* immediate return'—to the devil," replied the Adjutant.

"Yes-every time," he continued. "He will pretend that fighting Germans is a more urgent and important matter than returning pots. He will lay aside no plans of battle and schemes of strategy to attend to the pots. He will detail no force of trusty soldiers to convoy them to the coast.... He will refuse to keep them prominently before his vision.... In short, he will hang on to the damn things.... And when the war is o'er and he returns, he'll swear he never had a single cooking-pot in Africa, and in any case they are his own private property, and always were...."

"I shall have to keep on reminding him about them," observed Bertram, endeavouring to separate the grain of truth from the literal "chaff" of the Adjutant-who seemed to be talking rapidly and with bitter humour, to keep himself from thinking of his cruel and crushing disappointment, or to hide his real feelings.

"If you go nightly to his tent, and, throwing yourself prostrate at his feet, clasp him around the knees, and say: '*Oh, sir, think of poor pot-less Colonel Frost*,' he will reply: '*To hell with Colonel Frost!* . . .' Yes-every time. . . . Until, getting impatient of your reproachful presence, he will say: '*You mention pots again and I'll fill you with despondency and alarm. . .*' He'll do it, too-he's quite good at it."

"Rather an awkward position for me," ventured Bertram.

"Oh, quite, quite," agreed Murray. "Colonel Frost will wire that unless you return his pots, he'll break you-and Colonel Rock will state that if you so much as hint at pots, *he'll* break you. . . . But that's neither here nor there-the Correspondence is the thing. It will begin when you are broke by one of the two-and it will be but waxing in volume to its grand climacteric when the war is forgotten, and the pots are but the dust of rust. . . . A great thought. . . Yes. . ."

Bertram stared at the Adjutant. Had he gone mad? Fever? A touch of the sun? It was none of these things, but a rather terrible blow, a blighting and a shattering of his almost-realised hopes-and he must either talk or throw things about, if he were not to sit down and blaspheme while he drank himself into oblivion. . . .

For a time they regarded the pots in awed contemplative silence and felt themselves but ephemeral in their presence, as they thought of the Great Correspondence, but yet with just a tinge of that comforting and sustaining *quorum pais magna fui* feeling, to which Man, the Mighty Atom, the little devil of restless interference with the Great Forces, is ever prone.

In chastened silence they returned to the Adjutant's office, and Bertram sat by his desk and watched and wondered, while that official got through the rest of his morning's work and dealt faithfully with many-chiefly sinners.

He then asked the Native Adjutant, who had been assisting him, to send for Jemadar Hassan Ali, who was to accompany Bertram and the draft on the morrow, and on that officer's arrival he presented him to the young gentleman.

As he bowed and shook hands with the tall, handsome Native Officer, Bertram repressed a tendency to enquire after Mrs. Ali and all the little Allies, remembering in time that to allude directly to a native gentleman's wife is the grossest discourtesy and gravest immorality. All he could find to say was: "*Salaam, Jemadar Sahib*! *Sub achcha hai?*" [150] which at any rate appeared to serve, as the Native Officer gave every demonstration of cordiality and pleasure. What he said in reply, Bertram did not in the least understand, so he endeavoured to put on a look combining pleasure, comprehension, friendliness and agreement-which he found a slight strain- and remarked: "*Béshak! Béshak!*" [151] as he nodded his head. . . .

The Jemadar later reported to his colleagues that the new Sahib, albeit thrust in over the heads of tried and experienced Native Officers, appeared to *be* a Sahib, a gentleman of birth, breeding, and good manners; and evidently possessed of far more than such slight perception and understanding as was necessary for proper appreciation of the worth and virtues of Jemadar Hassan Ali. Also that he was but a hairless-faced babe-but doubtless the Sircar knew what it was about, and was quite right in considering that a young boy of the Indian Army Reserve was fitter to be a Second-Lieutenant in the *pultan*, than was a Jemadar of fifteen years' approved service and three medals. One of his hearers laughed sarcastically, and another grunted approval, but the Subedar-Major remarked that certain opinions, however tenable, were, perhaps, better left unvoiced by those who had accepted service under the Sircar on perfectly clear and definite terms and conditions.

When the Jemadar had saluted and left the office, Murray turned upon Bertram suddenly, and, with a concentrated glare of cold ferocity, delivered himself.

"Young Greene," quoth he, "yesterday I said you were a Good Egg and a desirable. I called you Brother, and fell upon your neck, and I welcomed you to my hearth. I overlooked your being the son of a beknighted General. I looked upon you and found you fair and good-as a 'relief.' You were a stranger, and I took you in. . . . Now you have taken *me* in-and I say you are a cuckoo in the nest, a viper in the back-parlour, a worm in the bud, a microbe in the milk, and an elephant in the ointment. . . . You are a —a —".

"I'm *awfully* sorry, Murray," interrupted the unhappy Bertram. "I'd do *anything* —"

"Yes-and any *body*," continued the Adjutant. "I say you are a pillar of the pot-houses of Gomorrah, a fly-blown turnip and a great mistake. Though of apparently most harmless exterior and of engaging manners, you are an orange filled with ink, an addled egg of old, and an Utter Improbability. I took you up and you have done me down. I took you out and you have done me in. I took you in and you have done me out-of my chance in life. . . . Your name is now as a revolting noise in my ears, and your face a repulsive sight, a thing to break plates on . . . and they 'call you *Cupid*'!"

"I can't tell you how distressed I am about it, Murray," broke in the suffering youth. "If only there were anything I could do so that you could go, and not I —"

"You can do nothing," was the cold reply. "You can not even, in mere decency, die this night like a gentleman. . . . And if you did, they'd only send some other pale Pimple to take the bread out of a fellow's mouth. . . . This is a civilians' war, mark you; they don't want professional soldiers for a little job like this. . . ."

"It wasn't *my* fault, Murray," protested Bertram, reduced almost to tears by his sense of wicked unworthiness and the injustice to his kind mentor of yesterday.

"Perhaps not," was the answer, "but why were you ever *born*, Cupid Greene, that's what I ask? You say it isn't your fault-but if you'd never been born . . . Still, though I can never forget, I forgive you, and would share my last pot of rat-poison with you cheerfully. . . . Here-get out your note-book," and he proceeded to give the boy every "tip" and piece of useful advice and information that he could think of as likely to be beneficial to him, to the men, to the regiment, and to the Cause.

Chapter III
Preparations

That night Bertram could not sleep. The excitement of that wonderful day had been too much for his nerves, and he lay alternating between the depths of utter black despair, fear, self-distrust and anxiety on the one hand, and the heights of exultation, hope, pride, and joy on the other.

At one moment he saw himself the butt of his colleagues, the contempt of his men, the *bête noir* of his Colonel, the shame of his Service, and the disgrace of his family.

At another, he saw himself winning the approval of his brother officers by his modesty and sporting spirit, the affection and admiration of his men by his kindness and firmness, the goodwill of his Colonel by his obvious desire to learn and his keen enthusiasm in his duty, the respect of his Service for winning a decoration, and the loving regard of the whole clan of Greene for his general success as a soldier.

But these latter moments were, alas, far less realistic and convincing than the others. In them he merely hoped and imagined-while in the black ones he felt and *knew*. He could not do otherwise than realise that he was utterly inexperienced, ignorant, untried and incompetent, for it was the simple fact. If *he* could be of much use, then what is the good of training men for years in colleges, in regiments, and in the field, to prepare them to take their part in war?

He knew nothing of either the art or the science of that great and terrible business. He had neither the officer's trained brain nor the private soldier's trained body; neither the theory of the one nor the practice of the other. Even if, instead of going to the Front to-morrow as an officer, he had been going in a British regiment as a private, he would have been equally useless. He had never been drilled, and he had never used a weapon of any kind. All he had got was a burning desire to be of use, a fair amount of intelligence, and, he hoped, the average endowment of courage. Even as to this last, he could not be really certain, as he had never yet been tried-but he was very strongly of opinion that the dread of showing himself a coward would always be far stronger than the dread of anything that the enemy could do to his vile body. His real fear was that he should prove incompetent, be unequal to emergency, and fail those who relied upon him or trusted in him. When he thought of that, he knew Fear, the cold terror that causes a fluttering of the heart, a dryness of the mouth, a weakness of the knees, and a sinking of the stomach.

That was the real dread, that and the fear of illness which would further decrease capacity and usefulness. What were mere bullets and bayonets, wounds and death, beside revealed incompetence and failure in duty?

Oh, that he might have luck in his job, and also keep in sufficient health to be capable of his best-such as it was.

When Hope was in the ascendant, he assured himself that the greatest work and highest duty of a British officer in a Native regiment was to encourage and enhearten his men; to set them a splendid example of courage and coolness; to hearten them up when getting depressed; to win their confidence, affection and respect, so that they would cheerfully follow him anywhere and "stick it" as long as he did, no matter what the hardship, danger, or misery. These things were obviously a thousand times more important than parade-ground knowledge and such details as correct alignment, keeping step, polishing buttons, and so forth-important as these might be in their proper place and season. And one did not learn those greater things from books, nor on parade, nor at colleges. A man as ignorant as even he of drill, internal economy, tactics and strategy, might yet be worth his rations in the trenches, on the march, yes, or in the wild, fierce bayonet-charge itself, if he had the attributes that enable him to encourage, uplift, enhearten and give confidence.

And then his soaring spirit would swiftly stoop again, as he asked himself: "And have *I* those qualities and attributes?" and sadly replied: "Probably not-but what is, at any rate, certain, is the fact that I have no knowledge, no experience, no understanding of the very alphabet of military lore, no slightest grasp of the routine details of regimental life, discipline, drill, regulations, internal economy, customs, and so forth-the things that are the elementary essentials of success to a body of armed men proceeding to fight." . . . And in black misery and blank despair he would groan aloud: "*I cannot go. I cannot do it.*" . . . He was very young, very much a product of modern civilisation, and a highly specialised victim of a system and a generation that had taken too little account of naked fact and elemental basic tendency—a system and a generation that pretended to believe that human nature had changed with human conditions. As he realised, he had, like a few million others, been educated not for Life and the World-As-It-Is, but for examinations and the world as it is not, and never will be. . . .

He tossed and turned through the long hot night on the little hard camp-bed, listening to Murray's regular breathing and the scampering of the rats as they disported themselves on the other side of the canvas ceiling cloth and went about their unlawful occasions. . . .

He reviewed the events of that epoch-making day from the arrival of the telegram to his getting into bed. . . . A memorable morning, a busy afternoon and evening, a rotten night-with a beastly climax-or anti-climax. . . . Would he never get to sleep on this hard, narrow bed? . . . What would he be fit for on the dreadful morrow if he slept not at all? . . . What a day it had been! Rather amusing about those cooking-pots. It wouldn't be very amusing for *him* if the situation developed as Murray had prophesied. . . . Rather a good bit of work that he had put in between lunch and dinner with the drill-book and a box of matches. Matches made good sections, companies, and battalions for practising drill-manœuvres on a desk-but it would he a different thing to give the orders correctly and audibly to hundreds of men who watched one with inscrutable eyes. . . . How he wished he had declined the invitation of Bludyer to accompany him and Macteith to the theatre. . . . They had proceeded in a car to the Club and there picked up some other fellows. The play was *The Girl in the Taxi*, and Bertram sat ashamed, humiliated and angry, as a third-rate company of English actors and actresses performed their sorry parts in a travesty of European life and manners, before the avid eyes of hundreds of natives. There they sat, with faces contemptuous, sensual, blank, eager, gleeful or disgusted, according to their respective conditions and temperaments-the while they gathered from the play that English life is a medley of infidelity, dissipation, intrigue and vulgarity.

And, after the play, Macteith had said: "Let's go to the Home-from-Home for a 'drink-and-a-little-music—what-what'?"

Bertram had thought it a somewhat strange proceeding to go to a Home, at eleven o'clock at night, for music, and he would greatly have preferred to go to bed. However, he could not very well say that they must take him back to bed first, nor announce his intention of leaving the party and walking home. . . .

. . . Macteith having given instructions to the Eurasian chauffeur, the taxi sped away and, skirting the sea-shore, turned off into a quiet avenue of giant palms, in which stood detached bungalows of retiring and unobtrusive mien. Into the compound of one of these the taxi turned, and a bell rang loudly, apparently of its own volition. As they got out of the car, a lady came out to the brilliantly lighted verandah from the drawing-room which opened on to it. Bertram did not like the look of this lady at all. Her face reminded him of that of a predatory animal or bird, with its fierce eyes, thin, hard lips and aquiline nose. Nor, in his estimation, did the obvious paint and powder, the extreme-fashioned satin gown, and the profusion of jewellery which she wore, do anything to mitigate the unfavourable impression received at first sight of her face. . . . Really the last person one would have expected to find in charge of a Home. . . . Nor was Macteith's greeting of "Hullo, Fifi, my dear! Brought some of the Boys along," calculated to allay a growing suspicion that this was not really a Home at all.

Entering the drawing-room with the rest, Bertram beheld a bevy of ladies sitting in an almost perfect circle, each with a vacant chair beside her. Some of them were young, and some of them presumably had been. All were in evening dress and in the exaggerated extreme of fashion. All seemed to be painted and powdered, and all looked tired and haggard. Another attribute common to the whole party was that they all seemed to be foreigners-judging by their accents as they welcomed Macteith and some of the others as old acquaintances.

Bertram liked the look of these ladies as little as he did that of the person addressed as "Fifi," and he hoped that the party would not remain at the house long. He was tired, and he felt thoroughly uncomfortable, as noisy horse-play and badinage began, and waxed in volume and pungency. A servant, unbidden, entered with a tray on which stood three bottles of champagne and a number of glasses. He noticed that the bottles had been opened, that the corks and gold-foil looked weary and experienced, and that the wine, when poured out, was singularly devoid of bubbles and froth. He wished he had not come. . . . He did not want to drink alleged champagne at midnight. . . . There was no music, and the people were of more than doubtful breeding, taste and manners. . . . Macteith had actually got his arm round the waist of one woman, and she was patting his cheek as she gazed into his eyes. Another pair exchanged a kiss before his astonished gaze. He decided to walk out of the house, and was about to do so when the girl nearest to him seized his hand and said: "You seet daown 'ere an' spik to me, sare," as she pulled him towards the chair that stood vacant beside her. In an agony of embarrassment born of a great desire to refuse to stay another minute, and a somewhat unnecessary horror of hurting the young lady's feelings by a refusal, he seated himself with the remark: "Merci, mam'selle-mais il se fait tard. Il est sur les une heure . . ." as she appeared to be a French woman.

"Laissez donc!" was the reply. "Il est l'heure du berger," a remark the point of which he missed entirely. Finding that he knew French, she rattled on gaily in that tongue, until Bertram asked her from what part of France she came. On learning that she was from Alais in Provence, he talked of Arles, Nismes, Beaucaire, Tarascon, Avignon and the neighbourhood, thinking to please her, until, to his utter amazement and horror, she turned upon him with a vile, spitting oath, bade him be silent, and then burst into tears. Feeling more shocked, unhappy and miserable than he had ever felt before, he begged the girl to accept his regrets and apologies-as well as his farewell-and to tell him if he could in any way compensate her for the unintentional hurt he had somehow inflicted.

On her sullen reply of "Argent comptant porte médecine," Bertram dropped a fifty rupee note into her lap and literally fled from the house. . . .

. . . Yes —a rotten night with a beastly anti-climax to the wonderful day on which he had received . . . *he*, of all people in the world! . . . had received orders to proceed to the Front. . . . Bertram Greene on Active Service! How could he have the impudence-and it all began again and was revolved once more in his weary mind. . . .

Dawn brought something of hope and a little peace to the perturbed soul of the over-anxious boy.

Chapter IV
Terra Marique Jactatus

As he arrayed himself in all his war-paint, after his sleepless and unhappy night, Bertram felt feverish, and afraid. His head throbbed violently, and he had that distressing sensation of being remorselessly urged on, fatedly fury-driven and compelled to do all things with terrible haste and hurry.

Excitement, anxiety, sleeplessness and the conflicting emotions of hope and fear, were taking their toll of the nervous energy and vitality of the over-civilised youth.

He felt alarmed at his own alarm, and anxious about his own anxiety-and feared that, at this rate, he would be worn out before he began, a physical and mental wreck, fitter for a hospital-ship than a troop-ship, before ever he started.

"The lad's over-engined for his beam," observed Murray to himself, as he lay on his camp cot, drinking his *choti hazri* tea, and watching Bertram, who, with white face and trembling fingers, stood making more haste than speed, as he fumbled with straps and buckles. "Take it easy, my son," he said kindly. "There's tons of time, and then some. I'll see you're not late. . . ."

"Thanks, Murray," replied Bertram, "but —"

"Here-take those belts off at once," interrupted the Adjutant. "Take the lot off and lie down again-and smoke this cigarette. . . . *At once*, d'ye hear?" and the tone was such that Bertram complied without comment. He sank on to the camp-bed, swung up his long legs, with their heavy boots, shorts, and puttees and puffed luxuriously. He had intended to be a non-smoker as well as a teetotaller, now that he was "mobilised," but it would be as well to obey Murray now and begin his abstinence from tobacco when he got on board. He lay and smoked obediently, and soon felt, if not better, at least calmer, cooler and quieter.

"Blooming old tub won't start till to-night —you see'f she does," said Murray. "Sort of thing we always do in the Army. . . . *Always*. . . . Harry and hurry everybody on parade at seven, to catch a boat that doesn't profess to sail till two, and probably won't actually do it till midnight."

"I should die of shame if I were late for my first parade," said Bertram anxiously.

"You'd die of the Colonel, if you didn't of shame," was the reply. . . . "I'll see you're not late. You take things a bit easier, my son. Your King and Country want you in East Africa, not in a lunatic asylum —"

"*Pappa*! *What part did you take in the Great War?*" squeaked a falsetto voice from the door, and looking up, Bertram beheld Lieutenant Bludyer, always merry and bright, arrayed in crimson, scarlet-frogged pyjama coat, and pink pyjama trousers. On his feet were vermilion velvet slippers.

"I'll take a leading part in your dirty death," said the Adjutant, turning to the speaker, or squeaker.

"Thought this might be useful, Greene," continued Bludyer in his natural voice, as he handed Bertram a slab of thin khaki linen and a conical cap of a kind of gilded corduroy. "Make yourself a regimental *puggri* in the day of battle. Put the cap on your nut and wind the turban over it. . . . Bloke with a helmet and a white face hasn't an earthly, advancing with a line of Sepoys in *puggris*. The enemy give him their united attention until he is outed. . . ."

"Oh, thanks, awfully, Bludyer," began Bertram.

"So go dirty till your face is like Murray's, grow a hoary, hairy beard, an' wear a turban on your fat head," continued Bludyer. "Your orderly could do it on for you, so that it wouldn't all come down when you waggled. . . ."

"Thanks, most awfully. It's exceedingly kind of you, Bludyer," acknowledged Bertram, and proceeded to stuff the things into his haversack.

"Wow! Wow!" ejaculated Bludyer. "Nice-mannered lad and well brought up, ain't he, Randolph Murray?" and seating himself on that officer's bed, he proceeded to use the tea-cosy as a foot-warmer, the morning being chilly.

The Adjutant arose and proceeded to dress.

"Devil admire me!" he suddenly shouted, pointing at Bertram. "Look at that infernal lazy swine! Did you ever see anything like it, Bludyer? Lying hogging there, lolling and loafing in bed, as if he had all day to finish nothing in! . . . Here, get up, you idle hound, and earn your living. Dress for parade, if you can do nothing else."

And Bertram gathered that he might now get on with his preparations.

"Yes," added Bludyer, "you really ought to get on with the war, Greene. *Isn't* he a devil-may-care fellow, Murray? He don't give a damn if it snows," and adding that it was his flute-night at the Mission, and he now must go, the young gentleman remained seated where he was.

"You aren't hurrying a bit, Greene," he remarked, after eyeing Bertram critically for a few minutes. "He won't prosper and grow rich like that, will he, Randolph Murray? That is not how the Virtuous Apprentice got on so nicely, and married his master's aunt. . . . No. . . . And Samuel Smiles was never late for parade-of that I'm quite certain. No. '*Self*-help' was *his* motto, and the devil take the other fellow. . . . Let me fasten that for you. This strap goes under not over. . . ." And, with his experienced assistance, Bertram was soon ready, and feeling like a trussed fowl and a Christmas-tree combined, by the time he had festooned about him his sword, revolver, full ammunition-pouches, field-glasses, water-bottle, belt-haversack, large haversack, map-case, compass-pouch, whistle-lanyard, revolver-lanyard, rolled cape, and the various belts, straps and braces connected with these articles.

By the time the last buckle was fastened, he longed to take the whole lot off again for a few minutes, and have a really comfortable breathe. (But he *did* wish Miranda Walsingham could see him.)

* * *

In a corner of the parade-ground stood the Hundred, the selected draft which was to proceed to Africa to fill the gaps that war had torn in the ranks of the Hundred and Ninety-Eighth. On their flank the regimental band was drawn up in readiness to play them to the docks. The men wore khaki turbans, tunics, shorts, puttees and hob-nailed boots, and carried only haversacks, water-bottles, bandoliers, rifles and bayonets. The rest of their kit, each man's done up in a neat bundle inside his waterproof ground-sheet and striped cotton sleeping-*dhurrie*, had gone on in bullock-carts to await them at the wharf.

Around the Hundred stood or squatted the remainder of the battalion, in every kind and degree of dress and undress. Occasionally one of these would arise and go unto his pal in the ranks, fall upon his neck, embrace him once again, shake both his hands alternately, and then return to the eligible site whence, squatting on his heels, he could feast his eyes upon his *bhai*, his brother, his friend, so soon to be torn from him. . . . As the officers approached, these spectators fell back. Bertram's heart beat so violently that he feared the others would hear it. Was he going to have "palpitations" and faint, or throw a fit or something? He was very white, and felt very ill. Was his ignorance and incompetence to be exposed and manifested now? . . .

"Look fierce and take over charge, my son," said the Adjutant, as the small party of officers came in front of the draft.

"Company!" shouted Bertram, "Shun!"

That was all right. He had hit the note nicely, and his voice had fairly boomed. He had heard that men judge a new officer by his voice, more than anything.

The Hundred sprang to attention, and Bertram, accompanied by the Adjutant and Macteith, walked slowly down the front rank and up the rear, doing his best to look as though he were critically and carefully noting certain points, and assuring himself that certain essentials were in order. He was glad that he had not suddenly to answer such a question as "*What* exactly are you peering at and looking for?" He wished he had sufficient Hindustani to ask a stern but not unkindly question here and there, or to make an occasional comment in the manner of one from whom no military thing is hid. He suddenly remembered that he knew the Hindustani for "How old are you?" so he asked this question of a man whose orange-coloured beard would obviously have been white but for henna dye. Not in the least understanding the man's reply, he remarked "H'm!" in excellent imitation of the Colonel, and passed on.

"Not the absolute pick of the regiment, I should think, are they?" he remarked to Murray, as they returned to the front of the company.

"They are not," he said.

"Pretty old, some of them," added Bertram, who was privately hoping that he did not look such a fraudulent Ass as he felt.

Major Fordinghame strolled up and returned the salutes of the group of officers.

"This experienced officer thinks the draft is not the pure cream of the regiment, Major," said Murray, indicating Bertram.

"Fancy that, now," replied Major Fordinghame, and Bertram blushed hotly.

"I thought some of them seemed rather old, sir," he said, "but-er-perhaps old soldiers are better than young ones?"

"It's a matter of taste-as the monkey said when he chewed his father's ear," murmured Bludyer.

Silence fell upon the little group.

"And both have their draw-backs —as the monkey said when she pulled her twins' tails," he added pensively.

Bertram wondered what he had better do next.

The Native Officer of the draft came hurrying up, and saluted. Another Hindustani sentence floated into Bertram's mind. "You are late, Jemadar Sahib," said he, severely.

Jemadar Hassan Ali poured forth a torrent of excuse or explanation which Bertram could not follow.

"What do you do if a Havildar or Naik or Sepoy is late for parade?" he asked, or attempted to ask, in slow and barbarous Hindustani.

Another torrent of verbiage, scarcely a word of which was intelligible to him.

He put on a hard, cold and haughty look, or attempted to do so, and kept, perforce, an eloquent but chilling silence. Murray and the Major exchanged glances.

"Greene Sahib is *very* particular and *very* strict, Jemadar Sahib," said the Major. "You had better bear it in mind, and tell the men too. He'll stand no sort of nonsense from anybody. You'll find him very kind so long as he is satisfied, but if he isn't —well!" and the Major shrugged his shoulders expressively.

Bertram looked gratefully at the Major (for he understood "Englishman's Hindustani"), and as sternly as he could at the Jemadar, who saluted again and retired.

The Colonel rode up, and the officers sprang to attention.

"Everything ready, sir," said the Adjutant. "They can march off when you like."

"H'm!" said the Colonel, and stared at Bertram as though he honestly and unaffectedly did wonder why God made such things. He then wheeled his horse towards the waiting Hundred. "Men of the Hundred and Ninety-Ninth," said he in faultless Hindustani, "you are now going across the Black Water to fight the enemies of the King Emperor, and of yourselves. They would like to conquer your country and oppress you. You go to fight for your own homes and children, as well as for your Emperor. Bring honour to your regiment and yourselves. Show the *Germanis* and their *Hubshis* [152] what Indian Sepoys can do-both in time of battle and in time of hunger, thirst, and hardship. Before God I say I would give anything to come with you, but I have to do my duty here-for the present. We may meet again in Africa. Good-bye. Good luck. . . . Good-bye. . . ." The Jemadar called for three cheers for the Colonel, and the Hundred lustily cried: "*'Eep, 'Eep, 'Oorayee*." The remainder of the regiment joined in, and then cheered the Hundred. Meanwhile, the Colonel turned to Bertram.

"Good-by, young Greene. Good luck," he said, and leaning from his horse, wrung Bertram's hand as though it had been that of his only son.

Similarly did the others, with minor differences.

"Well-it's useless to weep these unavailing tears," sobbed Bludyer. "There's an end to everything, as the monkey said when he seized the tip of his mother's nose...."

"Farewell, my blue-nosed, golden-eyed, curly-eared Mother's Darling," said Macteith.

"Good luck, sonny. Write and let me know how you get on," said Murray. "You'll do. You've got the guts all right, and you'll very soon get the hang of things...."

"March 'em off, now," he added. "Chuck a chest, and don't give a damn for anybody," and Bertram carefully collected his voice, swallowed a kind of lump in his throat, bade his wildly beating heart be still, gave thought to the drill-book, and roared:

"Company!... 'Shun!... Slope *Arms*!... Form *fours*!... *Right*!... Quick *march*!"—the band struck up-and they were off.

Yes, he, Bertram Greene, pale clerkly person, poet and æsthete, was marching proudly, in full military attire, at the head of a hundred fighting-men —marching to the inspiring strains of the regimental band, to where the trooper waited on the tide! If his father could only see him! He was happy as he had never been before in his life, and he was proud as he never had been before.... If Miranda could only see him! He, Bertram Greene, was actually marching to war, with sword on thigh, and head held high, in sole command of a hundred trained fighting-men!

His heart beat very fast, but without pain now, and he was, for the moment, free of his crushing sense of inadequacy, inexperience and unworthiness. He was only conscious of a great pride, a great hope, and a great determination to be worthy, so far as in him lay the power, of his high fate....

No man forgets his first march at the head of his own force, if he forgets his first march in uniform. For Bertram this was both. It was his first march in uniform, and he was in whole and sole control of this party-like a Centurion of old tramping the Roman Road at the head of his hundred Legionaries-and Bertram felt he would not forget it if he lived till his years equalled the number of his men.

It was not a very long march, and it was certainly not a very picturesque one-along the cobbled Dock Road, with its almost innumerable cotton-laden bullock-carts —but Bertram trod on air through a golden dream city and was exalted, brother to the Knights of Arthur who quested for the Grail and went about to right the wrong and to succour the oppressed....

Arrived at the dock-gates, he was met and guided aright, by a brassarded myrmidon of the Embarkation Staff Officer, to where His Majesty's Transport *Elymas* lay in her basin beside a vast shed-covered wharf.

Beneath this shed, Bertram halted his men, turned them into line, and bade them pile arms, fall out, and sit them down in close proximity to their rifles.

Leaving the Jemadar in charge, he then went up the gangway of the *Elymas* in search of the said Embarkation Staff Officer, who, he had been told, would allot him and his men their quarters on the ship. As he gazed around the deserted forward well-deck, he saw an officer, who wore a lettered red band round his arm, hurrying towards him along the promenade deck, his hands full of papers, a pencil in his mouth, and a careworn, worried look upon his face.

"You Greene, by any chance?" he called, as he ran sideway down the narrow ladder from the upper deck.

"Yes, sir," replied Bertram, saluting as he perceived that the officer was a captain. "Just arrived with a draft of a hundred men from the Hundred and Ninety-Ninth," he added proudly.

"Good dog," was the reply, "keep the perishers out of it for a bit till I'm ready.... Better come with me now though, and I'll show you, *one*, where they're to put their rifles; *two*, where they're to put themselves; *three*, where they will do their beastly cooking; and *four*, where you will doss down yourself.... Don't let there be any mistakes, because there are simply millions more coming," and he led the way to a companion hatch in the after well-deck, and clattered down a ladder into the bowels of the ship, Bertram following him in his twists and turns with a growing sense of bewilderment.

He was very glad to hear that he and his merry men were not to have the ship to themselves, for there were a thousand and one points that he would be very glad to be able to refer to the decision of Authority, or the advice of Experience.

The Embarkation Officer, dripping and soaked and sodden with perspiration, as was Bertram himself, wound his devious way, along narrow passages, ladders and tunnels, to a kind of cage-like cloak-room fitted with racks.

"Your men'll come here in single file, by the way we have come," said he, "enter this armoury one by one, leave their rifles on these racks, and go up that ladder to the deck above, and round to the ladder leading out on the forward well-deck. You'll have to explain it carefully, and shepherd 'm along too, or there'll be a jam and loss of life and-worse-loss of time.... In the early days we managed badly on one occasion and got a crowd of Sikhs pushing against a crowd of Pathans...." He then led the disintegrating Bertram by devious paths to a dark oven-like and smelly place (which Bertram mentally labelled "the horizontal section of the fo'c'sle, three storeys down") in which the Hundred were to live, or to die-poor devils! There would hardly be standing room-and thence to the scene of their culinary labours. Lastly, when the bewildered youth was again feeling very ill, the Embarkation Officer retraced his steps, showed him certain water-taps for the use of his men, and led the way up and out to the blessed light of day, fresh air, and the comparative coolness of the deck. "Your cabin's along here," said he, entering a long corridor that debouched on to the well-deck. "Let's see, Number 43, I think. Yes. A two-berth cabin to yourself-and last trip we had three generals in a one-berth cabin, four colonels in a bath at once, and five common officers on top of one another in each chair at table.... Fact—I assure you.... Go in and chuck away all that upholstery-you can run about in your shirt-sleeves now, or naked if you like, so long as you wear a helmet to show you are in uniform.... Bye-bye—be a good boy," and he bustled away.

Bertram thankfully took the Embarkation Officer's advice, and cast off all impedimenta until he was clad only in khaki shirt, shorts, puttees and boots. He thought he could enter into the feelings of a butterfly as it emerges from the constricting folds of its cocoon.

He sat down for a minute on the white bed prepared for his occupation. The other was cumbered with his valise, sack, and strapped bundle, which had come down on the first of the bullock-carts and been brought on board at once. He looked round the well-appointed, spotless cabin, with its white paint and mahogany fittings, electric fans and lights. That one just beside his pillow would be jolly for reading in bed. Anyhow, he'd have a comfortable and restful voyage. What a blessing that he had a cabin to himself, and what a pity that the voyage took only about ten days.... Would life on a troop-ship be a thing of disciplined strenuousness, or would it be just a perfectly slack time for everybody?... It should be easy for him to hide his ignorance while on board-there couldn't be very much in the way of drill.... How his head throbbed, and how seedy and tired he felt!... He lay back on his bed and then sprang up in alarm and horror at what he had done. A pretty way to commence his Active Service!—and, putting on his heavy and uncomfortable helmet, he hurried to the wharf.

Going down the gangway, he again encountered the Embarkation Officer.

"Better let your men file on board with their rifles first, and then off again for their kits and bedding, and then back again to the quarters I showed you. Having pegged out their claims there, and each man hung his traps on the peg above his sleeping-mat, they can go up on the after well-deck and absolutely nowhere else. See? And no man to leave the ship again, on any pretence whatever. Got it?"

"Yes, sir," replied Bertram, and privately wondered if he would even find his way again to that cage-like cloak-room in the hold, and that "horizontal section of the fo'c'sle three storeys down."

But he *must* do this, his very first job, absolutely correctly, and without any bungling and footling. He must imagine that he was going in for an examination again-an examination this time in quite a new subject, "The art of getting men on board a ship, bedding them down, each with his own bundle of kit, in one place, and storing their rifles in another, without confusion or loss of time." *Quite* a new subject, and one in which previous studies, Classics, Literature, Philosophy, Art, were not going to be of any great value.

Perhaps it would be as well to take the Jemadar, Havildars and Naiks on a personally conducted tour to the armoury, quarters, cooking-places and taps, and explain the *modus operandi* to them as well as he could. One can do a good deal to eke out a scanty knowledge of the vernacular by means of signs and wonders-though sometimes one makes the signs and the other person wonders. . . .

Returning to the oven-like shed, resonant with the piercing howls of *byle-ghari-wallas*, [153]coolies, Lascars and overseers; the racking rattle and clang and clatter of chains, cranes, derricks and donkey-engines; the crashing of iron-bound wheels over cobble-stones, and the general pandemonium of a busy wharf, he beckoned the Jemadar to him and made him understand that he wanted a couple of Havildars and four Naiks to accompany him on board.

Suddenly he had a bright idea. (Good old drill-book and retentive memory of things read, heard, or seen!) . . . "Why have you set no sentry over the arms, Jemadar Sahib? It should not be necessary for me to have to give the order," he said as well as he could in his halting Hindustani.

The Jemadar looked annoyed-and distinctly felt as he looked. Half the men had heard the reproof. He, an old soldier of fifteen years' service, to be set right by a child like this! And the annoying part of it was that the amateur was right! Of course he should have put a sentry over the arms. It was probably the first time he had omitted to do so, when necessary, since he had first held authority . . . and he raged inwardly. There are few things that annoy an Indian more than to be "told off" before subordinates, particularly when he is obviously in the wrong. Was this youthful Greene Sahib a person of more knowledge and experience than had been reported by the Adjutant's Office *babu*? The *babu* had certainly described him as one whom the other officers laughed at for his ignorance and inexperience. Had not the worthy Chatterji Chuckerbutti related in detail how Macteith Sahib had called upon his gods and feigned great sickness after offensively examining Greene Sahib through his field-glasses? Strange and unfathomable are the ways of Sahibs, and perhaps the true inwardness of the incident had been quite otherwise? It might have been an honorific ceremony, in fact, and Macteith Sahib might have feigned sickness at his own unworthiness, according to etiquette? . . . After all, the military salute itself is only a motion simulating the shading of one's eyes from the effulgent glory of the person one salutes; and the Oriental bowing and touching the forehead is only a motion simulating taking up dust and putting it on one's head. . . . Yes-the *babu* may have been wrong, and Macteith Sahib may really have been acclaiming Greene Sahib his superior, and declaring his own miserable unworthiness. . . . One never knew with Sahibs. Their minds are unreadable, and one can never get at what they are thinking, or grasp their point of view. One could only rest assured that there is always method in their madness-that they are clever as devils, brave as lions, and-averse from giving commissions as lieutenants, captains, majors, and colonels to Indian Native Officers. . .

"Get a move on, Jemadar Sahib," said the voice of Greene Sahib curtly, in English, and the Jemadar bustled off to set the sentry and call the Havildars and Naiks-rage in his heart. . . .

More easily than he had expected, Bertram found his way, at the head of the party, to the required places, and showed the Jemadar and Non-commissioned Officers how the men should come and depart, in such manner as to avoid hindering each other and to obviate the possibility of a jam.

The Jemadar began to ask questions, and Bertram began to dislike the Jemadar. He was a talker, and appeared to be what schoolboys call "tricky." He knew that Bertram had very little Hindustani, and seemed anxious to increase the obviousness of the fact.

Bertram felt unhappy and uncomfortable. He wished to be perfectly courteous to him as a Native Officer, but it would not do to let the man mistake politeness for weakness, and inexperience for inefficiency. . . . Was there a faint gleam of a grin on the fellow's face as he said: "I do not understand," at the end of Bertram's attempt at explanation?

"Do *you* understand?" the latter said, suddenly, turning to the senior Havildar, the man who had turned out the Guard for him on his first approach to the Lines on that recent day that seemed so long ago.

"*Han,* [154] *Sahib,*" replied the man instantly and readily. "*Béshak!*" [155]

"Then you'd better explain to the Jemadar Sahib, who does not," said Bertram with a click of his jaw, as he turned to depart.

The Jemadar hastened to explain that he *fully* understood, as Bertram strode off. Apparently complete apprehension had come as soon as he realised that his dullness was to be enlightened by the explanation of the quicker-witted Havildar. He gave that innocent and unfortunate man a look of bitter hatred, and, as he followed Bertram, he ground his teeth. Havildar Afzul Khan Ishak should live to learn the extreme unwisdom of understanding things that Jemadar Hassan Ali professed not to understand. As for Second-Lieutenant Greene-perhaps he should live to learn the unwisdom of quarrelling with an experienced Native Officer who was the sole channel of communication between that stranger and the Draft at whose head he had been placed by a misguided Sircar. . . .

Returning to the wharf, and conscious that he had a splitting head, a sticky mouth, shaking limbs, sore throat and husky voice, Bertram roared orders to the squatting Sepoys, who sprang up, fell in, unpiled arms, and marched in file up the gangway and down into the bowels of the ship, shepherded and directed by the Non-commissioned Officers whom he had posted at various strategic points. All went well, and, an hour later, his first job was successfully accomplished. His men were on board and "shaking down" in their new quarters. He was free to retire to his cabin, bathe his throbbing head, and lie down for an hour or so.

* * *

At about midday he arose refreshed, and went on deck, with the delightful feeling that, his own labours of the moment accomplished, he could look on at the accomplishment of those of others. Excellent! . . . And for many days to come he would be free from responsibility and anxiety, he would have a time of rest, recuperation, and fruitful thought and study. . . . Throughout the morning detachments of Sepoys of the Indian Army and Imperial Service Troops continued to arrive at the wharf and to embark. Bertram was much interested in a double-company of Gurkhas under a Gurkha Subedar, their yellowish Mongolian faces eloquent of determination, grit, and hardiness.

They contrasted strongly with a company of tall, hairy Sikhs, almost twice their size, man for man, but with evidences of more enthusiasm than discipline in their bearing. Another interesting unit was a band of warriors of very mixed nationality, under a huge Jemadar who looked a picture of fat contentment, his face knowing no other expression than an all-embracing smile. It was whispered later that this unit saw breech-loading rifles for the first time, on board the *Elymas*, having been more familiar, hitherto, with jezails, jingals, match-locks, flintlocks, and blunderbusses. Probably a gross exaggeration, or an invention of Lieutenant Stanner, of the Hundred and Ninety-Eighth, who gave them the name of "The Mixed Pickles."

All three of these detachments were Imperial Service Troops-that is to say, were in the service of various Indian Rajahs-but were of very different value, both the Gurkhas and the Sikhs being as good material as could be found among native troops anywhere in the world.

To Bertram, the picture of the little Gurkha Subedar, the tall Sikh Subedar, and the burly Jemadar of the Mixed Pickles, was a very interesting one, as the three stood together on the wharf, eyeing each other like three strange dogs of totally different breeds-say, a fighting terrier, a wolf-hound and a mastiff.

With a snap and a slick, and a smart "*One two,*" a company of British Infantry arrived and embarked. Beside the Mixed Pickles they were as a Navy motor-launch beside a native bunderboat. At them they smiled amusedly, at the Sikhs they stared, and at the Gurkhas they grinned appreciatively.

The news having spread that the *Elymas* would not start until the morrow, various visitors came on board, in search of friends whom they knew to be sailing by her. Captain Stott,

R.A.M.C., came over from the *Madras* hospital ship, in search of Colonel Haldon. Murray and Macteith came down to see Stanner, of the Hundred and Ninety-Eighth, and one Terence Brannigan, of the Baluchis. . . .

"Who's the chap on your right, Colonel?" asked Captain Stott, of gentle and kindly old Colonel Haldon at dinner that evening. "Rather an unusual face to be 'in' khaki-or one would have said so before the war," and he indicated Bertram.

"Dunno," was the reply. "Stranger to me. Nice-lookin' boy. . . . Looks a wee-trifle more like a chaplain than a butcher, as you say," though Captain Stott had not said that at all.

Seeing Bertram talking to Murray and Macteith after dinner, Captain Stott asked the latter who he was, for physiognomy and character-study were a hobby of his.

Macteith told him what he knew, and added: "And they're sending *that* half-baked milksop to British East" (and implied: "While *I*, Lieutenant and Quartermaster Reginald Macteith, remain to kick my heels at the depot.")

Next day the *Elymas* began her voyage, a period of delightful *dolce far niente* that passed like a dream, until one wonderful evening, the palm-clad shores of Africa "arose from out of the azure sea," and, with a great thrill of excitement, hope, anxiety and fear Bertram gazed upon the beautiful scene, as the *Elymas* threaded the lovely Kilindini Creek which divides the Island of Mombasa from the mainland.

Chapter V
Mrs. Stayne-Brooker

And on those same palm-clad shores that arose from out the azure sea, an unhappy woman had been expiating, by long years of bitter suffering, in tears and shame and humiliation, the madness of a moment. . . .

Mrs. Stayne-Brooker's life in German East Africa was, if possible less happy than her life in the British colony. The men she met in Nairobi, Mombasa, Zanzibar, Witu or Lamu, though by no means all gentlemen, all treated her as a gentlewoman; while the men she met in Dar-es-Salaam, Tanga, Tabora, Lindi or Bukoba, whether "gentlemen" or otherwise, did not. In British East Africa her husband was treated by planters, Government officials, sportsmen, and Army men, as the popular and cheery old Charlie Stayne-Brooker —a good man in the club-bar, card-room and billiard-room, on the racecourse, at the tent club, and on shooting trips. With several Assistant District Commissioners and officers of the King's African Rifles he was very intimate. In German East Africa he was treated differently-in a way difficult to define. It was as though he were a person of importance, but *déclassé* and contemptible, and this impression she gained in spite of her knowing no German (a condition of ignorance upon which her husband insisted). The average German official and officer, whether of the exiled Junker class, or of plebeian origin, she loathed-partly because they seemed to consider her "fair game," and made love to her, in more or less broken English, without shame or cessation. Nor did it make life easier for the poor lady that her husband appeared to take delight in the fact. She wondered whether this was due to pride in seeing a possession of his coveted by his "high-well-born," and other, compatriots, or to a desire to keep ever before her eyes a realisation of what her fate would be if he cast her off, or she ran away from him.

Worst of all was life in the isolated lonely house on his coffee and rubber plantation, where for months on end she would never see a white face but his, and for weeks on end, when he was away on his mysterious affairs, no white face at all. . . . And at the bottom of his compound were *bandas*, grass huts, in an enclosure, wherein dwelt native women. . . .

One night, in the year 1914, she sat alone in the silent lonely house, thinking of her daughter Eva at Cheltenham, of her happy, if hapless, girlhood in her father's house, of her brief married life with an honourable English gentleman (oh, the contrast!), and wondering how much longer she could bear her punishment. . . Suddenly and noiselessly appeared in the verandah her husband's chief factotum, head house-boy, and familiar, one Murad, an Arab-Swahili, whom she feared and detested.

"*Bwana* coming," said he shortly, and as noiselessly disappeared.

Going out on to the verandah, she saw her husband and a few "boys" (gun-bearers, porters, and servants) coming through the garden. It was seven weeks since she had seen or heard anything of him.

"Pack," was his greeting, "at once. You start on *safari* to the railway as soon as possible, or sooner. You are going to Mombasa. I have cabled to Eva to come out by the next boat. . . . P. and O. to Aden, and thence to Mombasa. . . . She should be here in three weeks or so . . ." and he went off to bath and change. At dinner he informed her that she was to settle at Mombasa with Eva, make as many new friends as possible, entertain, and generally be the most English of English matrons with the most English of English daughters-the latter fresh from boarding-school in England. . . . Dear old Charlie Stayne-Brooker, it was to be known, had gone to Bukoba, to the wonderful sleeping-sickness hospital, for diagnosis of an illness. Nothing serious, really, of course-but one couldn't be too careful when one had trouble with the glands of the neck, and certain other symptoms, after spending some time in that beastly tsetse-fly country. . . . She was to give the impression that he had made light of it, and quite "taken her in" —wouldn't dream of allowing his wife and daughter to go up there. People were to form the opinion that poor old Charlie might be in a worse way than his wife imagined.

And if such a thing as war broke out; *if* such a thing came to pass, mark you; her house in Mombasa was to be a perfect Home-from-Home for the officers of the British Expeditionary Force which would undoubtedly be dispatched from India. It would almost certainly be the Nth Division from Bombay-so she need not anticipate the pleasure of receiving her late husband and his friends. . . . Further instructions she would receive in the event of war, but meanwhile, and all the time, her business was to demonstrate the utter Englishness of the Stayne-Brooker family, and to keep her eyes and ears open. What General or Staff-Officer will not "talk" to a beautiful woman-of the right sort? Eh? Ha-Ha! That was her business in Mombasa now — *and ten times more so if war broke out* —to be a beautiful woman-of the right sort, tremendously popular with the people who know things and do things. Moreover, Eva, her daughter, was to be trained right sedulously to be a beautiful woman-of the right sort. . . . Staff-officers in her pocket. Eh? Ha-Ha! . . . And, sick at heart, loving her daughter, loathing her husband, and loathing the unspeakable rôle he would force upon her, Mrs. Stayne-Brooker travelled to Mombasa, met her daughter with mingled joy and terror, happiness and apprehensive misery, and endeavoured to serve two masters-her conscience and her husband.

Chapter VI
Mombasa

"If you'd like to go ashore and have a look at Mombasa after tiffin, Mr. Greene," said the fourth officer of the *Elymas* to Bertram, the next morning, as he leant against the rail and gazed at the wonderful palm-forest of the African shore, "some of us are going for a row-to stretch our muscles. We could drop you at the Kilindini *bunder*."

"Many thanks," replied Bertram. "I shall be very much obliged," and he smiled his very attractive and pleasant smile.

This was a welcome offer, for, privately, he hated being taken ashore from a ship by natives of the harbour in which the ship lay. One never knew exactly what to pay the wretches. If one asked what the fare was, they always named some absurd amount, and if one used one's common sense and gave them what seemed a reasonable sum they were inevitably hurt, shocked, disappointed in one, indignantly broken-hearted, and invariably waxed clamorous, protestful, demanding more. It had been the same at Malta, Port Said and Aden on his way out to India. In Bombay harbour he had once gone for a morning sail in a bunderboat, and on their return, the captain of the crew of three had demanded fifteen rupees for a two-hour sail. A pound for two hours in a cranky sailing-boat! —and the scoundrels had followed him up the steps clamouring vociferously, until a native policeman had fallen upon them with blows and curses. . . . How he wished he was of those men who can give such people their due in such a manner that they receive it in respectful silence, with apparent contentment, if not gratitude. Something in the eye and the set of the jaw, evidently-and so was glad of the fourth officer's kind suggestion.

He would have been still more glad had he heard the fourth officer announce, at table, to his colleagues: "I offered to drop that chap, Lieutenant Greene, at Kilindini this afternoon, when we go for our grind. He can take the tiller-ropes. . . . I like him the best of the lot-no blooming swank and side about him."

"Yes," agreed the "wireless" operator, "he doesn't talk to you as though he owned the earth, but was really quite pleased to let you stand on it for a bit. . . . I reckon he'll do all right, though, when he gets-down-to-it with the Huns-if he doesn't get done in. . . ."

And so it came to pass that Bertram was taken ashore that afternoon by some half-dozen officers and officials (including the doctor, the purser, and the Marconi operator) of the *Elymas* —worthy representatives of that ill-paid, little-considered service, that most glorious and beyond-praise, magnificent service, the British Mercantile Marine-and, landing in state upon the soil of the Dark Continent, knew "the pleasure that touches the souls of men landing on strange shores."

Arrived at the top of the stone steps of the Kilindini quay, Bertram encountered Africa in the appropriately representative person of a vast negro gentleman, who wore a red fez cap (or tarboosh), a very long white calico night-dress and an all-embracing smile.

"*Jambo*!" quoth the huge Ethiopian, and further stretched his lips an inch nearer to his ears on either side.

Not being aware that the African "*Jambo*" is equivalent to the Indian "*Salaam*," and means "Greeting and Good Health," or words to that effect, Bertram did not counter with a return "*Jambo*," but nodded pleasantly and said: "Er-good afternoon."

Whereupon the ebon one remarked: "Oh, my God, sah, ole chap, thank you," to show, in the first place, that he quite realised the situation (to wit, Bertram's excusable ignorance of Swahili-Arabic), and that he was himself, fortunately, a fluent English scholar. Bertram stared in amazement at the pleasant-faced, friendly-looking giant.

"*Bwana* will wanting servant, ole chap," continued the negro, "don't it? I am best servant for *Bwana*. Speaking English like hell, sah, please. Waiting here for *Bwana* before long time to come. Good afternoon, thank you, please, Master, by damn, ole chap. Also bringing letter for *Bwana*. . . . You read, thanks awfully, your mos' obedient servant by damn, oh, God, thank you, sah," and produced a filthy envelope from some inner pocket of the aforementioned night-dress, which, innocent of buttons or trimming, revealed his tremendous bare chest.

Bertram felt uncomfortable, and, for a moment, again wished that he was one of those men-with-an-eye-and-a-jaw who could give a glare, a grunt, and a jerk of the head which would cause the most importunate native to fade unobtrusively away.

On the one hand, he knew it would be folly to engage as a servant the first wandering scoundrel who accosted him and suggested that he should do so; while, on the other, he distinctly liked this man's cheery, smiling face, he realised that servants would probably be at a decided premium, and he recognised the extreme desirability of having a servant, if have one he must, who spoke English, however weird, and understood it when spoken. Should he engage the man then and there? Would he, by so doing, show himself a man of quick decision and prompt action-one of those forceful, incisive men he so admired? Or would he merely be acting foolishly and prematurely, merely exhibiting himself as a rash and unbalanced young ass? Anyhow, he would read the "chits" which the filthy envelope presumably contained. If these were satisfactory, he would tell the man that the matter was under consideration, and that he might look out for him again and hear his decision.

As Bertram surmised, the envelope contained the man's "chits," or testimonials. The first stated that Ali Sloper, the bearer, had been on *safari* with the writer, and had proved to be a good plain cook, a reliable and courageous gun-carrier, a good shot, and an honest, willing worker. The second was written by a woman whose house-boy Ali Suleiman had been for two years in Mombasa, and who stated that she had had worse ones. The third and last was written at the Nairobi Club by a globe-trotting Englishman named Stayne-Brooker, who had employed the man as personal "boy" and headman of porters, on a protracted lion-shooting trip across the Athi and Kapiti Plains and found him intelligent, keen, cheery, and staunch. (*Where had he heard the name Stayne-Brooker before-or had he dreamed it as a child?*) Certainly this fellow was well-recommended, and appeared to be just the man to take as one's personal servant on active service. But *did* one take a servant on active service? One could not stir, or exist, without one in India, and officers took syces and servants with them on frontier campaigns-but Africa is not India.... However, he could soon settle that point by asking.

"I'll think about it," he said, returning the chits. "I shall be coming ashore again to-morrow.... How much pay do you want?"

"Oh, sah! Master not mentioning it!" was the reply of this remarkable person. "Oh, nothing, nothing, sah! *Bwana* offering me forty rupees a mensem, I say 'No, sah! Too much.'... Master not mention it."

"It might not be half a bad idea to mention it, y'know," said Bertram, smiling and turning to move on.

"Oh, God, sah, thank you, please," replied Ali Sloper, *alias* Ali Suleiman. "I do not wanting forty. I am accepting thirty rupees, sah, and am now your mos' obedient servant by damn from the beginning for ever. And when *Bwana*, loving me still more, can pay more, ole chap. God bless my thank-you soul" —and "fell in" behind Bertram as though prepared to follow him thence to the end of the world or beyond.

Bertram gazed around, and found that he was in a vast yard, two sides of which were occupied by the largest corrugated-iron sheds he had ever seen in his life. One of these appeared to be the Customs shed, and into another a railway wandered. Between two of them, great gates let a white sandy road escape into the Unknown. On the stone quay the heat, shut in and radiated by towering iron sheds, was the greatest he had ever experienced, and he gasped for breath and trickled with perspiration. He devoutly hoped that this was not a fair sample of Africa's normal temperature. Doubtless it would be cooler away from the quay, which, with the iron sheds, seemed to form a Titanic oven for the quick and thorough baking of human beings. It being Sunday afternoon, there were but few such, and those few appeared to be thoroughly enjoying the roasting process, if one might judge from their grinning faces and happy laughter. They were all Africans, and, for the most part, clad in long, clean night-dresses and fez caps. Evidently Ali Sloper or Suleiman was dressed in the height of local fashion. On a bench, by the door of the Customs shed, lounged some big negroes in dark blue tunics and shorts, with blue puttees between bare knees and bare feet. Their tall tarbooshes made them look even taller than they were, and the big brass plates on their belt-buckles shone like gold. Bertram wondered whether the Germans had just such brawny giants in their Imperial African Rifles, and tried to imagine himself defeating one of them in single combat. The effort was a failure.

At the gates was a very different type of person, smarter, quicker, more active and intelligent-looking, a Sikh Sepoy of the local military police. The man sprang to attention and saluted with a soldierly promptness and smartness that were a pleasure to behold.

Outside the dock, the heat was not quite so intense, but the white sandy road, running between high grass and palms, also ran uphill, and, as the perspiration ran down his face, Bertram wished he might discover the vilest, most ramshackle and moth-eaten *tikka-ghari* that ever disgraced the streets of Bombay. That the hope was vain he knew, and that in all the island of Mombasa there is no single beast of burden, thanks to the tsetse fly, whose sting is death to them. . . . And the Mombasa Club, the Fort, and European quarter were at the opposite side of the island, four miles away, according to report. Where were these trolley-trams of which he had heard? If he had to walk much farther up this hill, his uniform would look as though he had swum ashore in it.

"Master buck up like hell, ole chap, thank you," boomed a voice behind. "Trolley as nearer as be damned please. Niggers make push by Jove to Club, thank God," and turning, Bertram beheld the smiling Ali beaming down upon him as he strolled immediately behind him.

"Go away, you ass," replied the hot and irritated Bertram, only to receive an even broader smile and the assurance that his faithful old servant would never desert him-not after having been his devoted slave since so long a time ago before and for ever more after also. And a minute or two later the weary warfarer came in sight of a very narrow, single tram-line, beside the road. Where this abruptly ended stood a couple of strange vehicles, like small, low railway-trolleys, with wheels the size of dinner-plates. On each trolley was a seat of sufficient length to accommodate two people, and above the bench was a canvas roof or shade, supported by iron rods. From a neighbouring bench sprang four men, also clad in night-dresses and fez caps, who, with strange howls and gesticulations, bore down upon the approaching European.

"*Hapa,* [156] *Bwana!*" they yelled. "*Trolley hapa,*" and, for a moment, Bertram thought they would actually seize him and struggle for possession of his body. He determined that if one of the shrieking fiends laid a hand upon him, he would smite him with what violence he might. The heat was certainly affecting his temper. He wondered what it would feel like to strike a man—a thing he had never done in his life. But, on reaching him, the men merely pointed to their respective trolleys and skipped back to them, still pointing, and apparently calling Heaven to witness their subtle excellences and charms.

As Bertram was about to step on to the foremost trolley, the men in charge of the other sprang forward with yelps of anguish, only to receive cause for louder yelps of deeper anguish at the hands of Ali, who, with blows and buffets, drove them before him. Bertram wondered why the pair of them, each as big as their assailant, should flee before him thus. Was it by reason of Ali's greater moral force, juster cause, superior social standing as the follower of a white man, or merely the fact that he took it upon him to be the aggressor. Probably the last. Anyhow-thank Heaven for the gloriously cool and refreshing breeze, caused by the rapid rush of the trolley through the heavy air, as the trolley-"boys" ran it down the decline from the hill-top whence they had started.

As soon as the trolley had gained sufficient momentum, they leapt on to the back of the vehicle, and there clung until it began to slow down again. Up-hill they slowly pushed with terrific grunts, on the level they maintained a good speed, and down-hill the thing rattled, bumped and bounded at a terrific pace, the while Bertram wondered how long it would keep the rails, and precisely what would happen if it jumped them. Had he but known it, there was a foot-brake beneath the seat, which he should have used when going down-hill. 'Twas not for the two specimens of Afric's ebon sons, who perched and clung behind him, to draw his attention to it. Was he not a *Bwana*, a white man, and therefore one who knew all things? And if he wanted to break his neck had he not a right so to do? And if they, too, should be involved in the mighty smash, would not that fact prove quite conclusively that it was their *kismet* to be involved in the smash, and therefore inevitable? Who shall avoid his fate? . . . And so, in blissful ignorance, Bertram swooped down-hill in joyous, mad career. He wished the pace were slower at times, for everything was new and strange and most interesting. Native huts, such as he had seen in pictures (labelled "kaffir-kraals") in his early geography book, alternated with official-looking buildings, patches of jungle; gardens of custard-apple, mango, paw-paw, banana, and papai trees; neat and clean police-posts, bungalows, cultivated fields, dense woods and occasional mosques, Arab houses, go-downs, [157] temples, and native infantry "lines."

On the dazzlingly white road (which is made of coral and nothing else) were few people. An occasional Indian Sepoy, a British soldier, an *askari* of the King's African Rifles, an official *peon* with a belt-plate as big as a saucer (and bearing some such legend as *Harbour Police* or *Civil Hospital*), a tall Swahili in the inevitable long night-dress and tarboosh, or a beautifully worked skull cap, a file of native women clad each in a single garment of figured cotton which extended from arm-pit to ankle, leaving the arms and shoulders bare. The hairdressing of these ladies interested Bertram, for each head displayed not one, but a dozen, partings, running from the forehead to the neck, and suggesting the seams on a football. At the end of each parting was a brief pigtail bound with wire. Bertram wondered why these women always walked one behind the other in single file, and decided that it was an inherited and unconscious instinct implanted by a few thousand years of use of narrow jungle-paths from which they dared not stray as the armed men-folk did. . . .

After half an hour or so of travelling this thrillingly interesting road, Bertram perceived that they were drawing near to the busy haunts of men. From a church, a congregation of Goanese or else African-Portuguese was pouring. The scene was a very Indian one-the women, with their dusky faces and long muslin veils worn *sari*-fashion over their European dresses of cotton or satin; the men, with their rusty black suits or cotton coats and trousers and European hats or solar *topis*. One very venerable gentleman, whose ancestors certainly numbered more Africans than Portuguese, wore a golfing suit (complete, except for the stockings), huge hob-nailed boots, and an over-small straw-yard with a gay ribbon. A fine upstanding specimen of the race, obviously the idol of his young wife, who walked beside him with her adoring gaze fixed upon his shining face, began well with an authentic silk hat, continued excellently with a swallow-tailed morning-coat, white waistcoat, high collar and black satin tie, but fell away from these high achievements with a pair of tight short flannel tennis-trousers, grey Army socks, and white canvas shoes.

"An idol with feet of pipe-clay," smiled Bertram to himself, as his chariot drove heavily through the throng, and his charioteers howled "*Semeele! Semeele!*" at the tops of their voices.

Soon the tram-line branched and bifurcated, and tributary lines joined it from garden-enclosed bungalows and side turnings. Later he discovered that every private house has its own private tram-line running from its front door down its drive out to the main line in the street, and that, in Mombasa, one keeps one's own trolley for use on the public line, as elsewhere one keeps one's own carriage or motor-car.

On, past the Grand Hotel, a stucco building of two storeys, went the rumbling, rattling vehicle, past a fine public garden and blindingly white stucco houses that lined the blindingly white coral road, across a public square adorned with flowering shrubs and trees, to where arose a vast grey pile, the ancient blood-drenched Portuguese fort, and a narrow-streeted, whitewashed town of tall houses and low shops began.

Here the trolley-boys halted, and Bertram found himself at the entrance of the garden of the Mombasa Club, which nestles in the shadow of its mighty neighbour, the Fort-where once resided the Portuguese Governor and the garrison that defied the Arab and kept "the Island of

Blood" for Portugal, and where now reside the Prison Governor and the convicts that include the Arab, and keep the public gardens for the public.

Boldly entering the Club, Bertram left his card on the Secretary and Members (otherwise stuck it on a green-baize board devoted to that purpose), and commenced a tour of inspection of the almost empty building. Evidently Society did not focus itself until the cool of the evening, in Africa as in India, and evidently this club very closely resembled a thousand others across the Indian Ocean from Bombay to Hong Kong, where the Briton congregates in exile. The only difference between this and any "station" club in India appeared to be in the facts that the servants were negroes and the trophies on the walls were different and finer. Magnificent horns, such as India does not produce, alternated with heads of lion and other feral beasts. Later Bertram discovered another difference in that the cheery and hospitable denizens of the Mombasa Club were, on the whole, a thirstier race than those of the average Indian club, and prone to expect and desire an equal thirst in one their guest. He decided that it was merely a matter of climate—a question of greater humidity.

Emerging from an airy and spacious upstairs bar-room on to a vast verandah, his breath was taken away by the beauty of the scene that met his eye, a scene whose charm lay chiefly in its colouring, in the wonderful sapphire blue of the strip of sea that lay between the low cliff, on which the club was built, and the bold headland of the opposite shore of the mainland, the vivid emerald green of the cocoa-palms that clothed that same headland, the golden clouds, the snowy white-horses into which the wind (which is always found in this spot and nowhere else in Mombasa) whipped the wavelets of the tide-rip, the mauve-grey distances of the Indian Ocean, with its wine-dark cloud-shadows, the brown-grey of the hoary fort (built entirely of coral), the rich red of tiled roofs, the vivid splashes of red, orange, yellow and purple from flowering vine and tree and shrub—a wonderful colour-scheme enhanced and intensified by the dazzling brightness of the sun and the crystal clearness of the limpid, humid air. . . . And in such surroundings Man had earned the title of "The Island of Blood" for the beautiful place-and, once again, as in those barbarous far-off days of Arab and Portuguese, the shedding of blood was the burden of his song and the high end and aim of his existence. . . . Bertram sank into a long chair, put his feet up on the mahogany leg-rests, and slaked the colour-thirst of his æsthetic soul with quiet, joyous thankfulness. . . . Beautiful! . . .

What would his father say when he knew that his son was at the Front? . . .

What was Miranda doing? Nursing, probably. . . . What would *she* say when she knew that he was at the Front? . . . Dear old Miranda. . . .

Where had he heard the name, *Stayne-Brooker*, before? *Had* he dreamed it in a nightmare as a child-or had he heard it mentioned in hushed accents of grief and horror by the "grown-ups" at Leighcombe Priory? . . . Some newspaper case perhaps. . . . He had certainly heard it before. . . . He closed his eyes. . . .

A woman strolled by with a selection of magazines in her hand, and took a chair that commanded a view of his. Presently she noticed him. . . . A new-comer evidently, or she would have seen him before. . . . What an exceedingly nice face he had-refined, delicate. . . . Involuntarily she contrasted it with the face of the evil and sensual satyr to whom she was married. . . . She would like to talk to him. . . .

Bertram opened his eyes, and Mrs. Stayne-Brooker became absorbed in the pages of her magazine. . . .

What a beautiful face she had, and *how* sad and weary she looked . . . drawn and worried and anxious. . . . Had she perhaps a beloved husband in the fighting-line somewhere? He would like to talk to her-she looked so kind and so unhappy. . . . A girl, whose face he did not see, came and called her away. . .

Chapter VII
The Mombasa Club

As Bertram lay drinking in the beauty of the scene, the Club began to fill, and more particularly that part of it devoted to the dispensation and consumption of assorted alcoholic beverages. Almost everybody was in uniform, the majority in that of the Indian Army (as there was a large base camp of the Indian Expeditionary Force at Kilindini), and the remainder in those of British regiments, the Navy, the Royal Indian Marine, the Royal Engineers, the Royal Army Medical Corps, Artillery, local Volunteer Corps, and the "Legion of Frontiersmen." A few ladies adorned the lawn and verandahs. Two large and weather-beaten but unascetic-looking men of middle age sat them down in chairs which stood near to that of Bertram. They were clad in khaki tunics, shorts and puttees, and bore the legend "C.C." in letters of brass on each shoulder-strap.

"Hullo!" said the taller of them to Bertram, who was wondering what "C.C." might mean. "Just come ashore from the *Elymas*? Have a drink?"

"Yes," replied he; "just landed. . . . Thanks-may I have a lime-squash?"

"What the devil's that?" asked the other, and both men regarded him seriously and with a kind of shocked interest. "Never heard of it."

"Don't think they keep it here," put in the shorter of the two men. "How d'you make it?"

"Lemon-juice, soda-water, and sugar," replied Bertram, and felt that he was blushing in a childish and absurd manner.

Both men shook their heads, more in sorrow than in anger. They looked at each other, as might two physicians at the bedside of one whose folly has brought him to a parlous pass.

"Quite new to Africa?" enquired the taller.

"Yes. Quite," confessed Bertram.

"Ah! Well, let me give you a word of advice then," continued the man. "*Don't touch dangerous drinks*. Avoid all harmful liquor as you would poison. It is poison, in this climate. Drink is the curse of Africa. It makes the place the White Man's Grave. You can't be too careful. . . . Can you, Piggy?" he added, turning to his friend.

"Quite right, Bill," replied "Piggy," as he rang a little bell that stood on a neighbouring table. "Let's have a 'Devil's Own' cocktail and then some beer for a start, shall we? . . . No-can't be too careful. . . . Look at me f'r example. Been in the country quarter of a century, an' never exceeded once! Never *tasted* it, in fact."

"What-alcohol?" enquired Bertram.

"No. . . . I was talking about harmful liquor," replied Piggy patiently. "Things like —*what* did you call it? . . . Chalk-squash?"

"Lime-squash," admitted Bertram with another glowing blush.

"Give it up, Sonny, give it up," put in Bill. "Turn over a new leaf and start afresh. Make up your mind that, Heaven helping you, you'll never touch a drop of the accursed poison again, but forswear slops and live cleanly; totally abstaining from-what is it? —soda-crunch? —fruit-juice, ginger-beer, lemonade, toast-water, barley-water, dirty-water, raspberryade, and all such filthy decoctions and inventions. . . ."

"Yes-give the country a chance," interrupted Piggy. "Climate's all right if you'll take reasonable care and live moderately," and he impatiently rang the little bell again. "'Course, if you *want* to be ill and come to an early and dishonourable grave, drink all the rot-gut you can lay hands on-and break your mother's heart. . . ."

Piggy lay back in his chair and gazed pensively at the ceiling. So did Bill. Bertram felt uncomfortable. "Dear, dear, dear!" murmured Bill, between a sigh and a grunt. "Chalk-powder and lemonade! . . . what a nerve! . . . Patient, unrecognised, unrewarded heroism. . . ."

"Merciful Heaven," whispered Piggy, "slaked-lime and ginger-beer! . . What rash, waste courage and futile bravery. . . ." And suddenly leapt to his feet, swung the bell like a railway porter announcing the advent of a train, and roared "*Boy!*" until a white-clad, white-capped Swahili servant came running.

"*N'jo*, Boy!" he shouted. "Come here! . . . Lot of lazy, fat *n'gombe*. [158] . . . Three 'Devil's Own' cocktails, *late hapa*," [159] and as, with a humble "*Verna, Bwana*," the servant hurried to the bar, grumbling.

"And now he'll sit and have a *shauri* [160] with his pals, while we die of thirst in this accursed land of sin and sorrow. . . . Beastly *shenzis*. [161] . . ."

"You don't like Africa?" said Bertram, for the sake of something to say.

"Finest country on God's earth. . . . The *only* country," was the prompt reply.

"I suppose the negro doesn't make a very good servant?" Bertram continued, as Piggy rumbled on in denunciation.

"Finest servants in the world," answered that gentleman. "The *only* servants, in fact. . . ."

"Should I take one with me on active service?" asked Bertram, suddenly remembering Ali Suleiman, *alias* Sloper.

"If you can get one," was the reply. "You'll be lucky if you can. . . . All snapped up by the officers of the Expeditionary Force, long ago."

"Yes," agreed Bill. "Make all the difference to your comfort if you can get one. Don't take any but a Swahili, though. . . . You can depend on 'em, in a tight place. The good ones, that is. . . ."

A big, fat, clean-shaven man, dressed in white drill, strolled up to the little group. He reminded Bertram of the portraits of Mr. William Jennings Bryan who had recently visited India, and in three days unhesitatingly given his verdict on the situation, his solution of all political difficulties, and his opinion of the effete Britisher-uttering the final condemnation of that decadent.

"Hello! Hiram Silas P. Pocahantas of Pah," remarked Piggy, with delicate pleasantry, and the big man nodded, smiled, and drew up a chair.

"The drinks are on me, boys," quoth he. "Set 'em up," and bursting into song, more or less tunefully, announced —

"I didn't raise my boy to be a soldier,"

whereat Bill hazarded the opinion that the day might unexpectedly and ruddily dawn when he'd blooming well wish he bally well *had*, and that he could join them in a cocktail if he liked-or he could bung off if he didn't. Apparently William disapproved of the American's attitude, and that of his Government, toward the War and the Allies' part therein; for, on the American's "allowing he would *con*sume a highball" and the liquor arriving, he drank a health to those who are not too proud to fight, to those who do not give themselves airs as the Champions of Freedom, and then stand idly by when Freedom is trampled in the dust, and to those whose Almighty God is not the Almighty Dollar!

Expecting trouble, Bertram was surprised to find that the American was apparently amused, merely murmured "Shucks," and, in the midst of a violent political dissertation from Bill, ably supported by Piggy, went to sleep with a long thin cigar in the corner of his long thin mouth. He had heard it all before.

Bertram found his Devil's Own cocktail an exceedingly potent and unpleasant concoction. He decided that his first meeting with this beverage of the Evil One should be his last, and when Piggy, suddenly sitting up, remarked: "What's wrong with the drinks?" and tinkled the bell, he arose, said a hurried farewell in some confusion, and fled.

"'Tain't right to send a half-baked lad like that to fight the Colonial German," observed Bill, idly watching his retreating form.

"Nope," agreed the American, waking up. "I *was* going to say it's adding insult to injury-but you ain't injured Fritz any, yet, I guess," and went to sleep again before either of the glaring Englishmen could think of a retort.

Ere Bertram left the Club, he heard two pieces of "inside" military information divulged quite openly, and by the Staff itself. As he reached the porch, a lady of fluffy appearance and kittenish demeanour was delaying a red-tabbed captain who appeared to be endeavouring to escape.

"And, oh, Captain, *do* tell me what 'A.S.C.' and 'C.C.' mean," said the lady. "I saw a man with 'A.S.C.' on his shoulders, and there are two officers with 'C.C.,' in the Club. . . . *Do* you know what it means? I am *so* interested in military matters. Or is it a secret?"

"Oh, no!" replied the staff-officer, as he turned to flee. "'A.S.C.' stands for Ally Sloper's Cavalry, of course, and 'C.C.' for Coolie Catchers. . . . They are slave-traders, really, with a Government contract for the supply of porters. They get twenty rupees for each slave caught and delivered alive, and ten for a dead one, or one who dies within a week."

"What do they want the *dead* ones for?" she whispered.

"*That* I dare not tell you," replied the officer darkly, and with a rapid salute, departed.

Emerging from the Club garden on to the white road, Bertram gazed around for his trolley-boys and beheld them not.

"All right, ole chap," boomed the voice of Ali, who suddenly appeared beside him. "I looking after *Bwana*. Master going back along shippy? I fetch trolley now and see *Bwana* at Kilindini, thank you, please sah, good God," and he disappeared in the direction of the town, returning a couple of minutes later with the trolley.

"Master not pay these dam' thieves too much, ole chap," he remarked. "Two journey and one hour wait, they ask five rupees. Master give two-an'-a-puck."

"How much is a 'puck'?" enquired Bertram, ever anxious to learn.

"Sah?" returned the puzzled Ali.

"What's a puck?" repeated Bertram, and a smile of bright intelligence engulfed the countenance of the big Swahili.

"Oh, yessah!" he rumbled. "Give two rupee and what *Bwana* call 'puck-in-the-neck.' All the same, biff-on-the-napper, dig-in-the-ribs, smack-in-the-eye, kick-up-the —"

"*Oh*, yes, I see," interrupted Bertram, smiling-but at the back of his amusement was the sad realisation that he was not of the class of *bwanas* who can gracefully, firmly and finally present two-and-a-puck to extortionate and importunate trolley-boys.

He stepped on to the trolley and sat down, as Ali, saluting and salaaming respectfully, again bade him be of good cheer and high heart, as he would see him at Kilindini.

"How will you get there? Would you like to ride?" asked the kind-hearted and considerate Bertram (far too kind-hearted and considerate for the successful handling of black or brown subordinates and inferiors).

"Oh, God, sah, no, please," replied the smiling Ali. "This Swahili slave cannot sit with *Bwana*, and cannot run with damn low trolley-boys. Can running by self though like gentleman, thank you, please," and as the trolley started, added: "So long, ole chap. See Master at Kilindini by running like hell. Ta-ta by damn!" When the trolley had disappeared round a bend of the road, he generously kilted up his flowing night-dress and started off at the long loping trot which the African can maintain over incredible distances.

Arrived at Kilindini, Bertram paid the trolley-boys and discovered that, while they absorbed rupees with the greatest avidity, they looked askance at such fractions thereof as the eight-anna, four-anna, and two-anna piece, poking them over in their palms and finally tendering them back to him with many grunts and shakes of the head as he said:

"Well, you'll *have* to take them, you silly asses," to the uncomprehending coolies. "*That* lot makes a rupee-one half-a-rupee and two quarters, and that lot makes a rupee-four two-anna bits and two four-annas, doesn't it?"

But the men waxed clamorous, and one of them threw his money on the ground with an impudent and offensive gesture. Bertram coloured hotly, and his fist clenched. He hesitated; ought he. . . . *Smack*! *Thud*! and the man rolled in the dust as Ali Sloper, *alias* Suleiman, sprang upon him, smote him again, and stood over him, pouring forth a terrific torrent of violent vituperation.

As the victim of his swift assault obediently picked up the rejected coins, he turned to Bertram.

"These dam' niggers not knowing *annas*, sah," he said, "only *cents*. This not like East Indiaman's country. Hundred cents making one rupee here. All shopkeepers saying, 'No damn good' if master offering annas, please God, sah."

"Well—I haven't enough money with me, then—" began Bertram.

"I pay trolley-boys, sah," interrupted Ali quickly, "and Master can paying me to-morrow—or on pay-day at end of mensem."

"But, look here," expostulated Bertram, as this new-found guide, philosopher and friend sent the apparently satisfied coolies about their business. "I might not see you to-morrow. You'd better come with me to the ship and—"

"Oh, sah, sah!" cried the seemingly hurt and offended Ali, "am I not *Bwana's* faithful ole servant?" and turning from the subject as closed, said he would produce a boat to convey his cherished employer to his ship.

"Master bucking up like hell now, please," he advised. "No boat allowed to move in harbour after six pip emma, sah, thank God, please."

"Who on earth's Pip Emma?" enquired the bewildered Bertram, as they hurried down the hill to the quay.

"What British soldier-mans and officer-*bwanas* in Signal Corps call 'p.m.,' sah," was the reply. "Master saying 'six p.m.,' but Signal *Bwana* always saying 'six pip emma'—all same meaning but different language, please God, sah. P'r'aps German talk, sah? I do'n' know, sah."

And Bertram then remembered being puzzled by a remark of Maxton (to the effect that he had endeavoured to go down to his cabin at "three ack emma" and being full of "beer," had fallen "ack over tock" down the companion), and saw light on the subject. Truly these brigade signaller people talked in a weird tongue that might seem a foreign language to an uninitiated listener.

At the pier he saw Commander Finnis, of the Royal Indian Marine, and gratefully accepted an offer of a joy-ride in his launch to the good ship *Elymas*, to which that officer was proceeding.

"We're disembarking you blokes to-morrow morning," said he to Bertram, as they seated themselves in the stern of the smart little boat. "Indian troops going under canvas here, and British entraining for Nairobi. Two British officers of Indian Army to proceed by tug at once to M'paga, a few hours down the coast, in German East. Scrap going on there. Poor devils will travel on deck, packed tight with fifty sheep and a gang of nigger coolies. . . . *Some whiff!*" and he chuckled callously.

"D'you know who are going?" asked Bertram eagerly. Suppose he should be one of them-and in a "scrap" by this time to-morrow! How would he comport himself in his first fight?

"No," yawned the Commander. "O.C. troops on board will settle that."

And Bertram held his peace, visualising himself as collecting his kit, hurrying on to a dirty little tug to sit in the middle of a flock of sheep while the boat puffed and panted through the night along the mysterious African shore, landing on some white coral beach beneath the palms at dawn, hurrying to join the little force fighting with its back to the sea and its face to the foe, leaping into a trench, seizing the rifle of a dying man whose limp fingers unwillingly relaxed their grip, firing rapidly but accurately into the —

"Up you go," quoth Commander Finnis, and Bertram arose and stepped on to the platform at the bottom of the ladder that hospitably climbed the side of His Majesty's Troop-ship *Elymas*.

Chapter VIII
Military and Naval Manœuvres

However nonchalant in demeanour, it was an eager and excited crowd of officers that stood around the foot of the boat-deck ladder awaiting the result of the conference held in the Captain's cabin, to which meeting-place its proprietor had taken Commander Finnis before requesting the presence of Colonel Haldon, the First Officer, and the Ship's Adjutant, to learn the decision and orders of the powers-that-be concerning all and sundry, from the ship's Captain to the Sepoys' cook.

Who would Colonel Haldon send forthwith to M'paga, where the scrap was even then in progress (according to Lieutenant Greene, quoting Commander Finnis)? What orders did the papers in the fateful little dispatch-case, borne by the latter gentleman, contain for the various officers not already instructed to join their respective corps? Who would be sent to healthy, cheery Nairobi? Who to the vile desert at Voi? Who to interesting, far-distant Uganda? Who to the ghastly mangrove-swamps down the coast by the border of German East? Who to places where there was real active service, fighting, wounds, distinction and honourable death? Who to dreary holes where they would "sit down" and sit tight, rotting with fever and dysentery, eating out their hearts, without seeing a single German till the end of the war. . . .

Bertram thought of a certain "lucky-dip bran-tub," that loomed large in memories of childhood, whence, at a Christmas party, he had seen three or four predecessors draw most attractive and delectable toys and he had drawn a mysterious and much-tied parcel which had proved to contain a selection of first-class coke. What was he about to draw from Fate's bran-tub to-day?

When the Ship's Adjutant, bearing sheets of foolscap, eventually emerged from the Captain's cabin, ran sidling down the boat-deck ladder and proceeded to the notice-board in the saloon-companion, followed by the nonchalantly eager and excited crowd, as is the frog-capturing duck by all the other ducks of the farm-yard, Bertram, with beating heart, read down the list until he came to his own name-only to discover that Fate had hedged.

The die was not yet cast, and Second-Lieutenant B. Greene would disembark with detachments, Indian troops, and, at Mombasa, await further orders.

Captain Brandone and Lieutenant Stanner would proceed immediately to M'paga, and with wild cries of "Yoicks! Tally Ho!" and "Gone away!" those two officers fled to their respective cabins to collect their kit.

Dinner that night was a noisy meal, and talk turned largely upon the merits or demerits of the places from Mombasa to Uganda to which the speakers had been respectively posted.

"Where are you going, Brannigan?" asked Bertram of that cheery Hibernian, as he seated himself beside him.

"Where am Oi goin', is ut, me bhoy?" was the reply. "Faith, where the loin-eating man-Oi mane the man-eating loins reside, bedad. Ye've heard o' the man-eaters of Tsavo? That's where Oi'm goin', me bucko-to the man-eaters of Tsavo."

Terence had evidently poured a libation of usquebagh before dining, for he appeared wound up to talk.

"Begorra-if ut's loin-eaters they are, it's Terry Brannigan'll gird up *his* loins an' be found there missing entoirely. . . . Oi'd misloike to be 'aten by a loin, Greene . . ." and he frowned over the idea and grew momentarily despondent.

"'Tis not phwat I wint for a sojer for, at all, at all," he complained, and added a lament to the effect that he was not as tough as O'Toole's pig. But the mention of this animal appeared to have a cheering effect, for he burst into song.

"Ye've heard of Larry O'Toole,
O' the beautiful town o' Drumgool?
Faith, he had but wan eye
To ogle ye by,
But, begorra, that wan was a jool. . . ."

After dinner, Bertram sought out Colonel Haldon for further orders, information and advice.

"Everybody clears off to-morrow morning, my boy," said he, "and in twenty-four hours we shall be scattered over a country as big as Europe. You'll be in command, till further orders, of all native troops landed at Mombasa. I don't suppose you'll be there long, though. You may get orders to bung off with the Hundred and Ninety-Ninth draft of the Hundred and Ninety-Eighth, or you may have to see them off under a Native Officer and go in the opposite direction yourself. . . . Don't worry, anyway. You'll be all right. . . ."

That night Bertram again slept but little, and had a bad relapse into the old state of self-distrust, depression and anxiety. This sense of inadequacy, inexperience and unworth was overwhelming. What did he know about Sepoys that he should, for a time, be in sole command and charge of a mixed force of Regular troops and Imperial Service troops which comprised Gurkhas, Sikhs, Pathans, Punjabi Mahommedans, Deccani Marathas, Rajputs, and representatives of almost every other fighting race in India? It would be bad enough if he could thoroughly understand the language of any one of them. As it was, he had a few words of cook-house Hindustani, and a man whom he disliked and distrusted as his sole representative and medium of intercourse with the men. Suppose the fellow was rather his *mis*-representative? Suppose he fomented trouble, as only a native can? What if there were a sudden row and quarrel between some of the naturally inimical races —a sort of inter-tribal shindy between the Sikhs and the Pathans, for example? Who was wretched little "Blameless Bertram," to think he could impose his authority upon such people and quell the riot with a word? What if they defied him and the Jemadar did not support him? What sort of powers and authority had he? . . . He did not know. . . . Suppose there *were* a row, and there was real fighting and bloodshed? It would get into the papers, and his name would be held up to the contempt of the whole British Empire. It would get into the American papers too. Then an exaggerated account of it would be published in the Press of the Central Powers and their wretched allies, to show the rotten condition of the Indian Army. The neutral papers would copy it. Soon there would not be a corner of the civilised world where people had not heard the name of Greene, the name of the wretched creature who could not maintain order and discipline among a few native troops, but allowed some petty quarrel between two soldiers to develop into an "incident." Yes-that's what would happen, a "regrettable incident." . . . And the weary old round of self-distrust, depreciation and contempt went its sorry cycle once again. . . .

Going on deck in the morning, Bertram discovered that supplementary orders had been published, and that all native troops would be disembarked under his command at twelve noon, and that he would report, upon landing, to the Military Landing Officer, from whom he would receive further orders. . . . Troops would carry no ammunition, nor cooked rations. All kits would go ashore with the men. . . .

Bertram at once proceeded to the companion leading down to the well-deck, called a Sepoy of the Hundred and Ninety-Ninth, and "sent his salaams" to the Jemadar of that regiment, to the Subedar of the Gurkhas, the Subedar of the Sherepur Sikhs and the Jemadar of the Very Mixed Contingent.

To these officers he endeavoured to make it clear that every man of their respective commands, and every article of those men's kit, bedding, and accoutrements, and all stores, rations and ammunition, must be ready for disembarkation at midday.

The little Gurkha Subedar smiled brightly, saluted, and said he quite understood-which was rather clever of him, as his Hindustani was almost as limited as was Bertram's. However, he had grasped, from Bertram's barbarous and laborious "*Sub admi . . . sub saman . . . sub chiz . . . tyar . . . bara badji . . . ither se jainga . . .*" that "all men . . . all baggage . . . all things . . . at twelve o'clock . . . will go from here" —and that was good enough for him.

"Any chance of fighting to-morrow, Sahib?" he asked, but Bertram, unfortunately, did not understand him.

The tall, bearded Sikh Subedar saluted correctly, said nothing but "*Bahut achcha, Sahib*," and stood with a cold sneer frozen upon his hard and haughty countenance.

The burly Jemadar of the Very Mixed Contingent, or Mixed Pickles, smiled cheerily, laughed merrily at nothing in particular, and appeared mildly shocked at Bertram's enquiry as to whether he understood. Of *course*, he understood! Was not the Sahib a most fluent speaker of most faultless Urdu, or Hindi, or Sindhi, or Tamil or something? Anyhow, he had clearly caught the words "all men ready at twelve o'clock" —and who could require more than a nice clear *hookum* like that.

Jemadar Hassan Ali looked pained and doubtful. So far as his considerable histrionic powers permitted, he gave his rendering of an honest and intelligent man befogged by perfectly incomprehensible orders and contradictory directions which he may not question and on which he may not beg further enlightenment. His air and look of "*Faithful to the last I will go forth and strive to obey orders which I cannot understand, and to carry out instructions given so incomprehensibly and in so strange a tongue that Allah alone knows what is required of me*" annoyed Bertram exceedingly, and having smiled upon the cheery little Subedar and the cheery big Jemadar, and looked coldly upon the unpleasant Sikh and the difficult Hassan Ali, he informed the quartette that it had his permission to depart.

As they saluted and turned to go, he caught a gleam of ferocious hatred upon the face of the Gurkha officer whom the Sikh jostled, with every appearance of intentional rudeness and the desire to insult. Bertram's sympathy was with the Gurkha and he wished that it was with him and his sturdy little followers that he was to proceed to the front. He felt that they would follow him to the last inch of the way and the last drop of their blood, and would fight for sheer love of fighting, as soon as they were shown an enemy.

After a somewhat depressing breakfast, at which he found himself almost alone, Bertram arrayed himself in full war paint, packed his kit, said farewell to the ship's officers and then inspected the troops, drawn up ready for disembarkation on the well-decks. He was struck by the apparent cheerfulness of the Gurkhas and the clumsy heaviness of their kit which included a great horse-collar roll of cape, overcoat or ground-sheet strapped like a colossal cross-belt across one shoulder and under the other arm; by the apparent depression of the men of the Very Mixed Contingent and their slovenliness; by what seemed to him the critical and unfriendly stare of the Sherepur Sikhs as he passed along their ranks; and by the elderliness of the Hundred and Ninety-Ninth draft. Had these latter been perceptibly aged by their sea-faring experiences and were they feeling terribly *terra marique jactati*, or was it that the impossibility of procuring henna or other dye had caused the lapse of brown, orange, pink and red beards and moustaches to their natural greyness? Anyhow, they looked distinctly old, and on the whole, fitter for the ease and light duty of "employed pensioner" than for active service under very difficult conditions against a ferocious foe upon his native heath. His gentle nature and kindly heart led Bertram to feel very sorry indeed for one bemedalled old gentleman who had evidently had a very bad crossing, still had a very bad cough, and looked likely to have another go of fever before very long.

As he watched the piling-up of square-sided boxes of rations, oblong boxes of ammunition, sacks, tins, bags and jars, bundles of kit and bedding, cooking paraphernalia, entrenching tools, mule harness, huge zinc vessels for the transport of water, leather *chhagals* and canvas *pakhals* or waterbags, and wished that his own tight-strapped impedimenta were less uncomfortable and heavy, a cloud of choking smoke from the top of the funnel of some boat just below him, apprised him of the fact that his transport was ready. Looking over the side he saw a large barge, long, broad, and very deep, with upper decks at stem and stern, which a fussy little tug had just brought into position below an open door in the middle of the port side of the *Elymas*. It was a long way below it too, and he realised that unless a ladder were provided every man would have to drop from the threshold of the door to the very narrow edge of the barge about six feet below, make his way along it to the stern deck, and down a plank on to the "floor" of the barge itself. When his turn came he'd make an ass of himself-he'd fall-he knew he would!

He tried to make Jemadar Hassan Ali understand that two Havildars were to stand on the edge of the barge, one each side of the doorway and guide the errant tentative feet of each man as he lowered himself and clung to the bottom of the doorway. He also had the sacks thrown where anyone who missed his footing and fell from the side of the barge to the bottom would fall upon them and roll, instead of taking the eight feet drop and hurting himself. When this did happen, the Sepoys roared with laughter and appeared to be immensely diverted. It occurred several times, for it is no easy matter to lower oneself some six feet, from one edge to another, when heavily accoutred and carrying a rifle. When every man and package was on board, Bertram cast one last look around the *Elymas*, took a deep breath, crawled painfully out backwards through the port, clung to the sharp iron edge, felt about wildly with his feet which were apparently too sacred and superior for the Havildars to grab and guide, felt his clutching fingers weaken and slip, and then with a pang of miserable despair fell-and landed on the side of the barge a whole inch below where his feet had been when he fell. A minute later he had made his way to the prow, and, with a regal gesture, had signified to the captain of the tug that he might carry on.

And then he sat him down upon the little piece of deck and gazed upon the sea of upturned faces, black, brown, wheat-coloured, and yellow, that spread out at his feet from end to end and side to side of the great barge.

Of what were they thinking, these men from every corner of India and Nepal, as they stood shoulder to shoulder, or squatted on the boxes and bales that covered half the floor of the barge? What did they think of him? Did they really despise and dislike him as he feared, or did they admire and like and trust him-simply because he was a white man and a Sahib? He had a suspicion that the Sikhs disliked him, the Mixed Contingent took him on trust as an Englishman, the Hundred and Ninety-Ninth kept an open mind, and the Gurkhas liked him-all reflecting really the attitude of their respective Native Officers. . . .

In a few minutes the barge was run alongside the Kilindini quay, and Bertram was, for the second time, climbing its stone stairs, in search of the Military Landing Officer, the arbiter of his immediate destiny.

As he reached the top of the steps he was, as it were, engulfed and embraced in a smile that he already knew-and he realised that it was with a distinct sense of pleasure and a feeling of lessened loneliness and unshared friendless responsibility that he beheld the beaming face of his "since-long-time-to-come" faithful old retainer Ali Suleiman.

"God bless myself please, thank you, *Bwana*," quoth that gentleman, saluting repeatedly. "*Bwana* will now wanting Military Embarkation Officer by golly. I got him, sah," and turning about added, "*Bwana* come along me, sah, I got him all right," as though he had, with much skill and good luck, tracked down, ensnared, and encaged some wary and wily animal. . . .

At the end of the little stone pier was a rough table or desk, by which stood a burly officer clad in slacks, and a vast spine-pad of quilted khaki. On the tables were writing-materials and a mass of papers.

"Mornin'," remarked this gentleman, turning a crimson and perspiring face to Bertram. "I'm the M.L.O. You'll fall your men in here and they'll stack their kits with the rations and ammunition over there. Then you must tell off working-parties to cart the lot up to the camp. I've only got two trucks and your fatigue-parties'll have to man-handle 'em. You'll have to ginger 'em up or you'll be here all day. I don't want you to march off till all your stuff's up to the camp. . . . Don't bung off yourself, y'know. . . . Right O. Carry on. . . ." Bertram saluted.

Another job which he must accomplish without hitch or error. The more jobs he *could* do, the better. What he dreaded was the job for the successful tackling of which he had not the knowledge, ability or experience.

"Very good, sir," he replied. "Er-where *are* the trolleys?" for there was no sign of any vehicle about the quay.

"Oh, they'll roll up by and by, I expect," was the reply. Bertram again saluted and returned to the barge. Calling to the Native Officers he told them that the men would fall in on the bunder and await further orders, each detachment furnishing a fatigue-party for the unloading of the impedimenta. Before very long, the men were standing at ease in the shade of a great shed, and their kits, rations and ammunition were piled in a great mound at the wharf edge.

And thus, having nothing to do until the promised trucks arrived, Bertram realised that it was terribly hot; suffocatingly, oppressively, dangerously hot; and that he felt very giddy, shaky and faint.

The sun seemed to beat upward from the stone of the quay and sideways from the iron of the sheds as fiercely and painfully as it did downward from the sky. And there was absolutely nowhere to sit down. He couldn't very well squat down in the dirt. . . . No-but the men could-so he approached the little knot of Native Officers and told them to allow the men to pile arms, fall out, and sit against the wall of the shed-no man to leave the line without permission.

Jemadar Hassan Ali did not forget to post a sentry over the arms on this occasion. For an hour Bertram strolled up and down. It was less tiring to do that than to stand still. His eyes ached most painfully by reason of the blinding glare, his head ached from the pressure on his brows of his thin, but hard and heavy, helmet (the regulation pattern, apparently designed with an eye to the maximum of danger and discomfort) and his body ached by reason of the weight and tightness of his accoutrements. It was nearly two o'clock and he had breakfasted early. Suppose he got sunstroke, or collapsed from heat, hunger, and weariness? What an exhibition! When would the men get their next meal? Where were those trolleys? It was two hours since the Military Landing Officer had said they'd "roll up by and by." He'd go and remind him.

The Military Landing Officer was just off to his lunch and well-earned rest at the Club. He had been on the beastly bunder since six in the morning-and anybody who wanted him now could come and find him, what?

"Excuse me, sir," said Bertram as Captain Angus flung his portfolio of papers to his orderly, "those trucks haven't come yet."

"*Wha'* trucks?" snapped the Landing Officer. He had just told himself he had *done* for to-day—and he had had nothing since half-past five that morning. People must be reasonable-he'd been hard at it for eight solid hours damitall y'know.

"The trucks for my baggage and ammunition and stuff."

"Well, *I* haven't got 'em, have I?" replied Captain Angus. "Be reasonable about it. . . I can't *make* trucks. . . Anybody'd think I'd stolen your trucks. . . . You must be *patient*, y'know, and *do* be reasonable. . . . *I* haven't got 'em. Search me."

The Military Landing Officer had been on his job for months and had unconsciously evolved two formulæ, which he used for his seniors and juniors respectively, without variation of a word. Bertram had just heard the form of prayer to be used with Captains and unfortunates of lower rank, who showed yearnings for things unavoidable. To Majors and those senior thereunto the crystallised ritual was:

"Can't understand it, sir, at all. I issued the necessary orders all right-but there's a terrible shortage. One must make allowances in these times of stress. It'll turn up all right. *I'll* see to it . . ." etc., and this applied equally well to missing trains, mules, regiments, horses, trucks, orders, motor-cars or anything else belonging to the large class of Things That Can Go Astray.

"You told me to wait, sir," said Bertram.

"Then why the devil *don't you?*" said Captain Angus.

"I am, sir," replied Bertram.

"Then what's all this infernal row about?" replied Captain Angus.

Bertram felt that he understood exactly how children feel when, unjustly treated, they cannot refrain from tears. It was *too* bad. He had stood in this smiting sun for over two hours awaiting the promised trucks-and now he was accused of making an infernal row because he had mentioned that they had not turned up! If the man had told him where they were, surely he and his three hundred men could have gone and got them long ago.

"By the way," continued Captain Angus, "I'd better give you your route-for when you *do* get away-and you mustn't sit here all day like this, y'know. You must ginger 'em up a bit" (more formula this) "or you'll all take root. Well, look here, you go up the hill and keep straight on to where a railway-bridge crosses the road. Turn to the left before you go under the bridge, and keep along the railway line till you see some tents on the left again. Strike inland towards these, and you'll find your way all right. Take what empty tents you want, but don't spread yourself *too* much-though there's only some details there now. You'll be in command of that camp for the present. . . . Better not bung off to the Club either-you may be wanted in a hurry. . . . I'll see if those trucks are on the way as I go up. Don't hop off till you've shifted all your stuff. . . So long! . . ." and the Military Landing Officer bustled off to where at the Dock gates a motor-car awaited him. . . .

Before long, Bertram found that he must either sit down or fall down, so terrific was the stifling heat, so heavy had his accoutrements become, and so faint, empty and giddy did he feel.

Through the open door of a corrugated-iron shed he could see a huge, burly, red-faced European, sitting at a little rough table in a big bare room. In this barn-like place was nothing else but a telephone-box and a chair. Could he go in and sit on it? That dark and shady interior looked like a glimpse of heaven from this hell of crashing glare and gasping heat. . . . Perhaps confidential military communications were made through that telephone though, and the big man, arrayed in a singlet and white trousers, was there for the very purpose of receiving them secretly and of preventing the intrusion of any stranger? Anyhow-it would be a minute's blessed escape from the blinding inferno, merely to go inside and ask the man if he could sit down while he awaited the trucks. He could place the chair in a position from which he could see his men. . . . He entered the hut, and the large man raised a clean-shaven crimson face, ornamented with a pair of piercing blue eyes, and stared hard at him as he folded a pinkish newspaper and said nothing at all, rather disconcertingly.

"May I come in and sit down for a bit, please?" said Bertram. "I think I've got a touch of the sun."

"Put your wacant faice in that wacant chair," was the prompt reply.

"Thanks-may I put it where I can see my men?" said Bertram.

"Putt it where you can cock yer feet on this 'ere table an' lean back agin that pertition, more sense," replied the large red man, scratching his large red head. "*You* don' want to see yore men, you don't," he added. "They're a 'orrid sight. . . . All natives is. . . . You putt it where you kin get a good voo o' *me*. . . . Shed a few paounds o' the hup'olstery and maike yerself atome. . . . Wisht I got somethink to orfer yer-but I ain't. . . . Can't be 'osspitable on a basin o' water wot's bin washed in-can yer?"

Bertram admitted the difficulty, and, with a sigh of intense relief, removed his belt and crossbelts and all that unto them pertained. And, as he sank into the chair with a grateful heart, entered Ali Suleiman, whom he had not seen for an hour, bearing in one huge paw a great mug of steaming tea, and in the other a thick plate of thicker biscuits.

Bertram could have wrung the hand that fed him. Never before in the history of tea had a cup of tea been so welcome.

"Heaven reward you as I never can," quoth Bertram, as he drank. "Where on earth did you raise it?"

"Oh, sah!" beamed Ali. "Master not mentioning it. I am knowing cook-fellow at R.E. Sergeants' Mess, and saying my frien' Sergeant Jones, R.E., wanting cup of tea and biscuits at bunder P.D.Q."

"P.D.Q.?" enquired Bertram.

"Yessah, all 'e same 'pretty dam quick' —and bringing it to *Bwana* by mistake," replied Ali, the son of Suleiman.

"But *isn't* there some mistake?" asked the puzzled youth. "I don't want to . . ."

"Lookere," interrupted the large red man, "*you* don' wanter discover no mistakes, not until you drunk that tea, you don't. . . . You push that daown yore neck and then give that nigger a cent an' tell 'im to be less careful nex' time. You don' wanter *dis*courage a good lad like that, you don't. Not 'arf, you do."

433

"But-Sergeant Jones's tea" began Bertram, looking unhappily at the half-emptied cup.

"*Sergeant Jones's tea!*" mimicked the rude red man, in a high falsetto. "*If* ole Shifter Jones drunk a cup o' tea it'd be in all the paipers nex' mornin', it would. Not arf it wouldn't. Don' believe 'e ever tasted tea, I don't, an' if he *did* —"

But at this moment a white-clad naval officer of exalted rank strode into the room, and the large red man sprang to his feet with every sign of respect and regard. Picking up a Navy straw hat from the floor, the latter gentleman stood at attention with it in his hand. Bertram decided that he was a naval petty officer on some shore-job or other, perhaps retired and now a coast-guard or Customs official of some kind. Evidently he knew the exalted naval officer and held him, or his Office, in high regard.

"Get my message, William Hankey?" he snapped.

"Yessir," replied William Hankey.

"Did you telephone for the car at once?"

"Nossir," admitted Hankey, with a fluttering glance of piteous appeal.

The naval officer's face became a ferocious and menacing mask of wrath and hate, lit up by a terrible glare. Up to that moment he had been rather curiously like Hankey. Now he was even more like a very infuriated lion. He took a step nearer the table, fixed his burning, baleful eye upon the wilting William, and withered him with the most extraordinary blast of scorching invective that Bertram had ever heard, or was ever likely to hear, unless he met Captain Sir Thaddeus Bellingham ffinch Beffroye again.

"You blundering bullock," quoth he; "you whimpering weasel; you bleating blup; you miserable dog-potter; you horny-eyed, bleary-nosed, bat-eared, lop-sided, longshore loafer; you perishing shrimp-peddler; you Young Helper; you Mother's Little Pet; you dear Ministering Child; you blistering bug-house body-snatcher; you bloated bumboat-woman; you hopping hermaphrodite-what d'ye mean by it? Eh? . . . *What d'ye mean by it*, you anæmic Aggie; you ape-faced anthropoid; you adenoid; you blood-stained buzzard; you abject abortion; you abstainer; you sickly, one-lunged, half-baked, under-fed alligator; you scrofulous scorbutic; you peripatetic pimple; you perambulating pimp-faced poodle; what about it? Eh? *What about it?*"

Mr. William Hankey stood silent and motionless, but in his face was the expression of one who, with critical approval, listens and enjoys. Such a look may be seen upon the face of a musician the while he listens to the performance of a greater musician.

Having taken breath, the Captain continued: "What have you got to say for yourself, you frig-faced farthing freak, you? Nothing! You purple poultice-puncher; you hopeless, helpless, herring-gutted hound; you dropsical drink-water; you drunken, drivelling dope-dodger; you mouldy, mossy-toothed, mealy-mouthed maggot; you squinny-faced, squittering, squint-eyed squab, you-what have you got to say for yourself? Eh? . . . *Answer me*, you mole; you mump; you measle; you knob; you nit; you noun; you part; you piece; you portion; you bald-headed, slab-sided, jelly-bellied jumble; you mistake; you accident; you imperial stinker; you poor, pale pudding; you populous, pork-faced parrot-why don't you speak, you doddering, dumb-eared, deaf-mouthed dust-hole; you jabbering, jawing, jumping Jezebel, why don't you answer me? Eh? *D'ye hear* me, you fighting gold-fish; you whistling water-rat; you Leaning Tower of Pisa-pudding; you beer-belching ration-robber; you pink-eyed, perishing pension-cheater; you flat-footed, frog-faced fragment; you trumpeting tripe-hound? Hold your tongue and listen to me, you barge-bottom barnacle; you nestling gin-lapper; you barmaid-biting bun-bolter; you tuberculous tub; you mouldy manure-merchant; you moulting mop-chewer; you kagging, corybantic cockroach; you lollipop-looting lighterman; you naval know-all. *Why didn't you telephone for the car?*"

"'Cos it were 'ere all the time, sir," replied Mr. William Hankey, perceiving that his superior officer had run down and required rest.

"*That's* all right, then," replied Captain Sir Thaddeus Bellingham ffinch Beffroye pleasantly, and strode to the door. There he turned, and again addressed Mr. Hankey.

"Why couldn't you say so, instead of chattering and jabbering and mouthing and mopping and mowing and yapping and yiyiking for an hour, Mr. Woozy, Woolly-witted, Wandering William Hankey?" he enquired.

The large red man looked penitent.

"Hankey," the officer added, "you are a land-lubber. You are a pier-head yachtsman. You are a beach pleasure-boat pilot. You are a canal bargee."

Mr. Hankey looked hurt, *touché*, broken.

"Oh, *sir*!" said he, stricken at last.

"William Hankey, you are a *volunteer*," continued his remorseless judge.

Mr. Hankey fell heavily into his chair, and fetched a deep groan.

"William Hankey-Pankey —you are a *conscientious objector*," said the Captain in a quiet, cold and cruel voice.

A little gasping cry escaped Mr. Hankey. He closed his eyes, swayed a moment, and then dropped fainting on the table, the which his large red head smote with a dull and heavy thud, as the heartless officer strode away.

A moment later Mr. Hankey revived, winked at the astonished Bertram, and remarked:

"I'd swim in blood fer 'im, I would, any day. I'd swim in beer wi' me mouf shut, if 'e ast me, I would. . . . 'E's the pleasant-manneredest, kindest, nicest bloke I was ever shipmates wiv, 'e is. . ."

"His bark is worse than his bite, I suppose?" hazarded Bertram.

"Bark!" replied Mr. Hankey. "'E wouldn' bark at a blind beggar's deaf dog, 'e wouldn't. . . . The ship's a 'Appy Ship wot's got *'im* fer Ole Man. . . . Why-the matlows do's liddle things jest to git brought up before 'im to listen to 'is voice. . . . Yes. . . . Their Master's Voice. . . . Wouldn' part brass-rags wiv 'im for a nogs'ead o' rum. . . ."

Feeling a different man for the tea and biscuits, Bertram thanked Mr. Hankey for his hospitality, and stepped out on to the quay, thinking, as the heat-blast struck him, that one would experience very similar sensations by putting his head into an oven and then stepping on to the stove. In the shade of the sheds the Sepoys sprawled, even the cheery Gurkhas seemed unhappy and uncomfortable in that fiery furnace.

Bertram's heart smote him. Had it been the act of a good officer to go and sit down in that shed, to drink tea and eat biscuits, while his men . . . ? Yes, surely that was all right. He was far less acclimatised to heat and glare than they, and it would be no service to them for him to get heat-stroke and apoplexy or "a touch of the sun." They had their water-bottles and their grain-and-sugar ration and their cold *chupattis*. They were under conditions far more closely approximating to normal than he was. Of course it is boring to spend hours in the same place with full equipment on, but, after all, it was much worse for a European, whose thoughts run on a cool club luncheon-room; a bath and change; and a long chair, a cold drink and a novel, under a punkah on the club verandah thereafter. . . . Would those infernal trucks *never* come? Suppose they never did? Was he to stay there all night? He had certainly received definite orders from the "competent military authority" to stay there until all his baggage had been sent off. Was that to relieve the competent military authority of responsibility in the event of any of it being stolen? . . . Probably the competent military authority was now having his tea, miles away at the Club. What should he do if no trucks had materialised by nightfall? How about consulting the Native Officers? . . . Perish the thought! . . . They'd have to stick it, the same as he would. The orders were quite clear, and all he had got to do was to sit tight and await trucks-if he grew grey in the process.

Some six hours from the time at which he had landed, a couple of small four-wheeled trucks were pushed on to the wharf by a fatigue-party of Sepoys from the camp; the Naik in charge of them saluted and fled, lest he and his men be impounded for further service; and Bertram instructed the Gurkha Subedar to get a fatigue-party of men to work at loading the two trucks to their utmost capacity, with baggage, kit, and ration-boxes. It was evident that the arrival of the trucks did not mean the early departure of the force, for several journeys would be necessary for the complete evacuation of the mound of material to be shifted. Having loaded the trucks, the fatigue-party pushed off, and it was only as the two unwieldy erections of baggage were being propelled through the gates by the willing little men, that it occurred to Bertram to enquire whether they had any idea as to where they were going.

Not the slightest, and they grinned cheerily. Another problem! Should he now abandon the force and lead the fatigue-party in the light of the Military Landing Officer's description of the route, or should he endeavour to give the Gurkha Subedar an idea of the way, and send him off with the trucks? And suppose he lost his way and barged ahead straight across the Island of Mombasa? That would mean that the rest of them would have to sit on the wharf all night-if he obeyed the Military Landing Officer's orders. . . . Which he *must* do, of course. . . . Bertram was of a mild, inoffensive and quite unvindictive nature, but he found himself wishing that the Military Landing Officer's dinner might thoroughly disagree with him. . . . His own did not appear likely to get the opportunity. . . . He then and there determined that he would never again be caught, while on Active Service, without food of some kind on his person, if he could help it-chocolate, biscuits, something in a tablet or a tin. . . . Should he go and leave the Native Officer in command, or should he send forth the two precious trucks into the gathering gloom and hope that, dove-like, they would return? . . .

And again the voice of Ali fell like balm of Gilead, as it boomed, welcome, opportune and cheering.

"Sah, I will show the Chinamans the way to camp and bring them back P.D.Q.," quoth he.

"Oh! Good man!" said Bertram. "Right O! But they're not Chinamen-they are Gurkha soldiers. . . . Don't you hit one, or chivvy them about. . . ."

"Sah, I am knowing all things," was the modest reply, and the black giant strode off, followed by the empiled wobbling waggons.

More weary waiting, but, as the day waned, the decrease of heat and sultriness failed to keep pace with the increasing hunger, faintness and sickness which made at least one of the prisoners of the quay wish that either he or the Emperor of Germany had never been born. . . .

Journey after journey having been made, each by a fresh party of Gurkhas (for Bertram, as is customary, used the willing horse, when he saw that the little hill-men apparently liked work for its own sake, as much as the other Sepoys disliked work for any sake), the moment at last arrived when the ammunition-boxes could be loaded on to the trucks and the whole force could be marched off as escort thereunto, leaving nothing behind them upon the accursed stones of that oven, which had been their gaol for ten weary hours.

Never was the order, "Fall in!" obeyed with more alacrity, and it was with a swinging stride that the troops marched out through the gates in the rear of their British officer, who strode along with high-held head and soldierly bearing, as he thanked God there was a good moon in the heavens, and prayed that there might soon be a good meal in his stomach.

Up the little hill and past the trolley "terminus" the party tramped, and the hot, heavy night seemed comparatively cool after the terrible day on the shut-in, stone and iron heat-trap of the quay. . . . As he glanced at the diamond-studded velvet of the African sky, Bertram thought how long ago seemed that morning when he had made his first march at the head of his company. It seemed to have taken place, not only in another continent, but in another age. Already he seemed an older, wiser, more resourceful man. . . .

"*Bwana* turning feet to left hands here," said Ali Suleiman from where, abreast of Bertram, he strode along at the edge of the road. "If *Bwana* will following me in front, I am leading him behind"—with which clear and comprehensible offer, he struck off to the left, his long, clean night-shirt looming ahead in the darkness as a pillar of cloud by night. . . .

Again Bertram blessed him, and thanked the lucky stars that had brought him across his path. He had seen no railway-bridge nor railway-line; he could see no tents, and he was exceedingly thankful that it was not his duty to find, by night, the way which had seemed somewhat vaguely and insufficiently indicated for one who sought to follow it by day. Half an hour later he saw a huge black mass which, upon closer experience, proved to be a great palm grove, in the shadow of which stood a number of tents.

* * *

In a remarkably short space of time, the Sepoys had occupied four rows of the empty tents, lighted hurricane lamps, unpacked bedding and kit bundles, removed turbans, belts and accoutrements, and, set about the business of cooking, distributing, and devouring their rations.

The grove of palms that had looked so very inviolable and sacredly remote as it stood untenanted and silent in the brilliant moonlight, now looked and smelt (thanks to wood fires and burning ghee) like an Indian bazaar, as Sikhs, Gurkhas, Rajputs, Punjabis, Marathas, Pathans and "down-country" Carnatics swarmed in and out of tents, around cooking-fires, at the taps of the big railway water-tank, or the kit-and-ration dump-the men of each different race yet keeping themselves separate from those of other races. . . .

As the unutterably weary Bertram stood and watched and wondered as to what military and disciplinary conundrums his motley force would provide for him on the morrow, his ancient and faithful family retainer came and asked him for his keys. That worthy had already, in the name of his *Bwana*, demanded the instant provision of a fatigue-party, and directed the removal of a tent from the lines to a spot where there would be more privacy and shade for its occupant, and had then unstrapped the bundles containing his master's bed, bedding and washhand-stand, and now desired further to furnish forth the tent with the suitable contents of the sack. . . .

And so Bertram "settled in," as did his little force, save that he went to bed supperless and they did not. Far from it-for a goat actually strayed bleating into the line and met with an accident-getting its silly neck in the way of a *kukri* just as its owner was, so he said, fanning himself with it (with the *kukri*, not the goat). So some fed full, and others fuller.

Next day, Bertram ate what Ali, far-foraging, brought him; and rested beneath the shade of the palms and let his men rest also, to recover from their sea-voyage and generally to find themselves. . . . For one whole day he would do nothing and order nothing to be done; receive no reports, issue no instructions, harry nobody and be harried by none. Then, on the morrow, he would arise, go on the warpath in the camp, and grapple bravely with every problem that might arise, from shortage of turmeric to excess of covert criticism of his knowledge and ability.

But the morrow never came in that camp, for the Base Commandant sent for him in urgent haste at eventide, and bade him strain every nerve to get his men and their baggage, lock, stock and barrel, on board the *Barjordan*, just as quickly as it could be done (and a dam' sight quicker), for reinforcements were urgently needed at M'paga, down the coast.

Followed a sleepless nightmare night, throughout which he worked by moonlight in the camp, on the quay, and on the *Barjordan's* deck, reversing the labours of the previous day, and re-embarking his men, their kit, ammunition, rations and impedimenta-and in addition, two barge-loads of commissariat and ordnance requisites for the M'paga Brigade.

At dawn the last man, box, and bale was on board and Bertram endeavoured to speak a word of praise, in halting Hindustani, to the Gurkha Subedar, who, with his men, had shown an alacrity and gluttony for work, beyond all praise. All the other Sepoys had worked properly in their different shifts-but the Gurkhas had revelled in work, and when their second shift came at midnight, the first shift remained and worked with them!

Having gratefully accepted coffee from Mr. Wigger, the First Officer, Bertram, feeling "beat to the world," went down to his cabin, turned in, and slept till evening. When he awoke, a gazelle was gazing affectionately into his face.

He shut his eyes and shivered. . . . Was this sunstroke, fever, or madness? He felt horribly frightened, his nerves being in the state natural to a person of his temperament and constitution when overworked, underfed, affected by the sun, touched by fever, and overwrought to the breaking-point by anxiety and worry.

He opened his eyes again, determined to be cool, wise and brave, in face of this threatened breakdown, this hallucination of insanity.

The gazelle was still there-there in a carpeted, comfortable cabin, on board a ship, in the Indian Ocean. . . .

He rubbed his eyes.

Then he put out his hand to pass it through the spectral Thing and confirm his worst fears. The gazelle licked his hand, and he sat up and said: "Oh, damn!" and laughed weakly.

The animal left the cabin, and he heard its hoofs pattering on the linoleum.

Later he found it to be a pet of the captain of the *Barjordan*, Captain O'Connor.

Next morning the ship anchored a mile or so from a mangrove swamp, and the business of disembarkation began again, this time into the ship's boats and some sailing dhows that had met the *Barjordan* at this spot.

When all the Sepoys and stores were in the boats and dhows, he put on the *puggri* which Bludyer had given him, with the assistance of Ali Suleiman and the Gurkha Subedar, looked at himself in the glass, and wished he felt as fine and fierce a fellow as he looked. . . . He then said "Farewell" to kindly Captain O'Connor and burly, energetic Mr. Wigger-both of whom he liked exceedingly-received their hearty good wishes and exhortations to slay and spare not, and went down on the motor-launch that was to tow the laden boats to the low gloomy shore-if a mangrove swamp can be called a shore. . . .

One more "beginning" —or one more stage on the road to War! Here was *he*, Bertram Greene, armed to the teeth, with a turban on his head, about to be landed-and left-on the shores of the mainland of this truly Dark Continent. He was about to invade Africa! . . .

If only his father and Miranda could see him *now*!

Chapter IX
Bertram Invades Africa

Bertram waded ashore and looked around.

Through a rank jungle of high grass, scrub, palms, trees and creepers, a narrow mud path wound past the charred remnants of a native village to where stood the shell-scarred ruins of a whitewashed *adobe* building which had probably been a Customs-post, treasury, post-office and Government Offices in general. . . . He was on the mainland of the African Continent, and he was on enemy territory in the war area! How far away was the nearest German force? What should he do if he were attacked while disembarking? How was he to find the main body of his own brigade? What should he do if there were an enemy force between him and them? And what was the good of asking himself conundrums, instead of concentrating every faculty upon a speedy and orderly disembarkation?

Turning his back upon the unutterably dreary and depressing scene, as well as upon all doubts and fears and questions, he gave orders that the Gurkhas should land first. His only object in this was to have what he considered the best fighting men ashore first, and to form them up as a covering force, ready for action, in the event of any attack being made while the main body was still in the confusion, muddle and disadvantage of the act of disembarkation. And no bad idea either-but the Subedar of the Sherepur Sikhs saw, or affected to see, in this Gurkha priority of landing, an intentional and studied insult to himself, his contingent, and the whole Sikh race. He said as much to his men, and then, standing up in the bows of the boat, called out:

"Sahib! Would it not be better to let the Sherepur Sikh Contingent land first, to ensure the safety of-er-those beloved of the Sahib? There might be an attack. . . ."

Not understanding in the least what the man was saying, Bertram ignored him altogether, though he disliked the sound of the laughter in the Sikh boat, and gathered from the face of the Gurkha Subedar that something which he greatly resented had been said.

"*Khabadar* . . . *tum!*" [163] the Gurkha hissed, as he stepped ashore, and, with soldierly skill and promptness, got his men formed up, in and around the ruined building and native village, in readiness to cover the disembarkation of the rest. Five minutes after he had landed, Bertram found it difficult to believe that a hundred Gurkha Sepoys were within a hundred yards of him, for not one was visible. At the end of a couple of hours the untowed dhows had arrived, all troops, ammunition, supplies and baggage were ashore, the boats had all departed, and Bertram again found himself the only white man and sole authority in this mixed force, and felt the burden of responsibility heavy upon him.

The men having been formed up in their respective units, with the rations, ammunition, and kit dump in their rear, Bertram began to consider the advisability of leaving a strong guard over the latter, and moving off in search of the brigade camp. Would this be the right thing to do? Certainly his force was of no earthly use to the main body so long as it squatted in the mud where it had landed. Perhaps it was urgently wanted at that very moment, and the General was praying for its arrival and swearing at its non-arrival—every minute being precious, and the fate of the campaign hanging upon its immediate appearance. It might well be that an attack in their rear by four hundred fresh troops would put to flight an enemy who, up to that moment, had been winning. He would not know the strength of this new assailant, nor whether it was to be measured in hundreds or in thousands. Suppose the General was, at that very moment, listening for his rifles, as Wellington listened for the guns of his allies at Waterloo! And here he was, doing nothing-wasting time. . . . Yes, but suppose this dense bush were full of scouts and spies, as it well might be, and probably was, and supposing that the ration and ammunition dump was captured as soon as he had marched off with his main body? A pretty start for his military career-to lose the ammunition and food supply for the whole force within an hour or two of getting it ashore! His name would be better known than admired by the British Expeditionary Force in East Africa. . . . What would Murray have done in such a case? . . . Suppose he "split the difference" and neither left the stores behind him nor stuck in the mud with them? Suppose he moved forward in the direction of the Base Camp, taking everything with him? But that would mean that every soldier in the force would be burdened like a coolie-porter—and, moreover, they'd have to move in single file along the mud path that ran through the impenetrable jungle. Suppose they were attacked? . . .

Bertram came to the conclusion that it may be a very fine thing to have an independent command of one's own, but that personally he would give a great deal to find himself under the command of somebody else-be he never so arrogant, unsympathetic and harsh. Had Colonel Frost suddenly appeared he would (metaphorically) have cast himself upon that cold, stern man's hard bosom in transports of relief and joy. . . . He was going to do his very best, of course, and would never shirk nor evade any duty that lay before him-but-he felt a very lonely, anxious, undecided lad, and anxiety was fast becoming nervousness and fear-fear of doing the wrong thing, or of doing the right thing in the wrong way. . . . Should he leave a strong guard over the stores and advance? Should he remain where he was, and protect the stores to the last? Or should he advance with every man and every article the force possessed? . . .

Could the remainder carry all that stuff if he told off a strong advance-guard and rear-guard? And, if so, what could a strong advance-guard or rear-guard do in single file if the column were attacked in front or rear? How could he avoid an ambush on either flank by discovering it in time-in country which rendered the use of flank guards utterly impossible? A man could only make his way through that jungle of thorn, scrub, trees, creepers and undergrowth by the patient and strenuous use of a broad axe and a saw. A strong, determined man might do a mile of it in a day. . . . Probably no human foot had trodden this soil in a thousand years, save along the little narrow path of black beaten mud that wound tortuously through it. Should he send on a party of Gurkhas with a note to the General, asking whether he should leave the stores or attempt to bring them with him? The Gurkhas were splendid jungle-fighters and splendidly willing. . . . But that would weaken his force seriously, in the event of his being attacked. . . . And suppose the party were ambushed, and he stuck there waiting and waiting, for an answer that could never come. . . .

With a heavy sigh, he ran his eye over the scene-the sullen, oily water, the ugly mangrove swamp of muddy, writhing roots and twisted, slimy trunks, the dense, brooding jungle, the grey, dull sky-all so unfriendly and uncomfortable, giving one such a homeless, helpless feeling. The Gurkhas were invisible. The Sherepur Sikhs sat in a tight-packed group around their piled arms and listened to the words of their Subedar, the men of the Hundred and Ninety-Ninth squatted in a double row along the front of the *adobe* building, and the Very Mixed Contingent was just a mob near the ration-dump, beside which Ali Suleiman stood on guard over his master's kit. . . . Suppose there were a sudden attack? But there couldn't be? An enemy could only approach down that narrow path in single file. The impenetrable jungle was his friend until he moved. Directly he marched off it would be his terrible foe, the host and concealer of a thousand ambushes.

He felt that he had discovered a military maxim on his own account. *Impenetrable jungle is the friend of a force in position, and the enemy of a force on the march.* . . . Anyhow, the Gurkhas were out in front as a line of sentry groups, and nothing could happen to the force until they had come into action. . . . Should he —

"*Sahib*! *Ek Sahib ata hai.* . . . *Bahut hubshi log ata hain*," said a voice, and he sprang round, to see the Gurkha Subedar saluting.

What was that? "*A sahib is coming.* . . . *Many African natives are coming!*" . . . Then they *were* attacked after all! A German officer was leading a force of *askaris* of the Imperial African Rifles against them-those terrible Yaos and Swahilis whom the Germans had disciplined into a splendid army, and whom they permitted to loot and to slaughter after a successful fight. . . .

His mouth went dry and the backs of his knees felt loose and weak. He was conscious of a rush of blood to the heart and a painful, sinking sensation of the stomach. . . . It had come. . . . The hour of his first battle was upon him. . . .

He swallowed hard.

"*Achcha*, [164] *Subedar Sahib*," he said with seeming nonchalance, "*shaitan-log ko maro. Achcha kam karo*,"[165] and turning to the Sherepur Sikhs, the Hundred and Ninety-Ninth and the Very Mixed Contingent bawled: "*Fall in!*" in a voice that made those worthies perform the order as quickly as ever they had done it in their lives.

"*Dushman nahin hai,* [166] *Sahib*," said the Gurkha Subedar-as he realised that Bertram had ordered him "to kill the devils"—and explained that the people who approached bore no weapons.

Hurrying forward with the Subedar to a bend in the path beyond the burnt-out native village, Bertram saw a white man clad in khaki shirt, shorts and puttees, with a large, thick "pig-sticker" solar-topi of pith and quilted khaki on his head, and a revolver and hunting-knife in his belt. Behind him followed an apparently endless column of unarmed negroes. Evidently these were friends-but there would be no harm in taking all precautions in case of a ruse.

"Be ready," he said to the Subedar.

That officer smiled and pointed right and left to where, behind logs, mounds, bushes, and other cover, both natural and hastily prepared, lay his men, rifles cuddled lovingly to shoulder, fingers curled affectionately round triggers, eyes fixed unswervingly upon the approaching column, and faces grimly expectant. So still and so well hidden were they, that Bertram had not noticed the fact of their presence. He wondered whether the Subedar had personally strewn grass, leaves and brushwood over them after they had taken up their positions. He thought of the Babes in the Wood, and visualised the fierce little Gurkha as a novel kind of robin for the work of burying with dead leaves. . . .

He stopped in the path and awaited the arrival of the white man.

"Good morning, Mr. Greene," said that individual, as he approached. "Sorry if I've kept you waiting, but I had another job to finish first."

Bertram stared in amazement at this person who rolled up from the wilds of the Dark Continent with an unarmed party, addressed him by name, and apologised for being late! He was a saturnine and pessimistic-looking individual, wore the South African War ribbons on his breast, and the letters C.C. on his shoulders, and a lieutenant's stars.

"Good morning," replied Bertram, shaking hands. "I'm awfully glad to see you. I was wondering whether I ought to push off or stay here. . . ."

"No attractions much here," said the new-comer. "I should bung off. . . . Straight along this path. Can't miss the way."

"Is there much danger of attack?" asked Bertram.

"Insects," replied the other.

"Why not by Germans?" enquired Bertram.

"River on your left flank," was the brief answer of the saturnine and pessimistic one.

"Can't they cross it by bridges?"

"No; owing to the absence of bridges. I'm the only Bridges here," sighed Mr. Bridges, of the Coolie Corps.

"Why not in boats then?"

"Owing to the absence of boats."

"Might not the Germans open fire on us from the opposite bank then?" pursued the anxious Bertram, determined not to begin his career in Africa with a "regrettable incident," due to his own carelessness.

"No; owing to the absence of Germans," replied Mr. Bridges. "Where's your stuff? I've brought a thousand of my blackbirds, so we'll shift the lot in one journey. If you like to shove off at once, I'll see nothing's left behind. . . ." And then, suddenly realising that there was not the least likelihood of attack nor cause for anxiety, and that all he had to do was to stroll along a path to the camp, where all responsibility for the safety of men and materials would be taken from him, Bertram relaxed, and realised that the heat was appalling and that he felt very faint and ill. His kit had suddenly grown insupportably heavy and unsufferably tight about his chest; his turban gave no shade to his eyes nor protection to his temples and neck, and its weight seemed to increase by pounds per minute. He felt very giddy, blue lights appeared before his eyes, and there was a surging and booming in his ears. He sat down, to avoid falling.

"Hullo! Seedy?" ejaculated Bridges, and turned to a big negro who stood behind him, and appeared to be a person of quality, inasmuch as he wore the ruins of a helmet, a khaki shooting-jacket much too small for him, and a whistle on a string. ("Only that and nothing more.")

"Here, MacGinty-my-lad," said Bridges to this gentleman, "*m'dafu late hapa*," and with a few whistling clicks and high-pitched squeals, the latter sped another negro up a palm tree. Climbing it like a monkey, the negro tore a huge yellow coco-nut from the bunch that clustered beneath the spreading palm leaves, and flung it down. This, Mr. MacGinty-my-lad retrieved and, with one skilful blow of a *panga*, a kind of *machete* or butchers' axe, decapitated.

"Have a swig at this," said Bridges, handing the nut to Bertram, who discovered it to contain about a quart of deliciously cool, sweet "milk," as clear as distilled water.

"Thanks awfully, Bridges," said he. "I think I had a touch of the sun. . . ."

"Had a touch of breakfast?" enquired the other.

"No," replied Bertram.

"Hence the milk in the coco-nut," said Bridges, and added, "If you want to live long and die happy in Africa, you *must* do yourself well. It's the secret of success. You treat your tummy well-and often-and it'll do the same for you. . . . If you don't, well, you'll be no good to yourself nor anyone else."

"Thanks," said the ever-grateful Bertram, and arose feeling much better.

"Fall in, Subedar Sahib," said he to the Gurkha officer, and the latter quickly assembled his men as a company in line.

The Subedar of the Sherepur Sikhs approached and saluted. "We want to be the advance-guard, Sahib," he said.

"Certainly," replied Bertram, and added innocently, "There is no enemy between here and the camp."

The Sikh flashed a glance of swift suspicion at him. . . . Was this an intentional *riposte*? Was the young Sahib more subtle than he looked? Had he meant "The Sikhs may form the advance-guard *because* there is no fear of attack," with the implication that the Gurkhas would again have held the post of honour and danger if there had been any danger?

"I don't like the look of that bloke," observed Bridges, as the Sikh turned away, and added: "Well—I'll handle your stuff now, if you'll bung off," and continued his way to the dump, followed by Mr. MacGinty and a seemingly endless file of very tall, very weedy, Kavirondo negroes, of an unpleasant, scaly, greyish-black colour and more unpleasant, indescribable, but fishlike odour. These worthies were variously dressed, some in a *panga* or *machete*, some in a tin pot, others in a gourd, a snuff-box, a tea-cup, a saucepan or a jam-jar. Every man, however, without exception, possessed a red blanket, and every man, without exception, wore it, for modesty's sake, folded small upon his head-where it also served the purpose of a porter's pad, intervening between his head and the load which it was his life's work to bear thereupon. . . . When these people conversed, it was in the high, piping voices of little children, and when Bridges, Mr. MacGinty-my-lad, or any less *neapara* (head man), made a threatening movement towards one of them, the culprit would forthwith put his hands to his ears, draw up one foot to the other knee, close his eyes, cringe, and emit an incredibly thin, small squeal, a sound infinitely ridiculous in the mouth of a man six feet or more in stature. . . . When the last of these quaint creatures had passed, Bertram strode to where the Sherepur Sikhs had formed up in line, ready to march off at the head of the force. The Subedar gave an order, the ranks opened, the front rank turned about, and the rifles, with bayonet already fixed, came down to the "ready," and Bertram found himself between the two rows of flickering points.

"*Charge magazhinge*," shouted the Subedar, and Bertram found an odd dozen of rifles waving in the direction of his stomach, chest, face, neck and back, as their owners gaily loaded them. . . . Was there going to be an "accident"? . . . Were there covert smiles on any of the fierce bearded faces of the big men? . . . Should he make a dash from between the ranks? . . . No-he would stand his ground and look displeased at this truly "native" method of charging magazines. It seemed a long time before the Subedar gave the orders, "Front rank-about turn. . . . Form fours. . . . Right," and the company was ready to march off.

"All is ready, Sahib," said the Subedar, approaching Bertram. "Shall I lead on?"

"Yes, Subedar Sahib," replied Bertram, "but why do your men face each other and point their rifles at each other's stomachs when they load them?"

His Hindustani was shockingly faulty, but evidently the Subedar understood.

"They are not afraid of being shot, Sahib," said he, smiling superiorly.

"Then it is a pity they are not afraid of being called slovenly, clumsy, jungly recruits," replied Bertram-and before the scowling officer could reply, added: "March on-and halt when I whistle," in sharp voice and peremptory manner.

Before long the little force was on its way, the Gurkhas coming last-as the trusty rear-guard, Bertram explained-and, after half an hour's uneventful march through the stinking swamp, reached the Base Camp of the M'paga Field Force-surely one of the ugliest, dreariest and most depressing spots in which ever a British force sat down and acquired assorted diseases.

Chapter X
M'paga

Halting his column, closing it up, and calling it to attention, Bertram marched past the guard of King's African Rifles and entered the Camp. This consisted of a huge square, enclosed by low earthen walls and shallow trenches, in which were the "lines" of the Indian and African infantry, composing the inadequate little force which was invading German East Africa, rather with the idea of protecting British East than achieving conquest. The "lines" of the Sepoys and *askaris* consisted of rows of tiny low tents, while along the High Street of the Camp stood hospital tents, officers' messes, the General's tent, and that of his Brigade Major, and various other tents connected with the mysteries of the field telegraph and telephone, the Army Service Corps' supply and transport, and various offices of Brigade and Regimental Headquarters. As he passed the General's tent (indicated by a flagstaff and Union Jack), a tall lean officer, with a white-moustached, keen-eyed face, emerged and held up his hand. Seeing the crossed swords of a General on his shoulder-straps, Bertram endeavoured to rise to the occasion, roared: "*Eyes right,*" "*Eyes front,*" and then "*Halt,*" saluted and stepped forward.

The General shook hands with him, and said: "Glad to see you. Hope you're ready for plenty of hard work, for there's plenty for you. . . . Glad to see your men looking so businesslike and marching so smartly. . . . All right-carry on. . . ."

Bertram would gladly have died for that General on the spot, and it was positively with a lump (of gratitude, so to speak) in his throat that he gave the order "*Quick march,*" and proceeded, watched by hundreds of native soldiers, who crawled out of their low tents or rose up from where they lay or squatted to clean accoutrements, gossip, eat, or contemplate Infinity.

Arrived at the opposite entrance of the Camp, Bertram felt foolish, but concealed the fact by pretending that he had chosen this as a suitable halting place, bawled: "*Halt,*" "*Into line—left turn,*" "*Stand at ease,*" "*Stand easy,*" and determined to wait events. He had carried out his orders and brought the troops to the Camp as per instructions. Somebody else could come and take them if they wanted them. . . .

As he stood, trying to look unconcerned, a small knot of British officers strolled up, headed by a tall and important-looking person arrayed in helmet, open shirt, shorts, grey stockings and khaki canvas shoes.

"Greene?" said he.

"Yes, sir," said Bertram, saluting.

"Brigade Major," continued the officer, apparently introducing himself. "March the Hundred and Ninety-Ninth on and report to Colonel Rock. The Hundred and Ninety-Eighth are outside the perimeter," and he pointed to where, a quarter of a mile away, were some grass huts and rows of tiny tents. "The remainder will be taken over by their units here, and your responsibility for them ceases."

Bertram, very thankful to be rid of them, marched on with the Hundred, and halted them in front of the low tents, from which, with whoops of joy, poured forth the warriors of the Hundred and Ninety-Eighth in search of any *bhai*, pal, townee, bucky, or aunt's cousin's husband's sister's son —(who, as such, would have a strong claim upon his good offices) —in the ranks of this thrice-welcome reinforcement.

Leaving the Hundred in charge of Jemadar Hassan Ali to await orders, Bertram strode to a large grass *banda*, or hut, consisting of three walls and a roof, through the open end of which he could see a group of British officers sitting on boxes and stools, about a long and most uneven, undulating table of box-sides nailed on sticks and supported by four upright logs.

At the head of this table, on which were maps and papers, sat a small thick-set man, who looked the personification of vigour, force and restless activity. Seeing that this officer wore a crown and star on his shoulder-strap, Bertram went up to him, saluted, and said:

"Second-Lieutenant Greene, I.A.R., sir. I have brought a hundred men from the Hundred and Ninety-Ninth, and nine cooking-pots —which Colonel Frost wishes to have returned at once. . . ."

"The men or the cooking-pots, or both?" enquired Colonel Rock, whose habit of sarcastic and savage banter made him feared by all who came in contact with him, and served to conceal a very kindly and sympathetic nature.

"The cooking-pots, sir," replied Bertram, blushing as the other officers eyed him critically and with half-smiles at the Colonel's humour. Bertram felt, a little cynically, that such wit from an officer of their own rank would not have seemed so pleasingly humorous to some of these gentlemen, and that, moreover, he had again discovered a Military Maxim on his own account. *The value and humorousness of any witty remark made by any person in military uniform is in inverse ratio to the rank and seniority of the individual to whom it is made.* In other words, a Colonel must smile at a General's joke, a Major must grin broadly, a Captain laugh appreciatively, a Subaltern giggle right heartily, a Warrant Officer or N.C.O. explode into roars of laughter, and a private soldier roll helpless upon the ground in spasms and convulsions of helpless mirth.

Hearing a distinct snigger from the end of the table, Bertram glanced in that direction, said to himself, "You're a second-lieutenant, by your appreciative giggle," and encountered the sneering stare of a vacant-faced youth whom he heartily disliked on sight.

"Wants the cooking-pots back, but not the men, eh?" observed the Colonel, and, turning to the officer who sat at his left hand, a tall, handsome man with a well-bred, pleasant, dark face, who was Adjutant of the Hundred and Ninety-Ninth, added:

"Better go and see if there's good reason for his not wanting them back, Hall. . . . Colonel Frost's a good man at selling a horse-perhaps he's sold us a pup. . . ."

More giggles from the vacant faced youth as Captain Hall arose and went out of the shed of grass and sticks, thatched on a framework of posts, which was the Officers' Mess of the Hundred and Ninety-Eighth Regiment.

Feeling shy and nervous, albeit most thankful to be among senior officers who would henceforth relieve him of the lonely responsibility he had found so trying and burdensome, Bertram seized the opportunity of the Adjutant's departure to escape, and followed that officer to where the Hundred awaited the order to dismiss.

"Brought a tent?" asked Captain Hall, as they went along.

"No," replied Bertram. "Ought I to have done so?"

"If you value your comfort on these picnics," was the answer. "You'll find it a bit damp o' nights when it rains, in one of these grass huts. . . . You can pig in with me to-night, and we'll set a party of Kavirondo to build you a *banda* to-morrow if you're staying on here."

"Thanks awfully," acknowledged Bertram. "Am I likely to go on somewhere else, though?"

"I did hear something about your taking a provision convoy up to Butindi the day after tomorrow," was the reply. "One of our Majors is up there with a mixed force of Ours and the Arab Company, with some odds and ends of King's African Rifles and things. . . . Pity you haven't a tent."

After looking over the Hundred and committing them to the charge of the Subedar-Major of the Hundred and Ninety-Eighth, Captain Hall invited Bertram "to make himself at home" in his hut, and led the way to where a row of green tents and grass huts stood near the Officers' Mess. On a Roorkee chair, at the door of one of these, sat none other than the Lieutenant Stanner whom Bertram had last seen on the deck of *Elymas*. With him was another subaltern, one of the Hundred and Ninety-Eighth.

"Hullo, Greene-bird!" cried Stanner. "Welcome home. Allow me to present you to my friend Best. . . . He is Very Best to-day, because he has got a bottle of whisky in his bed. He'll only be Second Best to-morrow, because he won't have any by then. . . . Not if he's a gentleman, that is," he added, eyeing Best anxiously.

That officer grinned, arose, and entering the hut, produced the whisky, a box of "sparklets," a kind of siphon, and a jug of dirty water.

"You already know Hall?" continued Stanner, the loquacious. "I was at school with his father. He's a good lad. Address him as Baronial Hall when you want something, Music Hall when you're feeling girlish, Town Hall when he's coming the pompous Adjutant over you, and Mission Hall when you're tired of him."

"Don't associate with him, Greene. Come away," said Captain Hall. "He'll teach you to play shove-ha'penny, to smoke, and to use bad language," but as Best handed him a whisky-and-dirty-water, feebly aerated by a sparklet, he tipped Stanner from his chair, seated himself in it, murmured, "When sinners entice thee, consent thou some," and drank.

"Why are you dressed like that? Is it your birthday, or aren't you very well?" enquired Stanner suddenly, eyeing Bertram's lethal weapons and Sepoy's turban. Bertram blushed, pleaded that he had nowhere to "undress," and had only just arrived. Whereupon the Adjutant, remarking that he must be weary, arose and took him to his hut.

"Get out of everything but your shirt and shorts, my son," said he, "and chuck that silly *puggri* away before you get sunstroke. All very well if you're going into a scrap, but it's as safe as Piccadilly round here." Bertram, as he sank into the Adjutant's chair, suddenly realised that he was more tired than ever he had been in his life before.

"Where *Bwana* sleeping to-night, sah, thank you, please?" boomed a familiar voice, and before the tent stood the faithful Ali, bowing and saluting-behind him three tall Kavirondo carrying Bertram's kit. Ali had commandeered these men from Bridges' party, and had hurried them off far in advance of the porters who were bringing in the general kit, rations, and ammunition. By means best known to himself he had galvanised the "low niggers" into agility and activity that surprised none more than themselves.

"Oh-it's my servant," said Bertram to the Adjutant. "May he put my bed in here, then?"

"That's the idea," replied Captain Hall, and, in a few minutes, Bertram's camp-bed was erected and furnished with bedding and mosquito net, his washhand-stand was set up, and his canvas bucket filled with water. Not until everything possible had been done for his master's comfort did Ali disappear to that mysterious spot whereunto native servants repair beyond the ken of the master-folk, when in need of food, leisure and relaxation.

Having washed, eaten and slept, Bertram declared himself "a better and wiser man," and asked Hall if he might explore the Camp, its wonders to admire. "Oh, yes," said Hall, "but don't go into the gambling dens, boozing-kens, dancing-saloons and faro tents, to squander your money, time and health."

"*Are* there any?" asked Bertram, in wide-eyed astonishment.

"No," replied Hall.

Bertram wished people would not be so fond of exercising their humour at his expense. He wondered why it was that he was always something of a butt. It could not be that he was an absolute fool, or he would not have been a Scholar of Balliol. He sighed. *Could* one be a Scholar of Balliol and a fool? . . .

"You might look in on the General, though," continued Hall, "and be chatty. . . . It's a very lonely life, y'know, a General's. I'm always sorry for the poor old beggars. Yes-he'd be awfully glad to see you. . . . Ask you to call him Willie before you'd been there a couple of hours, I expect."

"D'you mean I ought to call on the General formally?" asked Bertram, who knew that Hall was "ragging" again, as soon as he introduced the "Willie" touch.

"Oh, don't be too formal," was the reply. "Be matey and cosy with him. . . . I don't suppose he's had a really heart-to-heart chat with a subaltern about the things that *really* matter-the Empire (the Leicester Square one, I mean); Ciro's; the girls; George Robey, George Graves, Mr. Bottomley, Mrs. Pankhurst and the other great comedians-since I dunno-when. He'd *love* to buck about what's doing in town, with *you*, y'know. . . ."

Bertram sighed again. It was no good. *Everybody* pulled his leg and seemed to sum him up in two minutes as the sort of green ass who'd believe anything he was told, and do anything that was suggested.

"I say, Hall," he said suddenly, "I'm a civilian, y'know, and a bit of a fool, too, no doubt. I am absolutely ignorant of all military matters, particularly those of etiquette. I am going to ask you things, since you are Adjutant of the corps I'm with. If you score off me, I think it'll be rather a cheap triumph and an inglorious victory, don't you? . . . I'm not a bumptious and conceited ass, mind-only an ignorant one, who fully admits it, and asks for help. . . ."

As the poet says, it is a long lane that has no public-house, and a long worm that has no turning.

Hall stared.

"Well said, Greene," quoth he, and never jested at Bertram's expense again.

"Seriously-should I leave a card on the General?" continued Bertram.

"You should not," was the reply. "Avoid Generals as you would your creditors. They're dangerous animals in peace-time. On manœuvres they're ferocious. On active service they're rapid. . . ."

"Any harm in my strolling round the Camp?" pursued Bertram. "I'm awfully interested, and might get some ideas of the useful kind."

"None whatever," said Hall. "No reason why you shouldn't prowl around like the hosts of Midian till dinner-time. There's nothing doing in the Hundred and Ninety-Eighth till four a.m. to-morrow, and you're not in that, either."

"What is it?" asked Bertram.

"Oh, a double-company of Ours is going out to mop up a little post the Germans have established across the river. We're going to learn 'em not to do such," said Hall.

"D'you think I might go?" asked Bertram, wondering, even as he spoke, whether it was his voice that was suggesting so foolish a thing as that Bertram Greene should arise at three-thirty in the morning to go, wantonly and without reason, where bullets were flying, bayonets were stabbing, and death and disablement were abroad.

"Dunno," yawned Hall. "Better ask the Colonel. What's the matter with bed at four ack emma? That's where I'd be if I weren't in orders for this silly show."

As Bertram left the tent on his tour of exploration he decided that he would ask the Colonel if he might go with the expedition, and then he decided that he would do nothing so utterly foolish. . . . No, of course he wouldn't. . . .

Yes, he would. . . .

Chapter XI
Food and Feeders

Rightly or wrongly, Bertram gathered the impression, as he strolled about the Camp, that this was not a confident and high-spirited army, drunk with the heady fumes of a debauch of victory. The demeanour of the Indian Sepoys led him to the conclusion, just or unjust, that they had "got their tails down." They appeared weary, apprehensive, even despondent, when not merely apathetic, and seemed to him to be distinctly what they themselves would call *mugra* —pessimistic and depressed.

The place alone was sufficient to depress anybody, he freely admitted, as he gazed around at the dreary grey environs of this little British *pied-à-terre* —grey thorn bush; grey grass; grey baobab trees (like hideous grey carrots with whiskerish roots, pulled up from the ground and stood on end); grey shell-strewn mud; grey bushwood; grey mangroves; grey sky. Yes, an inimical minatory landscape; a brooding, unwholesome, sinister landscape; the home of fever, dysentery, disease and sudden death. And over all hung a horrible sickening stench of decay, an evil smell that seemed to settle at the pit of the stomach as a heavy weight.

No wonder if Indians from the hills, deserts, plains and towns of the Deccan, the Punjab, Rajputana, and Nepal, found this terrible place of most terrific heat, foul odour, bad water and worse mud, enervating and depressing. . . . Poor beggars-it wasn't *their* war either. . . . The faces of the negroes of the King's African Rifles were inscrutable, and, being entirely ignorant of their ways, manners, and customs, he could not tell whether they were exhibiting signs of discouragement and depression, or whether their bearing and demeanour were entirely normal. Certainly they seemed a stolid and reserved folk, with a kind of dignity and self-respecting aloofness that he had somehow not expected. In their tall tarbooshes, jerseys, shorts and puttees, they looked most workman-like and competent soldiers. . . . Certainly they did not tally with his preconceived idea of them as a merry, care-free, irresponsible folk who grinned all over their faces for sheer light-heartedness, and spent their leisure time in twanging the banjo, clacking the bones, singing rag-time songs and doing the cake-walk. On duty, they stood like ebon statues and opened not their mouths. Off duty they squatted like ebon statuettes and shut them. Perhaps they did not know that England expects every nigger to do his duty as a sort of born music-hall, musical minstrel-or perhaps they *were* depressed, like the Sepoys, and had laid aside their banjoes, bones, coon-songs and double-shuffle-flap-dancing boots until brighter days? . . . Anyhow, decided Bertram, he would much rather be with these stalwarts than against them, when they charged with their triangular bayonets on their Martini rifles; and if the German *askaris* were of similar type, he cared not how long his first personal encounter with them might be postponed. . . . Nor did the Englishmen of the Army Service Corps, the Royal Engineers, the Signallers and other details, strike him as light-hearted and bubbling with the *joie de vivre*. Frankly they looked ill, and they looked anxious. . . .

Strolling past the brushwood-and-grass hut which was the R.A.M.C. Officers' Mess, he heard the remark:

"They've only got to leave us here in peace a little while for us all to die natural deaths of malaria or dysentery. The wily Hun knows *that* all right. . . . No fear-we shan't be attacked here. No such luck."

"Not unless we make ourselves too much of a nuisance to him," said another voice. "'Course, if we go barging about and capturing his trading posts and 'factories,' and raiding his *shambas*, he'll come down on us all right. . . ."

"I dunno what we're doing here at all," put in a third speaker. "You can't invade a blooming *continent* like German East with a weak brigade of sick Sepoys. . . . Sort of bloomin' Jameson's Raid. . . . Why-they could come down the railway from Tabora or Kilimanjaro way with enough European troops alone to eat us alive. What are we here, irritating 'em at all for, *I* want to know? . . ."

"Why, to maintain Britain's glorious traditions-of sending far too weak a force in the first place," put in the first speaker. "They'll send an adequate army later on, all right, and do the job in style. We've got to demonstrate the necessity for the adequate army first, though. . . ."

"Sort of bait, like," said another, and yawned. "Well, we've all fished, I expect. . . . Know how the worm feels now. . . ."

"I've only fished with flies," observed a languid and euphuistic voice.

"*What* an honour for the 'appy fly!" replied the worm-fisherman, and there was a guffaw of laughter.

Bertram realised that he was loitering to the point of eavesdropping, and strolled on, pondering many things in his heart. . . .

In one corner of the great square of mud which was the Camp, Bertram came upon a battery consisting of four tiny guns. Grouped about them stood their Sepoy gunners, evidently at drill of some kind, for, at a sudden word from a British officer standing near, they leapt upon them, laboured frantically for five seconds, stood clear again, and, behold, each gun lay dismembered and prone upon the ground-the wheels off, the trail detached, the barrel of the gun itself in two parts, so that the breech half was separate from the muzzle half. At another word from the officer the statuesque Sepoys again sprang to life, seized each man a piece of the dismembered gun, lifted it above his head, raised it up and down, replaced it on the ground and once more stood at attention. Another order, and, in five seconds, the guns were reassembled and ready to fire.

"A mountain-battery of screw guns, so called because they screw and unscrew in the middle of the barrel," said Bertram to himself, and concluded that the drill he had just witnessed was that required for putting the dissected guns on the backs of mules for mountain transport, and rebuilding them for use. Certainly they were wonderfully nippy, these Sepoys, and seemed, perhaps, rather more cheery than the others. One old gentleman who had a chestful of medal-ribbons raised and lowered a gun-wheel above his head as though it had been of cardboard, in spite of his long grey beard and pensioner-like appearance.

Bertram envied the subaltern in command of this battery. How splendid it must be to know exactly what to do and to be able to do it; to be conscious that you are adequate and competent, equal to any demand that can be made upon you. Probably this youth was enjoying this campaign in the mud and stench and heat as much as he had ever enjoyed a picnic or tramping or boating holiday in England. . . . Lucky dog. . . .

At about seven o'clock that evening, Bertram "dined" in the Officers' Mess of the Hundred and Ninety-Eighth. The rickety hut, through the walls of which the fires of the Camp could be seen, and through the roof of which the great stars were visible, was lighted, or left in darkness, by a hurricane-lamp which dangled from the ridge-pole. The officers of the corps sat on boxes, cane-stools, shooting-seats, or patent "weight-less" contrivances of aluminium and canvas. The vacant-faced youth, whose name was Grayne, had a bicycle-saddle which could be raised and lowered on a metal rod. He was very proud of it and fell over backwards twice during dinner. Bertram would have had nothing whatever to sit on had not the excellent and foresighted Ali discovered the fact in time to nail the two sides of a box in the shape of the letter T by means of a stone and the nails still adhering to the derelict wood. On this Bertram balanced himself with less danger and discomfort than might have been expected, the while he viewed with mixed feelings Ali's apologies and promise that he would steal a really nice stool or chair by the morrow.

On the mosaic of box-sides that formed the undulating, uneven, and fissured table-top, the Mess servant places tin plates containing a thin and nasty soup, tasting, Bertram thought, of cooking-pot, dish-cloth, wood-smoke, tin plate and the thumb of the gentleman who had borne it from the cook-house, or rather the cook-hole-in-the-ground, to the Mess hut. The flourish with which Ali placed it before his "beloved ole marstah" as he ejaculated "Soop, sah, thick an' clear thank-you please" went some way to make it interesting, but failed to make it palatable.

Although sick and faint for want of food, Bertram was not hungry or in a condition to appreciate disgraceful cooking disgustingly served.

As he sat awaiting the next course, after rejecting the thick-an'-clear "soup," Bertram took stock of the gentlemen whom, in his heart, he proudly, if shyly, called his brother-officers.

At the head of the table sat the Colonel, looking gloomy and distrait. Bertram wondered if he were thinking of the friends and comrades-in-arms he had left in the vile jungle round Tanga-his second-in-command and half a dozen more of his officers-and a third of his men. Was he thinking of his School-and Sandhurst-and life-long friend and trusted colleague, Major Brett-Boyce, slain by the German *askaris* as he lay wounded, propped against a tree by the brave and faithful dresser of the subordinate medical service, who was murdered with him in the very midst of his noble work, by those savage and brutal disciples of a more savage and brutal *kultur*?

Behind him stood his servant, a tall Mussulman in fairly clean white garments, and a big white turban round which was fastened a broad ribbon of the regimental colours adorned with the regimental crest in silver.

"Tell the cook that he and I will have a quiet chat in the morning, if he'll be good enough to come to my tent after breakfast-and then the provost-marshal shall show him a new game, perhaps," said the Colonel to this man as he finished his soup.

With the ghost of a smile the servant bowed, removed the Colonel's plate and departed to gloat over the cook, who, as a Goanese, despised "natives" heartily and without concealment, albeit himself as black as a negro.

Returning, the Colonel's servant bore a huge metal dish on which reposed a mound of most repulsive-looking meat in lumps, rags, shreds, strings, tendrils and fibres, surrounded by a brownish clear water. This was a seven-pound tin of bully-beef heated and turned out in all its native ugliness, naked and unadorned, on to the dish. Like everyone else, Bertram took a portion on his plate, and, like everyone else, left it on his plate, and, like everyone else, left it after tasting a morsel-or attempting to taste, for bully-beef under such conditions has no taste whatever. To chew it is merely as though one dipped a ball of rag and string into dirty water, warmed it, put it in one's mouth, and attempted to masticate it. To swallow it is moreover to attain the same results-nutrient, metabolic and sensational-as would follow upon the swallowing of the said ball of rags and string.

The morsel of bully-beef that Bertram put in his mouth abode with him. Though of the West it was like the unchanging East, for it changed not. He chewed and chewed, rested from his labours, and chewed again, in an honest and earnest endeavour to take nourishment and work out his own insalivation, but was at last forced to acknowledge himself defeated by the stout and tough resistance of the indomitable lump. It did not know when it was beaten and it did not know when it was eaten; nor, had he been able to swallow it, would the "juices" of his interior have succeeded where those of his mouth, aided by his excellent teeth, had failed. In course of time it became a problem-another of those small but numerous and worrying problems that were fast bringing wrinkles to his forehead, hollows to his cheeks, a look of care and anxiety to his eyes, and nightmares to his sleep. He could not reduce it, he could not swallow it, he could not publicly reject it. What *could* he do? . . . A bright idea. . . . Tactics. . . . He dropped his handkerchief-and when he arose from stooping to retrieve it, he was a free man again. A few minutes later a lump of bully-beef undiminished, unaffected and unfrayed, travelled across the mud floor of the hut in the mandibles of an army of big black ants, to provide them also with a disappointment and a problem, and, perchance, with a bombproof shelter for their young in a subterranean dug-out of the ant-hill. . . .

Bertram again looked around at his fellow-officers. Not one of them appeared to have reduced the evil-looking mass of fibrous tissue and gristle that lay upon his plate-nor, indeed, did Bertram, throughout the campaign, ever see anyone actually eat and swallow the disgusting and repulsive muck served out to the officers and European units of the Expeditionary Force-hungry as they often were.

To his foolish civilian mind it seemed that if the money which this foul filth cost (for even bully-beef costs money-ask the contractors) had been spent on a half or a quarter or a tithe of the quantity of *edible* meat-such as tinned ox-tongue —sick and weary soldiers labouring and suffering for their country in a terrible climate, might have had a sufficiency of food which they could have eaten with pleasure and digested with benefit, without costing their grateful country a penny more. . . .   Which is an absurd and ridiculous notion expressed in a long and involved sentence. . . .

Next, to the Colonel, eyeing his plate of bully-beef through his monocle and with patent disgust, sat Major Manton, a tall, aristocratic person who looked extraordinarily smart and dapper. Hair, moustache, finger-nails and hands showed signs of obvious care, and he wore tunic, tie and, in fact, complete uniform, in an assembly wherein open shirts, bare arms, white tennis shoes, slacks, shorts, and even flannel trousers were not unknown. Evidently the Major put correctness before comfort-or, perhaps, found his chief comfort in being correct. He spoke to no one, but replied suavely when addressed. He looked to Bertram like a man who loathed a rough and rude environment having the honour or pleasure or satisfaction of knowing that he noticed its existence, much less that he troubled to loathe it. Bertram imagined that in the rough and tumble of hand-to-hand fighting, the Major's weapon would be the revolver, his aim quick and clean, his demeanour unhurried and unflurried, the expression of his face cold and unemotional.

Beside him sat a Captain Tollward in strong contrast, a great burly man with the physiognomy and bull-neck of a prize-fighter, the hands and arms of a navvy, and the figure of a brewer's dray-man. Frankly, he looked rather a brute, and Bertram pictured him in a fight-using a fixed bayonet or clubbed rifle with tremendous vigour and effect. He would be purple of face and wild of eye, would grunt like a bull with every blow, roar to his men like a charging lion, and swear like a bargee between whiles. . . .   "Thank God for all England's Captain Tollwards this day," thought Bertram as he watched the powerful-looking man, and thought of the gladiators of ancient Rome.

Stanner was keeping him in roars of Homeric laughter with his jests and stories, no word of any one of which brought the shadow of a smile to the expressionless strong face of Major Manton, who could hear every one of the jokes that convulsed Tollward and threatened him with apoplexy. Next to Stanner sat Hall, who gave Bertram, his left-hand neighbour, such information and advice as he could, anent his taking of the convoy to Butindi, should such be his fate.

"You'll see some fighting up there, if you ever get there," said he. "They're always having little 'affairs of out-posts' and patrol scraps. You may be cut up on the way, of course. . . . If the Germans lay for you they're bound to get you, s' far as I can see. . . . How *can* you defend a convoy of a thousand porters going in single file through impenetrable jungle along a narrow path that it's practically impossible to leave? . . . You can have an advance-guard and a rear-guard, of course, and much good may they do you when your *safari* covers anything from a couple of miles to three or four. . . . What are you going to do if it's attacked in the middle, a mile or so away from where you are yourself? . . . What are you going to do if they ambush your advance-guard and mop the lot up, as they perfectly easily could do, at any point on the track, if they know you're coming-as of course they will do, as soon as we know it ourselves. . . . "

"You fill me with despondency and alarm," said Bertram, with a lightness that he was far from feeling, and a sinking sensation that was not wholly due to emptiness of stomach.

Suddenly he was aware that a new stench was contending with the familiar one of decaying vegetation, rotting shell-fish, and the slime that was neither land nor water, but seemed a foul grease formed by the decomposition of leaves, grasses, trees, fish, molluscs and animals in an inky, oily fluid that the tides but churned up for the freer exhalation of poisonous miasma, and had not washed away since the rest of the world arose out of chaos and darkness, that man might breathe and thrive. . . .   The new smell was akin to the old one but more penetrating, more subtly vile, more *vulgar*, than that ancient essence of decay and death and dissolution, and-awaking from a brown study in which he saw visions of himself writhing beneath the bayonets of a dozen gigantic savages, as he fell at the head of his convoy-he perceived that the new and conquering odour proceeded from the cheese. On a piece of tin, that had been the lid of a box, it lay and defied competition, while, with the unfaltering step of a strong man doing right, because it is his duty, Ali Suleiman bore it from *bwana* to *bwana* with the booming murmur: "Cheese, please God, sah, thank you." To the observant and thoughtful Bertram its reception by each member of the Mess was interesting and instructive, as indicative of his character, breeding, and personality.

The Colonel eyed it with a cold smile.

"Yes. Please God it *is* only cheese," he remarked, "but take it away-quick."

Major Manton glanced at it and heaved a very gentle sigh. "No, thank you, Boy," he said.

Captain Tollward sniffed hard, turned to Stanner, and roared with laughter.

"What ho, the High Explosive!" he shouted, and "What ho, the Forty Rod Gorgonzola-so called because it put the battery-mules out of action at that distance. . . . Who unchained it, I say? Boy, where's its muzzle?" and he cut himself a generous slice.

Stanner buried his nose in his handkerchief and waved Ali away as he thrust the nutritious if over-prevalent delicacy upon his notice.

"Take it to Bascombe *Bwana* and ask him to fire it from his guns," said he. "Serve the Germans right for using poison-gas and liquid fire. . . . Teach 'em a lesson, what, Tollward?"

"Don't be dev'lish-minded," replied that officer when laughter permitted him to speak. "You're as bad as the bally Huns yourself to suggest such an atrocity. . . ."

"Seems kinder radio-active," said Hall, eyeing it with curiosity. "Menacing . . ." and he also drove it from him.

Bertram, as one who, being at war, faces the horrors of war as they come, took a piece of the cheese and found that its bite, though it skinned the roof of his mouth, was not as bad as its bark. Grayne affected to faint when the cheese reached him, and the others did according to their kind.

Following in the tracks of Ali came another servant, bearing a wooden box, which he tendered to each diner, but as one who goeth through an empty ritual, and without hope that his offering will be accepted. In the box Bertram saw large thick biscuits exceedingly reminiscent of the dog-biscuit of commerce, but paler in hue and less attractive of appearance. He took one, and the well-trained servant only dropped the box in his surprise.

"What are you going to do with *that*?" enquired Hall.

"Why!—eat it, I suppose," said Bertram.

"People don't eat *those*," replied Hall.

"Why not?" asked Bertram.

"Try it and see," was the response.

Bertram did, and desisted not until his teeth ached and he feared to break them. There was certainly no fear of breaking the biscuit. Was it a sort of practical joke biscuit—a rather clever imitation of a biscuit in concrete, hardwood, or pottery-ware of some kind?

"I understand why people do not eat them," he admitted.

"Can't be done," said Hall. "Why, even the Kavirondo who eat live slugs, dead snakes, uncooked rice, raw flesh or rotten flesh and any part of any animal there is, do not regard those things as food. . . . They make ornaments of them, tools, weapons, missiles, all sorts of things. . . ."

"I suppose if one were really starving one could live on them for a time," said the honest and serious-minded Bertram, ever a seeker after truth.

"Not unless one could get them into one's stomach, I suppose," was the reply; "and I don't see how one would do it. . . . I was reduced to trying once, and I tried hard. I put one in a basin and poured boiling water on it. . . . No result whatever. . . . I left it to soak for an hour while I chewed and chewed a piece of bully-beef. . . . Result? . . . It was slightly darker in colour, but I could no more bite into it than I could into a tile or a book. . . ."

"Suppose you boiled one," suggested Bertram.

"Precisely what I did," said Hall, "for my blood was up, apart from the fact that I was starving. It was a case of Hall *versus* a Biscuit. I boiled it-or rather watched the cook boil it in a *chattie*. . . . I gave it an hour. At the end of the hour it was of a slightly still darker colour-and showed signs of splitting through the middle. But never a bit could I get off it. . . . 'Boil the dam' thing all day and all night, and give it me hot for breakfast,' said I to the cook. . . . As one who patiently humours the headstrong, wilful White Man, he went away to carry on the foolish struggle. . . ."

"What was it like in the morning?" enquired Bertram, as Hall paused reminiscent, and chewed the cud of bitter memory.

"Have you seen a long-sodden boot-sole that is resolving itself into its original layers and laminæ?" asked Hall. "Where there should be one solid sole, you see a dozen, and the thing gapes, as it were, showing serried rows of teeth in the shape of rusty nails and little protuberances of leather and thread?"

"Yes," smiled Bertram.

"That was my biscuit," continued Hall. "At the corners it gasped and split. Between the layers little lumps and points stood up, where the original biscuit holes had been made when the dreadful thing was without form, and void, in the process of evolution from cement-like dough to brick-like biscuit. . . ."

"Could you eat it?" asked Bertram.

"Could *you* eat a boiled boot-sole?" was the reply. "The thing had turned from dry concrete to wet leather. . . . It had exchanged the extreme of brittle durability for that of pliant toughness. . . . *Eat* it!" and Hall laughed sardonically.

"What becomes of them all, then, if no one eats them?" asked Bertram.

"Oh-they have their uses, y' know. Boxes of them make a jolly good breastwork. . . The Army Service Corps are provided with work-taking them by the ton from place to place and fetching them back again. . . . I reveted a trench with biscuits once. . . . Looked very neat. . . . Lonely soldiers, in lonely outposts, do GOD BLESS OUR HOME and other devices with them-and you can make really attractive little photo-frames for 'midgets' and miniature with them if you have a centre-bit and carving tools. . . The handy-men of the R.E. make awf'ly nice boxes of children's toy-building-bricks with them, besides carved *plaques* and all sorts of little models. . . . I heard of a prisoner who made a complete steam-engine out of biscuits, but I never saw it myself. . . . Oh, yes, the Army would miss its biscuits-but I certainly never saw anybody eat one. . . ."

Nor did Bertram, throughout the campaign. And here again it occurred to his foolish civilian mind that if the thousands of pounds spent on wholly and utterly inedible dog-biscuit had been spent on the ordinary biscuits of civilisation and the grocer's shop, sick and weary soldiers, working and suffering for their country in a terrible climate, might have had a sufficiency of food that they could have eaten with pleasure and digested with benefit, without costing their grateful country a penny more.

"Which would be the better," asked Bertram of himself—"to send an army ten tons of 'biscuit' that it cannot eat, or one ton of real biscuit that it can eat and enjoy?"

But, as an ignorant, simple, and silly civilian, he must be excused. . . .

Dessert followed, in the shape of unripe bananas, and Bertram left the table with a cupful of thin soup, a small piece of cheese, and half a crisp, but pithy and acidulous banana beneath his belt. As the Colonel left the hut he hurried after him.

"If you please, sir," said he, "may I go out with the force that is to attack the German post to-morrow?"

Having acted on impulse and uttered the fatal words, he regretted the fact. Why should he be such a silly fool as to seek sorrow like this? Wasn't there danger and risk and hardship enough-without going out to look for it?

"In what capacity?" asked Colonel Rock, and added: "Hall is in command, and Stanner is his subaltern."

"As a spectator, sir," said Bertram, "and I might-er-be useful perhaps-er-if—"

"Spectator!" mused the Colonel. "Bright idea! We might *all* go, of course. . . . Two hundred men go out on the job, and a couple of thousand go with 'em to whoop 'em on and clap, what? Excellent notion. . . . Wonder if we could arrange a 'gate,' and give the gate-money to the Red Cross, or start a Goose Club or something. . ." and he turned to go into his tent.

Bertram was not certain as to whether this reply was in the nature of a refusal of his request. He hoped it was.

"May I go, sir?" he said.

"You may not," replied the Colonel, and Bertram felt very disappointed.

Chapter XII
Reflections

That night Bertram was again unable to sleep. Lying awake on his hard and narrow bed, faint for want of food, and sick with the horrible stench of the swamp, his mind revolved continually round the problem of how to "personally conduct" a convoy of a thousand porters through twenty miles of enemy country in such a way that it might have a chance if attacked. After tossing and turning for hours and vainly wooing sleep, he lay considering the details of a scheme by which the armed escort should, as it were, circulate round and round from head to tail of the convoy by a process which left ten of the advance-guard to occupy every tributary turning that joined the path and to wait at the junction of the two paths until the whole convoy had passed and the rear-guard had arrived. The ten would then join the rear-guard and march on with them. By the time this had been repeated sufficiently often to deplete the advance-guard, the convoy should halt while the bulk of the rear-guard marched up to the head of the column again and so *da capo*. It would want a lot of explaining to whoever was in command of the rear-guard, for it would be impossible for him, himself, to struggle up and down a line miles long—a line to which anything might happen, at any point, at any moment. . . . He could make it clear that at any turning he would detail ten men from the advance-guard, and then, when fifty had been withdrawn for this flanking work, he would halt the column so that the officer commanding the rear-guard could send fifty back. . . . Ten to one the fool would bungle it, and he might sit and await the return of the fifty until the crack of doom, or until he went back and fetched them up himself. And as soon as he had quitted the head of the column there would be an attack on it! . . . Yes-or perhaps the ass in command of the ten placed to guard the side-turnings would omit to join the rear-guard as it passed-and he'd roll up at his destination, with a few score men short. . . . What would be done to him if he—

Bang! . . .

Bertram's heart seemed to leap out of his body and then to stand still. His bones seemed to turn to water, and his tongue to leather. Had a shell burst beneath his bed? . . . Was he soaring in the air? . . . Had a great mine exploded beneath the Camp, and was the M'paga Field Force annihilated? . . . Captain Hall sat up, yawned, put his hand out from beneath the mosquito curtain of his camp-bed and flashed his electric torch at a small alarm-clock that stood on a box within reach.

"What was that explosion?" said Bertram as soon as he could speak.

"Three-thirty," yawned Hall. "Might as well get up, I s'pose. . . . Wha'? . . . 'Splosion? . . . Some fool popped his rifle off at nothing, I sh'd say. . . . Blast him! Woke me up. . ."

"It's not an attack, then?" said Bertram, mightily relieved. "It sounded as though it were right close outside the hut. . . ."

"Well-you don't attack with *one* rifle shot-nor beat off an attack with *none*. I don't, at least," replied Hall. . . "Just outside, was it?" he added as he arose. "Funny! There's no picket or sentry there. You must have been dreaming, my lad."

"I was wide awake before it happened," said Bertram. "I've been awake all night. . . . It was so close, I—I thought I was blown to bits. . . ."

"'Oo wouldn' sell 'is liddle farm an' go ter War," remarked Hall in Tommy vein. "It's a wearin' life, being blowed outer yer bed at ar' pars free of a mornin', ain't it, guv'nor?"

A deep and hollow groan, apparently from beneath Bertram's bed, almost froze that young gentleman's blood.

Pulling on his slippers and turning on his electric torch, Hall dashed out of the hut. Bertram heard him exclaim, swear, and ask questions in Hindustani. He was joined by others, and the group moved away. . . .

"Bright lad nearly blown his hand off," said Hall, re-entering the hut and lighting a candle-lamp. "Says he was cleaning his rifle. . . ."

"Do you clean a rifle while it is loaded, and also put one hand over the muzzle and the other on the trigger while you do it?" asked Bertram.

"*I* don't, personally," replied Captain Hall, shortly. He was loath to admit that this disgrace to the regiment had intentionally incapacitated himself from active service, though it was fairly obvious.

"I wish he'd gone somewhere else to clean his rifle," said Bertram. "I believe the thing was pointed straight at my ear. I tell you—I felt as though a shell had burst in the hut."

"Bullet probably came through here," observed Hall nonchalantly as he laced his boots. (Later Bertram discovered that it had actually cut one of the four sticks that supported his mosquito curtain, and had torn the muslin thereof.)

Sleep being out of the question, Bertram decided that he might as well arise and watch the setting-forth of the little expedition.

"Going to get up and see you off the premises," said he.

"Stout fella," replied Hall. "I love enthusiasm-but it'll wear off. . . . The day'll come, and before long, when you wouldn't get out of bed to see your father shot at dawn. . . . Not unless you were in orders to command the firing-party, of course," he added. . .

Bertram dressed, feeling weak, ill and unhappy. . . .

"Am I coming in, sah, thank you?" said a well-known voice at the doorless doorway of the hut.

"Hope so," replied Bertram, "if that's tea you've got."

It was. In a large enamel "tumbler" was a pint of glorious hot tea, strong, sweet and scalding.

"Useful bird, that," observed Hall, after declining to share the tea, as he was having breakfast at four o'clock over in the Mess. "I s'pose you hadn't ordered tea at three forty-five, had you?"

Bertram admitted that he had not, and concealed the horrid doubt that arose in his mind-born of memories of Sergeant Jones's tea at Kilindini-as to whether he was not drinking, under Hall's very nose, the tea that should have graced Hall's breakfast, due to be on the table in the Mess at that moment. . . .

If Captain Hall found his tea unduly dilute he did not mention the fact when Bertram came over to the Mess *banda*, and sat yawning and watching him-the man who could nonchalantly sit and shovel horrid-looking porridge into his mouth at four a.m., and talk idly on indifferent subjects, a few minutes before setting out to make a march in the darkness to an attack at dawn. . . .

Ill and miserable as he felt, Bertram forgot everything in the thrilling interest of watching the assembly and departure of the little force. Out of the black darkness little detachments appeared, sometimes silhouetted against the red background of cooking fires, and marched along the main thoroughfare of the Camp to the place of assembly at the quarter-guard. Punctual to the minute, the column was ready to march off, as Captain Hall strolled up, apparently as unconcerned as if he were in some boring peace manœuvres, or about to ride to a meet, instead of to make a cross-country night march, by compass, through an African jungle-swamp to an attack at dawn, with the responsibility of the lives of a couple of hundred men upon his shoulders, as well as that of making a successful move on the chess-board of the campaign. . . .

At the head of the column were a hundred Sepoys of the Hundred and Ninety-Eighth, under Stanner. In the light of the candle-lantern which he had brought from the *banda*, Bertram scrutinised their faces. They were Mussulmans, and looked determined, hardy men and fine soldiers. Some few looked happily excited, some ferocious, but the prevailing expression was one of weary depression and patient misery. Very many looked ill, and here and there he saw a sullen and resentful face. On the whole, he gathered the impression of a force that would march where it was led and would fight bravely, venting on the foe its anger and resentment at his being the cause of their sojourning in a stinking swamp to rot of malaria and dysentery.

How was Stanner feeling, Bertram wondered. He was evidently feeling extremely nervous, and made no secret of it when Bertram approached and addressed him. He was anything but afraid, but he was highly excited. His teeth chattered as he spoke, and his hand shook when he lit a cigarette.

"Gad! I should hate to get one of their beastly expanding bullets in my stomach," said he. "They fire a brute of a big-bore slug with a flat nose. Bad as an explosive bullet, the swine," and he shuddered violently. "Stomach's the only part I worry about, and I don't give a damn for bayonets. . . . But a bullet through your stomach! You live for weeks. . . ."

Bertram felt distinctly glad to discover that a trained regular officer, like Stanner, could entertain these sensations of nervous excitement, and that he himself had no monopoly of them. He even thought, with a thrill of hope and confidence, that when his turn came he would be less nervous than Stanner. He knew that Stanner was not frightened, and that he did not wish he was snug in bed as his brother-officers were, but he also knew that Bertram Greene would not be frightened, and hoped and believed he would not be so palpably excited and nervous. . . .

Behind the detachment of the Hundred and Ninety-Eighth came a machine-gun team of *askaris* of the King's African Rifles, in charge of a gigantic Sergeant. The dismounted gun and the ammunition-boxes were on the heads of Swahili porters.

Bertram liked the look of the Sergeant. He was a picture of quiet competence, reliability and determination. Although a full-blooded Swahili, his face was not unhandsome in a fierce, bold, and vigorously purposeful way, and though he had the flattened, wide-nostrilled nose of the negro, his mouth was Arab, thin-lipped and clear cut as Bertram's own. There was nothing bovine, childish nor wandering in his regard, but a look of frowning thoughtfulness, intentness and concentration.

And Sergeant Simba was what he looked, every inch a soldier, and a fine honourable fighting-man, brave as the lion he was named after; a subordinate who would obey and follow his white officer to certain death, without question or wavering; a leader who would carry his men with him by force of his personality, courage and leadership, while he could move and they could follow. . . . Beside Sergeant Simba, the average German soldier is a cur, a barbarian, and a filthy brute, for never in all the twenty years of his "savage" warfare has Sergeant Simba butchered a child, tortured a woman, murdered wounded enemies, abused (nor used) the white flag, fired on the Red Cross, turned captured dwelling-places into pig-styes and latrines in demonstration of his *kultur* —nor, when caught and cornered, has he waggled dirty hands about cunning, cowardly head with squeal of *Kamerad*! *Kamerad*! . . . Could William the Kultured but have officered his armies with a hundred thousand of Sergeant Simba, instead of with his high-well-born Junkers, the Great War might have been a gentleman's war, a clean war, and the word *German* might not have become an epithet for all time, nor the "noble and knightly" sons of ancient houses have received commissions as Second Nozzle-Holder in the Poison-Gas Grenadiers, Sub Tap-Turner in a Fire-Squirting Squadron, or Ober Left-behind to Poison Wells in the Prussic (Acid) Guard. . . .

As Bertram watched this sturdy-looking Maxim-gun section, with their imperturbable, inscrutable faces, an officer of the King's African Rifles emerged from the circumambient gloom and spoke with Sergeant Simba in Swahili. As he departed, after giving his orders and a few words of advice to Sergeant Simba, he raised his lantern to the face of the man in charge of the porters who carried the gun and ammunition. The man's face was instantly wreathed in smiles, and he giggled like a little girl. The officer dug him affectionately in the ribs, as one smacks a horse on dismounting after a long run and a clean kill, and the giggle became a cackle of elfin laughter most incongruous. Evidently the man was the officer's pet butt and prize fool.

"*Cartouchie n'gapi?*" asked the officer.

"Hundrem millium, *Bwana*," replied the man, and as the officer turned away with a laugh, Bertram correctly surmised that on being asked how many cartridges he had got, the man had replied that he possessed a hundred million.

Probably he spoke in round numbers, and used the only English words he knew. . . . The African does not deal in larger quantities than ten-at-a-time, and his estimates are vague, and still more vague is his expression of them. He will tell you that a place is "several nights distant," or perhaps that it is "a few rivers away." It is only just, however, to state that he will cheerfully accept an equal vagueness in return, and will go to your tent with the alacrity of clear understanding and definite purpose, if you say to him: "Run quickly to my tent and bring me the thing I want. You will easily distinguish it, as it is of about the colour of a flower, the size of a piece of wood, the shape of elephant's breath, and the weight of water. *You* know—it's as long as some string and exactly the height of some stones. You'll find it about as heavy as a dead bird or a load on the conscience. That thing that looks like a smell and feels like a sound. . . ." He may bring your gun, your tobacco-pouch, your pyjamas, your toothbrush, or one slipper, but he will bring *something*, and that without hesitation or delay, for he immediately and clearly grasped that that particular thing, and none other, was what you wanted. He recognised it from your clear and careful description. It was not as though you had idly and carelessly said: "Bring me my hat" (or my knife or the matches or some other article that he handled daily), and left him to make up his mind, unaided, as to whether you did not really mean trousers, a book, washhand-stand, or the pens, ink, and paper of the gardener's aunt. . . .

Behind the Swahili was a half-company of Gurkhas of the Kashmir Imperial Service Troops. As they stood at ease and chatted to each other, they reminded Bertram of a class of schoolboys waiting to be taken upon some highly pleasurable outing. There was an air of cheerful excitement and joyous expectancy.

"*Salaam, Subedar Sahib*," said Bertram, as the fierce hard face of his little friend came within the radius of the beams of his lantern.

"*Salaam, Sahib*," replied the Gurkha officer, "*Sahib ata hai?*" he asked.

"*Nahin*," replied Bertram. "*Hamara Colonel Sahib hamko hookum dea ki 'Mut jao,*'" and the Subedar gathered that Bertram's Colonel had forbidden him to go. He commiserated with the young Sahib, said it was bad luck, but doubtless the Colonel Sahib in his wisdom had reserved him for far greater things.

As he strolled along their flank, Bertram received many a cheery grin of recognition and many a "*Salaam, Sahib*," from the friendly and lovable little hill-men.

In their rear, Bertram saw, with a momentary feeling that was something like the touch of a chill hand upon his heart, a party of Swahili stretcher-bearers, under an Indian of the Subordinate Medical Department, who bore, slung by a crossbelt across his body, a large satchel of dressings and simple surgical appliances. . . . Would these stretcher-bearers come back laden-sodden and dripping with the life-blood of men now standing near them in full health and strength and vigour of lusty life? Perhaps this fine Sergeant, perhaps the Subedar-Major of the Gurkhas? Stanner? Hall? . . .

Suddenly the column was in motion and passing through the entrance by which Bertram had come into the Camp-was it a month ago or only yesterday?

Without disobeying the Colonel, he might perhaps go with the column as far as the river? There was a water-picket there permanently. If he did not go beyond the picket-line, it could not be held that he had "gone out" with the force in face of the C.O.'s prohibition.

Along the narrow lane or tunnel which wound through the impenetrable jungle of elephant-grass, acacia scrub, live oak, baobab, palm, thorn, creeper, and undergrowth, the column marched to the torrential little river, thirty or forty yards wide, that swirled brown, oily, and ugly, between its reed-beds of sucking mud. Here the column halted while Hall and Stanner, lantern in hand, felt their slow and stumbling way from log to log of the rough and unrailed bridge that spanned the stream. On the far side Hall waited with raised lantern, and in the middle stayed Stanner and bade the men cross in single file, the while he vainly endeavoured to illuminate each log and the treacherous gap beside it. Before long the little force had crossed without loss —(and to fall through into that deep, swift stream in the darkness with accoutrements and a hundred rounds of ammunition was to be lost for ever) —and in a minute had disappeared into the darkness, swallowed up and lost to sight and hearing, as though it had never passed that way. . . .

Bertram turned back to Camp and came face to face with Major Manton.

"Morning, Greene," said he. "Been to see 'em off? Stout fella." And Bertram felt as pleased and proud as if he had won a decoration. . . .

The day dawned grey, cheerless and threatening over a landscape as grey, cheerless and threatening as the day. The silent, menacing jungle, the loathsome stench of the surrounding swamp, the heavy, louring sky, the moist, suffocating heat; the sense of lurking, threatening danger from savage man, beast and reptile, insect and microbe; the feeling of utter homelessness and rough discomfort, combined to oppress, discourage and disturb. . . .

Breakfast, eaten in silence in the Mess *banda*, consisted of porridge that required long and careful mastication by any who valued his digestion; pieces of meat of dull black surface and bright pink interior, also requiring long and careful mastication by all who were not too wearied by the porridge drill; and bread.

The bread was of interest-equally to the geologist, the zoologist, the physiologist, the chemist, and the merely curious. To the dispassionate eye, viewing it without prejudice or partiality, the loaf looked like an oblate spheroid of sandstone-say the Old Red Sandstone in which the curious may pick up a mammoth, aurochs, sabre-toothed tiger, or similar ornament of their little world and fleeting day-and to the passionate hand hacking *with* prejudice and partiality (for crumb, perhaps), it also felt like it. It was Army Bread, and quite probably made since the outbreak of the war. The geologist, wise in Eras —*Paleolithic, Pliocene, Eocene, May-have-been* —felt its challenge at once. To the zoologist there was immediate appeal when, by means of some sharp or heavy tool, the outer crust had been broken. For that interior was honey-combed with large, shiny-walled cells, and every cell was filled with a strange web-like kind of cocoon of finest filaments, now grey, now green, to which adhered tiny black specks. Were these, asked the zoologist, the eggs of insects, and, if so, of what insects? Were they laid before the loaf petrified, or after? If before, had the burning process in the kiln affected them? If after, how did the insect get inside? Or were they possibly of vegetable origin-something of a fungoid nature-or even on that strange borderland 'twixt animal and vegetable where roam the yeasty microbe and boisterous bacillus? Perhaps, after all, it was neither animal nor vegetable, but mineral? . . . So ponders the geologist who incurs Army Bread in the wilds of the earth.

The physiologist merely wonders once again at the marvels of the human organism, that man can swallow such things and live; while the chemist secretes a splinter or two, that he may make a qualitative and quantitative analysis of this new, compound, if haply he survive to return to his laboratory.

To the merely curious it is merely curious-until he essays to eat it-and then his utterance may not be merely precious. . . .

After this merry meal, Bertram approached the Colonel, saluted, and said:

"Colonel Frost, of the Hundred and Ninety-Ninth, ordered me to be sure to request you to return his nine cooking-pots at your very earliest convenience, sir, if you please."

Colonel Rock smiled brightly upon Bertram.

"He always was a man who liked his little joke," said he. . . . "Remind me to send him —"

"Yes, sir," interrupted Bertram, involuntarily, so pleased was he to think that the Pots of Contention were to be returned after all.

". . . A Christmas-card —will you?" finished Colonel Rock.

Bertram's face fell. He thought he could hear, afar off, the ominous sound of the grinding of the mill-stones, between the upper and the nether of which he would be ground exceeding small. . . . Would Colonel Frost send him a telegram? What would Colonel Rock say if he took it to him? Could he pretend that he had never received it. Base thought! If he received one every day? . . .

Suppose he were wounded. Could he pretend that his mind and memory were affected-loss of memory, loss of identity, loss of cooking-pots? . . .

"By the way," said the Colonel, as Bertram saluted to depart, "you'll leave here to-morrow morning with a thousand porters, taking rations and ammunition to Butindi. You will take the draft from the Hundred and Ninety-Ninth as escort, and report to Major Mallery there. Don't go and get scuppered, or it'll be bad for them up at Butindi. . . . Start about five. Lieutenant Bridges, of the Coolie Corps, will give you a guide. He's been up there. . . . Better see Captain Brent about it to-night. He'll hand over the thousand porters in good condition in the morning. . . . The A.S.C. people will make a separate dump of the stuff you are to take. . . . Make sure about it, so that you don't pinch the wrong stuff, and turn up at Butindi with ten tons of Number Nine pills and other medical comforts. . . ."

Bertram's heart sank within him, but he strove to achieve a look that blent pleasure, firmness, comprehension, and wide experience of convoy-work into one attractive whole. Wending his way to his *banda*, Bertram found Ali Suleiman making work for himself and doing it.

"I am going to Butindi at five to-morrow morning," he announced. "Have you ever been that way?"

"Oh, yes, sah, please God, thank you," replied Ali. "I was gun-bearer to a *bwana*, one 'Mericani gentlyman wanting to shoot sable antelope-very rare inseck-but a lion running up and bite him instead, and shocking climate cause him great loss of life."

"Then you could be guide," interrupted Bertram, "and show me the way to Butindi?"

"Yes, sah," replied Ali, "can show *Bwana* everythings. . . . *Bwana* taking much quinine and other *n'dawa* [167] there though. Shocking climate causing *Bwana* bad *homa*, bad fever, and perhaps great loss of life also. . . ."

"D'you get fever ever?" asked Bertram.

"Sometimes, sah, but have never had loss of life," was the reassuring answer. . . .

That morning and afternoon Bertram spent in watching the work of the Camp, as he had no duties of his own, and towards evening learnt of the approach of the expedition of the morning. . . .

The column marched along with a swing, evidently pleased with itself, particularly the Swahili detachment, who chanted a song consisting of one verse which contained but one line. "*Macouba Simba na piga mazungo*," [168] they sang with wearying but unwearied regularity and monotony. At their head marched Sergeant Simba, looking as fresh as when he started, and more like a blackened European than a negro.

The Subedar and his Gurkhas had been left to garrison the outpost, but a few had returned on the stretchers of the medical detachment.

Bertram, with sinking heart and sick feelings of horror, watched these blood-stained biers, with their apparently lifeless burdens, file over the bridge, and held his breath whenever a stretcher-bearer stumbled on the greasy logs.

As the last couple safely crossed the bridge and laid their dripping stretcher down for a moment, the occupant, a Gurkha rifleman, suddenly sat up and looked round. His face was corpse-like, and his uniform looked as though it had just been dipped in a bath of blood. Painfully he rose to his feet, while the Swahili bearers gaped in amazement, and tottered slowly forward. Reeling like a drunken man, he followed in the wake of the disappearing procession, until he fell. Picking up the empty stretcher, the bearers hurried to where he lay-only to be waved away by the wounded man, who again arose and reeled, staggering, along the path.

Bertram met him and caught his arm as he collapsed once more.

"*Subr karo*," said Bertram, summoning up some Hindustani of a sort. "*Stretcher men baitho.*" [169]

"*Nahin, Sahib*," whispered the Gurkha; "*kuch nahin hai.*" [170] He evidently understood and spoke a little of the same kind. No. It was nothing. Only seven holes from Maxim-gun fire, that had riddled him as the German N.C.O. sprayed the charging line until a *kukri* halved his skull. . . . It was nothing. . . . No-it would take more than a *Germani* and his woolly-haired *askaris* to put Rifleman Thappa Sannu on a stretcher. . . .

Bertram's hand seemed as though it were holding a wet sponge. He felt sick, and dreaded the moment when he must look at it and see it reeking red.

"*Mirhbani, Sahib*," whispered the man again. "*Kuch nahin hai. Hamko mut pukkaro.*" [171]

He lurched free, stumbled forward a dozen yards, and fell again.

There was no difficulty about placing him upon the stretcher this time, and he made no remonstrance, as he was dead.

Bertram went to his *banda*, sat on the edge of his bed, and wrestled manfully with himself.

By the time Hall had made his report to the Colonel and come to the hut for a wash and rest, Bertram had conquered his desire to be very sick, swallowed the lump in his throat, relieved the stinging in his eyes, and contrived to look and behave as though he had not just had one of the most poignant and disturbing experiences of his life. . . .

"Ripping little show," said Captain Hall, as he prepared for a bath and change. "The Gurkhas did in their pickets without a sound. Gad! They can handle those *kukris* of theirs to some purpose. Sentry on a mound in the outpost pooped off for some reason. They must just have been doing their morning Stand-to. . . . All four sides of the post opened fire, and we were only attacking on one. . . . They'd got a Maxim at each corner. . . . Too late, though. One hurroosh of a rush before they knew anything, and we were in the *boma* with the bayonet. Most of them bunked over the other side. . . . Got three white men, though. A Gurkha laid one out-on the Maxim, he was-and the Sergeant of the Swahilis fairly spitted another with his bayonet. . . . Third one got in the way of my revolver. . . I don't s'pose the whole thing lasted five minutes from the time their sentry fired. . . . The Hundred and Ninety-Eighth were fine. Lost our best Havildar, though. He'd have been Jemadar if he'd lived. He was leading a rush of his section in fine style, when he 'copped a packet.' Stopped one badly. Clean through the neck. One o' those beastly soft-nosed slugs the swine give their *askaris* for 'savage' warfare. . . . As if a German knew of any other kind. . . ."

"Many casualties?" asked Bertram, trying to speak lightly.

"No-very few. Only eleven killed and seven wounded. Wasn't time for more. Shouldn't have had that much, only the blighter with the Maxim was nippy enough to get going with it while we charged over about forty yards from cover. The Gurkhas jumped the ditch like greyhounds and over the parapet of the inner trench like birds. . . . You *should* ha' been there. . . . They never had a chance. . . ."

"Yes," said Bertram, and tried to visualise that rush at the belching Maxim.

"Didn't think much of their *bundobust*," continued Hall. "Their pickets were pretty well asleep and the place hadn't got a yard of barbed wire nor even a row of stakes. They hadn't a field of fire of more than fifty yards anywhere. . . . Bit provincial, what? . . ."

While Hall bathed, Bertram went in search of Captain Brent of the Coolie Corps.

Dinner that night was a vain repetition of yesterday's, save that there was more soup and cold bully-beef gravy available, owing to the rain.

The roof of the *banda* consisting of lightly thatched grass, reeds, twigs, and leaves, was as a sieve beneath the tropical downpour. There was nothing to do but to bear it, with or without grinning. Heavy drops in rapid succession pattered on bare heads, resounded on the tin plates, splashed into food, and, by constant dropping, wore away tempers. By comparison with the great heat of the weather, the rain seemed cold, and the little streams that cascaded down from pendent twig or reed were unwelcome as they invaded the back of the neck of some depressed diner below.

A most unpleasant looking snake, dislodged or disturbed by the rain, fell with sudden thud upon the table from his lodging in the roof. Barely had it done so when it was skewered to the boards by the fork of Captain Tollward. "Good man," said Major Manton, and decapitated the reptile with his knife.

"Just as well to put him out of pain," said he coolly; "it's a *mamba*. Beastly poisonous," and the still-writhing snake was removed with the knife and fork that had carved him. "Lucky I got him in the neck," observed Tollward, and the matter dropped.

Bertram wondered what he would have done had a small and highly poisonous serpent suddenly flopped down with a thump in front of his plate. Squealed like a girl perhaps?

461

Before long he was sitting huddled up beneath a perfect shower-bath of cold drops, with his feet in an oozy bog which soon became a pool and then a stream, and by the end of "dinner" was a torrent that gurgled in at one end of the Mess *banda*, and foamed out at the other. In this filthy water the Mess servants paddled to and fro, becoming more and more suggestive of drowned birds, while the yellowish khaki-drill of their masters turned almost black as it grew more sodden. One by one the lamps used by the cook and servants went out. That in the *banda* went out too, and the Colonel, who owned a tent, followed its example. Those officers who had only huts saw no advantage in retiring to them, and sat on in stolid misery, endeavouring to keep cigarettes alight by holding them under the table between hasty puffs.

Having sat-as usual-eagerly listening to the conversation of his seniors-until the damp and depressed party broke up, Bertram splashed across to his *banda* to find that the excellent Ali had completely covered his bed with his water-proof ground-sheet, had put his pyjamas and a change of underclothing into the bed and the rest of his kit under it. He had also dug a small trench and drain round the hut, so that the interior was merely a bog instead of a pool. . . .

Bertram then faced the problem of how to undress while standing in mud beneath a shower-bath, in such a manner as to be able to get into bed reasonably dry and with the minimum of mud upon the feet. . . .

As he lay sick and hungry, cold and miserable, with apparently high promise of fever and colic, listening to the pattering of heavy drops of water within the hut, and the beating of rain upon the sea of mud and water without, and realised that on the morrow he was to undertake his first really dangerous and responsible military duty, his heart sank. . . . Who was *he* to be in sole charge of a convoy upon whose safe arrival the existence of an outpost depended? What a *fool* he had been to come! Why should *he* be lying there half starving in that bestial swamp, shivering with fever, and feeling as though he had a very dead cat and a very live one in his stomach? . . . Raising his head from the pillow, he said aloud: "I would not be elsewhere for anything in the world. . . ."

Chapter XIII
Baking

When Bertram was awakened by Ali at four o'clock the next morning, he feared he would be unable to get up. Had he been at home, he would have remained in bed and sent for the doctor. His head felt like lead, every bone in his body ached, and he had that horrible sense of internal *malaise*, than which few feelings are more discouraging, distressing and enervating.

The morning smelt horrible, and, by the light of the candle-lamp, the floor was seen to have resigned in favour of the flood. Another problem: Could a fair-sized man dress himself on a tiny camp-bed beneath a small mosquito curtain? If not, he must get out of bed into the water, and paddle around in that slimy ooze which it hid from the eye but not from the nose. Subsidiary problem: Could a man step straight into a pair of wet boots, so as to avoid putting bare feet into the mud, and then withdraw alternate feet from them, for the removal of pyjamas and the putting-on of shorts and socks, while the booted foot remained firmly planted in the slush for his support?

Or again: Sitting precariously on the edge of a canvas bed, could an agile person, with bare feet coyly withdrawn from contact with the foulness beneath, garb his nether limbs to the extent that permitted the pulling-on of boots? . . .

He could try anyhow. . . . After much groping and fumbling, Bertram pulled on his socks and shorts, and then, still lying on his bed, reached for his boots. These he had left standing on a dry patch beneath his bed, and now saw standing, with the rest of his kit, in a couple of inches of filthy water. Balancing himself on the sagging edge of the strip of canvas that served as bed-laths, palliasse and mattress, he struggled into the resisting and reluctant boots, and then boldly entered the water, pleased with the tactics that had saved him from touching it before he was shod. . . . It was not until he had retrieved his sodden puttees and commenced to put them on, that he realised that he was still wearing the trousers of his pyjamas!

And then it was that Bertram, for the first time in his life, furiously swore-long and loud and heartily. Let those who say in defence of War that it rouses man's nobler instincts and brings out all that is best in him, note this deplorable fact.

Could he keep them on, or must he remove those clinging, squelching boots and partially undress again?

Striped blue and green pyjamas, showing for six inches between his shorts and his puttees, would add a distinctly novel touch to the uniform of a British officer. . . . No. It could not be done. Ill as he felt, and deeply as he loathed the idea of wrestling with the knots in the sodden boot-laces of those awful boots, he must do it-in spite of trembling hands, swimming head, and an almost unconquerable desire to lie down again.

And then-alas! for the moral maxims of the copy-books, the wise saws and modern instances of the didactic virtuous-sheer bad temper came to his assistance. With ferocious condemnations of everything, he cut his boot-laces, flung his boots into the water, splashed about violently in his socks, as he tore off the offending garments and hurled them after the boots, and then completed his dressing with as little regard to water, mud, slime, filth, and clay as though he were standing on the carpet of his dressing-room in England.

"*I'm fed up!*" quoth he, and barged out of the *banda* in a frame of mind that put the Fear of God and Second-Lieutenant Bertram Greene into all who crossed his path. . . . (*Cupid* forsooth!)

The first was Ali Suleiman, who stood waiting in the rain, until he could go in and pack his master's kit.

"Here-you-pack my kit sharp, and don't stand there gaping like a fish in a frying-pan. Stir yourself before I stir *you*," he shouted.

The faithful Ali dived into the *banda* like a rabbit into its hole. Excellent! This was the sort of *bwana* he could reverence. Almost had he been persuaded that this new master was not a real gentleman-he was so gentle. . . .

Bertram turned back again, but not to apologise for his harsh words, as his better nature prompted him to do.

"Where's my breakfast, you lazy rascal?" he shouted.

"On the table in Mess *banda*, please God, thank you, sah," replied Ali Suleiman humbly, as one who prays that his grievous trespasses may be forgotten.

"Then why couldn't you say so, you-you-you —" and here memories of the Naval Officer stole across his subconsciousness, "you blundering burden, you posthumous porridge-punter, you myopic megalomaniac, you pernicious, piebald pacifist. . . ."

Ali Suleiman rolled his eyes and nodded his head with every epithet.

"Oh, my God, sah," said he, as Bertram paused for breath, "I am a dam man mos' blasted sinful" —and, so ridiculous a thing is temper, that Bertram neither laughed nor saw cause for laughter.

Splashing across to the Mess *banda*, he discovered a battered metal teapot, an enamelled tumbler, an almost empty tin of condensed milk, and a tin plate of very sad-looking porridge. By the light of a lamp that appealed more to the olfactory and auditory senses than to the optic, he removed from the stodgy mess the well-developed leg of some insect unknown, and then tasted it —(the porridge, not the leg).

"*Filthy muck*," he remarked aloud.

"Sahib calling me, sir?" said a voice that made him jump, and the Cook's Understudy, a Goanese youth, stepped into the circle of light-or of lesser gloom.

"Very natural you should have thought so," answered Bertram. "I said *Filthy Muck*."

"Yessir," replied the acting deputy assistant adjutant cooklet, proudly, "I am cooking breakfast for the Sahib."

"*You* cooked this?" growled Bertram, and half rose, with so menacing an expression and wild an eye that the guilty fled, making a note that this was a Sahib to be properly served in future, and not, as he had foolishly thought him, a poor polite soul for whom anything was good enough. . . .

Pushing the burnt and nauseating horror from him, Bertram essayed to pour out tea, only to find that the fluid was readily procurable from anywhere but the spout. A teapot that will not "pour out" freely is an annoyance at the best of times, and to the most placid of souls. (The fact that tea through the lid is as good as tea through the spout is more than counter-balanced by the fact that tea in the cup is better than tea on the table-cloth. And it is a very difficult art, only to be acquired by patient practice, to pour tea into the cup and the cup alone, from the top of a spout-bunged teapot. Try it.)

Bertram's had temper waxed and deepened.

"*Curse the thing!*" he swore, and banged the offending pot on the table, and, forgetting his nice table-manners, blew violently down the spout. This sent a wave of tea over his head and scalded him, and there the didactic virtuous, and the copy-book maxims, scored.

Sorely tempted to call to the cooklet in honeyed tones, decoy him near with fair-seeming smiles, with friendly gestures, and then to fling the thing at his head, he essayed to pour again.

A trickle, a gurgle, a spurt, a round gush of tea-and the pale wan skeletal remnants of a once lusty cockroach, sodden and soft, leapt into the cup. Swirling round and round, it seemed giddily to explore its new unresting-place, triumphant, as though chanting, with the Ancient Mariner, some such pæan as

> "I was the first that ever burst
> Into this silent tea. . . ."

Heaven alone knew to how many cups of tea that disintegrating corpse had contributed of its best before the gusts of Bertram's temper had contributed to its dislodgment.

(Temper seems to have scored a point here, it must be reluctantly confessed.)

Bertram arose and plunged forth into the darkness, not daring to trust himself to call the cook.

Raising his clenched hands in speechless wrath, he drew in his breath through his clenched teeth-and then slipped with catastrophic suddenness on a patch of slimy clay and sat down heavily in very cold water.

He arose a distinctly dangerous person. . . .

Near the ration-dump squatted a solid square of naked black men, not precisely savages, raw *shenzis* of the jungle, but something between these and the Swahilis who work as personal servants, gun-bearers, and the better class of *safari* porters. They were big men and looked strong. They smelt stronger. It was a perfectly indescribable odour, like nothing on earth, and to be encountered nowhere else on earth-save in the vicinity of another mass of negroes.

In the light of a big fire and several lanterns, Bertram saw that the men were in rough lines, and that each line appeared to be in charge of a headman, distinguished by some badge of rank, such as a bowler hat, a tobacco tin worn as an ear-ring, a pair of pink socks, or a frock coat. These men walked up and down their respective lines and occasionally smote one of their squatting followers, hitting the chosen one without fear or favour, without rhyme or reason, and apparently without doing much damage. For the smitten one, without change of expression or position, emitted an incredibly thin piping squeal, as though in acknowledgment of an attention, rather than as if giving natural vent to anguish. . . .

Every porter had a red blanket, and practically every one wore a *panga*. The verbs are selected. They *had* blankets and they *wore* pangas. The blankets they either sat upon or folded into pads for insertion beneath the loads they were to carry upon their heads. The *pangas* were attached to strings worn over the shoulder. This useful implement serves the African as toothpick, spade, axe, knife, club, toasting-fork, hammer, weapon, hoe, cleaver, spoon, skinning-knife, and every other kind of tool, as well as being correct jungle wear for men for all occasions, and in all weathers. He builds a house with it; slays, skins and dismembers a bullock; fells a tree, makes a boat, digs a pit; fashions a club, spear, bow or arrow; hews his way through jungle, enheartens his wife, disheartens his enemy, mows his lawn, and makes his bed. . . .

Not far away, a double company of the Hundred and Ninety-Eighth "stood easy." The fact that they were soaked to the skin did nothing to give them an air of devil-may-care gaiety.

The Jemadar in command approached and saluted Bertram, who recognised the features of Hassan Ali.

"It's *you*, is it!" he grunted, and proceeded to explain that the Jemadar would command the rear-guard of one hundred men, and that by the time it was augmented to a hundred and fifty by the process of picking up flankers left to guard side-turnings, the column would be halted while fifty men made their way up to the advance-guard again, and so on.

"D'you understand?" concluded Bertram.

"*Nahin, Sahib*," replied the Jemadar.

"*Then fall out*," snapped Bertram. "I'll put an intelligent private in command, and you can watch him until you do," and then he broke into English: "I've had about enough of you, my lad, and if you give me any of your damned nonsense, I'll twist your tail till you howl. Call yourself an *officer*! . . ." and here the Jemadar, saluting repeatedly, like an automaton, declared that light had just dawned upon his mind and that he clearly understood.

"And so you'd better," answered Bertram harshly, staring with a hard scowl into the Jemadar's eyes until they wavered and sank. "So you'd *better*, if you want to keep your rank. . . . March one hundred men down the path past the Officers' Mess, and halt them a thousand yards from here. . . . The coolies will follow. You will return and fall in behind the coolies with the other hundred as rear-guard. See that the coolies do not straggle. March behind your men-so that you are the very last man of the whole convoy. D'you understand?"

Jemadar Hassan Ali did understand, and he also understood that he'd made a bad mistake about Second-Lieutenant Greene. He was evidently one of those subtle and clever people who give the impression that they are not *hushyar*, [172] that they are foolish and incompetent, and then suddenly destroy you when they see you have thoroughly gained that impression.

Respect and fear awoke in the breast of the worthy Jemadar, for he admired cunning, subtlety and cleverness beyond all things.... He marched a half of his little force off into the darkness, halted them some half-mile down the path (or rivulet) that led into the jungle, put them in charge of the senior Havildar and returned.

Meanwhile, Lieutenant Bridges, in a cloak and pyjamas, had arrived, yawning and shivering, to superintend the loading up of the porters. At an order, given in Swahili, the first line of squatting Kavirondo arose and rushed to the dump.

"Extraordinary zeal!" remarked Bertram to Bridges.

"Yes-to collar the lightest loads," was the illuminating reply.

The zeal faded as rapidly as it had glowed when he coldly pointed with the *kiboko*, which was his badge of office and constant companion, to the heavy ammunition-boxes.

"I should keep that near the advance-guard and under a special guard of its own," said he.

"I'm going to-naturally," replied Bertram shortly, and added: "Hurry them along, please. I want to get off to-day."

Bridges stared. This was a much more assured and autocratic person than the mild youth he had met at the water's edge a day or two ago.

"Well-if you like to push off with the advance-guard, I'll see that a constant stream of porters files off from here, and that your rear-guard follows them," said he.

"Thanks —I'll not start till I've seen the whole convoy ready," replied Bertram.

Yesterday he'd have been glad of advice from anybody. Now he'd take it from no one. Orders he would obey, of course-but "a poor thing but mine own" should be his motto with regard to his method of carrying out whatever he was left to do. They'd told him to take their beastly convoy; they'd left him to do it; and he'd do it as he thought fit.... Curse the rain, the mud, the stench, the hunger, sickness and the beastly pain that nearly doubled him up and made him feel faint....

Grayne strolled over.

"Time you bunged off, my lad," quoth he, loftily.

"If you'll mind your own business, I shall have the better chance to mind mine," replied Bertram, eyeing him coldly-and wondering at himself.

Grayne stared open-mouthed, and before he could speak Bertram was hounding on a lingering knot of porters who had not hurried off to the line as soon as their boxes of biscuit were balanced on their heads, but stood shrilly wrangling about something or nothing.

"*Kalele! Kalele!*" shouted Bertram, and sprang at them with raised fist and furious countenance, whereat they emitted shrill squeals and fled to their places in the long column.

He had no idea what "*Kalele!*" meant, but had heard Bridges and the headman say it. Later he learnt that it meant "Silence!" and was a very useful word....

Ali Suleiman approached, seized three men, and herded them before him to fetch Bertram's kit. Having loaded them with it, he drove them to the head of the column and stationed them in rear of the advance-guard.

Returning, he presented Bertram with a good, useful-looking cane.

"*Bwana* wanting a *kiboko*," said he. "*Shenzis* not knowing anything without *kiboko* and not feeling happy in mind. Not thinking *Bwana* is a real master."

Yesterday Bertram would have chidden Ali gently, and explained that kind hearts are more than coronets and gentle words than cruel whips. To-day he took the cane, gave it a vicious swish, and wished that it were indeed a *kiboko*, one of those terrible instruments of hippopotamus hide, four feet in length, as thick as a man's wrist at one end, tapering until it was of the thinness of his little finger at the other....

A big Kavirondo seized a rum jar. His bigger neighbour dropped a heavy box and tried to snatch it from him. He who had the lighter jar clung to it, bounded away, and put it on his head. The box-wallah, following, gave him a sudden violent blow in the back, jerking the jar from his head.

Raising his cane, Bertram brought it down with all his strength on the starboard quarter of the box-wallah as he stooped to grab the jar. With a wild yelp, he leapt for his box and galloped to his place in the column.

"Excellent!" said Bridges, "you'll have no trouble with the *safari* people, at any rate."

"I'll have no trouble with anybody," replied Bertram with a quiet truculence that surprised himself, "not even with a *Balliol* negro."

Bridges decided that he had formed his estimate of Lieutenant Greene too hastily and quite wrongly. He was evidently a bit of a tough lad when he got down to it. Hot stuff. . . .

At last the dump had disappeared completely, and its original components now swayed and turned upon the heads of a thousand human beasts of burden—human in that they walked erect and used fire for cooking food; beasts in that they were beastly and beast-like in all other ways. Among them, and distinguished by being feebler of physique, and, if possible, feebler of mind, was a party of those despised savages, the Kikuyu, rendered interesting as providing the great question that shook the Church of England to its foundations, and caused Lord Bishops to forget the wise councils of good Doctor Watts' hymn. (It is to be feared that among the even mightier problems of the Great War, the problem of the spiritual position and ecclesiastical condition of the Communicating Kikuyu has been temporarily lost sight of. Those who know the gentleman, with his blubber-lipped, foreheadless face, his teeth filed to sharp points, his skin a mass of scar patterns, done with a knife, and his soulless, brainless animalism and bestiality, would hate to think he was one short on the Thirty-Nine Articles or anything of that sort.)

Bertram gave a last injunction to Jemadar Hassan Ali, said farewell to Bridges, and strode to the head of the column. Thence he sent out a "point" of a Havildar and three men, and waited to give the word to advance, and plunge into the jungle, the one white man among some fifteen hundred people, all of whom looked to him, as to a Superior Being, for guidance and that competent command which should be their safeguard.

As the point disappeared he turned and looked along the apparently endless line, cried "*Quick March*," and set off at a smart pace, the first man of the column.

He was too proud and excited to realise how very ill he felt, or to be ashamed of the naughty temper that he had so clearly and freely exhibited.

Chapter XIV
The Convoy

Bertram never forgot this plunge into the primeval jungle with its mingled suggestions of a Kew hot-house, a Turkish bath, a shower bath, a mud bath and a nightmare.

His mind was too blunted with probing into new things, his brain too dulled by the incessant battering of new ideas, too drunk with draughts of strange mingled novelty, too covered with recent new impressions for him to be sensitive to fresh ones.

Had an elephant emerged from the dripping jungle, wagged its tail and sat up and begged, he would have experienced no great shock of surprise. He, a town-bred, town-dwelling, pillar of the Respectable, the Normal and the Established, was marching through virgin forest at the head of a thousand African porters and two hundred Indian soldiers and their camp-followers, surrounded by enemies-varying from an *ex*-Prussian Guard armed with a machine-gun to a Wadego savage armed with a poisoned arrow-to the relief of hungry men in a stockaded outpost! . . . What further room was there for marvels, wonders, and surprises? As he tramped, splashed, slipped and stumbled along the path, and the gloom of early morning, black sky, mist, and heavy rain slowly gave way to dawn and daylight, his fit of savage temper induced by "liver," hunger, headache and disgust, slowly gave way, also, to the mental inertia, calm, and peace, induced by monotonous exercise. The steady dogged tramp, tramp, tramp, was an anodyne, a sedative, a narcotic that drugged the mind, rendering it insensitive to the pains and sickness of the body as well as to its own worries, anxieties and problems. . . .

Bertram felt that he could go on for a very long time; go on until he fell; but he knew that when he fell it would be quite impossible for him to get up again. Once his legs stopped moving, the spell would be broken, the automaton would have "run down," and motion would cease quite finally. . . .

As daylight grew, he idly and almost subconsciously observed the details of his environment. This was better than the mangrove-thicket of the swamp, in a clearing of which the base camp lay. It was the densest of dense jungle through which the track ran, like a stream through a cañon, but it was a jungle of infinite variety. Above the green impenetrable mat of elephant grass and nameless tangle of undergrowth, scrub, shrub, liana, bush, creeper, and young trees, stood, in solid serried array, great trees by the million, palm, mango, baobab, acacia, live oak, and a hundred other kinds, with bamboo and banana where they could, in defiance of probability, squeeze themselves in. Some of the trees looked like the handiwork of prentice gods, so crude and formless were they, their fat trunks tapering rapidly from a huge ground-girth to a fine point, and putting forth little abortive leafless branches suggestive of straggly hairs. Some such produced brilliant red blossoms, apparently on the trunk itself, but dispensed with the banality of leaves and branches. Some great knotted creepers seemed to have threaded themselves with beads as big as a man's head, and the fruit of one arboreal freak was vast sausages.

Through the aerial roadways of the forest, fifty feet above the heads of the *safari*, tribes of monkeys galloped and gambolled as they spied upon it and shrieked their comment.

Apparently the varied and numerous birds held views upon the subject of *safaris* also, and saw no reason to conceal them.

One accompanied the advance-guard, piping and fluting: "*Poli-Poli*! *Poli-Poli*!" which, as Ali Suleiman informed Bertram, is Swahili for "Slowly! *Slowly!*"

Another bird appeared to have fitted up his home with a chime of at least eight bells, for, every now and then, a sweet and sonorous tolling rang through the jungle. One bird, sitting on a branch a few feet from Bertram's head, emitted two notes that for depth of timbre and rich sonorous sweetness could be excelled by no musical instrument or bell on earth. He had but the two notes apparently, but those two were marvellous. They even roused Bertram to the reception of a new impression and a fresh sensation akin to wonder.

From many of the overhanging trees depended the beautifully woven bottle-like nests of the weaver-bird. Brilliant parrots flashed through the tree-tops, incredible horn-bills carried their beaks about, the hypocritical widower-bird flaunted his new mourning, the blue starling, the sun-bird, and the crow-pheasant, with a score of other species, failed to give the gloomy, menacing jungle an air of brightness and life, seemed rather to emphasise its note of gloom, its insistence upon itself as the home of death where Nature, red in tooth and claw, pursued her cycle of destruction with fierce avidity and wanton masterfulness. . . .

Suddenly a whistle rang out-sharp, clear, imperative. Its incisive blow upon the silence of the deadly jungle startled Bertram from his apathy. His tired wits sprang to life and activity, urged on his weary flagging muscles. He wheeled round and faced the Sepoys just behind him, even as the blast of the whistle ceased.

"*Halt*! *Baitho*!" [173] he shouted-gave the drill-book sign to lie down-and waited, for a second that seemed like a year, to feel the withering blast of fire that should tear through them at point-blank range. . . . Why did it not come? . . . Why did no guttural German voice shout an order to fire? . . . . He remained standing upright, while the Sepoys, crouching low, worked the bolts of their rifles to load the latter from their magazines. He was glad to see that they made ready thus, without awaiting an order, even as they sank to the ground. Would it not be better to march in future with a cartridge in the chamber and the cut-off of the magazine open? . . . Accidents? . . . Not if he made them march with rifles at the "slope." . . . Better the risk of an accident than the risk of being caught napping. . . . Why did not the accursed German give the order to fire? . . . Was it because Bertram had got his men crouching down so quickly? . . . Would the crashing volley thunder out, the moment they arose? . . . They could not stay squatting, kneeling and lying in the mud for ever. . . . Where was the ambush? . . . Had they Maxims in trees, commanding this path? . . . Were the enemy massed in a clearing a foot or two from the road, and separated from it only by a thin screen of foliage? . . . What should he do if there were a sudden bayonet-charge down the path, by huge ferocious *askaris*? . . . You can't meet a charge with efficient rifle-fire when you are in single file and your utmost effort at deployment would get two, or possibly three crowded and hampered men abreast. . . . On the other hand, the enemy would not be charging under ideal conditions either. . . . More likely a machine-gun would suddenly nip out, from concealment beside the path, and wither the column away with a blast of fire at six hundred rounds a minute. . . . Perhaps the "point" marching on ahead would have the sense and the courage and the time to get into the gun-team with their bayonets before it got the gun going? . . . *Why did not the enemy fire?* . . . He would go mad if they didn't do so soon. . . . Were they playing with him, as a cat plays with a mouse? . . .

The whistle rang out again, harsh, peremptory, fateful-and then Ali Suleiman laughed, and pointed at a small bird. As he did so, the bird whistled again, with precisely the note of a police-whistle blown under the stress of fear, excitement or anger, a clamant, bodeful, and insistent signal.

Bertram would have welcomed warmly an opportunity to wring little birdie's neck, in the gust of anger that followed the fright.

Giving the signal to rise and advance, Bertram strode on, and, still under the stimulus of alarm, forgot that he was tired.

He analysed his feelings. . . . Was he frightened and afraid? Not at all. The whistle had "made him jump," and given him a "start," of course. The waiting for the blast of fire, that he knew would follow the signal, had been terribly trying —a torture to the nerves. The problem of what to do, in response to the enemy's first move, had been an agonising anxiety-but he would certainly have done something-given clear orders as to object and distance if there had been anything to fire at; used his revolver coolly and set a good example if there had been a charge down the path; headed a fierce rush at the Maxim if one had come out of cover and prepared to open fire. . . . No-he decidedly was not frightened and afraid. . . He was glad that he had remained erect, and, with his hand on his revolver, had, with seeming coolness, scanned the surrounding trees and jungle for signs of an ambushed enemy. . . .

The road forked, and he turned to Ali Suleiman, who had marched near him from the start, in the proud capacity of guide.

"Which of these paths?" said he.

"The left hands, sah, please God," was the reply; "the right is closed also."

"What d'you mean?" asked Bertram, staring down the open track that branched to the right.

"See, *Bwana*," replied Ali, pointing to a small branch that lay in the middle of the path, with its broken end towards them and its leaves away from them. "Road closed. I 'spec *askari* patrol from Butani putting it there, when they know *Bwana* coming, thank God, please."

Apparently this twig, to the experienced eye, was precisely equivalent to a notice-board bearing the legend, *No Thoroughfare*. Bertram signalled a halt and turned to the Havildar at the head of the advance-guard.

"Take ten men and patrol down that path for a thousand yards," said he. "Then march back, wait for the rear-guard, and report to the Jemadar Sahib."

The man saluted, and Bertram saw him and his patrol move off, before he gave the order for the column to advance again. . . . That should secure the *safari* from attack down *that* path, anyhow. Ten determined men could hold up any number for any length of time, if they did the right thing. . . . These beastly bush fighting conditions cut both ways. . . . Yes-then suppose a small patrol of enemy *askaris* were on this track in front of him, and decided to hold the convoy up, what could he do?

To advance upon them, practically in single file, would be like approaching a long stick of sealing-wax to the door of a furnace-the point would melt and melt until the whole stick had disappeared without reaching the fire. . . . Of course, if there was a possibility of getting into the jungle, he would send out parties to take them in flank as he charged down the path. But that was just the point-you *couldn't* get more than a few yards into the jungle in the likeliest places, and, when you'd done that, you'd be utterly out of touch with your right and left-hand man in no time-not to mention the fact that you'd have no sense of direction or distance. . . .

No. . . . He'd just head a charge straight for them, and if it were a really determined one and the distance not too great, enough of the advance-guard might survive to reach them with the bayonet. . . . Evidently, if there were any rules at all in this jungle warfare, one would be that the smaller of the two forces should dispose itself to bring every rifle to bear with magazine fire, and the larger should make the swiftest charge it possibly could. If it didn't—a dozen men would be as good as a thousand-while their ammunition held out. . . . What an advantage over the Indian Sepoy, with his open order *maidan* [174] training, the *askari*, bred and born and trained to this bush-fighting, would have! The German *ought* to win this campaign with his very big army of indigenous soldiers and his "salted" Colonials. What chance had the Sepoy or the British Regular in these utterly strange and unthought-of conditions? . . . As well train aviators and then put them in submarines as train the Indian Army for the frontier and the plains and then put them in these swamps and jungles where your enemy is invisible and your sole "formation" is single file. What about the sacred and Medean Law: *Never fire until you can see something to fire at?* They'd never fire at all, at that rate, with an enemy who habitually used machine-guns from tree-tops and fired from dense cover-and small blame to him. . . .

A sound of rushing water, and a few minutes later the path became the edge of a river-bank beneath which the torrent swirled. It looked as though its swift erosion would soon bring the crumbling and beetling bank down, and the path would lead straight into the river. He must mention the fact at Butindi.

He stared at the jungle of the opposite bank, apparently lifeless and deserted, though menacing, secretive and uncanny. An ugly place. . . . Suppose the Germans bridged the river just here. . . . He found that he had come to a halt and was yearning to sit down. . . . He must not do that. He must keep moving. But he did not like that gap in the path where, for some yards, it ran along the edge of the bank. It was a gap in the wall, an open door in the house, a rent in the veil of protection. The jungle seemed a friend instead of a blinding and crippling hindrance, impediment, and obstacle, now that the path lay open and exposed along that flank. Suppose there were an ambush in the jungle on the other side of the narrow rushing river, and a heavy fire was opened upon his men as they passed? He could not get at an enemy so placed, nor return their fire for long, from an open place, while they were in densest cover. They could simply prohibit the passing of the *safari*.... Anyhow, he'd leave a force there to blaze like fury into the jungle across the river if a shot were fired from there.

"Naik," said he, to a corporal, "halt here with twenty men and line the edge of the bank. If you are fired at from across the river, pour in magazine fire as hard as you can go-and make the porters *run* like the devil across this gap." He then translated, as well as he could, and marched on. He had done his best, anyhow.

For another hour he doggedly tramped on. The rain ceased, and the heat grew suffocating, stifling, terrible to bear. He felt that he was breathing pure steam, and that he must climb a tree in search of air-do *something* to relieve his panting lungs.... He tore his tunic open at the throat.... *Help*! he was going to faint and fall.... With a great effort he swung about and raised his hand for the "halt" and lowered it with palm horizontal downward for the "lie down."... If the men were down themselves they would not realise that he had fallen.... It would not do to fall while marching at their head, to fall and lie there for the next man to stumble over him, to set an example of weakness.... The officer should be the last man to succumb to anything-but wounds-in front....

He sank to the ground, and feeling that he was going to faint away, put his head well down between his knees, and, after a while, felt better.

"*Bwana* taking off tunic and belts," said Ali Suleiman, "and I carry them. *Bwana* keep only revolver, by damn, please God, sah."

A bright idea! Why not? Where was the sense in marching through these foul swamps and jungles as though it were along the Queen's Road at Bombay? And Ali, who would rather die than carry a load upon his head, like a low *shenzi* of a porter, would be proud to carry his master's sword and personal kit.

In his shirt-sleeves, with exposed chest, Bertram felt another man, gave the signal to advance, and proceeded free of all impedimenta save his revolver....

Suddenly the narrow, walled-in path debouched into a most beautiful open glade of trees like live oaks. These were not massed together; there was no undergrowth of bush; the grass was short and fine; the ground sloping slightly upward was gravelly and dry-the whole spot one of Africa's freakish contrasts.

Bertram determined to halt the whole *safari* here, get it "closed up" into something like fours, and see every man, including the rear-guard, into the place before starting off again.

With the help of Ali, who interpreted to the headmen, he achieved his object, and, when he had satisfied himself that it was a case of "all present and correct," he returned to the head of the column and sat him down upon the trunk of a fallen tree....

Everybody, save the sentries, whom he had posted about the glade, squatted or lay upon the ground, each man beside his load....

Though free now of the horrible sense of suffocation, he felt sick and faint, and very weary. Although he had not had a proper meal since he left the *Barjordan*, he was not hungry-or thought he was not.... Would it be his luck to be killed in the first fight that he took part in? His *good* luck? When one is ill and half starved, weary beyond words, and bearing a nightmare burden of responsibility in conditions as comfortless and rough as they can well be, Death seems less a grisly terror than a friend, bearing an Order of Release in his bony hand....

Ali stood before him unbuckling his haversack.

"Please God, sah, I am buying *Bwana* this chocolates in Mombasa when finding master got no grubs for emergency rasher," said he, producing a big blue packet of chocolate.

"Good man!" replied Bertram. "I meant to get a stock of that myself...."

He ate some chocolate, drank of the cold tea with which the excellent Ali had filled his water-bottle, and felt better.

After an hour's rest he gave the order to fall in, the headmen of the porters got their respective gangs loaded up again, and the *safari* wound snake-like from the glade along the narrow path once more, Bertram at its head. He felt he was becoming a tactical soldier as he sent a lance-naik to go the round of the sentries and bid them stand fast until the rear-guard had disappeared into the jungle, when they were to rejoin it.

On tramped the *safari*, hour after hour, with occasional halts where the track widened, or the jungle, for a brief space, gave way to forest or *dambo*. Suddenly the head of the column emerged from the denser jungle into an undulating country of thicket, glade, scrub, and forest. Bertram saw the smoke of campfires far away to the left; and with one accord the porters commenced to beat their loads, drum-wise, with their *safari* sticks as they burst into some tribal chant or pæan of rejoicing. The convoy had reached Butindi in safety.

Chapter XV
Butindi

Half a mile beyond a village of the tiniest huts-built for themselves by the Kavirondo porters, and suggesting beehives rather than human habitations-Bertram beheld the entrenched and stockaded *boma*, zariba, or fort, that was to be his home for some months.

At that distance, it looked like a solid square of grass huts and tents, surrounded by a high wall. He guessed each side to be about two hundred yards in length. It stood in a clearing which gave a field of fire of some three hundred yards in every direction.

Halting the advance-guard, he formed it up from single file into fours; and, taking his kit from Ali, resumed it. Giving the order to march at "attention," he approached the *boma*, above the entrance to which an officer was watching him through field-glasses.

Halting his men at the plank which crossed the trench, he bade them "stand easy," and, leaving them in charge of a Havildar, crossed the little bridge and approached the gateway which faced sideways instead of outwards, and was so narrow that only one person at a time could pass through it.

Between the trench and the wall of the *boma* was a space some ten yards in width, wherein a number of small men in blue uniform, who resembled neither Indians nor Africans, were employed upon the off-duty duties of the soldier-cleaning rifles and accoutrements, chopping wood, rolling puttees, preparing food, washing clothing, and pursuing trains of thought or insects.

Against the wall stood the long lean-to shelters, consisting of a roof of plaited palm-leaf, supported by poles, in which they lived. By the entrance was a guard-house, which suggested a rabbit-hutch; and a sentry, who, seeing the approach of an armed party, turned out the guard. The Sergeant of the Guard was an enormous man with a skin like fine black satin, a skin than which no satin could be blacker nor more shiny. He was an obvious negro, Nubian or Soudanese, but the men of the guard were small and fair, and wore blue turbans, of which the ornamental end hung tail-wise down their backs. Beneath their blue tunics were unpleated kilts or skirts, of a kind of blue tartan, reaching to their knees. They had blue puttees and bare feet.

Saluting the guard, Bertram entered the *boma* and found himself in the High Street of a close-packed village of huts and tents, which were the dwelling-places of the officers, the hospital and sick-lines, the commissariat store, the Officers' Mess, the cook-house, orderly-room, and offices.

In the middle of the High Street stood four poles which supported a roof. A "table" of posts and packing-case boards, surrounded by native bedsteads of wood and string-by way of seats-constituted this, the Officers' Mess, Club, Common Room and Bar. A bunch of despondent-looking bananas hanging from the ridge-pole suggested food, and a bath containing a foot of water and an inch of mud suggested drink and cholera.

About the table sat several British officers in ragged shirts and shorts, drinking tea and eating native *chupatties*. They looked ill and weary. The mosaic of scraps of stencilled packing-case wood, the tin plates, the biscuit-box "sugar-basin," the condensed milk tin "milk-jug," the battered metal teapot and the pile of sodden-looking *chupatties* made as uninviting an afternoon tea ménage as could be imagined, particularly in that setting of muddy clay floor, rough and dirty *angarebs*, and roof-and-wall thatch of withered leaves and grass. A typical scene of modern glorious war with its dirt, discomfort and privation, its disease, misery and weary boredom. . . .

Bertram approached the rickety grass hut and saluted.

A very tall man, with the face and moustache of a Viking, rose and extended his hand.

"How do, Greene?" said he. "Glad to see you. . . . Hope you brought the rum ration safe. . . . Take your bonnet off and undo your furs. . . . Hope that pistol's not loaded. . . . Nor that sword sharp. . . . Oughtn't to go about with nasty, dangerous things like that. . . . Hope the rum ration's safe. . . . Have some tea and a bloater. . . . Berners, go and do Quartermaster, like a good lad. . . . Have some rum and a bloater, Greene. . . ."

"Thank you, sir," said Bertram, noting that the big man had a crown on one shoulder of his shirt and a safety-pin spanning a huge hole on the other. His great arms and chest were bare, and a pair of corduroy riding-breeches, quite unfastened at the knee and calf, left an expanse of bare leg between their termination and the beginning of grey, sagging socks. Hob-nailed boots, fastened with string, completed his attire. He looked like a tramp, a scarecrow, and a strong leader of men.

"'Fraid you'll have to drink out of a condensed milk tin, until your kit turns up. . ." said a pale and very handsome youth. "You get a flavour of milk, though," he added with an air of impartiality, "as well as of tin and solder. . . . They burn your fingers so damnably, though, when you go to pick 'em up. . . . Or why not drink out of the teapot, if everyone has finished? . . . Yes—I'll drop in a spot of condensed milk."

"No-damn it all, Vereker," put in the Major, "let's do him well and create an impression. Nothing like beginning as you don't mean to go on-or can't possibly go on. . . . He can have The Glass this evening. And some fresh tea. And his own tin of condensed. . . . And a bloater. Hasn't he brought us rum and hope? . . ."

The pale and handsome Vereker sighed.

"You create a *false* impression, sir," he said, and, taking a key from his neck, arose and unlocked a big chop-box that stood in a corner of the *banda*. Thence he produced a glass tumbler and set it before Bertram.

"There's The Glass," said he. "It's now in your charge, present and correct. I'll receive it from you and return the receipt at 'Stand-to.' . . ."

Bertram gathered that the tumbler was precious in the Major's sight, and that honour was being shown him. He had a faint sense of having reached Home. He was disappointed when a servant brought fresh tea, a newly-opened tin of milk, and the lid of a biscuit-box for a plate, to discover that the banana which reposed upon it was the "bloater" of his hopes and the Major's promise.

"For God's sake use plenty of condensed milk," said that gentleman, as Bertram put some into the glass, preparatory to pouring out his tea. Bertram thought it very kind and attentive of him-until he added: "And pour the tea *on* to it, and not down the side of the glass. . . . That's how the other tumbler got done in. . . ."

As he gratefully sipped the hot tea and doubtfully munched a *chapatti*, Bertram took stock of the other members of the Mess. Beside Major Mallery sat a very hard-looking person, a typical fighting-man with the rather low forehead, rather protruding ears, rather high cheek-bones, heavy jaw and jutting chin of his kind. He spoke little, and that somewhat truculently, wore a big heavy knife in his belt, looked like a refined prize-fighter, and answered to the name of Captain Macke.

Beside him, and in strong contrast, sat a young man of the Filbert genus. He wore a monocle, his nails were manicured, he spoke with the euphuism and euphemism of a certain Oxford type, he had an air of languor, boredom and acute refinement, was addressed as Cecil Clarence, when not as Gussie Augustus Gus, and seemed to be one of the very best.

On the same string bed, and in even stronger contrast, sat a dark-faced Indian youth. On his shoulder-straps were the letters I.M.S. and two stars. A lieutenant of the Indian Medical Service, and, as such, a member of this British Officers' Mess. Bertram wondered why the fact that he had been to England and read certain books should have this result; and whether the society of the Subedar-Major of the regiment would have been preferred by the British officers. The young man talked a lot, and appeared anxious to show his freedom from anxiety, and his knowledge of English idiom and slang. When he addressed anyone by the nickname which intimate pals bestowed upon him, Bertram felt sorry for this youth with the hard staccato voice and raucous, mirthless laugh. Cecil Clarence said of him that "if one gave him an inch he took an 'ell of a lot for granted." His name was Bupendranath Chatterji, and his papa sat cross-legged and bare-footed in the doorway of a little shop in a Calcutta bazaar, and lent moneys to the poor, needy and oppressed, for a considerable consideration.

"'Bout time for Stand-to, isn't it?" said the Major, consulting his wrist-watch. "Hop it, young Clarence. . . . You might come round with me to-night, Greene, if you've finished tea. . . . Can't offer you another bloater, I'm afraid. . . ."

The other officers faded away. A few minutes later a long blast was blown on a whistle, there were near and distant cries of "Stand-to," and Cecil Clarence returned to the Mess *banda*. He was wearing tunic and cross-belt. On his cheerful young face was a look of portentous solemnity as he approached the Major, halted, saluted, stared at him as at a perfect stranger, and said: "Stand-to, sir. All present and correct."

Over the Major's face stole a similar expression. He looked as one who has received sudden, interesting and important but anxious news.

"Thank you," said he. "I'll-ah-go round. Yes. Come with me, will you? . . ." Cecil Clarence again saluted, and fell in behind the Major as he left the *banda*. Bertram followed. The Major went to his tent and put on his tunic and cross-belt. These did little to improve the unfastenable riding-breeches, bare calves and grey socks, but were evidently part of the rite.

Proceeding thence to the entrance to the *boma*, the Major squeezed through, was saluted by the guard, and there met by an English officer in the dress of the small men whom Bertram had noticed on his arrival. His white face looked incongruous with the blue turban and tartan petticoat. "All present and correct, sir," said he. Half his men were down in the trench, their rifles resting in the loop-holes of the parapet. These loop-holes were of wicker-work, like bottomless waste-paper baskets, and were built into the earthwork of the parapet so that a man, looking through one, had a foot of earth and logs above his head. The other half of his blue-clad force was inside the *boma* and lining the wall. This wall, some eight feet in height, had been built by erecting two walls of stout wattle and posts, two feet apart, and then filling the space between these two with earth. Along the bottom of the wall ran a continuous fire-step, some two feet in height, and a line of wicker-work loop-holes pierced it near the top. In the angle, where this side of the *boma* met the other, was a tower of posts, wattle and earth, some twelve feet in height, and on it, within an earth-and-wattle wall, and beneath a thatched roof, was a machine-gun and its team of King's African Rifles *askaris*, in charge of an English N.C.O. On the roof squatted a sentry, who stared at the sky with a look of rapt attention to duty.

"How are those two men, Black?" asked the Major, as the N.C.O. saluted.

"Very bad, sir," was the reply. "They'll die to-night. I'm quite sure the Germans had poisoned that honey and left it for our *askari* patrols to find. I wondered at the time that they 'adn't skoffed it themselves. . . . And it so near their *boma* and plain to see, an' all. . . . I never thought about poison till it was too late. . . ."

"Foul swine!" said the Major. "I suppose it's a trick they learnt from the *shenzis*, this poisoning wild honey? . . ."

"More like they taught it 'em, sir," was the reply. "There ain't no savage as low as a German, sir. . . . I lived in German East, I did, afore the war. . . . I *know* 'em. . . ."

The next face of the *boma* was held by the Hundred and Ninety-Eighth. Captain Macke met the Major and saluted him as a revered stranger. He, too, wore tunic and cross-belt and a look of portentous solemnity, such as that on the faces of the Major, Cecil Clarence, and, indeed, everybody else. Bertram, later, labelled it the Stand-to face and practised to acquire it.

"How many sick, Captain Macke?" enquired the Major.

"Twenty-seven, sir," was the reply. Bertram wondered whether they were "present" in the spirit and "correct" in form.

"All fever or dysentery-or both, I suppose?" said the Major.

"Yes-except one with a poisoned foot and one who seems to be going blind," was the reply.

As they passed along, the Major glanced at each man, looked into the canvas water-tanks, scrutinised the residential sheds beneath the wall-and, in one of them discovered a scrap of paper! As the ground was covered with leaves, twigs, and bits of grass, as well as being thick with mud, Bertram did not see that this piece of paper mattered much. This only shows his ignorance. The Major pointed at it, speechless. Captain Macke paled-with horror, wrath or grief. Gussie Augustus Gus stooped and stared at it, screwing his monocle in the tighter, that he might see the better and not be deceived. Vereker turned it over with his stick, and only then believed the evidence of three of his senses. The Jemadar shook his head with incredulous but pained expression. He called for the Havildar, whose mouth fell open. The two men were very alike, being relatives, but while the senior wore a look of incredulous pain, the junior, it seemed to Bertram, rather wore one of pained incredulity. That is to say, the Jemadar looked stricken but unable to believe his eyes, whereas the Havildar looked as though he could not believe his eyes but was stricken nevertheless.

All stared hard at the piece of paper. . . . It was a poignant moment. . . . No one moved and no one seemed to breathe. Suddenly the Havildar touched a Naik who stood behind his men, with his back to the group of officers, and stared fixedly at Nothing. He turned, beheld the paper at which the Havildar's accusing finger pointed, rigid but tremulous. . . . What next? The Naik pocketed the paper, and the incident was closed.

Bertram was glad that he had witnessed it. He knew, thenceforth, the proper procedure for an officer who, wearing the Stand-to face, sees a piece of paper.

The third wall of the *boma* was occupied by a company of Dogras of an Imperial Service Corps, under a Subedar, a fine-looking Rajput, and a company of Marathas of the Hundred and Ninety-Eighth, under the Subedar-Major of that regiment. Bertram was strongly attracted to this latter officer, and thought that never before had he seen an Indian whose face combined so much of patient strength, gentle firmness, simple honesty, and noble pride.

He was introduced to Bertram, and, as they shook hands and saluted, the fine old face was lit up with a smile of genuine pleasure and friendly respectfulness. A man of the old school who recognised duties as well as "rights"—and in whose sight "*false to his salt*" was the last and lowest epithet of uttermost degradation.

"You'll have charge of this face of the fort to-morrow, Greene," said the Major, as they passed on. "Subedar-Major Luxman Atmaram is a priceless old bird. He'll see you have no trouble. . . . Don't be in a hurry to tell him off for anything, because it's a hundred to one you'll find he's right."

Bertram smiled to himself at the thought of his being the sort to "tell off" anybody without due cause and was secretly pleased to find that Major Mallery had thought such a thing possible. . . .

The remaining side of the fort was held by Gurkhas, and Bertram noted the fact with pleasure. He had taken a great fancy to these cheery, steady people. Another machine-gun, with its team of *askaris* of the King's African Rifles, occupied the middle of this wall.

"Don't cough or sneeze near the gun," murmured Vereker to Bertram, "or it may fall to pieces again. The copper-wire is all right, but the boot-lace was not new to begin with."

"What kind of gun is it?" he asked.

"It was a Hotchkiss once. It's a Hot-potch now," was the reply. "Don't touch it as you pass," and the puzzled Bertram observed that it was actually bound with copper-wire at one point and tied with some kind of cord or string at another.

By the hospital—a horrible pit with a tent over it-stood the Indian youth and a party of Swahili stretcher-bearers.

Bertram wondered whether it would ever be his fate to be carried on one of those blood-stained stretchers by a couple of those negroes, laid on the mud at the bottom of that pit, and operated on by that young native of India. He shuddered. Fancy one's life-blood ebbing away into that mud. Fancy dying, mangled, in that hole with no one but a Bupendranath Chatterji to soothe one's last agonies. . . .

Having completed his tour of inspection, Major Mallery removed the Stand-to face and resumed his ordinary one, said: "They can dismiss," to Captain Macke and the group of officers, and tore off his cross-belt and tunic.

All his hearers relaxed their faces likewise, blew their whistles, cried "Dismiss!" in the direction of their respective Native Officers, and removed their belts and tunics almost as quickly as they had removed their Stand-to faces.

They then proceeded to the Bristol Bar.

Chapter XVI
The Bristol Bar

"Come along to the Bristol Bar and have a drink, Greene," said Cecil Clarence, *alias* Gussie Augustus Gus, emerging from his *banda*, into which he had cast his tunic and Sam Browne belt.

"Thanks," replied Bertram, wondering if there were a Jungle Hotel within easy reach of the *boma*, or whether the outpost had its own Place, "licensed for the sale of beer, wine, spirits, and tobacco, to be consumed on the premises. . . ."

In the High Street, next door to the Officers' Mess, were two green tents, outside one of which stood a rough camp-table of the "folding" variety, a native string bed, and a circle of Roorkee chairs, boxes and stools. On an erection of sticks and withes, resembling an umbrella stand, stood an orderly array of fresh coco-nuts, the tops of which had been sliced off to display the white interior with its pint or so of sweet, limpid milk.

Emerging from the tent, an Arab "boy" in a blue turban, blue jacket buttoning up to the chin, blue petticoat and puttees, placed bottles of various kinds on the table, together with a "sparklet" apparatus and a pannikin of water. The Bristol Bar was open. . . . From the other tent emerged an officer in the blue uniform of the little fair men.

He eyed the muddy ground, the ugly grey *bandas* of withered grass and leaves, the muddy, naked Kavirondo-piling their loads on the commissariat dump, and the general dreary, cheerless scene, with the cold eye of extreme distaste and disfavour.

"*Yah!*" said he. He eyed the bottles on the table.

"*Ah!*" said he, and seated himself behind the Bristol Bar.

"Start with a Ver-Gin, I think, as I've been such a good boy to-day," he murmured, and, pouring a measure of Italian vermuth into an enamelled mug, he added a smaller allowance of gin.

"Wish some fool'd roll up so that I can get a drink," he grumbled, holding the mug in his hand.

It did not occur to him to "*faire Suisse*," as the French say-to drink alone. He must at least say "Chin-chin" or "Here's how" to somebody else with a drink in his hand. Had it been cocoa, now, or something of that sort, one might drink gallons of it without a word to a soul. One could lie in bed and wallow and soak, lap it up like a cat or take it in through the pores-but this little drop of alcohol must not be drunk without a witness and a formula. So Lieutenant Forbes possessed his soul in impatience.

A minute later, from every *banda* and tent, from the Officers' Mess and from all directions, came British officers, bearing each man in his hands something to drink or something from which to drink.

The Major bore The Glass, and, behind him, the Mess butler carried a square bottle of ration whisky. He was followed by a Swahili clasping to his bosom a huge jar of ration rum, newly arrived. "Leesey" Lindsay, of the Intelligence Department, brought a collapsible silver cup, which, as he said, only wanted knowing. It leaked and it collapsed at inappropriate moments, but, on the other hand, it *did* collapse, and you could put it in your pocket-where it collected tobacco dust, crumbs, fluff, and grit. Vereker carried a fresh coco-nut and half a coco-nut shell. This latter he was going to carve and polish. He said that coco-nut shells carved beautifully and took a wonderful polish. . . . His uncle, an admiral, had one which he brought from the South Sea Islands. It was beautifully carved and had taken a high polish-from someone or other. A cannibal chief had drunk human blood from it for years. . . . Vereker was going to drink whisky from his for years, and keep it all his life-carving and polishing it between whiles. . . . "Yes. I used that as a drinking-cup all through my first campaign. It nearly fell on my head in the first battle I ever fought. Cut off the tree by a bullet. Carved and polished it myself," he would be able to say, in years to come. Meanwhile it looked a very ordinary half-shell of the common coco-nut of commerce as known to those who upon Saints' Days and Festivals do roll, bowl, or pitch. . . .

Captain Macke brought a prepared siphon of "sparklet" water and his ration whisky. Gussie Augustus Gus walked delicately, bearing a brimming condensed milk tin, and singing softly—

> "Dear, sweet Mother,
> Kind and true;
> She's a boozer,
> Through and through . . . .
> But roll your tail,
> And roll it high,
> And you'll be an angel
> By and by. . . ."

Lieutenant Bupendranath Chatterji brought a harsh laugh and an uncultivated taste, but a strong liking, for assorted liquors, preferably sweet. The officer who had been in command of the side of the fort occupied by the men in blue entered the tent and, having removed his belt, seated himself beside Lieutenant Forbes, behind the bar.

"Good evening, Major," said he; "won't you come and have a drink? . . . Do!"

Regarding The Glass with a look of surprise, and as though wondering how the devil it came to be there, the Major considered the invitation.

"Thanks!" said he. "Don't mind if I *do* sit down for a moment." And he placed The Glass upon the table. Strangely enough, his own Roorkee chair was already in the centre of the circle facing the said table, as it had been any evening at this time for the last fifty nights. The Mess butler put the rum and whisky beneath his chair. "Let me introduce Lieutenant Greene, attached to Ours. Wavell . . ." said he. . . . "Captain Wavell of Wavell's Arabs, Greene," and Bertram shook hands with a remarkable and romantic soldier of fortune, explorer and adventurous knight-errant, whom he came to like, respect, and admire with the greatest warmth. The others drifted up and dropped in, accidentally and casually, as it were, until almost all were there, and the Bristol Bar was full; the hour of the evening star and the evening drink had arrived; *l'heure d'absinthe, l'heure verte* had struck; the sun was below the yard-arm; now the day was over, night was drawing nigh, shadows of the evening stole across the sky; and, war or no war, hunger, mud, disease and misery, or no hunger, mud, disease and misery, the British officer was going to have his evening cocktail, his evening cheroot, and his evening "buck" at the club bar-and to the devil with all Huns who'd interfere with his sacred rights and their sacred rites.

"Here's the best, Major," said Forbes, and drank his ver-gin with gusto and appreciation. His very fine long-lashed eyes beneath faultlessly curving eyebrows-eyes which many a woman had enviously and regretfully considered to be criminally wasted on a mere man-viewed the grey prospect with less disgust. The first drink of the day provided the best minute of the day to this exile from the cream of the joys of Europe; and he eyed the array of bottles with something approaching optimism as he considered the question of what should be his drink for the evening.

"Cheerioh!" responded the Major, and took a pull at the whisky and slightly-aerated water in The Glass. "Here's to Good Count Zeppelin-our finest recruiting agent, and Grandpa Tirpitz-who'll bring America in on our side. . . ."

"What'll you drink, Greene?" asked Wavell. "Vermuth? Whisky? Rum? Gin? Try an absinthe? Or can I mix you a Risky-rum and whisky, you know-or a Whum-whisky and rum, of course?"

"They're both helpful and cheering," added Forbes.

"Let me make you a cock-eye," put in Gussie Augustus Gus. "Thing of my own. Much better than a mere cocktail. Thought of it in bed last night while I was sayin' my prayers. This is one," and he raised his condensed milk tin. "Cross between milk-punch, cocktail, high-ball, gin-sling, rum-shrub, and a bitters. . . . Go down to posterity as a 'Gussie' —along with the John Collins and Elsie May. . . . Great thought. . . . Let us pause before it. . . ."

"What's in it?" asked Captain Macke.

"Condensed milk," replied Augustus, "ration lime-juice, ration rum, ration whisky, medical-comfort brandy, vermuth, coco-nut milk, angostura, absinthe, glycerine. . . ."

"And a damn great flying caterpillar," added the Major as a hideous insect, with a fat, soft body, splashed into the pleasing compound.

"Dirty dog!" grumbled Augustus, fishing for the creature. "Here, don't play submarines in the mud, Eustace-be a sport and swim. . . . I can drink down to him, anyhow," he added, failing to secure the enterprising little animal with a finger and thumb that groped short of the bottom stratum of his concoction. "Got his head stuck in the toffee-milk at the bottom." Bertram declined a "Gussie," feeling unworthy, also unable.

"Have you tried rum and coco-nut milk?" asked Wavell. "It's a kind of local industry since we've been here. The Intelligence Department keeps a Friendly Tribe at work bringing in fresh coco-nuts, and our numerous different detachments provide fatigue-parties in rotation to open them. . . . Many a worse drink than half a tumbler of ration rum poured into the coco-nut. . . ."

"Point of fact—I'm a teetotaller just at present," replied Bertram, sadly but firmly. "May I substitute lime-juice for rum? . . ."

Vereker screwed in his monocle and regarded him. Not with astonishment or interest, of course, for nothing astonished or interested him any more. He was too young and wise for those emotions. But he regarded him.

"What a dreadful habit to contract at your age, Greene," observed Augustus, slightly shocked. "Y'ought to pull yourself together, y'know. . . . Give it up. . . . Bad. . . . Bad. . ." and he shook his head.

"What's it feel like?" asked Captain Macke.

"You've been getting into bad company, my lad," said Major Mallery.

"Oah! Maan, maan! You must not do thatt!" said Mr. Chatterji.

"I've got some ration lime-juice here," said Wavell, "but I really don't advise it as a drink in this country. It's useful stuff to have about when you can't get vegetables of any sort-but I believe it thins your blood, gives you boils, and upsets your tummy. . . . Drop of rum or whisky in the evening . . . do you more good."

Bertram's heart warmed to the kindly friendliness of his voice and manner-the more because he felt that, like himself, this famous traveller and explorer was of a shy and diffident nature.

"Thanks. I'll take your advice then," he said, and reflected that what was good enough for Wavell was good enough for him, in view of the former's unique experience of African and Asiatic travel. "I'll try the rum and coco-nut milk if I may," he added.

"Three loud cheers!" remarked Augustus. "Won't mother be pleased! . . . I'm going to write a book about it, Greene, if you don't mind. . . . 'The Redemption of Lieutenant Greene' or somethin'. . . . *You* know-how on the Eve of Battle, in a blinding flash of self-illuminating introspection, he saw his soul for the Thing it was, saw just where he stood-on the brink of an Abyss. . . . And repented in time. . . . Poignant. . . . Repented and drank rum. . . . Searching."

"Probably Greene's pulling our legs the whole time, my good ass," put in Vereker. "Dare say he's really a frightful drunkard. Riotous reveller and wallowing wassailer. . . . He's got rather a wild eye. . . ."

Bertram laughed with the rest. It was impossible to take offence, for there was nothing in the slightest degree offensive about these pleasant, friendly people.

Berners joined the group and saluted the Major. "Ammunition and ration indents all present and correct, sir," said he.

"Rum ration all right?" asked the Major. "How do you know the jars aren't full of water?"

"P'raps he'd better select one at random as a sample and bring it over here, Major," suggested Macke. And it was so. . . .

Another officer drifted in and was introduced to Bertram as Lieutenant Halke of the Coolie Corps, in charge of the Kavirondo, Wakamba, and Monumwezi labourers and porters attached to the Butindi garrison.

He was an interesting man, a big, burly planter, who had been in the colony for twenty years. "I want your birds to dig another trench to-morrow, Halke," said the Major. "Down by the water-picket."

"Very good, sir," replied Halke. "I'm glad that convoy rolled up safely to-day. Their *posho* [175] was running rather low . . ." and the conversation became technical.

Bertram felt distinctly better for his rum and milk. His weariness fell from him like a garment, and life took on brighter hues. He was not a wretched, weary lad, caught up in the maelstrom of war and flung from pleasant city streets into deadly primeval jungles, where lurked Death in the form of bacillus, savage beast, and more savage and more beastly Man. Not at all. He was one of a band of Britain's soldiers in an outpost of Empire on her far-flung battle-line. . . . One of a group of cheery comrades, laughing and jesting in the face of danger and discomfort. . . . He had Answered His Country's Call, and was of the great freemasonry of arms, sword on thigh, marching, marching. . . . Camp-fire and bivouac. . . . The Long Trail. . . . Beyond the Ranges. . . . Men who have Done Things. . . . A sun-burnt, weather-beaten man from the Back of Beyond. . . . Strong, silent man with a Square Jaw. . . . Romance. . . . Adventure. . . . Life. He drank some more of his rum and felt very happy. He nodded, drooped, snored—and nearly fell off his stool. Wavell smiled as he jerked upright again, and tried to look as though he had never slept in his life.

"So Pappa behaved nasty," Gussie Augustus Gus was saying to a deeply interested audience. "He'd just been turned down himself by a gay and wealthy widowette whom he'd marked down for his Number 2. When I said, 'Pappa, I'm going to be married on Monday, please,' he spake pompous platitudes, finishing up with: '*A young man married is a young man marred.*' . . . 'Yes, Pappa,' says I thoughtlessly, '*and an old man jilted is an old man jarred.*' . . . Caused quite a coolness. So I went to sea." Augustus sighed and drank—and then almost choked with violent spluttering and coughing.

"That blasted Eustace!" he said, as he suddenly and vehemently expelled something.

"Did you marry her?" asked Vereker, showing no sympathy in the matter of the unexpected recovery of the body of Eustace.

"No," said Augustus. "Pappa did." . . .

"That's what I went to see," he added.

"Don't believe you ever had a father," said Vereker.

"I didn't," said Gussie Augustus Gus. "I was an orphan. . . . Am still. . . . Poignant. . . . Searching. . . ."

Lieutenant Bupendranath Chatterji listened to this sort of thing with an owlish expression on his fat face. When anybody laughed he laughed also, loudly and raucously.

It was borne in upon Bertram that it took more than fever, hunger, boredom, mud, rain and misery to depress the spirits of the officers of the garrison of Butindi. . . .

"*Khana tyar hai,* [176] *Sahib,*" announced the Major's butler, salaaming.

"Come and gnaw ropes and nibble bricks, Greene," said the officer addressed, and with adieux to Wavell and Forbes, who ran a mess of their own, the guests departed from the Bristol Bar and entered the Officers' Mess. Here Bertram learnt the twin delights of a native bedstead when used as a seat. You can either sit on the narrow wooden edge until you feel as though you have been sitting on a hot wire for a week, or you can slide back on to the string part and slowly, slowly disappear from sight, and from dinner.

"This water drawn from the river and been standing in the bath all day, boy?"

"*Han,* [177] *Sahib,*" replied that worthy.

"Alum in the water?"

"*Han, Sahib.*"

"Water then filtered?"

"*Han, Sahib.*"
"Water then boiled?"
"*Han, Sahib.*"
"*Pukka* boiled?"
"*Han, Sahib*, all bubbling."
"Filtered again? You saw it all done yourself?"
"*Han, Sahib.*"
"That's all right, then," concluded the Major.

This catechism was the invariable prelude to the Major's use of water for drinking purposes, whether in the form of *aqua pura*, whisky and water, or tea. For the only foe that Major Mallery feared was the disease-germ. To bullet and bayonet, shrapnel and shell-splinter, he gave no thought. To cholera, enteric and dysentery he gave much, and if care with his drinking water would do it, he intended to avoid those accursed scourges of the tropics. Holding up the glass to the light of the hurricane lamp which adorned the clothless table of packing-case boards, he gazed through it—as one may do when caressing a glass of crusted ruby port—and mused upon the wisdom that had moved him to make it the sole and special work of one special man to see that he had a plentiful supply of pure fair water.

He gazed. . . . And slowly his idle abstracted gaze became a stare and a glare. His eyes protruded from his head, and he gave a yell of gasping horror and raging wrath that drew the swift attention of all—

While round and round in the alum-ised, filtered, boiled and re-filtered water, there slowly swam—a little fish.

* * *

Dinner was painfully similar to that at M'paga, save that the party, being smaller, was more of a Happy Family. It began with what Vereker called "Chatty" soup (because it was "made from talkative meat, in a chattie"), proceeded to inedible bully-beef, and terminated with dog-biscuit and coco-nut—unless you chose to eat your daily banana then.

During dinner, another officer, who had been out all day on a reconnaissance-patrol, joined the party, drank a pint of rum-and-coco-nut milk and fell asleep on the bedstead whereon he sat. He looked terribly thin and ill.

Macke punched him in the ribs, sat him up, and banged the tin plate of cold soup with his knife till the idea of "dinner" had penetrated the sleepy brain of the new-corner. "Feed yer face, Murie," he shouted in his ear.

"Thanks awf'ly," said that gentleman, took up his spoon, and toppled over backwards on to the bed with a loud snore.

"Disgustin' manners," said Gussie Augustus Gus.

"I wish we had a siphon of soda-water. I'd wake him all right."

"Set him on fire," suggested Vereker.

"He's too beastly wet, the sneak," complained Gussie.

"Oah, he iss sleepee," observed Lieutenant Bupendranath Chatterji.

Vereker regarded him almost with interest.

"What makes you think so?" he asked politely. In the laugh that followed, the sleeper was forgotten and remained where he was until Stand-to the following morning. He was living on quinine and his nerves-which form an insufficient diet in tropical Africa.

"Where *Bwana* sleeping to-night, sah, please Mister?" whispered Ali, as, dinner finished, Bertram sat listening with deep interest to the conversation.

Pipes alight, and glasses, mugs and condensed milk tins charged, the Mess was talking of all things most distant and different from jungle swamps and dirty, weary war. . . .

"Quite most 'sclusive Society in Oxford, I tell you," Gussie was saying. "Called ourselves *The Astronomers*. . . ."

"What the devil for? Because you were generally out at night?" asked Macke.

"No-because we studied the Stars-of the Stage," was the reply. . . .

"Rotten," said Vereker, with a shiver. "You sh'd have called yourselves *The Botanists*," he added a minute later.

"Why?"

"Because you culled Peroxide Daisies and Lilies of the Ballet."

"Ghastly," observed Gussie, with a shudder. "And *cull* is a beastly word. One who culls is a cully. . . . How'd you like to be called *Cully*, Murie?" he shouted in that officer's ear. Receiving no reply, he pounded upon the sleeper's stomach with one hand while violently rolling his head from side to side with the other.

Murie awoke.

"Whassup?" he jerked out nervously.

"How'd you like to be called *Cully*?" shouted Gussie again.

Murie fixed a glassy eye on him. His face was chalky white and his black hair lay dank across his forehead.

"Eh?" said he.

Gussie repeated his enquiry.

"Call me anything-but don't call me early," was the reply, as he realised who and where he was, and closed his eyes again.

"*You're* an ornament to the Mess. *You* add to the gaiety of nations. *You* ought to be on the halls," shouted the tormentor. "You're a refined Society Entertainer. . . ."

"Eh?" grunted Murie.

"Come for a walk in the garden I said," shouted Augustus. "Oh, you give me trypanosomiasis to look at you," he added.

"You go to Hell," replied Murie, and snored as he finished speaking.

Bertram felt a little indignant.

"Wouldn't it be kinder to let him sleep?" he said.

"No, it wouldn't," was the reply. "He'll sleep there for an hour, and then go over to his hut and be awake all night because he's had no dinner."

"I beg your pardon," said Bertram-and asked the Major where he was to sleep that night.

"On your right side, with your mouth shut," was the reply; to which Augustus added:

"Toe of the right foot in line with the mouth; thumb in rear of the seam of the pyjamas; heel of the left foot in the hollow of the back; and weight of the body on the chin-strap —as laid down in the drill-book."

"Haven't you a tent?" asked the Major, and, in learning that Bertram had not, said that a *banda* should be built for him on the morrow, and that he could sleep on or under the Mess table that night. . . .

When the Major had returned to his tent with the remark "All lights out in fifteen minutes," Ali set up Bertram's bed in the Mess *banda*, and in a few minutes the latter was alone. . . . As he sat removing his boots, Bertram was surprised to see Gussie Augustus Gus return to the Mess, carrying a native spear and a bundle of white material. Going to where Murie lay, he raised the spear and drove it with all his force-apparently into Murie's body! Springing to his feet, Bertram saw that the spear was stuck into the clay and that the shaft, protruding through the meshes of the bed string, stood up beside Murie. Throwing the mosquito-net over the top of it, Gussie enveloped the sleeper in its folds, as well as he could, and vanished.

Chapter XVII
More Baking

Bertram was awakened at dawn by the bustle and stir of Stand-to. He arose and dressed, by the simple process of putting on his boots and helmet, which, by reason of rain, wind, mud and publicity, were the only garments he had removed. Proceeding to that face of the fort which was to be his special charge, he found that one half of its defenders were lining its water-logged trench, and the other half, its wall. It was a depressing hour and place. Depressing even to one who had not slept in his wet clothes and arisen with throbbing head, horrible mouth, aching limbs and with the sense of a great sinking void within.

Around the fort was a sea of withering brushwood, felled trees, scrub and thorn, grey and ugly: inside the fort, a lake of mud. Burly Subedar-Major Luxman Atmaram seemed cheery and bright, so Bertram endeavoured to emulate him.

The Major, accompanied by Vereker (who called himself Station Staff Officer, Aide-de-camp to the O.C. Troops, Assistant Provost Marshal, and other sonorous names), passed on his tour of inspection. Bertram saluted.

"Good morning, sir," said he.

"Think so?" said the Major, and splashed upon his way.

"Good morning, Vereker," said Bertram, as that gentleman passed.

"Nothing of the sort. Wrong again," replied Vereker, and splashed upon *his* way.

Both were wearing the Stand-to face, and looked coldly upon Bertram, who was not.

After "Dismiss," Bertram returned to the Mess *banda*.

"Good morning, Greene," said the Major, and:

"Good morning, Greene," echoed Vereker.

Bertram decided that his not being properly dressed in the matter of the Stand-to face, was overlooked or condoned, in view of his youth and inexperience. . . . The vast metal teapot and a tray of dog-biscuits made their appearance.

"I'm going to have my bloater now," said Berners, plucking a banana from the weary-looking bunch. "Will someone remind me that I have had it, if I go to take another?"

"I will," volunteered Augustus. "Any time you pluck a bloater and I hit you on the head three times with the tent-peg mallet, that means 'Nay, Pauline.' See?" . . .

"What's the Programme of Sports for to-day, sir?" asked Berners of the Major, as he cleansed his fingers of over-ripe banana upon Augustus's silky hair.

"Macke takes a strong Officer's Patrol towards Muru," replied the Major. "Halke starts getting the trenches deepened a bit. You can wrestle with commissariat and ammunition returns, and the others might do a bit of parade and physical jerks or something this morning. I'm going to sneak round and catch the pickets on the hop. You'd better come with me, Greene, and see where they're posted. Tell the Subedar-Major what you want your men to do. Wavell's taking his people for a march. Murie will be in charge of the fort. . . ."

"Murie has temperature of one hundred and five," put in Lieutenant Bupendranath Chatterji. "He has fever probably."

"Shouldn't be at all surprised," observed the Major dryly. "What are you giving him?"

"Oah, he will be all right," was the reply.

"I've got three fresh limes I pinched from that *shamba*,"[178] said Augustus. "If he had those with a quart of boiling water and half a tin of condensed milk, he might be able to do a good sweat and browse a handful of quinine."

"No more condensed milk," said Berners. "Greene had the last tin last night, and the hog didn't bring any with him."

"I shall be delighted to contribute the remainder of it," said Bertram, looking into his tin. "There's quite three-quarters of it left."

"Good egg," applauded Augustus. "If you drink your tea from the tin, you'll get the flavour of milk for ever so long," and Ali having been despatched to the cook-house for a kettle of boiling water, Augustus fetched his limes and the two concocted the brew with their condensed milk and lime-juice in an empty rum-jar.

"What about a spot of whisky in it?" suggested Vereker.

"Better without it when fever is violent," opined the medical attendant, and Augustus, albeit doubtfully, accepted the *obiter dicta*, as from one who should know.

"Shall I shove it into him through the oil-funnel if he is woozy?" he asked, and added: "Better not, p'r'aps. Might waste half of it down his lungs and things . . ." and he departed, in search of his victim.

As Bertram left the *boma* in company of the Major, he found it difficult to realise that, only a few hours earlier he had not set eyes on the place. He seemed to have been immured within its walls of mud and wattle for days, rather than hours.

About the large clearing that lay on that side of the fort, Sepoys, servants, porters and *askaris* came and went upon their occasions; the stretcher-bearers, gun-teams, and a company of Gurkhas were at drill; and in the trenches, the long, weedy bodies of the Kavirondo rose and fell as they dug in the mud and clay. Near the gate a doleful company of sick and sorry porters squatted and watched a dresser of the Indian Subordinate Medical Department, as he sprinkled iodoform from a pepperbox on to the hideous sores and wounds of a separate squad requiring such treatment. The sight of an intensely black back, with a huge wound of a glowing red, upon which fell a rain of brilliant yellow iodoform, held Bertram's spell-bound gaze, while it made him feel exceedingly sick. Those patients suffering from ghastly sores and horrible festering wounds seemed gay and lighthearted and utterly indifferent, while the remainder, suffering from *tumbo*, [179] fever, cold in the head, or world-weariness, appeared to consider themselves at the last gasp, and each, like the Dying Gladiator, did lean his head upon his hand while his manly brow consented to Death, but conquered agony.

"The reason why the African will regard a gaping wound, or great festering sore, with no more than mild interest, while he will wilt away and proceed to perish if he has a stomach-ache is an interestin' exemplification of *omne ignotum pro magnifico*," remarked the Major.

Bertram stared at his superior officer in amazement. The tone and language were utterly different from those hitherto connected, in Bertram's experience, with that gentleman. Was this a subtle mockery of Bertram as a civilian Intellectual? Or was it that the Major liked to be "all things to all men" and considered this the style of conversation likely to be suitable to the occasion?

"Yes, sir?" said Bertram, a trifle shortly.

"Yes," continued Major Mallery. "He believes that all internal complaints are due to Devils. A stomach-ache is, to him, painful and irrefragible proof that he hath a Devil. One has entered into him and abideth. It's no good telling him anything to the contrary-because he can *feel* It there, and surely he's the best judge of what he can feel? So any internal complaint terrifies him to such an extent that he dies of fright-whereas he'll think nothing of a wound that would kill you or me. . . ."

Here, apparently, the Major's mocking fancy tired, or else his effort to talk "high-brow" to an Intellectual could be no further sustained, for he fell to lower levels with the remark:

"Rum blokes. . . Dam' funny. . ." and fell silent.

A well-trodden mud path led down to the river, on the far side of which was the water-picket commanding the approach, not to a ford, but to the only spot where impenetrable jungle did not prevent access to the river. . . .

"Blighters nearly copped us badly down here before we built the fort," said the Major. "Look in here . . ." and he parted some bushes beside the path and disappeared. Following him, Bertram found himself in a long, narrow clearing cut out of the solid jungle and parallel with the path.

"They had a hundred men at least, in here," said Major Mallery, "and you might have come along the path a hundred times without spotting them. There was a machine-gun up that tree, to deal with the force behind the point of ambush, and a big staked pit farther down the path to catch those in front who ran straight on.... Lovely trap.... They used to occupy it from dawn to sunset every day, poor fellers...."

"What happened?" asked Bertram.

"Our Intelligence Department learnt all about it from the local *shenzis*, and we forestalled them one merry morn. They were ambushed in their own ambush.... The *shenzi* doesn't love his Uncle Fritz a bit. No appreciation of *Kultur*-by-*kiboko*. He calls the Germans '*the Twenty-Five Lashes People*,' because the first thing the German does when he goes to a village is to give everybody twenty-five of the best, by way of introducing himself and starting with a proper understanding. Puts things on a proper footing from the beginning...."

"Their *askaris* are staunch enough, aren't they?" asked Bertram.

"Absolutely. They are well paid and well fed, and they are allowed to do absolutely as they like in the way of loot, rape, arson and murder, once the fighting is over.... They flog them most unmercifully for disciplinary offences-and the nigger understands that. Also they leave the defeated foe-his village, crops, property, women, children and wounded-to their mercy-and the nigger understands *that* too.... Our *askaris* are not nearly so contented with our milder punishments, cumbrous judicial system, and absolute prohibition of loot, rape, arson and the murder of the wounded. Yes-the German *askari* will stick to the German so long as he gets the conqueror's rights whenever he conquers-as is the immemorial law and custom of Africa... . 'What's the good of fighting a cove if you're going to cosset and coddle him directly you've won, and give him something out of the poor-box—instead of dismembering him?' says he... . You might say the *askari*-class is to the Native what the Junker-class is to the peasant, in Germany."

And conversing thus, the two officers visited the pickets and the sentries, who sat on *machans* in the tops of high trees and, in theory at any rate, scoured the adjacent country with tireless all-seeing eye.

Returning to the fort, Bertram saw the materials for his own private freehold residence being carried to the eligible site selected for its erection by the united wisdom of the Station Staff Officer and the Quartermaster. It was built and furnished in less than an hour by a party of Kavirondo, who used no other tools than their *pangas*, and it consisted of a framework of stout saplings firmly planted in the ground, wattle, and thatched leaves, twigs and grass. It had a window-frame and a doorway, and it kept out the sun and the first few drops of a shower of rain. If a *banda* does little else, it provides one's own peculiar place apart, where one can be private and alone.... On the table and shelf-of sticks bound together with strips of bark-Ali set forth his master's impedimenta, and took a pride in the Home....

Finding that the spine-pad of quilted red flannel-which Murray had advised him to get and to wear buttoned on to the inner side of his shirt, as a protection against the sun's actinic rays-was soaked with perspiration, Bertram gave it to Ali that it might be dried. What he did not foresee was that his faithful retainer would tie a long strip of bark from the new *banda* to the opposite one across the "street," and pin the red flannel article to flap in the breeze and the face of the passer-by....

"Oh, I say, you fellers, look here!" sang out the voice of Gussie Augustus Gus, as Bertram was finishing his shave, a few minutes later. "Here's that careless fellow, Greene, been and left his chest-protector off!... It's on the line to air, and I *don't* know what he's doing without it." The voice broke with anguish and trouble as it continued: "Perhaps running about with nothing on at all.... On his chest, I mean...."

There was a laugh from neighbouring *bandas* and tents where Vereker, Berners, Halke and "Leesey" Lindsay were washing by their cottage doors, preparatory to breakfast.

Bertram blushed hotly in the privacy of his hut. *Chest-protector*! Confound the fellow's impudence-and those giggling' idiots. He had half a mind to put his head out and remark; "The laughter of fools is as the crackling of thorns beneath a pot," and in the same moment wiser counsels prevailed.

Thrusting a soapy face out of the window, he said, in a tone expressive more of sorrow than of anger:

"I am surprised at *you*, Clarence! . . . To laugh at the infirmities of your elders! . . . Is it *my* fault I have housemaid's knee?"

To which Augustus, with tears in his eyes and voice, replied:

"Forgive me, Pappa. I have known trouble too. *I* had an Aunt with a corn. . . . *She* wore one. . . . Pink, like yours. . . . Poignant. . . . Searching. . . ."

This cheerful and indefatigable young gentleman had, in his rôle of Mess President, found time, after parade and kit-inspection that morning, to prepare a breakfast *menu*. Consulting it, Bertram discovered promise of

1. *Good Works*. Taken out of some animal, or animals, unknown. Perhaps Liver. Perhaps not. Looks rather poignant.

2. *Shepherd's Bush* (or is it Plaid or Pie?) or Toed-in-the-Hole. Same as above, bedded down in manioc. Looks very poignant.

3. There were *Sausages on Toast*, but they are in bad odour, uppish, and peevish to the eye, and there is no bread.

4. *Curried Bully-beef*. God help us. And Dog-biscuit.

5. *Arm of monkey*. No 'arm in that? *But* —One rupee reward is offered for a missing Kavirondo baby. Answers to the name of Horatio, and cries if bitten in the stomach. . . . Searching.

"Great news," quoth the author of this document, seating himself on the bed-frame beside Bertram and eyeing a plate of Good Works without enthusiasm. "There's to be a General Court-Martial after breakfast. You and I and Berners. Leesey Lindsay is prosecuting a bloke for spying and acting as guide to German raiding parties-him bein' a British subjick an' all. . . Splendid! . . . Shall we hang him or shoot him? . . ."

"*I* am Provost-Marshal," put in Vereker, "and *I* shall hang him. I know exactly how to hang, and am a recognised good hanger. Anyhow, no one has complained. . . . Wish we had some butter. . . ."

"Whaffor?" asked Augustus.

"Grease the rope," was the reply. "They like it. Butter is awfully good."

"Put the knot under the left ear, don't you?" asked Augustus.

"*I* do," answered Vereker. "Some put it under the right. . . . I have seen it at the back. Looks bad, though. Depressin'. Bloke hangs his head. Mournful sight. . . ."

"Got any rope?" enquired Augustus.

"No! . . . How thoughtless of me! . . . Never mind-make up something with strips of bark. . . . Might let the bloke make his own-only himself to blame, then, if it broke and he met with an accident."

"I *have* heard of suicides-and-people hanging themselves with their braces," observed Augustus.

"Wadego *shenzis* don't have braces," replied Vereker.

"No, but Greene does. I'm perfectly sure he'd be delighted to lend you his. He's kindness itself. Or would you rather he were shot, Greene? We must remember there's no blood about a hanging, whereas there's lots the other way —'specially if it's done by *askaris* with Martinis. . . . On the other hand, hanging lasts longer. I dunno *what* to advise for the best. . . ."

"Suppose we try him first," suggested Bertram.

"Of course!" was the somewhat indignant reply. "I'm surprised at *you*, Greene. You wouldn't put him to the edge of the sword without a trial, would you?"

"No, Greene," added Vereker. "Not goin' to waste a good *shenzi* like that. We're goin' to have a jolly good Court-Martial out of him before we do him in. . . . And I shall hang him, Clarence-rope or no rope."

"May I swing on his feet, Vereker?" begged Augustus. "*Do* let me! . . . Be a sport. . . ."

"Everything will be done properly and nicely," was the reply, "and in the best style. There will be no swinging on the prisoner's legs while *I'm* M.C. . . . Not unless the prisoner himself suggests it," he added.

"How'll we tell him of his many blessin's, and so on?" enquired Berners.

"There's an Arab blighter of Lindsay's who professes to know a tongue spoken by a porter who knows Wadego. The bloke talks to the porter in Wadego, the porter talks to the Arab in the Tongue, the Arab talks to Wavell in Arabic, and Wavell talks to us in any language we like-French, German, Swahili, Hindustani, Latin, Greek, American, Turkish, Portuguese, Taal or even English. He knows all those. . . ."

"Let's ask him to talk them all at once, while we smoke and quaff beakers of rum," suggested Augustus. "And I *say* —couldn't we torture the prisoner? I know lots of ripping tortures."

"Well, I'm not going to have him ripped," vetoed Vereker. "You gotter hand him over to the Provost-Marshal in good condition. . . Fair wear and tear of trial and incarceration allowed for, of course. . . . Bound to be *some* depreciation, I know."

"What's 'to incarcerate' mean, exactly?" enquired Augustus.

"Same as 'incinerate.'"

"Can we do it to him by law?" asked Augustus.

"You read the Orders, my lad," replied Vereker. "On the notice-board in the Orderly Room. That post's the Orderly Room. Written and signed by the Station Staff Officer. And look up Field and General Court-Martials in the King's Regulations and you'll know what your Powers are."

"I say, Berners. Let me find you the least contrary of those turned sausages, and have it nicely fried for you," begged Augustus. "You'd hardly taste anything awkward about it if you had some lemon-peel done with it. Plenty of lemon-peel and some coco-nut. I'll find the peel I threw away this morning. . . . *Do*."

"This is very kind and thoughtful of you, Gussie. What's the idea?" replied Berners.

"I want to propitiate you, Berners. You'll be President of the Court-Martial."

"And?"

"I want you to promise you won't have the prisoner found Guilty unless Vereker promises to let me swing on his feet. . . . I've *never* once had the chance. . . . And now my chance has come. . . . And Vereker feels thwartful. . . . It's due to his having a boil-and no cushion with him. . . . Be a good soul, Berners. . . "

"Let's see the sausages," said the President-elect.

"That's done it," admitted Augustus, and dropped the subject with a heavy sigh.

Bertram noticed that, in spite of his flow of cheery nonsense, Augustus ate nothing at all and looked very ill indeed. He remembered a sentence he had read in a book on board the *Elymas*:

"Comedy lies lightly upon all things, like foam upon the dark waters. Beneath are tragedy and the tears of time."

Chapter XVIII
Trial

After breakfast Bertram attended Court, which was a table under a tree, and took his seat on the Bench, an inverted pail, as a Ruler and a Judge, for the first and last time in his life. He felt that it was a strange and terrible thing that he should thus be suddenly called upon to try a man for his life.

Suppose that his two fellow-judges, Berners and Clarence, disagreed as to the death-sentence, and he had to give his verdict, knowing that a man's life depended on it! . . .

A couple of *askaris* of the King's African Rifles, police-orderlies of "Leesey" Lindsay's, brought in the prisoner. He was a powerful and decidedly evil-looking negro, clad in a striped petticoat. He had more of the appearance of furtive intelligence than is usual with *shenzis* of his tribe. Bertram decided that he carried his guilt in his face and had trickster and traitor written all over it. He then rebuked himself for pre-judging the case and entertaining prejudice against an untried, and possibly innocent, man.

"Guilty," said Augustus Gus. "Who's coming for a walk?"

"I'm President of this Court," replied Berners. "Who asked you to open your head? If I'm not sure as to his guilt, I may consult you later. Or I may not."

"Look here, Berners-let's do the thing properly," was the reply. "There's a Maxim-or is it a Hotchkiss-of English Law which says that a man is to be considered Guilty until he is proved to be Innocent. Therefore we start fair. He is Guilty, I say. Now we've got to prove him Innocent. Do be a sport, and give the poor blighter a show."

"I b'lieve it's the other way about," said Berners.

"Oh, indeed!" commented Augustus. "You'd say the feller's innocent and then start in to prove him guilty, would you? . . . Dirty trick, I call it. Filthy habit."

Wavell appeared at the entrance to his tent, holding a green, silk-covered book in his hand. The cover was richly embroidered and had a flap, like that of an envelope, provided with strings for tying it down. It was a copy of the Koran, and on it all witnesses were sworn, repeating an oath administered by Wavell in Arabic. . . .

"Ready?" asked he of the President, and proceeded with great patience, skill and knowledge of languages and dialects, to interpret the statements of Wadegos, Swahilis, Arabs, and assorted Africans. Occasionally it was beyond his power, or that of any human being, to convey the meaning of some simple question to a savage mind, and to get a rational answer.

For the prosecution, Lindsay, who was down with dysentery, had produced fellow-villagers of the accused, from each of whom Wavell obtained the same story.

Prisoner was enamoured of a daughter of the headman of the village, and, because his suit was dismissed by this gentleman, he had led a German raiding-party to the place, and, moreover, had shown them where hidden treasures were *cached*, and where fowls, goats, and cattle had been penned in the jungle, and where grain was stored. Also, he had "smelt out" enemies of the *Germanis* among his former neighbours, wicked men who, he said, had led English raiding-parties into the country of the *Germanis*, and had otherwise injured them. These enemies of the *Germanis* were all, as it happened, enemies of his own. . . . When this raiding-party of *askaris*, led by half a dozen *Germanis*, had burnt the village, killed all the villagers who had not escaped in time, and carried off all they wanted in the way of livestock, women, grain and gear, they had rewarded accused with a share of the loot. . . .

"Do they all tell the same tale in the same way, as though they had concocted it and learnt it by heart?" asked Bertram.

"No," replied Wavell. "I didn't get that impression."

"Let's question them one by one," said Berners.

A very, very old man, a sort of "witch-doctor" or priest, by his ornaments, entered the witness-box—otherwise arose from the group of witnesses and stood before the Court-to leeward by request.

"Hullo, Granpa! How's things?" said Augustus.

The ancient ruin mumbled something in Swahili, and peered with horny eyes beneath rheumy, shrivelled lids at the Court, as he stood trembling, his palsied head ashake.

"Don't waggle your head at *me*, Rudolph," said Augustus severely, as the old man fixed him with a wild and glassy eye. "*I'm* not going to uphold you. . . . Pooh! *What* an odour of sanctity! You're a *high* priest, y'know," and murmured as he sought his handkerchief, "Poignant! . . . Searching. . . ."

The old man repeated his former mumble.

"He says he did not mean to steal the tobacco," interpreted Wavell.

"Sort of accident that might happen to anybody, what?" observed Augustus. "Ask him if he knows the prisoner."

The question was put to him in his own tongue, and unfalteringly he replied that he had not meant to steal the tobacco-had not *really* stolen it, in fact.

Patiently Wavell asked, and patiently he was answered. "Do you know the prisoner?"

"I never steal."

"Do you know this man?"

"Tobacco I would never steal."

"What is this man's name?"

"Tobacco."

"Have you ever seen that man before?"

"What man?"

"This one."

"Yes. He is the prisoner."

"When have you seen him before?"

"Last night."

"When, before that?"

"He ate rice with us last night. He is the prisoner."

"Do you know him well?"

"Yes, I know he is the prisoner. *He* stole the tobacco."

"Have you known him long?"

"No. He is only a young man. He steals tobacco."

"Does he come from your village?"

"Yes."

"Have you known him all his life?"

"No, because he went and spent some time in the *Germanis'* country. I think he went to steal tobacco."

"Did he come back alone from the *Germanis'* country?"

"No. He brought *askaris* and *muzangos*. [180] They killed my people and burnt my village."

"You are sure it was this man who brought them?"

"Is he not a prisoner?"

Suddenly an ancient hag arose from the group of witnesses and bounded into Court. At the feet of Wavell she poured forth a torrent of impassioned speech.

"Cheer up, Auntie!" quoth Augustus, and as the woman ceased, added: "Ask her if she'd come to Paris for the week-end."

"What does she say?" enquired the President of the Court.

"In effect-that she will be security for *witness's* good behaviour, as he is her only child and never steals tobacco. He only took the tobacco because he wanted a smoke. He is ninety years of age, and a good obedient son to her. It is her fault for not looking after him better. She hopes he will not be hung, as she is already an orphan, and would then be a childless orphan. . . . She undertakes to beat him with a *runga*." [181]

"Does she identify prisoner as the man who led the German raiding-party?" asked Bertram, after Augustus had called for three loud cheers for the witness, had been himself called to order by the President, and had threatened that he would not play if further annoyed by that official.

Again, in careful Swahili, Wavell endeavoured to find traces of evidence for or against the accused.

"Do you know this man?"

"Yes, *Bwana*."

"Who is he?"

"The prisoner, *Bwana Macouba* (Great Master)."

"Why is he a prisoner?"

"Because he brought the *Germanis* to Pongwa, oh, *Bwana Macouba Sana* (Very Great Master)."

"How do you know he brought the *Germanis* to Pongwa?"

"Because he has been made prisoner for doing so, oh, *Bwana Macouba Kabeesa Sana* (Very Greatest Master)."

"Do you know anything about him?"

"He is the man who stole the tobacco which my little boy took."

All being translated and laid before the Court, it was decided that, so far, prisoner was scarcely proven guilty.

"Let's ask him whether he would like to say anything as to the evidence of the last two witnesses," suggested Bertram.

"He doesn't understand Swahili," objected Berners.

"I feel sure he does," replied Bertram. "I have been watching his face. He half grinned when they talked about tobacco, and looked venomous when they talked about him."

"Do you understand Swahili?" asked Wavell, suddenly, of the prisoner.

"No, not a word," replied that individual in the same tongue.

"Can you speak it?"

"No, not a word," he reaffirmed in Swahili.

"Well-did the last two witnesses tell the truth about you?"

"They did not. I have never seen them before. They have never seen me before. I do not know where Pongwa is. I think this is a very fine trial. I like it."

Other witnesses swore that the accused had indeed done the treacherous deed. One swore with such emphasis and certainty that he carried conviction to the minds of the Court-until it was discovered that witness was swearing that prisoner had stolen a bundle of leaf-tobacco from the son of the woman who was an orphan. . . .

The Court soon found that it could tell when a point was scored against the defendant, without waiting for translation, inasmuch as he always seized his stomach with both hands, groaned, rolled his eyes, and cried that he was suffering horribly from *tumbo*, when evidence was going unfavourably.

At length all witnesses had been examined, even unto the last, who swore he was the prisoner's brother, and that he saw the prisoner leading the *Germanis* and, lo, it wasn't his brother at all, and concluded with: "Yes-this is true evidence. I have spoken well. I can prove it, for I can produce the *sufuria*[182] which prisoner gave me to say that I am his brother, and to speak these truths. He is my innocent brother, and was elsewhere when he led the *Germanis* to Pongwa."

"Let's give him something out of the poor-box," suggested Augustus when this speech was interpreted, and then marred this intimation of kindly feelings by adding: "and then hang the lot of them."

"Has the prisoner anything to say?" asked the President.

The prisoner had.

"This is a good trial," quoth he, in Swahili. "I am now an important man. All the witnesses are liars. I have never seen any of them before. I do not associate with such. I have never seen Pongwa, and I have never seen a *Germani*. I will tell . . ."

Wavell looked at him suddenly, but made no movement.

"*Noch nichte!*" said he in German, very quietly.

The man stopped talking at once.

"You understand German. You speak German!" said Wavell, in that language, and pointing at him accusingly. "Answer quickly. You speak German."

"*Ganz klein wenig* —just a very little," replied the prisoner, adding in English: "I am a very clever man" —and then, in German: "*Ich hab kein Englisch.*"

"Prisoner has never seen a *Germani* —but he understands German!" wrote Bertram in his notes of the trial. "Also Swahili and English."

"Please ask him if he hasn't had enough trial now, and wouldn't he like to be hanged to save further trouble," said Augustus.

"*Tiffin tyar hai,* [183] *Sahib,*" said the Mess butler, approaching the President, and the Court adjourned.

The afternoon session of the Court proved dull up to the moment when the lady who was an orphan and the mother of the ninety-year-old, bounded into Court with a scream of:

"Ask him where he got his petticoat!"

Apparently this was very distressful to the defendant, for he was instantly seized with violent stomachic pains.

"Poignant! . . . Searching! . . ." murmured Augustus.

"Where did you get that *'Mericani*?" asked Wavell of the prisoner, pointing to his only garment.

"He got it from the *Germanis*. It was part of his share of the loot," screamed the old lady. "It is from my own shop. I know it by that mark," and she pointed to a trade-mark and number stencilled in white paint upon the selvedge of the loin-cloth.

Terrible agonies racked the prisoner as he replied: "She is a liar."

"Trade-mark don't prove much," remarked the President. "My pants and vest might have same trade-mark as the Kaiser's —but that wouldn't prove he stole them from me."

The sense of this remark was conveyed to the witness.

"Then see if a mark like *this* is not in the corner of that piece of *'Mericani,*" said the old lady, and plucking up her own wardrobe, showed where a small design was crudely stitched.

The *askaris* in charge of the prisoner quickly demonstrated that an identical "laundry-mark" ornamented his also. Presumably the worthy woman's secret price-mark, or else her monogram.

Terrific agonies seized the prisoner, and with a groan of "*Tumbo,*" he sank to the ground.

A kick from each of the *askaris* revived him, and he arose promptly and took a bright interest in the subsequent proceedings, which consisted largely in the swearing by several of the villagers that they had seen the *Germanis* loot the old lady's store and throw some pieces of the *'Mericani* to the accused. Two of the witnesses were wearing petticoats which they had bought from the female witness, and which bore her private mark. . . .

"Gentlemen," said the President at length, "I should like your written findings by six o'clock this evening, together with the sentence you would impose if you were sole judge in this case. The Court is deeply indebted to Captain Wavell for his courteous and most valuable assistance as interpreter. The witnesses may be discharged, and the prisoner removed to custody. . . . Clear the blasted Court, in fact, and come to the Bristol Bar. . . ."

"Oh, hang it all, Berners," objected Augustus, "let's hang him *now*. We can watch him dangle while we have tea. . . ." But the Court had risen, and the President was asking where the devil some bally, fat-headed fool had put his helmet, eh? . . .

For an hour Bertram sat in his *banda* with throbbing, aching head, considering his verdict. He believed the man to be a spy and a treacherous, murderous scoundrel-but what was really *proven*, save that he knew German and wore a garment marked similarly to those of three inhabitants of Pongwa? Were these facts sufficient to warrant the passing of the death sentence and to justify Bertram Greene, who, till a few days ago, was the mildest of lay civilians, to take the responsibility of a hanging judge and imbrue his hands with the blood of this man? If all that was suspected of him were true, what, after all, was he but a savage, a barbarous product of barbaric uncivilisation? . . . What right had anyone to apply the standards of a cultured white man from London to a savage black man from Pongwa? . . . A savage who had been degraded and contaminated by contact with Germans moreover. . . .

After many unsatisfactory efforts, he finally wrote out his judgment on leaves torn from his military pocket-book, and proposed, as verdict, that the prisoner be confined for the duration of the war as a spy, and receive twenty-five strokes of the *kiboko* for perjury. . . .

On repairing to Berners' hut at the appointed time, he found that Clarence had written a longer and better judgment than his own, and had proposed as sentence that the accused be detained during the King's pleasure at Mombasa Gaol, since it was evident that he had dealings with Germans and had recently been in German East Africa. He found the charge of leading a German raiding-party Not Proven.

The sentence of the President was that prisoner should receive twenty lashes and two years' imprisonment, for receiving stolen goods, well knowing them to be stolen, and for committing perjury.

"And that ought to dish the lad till the end of the war," observed he, "whereafter he'll have precious small use for his German linguistic lore-unless he goes to Berlin for the Iron Cross or a Commission in the Potsdammer Poison-Gas Guards, or somethin', what?"

Chapter XIX
Of a Pudding

There was a sound of revelry by night, at the Bristol Bar. A Plum Pudding had arrived. Into that lonely outpost, where men languished and yearned for potatoes, cabbage, milk, cake, onions, beer, steaks, chocolate, eggs, cigarettes, bacon, fruit, coffee, bread, fish, jam, sausages, honey, sugar, ham, tobacco, pastry, toast, cheese, wine and other things of which they had almost forgotten the taste, a Plum Pudding had drifted. When it had begun to seem that food began and ended with coco-nut, maize, bully-beef and dog-biscuit—a Plum Pudding rose up to rebuke error.

At least, it was going to do so. At present it lay, encased in a stout wooden box and a soldered sarcophagus of tin, at the feet of the habitués of the Bristol Bar, what time they looked upon the box and found it good in their sight. . . .

"You'll dine with us and sample it, I hope, Wavell?" said the Major, eyeing the box ecstatically.

"Thanks," was the reply. "Delighted. . . . May I bring over some brandy to burn round it?"

"Stout fella," said the Major warmly.

"Do we eat it as it is-or fry it, or something, or what?" he added. "I fancy you bake 'em. . . ."

"I believe puddings are boiled, sir," remarked Bertram.

"Yes—I b'lieve you're right, Greene," agreed Major Mallery. . . . "I seem to know the expression, 'boiled plum-pudding.' . . . Yes-boiled plum-pudding. . . ."

"Better tell the cook to boil the bird at once, hadn't we?" suggested Captain Macke.

"Yes," agreed Vereker. "I fancy I've heard our housekeeper at home talk about boiling 'em for *hours*. Hours and hours. . . . Sure of it."

"But s'pose the beastly thing's *bin* boiled already-what then?" asked Augustus. "Bally thing'd *dissolve*, I tell you. . . . Have to drink it. . . ."

"Very nice, too," declared Halke.

"I'd sooner eat pudding and drink brandy, than drink pudding and burn brandy," stated Augustus firmly. "What would we boil it in, anyhow?" he added. "It wouldn't go in a kettle, an' if you let it loose in a dam' great *dekchi* or something, it'd all go to bits. . . ."

"Tie it up in a shirt or something," said Forbes. . . . "What's your idea, Greene-as a man of intellect and education?"

"I'd say boil it," replied Bertram. "I don't believe they *can* be boiled too much. . . . I fancy it ought to be tied up, though, as Clarence suggests, or it might disintegrate, I suppose."

"Who's got a clean shirt or vest or pants or something?" asked the Major. "Or could we ram it into a helmet and tie it down?"

It appeared that no one had a *very* clean shirt, and it happened that nobody spoke up with military promptitude and smart alacrity when Lieutenant Bupendranath Chatterji offered to lend his pillow-case.

"I know," said the Major, in a tone of decision and finality. "I'll send for the cook, tell him there's a plum-pudding, an' he can dam' well serve it hot for dinner as a plum-pudding *ought* to be served-or God have mercy on him, for we will have none. . . ."

And so it was. Although at first the cook protested that the hour being seven and dinner due at seven-thirty, there was not time for the just and proper cooking of a big plum-pudding. But, "To hell with that for a Tale," said the Major, and waved pudding and cook away, with instructions to serve the pudding steaming hot, in half an hour, with a blaze of brandy round it, a sprig of holly stuck in it, and a bunch of mistletoe hung above it.

"And write '*God Bless Our Home*' on the *banda* wall," he added, as a happy after-thought. The cook grinned. He was a Goanese, and a good Christian cheat and liar.

The Bristol Bar settled down again to talk of Home, hunting, theatres, clubs, bars, sport, hotels, and everything else-except religion, women and war. . . .

"Heard about the new lad, Major?" asked Forbes. "Real fuzzy-wuzzy dervish Soudanese. Lord knows how he comes to be in these parts. Smelt war like a camel smells water, I suppose. . . . Got confused ideas about medals though. . . . Tell the tale, Wavell."

"Why-old Isa ibn Yakub, my Sergeant-Major —you know Isa, six-feet-six and nine medals, face like black satin"—began Wavell, "brought me a stout lad-with grey hair-who looked like his twin brother. Wanted to join my Arab Company. He'd come from Berbera to Mombasa in a dhow, and then strolled down here through the jungle. . . . Conversation ran somewhat thus:

"'You want to enlist in my Arab Company, do you? Why?'

"'I want to fight.'

"'Against the *Germanis*?'

"'Anybody.'

"'You know what the pay is?'

"'Yes. It is enough. But I also want my Omdurman medal-like that worn by Isa ibn Yakub.'

"'Oh-you have fought before? And at Omdurman.'

"'Yes. And I want my medal.'

"'You are sure you fought at Omdurman?'

"'Yes. Was I not wounded there and left for dead? Look at this hole through my side, below my arm. I want my medal-like that of Isa ibn Yakub.'

"'How is it that you have not got it, if you fought there as you say?'

"'They would not give it to me. I want you to get it for me.'

"'I do not believe you fought at Omdurman at all.'

"'I did. Was I not shot there?'

"'Were you in a Soudanese Regiment?'

"'No.'

"'What then?'

"'In the army of Our Lord the Mahdi. And I was shot in front of the line of British soldiers who wear petticoats! . . .'"

"Did you take him?" asked the Major, as the laugh subsided.

"Rather!" was the reply. "A lad who fought against us and expects us to give him a medal for it, evidently thinks we are sportsmen, and probably is one himself. I fancy he's done a lot of mixed fighting at different times. . . . Says he knew Gordon. . . ."

The cook, Mess butler, and a deputation of servants approached, salaamed as one man, and held their peace.

"What's up?" asked the Major. "Anyone dead?"

"The Pudding, sah," said the cook, and all the congregation said, "The Pudding."

A painful brooding silence settled upon the Bristol Bar.

"If you've let pi-dogs or *shenzis* or kites eat that pudding, they shall eat you-alive," promised the Major-and he had the air of one whose word is his bond.

"Nossir," replied the cook. "Pudding all gone to damn. Sahib come and see. I am knowing nothing. It is bad."

"*What?*" roared the Major, and rose to his feet.

"Sah, I am a poor man. You are my father and my mother," said the cook humbly, and all the congregation said that they were poor men and that the Major was their father and their mother.

The Major said that the congregation were liars.

"*Bad?*" stammered Forbes. "Puddings can't go *bad*. . . ."

"Oh, Mother, Mother!" said Augustus, and cried, his head upon his knees.

"Life in epitome," murmured Vereker. "*Tout lasse; tout passe; tout casse.*"

"Strike me blind!" said Halke.

"Feller's a purple liar. . . . Must be," opined Berners.

"Beat the lot of them," suggested Macke. "Puddings keep for ever if you handle 'em properly."

"Yes-the brutes haven't treated it kindly," said Augustus, wiping his eyes. "Here, Vereker, you're Provost-Marshal. Serve them so that *they* go bad-and see how they like it."

"It may just have a superficial coating of mould or mildew that can be taken off," said Bertram.

"Let's go an' interview the dam' thing," suggested Augustus. "We can then take measures-or rum."

The Bristol Bar was deserted in the twinkling of an eye as, headed by the Major, the dozen or so of British officers sought out the Pudding, that they might hold an inquest upon it. . . .

Near the cooking-fire in the straw shed behind the Officers' Mess *banda*, upon some boards beside a tin sarcophagus, lay a large green ball, suggestive of a moon made of green cheese.

In silent sorrow the party gazed upon it, stricken and stunned. And the congregation of servants stood afar off and watched.

Suddenly the Major snatched up the gleaming *panga* that had been used for prising open the case and for cutting open the tin box in which the green horror had arrived.

Raising the weapon above his head, the Major smote with all his might. Right in the centre of the Pudding the heavy, sharp-edged blade struck and sank. . . . The Pudding fell in halves, revealing an interior even greener and more horrible than the outside, as a cloud of greenish, smoke-like dust went up to the offended heavens. . . .

"Bury the damned Thing," said the Major, and in his wake the officers of the Butindi garrison filed out, their hearts too full, their stomachs too empty for words.

And the servants buried the Pudding, obeying the words of the Major.

But in the night the Sweeper arose and exhumed the Pudding and ate of it right heartily. And through the night of sorrow he groaned. And at dawn he died. This is the truth.

* * *

Dinner that night was a silent meal, if meal it could be called. No man dared speak to his neighbour for fear of what his neighbour might reply. The only reference to the Pudding was made by Augustus, who remarked, as a servant brought in a dish of roasted maize-cobs, where the Pudding should have come-chicken-feed where should have been Food of the Gods —"I am almost glad poor Murie and Lindsay are so ill that they couldn't possibly have eaten any Pudding in any case. . . . Seems some small compensation to 'em, don't it, poor devils. . . ."

"I do not think Murie will get better," observed Lieutenant Bupendranath Chatterji. "Fever and dysentery, both violent, and I have not proper things. . . ."

The silence seemed to deepen as everybody thought of the two sick men, lying in their dirty clothes, on dirty camp-beds, in leaky grass huts, with a choice of bully-beef, dog-biscuit, coconut and maize as a dysentery diet.

Whose turn next? And what sort of a fight could the force put up if attacked by Africans when all the Indians and Europeans were ill with fever and dysentery? Heaven bless the Wise Man who had kept the African Army of British East Africa so small and had disbanded battalions of the King's African Rifles just before the war. What chance would Indians and white men, who had lived for months in the most pestilential swamp in Africa, have against salted Africans led by Germans especially brought down from the upland health-resorts where they lived? . . .

"Can you give me a little quinine, Chatterji?" asked Augustus. "Got any calomel? I b'lieve my liver's as big as my head to-day. I feel a corner of it right up between my lungs. Stops my breathing sometimes. . . ."

"Oah, yees. Ha! Ha!" said the medical gentleman. "I have a few tablets. I will presently send you some also. . . ."

Next morning Augustus came in last to breakfast.

"Thanks for the quinine tablets, Chatterji," said he. "The hospital orderly brought them in his bare palm. I swallowed all ten, however. What was it-twenty grains?"

"Oah! That was calomel!" replied the worthy doctor, and Augustus arose forthwith and retired, murmuring: "Poignant! *Searching*!"

He had once taken a quarter of a grain of calomel, and it had tied him in knots.

When Bertram visited Murie, Lindsay and Augustus in their respective huts, Augustus seemed the worst of the three. With white face, set teeth, and closed eyes, he lay bunched up, and, from time to time, groaned, "Oh, poignant! *Searching!* . . ."

It being impossible for him to march, it fell to Bertram to take his duty that day, and lead an officers' patrol to reconnoitre a distant village to which, according to information received by the Intelligence Department, a German patrol had just paid a visit. For some reason the place had been sacked and burnt.

It was Bertram's business to discover whether there were any signs of a *boma* having been established by this patrol; to learn anything he could about its movements; whence it had come and whither it had gone; whether the massacre were a punishment for some offence, or just the result of high animal (German) spirits; whether there were many *shambas*, of no further use to slaughtered people, in which the raiders had left any limes, bananas, papai or other fruits, vegetables, or crops; whether any odd chicken or goat had been overlooked, and was wanting a good home; and, in short, to find out anything that could be found out, see all that was to be seen, do anything that might be done. . . . As he marched out of the Fort at the head of a hundred Gurkhas, with a local guide and interpreter, he felt proud and happy, quite reckless, and absolutely indifferent to his fate. He would do his best in any emergency that might arise, and he could do no more. He'd leave it at that.

He'd march straight ahead with a "point" in front of him, and if he was ambushed, he was ambushed.

When they reached the village, he'd deploy into line and send scouts into the place. If he was shot dead —a jolly good job. If he were wounded and left lying for the German *askaris* to find-or the wild beasts at night . . . he turned from the thought.

Anyhow, he'd got good cheery, sturdy Gurkhas with him, and it was a pleasure and an honour to serve with them.

One jungle march is precisely like another-and in three or four hours the little column reached the village, deployed, and skirmished into it, to find it a deserted, burnt-out ruin. *Kultur* had passed that way, leaving its inevitable and unmistakable sign-manual. The houses were only blackened skeletons; the gardens, wildernesses; the byres, cinder-heaps; the fruit-trees, withering wreckage. What had been pools of blood lay here and there, with clumps of feathers, burnt and broken utensils, remains of slaughtered domestic animals and chickens.

Kultur had indeed passed that way. To Bertram it seemed, in a manner, sadder that this poor barbarous little African village should be so treated than that a walled city of supermen should suffer. . . "Is there not more cruelty and villainy in violently robbing a crying child of its twopence than in snatching his gold watch from a portly stockbroker?" thought he, as he gazed around on the scene of ruin, desolation and destruction.

To think of Europeans finding time, energy, and occasion to effect *this* in such a spot, so incredibly remote from their marts and ways and busy haunts! Christians! . . .

Having posted sentries and chosen a spot for rally and defence, he sent out tiny patrols along the few jungle paths that led to the village, and proceeded to see what he could, as there was absolutely no living soul from whom he could learn anything. There was little that the ablest scoutmaster could deduce, save that the place had been visited by a large party of mischievously destructive and brutal ruffians, who wore boots. There was nothing of use or of value that had not been either destroyed or taken. Even papai trees that bore no fruit had been hacked down, and the *panga* had been laid to the root of tree and shrub and sugar-cane. Not a plantain, lime, mango, or papai was to be seen.

Bertram entered one of the least burnt of the well-made huts of thatch and wattle. There was what had been blood on the earthen floor, blackened walls, charred stools, bed-frames and domestic utensils. He felt sick. . . . In a corner was a child's bed of woven string plaited over a carved frame. It would make a useful stool or a resting-place for things which should not lie on the muddy floor of his *banda*. He picked it up. Underneath it was a tiny black hand with pinkish finger-tips. He dropped the bed and was violently sick. *Kultur* had indeed passed that way. . . .

Hurrying out into the sunlight, as soon as he was able to do so, he completed his tour of inspection. There was little of interest and nothing of importance.

Apparently the hamlet had boasted an artist, a sculptor, some village Rodin, before the Germans came to freeze the genial current of his soul. . . . As Bertram studied the handiwork of the absent one, his admiration diminished, however, and he withdrew the "Rodin." The man was an arrant, shameless plagiarist, a scoundrelly pick-brain imitator, a mere copying ape, for, seen from the proper end, as it lay on its back, the clay statue of a woman, without form and void, boneless, wiggly, semi-deliquescent, was an absolutely faithful and shameless reproduction of the justly world-famous Eppstein Venus.

"The man ought to be prosecuted for infringement of copyright," thought Bertram, "if there is any copyright in statues. . . ."

The patrols having returned with nothing to report, Bertram marched back to Butindi and reported it.

Chapter XX
Stein-Brücker Meets Bertram Greene-and Death

And so passed the days at Butindi, with a wearisome monotony of Stand-to, visiting the pickets, going out on patrol, improving the defences of the *boma*, foraging, gathering information, reconnoitring, trying to waylay and scupper enemy patrols, communicating with the other British outposts, surveying and map-making, beating off half-hearted attacks by strong raiding-patrols —all to the accompaniment of fever, dysentery, and growing weakness due to malnutrition and the terrible climate.

To Bertram it all soon became so familiar and normal that it seemed strange to think that he had ever known any other kind of life. His chief pleasure was to talk to Wavell, that most uncommon type of soldier, who was also philosopher, linguist, student, traveller, explorer and ethnologist.

From the others, Bertram learnt that Wavell was, among other things, a second Burton, having penetrated into Mecca and Medina in the disguise of a *haji*, a religious pilgrim, at the very greatest peril of his life. He had also fought, as a soldier of fortune, for the Arabs against the Turks, whom he loathed as only those who have lived under their rule can loathe them. He could have told our Foreign Office many interesting things about the Turk. (When, after he had been imprisoned and brutally treated by them at Sanaa, in the Yemen, he had appealed to our Foreign Office, it had sided rather with the Turk indeed, confirming the Unspeakable One's strong impression that the English were a no-account race, even as the Germans said.) So Wavell had fought against them, helping the Arabs, whom he liked. And when the Great War broke out, he had raised a double company of these fierce, brave, and blood-thirsty little men in Arabia, and had drilled them into fine soldiers. Probably no other Englishman-or European of any sort-could have done this; but then Wavell spoke Arabic like an Arab, knew the Koran almost by heart, and knew his Arabs quite by heart.

That he showed a liking for Bertram was, to Bertram, a very great source of pride and pleasure. When Wavell went out on a reconnoitring-patrol, he went with him if he could get Major Mallery's permission, and the two marched through the African jungle discussing art, poetry, travel, religion, and the ethnological problems of Arabia-followed by a hundred or so Arabs-Arabs who were killing Africans and being killed by Africans, often of their own religion and blood, because a gang of greedy materialists, a few thousand miles away, was suffering from megalomania. . . .

Indeed to Bertram it was food for much thought that in that tiny *boma* in a tropical African swamp, Anglo-Indians, Englishmen, Colonials, Arabs, Yaos, Swahilis, Gurkhas, Rajputs, Sikhs, Marathas, Punjabis, Pathans, Soudanese, Nubians, Bengalis, Goanese, and a mob of assorted *shenzis* of the primeval jungle, should be laying down their lives because, in distant Berlin, a hare-brained Kaiser could not control a crowd of greedy and swollen-headed military aristocrats.

* * *

"Your month's tobacco ration, Greene," said Berners one morning, as he entered Bertram's hut, "and *don't* leave your boots on the floor to attract jigger-fleas —unless you *want* blood-poisoning and guinea-worm —or is it guinea-fowl? Hang them on the wall. . . . And look between your toes every time you take 'em off. Jigger-fleas are, hell, once they get under the skin and lay their eggs. . ." and he handed Bertram some cakes of perfectly black tobacco.

"But, my dear chap, I couldn't smoke *that*," said Bertram, eyeing the horrible stuff askance.

"Of course you can't *smoke* it," replied Berners.

"What can I do with it, then?" he asked.

"Anything you like. . . . I don't care. . . . It's your tobacco ration, and I've issued it to you, and there the matter ends. .. . You can revet your trench parapet with it if you like-or give it to the Wadegos to poison their arrows with. . . . Jolly useful stuff, really. . . . Sole your boots, tile the roof of your *banda*, make a parquet floor round your bed, put it in Chatterji's tea, make a chair seat, lay down a pathway to the Mess, make your mother a teapot-stand, feed the chickens-oh, lots of things. But you can't *smoke* it, of course. . . . You expect too much, my lad. . . ."

"Why do they issue it, then?" asked Bertram.

"Same reason that they issue inedible bully-beef and unbreakable biscuits, I s'pose-contractors must *live*, mustn't they? . . . Be reasonable. . . ."

And again it seemed to the foolish civilian mind of this young man that, since tons of this black cake tobacco (which no British officer ever has smoked or could smoke) cost money, however little-there would be more sense in spending the money on a small quantity of Turkish and Virginian cigarettes that *could* be smoked, by men accustomed to such things, and suffering cruelly for lack of them. Throughout the campaign he saw a great deal of this strong, black cake issued (to men accustomed to good cigarettes, cigars or pipe-mixture), but he never saw any of it smoked. He presented his portion to Ali, who traded it to people of palate and stomach less delicate than those the British Government expects the British officer to possess. . . .

"You look seedy, Greene," observed the Major that same evening, as Bertram dragged himself across the black mud from his *banda* to the Bristol Bar-wondering if he would ever get there.

"Touch of fever, sir. I'm all right," replied he, wishing that everyone and everything were not so nebulous and rotatory.

He did not mention that he had been up all night with dysentery, and had been unable to swallow solid food for three days. (Nor that his temperature was one hundred and four-because he was unaware of the fact.) But he knew that the moment was not far off when all his will-power and uttermost effort would be unable to get him off his camp-bed. He had done his best-but the worst climate in the world, a diet of indigestible and non-nutritious food, taken in hopelessly inadequate quantities; bad water; constant fever; dysentery; long patrol marches; night alarms; high nerve-tension (when a sudden bang followed by a fusillade might mean a desultory attention, a containing action while a more important place was being seriously attacked, or that final and annihilating assault of a big force which was daily expected); and the monotonous, dirty, dreary life in that evil spot, had completely undermined his strength. He was "living on his nerves," and they were nearly gone. "You look like an old hen whose neck has been half-wrung for to-morrow's dinner before she was found to be the wrong one, and reprieved," said Augustus. "You let me make you a real, rousing cock-eye, and then we'll have an *n'goma* [184]-all the lot of us. . . ."

But finding Bertram quite unequal to dealing with a cock-eye or sustaining his part in a tribal dance that should "astonish the natives," he helped Bertram over to his *banda*, took off his boots and got him a hot drink of condensed milk and water laced with ration rum.

In the morning Bertram took his place at Stand-to and professed himself equal to performing his duty, which was that of making a reconnoitring-patrol as far as Paso, where there was another outpost. . . .

Here he arrived in time for tea, and had some with real fresh cow's milk in it; and had a cheery buck with Major Bidwell, Captains Tucker and Bremner, and Lieutenants Innes (another Filbert), Richardson, Stirling, Carroll, and Jones-stout fellows all, and very kind to him. He was very sorry indeed when it was time for him to march back again with his patrol.

He started on the homeward journey, feeling fairly well, for him; but he could never remember how he completed it. . . .

The darkness gathered so rapidly that he had a suspicion that the darkness was within him. Then he found that he was continually running into trees or being brought up short by impenetrable bush that somehow sprang up before him. . . . Also he was talking aloud, and rather surprised at his eloquence. . . . Then he was lying on the ground-being put on his feet again-falling again . . . trying to fight a bothering swarm of *askaris* with a quill pen, while he addressed the House of Commons on the iniquity of allowing Bupendranath Chatterji to be in medical charge of four hundred men with insufficient material to deal with a street accident. . . . Marching again, falling again, being put on his feet again. . . .

* * *

After two days on his camp-bed he was somewhat better, and on the next day he found himself in sole command of the Butindi outpost and a man of responsibility and pride. Urgent messages had taken Major Mallery with half the force in one direction, and Captain Wavell with half the remainder in another.

Suppose there should be an attack while he was in command! He half hoped there would be. . . .

Towards evening an alarm from a sentry and the turning out of the guard brought him running to the main gate, shouting "Stand-to!" as he ran.

Through his glasses he saw that a European and a small party of natives were approaching the *boma*. . . .

The new-comer was an Englishman of the name of Desmont, in the Intelligence Department, who had just made a long and dangerous tour through the neighbouring parts of German East in search of information. Apparently Butindi was the first British outpost that he had struck, as he asked endless questions about others-apparently with a view to visiting them *en route* to the Base Camp. Bertram extended to him such hospitality as Butindi could afford, and gave him all the help and information in his power. He had a very strong conviction that the man was disguised (whether his huge beard was false or not), but he supposed that it was very natural in the case of an Intelligence Department spy, scout, or secret agent. Anyhow, he was most obviously English. . . .

While he sat in the Officers' Mess and talked with the man —a most interesting conversation- Ali Suleiman entered with coco-nuts and a rum-jar. Seeing the stranger, he instantly wheeled about and retired, sending another servant in with the drinks. . . .

After a high-tea of coco-nut, biscuit, bully-beef, and roasted mealie-cobs, Desmont, who looked worn out, asked if he might lie down for a few hours before he "moved off" again. Bertram at once took him to his own *banda* and bade him make himself at home. Five minutes later came Ali with an air of mystery to where Bertram paced up and down the "High Street," and asked if he might speak with him.

"That man a *Germani*, sah!" quoth he. "Spy-man he is. Debbil-man. His own name *not* Desmont *Bwana*, and he is big man in Dar-es-Salaam and Tabora, and knowing all the big *Germani bwanas*. I was his gun-boy and I go with him to *Germani* East. . . . *Bwana* go and shoot him for dead, sah, by damn!"

Bertram sat down heavily on a chop-box.

"*What?*" gasped he.

"Yessah, thank you please. One of those porters not a *shenzi* at all. He Desmont *Bwana's* head boy Murad. Very bad man, sah. Master look in this spy-man's chop-boxes. *Germani* uniform in one-under rice and posho. Master see. . . ."

"You're a fool, Ali," said Bertram.

"Yessah," said Ali, "and Desmont *Bwana* a *Germani* spy-man. Master go an' shoot him for dead while asleep-or tie him to tree till Mallery *Bwana* coming. . . ."

Now what was to be done? Here was a case for swift action by the "strong silent man" type of person who thought like lightning and acted like some more lightning.

If he did nothing and let the man go when he had rested, would his conduct be that of a fool and a weakling who could not act promptly and efficiently on information received-conduct deserving the strongest censure? . . .

And if he arrested and detained one of their own Intelligence Officers, on the word of a native servant, would he ever hear the last of it?

"*Bwana* come and catch this bad man Murad," suggested Ali. "*Bwana* say, '*Jambo*, Murad *ibn Mustapha*! How much rupees Desmont Bwana paying you for spy-work?' and *Bwana* see him jump! By damn, sah! *Bwana* hold revolver ready." . . .

"Does the man know English then?" asked the perturbed and undecided Bertram.

"Yessah-all the same better as I do," was the reply. "And he pretending to be poor *shenzi* porter. He knowing *Germani* too. . . ."

At any rate, he might look into *this*, and if anything suspicious transpired, he could at least prevent Desmont from leaving before Mallery returned.

"Has he seen you?" asked Bertram.

"No, sah, nor has Desmont *Bwana*," was the reply-and Bertram bade Ali show him where the porters were.

They were outside the *boma*, squatting round a cooking-fire near the "lines" of the Kavirondo porters.

Approaching the little group, Bertram drew his revolver and held it behind him. He did not know why he did this. Possibly subconscious memory of Ali's advice, perhaps with the expectation that the men might attack him or attempt to escape; or perhaps a little pleasant touch of melodrama. . . .

"*Jambo, Murad ibn Mustapha!*" he said suddenly. "*Desmont Bwana wants you at once. Go quickly.*"

A man arose immediately and approached him. "Go back and sit down," said Bertram, covering the man with his revolver and speaking in German. He returned and sat down. Evidently he understood English and German and answered to the name of Murad ibn Mustapha! . . .

Ali had spoken the truth and it was now up to Bertram Greene to act wisely, promptly and firmly. This lot should be kept under arrest anyhow. But might not all this be part of Desmont's game as a scout, spy and secret service agent of the British Intelligence Department. Yes, *or* of the German Intelligence Department.

If there was a German uniform in one of the chop-boxes, it might well be a disguise for him to wear in German East. Or it might be his real dress. Anyhow-he shouldn't leave the outpost until Major Mallery returned. .

. . And that was a weak shelving of responsibility. He was in command of the post, and Major Mallery and the other officers with him might be scuppered. It was quite possible that neither the Major's party nor Captain Wavell's might ever get back to Butindi. He strolled over to his *banda* and looked in.

Desmont was evidently suffering from digestive troubles or a bad conscience, for his face was contorted, he moved restlessly and ground his teeth.

Suddenly he screamed like a woman and cried:

"*Ach! Gott in Himmel! Nein, Nein! Ich . . .*"

Bertram drew his revolver. The man was a German. Englishmen don't talk German in their sleep.

The alleged Desmont moaned.

"*Zu müde*," he said. "*Zu müde.*" . . .

Bertram sat down on his camp-stool and watched the man.

* * *

The Herr Doktor Karl Stein-Brücker had made a name for himself in German East, as one who knew how to manage the native. This in a country where they all pride themselves on knowing how to manage the native-how to put the fear of Frightfulness and *Kultur* into his heart. He had once given a great increase to a growing reputation by flogging a woman to death, on suspicion of unfaithfulness. He had wielded the *kiboko* with his own (literally) red right hand until he was aweary, and had then passed the job on to Murad ibn Mustapha, who was very slow to tire. But even he had had to be kept to it at last. . . .

"*Noch nichte!*" had the Herr Doktor said, "*Not yet!*" as Murad wished to stop, and

"*Ganz klein wenig!*" as the brawny arm dropped. "*Just a little more.*" . . .

It had been a notable and memorable punishment-but the devil of it was that whenever the Herr Doktor got run down or over-ate himself, he had a most terrible nightmare, wherein Marayam, streaming with blood, pursued him, caught him, and flogged him. And when she tired, he was doomed to urge her on to further efforts. After screaming with agony, he must moan "*Zu müde! Zu müde!*" and then-when she would have stopped —"*Noch nichte!*" and "*Ganz klein wenig!*" so that she began afresh. Then he must struggle, break free, leap at her-and find himself sweating, weeping and trembling beside his bed.

Presently the moaning sleeper cried "*Noch nichte!*" and a little later "*Ganz klein wenig!*" —and then with a scream and a struggle, leapt from the camp cot and sprang at Bertram, whose revolver straightway went off. With a cough and a gurgle the *soi-disant* Desmont collapsed with a ·450 service bullet through his heart.

When Major Mallery returned at dawn he found a delirious Second-Lieutenant Greene (and a dead European, and a wonderful tale from one Ali Suleiman. . . .)

With a temperature of 105·8 he did not seem likely to live. . . .

Whether Bertram Greene lived or died, however, he had, albeit ignorantly, avenged the cruel wrong done to his father. . . . He-the despised and rejected one-had avenged Major Hugh Walsingham Greene. Fate plays some queer tricks and Time's whirligig performs some quaint gyrations!

Part III
The Baking of Bertram By Love

Chapter I
Mrs. Stayne-Brooker Again

Luckily for himself, Second-Lieutenant Bertram Greene was quite unconscious when he was lifted from his camp-bed into a stretcher by the myrmidons of Mr. Chatterji and dispatched, carriage paid, to M'paga. What might happen to him there was no concern of Mr. Chatterji's — which was the important point so far as that gentleman was concerned.

Unconscious he remained as the four Kavirondo porters, the stretcher on their heads, jogged along the jungle path in the wake of Ali and the three other porters who bore his baggage. Behind the stretcher-bearers trotted four more of their brethren who would relieve them of their burden at regular intervals.

Ali was in command, and was also in a hurry, for various reasons, including prowling enemy patrols and his master's dire need of help. He accordingly set a good pace and kept the "low niggers" of his party to it by fabulous promises, hideous threats, and even more by the charm of song-part song in fact. Lifting up his powerful voice he delivered in deep diapason a mighty

"*Ah-Nah-Nee-Nee! Ah-Nah-Nee-Nee!*"

to which all the congregation responded

"*Umba Jo-eel! Umba Jo-eel*"

as is meet and right to do.

And when, after a few hundred thousand repetitions of this, in strophe and antistrophe, there seemed a possibility that restless and volatile minds desiring change might seek some new thing, Ali sang

"*Hay-Ah-Mon-Nee! Hay-Ah-Mon-Nee!*"

which is quite different, and the jogging, sweating congregation, with deep earnestness and conviction, took up the response:

"*Tunk-Tunk-Tunk-Tunk!*"

and all fear of the boredom of monotony was gone-especially as, after a couple of hours of this, you could go back to the former soulful and heartsome Threnody, and begin again. But if they got no forrader with the concert they steadily got forrader with the journey, as their loping jog-trot ate up the miles.

And, in time to their regular foot-fall and chanting, the insensible head of the white man rolled from side to side unceasingly. . . .

Unconscious he still was when the little party entered the Base Camp, and Private Henry Hall remarked to Private John Jones:

"That there bloke's gone West all right but 'e ain't gone long. . . . You can see 'e's dead becos 'is 'ead's a waggling and you can see 'e ain't bin dead *long* becos 'is 'ead's a waggling. . . ."

And Private John Jones, addressing the speaker as Mister Bloomin'-Well Sherlock 'Olmes, desired that he would cease to chew the fat.

Steering his little convoy to the tent over which the Red Cross flew, Ali handed over his master and the cleft stick holding Major Mallery's letter, to Captain Merstyn, R.A.M.C., and then stood by for orders.

It appeared that the *Barjordan* was off M'paga, that a consignment of sick and wounded was just going on board, and that Second-Lieutenant Greene could go with them. . . .

That night Bertram was conveyed out to sea in a dhow (towed by a petrol-launch from the *Barjordan*), taken on board that ship, and put comfortably to bed. The next night he was in hospital at Mombasa and had met Mrs. Stayne-Brooker.

* * *

As, thanks to excellent nursing, he very slowly returned to health and strength, Bertram began to take an increasing interest in the very charming and very beautiful woman whom he had once seen and admired at the Club, who daily took his temperature, brought his meals, administered his medicine, kept his official chart, shook up his pillows, put cooling hands upon his forehead, found him books to read, talked to him at times, attended the doctor on his daily visits, and superintended the brief labours of the Swahili youth who was ward-boy and house-maid on that floor of the hospital.

Before long, the events of the day were this lady's visits, and, on waking, he would calculate the number of hours until she would enter his room and brighten it with her presence. He had never seen so sweet, kind, and gentle a face. It was beautiful too, even apart from its sweetness, kindness and gentleness. He was very thankful when he found himself no longer too weak to turn his head and follow her with his eyes, as she moved about the room. It was indescribably delightful to have a woman, and such a woman, about one's sick bed-after negro servants, Indian orderlies, *shenzi* stretcher-bearers, and Bengali doctors. How his heart swelled with gratitude as she laid her cool hand on his forehead, or raised his head and gave him a cooling drink. . . . But how sad she looked! . . . He hated to see her putting up the mosquito-curtains that covered the big frame-work, like the skeleton of a room, in which his bed stood, and which, at night, formed a mosquito-proof room-within-a-room, and provided space for his bedside chair, table and electric-lamp, as well as for the doctor and nurse, if necessary.

One morning he sat up and said:

"*Please* let me do that, Sister —I hate to see you working for me-though I love to see *you* . . ." and then had been gently pushed back on to his pillow as, with a laugh, Mrs. Stayne-Brooker said:

"That's what I'm here for-to work I mean," and patted his wasted hand. (He *was* such a dear boy, and so appreciative of what one could do for him. It made one's heart ache to see him such a wasted skeleton.)

The time came when he could sit in a long chair with leg-rest arms, and read a book; but he found that most of his time was spent in thinking of the Sister and in the joys of retrospection and anticipation. He had to put aside, quite resolutely, all thought of the day when he would be declared fit for duty and be "returned to store." Think of a *banda* at Butindi and of this white room with its beautiful outlook across the strait to the palm-feathered shore; think of Ali as one's cup-bearer and of this sweet angelic Englishwoman. . . . Better not think of it at all. . . .

It was quite a little shock to him, one day, to notice that she wore a wedding-ring. . . . He had never thought of that. . . . He felt something quite like a little twinge of jealousy. . . . He was sure the man must be a splendid fellow though, or she would never have married him. . . . How old would she be? It was no business of his, and it was not quite gentlemanly to speculate on such a subject-but somehow he had not thought of her as "an old married woman." Not that married women are necessarily older than unmarried women. . . . A silly expression —"old" married women. He had imagined her to be about his own generation so to speak. Possibly a *little* older than himself-in years-but years don't make age really. . . . Fancy her being married! Well, well, well! . . . But what did that matter-she was just as much the charming and beautiful woman for whom he would have laid down his life in sheer gratitude. . . .

* * *

A man gets like this after fever. He is off his balance, weak, neurasthenic, and devoid of the sense of proportion. He waxes sentimental, and is to be forgiven.

* * *

But there is not even this excuse for Mrs. Stayne-Brooker.

* * *

She began by rather boring her daughter, Eva, about her new patient-his extreme gratitude, his charming ways and thoughts, his true gentleness of nature, his delightful views, the *niceness* of his mind, the likeableness of him. . . . She wondered aloud as to whether he had a mother-she must be a very nice woman. She wondered in silence as to whether he had a wife-she must be a very happy woman. . . . How old was he? . . . It was so hard to tell with these poor fellows, brought in so wasted with fever and dysentery; and rank wasn't much guide to age nowadays. He *might* be. . . . Well-he'd be up and gone before long, and she'd never see him again, so what was the good of wondering. . . . And she continued to wonder. . . . And then, from rather boring Miss Stayne-Brooker with talk about Lieutenant Greene she went to the extreme, and never mentioned him at all.

For, one day, with an actual gasp of horrified amazement, she found that she had suddenly realised that possibly the poets and novelists were not so wrong as she had believed, and that there *might* be such a thing as the Love-they hymned and described-and that Peace and Happiness might be its inseparable companions. . . . She would read her Browning, Herrick, Swinburne, Rosetti again, her Dante, her Mistral, and some of those plays and poems of Love that the world called wonderful, beautiful, true, for she had an idea that she might see glimmerings of wonder, beauty and truth in them —*now*. . . .

But then-how absurd! —at *her* age. Of course she would not read them again! At *her* age! . . .

And proceeded to do so at *her* Dangerous Age. . . .

Strange that *his* name should be Green or Greene-he was the fifth person of that name whom she had met since she left Major Walsingham Greene, eighteen years ago. . . .

Chapter II
Love

All too soon for two people concerned, Doctor Mowbray, the excellent Civil Surgeon of Mombasa, in whose hospital Bertram was, decided that that young gentleman might forthwith be let loose on ticket-of-leave between the hours of ten and ten for a week or two, preparatory to his discharge from hospital for a short spell of convalescence-leave before rejoining his regiment. . . .

"I'll call for you and take you for a drive after lunch," said Mrs. Stayne-Brooker, "and then you shall have tea with me, and we'll go over to the Club and sit on the verandah. You mustn't walk much, your first day out."

"I'm going to run miles," said Bertram, smiling up into her face and taking her hand as she stood beside his chair —a thing no other patient had dared to do or would have been permitted to do. ("He was such a dear boy-one would never dream of snubbing him or snatching away a hand he gratefully stroked-it would be like hitting a baby or a nice friendly dog. . . .")

"Then you'll be ill again at once," rejoined Mrs. Stayne-Brooker, giving the hand that had crept into hers a little chiding shake.

"Exactly . . . and prolong my stay here. . ." said Bertram, and his eyes were very full of kindness and gratitude as they met eyes that were also very full.

("What a sweet, kind, good woman she was! And what a cruel wrench it would be to go away and perhaps never see her again. . . .")

He went for his drive with Mrs. Stayne-Brooker in a car put at her disposal, for the purpose, by the Civil Surgeon; and found he was still very weak and that it was nevertheless good to be alive.

At tea he met Miss Stayne-Brooker, and, for a moment, his breath was taken away by her beauty and her extraordinary likeness to her mother.

He thought of an opened rose and an opening rose-bud (exactly alike save for the "open" and "opening" difference), on the same stalk. . . . It was wonderful how alike they were, and how young Mrs. Stayne-Brooker looked-away from her daughter. . . . The drive-and-tea programme was repeated almost daily, with variations, such as a stroll round the golf-course, as the patient grew stronger. . . . And daily Bertram saw the very beautiful and fascinating Miss Stayne-Brooker and daily grew more and more grateful to Mrs. Stayne-Brooker. He was grateful to her for so many things-for her nursing, her hospitality, her generous giving of her time; her kindness in the matter of lending him books (the books she liked best, prose works *and* others); her kind interest in him and his career, ambitions, tastes, views, hopes and fears; for her being the woman she was and for brightening his life as she had, not to mention saving it; and, above all, he was grateful to her for having such a daughter. . . . He told her that he admired Miss Stayne-Brooker exceedingly, and she did not tell him that Miss Stayne-Brooker did not admire him to the same extent. . . . She was a little sorry that her daughter did not seem as enthusiastic about him as she herself was, for we love those whom we admire to be admired. But she realised that a chit of a girl, fresh from a Cheltenham school, was not to be expected to appreciate a man like this one, a scholar, an artist to his finger-tips, a poet, a musician, a man who had read everything and could talk interestingly of anything —a man whose mind was a sweet and pleasant storehouse —a *kind* man, a gentleman, a man who, thank God, *needed* one, and yet to whom one's ideas were of as much interest as one's face and form. Of course, the average "Cheerioh" subaltern, whose talk was of dances and racing and sport, would, very naturally, be of more interest to a callow girl than this man whose mind (to Mrs. Stayne-Brooker) a kingdom was, and who had devoted to the study of music, art, literature, science, and the drama, the time that the other man had given to the pursuit of various hard and soft balls, inoffensive quadrupeds, and less inoffensive bipeds.

Thus Mrs. Stayne-Brooker, addressing, in imagination, a foolishly unappreciative Eva Stayne-Brooker.

* * *

As she and her daughter sat at dinner on the verandah which looked down on to Vasco da Gama Street, one evening, a month later, her Swahili house-boy brought Mrs. Stayne-Brooker a message. . . . A *shenzi* was without, and he had a *chit* which he would give into no hands save those of Mrs. Stayne-Brooker herself.

It was the escaped Murad ibn Mustapha, in disguise.

On hearing his news, she did what she had believed people only did in books. She fell down in a faint and lay as one dead.

* * *

Miss Stayne-Brooker tried to feel as strongly as her mother evidently did, but signally failed, her father having been an almost complete stranger to her. She was a little surprised that the blow should have been so great as to strike her mother senseless, for there had certainly been nothing demonstrative about her attitude to her husband-to say the least of it. She supposed that married folk got like that . . . loved each other all right but never showed it at all. . . . Nor had what she had seen of her father honestly impressed her with the feeling that he was a *very* lovable person. Neither before dinner nor after it-when he was quite a different man. . . .

Still-here was her mother, knocked flat by the news of his death, and now lying on her bed in a condition which seemed to vary between coma and hysteria. . . .

Knocked flat—(and yet, from time to time, she murmured, "Thank God! Oh, thank God!"). Queer!

* * *

When Mr. Greene called next day, Miss Eva received him in the morning-sitting-drawing-room and told him the sad news. Her father had died. . . . He was genuinely shocked.

"Oh, your poor, *poor* mother!" said he. "I am grieved for her"—and sat silent, his face looking quite sad. Obviously there was no need for sympathy with Miss Eva as she frankly confessed that she scarcely knew her father and felt for him only as one does for a most distant relation, whom one has scarcely ever seen.

With a request that she would convey his most heart-felt condolence and deepest sympathy to her mother, he withdrew and returned to the Mombasa Hotel, where he was now staying, an ex-convalescent awaiting orders. . . He had hoped for an evening with Eva. That evening the *Elymas* steamed into Kilindini harbour and Bertram, strolling down to the pier, met Captain Murray, late Adjutant of the One Hundred and Ninety-Ninth, and Lieutenant Reginald Macteith, both of whom had just come ashore from her.

He wrung Murray's hand, delighted to see him, and congratulated him on his escape from regimental duty, and shook hands with Macteith.

"By Jove, Cupid, you look ten years older than when I saw you last," said Murray, laying his hand on Bertram's shoulder and studying his face. "I should hardly have known you. . . ."

"Quite a little man now," remarked Macteith, and proceeded to enquire as to where was the nearest and best Home-from-Home in Mombasa, where one could have A-Drink-and-a-Little-Music-what-what?

"I am staying at the Mombasa Hotel," said Bertram coldly, to which Macteith replied that he hoped it appreciated its privilege.

Bertram felt that he hated Macteith, but also had a curious sense that that young gentleman had either lost in stature or that he, Bertram, had gained. . . . Anyhow he had seen War, and, so far, Macteith had not. He had no sort of fear of anything Macteith could say or do-and he'd welcome any opportunity of demonstrating the fact. . . . Dirty little worm! Chatting gaily with Murray, he took them to the Mombasa Club and there found a note from Mrs. Stayne-Brooker asking him to come to tea on the morrow.

* * *

"I won't attempt to offer condolence nor express my absolute sympathy, Mrs. Stayne-Brooker," said Bertram as he took her hand and led her to her favourite settee.

"Don't," said she.

"My heart aches for you, though," he added.

"It need not," replied Mrs. Stayne-Brooker, and, as Bertram looked his wonder at her enigmatic reply and manner, she continued:

"I will not pretend to *you*. I will be honest. Your heart need not ache for me at all-because mine sings with relief and gratitude and joy. . . ."

Bertram's jaw fell in amazement. He felt inexpressibly shocked.

Or was it that grief had unhinged the poor lady's mind?

"I am going to say to you what I have never said to a living soul, and will never say again. . . . I have never even said it to myself. . . . *I hated him most utterly and most bitterly.* . . ."

Bertram was more shocked than he had ever been in his life. . . This was terrible! . . . He wanted to say, "Oh, hush!" and get up and go away.

"I could not *tell* you how I hated him," continued Mrs. Stayne-Brooker, "for he spoilt my whole life. . . . I am not going into details nor am I going to say one word against him beyond that. I repeat that he *made* me loathe him-from my very wedding-day . . . and I leave you to judge. . . ."

Bertram judged.

He was very young-much younger than his years-and he judged as the young do, ignorantly, harshly, cruelly. . . .

What manner of woman, after all, was this, who spoke of her dead husband? Of her own husband-scarcely cold in his grave. Of her *husband* of all people in the world! . . . He could have wept with the shame and misery of it, the disillusionment, the shattering blow which she herself had dealt at the image and idol that he had set up in his heart and gratefully worshipped.

He looked up miserably as he heard the sound of a sob in the heavy silence of the room. She was weeping bitterly, shaken from head to foot with the violence of her-her-what could it be? not grief for her husband of course. Did she weep for the life that he had "spoilt" as she expressed it? Was it because of her wasted opportunities for happiness, the years that the locust had eaten, the never-to-return days of her youth, when joy and gaiety should have been hers?

What could he say to her? —save a banal "Don't cry"? There was nothing to say. He did not know when he had felt so miserable and uncomfortable. . . .

"It is over," she said suddenly, and dried her tears; but whether she alluded to the unhappiness of her life with her husband, or to her brief tempest of tears, he did not know.

What could he say to her? . . . It was horrible to see a woman cry. And she had been *so* good to him. She had revived his interest in life when through the miasma of fever he had seen it as a thing horrible and menacing, a thing to flee from. How could he comfort her? She had made no secret of the fact that she liked him exceedingly, and that to talk to him of the things that matter in Life, Art, Literature, Music, History, was a pleasure akin to that of a desert traveller who comes upon an inexhaustible well of pure water. Perhaps she liked him so well that he could offer, acceptably, that Silent Sympathy that is said to be so much finer and more efficacious than words. . . . Could he? . . Could he? . . .

Conquering his sense of repulsion at her attitude toward her newly dead husband, and remembering all he owed to her sweet kindness, he crossed to her settee, knelt on one knee beside her, took her hand, and put it to his lips without a word. She would understand-and he would go.

With a little sobbing cry, Mrs. Stayne-Brooker snatched her hand from him, and, throwing her arms about his neck, pressed her lips to his-her face was transfigured as with a great light-the light of the knowledge that the poets had told the great and wondrous truth when they sang of Love as the Greatest Thing-and sung but half the truth. All that she longed for, dreamed of, yearned over-and disbelieved-was true and had come to pass. . . .

She looked no older than her own daughter-and forgot that she was a woman of thirty-seven years, and that the man who knelt in homage (the moment that she was free to receive his homage!) *might* be but little over thirty.

She did not understand-but perhaps, in that moment, received full compensation for her years of misery, and her marred, thwarted, wasted womanhood.

Oh, thank God; thank God, that he loved her . . . she could not have borne it if . . .

* * *

Glad that he had succeeded in comforting her, slightly puzzled and vaguely stirred, he arose and went out, still without a word.

* * *

Returning to his hotel, he found a telegram ordering him to proceed "forthwith" to a place called Soko Nassai *via* Voi and Taveta, and as "forthwith" means the next train, and the next train to Voi on the Uganda Railway went in two hours, he yelled for Ali, collected his kit, paid his Club bill and got him to the railway station without having time or opportunity to make any visits of farewell. That he had to go without seeing Miss Eva again troubled him sorely, much more so than he would have thought possible.

In fact he thought of her all night as he lay on the long bed-seat of his carriage in a fog of fine red dust, instead of sleeping or thinking of what lay before him at Taveta, whence, if all or any of the Club gossip were true, he would be embarking upon a very hard campaign, and one of "open" fighting, too. This would be infinitely more interesting than the sit-in-the-mud trench warfare, but it was not of this that he found himself thinking so much as of the length and silkiness of Miss Eva's eyelashes, the tendrils of hair at her neck, the perfection of her lips, and similar important matters. He was exceedingly glad that he was going to be attached to a Kashmiri regiment, because it was composed of Dogras and Gurkhas, and he liked Gurkhas exceedingly, but he was ten thousand times more glad that there was a Miss Eva Stayne-Brooker in the world, that she was in Mombasa, that he could think of her there, and, best of all, that he could return and see her there when the war was o'er-and he sang aloud:

"When the war is o'er,
We'll part no more."

No-damn it all-one couldn't sing "at Ehren on the Rhine," after the German had shown his country to be the home of the most ruffianly, degraded, treacherous and despicable brute the world has yet produced; and, turning over with an impatient jerk, he tipped a little mound of drifted red dust and sand into his mouth and his song turned to dust and ashes and angry spluttering. *Absit omen.*

At Taveta, a name on a map and a locality beneath wooded hills, Bertram found a detachment of his regiment, and was accepted by his brother-officers as a useful-looking and very welcome addition to their small Mess. He was delighted to renew acquaintance with Augustus and with the Gurkha Subedar-whom he had last seen at M'paga. Here he also found the 29th Punjabis, the 130th Baluchis, and the 2nd Rhodesians. In the intervals of thinking of Miss Eva, he thought what splendid troops they looked, and what a grand and fortunate man he was to be one of their glorious Brigade.

When he smelt the horrible fever smell of the pestilential Lumi swamp, he hoped Miss Eva would not get fever in Mombasa.

When he feasted his delighted eyes on Kilimanjaro, on the rose-flushed snows and glaciers of Kibo and Mawenzi, their amazing beauty was as the beauty of her face, and he walked uplifted and entranced.

When the daily growing Brigade was complete, and marched west through alternating dense bush and open prairie of moving grass, across dry sandy nullahs or roughly bridged torrents, he marched with light heart and untiring body, neither knowing nor caring whether the march were long or short.

When Gussie Augustus Gus said it was dam' hot and very thoughtless conduct of Jan Smuts to make innocent and harmless folk walk on their feet at midday, Bertram perceived that it *was* hot, though he hadn't noticed it. His spirit had been in Mombasa, and his body had been unable to draw its attention to such minor and sordid details as dust, heat, thirst, weariness and weakness.

The ice-cold waters of the Himo River, which flows from the Kilimanjaro snows to the Pangani, reminded him of the coolness of her firm young hands.

As the Brigade camped on the ridge of a green and flower-decked hill looking across the Pangani Valley, to the Pare Hills, a scene of fertile beauty, English in its wooded rolling richness, he thought of her with him in England; and as the rancid smell of a frying *ghee*, mingled with the acrid smell of wood smoke, was wafted from where Gurkha, Punjabi, Pathan and Baluchi cooked their *chapattis* of *atta*, he thought of her in India with him. . . .

Day after day the Brigade marched on, and whether it marched between impenetrable walls of living green that formed a tunnel in which the red dust floated always, thick, blinding and choking, or whether it marched across great deserts of dried black peat over which the black dust hung always, thicker, more blinding and more choking-it was the same to Second-Lieutenant Bertram Greene, as he marched beside the sturdy little warriors of his regiment. His spirit marched through the realms of Love's wonderland rather than through deserts and jungles, and the things of the spirit are more real, and greater than those of the flesh.

For preference he marched alone, alone with his men that is, and not with a brother officer, that he might be spared the necessity of conversation and the annoyance of distraction of his thoughts. For miles he would trudge beside the Subedar in companionly silence. He grew very fond of the staunch little man to whom duty was a god. . . .

When the Brigade reached Soko Nassai it joined the Division which (co-operating with Van Deventer's South African Division, then threatening Tabora and the Central Railway from Kondoa Irangi) in three months conquered German East Africa-an almost adequate force having been dispatched at last. It consisted of the 2nd Kashmir Rifles, 28th Punjabis, 130th Baluchis, the 2nd Rhodesians, a squadron of the 17th Cavalry, the 5th and 6th Batteries of the S.A. Field Artillery, a section of the 27th Mountain Battery, and a company of the 61st Pioneers, forming the First East African Brigade. There were also the 25th Royal Fusiliers, the M.I. and machine-guns of the Loyal North Lancashire Regiment, the East African Mounted Rifles, a Howitzer Battery of Cornwall Territorials, "Z" Signalling Company, a "wireless" section, and a fleet of armoured cars. In reserve were the 5th and 6th South Africans.

Few divisions have ever done more than this one did-under the greatest hardships in one of the worst districts in the world.

Its immediate task was to clear the Germans from their strong positions in the Pare and Usambara Mountains, and to seize the railway to Tanga on the coast, a task of all but superhuman difficulty, as it could only be accomplished by the help of a strong force making a flanking march through unexplored roadless virgin jungle, down the Pangani valley, the very home of fever, where everything would depend upon efficient transport-and any transport appeared impossible. How could motor transport go through densest trackless bush, or horse and bullock transport where horse-sickness and tsetse fly forbade?

The First Brigade made the Pangani march and turning movement, performing the impossible, and with it went Second-Lieutenant Bertram Greene, head in air and soul among the stars, his heart full of a mortal tenderness and caught up in a great divine uplifting,

Chapter III
Love and War

As he marched on, day after day, his thoughts moving to the dogged tramp of feet, the groan of laden bullock-carts, the creak of mule packs, the faint rhythmic tap of tin cup on a bayonet hilt, the clank of a swinging chain end, through mimosa thorn and dwarf scrub, dense forest, mephitic swamp or smitten desert, ever following the river whose waters gave life and sudden death, the river to leave which was to die of thirst, and to stay by which was to die of fever, this march which would have been a nightmare of suffering, was merely a dream—a dream from which he would awake to arise and go to Mombasa. . . .

"I always thought you had guts, Greene," said Augustus coarsely, one night, as they laid their weary bones beneath a tarpaulin stretched between two carts. "I always thought you had 'em beneath your gentle-seeming surface, so to speak-but dammy, you're *all* guts. . . . You're a blooming whale, to march. . . . Why the devil don't you growl and grumble like a Christian gentleman, eh? . . . I hate you 'strong silent men.' . . . Dammitall-you march along with a smug smile on your silly face! . . . You're a perfect tiger, you know. . . . Don't like it. . . . Colonel will be saying your 'conduct under trying circumstances is an example and inspiration to all ranks.' . . . Will when you're dead anyhow. . . . Horrid habit. . . . You go setting an example to *me*, and I'll bite you in the stomach, my lad. . . ."

Bertram laughed and looked out at the great stars-blue diamonds sprinkled on black velvet- and was very happy.

Was he tired? Everybody else was, so he supposed he must be.

Was he hungry? Yes-for the sight of a face. . . . Oh, the joy of shutting his eyes and calling it to memory's eye, and of living over again every moment spent in her presence!

He realised, with something like amazement, that Love grows and waxes without the food and sustenance of the loved one's real presence. He loved her more than he had done at Mombasa. Had he really *loved* her at Mombasa at all? Certainly not as he did now-when he thought of nothing else, and performed all his duties and functions mechanically and was only here present in the mere dull and unfeeling flesh. . . .

As the column halted where, across an open glade, the menacing sinister jungle might at any moment burst into crackling life, as machine-gun and rifle-fire crashed out to mow men down, he felt but mild interest, little curiosity and no vestige of fear. He would do his duty to the utmost, of course, but-how sweet to get a wound that would send him back to where she was!

As the column crossed the baked mud of former floods, and his eye noted the foot-prints, preserved in it, of elephant, lion, large and small antelope, rhinoceros and leopard, these wonders moved him to but faint interest, for he had something a thousand times more interesting to think of. Things that would have thrilled him before this great event, this greatest event, of his life-such as the first complete assembling of the Brigade in the first sufficient open space it had yet encountered-by the great spare rock, Njumba-ya-Mawe, the House of Stone, on which General Jan Smuts himself climbed to see them pass; the sight of his own Kashmiris cutting a way straight through the bush with their *kukris*; the glimpses of animals he had hitherto only seen in zoological gardens; the faint sound of far-distant explosions where the retiring Germans were blowing up their railway culverts and bridges; the sight of deserted German positions with their trenches littered with coco-nut shells, husks, and mealie-cobs, their cunning machine-gun positions, and their officers' *bandas* littered with empty tins and bottles; the infernal hullabaloo when a lion got within the perimeter one night and stampeded the mules; the sudden meeting with a little band of ragged emaciated prisoners, some German patrol captured by the Pathan *sowars* of the 17th or the Mounted Infantry of the Lancashires; the passing, high in air, of a humming yellow aeroplane; the distant rattle of machine-guns, like the crackling of a forest fire, as the advance-guard came in sight of some retiring party of Kraut's force; the hollow far-off boom of some big gun brought from the *Konigsberg*—dismantled and deserted in the Rufigi river-as it fired from Sams upon the frontal feint of the 2nd Brigade's advance down the railway or at the column of King's African Rifles from M'buyini-these things which would have so thrilled him once, now left him cold-mere trifles that impinged but lightly on his outer consciousness. . . .

"You're a blasé old bloke, aren't you, Greene?" said the puzzled Augustus. "Hardened old warrior like you can't be expected to take much interest in a dull game like war, unless they let you charge guns and squares with cavalry, what? Sport without danger's no good to you, what? You wait till you find a dam' great Yao *askari* looking for your liver with a bayonet, my lad. . . . See you sit up and take notice then, what? Garn! You patient, grinning Griselda . . ." and so forth.

But, one evening, as the column approached the South Pare Mountains, near Mikocheni, Bertram "sat up and took notice," very considerable notice, as with a rush and a roar and a terrific explosion, a column of black smoke and dust shot up to the sky when a shell burst a few score yards away-the first of a well-placed series of four-point-one high explosive shells.

The column halted and lay low in the bush. Further progress would be more wholesome in the dark.

"Naval guns: over seven miles away: dam' good shootin'," quoth Augustus coolly, and with the air of a connoisseur, adding, "and we've got nothing that could carry half-way to 'em. I'm goin' 'ome. . . ."

Bertram, everything driven from his mind but the thought that he was under fire, was rejoiced to find himself as cool as Augustus, who suddenly remarked, "I'm not as 'appy as you look, and I don't b'lieve you are either" —as the column hurriedly betook itself from the position-betraying dust of the open to the shelter of the scrub that lay between it and the river, the river so beautiful in the rose-glow and gold of evening, and so deadly to all who could not crawl beneath the sheltering mosquito curtains as the light faded from the sinister-lovely scene.

* * *

Next day the column found one of the enemy's prepared positions in the dense bush, and it was not, as hitherto, a deserted one. The first intimation was, as usual in the blind, fumbling fighting of East Africa, a withering blast of Maxim fire, and terribly heavy casualties for a couple of minutes.

At one moment, nothing at all-just a weary, plodding line of hot, weary and dusty men, crossing a *dambo*, all hypnotised from thought of danger by fatigue, familiarity and normal immunity; at the next moment, slaughter, groans, brief confusion, burst upon burst of withering fire, a line of still or writhing forms.

It is an inevitable concomitant of such warfare, wherein one feels for one's enemy rather than looks for him, and a hundred-mile march is a hundred-mile ambush.

This particular nest of machine-guns and large force of *askaris* was utterly invisible at a few yards' range, and, at a few yards' range, it blasted the head and flank of the column.

Instinctively the war-hardened Sepoys who survived dropped to earth and opened fire at the section of bush whence came the hail of death —a few scattered rifles against massed machine-guns and a battalion of highly trained *askaris*, masters of jungle-craft. As, still firing, they crawled backward to the cover of the scrub on the side of the glade opposite to the German position, the companies who had been marching behind them deployed and painfully skirmished toward the concealed enemy, halting to fire volleys into the dense bush in the probable direction, striving to keep touch with their flanking companies, to keep something like a line, to keep direction, to keep moving forward, and to keep a sharp look-out for the enemy who, having effected their surprise and caught the leading company in the open, had vanished silently, machine-guns and all, from the position which had served their purpose. . . .

A few feet in advance of his men as they skirmished forward, extended to one pace interval, Bertram, followed by the Subedar, crossed the line of dead and wounded caught by the first blast of fire. He saw two men he knew, lieutenants of the 130th Baluchis, who had evidently been made a special target by the concealed riflemen and machine-gunners. He saw another with his leg bent in the middle at right-angles —and realised with horror that it was bent *forward*. Also that the wounded man was Terence Brannigan. . . .

He feared he was going to be sick, and shame himself before his Gurkhas as his eye took in the face of a Baluchi whose lower jaw had been removed as though by a surgeon's knife. He noted subconsciously how raven-blue the long oiled hair of these Pathans and Baluchis shone in the sun, their *puggris* having fallen off or been shot away. The machine-guns must have over-sighted and then lowered, instead of the reverse, as everybody seemed to be hit in the head, neck or chest except Brannigan, whose knee was so shattered that his leg bent forward until his boot touched his belt-with an effect as of that of a sprawled rag doll. Probably he had been hit by one of the great soft-nosed slugs with which the swine armed their *askaris*. The hot, heavy air reeked with blood. Some of the wounded lay groaning; some sat and smiled patiently as they held up shattered arms or pressed thumbs on bleeding legs; some rose and staggered and fell, rose and staggered and fell, blindly going nowhere. One big, grey-eyed Pathan lustily sang his almost national song, "*Zakhmi Dil*" —"The Wounded Heart," but whether in bravado, delirium, sheer *berserk* joy of battle, or quiet content at getting a wound that would give him a rest, change and privileges, Bertram did not know.

"*Stretcher-bearer log ainga bhai*," [185] said Bertram, as he passed him sitting there singing in a pool of blood.

"*Béshak Huzoor*," replied the man with a grin, "*ham baitha hai*," [186] and resumed his falsetto nasal dirge. Another, crouching on all fours with his face to the ground, suddenly raised that grey-green, dripping face, and crawled towards him. Bertram saw that he was trailing his entrails as he moved. To avoid halting and being sick at this shocking sight, he rushed forward to the edge of the scrub whence all this havoc had been wrought, his left hand pressed over his mouth, all his will-power concentrated upon conquering the revolt of his stomach.

Thinking he was charging an enemy, his men dashed forward after him, only to find the place deserted. Little piles of empty cartridge-cases marked the places where the machine-guns had stood behind natural and artificial screens. One tripod had been fixed on an ant-hill screened by bushes, and must have had a fine field of fire across the glade. How far back had they gone-and then, in which direction? How long would it be before the column would again expose a few hundred yards of its flank to the sudden blast of the machine-guns of this force and the withering short-range volleys of its rifles? Would they get away now and go on ahead of the column and wait for it again, or, that being the obvious thing, would they move down toward the tail of the column, and attack there? Or was it just a rear-guard holding the Brigade up while Kraut evacuated Mikocheni? . . . Near and distant rifle and machine-gun fire, rising to a fierce crescendo and dying away to a desultory popping, seemed to indicate that this ambush was one of many, or that the Brigade was fighting a regular battle. . . . Probably a delaying action by a strong rear-guard. . . . Anyhow, his business was to see that his men kept direction, kept touch, kept moving forward slowly, and kept a sharp look-out. . . . Firing came nearer on the right flank. That part of the line had seen something-or been fired on, evidently-and suddenly he came to the edge of the patch or belt of jungle and, looking across another glassy glade, he saw a white man striking, with a whip or stick, at some *askaris* who were carrying off a machine-gun. Apparently he was hurrying their retirement. Quickly Bertram turned to the grim little Subedar and got a section of his men to fire volleys at the spot, but there was no sign of life where, a minute earlier, he had certainly seen a German machine-gun team. . . .

He felt very cool and very strong, but knew that this great strength might fail him at any moment and leave him shaking and trembling, weak and helpless. . . .

He must line this edge of the jungle and examine every bush and tree of the opposite edge, across the glade, before adventuring out into its naked openness.

Suppose a dozen machine-guns were concealed a few yards within that sinister sullen wall. He bade the Subedar halt the whole line and open rapid fire upon it with a couple of sections. If he watched through his glasses carefully, he might see some movement in those menacing depths and shadows, movement induced by well-directed fire-possibly he might provoke concealed machine-gunners or *askaris* to open fire and betray their positions. If so, should he lead his men in one wild charge across the glade, in the hope that enough might survive to reach them? If only the Gurkhas could get there with their *kukris*, the guns would change hands pretty speedily. . . . It would be rather a fine thing to be "the chap who led the charge that got the Maxims." . . .

"*Gya, Sahib*," said the Subedar as he stared across the glade. "*Kuch nahin hai.*" [187]

Should he move on? And if he led the line out into a deathtrap? . . . He could see nothing of the companies on the left and right flank, even though this was thin and penetrable bush. How would he feel if he gave the order to advance and, as soon as the line was clear of cover, it was mown down like grass?

Bidding the Subedar wait, he stepped out and, with beating heart, advanced across the open. . . . He couldn't talk to the Gurkhas, but he could show them that a British officer considered their safety before his own. He entered the opposite scrub, his heart in his mouth, his revolver shaking wildly in his trembling hand, but an exhilarating excitement thrilling him with a kind of wild joy. . . . He rather hoped he would be fired at. He wished to God they would break the horrible stillness and open fire. . . . He felt that, if they did not soon do so, he would scream and blaspheme or run away. . . .

Nothing there. No trenches. No suspicious broken branches or withering bushes placed *en camouflage*. He wheeled about, re-entered the glade, and gave the signal for his men to advance. They crossed the glade. Again they felt their way, tore, pushed, writhed, forced their way, through a belt of thin jungle, and again came upon a narrow glade and, as the line of jungle-bred, jungle-trained Gurkhas halted at its edge, a horde of *askaris* in a rough double line dashed out from the opposite side and, as the Gurkhas instinctively opened independent magazine fire, charged yelling across, with the greatest *élan* and ferocity. Evidently they thought they were swooping down upon the scattered remnants of the company that had headed the column, or else were in great strength, and didn't care what they "bumped into," knowing that their enemy had no prepared positions and death-traps for them to be caught in. . . .

As he stood behind a tree, steadily firing his revolver at the charging, yelling *askaris* now some forty yards distant, Bertram was aware of another line, or extended mob, breaking like a second wave from the jungle, and saw a couple of machine-gun teams hastily fling down their boxes and set up their tripods. He knew that a highly trained German gunner would sit behind each one and fire single shots or solid streams of bullets, according to his targets and opportunities. Absolute artists, these German machine-gunners and, ruffianly brutal bullies or not, very cool, brave men.

So was he cool and brave, for the moment-but how soon he would collapse, he did not know. He had emptied his revolver, and he realised that he had sworn violently with every shot. . . . He reloaded with trembling fingers, and, looking up, saw that the fight was about to become a hand-to-hand struggle. Firing rapidly, as the *askaris* charged, the Gurkhas had thinned their line, and the glade was dotted with dozens of their dead and wounded-but the survivors, far outnumbering the Gurkhas, were upon them-and, with shrill yells, the little men rose and rushed at their big enemies *kukri* in hand.

The Subedar dashed at a huge non-commissioned officer who raised his fixed bayonet to drive downward in a kind of two-handed spear-thrust at the little man. Bertram thought the Gurkha was killed but, as he raised his revolver, he saw the Subedar duck low and slash with incredible swiftness at the negro's thigh and again at his stomach. In the very act of springing sideways he then struck at the *askari's* wrist and again at his neck. The little man was using his national weapon (the *kukri*, the Gurkha's terrible carved knife, heavy, broad and razor-edged, wherewith he can decapitate an ox) when it came to fighting-no sword nor revolver for him-and the negro fell, with four horrible wounds, within four seconds of raising his rifle to stab, his head and hand almost severed, his thigh cut to the bone and his abdomen laid open.

"Sha-bas!" [188]yelled Bertram, seeing red, and going mad with battle lust, and shouting "Maro! Maro!" [189]at the top of his voice, rushed into the hacking, hewing, stabbing throng that, with howls, grunts, and screams, swayed to and fro, but gradually approached the direction whence the Gurkhas had advanced. . . .

And the two artists behind the machine-guns, the two merry manipulators of Death's brass band, sat cool and calm, playing delicate airs upon their staccato-voiced instruments-here a single note and there a single note, now an arpeggio and now a run as they got their opportunity at a single man or a group, a charging section or a firing-line. Where a whirling knot of clubbing, thrusting, slashing men was seen to be more foe than friend they treated it as foe and gave it a whole *rondo*—these heralds and trumpeters of Death.

And, as Bertram rushed out into the open, each said "Offizier!" and gave him their undivided attention.

"Shah-bas! Subedar Sahib," he yelled; "Maro! Maro!" and the Gurkhas who saw and heard him grinned and grunted, slashing and hacking, and thoroughly enjoying life. . . . (This was worth all the marching and sweating, starving and working. . . . *This* was something like! A *kukri* in your hand and an enemy to go for!)

Firing his revolver into the face of an *askari* who swung up his clubbed rifle, and again into the chest of one who drove at him with his bayonet, he shouted and swore, wondering at himself as he did so.

And then he received a blow on his elbow and his revolver was jerked from his open, powerless hand. Glancing at his arm he saw it was covered with blood, and, at the same moment, a gigantic *askari* aimed a blow at his skull—a blow that he felt would crush it like an egg . . . and all he could do was to put his left arm across his face . . . and wait . . . for a fraction of a second. . . . He saw the man's knees crumple. . . . Why had he fallen instead of delivering that awful blow?

The nearer machine-gunner cursed the fallen man and played a trill of five notes as he got a clear glimpse of the white man. . . .

Someone had kicked his legs from under Bertram-or had they thrown a stone-or what? He was on the ground. He felt as though a swift cricket-ball had hit his shin, and another his knee, and his right arm dropped and waggled aimlessly-and when it waggled there was a grating feeling (which was partly a grating sound) horrible to be heard. . . . And he couldn't get up. . . .

He felt very faint and could see nothing, by reason of a blue light which burnt dully, but obscured his vision, destroying the sunlight. Darkness, and a loud booming and rushing sound in his ears. . . .

Then he felt better and, half raising himself on his left hand, saw another line emerge from the scrub and charge. . . . Baluchis and Gurkhas, friends . . . thank God!! And there was Augustus. He'd pass him as, just now, he had passed Terence Brannigan and the two other Baluchi subalterns. Would Augustus feel sick at the sight of him, as *he* had done? . . .

With a wild yell, the big Baluchis and little Gurkhas charged, and the line was borne back toward the machine-gunners, who disappeared with wonderful dispatch, in search of a desirable and eligible pitch, preferably on a flank, for their next musical performance.

"Hullo, Priceless Old Thing, stopped one?" asked Augustus, pausing in his rush.

"Bit chipped," Bertram managed to say.

"Oh, poignant! Search—" began Augustus . . . and fell across Bertram, causing him horrible agony, a bullet-hole the size of a marble in his forehead, the back of his head blown completely out.

Bertram fainted as his friend's brains oozed and spread across his chest.

Having dodged and manoeuvred to a flank position, one of the machine-gunners played a solo to the wounded while waiting a more favourable moment and target. His fellow sons of *kultur* wanted no wounded German *askaris* on their hands, and of course the wounded Sepoys and British were better dead. Dead men don't recover and fight again. . . . So he did a little neat spraying of twitching, writhing, crawling, wriggling or staggering individuals and groups. Incidentally he hit the two British officers again, riddling the body which was on top of the other, putting one bullet through the left arm of the underneath one. . . . Then he had to scurry off again, as the fighting-line was getting so far towards his left that he might be cut off. . . . Anyhow he'd had a very good morning and felt sure his "good old German God" must be feeling quite pleased about it.

Chapter IV
Baked

§1

When he recovered consciousness, Bertram found himself lying on a stretcher in a little natural clearing in the bush—a tiny square enclosed by acacia, sisal, and mimosa scrub. On a candelabra tree hung a bunch of water-bottles, a helmet, some haversacks, a tunic, and strips of white rag.

An officer of the Royal Army Medical Corps and a *babu* of the Indian Subordinate Medical Service were bending over a medical pannier. Stretcher-bearers brought in another burden as he turned his head to look round. It was a Native Officer. On top of his head was an oblong of bare-shaven skull-some caste-mark apparently. Following them with his eyes Bertram saw the stretcher-bearers place the unconscious (or dead) man at the end of a small row of similar still forms.... There was Brannigan.... There was a man with whom he had shared a tent for a night at Taveta.... What was his name?... There were the two Baluchi subalterns.... Was that the dead row-the mortuary, so to speak, of this little field ambulance? Was he to join it?

The place stunk of blood, iodine and horrors. He could move neither hand nor foot, and the world seemed to be a Mountain of Pain upon the peak of which he was impaled....

The continued rattle of firing was coming nearer, surely? It was-much nearer. The stretcher-bearers brought in another casualty, the stretcher dripping blood. No "walking wounded" appeared to come to this particular dressing-station.

The firing was getting quite close, and the sound of the cracking of branches was audible. Leaves and twigs, cut from the trees by the bullets, occasionally fell upon the mangled and broken forms as though to hide them....

"Sah-they are coming!" said the *babu* suddenly. His face was a mask of fear, but he continued to perform his duties as dresser, as well as his shaking hands would permit.

Suddenly a ragged line of Gurkhas broke into the clearing, halting to fire, retreating and firing again, fighting from tree to tree and bush to bush.... The mixed, swaying and changing battle-line was going to cross the spot where the wounded lay.... Those of them who were conscious knew what *that* meant...

So did the medical officer, and he shouted to the stretcher-bearers, *babu*, mule-drivers, porters, everybody, to carry the wounded farther into the bush-quick-quick....

As his stretcher was snatched up, Bertram-so sick with pain, and the cruel extra agony of the jolts and jars, that he cared not what befell him-saw a group of *askaris* burst into the clearing, glare around, and rush forward with bayonets poised. He shut his eyes as they reached the other stretchers....

§2

On the terrible journey down the Tanga Railway to M'buyuni, between Taveta and Voi, Bertram kept himself alive with the thought that he would eventually reach Mombasa....

He had forgotten Eva only while he was in the fight and on the stretcher, but when he lay on the floor of the cattle-truck he seemed to wake from a night of bad dreams-to awake again into the brightness and peace of the day of Love.

Of course, the physical agony of being jolted and jerked for a hundred and fifty miles, throughout which every bump of every wheel over every railway joint gave a fresh stab of pain to each aching wound and his throbbing head, was a terrible experience-but he would rather have been lying on the floor of that cattle-truck bumping towards Mombasa, than have been marching in health and strength away from it.

Every bump that racked him afresh meant that he was about forty feet nearer to M'buyuni which was on the line to Voi which is on the line to Mombasa.

What is the pain of a shattered right elbow, a broken left arm, a bullet hole in the right thigh and another in the left calf, when one is on the road to where one's heart is, and one is filled with the divine wonder of first love?

He could afford to pity the poor uninjured Bertram Greene of yesterday, marching farther and farther from where all hope, happiness, joy, peace and plenty lay, where love lay, and where alone in all the world could he know content. . . .

She would not think the less of him that he had temporarily lost the use of his hands and, for a time, was lame. . . . He had done his duty and was out of it! Blessed wounds! . . .

§3

In the hospital at M'buyuni the clean bullet-holes in the flesh of his legs healed quickly. Lucky for him that they had been made by nickel Maxim-bullets and not by the horrible soft-nosed slugs of the *askaris'* rifles. The bone-wounds in his arms were more serious, and he could walk long before he could use his hands.

His patient placidity was remarkable to those who came in contact with him-not knowing that he dwelt in a serene world apart and dreamed love's young age-old dream therein.

Every day was a blessed day in that it brought him much nearer to the moment when he would see her face, hear her voice, touch her hand. What unthinkably exquisite joy was to be his-and was his *now* in the mere contemplation of it!

His left arm began to do well, but the condition of his right arm was less satisfactory.

"Greene, my son," said the O.C. M'buyuni Stationary Hospital to him one day, "you're for the Hospital Ship *Madras*, her next trip. Lucky young dog. Wish I was. . . . Give my love to Colonel Giffard and Major Symons when you get on board. . . . You'll get a trip down to Zanzibar, I believe, on your way to Bombay. . . . You'll be having tea on the lawn at the Yacht Club next month-think of it!"

Bertram thought of something else and radiated joy.

"Aha! That bucks you, does it? Wounded hero with his arm in a sling at the Friday-evening-band-night-tea-on-the-lawn binges, what?"

Bertram smiled.

"Could I stay on in Mombasa a bit, sir?" he asked.

The O.C. M'buyuni Stationary Hospital stared.

"Eh?" said he, doubting that he could have heard aright. Bertram repeated the question, and the O.C., M.S.H., felt his pulse. Was this delirium?

"No," he said shortly in the voice of one who is grieved and disappointed. "You'll go straight on board the *Madras* —and damned lucky too. . . . You don't deserve to. . . . I'd give . . ."

"What is the procedure when I get to Bombay?" asked Bertram, as the doctor fell into a brown study.

"You'll go before a Medical Board at Colaba Hospital. They may detain you there, give you a period of sick leave, or invalid you out of the Service. Depends on how your right arm shapes. . . . You'll be all right, I think."

"And if my arm goes on satisfactorily I shall be able to come back to East Africa in a month or two perhaps?" continued Bertram.

"Yes. Nice cheery place, what?" said the Medical Officer and departed. He never could suffer fools gladly and he personally had had enough, for the moment, of heat, dust, stench, monotony, privation, exile, and overwork. . . . *Hurry* back to East Africa! . . . Zeal for duty is zeal for duty-and lunacy's lunacy. . . . But perhaps the lad was just showing off and talking through his hat, what?

§4

The faithful Ali, devoted follower of his old master's peregrinations, saw the muddy, blood-stained greasy bundles, which were that master's kit, safe on board the *Madras* from the launch which had brought the party of wounded officers from the Kilindini pier. Personally he conducted the bundles to the cabin reserved for Second-Lieutenant B. Greene, I.A.R., and then sought their owner where he reclined in a *chaise longue* on deck, none the better for his long journey on the Uganda Railway.

"I'm coming back, Ali," said he as his retainer, a monument of restrained grief, came to him.

"Please God, *Bwana*," was the dignified reply.

"What will you do while I am away?" he asked, for the sake of something to say.

"Go and see my missus and childrens, my little damsels and damsons at Nairobi, sah," was the sad answer. "When *Bwana* sailing now?"

"Not till this evening," answered Bertram, "and the last thing I want you to do for me is to take these two *chits* to Stayne-Brooker Mem-Sahib and Stayne-Brooker Miss-Sahib as quickly as you can. You'll catch them at tiffin if you take a trolley now from Kilindini. They *must* have them quickly. . . . If they come to see me before the ship sails at six, there'll be an extra present for one Ali Suleiman, what?"

"Oh, sah! *Bwana* not mentioning it by golly," replied Ali and fled.

Mrs. Stayne-Brooker was crossing from the Hospital to Vasco da Gama Street for lunch when, having run quicker than any trolley ever did, he caught sight of her, salaamed and presented the two *chits*, written for Bertram by a hospital friend and companion of his journey, as soon as they got on board. She opened the one addressed to herself.

"*My Dear Mrs. Stayne-Brooker,*"

'it ran, "*I have just reached the Madras, and sail at six this evening. I cannot tell you how much I should like to see you, if you could take your evening drive in this direction and come on board. How I wish I could stay and convalesce in Mombasa! Very much more than ever words could possibly express. It is just awful to pass through like this.*

"*I do hope you can come.*
"*Your ever grateful and devoted*
"*Bertram Greene.*"

The worthy Ali, panting and perspiring, thought the lady was going to fall.

"*Bertram!*" she whispered, and then her heart beat again, and she regained control of her trembling limbs.

"You are Greene *Bwana's* boy!" she said, searching Ali's bedewed but beaming countenance. "Is he-is he ill-hurt-wounded?" (She did not know that the man had been in her husband's service.)

"Yes, Mem," was the cheerful reply. "Shot in all arms and legs. Also quite well, thank you."

"Go and tell him I will come," she said. "Be quick. Here —*baksheesh*. . . . Now, *hurry*."

"Oh, Mem! Mem-Sahib not mentioning it, thank you please," murmured Ali as his huge paw engulfed the rupees. Turning, he started forthwith upon the four-mile return run.

Putting the note addressed to her daughter on the lunch-table, beside her plate, she hurried into her room, crying for joy, and, with trembling hands, made her toilette. She must look her best-look her youngest.

He was back! He was safe! He was alive! Oh, the long, long night of silence through the black darkness of which she had miserably groped! The weary, weary weeks of waiting and wondering, hoping and fearing, longing and doubting! But her prayers had been answered-and she was about to *see* him. . . . And if he were shattered and broken? She could almost find it in her heart to hope he was-that she might spend her life in guarding, helping, comforting him. He would *need* her, and oh, how she yearned to be needed, she who had never yet been really needed by man, woman, or child. . . .

"Mother!" said Miss Stayne-Brooker, as she went in to lunch. "*What* a bright, gay girlie you look! . . . Here's a note from that Mr. Greene of yours. He says:

'*Dear Miss Stayne-Brooker,*
'*I am passing through Mombasa, and am now on board the Madras. I can't come and see*

you-do you think you'd let your mother bring you to see me' —he's crossed that out and put '*see the Hospital Ship Madras*' —'*it might interest you. I have written to ask if she'd care to come. Do-could you?*

'*Always your grateful servant,*
'*Bertram Greene.*'

But I am playing golf with Reggie and having tea with him at the Club, you know."

"All right, dear. I'll go and see the poor boy."

"That's right, darling. You won't mind if I don't, will you? . . . He's *your* friend, you know."

"Yes," said Mrs. Stayne-Brooker, "he's *my* friend," and Miss Stayne-Brooker wondered at the tone of her mother's voice. . . . (Poor old Mums; she made quite a silly of herself over this Mr. Greene!)

§5

Having blessed and rewarded the worthy Ali, returned dove-like to the *Madras*, Bertram possessed his soul with what patience he could, and sought distraction from the gnawing tooth of anxiety by watching the unfamiliar life of a hospital-ship. . . .

Suppose Eva Stayne-Brooker could not come! Suppose the ship sailed unexpectedly early! . .

He could not sit still in that chair and wait, and wait. . . .

A pair of very pretty nurses, with the sallow ivory complexion, black hair and large liquid eyes of the Eurasian, walked up and down.

Another, plain, fat, and superiorly English, walked apart from them.

Two very stout Indian gentlemen, in the uniform of Majors of the Indian Medical Service, promenaded, chattering and gesticulating. The Chief Engineer (a Scot, of course), leaning against the rail and smoking a black Burma cheroot, eyed them with a kind of wonder, and smiled tolerantly upon them. . . . Travel and much time for philosophical reflection had confairrmed in him the opeenion that it tak's all sorrts to mak' a Univairse. . . .

From time to time, a sick or wounded man was hoisted on board, lying on a platform that dangled from four ropes at the end of a chain and was worked by a crane. From the launch to the deck of the ship he was slung like so much merchandise or luggage, but without jar or jolt. Or a walking-wounded or convalescent sick man would slowly climb the companion that sloped diagonally at an easy angle along the ship's side from the promenade-deck to the water.

On the fore and aft well-decks, crowds of sick or wounded Sepoys crouched huddled in grey blankets, or moved slowly about with every evidence of woe and pain. It takes an Indian Sepoy to do real justice to illness of any kind. He is a born actor and loves acting the dying man better than any part in life's drama. This is not to say that he is a malingerer or a weakling-but that when he is sick he *is* going to get, at any rate, the satisfaction of letting everybody know it and of collecting such sympathy and admiration as he can.

"No, there is no one so sick as a sick Indian," smiled Bertram to himself.

In contrast was the demeanour of a number of British soldiers sitting and lying about the deck allotted to them, adjoining but railed off from that of the officers.

Laughter and jest were the order of the day. One blew into a mouth-organ with more industry than skill; another endeavoured to teach one of the ship's cats to waltz on its hind legs; some played "brag" with a pack of incredibly dirty little cards; and others sat and exchanged experiences, truthfully and otherwise.

Near to where Bertram stood, a couple sprawled on the deck and leaned against a hatch. The smaller of the two appeared to be enjoying the process of annoying the larger, as he tapped his protruding and outlying tracts with a *kiboko*, listening intently after each blow in the manner of a doctor taking soundings as to the thoracic or abdominal condition of a patient.

An extra sharp tap caused the larger man to punch his assailant violently in the ribs, whereupon the latter threw his arms round the puncher's neck, kissed him, and stated, with utter disregard for facts:

"'Erb! In our lives we was werry beautiful, an' in our deafs we wos not diwided." (Evidently a reminiscence of the Chaplain's last sermon.)

But little mollified by the compliment, Herbert smote again, albeit less violently, as he remarked with a sneer:

"Ho, yus! You wouldn't a bin divided all right if you'd stopped one o' them liddle four-point-seven shells at Mikocheni, you would. Not 'arf, you wouldn't. . . ."

But for crutches, splints, slings and bandages, no one would have supposed this to be a collection of sick and wounded men, wreckage of the storm of war, flotsam and jetsam stranded here, broken and useless. . . .

Bertram returned to his chair and tried to control his sick impatience and anxiety. Would she come? What should he say to her if she did? . . . Should he "propose" —(beastly word)? He had not thought much about marriage. . . . To see her and hear her voice was what he really wanted. Should he tell her he loved her? . . . Surely that would be unnecessary.

And then his heart stood still, as Mrs. Stayne-Brooker stepped from the companion-platform on to the deck, and came towards him-her face shining and radiant, her lips quivering, her eyes suffused.

He realised that she was alone, and felt that he had turned pale, as his heart sank like lead. But perhaps *she* was behind. . . . Perhaps she was in another boat. . . . Perhaps she was coming later. . . .

He rose to greet her mother-who gently pushed him back on the long cane couch-chair and rested herself on the folding stool that stood beside it.

Still holding his left hand, she sat and tried to find words to ask of his hurts, and could say nothing at all. . . . She could only point to the sling, as she fought with a desire to gather him to her, and cry and cry and cry for joy and sweet sorrow.

"Yes," said Bertram, "but that's the only bad one. . . . Shan't lose the use of it, I expect, though. . . . Would she-would a woman-think it cheek if a maimed man-would she mind his being-if she really . . . ?"

"Oh, my dear, my dear! Don't! Oh, don't!" Mrs. Stayne-Brooker broke down. "She'd love him ten thousand times more-you poor, foolish . . ."

"Will she come?" he interrupted. "And dare I tell her I . . ."

And Mrs. Stayne-Brooker understood.

She was a brave woman, and Life had taught her not to wear her poor heart upon her sleeve, had taught her to expect little (except misery), and to wear a defensive mask.

"*Eva is engaged to marry Mr. Macteith*," she said in a toneless voice, and rose to go-to go before she broke down, fainted, became hysterical, or went mad. . . .

Had two kind people ever dealt each other two such blows?

She looked at his face, and knew how her own must look. . . .

Why *should* God treat her so? . . . To receive so cruel a wound and to have to deal one as cruel to the heart she so loved! . . .

He looked like a corpse-save that his eyes stared through her, burning her, seeing nothing. She must go, or disgrace herself-and him. . . . She felt her way, blindly fumbling, to the companion, realising even then that, when the stunned dullness immediately following this double blow gave place to the keen agony that awaited her recovery of her senses, there would be one spot of balm to her pain, there would be one feeble gleam of light in the Stygian darkness of her life-she would not be aching and yearning for the passionate love of her own son-in-law! . . .

And, were this veracious chronicle a piece of war-fiction woven by a romancer's brain, Bertram Greene would have been standing on the deck that evening, looking his last upon the receding shores of the country wherein he had suffered and done so much.

On his breast would have been the Victoria Cross, and by his side the Woman whom he had Also Won.

She would have murmured "Darling!" . . . He would have turned to her, as the setting sun, ever obliging, silhouetted the wonderfully lovely palms of the indescribably beautiful Kilindini Creek, and said to her:

"*Darling, life is but beginning.*"

* * *

Facts being facts, it is to be stated that Bertram sat instead of standing, as the *Madras* moved majestically down the Creek; that on his breast, instead of the Cross, a sling with a crippled arm; and by his side, instead of the Woman, a Goanese steward, who murmured:

"Master having tea out here, sir, please?" and to whom Bertram turned as the setting sun silhouetted the palms and said: "*Oh, go to hell!*" (and then sincerely apologised.)

* * *

Captain Stott passed and recognised him, in spite of changes. He noted the hardened face, the line between the eyes, the hollowed cheeks, the puckers and wrinkles, the steel-trap mouth, and wondered again at how War can make a boy into a Man in a few months. . . .

There was nothing "half-baked" about *that* face.

* * *

And so, in ignorance, the despised and rejected boy again avenged his father, this time upon the woman who had done him such bitter, cruel wrong.

Chapter V
Finis

After war, peace; after storm, calm; after pain, ease. . . .

Almost the first people whom he met in the Bombay Yacht Club after visiting the Colaba Hospital and being given six months' leave by the Medical Board, were his father and Miranda Walsingham.

Major Walsingham Greene had been severely wounded in Mesopotamia-but he had at last won decoration, promotion, recognition. He was acting Brigadier-General when he fell-and it was considered certain that he would get the Victoria Cross for which he had been recommended.

When he beheld his son, in khaki, war-worn and wounded (like himself, like his father and grandfather, like a true Greene of that ilk), his cup was full and he was a happy man-at last.

And Miranda! She could scarcely contain herself. She almost threw her arms round her old playmate's neck, then and there, in the middle of the Yacht Club lawn. . . . How splendid he looked! Who said her Bertram might make a scholar and a gentleman-but would never make a *man*?

Oh, joy! She had come out to bring home her "Uncle" Hugh and generally look after him-and now there were *two* patients to look after.

* * *

It was a happy voyage Home, and a very happy six months at Leighcombe Priory thereafter. . . .

And when acting Brigadier-General Walsingham Greene and his son returned to India, Miranda Walsingham went with them as Mrs. Bertram Greene.

But Bertram was no longer "Cupid" —he seemed to have left "Cupid" in Africa.

Short Story Collections:

STEPSONS OF FRANCE

To
THE AUTHOR OF "SALAAM"

"Soldats de la Légion,
De la Légion Étrangère,
N'ayant pas de nation,
La France est votre Mère."

WAR-SONG OF THE LEGION.

I. Ten Little Legionaries

At the Depôt at Sidi-bel-Abbès, Sergeant-Major Suicide-Maker was a devil, but at a little frontier outpost in the desert, he was *the* devil, the increase in his degree being commensurate with the increase in his opportunities. When the Seventh Company of the First Battalion of the Foreign Legion of France, stationed at Aïnargoula in the Sahara, learned that Lieutenant Roberte was in hospital with a broken leg, it realized that, Captain d'Armentières being absent with the Mule Company, chasing Touaregs to the south, it would be commanded for a space by Sergeant-Major Suicide-Maker—in other words by The Devil.

Not only would it be commanded by him, it would be harried, harassed, hounded, bullied, brow-beaten, and be-devilled; it would be unable to call its soul its own and loth to so call its body.

On realizing the ugly truth, the Seventh Company gasped unanimously and then swore diversely in all the languages of Europe and a few of those of Asia and Africa. It realized that it was about to learn, as the Bucking Bronco remarked to his friend John Bull (once Sir Montague Merline, of the Queen's African Rifles), that it had been wrong in guessing it was already on the ground-floor of hell. Or, if it had been there heretofore, it was now about to have a taste of the cellars.

Sergeant-Major Suicide-Maker had lived well up to his reputation, even under the revisional jurisdiction and faintly restraining curb of Captain d'Armentières and then of Lieutenant Roberte.

Each of these was a strong man and a just, and though anything in the world but mild and indulgent, would not permit really unbridled vicious tyranny such as the Sergeant-Major's unsupervised, unhampered sway would be. Under their command, he would always be limited to the surreptitious abuse of his very considerable legitimate powers. With no one above him, the mind shrank from contemplating the life of a Legionary in Aïnargoula, and from conceiving this worthy as absolute monarch and arbitrary autocrat.

The number of men undergoing *cellule* punishment would be limited only by standing room in the cells-each a miniature Black Hole of Calcutta with embellishments. The time spent in drilling at the *pas gymnastique*[190] and, worse, standing at "attention" in the hottest corner of the red-hot barrack-yard would be only limited by the physical capacity of the Legionaries to run and to stand at "attention." Never would there be "*Rompez*"[191] until some one had been carried to hospital, suffering from heatstroke or collapse. The alternatives to the maddening agony of life would be suicide, desertion (and death from thirst or at the hands of the Arabs), or revolt and the Penal Battalions-the one thing on earth worse than Legion life in a desert station, under a half-mad bully whose monomania was driving men to suicide. *Le Cafard*, the desert madness of the Legion, was rampant and chronic. Ten legionaries under the leadership of a Frenchman calling himself Blondin, and who spoke perfect English and German, had formed a secret society and hatched a plot. They were going to "remove" Sergeant-Major Suicide-Maker and "go on pump," as the legionary calls deserting.

Blondin (a pretty, black-eyed, black-moustached Provençal, who looked like a blue-jowled porcelain doll) was an educated man, brilliantly clever, and of considerable personality and force of character. Also he was a finished and heartless scoundrel. His nine adherents were Ramon Diego, a grizzled Spaniard, a man of tremendous physical strength and weak mind; Fritz Bauer, a Swiss, also much stronger of muscle than of brain; a curious Franco-Berber half-caste called Jean Kebir, who spoke perfect Arabic and knew the Koran by heart (*Kebir* is Arabic for "lion," and a lion Jean Kebir was, and Blondin had been very glad indeed to win him over, as he would be an invaluable interpreter and adviser in the journey Blondin meant to take); Jacques Lejaune, a domineering, violent ruffian, a former merchant-captain, who could steer by the stars and use a compass; Fritz Schlantz, a wonderful marksman; Karl Anderssen, who had won the *médaille* for bravery; Mohamed the Turk-just plain Mohamed (very plain); Georges Grondin the musician who was a fine cook; and finally the big Moorish negro, Hassan Moghrabi, who understood camels and horses.

The Society had been larger, but Franz Joseph Meyr the Austrian had killed Dimitropoulos the Greek, had deserted alone, and been filleted by the Touaregs. Also Alexandre Bac, late of Montmartre, had hanged himself, and La Cigale had gone too hopelessly mad.

It had been for a grief unto Monsieur Blondin that he could by no means persuade old Jean Boule to join. On being sworn to secrecy and "approached" on the subject, ce bon Jean had replied that he did not desire to quit the Legion (*Bon sang de Dieu!*), and, moreover, that if he went "on pump," his friends les Légionnaires Rupert, 'Erbiggin, and le Bouckaing Bronceau would go too-and he did not wish to drag them into so perilous a venture as an attempt to reach the Moroccan coast across the desert from Aïnargoula. Moreover, if he came to know anything of the plot to kill the Sergeant-Major he would certainly warn him, if it were to be a mere stab-in-the-back assassination affair, some dark night. A fair fight is a different thing. If Blondin met the Sergeant-Major alone, when both had their sword-bayonets—that was a different matter....

Monsieur Blondin sheered off, and decided that the less Jean Boule knew of the matter, the better for the devoted Ten....

"Ten little Légionnaires
Going 'on pump,'
Got away safely
And gave *les autres* the pump,"

sang Monsieur Blondin, who was very fond of airing his really remarkable knowledge of colloquial English, British slang, clichés, rhymes, and *guinguette* songs. Not for nothing had he been a Credit Lyonnais bank-clerk in London for six years. Being a Provençal, he added a pronounced *galégeade* wit to his *macabre* Legion-humour.

One terrible day the Sergeant-Major excelled himself-but it was not, as it happened, one of the Ten who attempted to "remove" him.

Having drilled the parade of "defaulters" almost to death, he halted the unfortunate wretches with their faces to a red-hot wall and their backs to the smiting sun, and kept them at "attention" until Tou-tou Boil-the-Cat, an evil liver, collapsed and fell. He was allowed to lie. When, with a crash, old Tant-de-Soif went prone upon his face, paying his dues to Alcohol, the Sergeant-Major gave the order to turn about, and then to prepare to fire. When the line stood, with empty rifles to the shoulder, as in the act of firing, he kept it in the arduous strain of this attitude that he might award severe punishment to the owner of the first rifle that began to quiver or sink downward. As he did so, he lashed and goaded his victims mercilessly and skilfully.

At last, the rifle of poor young Jean Brecque began to sway and droop, and the Sergeant-Major concentrated upon the half-fainting lad the virulent stream of his poisonous vituperation. Having dealt with the subject of Jean, he began upon that of Jean's mother, and with such horrible foulness of insult that Jean, whose mother was his saint, sprang forward and swung his rifle up to brain the cowardly brute with the butt. As he bounded forward and sprang at the Sergeant-Major, that officer coolly drew his automatic pistol and shot Jean between the eyes.

Had Blondin acted then, his followers, and the bulk of the parade, would have leapt from their places and clubbed the Sergeant-Major to a jelly. But Monsieur Blondin knew that the Sergeant-Major had seven more bullets in his automatic, also that the first man who moved would get one of them, and suicide formed no part of his programme.

"Not just anyhow and anywhere in the trunk, you will observe, scélérats," remarked the Suicide-Maker coolly, turning Jean over with his foot, "but neatly in the centre of the face, just between the eyes. My favourite spot. *Cessez le feu! Attention! Par files de quatre. Pas gymnastique....En avant....Marche!*"...

The plan was that the Ten, stark naked-so as to avoid any incriminating stains, rents, or other marks upon their garments-should, bayonet in hand, await the passing of the "Suicide-Maker" along a dark corridor that evening. Having dealt with him quietly, but faithfully, they would dress, break out of the post, and set their faces for Morocco at the *pas gymnastique*.

As for Monsieur Blondin, he was determined that this should be no wretched abortive stroll into the desert, ending in ignominious return and surrender for food and water; in capture by *goums*[192] in search of the 25 franc reward for the return of a dead or alive deserter; nor in torture and death at the hands of the first party of nomad Arabs that should see fit to fall upon them. Blondin had read the *Anabasis* of one Xenophon, and an *Anabasis* to Maroc he intended to achieve on the shoulders, metaphorically speaking, of the faithful nine. Toward the setting sun would he lead them, across the Plain of the Shott, through the country of the Beni Guil, toward the Haut Atlas range, along the southern slopes to the Adrar Ndren, and so to Marakesh and service with the Sultan, or to escape by Mogador, Mazagan, or Dar-el-Beida. No more difficult really than toward Algiers or Oran, and, whereas capture in that direction was certain, safety, once in Morocco, was almost equally sure. For trained European soldiers were worth their weight in silver to the Sultan, and, in his service, might amass their weight in gold. A Moorish villa (and a harem) surrounded by fig-orchards, olive-fields, vineyards, palm-groves, and a fragrant garden of pepper-trees, eucalyptus, walnut, almond, oleander, orange and lemon, would suit Monsieur Blondin well. Oh, but yes! And the Ouled-Nael dancing-girls, Circassian slaves, Spanish beauties....

The first part of the plan failed, for *ce vieux sale cochon* of a Jean Boule came along the corridor, struck a match to light his cigarette, saw the crouching, staring, naked Ten, and, being a mad Englishman and an accursed dog's-tail, saved the life of the Sergeant-Major. That the Ten took no vengeance upon Jean Boule was due to their lack of desire for combat with the mighty *Americain*, le Bouckaing Bronceau, and with those tough and determined fighters, les Légionnaires Rupert and 'Erbiggin. All four were masters of *le boxe*, and, if beaten, knew it not....

The Ten went "on pump" with their wrongs unavenged, save that Blondin stole the big automatic-pistol of the Sergeant-Major from its nail on the wall of the orderly-room.

They took their Lebel rifles and bayonets, an accumulated store of bread and biscuits, water, and, each man, such few cartridges as he had been able to steal and secrete when on the rifle-range, or marching with "sharp" ammunition.

Getting away was a matter of very small difficulty; it would be staying away that would be the trouble. One by one, they went over the wall of the fort, and hid in ditches, beneath culverts, or behind cactus-bushes.

At the appointed rendezvous in the *village Négre*, the Ten assembled, fell in, and marched off at the *pas gymnastique*, Blondin at their head. After travelling for some hours, with only a cigarette-space halt in every hour, and ere the stars began to pale, Blondin gave the order "*Campez!*" and the little company sank to the ground, cast off accoutrements and capotes, removed boots, and fell asleep. Before dawn Blondin woke them and made a brief speech. If they obeyed him implicitly and faithfully, he would lead them to safety and prosperity; if any man disobeyed him in the slightest particular, he would shoot him dead. If he were to be their leader, as they wished, he must have the promptest and most willing service and subordination from all. There was a terrible time before them ere they win to the Promised Land, but there was an infinitely worse one behind them—so let all who hoped to attain safety and wealth look to it that his least word be their law.

And the Ten Bad Men, desperate, unscrupulous, their hand against every man's, knowing no restraint nor law but Expedience, set forth on their all but hopeless venture, trusting ce cher Blondin (who intended to clamber from this Slime-pit of Siddim on their carcasses, and had chosen them for their various utilities to his purpose).

At dawn, Blondin leading, caught sight of a fire as he topped a ridge, sank to earth, and was at once imitated by the others.

He issued clear orders quickly, and the band skirmished toward the fire, *en tirailleur*, in a manner that would have been creditable to the Touaregs themselves. It was a small Arab douar, or encampment, of a few *felidj* (low camel-hair tents), and a camel-enclosure. Blondin's shot, to kill the camel-sentry and bring the Arabs running from their tents, was followed by the steady, independent-firing which disposed of these unfortunates.

His whistle was followed by the charge, which also disposed of the remainder and the wounded, and left the Ten in possession of camels, women, food, weapons, tents, Arab clothing, and money. Fortune was favouring the brave! But the Ten were now Nine, for, as they charged, the old sheikh, sick and weak though he was, fired his long gun into the chest of Karl Anderssen at point-blank range....

An hour later the *djemels* were loaded up with what Blondin decided to take, the women were killed, and the Nine were again *en route* for Maroc, enhearted beyond words. There is a great difference between marching and riding, between carrying one's kit and being carried oneself, and between having a little dry bread and having a fine stock of goat-flesh, rice, raisins, barley, and dates when one is crossing the desert.

In addition to the *djemels*, the baggage-camels, there were five *mehara* or swift riding-camels, and, on four of these, Monsieur Blondin had mounted the four men he considered most useful to his purposes-to wit, Jean Kebir, the Berber half-caste who spoke perfect Arabic as well as the *sabir* or lingua-franca of Northern Africa, and knew the Koran by heart; Hassan Moghrabi, the Moorish negro, who understood camels and horses; Mohamed the Turk, who also would look very convincing in native dress; and Jacques Lejaune, who could use a compass and steer by the stars, and who was a very brave and determined scoundrel.

When allotting the *mehara* to these four, after choosing the best for himself, Blondin, hand on pistol, had looked for any signs of discontent from Ramon Diego, Fritz Bauer, Fritz Schlantz, or Georges Grondin, and had found none. Also when he ordered that each man should cut the throat of his own woman, and Hassan Moghrabi should dispose of the three superfluous ones, no man demurred. The Bad Men were the less disposed to refuse to commit cold-blooded murder because the stories of the tortures inflicted upon the stragglers and the wounded of the Legion are horrible beyond words-though not more horrible than the authentic photographs of the tortured remains of these carved and jointed victims, that hang, as terrible warnings to deserters, in every *chambrée* of the *casernes* of the Legion. They killed these women at the word of Blondin-but they knew that the women would not have been content with the mere killing of *them*, had they fallen into the hands of this party of Arabs.

As, clad in complete Arab dress, they rode away in high spirits, le bon Monsieur Blondin sang in English, in his droll way —

> "Ten little Légionnaires
> Charging all in line —
> A naughty Arab shot one
> And then-there were *Nine*."

The Nine rode the whole of that day and, at evening, Blondin led them into a *wadi* or canyon, deep enough for concealment and wide enough for comfort. Here they camped, lit fires, and Georges Grondin made a right savoury stew of kid, rice, raisins, barley, dates, and bread in an Arab *couscouss* pot. The Nine slept the sleep of the just and, in the morning, arose and called ce bon Blondin blessed. With camels, food, cooking-pots, sleeping-rugs, tents, clothing, extra weapons, and much other useful loot, hope sprang strong as well as eternal in their more or less human breasts.

Blondin led them on that day until they had made another fifty miles of westing, and halted at a little oasis where there was a well, a *kuba* (or tomb of some marabout or other holy person), and a small *fondouk* or caravan rest-house. Jean Kebir having reconnoitred and declared the *fondouk* empty, and the place safe, they watered their camels, occupied the *fondouk*, and, after a pleasant evening and a good supper, slept beneath its hospitable and verminous shelter-four of the party being on sentry-go, for two hours each, throughout the night.

At this place, the only human beings they encountered were a horrible disintegrating lump of disease that hardly ranked as a human being at all, and an ancient half-witted person who appeared to combine the duties of verger and custodian of the *kuba* with those of caretaker and host of the *fondouk*. Him, Jean Kebir drove into the former building with horrible threats. Fortunately for himself, the aged party strictly conformed to the orders of Kebir, for Blondin had given the Berber instructions to dispatch him forthwith to the joys of Paradise if he were seen outside the tomb. Next day, as the party jogged wearily along, Blondin heard an exclamation from Jean Kebir and, turning, saw him rein in his *mehari* and stare long and earnestly beneath his hand toward the furthermost sand-hills of the southern horizon. On one of these, Blondin could make out a speck. He raised his hand, and the little cavalcade halted.

"What is it?" he asked of Kebir.

"A Targui scout," was the reply. "We shall be attacked by Touaregs—*now* if they are the stronger party, to-night in any case-unless we reach some *ksar*[193] and take refuge....That might be more dangerous than waiting for the Touaregs, though."

"How do you know the man is a Targui?" asked Blondin.

"I do not know *how* I know, but I do know," was the reply. "Who else would sit all day motionless on a *mehari* on top of a sand-hill but a Targui? The Touareg system is to camp in a likely place and keep their horses fresh while a chain of slaves covers a wide area around them. In bush country they sit up in trees, and in the desert they sit on camels, as that fellow is doing. Directly they spot anything, they rush off and warn their masters, who then gallop to the attack on horseback if they are in overwhelming strength, or wait until night if they are not."

Even as he spoke the watcher disappeared.

"Push on hard," ordered Blondin, and debated as to whether it would be better for the *mehari*-mounted five to desert the *djemel*-mounted four and escape, leaving them to their fate, or to remain, a band of nine determined rifles. Union is strength, and there is safety in numbers-so he decided that the speed of the party should be that of the well-flogged *djemels*.

"Goad them on, *mes enfants*," cried he to Diego, Bauer, Schlantz, and Grondin. "I will never desert you-but you must put your best leg foremost. We are nine, and they may be ninety or nine hundred, these *sacrés chiens* of Touaregs." An hour of hard riding, another-with decreasing anxiety, and suddenly Blondin's sharp, clear order:

"*Halte!...Formez le carré!...Attention pour les feux de salve!*" as, with incredible rapidity, an avalanche of horsemen appeared over a ridge and bore down upon them in a cloud of dust, with wild howls of "*Allah Akbar*"..."*Lah illah il Allah!*" and a rising united chant "*Ul-ul-ul-ul Ullah Akbar.*"

Swiftly the trained legionaries dismounted, knelt their camels in a ring, took cover behind them, and, with loaded rifles, awaited their leader's orders. Coolly Blondin estimated the number of this band of The-Forgotten-of-God, the blue-clad, Veiled Men of the desert....Not more than twenty or thirty. They would never have attacked had not their scout taken the little caravan to be one of traders, some portion of a migrating tribe, or, perchance, a little gang of smugglers, traders of the Ouled-Ougouni or the Ouled-Sidi-Sheikhs, or possibly gun-running Chambaa taking German rifles from Tripoli to Morocco—a rich prey, indeed, if this were so. Each Chambi would fight like Iblis himself though, if Chambaa they were, for such are fiends and devils, betrayers of hospitality, slayers of guests, defilers of salt, spawn of Jehannum, who were the sons and fathers of murderers and liars. Moreover, they would be doubly watchful, suspicious, and resolute if they, French subjects, were smuggling German guns across French territory into Morocco under the very nose of the Bureau Arabe....However, there were but nine of them, in any case, so *Ul-ul-ul-ul-ul Ullah Akbar*!

"Don't fire till I do-and then at the horses, and don't miss," shouted Blondin.

The avalanche swept down, and lances were lowered, two-handed swords raised, and guns and pistols presented-for the Touareg fires from the saddle at full gallop.

Blondin waited.

Blondin fired....The leading horse and rider crashed to the ground and rolled like shot rabbits. Eight rifles spoke almost simultaneously, and seven more men and horses spun in the dust. At the second volley from the Nine, the Touaregs broke, bent their horses outward from the centre of the line, and fled. All save one, who either could not, or would not, check his maddened horse. Him Blondin shot as his great sword split the skull of Fritz Bauer, whose poor shooting, for which he was notorious, had cost him his life. "*Cessez le feu*," cried Blondin, as one or two shots were fired after the retreating Arabs. "They won't come back, so don't waste cartridges.... See what hero can catch me a horse."

As he coolly examined the ghastly wound of the dying Fritz Bauer, he observed to the faithful Jean Kebir "*Habet!*" and added —

> "Nine little Légionnaires —
> But one fired late
> When a Touareg cut at him —
> And so there were *Eight*."

"*Eh bien, mon Capitaine?*" inquired Kebir.

"*N'importe, mon enfant!*" smiled Monsieur Blondin, and turned his attention to the property and effects of the dying man....

"We shall hear more of these Forsaken-of-God before long," observed Jean Kebir when the eight were once more upon their way.

They did. Just before sunset, as they were silhouetted against the fiery sky in crossing a sand-hill ridge, there was a single shot, and Georges Grondin, the cook, grunted, swayed, observed "*Je suis bien touché*"," and fell from his camel.

Gazing round, Blondin saw no signs of the enemy. The plain was empty of life-but there might be hundreds of foemen behind the occasional aloes, palmettos, and Barbary cacti; crouching in the *driss*, or the thickets of lentisks and arbutus and thuyas. Decidedly a place to get out of. If a party of Touaregs had ambushed them there, they might empty every saddle without showing a Targui nose....

A ragged volley was fired from the right flank.

"Ride for your lives," he shouted, and set an excellent example to the other seven.

"What of Grondin?" asked Kebir, bringing his *mehari* alongside that of Blondin.

"Let the dead bury their dead," was the reply. (Evidently the fool had not realized that the *raison d'être* of this expedition was to get one, Jean Blondin, safe to Maroc!)

An hour or so later, in a kind of little natural fortress of stones, boulders, and rocks, they encamped for the night, a sharp watch being kept. But while Monsieur Blondin slept, Jean Kebir, who was attached to Georges Grondin, partly on account of his music and partly on account of his cookery, crept out, an hour or so before dawn, and stole back along the track, in the direction from which they had come.

He found his friend at dawn, still alive; but as he had been neatly disembowelled and the abdominal cavity filled with salt and sand and certain other things, he did not attempt to move him. He embraced his cher Georges, bade him farewell, shot him, and returned to the little camp.

As the cavalcade proceeded on its way, Monsieur Blondin, stimulated by the brilliance and coolness of the glorious morning, and by high hopes of escape, burst into song.

> "Eight little Légionnaires
> Riding from 'ell to 'eaven,
> A wicked Targui shot one —
> And then there were *Seven*,"

improvised he.

Various reasons, shortness of food and water being the most urgent, made it desirable that they should reach and enter a small *ksar* that day.

Towards evening, the Seven beheld what was either an oasis or a mirage —a veritable eye-feast in any case, after hours of burning desolate desert, the home only of the horned viper, the lizard, and the scorpion.

It proved to be a small palm-forest, with wells, irrigating-ditches, cultivation, pigeons, and inhabitants. Cultivators were hoeing, blindfolded asses were wheeling round and round *noria* wells, veiled women with red *babooshes* on their feet bore brightly coloured water-vases on their heads. Whitewashed houses came into view, and the cupola of an adobe-walled *kuba*.

Jean Kebir was sent on to reconnoitre and prospect, and to use his judgment as to whether his six companions-good men and true, under a pious vow of silence-might safely enter the oasis, and encamp.

While they awaited his return, naked children came running towards them clamouring for gifts. They found the riders dumb, but eloquent of gesture-and the gestures discouraging.

Some women brought clothes and commenced to wash them in an irrigation stream, on some flat stones by a bridge of palm trunks. The six sat motionless on their camels.

A jet-black Haratin boy brought a huge basket of Barbary figs and offered it-as a gift that should bring a reward. At a sign from Blondin, Mohamed the Turk took it and threw the boy a *mitkal*.

"Salaam," said he.

"*Ya, Sidi, Salaam aleikoum,*" answered the boy, with a flash of perfect teeth.

Blondin glared at Mohamed. Could not the son of a camel remember that the party was dumb-pious men under a vow of silence? It was their only chance of avoiding discovery and exposure as accursed Roumis[194] when they were near the habitations of men.

A burst of music from tom-tom, derbukha, and raita broke the heavy silence, and then a solo on the raita, the "Muezzin of Satan," the instrument of the provocative wicked voice. Some one was getting born, married, or buried, apparently.

Fritz Schlantz, staring open-mouthed at cyclamens, anemones, asphodels, irises, lilies, and crocuses between a little cemetery and a stream, was, for the moment, back in his Tyrolese village. He shivered....

Jean Kebir returned. He recommended camping on the far side of the village at a spot he had selected. There were strangers, heavily armed with yataghans, lances, horse-pistols, flissas, and *moukalas* in the *fondouk*. In addition to the flint-lock moukalas there were several repeating rifles. They were all clad in *burnous* and *chechia*, and appeared to be half-trader, half-brigand Arabs of the Table-land, perhaps Ouled-Ougouni or possibly Ait-Jellal. Anyhow, the best thing to do with them was to give them a wide berth.

The Seven passed through the oasis and, camping on the other side, fed full upon the proceeds of Kebir's foraging and shopping.

That night, Fritz Schlantz was seized with acute internal pains, and was soon obviously and desperately ill.

"Cholera!" said Monsieur Blondin on being awakened by the sufferer's cries and groans. "Saddle up and leave him."

Within the hour the little caravan had departed, Jacques Lejaune steering by the stars. To keep up the spirits of his followers Monsieur Blondin sang aloud.

First he sang —

> "Des marches d'Afrique
> J'en ai pleine le dos.
> On y va trop vite.
> On n'y boit que de l'eau.
> Des lauriers, des victoires,
> De ce songe illusoire
> Que l'on nomine 'la gloire,'
> J'en ai plein le dos,"

and then *Derrière l'Hôtel-Dieu*, and *Père Dupanloup en chemin de fer*. In a fine tenor voice, and with great feeling, he next rendered *L'Amour m'a rendu fou*, and then, to a tune of his own composition, sang in English —

> "Seven little Légionnaires
> Eating nice green figs,
> A greedy German ate too much —
> And then there were *Six*."

Day after day, and week after week, the legionaries pushed on, sometimes starving, often thirsty, frequently hunted, sometimes living like the proverbial *coq en pâte*, or, as Blondin said, "Wee peegs in clover," after ambushing and looting a caravan.

Between Amang and Illigh lie the bones of Jacques Lejaune, who was shot by Blondin. As they passed out of the dark and gloomy shade of a great cedar forest, there was a sudden roar, and a lioness flung herself from a rock upon Lejaune's camel. Lejaune was leading as the sun had set. Blondin, who was behind him, fired quickly, and the bullet struck him in the spine and passed out through his shattered breast-bone. He had been getting "difficult" and too fond of giving himself airs on the strength of his navigating ability, and, moreover, Monsieur Blondin had learnt to steer by the stars, having located the polar star by means of the Great Bear.

It was a sad "accident," but Blondin had evidently recovered his spirits by morning, as he was singing again.

He sang—

> "Six little Légionnaires
> Still all alive,
> But one grew *indiscipliné* —
> And then there were *Five*."...

Distinctly of a *galégeade* wit and a *macabre* humour was Monsieur Blondin, and even as his eye roamed over the scrubby hill-sides and he thought fondly of the *mussugues*, the cistus-scrub hillocks of his dear Provence, he calculated the total sum of money now divided among the said Five, and reflected that division, where money is concerned, is deplorable. Also, as he gazed upon the tracts of thorn that recalled the *argeras* of Hyères, he decided that, all things considered, it would be as well for him to reach Marakesh alone. He understood the principle of rarity-value, and knew that either one of two new-comers would not fetch a quarter of the price of a single new-comer to a war-harassed Sultan whose crying need was European drill-sergeants and centurions.

Jean Blondin would rise to be a second Kaid McLeod, and would amass vast wealth to boot....

At Ait-Ashsba, bad luck overtook Ramon Diego. At the *fondouk* he smote a burly negro of Sokoto who jostled him. The negro, one of a band of departing wayfarers, was a master of the art of *rabah*, the native version of *la savate*, and landed Ramon a most terrible kick beneath the breast-bone. As he lay gasping and groaning for breath, the negro whipped out his razor-edged yataghan and bent over the prostrate man. Holding aloof, Blondin saw the negro spit on the back of Ramon Diego's neck, and with his finger draw a line thereon. Stepping swiftly back, the gigantic black then smote with all his strength, and the head of Ramon Diego rolled through the doorway and down the stony slope leading from the *fondouk*. As the negro mounted his swift Filali camel, Blondin investigated the contents of a leather bag which Ramon always wore at the girdle, beneath his *haik*. On being told of the mishap, Jean Kebir was all for pursuit and vengeance. This, Blondin vetoed sternly. There were now only four of them, and henceforth they must walk delicately and be *miskeen*, modest, humble men. Only four now!

> "Five little Légionnaires,
> Each man worth a score;
> But a big nigger 'it one —
> And then there were *Four*,"

sang Monsieur Blondin.

But what a four! Jean Kebir, the genuine local article, more or less; Hassan Moghrabi, near his native heath and well in the picture; Mohamed the Turk, a genuine Mussulman, able to enter any mosque or *kuba* and display his orthodoxy; and himself, a pious man hooded to the eyes, under a vow of silence.

In due course, the Four reached the Adrar highlands, and tasted of the hospitality of this grim spot, with its brigands' *agadirs* or castles of stone. Having no *mezrag*, no token of protection from some Chief of Many Tents, and the thrifty Blondin refusing Kebir's request to be permitted to buy one, they had to trust to speed and secrecy. As it was, a band swooping down upon them from an *agadir* (obviously of Phoenician origin), pursued them so closely and successfully, that Mohamed, the worst mounted, bringing up the rear, was also brought to earth by a lance thrust through his back and ended his career hanging by the flesh of his thigh from a huge hook which protruded from the wall above the door of the *agadir*.

Though greatly incensed at the loss of the Turk's camel and cash, Monsieur Blondin was soon able to sing again.

> "Four little Légionnaires
> Out upon the spree,
> The Adrar robbers caught one —
> And soon there were *Three*,"...

he chanted merrily.

As the Three watched some hideous Aissa dervishes dancing on glowing charcoal, skewering their limbs and cheeks and tongues, eating fire, and otherwise demonstrating their virtue one night, near El Goundafi, a *djemel*, thrusting forth his head and twisting his snaky neck, neatly removed the right knee-cap of Hassan Moghrabi, and he was of no further use to Monsieur Blondin. He was left behind, and died in a ditch some three days later, of loss of blood, starvation, gangrene, and grief.

Clearly Jean Blondin was reserved for great things. Here were the Ten reduced to Two, and of those two he was one-and intended to be the only one when he was safe in Maroc. Singing blithely, he declared that —

> "Three little Légionnaires
> Nearly travelled through,
> When a hungry camel ate one —
> And now there are but *Two*."...

On through the beautiful Adrar, past its forests of arbutus, lentisk, thuya, figs, pines, and palmettos to its belt of olive groves, walnut, and almond; on toward Djebel Tagharat, the Lord of the Peaks, the Two-Headed. On through the Jibali country, called the "Country of the Gun" by the Arabs, as it produces little else for visitors, toward the Bled-el-Maghzen, the "Government's Territory," experiencing many and strange adventures and hair-breadth escapes. And, all the way, Jean Kebir served his colleague and leader well, and often saved him by his ready wit, knowledge of the country and the *sabir*, and his good advice.

And in time they reached the gorge of Wad Nafiz, and rode over a carpet of pimpernels, larkspur, gladiolus, hyacinths, crocuses, wasp-orchids, asphodels, cyclamens, irises, and musk-balsams; and Blondin realized that it was time for Jean Kebir to die, if he were to ride to Marakesh alone and to inherit the whole of what remained of the money looted in the fifteen-hundred-mile journey, that was now within fifteen hours of its end....

He felt quite sad as he shot the sleeping Jean Kebir that night, but by morning was able to sing —

>"Two little Légionnaires
Travelling with the sun,
Two was one too many —
So now there is but *One*,"

and remarked to his camel, *"'Finis coronat opus,' mon gars."*...

Even as he caught sight, upon the horizon, of the sea of palms in which Marakesh is bathed, he was aware of a rush of yelling, gun-firing, white-clad lunatics bearing down upon him.... A Moorish *harka*! Was this a *lab-el-baroda*, a powder-play game-or what? They couldn't be shooting at *him*....What was that Kebir had said? ..."The Moors are the natural enemies of the Arabs. We must soon get Moorish garb or hide" —when ...a bullet struck his camel and it sprawled lumberingly to earth. Others threw up spouts of dust. Blondin sprang to his feet and shouted. Curse the fools for thinking him an Arab! *Oh, for the faithful Jean Kebir to shout to them in the* sabir *lingua franca!* ...A bullet struck him in the chest. Another in the shoulder. He fell.

As the Moors gathered round to slice him in strips with flissa, yataghan, and sword, they found that their prey was apparently expending his last breath in prayers and pæans to Allah. He gasped:

>"One little Légionnaire,
To provide *le bon Dieu* fun,
Was killed because he killed his friend —
And now there are *None*."...

There were.

Decidedly of a *galégeade* wit and a *macabre* humour to the very last-ce bon Jean Blondin. *"Que voulez-vous? C'est la Legion!"*...

II. À La Ninon De L'Enclos

It was one of La Cigale's good days, and the poor "Grasshopper" was comparatively sane. He was one of the most remarkable men in the French Foreign Legion in that he was a perfect soldier, though a perfect lunatic for about thirty days in the month. When not a Grasshopper (or a Japanese lady, a Zulu, an Esquimaux dog or a Chinese mandarin) he was a cultured gentleman of rare perception, understanding, and sympathy. He had been an officer in the Belgian Corps of Guides, and military attaché at various courts....

From a neighbouring group talking to Madame la Cantinière, in the canteen, came the words, clearly heard, "*Ah! Oui! Oui! Dans la Rue des Tournelles.*"...

"Now, why should the words 'Rue des Tournelles' bring me a distinct vision of the Café Marsouins in Hanoï by the banks of the Red River in Tonkin?" asked the Grasshopper a minute later, in English.

"Can't tell you, Cigale; there is no such *rue* in Hanoï," replied Jean Boule.

"No, *mon ancien*," agreed the Grasshopper, "but there was Fifi Fifinette's place. Aha! I have it!"

"Then give us a bit of it, Cocky," put in 'Erb (le Légionnaire 'Erbiggin-one, Herbert Higgins from Hoxton).

"Yep-down by the factory, near Madame Ti-Ka's joint, it were," observed the Bucking Bronco.

"Aha! I have it. I remember me why the words 'Rue des Tournelles' reminded me all suddenly of the Café Marsouins in Hanoï," continued the Grasshopper. "It was there that I heard from Old Dubeque the truth of the story of Ninon Dürlonnklau, who was Fifi Fifinette's predecessor. She was a reincarnation of Ninon de l'Enclos, and of course Ninon dwelt in the Rue des Tournelles in Old Paris a few odd centuries back."

"Did they call the gal Neenong de Longclothes because she wore tights, Ciggy?" inquired 'Erb.

"Put me wise to Neenong's little stunts before I hit it for the downy,"[195] requested the Bucking Bronco.

"Ninon de l'Enclos was a lady of the loveliest and frailest," said the Grasshopper. "Oh! but of a charm. *Ravissante*! She was, in her time, the well-beloved of Richelieu, Captain St. Etienne, the Marquis de Sevigné, Condé, Moissins, the Duc de Navailles, Fontenelle, Des Yveteaux, the Marquis de Villarceaux, St. Evrémonde, and the Abbé Chaulieu. On her eightieth birthday she had a devout and impassioned lover. On her eighty-fifth birthday the good Abbé wrote to her, 'Cupid has retreated into the little wrinkles round your undimmed eyes.'"...

"*Some* girl," opined the Bucking Bronco.

"And she lived in the Rue des Tournelles, and so the mention of that street called the Café Marsouins of Hanoï in Tonkin to my mind (for there did I hear the truth of the fate of Ninon Dürlonnklau, the predecessor of Fifi Fifinette whom some of us here knew)....

"And the chevalier de Villars, the son of Ninon de l'Enclos, was her lover also, not knowing that Ninon was his mother, nor she that de Villars was her son-until too late. Outside her door a necromancer prophesied the death of de Villars to his face. An hour later Ninon knew by a birth-mark that de Villars was her son, and cried aloud, 'You are my son!' So he fulfilled the prophecy of the necromancer. He drove his dagger through his throat-just where this birth-mark was. What you call *mole*, eh? ...Shame and horror? No ...Love. They who loved Ninon de l'Enclos *loved*. Her arms or those of death. No other place for a lover of Ninon. You Anglo-Saxons could *never* understand....

"And in Hanoï lived her reincarnation, Ninon Dürlonnklau, supposed to be the daughter of one Dürlonnklau, a German of the Legion, and of a perfect flower of a Lao woman. And, mind you, *mes amis*, there is nothing in the human form more lovely than a beautiful Lao girl from Upper Mekong.

"And *this* Ninon! Beautiful? Ah, my friends-there are no words. Like yourselves, I seek not the bowers of lovers-but I have the great love of beauty, and I have seen Ninon Dürlonnklau. Would I might have seen Ninon de l'Enclos that I might judge if she were one half so lovely and so fascinating. And when I first beheld the Dürlonnklau she was no *jeune fille*....

"She had been the well-beloved of governors, generals, and officials and officers-and there had been catastrophes, scandals, suicides ... the usual *affaires* —before she became the hostess of legionaries, marsouins,[196] sailors....

"She had herself not wholly escaped the tragedy and grief that followed in her train, for at the age of seventeen she had a son, and that son was kidnapped when at the age that a babe takes the strongest grip upon a mother's heart and love and life.... And after a madness of grief and a long illness, she plunged the more recklessly into the pursuit of that pleasure and joy that must ever evade the children of pleasure, *les filles de joie*."

'Erb yawned cavernously.

"Got a gasper, Farver?" he inquired of John Bull.

The old soldier produced a small packet of vile black Algerian cigarettes from his *képi*, without speaking.

"Quit it, Dub!" snapped the deeply interested Bucking Bronco. "*Pro*duce silence, and then some, or beat it."[197]

"Awright, Bucko," mocked the unabashed 'Erb, imitating the American's nasal drawl and borrowing from his vocabulary. "You ain't got no call ter git het up none, thataway. Don't yew git locoed an rip-snort —'cos I guess I don' stand fer it, any."

"Stop it, 'Erb," said John Bull, and 'Erb stopped it. There would be trouble between these two one hot day....

"The Legion appropriated her to itself at last," continued the Grasshopper, "and picketed her house. Marsouins, sailors, *pékins*[198] —all ceased to visit her. It was more than their lives were worth, and there were pitched battles when whole *escouades* of *ces autres* tried to get in, before it was clearly understood that Ninon belonged to the Legion. And this was meat and drink to Ninon. She loved to be La Reine de la Légion Étrangère. This was not Algiers, mark you, and she had been born and bred in Hanoï. She had not that false perspective that leads the women of the West to prefer those of other Corps to the sons of La Légion. And there were one or two moneyed men hiding in our ranks just then. She loved one for a time and then another for a time, and frequently the previous one would act rashly. Some took their last exercise in the Red River. An unpleasant stream in which to drown.

"Then came out, in a new draft, young Villa, supposed to be of Spanish extraction-but he knew no Spanish. I think he was the handsomest young devil I have ever seen. He had coarse black hair that is not of Europe, wild yellow eyes, and a curious, almost gold complexion. He was a strange boy, and of a temperament decidedly, and he loved flowers as some women do-especially ylang-ylang, jasmine, magnolia, and those of sweet and sickly perfume. He said they stirred his blood, and his pre-natal memories....

"And one night old Dubeque took him to see La Belle Dürlonnklau.

"As he told it to me I could see all that happened, for old Dubeque had the gift of speech, imagination, and the instinct of the drama.... Old Dubeque-the drunken, depraved scholar and *gentilhomme*.

"Outside her door a begging soothsayer whined to tell their fortunes. It was the Annamite New Year, the Thêt, when the native *must* get money somehow for his sacred jollifications. This fellow stood making the humble *laï* or prolonged salaam, and at once awoke the interest of young Villa, who tossed him a piastre.

"Old Dubeque swears that, as he grabbed it, this *diseur de bonne aventure*, a scoundrel of the Delta, said, 'Missieu French he die to-night,' or words to that effect in pigeon-French, and Villa rewarded the Job-like Annamite with a kick.... They went in....

"As they entered the big room where were the Mekong girls and Madame Dürlonnklau, the boy suddenly stopped, started, stared, and stood with open mouth gazing at La Belle Ninon.

He had eyes for no one else. She rose from her couch and came towards him, her face lit up and exalted. She led him to her couch and they talked. Love at first sight! *Love* had come to that so-experienced woman; to that wild *farouche* boy. Later they disappeared into an inner room....

"Old Dubeque called for a bottle of wine, and drank with some of the girls.

"He does not know how much later it was that the murmur of voices in Madame's room ceased with a shriek of *'Mon fils,'* a horrid, terrific scream, and the sound of a fall.

"Old Dubeque was not so drunk but what this sobered him. He entered the room.

"Young Villa had fulfilled the prophecy of the necromancer. He had driven his bayonet through his throat-just where a large birthmark was. What you call *mole*, eh? It was exposed when his shirt-collar was undone....Ninon Dürlonnklau lived long, may be still alive-anyhow, I know she lived long-in a *maison de santé*. Yes —a reincarnation....

"That is of what the words *la Rue de Tournelles* reminded me."

"'Streuth!" remarked le Légionnaire 'Erbiggin, and scratched his cropped head.

III. An Officer And—a Liar

Little Madame Gallais was always a trifle inclined to the occult, to spiritualism, and to dabbling in the latest thing psychic and metaphysical. At home, in Marseilles, she was a prominent member and bright particular star of a Cercle which was, in effect, a Psychical Research Society. She complained that one of the drawbacks of accompanying her husband on Colonial service was isolation from these so interesting pursuits and people.

Successful and flourishing occultism needs an atmosphere, and it is difficult for a solitary crier in the wilderness to create one. However, Madame Gallais did her best. She could, and would, talk to you of your subliminal self, your subconscious ego, your true psyche, your astral body, and of planes. On planes she was quite at home. She would ask gay and sportive *sous-lieutenants*, fresh from the boulevards of Paris, as to whether they were mediumistic, or able to achieve clairvoyant trances. It is to be recorded that, at no dance, picnic, garden-party, "fiv' o'clock," or dinner did she encounter a French officer who confessed to being mediumistic or able to achieve clairvoyant trances.

Nor was big, fat Adjudant-Major Gallais any better than the other officers of the Legion and the *Infanterie de la Marine* and the *Tirailleurs Tonkinois* who formed the circle of Madame's acquaintance in Eastern exile. No-on the contrary, he distinctly inclined to the materialistic, and preferred red wines to blue-stockings—(not blue silk stockings, *bien entendu*). For mediums and ghost-seers he had an explosive and jeering laugh. For vegetarians he had a contempt and pity that no words could express.

A teetotaller he regarded as he did a dancing dervish.

He had no use for ascetics and self-deniers, holding them mad or impious.

No, it could not be said that Madame's husband was mediumistic or able to achieve clairvoyant trances, nor that he was a tower of strength and a present help to her in her efforts to create the atmosphere which she so desired.

When implored to gaze with her into the crystal, he declared that he saw things that brought the blush of modesty to the cheek of Madame.

When begged to take a hand at "planchette" writing, he caused the innocent instrument to write a naughty *guinguette* rhyme, and to sign it Eugénie Yvette Gallais.

When besought to witness the wonders of some fortune-teller, seer, astrologer or yogi, he put him to flight with fearful grimaces and gesticulations.

And this was a great grief unto Madame, for she loved astrologers and fortune-tellers in spite of all, or rather of nothing. And yet *malgré* the fat Adjudant-Major's cynicism and hardy scepticism, the very curious and undeniable fact remained, that Madame had the power to influence his dreams. She could, that is to say, make him dream of her, and could appear to him in his dreams and give him messages. The Adjudant-Major admitted as much, and thus there is no question as to the fact. (Indeed, when Madame died in Marseilles many years later, he announced the fact to us in Algeria, more than forty-eight hours before he received confirmation of what he knew to be the truth of his dream.)

Two people less alike than the gallant Adjudant-Major and his wife you could not find. Perhaps that is why they loved each other so devotedly.

"I wonder if my boy will be mediumistic," murmured little Madame Gallais, as she hung fondly over the cot in which reposed little Edouard André. "Oh, to be able to hold communion with him when we are parted and I am in the spirit-world."

"Give the little *moutard* plenty of good meat," said the big man. "We want *le petit Gingembre* to be a heavy-weight—a born and bred cuirassier."...

"*Mon ange*, do you see any reason why twin souls, united in the bonds of purest love and closest relationship, should not be able to communicate quite freely when far apart?" Madame Gallais would reply.

"Save postage, in effect?" grinned the Adjudant-Major.

"I mean by medium of rappings, 'planchette,' dreams-if not by actual appearance and communication in spirit guise?"

"Spirit guys?" queried the stronger and thicker vessel.

"Yes, my soul, spirit guise."

"Oh, ah, yes....Better not let me catch the young devil in spirit guise, or I'll teach him to stick to good wine and carry it like a gentleman....He must learn his limit....How soon do you think we could put him into neat little riding-breeches? ...Cavalry for him....Not but what the Legion is the finest regiment in the world....Still Cuirassiers for him."

"My Own! Let the poor sweet angel finish with his first petticoats before we talk of riding-breeches....And how, pray, would the riding-breeches accord with his so-beautiful long curls. They would not, *mon ange, nest ce pas?*"...

"No-but surely the curls can be cut off in a very few moments, can't they?" argued the Major, with the conscious superiority of the logical sex.

But she, of the sex that needs no logic, only smiled and replied that she would project herself into her son's dreams every night of his life.

And in the fulness of time, Edouard André having arrived at boy's estate, the curse of the Colonial came upon little Madame Gallais, and she had to take her son home to France and leave him there with her heart and her health and her happiness. She, in her misery, could conceive of only one fate more terrible-separation from her large, dull husband, whom she adored for his strength, placidity, courage, adequacy, and, above all, because he adored her. Separation from him would be death, and she preferred the half-death of separation from *le petit Gingembre*.

She wrote daily to him on her return to Indo-China—printing the words large and clear for his easier perusal and, at the end of each weekly budget, she added a postscript asking him whether he dreamed of mother often. She also wrote to her own mother by every mail, each letter containing new and fresh suggestions for his mental, moral, and physical welfare, in spite of the fact that the urchin already received the entire devotion, care, and love of the little household at Marseilles.

Their unceasing, ungrudging devotion, care and love, however, did not prevent a gentle little breeze from springing up one summer evening, from bulging the bedroom window-curtain across the lighted gas-jet, and from acting as the first cause of poor little Edouard André being burnt to death in his bed, before a soul was aware that the tall, narrow house was on fire.

Big Adjudant-Major Gallais was in a terrible quandary and knew not what to do. He had but little imagination, but he had a mighty love for his wife-and she was going stark, staring mad before his haggard eyes....And, if she died, he was going to take ship from Saigon and just disappear overboard one dark night, quietly and decently, like a gentleman, with neither mess, fuss, nor post-mortem *enquête*.

But there was just a ghost of a chance, a shadow of a hope-this "planchette" notion that had come to him suddenly in the dreadful sleepless night of watching....It could not make things worse-and it might bring relief, the relief of tears. If she could weep she could sleep. If she could sleep she could live, perhaps-and the Major swallowed hard, coughed fiercely, and scrubbed his bristly head violently with both big hands.

It would be a lying fraud and swindle; but what of that if it might save her life and reason-and he was prepared to forge a cheque, cheat at cards, or rob a blind Chinese beggar of his last *sabuk*, to give her a minute's comfort, rest, and peace....For clearly she must weep or die, sleep or die, unless she were to lose her reason-and while she was in an asylum he could not take that quiet dive overboard so that they could all be together again in the keeping and peace of *le bon Dieu*....Rather death than madness, a thousand times....But if she died and he took steps to follow her-was there not some talk about suicides finding no place in Heaven?

Peste! What absurdity! For surely *le bon Père* had as much sense of fair-play and mercy as a battered old soldier-man of La Legion? But it had not come to that yet. The Legion does not surrender-and the Adjudant-Major of the First Battalion of The Regiment had still a *ruse de guerre* to try against the enemy. He would do his best with this "planchette" swindle, and play it for what it was worth. While there is life there is hope, and he had been in many a tight place before, and fought his way out.

To think of Edouard André Lucien Gallais playing with "planchette"! She had often begged him to join hands with her on its ebony board, and to endeavour to "get into communication" with the spirits of the departed-but he had always acted the *farceur*.

"Ask the sacred thing to tip us the next Grand Prix winner," he had said, or "But, yes —I would question the kind spirits as to the address of the pretty girl I saw at the station yesterday," and then he would cause the innocent machine to say things most unspiritual. Well-now he would see what sort of lying cheat he could make of himself. To lie is not gentlemanly-but to save life and reason is. If to lie is to blacken the soul-let the soul of Adjudant-Major Gallais be black as the blackest *ibn Eblis*, if thereby an hour's peace might descend upon the tortured soul of his wife. The good Lord God would understand a gentleman-being one Himself..

And the Major, large, heavy, and slow-witted, entered his wife's darkened room, and crept toward the bed whereon she lay, dry-eyed, talking aloud and monotonously.

"... To play such a trick on me! May Heaven reward those who play tricks. Of course, it is a hoax-but why does not mother cable back that there never was any fire at all, and that she knows nothing about the telegram? ... How could *le petit Gingembre* be dead, when there he is, in the photo, smiling at me so prettily, and looking so strong and well? What a fool I am! Anyone can play tricks on me. People do.... I shall tell my husband. He would never play a trick on me, nor allow such a thing.... A trick! A hoax! ... Of course, one can judge nothing from the handwriting of a telegram. Anybody could forge one. A letter would be so difficult to forge.... The sender of that wicked cable said to himself, 'Madame Gallais cannot pretend that the message does not come from her mother on grounds of the handwriting being different from that of her mother-because the writing is never that of the sender, but that of the telegraph-clerk. She will be deceived and think that her mother has really sent it.' ... How unspeakably cruel and wicked! No, a letter could not be forged, and that is why there is no letter. Let them wait until my husband can get at them. *Mon petit Gingembre*! And it is his birthday in a month.... What shall I get for him? I cannot make up my mind. One cannot get just what one wants out here, and if one sends the money for something to be bought at Home, it is not the same thing-it does not seem to the child as though his parents sent it at all. How lucky I am to have mother to leave him to. She simply worships him, and he couldn't have a happier time, nor better treatment, if I were there myself. No-that's just it-the happier a child is the less it needs you, and you wouldn't have it unhappy so that it *did* want you. How the darling will..." and then again rose the awful wailing cry as consciousness of the terrible truth, the cruel loss, the horrible fate, and the sensation of utter impotence of the bereaved, surged over the wearied, failing brain. She must cry or die.

The Major sat beside her and gently patted her, in his dull yearning to help, to relieve the dreadful agony, to do something.

A gust of rebellious rage shook him, and he longed to fight and to kill. Why was he smitten thus, and why was there no tangible opponent at whom he could rush, and whom he could hew and hack and slay? He rose to his feet, with clenched fists uplifted, and purpling face.

"Be calm," he said, and took a hold upon himself.

Useless to attempt to fight Fate or the Devil or whatever it was that struck you from behind like this, stabbed you in the back, turned life to dust and ashes.... He must grin and bear it like a man. Like a man-and what of the woman?

"He's happy now, *petit*, our *petit Gingembre*," said the poor wretch.

"He's just a jolly little angel, having a fête-day of a time. He's not weeping and unhappy. Not he, *peaudezébie!*"

"Burning!" screamed the woman. "My baby is burning! My *petit Gingembre* is burning, and no one will help him.... My baby is burning and Heaven looks on! Oh, mother! —Annette! —Marie! —Grégoire! —rush up to the bedroom! ... Quick-he is burning! The curtain is on fire.

The blind has caught.... The dressing-table is alight.... The blind has fallen on the bed. His pillow is smouldering. He is suffocating. The bed is on fire..." and scream followed heartrending scream. The stricken husband seized the woman's hands and kissed them.

"No, *petit*, he never woke. He never felt anything. He just passed away to *le bon Dieu* in his sleep, without pain or fright, or anything. He just died in his sleep. There is no pain at all about that sort of suffocation, you know," he said.

"Oh, if I could but think so!" moaned the woman. "If I could only for a moment think so! ... Burning to death and screaming for mother.... Edouard! Shoot me-shoot me! Or let me..."

"See, Beloved of my Soul," urged her husband, gently shaking her. "I do solemnly swear that I know he was not hurt in the least. He never woke. I happen to know it. I am not saying it to comfort you. I know it."

"How could you know, Edouard? ... Oh, my little baby, my little son! Oh, wake me from this awful *cauchemar*, Edouard. Say I am dreaming and am going to wake."

"The little chap's gone, darling, but he went easy, and he's well out of this cursed world, anyhow. He'll never have suffering and unhappiness... And he had such a happy little life."...

Then, for the first time in his career, the Major waxed eloquent, and, for the first time in his life, lied fluently and artistically. "I wonder if you'll believe me if I tell you how I *know* he wasn't hurt," he continued. "It's the truth, you know. I wouldn't lie to you, would I?"

"No, you wouldn't deceive me, and you haven't the wit if you would," replied his wife.

"No, dearest, that's just it. I wouldn't and couldn't, as you say. Well, look here, last night the little chap appeared to me. *Le petit Gingembre* himself! Faith of a gentleman, he did.... I may have been asleep, but he appeared to me as plain as you are now.... As pretty, I mean," he corrected with a heavy, anxious laugh and pat, peering into the drawn and disfigured face to see if his words reached the distraught mind, "and he said, 'Father, I want to speak to mother, and she cannot hear because she cries out and screams and sobs. It makes nae so wretched that I cannot bear it.'"

The man moistened parched lips with a leathery tongue.

"And he said, 'Tell her I was not hurt a little bit-not even touched by the flames. I just slept on, and knew nothing.... And I couldn't be happy, even in Heaven, while she grieves so.'"

The woman turned to him.

"Edouard, you are lying to me-and I am grateful to you. It is as terrible for you as for me," and she beat her forehead with clenched fists.

"Eugénie!" cried her husband, "Do you call me a liar! *Me*? Did I not give you my word of honour?"

"Aren't you lying, Edouard? *Aren't* you? ... Don't deceive me, Edouard André Gallais!" and she seized his wrist in a grip that hurt him.

"I take my solemn oath I am not lying," lied the Major. "Heaven smite me if I am. I swear I am speaking the absolute truth. *Nom de nom de Dieu!* Would I lie to you?"

He must convince her while she had the sanity to understand him.... "I believe you, Edouard. You are not deceiving me. Oh, thank God! I humbly thank the good merciful Father. And it was-it was —a real and actual communication, Edouard-and vouchsafed to you, the scoffer at spirit communication."

"Yes, but that's not all, my Eugénie. The little chap said, 'I cannot come to mother while she cries out and moans. Tell her to talk with me by "planchette," you joining with her.' He did," lied the Major.

"Oh! Oh! Edouard! Quick! Where is it? ... Oh, my baby!" cried Madame Gallais, rising and rushing to a cabinet from which she produced a heart-shaped ebony board some ten inches long and six broad, having at the wide end two legs, an inch or so in length terminating in two swivelled ivory wheels, and, at the other end, a pencil of the same length as the legs.

Seating herself at her writing-table, she placed the instrument on a large sheet of paper, while her husband brought a chair to her side.

Both placed their hands lightly on the broad part of the board and awaited results.

The pencil did not stir.

Minute after minute passed.

The Adjudant-Major was a cunning man of war, and he was using all his cunning now.

The woman uttered a faint moan as the tenth minute ebbed away.

"Patience, Sweetheart," said he. "It's worth a fair trial and a little patience, isn't it?"

"Patience!" was the scornful reply. "I'll sit here till I die-or I'll hear from my boy.... You *didn't* lie to me, Edouard?"

The pencil stirred-stirred, moved, and stopped.

The woman groaned.

The pencil stirred again. Then it moved-moved and wrote rapidly, improving in pace and execution as the Major gained practice in pushing it without giving the slightest impression of using "undue influence."

His wife firmly and fanatically believed that the spirit of her child was actually present and utilizing, through their brains, the muscles of their arms, to convey to the paper the message it could neither speak nor write itself.

Presently the pencil ceased to move, and, after another period of patient waiting, the stricken mother took the paper from beneath the instrument and read the "message" of the queer, wavering writing, feeble, unpunctuated, and fantastic, but quite legible, although conjoined.

"My Dearest Maman," it ran. "Why do you grieve so for me and make me so unhappy? How can I be joyous when you are sad? Let me be happy by being happy yourself. I cannot come to you while you mourn. Be glad, and let me be glad and then you must be more happy still, because I am happy. I never felt any pain at all. I just awoke to find myself here, where all would be joy for me, except for your grief. I have left a world of pain, to wait a little while for you where we shall be together in perfect happiness for ever. Let me be happy, dearest Maman, by being resigned, and then happy, yourself. When you are at peace I can come to you always in your dreams, and we can talk together. Give me happiness at once, darling Mother. Please do. Your *Petit Gingembre*" ...which was not a bad effort for an unimaginative and dull-witted man.

He had his instant reward, for on finishing the reading of the "message," Madame Gallais threw her arms round his neck and burst into tears-the life-giving, reason-saving, blessed relief of tears.

An hour later she slept, for the first time in five days, holding her husband's big hand as he sat by her bed.

When she stirred and relinquished it, the next morning, the Major arose and went out.

"What a sacred liar I am!" quoth he. "Garçon, bring me an *apéritif*."

It is notorious that a tangled web we weave when first we practise to deceive. And Major Gallais practised hard. Two and three and four times daily did he manufacture "messages" from the dead child, and strive, with his heart in his mouth, to make the successful cheat last until the first wild bitterness of his wife's grief had worn off.

His hair went grey in the course of a month.

The mental strain of invention, the agony of rasping his own cruel wound by this mockery-for he had loved *le petit Gingembre* as much as the child's mother had done-and the constant terror lest some unconvincing expression or some unguarded pressure on the "planchette" should betray him, were more exhausting and wearing than two campaigns against the "pirates" of Yen Thé.

But still he had his reward, for his wife's sane grief, heavy though it was and cruel, was a very different thing from the mad abandonment and wild insanity of those dreadful days before he had his great idea.

Many and frequent still were the dreadful throes of weeping and rebellions against Fate-but "planchette" could always bring distraction and comfort to the tortured mind, and the soothing belief in real presence and a genuine communion.

But there was no anodyne for the man's bitter grief, and the "planchette" became a hideous nightmare to him. Even his work was no salvation to him, for though the *Adjudant-Major* is a regimental staff officer, corresponding somewhat to our Adjutant —(the "Adjutant" is a non-com. in the French army) —and a very busy man, Gallais found that his routine duties were performed mechanically, and by one side of his brain as it were, while, undimmed, in the fore-front of his mind, blazed the baleful glare of a vast "planchette," in the flames of which his little son roasted and shrieked.

And still the daily tale of "messages" must be invented, and daily grew a greater and more distressing burden and terror.

How much longer could he go on, day after day, and several times a day, producing fresh communications, conversations, messages, ideas? How much longer could he go on inventing plausible and satisfactory answers to the questions that his wife put to the "spirit" communicant? How could Adjutant-Major Gallais of La Légion Étrangère describe Heaven and the environment, conditions, habits, conduct and conversations of the inhabitants of the Beyond? How much longer would he be able to use the jargon of his wife's books on Occultism and Spiritualism, study them as he might, without rousing her suspicions? The swindle could not have lasted a day had she not been only too anxious to believe, and only too ready to be deceived.

What would be the end of it all? What would his wife do if she found out that he had cheated her? Would she ever forgive him? Would she leave him? Would the shock of the disappointment kill her? Would she ever believe him again?

What *could* the end of it be?

He must stick it out-for life, if need be-and he was not an imaginative man.

What would be the end?

The end was-that she felt she must go home to France and see her boy's grave, tend it, pray by it, and give such comfort as she could to her poor mother, almost as much to be pitied as herself.

Gallais encouraged the idea. The change would be good for her, and he would be able to join her in a few months. Also this terrible "planchette" strain would cease for him, and he might recover his sleep and appetite....

"To think that we shall be parted, this time to-morrow, my dearest Edouard," wept Madame Gallais, as they sat side by side in their bed-sitting-room, in the *Hôtel de la République* at Saigon. "I on the sea and you on your way back alone. If every thing were not arranged, I would not go. Let us have a last 'planchette' with our son, and get to bed. We are having *petit déjeuner* at five, you know."

The Major racked his brain for something to write, as Madame went to her dressing-case for the little instrument (to the Major, an instrument of torture) —racked his brain for something he had not said before, and racked in vain. He grew hotter and hotter and broke into a profuse perspiration as she seated herself beside him. *Nom de nom de Dieu de Dieu de sort*! What could he write? Why had his brain ceased to operate?

Nombril de Belzébuth! Could he not make up one more lie after carrying on for weeks-weeks during which his waking hours-riding, drilling, marching along the muddy causeways between the rice-fields, working in his office, inspecting, eating, and drinking-had been devoted to hatching "messages," conversations, communications and lies, till he had lost health, weight, sleep, and appetite....

No....He could not write a single word, for his mind was absolutely blank.

Minutes passed.

Sweating, cursing, and praying, the unfortunate man sat in an agony of misery, and could not write a single word.

Would not *le bon Dieu* help him? Just this one last time?...

Minutes passed.

Not to have saved his life, not to have saved the life of his wife, not to have brought back *le petit Gingembre*, could the poor tortured wretch have written a single word....What would his wife do when she discovered the cheat-for if no words came during the next minute or two he knew he must spring to his feet, make full confession, and throw himself upon his wife's mercy.

That or go mad.

549

What would she do? .... Leave him for ever? ... Spit upon him and call him "Liar," "Cheat," and "Heartless, cruel villain"?

Would the dreadful reaction and shock kill her? —deprive her of reason?

Suddenly he perceived that, with hands which were acres in extent, he was endeavouring to move a "planchette" the size of Indo-China —a "planchette" that was red-hot and of which the fire burnt into his brain. Its smoke and fumes were choking him; its fierce white light was blinding him; the thing was killing him.

By the time, several weeks later, that little Madame Gallais had nursed her husband back to sanity and consciousness, the first bitterness of grief was past and she herself could play the comforter.

"Oh, my Edouard," she wept upon his shoulder when first the brain-fever left him and he knew her, "we have lost our little Gingembre-but you have me, and, oh, my brave hero-husband, I have you. I shall weep no more."...

"Planchette" stands on Madame's desk-but she does not use it.

IV. The Dead Hand

Chubby, cherubic, and cheerful, with the pure, wholesome blood of his native Provence yet glowing in his cheeks, Extreme Youth was the only trouble really-and there are many worse diseases-of Lieutenant Archambaut Thibaut d'Amienville of the Chasseurs d'Afrique, of the glorious XIXth Army Corps of La République Française.

As he sat back from the table, fingering his glass, he looked exceedingly handsome, dashing, and romantic in his beautiful pale blue uniform. But he had not found his level, and he was making some bad breaks. It does not always conduce to modesty and diffidence in a young man that his papa is a very prominent and powerful politician, and his mother a leader of Paris Society. As the deft native waiters, arrayed in spotless white, moved the table-cloth and set forth fresh glasses, ash-trays, shapely bottles and cigarette-boxes on the shining mahogany that reflected the electric lights like a mirror, he rushed in once again. There was no squashing him.

One has heard of people being young enough to know better-young enough, that is, to have high ideals, generosity, and purity of motive-but Lieutenant Archambaut Thibaut d'Amienville was young enough to know best. He was so young, so wise, and so well informed that he was known as *Général* and not *Lieutenant* d'Amienville among his intimates. And he was at the moment giving generously and freely to his seniors of the stores of his wisdom and knowledge.

Captain Gautier d'Armentières, of the First Battalion of La Légion Étrangère, scarred and war-worn hero of Tonquin, Dahomey, and Madagascar, beloved as few officers are beloved by the wild and desperate men he led, fine soldier and fine gentleman, remarked to the officer on his left —a gorgeous Major of Spahis, resplendent in scarlet cloak (huddled in which he shivered with fever), *ceinturon*, and full baggy trousers:

"So you are going to have another try for a lion?" But the Major had no time to reply for "Général" d'Amienville had caught the ultimate word. (He had promised his mamma a select consignment of lion-skins of his own procuring when he left for the wilds of Algiers and the Soudan, and she had helped in the purchase of the battery of sporting weapons that he had bought at the gun-shop in the Rue de la Paix, guiding his taste to the choice of "pretty ones with nice water-marking on the barrels," and dainty ornament in the way of engraving, chasing, damascening and mounting.)

"Lion?" said he quickly. "What you want for lion, d'Armentières, is impact, concussion, force-er-weight, a-ah-stunning blow....It is absolutely useless, you know, for you to go and drill him through and through with neat little holes of which he is unaware, and which trouble him not at all....None of your Mausers or Lebels, you know."...

Eight pairs of eyes regarded the young gentleman without enthusiasm or affection; nay, with positive coldness.

The strong and clever face of one of the party, a Captain of Zouaves, looked somewhat Machiavellian, as, with a cold smile, he encouragingly murmured "Yes?"

Colonel Leon Lebrun, famous chief of Tirailleurs and old enough to have been the young gentleman's grandfather, assumed a Paul-at-the-feet-of-Gamaliel air, and with humility also said "Yes?"

"Yes," continued d'Amienville, "never take one of these small-bore toys, no matter what the muzzle-velocity. Get something with a good fat bore and a good fistful of cordite. Then you know where you are and what you are doing....I'd as soon go with my automatic pistol as with a small-bore....And never go on foot-especially in those reedy places. And never touch a *tablier* —what the English call a *machan* when they put them up for tiger in their Indian colonies.... No good....Suicide in fact....What you want to do is to have a platform-like a sentry's *vue* —strongly lashed in the branches of a convenient high tree, near the 'kill,' put a mattress on it, and make yourself comfortable."

"And if, in effect, there be no tree?" respectfully inquired Médecin-Major Parme, twirling his huge moustache without revealing the expression on his thin lips.

"Oh-er-well, then, of course, you might-er-well, perhaps dig a pit and fence yourself round. You might, in fact, have a sort of cage....Just as good for keeping wild beasts out as for keeping them in."

"Excellent!" murmured the Colonel.

"Now *I* should never have thought of going lion-hunting in a cage. But original! Original! Of a cleverness! ...How many lions have you shot?"

The flush of embarrassment deepened that of youth and juiciness in the plump cheek of the young officer.

"Oh-er-well, I have never actually *shot* any, you know," he replied, in some confusion, but still with a suggestion of having done something very similar-of having ridden them down with a hog-spear, or caught them on a rod and line.

"*Haven't* you?" asked Captain d'Armentières in apparent surprise. From the discomfort of his confession the youth quickly recovered with the attempted *tu quoque* —

"Have *you*?"

"Yes," admitted the Captain, hesitatingly.

"*Oh?* —and when did you shoot one, pray?" inquired d'Amienville, with a sceptical note, sufficiently impertinent to be irritating.

The Captain's uniform of dark blue and red was a very modest affair beside that of the young Chasseur-and, *nom de Dieu!* who was *he* to attempt a sneer at the son of Madame d'Amienville-not to mention of Monsieur d'Amienville, politician of international fame and importance?

The young officer raised his absinthe to the light, crossed a leg, admired a neat boot, and glanced a trifle disdainfully at the grizzled, unfashionable old *barbare* of whom the elegant salons of Paris had never heard. (A mere St. Maizent man snubbing an alumnus of St. Cyr!)

"My last, about this time last year," was the reply.

"Your *last*? And how many, pray, have you shot?" asked d'Amienville languidly.

"*Eighty-three*," replied the officer of the Legion, fixing a bleak and piercing grey eye upon the youth.

Wry smiles wreathed the faces of the audience, and the "Général" changed the subject forthwith. As the fresh and verdant one was their fellow-guest (of d'Armentières), the others forebore to laugh aloud.

Drawing a bow at a venture, the Lieutenant had a shot at the horse, he having just purchased his very first pony.

"Excellent riding country, this," he observed patronizingly to his neighbour, a hard-bitten, saturnine officer, hawk-eyed, hawk-nosed, and leathern-cheeked. "I shall do a lot of it....Very keen on riding and awfully fond of horses. I love the *chasse au renard*....Ah! Horses! I know something about them too....A thing most useful-to understand horses. It is not given to all.... Incredible lot to learn though....A difficult subject....Difficult."...

"Very," acquiesced the neighbour, finding himself the more immediate recipient of the information.

"But yes-very. Any time you may be thinking of buying, let me know, and I shall be charmed to place my knowledge and experience at your disposal. Charmed. Yes, I will look the beast over....Always best to take advice when buying a horse. Terrible rogues these Arabs. You are certain to be swindled if you rely on your own judgment. Cunning fellows these native *piqueurs*. Hide any defect from inexperienced eyes-bad hoofs, sand-crack, ring-bone, splint, wind-galls, *souffle*, sight, teeth, age, vice-anything. Charmed to give you my opinion at any time.... Try him for you too."...

"Most extremely amiable of you, I'm sure. Most kind. A thousand thanks. I realize I have a terrible lot to learn about horses yet," replied the favoured one.

"Yes, they take a lot of knowing," replied the "Général," and, as the man rose, bade farewell to his host, saluted the company, and departed to catch the ten-fifteen to Oran, that young but knowing gentleman observed generously:

"An agreeable fellow that—a most amiable person. Who is he?"

"Vétérinaire-Colonel Blois!" replied d'Armentières. "Probably the cleverest veterinary-surgeon in the army.... You may know his standard work." ... But Lieutenant d'Amienville again changed the subject hastily, and then scolded a servant for not bringing him what he had not ordered. Thereafter he was silent for nearly five minutes.

Some one mentioned Adjudant-Major Gallais and his curious end. (He dreamed that he saw his wife murdered by burglars in their little flat at Marseilles, was distraught until news came that such a tragedy had actually happened at the very time of the dream, and at once shot himself.)

"A very remarkable case of coincidence, to say the least of it," observed Captain d'Armentières. "Personally I should be inclined to call it something more."

But Lieutenant d'Amienville was a modern of the moderns, an agnostic, a sceptic.

"All bosh and rubbish," quoth he. "*Sottise*.... There is no such thing as this occultism, spiritualism, telepathy, and twaddle. To the devil with supraliminal, transliminal, subliminal, astral, and supernatural. There *is* no supernatural."...

"So?" murmured a dapper little man in scarlet breeches and a black tunic which had the five-*galon*ed sleeve of a Colonel.

"All nonsense," continued the young gentleman. "All this that one hears about mysterious and inexplicable occurrences is always second-hand. Second-hand and third person.... Third person singular-very singular. Ha! Ha!...Yes, all rot and rubbish. Now, has anyone of *us* here ever had an experience of the supernatural sort? Not one, I'll be bound. Not one.... But we all know somebody who has. It's always the way."...

"Well," remarked Captain d'Armentières, "I was once throttled by a Dead Hand-if you would call that an experience."

"I was speaking seriously," replied the Lieutenant loftily.

"So was I," answered the Captain coldly.

"What do you mean?" queried the youth, fearing the, to him, worst thing on earth-ridicule.

"Precisely what I say," was the quiet reply. "I was once seized by the throat, and all but killed, by a Dead Hand, in the middle of the night as I lay in bed....I give you my word of honour-and I request-and advise-you not to cast any doubt on my statement."

The pointed jaw of Lieutenant d'Amienville dropped, and he stared round-eyed and openmouthed at the officer of the Legion, apparently sane and obviously sober, who could say such things seriously.... Could it be a case of this *cafard* of which he had heard so much? No —*le cafard* is practically confined to the rank and file-and this man was, moreover, as cool as a cucumber and as normal as the night. He glanced round the table at his fellow-guests. They looked expectant and interested. This *vieux moustache* was evidently a man of standing and consideration among them.

"Tell us the story, *mon gars*," said the Major of Spahis, pouring cognac into his coffee.

"Do," added the Captain of Zouaves.

"Let's go out into the garden and have it," proposed the Colonel of Tirailleurs Algériens, half rising. "May we, d'Armentières?"

"Yes —I must hear this," acquiesced the young Lieutenant with an air of open-mindedness, but reserved judgment.

"Come on, by all means," answered d'Armentières. "I should have thought of it before, Colonel"; and the party rose and strolled across the veranda out into the garden of the *Cercle Militaire*.

Légionnaire Jean Boule, or John Bull, standing at the gate leading into the high-road, and awaiting his officer as patiently as a good orderly should, thought the scene extraordinarily stage-like and theatrical, albeit he had seen it many times before.

The brilliant moonlight on the tall and beautiful plane-trees, the cypress and the myrtle, the orange, magnolia, wistaria, bougainvillea, the ivy-draped building of the *Cercle* with its hundreds of lights, the gorgeous scarlet of the Spahi, the pale blue of the Chasseur, the yellow and blue of the Tirailleur, the scarlet and black of the Legionary, and the other gay uniforms made up a picture as unreal as beautiful.

Gazing upon it, he thought of days when he, too, sat in such groups in such club-gardens when Life went very well.

In the distance, the famous band of the Legion was playing Gounod's *Serenade*—probably in the Public Gardens outside the Porte de Tlemçen....

"*En avant, mon choux*," said the Médecin-Major, as the party settled into wicker chairs, and the bare-footed, silent servants ministered to its needs with cigarettes, cheroots, and weird liqueurs.

"And forthwith," added the Colonel, puffing a vast cloud as he lay back and gazed sentimentally at the moon.

"Well-as you like, gentlemen-but it was nothing. Just a queer little experience. It won't interest you much, I'm afraid," said d'Armentières.

Then Lieutenant d'Amienville commenced a dissertation upon auto-suggestion, illusion, and self-deception, but the remainder of Captain d'Armentières' guests intimated clearly to their host that they wanted his story, and wanted it at once.

"Have it for what it is worth, then," said that officer. "But I request Lieutenant d'Amienville clearly to understand that what I am about to tell you is *the absolute truth*—the plain and simple tale of what actually occurred to me personally. Moreover, should he, while believing in the honesty of my belief, doubt the trustworthiness of my observations and conclusions, I may mention that my *ordonnance* will be found waiting near the gate-and may be called and questioned. For he was concerned in the matter, and not only saw the marks upon my throat, but actually touched the Dead Hand which all but choked the life out of me."

The voice of the "Général" was stilled within him, but his face was very eloquent indeed. "It happened in Haiphong," continued the quiet, cultured voice of the weary-looking man, "when the Legion sent big drafts out to Tonkin in '83. I was commanding a detachment then, with the rank of Lieutenant. We had disembarked at the mouth of the Red River into two old three-decker river-gunboats, and I had had an infernally busy day-what with the debarkation from the ship and then again at Haiphong, after the six-hour journey up the river. On top of all I had high fever.

"Now, before getting into bed that night, I turned out the lamp that hung on a nail on the wall, and then lay down, finished my cigarette, and turned out the tiny hand-lamp which I had brought in from the bathroom and placed on the little *petit-déjeuner* table beside my bed, noting, as I did so, that the matches were beside it. I always lock my door at night and sleep without a light, but with the means of getting a light easily accessible. Funny things are apt to occur at night in some parts of the shiny East....I expect they've got electric light in Haiphong by now....Well, in two minutes I was sound asleep-sleeping the sleep of the just and enjoying the reward of my good conscience, virtuous life, and hard work."

..."*Va ten, blagueur,*" murmured Colonel Lebrun with a smile.

"An hour or two later, I awoke suddenly-awoke to the knowledge that I was being murdered, was dying, and, in effect, very nearly dead. Some one had me by the throat and was choking my life out with as deadly and scientific a grip as ever fastened upon a man's neck....The human mind is curiously constituted, and, even in that moment, I tried to remember the name of a book about the garotters of India, the 'Thugs'—a book I had read many years before, when studying English-written by a Colonel of the Army of India....'Chinese garotters,' thinks I to myself, and realized that I was in for it, for I could no more yell for assistance than I could fly. There was my orderly sleeping on a rug in a little ante-chamber a few feet from me, and I could not call to him. I must face my fate alone and live or die without help from outside. I was terrified."....

One or two of his audience glanced at the medals and decorations on the speaker's breast (they included the *Croix de Guerre* and the *Médaille Militaire*) and smiled.

"I should have felt for his eyes and blinded him!" announced Lieutenant d'Amienville.

..."Simultaneously with the awakening to the knowledge that I was being throttled by some silent, motionless, invisible assailant, came my attempt to strike him, of course-to spring up, and to grapple with him; but, simultaneously again with the attempt, came the knowledge that my right arm was absolutely useless beneath his weight, and that I was pinned to the pillow, like a butterfly to a cork, by the weight and power of the hand that had me in its grip. Finding my right immovable, I naturally struck out with my left and hit again and again with all my strength-to find that I struck *nothing* —until, being at my last gasp, I grabbed at the hand that was choking me and strove to tear it from my throat.

"Even at that terrible moment I was startled at the extraordinary coldness of the hand I grasped. It was as deadly cold as it was horribly strong, and as brain reeled and senses failed, I seemed to visualize a terrible marble statue endowed with life and superhuman strength, leaning its cruel weight upon the frozen hand that clutched my throat. And I could not seize or even touch any part of this horrible assailant but the Hand....And I tell you the thing was dead-dead and cold....I was dying-throttled by a Dead Hand, and that is the simple truth."...

None of the party moved or spoke-not even d'Amienville. That, and the fact that scarcely a cigar or cigarette remained alight, were remarkable tributes to d'Armentières' dramatic and convincing way of speech. And those of the party who knew him well, also knew him to be incapable of telling a lie, when he had given his word that what he said was the truth.

..."Well, I have never believed in taking things lying down, so I tried once again to get up, and, putting all my heart and soul and strength into a mighty heave, I strove to throw my assailant off before I lost consciousness completely....In vain....

"All this takes time in the telling, but it must have taken mighty little time in the doing, for I was almost dead from suffocation when I first awoke.

"As I strained and tore at the hand, I struggled to rise. My body writhed, but my right arm budged not a fraction of an inch, and the grip on my throat perceptibly tightened, though I thought the limit had surely been reached....I must get one breath, or ears and eyes and brain must burst....Surely I was black in the face and my eyeballs were on my cheek-bones?...I lived a lifetime in a second....So this was the end and the finish of Gautier d'Armentières, was it? Here were to end all dreams of military glory and distinction, all visions of fine, quick death in action against the foes of La France?...A dog's death! To be slowly suffocated in my bed-choked to death by a cold Dead Hand, a Hand without a tangible body....

"As my frame was convulsed and my senses finally reeled in unconsciousness or death, I made my last wild attempt, and probably put forth such a violent concentration of co-ordinated effort as never before in my life-and, with a gasp and sob of thankfulness, I flung my assailant off!

"And, as he fell, he stabbed me in the arm.

"Yes-with the last vestige of my strength I flung it off, and the crash of falling lamp and table was the sweetest sound I ever heard, and the pain of the stab in my arm was absolutely welcome....For I don't mind confessing that I prefer human, or rather *real*, antagonists when I have to fight-and when lamp and table smashed to the ground under its weight, and I felt myself knifed, I knew that this cold, dead hand belonged to something actual and tangible-something alive, something human....

"But I have never touched anything that seemed more dead and cold, for all that.

"Well, my assailant was hardly on the ground before I was there too, for, although my right arm was absolutely useless from the stab, I meant to have him somehow. I hate being choked at night when I am getting my due and necessary sleep, and I wanted him badly. I was really annoyed about it all....

"But he wasn't there, and, as I sprang to my feet and struck and grabbed and clutched, I clutched and grabbed and struck-precisely nothing!

"My terror returned tenfold. Was the Thing supernatural after all? I had fallen practically on top of it and actually holding it-and it *was not*....But-nonsense! The most violent and virulent Oriental djinn, spirit, ghost, devil, afrit, *esprit malin*, or demon, does not stab one, even if it throttles-as some of them are said to do....

"I crouched still and silent with restrained breathing, hoping to hear other breathing or some movement.

"Perfect silence and stillness!

"I burst into a cold perspiration-as I imagined the thing to be behind me, and about to seize my neck again in its frozen, vice-like grip.

"I whirled around with extended arms, and then, rising to my feet, struck out in every direction, dealing *coups de savate* when my arms tired. And then again I crouched and listened and waited-with my hands at my throat.

"Perfect silence and stillness!

"And, do you know, my friends, it positively never occurred to me to cry out for help! ... I suppose my faculties were all so engrossed in this strange struggle that no corner of my brain was free to think, '*One shout and Jean Boule will burst in your door, sword-bayonet in hand.*'"...

"More likely you wanted to see it out all by your little self, *mon ancien*," smiled Colonel Lebrun.

"But no, I assure you. I never thought to shout for help....And then, as I put a hand to the floor, I touched the matches that had fallen with the table. And I thanked *le bon Dieu*.... With trembling fingers I struck a light-wondering what would be revealed to my staring eyes, and whether the light would be the signal for my death-blow. Should I get it in the back-or across the neck? Was it a common Chinese 'pirate'? I hoped so, ... but they do not have dead hands and intangible bodies.

"The match flared....

"The room was empty....

"Absolutely empty. And, look you, my friends, the door was still locked on the inside; there was no fireplace and chimney, and not so much as a cat could have escaped by the window without knocking down the articles which stood on the inner ledge of it-some little brass ornaments, a crude vase, and one or two framed photographs or pictures. I went cold all over. What had throttled me? What had stabbed me? Where was the cold Dead Hand which I had grasped?...

"I lit the wall-lamp.

"There lay the table, overturned in the struggle. There lay the little lamp which I had carried in from the neighbouring bathroom. Its glass chimney was shattered and oil was running from its brass reservoir. And there, in my right arm, was the great, gaping stab.

"Going to the mirror, I saw at a glance that there were marks of fingers on my throat....*And I knew that nothing bigger than a rat could have left the room!*

"I felt that I had had enough of mystery in solitude, and remembered my orderly. I was weak and faint from the awful struggle, and a little sick from the stab....Also, my friends, I was frightened....A murderous foe who can throttle and stab, does not lock the door on the inside as he leaves the room, look you, and neither does he climb through a small window in silence without disturbing bric-a-brac upon the sill....

"I unlocked the door, and shouted to my Jean Boule. He replied on the instant, and came running.

"He must have thought me mad when he heard my tale-until I directed his attention to the stab in my arm and the finger-marks on my neck....

"He stared at the debris on the floor, at the undisturbed ornaments on the window-ledge, at the door, and finally at the marks on my person.

"'Why does not Monsieur le Capitaine bleed?' said he suddenly. 'Has he used anything to stop the hæmorrhage so successfully?' and he took my arm in his hands.

"Sure enough-no drop of blood had flowed from the deep stab in my forearm.

"'Why, the arm is dead,' cried Jean Boule, as he felt it. 'What have you been doing to it, mon Capitaine? ...Excuse me' ...and he placed a thumb on each side of the stab, opened it, and peered. Then he laughed in his quiet gentlemanly way, and glanced at the smashed lamp.

"'I thought so,' he said. 'Glass. No circulation. The hand dead,' and he laughed again.

"'What do you mean, Légionnaire?' I asked, nettled by his amusement.

"'Why-Monsieur le Capitaine has had a great and terrible fight *with himself* —and won. He went to sleep on his right side with his right arm raised and bent over his neck-and the arm also went to sleep as the circulation ceased, owing to the position-and Monsieur le Capitaine got hold of his throat and choked himself. Then he had nightmare, *cauchemar*, turned on his back, and woke up choking, and it was some time before he could budge the cold, stiff arm.... When he did, he flung it straight on to the lamp, broke the thing, and cut himself to the bone.'...

"And so it was!...

"But I contend that *I have been throttled by a Dead Hand*, d'Amienville."...

Lieutenant d'Amienville made a strange noise in his throat and then rose and escaped from the circle of mocking eyes.

It was felt that Captain d'Armentières had not only moved an immovable arm, but had, as the droll English say, "pulled" an unpullable leg.

V. The Gift

It was Guest Night at the Spahis' mess.

"What *I* complain of is the utter absence of gratitude among natives," said "Général" Archambaud Thibaud d'Amienville of the Chasseurs d'Afrique of the XIXth Army Corps of La République Française. "It is highly significant that there is no word for 'Thank you' in the vernacular, isn't it? ...If you do a native a good turn, he either wonders what you want of him, or else casts about in his mind for the reason why you want to propitiate him. If you had cause to punish one of your Spahis and did not do it, he would think you were afraid to. Kindness is in their eyes pure weakness. If you forego vengeance, it must be because you think the offender may avenge that vengeance. No, gratitude doesn't flourish under a tropical sun." ...Lieutenant d'Amienville was very young and therefore very cynical.

"Is it a plant of very hardy growth under a temperate one?" inquired Captain Gautier d'Armentières of the First Battalion of the Legion. "I seem to have heard complaints, and I fancy that poets from the days of Homer to those of this morning have had something to say about it."

"Quite so," agreed Médecin-Major Parme; "but pass me the matches, and I will promise a brief pang of gratitude.... Quite so.... If a fellow does you a really good turn, he is strongly inclined to like you for evermore, and you are equally strongly disposed to regard him as a nuisance, and his mouldy face as a reminder of the time when you had to *faire la lessive*[199] or were in some fearful scrape....I could name a certain absinthe-sodden old Colonel who absolutely loathes me for having saved him, body and soul, some years ago, when he had been betting (and, of course, losing, as all people who bet do) and had then gone to Monte Carlo to put everything right at the gaming-tables! What made it worse was the fact that the departed francs were rather the property of Madame la République than of the Colonel. And Madame prefers to do her own gambling. His position, one Sunday night, was that Monday morning must find him with gold in his pocket or lead in his brain. I found the gold, as I had been at school with him, and had stayed with his people a lot, ...but I am sure he merely remembers a very shady passage in his career every time he sees me, and loathes me in consequence. He paid the debt off long ago, too."

"I believe you are right," agreed Colonel Lebrun. "One uses the expression '*debt* of gratitude,' and nobody really likes being in debt....The gratitude is rarely paid though. I suppose it is because the creditor of gratitude occupies the higher ground, and one resents being on the lower."

"I certainly once lost a friend by doing him a kindness," put in Adjudant-Major Berthon of the Legion, who was also dining at the Spahis' mess. "This was a loan case, too, and a slight coolness ending in a sharp frost followed immediately upon it....And it wasn't my fault the coolness arose, I am sure."

"Of course the benefactor always likes the beneficiary better than the beneficiary likes the benefactor," said the cynical "Général" d'Amienville, "and the kind action always dwells longer in the mind of the doer than in that of the receiver. Far longer. Always."

"Not always," observed Captain d'Armentières. "Only yesterday..."

"*Always*," contradicted d'Amienville.

"I was about to say," continued d'Armentières, "that, only yesterday, I reminded a man of a good turn he did me years ago, and he had clean forgotten it....And it was a deed I could not forget if I lived to be a hundred years old."

"I simply don't believe a man could give you half of his kingdom, or save your valuable life or honour, and forget all about it," replied the "Général."

"I did not say he gave me a half of his kingdom or saved my valuable life or honour," was the quiet answer. "I said he did me a good turn and had absolutely forgotten the incident though I have not, and never shall. I feel the deepest gratitude towards him and always will. I should be very glad of an opportunity of proving the fact."...

"A very noble sentiment," sneered the young gentleman.

"No," said d'Armentières patiently. "I am not concerned to exhibit my high morality, fine nature, and noble sentiments, but am stating an example in opposition to your theory; a fact of memory-the respective memories of benefactor and beneficiary. He had forgotten doing the kindness, while I had remembered receiving it."

"What was the nature of the action, if one might inquire?" put in Médecin-Major Parme.

"Yes, what did he do, *mon salop*?" added Colonel Lebrun. "Surrender the beauteous damsel whom you both loved, with the hiccuping cry, 'Take her. She is thine,' and thenceforth hide a breaking heart beneath a writhing brow or a wrinkling tunic or something?"

"Did he leap into the raging flood, or only place his huge fortune at your disposal? What was the noble deed?" asked Adjudant-Major Berthon.

"It was a gift," replied d'Armentières, smiling. "A free, unsolicited, unexpected, magnificent gift."

"And he had *forgotten* it?" asked d'Amienville, with cold incredulity.

"Absolutely. But I never shall," said d'Armentières.

"And pray, what was this magnificent gift?" sneered d'Amienville. "A priceless horse, a mistress, an estate, a connoisseur's collection, an invaluable secret, your freedom-or what? What wonderful thing did he present to you and forget?"

"A sausage," was the grave answer.

The Spahis roared with laughter at their unpopular brother-officer. He was their guest, but they could not forbear to laugh. A very little goes a long way in the matter of wit in a bored mess, exiled from Home and the larger interests of life.

The "Général" coloured hotly, and remarked that some people were doubtless devilish funny-in season and out of season.

"I assure you it is my misfortune and not my fault if I am funny," was the grave statement of the Legionary. "I have been the recipient of other kindnesses, but not one of them has made such a mark on the tablets of my memory as that sausage."

"They do make marks, I know," observed Médecin-Major Parme. "My wife threw one at me once, just as I was going out to call on the Commander-in-Chief-in-Algeria. He noticed the mark before I did."

"Tell us the touching tale," put in Colonel Lebrun. "Were you on a raft in mid-ocean with one sausage between you and death, and did he say, 'Thy belly is greater than mine,' or 'Your bird,' or something?"

"Surely he'd remember that," observed the sapient d'Amienville.

"No. 'Twas thus," said d'Armentières. "You Spahis don't, for your sins, get sent to Indo-China. We do. And it can be more truly damnable along the Red River than in any desert station in the Sahara. You *have* got the sun, though you grumble at it, and too much heat is always better and less depressing than too little, to my way of thinking. What did Dante know of Hell when he had never been in a place consisting wholly of muddy water and watery mud-with nothing else for hundreds of square miles-except fever, starvation, dysentery, and the acutest craving for suicide? Yes. A low black sky of wet cotton wool, a vast river of black, muddy water, and its banks vast expanses of black watery mud. Nothing else to see-but much to feel. I was a young soldier then —a private of the Legion in my first year."...

Captain d'Armentières paused. No one moved or spoke. It was not easy to "get him going" — but it was worth a lot of trouble, for d'Armentières was a man of very great experience, very great courage, and very great ability. Soldier, philosopher, reformer, hero, thinker, and something of a saint.

"Yes-you can go for weeks along the Red River of Tonkin, in an old stinking sampan, drenched, chilled to the bone, shivering, until you envy the Annamese boatmen in their straw hut in the stern-and see nothing but clouds, water, and mud, save when the unceasing rain is too heavy for you to see anything at all. If God is very good, you *may* perhaps see a castor-oil plant sailing along in the water to tell that there are other human beings somewhere in the terrible world of mud, water, fog, clouds, and rain-Annamese peasants who have sown castor-oil plants in the mud, apparently for the pleasure of seeing that accursed river change its course in order to engulf them.

"I remember wondering why I, why any single one of my Company, consented to live another day.... You Spahis and Chasseurs, Zouaves and Tirailleurs Algériens, Turcos and others of the XIXth Army Corps talk of your desert hardships-thirst, *cafard*, Arabs, heat, *ennui*....Pah! I have tried both, and I'd serve a year in the Sahara rather than a week in the Annam jungles in the rains. I remember asking the man to whom I have been referring, my benefactor, an Englishman calling himself John Bull, or Jean Boule, why *he*, for example, went on living.

"'I don't know,' he replied, 'Partly hope of better things, I suppose. Partly a feeling that suicide is cowardice, and partly the strongest instinct of the human mind-that of self-preservation.'

"And yet, he was obviously a very unhappy man-as any refined person of breeding and education must be, in the ranks of the Legion. I pondered this until, night falling, the boatmen steered for the shore and anchored our junk. The happy souls then shut themselves in their straw hut and caroused on *shum-shum*, the poor man's absinthe in China-an awful rice-spirit — while we huddled, foodless, sodden, and frozen in that ceaseless rain, fog, and bitter wind.... Who would not drink himself insensible and unconscious when there was nothing of which to be sensible and conscious but misery of the acutest? ... It always interests me to hear the comfortably-placed rail against the drunkenness of the poor and wretched....What would not the smuggest bourgeois Bonpère not have given, had he been with us that night, to drown his shuddering soul in the vilest form of alcohol, and escape that bitter fog, fever, hunger, sickness, and awful ache; the mosquitoes, stench, pain, and homeless, lonely misery....When the 'Black Flags' came, with the full moon, I was glad, I would have consented to fall into their hands alive rather than not die-and they could have taught the Holy Inquisition a whole language and literature of torture of which the Inquisition only knew the alphabet....Yes. I knew I had malarial fever, and I feared I had yellow fever. I knew I had dysentery, and I feared I had cholera. I knew I had an appalling cold and cough, and I feared I had consumption. I can now smile at myself as I was then-but I can also make allowances, for I was a starving, fever-wrecked child of seventeen-nearly dead with dysentery....The bullets of the Black Flags were striking all around us, and it was a case of attacking them for our own safety. They were so close and had the range so well that I suspected our boatmen. I remember old Ivan Plevinski suddenly grunted hideously, heaved himself to his feet, removed his *képi*, and bowed toward the bank. '*Merci, messieurs,*' he gasped, '*Milles remerciments. Je vous renter cie. Slav a Bogu,*[200]' and died. I envied old Ivan Plevinski, and, judging by his way of life, decided that it would not be from cold that he would suffer in the Hereafter....

"Meanwhile, John Bull, by right of his superior ability, experience, personality, and force, had taken command, and the sampan was being poled and hauled ashore. I tried to take a hand at heaving-in the anchor-rope, but fell on it from sheer weakness and was kicked clear of it. As the junk grounded in the mud, the Legionaries sprang over the side, led by John Bull, and struggled through the mud toward the swamp-jungle whence the bullets came. I staggered as far as I could, and then fell and began slowly to sink in the black clayey mud. No —I was not afraid, only very glad to die. And half delirious, watched the fight in the moonlight. I remember being bitterly disappointed that I could not distinguish the features of a man who, on his half-engulfed arms and knees, was vomiting blood just in front of me. I did so want to know who had 'got it,' for he also would accompany me and Ivan Plevinski to the Judgment Seat. I wondered what St. Peter would say if the fellow vomited blood on the doorstep of the Gates of Heaven. Then I became unconscious, delirious....The junk following ours-in which was Lieutenant Egrier, as he then was-came ashore, took the 'pirates' in flank, and drove them off....

"All this leading up to the Sausage of Contention" (with a little bow and smile in the direction of Lieutenant d'Amienville, fingering his wine-glass and endeavouring to maintain a cynical smile)...."You know Egrier's bluff, jolly way. 'What would you like, Jean Boule-recommendation for the *Croix de Guerre* or one of my tinned sausages,' he cried, as he approached Jean, who was pulling me out of the mud. I had broken into a perspiration, and was my own man again by then, and desperately anxious to live. (What was wrong with a world that held 'recommendations,' the *Croix de Guerre*, the *Médaille Militaire*, promotion, a career of glory fighting for La Belle France?)

"'A sausage, mon Lieutenant,' replied Jean Boule, laying me on a bed he had made of mangrove twigs, straw from the boat, and his *capote*.

"'Wise philosopher,' laughed Egrier. 'You shall have two-one for distinguished conduct in the field and one for wisdom.'

"He was as good as his word. Before our sampans resumed their way to Phu-lang-Thuong, he gave Jean two sausages from the tin he opened. As I live, that gaunt, starving man cooked them both, gave one to me, and made the rest of our boat-load cast lots for the other.

"I met him recently. He is still *Soldat deuxième classe*, for he has consistently refused promotion. When I shook him by the hand, he remembered me, but he had absolutely and completely forgotten the episode of the sausage.

"I have not-and I regard his gift to me that day on the Red River in Tonkin as one of the noblest ever given....He is my orderly now....Have you ever starved, d'Amienville? ...No?"...

VI. The Deserter

As she stood on the deck beside her lover-husband and gazed upon the thrillingly beautiful panorama of Marseilles, there was assuredly no happier woman in the world. As he looked at the rapt face and wide-opened glorious eyes of the lovely girl beside him there can scarcely have been a man as happy.

They had been married in England a week earlier, were on their way to his vast house and vaster estate in Australia, and had come round by sea, instead of suffering the miseries of the "special" across France (which saves a week to leave-expired returning Anglo-Indians).

Happy! Her happiness was almost a pain. As a child she had childishly adored him; and now he had returned from his wanderings, after a decade of varied, strenuous life-to adore her. Life was too impossibly, hopelessly wonderful and beautiful....He, who had been everywhere, done everything, been everything-soldier, sailor, rancher, planter, prospector, hunter, explorer-had come Home for a visit, and laid his heart at the feet of a country mouse. Happy! His happiness frightened him. After more than ten years of the roughest of roughing it, he had "made good" (exceeding good), and on top of good fortune incredible, had, to his wondering bewilderment, won the love of the sweetest, noblest, fairest, and most utterly lovable and desirable woman in the world. She whom he had left a child had grown into his absolute ideal of Woman, and had been by some miracle reserved for him.

And which would now know the greater joy in their travels-he in showing her the fair places of the earth and telling her of personal experiences therein, or she in being shown them by this adored hero who had come to make her life a blessed dream of joy? Not that the fair places of the earth were necessary to their happiness. They could have spent a happy day in London on a wet Sunday, or at the end of Southend pier on a Bank Holiday, or in a prison-cell for that matter-for the mind of each to the other a kingdom was.

"Would you like to go ashore? ... 'Madame, will you walk and talk with me,' in the *Cannebière*?" he asked.

"Of *course*, we must go ashore, Beloved Snail," was the reply. "I have no idea what the *Cannebière is* —but," and she hugged his arm and whispered, "you can always 'give me the keys of Heaven,' and walk and talk with me There." (He was "Beloved Snail" when he was a Bad Man and late for meals; "Bill" when he was virtuous or forgiven.)

The ship being tied up, and a notice having guaranteed that she would on no account untie before midnight, this foolish couple, who utterly loved each other, walked down the gangway, passed the old lady who sells balloons and the old gentleman who sells deck-chairs, the young lady who sells glorious violets and the young gentleman who sells un-glorious "field"-glasses; through the echoing customs-shed and out to where, beside a railway-line, specimens of the genus *cocher* lie in wait for those who would drive to the boulevards and in hope for those who know not that four francs is ample fare.

To the sights of Marseilles he took her, enjoying her enjoyment as he had enjoyed few things in his life, and then in the *Cannebière* dismissed the fiacre.

"In Rome you must roam like the Romans," he observed. "In Marseilles you must sit on little chairs in front of a café and see the World and his Wife (or Belle Amie) go by."

"Fancy sitting outside a public-house in Regent Street or the Strand and watching Londoners go by!" said the girl. "Isn't it extraordinary what a difference in habits and customs one finds by travelling a few miles? Think of English officers sitting, in uniform, on the pavement, like those are, and drinking in public," ...and she pointed to a group of French officers so engaged. "Do let's go and sit near them," she added. "I have never seen soldiers dressed in pale blue and silver, and all the colours of the rainbow....Aren't they pretty-dears!"...

"Their uniforms look quaint to the insular eye, madam, I admit," he replied, as he led the way to an unoccupied table near the brilliant group, "but they are not toy soldiers by any means. They all belong to regiments of the African Army Corps, the Nineteenth, and there isn't a finer one on earth."

"Darling, you know *everything*," smiled his wife. "Fancy knowing a thing like that now! I wonder how many other Englishmen know anything about this African Army and that it is the Ninety-Ninth. Now *how* do you know?"

It was his turn to smile, and he did so somewhat wryly.

"What will you have?" he asked, as an aproned *garçon* hovered around. "Coffee or *sirop* or–how would you like to be devil-of-a-fellow and taste a sip of absinthe? ...You'll hate it."

"No, thank you, Bill-man. Is the syrup golden-syrup or syrup-of-squills or what? No, I'll have some coffee and see if it is."

"Is what?"

"Coffee."...

Meanwhile an elderly, grizzled officer, with a somewhat brutal face, was staring hard and rudely at the unconscious couple. He wore a dark blue tunic with red-tabbed and gold-braided collar and cuffs, scarlet overalls, and a blue and red *képi*. So prolonged was his unshifting gaze, so fierce his frown, and so obvious his interest, that his companions noticed the fact.

"Is the old hog smitten with *la belle Anglaise*, I wonder, or what?" murmured a handsome youth in the beautiful pale blue uniform of the Chasseurs d'Afrique to an even more gorgeous officer of Spahis.

"I have never known Legros take the faintest interest in women," replied the other. "There will be a beastly *fracas* if the husband glances this way. He'll promise Legros to *ponch ees 'ead* if he thinks he's being rude–as he is."

Certainly the elderly and truculent-looking officer was being rude, for not only was he staring with a hard, concentrated glare, but he was leaning as far forward as he could, the better to do it. Anyone–man, woman, or child–being conscious of this deliberate, searching gaze, must resent it. It was that of a gendarme, examining the face of a criminal and endeavouring to "place" him and recollect the details of his last encounter with him, or of a *juge d'instruction* examining a criminal in that manner which does not find favour in England.

"It is as good as sitting in the stalls of a theatre, sitting here and seeing all these varied types go by, isn't it, Bill?" observed the girl. "Oh, *do* look at *that* —that boy in brown velvet and a forked beard!"

"We are sitting in the Stalls of the Theatre of Life, my child," was the sententious reply, but in reality they were sitting nearer to the Pit.

The brutal-looking officer scratched the back of his neck slowly up and down with the forefinger of his left hand, a sure sign that he was wrestling with an elusive reminiscence. For a moment he took his eyes from the face of the Englishman and looked sideways at the pavement, cudgelling his brains, ransacking the cells of his memory. With a muttered oath at failure to recapture some piece of long-stored information, he put his hand into the inside pocket of his tunic and produced a tiny flat case. From this he took a pair of pince-nez and adjusted them upon the bridge of his broad, short nose. From the slowness and clumsiness of his movements it was evident that he had only just taken to glasses, or else wore them very seldom.

The latter was the case, as Lieutenant Legros considered spectacles of any kind a most unmilitary and *pékinesque* adjunct to uniform.

A quiet, gentlemanly-looking officer, a Captain, wearing a similar uniform to that of Legros, observed the action.

"Evidently something interests our friend beyond ordinary," he remarked, and followed the look that the elderly Lieutenant again fixed upon the Englishman, whom the Captain now noticed for the first time.

Sitting with his back to the road, and almost facing Legros, he got a better view of the Englishman's features than did that deeply interested officer, who, without reply, continued his searching scrutiny. Evidently a person of great powers of concentration. As his glance fell upon the young couple, the Captain started slightly and then looked away.

"Who's for a stroll?" he remarked, half rising. But his suggestion was not adopted, for glasses were charged, cigarettes alight, the shade of the café and awning very agreeable, and the sunshine hot without.

"Have an *apéritif* first, *mon ami*, and be restful," said a Zouave officer, and tinkled the little table-bell loudly.

The Englishman half-consciously turned toward the sound, and looked away again without noticing the baleful, steady glare fixed upon him through the glasses of the Lieutenant.

"*Dame!*" grunted that officer, and smote his brow in an agony of exasperation at the failure of his memory.... Curse it! Was he getting old? He had the fellow's name and the circumstances of his case on the tip of his tongue, so to speak-at the tips of his fingers, as it were-and he could not say the word he was bursting to say; could not lay his twitching mental fingers on the details.... He knew.... He was right.... He would have it in a minute.

A paper-boy passed the long front of the café and shouted some wholly unintelligible word as he gazed over the serried ranks of chairs and loungers.

"What does he say, Bill?" asked the girl. "It sounds like *Barin*. How ill the poor lad looks! Fancy having to sell papers for a living when you are starving and horribly ill, as he obviously is," and as her hand stole to her charitable purse, she gratefully thought of the utter security, peace, comfort, and health of *her* life-now that Bill had linked it to his.... What was the phrase? ... Yes-she had "hitched her wagon to a star"; her poor little homely wagon to the glorious and brilliant star of her Bill's career.... The inquisitorial Lieutenant used the paper-boy for the purposes of his tactics. Rising, he made his way between the chairs and the groups of *apéritif*-drinking citizens, to where the boy stood, bought a paper, and returned by a route which brought him full face-to-face with the Englishman. Recognition was instantaneous and mutual. The brutal countenance of the elderly Lieutenant was not improved by a sardonic smile and look of mean and petty triumph as he thrust an outstretched index-finger in the Englishman's face and harshly grunted.

"Henri Rrrobinson!" and then laughed a sneering, hideous cackle.

Staring in utter bewilderment from the French officer to her husband, the girl saw with horror that his jaw had dropped, his mouth and eyes were gaping wide, and he had gone as white as a sheet.

"Sergeant Legros!" he whispered.

"Lieutenant Legros," grunted the other.

What had happened? What in the name of the Merciful Father was this? Was she dreaming? Her husband looked deathly. He seemed paralysed with fright.

The Lieutenant half turned, and shouted to a couple of sombre and mysterious-looking gens d'armes who had been standing for some time on the little "island" under the big lamp-post in the middle of the road. As they approached, the Englishman rose to his feet.

"Listen, darling!" he hissed. "Get out of this quick-to the ship. Take a *fiacre* and say '*P. and O. bateau.*' I'll join you all right. They have..."

The Lieutenant put a heavy hand on his shoulder and swung him round.

"Arrest this man," said he to the gens d'armes, "and take him to Fort St. Jean. He is a deserter, one Henri Rrrobinson, from the First Battalion of the Foreign Legion. Deserted from Sidi-bel-Abbès eight years ago. But *I* knew the dog. Aha!"

The group of officers whom Legros had just left, joined the gathering crowd.

"Poor devil!" said Captain d'Armentières. He too had recognized the *soi-disant* Henry Robinson.... "Poor girl!" he added. "Poor little soul!" She looked like une *nouvelle mariée* too. Of course Legros had only done his duty-curse him. Curse him a thousand times for a black-guardly, brutal ruffian. The girl was going to faint.... Her wedding-ring looked brand-new. "If this is his wedding-night, he'll spend it in the *salle de police* of Fort St. Jean," he reflected. "If he is on his honeymoon, he'll spend it in the *cellules* until the General Court-Martial at Oran gives him a few years *rabiau* with the Zephyrs. If he survives that, which is improbable, he will finish his five years of Legion service. No-she won't see much of him during the next decade.... Poor little soul!"

The gens d'armes duly arrested the deserter. He caught the eye of the Captain.

"Captain d'Armentières," said he, "you are a French gentleman. This lady is my wife. We have been married a week. I beg of you to see her safe on board the P. and O. steamer *Maloja*, which we have just left, for an hour's visit here."

"I will do so," said d'Armentières.

A fat and kindly Frenchman, who understood English, translated for the benefit of the crowd. It became intensely sympathetic-at least with the girl. The French, for some reason, imagine their Foreign Legion to be composed of Germans, and the French do not love Germans.... And then, having commended his wife to d'Armentières (whom he had liked and admired in the past when he had played the fool's prank of joining the Legion "for a lark"), he thought rapidly and clearly....

If they once got him inside Fort St. Jean (the clearing-house for drafts and details going to, and coming from, Algeria-recruits, convalescents, leave-expired, all sorts; Legionaries, Zouaves, Turcos, Spahis, Tirailleurs) he was done. In a short time he would be a convict, in military-convict dress, enduring the living-death of existence in the Zephyrs, the terrible Disciplinary Battalion, compared with whose lot that of the British long-sentence convict at Dartmoor, Portland, or Wormwood Scrubbs is a bed of roses in the lap of luxury. After that-back to the Legion *if* he were alive to finish his five years, of which there were four unexpired. And his wife-stranded, without money, in Marseilles, unless d'Armentières got her to the ship. And what would she do then-at the end of the voyage? ...God help them! ...A few minutes ago-happiness unspeakable, safety, security, peace, all life before them. Now-in a few minutes he would be in gaol and his adored, adoring wife a deserted, friendless stranger in a strange land.... Would they *allow* d'Armentières to take her to the ship? Would they want her to give evidence-put her in some kind of prison until the Court-Martial sat? Suppose d'Armentières had not been there, and she had been left to the tender mercies of Legros-or utterly deserted, fainting on a café chair....

Well, things couldn't be much worse (or *could* they) if he "resisted the police," assaulted the duly-appointed officers of the law in the execution of their duty, and made a break for liberty. No, things couldn't be worse. Neither he nor she would survive the next ten years. And there was a *chance*, or the ghost of a shadow of a chance. The deck of the *Maloja* was English soil, and they could not lay a finger on him there. If only she were safe on board, he'd make the attempt. There was a chance-and he had always taken the sporting chance, all his life....And this vile cur of a Legros! He had many a score to pay off to Sergeant Legros-the prize bully of the XIXth Army Corps. Now *this*! If he could only have his hands at the throat of Legros. As these thoughts flashed through his brain, "May I say farewell to my wife and see her into a *fiacre* with you, Captain d'Armentières?" he asked. He appeared to be as cool as he was pale. The Captain was the senior officer present.

"Yes," he said. "I will drive her as quickly as possible to the ship," and willing hands helped the fainting girl into the *fiacre*....Was she dying? As she lost her hold and sank into the bottomless depths of unconsciousness she was finally aware that her husband winked at her violently. That wink in a face which was a pallid, tragic mask, was the most dreadful and heartrending thing she had ever seen. Anyhow, it meant some kind of reassurance which he could not put into words without disclosing some plan to his captors. She fainted completely, in the act of wondering whether this was merely that he was putting a good face on it and pretending for her benefit, or whether he really had a plan. Anyhow she was to go to the ship-and, in any case, she was dying of a broken heart....

As he watched his wife driven rapidly away, the Englishman formulated his plans.

He would delay as long as he could in order that his wife might be on board the ship before he reached it, if ever he did.

He would go quietly and willingly-but as slowly as possible-while the road to Fort St. Jean was the road to the ship. He would then break away from his pursuers and run for it. He would show them what an old Oxford miler and International Rugger forward could do in the way of running and dodging, and, perchance, what sort of a fight an amateur champion heavy-weight could put up.

But strategy first, strength and skill afterwards, for he was playing a terrible game, with his wife's happiness at stake, not to mention his own liberty. With a groan, he artistically smote his knees together and sank to the ground. That would gain a little time anyhow, and they'd hardly carry him to Fort St. Jean, nor waste a cab-fare on the carcase of a Legionary.

He wasn't quite certain as to the nearest way from the *Cannebière* to Fort St. Jean, but he remembered that it was down by the waterfront. Yes, he could again see its quaint old tower, like a lighthouse, and its drawbridged moat, as he closed his eyes. Part of the way to it would be the way to the P. and O. wharf at Mole C, or whatever it was, anyhow. Would they take him by tram? That might complicate matters. If they were going to do that, should he make his break for liberty at once, or on the journey, or at the end of it? It would be comparatively easy to make a dash before or after the tram-ride, but they'd surely never let him escape them from a crowded tram. Would they handcuff him? If so, that would settle it. He'd fight and run the moment handcuffs were produced. You can't run in handcuffs, although you think you can. Would they shoot? It would be Hell to be winged in sight of the ship. Was the P. and O. wharf British soil, as well as the ship?

Almost certainly not.

Lieutenant Legros kicked him in the ribs.

"Get up, *tricheur*," he shouted. He was in his element, and fairly gloated over his victim, who only groaned and collapsed the more.

To those of the crowd who realized that he was an Englishman, he was an object of pity; to those who concluded that, being a Legionary, he was a German, he was merely an object of interest.

The officers who had been sitting with Legros departed in some disgust, and the crowd changed, eddied, and thinned....Only a sick man being attended to by a couple of gens d'armes!

These latter grew a little impatient. The sooner they could dispose of this fine fellow the better, but they certainly weren't going to march to Fort St. Jean at the request of a Lieutenant of Légionaries. Let the army do its own dirty work. They'd run him in all right to the nearest lock-up, and he could be handed over to the military authorities, to be dealt with, whenever they liked to fetch him. To the devil with all Légionnaires, be they deserters or Lieutenants!

"He had better be taken to the police-station on a stretcher, mon Lieutenant," suggested one of them. "It would appear that he has fainted."

"Stretcher!" roared Legros, and spat. "Pah! That is not how we deal with swine of Légionnaires who sham sick. Stretcher! Drag him face downward by one toe at the tail of a dust-cart more likely!"

Oho! Police-station, was it? Not Fort St. Jean immediately. And where might the nearest police-station be, wondered the prostrate Englishman. He must not let them get him there. The boat would sail at midnight, whether he were on board or not-and once the cell door closed on him it would not open till the morning.

Perhaps he had better take his leave at once. Unless they went in the direction of the docks for some part of the way it would be a cruelly punishing run....Just as bad for them though, and he'd back himself against any of these beefy old birds for a four-mile race....His wife must be half-way there by now-more, if d'Armentières urged the *cocher*, as he would.

Was it likely that d'Armentières would collect a guard of gens d'armes, dock police, soldiers, or customs officials at the wharf gate or the ship's gangway, and lie in wait to see if he tried to get on board? No —d'Armentières was not that sort.

(He was not, and when, later, Lieutenant Legros was reduced to the rank of sergeant for what was practically the brutal murder of a Legionary, Captain d'Armentières thought of this incident and rejoiced.)

And if he did-let them stop him if they could. He'd break through the scrum of them all right. Lay some of them out too.

What was Legros saying? Urging the gens d'armes to boot him up and lug him off by the scruff of his neck, eh?

He groaned again, sat up with difficulty, shakily and painfully rose to his feet, then smote Legros a smashing blow between the eyes, butted the gendarme who stood on his right, and with a dodge, a jump, and a wriggle was away and running like a hare.

To the end of his life he never forgot that race for life, and for more than life. Scores of times he lived through it again in terrible nightmares and suffered a thousand times more than he did on the actual run itself. For then he was quite cool, steady, and unafraid. He imagined himself to be running with the ball at Blackheath or Richmond, threading his way through the hostile fifteen, dodging, leaping, handing-off. But there were one or two differences. In Rugger you may not drive your clenched fist with all your might into the face of any man who springs at you.... Nor do you run for miles over cobbles....

It was really surprisingly easy. Once he had got clear and put a few yards between himself and the uninjured gendarme, it was even betting that he'd win-provided his wind held and he didn't get the stitch, and that he did not slip and fall on the cursed stones. For the folk behind he cared nothing, and with such in front as grasped the situation in time to do something, he could deal. Some he dodged, some he handed-off as at Rugger, and some he hit. These last were slower to rise than those he handed-off, or caused to fall by dodging them as they sprang at him.

When he turned a sharp corner he was so well ahead of the original pursuers that he was merely a man running, and that is not in itself an indictable offence. Certainly people stopped and stared at the sight of an obvious foreigner running at top speed, but he might have a boat to catch, he might be pursuing a train of thought or his lost youth and innocence. *Que voulez-vous?* Besides, he might be English, and therefore mad.

And then the blue-faced, panting gendarme would round the corner at the head of such *gamins*, loafers, police agents, and other citizens as saw fit to run on a hot afternoon. Whereupon people in this sector of street would look after the runaway and some run after him as well. So the pursuing crowd continually changed, as some left it and others joined it, until there remained of the old original firm scarcely any but the distressed and labouring gendarme-who, at last, himself gave up, reeled to the wall, and whooping and gasping for breath, prepared to meet his Maker.

Before the poor man had decided that this event was not yet, the Englishman had dashed round another corner and actually leapt on to an electric tram in full flight toward the *quais*!

Ciel! How mad were these English! Fancy a man running like that now, just to catch a tram. No, he would not go inside; he preferred to stand on the platform, and stand there he would.

He did, and anon, the tram having stopped at his polite request to the conductor, he strolled on to the P. and O. wharf and marched up the gangway of the good ship *Maloja*.

A steward informed him that his wife were ill, 'aving been brought aboard by a French gent and took to 'er cabing. She were still lying down....

She was, at that moment, very ill indeed, mentally and physically.

But not for long, when his arms had assured her that they were not those of a vision and a ghost....

If you ever travel Home with them, you'll find they don't go ashore at Marseilles. No, they don't like the place-prefer to stay on board, even through the coaling.

VII. Five Minutes

Le Légionnaire Jacques Bonhomme (as he called himself) was dying, and Sergeant Baudré, in charge of the convoy of wounded, proceeding from the nasty, messy fighting at Hu-Thuong to the base hospital at Phulang-Thuong, kindly permitted a brief halt that he might die in peace.

The good Sergeant Baudré could not accord more than an hour to the Legionary for his dying arrangements, because he had been instructed by his captain to get back as quickly as possible, and Phulang-Thuong lies only twenty-four miles south of Hu-Thuong.

Sergeant Baudré had other reasons also. For one, he was apprehensive of attack by some wandering band of De Nam's "pirates," and the outlaw brigands who served Monsieur De Nam, mandarin of the deposed Emperor of Annam, Ham-Nghi, were men whose courage and skill in fighting were only excelled by their ingenuity and pitilessness in torturing such of their enemies as fell into their hands. No, Sergeant Baudré had seen the remains of some of the prisoners of these "Black Flags," and he shuddered yet whenever he thought of them.

And what could he do, strung out over a mile, with a weak escort of Tirailleurs Tonkinois to provide his point, cover-point, and main body with the wounded, and an *escouade* of Legionaries for his rearguard? The sooner he got to Phulang-Thuong, the better. Returning, unhampered by the wounded, he could take care of himself, and any band of "Black Flags" who chose to attack him could do so. They should have a taste of the fighting qualities of Sergeant Baudré and his Legionaries. As it was-Sergeant Baudré shrugged his shoulders and bade Legionary Jacques Bonhomme die and be done with it.

"I thank you, Sergeant," murmured the dying man. "May I speak with le Légionnaire Jean Boule, if he is with the squad?"

The Sergeant grunted. He ran his eye along the halted column. Would those Tirailleurs Tonkinois stand, if there were a sudden rush of howling devils from the dense jungle on either side of the track? And why should they be allowed to take their women about with them everywhere, so that these should carry their kit and accoutrements for them? Nobody carried Sergeant Baudré's hundred-weight of kit when he marched. Why should these Annamese be pampered thus? Should he send the squad of Legionaries to the head of the column when they advanced again? It would be just his luck if the column was attacked in front while the Legionaries were in the rear, or *vice versâ*.

Sergeant Baudré strolled toward the rear. He would get the opinion of "Jean Boule" in the course of a little apparently aimless conversation. He had been an officer before he joined the Legion, and these English knew all there is to know about guerilla fighting....

From his remarks and replies it was clear to the good Sergeant that the Englishman considered that any attack would certainly come from the rear.

"Without doubt," agreed Sergeant Baudré. "That is why I keep the *escouade* as rear-guard."

"By the way," he added, "Légionnaire Bonhomme wishes to say '*Au 'voir*' to you. He is off in a few minutes. Go and tell him to hurry up. We march again as soon as we have fed. He is the first stretcher in front of the Tirailleurs' women."

Légionnaire John Bull hurried to the spot. He knew that poor Jacques Bonhomme's number was up. It was a marvel how he had hung on, horribly wounded as he was-shot, speared, and staked, all at once, and all in the abdomen. He had been friendly with Jacques-an educated man and once a gentleman.

A glance showed him that he was too late. The man was delirious and semi-conscious. If he had any message or commission, it would never be put into words now.

The Englishman sat on the ground beside the stretcher and took the hand of the poor wretch. Possibly some sense of sympathy, company, friendship, or support might penetrate to, and comfort, the stricken soul.

After a while the over-bright eyes turned toward him.

"Any message, Jacques, *mon ami?*" he whispered, stroking the hand he held.

But Jacques Bonhomme talked on in the monotonous way of the fever-smitten, though with a strange consecutiveness. John Bull listened carefully, in the hope that some name, rank, office, or address might be mentioned and give a clue to relatives or the undelivered message or last commission.

..."Only five minutes in each year! Morel tells me there are five hundred and twenty-five thousand and six hundred minutes in each year, and I believe him implicitly, for he is the finest mathematical professor the Sorbonne ever had. I believe him implicitly. He is no Classic, but he has good points and can do wonderful things with figures. Wonderful feats! He knows all about things like the Metric System, Decimals, and Vulgar Fractions and similar things of which one hears but never encounters. He can not only add up columns of francs and centimes, such as are found in the bills which tradesmen are fond of writing, even when they have received payment, but he can deal with things like pounds, shillings, and pence; dollars and cents; yen and sabuks; or rupees, annas, and pice, not only with marvellous accuracy, but with incredible rapidity. This makes him an invaluable travelling companion for a Classic who knows none of these things-apart from the fact that he can also find out the times of trains and steamers from railway and shipping guides. It is wonderful to see him seize a book, scan it for a moment, and then say unhesitatingly that a train will leave the Gare de Lyon at a certain hour on a certain day, that it will just catch a ship at Marseilles on the next day, and that this ship will just catch another at Aden, so many days later, and that this one will land you in Japan at a certain hour on a certain day. And yet he is not a bit proud of these things-no prouder than I am of my little metrical translation of the Satires and Odes of Horace into Greek. And he thinks I travel with him for the sake of his delightful company! A man who cannot utter a hackneyed Latin quotation without some horrible false quantity. Poor Morel!...

"And this piece of information as to the number of minutes in a year is one of the most useful calculations he ever did on my behalf, except the one he did in answer to my query as to how many waking minutes there are-how many minutes in what one might call an active or waking year. That is to say, counting only the minutes when one is not asleep. He tells me there are three hundred and seventy-two thousand and three hundred waking minutes in the year for a man who averages seven hours sleep a day, or rather night-for he never sleeps in the day. How he knows I cannot tell, but I believe him absolutely, for he is as truthful as he is clever. So now I know that if I subtract five from this last appalling total I can tell how many minutes of the year I spend in thinking of the other five. After arriving at an aggravating variety of results, I again sought the good Morel's help, and he assures me that, subtracting five from the last total with which he furnished me, I have three hundred and seventy-two thousand and two hundred and ninety-five minutes.

"Thus I can now tell you clearly, that I spend three hundred and seventy-two thousand and two hundred and ninety-five minutes of the year in thinking of the other five-the five I spend with *Her*....

"That is my point-do you understand?

"But although these magnificent figures give me much gratification, they cannot be taken as what Morel calls 'final,' for though during the majority of those minutes I am thinking of the other five consciously, I am only thinking of them subconsciously during the remainder, when I am lecturing, writing Greek hexameters, or reconstructing Greece and Rome for bored students who care for none of these things so long as they pass their absurd examinations-for we have not the spirit of study any more in France, but only the letter, thanks to those same examinations that prohibit thought, research, reading and culture absolutely. Moreover the figures are also what Morel calls 'vitiated,' by the fact that a vast number of my sleeping moments are also given to dreaming of those five, and dreaming, as any philosopher will tell you, is far better and finer than thinking. Morel stoutly denies this-but that one would expect from so uneducated and uncultured a man. What I want to know is whether you think I might balance the waking moments when I can only think of her subconsciously against the sleeping moments when I am actually dreaming of her, and consider that the total of three hundred and seventy-two thousand and two hundred and ninety-five is approximately correct? The matter is of the first importance to me. I hate figures, as a rule, for they give me a headache, but in this one instance I want them correct. As I am so often told that I must be more scientific, accurate, and exact, I have tried to express myself mathematically and can do no better. To me it seems that I might just as well have said, 'I spend all the year in thinking of five minutes of it'—but I suppose some queer child of the new generation of Frenchmen would at once point out that I spend nearly a third of my time in sleeping, and much of it in working....My head is in a dreadful whirl and muddle about it though....

"Every year she goes to the tiny Breton village of Poldac for one week. I suppose she feels that she must have one week's rest and communion with her own soul if she is to live. On the first day of every July she goes, and her train stops at Pennebecque for five minutes. As you have guessed, I go to Pennebecque every year for that five minutes. It is the longest stop that the train makes....And the setting of the scene is so wonderful, it is worthy to frame such a picture. I would not see her in the dust and noise and bustle of the Gare de l'Ouest, or at any ugly little wayside station. Yes, I go to Pennebecque to see her for five minutes every year. The only other train that passes through that tiny place does so at night. So I arrive over-night and sit on a seat and wait, almost too happy and exalted to breathe....

"I have sat on that seat, for the last night of June, for seven years. And I have striven not to pray that the Marquis might die. And yet would not he be better dead-the poor, lolling-tongued, squint-eyed, half-witted Marquis? Think of that marvel of beauty, grace, goodness, and wit, the Marquise de Montheureux, making herself the nurse, the attendant, the keeper, of a lunatic!

"Yes, but for that one week in the year she is never out of his sight, night or day. If she but turns her back he weeps and sobs aloud. She tends that great, slobbering, dribbling lout, that mindless, soulless clod-no more sentient nor responsive than a hippopotamus-as the most devoted of young mothers tends and nurses her firstborn....

"For one week in the year she lives her own life, and for five minutes in the year I see her. For six months I do nothing but look forward to that five minutes, and for six months again I do nothing but look back upon it.

"The first time, she did not see me, or did not recognize me as the man whom she had seen at the neighbouring château of the de Grandcourts-where I was tutor to the young Comte.

"The second time I ventured to bow, having debated the matter for a year, and she bowed and smiled, with the remark that only the other day the Comtesse de Grandcourt was speaking of me and my good influence over the headstrong and rather wild boy who had been in my charge.

"The next year she spoke to me and commented on the curious coincidence of my being there again. She is of the real and true *noblesse*, you see, and has the kind, gentle, and unassuming manner of the genuine aristocrat. *Noblesse oblige*. She was as sweetly, graciously kind to the village curé, to her own servants, or to me, as she was to de Grandcourt himself. She was a noble, and her nobility was made patent by her nobleness. It is your bourgeois 'noble' whose nobility has to be advertised by gilt and plush and display and rudeness to 'inferiors.'

"The fourth year she did not remark on the 'coincidence' of my presence at the station. She understood. And she accepted the bunch of roses I took. Oh, the sleepless nights I passed in the agony of that struggle to decide whether to take the roses!

"The year she did not come was rather terrible. I did not know what an eternity could be covered by two years. The bellowing calf of a Marquis was 'ill,' forsooth, and she never left his bedside....Curse him! Had he not even the sense and understanding to see what he was making of her life, and to die like a man?

"*Bon Dieu*! Surely *to die* is easy-it is living that is so hard. But no-Monsieur le Marquis de Montheureux could not die. He must go on living, even though he could not wash his own face nor feed himself....

"The sixth year she gave me so beautiful and kind and understanding a smile! She knew that I lived but for that five minutes. How I sang through the next twelve months! She knew.

She understood. She smiled at me. Why should I not love her? It did neither her nor anyone else any harm, and it made my life-well-glorious, and gave it all the fineness and fulness that it possessed.

"For I simply did everything as though she were watching me, and as though account were to be rendered to her instead of to God. Was this an offence against *Le Bon Dieu?*...

"Sin? I dare to think for myself in religious matters. And I say that what is absolutely good must be of God-and if it isn't, I can't help it. And I lived as though she were watching me.

"The seventh year she gave me her hand. Had my heart been other than strong I should have died....For twelve months I pondered the possibility of daring to put my lips to it, should she give me her hand again. Whenever she encountered de Grandcourt, he used to bow in the ancient grand manner, sweeping the ground with his hat, as though it were a great *mousquetaire* head-dress, and as she swept him a mock curtsey in return he could kiss her hand. Why should not I? No de Grandcourt could honour her more nor love her as much....

"That eighth year, I, poor fool, had determined that, if she again gave me her hand, I would kiss it. What Emperor then could have the pride and glory of the man who had kissed the hand of the Marquise de Montheureux? Would I, Cæsar Maximilien Raoul de Baillieul, then change with any king on earth?

"The day came, and I sat in the usual place, awaiting her, and picturing her. She would wear, this year, a silken dust-cloak of a lavender tint, and her glorious hair would be uncovered. One hand would be bare, the other gloved in a shade of lavender. I felt certain of these details.

"The train came at last, and yet all too soon. When she had come and gone there would be twelve months to live through, before I might see her again.

"I went to the window of the nearest first-class carriage.

"There she sat alone, and, as I approached, the beautiful slow smile, to me the loveliest thing on earth, warmed her glorious face.

"She was arrayed in lavender-coloured silk, her head was bare and so was her hand. She extended it towards me. With heart beating as though I had just run a race, I stepped to the window —*and she was not*. The carriage was empty, and as I clung to the handle, a little faint, her maid, dressed in deep mourning, came to a neighbouring window and looked out....

"Madame la Marquise had died of typhoid which had broken out in Montheureux village. She would stay and work among her stricken people. The Marquis had died within twenty-four hours. No, not of the disease. Of grief. He had grasped that she was dead, and that he would never see her again. The maid was on her way to Poldec to arrange about Madame's cottage and property there.

"It appears that I fell there as one dead and lay ill for weeks.

"But no, I must not commit suicide or I might not enter the Heaven where she is ... the Heaven that our Wise Men decided does not exist, when they turned God out of France.... But I must crucify myself in some way or go mad. Physical pain and strife and stress alone can save me.

"I shall enlist in the Foreign Legion. Perhaps I shall earn an honourable death against the enemies of France.

"Oh, Rose of the World. Rosemonde, Rosemonde, Rosemonde ——"

"Finished?" quoth Sergeant Baudré, approaching. "Dump him in that rice-mud. He'll be more useful dead than he ever was alive."

VIII. "Here Are Ladies"

A sluggish, oily river with mangrove-swamp banks; a terrible September day with an atmosphere of superheated, poisonous steam; and the two French gunboats, *Corail* and *Opale*, carrying a detachment of the French Foreign Legion, part of an expeditionary force entrusted with the task of teaching manners, and an enhanced respect for Madame la République, to Behanzin, King of Dahomey.

The Legionaries standing, squatting, and lying on the painfully hot iron decks, were drenched in perspiration. The light flannel active-service kits, served out to them at Porto Novo, clung wetly to their bodies. From under the big ugly pith helmets of dirty white, dirty white faces showed cadaverous and wan. For a month they had forced their way through the West African jungle, sometimes achieving as much as a mile an hour through the sucking mud of a swamp; sometimes thrusting their stifling, choking way through elephant grass eight to ten feet in height; and again fighting through dense tangled bush with chopper, *coupe-coupe*, and axe. They had travelled "light," with only rifle and bayonet and one hundred and fifty rounds of ammunition, but even this lightness had been too heavy for some. The more coffee and quinine for the rest! To give variety to the sufferings of fatigue, fever, hunger, thirst, and dysentery, the Dahomeyans frequently attacked in the numerical superiority of a hundred to one. No mean opponents either, with their up-to-date American rifles and batteries of Krupp guns for long range work, and their spears and machetes for the charge.

As usual, the Legion was marking its trail with the generous distribution of the graves of its sons.

And now the VIIth Company had left swamp and jungle for the floating ovens *Corail* and *Opale*. Terrific heat, but no sunshine; the "landscape" minatory, terrible; life, the acme and essence of discomfort and misery. Even the Senegalese boatmen seemed affected and depressed.

"Say, John! Is this-yer penny-steamboat trip fer the saloobrity of our healths?" asked the Bucking Bronco, in a husky voice, of his neighbour le Légionnaire Jean Boule or John Bull. The old soldier wiped the sweat from his face with his sleeve.

"I overheard Commandant Faraux telling Colonel Dodds that there is a ford up here somewhere, and that it must be found and seized," he answered wearily. "I expect we're looking for it now."

"Well, *I* ain't got it. Search me!" said the American. "I allow Ole Man Farrow's got another think comin' if he..."—a ragged crash of musketry from the bank a hundred yards distant, and the ironwork of the *Opale* rang again under a hail of bullets.

In ten seconds the Légionaries were lining the sand-bagged bulwarks with loaded rifles at the "ready."

"Oh, the fools-the silly bunch o' boobs!" murmured the Bucking Bronco. "I allow thet's torn it! The pie-faced pikers hev sure wafted the bloom off the little secret."

"Yes," agreed John Bull, "you'd have thought even Behanzin's generals would have had the sense to lie low and not announce themselves until we'd got our column fairly tied up in the middle of the ford."...

The roar of Hotchkiss guns and Lebel rifles from the two boats drowned his further remarks, as well as the irregular crashings of the bursts of Dahomeyan musketry....

The debarkation of the VIIth Company was unhindered, the ford seized, and the safe passage of the Expeditionary Force guaranteed, the Dahomeyans having retired.

"Waal!" remarked the Bucking Bronco to his friend as half the VIIth Company moved off next morning, as Advance Guard. "Strike me peculiar ef thet ain't the softest cinch I seen ever. Guess Ole Man Behanzin ain't been to no West Point Academy. They say his best men is women-an' I kin believe it!"

"Amazons," remarked Jean Boule. "I pray we don't come across any. Fancy shooting at women."

"You smile your kind, fatherly smile at 'em, John, an' I allow they'll come an' eat outer yer hand.... Are they really fightin'-*gals*, with roof-garden hats an' shirt-waists, and mittens on their pasterns? ... Gee-whiz! Guess I'll take a few prisoners an' walk with a proud tail!"

"They're women, all right," was the reply, "and I believe they are as dangerous as dervishes-apart from any question of one's not shooting to kill when they charge.... If all I've heard about them is true, chivalry is apt to be a trifle costly."

"Waal, John, as Légionnaires, we ain't habituated to luxury any, and can't afford nawthen costly. Ef any black gal lays fer me with an axe-it's a smackin' fer hers."

"Yes-but what are we going to do if an Amazon regiment opens an accurate and steady fire on us with Winchester repeaters and then charges with the bayonet?"

"Burn the trail for Dixie," grinned the American. "I guess we'd hit the high places some, an' roll our tails for Home. *Gee*-Whillikins! Charged by gals!"

"That's all very well," grumbled the Englishman, "but the Legion doesn't run, either from men or from women. If an Amazon regiment charges us, we've got to fight.... It would be ghastly."

Even as he spoke the deadly silent forest suddenly gave birth to thousands of black shadows, all moving swiftly and noiselessly, and from all directions, upon the tiny column of the Advance Guard.

With one accord, at some signal, they halted, rested the butts of their rifles on their thighs, fired, and then, howling like devils, charged with great *élan*, led by a number of tall, muscular women, handsome and finely made.

"*Gals!*" gasped the American, as the column instinctively halted, faced outwards in two ranks, and poured magazine fire into the dense masses of the charging savages.

"*Look* at her!" he cried, and pointed to a young woman, who, bare to the waist, and wearing a fez cap, a short blue cotton kilt, and a leather belt and cartridge-cases, came bounding straight toward him. In her right hand she brandished a thick-backed, heavy chopping-sword like a *coupe-coupe* or machete, and in her left carried a bright new repeating-carbine. Nothing could have been more dashing, courageous, and inspiring than the leading of this Fury, as she rushed straight for the levelled rifles of the Legionaries, waving her men on and yelling mingled words of encouragement, threat, and taunt at them as she strove to bring them to the consummation of the charge.

Her efforts were in vain, however. The Dahomeyan male warrior is not of very heroic stuff, and does his best fighting in a surprised camp, a broken square, or against a scattered line. His *métier* is the ambush, the rush at dawn, the hacking and hewing hundred-to-one fight in dense jungle where the foe cannot form or charge, the tree-top sniping, the trampling flat of a worn-out enemy by sheer weight of numbers.

Before the steady fire of an unbroken line he generally wilts away, and vanishes shadow-like into the impenetrable depths of his native jungle, to try another surprise, another ambush, another dawn-rush of ten thousand men, at the next opportunity.

As usual, beneath the accurate fire that mowed them down in swathes, the Dahomeyans broke and fled, slowly followed by their Amazon leaders, who shrilly cursed, and fiercely struck at, the retiring faint-hearts.

Just as the "cease-fire" whistle blew, the woman who had been charging at the Bucking Bronco and John Bull (and who had stood screaming at her followers as they halted, faltered, and broke) threw up her arms and fell.

"That weren't *me*," quoth the Bucking Bronco, "an' I hope it was a dod-gasted accident. She was some gal, that gal. Let's have a look at her if we ain't agoin' to charge nor nawthen."

The officer commanding the Advance Guard was certainly not going to charge. He was only too thankful to have beaten off the sudden and well-executed attack. How marvellously the brutes had materialized from the apparently uninhabited forest, still silent and gloomy as the tomb. But what *fools*! That force alone, properly handled, and attacking while the column was in the middle of the wide deep ford, might have told a very different story.

"Bugler," called he, "blow the 'alarm' and the 'regimental-call' till your veins crack and your lungs burst....No-turn toward the river, *sot*, I want the main body to hear....Sergeant-Major, send two of the strongest running back with this."...

They were the last words he spoke. The Amazons themselves were charging this time —a whole regiment-and no regiment in this world ever charged with greater dash, courage, violence, and determination. Firing as they came, and utterly disregarding the steady magazine-fire of the Legionaries, they swept down upon them like an avalanche-like cavalry-and burst upon the little line, through it, and over it, like a hailstorm across a wheatfield.

Rushing at Captain Roux, one fired her Spencer carbine into his chest, while another drove a spear into his abdomen. As he fell, a third stooped and deliberately hacked off his head with her chopping-knife. There was no question of "sparing women" as these furies, each as big and strong and well-armed as any Legionary, hacked, hewed, and thrust, or, kneeling a few yards from their victims, gave them the contents of the magazines of their carbines.

While parrying the fierce thrusts of one stalwart virago, John Bull, struck on the head from behind by two assailants at once, fell to the ground, even as his eye had subconsciously taken in and registered upon his brain a picture of his mighty friend swinging his rifle round and round his head by the muzzle, the butt describing a circle within which he stood unhurt as to his body, though apparently shocked in mind, to judge from his roar of "Scat! ye shameless jumpin' Jezebels!"

Without thought of defending himself, the bugler continuously blew the "alarm" and the "regimental call" (in the hope that it might carry back to the main body, which apparently had delayed longer at the ford than had been expected) until he went down with a bullet through his leg and another in his shoulder, two of seven fired at him from a score paces distance by a young Amazon. A minute later, the man rose to his knees and blew with almost undiminished strength, until the same young woman riddled his chest, at point-blank range, with another magazineful.

Recovering consciousness, John Bull saw a gigantic Amazon make a dive at the knees of the Bucking Bronco, ducking beneath the whirling rifle-butt. A moment later he was down, but, instead of being hacked to pieces, was borne away, kicking and cursing, by a dozen powerful women.

Knowing what that meant, he would rather have seen his friend killed before his eyes.... As another wave of faintness swept over him, he heard the distant strains of "Tiens! Voilà du boudin" —the March of the Legion, and knew that the buglers of the column were sending the encouraging notes ahead of their straining bodies, as the remainder of the force hurried to the rescue. Poor Bugler Langout's message had carried on the heavy air, which seems to blanket the sound of rifle fire while transmitting that of a whistle, bugle, or war-drum to a surprising distance.

Heavy fire from the debouching troops saved the few survivors of the Advance Guard-but it was not until the whole column had fought a tough action in company squares, that the Amazons and the rallied and reinforced Dahomeyans acknowledged defeat, for that day at any rate, and disappeared shadow-like into the jungle as suddenly as they had come.

John Bull and the assistant-surgeon decided that the butt-end of a carbine had struck the former on the head, and that almost simultaneously a chopping-sword had struck the butt of the carbine while it was in contact with his skull, inasmuch as his head bore no cut, there were splinters of wood in his hair, and a carbine with a hacked stock lay beside him when he was picked up and examined. He had nearly been handed over to the burial-party instead of to the carriers, and, when he realized that the Bucking Bronco had been carried off, he almost wished that this had actually happened. Most horrible stories of the fate of prisoners of the Dahomeyans were current throughout the expeditionary force, though no proofs of their truth had yet materialized.

When a list of the killed, wounded, and missing was made out, it was found that the Sergeant-Major had disappeared also, and one of the survivors remembered seeing him borne off in a surging crowd of Amazons, "like a band of big black ants carrying off an injured wasp," as he graphically described it.

That night John Bull, old Tant de Soif, the Grasshopper, Jan Minnaerts, Black Gaspard, Achille Mattel, and one or two more of the *escouade* to which the Bucking Bronco belonged, volunteered to go out as a scouring-party to reconnoitre for the enemy, and, incidentally, to try to discover some traces of their missing comrade and the *sous-officier.*

"Let Jean Boule be in charge," said Lieutenant Roberte, commanding the remnants of the VIIth Company, *vice* Captain Roux, killed in action, "he has some sense, and can use the stars. If you fall into the hands of the enemy, I shall punish you severely-give you all a taste of the *crapaudine* perhaps. *Bonne chance, mes enfants.*"...

* * *

"We must turn back, *mon ami,*" said Martel to John Bull at last.

"But yes," agreed old Tant de Soif, "it is useless to throw good meat after bad.... They have died their deaths by now-or are being taken to the sacred city of Kana for sacrifice."

"I smell smoke," suddenly said the Grasshopper, wrinkling his delicate nostrils. *"Nom de Dieu!"* he added, "and burning flesh."

It soon became more than evident that he was right. Either they were approaching the spot where flesh was being burnt, or a faint breeze had sprung up and wafted the foul smell in their direction.

Treading like Dahomeyans themselves, they turned from the jungle track they had discovered, along another that lay plain in the moonlight across a little open glade, and seemed to lead in the direction of the smell. Thousands of bare feet must recently have made the path-the feet of men hurrying along in single file....

* * *

Although scarcely recognizable as a human being, the Sergeant-Major, a huge stalwart Alsatian, was still alive.

Steel and fire had been used with remarkable skill, that so much could have been done and the spark of life still kept in the unspeakably tortured, defiled, and mangled body. A score of Amazons were at work upon him.

The Bucking Bronco, stark naked, but apparently uninjured, was bound to a young palm. Either he was merely awaiting his turn and incidentally suffering the ghastly ordeal of seeing the tortures of the Sergeant-Major and enduring the agonies of anticipation, or else he was being reserved as an acceptable offering to King Behanzin and a candidate for the wicker torture-baskets of the sacrificial slaughter-house of Kana.

"A volley when I shout," whispered John Bull, "then a yell and the bayonet."

A few seconds later he was killing women, driving his bayonet into their bodies until the curved hilt struck with a thud. The thuds gave him infinite pleasure-and then he was violently sick. Surprised by the sudden volley, ignorant of the strength of their assailants, and only partly armed, the Amazons broke and scattered into the jungle. While John Bull, with shaking hands, prized at the Bucking Bronco's bonds with his sword-bayonet, old Tant de Soif put a merciful bullet into the brain of the Sergeant-Major and then busied himself about collecting the dismembered fragments of that unfortunate.

"For all the world like picking up an old woman's packages when she has slipped up on a banana-skin," quoth he. He was a quaint old gentleman, a *vieux moustache* who had seen many queer things in his forty years of assorted service in the Line, the Infanterie de la Marine, and the Legion.

"We daren't stay to bury him," said Martel; "they'll rally and return in a minute."

As the little party retreated at the *pas gymnastique,* the Bucking Bronco remarked to his friend, panting ahead of him, "Say, John! I allow I'm a what-is-it henceforth-an'-a-dern-sight-more. You know—a Miss-Hog-you-beast."

"A *what?*"

"A Miss-Hog-you-beast."
"Yes! What some people call a misogynist. I don't blame you!"

IX. The Macsnorrt

The MacSnorrt was on the downward path, and had been for many years. Physically, mentally, and morally he was deteriorating; and as for the other aspects-social, financial, and worldly-he had been Chief Engineer on a Cunarder, and he was now the blackest of the black sheep of the VIIIth Company of the First Battalion of the Legion. From sitting at meals with the passengers in the First Saloon of a great liner, he had come to sitting with assorted blackguards over their tin *gamelles* of *soupe*; from drawing hundreds per annum, he had come to drawing a half-penny per day; his brain was failing from lack of use and excess of absinthe and mixed alcoholic filth, his superb health and strength were undermined, and he was becoming a Bad Man.

The history of his fall is told in one short word-Drink; and drink had turned a fine, useful, and honourable man into a degraded ruffian. The man who had thought of fame, wealth, inventions, patents, knighthood-now thought of the successful shikarring of the next drink, or the stealing of the wherewithal to get it. Whether this poor soul were married and the father of a family, I never knew, and did not care to ask, but it is quite probable that he was. Such men usually are. Let us hope he was not. Sober, he was a truculent, morose, and savage ruffian-ashamed of his ashamedness, hating himself and everybody else, dangerous and vile; a bad soldier till the fighting began, and then worth two. Drunk, he was exceedingly amusing, and one caught glimpses of the kindly, witty, and genial original.

* * *

The best of soldiers, be he Maréchal or *Soldat deuxième classe*, as was the MacSnorrt, may be overcome by a combination and alliance of foes, any one of whom he could defeat alone.

As the MacSnorrt endeavoured to make clear to Captain d'Armentières next day, it was merely the conjunction against him of a good dinner, Haiphong, the stupeedity of the Annamese male in wearing a chignon and a petticoat like a wumman, *shum-shum*, sunstroke, and his own beautiful but ardent disposition, that had been his undoing. With any one of these he could have coped; by their unholy alliance he had been-he freely admitted it-completely defeated.

Captain d'Armentières heard him with courtesy, and awarded him eight days' *salle de police* and the *peloton de chasse* with sympathy.

He had known of similar fortuitous concatenations of adverse circumstance before in connection with le Légionnaire MacSnorrt.

It was the Captain's *ordonnance*, one Jean Boule, who had, luckily for that reveller, discovered the MacSnorrt and encompassed his capture by a strong picket.

Passing a pagoda one night, he had heard, uplifted in monologue, a rich voice whose accents, or accent, he had heard before, that of the MacSnorrt, the Bad Man of the VIIIth Company, recently arrived in a draft from Sidi-bel-Abbès to reinforce the VIIth after certain painful dealings with the Pavilions Noirs, the "pirates" of the Yen Thé.

Mingled with, but far from subduing the vinous voice and hiccups of the MacSnorrt, were the angry murmurings, quick whispers, and the lisping and clicking voices of a native Annamese and Chinese crowd.

Was the fool interfering with those so-tender "religious susceptibilities," and intruding upon priests and their flock in search of moral consolation and fortification? He had no business in there at all.

Following the wall and rounding a corner, Jean Boule came to a gate. Pushing it open gently, he looked in.

Reclining majestically upon the ground, his back against the wall, was the MacSnorrt. In his vast left paw was a bottle of *shum-shum*, the deadly, maddening spirit distilled from rice. Clasped by his mighty right arm to his colossal bosom, the MacSnorrt held —a *doi* or Sergeant of Tirailleurs Tonkinois![201]

The little man, his lacquered hat, with its red bonnet-strings on one side, his chignon in grave disarray, looked even more like a devil than was his normal wont, as he struggled violently to escape from his degrading and undignified situation.

It was clear that, if the Annamese could get at his bayonet, there would be a vacancy at the head of the clan of MacSnorrt and at the tail of the VIIIth Company of the Legion.

"Lie ye still, lassie," adjured the gigantic Legionary, as his captive struggled again vainly, for the great right arm was not only round his waist, but round both his arms, and he could only pick at the handle of his bayonet with ineffectual finger-tips.

"Lie ye still, ye wee prood besom, or I'll e'en tak' ane o' the ither lasses to ma boosom," threatened the MacSnorrt, but softened the apparent harshness of the threat by a warm lingering kiss upon the yellow cheek of the murderously savage soldier.

He then applied the *shum-shum* bottle to his lips, poured a libation of the crude and poisonous spirit, and then frankly explained to his captive that he had not selected "her" from among the other "sonsie lassies" by reason of any superior beauty, but simply because he liked her saucy fancy-dress—quite like a *vivaandière*, and he had always had a tender spot in his heartt o' hearrts for a *vivaandière*.

The enraged and half-demented Sergeant screamed to the little crowd of priests, loafers, coolies and Haiphong citizens to knife the foreign devil, or, taking his bayonet, to drive it in under his ear.... The crowd allowed "I dare not" to wait upon "I would"—for the moment.

"Aye! ... Oo-aye! It's not Jock MacSnorrt that could reseest the blaandishments o' onny little deevil o' a *vivaandière*," confessed the aged roué.... "It was for the sake o' the *vivaandières* I joined the French airrmy, ye'll ken-when I was an innocent slip o' a laddie.... Romaantic!...

"Aye-an' they're mostly fat auld runts wi' twa chins," he added, with a sudden fall to pessimism and confession of disillusionment.

"'Tis the ruin o' the British Airrmy, ye'll ken," he confided to the ugly crowd that gradually closed in around him, "that they hae no *vivaandières* to comfort the puir laddies.... Hae the Gorrdons onny *vivaandières*, I'll ask ye? The Seaforrths? The Caamerons? The Heelan' Light Infantry? The Royal Scots? ... They hanna. It a' comes o' such matters being in the han's o' the Southrons-the drunken an' lasceevious deils. Look at the Navy.... Is there a ship o' them a'— fra' battleship to river gunboat-that has a *vivaandière*, I'm speirin' ye, lassie? There isna.... An' theenk o' the graan' worrk they could do for the puir wounded-instead o' they bluidy-minded, sick-bay orrderly deevils!

"Losh, maan! Contemplaate it!

"Eh, Wooman in oor 'oors o' ease
A settin' lightly on oor knees....

"Lie still, ye haverin', snoot-cockin' besom-an' I'll tell ye a' aboot the horrors o' a naval engagement-an' I seen hunnerds. I'll tell ye a' aboot the warrst o' the lot-when I lossed ma guid right arrm. Then conseeder what a deeference ane bonnie *vivaandière* lassie might ha' made..." A violent struggle from the insanely incensed and ferocious *doi*.

"Wull ye bide quiet, ma bonnie wean? Or shall I send ye awa' oot into the cauld warrld to airrn yere ain leevin'? Ye're awfu' sma' for sic a fate, ye'll ken, ma bairnie! An' this is no Sauchiehall Street, I'm tellin' ye.... Did ye see the wee-bit gunboats we came in, the morrn? Well, imaagine ane o' they ten times increased and multiplied, an', in fact, made a hantle bigger. I sairved in ane o' yon, but I shall not disclose in what capaacity-save an' except that it was honourable to me on the ane side an' to her Majesty on the ither.... *Wull* ye bide quiet like a respeckitable *tai-tai* or I'll hae ye awa'....

"Eh! maan, a naval engagement's graand. Watter everywheer! On board, I mean. Everywheer. Gaallons o' it."...

"May a cat tread on your heart!" hissed the struggling *doi*. "May dragons tear you! May the bellies of mud-fish be your grave! May you be cast on a Mountain of Knives."...

"What did ye say, lassie? *Why* do they want watter on booarrd? *To hide the awfu' things that fall aboot!* Eyes, arrms, legs, noses, ears, toes, fingers-ye wouldna hae them lying there plain for the eye o' man to see? No! Gaallons o' watter...."

"Bide ye quiet, *kuniang*, or ye won't be a *kuniang* much longer, I'm thinkin'. Aye! Dozens o' gaallons o' watter. Everywheer. Hoses playin' a' aboot the plaace. Pumps squirrtin' it. Inches o' it on the decks. An' *blood*! Ma certie! Lassie-ye'd never believe. Hunnerds o' gaallons o' watter, an' as the shells burrst a' aroond-what falls into the watter in a pairrfect hail?"...

"Devils draw your entrails!" panted the writhing *doi*.

"Eh? Bullets, d'ye say? That's wheer ye're wrang, lassie. Na! Na! —Eyes, arrms, legs, noses, ears, toes, fingers! Ye'd scarcely credit it. An' thousands o' gaallons o' watter! Juist to hide the awfu' sichts and sounds.... There'll be a gun-team working their gun in watter. Thousan's o' gaallons o' watter. Feet deep. An' a maan wull stoop to fish up a shell for the gun-an' what'll he bring up belike?"

"Be the graves of your ancestors torn open by pariah dogs and their bones devoured!" cursed the Sergeant, getting one arm free at last.

"Bring up a shell, d'ye say, ma wean? More likely an eye or an arrm or a leg, or a nose or an ear or a toe or a finger frae beneath that fearfu' flood.... Oo-aye! Meelions o' gaallons o' water! Feet deep. An' the bed o' that awfu' sea, a wrack o' spare-parts o' the human forrm divine! Meelions o' gaallons o' watter. Yarrds deep on the decks. They always hae it the like o' that in a naval engagement. Aye —I seen hunnerds ..." and the *doi* had got at his bayonet at last. Then the *bonze* struck heavy blows upon the big bell hanging near in its bamboo-frame support, and the crowd closed in. If the *doi* struck, they would hack and tear this foreign devil to pieces.

With a *weeeep* of steel on steel the bayonet cleared the scabbard and the *doi* struck at his captor's throat as John Bull sprang forward. But the sound of the drawing of the bayonet had an extraordinary effect on the MacSnorrt-and it was with the weapon held only in his left hand that the *doi* struck-and missed. Seizing him by the throat with both huge hands the Légionnaire scrambled to his feet and used him as a battering-ram in his headlong roaring drive at the closing knife-drawing crowd.

With a yell of "Ye dommed dirrty Jael!" he wrenched the bayonet from the little Annamese and flung him head-long as the crowd gave back.

John Bull sprang to his side, and the two in a whirling, punching, struggling plunge fought their way to the gate, burst through it-and were promptly arrested by the picket, opportunely passing.

With these new enemies the MacSnorrt did further battle, until a tap on the head from a Gras rifle in the skilful hands of Sergeant Legros brought him to that state in which he was perhaps best-unconsciousness.

X. "Belzébuth"

We were heavy sportsmen (à l'Anglaise) at Bellevue at that time. Not only did we lay out a race-course, but we imported hounds and performed the *Chasse au renard*. We got up point-to-point races and paperchases. There were actually Ladies' races, and some folk went so far as to talk about pig-sticking.

"Of course, Madame Merlonorot will ride when she comes out to Algeria?" asked Madame Paës.

"*Dieu*! Rather!" replied Colonel Merlonorot of the Zouaves. "I am on the look-out for a good thing for her now. She wants all the equine perfections embodied in one Arab pony. Won't keep a string.... Too much bother.... Must have won a good race or two, must have been hunted by a lady, must hack quietly in both saddles, must trap, and be trusted to take no exception to camels, Arab music, whirling dervishes, or fireworks. Also he must make the promenade in the governess-cart upon occasion! What?"

"It's a far cry from the race-course to the governess-cart, isn't it?" inquired Madame Paës.

"Yes. But she'll expect me to produce all that in the next month-and not to spend more than about three thousand francs! ... Let's know if you hear of anything that might meet most of the requirements-and available within the month, will you, dear Madame? Must be a racer, though-and that limits the field when you're looking for a hack.... She's great on Ladies' Point-to-Points, Hunt-races, *Chasse au renard*, and everything you can do on a horse. She would play *le polo* and would pursue the pig with a spear if I would consent!"

"I will remember, Colonel-and I have an idea.... Three thousand francs for a pony that meets all the specifications?"

"About that, and a thousand thanks. Must be young, thoroughbred, and something to look at-and be vetted sound all over, of course."...

Three thousand francs! It would mean Home this year instead of next. Paris in Spring! It would mean avoiding the awful prostrating heat of *la canicule* for the babies-neither of them robust, both of them showing the signs of French babyhood kept too long in Africa's forcing-house. It might mean life to one or both of them, especially with the usual cholera, smallpox, typhoid, and dysentery epidemics about, as they grew weaker. And Guillaume needed his long-overdue leave badly. He was overworked, run down, ill, and his temper-never very good-was getting unbearable. Fancy having leave and being too poor to take it! What a shame it was that the condition of the majority of married junior officers of the XIXth Army Corps should be one of cruel grinding poverty, pitiful shifts to keep up appearances, and a weary, heart-breaking struggle to make ends meet. Well, one must "drag the lengthening chain" and, having once clasped it on, must take the consequences. One can't start life afresh in France at thirty odd-and, well, one can always hope, or nearly always. And one might win a prize in the Lottery. (Think of it! One's chief hope for a brighter future, a chance of winning a prize in the Lottery!) ... Three thousand francs!

But young Belzébuth had never run a race in his life and never taken part in the *Chasse au renard* nor the pursuit of the spear-threatened pig, unless, perhaps, when he had had an English master in Maroc. Still, he was a real picture, was rising seven, sound as a bell, quiet as a mouse, and undoubtedly thoroughbred.

He hacked in both saddles and was a fast and steady trapper-and took the babies for an airing daily. Certainly he had a turn of speed-and there was simply no tiring him.

He would take Guillaume (a very bad and nervous rider) for a ride in the morning, and in the trap to the barracks after breakfast. He would bring him home to lunch, and then take the babies for their drive in the evening.

Sometimes he would finish up the day by taking the trap to a distant villa when a dinner-party was toward. And when Guillaume was away on manoeuvres or marches, Madame Paës, horse-woman born and bred, got her only riding.

Three thousand francs! And Guillaume had bought him for two hundred francs when Lieutenant d'Amienville-who ought not to be allowed to keep a pig or a pariah dog, much less a horse-went away. Starved, neglected, and dying for want of work, Belzébuth had looked a bad bargain at 200 fcs. A man ought not to go unprosecuted who buys a horse and uses a motor-car, leaving the horse to the mercy of a rascally *homard* who feeds it on offal and never takes it out of the stall. Her heart had ached when she had seen the staring coat, blear eye, and overgrown hoofs of the walking skeleton that Lieutenant d'Amienville swore had cost him, raw, a couple of thousand francs. She could have hung her sun-hat on him in a dozen places. But she knew a good horse when she saw one. Had not her father run his own horses at Longchamps and Auteuil before he went bankrupt?

And, under her care, Belzébuth had soon changed into a picture of bright, sleek, healthy happiness, and had served them exceedingly well.

Could she make him worth three thousand francs before Guillaume returned from manoeuvres, sell him to Colonel Merlonorot (her father's old comrade), and put the money into Guillaume's hand, saying, "Book the passages for Marseilles to-morrow, *mon ange*."

Could she? For, the utmost screwing and scraping, the most optimistic view of the saleable value of the few goods and chattels, the estimating the cheapest and nastiest journey to Paris-left a gaping chasm of a good thousand francs between hope and realization of a holiday in La Ville Lumière. No, nothing could bridge it-unless Belzébuth would fetch three thousand francs instead of the three or four hundred they had expected. Five hundred was the highest Guillaume had ever dreamed of-and that was after a cheery dinner at some Mess and a little champagne.

Even five hundred would be a profit of a hundred and fifty per cent. she believed.

Yes-four hundred would be cent. per cent., and five would be half as much again.

What would three thousand be on two hundred? Fifteen per cent.? No, of course not. Fifteen hundred per cent.? It sounded impossible.

And of course it was impossible.

Still-she would add five pounds of *avoine* daily to Belzébuth's *blé* and *son*, and start training him while Guillaume was away. She would join the club of the *Chasse au renard* at once, and she would enter for the Ladies' Race in the Desert Point-to-Point, which would be run just three weeks hence at Bellevue.

But what a terrible plunge! A hundred francs to the *cercle*, and Heaven alone knew what oats were fetching. Or perhaps she could hunt three or four times only, and pay a small donation or something? And she could certainly avoid getting the Beaune that Médecin-Major Parme had ordered her to take, since she had had malarial fever, and use the money for oats. But what a speculation! It is an ill-wind that blows no good at all-the fever had reduced her weight, and she could ride at about seven stone now.

But what would Guillaume say of the wasted money-if she failed? Well, it wouldn't be all waste, for Belzébuth's value would go up, in any case, if she hunted him well and he got a place in the Point-to-Point.

The proverbs say that where there is a will there is a way, and that Heaven helps those that help themselves.

She would simply *live* to sell Belzébuth to dear rich old Colonel Merlonorot for three thousand francs, as a racer, hunter, hack in both saddles, bright trapper, and confidential nursery-pony! For the next month she would give mind, soul, and body to winning the Desert Point-to-Point....

* * *

Belzébuth was taken for a long quiet ride next morning, and for another in the evening, and his mistress personally superintended his feed and toilet.

Next day he was introduced to a new and glorious place where the going was beautiful and you went straight ahead between railings, with plenty of room and no obstacles.

He took his furlong burst on the race-course at a good pace, and improved daily at two, three, and four furlongs.

Madame Paës' notions of training were original, but based on the sound principle, "Train for what you have to do by repeatedly doing it-and work up gradually to the first doing."

After a week Belzébuth was doing his mile on the race-course and doing it uncommon well (as one or two observers noted). Also he went down the lane of jumps cleverly and willingly, beautifully schooled.

One morning, Colonel Merlonorot noticed Madame Paës at the meet, on a very likely-looking bay Arab-good in the legs, well ribbed up, high in the withers, and with a blood look about him. ("He liked the look of that beast. *Nom d'un pipe*, he did!")

Madame Paës had not hunted since she had scrambled about with the North Devons in Angleterre—a long-legged, long-haired Diana of fourteen (at a Devonshire school) on a fat pony.

She was now a tiny, slim, pale, big-eyed Diana of twenty-four—and as good as a jockey. But she looked as though she had been too long in Exile (which was exactly the case), and fitter for a deck-chair on a homeward-bound liner than for a saddle in the hunting-field....

When would they get off? How would Belzébuth behave? Would he belie his nursery mildness and go *fou* when it was a case of full cry and all away? Would the unwonted oats and the rousing on the race-course and over the jumps react unfavourably now for the weak-backed, weary rider? He was certain to be *méchant*, and might buck or bolt. Would trembling hands and aching arms be unable to hold him? How her back ached, too! ...Dear old Belzébuth, be good! It's for the babies and Guillaume....God knew she'd sooner be in bed than in the midst of this gay throng of strong and happy men and women, well-content, well-clad, well-fed....

Well-fed! A melancholy fact. Madame Paës, wife of a French commissioned officer, was not well fed. A woman of the unselfish sort does not buy costly tonic-foods, dainties, and wines, and eat the money that is sorely needed for other things. For plain food she had no appetite. To people who have been brought up in a château atmosphere, an income-which to *ci-devant* dwellers in Montmartre or the bourgeois suburbs is wealth-may be degrading poverty.

The Paës had expenses which it was due to their honour and proper pride to have-and which are not due to the honour and proper pride of the bourgeoisie....And these expenses and the health of Guillaume and the babies came before food and clothes for Madame Paës, in Madame Paës' opinion.

A note of music from the clump of jungle that had swallowed up the hounds. A crash of the grand wild music. A line! Hounds are off and the first "run" is on.

Belzébuth commenced by a series of bounds, the outcome of a high and joyous heart, good feeding, and good condition. He felt a touch of the curb, arched his back in protest, and went along at a smart canter, a vision of dainty horse-flesh.

The jackal got into a vineyard, was put out again, and had to make for open country.

It was fine going, and Madame Paës let Belzébuth go. He went-and in five minutes the first rider behind the Master was Madame Paës, and she was holding Belzébuth in, or he would have passed the Master's big Syrian-Barb who was doing his possible under Colonel de Longueville's fifteen stone.

When the end came, Madame Paës was in at the death, lengths ahead of the second arrival, and minutes ahead of the field. Belzébuth had hardly turned a hair, and the Master presented the rider with the brush and a compliment. Madame Paës took her pony home, the while the field jogged on to the next likely cactus covert.

In another week Belzébuth was doing two kilometres on the race-course, morning and evening.

At the next meet, a very long run (twenty-two kilometres, the Master said) was finished by a field of four arriving thus: the Master and Madame Paës together; Captain Dutoit of the Spahis, seconds later; fourth man, Major Bruil of the Chasseurs d'Afrique, minutes later. Rest nowhere-and strung out for miles. Belzébuth had been held, while the other horses had been spurred.

Belzébuth hunted twice more, and the hunt-correspondent of the "Depêche Algérienne" singled him out for high praise.

Madame Paës dropped race-course practice and hunting, and let him do exercise walks in the compound on one day, and a point-to-point run on another.

Riding out alone to some scrubby, sandy jungle, she would endeavour to estimate a two-kilometre distance, note a clump of palms, a tree, a hut, a hillock, and other natural landmarks, and then ride from one to the other at Belzébuth's best speed.

Once she had a narrow escape of settling the question of Belzébuth's value, and all other values, finally. Emerging at a furious gallop from a cactus-strewn area, in which pace could only be maintained and disaster avoided by skilful "bending," she came upon a beautiful smooth patch with a gentle rise ending in —a wadi or gully, thirty feet deep and fifty wide. She realized the fact in time to bring Belzébuth round in a curve that missed the precipice by inches.

On the Wednesday before the Saturday on which the race would be run, Madame Paës took Belzébuth out for his last training gallop. In the middle of it she put him at a *terrasse*, a "bund," or low earthen embankment, round what had once been a cultivated field.

The three-foot banks Belzébuth preferred to clear. The four-foot variety he liked to treat as on-and-offs —alighting on the two-foot top and leaving it like a bird.

This particular bank was a delusion and a snare.

Though fair-seeming to the eye on Madame Paës' side of it, on the other it was eroded, crumbling, beetling.

Belzébuth landed beautifully on the top-and horse and rider went down in a cloud of dust and an avalanche of clods and stones.

The horse turned a complete somersault across the woman.

But the flood that had caused the erosion had made some amends by scooping a channel at the base of the undermined bank, and instead of breaking every bone in Madame Paës' body and crushing her chest, Belzébuth's weight forced her into this channel and rested on its sides.

He arose and stood steady as a troop-horse.

His mistress lay still and white.

Soon she stirred, sat up-and straightened her tricorne hat. Then, too shaken to stand, sick and faint, giddy and stunned, not knowing whether she was seriously injured, she crawled to Belzébuth and examined his knees.

"*Oh! Thank God!*" she whispered, on finding that, instead of being broken as she had expected, they were unmarked.

What did her own injuries matter so long as Belzébuth's knees were right?

A blemish there-and two hundred francs was his price.

An hour later, Madame Paës, looking like death on a bay horse, rode into the compound of her villa and went straight to bed.

Next day she could not move.

On the Friday she was better, but unable to get up.

On Saturday she would leave her bed and, if necessary, be carried downstairs, driven to the starting-point, and lifted on to Belzébuth.

Who could ride him for her at seven stone-and ride him as she would? Nobody.

All Bellevue was *en route* for the scene of the famous Bellevue Point-to-Point races, consisting of team-races for horses, another for ponies, a handicap, and an open race for quadrupeds of any size and bipeds of any weight.

Then came the Ladies' Point-to-Point, over two and a half kilometres of fairly good course and a few jumps.

The ordinary course was a stiff one, and so arranged that a really bold and resolute rider could shorten the distance on the average man by taking *wadis*, and the other "places" that discretion would ride round.

The Ladies' Course included nothing that gave the stout heart and strong seat a marked advantage. So much the worse for Madame Paës, who was out, not so much to win a race and glory, as to win health and happiness, possibly life itself, for her children and husband.

A large crowd, on horseback for the most part, surrounded the tents (where the officers of the *Chasseurs d'Afrique* were "At Home"), the starting-point, and neighbouring winning-post.

Madame Paës lay in a long chair, with closed eyes-while the men's four races were run-limp, relaxed, and weary to death.

Oh, for a cushion to put under her weak and aching back! —and oh, for a *petit verre* of *eau de vie* to give her heart and strength! But her idolized Guillaume (a prig of the first water and petty domestic tyrant) did not "approve" of alcohol for ladies. There were so many things of which Guillaume did not "approve" for other people, though he appeared to approve of most things for Guillaume.

At last! The bell for the Ladies' Point-to-Point, the most popular and famous race in the Colony.

Madame Paës mounted Belzébuth and walked him to the starting-point.

Nine competitors.

Colonel Lebrun's wife on the pride of the Chasseurs (but a heavy, bumping, mouth-sawing rider who would spoil any horse's chance).

Madame Maxin on a characterless, unreliable racer.

Little Angélique Dandin, on her brother's one and only pony.

Madame Malherbe, cool, quiet, neat, and businesslike, on a light and dainty black mare with slender legs but powerful quarters.

Major Parme's wife on the best horse that her money could buy-but a woman who thought far more of hat, habit, and figure than of seat and hands.

Madame Deville, riding (astride) her husband's charger and intending to win if spur and quirt would do it.

Colonel de Longueville's wife, a fine horse-woman, handsome, smart, and clever, on the pick of her husband's racing-stable. And a couple of quidnuncs.

A bad field to beat.

Betting was on Madame Maxin if her horse "behaved." If he didn't, Madame de Longueville must win in a common canter.

Strangers liked the look of Madame Malherbe, but local wisdom knew her mare couldn't live with the other two.

General Blanc, starter, drew the attention of the ladies to a pair of red flags half a kilometre away, a pair of blue ones to the right of these and half a kilometre from them, another pair of red to the right of the "field," and a pair of white, at present behind their backs and some three furlongs distant.

"You must pass between the red flags, then between the blue, then the red, and lastly between the white, and finish here," said he. "There is nothing serious in the way of ditch or wall. Pick your own route-and any competitor not passing between the flags is, of course, disqualified."

A silly question from Madame Lebrun-politely answered.

All ready? ...The flag falls.

Madame Paës thanked Heaven they were away at last.

A hundred yards from the starting-point is a brush-wood jump which must be taken-or a large patch of dense cactus-jungle skirted to the left or right.

Should she try and take it first of all?

She hated jumping in company. Yes. A flick told Belzébuth he might stretch himself for a bit, and he cleared the jump ten lengths ahead of the next horse.

"*Nom de Dieu*! It's an 'outsider's year,'" said General Blanc. "Bar accidents, that's the winner. Who is she?"

Madame Lebrun's horse-with a round dozen stone hanging on his mouth-refused; the lady and the animal parted company, and the subsequent proceedings interested them no more.

Madame Parme elected to skirt the jungle, and was out of the race from that moment.

A quidnunc took alarm at the pace and pulled with all her strength.

The virtueless and evil-reputed racer drew level with Belzébuth, Madame Maxin spurring, and Madame de Longueville passed both.

Madame Paës was holding Belzébuth in from the moment he had cleared the first jump.

Madame Deville began flogging, like a jockey, in the first quarter-mile of the race, and passed Madame de Longueville with a spurt. Shortly after she took fifth place and kept it....

Between the first flags passed Madame de Longueville with the wicked racer at her girth and Belzébuth at her tail, Madame Malherbe a dozen lengths behind, and Madame Deville thirty.

Angelique Dandin came later in the day, having lost her way. Neither quidnunc continued her wild career to this point....

Gradually the distance between the leading three and the following two lengthened-and, for a kilometre, Madame Paës, Madame de Longueville, and Madame Maxin ran neck and neck.

Suddenly the bad-charactered racer took a line of his own, missed the next flags by a few metres, and bolted into the desert. At the second flags, Madame de Longueville led, Belzébuth consenting-or, rather, being made to consent; Madame Malherbe, creeping up, passed the flags three lengths behind, and Angelique Dandin, catching Madame Deville, led her through, a score lengths in rear....

Madame Paës was filled with hope.

Should she let Belzébuth out yet? No, not till the last flags-if she could live so long-if her heart would beat instead of stabbing-if her brain would not reel so-if the blue mist would clear from her eyes.

(Those who had climbed to points of vantage shouted that Madame de Longueville would win in a walk-had led from the start-was going strong-except for that dark horse which seemed to manage to hang on....)

A fairish jump ahead-should she pass Madame de Longueville? No, let her take it first, and let Belzébuth save himself for the three-furlong run home.

At the last flags Madame de Longueville led by twenty lengths, Madame Paës second, Madame Malherbe third, Angelique Dandin a neck behind, and Madame Deville, still flogging, a safe fifth.

And then Madame Paës gave Belzébuth a sharp flick, raised her bridle hand, and called to him.

The roar of applause and welcome to Madame de Longueville died down with curious suddenness as Belzébuth sprang forward, passed Madame de Longueville's lathered grey Arab as though he were standing, forged rapidly and steadily ahead, and, finishing in a quiet canter, won the race by a good furlong. Madame Paës reeled in the saddle and fell heavily into the arms of Colonel Merlonorot, who came forward to help her to dismount.

"Splendid! Splendid!" said he. *"Mon Dieu!* If I hadn't just bought my wife a horse, I'd ask if that pony of yours is for sale. You should run him at Longchamps!"

..."*If I hadn't just bought my wife a horse*" ...what was he saying? *"If I hadn't just bought my wife a horse*, I'd ask if that pony of yours is for sale."...

Then it was all for nothing-and money wasted!

Madame Paës fainted quietly and privately in a comfortable chair at the back of the empty reception-tent of the Spahis.

Colonel Merlonorot drove her home in his uncomfortable high dogcart —(quite *à l'Anglaise*).

Just time to change and rest before Guillaume arrived....

He burst into her room, looking fagged, white, and weary-and his greeting, after five weeks' absence, was —

"What on earth have you been doing with my horse? It's as lame as a tree, and the valet has got its near fore in a bucket of hot water....It's a shame, I say....The only horse I have got, and you can't take a little care of it! What am I to do to-morrow? I suppose it doesn't trouble you that I must cycle to barracks in the sun? ...*Peste*! ...*Nom d'un Nom*! ..." and much more.

Poor Guillaume! He was so overworked and ill-but she wept bitterly, and, lying awake all night, wished she were dead. But a note was handed in at breakfast, next morning, from Colonel de Longueville, which ran:

"DEAR MADAME,

"I should like to offer my very hearty congratulations on your, and your pony's performance yesterday, and to ask whether your husband would take 4,000 fcs. for him.

"I gave that for the pony that Belzébuth left standing yesterday-so it's not a very brilliant offer. I should train him for bigger things.

"With my most distinguished regards and compliments,
"HENRI DE LONGUEVILLE,

"Colonel."

Madame Paës, being very weak and tired, wept again.

XI. The Quest

Ex-No. 32867, *Soldat première classe*, shuffled out of the main gate of the barracks of the First Battalion of La Légion Étrangère at Sidi-bel-Abbès for the last time, and without a farewell glance at that hideous yellow building. He had once been Geoffry Brabazon-Howard, Esquire, of St. James's Street and the United Service Club, but no one would have thought it of the stooping, decrepit creature in the ill-fitting blue suit of ready-made (and very badly made) mufti, the tam-o'-shanter cap and blue scarf, from the *fourrier-sergent's* store. He looked more like a Basque bear-leader whose bear has been impounded, or an Italian organ-grinder who has had to pawn his organ-save that the rather vacant eye in the leathern face was grey and the hair, beneath the *beret*, of a Northern fairness. A careful observer (such as a mother or wife, had he had one to observe him) would have noticed that his hands shook like those of an old man, that his eyes were heavy and blood-shot, as though from sleeplessness, and that his legs did not appear to be completely under control. A casual passer-by might have supposed him to be slightly drunk, or recovering from a drunken bout.

He had that day received his discharge from the Legion, his bonus as holder of the *médaille* and *croix*, his papers and travelling-warrant to any place in France, the blessing of his Captain, and the cheery assurance of Médecin-Major Parme that he was suffering from cerebro-spinal sclerosis, and would gradually but surely develop into a paralysed lunatic.

Certainly he felt very ill. He was in no great pain, and he regretted the fact. He would far rather have felt the acutest pain than the strange sensation that there was a semi-opaque veil between himself and his fellow-men, that he lived quite alone and unapproachable in a curious cloud, and that, although he slept but little, he lived in a dream. He was also much distressed by the feeling that his hands were as large and thick as boxing-gloves, that his feet had soles of thick felt, and that he had *fourmis* (pins-and-needles) in his legs. He would gladly have exchanged the terrible feeling of weakness (and imminent collapse) in the small of his back for any kind of pain. And, above all things, he wanted *rest*. Not sleep! Heaven forbid. Sleep was the portal of a Hell unnameable and unimaginable, and the worst of it was that insomnia led to the very same place, and one lived on the horns of a dilemma. If one did things to keep oneself awake, they either lost their efficacy and one slept (and fell into Hell) or one got insomnia (and crawled there with racking, bursting head and eyes that burnt the brain).

Rest! That was it. Well-he had done his five years in the Legion and got his discharge. Why shouldn't he rest? He would rest forthwith, before he set out upon his Quest, the last undertaking of his life.

He sat down on the *pavé* in the shade of the Spahis' barracks and leant against the wall. In five seconds he was asleep.

Later, two gens d'armes passed. One turned back and kicked him. "Get out of this," said he tersely.

Ex-No. 32867 of the Première Légion Étrangère staggered to his feet with what speed he might.

"I *beg* your pardon," said he in English. "I am afraid...." and then he realized who and what and where he was.

Mechanically he walked back to barracks and made to enter the great main gate. The sentry stopped him, and the Sergeant of the Guard came up.

"By no means, verminous *pekin*,"[202] quoth Sergeant Legros. "Is this a doss-house for every dirty tramp of a broken-down *pèkin* that chooses to enter and defile it?" and he ordered the sentry to fling the thing out. "But that a French bayonet must not be used as a stable-fork, I would..." he began again, but *Ex*-No. 32867 perceived that this was not the place of Rest, and shuffled away again.

Sergeant Legros spat after him. If there was one thing he hated more than a Legionary, it was a time-expired man, a vile dog who had survived his treatment and escaped his clutches....

Ex-No. 32867 passed along the barrack wall, his eyes staring vaguely ahead. If he might not sit on the ground and could not get back to his *chambrée* and cot, where could he go for rest? He could not set forth upon his Quest until he had rested. His back was too near the breaking-point, his knees too weak, his feet too uncertain. There were seats in the gardens by the Porte de Tlemçen, if he could get so far. But in the Place Sadi Carnot he suddenly found that he had sat down. Well-he would....He fell asleep at once....

The gendarme seemed very suspicious, but that is only natural in a gendarme. Yes-the papers were apparently in order, but he would do well to remember that the gendarme had his eye upon him. He could go, this time-so, *Marche!*—and sit down no more for a siesta in the middle of the road....

Where was it he had been going for a rest? ...A bright idea—*Carmelita's*! She would let him rest, and, if not too busy, would see that he did not fall asleep and go to Hell....

"Bon jour, mon ami!" cried Carmelita, as he entered the little Café de la Legion. "Che cosa posse offrirve? Seet daown. What you drink?"

Ex-No. 32867 raised his *beret*, bowed, smiled, and fell asleep across a table. Carmelita raised puzzled brows. Drunk at this time of day? She pulled him backward on to the wooden bench, untied his scarf, and, going to her room behind the bar, returned with an old cushion which she thrust beneath his head. He at once sat up, thanked her politely, and walked out of the café.

"Eh! Madonna! These English," shrugged Carmelita, and resumed her work. If one stopped to notice the eccentricities of every half-witted Légionnaire, one might spend one's life at it....

Ex-No. 32867 strolled slowly along to the railway-station, showed his papers to the Sergeant of the Guard on duty there, sat him down, and went to sleep. Five minutes later he arose, approached the ticket-office, tried hard for a minute to penetrate the half-opaque veil that hung between him and his fellow-men, and then sat down beneath the *guichet* and went to sleep....

The station-master was doing his best to make it clear that he hated filth, dust, dead leaves, stray pariah dogs, discharged Legionaries, and similar kinds of offal to remain unswept from the clean floor of his station.

The awakened man peered hard through the half-opaque veil that hung between him and the great man, made a mighty effort of concentration, and then said quite distinctly:

"I want a third single to Oran. I am starting on my Quest, after waiting five years."

"Then wait another five hours, Mr. Discharged Legionary," said the functionary, "and come again at 9.20 for your third single to Oran-if you are not too drunk. Meanwhile, you cannot sleep here, unless it is in the permanent-way with your ugly neck across a rail."

The time-expired considered this.

"No, I go on a Quest," said he, and the station-master, with a gesture of a spatulate thumb in the direction of the door, indicated that the sooner the son of a camel commenced it the better for all concerned.

He was an unsympathetic person-but then he was held responsible when unconsidered trifles of Government property were stolen from the station precincts. And it is well known that a Legionary will steal the wall-paper from your wall while your back is turned, cut it up small, and try to sell it back to you as postage-stamps as soon as darkness sets in.

Ex-No. 32867 got to his feet once more, marched mechanically to barracks, was somewhat roughly handled by the guard at the order of Sergeant Legros, and, having staunched the bleeding from his nose, split lip, and cut cheek with the lining of his *beret*, made his way to the Café de la Legion. Entering, he bowed to Carmelita with a dignified flourish of his pulpy *beret*, fell at full length on the floor, and went to sleep.

"Queer, how differently drink takes different people," mused Carmelita, as she again applied the cushion to supporting the battered head-and yet she had hitherto known this Guillaume Iyoné or Dhyoni (or William Jones!) of the IIIrd Company, as a soldier of the soberest and quietest. Quite like old Jean Boule of the VIIth. Doubtless he had been "wetting his discharge papers." Apparently he had done it to the point of drowning them.

At *l'heure verte, l'heure de l'absinthe*, the café began to fill, and for a time the sleeper was undisturbed by the *va et vient* of Carmelita's customers....

"'Ullo, Cocky!" remarked le Légionnaire 'Erbiggin ("'Erb"), entering with his compatriots Rupert and John Bull, followed by the Grasshopper and the Bucking Bronco. "Gorn to yer pore 'ed, 'as it? Come *hup* —an' 'ave s'more," and he sought to rouse the sleeper.

"Strike me strange ef it 'ent thet *com*-patriot o' yourn, John," said the Bucking Bronco. "Willie the Jones, o' the IIIrd Company.... Guess he's got a hard cider jag. Didn't know he ever fell off the water-cart any."

"William Jones" sat up.

"Really, I *beg* your pardon," he said, "I thought I..." and then peered through the heavy blanketing veil that was daily thickening between him and his fellow-men.

"He's no more drunk than I am," said John Bull...."I suppose he's just discharged. I thought he was in hospital....Looks as though he ought to be, anyhow."

"I have rested, and I must begin my Quest," said "William Jones," *Ex*-No. 32867. "I have a glorious Quest to undertake, and I have little time. I..."

"Yus. *Ingk*quest's abaht your mark, Cocky," observed 'Erb. "Crowner's ingkquest."

"Help me up," added the sick man. "I must begin my Quest."

"*De sot homme, sot songe*," murmured La Cigale, shaking his head mournfully. "I too have Quests, but they tangle and jangle in my brain-and folk say I am mad or drunk.... Some will say you are mad, *mon ami*, and some will say you are drunk."

"Are you going to England?" asked John Bull, as he helped the man to his feet.

"England? ...England? ...Oh, yes. I am going to England. Where *should* I go? She lives in England," was the reply.

"Have you friends?"

"She is my Friend. Of Friendship she is the Soul and the Essence."

"*Chacun aime comme il est*," remarked the Grasshopper. "This is a gentleman," and added, "*Il n'y a guere de femme assez habile pour connaître tout le mal qu'elle fait.*"

"I allow we oughter take him daown town to the railway deepôt and see him on the cars," put in the Bucking Bronco. "Ef we don't tote him thar an' tell him good-bye, it's the looney-house for his. He'll set down in the bazaar and go as *maboul*[203] as a *kief*[204]-smoker."...

"I was going to say we'd better see him off," agreed John Bull. "If he gets to England, he'll have more chance than as a discharged Legionary in Algiers-or France either. Wish we could get an address from him. We could tie a label on him."

But they could not, and after the Bucking Bronco had procured him food from Carmelita's "pie-foundry," as he termed her modest *table d'hôte*, they took him to the station and, under the cold eye of the Sergeant of the Guard at the platform gate, saw him off....

As one in a dream, as one seeing through a glass darkly and beholding men as trees walking, *Ex*-No. 32867, William Jones, *alias* Geoffry Brabazon-Howard, Esquire, made his way to London. There is a providence that watches over children and drunken men, and *Ex*-No. 32867 was as a compound of both. He knew he was exceeding ill and quite abnormal in some directions, such as never being *quite* certain as to whether he was really doing and experiencing things, or was dreaming; but what he did not realize was that, concurrently with severe insomnia, he was liable at any moment to fall suddenly asleep for a few minutes, wherever he might be, and whatever he might be doing. He was aware that he had brief periods of "abstraction," but was quite unaware that they were periods of profound slumber. Unfortunately they only endured for a few seconds or a few minutes, and, though serving to place him in endless dangerous, ridiculous, and awkward situations, did not amount to anything approaching a "living-wage" of sleep-rarely to more than an hour in the twenty-four and generally to much less.

At times he was, for a few hours perhaps, entirely normal, to all appearances; and could talk, behave, and transact business in such a way that no casual observer would be aware of anything unusual in the man. He himself, however, when at his best, was still aware of the isolating-medium in which he moved and lived and had his being; the slowly thickening cloud, the imponderating veil, that shut him in, and cut him off, with increasing certainty and speed.

What would happen when he could no longer pierce and penetrate this fog, or wall, of cloudy glass; this vast extinguisher of sombre web, and could hold no communication with the outer world?

Was he becoming an idiot before becoming a paralytic, and thus having the gross presumption to reverse the order of things foretold by Médecin-Major Parme?

On arrival at Charing Cross, he had strolled idly through the streets of London, slept on a bench in Leicester Square; had thought he was in the public gardens outside the Porte de Tlemçen at Sidi-bel-Abbès, and hoped that the Legion's famous band would come and play its sad music in that sad place; and, being "moved on," had wandered away, dazed and bewildered, going on and on until he reached Hammersmith. Here he found his way into one of those Poor Man's Hotels, a Rowton House-vaguely under the impression that it was some kind of barrack.

Here he had a glorious time of Rest, broken only by the occasional misfortune of having a night's sleep, or rather a nightmare in the unnameable Hell to keep out of which he exerted all his failing faculties. And at the Hammersmith Rowton House he became an object of the intensest interest to such of his fellow-inhabitants of that abode of semi-starvation and hopeless misery as were not too deeply engulfed in their own struggle with despair and death to notice anything at all.

For "William Jones" began to blossom forth into a "toff," a perfect dook, until it was the generally accepted theory that he was a swell-mobsman just out of gaol, and now working the West End in the correct garb of that locality.

Little by little the man had replaced his old clothes by new, his *beret* by a correct hat, his scarf by the usual neck-wear of an English gentleman, his *fourrier-sergent's* suit of mufti by a Conduit Street creation, his rough boots by the most modish of cloth-topped kid; and generally metamorphosed William Jones, late of the Foreign Legion, into Geoffry Brabazon-Howard, Esq., late of St. James's Street and the United Service Club.

In one of his hours of mental clarity and vigour, he had called at his bank and drawn the sum of ninety pounds, left at current-account there when he disappeared into the Legion; and in another such hour (and in his new clothes) had called at his Club, seen the secretary, and arranged for the revival of his lapsed membership.

It had taken both the bank-manager and the secretary some time to recognize him, but they had done so eventually, and had been shocked to think of what the man must have been through to have changed as he had, and to look as he did.

He had been through a good deal. In addition to the very real hardships of campaigning in the Sahara as a private of the Legion, he had had black-water fever and dysentery, had been wounded in the abdomen by an Arab lance, carried away by the Arabs while unconscious from loss of blood from this wound, and kept until he should recover consciousness and be eligible for torture. (It is pointless to torture a practically dead person.) The badness of his wound had saved his life, for by the time he had sufficiently recovered to be interesting to his captors, they were attacked and routed, and "William Jones" had been restored to the bosom of his company only slightly tortured after all. The shock to an enfeebled man, who was also suffering from a hideous wound, had been considerable, however.

Thereafter, enteric had done little to improve his health, and his resultant slowness and stupidity had earned him the special attention of Sergeant-Major Suicide-Maker and Sergeant Legros.

So there is little wonder that his banker and club-secretary were shocked at the change in him, and wondered how many days or weeks he had to live.

And to the secretary, who saw him almost daily, it was clear that the poor chap was sometimes queer in the head too-and no wonder, looking as awfully ill as he did.

For example, one day he would walk into the Club, sit down on the Hall-Porter's stool, and go to sleep immediately!

Another day he would do the same thing on the stairs, or even the front steps.

If he sat down in a smoking-room arm-chair and fell asleep, as is a member's just and proper right, he would spring up if anyone approached, say, "I really *beg* your pardon. I am afraid I..." and walk straight out of the Club.

What would the worthy secretary have thought had he known that Geoffry Brabazon-Howard, Esquire (once of the Black Lancers), walked daily to the Club from the Hammersmith Rowton House in the morning and back to that same retreat in the evening; and that such food as he ate, was eaten in his cubicle there, or at a coffee-stall? At a Rowton House one has the "use of the fire" in the basement for one's cooking purposes, but Geoffry was a most indifferent cook, and it is difficult to purchase really cookable provisions on a sum of fourpence a day. For this was the amount that he had decided upon as the irreducible minimum to be expended on food if he were to keep up the strength required for the daily journey to the West End and back. After paying for his clothes and setting aside his club fees, he would have enough to live on at this rate, until the London season and through it, if he were very, very careful. He would have to renew some of his clothing, perhaps, later on-boots, linen, ties-and there were always incidental and unavoidable expenses. However, with great care and a little luck, he could last to the end of the season and pursue his Quest. And this great absorbing Quest, which had made him expend his all in fine clothing, club membership, and the appearance of being a "person of quality" and a gentleman of means and leisure?

Merely to come face to face with, to meet on terms of equality, to have just one encounter and conversation with—a woman.

Before he died he must see, and speak to, Peggy once again-to Lady Margaret Hillier-because of whom he had vanished into the French Foreign Legion, and of whom he had thought daily and nightly ever since.

He had had a thin time, he was near the end of his tether, life held nothing for him, and he had no desire to prolong it-but before he lay down for the last time he *would* see Peggy again, hear her voice, feast his eyes on her beautiful face, and his ears on the sound of her words and laughter, yea, feast his very soul upon the banquet that it had dreamed of-and then he would have no further use for clubs, fine clothes, a penny chair in the Park, nor anything else.

The ass was quite mad, you perceive....

Now one *can* live on fourpence a day, and for a very long time too. If one starts in robust health and strength, one can maintain an appearance of health and the power to work for a quite surprising period. But if one is really very ill, on the verge of a nervous collapse, and badly in need of a rest-cure with special diet, tonic, and drugs-fourpence a day is not enough.

They give you a surprisingly filling meal at certain coffee-shops and cocoa-houses (like Pearce-and-Plenty or Lockhart's) for fourpence, but one meatless meal per diem is not enough. It is, on the whole, better to have two penny-worth at dawn and two pennyworth at sunset, and a good drink of water at midday. Better still is it, if you are really experienced in the laying-out of money, to have a pennyworth at dawn, two pennyworth at midday and a penny-worth at sunset. (You can go to bed with a full stomach by supping on a quart of water.)

But Geoffry had not complete liberty in the matter. One cannot go for a twopenny mid-day meal in a silk hat, faultless morning coat buttoned over the white waistcoat of a blameless laundress, and in patent cloth-topped boots. Geoffry was, by force of circumstances, debarred this thrice-a-day system of feeding, and was constrained to breakfast (in rags) at an early coffee-stall and to dine at the same, in the same decrepit clothing, late at night. After breakfast he would return to his cubicle, dress for the Club, and creep forth, still in the early hours of the morning. (One attracts attention if, in the broad light of naked day, one issues from a Rowton House in the correct garb of Pall Mall and Piccadilly.) At night he would undress, carefully fold his immaculate clothes, don his rags, and sally forth to dine on twopence. The coffee-stall keeper regarded him as a broken-down torf and eke a balmy, but coffee-stall keepers are a race blasé of freaks, social, moral, and mental.

Between these meals Geoffry Brabazon-Howard pursued his Quest. He went to his Club and listened eagerly for "society" gossip, and read "society" papers (of the kind that inform the public when Lady Diana Blathers dines at the Fritz, and photographs her inhaling the breath of an abortive animal, apparently a bye-product of the dog-industry; announces the glad tidings that Mrs. Bobbie Snobbie has returned to Town; or that the Earl of Spunge was seen scratching his head in Bond Street yesterday). Having sought in vain for news of Lady Margaret Hillier, he slowly paraded the fashionable shopping thoroughfares, and then, utterly weary, turned into the Park, selected an eligible site for seeing the pedestrians, carriage-exercisers, and riders, and sat for hours watching and waiting, hoping against hope-as he thought. In point of fact he spent a great portion of this time in dropping asleep and being awakened by nearly falling off the chair. He was sometimes tempted to expend this chair-penny in food, but restrained the base cravings of his lower nature. He pictured himself arrayed in the correctest of dress, nonchalantly seated on a Park chair, gaily observing the gyrations of the giddy throng of fashionable human ephemeræ-suddenly seeing Peggy, and rising, accosting her with graceful badinage, airy flippancy, and casual interest. Peggy would laugh and talk amusingly and lightly, he would beg her to come and lunch with him at the Club, or take tea if such were the hour; he would feast his eyes and ears and soul as he had promised himself-and *then*? —then he would lay down his arms and cease to fight this relentless Foe-sickness, disease, and death-that besieged him day and night, and sought to prevent his walk to the Club, sought to thwart the pursuit of his Quest. Having seen Peggy again, heard her laugh and speak, looked into her hopelessly perfect and wonderful eyes, he would surrender the fortress he no longer wished to hold, and would permit the Enemy to enter-trusting that *le bon Dieu, Le Bon Général*, would see to it that, for a broken old soldier, death was annihilation, peace, and rest....

Daily he grew thinner, as a sick man living on fourpence a day must, and frequently he would finger the sovereign that always lay in his waistcoat pocket-ready for the day when Peggy should lunch at the Club with him. It is not wholly easy to keep a sovereign intact while you slowly starve and every fibre of your being craves for tobacco, for brandy, for food-as you smell choice Havanas in the Club smoking-room, see fat, healthy men drinking their whiskies and brandies, and when you are violently smitten by rich savours of food as you pass the door of the dining-room.

The fragrance of coffee and eggs-and-bacon! The glimpse of noble barons of beef on the sideboard! The sight of tea-and-toast at four in the afternoon when you have had nothing since four in the morning! But the sovereign remained intact. With that he and Peggy could have an excellent lunch-without wine-and Peggy never touched wine....

* * *

He started to his feet.

"I really *beg* your pardon! I am afraid I..." A stranger had awakened him as he slept in a smoking-room arm-chair.... He did not recollect how he came to do such a thing when he should have been in the Park.... *What* was the man saying—"Ill?"

"I was afraid you were ill. To tell the truth, I jolly well thought you were dead for the moment. Let me drive you to my doctor's. Splendid chap. Just going that way.... No-don't run away."

"Most awfully kind," replied Geoffry, peering through the veil, "but I'm *quite* all right. Just a bit tired, you know. I am going to have a real Rest soon.... At present I have a Quest."

The poor devil looked absolutely *starved*, thought Colonel Doddington. Positively ghastly.

"Come and have some lunch with me," he said, "and let me tell you about this doctor of mine, anyhow."

Geoffry flushed-though it was remarkable that there was sufficient blood in so meagre a body and feeble a heart for the purpose.

Lunch! A four-course lunch in a beautiful room-silver, crystal, fine napery, good service-perhaps wine, certainly alcohol of some sort, and real coffee....

It was a cruel temptation. But he put it from him. After all, one was a gentleman, and a gentleman does not accept hospitality which he cannot return, from a stranger.

"Awfully sorry-but I *must* go," he replied. "I'm feeding out." He was-late that night, on twopence.

He fled, and outside mopped his brow. It *had* been a terrible temptation and ordeal. For two pins he would go back and have a brandy-and-soda at the cost of two days' food. No, he dared not risk collapse-and two days' complete starvation would probably mean collapse. Collapse meant expense too, and money was time to him. The expenditure of more than fourpence a day would shorten the time of his Quest. A day lost, was a chance lost. She might pass through London at that very time, if he lay ill in the Hammersmith Rowton House.

That night he had to take a 'bus home or lie down in the street. Next day, dressing took so long and his walk to the Club was so painful and slow, that he had to omit the Bond Street, Regent Street, and Piccadilly walk, and go straight to the Park.

There he had shocking luck. A zealous but clumsy policeman rendered him First Aid to the Fainting with such violence that he spoilt the collar and shirt-front that should have lasted another two days. Why could not the worthy fool have left him to come out of his faint alone? He went *into* it alone, all right. And there was an accursed, gaping crowd. Nor could he give the policeman two pennies, and so gave him nothing-which was very distressing. A most unlucky day!

Well-the days of his Quest were numbered, and the number was lessened.

Next day he found the Enemy very powerful and the tottering fortress closely beset. He would be hard put to it to walk to the Club-but come! —an old Legionary who had done his fifty kilometres a day under a hundred-weight kit, over loose sand, with the thermometer at 120° in the shade; and who had lived on a handful of rice-flour and a mouthful of selenitic water in the Sahara-surely he was not going to shirk a stroll from Hammersmith Broadway to Pall Mall and round the Town to the Park?

He had got as far as Devonshire House, when a lady, who was driving from the Berkeley Hotel, where she had been lunching, to the Coburg Hotel, where she was to have tea with friends who were taking her on to Ranelagh, suddenly saw him and thought she saw a ghost. As her carriage crawled through the crush into Berkeley Street it brought her within a yard of him.

She turned very pale and lay back on the cushions. Immediately she sat upright again, and then leaned towards him. It *could* not be! Not this poor wreck, this shattered ruin-her splendid *Geoff* —the Geoff who had seemed to love her, five years ago, and had suddenly dropped her, and so been the cause of her marrying in haste and repenting in even greater haste, to the day of her widowhood.

"*Geoff!*" she said.

He raised his hat with a trembling hand and his face was transfigured.... Was he dying on his feet, wondered the woman.

"Get in, Geoff," she said, and the footman half-turned and then jumped down.

Geoffry Brabazon-Howard, with a great and almost final effort, stepped into the victoria.

"Will you come to lunch with me at..." he began, and then burst into tears.

Later, it was the woman who wept, tears of joy and thankfulness, after the agonizing suspense when the great specialist staked his reputation on his plain verdict that the man was not organically diseased. He was in a parlous state, no doubt, practically dying of starvation and nervous exhaustion-but nursing could save him.

Nursing did-the nursing of Lady Peggy Brabazon-Howard.

XII. "Vengeance Is Mine..."

As Jean Rien expressed it, he was *bien touché*; as le Légionnaire 'Erbiggin put it, he had got it in the neck; as the Bucking Bronco "allowed," his monica was up; as Jean Boule saw, he was dying.

One cannot blame him, since an Arab lance had pinned him to the ground and an Arab *flissa* had nearly severed his arm from his shoulder.

Jean Rien evidently blamed himself however, and for many things-chief among them a little matter of parricide, it seemed to Jean Boule, as he bent over him in his endeavour to comfort and to soothe.

"In much pain, *mon ami?*" the old soldier asked, as he moistened the dying man's lips and forehead.

"Little of body, but in great pain of mind....I would confess to you, Père Boule....I would ease my soul....I would ask if you think I am a murderer....I have not blamed myself until now that I am dying....Now I am afraid....Look you, Père Jean Boule, I was brought up by my mother (*le bon Dieu* rest and bless her soul) with one purpose in life, with one end to fulfil, with one deed to do. Nothing earlier can I remember than her making me repeat after her the words of a promise and an oath. Night after night, as I went to bed, morning after morning, as I arose, I said my prayers at her knee, and followed them by this promise and this oath which she had taught me. Never did we sit down to a meal, never did we rise from one, without this formula. From my very birth I was dedicated, and my life was devoted and avowed, to the fulfilment of this promise, the keeping of this oath....Hear it....'*I, Jean-Without-A-Name, son of Marie Duval and Ober-Leutnant von Schlofen of the Hundred and Thirty-ninth Pomeranian Regiment, do most solemnly swear, that from my seventeenth birthday I will devote the whole of my mind and will, my strength and skill, my time and my money, to finding the man who in 1870 was Ober-Leutnant von Schlofen and who is my father, the torturer of my mother and the murderer of my mother's beloved husband, Jacques Duval. I do most solemnly swear that, having found him, I will call him "Father," I will torture him, as he tortured my mother, and I will kill him even as he killed him who should have been my father, so help me God and the Blessed Virgin. Amen.*'...

"Yes, my friend, morning, noon, and night I repeated this after my mother, and at the conclusion of each repetition this poor soul, who loved and hated me, and whose heart was buried in the pit in which lay Jacques Duval and many more, would kiss me on the brow, and say, 'Thou art the instrument of God's vengeance.' For sixteen years she did this, and on my seventeenth birthday gave me a knife that had belonged to Jacques Duval, together with her savings of seventeen years. The knife had killed poor Jacques, and the money was to help in his avenging by means of the knife....Mad? Yes, mad as ever a human being was, poor soul....But think of what she saw and suffered....Married a week before war broke out, her husband torn from her arms to march away to fight, perhaps to be maimed and mangled, perhaps to die....Months of solitude....Rumours....Hopes....Soul-sickening fears....Can you not see her in their little house-where they were to have been so happy-waiting, hoping, fearing? And then, one dark night, a heavy tramp of soldiers, screams, red-reflections lighting up the clean little room in which she slept, and then-blows on her door, harsh guttural shouts, and the crash of the burst-in door....

"For a fortnight the Herr Ober-Leutnant von Schlofen, in command of the detachment that had occupied the little village, made her house his headquarters, and as, from the first moment, she had defended herself tooth and nail, Marie Duval spent that time, bound hand and foot, and locked in her little room. At first, when she was untied, that she might eat and drink, she refused, but when pain, horror, grief, and every other anguished feeling had merged into a very madness of passion for revenge, she ate and drank, that she might have strength to slay....

"And the night that her teeth met in the Herr Ober-Leutnant's throat, her Jacques came back wounded, and they caught him and brought him to this foul and filthy von Schlofen swine of Germany....

"On learning they were husband and wife, von Schlofen confronted them in their bonds-she, half-dead with shame, exhaustion, and misery; he half-dead with wounds and the brutality of his captors. Then, while two of his vile bloodhounds held the woman, four others flung the man face downward over the kitchen table, placed a pail beneath his head, and von Schlofen cut his throat from ear to ear with that same knife....

"Thereafter they flogged Marie Duval with the Herr Ober-Leutnant's switch that she might learn obedience and gratitude, and that he might find her tamer....

"Mad? Oh yes, quite more than a little mad, this poor Marie Duval....And when I was born, she dedicated me, as I say, her instrument of vengeance, so that on my seventeenth birthday I took train for Strasburg and the beginning of my quest. I had no great difficulty in tracking down this von Schlofen, who had become Colonel of the Hundred and Thirty-ninth Pomeranian Regiment, and then retired to his large estates in Silesia.

"When not hunting the boar and the deer there, he spent most of his time in an ancient, gloomy house in Thorn. And in Thorn I took up my abode and worked at my trade of carpenter....

"I shall never forget my first sight of the man who was my father and my quarry; the man who gave me birth and whom I had been brought up, by the loving mother who hated me, to kill with the knife that had killed the man who should have been my father. My heart beat so fast that I feared I should faint or suffocate and die with my life's purpose unaccomplished. I gripped the haft of the knife beneath my blouse, the haft of the knife whose blade this barbarous German brute had driven into the throat of Jacques Duval, and which I was to drive into his own fat neck as I had been taught and trained to do....Oh yes, taught and trained. Did I tell you how Madame ma mère daily practised my hand at knife-strokes? Never a pig was killed within miles of our village but I must be taken to see the doing of it, while I was a child, and to do it myself when old enough.

"No opportunity was I allowed to lose of driving my knife to the hilt in any dead animal, into anything in which a knife could be driven.

"I can hear her thin and bitter voice at this moment, see the wild glare in her eye as she gloated beside me while I stuck some neighbour's pig and the blood gushed warm into the blood-tub.

"'Ohé,' she would cry. 'Gobbets of flesh and gouts of gore! So shalt thou bleed the foulest pig in all that Prussian sty, thine own father, thou accursed little devil. God and the Blessed Virgin reward and bless thee, my angel.'...

"Oui, mon vieux, a strange upbringing for a child, hein?

"And when I first beheld him, my father, the foulest pig in all that Prussian sty, I looked at the spot beneath his ear where I should strike and bleed him as he bled Jacques Duval-ere I cut his throat from ear to ear, as he cut the throat of Jacques Duval."...

Jean Rien closed his eyes and fell silent.

"Well, 'e might 'a finished 'is tile afore 'e 'opped it," remarked le Légionnaire 'Erbiggin, with apparent callousness, belied by his sympathetic, unhappy countenance. "So fur as I could onnerstan' 'im, 'e wos agoin' ter do 'is pore ol' farver in.....'Ere, give 'im a suck o' this *bapédi*," he added, as he produced a small medicine bottle half-full of the fiery fig-spirit.

"No," replied John Bull; "only increase the bleeding, if he is not dead. All the better if he has fainted."

Jean Rien opened his eyes.

"I can scarcely see you, Père Jean Boule," he murmured. "It is as dark as it was in that room where he lay when at last I had him at my mercy....Yes, at length, after months of weary waiting for my opportunity, months of practice at the burglars' trade, months of scheming and study of the big house where the Pettenkoferstrasse joins the Baseler Alee, he lay before me on his bed, the moon shining on his white face. The hour for which I had been in training for two-and-twenty years had struck. I crept from the window, by which I had entered, to the door, and turned the key, praying that the noise might not awake him. It did not.

"I crept back to the bedside, raised my knife on high, shouted '*My Father*,' thrust his big head over to one side and, as I had done a thousand times in the course of my training, drove the knife home to the very hilt-and even as, in the one motion, my left hand turned his head and my right hand stabbed, I knew that I had struck a stark, rigid corpse! ... He was dead and cold! ... I laughed aloud." ...

Jean Rien laughed aloud and died.

XIII. Sermons in Stones

It was a truly terrible night, and, to add to his own troubles and sufferings, John Bull had a great and growing anxiety as to the state of his beloved comrade, the Bucking Bronco. For that gentleman was undoubtedly working up for a "go" of *le cafard*, the desert madness of the Legion that so often ends in suicide, murder, or some military "crime," the punishment for which may be death, or the worse-than-death of the Zephyrs.

So awful was the heat of the barrack-room, and so charged was the atmosphere with electricity and human passion and misery, that even 'Erb had succumbed, and, in a fit of rage, akin to sheer madness, had dashed his beloved mouth-organ upon the ground and stamped it shapeless, his face contorted with demoniac rage. Thereafter, he set himself to tease and enrage the big American whose mind was as much slower, as his soul and body were greater, than those of the little Cockney.

As he leant across Reginald Rupert's bed to reach his sack of cleaning-rags, John Bull whispered to that legionary, "The Bronco'll run amuck to-night if we don't watch it. He has already said he's going 'on pump' and also that he's going to 'lean agin the Sergeant-Major till he moults'! If 'Erb 'gits his goat,' he'll kill him, and then shoot himself."

"Spin a yarn, Bull," advised Rupert.... "If 'Erb gets impossible, I'll knock him out and we'll put him to bed. I'm with you, Old Thing."

Before the old soldier could reply, a loud crash caused him to spring round. The Bucking Bronco had flung his rifle against the white-washed wall.

"The Devil admire me if ever I clean that gosh-dinged, dod-gasted gas-pipe again," he growled, and added, "Yep! An' if any yaller-dog hobo of a *Caporal* gits fresh with me, I'll wipe his denied dial with it!"

"You know Seven Dials, Buck?" queried 'Erb innocently.

"Yep," was the reply.

"Then stuff four of 'em up yer shirt. Yah!" jeered 'Erb.

"You ain't offended, matey, are yer?" he added, in a tone of contrite concern.

"Nope," said the American, staring hard.

"Then stuff up the remainin' three!" yelped his tormentor, and laughed insultingly.

The huge American rose to his feet menacingly, but as Rupert stepped between him and 'Erb, he sat down again.

"Wot I complains of is that all the Seven Dials rolled inter one wouldn't make anything as ugly as *your* dial," he grumbled. "Why don' youse take it to a dime-show mooseum? It's like them faces them Chinese guys paints on their shields to terrify their enner-mies. Why should you be allowed to bring it into this shack an' spile my slumbers? It makes me tired, an' I feel it's my painful dooty to change it some."...

"'Streuth!" shrilled 'Erb. "'Ark at 'im! An' 'im on'y alive becos 'e ain't never see 'isself in a lookin'-glass! 'Ere, fetch a mirror, somebody, and let 'im commit sooicide wiv a single squint in it-if it don't break afore 'e can realize the orful troof."...

"Shut up, 'Erb," interrupted John Bull. "You fellows must help me, I want to talk. If I don't, I shall get *cafard* —and do something that'll put me in the Sergeant-Major's hands. I'm going to spin a yarn.... What's the most remarkable thing you've ever seen, 'Erb?"

"The Buckin' Bronco's silly faice, Farver," replied that gentleman.

The Bucking Bronco rose and began removing his shirt as if for battle.

'Erb reached for his bayonet.

Precisely how most *cafard* tragedies begin.

Rupert passed him a rag.

"It does want a bit of a polish," he said.

"That's right, Buck, you'll be cooler without that," remarked John Bull, and added:

"Look here, I'm going to clean your rifle to-night —and you can do mine to-morrow night."

"Please yerself, Johnnie," was the reply, "I'm done with chores in this outfit. I'm going to strip stark, and then I'm agoin' to march to Sidi-bel-Abbès —soon as I twisted ole Suicide-Maker's head 'round three times and catch who you can.' His body remains at attention facin' front while his head goes round-see? ...Guess I'm *locoed* to-night. Anyhaow, I'm gwine to strip naked and go 'on pump' and see Carmelita." (Carmelita was six hundred miles to the north.)

"Well, put a turban on yer 'ead, fer modesty's saike, if you're a callin' on lidies," sneered 'Erb.

"What's the most remarkable thing *you've* ever seen, Bull?" asked Rupert, taking his cue. "That night when it was a case of pearls or impalement must have been about your most exciting time, what?"

"You never tole us nothin' abaht that, Farver. Wot was it?" inquired 'Erb, rising to the fly.

"Oh-rather a queer night I once spent," replied John Bull, "but it wasn't the queerest experience I ever had."

"Well, wot was the rummiest start you ever seen, then?" pursued 'Erb.

"Oh, just some stones-and what they did," was the reply.

"Git busy at 'em both, Johnnie, the pearls an' the other stones," said the Bucking Bronco, and added, "It looks like hell, you cleanin' my gun. Push it here."

Only too glad to see his friend employed, the old Legionary handed the rifle and rag to him and gave him a cigarette.

"There isn't much to the pearl yarn," he said. "It was before you joined, Buck. We were doing some unpeaceful penetration down south, and I was laid out in an Arab charge. They rode right through us, and I got a kick on the head that put me to sleep for hours. When I sat up, the Arabs were looting the dead and killing the wounded-who hadn't already killed themselves. I suppose I was the only one not too badly wounded to be of any use for affording sport under torture. Anyhow I was the only man marched off to the *douar* —a very large one indeed, being that of the Sheikh Abou Moustapha ben Isa Bahr-el-Man-deb, the great Arab guerilla leader-and by the time I got there, I was as glad to see the place as if it had been my home. A *mehari* camel goes at a good pace-and I wasn't on its back."

"Dragged?" queried 'Erb.

"Well, I ran as long as I could, of course, but the sand was very loose and fine. When we stopped, and everybody who wanted a whack at me had finished, I was tied to a palm-tree, and a negro gentleman with a long gun, a sword, three daggers and a flint-lock pistol, was set to see I didn't get into mischief. In the evening a gang of them came and untied me and led me into the *douar* of low black tents. I thought I was 'for it' then, and could not keep my mind off the barrack-room photos of mutilated Legionaries. They took me to Sheikh Abou, however, where he sat on a carpet in front of his tent, drinking coffee and smoking cigarettes like a Christian. He was a fine-looking old bird, and spoke very fair French.

"'Bon soir, chien,' says he.

"'Bon soir, chat,' says I.

"'Pourquoi "*chat*"?' says he.

"'Parce que,' says I.

"I also explained that the French dog hunts the Arab cat, but he scored with a quiet smile and the remark that it rather looked as though the alleged cat was going to hunt the dog of an Unbeliever. My attempt at driving him into a rage and earning a swift death failed altogether. He was too big a man really, too balanced, too scholarly, too philosophic, for petty rages and quick stabs.

"'Are you unwounded, dog?' he asked.

"'By the weapons of soldiers,' I replied. 'Only bruised by the *matracks* of brave Arab gentlemen who strike manacled prisoners of war.'

"'What do the Franzawi do to Arab prisoners?' he returned.

"'They don't bind them and beat them,' I said.

"'What do they do to Arab women?' was his next question.

"'What did they do to your daughter?' I asked in turn. I knew that she had been sent straight to him, with a courteous letter, as soon as our general knew who she was.

"'True,' owned the Sheikh. 'See here, dog. My son, the bravest and handsomest man who ever sat a horse, was shot in cold blood by you Franzawi. My daughter was treated as a princess-which she is-and sent safely back to me. At dawn to-morrow, I shall either avenge the death of my son or else reward the kindness to my daughter.'

"He then gave orders to some of the gang, and they cut down a young palm that grew in front of his tent, leaving a stump a couple of feet high. This they trimmed with axes and knives to a point like that of a spear.

"While they were doing this, he went into his tent and came out again with a tiny bag of soft leather. Out of this he tipped some very decent pearls on to the carpet in front of him.

"'See these pearls,' said he. 'In the morning you shall have them as well as a camel and a guide to take you to your camp, *if* I find that gratitude for my daughter's safety is stronger than the desire to avenge my son's murder. Should this not be the case, however, you will be impaled upon that stump like a date on a dagger, and with your face to the sun-after your eyelids have been removed. Go and ponder Life, Death, Kismet, the Goodness of Allah-and the relative values of Pearls and Impalement. After all-wealth is a snare and a delusion whilst Death may be annihilation and peace-even for a dog of a *giaour*.'

"'Which do you think it will be-pearls or death, Sheikh?' I asked.

"'*Mektoub rebib! Inshallah!*[205] ...I positively do not know. *Barca!*[206] replied the old gentleman-and I was taken back to my tree and given a gourd of water and a few dates.

"I had a merry night, I assure you! I wasn't to die then, however, for, towards dawn, the negro fell asleep, and as they had left me unbound, after giving me the food and water, I grabbed his bag of dates and grain, and did the record long-distance run of my life, most of it over that stony out-crop that takes no footprints. I put in the day in a cave, ran all the next night, and next day reached Sefraina-an outpost of ours."

"'Streuth!" murmured 'Erb, "an' *that* wasn't your rummiest go, Farver? You seen some queer things, you 'ave, since you bin a Legendary!"

"No, the most truly extraordinary thing that ever happened to me took place before I joined the Legion. It was in India."

"What about them stones, John?" queried the Bucking Bronco, wiping his streaming brow with the rag that he had just used for cleaning his rifle.

"That's what I'm going to tell you about," was the reply.

"I was a youngster then, and I had got leave from my ship to go and see my brother who was commanding-who was-er-up country. We were lying in Bombay harbour and going into dock for some repairs or other. It took me a couple of days to get to where my brother was stationed-up in some very hilly country. As my train dropped down a steep incline into the place where I was to get out, I noticed that a branch line ran off to the left and climbed the side of a very steep rock and there ended abruptly. I asked my brother what this was, and he told me that sometimes a truck or two would break away at the end of a climbing train and come rushing down the incline, which was many miles in length. As it approached the station it could be switched off on to this steeply rising branch line and expend its momentum in running up it, instead of dashing into the first train it met on the main line. And thereby hung a quaint and interesting tale. Some months before my visit, a naked Holy Man had rolled up, with his hair plastered with mud and tow, his body smeared all over with ashes, and his soul too lofty and enlightened to let his gross body do a job of work of any sort. He staked out a claim under this great rock near the line, planted himself in the middle of the patch of hand-patted dirt that was to be his home, and there squatted all day long, with his begging-bowl and an ugly-looking steel spike. The neighbouring villagers fed him of course, and, like wise men, propitiated him in every way and gave him anything he wanted-for, judging by his filthiness, nakedness, and laziness, he must be a very holy man indeed, must have acquired great merit, and be very potent to upset the apple-cart of anyone who thwarted him. Also he worked divers miracles, and caused a brazen image of Kali to arise from the earth at his feet. This he put in a circle of red-painted stones-and straightway there was a sacred shrine and the foundations of a great place of pilgrimage and the site of a holy temple.

"But when June drew near, the villagers warned the Holy Man that the rains would break soon and he'd get uncommon damp when it rained. The holy one replied that he would build him a hut perchance.

"The villagers smiled, and said it rained three inches a day for months on end in those parts, when the monsoon broke. 'My hut shall be of stone,' said His Holiness.

"The villagers laughed outright. Where was there stone enough to make a grindstone, let alone a house, in those grassy jungle parts?

"'Stone for my house shall fall at my feet from heaven,' said the holy one. Whereat the villagers stared in round-eyed wonder. His Holiness was going it! Wasn't he biting off a bit more than he could chew? This was a plain issue and no blooming oracle-mongering about it. Either stone would fall or it would not-and the probabilities were strongly in favour of the *not*. Still he had done some good hefty miracles, some of which might not have been bunkum. '*Nous verrons!*' said the headman, in his own vernacular.

"And, a week before the rains broke, a truck or two laden with cut stone broke away from a train, careered gaily down the long incline, were duly switched off on to the safety-siding, and, being unusually heavy and swift, ran clean over the end and shot a truck-load or two of dressed stone at the feet of the Holy Man!

"'*Voilà!*' (or the equivalent thereof) said he to the villagers, and smiled patronizingly. You bet they turned to and built His Holiness as eligible a family residence as Holy Man could desire, and with the remainder of the stones they built him a nice stone platform to squat on in the sun, and think his great thoughts.

"I know this is all true, because my brother was told of His Holiness's daring prophecy long before the stones were safely delivered. When I heard the story from him, of course I must needs ride over and have a look at this local lion.

"I arrived at a moment of domestic crisis apparently, for from the hut of this celibate saint came the screams of a woman and the sounds of a real handsome hiding. Being young and foolish, I concluded that the lowing lady was getting the handsome hiding and that I had better take a hand. I barged in and found I was right. His reverence dropped the stick and picked up his spear-headed staff, but I gave him a soother on the point of the chin and cleared out, preceded by the lady, who sprinted like a hare.

"I rode off rather pleased with my silly young self, and half an hour later was crossing a perfectly level stretch of grass, when suddenly, just as I bent to dismount to tighten my girth, a great stone missed my head by a hair's-breadth and struck the ground with a mighty nasty thud. The fraction of a second earlier, it would have got me. I stared at it in amazement, and looked all round. There wasn't another stone for miles, nor, except for a clump of feathery bamboos, a tree, nor a building, a wall, a hollow, nor a fold in the ground where anyone could be hiding. Absolutely nothing but level grass and a clump of bamboos that could not conceal a small monkey-much less a man.

"I was too astounded to move for a minute or two. Then I rode round and round in widening circles, quartering the ground until I had established, beyond all doubt, the fact that whoever threw the stone had thrown it at least four hundred yards-and the man never lived who could have thrown it forty.

"I went back and examined it-and realized, with no added comfort, that it was a stone from my holy friend's house or platform! I remounted my horse-who was trembling and sweating as though he could see a tiger-and started to ride back. If *that* was his game! ... And as I bent my head to light the cigarette I badly needed, another stone grazed my *topi*. Like the first, it hit the turf with a thud that was sickening to hear. Then I was frightened, I admit, as well as enraged. Again I circled round, this time galloping hard in a frenzy of anger and fear. If either of those stones had hit me, I should have been killed-and there wasn't a sign of a human being nor of a place where one could have hidden! And a blight seemed to have come over the day, chilling my very soul, and making me feel as though I were a child in a nightmare.

"I *knew* there would be another, and that the third one would not miss me. I shall never forget the feeling of utter helplessness, wrath, and terror that possessed me. What could I do? There *was* nothing to do, and at any moment the blow might fall-literally a bolt from the blue. And then I pulled myself together, thought of my fellow midshipmen, and imagined the eyes of the whole of my ship's company to be upon me.

"Tactics for ever! Dismounting and unbuckling the girth, I took off my saddle and, holding the end of the girth in my hand, pulled the big heavy saddle up and put it on my head and neck. Retaining it there with one hand, I set spurs to my horse, and rode hell-for-leather.

"And that's all I know about it-until I came to my senses and found myself lying in bed in my brother's bungalow!

"They told me the horse had come home riderless and unsaddled-and they at once concluded I had come a cropper, as I had remarked, on starting, that it was 'so long since I had seen a horse that I hardly knew the stem from the stern, nor how to sit amidships and hold the rudder lines.'

"My brother had ridden out and found me lying unconscious.

"'You must have taken a frightful toss,' he said, 'but how the deuce did you come to get the saddle smashed? How did it come to be off the horse? It looked as though some one had hit it with a huge sledge-hammer.'

"'Or a stone,' said I.

"'Yes,' said he. 'Why a stone?'

"I told him exactly what had happened, and he laughed.

"Falling on your head has made you dream dreams and see visions,' said he. He did *not* laugh a fortnight later when he and I went over the ground and found the three stones-in that stoneless place. When we went on, to call on the Holy Man, we learned that the gentleman had gone for a walk-to Benares, a thousand miles away."...

"Strike me pecooliar!" murmured the Bucking Bronco. "That tale made outer whole cloth, John?"

"It's every word of it true," was the reply.

"Well, you go to bed, Sonny; yore pore brain's about biled I allow," counselled the American; and, exchanging a glance with Rupert, the old Legionary allowed himself to be helped on to his cot and soothed.

"We'll fan pore ole Farver wiv a noos-paper till he goes ter sleep," said 'Erb, getting an old *Echo d'Oran* from his shelf. "He's fair off 'is ole napper to-night."

And when the eyes of Jean Boule closed, apparently in slumber, the others silently sought their respective red-hot beds.

XIV. Moonshine

La Cigale, the Mad "Grasshopper" of the VIIth Company, was solemnly dancing by the light of the moon. He was a fine soldier and a hopeless lunatic, and had once been a Belgian Officer (Corps of Guides, the most aristocratic in the Belgian Army) and military attaché at various Embassies. No one knew his story, not even le Légionnaire Jean Boule, whom he loved and who, through great suffering, had attained great understanding and sympathy.[207]

This same gentleman, accompanied by the Bucking Bronco, Reginald Rupert, and 'Erb, was even now looking for him, knowing that he was always worse at the period of full moon and apt to do strange things.

They found him-solemnly dancing by the light of the moon-on a patch of green turf by the palms of the oasis.

"Doin' a bloomin' fandango on the light fantastic toe-all on 'is little own!" observed 'Erb.

"Funny how the moon affects madmen," said Rupert.

"Yes," agreed John Bull. "Ancient idea too. *Luna* the moon, *lunatic*. Evidently some connection."

"Shall we butt in an' put the kibosh on it?" asked the Bucking Bronco.

"No," replied John Bull. "Let's settle down and have a smoke. We'll see him to bed when he's tired of dancing. If he wearies himself out there'll be more chance of some sleep for us.... We can't leave him to himself to-night."

"Nope," agreed the Bucking Bronco. "Remember the night he went *loco* once and for all? When the grasshopper jumped into his *soupe*."

"Yes; but it wasn't the locust in his *gamelle* that was really the last straw. He'd have had permanent *cafard* from that day, anyhow....Look! —he's stopped."...

The Grasshopper, hearing voices, had ceased his posturing, bowing, and dancing. Crouching low, he progressed toward the shadow of the palms by long leaps.

"Hullo, *mon ami*!" cried John Bull; "come and have a smoke."

"*She* always danced like that to the Chaste Huntress of the skies when she showed mortals her full face," said La Cigale, as he flung himself down by his friend.

"'Oo did?" queried 'Erb.

"Diane de Valheureux," was the reply. "That is why Delacroix killed her. That Delacroix of the artillery."

"I could onnerstand 'im killin' 'er if she *sung*, but I don' see wot 'e wanted to kill her for fer dancin'," observed 'Erb. "Too bloomin' pertickler, *I* calls it."

"He was jealous," replied La Cigale, as he pressed his thin hands over his forehead and smouldering eyes.

"Diane was born at the full of the moon out in the beautiful garden of her father's château. It was her mother's whim —a woman of fire and moonbeams and wild fancies and poesies herself: Pan's own daughter.

"And from the day she could walk, Diane must go out and dance in the light of the full moon.

"I loved Diane. Also did Delacroix. He was mad for love of her. I was sane for love of her, since my love showed me all Beauty and Harmony and the utter worthlessness of the baubles that men strive for.

"She loved me —I think. If she did not, certainly she loved no one else. I understood, you see. And, on one evening, given by God, she let me dance with her in the forest while Diana smiled full-face from Heaven.

"And her parents gave her to Delacroix, who had great possessions and a soul that values great possessions at their untrue value. The soul of a pedlar-the base suspicious mind of a ferret.

"After she was married-and broken-hearted —she still had one joy. She could still dance with the fairies in a glade of the forest at full moon. She *could*, do I say? She could not do otherwise when Diana and Pan and the Old Gods called-this night-born elf of night, moonlight, and the open sky and earth. And, returning from her midnight dance with the fairies, by the light of the

Harvest Moon, she found that the husband whom she had left snoring, sat glowering-awaiting her-his mind a seething cesspool of foul suspicions.

"He killed her-of course. Such things as Fairy Dianes *are* killed by such other things as Hog Delacroix. And my heart broke. As your fine poet says, I think:

> 'There came a mist and a blinding rain,
> And life was never the same again.'

Never. Nor had I the satisfaction of dealing with Delacroix. The brave soul fled and disappeared."

"You'll cop 'im yet, Ciggy," interrupted 'Erb. "Cheer up, Ole Cock. We'll all lay fer 'im, an' do 'im in proper, one o' these dark nights."

"I have settled accounts with him, now, I thank you," continued La Cigale. "I suddenly came face to face with him on board the troopship *L'Orient* at Oran. It was when the Legion sent drafts to Tonkin, to fight the Black Flags.

"I was on sentry, and looking up, as a man came along the gangway, beheld the evil face of Delacroix!

"By the time I had recovered my wits, and realized that it was he in the flesh, and not his ghost, he had passed on and was swallowed up by the part of the ship devoted to officers.

"I saw no more of him until it was again my turn for sentry duty. By this time we were at Port Said, and as desertion was easy here-since a man had but to dive overboard and swim a few yards or even rush down a gangway when we were coaling-all sentries were given ball-cartridge and strict orders to shoot any soldier attempting to leap overboard or make a burst for the coal-wharf and British soil. (Once ashore, he must not be touched, or there would be trouble with England-and he might, with impunity, stand on the quay and deride us.)

"It was not likely that any of the French regulars would desert-artillery, line, or *marsouins* —but there would have been but few of the Legion who would not have made the promenade ashore but for these precautions.

"And as I stood there-my loaded Lebel in my hands-who should approach the head of the gangway over which I stood sentry, but this Delacroix, this thing whose foul hands-the very hands there before my eyes-had choked the life out of my Diane!

"Should I blow out his vile brains, or should I give myself the joy unspeakable of plunging my bayonet into his carcase?

"Neither. Too brief a joy for me-too brief an agony for him.

"As he passed, I held my hand with an effort that made me pale.

"The third time I saw him was in the Indian Ocean as we headed south for our next stopping-place, Singapore.

"He was leaning on the rail of the officers' promenade-deck, smoking a cigar after his comfortable lunch. The deck was empty. I ran lightly up the companion from our troop-deck, polluted the promenade-deck with my presence, sprang at him, seized him from behind, flung him overboard, and sprang after him with a cry of '*Diane*'!

"I must watch him drown; I must shout that name in his ear as he died. I must be with him at the last, and my hands must be at the throat of the foul dog. Not mine to fling him overboard and be clapped in irons while they threw him life-belts, and then lowered boats!

"Swimming with powerful strokes to where he had struck the water, I waited till he came up, and then seized him by the throat and strove to choke the life out of him as he had done to Diane. He struck at me wildly, and I thrust his head again beneath the water. But, yes! with a shout of 'Diane!' I dragged him below and swam downward as deeply as I could go. With bursting lungs I swam upward again and gloated upon his purpling face, and then-down, down, down, down, once more....

"When they dragged me into the boat, I was senseless and he was dead. I had swum with him for nearly an hour.

"When I recovered on board the ship, I was the hero of the hour-the man who had sprung into the sea, without stopping to divest himself of so much as his boots, to save an Officer....

"What am I saying? ...I am sleepy....Bon soir, mes amis," and the Grasshopper rose and retired toward the tents.

"*Some* story!" remarked the Bucking Bronco, as the four followed. "Wouldn't thet jar you! Sure it's the mos' interestin' an' wonderfullest yarn I heerd him tell yet. Ain't it, John?"

"M —m ...yes....It is the more interesting and wonderful," was the reply of John Bull, as he thoughtfully flicked the ash from the end of his cigarette, "by reason of the fact that I happen to know-that the Grasshopper cannot swim a stroke."

XV. The Coward of the Legion

Jean Jacques Dubonnet had distinguished himself that day, and he lay on his bed that night and cried. His companion, old Jean Boule, in that little hut of sticks and banana-leaves, had just been congratulating him on the fact that he had almost certainly won himself the *croix de guerre* or the *médaille militaire* for his distinguished bravery. And he had burst into tears, his body shaken with great rending sobs.

John Bull was not only a gentleman; he was a person of understanding and sympathy, and he had suffered enough, and seen enough of suffering, to feel neither surprise, disgust, nor contempt.

"God! Oh, God! I am a coward. I am a branded coward!" blubbered the big man on the creaking bed of boughs and boxes.

Was this fever, reaction, drink, *le cafard*, or what?

Certainly Dubonnet had played the man, and shown great physical courage that day against the Sakalaves, the brave Malagasy savages who have given Madame la République a good deal of trouble and annoyance, and filled many a shallow grave with the unconsidered carcasses of *Marsouins*[208] and Légionnaires in the red soil of Madagascar. As the decimated Company had slowly fallen back from the ambush in the dense plantations of the lovely Boueni palms, Lieutenant Roberte had fallen, shot through the body by a plucky Sakalave who had deliberately rested his prehistoric musket on his thigh and discharged it at a dozen yards range, himself under heavy fire. With insulting howls of "*Taim-poory, taim-poory,*" half a dozen of the enemy had sprung at the fallen man, when Dubonnet, rushing from cover, had shot two in quick succession, bayoneted two others, kicked violently in the face a fifth, who stooped over the Lieutenant with a *coupe-coupe*, and then, swinging his Lebel by the butt, had put up so good a fight that he had driven the savages back and had then partly dragged and partly carried his officer with him, to where the Company could rally, re-form, and make their stand to await reinforcements. Undeniably Dubonnet had risked his life to save that of his officer, and had fought with very great courage and determination or he could never have reached the rallying-place with an unconscious man, when so many of his comrades could not reach it at all.

Yet there he lay, weeping like a child, and calling upon his Maker to ease his guilty bosom of the burden it had borne so long-the knowledge that he was a "branded" coward.

It was terribly, cruelly hot in the tiny hut, and, to John Bull, who arose from his camp-bed of packing-case boards, it seemed even hotter outside, as he went to fetch the hollow bamboo water-"bottle" which hung from the tree under which the hut was built. Was it possible that the Madagascan moon gave out heat-rays of its own, or reflected those of the sun as it did the rays of light? It really seemed hotter in the moonlight than out of it.... Carrying the bamboo water-receptacle, a cylinder as tall as himself-really a pipe with one end sealed with gum, wax, or clay, when a joint of the stem does not serve the purpose-the Englishman passed in through the doorless door-way and delivered an ultimatum.

"Whatever may be the trouble, *mon ami*, weeping will not help it. Enough! ... Sit up and tell me all about it, or I'll wash you off that bed like the insect you're pretending to be.... Now then—a drink or a drenching?"

"Give me a drink for the love of God!" said Dubonnet, sitting up. "Absinthe, rum, cognac-anything," and he clutched at the breast of his canvas shirt as though he feared it might open and expose his breast.

"Yes. Good cold water," replied John Bull.

"Cold water!" mocked the other between sobs. "Cold Englishman! *Cold water!*" and he bowed his head on his knees and groaned and wept afresh.

The old soldier carefully poured water from the open end of the great pipe into a *gamelle*, and offered it to the other, who drank feverishly. "Are you wounded in the chest, there?" he asked.

This *cafard*, the madness that comes upon soldiers who eat out their hearts in the monotony of exile and wear out their stomachs and brains in the absinthe-shop, takes strange forms and reduces its victims to queer plights. How should le Légionnaire Jean Jacques Dubonnet, *Soldat première classe*, recommended for decoration for bravery in the field, be a coward?

"Oh, merciful God-help me to bear it. I am a Coward—a branded Coward!" wailed the huddled figure on the rickety, groaning bed.

"See here, comrade," said John Bull, overcoming a certain slight, but perceptible, repugnance, and placing an arm across the bowed and quivering shoulders, "I am no talker, as you are aware. If it would give you any relief to tell me all about it-rest assured that no word of it will ever be repeated by me. It may ease you. I may be able to help or comfort. Many Légionnaires, some on their death-beds, have felt the better for telling me of their troubles....But do not think I want to pry."...

Swiftly the wretched man turned, flung his arms about the Englishman's neck, and kissed him.

John Bull forbore to shudder. (Heavens! How different is the excellent French *poilu* from the British Tommy!) But if he could bring peace and the healing, soothing sense of confession, if not of anything approaching absolution, to this tortured soul, the night would have been well spent-better spent than in sleep, though he was very, very tired.

"I will tell you, *mon ami*, and will pray to you then to give me comfort or a bullet in the temple. A little accident as you clean your rifle! *I* cannot do it. I *dare* not do it-and no bullet will touch me in battle-as you have seen to-day. I live to die, and am too big a coward to take my life....I am a branded coward....See! See!" and he tore open the breast of his shirt. At once he closed it again, and hugged himself.

"No, no! I will tell you first," he cried. The madness of *le cafard*, no doubt. The man had only recently been drafted to the VIIth Company from the depôt, and had appeared a morose, surly, and unattractive person, friendless and undesirous of friends. Accident had made him the stable-companion of the Englishman in this little damp fever-stricken hell in the reeking corner of the Betsimisarake district, in which the remains of the Company were pinned....

The deplorable and deploring Dubonnet thrust his grimy fists into his eyes and across the end of his amorphous nose, as, with a sniff which militated against the romantic effect of the declaration, he said, "I swear I loved her. I loved her madly. It was my unfortunate and uncontrollable love that caused the trouble in the first place....But it was her fault too, mind you! Why couldn't she have *told* me she had a husband, away at Lyons, finishing his military service—a husband whom she had not seen for six months, and whom she would not see for another six?...Too late the fool confessed it—a month before he was coming, and a couple of months before something else was coming! And he famous, as I learned too late, for having all the jealous hate of Hell in his heart, if she so much as looked at another man. He, a porter of the Halles, notorious for his quarrelsomeness and for his fearful strength and savage temper. She hated him nearly as much as she feared him-and me, me she loved to distraction. And I her.... Believe me, she was the loveliest flower-seller in Paris-with a foot and ankle, an eye, a figure, ravishing, I tell you...and he would break her neck when he saw how she was and stab me to the heart. *She* would never have told him it was I she loved, but those others would-for dozens knew that she was my *amie*, and many in my gang did not love me. I am not of those whom men love-but women, ah!—and there were jealous ones in our *ruelle* who would have gone far to see her beauty spoiled and my throat cut....It was all her fault, I say! Did she not deceive me in hiding the fact that she had a husband? She deceived us all. But when this *scélérat* should turn up from Lyons, and find her at her pitch or in the flower-market, would any of them have held their tongues?...Can you not see it?...The crowd at the door, the screams as he entered and dragged her out into the gutter by the hair, his foot on her throat...and, afterwards-his knife at my breast....Would any of the gang have stood by me? No, they would have licked their chops and goaded him on...and, oh God, I am a *coward*....I can fight when my blood is up and I have to struggle for my life....I can fight as one of a regiment, a company, a crowd, all fighting side by side, each defending the other by fighting the common foe....I can take my part in a mélée and I can do deeds then that I do not know I have done till afterwards....I can fight when the tiger in me is aroused and has smelt blood-but I am a *coward* if I am alone. I, alone, dare not fight one man alone.... Were I being tracked alone through the jungle here by but one of the six men I attacked to-day, my knees would knock together and my legs would refuse to bear me up. I should flee if they would carry me, flee shrieking, but they would not bear me a hundred metres. They would collapse, and I should lie shuddering with closed eyes, awaiting the blow. I can hunt-with the pack-but I cannot be hunted. No. When our band waylaid the greasy bourgeois as he lurched homeward from his restaurant in the Place Pigalle or his Montmartre cabaret, I was as good an *apache* as any in the gang, and struck my blow with the best; but if it was a case of a row with the *agents de police*, and we were being individually shadowed, my heart turned to water, and I lay in bed for days. In a fair fight between about equal numbers of anarchists and *apaches* on the one hand, and *messieurs les agents* on the other, if it came upon us suddenly as they raided our rookery, I could play a brave man's part in the rush for the street; but I cannot be the hunted one —I cannot fight alone with none on either side of me. Oh God, I am a coward," and the wretch again buried his face in his knees and wept and sobbed afresh.

A common, cowardly gutter-hooligan apparently; an *apache*, a Paris street-wolf, and, like all wolves, braver in the pack than when alone; but in John Bull's gaze there was more of pity than anything. Suppose he, John Bull, had been born in a foul corner of some filthy cellar beneath a Paris slum? Would he have been so different? Was the *man* to blame, or the Fate that gave him the ancestry and environment that had made him precisely what he was?

"You will be called out before the battalion and decorated with the cross or the *médaille, mon ami*, for your heroism to-day. Put the past behind, and let your life re-date from the day the Colonel pins the decoration on your breast. Begin afresh. You will carry about with you always the visible sign and recognition that you are a hero-there on your breast, I say."...

With a shriek of *"What do I bear on my breast now?"* the ex-*apache* tore open his shirt and exposed two strips of strong linen sticking-plaster, each some ten inches long and two inches wide, that lay stuck horizontally across his broad chest.

What was this? Had he two ghastly gashes beneath the plaster? Had all that he had been saying been merely the delirium of a badly-wounded man? Seizing their ends, the *apache* tore them violently from his skin, and, by the light of the little lamp, John Bull saw, deeply branded, and most skilfully tattooed in the ineradicable burns, the following words (in French):

J. J. DUBONNET
LIAR AND COWARD

The Englishman recoiled in horror, and the other thought it was in contempt.

"Where are your fine phrases *now?*" he snarled, with concentrated bitterness. "'*You will carry about with you always the visible sign and recognition that you are a hero*,'" he mocked. "I do indeed! ...Oh God, take it from me. Let me sleep and wake to find it gone, and I will become a monk and wear out my life in prayer," ...and he threw himself face-downward on the bed and tore the covering of his straw pillow with his teeth.

"See, *mon ami*," said John Bull, "the *médaille* will be above that. It will be superimposed. It will bury that beneath it. Let it bury it for ever. That is of the past-the *médaille* is of to-day and the glorious future. That is man's revenge-the cruel punishment and vengeance of an injured brute. The médaille is man's reward-the glad recognition of those who admire courage."...

"It is not the husband's work," growled Dubonnet. "He never caught me. My own gang did that-my comrades-my *friends*! Think of their loathing and contempt, their hatred and disgust, that they could do that to a man and leave him to live. Think of it! ...And I dare not kill myself and meet *her*. I am a coward. I fear Death himself, and I fear her reproachful eyes still more....I *am* a coward and I *am* a liar. I broke my faith and word and trust to her-and I feared the death that she welcomed because *I* was by her side to share it. She drank the poison in her glass, threw herself into my arms, and bade me drink mine and come with her to the Beyond, where no brutal, hated husband could drag her from me to his own loathed arms....And I did not. I could not. She died in my arms with those great reproachful eyes on mine, and whispered, 'Come with me, my Beloved. I am afraid to go alone.' And when I would not, she cursed me and died. And I let her go alone—I, who had planned our double suicide, our glorious and romantic suicide in each other's arms-that we might not have to part, might not have to face her husband's wrath, might be together for all time, though it were in hell....Before she drank, she blessed me. Before she died, she cursed me-and still I could not drink....And now I have not the courage to go on living, and I have not the courage to take my life....And they are going to brand me as a hero, are they? ... *That* on my coat and *this* beneath it!" and peals of hysterical laughter rang out on the still night.

"Yes—*that* on your coat," said the Englishman. "Does it count for nothing? Let the one balance the other. Put the past behind you and start afresh....Can you bear pain? Physical pain, I mean?"

"Is not all my life a pain?—did I not have to bear the pain of being branded with a red-hot iron? What is physical pain compared with what I bear night and day-remorse, self-loathing, the fear of the discovery of *this* by my comrades? How much longer will it be before some prying swine sees these strips and refuses to believe they hide wounds-laughs at my tale of attempted suicide in a fit of *cafard*—*hara-kiri*—self-mutilation with a knife."...

"Because, if you can face the pain, we can obliterate that. We can remove the record of shame, and you can wear the record of courage and duty without fear of discovery of the..."

"*What* do you say?" cried Dubonnet, as the words penetrated his anguished and self-centred mind. "*What*? Remove it? *How*—in the name of God?"

"Burn it out as it was burnt in," was the cool reply. "I will do it for you if you ask me to.... The pain will be ghastly and the mark hideous-but it will *be* a mark and nothing else. Anyone seeing it will merely see that you have been severely burnt-and they'll be about right."

Dubonnet sat up.

"You could and would do that?" he said.

"Yes. I should make a flat piece of iron red-hot and lay it firmly across the writing. It would depend on you whether it were successful or not, and would be a good test of nerve and courage. Have it done-and make up your mind that cowardice and treachery were burnt out with the words. Then start life afresh and win another decoration."...

"There are anæsthetics," whimpered Dubonnet. "Chloroform."...

"Not for Legionaries in Madagascar," was the reply. "Unless you'd like to go to Médecin-Major Parme with your story and ask him to operate, to oblige a young friend?"

Dubonnet shivered, and then spat. "*Médecin-Major Parme!*" he growled.

"If you like to wait a few weeks or months or years, you may have the opportunity and the money to buy chloroform," continued the Englishman, "or the means for making local injections of cocaine or something; but I suggest you make a kind of sacrament of the business-have the damnable thing burnt out precisely as it was burnt in, and as you clench your teeth on the bullet in manly silence and soldierly stoicism, realize it is *the past* that is being burnt also, and that the good fire is burning out all that makes you hate yourself and hate life. Let it be symbolic."

John Bull knew his man. He had met his type before. Too much imagination; too little ballast; the material for a first-class devil, or a first-class man; swayed and governed by his symbols, shibboleths, and prejudices; the slave and victim of an *idée fixe*....If he could get him to undergo this ordeal, he would emerge from it a new man—a saved man. An anæsthetic would spoil the whole moral effect. If he would face the torture and bear it, he would regard himself as a brave man, just as surely as he now regarded himself as a coward. He would recover his self-respect, and he would *be* brave because he believed himself to be brave. It would literally be his regeneration and salvation.

"It would hurt no more in the undoing than it did in the doing," he continued.

The poor wretch shuddered.

"She had written a few words of farewell to one or two," he said, "and told how we were going to die together, and when and where.... Her mother and some others burst in and found me with her body in my arms and my untasted poison beside me....I went mad. I raved. I denounced myself. A vile woman who had once loved me, jeered at me and bade me drink my share and rid the world of myself....I could not....My own gang bound me on my bed, and one of them brought an old chisel and the half of an iron pipe split lengthways. With the straight edge and the semicircular one, they did their work. I was their prisoner for-ah! *how long*? And then they tattooed the scars-not satisfied with their handiwork as it was....Before her husband found me I had fled to the shelter of the Legion....I told the surgeon at Fort St. Jean that it was done by a rival gang because I had pretended to join them and did not. He gave me a roll of the sticking-plaster and advised me, for my comfort, to hide my '*endossement*' as he brutally called it."...

"Well, now get rid of it," interrupted John Bull. "The flat iron clamp, binding the corners of that packing-case, would be the very thing. You are *not* a coward. You proved that to-day. Prove it more highly to-night, and, when they decorate you, let there be a still more honourable decoration beneath-the scars of a great victory....Come on."...

When old Jean Jacques Dubonnet fell, many years later, at Verdun, the Colonel of his battalion, on hearing the news, remarked, "I have lost my bravest soldier."

The marks of a terrible burn on his chest were almost obliterated by German bullets and bayonets.

XVI. Mahdev Rao

The Legion's net is as wide as its meshes are close; and some rare, as well as queer, fish find their way into it.

Possibly the rarest that it ever contained was a Mahratta soldier who, during the Great War, found his way, always toward the rising sun, across a hundred miles of African jungle, until he reached the sea, and there, boarding a *dhow* at night, was carried across hundreds of miles of ocean.

The crew of the *dhow* was an interesting one, among its members being two French gentlemen, one an Intelligence Officer and the other a kindly priest, formerly of Goa-neither of whom was in anywise distinguishable from his sea-faring Arab colleagues.

The *dhow*, of a humble, unobtrusive and diffident disposition, had business at a lone coastal outpost where flies the *Tricouleur*, and where sins and suffers a small garrison, of Colonial Infantry and of the Legion....

Here the said priest, whose fairish knowledge of the Marathi tongue had enabled him to understand something of the soldier's story, was glad to assist him to attain his highest ambition-to fight against his personal and national enemies, once more.

As a trained soldier and a stout fellow, he found favour in the sight of the Commandant of the post, was duly enrolled as a soldier of France, and eventually found himself precisely where he desired to be....

* * *

Mahdev Rao Ramrao, son of Ramrao Krishnaji, was born in a little mud-walled village that nestles above its rice-fields on the slope of the Western Ghats, in the Deccan of India.

High up above the village, its outline clear-cut against the sky, was the fort, "*Den of the Tiger*," from which Mahdev Rao's forbears, led by Shivaji the Great, had swept down to harry the plains, to plunder towns, and to fight the invading Mussulman....

As he toddled about the crooked streets of tiny mud-built Nagaum, clutching the finger of his grandfather, Krishnaji Arjun, the little fat Mahdev Rao, clad in an embroidered velvet cap and a necklace, learned that he was a Pukka Bahadur, a mighty one, the son, grandson, great-grandson, and general descendant of soldiers, fierce fighting men-from the days of Shivaji the Great, three hundred years ago, to the days of Wellesley Sahib (who had fought in those very parts), Nicholson Sahib, Outram Sahib (whose Orderly, grandfather's own father had been), Havelock Sahib, Roberts Sahib, even unto the days of the Great Lat-Sahib Kitchener, the Elephant of War, whose shadow had destroyed the *Hubshis*[209] and their prophet the Mahdi....

And, as he grew up, Mahdev Rao understood that he was a *Kshattria*, of the caste next to the Brahmins themselves; that he was a cradle-ordained soldier, and that he had traditions to reverence and maintain. So he developed into a fine proud youth, self-respecting, ambitious, and religious beyond the conception of the vast majority of Europeans.

In due course, the day came when, as his father, his grandfather, and his great-grandfather had done, he sallied forth from Nagaum, and tramped to the recruiting-depôt at Belara to take service under the Sahibs as a Sepoy-to serve the King Emperor as his father and grandfather had served the Queen, and his other ancestors had served John Company or their own Rajah in due season. His intention was to be faithful to his salt; his ambition was to rise to be a Havildar, possibly a Jemadar, and conceivably a Subedar; his hope was to return to Nagaum full of honours, with medals and a pension, and to superintend the cultivation of the family plot of land (theirs since the days of Shivaji, the Scourge of the Deccan) and the upbringing of his sons and grandsons....But Fate willed otherwise, and affairs in Nagaum were affected by the fact that an egotistical megalomaniac was making a God in his own image, seven thousand miles away in Berlin....

* * *

As a white-clad recruit at Belara, life went very well for Mahdev Rao the Mahratta, and when he found himself a khaki-clad full private of the Old Hundredth Bombay Rifles, he found himself indeed.

He was that happy man, the man whose day is full of work that is his hobby, work that he loves, work that is his play. The Jemadar of his double-company was an old friend of his father, and his own Havildar was a Nagaum man. Him, Mahdev Rao cultivated with such words and gifts as are fitting-and highly politic. The Captain Sahib of his double-company was a *pukka* Sahib, a great *shikari*, horseman, athlete and soldier. The descendant of Pindaris could understand and admire the descendant of Norman freebooters and Elizabethan gentlemen-adventurers and soldiers of fortune. The Colonel Sahib, with his nine medal-ribbons, white moustache, and burning eye, was Mahdev Rao's idea and ideal of a Man. At an age when Mahdev Rao's people were getting a little senile and more than a little shaky, he seemed as young and active as a Mahdev himself-yea, though as old as Mahdev's grandfather. Sepoys who had seen him at work on the Frontier, when the Ghazis charged home like wounded tigers, spoke of him with bated breath. This was a Bahadur of Bahadurs, a *Man*. Oh, to die in battle under his approving eye! What bliss! ...The Adjutant Sahib, Mahdev disliked and feared, though he respected him. (It seems the painful duty of a good Adjutant to make himself disliked and feared, as it is his gratifying privilege to be respected.)...

And, by the time war broke out, in August, 1914, the Regiment was Mahdev Rao's happy home; the Colonel Sahib was, in his own expressive phrase, "his Father and his Mother," and his Mahratta comrades were his brothers.

Incidentally and severally, his *guru*, his Captain, Lieutenant, Subedar, Jemadar and Havildar were also his Father and his Mother; and the honour of his Regiment was the honour of Mahdev Rao. Even the Punjabi Mahommedans and Pathans of the other double-companies were worthy souls, inasmuch as they were part of the Regiment; and still more so the Sikhs, Rajputs, and Dogras; but, of course, the very salt of the Regiment, which was the salt of the Army, which was the salt of the Earth, was Mahdev Rao's double-company of Deccani Mahrattas.

When it was known, a few months later, that the Regiment was to go on Active Service, Mahdev Rao's cup of happiness was already full, by reason of the fact that he had that very day defeated Pandurang Bagu and became champion wrestler of the Regiment —a distinction which guarantees that its holder would give a little trouble to any wrestler in the world, be his nationality and eminence what it might....Judge of the swamping, seething overflow of the said cup of happiness when the news came, plain and indubitable, through the regimental babu, that the Old Hundredth Bombay Rifles were to proceed forthwith to the city of Bombay and embark for East Africa!

Here was news indeed! News of increased saving from pay, decreased expenses, a certain medal, the chances of decoration and promotion; and adventure, experience, change....Of course, to cross the Black Water was to lose caste, but the *guru* and the village priests would soon put that right and provide dispensation at not too exorbitant rates. Marvellous fellows, the Brahmins, at wangling a thing when there was money in it....

* * *

The ten days' journey from Bombay to Mombasa was very wonderful to Mahdev Rao, who had scarcely seen the sea before, and had never set foot on a ship or boat of any description....The problem of how it propelled itself without sails or wheels puzzled him exceedingly, and still more so the problem of how it found its way, day after day, night after night, from one spot on the coast of India to another spot on the coast of Africa. And not just any old spot, mark you, but a definite given place at which it would arrive at a stated time. Certainly the Sahibs up on the bridge could not see across the space of a ten days' journey with the most powerful of field-glasses....

It was a surprise to him to find that the shores of this new and strange continent were remarkably like those of India, and that the coconut groves of the Kilindini inlet, between the island of Mombasa and the mainland, might have come straight from Bombay...But then surprises came so thick and fast, that his mind, always more tenacious than acute, became dulled, and he ceased to be surprised at anything-even at the fact that he was expected to fight in jungle so dense that no human being could move through it, save along the foot-wide paths that wound and twisted from village to village or from ford to ford. But how was a man to fight in such country, and what was a double-company to do, accustomed as it was to attack in extended order, and taught never to fire a round until there was a visible enemy to fire at? How *could* it fight in single file, with an impenetrable wall of trees, creepers, bush and thorn on either side?...

The days between the debarkation at Mombasa and the occupation by his double-company of an advanced outpost (days of weary marching through jungle and swamp) passed like a dream, and Mahdev Rao settled down to the routine of this new strange life in a swamp-jungle, and soon felt as though he had never known any other.

It was not a pleasant life, for it was monotonous, unhealthy, and dull, the heat was terrific, food was not all it might have been, fever and dysentery were rife and, in his own phrase, "air and water were bad."

But Mahdev Rao was too keen a soldier to grumble. One did not expect Active Service to be like a furlough-trip to one's home, nor to have the comforts and luxuries of Nagaum, Belara or Bombay, in this enemy's country-the loathsome swamp where lived the *Hubshis* under the rule of their *Germani* masters (a kind of White Men, he gathered, who were not Sahibs).

So he trudged along cheerily when his half of the little garrison went marching on a reconnaissance into the enemy's country; did his sentry-go smartly; sat watching with keen untiring eyes on the *machan* in the tree-top, when such was his duty; and scouted warily along the jungle tracks when sent out with a comrade to patrol to the next outpost....

"That Mahdev Rao's a good lad," remarked Captain Delamere to Lieutenant Carr as they sat in the grass-hut "Officers' Mess" of the outpost, one evening, and tried to masticate the tinned string and encaustic tiles, served out to them under the name of bully-beef and biscuit.

"Always merry and bright, and chucks a chest when some of the other blokes begin to slouch and lag a bit."

"Yes," agreed Carr; "he'll make a damgood Havildar some day....Might make him a Lance-Naik now....Hardly the brains to go further than Havildar, I am afraid...but we c'd do with a few thousand Mahdev Raos out here."...

"We'll give him a stripe," said Delamere, as he tried to cut up some black-cake ration-tobacco (horrible cheap poison), with the one and only table-knife.

"Why the devil can't they issue tobacco a man can smoke, if they're going to issue a tobacco-ration at all?..." he growled, and added: "Yes-we'll give Mahdev Rao a stripe."...But it was some one else, and a very different person, who gave Mahdev Rao his stripes.

For, on the following day, he and Pandurang Bagu, patrolling to meet the patrol from the next outpost, were ambushed.

There was a sudden burst of fire from a tree-top, as well as from the bush before and behind them, and Pandurang Bagu went down with a heavy bullet of soft lead in his shattered hip-joint. Almost simultaneously, Mahdev Rao was felled by the blow of a rifle-butt, as he raised his rifle to fire at big khaki-clad *Hubshis*, in tall khaki grenadier-caps, who rushed at him in front.

"Good!" grunted the Swahili sergeant in charge of the squad. "That one will be able to talk. Kill the other."

Seven bayonets were plunged into Pandurang Bagu as, with trembling hands, he raised his rifle. As one does not get the pleasure of plunging one's bayonet into an enemy every day, the Swahilis and Yaos made the most of their opportunity, and Pandurang Bagu's life ebbed quickly out through dozens of wounds....The Sergeant was a happy man, and his ebon countenance was wreathed in smiles. He had been sent out, by the *Herr Offizier*, with orders to ambush a patrol and bring in at least one member of it alive-and he had succeeded to perfection.

One night's wait in a most admirable ambush; strict orders not to shoot the last man of the patrol-be there a dozen or be there but two-and to spring out at each end of the ambush and capture the survivor alive; five seconds of smart work as per programme, and the job was done.

And done very neatly-for there are few braver or more skilful soldiers in the world than these African Rifles, when fighting in their own unique jungle....

When Mahdev Rao recovered consciousness (which he did very quickly, thanks to his thick skull and thicker turban) he found himself a prisoner. His hands were bound behind his back, he was stripped almost naked, and his kit and accoutrements were being examined and looted by his captors.

He realized that he was bare-headed and that the long tuft of hair, left among the cropped stubble (that the gods might lift him into heaven, when his time came), was hanging down his back.

He ground his teeth at the shameful outrage these casteless sons of pariah-dogs had put upon him, in knocking his turban off and exposing his bare head. He rose to his knees and staggered to his feet, only to be knocked down again from behind.

"If you strike him senseless, you will have to carry him, Achmet Ali," said the Sergeant. "He has to be in the *boma*[210] by to-morrow morning, alive and able to answer the questions of the *Bwana Macouba*."[211] ...

"I am the hero who knocked him down first," said Achmet Ali, and straightway improvised a chant.

"I am the hero,
The swift-striking hero,
I am the hero
Who knocked him down first."

"Be also the hero that drives him along with a bayonet, then," interrupted the Sergeant, "and you'll be the hero whose head I will blow off if the dog escapes."

And, for the remainder of that day and all that night, the *askaris* drove Mahdev Rao (as the potter and *dhobi* of Nagaum drive their donkeys) with blows and curses.

Once, during one of the brief halts, food was offered him (cold boiled rice and a plantain), and he tried to give these foul Untouchables, these casteless carrion-scavengers, some faint idea of the unutterable pollution of the very thought of taking food from their defiling hands-the filthy *Hubshi* dogs!...

"He is too frightened to eat, poor heathen Infidel dog," remarked the Sergeant to Achmet Ali, as he turned towards Mecca and prostrated himself in prayer....

While fording a river, next morning, Mahdev Rao endeavoured to drown himself and the hero, to the boundless amusement of the rest of the squad. The hero revenged himself by making a pattern of cuts upon his captive's back with the point of his bayonet. But they were only about an inch long and quarter of an inch deep, and not likely to affect his value when questioned by the *Bwana Macouba* as to the number and disposition of the British forces.

* * *

The *Germani boma* was very similar to the one from which Mahdev Rao had come, but considerably larger. Dazed and starving as he was, he noted its strength, the height of its palisades, the depth of its trenches, the number of its machine-guns, and the strength of its garrison of native African Rifles (*askaris*) and *Germani* Europeans. He was surprised to see that the majority of the latter wore beards.... He had never before seen a European officer or soldier with a beard.... Obviously the *askaris* were well drilled and highly disciplined.

Also, everything about the place was well done. The huts were neater and stronger and better thatched than in his own *boma*, paths were more neatly made and kept, the earthworks were bigger and stronger. Evidently the *Germanis* had more coolie-labourers and got more work out of them, or else they gave more attention to these details. Certainly it was a very strong *boma*, and very strongly garrisoned. He had seen twelve machine-guns and two small quick-firers (something like Indian mountain-battery guns) already. He would have a lot to tell the Captain Sahib when he escaped and got back to the outpost.... But would they not take very especial care that he did not escape, after he had seen so much? ... And how was he to find his way back to his Company through that dense blind jungle, if he did escape? ... It had got to be done, anyhow-and then he could lead the Captain Sahib and the double-company to this place, and they could rush it at dawn, with much slaughter of black untouchable pariahs who kept a high-caste Indian bare-headed, offered him polluted food and water with their defiling hands, struck him, and generally behaved like the savages they were....

Doubtless, however, their *Germani* masters would punish them and do justice. Though not *pukka* Sahibs, they were White Men, and, as such, would have understanding and a sense of decency.

White Men do not offend against the religion of others; they understand caste and respect it; they know that prisoners of war are to be honourably treated.... Yes, they understand a high-caste man, and know the difference between a dog of a low-caste negro *askari* of Africa, and a high-caste *Kshattria* Sepoy of India; the difference between one who comes next to the Brahmins themselves and one who is utterly beyond the pale, a walking pollution to earth, air, and water, whose very shadow is a defilement and a desecration to what it falls upon.... Yes, it would be all right when he was brought face to face with their officers, even though they were *Germanis*....

He was hustled into a filthy grass hut in which were four negroes-spies, defaulters and guides, the last being kept in bonds with the criminals, by reason of their incurable desire to leave the service of their employers and captors....

Later he was haled forth-still bare-headed, bound, and half-naked —to where, beneath a tree, sat three Europeans, attended by a Sergeant and guard of *askaris*, and one or two nondescript persons, including a half-caste in European clothing, a clerk, and a servant. On a camp-table before the White Men were bottles of beer, glasses, a revolver, a heavy kiboko[212] of rhinoceros-hide, a map, and a notebook.

The central figure of the three (one Von Groener), who wore a khaki uniform, blue putties and a white-topped peaked cap, bade the half-caste ask the prisoner the name of his regiment, the number of men in his *boma*, and the number of machine-guns it contained-for a start.

The "half"-caste, a Negroid Goanese-Arab-Indian, put the questions in the barbarous Hindustani of the Goanese quarter of Dar-es-Salaam. Mahdev Rao, a Mahratta, always speaking Marathi in the Regiment, knew little more Hindustani than he did English.

"Tera pultan ka nam kya hai?" said the "interpreter." "Kitni admi tera boma men hain? Kitni tup-tup tup-tup bandook hain?"[213]

Madhev Rao had a fair idea as to what the man was driving at, but he looked stupid, and, in Marathi, replied:

"I do not understand."

Mr. Alonzo Gomez had never heard Marathi in his life.

"The man does not understand the language of India, *Herr Kommandant*," he said, in clumsy German, to the officer who sat in the centre.

"But that is absurd," replied that worthy. "If he comes from India he knows the language of India. Tell him I will *kiboko* the flesh from his bones if he tries to fool *me*."

"Bwana Sahib tumko kiboko diega,"[214] answered Gomez to the prisoner.

"I will try him in English," said the senior officer to the others. "The English give all drill-orders in English; therefore this animal understands English."

"Ja! Ja!" agreed the other two. "Ganz klein wenig."

"Hear, pig-dog," quoth the senior gentleman, "his battalion what his name calls? How large are man-number of it? How large are gun-machine-number of it? Isn't it?"

To Mahdev Rao, at least two of the gutturally pronounced words were familiar. "Sahib," he said in Marathi, "I am a Sepoy and a prisoner of war. I am not a spy. And I am very tired and thirsty."...

"The swine is contumacious," said the senior. "He understands both English and Hindustani. He is shamming. We will help him to find his wits-and his tongue," and he gave a curt order to the *askari* Sergeant. (Also to the Swahili servant-concerning the replenishment of the beer supply.) He was a handsome man of about forty, with a small forked beard, a cold blue eye, and a hard domineering expression. Once he had been an ornament of Berlin and Potsdam, an *Ober-Leutnant* of Grenadiers; but debt, drink, cards, and an unfortunate duel, had sent him into exile. In exile he had grown morose, bitter and savage, loathing and blaming everything and every one-except himself.

Of his companions, one was a ne'er-do-well relation of a German General and had been shipped to German East Africa to die of fever, beer, and dissipation; the other was an ex-*Feldwebel* of the Prussian Guard who had made money as an elephant-poacher and then done exceeding well as a trader and planter-well from the financial point of view *bien entendu*; from the moral point of view he had not done very well.

The three were not typical of their class, and were of wholly different fibre from their General (a great soldier and a gentleman).

They were three bad men, bad by the standards of the German colony-and the order that *Ober-Leutnant* von Groener had given, and that his colleagues had applauded, was that Mahdev Rao, prisoner of war, captured in uniform, upon his lawful occasions as a soldier, should be tied to a tree and flogged with the terrible rhinoceros-hide *kiboko* with which the German instils discipline into his native soldiers, servants, coolies, criminals, and lady "housekeepers."

Mahdev Rao was seized by the *askari* guard, and so tied that he was hugging, with arms and legs, the big tree beneath which the "court" was sitting.

In the hands of a huge, brawny, and most willing Sergeant of *askaris*, the five-foot *kiboko*, tapering from the thickness of a man's wrist to that of his little finger, supple as india-rubber, and tougher than anything in the world, is a most terrible instrument of torture and punishment. The "draw" of the scientific pulling-stroke (as of one who cuts through a stick with one slice of a knife) of the *kiboko*, lacerates and mangles, blood leaping at every blow....

By the time the three German gentlemen considered that Mahdev Rao was sufficiently exhorted, encouraged, and rebuked (for his contumaciousness), he was also senseless and apparently dead.... It was annoying, as the *Herr Ober-Leutnant* had hoped to obtain much interesting and useful information concerning the Indian Expeditionary Force, and to send it to Head-Quarters....

Mahdev Rao recovered consciousness in the same prison-hut. He was alone, and the fact that there was no one present to see such a fall from grace, aided the terrible pangs of thirst in inducing him to drink from the gourd of water that stood in the corner....Later, he ate a couple of plantains....As they were covered by their skins, the interior had not been defiled-or, at any rate, one could take a certain amount of comfort from such a theory and argument.

Later still, he bowed to the inevitable, and ate the cold boiled rice his *askari* gaoler brought him. It was a terrible thing to do-but life was dear-and revenge was dearer. He would live, at any cost, to be revenged upon that-that-swine, and son of swine-that offspring of pariah curs-that carrion-eating lump of defilement and pollution-who had had him, him, Sepoy Mahdev Rao of the Old Hundredth Bombay Rifles, flogged, publicly flogged, by black beasts of *Hubshis*....

Great as were his physical sufferings, his mental sufferings were a thousand times greater. His body felt pain: his mind felt agonizing tortures and excruciating torments unspeakable.... He ground his teeth, clenched his fists, and cried aloud in rage and horror-and then fell silent and still ... for no-he must not go mad, he must not lose strength, he must not die-until he had had his revenge....

Next day he was questioned again and flogged again....

At the end of a week the *Ober-Leutnant* decided to send him to Head-Quarters at Mombobora. There was a Missionary Father in the town, who had worked in India and would know the language perfectly. There was also a hospital, where they would patch the dog up, that he might be able to converse with the Father....Anyhow-since the Colonel seemed to think that he, the *Ober-Leutnant*, had shown little skill in his endeavours to get information from this Indian, let him see if he could do any better himself....

At Head-Quarters they learnt nothing from Mahdev Rao, though he learnt much from them concerning the difference between German and British methods of dealing with native prisoners who will not "talk."

He was not flogged, but he was abused, starved, bound, insulted, and finally herded with a chain-gang of negro criminals, and set to such work as road-sweeping and latrine-cleaning.

What this means to a man of caste, no one who has not lived in India can guess, and no one but a high-caste Indian can know. Nothing worse can happen to him.

And, from time to time, he was brought before the Missionary, who talked to him in excellent Marathi, promising him all kinds of rewards if he would describe the composition and disposition of the Expeditionary Force from India.... Were there Pathans and Gurkhas in it? ... Were there field-batteries? ... Were there Pioneer Corps? ... Had part of it gone by the Uganda Railway to Nairobi and the Lakes? ... Were the Sepoys loyal? ... If he returned to them with much money and more promises, would he be able to induce any of them to desert? ... What was the state of feeling in India? ... And much more, until Mahdev Rao, maddened, sullen, brutalized, barely sane, by reason of his wrongs, cruelties, and immeasurable degradations, would lift up his voice and curse the *padre*, the evil white *fakir*, until his guards smote him on the mouth and dragged him away—a naked, filthy wreck of a man....

Constantly he sought an opportunity of escape from the town, but found none.

He must have food, a weapon of some kind, and he must get more strength and recover his health, get rid of this fever, before he could take the opportunity if one offered. But when he was not road-sweeping or road-making with the chain-gang, he was otherwise working, always under the eye of an *askari* guard, who asked nothing better than an excuse to shoot him....

No-he must wait, and it was always possible that the *Germani* officer, who had flogged him, might come to this Head-Quarters, and save Mahdev Rao the journey to that gentleman's *boma*.

For Mahdev Rao's one idea now, his one reason for living, was to avenge himself upon *Ober-Leutnant* von Groener-the man who, instead of treating him as a prisoner of war, had had him publicly flogged, and had then sent him to this place where a high-caste Indian Sepoy was as a cannibal negro criminal, and was herded with them.... He did not wish to live. He did not wish to return to India-he was too eternally and utterly defiled, polluted, and out-caste for that. But he did not intend to die until he had met the *Germani* who had had him flogged, the man whom he regarded as the arch-type of his captors, the man who had brought him into this living death of defilement, the man who was the cause of all his woes....

To listen seriously to the Missionary Father's temptations to treachery never occurred to him. He was Sepoy Mahdev Rao of the Old Hundredth Bombay Rifles, a soldier of the King Emperor, and son of a long line of brave and honest fighting men, "true to salt," and loyal as hilt to blade....

* * *

One morning, with the rest of a road-sweeping gang, Mahdev Rao was working at a spot just outside the native "town" of Mombobora, where a little bridge crossed a muddy stream, more mud than stream, that lay between two tracts of cultivation....

A squad of *askaris* tramped past ... a doctor and two nurses ... a small herd of cattle ... a German lady in a kind of rickshaw ... an officer in a hammock slung from a stout bamboo pole, borne by four Kavarondo natives ... a file of negresses with water-jars upon their heads ... and then-did his eyes deceive him? —his Enemy, the man who had had him flogged!

* * *

... Strolling along, taking the morning air, came *Ober-Leutnant* Fritz von Groener, who had been summoned to Mombobora by the Colonel, and had arrived on the previous day.

As he reached the little bridge, a crouching man, a filthy, half-naked wretch of the road-gang, suddenly rose and sprang at him, drove him sideways and backwards, before he could raise his heavy whip or draw his automatic-and seized him in a grip, scientific and powerful, the hold of a champion wrestler, in whom was the strength of madness and the lust of revenge.

Before the lounging *askari* guard heard a sound of the struggle, the two, swaying and straining, fell against the low coping of the bridge, toppled over it, and splashed heavily into the liquid mud beneath-the German officer beneath the Indian soldier, whose hands were at his throat, whose knee was on his chest, and who, slowly, strongly, surely, thrust his head beneath the foul slime, and held it there as the writhing bodies sank and splashed in the watery mud....

It is probable that the *Herr Ober-Leutnant* was dead before Askari Mustapha Moussa, in charge of the road-gang, had realized that something was wrong, had reached the bridge-head and had made up what must be called his mind, that it was his duty to risk a shot at the "coolie."

Certainly he was dead enough when the hands of Mahdev Rao were at length torn from his throat, and the two were dragged from the mud into which they were disappearing....

* * *

Rumours of the approach of an enemy force caused much confusion that night, and Sepoy Mahdev Rao, sentenced to be shot at dawn, decided to view the dawn elsewhere than in Mombobora, or to die in an attempt to turn this confusion to good account....

XVII. The Merry Liars

A competition in lying was proceeding, and entries were good. (One Légionnaire told of his beloved pet rabbit which nibbled lead, ate cordite, swallowed a burning match-and then went out and shot its own, and its master's, supper.)

"Yep," growled the Bucking Bronco, as the little group of Legionaries, from all corners of the earth and all strata of human society, turned towards him, "I allow I can tell as big a lie as Ole Man Dobroffski-even if I *ain't* the Czar of Roosia's gran'pa's little gran'chile, Wilhelmine-Bungorfski-Poporf."

Père Jean Boule, "father" of the Second Battalion, and incidentally an English baronet, moved uneasily. The Bucking Bronco had always disliked the Russian aristocrat, and had never made any secret of the fact. If ever they fought, there would not be two survivors of that fight ... and the Bucking Bronco was his beloved and loving friend, and a mine of virtues, though a Bad Man-of the best sort. He had been, among other things, a miner, cowboy, tramp, lumberman, professional boxer, U.S.A. trooper, and ornament of a Wild West show, of which he was the trick revolver-shot.

"Ah...you allus was a purple liar, Buck," put in 'Erb, the Cockney, as the American produced a deplorable French pipe and some more deplorable French tobacco. (*How* his soul yearned for a corn-cob and some Golden Bar, or "the makings" and a bag of Bull Durham!)

"I give a guy a picky-back once," continued the Bucking Bronco, ignoring 'Erb, whom he usually treated as a mastiff treats a small cur.

"But how interesting!" murmured the ex-Colonel of the Imperial Guard, who called himself "Dobroffski."

"And it killed that guy, and it killed his gal, and it sent me bug-house —*loco* —for Devil-knows-how-long-an'-all," continued the American, ignoring Dobroffski as he had ignored 'Erb.

"What is it that it is, then-this *'bug-'ouse'* and this *'loco'*?" murmured le Légionnaire Alphonse Blanc, whose English included no American.

"Same as what you'd call 'dotty' —or 'off 'is onion' —'looney' —'balmy on the crumpet' —in yore silly lingo," explained 'Erb helpfully.

"*Fou*," murmured La Cigale, for the benefit of Blanc and Tant-de-Soif, whose knowledge of English was limited also. (La Cigale, the ex-Belgian officer, knew all there was to know about *démence*, poor soul.)

"Wot killed 'em? Was it the sight o' the faices you made-doin' the job o' work?" inquired 'Erb.

The Bucking Bronco leaned back against the wall of rough-hewn, thickly-mortared grey stones, spread his huge legs abroad, and blew a cloud of smoke. He was wearing his *capote* (the long blue great-coat) and red trousers tucked into black leggings, but he shivered as though cold.

"I can see that gal's face now," he said, staring out across the ocean of sand that surrounded the fort; and the enormous powerful man, with his long arms, big hands, leathern face, and heavy drooping moustache, looked ill and fell silent.

"Wish *I* could, Ole Cock," observed 'Erb. "Where's she 'iding?"

"And Bud Conklin's feet, too, a danglin' just above me face. Ole Bud Conklin, what I'd bin a road-kid with, an' took the trail with ever-since-when —ranchin'; gold-prospectin', with a rusty pan and a bag o' flour; ridin' the blind, right across the States; lumberin'; throwin' our feet fer a two-bit poke-out, in the towns; and trampin' through the alkali sage bush, as thirsty as a bitch with nine pups.

"Bud Conklin was a blowed-in-the-glass White Man, an' I was the death of him. Yes, Sir. And his gal —a little peach, named Mame Texas....I guess she begun life as 'Mame o' Texas,' never hevin' hed no parients-nawthen to speak of —'cos Dago Jake had lifted her outer Ole Pete Frisco's ranch when his gang shot th' ol' sinner up, down Texas way (an' *he* never hed no wife-nawthen to speak of) and burnt the place down.

"An' when she filled out and grow'd up a bit, Dago Jake he got that sot on the gal, he allowed as he'd give any man lead-pisenin' as looked at her twice; an' he beat her up every time he got a whisky-jag, so' she shouldn't look twice at nobody else.

"Marry her? No! There wasn't no sky-pilots around Hackberry Crossin' by the Frio River in them prickly-pear flats; an' Dago Jake dassn't show his ugly face near no church-bearin' city-even if he'd held with matterimony as a pastime.

"Nope! Nix on marryin' fer Jake.

"Then me an' Bud eventuates in Hackberry Crossin', travellin' mighty modest and unconspishus, after arguin' with a disbelievin' roller of a Ranger as allowed we'd found our pinto hosses before no one hadn't lost 'em.

"An' it was up to us to lose ourselves an' keep away with both feet after we'd collected that cracker-jack's hoss, an' gun likewise, and the financial events in the pockets of his pants.

"He was a sure annoyed boob when me an' Bud told him good-bye an' set his erring feet fer Quatana-having took his belt and pant-suspenders and bootlaces so's he'd hev to hold his pants up with one hand an' his boots on with the other. An' then we burnt the trail for Hackberry Crossin', day an' night, and went to earth at Dago Jake's, sech being Jake's perfession.

"Bud didn' look at Mame twice. Nope, once was enuff, but it lasted all the time she was in sight! ...Bud took it bad....He wrote po'try. An' he made me listen to it while we wolfed our mornin' *frijoles* an cawfy, or evenin' goat-mutton steaks an' canned termatoes, an' forty-rod whisky. Bud's fav'rite spasm begun: —

"'*O Mame, which art not in reach,*
O Mame, thou art a peach!
I fair must let a screech
Or else my heart it will be too full for speech.'

An' there was about twenty noo verses each day. He made 'em up outa his silly head while we lay doggo, up in the pear-thicket along the *arroyo* behint Jake's adobe.

"An' by the time the Sheriff, an' the Lootenant of Rangers, an' the Town Marshal o' Quatana begun to allow that no such suspicious characters as me an' Bud hadn't ever crossed the Frio at Hackberry Crossin', Bud was nearly as much in love with Mame as Mame was with Bud.

"They *hed* got it bad.

"And soon that low-lifer coyote of a Dago Jake, he begins to smell a rat, and afore long he smells a elephant. Bud wants to shoot him up, but Mame won't stand for it. She don't want Bud to swing fer a goshdinged tough like Jake. '*It would be man-slaughterin' murder,*' says she; '*besides which, Jake kin pull a gun as quick as greased lightnin'. Yew ain't got nawthen on Jake at that game,*' she says, '*wherefore I holds it onlawful and calc'lated to cause a breach of the peace-and o' yew likewise, Bud,*' an' she kisses him like hell, we-all being in the pear-thicket, an' me lookin' the other way like I was searchin' fer me lost youth an' innercence...."

"Wot abaht this 'ere picky-back, Buck?" interrupted 'Erb. "Thought you was agoin' to tell a thunderin' good lie abaht killing yer pal an' 'is donah, through playin' picky-backs with 'em."

Le Légionnaire Reginald Rupert, leaning forward from his place on the bench, smote 'Erb painfully in the ribs: William Jones crushed the little man's *képi* over his face: while La Cigale, in the voice of one who chides a dog, hissed "*Tais-toi, canaille!*" in an unwonted fit of anger at the unmannerly interruption.

"But what is it that it is, this peek-a-back?" whispered Alphonse Blanc to John Bull, as the Bucking Bronco turned his slow contemptuous regard upon 'Erb.

"As to say, *sur-le-dos*," replied the old Legionary, seizing the Cockney in a grip of iron as he prepared to deal faithfully with Rupert and Jones (who had been Captain Geoffry Brabazon-Howard of the Black Lancers).

* * *

"And the end of it was," continued the American, "that we made our get-away, the three of us, one night; mighty clever, we thought, until we heard Dago Jake laugh-at our very first campin' ground!...

"I'd kep' first watch, an' then Bud the next-and Mame, she must sit up and keep watch with him....'Fore long they was doin' it with their four eyes shut, being as tired as a greaser's mule, and aleanin' agin a tree, wrop in each other's arms....

"I ain't ablamin' 'em any.... *They* paid-most, anyhow....

"When I wakes up, hearing Dago Jake's pleasin' smile, he'd got 'em covered with his gun, an' half-a-dozen of his gang (blowed-in-glass-Bad-Men-from-Texas they was, too) had got me covered also likewise.

"'*First on you as moves, and I let some daylight into the dark innards o' that respectable young female as yore acuddlin', Bud Conklin,' says Jake. 'Git up and hands up.'*

"'*Do it smart, Buck,*' ses Bud, and we jumps up and puts our hands up, right there. I guess Bud hoped as how Jake might forgive the gal an' take her back-when he'd done with Bud....

"I'd hev reached for the hip-pocket o' me pants and pulled my gun-for I allow that no moss don't grow on me when I start in to deliver the goods with a gun-for all his bonehead bunch o' shave-tails, but I allowed Jake would shoot the gal up, all right; and that was where the outfit had got the bulge on us.... Yep, it was Jake's night to howl,...

"And right here's where the picky-back eventuates, Sonny," he added, addressing 'Erb.

"Yep. Mr. Fresh-Tough Coyote Dago Jake had thought out a neat cinch-cool as ice-with his black heart boilin' and bubblin' like pitch.... In about half no-time, me an' Bud was roped-up with raw-hide lariats-me like a trussed fowl and Bud with his hands only. They was bound fit to cut 'em off, but his legs was free-and all the time Dago Jake covers the gal, and asks in his dod-gasted greasy voice-like molasses gurglin' outer a bar'l (no, I didn't like Jake's voice) — whether she'd hev her ears shot off or be crippled fer life with a shot in each knee, if she stirred an inch, or me an' Bud tried to move hand or foot.... Yes, Sir, Jake fair gave me the fantods that bright an' shinin' morn.

"Then, when they'd done tyin' me an' Bud like parcels, they bound the gal to the tree what we'd been campin' under. They tied her hands behind her; they tied her feet an' knees together; and they tied her to that tree like windin' string round a bat-handle.... And then they puts a halter round Bud's neck an' ties the other end to a branch —*after settin' Bud up on my shoulders, with his legs one each side of my head an' his feet danglin' down on my chest*.... Yes, Sir.... And I calc'lated that if I *co*-lapsed, Bud's feet would still dangle-about a yard from the ground or a couple o' foot, when the rope stretched and gave a bit, or the bough bent a little.... And Mame stood face to face with us six feet away...."

* * *

The Bucking Bronco fell silent-and no member of the little group of Legionaries broke the silence. I could see from their faces that even Tant-de-Soif and Alphonse Blanc grasped the situation-while from La Cigale, Dobroffski, and the Japanese, scarcely a nuance of meaning was hid.

It was plain that John Bull, Reginald Rupert, and William Jones visualized the scene more clearly, and felt its poignant horror more fully than did 'Erb, ex-denizen of the foulest slums of London.

"'*Streuth!*'" 'Erb murmured at last, and scratched his head.

"And then, '*I fear I must now leave you for a spell, ladies an' gents,*' ses Dago Jake," continued the American, "after he'd smacked his lips some, an' pointed out our cleverness and beauty to the grinnin' outfit —'*but I'll look in a bit later on-say this day week or so, an' pay my respex*' —and the hull outfit rides off, laffin' fit to bust.

"And there was we-all —Bud hevin' as long to live as I could stand up under his weight; an' me an' Mame with as long to live as starvation 'ud let us.

"No, there wasn't no hope of nobody comin' along through them prickly-pear flats. That didn't eventuate to happen once in a month-apart from Dago Jake layin' hisself out to see that it didn't happen till we-all had got what was acomin' to us.

"He c'd fix it to detain anybody what might come to Hackberry Crossin' plannin' to follow the trail we'd took West-which was as onlikely as celluloid apples in Hell-an' nobody never come East along it, 'cos there was a better one.

"Nope-we'd chose that highly onpopulous thoroughfare apurpose, travellin' modest an' onconspishus as before, an' the more so for to avoid onpleasantness for Mame consevent upon pursuit by Dago Jake.

"And there wouldn't be no Ranger patrol along neether. If any come at all, it'd be along the trail we'd reckoned as Jake'd take when he found we'd vamoosed durin' his temp'r'y indisposition of whisky-jag....

"*Gee*-whillikins! what wouldn't I hev give fer that same Ranger, that Bud an' I had held up an' dispoiled contumelious, to happen along-even if it meant ten years striped pyjamas in the County Pen or in St. Quentin with hard labour, strait-jacket an' dungeons. I'd ha' fell upon his neck an' kissed him frequent an' free....Yep....And *then* some."...

The irrepressible 'Erb improved the occasion, as the big American ceased and seemed to stare into the past.

"Ah!" he moralized, "if you'd bin alivin' of a *honest* life an' keepin' out o' trouble wi' the plice, you'd never 'a come to trouble like *that*....It was all along o' yore interferin' wi' the copper as wanted to see the receipt for them 'osses, that you come ter grief."

"An' that's where yore wrong *agin*, Sonny," replied the Bucking Bronco with his big-dog-to-little-dog air of forbearance. "Though I allow youse an authority on avoidin' trouble with the perlice"—('Erb's presence in the Legion was consequent upon his hurried leaving of his country for his country's good)—"for it was entirely due to that same Ranger's ferocious pussonal interest in me that I'm alive to-day. He'd allowed he would trail me and Bud if it took the rest of his misspent life-an' arrest us lone-handed. He was that mad! Walkin' on foot without pant-suspenders is humiliatin' to a sensitive nature what has jest bin relieved of its gun."

He fell silent again, and nobody spoke or stirred.

"We talked a bit, at first," he continued after a long pause, "an' ole Bud Conklin showed his grit, cheering up Mame, an' sayin' Dago Jake was only playin' a trick on us. But the gal *knew* Dago Jake, an' soon she began to lose holt on herself....I ain't blamin' her any....She loved Bud Conklin, y'see....She cried, and struggled, and screeched, and I wished she'd stop-until she begun to laugh, and then I'd rather she'd cried and screeched.

"And '*Come up, ol' hoss*,' says Bud to me, when fust I staggered a bit-jest quiet like-jest like he'd said a thousand times when a tired pony stumbled under him.

"And by-an'-by he leans down an' whispers, '*I'd kick free of yer, pard, if it wan't for the gal.*'

"An' when I begins to tremble an' sway around, he leans down agin and says very quiet, '*Hold up till the gal faints or sleeps or su'think, Buck,*' he says. '*Hold up, ole pard....She'll go mad for life if I dances an' jerks afore her eyes!*' ...An' I know he weren't hevin' no daisy of a dandy time up there-and that he'd have kicked clear long ago but for the gal....

"Faint? Sleep? Not she....There she stood, face to face with us-havin' highstericks a spell; then laffin' a spell, then prayin' some....Then croonin' over Bud Conklin like he was her babby.... Whiles, she'd praise me fer standin' firm an' savin' her man-an' there was a spell when the pore thing thought I was God.

"One time, 'bout mid-day, Bud Conklin swore an' cursed at Dago Jake till I fair blushed to hear him-an' then I waded in and beat him holler at swearin', an' cursin' the name of Dago Jake....But *that* didn't cut no ice-nor cut our raw-hide lariats neither.

"In all them story-books about Red Injuns an' Deadwood Dicks an' such, the blue-eyed, golden-haired Hero *allus* busts his bonds. He figgers to bust 'em on time; then to find a saddled hoss standin' ready; likewise to pick up a new-loaded gun *and* a square meal by the road-side, before gallopin' a hundred miles to make a fuss o' the Villain and make a date with the Hero*ine*

—jest as that husky hoodlum's criminile *advances*, drugs, stranglin's and starvin's is gettin' irksome to the young female....

"I guess Dago Jake an' his outfit wasn't the guys as had roped up aforesaid Hero....Nit....But they *was* the guys as had roped up us, an' we didn't bust no bonds. Nary a bust. And once, towards evenin', I begun to sway so bad that I half dropped Bud, an' on'y got him straight on my shoulders agin, jest in time ... (an' I hear the screech that Mame let, *now*, sometimes.) '*Air you achokin' any, Bud?*' I ses. '*No, pard*,' ses he, '*I ain't chokin' none, but you couldn't git a cigarette-paper between my neck an' this derned lasso. I allow nex' time will give little Willie a narsty cough an' a crick in the neck.*'

"An' at the same time we notices that Mame was still an' quiet, with her eyes shut. '*Now, Buck*,' ses Bud, '*fall down an' roll clear....Better she sees me dead than watch me dyin'*.'

"'*Fall down, nawthen*,' says I. '*I'm agoin' to stand right here till the Day o' Jedgement; an' then I allow I'll donate Mister Tin-horn Dago Jake a tomato-eye.*' And right then Mame opens her eyes an' smiles sweet, up at Bud.

"'*Hevn't we played this silly game long enuff, Buddy?*' she says. '*I'm so tired....Let's go git married, like we planned*' —an' I heerd Bud cough. She shuts her eyes agin then-an' very slow an' careful I turns right round so's not to see her no more.

* * *

"An' I stood still till it was dark....

"So whether Mame died afore Bud or not-she didn't see him die, an' that there fact has kep' me from goin' bug-house like Cigale...

"*Her dead face an' Bud's boot-soles fer a day or two!* ...

"Yep. It were that Ranger as arrested us. A dead woman tied to a tree, a dead man danglin' from it, an' a dead man lyin' just below his feet-on'y he wasn't quite dead.

"He was a White Man, that Ranger. He was hoppin' mad when he figgers out what had happened, an' gives me rye-whisky, an' dopes me to sleep, an' lets me lie there some.

"He was young an' innercent, an' when he'd donated me some grub an' some more whisky, I talked to him eloquential. I *did* wanta tell Dago Jake good-bye, before the Ranger hiked me off to his Lieutenant, an' they rounded Jake an' his gang up. The Ranger allowed it was Bud what had held him up and trated him contumelious that day, an' thet as pore Bud had handed in his checks, an' I'd nearly done likewise, he was agoin' to fergit me....He on'y wanted me as witness agin Dago Jake and Co., for the murder of Mame an' Bud....

"An' as we jogs along I talks to him some more, an' in the end he lets me go to the adobe hut to tell Jake good-bye afore he arrests him.

* * *

"'Bout four o'clock a.m. in the early mornin' it was, and Jake sleepin' off a whisky-jag! ...But he sobers up right slick when I wakes him and he sees my pretty face....He didn't even reach for his gun-not that it was still there if he had. I allow he thought I'd come from hell for him.

"*I had.*

"Yep. I tells Dago Jake good-bye all-right —all-right. An' without usin' no gun, nor knife, nor no other lethial weepon. I takes my farewell o' that gentle Spani-*ard* with my bare hands, and then I walks outer the shack a-singin' —

"'Roll your tail an' roll it high,
Fer you'll be an angel by-an-by,'

an' walkin' with a proud tail accordin'.

"'How *is* Dago Jake?' ses the Ranger.

"'He *ain't*,' ses I...."

* * *

As usual it was 'Erb who spoke first.

"I b'lieve you bin tellin' the *troof*, Buck," said he, "an' that's disqualified in a bloomin' competition for 'oo can tell the biggest lie. My performin' rabbit wins, bless 'is liddle 'eart! Come along to the canteen, and..."

"I know a performin' train wot's got yore performin' jack rabbit skinned a mile," interrupted the American.

"Performin' *train*?" inquired 'Erb blankly.

"That's so," was the drawled reply. "You never seen such a slick train in Yurrup nor Africky.... I was makin' a quick get-away from that Ranger-an' he gallops on to the platform at the deepôt as this U.P.R. double-express fast train glides outa the station. I leans well over the side of the observation-car and plants a kiss upon his bronzed an' manly cheek....At least, I *begun* the kiss there, but where did that kiss *finish*?

"On the southern end of an ole cow abrowsin' beside the track *thirty-three miles down the line*! Some train, and some travellin' that! ...You an' yore performin' rabbit! You make me tired."

"'Streuth!" murmured 'Erb again, and scratched his cropped head, as was his custom when endeavouring to grapple with mysteries beyond his ken.

* * *

> "Soldats de la Legion,
> De la Légion Étrangère,
> N'ayant pas de nation,
> La France est votre Mère."

Footnotes

1. Store-room.
2. Footman and male "housemaid".
3. Gardener.
4. Groom.
5. Real, solid, permanent, proper, ripe, genuine.
6. Anna = a penny.
7. Strong, powerful chief.
8. Grass-man.
9. Carriage.
10. Bullock-carts.
11. A kind of starling.
12. Water-carriers.
13. Servant.
14. Camel-man.
15. Confined to barracks.
16. A famous Hussar regiment.
17. Teetotal.
18. Cigarettes.
19. When a non-commissioned officer does anything to risk losing his stripes he says he "chances his arm".
20. Permanent Military Police.
21. Summons before the Commanding Officer in Orderly Room.
22. Guard-room.
23. Infantry Regiments.
24. Cavalry Regiment.
25. Silent.
26. This actually happened some years ago at Bangalore. —AUTHOR.
27. News, information.
28. Camel.
29. By means of its "Decies Horizontal Screw Stabilizer," which enabled it to "hover" with only a very slight rise and fall.
30. Native bed-frame.
31. Baggage-camel.

32. Hindustani—enough, finished, complete.
33. Meat.
34. Food.
35. Garden. Cultivation.
36. An emphatic negative.
37. Deserters.
38. In the days of the high, tight stock and cravat, the recruit was supposed to be livid and blue in the face until he grew accustomed to them.
39. Civilians.
40. To drink alone; to sulk.
41. The week before Lent, or "mad week," when all good *mujiks* get drunk—or used to do.
42. A curious piece of Legion "French" meaning "Be quick."
43. "Get up. Come here. Take care! You ugly mule."
44. Penal battalion.
45. Time spent in prison or in the Penal Battalions—which does not count towards the five years period of service.
46. Untrue.
47. Lit., "to carry coals to Newcastle."
48. Guardian, watchman.
49. Written in 1913.–AUTHOR.
50. lit., tin-ware (medals and decorations).
51. On a sick bed.
52. Bayonet.
53. To bayonet.
54. Arab gens d'armes.
55. White man.
56. The postmaster.
57. Sleep.
58. Dog—and son of a dog.
59. Since increased to three, of course.
60. Untrue.
61. Deck-chair.
62. Chinese pariah dog.
63. Mark of the Zephyrs.
64. Last Post. So called (in the American Army) because it is the signal to leave the Canteen and turn off the beer-taps.

65. Bed.
66. Drink his beer.
67. Tramp, a rough.
68. Policemen.
69. Train conductors.
70. Wine.
71. Estates.
72. Baby.
73. Yes.
74. Without doubt.
75. Native cigarette.
76. School.
77. Mohammedan High School.
78. Clerk.
79. Examination.
80. Certificate.
81. An insulting and contemptuous gesture.
82. A class of negroes, much employed as sailors and boatmen, and called Seedeeboys.
83. Europe.
84. Bustard.
85. A kind of partridge.
86. Gazelle.
87. Bad characters.
88. Long staves.
89. Brass cup or vase.
90. Basin or pot.
91. Telegram.
92. Turban.
93. Bravo! Excellent!
94. Native cot or bed.
95. Carpet.
96. Camel-men.
97. Halting-enclosure, rest-house.
98. Order.
99. Tracker.

100. Bran.
101. Circuit, course.
102. A Mussulman greeting.
103. Meeting.
104. One hundred thousand.
105. Warm sheep-skin coats.
106. Kos = two miles.
107. Priest.
108. Infantry Regiment.
109. To *halal* is to make lawful, here to cut the throat of a living animal in order that its flesh may be eatable by good Mussulmans.
110. Small dug-out canoe.
111. Rhinoceros-hide whip.
112. Corfield?
113. Native boatswain.
114. Bullock carts.
115. Poor travellers' rest-house.
116. Who's there.
117. Come in.
118. Sun-helmet.
119. Written in 1912. —AUTHOR.
120. "Little presence," early breakfast, *petit déjeuner*.
121. Ghurka knives.
122. Note.
123. Plain; level tract of ground.
124. Public conveyance.
125. Bring.
126. To.
127. Finale, enough, the end.
128. Pig.
129. Go away.
130. An insulting epithet.
131. Hearty greeting.
132. Quarter-staff and sword.
133. Collector's Court and Office.

134. Dealers.
135. Money-lenders.
136. Bullock-carts.
137. At once.
138. Bowls.
139. Enough, stop.
140. Swine.
141. Look.
142. Jao = go (imperative).
143. Seize (imperative).
144. Plain.
145. Loin-cloth.
146. Good.
147. Make.
148. "I want the Colonel. Where is he?"
149. Cupboard.
150. "Is all well?"
151. "Without doubt."
152. Woolly ones. Negroes.
153. Bullock-cart men.
154. Yes.
155. Without doubt.
156. Here.
157. Store-sheds.
158. Oxen.
159. Bring here.
160. Talk, palaver.
161. Savages.
162. "Very good, sir."
163. "Be careful —*you!*"
164. "Good!"
165. "Kill the devils. Do well."
166. "It is not the enemy."
167. Medicine.
168. "Great Simba has killed a white man."

169. "Wait. Lie on the stretcher."
170. "It is nothing."
171. "Thanks. It is nothing. Do not hold me."
172. Clever and competent.
173. Sit down.
174. Open plain.
175. Food.
176. "Dinner is ready."
177. Yes.
178. Cultivation, garden.
179. Over-eating.
180. White men.
181. Club.
182. Cooking-pot.
183. "Lunch is ready."
184. Tribal dance.
185. "The stretcher-bearers will come, brother."
186. "No doubt, sir. I am waiting."
187. "Gone, sir. There is nothing."
188. "Bravo."
189. "Kill! Kill!"
190. The "double" march.
191. Dismiss.
192. Arab gens d'armes.
193. Fortified village.
194. Europeans.
195. Go to bed.
196. Colonial infantry.
197. Go away.
198. Civilians.
199. Sell up everything.
200. Glory to God.
201. Known as *Les Jeunes Filles* to the Legion, by reason of their long hair.
202. *Pèkin* = civilian.
203. Mad.

204. Hemp.
205. It is written! As God wills!
206. Enough.
207. *Vide* "The Wages of Virtue." John Murray.
208. Colonial Infantry (Infanterie de la Marine).
209. "Woolly ones" (negroes).
210. Enclosure; jungle fort.
211. Great Master.
212. Whip.
213. "What is the name of your regiment? How many men are there in your outpost? How many machine-guns?"
214. "The Master will flog you."

Printed in Great Britain
by Amazon